LORD PETER
TAKES THE CASE

WIMSEY, PETER DEATH BREDON, D.S.O.; *born* 1890, *2nd son* of Mortimer Gerald Bredon Wimsey, 15th Duke of Denver, and of Honoria Lucasta, *daughter of* Francis Delagardie of Bellingham Manor, Hants. *Married* 1935, Harriet Deborah Vane, *daughter of* Henry Vane M.D.; one *son* (Bredon Delagardie Peter) *born*,1936.

Educated: Eton College and Balliol College, Oxford (1st class honours, Sch. of Mod. Hist. 1912) ; served with H.M.Forces 1914/18 (Major, Rifle Brigade). *Author of*: "Notes on the Collecting of Incunabula," "The Murderer's Vade-Mecum," etc. *Recreations*: Criminology; bibliophily; music; cricket.

Clubs: Marlborough; Egotists'; Bellona. *Residences*: 110A, Piccadilly, W.; Bredon Hall, Duke's Denver, Norfolk.

Arms: Sable, 3 mice courant, argent; crest, a domestic cat couched as to spring, proper; motto: As my Whimsy takes me.

LORD PETER
TAKES THE CASE

· DOROTHY L. ·
SAYERS

Clouds of Witness ◆ Unnatural Death ◆ The Five Red Herrings
The Unpleasantness at the Bellona Club

Book-of-the-Month Club
New York

Unnatural Death

BIOGRAPHICAL NOTE

Communicated by PAUL AUSTIN DELAGARDIE

I AM ASKED by Miss Sayers to fill up certain lacunæ and correct a few trifling errors of fact in her account of my nephew Peter's career. I shall do so with pleasure. To appear publicly in print is every man's ambition, and by acting as a kind of running footman to my nephew's triumph I shall only be showing a modesty suitable to my advanced age.

The Wimsey family is an ancient one—too ancient, if you ask me. The only sensible thing Peter's father ever did was to ally his exhausted stock with the vigorous French-English strain of the Delagardies. Even so, my nephew Gerald (the present Duke of Denver) is nothing but a beef-witted English squire, and my niece Mary was flighty and foolish enough till she married a policeman and settled down. Peter, I am glad to say, takes after his mother and me. True, he is all nerves and nose—but that is better than being all brawn and no brains like his father and brother, or a bundle of emotions, like Gerald's boy, Saint-George. He has at least inherited the Delagardie brains, by way of safeguard to the unfortunate Wimsey temperament.

Peter was born in 1890. His mother was being very much worried at the time by her husband's behaviour (Denver was always tiresome, though the big scandal did not break out till the Jubilee year), and her anxieties may have affected the boy. He was a colorless shrimp of a child, very restless and mischievous, and always much too sharp for his age. He had nothing of Gerald's robust physical beauty, but he developed what I can best call a kind of bodily cleverness, more skill than strength. He had a quick eye for a ball and beautiful hands for a horse. He had the devil's own pluck, too : the intelligent sort of pluck that sees the risk before it takes it. He suffered badly from nightmares as a child. To his father's consternation he grew up with a passion for books and music.

His early school-days were not happy. He was a fastidious child, and I suppose it was natural that his school-fellows should call him " Flimsy " and treat him as a kind of comic turn. And he might, in sheer self-protection, have accepted the position and degenerated into a mere licensed buffoon, if some games-master at Eton had not discovered that he was a brilliant natural cricketer. After that, of course, all his eccentricities were accepted as wit, and Gerald underwent the salutary shock of seeing his despised younger brother become a bigger personality than himself. By the time he reached the Sixth Form, Peter had contrived to become the fashion—athlete, scholar, *arbiter elegantiarum— nec pluribus impar*. Cricket had a great deal to do with it— plenty of Eton men will remember the " Great Flim " and his performance against Harrow—but I take credit to myself for introducing him to a good tailor, showing him the way about Town, and teaching him to distinguish good wine from bad. Denver bothered little about him— he had too many entanglements of his own and in addition was taken up with Gerald, who by this time was making a prize fool of himself at Oxford. As a matter of fact Peter never got on with his father, he was a ruthless young critic of the paternal misdemeanours, and his sympathy for his mother had a destructive effect upon his sense of humour.

Denver, needless to say, was the last person to tolerate his own failings in his offspring. It cost him a good deal of money to extricate Gerald from the Oxford affair, and he was willing enough to turn his other son over to me. Indeed, at the age of seventeen, Peter came to me of his own accord. He was old for his age and exceedingly reasonable, and I treated him as a man of the world. I established him in trustworthy hands in Paris, instructing him to keep his affairs upon a sound business footing and to see that they terminated with goodwill on both sides and generosity on his. He fully justified my confidence. I believe that no woman has ever found cause to complain of Peter's treatment ; and two at least of them have since married royalty (rather obscure royalties, I admit, but royalty of a sort). Here again, I insist upon my due share of the credit ; however good the material one has to work upon it is ridiculous to leave any young man's social education to chance.

The Peter of this period was really charming, very frank,

modest and well-mannered, with a pretty, lively wit. In 1909 he went up with a scholarship to read History at Balliol, and here, I must confess, he became rather intolerable. The world was at his feet, and he began to give himself airs. He acquired affectations, an exaggerated Oxford manner and a monocle, and aired his opinions a good deal, both in and out of the Union, though I will do him the justice to say that he never attempted to patronise his mother or me. He was in his second year when Denver broke his neck out hunting and Gerald succeeded to the title. Gerald showed more sense of responsibility than I had expected in dealing with the estate ; his worst mistake was to marry his cousin Helen, a scrawny, over-bred prude, all county from head to heel. She and Peter loathed each other cordially ; but he could always take refuge with his mother at the Dower House.

And then, in his last year at Oxford, Peter fell in love with a child of seventeen and instantly forgot everything he had ever been taught. He treated that girl as if she was made of gossamer, and me as a hardened old monster of depravity who had made him unfit to touch her delicate purity. I won't deny that they made an exquisite pair—all white and gold—a prince and princess of moonlight, people said. Moonshine would have been nearer the mark. What Peter was to do in twenty years' time with a wife who had neither brains nor character nobody but his mother and myself ever troubled to ask, and he, of course, was completely besotted. Happily, Barbara's parents decided that she was too young to marry ; so Peter went in for his final Schools in the temper of a Sir Eglamore achieving his first dragon ; laid his First-Class Honours at his lady's feet like the dragon's head, and settled down to a period of virtuous probation.

Then came the War. Of course the young idiot was mad to get married before he went. But his own honourable scruples made him mere wax in other people's hands. It was pointed out to him that if he came back mutilated it would be very unfair to the girl. He hadn't thought of that, and rushed off in a frenzy of self-abnegation to release her from the engagement. I had no hand in that ;

I was glad enough of the result, but I couldn't stomach the means.

He did very well in France ; he made a good officer and the men liked him. And then, if you please, he came back on leave with his captaincy in '16, to find the girl married— to a hardbitten rake of a Major Somebody, whom she had nursed in the V.A.D. hospital, and whose motto with women was catch 'em quick and treat 'em rough. It was pretty brutal ; for the girl hadn't had the nerve to tell Peter beforehand. They got married in a hurry when they heard he was coming home, and all he got on landing was a letter, announcing the *fait accompli* and reminding him that he had set her free himself.

I will say for Peter that he came straight to me and admitted that he had been a fool. " All right," said I, " you've had your lesson. Don't go and made a fool of yourself in the other direction." So he went back to his job with (I am sure) the fixed intention of getting killed ; but all he got was his majority and his D.S.O. for some recklessly good intelligence work behind the German front. In 1918 he was blown up and buried in a shell-hole near Caudry, and that left him with a bad nervous breakdown, lasting, on and off, for two years. After that, he set himself up in a flat in Piccadilly, with the man Bunter (who had been his sergeant and was, and is, devoted to him), and started out to put himself together again.

I don't mind saying that I was prepared for almost anything. He had lost all his beautiful frankness, he shut everybody out of his confidence, including his mother and me, adopted an impenetrable frivolity of manner and a dilettante pose, and became, in fact, the complete comedian. He was wealthy and could do as he chose, and it gave me a certain amount of sardonic entertainment to watch the efforts of post-war feminine London to capture him. " It can't," said one solicitous matron, " be good for poor Peter to live like a hermit." " Madam," said I, " if he did, it wouldn't be." No ; from that point of view he gave me no anxiety. But I could not but think it dangerous that a man of his ability should have no job to occupy his mind, and I told him so.

In 1921 came the business of the Attenbury Emeralds. That affair has never been written up, but it made a good deal of noise, even at that noisiest of periods. The trial of the thief was a series of red-hot sensations, and the biggest sensation of the bunch was when Lord Peter Wimsey walked into the witness-box as chief witness for the prosecution.

That was notoriety with a vengeance. Actually, to an experienced intelligence officer, I don't suppose the investigation had offered any great difficulties ; but a " noble sleuth " was something new in thrills. Denver was furious ; personally, I didn't mind what Peter did, provided he did something. I thought he seemed happier for the work, and I liked the Scotland Yard man he had picked up during the run of the case. Charles Parker is a quiet, sensible, well-bred fellow, and has been a good friend and brother-in-law to Peter. He has the valuable quality of being fond of people without wanting to turn them inside out.

The only trouble about Peter's new hobby was that it had to be more than a hobby, if it was to be any hobby for a gentleman. You cannot get murderers hanged for your private entertainment. Peter's intellect pulled him one way and his nerves another, till I began to be afraid they would pull him to pieces. At the end of every case we had the old nightmares and shell-shock over again. And then Denver, of all people—Denver, the crashing great booby, in the middle of his fulminations against Peter's degrading and notorious police activities, must needs get himself indicted on a murder charge and stand his trial in the House of Lords, amid a blaze of publicity which made all Peter's efforts in that direction look like damp squibs.

Peter pulled his brother out of that mess, and, to my relief, was human enough to get drunk on the strength of it. He now admits that his " hobby " is his legitimate work for society, and has developed sufficient interest in public affairs to undertake small diplomatic jobs from time to time under the Foreign Office. Of late he has become a little more ready to show his feelings, and a little less terrified of having any to show.

His latest eccentricity has been to fall in love with that girl whom he cleared of the charge of poisoning her lover. She refused to marry him, as any woman of character would. Gratitude and a humiliating inferiority complex are no foundation for matrimony ; the position was false from the start. Peter had the sense, this time, to take my advice. " My boy," said I, " what was wrong for you twenty years back is right now. It's not the innocent young things that need gentle handling—it's the ones that have been frightened and hurt. Begin again from the beginning —but I warn you that you will need all the self-discipline you have ever learnt."

Well, he has tried. I don't think I have ever seen such patience. The girl has brains and character and honesty ; but he has got to teach her how to take, which is far more difficult than learning to give. I think they will find one another, if they can keep their passions from running ahead of their wills. He does realise, I know, that in this case there can be no consent but free consent.

Peter is forty-five now, it is really time he was settled. As you will see, I have been one of the important formative influences in his career, and, on the whole, I feel he does me credit. He is a true Delagardie, with little of the Wimseys about him except (I must be fair) that underlying sense of social responsibility which prevents the English landed gentry from being a total loss, spiritually speaking. Detective or no detective, he is a scholar and a gentleman ; it will amuse me to see what sort of shot he makes at being a husband and father. I am getting an old man, and have no son of my own (that I know of) ; I should be glad to see Peter happy. But as his mother says, " Peter has always had everything except the things he really wanted," and I suppose he is luckier than most.

PAUL AUSTIN DELAGARDIE

CONTENTS

PART I

THE MEDICAL PROBLEM

" But how I caught it, found it, or came by it,
What stuff 'tis made of, whereof it is born,
I am to learn."

MERCHANT OF VENICE

CHAPTER I

OVERHEARD

"The death was certainly sudden, unexpected, and to me mysterious."
Letter from Dr. Paterson to the Registrar in the case
of Reg. v. Pritchard.

"But if he thought the woman was being murdered——"

"My dear Charles," said the young man with the monocle, "it doesn't do for people, especially doctors, to go about 'thinking' things. They may get into frightful trouble. In Pritchard's case, I consider Dr. Paterson did all he reasonably could by refusing a certificate for Mrs. Taylor and sending that uncommonly disquieting letter to the Registrar. He couldn't help the man's being a fool. If there had only been an inquest on Mrs. Taylor, Pritchard would probably have been frightened off and left his wife alone. After all, Paterson hadn't a spark of real evidence. And suppose he'd been quite wrong—what a dust-up there'd have been !"

"All the same," urged the nondescript young man, dubiously extracting a bubbling-hot Helix Pomatia from its shell, and eyeing it nervously before putting it in his mouth, "surely it's a clear case of public duty to voice one's suspicions."

"Of *your* duty—yes," said the other. "By the way, it's not a public duty to eat snails if you don't like 'em. No, I thought you didn't. Why wrestle with a harsh fate any longer ? Waiter, take the gentleman's snails away and bring oysters instead. . . . No—as I was saying, it may be part of *your* duty to have suspicions and invite investigation and generally raise hell for everybody, and if you're mistaken nobody says much, beyond that you're a smart, painstaking officer though a little over-zealous. But doctors, poor devils ! are everlastingly walking a kind of social tight-rope. People don't fancy calling in a man who's liable to bring out accusations of murder on the smallest provocation."

" Excuse me."

The thin-faced young man sitting alone at the next table had turned round eagerly.

" It's frig¹·tfully rude of me to break in, but every word you say is absolutely true, and mine is a case in point. A doctor—you can't have any idea how dependent he is on the fancies and prejudices of his patients. They resent the most elementary precautions. If you dare to suggest a post-mortem, they're up in arms at the idea of ' cutting poor dear So-and-so up,' and even if you only ask permission to investigate an obscure disease in the interests of research, they imagine you're hinting at something unpleasant. Of course, if you let things go, and it turns out afterwards there's been any jiggery-pokery, the coroner jumps down your throat and the newspapers make a butt of you, and, whichever way it is, you wish you'd never been born."

" You speak with personal feeling," said the man with the monocle, with an agreeable air of interest.

" I do," said the thin-faced man, emphatically. " If I had behaved like a man of the world instead of a zealous citizen, I shouldn't be hunting about for a new job to-day."

The man with the monocle glanced round the little Soho restaurant with a faint smile. The fat man on their right was unctuously entertaining two ladies of the chorus ; beyond him, two elderly habitués were showing their acquaintance with the fare at the " Au Bon Bourgeois " by consuming a Tripes à la Mode de Caen (which they do very excellently there) and a bottle of Chablis Moutonne 1916 ; on the other side of the room a provincial and his wife were stupidly clamouring for a cut off the joint with lemonade for the lady and whisky and soda for the gentleman, while at the adjoining table, the handsome silver-haired proprietor, absorbed in fatiguing a salad for a family party, had for the moment no thoughts beyond the nice adjustment of the chopped herbs and garlic. The head waiter, presenting for inspection a plate of Blue River Trout, helped the monocled man and his companion and retired, leaving them in the privacy which unsophisticated people always seek in genteel tea-shops and never, never find there.

" I feel," said the monocled man, " exactly like Prince Florizel of Bohemia. I am confident that you, sir, have an interesting story to relate, and shall be greatly obliged if you will favour us with the recital. I perceive that you have finished your dinner, and it will therefore perhaps not be disagreeable to you to remove to this table and entertain us with your story while we eat. Pardon my Stevensonian manner—my sympathy is none the less sincere on that account."

" Don't be an ass, Peter," said the nondescript man. " My friend is a much more rational person than you might suppose to hear him talk," he added, turning to the stranger, " and if there's anything you'd like to get off your chest, you may be perfectly certain it won't go any farther."

The other smiled a little grimly.

" I'll tell you about it with pleasure if it won't bore you. It just happens to be a case in point, that's all."

" On *my* side of the argument," said the man called Peter, with triumph. " Do carry on. Have something to drink. It's a poor heart that never rejoices. And begin right at the beginning, if you will, please. I have a very trivial mind. Detail delights me. Ramifications enchant me. Distance no object. No reasonable offer refused. Charles here will say the same."

" Well," said the stranger, " to begin from the very

beginning, I am a medical man, particularly interested in the subject of Cancer. I had hoped, as so many people do, to specialise on the subject, but there wasn't money enough, when I'd done my exams., to allow me to settle down to research work. I had to take a country practice, but I kept in touch with the important men up here, hoping to be able to come back to it some day. I may say I have quite decent expectations from an uncle, and in the meanwhile they agreed it would be quite good for me to get some all-round experience as a G.P. Keeps one from getting narrow and all that.

" Consequently, when I bought a nice little practice at . . .—I'd better not mention any names, let's call it X, down Hampshire way, a little country town of about 5,000 people—I was greatly pleased to find a cancer case on my list of patients. The old lady——"

" How long ago was this ? " interrupted Peter.

" Three years ago. There wasn't much to be done with the case. The old lady was seventy-two, and had already had one operation. She was a game old girl, though, and was making a good fight of it, with a very tough constitution to back her up. She was not, I should say, and had never been, a woman of very powerful intellect or strong character as far as her dealings with other people went, but she was extremely obstinate in certain ways and was possessed by a positive determination not to die. At this time she lived alone with her niece, a young woman of twenty-five or so. Previously to that, she had been living with another old lady, the girl's aunt on the other side of the family, who had been her devoted friend since their school days. When this other old aunt died, the girl, who was their only living relative, threw up her job as a nurse at the Royal Free Hospital to look after the survivor— my patient—and they had come and settled down at X about a year before I took over the practice. I hope I am making myself clear."

" Perfectly. Was there another nurse ? "

" Not at that time. The patient was able to get about, visit acquaintances, do light work about the house, flowers and knitting and reading and so on, and to drive about the place—in fact, most of the things that old ladies do occupy their time with. Of course, she had her bad days of pain from time to time, but the niece's training was quite sufficient to enable her to do all that was necessary."

" What was the niece like ? "

" Oh, a very nice, well-educated, capable girl, with a great deal more brain than her aunt. Self-reliant, cool, all that sort of thing. Quite the modern type. The sort of woman one can trust to keep her head and not forget things. Of course, after a time, the wretched growth made its appearance again, as it always does if it isn't tackled at the very beginning, and another operation became necessary. That was when I had been in X about eight months. I took her up to London, to my own old chief, Sir Warburton Giles, and it was performed very successfully as far as the operation itself went, though it was then only too evident that a vital organ was being encroached upon, and that the end could only be a matter of time. I needn't go into details. Everything was done that could be done. I wanted the old lady to stay in town under Sir Warburton's eye, but she was vigorously opposed to this. She was accustomed to a country life and could not be happy except in her own home. So she went back to X, and I was able to keep her going with visits for treatment at the nearest large town, where there is an excellent hospital. She rallied amazingly after the operation and eventually was able to dismiss her nurse and go on in the old way under the care of the niece."

" One moment, doctor," put in the man called Charles, " you say you took her to Sir Warburton Giles and so on. I gather she was pretty well off."

" Oh, yes, she was quite a wealthy woman."

" Do you happen to know whether she made a will ? "

" No. I think I mentioned her extreme aversion to the idea of death. She had always refused to make any kind of will because it upset her to think about such things. I did once venture to speak of the subject in the most casual way I could, shortly before she underwent her operation, but the effect was to excite her very undesirably. Also she said, which was quite true, that it was quite unnecessary. ' You, my dear,' she said to the niece, ' are the only kith and kin I've got in the world, and all I've got will be yours some day, whatever happens. I know I can trust you to remember my servants and my little charities.' So, of course, I didn't insist.

" I remember, by the way—but that was a good deal later on and has nothing to do with the story——"

" *Please*," said Peter, " *all* the details."

" Well, I remember going there one day and finding my patient not so well as I could have wished and very much agitated. The niece told me that the trouble was caused by a visit from her solicitor—a family lawyer from her home town, not our local man. He had insisted on a private interview with the old lady, at the close of which she had appeared terribly excited and angry, declaring that everyone was in a conspiracy to kill her before her time. The solicitor, before leaving, had given no explanation to the niece, but had impressed upon her that if at any time her aunt expressed a wish to see him, she was to send for him at any hour of the day or night and he would come at once."

" And was he ever sent for ? "

" No. The old lady was deeply offended with him, and almost the last bit of business she did for herself was to take her affairs out of his hands and transfer them to the local solicitor. Shortly afterwards, a third operation became necessary, and after this she gradually became more and more of an invalid. Her head began to get weak, too, and

she grew incapable of understanding anything complicated, and indeed she was in too much pain to be bothered
about business. The niece had a power of attorney, and
took over the management of her aunt's money entirely."

" When was this ? "

" In April, 1925. Mind you, though she was getting a
bit ' gaga '—after all, she was getting on in years—her
bodily strength was quite remarkable. I was investigating
a new method of treatment and the results were extraordinarily interesting. That made it all the more annoying
to me when the surprising thing happened.

" I should mention that by this time we were obliged to
have an outside nurse for her, as the niece could not do
both the day and night duty. The first nurse came in April.
She was a most charming and capable young woman—
the ideal nurse. I placed absolute dependence on her. She
had been specially recommended to me by Sir Warburton
Giles, and though she was not then more than twenty-
eight, she had the discretion and judgment of a woman
twice her age. I may as well tell you at once that I became
deeply attached to this lady and she to me. We are engaged,
and had hoped to be married this year—if it hadn't been
for my damned conscientiousness and public spirit."

The doctor grimaced wryly at Charles, who murmured
rather lamely that it was very bad luck.

" My fiancée, like myself, took a keen interest in the
case—partly because it was my case and partly because
she was herself greatly interested in the disease. She looks
forward to being of great assistance to me in my life work
if I ever get the chance to do anything at it. But that's by
the way.

" Things went on like this till September. Then, for
some reason, the patient began to take one of those un-
accountable dislikes that feeble-minded patients do take
sometimes. She got it into her head that the nurse wanted
to kill her—the same idea she'd had about the lawyer,

you see—and earnestly assured her niece that she was being poisoned. No doubt she attributed her attacks of pain to this cause. Reasoning was useless—she cried out and refused to let the nurse come near her. When that happens, naturally, there's nothing for it but to get rid of the nurse, as she can do the patient no possible good. I sent my fiancée back to town and wired to Sir Warburton's Clinic to send me down another nurse.

" The new nurse arrived the next day. Naturally, after the other, she was a second-best as far as I was concerned, but she seemed quite up to her work and the patient made no objection. However, now I began to have trouble with the niece. Poor girl, all this long-drawn-out business was getting on her nerves, I suppose. She took it into her head that her aunt was very much worse. I said that of course she must gradually get worse, but that she was putting up a wonderful fight and there was no cause for alarm. The girl wasn't satisfied, however, and on one occasion early in November sent for me hurriedly in the middle of the night because her aunt was dying.

" When I arrived, I found the patient in great pain, certainly, but in no immediate danger. I told the nurse to give her a morphia injection, and administered a dose of bromide to the girl, telling her to go to bed and not to do any nursing for the next few days. The following day I overhauled the patient very carefully and found that she was doing even better than I supposed. Her heart was exceptionally strong and steady, she was taking nourishment remarkably well and the progress of the disease was temporarily arrested.

" The niece apologised for her agitation, and said she really thought her aunt was going. I said that, on the contrary, I could now affirm positively that she would live for another five or six months. As you know, in cases like hers, one can speak with very fair certainty.

" ' In any case,' I said, ' I shouldn't distress yourself too much. Death, when it does come, will be a release from suffering.'

" ' Yes,' she said, ' poor Auntie. I'm afraid I'm selfish, but she's the only relative I have left in the world.'

" Three days later, I was just sitting down to dinner when a telephone message came. Would I go over at once ? The patient was dead."

" Good gracious ! " cried Charles, " it's perfectly obvious——"

" Shut up, Sherlock," said his friend, " the doctor's story is not going to be obvious. Far from it, as the private said when he aimed at the bull's-eye and hit the gunnery instructor. But I observe the waiter hovering uneasily about us while his colleagues pile up chairs and carry away the cruets. Will you not come and finish the story in my flat ? I can give you a glass of very decent port. You will ? Good. Waiter, call a taxi. . . . 110A, Piccadilly."

CHAPTER II

MICHING MALLECHO

" By the pricking of my thumbs
Something evil this way comes."
Macbeth

THE APRIL NIGHT was clear and chilly, and a brisk
wood fire burned in a welcoming manner on the hearth.
The bookcases which lined the walls were filled with rich
old calf bindings, mellow and glowing in the lamp-light.
There was a grand piano, open, a huge chesterfield piled
deep with cushions and two arm-chairs of the build that
invites one to wallow. The port was brought in by an
impressive man-servant and placed on a very beautiful
little Chippendale table. Some big bowls of scarlet and
yellow parrot tulips beckoned, banner-like, from dark
corners.

The doctor had just written his new acquaintance down
as an æsthete with a literary turn, looking for the ingre-
dients of a human drama, when the man-servant re-entered.

" Inspector Sugg rang up, my lord, and left this message, and said would you be good enough to give him a call
as soon as you came in."

" Oh, did he ?—well, just get him for me, would you ?
This is the Worplesham business, Charles. Sugg's mucked
it up as usual. The baker has an alibi—naturally—he would
have. Oh, thanks. . . . Hullo ! that you, Inspector ? What
did I tell you ?—Oh, routine be hanged. Now, look here.
You get hold of that gamekeeper fellow, and find out from
him what he saw in the sand-pit. . . . No, I know, but I
fancy if you ask him impressively enough he will come
across with it. No, of course not—if you ask if he was there,

he'll say no. Say you know he was there and what did he see—and, look here! if he hums and haws about it, say you're sending a gang down to have the stream diverted. . . . All right. Not at all. Let me know if anything comes of it."

He put the receiver down.

" Excuse me, Doctor. A little matter of business. Now go on with your story. The old lady was dead, eh? Died in her sleep, I suppose. Passed away in the most innocent manner possible. Everything all ship-shape and Bristol-fashion. No struggle, no wounds, hæmorrhages, or obvious symptoms, naturally, what? "

" Exactly. She had taken some nourishment at 6 o'clock —a little broth and some milk pudding. At eight, the nurse gave her a morphine injection and then went straight out to put some bowls of flowers on the little table on the land-ing for the night. The maid came to speak to her about some arrangements for the next day, and while they were talking, Miss . . . that is, the niece—came up and went into her aunt's room. She had only been there a moment or two when she cried out, ' Nurse! Nurse! ' The nurse rushed in, and found the patient dead.

" Of course, my first idea was that by some accident a double dose of morphine had been administered——"

" Surely that wouldn't have acted so promptly."

" No—but I thought that a deep coma might have been mistaken for death. However, the nurse assured me that this was not the case, and, as a matter of fact, the possibility was completely disproved, as we were able to count the ampullæ of morphine and found them all satisfactorily accounted for. There were no signs of the patient having tried to move or strain herself, or of her having knocked against anything. The little night-table was pushed aside, but that had been done by the niece when she came in and was struck by her aunt's alarmingly lifeless appearance."

" How about the broth and the milk-pudding? "

" That occurred to me also—not in any sinister way, but to wonder whether she'd been having too much—distended stomach—pressure on the heart, and that sort of thing. However, when I came to look into it, it seemed very unlikely. The quantity was so small, and on the face of it, two hours were sufficient for digestion—if it had been that, death would have taken place earlier. I was completely puzzled, and so was the nurse. Indeed, she was very much upset."

" And the niece ? "

" The niece could say nothing but ' I told you so, I told you so—I knew she was worse than you thought.' Well, to cut a long story short, I was so bothered with my pet patient going off like that, that next morning, after I had thought the matter over, I asked for a post-mortem."

" Any difficulty ? "

" Not the slightest. A little natural distaste, of course, but no sort of opposition. I explained that I felt sure there must be some obscure morbid condition which I had failed to diagnose and that I should feel more satisfied if I might make an investigation. The only thing which seemed to trouble the niece was the thought of an inquest. I said—rather unwisely, I suppose, according to general rules—that I didn't think an inquest would be necessary."

" You mean you offered to perform the post-mortem yourself."

" Yes—I made no doubt that I should find a sufficient cause of death to enable me to give a certificate. I had one bit of luck, and that was that the old lady had at some time or the other expressed in a general way an opinion in favour of cremation, and the niece wished this to be carried out. This meant getting a man with special qualifications to sign the certificate with me, so I persuaded this other doctor to come and help me to do the autopsy."

" And did you find anything ? "

" Not a thing. The other man, of course, said I was a

fool to kick up a fuss. He thought that as the old lady was certainly dying in any case, it would be quite enough to put in, Cause of death, Cancer ; immediate cause, Heart Failure, and leave it at that. But I was a damned conscientious ass, and said I wasn't satisfied. There was absolutely nothing about the body to explain the death naturally, and I insisted on an analysis."

" Did you actually suspect—— ? "

" Well, no, not exactly. But—well, I wasn't satisfied. By the way, it was very clear at the autopsy that the morphine had nothing to do with it. Death had occurred so soon after the injection that the drug had only partially dispersed from the arm. Now I think it over, I suppose it must have been shock, somehow."

" Was the analysis privately made ? "

" Yes ; but of course the funeral was held up and things got round. The coroner heard about it and started to make inquiries, and the nurse, who got it into her head that I was accusing her of neglect or something, behaved in a very unprofessional way and created a lot of talk and trouble."

" And nothing came of it ? "

" Nothing. There was no trace of poison or anything of that sort, and the analysis left us exactly where we were. Naturally, I began to think I had made a ghastly exhibition of myself. Rather against my own professional judgment, I signed the certificate—heart failure following on shock, and my patient was finally got into her grave after a week of worry, without an inquest."

" Grave ? "

" Oh, yes. That was another scandal. The crematorium authorities, who are pretty particular, heard about the fuss and refused to act in the matter, so the body is filed in the churchyard for reference if necessary. There was a huge attendance at the funeral and a great deal of sympathy for the niece. The next day I got a note from one of my most influential patients, saying that my professional services would no longer be required. The day after that, I was avoided in the street by the Mayor's wife. Presently I found my practice dropping away from me, and discovered I was getting known as ' the man who practically accused that charming Miss So-and-so of murder.' Sometimes it was the niece I was supposed to be accusing. Sometimes it was ' that nice Nurse—not the flighty one who was dismissed, the other one, you know.' Another version was, that I had tried to get the nurse into trouble because I resented the dismissal of my fiancée. Finally, I heard a rumour that the patient had discovered me ' canoodling ' —that was the beastly word—with my fiancée, instead of doing my job, and had done away with the old lady myself out of revenge—though why, in that case, I should have refused a certificate, my scandal-mongers didn't trouble to explain.

" I stuck it out for a year, but my position became intolerable. The practice dwindled to practically nothing, so I sold it, took a holiday to get the taste out of my mouth —and here I am, looking for another opening. So that's that—and the moral is, Don't be officious about public duties."

The doctor gave an irritated laugh, and flung himself back in his chair.

" I don't care," he added, combatantly, " the cats ! Confusion to 'em ! " and he drained his glass.

" Hear, hear ! " agreed his host. He sat for a few moments looking thoughtfully into the fire.

" Do you know," he said, suddenly, " I'm feeling rather interested by this case. I have a sensation of internal gloating which assures me that there is something to be investigated. That feeling has never failed me yet—I trust it never will. It warned me the other day to look into my Income-tax assessment, and I discovered that I had been paying about £900 too much for the last three years. It urged me only last week to ask a bloke who was preparing to drive me over the Horseshoe Pass whether he had any petrol in the tank, and he discovered he had just about a pint—enough to get us nicely half-way round. It's a very lonely spot. Of course, I knew the man, so it wasn't *all* intuition. Still, I always make it a rule to investigate anything I feel like investigating. I believe," he added, in a reminiscent tone, " I was a terror in my nursery days. Anyhow, curious cases are rather a hobby of mine. In fact, I'm not just being the perfect listener. I have deceived you. I have an ulterior motive, said he, throwing off his side-whiskers and disclosing the well-known hollow jaws of Mr. Sherlock Holmes."

" I was beginning to have my suspicions," said the doctor, after a short pause. " I think you must be Lord Peter Wimsey. I wondered why your face was so familiar, but of course it was in all the papers a few years ago when you disentangled the Riddlesdale Mystery."

" Quite right. It's a silly kind of face, of course, but rather disarming, don't you think ? I don't know that I'd have chosen it, but I do my best with it. I do hope it isn't contracting a sleuth-like expression, or anything unpleasant. This is the real sleuth—my friend Detective-Inspector Parker of Scotland Yard. He's the one who really does the work. I make imbecile suggestions and he does the work of elaborately disproving them. Then, by a process of elimination, we find the right explanation, and the world says, ' My god, what intuition that young man has !' Well, look here—if you don't mind, I'd like to have a go at this. If you'll entrust me with your name and address and the names of the parties concerned, I'd like very much to have a shot at looking into it."

The doctor considered a moment, then shook his head.

" It's very good of you, but I think I'd rather not. I've got into enough bothers already. Anyway, it isn't professional to talk, and if I stirred up any more fuss, I should probably have to chuck this country altogether and end up as one of those drunken ship's doctors in the South Seas or somewhere, who are always telling their life-history to people and delivering awful warnings. Better to let sleeping dogs lie. Thanks very much, all the same."

" As you like," said Wimsey. " But I'll think it over, and if any useful suggestion occurs to me, I'll let you know."

" It's very good of you," replied the visitor, absently, taking his hat and stick from the man-servant, who had answered Wimsey's ring. " Well, good night, and many thanks for hearing me so patiently. By the way, though," he added, turning suddenly at the door, " how do you propose to let me know when you haven't got my name and address ? "

Lord Peter laughed.

" I'm Hawkshaw, the detective," he answered, " and you shall hear from me anyhow before the end of the week."

CHAPTER III

A USE FOR SPINSTERS

*" There are two million more females than males in England and Wales !
And this is an awe-inspiring circumstance."*

GILBERT FRANKAU

"WHAT DO YOU REALLY think of that story? " inquired Parker. He had dropped in to breakfast with Wimsey the next morning, before departing in the Notting Dale direction, in quest of an elusive anonymous letter-writer. " I thought it sounded rather as though our friend had been a bit too cocksure about his grand medical specialising. After all, the old girl might so easily have had some sort of heart attack. She was very old and ill."

" So she might, though I believe as a matter of fact cancer patients very seldom pop off in that unexpected way. As a rule, they surprise everybody by the way they cling to life. Still, I wouldn't think much of that if it wasn't for the niece. She prepared the way for the death, you see, by describing her aunt as so much worse than she was."

" I thought the same when the doctor was telling his tale. But what did the niece do? She can't have poisoned her aunt or even smothered her, I suppose, or they'd have found signs of it on the body. And the aunt *did* die—so perhaps the niece was right and the opinionated young medico wrong."

" Just so. And of course, we've only got his version of the niece and the nurse—and he obviously has what the Scotch call ta'en a scunner at the nurse. We mustn't lose sight of her, by the way. She was the last person to be with the old lady before her death, and it was she who administered that injection."

" Yes, yes—but the injection had nothing to do with it.

If anything's clear, that is. I say, do you think the nurse can have said anything that agitated the old lady and gave her a shock that way. The patient was a bit gaga, but she may have had sense enough to understand something really startling. Possibly the nurse just said something stupid about dying—the old lady appears to have been very sensitive on the point."

" Ah ! " said Lord Peter, " I was waiting for you to get on to that. Have you realised that there really is one rather sinister figure in the story, and that's the family lawyer."

" The one who came down to say something about the will, you mean, and was so abruptly sent packing."

" Yes. Suppose he'd wanted the patient to make a will in favour of somebody quite different—somebody outside the story as we know it. And when he found he couldn't get any attention paid to him, he sent the new nurse down as a sort of substitute."

" It would be rather an elaborate plot," said Parker, dubiously. " He couldn't know that the doctor's fiancée was going to be sent away. Unless he was in league with the niece, of course, and induced her to engineer the change of nurses."

" That cock won't fight, Charles. The niece wouldn't be in league with the lawyer to get herself disinherited."

" No, I suppose not. Still, I think there's something in the idea that the old girl was either accidentally or deliberately startled to death."

" Yes—and whichever way it was, it probably wasn't legal murder in that case. However, I think it's worth looking into. That reminds me." He rang the bell. " Bunter, just take a note to the post for me, would you ? "

" Certainly, my lord."

Lord Peter drew a writing pad towards him.

" What are you going to write ? " asked Parker, looking over his shoulder with some amusement.

Lord Peter wrote :

" Isn't civilisation wonderful ? "

He signed this simple message and slipped it into an envelope.

" If you want to be immune from silly letters, Charles," he said, " don't carry your monomark in your hat."

. . . .

" And what do you propose to do next ? " asked Parker. " Not, I hope, to send me round to Monomark House to get the name of a client. I couldn't do that without official authority, and they would probably kick up an awful shindy."

" No," replied his friend, " I don't propose violating the secrets of the confessional. Not in that quarter at any rate. I think, if you can spare a moment from your mysterious correspondent, who probably does not intend to be found, I will ask you to come and pay a visit to a friend of mine. It won't take long. I think you'll be interested. I—in fact, you'll be the first person I've ever taken to see her. She will be very much touched and pleased."

He laughed a little self-consciously.

" Oh," said Parker, embarrassed. Although the men were great friends, Wimsey had always preserved a reticence about his personal affairs—not so much by concealing as by ignoring them. This revelation seemed to mark a new stage of intimacy, and Parker was not sure that he liked it. He conducted his own life with an earnest middle-class morality which he owed to his birth and up-bringing, and, while theoretically recognising that Lord Peter's world acknowledged different standards, he had never contemplated being personally faced with any result of their application in practice.

" —rather an experiment," Wimsey was saying a trifle shyly ; " anyway, she's quite comfortably fixed in a little flat in Pimlico. You can come, can't you, Charles ? I really should like you two to meet."

" Oh, yes, rather," said Parker, hastily, " I should like to very much. Er—how long—I mean——"

" Oh, the arrangement's only been going a few months," said Wimsey, leading the way to the lift, " but it really seems to be working out quite satisfactorily. Of course, it makes things much easier for me."

" Just so," said Parker.

" Of course, as you'll understand—I won't go into it all till we get there, and then you'll see for yourself," Wimsey chattered on, slamming the gates of the lift with unnecessary violence—" but, as I was saying, you'll observe it's quite a new departure. I don't suppose there's ever been anything exactly like it before. Of course, there's nothing new under the sun, as Solomon said, but after all, I daresay all those wives and porcupines, as the child said, must have soured his disposition a little, don't you know."

" Quite," said Parker. " Poor fish," he added to himself, " they *always* seem to think it's different."

" Outlet," said Wimsey, energetically, " hi ! taxi ! . . . outlet—everybody needs an outlet—97A, St. George's Square—and after all, one can't really blame people if it's just that they need an outlet. I mean, why be bitter ? They can't help it. I think it's much kinder to give them an outlet than to make fun of them in books—and, after all, it isn't really difficult to write books. Especially if you either write a rotten story in good English or a good story in rotten English, which is as far as most people seem to get nowadays. Don't you agree ? "

Mr. Parker agreed, and Lord Peter wandered away along the paths of literature, till the cab stopped before one of those tall, awkward mansions which, originally designed for a Victorian family with fatigue-proof servants, have lately been dissected each into half a dozen inconvenient bandboxes and let off in flats.

Lord Peter rang the top bell, which was marked " CLIMPSON," and relaxed negligently against the porch.

"Six flights of stairs," he explained ; "it takes her some time to answer the bell, because there's no lift, you see. She wouldn't have a more expensive flat, though. She thought it wouldn't be suitable."

Mr. Parker was greatly relieved, if somewhat surprised, by the modesty of the lady's demands, and, placing his foot on the door-scraper in an easy attitude, prepared to wait with patience. Before many minutes, however, the door was opened by a thin, middle-aged woman, with a sharp, sallow face and very vivacious manner. She wore a neat, dark coat and skirt, a high-necked blouse and a long gold neck-chain with a variety of small ornaments dangling from it at intervals, and her iron-grey hair was dressed under a net, in the style fashionable in the reign of the late King Edward.

"Oh, Lord Peter ! How *very* nice to see you. Rather an *early* visit, but I'm sure you will excuse the sitting-room being a trifle in disorder. *Do* come in. The lists are *quite* ready for you. I finished them last night. In fact, I was just about to put on my hat and bring them round to you. I do *hope* you don't think I have taken an *unconscionable* time, but there was a quite *surprising* number of entries. It is *too* good of you to trouble to call."

"Not at all, Miss Climpson. This is my friend, Detective-Inspector Parker, whom I have mentioned to you."

"How do you do, Mr. Parker—or ought I to say Inspector ? Excuse me if I make mistakes—this is really the first time I have been in the hands of the police. I hope it's not rude of me to say that. Please come up. A great many stairs, I am afraid, but I hope you do not mind. I do so like to be *high up*. The air is so much better, and you know, Mr. Parker, thanks to Lord Peter's great kindness, I have such a *beautiful, airy* view, right over the houses. I think one can work so much *better* when one doesn't feel cribbed, cabined and confined, as Hamlet says. Dear me ! Mrs. Winbottle *will* leave the pail on the stairs, and always in that very dark corner. I am *continually* telling her about it. If you keep close to the banisters you will avoid it nicely. Only one more flight. Here we are. Please overlook the untidiness. I always think breakfast things look so *ugly* when one has finished with them—almost sordid, to use a nasty word for a nasty subject. What a pity that some of these clever people can't invent *self-cleaning* and *self-clearing* plates, is it not? But please *do* sit down ; I won't keep you a moment. And I know, Lord Peter, that you will not hesitate to smoke. I do so enjoy the smell of your cigarettes—quite delicious— and you are so *very* good about extinguishing the ends."

The little room was, as a matter of fact, most exquisitely neat, in spite of the crowded array of knick-knacks and photographs that adorned every available inch of space. The sole evidences of dissipation were an empty eggshell, a used cup and a crumby plate on a breakfast tray. Miss Climpson promptly subdued this riot by carrying the tray bodily on to the landing.

Mr. Parker, a little bewildered, lowered himself cautiously into a small arm-chair, embellished with a hard, fat little cushion which made it impossible to lean back. Lord Peter wriggled into the window-seat, lit a Sobranie and clasped his hands about his knees. Miss Climpson, seated upright at the table, gazed at him with a gratified air which was posi- tively touching.

" I have gone *very* carefully into all these cases," she began, taking up a thick wad of type-script. " I'm afraid, indeed, my notes are rather *copious*, but I trust the typist's bill will not be considered too heavy. My handwriting is very clear, so I don't think there can be any errors. Dear me ! such *sad* stories some of these poor women had to tell me ! But I have investigated most fully, with the kind assistance of the clergyman—a very nice man and so helpful—and I feel sure that in the majority of the cases your assistance will be *well bestowed*. If you would like to go through——"

" Not at the moment, Miss Climpson," interrupted Lord Peter, hurriedly. " It's all right, Charles—nothing whatever

to do with Our Dumb Friends or supplying Flannel to Unmarried Mothers. I'll tell you about it later. Just now, Miss
Climpson, we want your help on something quite different."

Miss Climpson produced a business-like notebook and sat
at attention.

"The inquiry divides itself into two parts," said Lord
Peter. "The first part, I'm afraid, is rather dull. I want
you (if you will be so good) to go down to Somerset House
and search, or get them to search, through all the death-
certificates for Hampshire in the month of November,
1925. I don't know the town and I don't know the name
of the deceased. What you are looking for is the death-
certificate of an old lady of 73 ; cause of death, cancer ;
immediate cause, heart-failure ; and the certificate will have
been signed by two doctors, one of whom will be either a
Medical Officer of Health, Police Surgeon, Certifying Surgeon under the Factory and Workshops Act, Medical Referee
under the Workmen's Compensation Act, Physician or Surgeon in a big General Hospital, or a man specially appointed
by the Cremation authorities. If you want to give any excuse
for the search, you can say that you are compiling statistics
about cancer ; but what you really want is the names of
the people concerned and the name of the town."

"Suppose there are more than one answering to the
requirements ?"

"Ah ! that's where the second part comes in, and where
your remarkable tact and shrewdness are going to be so
helpful to us. When you have collected all the " possibles,"
I shall ask you to go down to each of the towns concerned
and make very, very skilful inquiries, to find out which is
the case we want to get on to. Of course, you mustn't appear
to be inquiring. You must find some good gossipy lady
living in the neighbourhood and just get her to talk in a
natural way. You must pretend to be gossipy yourself—
it's not in your nature, I know, but I'm sure you can make
a little pretence about it—and find out all you can. I

fancy you'll find it pretty easy if you once strike the right
town, because I know for a certainty that there was a
terrible lot of ill-natured talk about this particular death,
and it won't have been forgotten yet by a long chalk."

" How shall I know when it's the right one ? "

" Well, if you can spare the time, I want you to listen
to a little story. Mind you. Miss Climpson, when you get
to wherever it is, you are not supposed ever to have heard
a word of this tale before. But I needn't tell you that. Now,
Charles, you've got an official kind of way of puttin' these
things clearly. Will you just weigh in and give Miss Climpson the gist of that rigmarole our friend served out to us
last night ? "

Pulling his wits into order, Mr. Parker accordingly
obliged with a digest of the doctor's story. Miss Climpson
listened with great attention, making notes of the dates and
details. Parker observed that she showed great acumen
in seizing on the salient points ; she asked a number of very
shrewd questions, and her grey eyes were intelligent. When
he had finished, she repeated the story, and he was able
to congratulate her on a clear head and retentive memory.

" A dear old friend of mine used to say that I should
have made a very good lawyer," said Miss Climpson,
complacently, " but of course, when I was young, girls
didn't have the education or the *opportunities* they get
nowadays, Mr. Parker. I should have liked a good education, but my dear father didn't believe in it for women.
Very old-fashioned, you young people would think him."

" Never mind, Miss Climpson," said Wimsey, " you've
got just exactly the qualifications we want, and they're
rather rare, so we're in luck. Now we want this matter
pushed forward as fast as possible."

" I'll go down to Somerset House at once," replied the
lady, with great energy, " and let you know the minute
I'm ready to start for Hampshire."

" That's right," said his lordship, rising. " And now we'll

just make a noise like a hoop and roll away. Oh ! and
while I think of it, I'd better give you something in hand
for travelling expenses and so on. I think you had better
be just a retired lady in easy circumstances looking for a
nice little place to settle down in. I don't think you'd
better be wealthy—wealthy people don't inspire confidence.
Perhaps you would oblige me by living at the rate of about
£800 a year—your own excellent taste and experience
will suggest the correct accessories and so on for creating
that impression. If you will allow me, I will give you a
cheque for £50 now, and when you start on your wander-
ings you will let me know what you require."

"Dear me," said Miss Climpson, "I don't——"

"This is a pure matter of business, of course," said
Wimsey, rather rapidly, "and you will let me have a note
of the expenses in your usual business-like way."

"Of course." Miss Climpson was dignified. "And I
will give you a proper receipt immediately.

"Dear, dear," she added, hunting through her purse,
"I do not appear to have any penny stamps. How extremely remiss of me. It is most *unusual* for me not to have
my little book of stamps—so handy I always think they are
—but only last night Mrs. Williams borrowed my last
stamps to send a very urgent letter to her son in Japan.
If you will excuse me a moment——"

"I think I have some," interposed Parker.

"Oh, thank you very much, Mr. Parker. Here is the
twopence. I *never* allow myself to be without pennies—
on account of the bathroom geyser, you know. Such a very
sensible invention, most *convenient*, and prevents *all* dispute
about hot water among the tenants. Thank you so much.
And now I sign my name *across* the stamps. That's right,
isn't it ? My dear father would be surprised to find his
daughter so business-like. He always said a woman should
never *need* to know anything about money matters, but
times have changed so greatly, have they not ? "

Miss Climpson ushered them down all six flights of stairs, volubly protesting at their protests, and the door closed behind them.

"May I ask——?" began Parker.

"It is not what you think," said his lordship, earnestly.

"Of course not," agreed Parker.

"There, I knew you had a nasty mind. Even the closest of one's friends turn out to be secret thinkers. They think in private thoughts which they publicly repudiate."

"Don't be a fool. Who *is* Miss Climpson?"

"Miss Climpson," said Lord Peter, "is a manifestation of the wasteful way in which this country is run. Look at electricity. Look at water-power. Look at the tides. Look at the sun. Millions of power units being given off into space every minute. Thousands of old maids, simply bursting with useful energy, forced by our stupid social system into hydros and hotels and communities and hostels and posts as companions, where their magnificent gossip-powers and units of inquisitiveness are allowed to dissipate themselves or even become harmful to the community, while the ratepayers' money is spent on getting work for which these women are providentially fitted, inefficiently carried out by ill-equipped policemen like you. My god! it's enough to make a man write to *John Bull*. And then bright young men write nasty little patronising books called 'Elderly Women,' and 'On the Edge of the Explosion'—and the drunkards make songs upon 'em, poor things."

"Quite, quite," said Parker. "You mean that Miss Climpson is a kind of inquiry agent for you."

"She is my ears and tongue," said Lord Peter, dramatically, "and especially my nose. She asks questions which a young man could not put without a blush. She is the angel that rushes in where fools get a clump on the head. She can smell a rat in the dark. In fact, she is the cat's whiskers."

"That's not a bad idea," said Parker.

" Naturally—it is mine, therefore brilliant. Just think.
People want questions asked. Whom do they send ? A man
with large flat feet and a note-book—the sort of man whose
private life is conducted in a series of inarticulate grunts. I
send a lady with a long, woolly jumper on knitting-needles
and jingly things round her neck. Of course she asks questions—everyone expects it. Nobody is surprised. Nobody is
alarmed. And so-called superfluity is agreeable and usefully
disposed of. One of these days they will put up a statue to
me, with an inscription :

> " ' To the Man who Made
> Thousands of Superfluous Women
> Happy
> without Injury to their Modesty
> or Exertion to Himself.' "

" I wish you wouldn't talk so much," complained his
friend. " And how about all those type-written reports ?
Are you turning philanthropist in your old age ? "

" No—no," said Wimsey, rather hurriedly hailing a taxi.
" Tell you about that later. Little private pogrom of my
own—Insurance against the Socialist Revolution—when it
comes. ' What did you do with your great wealth, com-
rade ? ' ' I bought First Editions.' ' Aristocrat ! à la lan-
terne ! ' ' Stay, spare me ! I took proceedings against 500
money-lenders who oppressed the workers.' ' Citizen, you
have done well. We will spare your life. You shall be pro-
moted to cleaning out the sewers.' Voilà ! We must move
with the times. Citizen taxi-driver, take me to the British
Museum. Can I drop you anywhere ? No ? So long. I am
going to collate a 12th century manuscript of Tristan, while
the old order lasts."

Mr. Parker thoughtfully boarded a westward-bound 'bus
and was rolled away to do some routine questioning, on
his own account, among the female population of Notting
Dale. It did not appear to him to be a milieu in which the
talents of Miss Climpson could be usefully employed.

CHAPTER IV

A BIT MENTAL

" A babbled of green fields."

King Henry V

Letter from Miss Alexandra Katherine Climpson to Lord Peter Wimsey.

> " C/o Mrs. Hamilton Budge,
> " Fairview, Nelson Avenue,
> " Leahampton, Hants.
> " April 29th, 1927.

" MY DEAR LORD PETER,

" You will be happy to hear, after my *two previous* bad shots (!), that I have found the *right* place at last. The Agatha Dawson certificate is the *correct* one, and the dreadful *scandal* about Dr. Carr is still very much alive, I am sorry to say for the sake of *human nature*. I have been fortunate enough to secure rooms in the *very next street* to Wellington Avenue, where Miss Dawson used to live. My landlady seems a very nice woman, though a *terrible gossip* !—which is *all to the good* ! ! Her charge for a very pleasant bedroom and sitting-room with *full board* is 3½ guineas weekly. I trust you will not think this *too extravagant*, as the situation is *just* what you wished me to look for. I enclose a careful statement of my expenses up-to-date. You will *excuse* the mention of *underwear*, which is, I fear, a *somewhat large* item ! but wool is so expensive nowadays, and it is necessary that every detail of my equipment should be suitable to my (supposed !) position in life. I have been careful to *wash* the garments through, so that they do not look *too new*, as this might have a *suspicious* appearance ! !

" But you will be anxious for me to (if I may use a vulgar expression) ' cut the cackle, and come to the horses ' (! !). On the day after my arrival, I informed Mrs. Budge that I was a great sufferer from *rheumatism* (which is quite true, as I have a sad legacy of that kind left me by, alas ! my *port-drinking* ancestors !)—and inquired what *doctors* there were in the neighbourhood. This at once brought forth a *long catalogue*, together with a *grand panegyric* of the sandy soil and healthy situation of the town. I said I should prefer an *elderly* doctor, as the *young men*, in my opinion, were *not to be depended on*. Mrs. Budge heartily agreed with me, and a little discreet questioning brought out the *whole story* of Miss Dawson's illness and the ' carryings-on ' (as she termed them) of Dr. Carr and *the nurse* ! ' I never did trust that first nurse,' said Mrs. Budge, ' for all she had her training at Guy's and ought to have been trustworthy. A sly, red-headed *baggage*, and it's my belief that all Dr. Carr's fussing over Miss Dawson and his visits all day and every day were just to get love-making with Nurse Philliter. No wonder poor Miss Whittaker couldn't stand it any longer and gave the girl the sack—none too soon, in my opinion. Not quite so attentive after that, Dr. Carr wasn't—why, up to the last minute, he was pretending the old lady was quite all right, when Miss Whittaker had only said the day before that she felt sure she was going to be taken from us.'

" I asked if Mrs. Budge knew Miss Whittaker personally. Miss Whittaker is *the niece*, you know.

" Not personally, she said, though she had met her in a social way at the Vicarage working-parties. But she knew all about it, because her maid was own sister to the maid at Miss Dawson's. Now is not that a *fortunate* coincidence, for you know how these girls *talk* !

" I also made careful inquiries about the *Vicar*, Mr. Tredgold, and was much gratified to find that he teaches *sound Catholic* doctrine, so that I shall be able to attend the

Church (S. Onesimus) without doing *violence* to my religious beliefs—a thing I could *not* undertake to do, *even in your interests*. I am sure you will *understand* this. As it happens, *all is well*, and I have written to my *very good friend*, the Vicar of S. Edfrith's, Holborn, to ask for an *introduction* to Mr. Tredgold. By this means, I feel sure of meeting *Miss Whittaker* before long, as I hear she is quite a ' pillar of the Church ' ! I do hope it is not *wrong* to make use of the Church of God to a *worldly* end ; but after all, you are only seeking to establish *Truth* and *Justice* !—and in so good a cause, we may perhaps permit ourselves to be a little bit *JESUITICAL* ! ! !

"This is all I have been able to do *as yet*, but I shall not be *idle*, and will write to you again as soon as I have *anything to report*. By the way, the *pillar-box* is *most conveniently placed* just at the corner of Wellington Avenue, so that I can easily *run out* and post my letters to you *myself* (away from *prying* eyes ! !)—and just take a little peep at Miss *Dawson's*—now Miss *Whittaker's*—house, ' The Grove,' at the same time.

"Believe me,
"Sincerely yours,
"ALEXANDRA KATHERINE CLIMPSON."

. . . .

The little red-headed nurse gave her visitor a quick, slightly hostile look-over.

" It's quite all right," he said apologetically, " I haven't come to sell you soap or gramophones, or to borrow money or enrol you in the Ancient Froth-blowers or anything charitable. I really am Lord Peter Wimsey—I mean, that really is my title, don't you know, not a Christian name like Sanger's Circus or Earl Derr Biggers. I've come to ask you some questions, and I've no real excuse, I'm afraid, for butting in on you—do you ever read the *News of the World*? "

Nurse Philliter decided that she was to be asked to go to

a mental case, and that the patient had come to fetch her in person.

" Sometimes," she said, guardedly.

" Oh—well, you may have noticed my name croppin' up in a few murders and things lately. I sleuth, you know. For a hobby. Harmless outlet for natural inquisitiveness, don't you see, which might otherwise strike inward and produce introspection an' suicide. Very natural, healthy pursuit—not too strenuous, not too sedentary ; trains and invigorates the mind."

" I know who you are now," said Nurse Philliter, slowly. " You—you gave evidence against Sir Julian Freke. In fact, you traced the murder to him, didn't you ? "

" I did—it was rather unpleasant," said Lord Peter, simply, " and I've got another little job of the same kind in hand now, and I want your help."

" Won't you sit down ? " said Nurse Philliter, setting the example. " How am I concerned in the matter ? "

" You know Dr. Edward Carr, I think—late of Lea-hampton—conscientious but a little lackin' in worldly wisdom—not serpentine at all, as the Bible advises, but far otherwise."

" What ! " she cried, " do *you* believe it was murder, then ? "

Lord Peter looked at her for a few seconds. Her face was eager, her eyes gleaming curiously under her thick, level brows. She had expressive hands, rather large and with strong, flat joints. He noticed how they gripped the arms of her chair.

" Haven't the faintest," he replied, nonchalantly, " but I wanted your opinion."

" Mine ? "—she checked herself. " You know, I am not supposed to give opinions about my cases."

" You have given it me already," said his lordship, grinning. " Though possibly I ought to allow for a little prejudice in favour of Dr. Carr's diagnosis."

" Well, yes—but it's not merely personal. I mean, my being engaged to Dr. Carr wouldn't affect my judgment of a cancer case. I have worked with him on a great many of them, and I know that his opinion is really trustworthy— just as I know that, as a motorist, he's exactly the opposite."

"Right. I take it that if he says the death was inexplicable, it really was so. That's one point gained. Now about the old lady herself. I gather she was a little queer towards the end—a bit mental, I think you people call it ? "

" I don't know that I'd say that either. Of course, when she was under morphia, she would be unconscious, or only semi-conscious, for hours together. But up to the time when I left, I should say she was quite—well, quite all there. She was obstinate, you know, and what they call a character, at the best of times."

" But Dr. Carr told me she got odd fancies—about people poisoning her ? "

The red-haired nurse rubbed her fingers slowly along the arm of the chair, and hesitated.

" If it will make you feel any less unprofessional," said Lord Peter, guessing what was in her mind, " I may say that my friend Detective-Inspector Parker is looking into this matter with me, which gives me a sort of right to ask questions."

" In that case—yes—in that case I think I can speak freely. I never understood about that poisoning idea. I never saw anything of it—no aversion, I mean, or fear of me. As a rule, a patient will show it, if she's got any queer ideas about the nurse. Poor Miss Dawson was always most kind and affectionate. She kissed me when I went away and gave me a little present, and said she was sorry to lose me."

" She didn't show any sort of nervousness about taking food from you ? "

" Well, I wasn't allowed to give her any food that last week. Miss Whittaker said her aunt had taken this funny notion, and gave her all her meals herself."

" Oh ! that's very interestin'. Was it Miss Whittaker, then, who first mentioned this little eccentricity to you ? "

" Yes. And she begged me not to say anything about it to Miss Dawson, for fear of agitating her."

" And did you ? "

" I did not. I wouldn't mention it in any case to a patient. It does no good."

" Did Miss Dawson ever speak about it to anyone else ? Dr. Carr, for instance ? "

" No. According to Miss Whittaker, her aunt was frightened of the doctor too, because she imagined he was in league with me. Of course, that story rather lent colour to the unkind things that were said afterwards. I suppose it's just possible that she saw us glancing at one another or speaking aside, and got the idea that we were plotting something."

" How about the maids ? "

" There were new maids about that time. She probably wouldn't talk about it to them, and anyhow, I wouldn't be discussing my patient with her servants."

" Of course not. Why did the other maids leave ? How many were there ? Did they all go at once ? "

" Two of them went. They were sisters. One was a terrible crockery-smasher, and Miss Whittaker gave her notice, so the other left with her."

" Ah, well ! one can have too much of seeing the Crown Derby rollin' round the floor. Quite. Then it had nothing to do with—it wasn't on account of any little—— "

" It wasn't because they couldn't get along with the nurse, if you mean that," said Nurse Philliter, with a smile. " They were very obliging girls, but not very bright."

" Quite. Well, now, is there any little odd, out-of-the-way incident you can think of that might throw light on the thing. There was a visit from a lawyer, I believe, that agitated your patient quite a lot. Was that in your time ? "

" No. I only heard about it from Dr. Carr. And he never heard the name of the lawyer, what he came about, or anything."

" A pity," said his lordship. " I have been hoping great things of the lawyer. There's such a sinister charm, don't you think, about lawyers who appear unexpectedly with little bags, and alarm people with mysterious conferences, and then go away leaving urgent messages that if anything happens they are to be sent for. If it hadn't been for the lawyer, I probably shouldn't have treated Dr. Carr's medical problem with the respect it ˙deserves. He never came again, or wrote, I suppose ? "

" I don't know. Wait a minute. I do remember one thing. I remember Miss Dawson having another hysterical attack of the same sort, and saying just what she said then —' that they were trying to kill her before her time.' "

" When was that ? "

" Oh, a couple of weeks before I left. Miss Whittaker had been up to her with the post, I think, and there were some papers of some kind to sign, and it seems to have upset her. I came in from my walk and found her in a dreadful state. The maids could have told you more about it than I could, really, for they were doing some dusting on the landing at the time and heard her going on, and they ran down and fetched me up to her. I didn't ask them about what happened myself, naturally—it doesn't do for nurses to gossip with the maids behind their employers' backs. Miss Whittaker said that her aunt had had an annoying communication from a solicitor."

" Yes, it sounds as though there might be something there. Do you remember what the maids were called ? "

" What was the name now ? A funny one, or I shouldn't remember it—Gotobed, that was it—Bertha and Evelyn Gotobed. I don't know where they went, but I daresay you could find out."

" Now one last question, and I want you to forget all

about Christian kindliness and the law of slander when you answer it. What is Miss Whittaker like ? "

An indefinable expression crossed the nurse's face.

" Tall, handsome, very decided in manner," she said, with an air of doing strict justice against her will, " an extremely competent nurse—she was at the Royal Free, you know, till she went to live with her aunt. I think she would have made a perfectly wonderful theatre nurse. She did not like me, nor I her, you know, Lord Peter—and it's better I should be telling you so at once, the way you can take everything I say about her with a grain of charity added—but we both knew good hospital work when we saw it, and respected one another."

" Why in the world didn't she like you, Miss Philliter ? I really don't know when I've seen a more likeable kind of person, if you'll 'scuse my mentionin' it."

" I don't know." The nurse seemed a little embarrassed. " The dislike seemed to grow on her. You—perhaps you heard the kind of things people said in the town ? when I left ?—that Dr. Carr and I—— Oh ! it really was damnable, and I had the most dreadful interview with Matron when I got back here. She *must* have spread those stories. Who else could have done it ? "

" Well—you *did* become engaged to Dr. Carr, didn't you ? " said his lordship, gently. " Mind you, I'm not sayin' it wasn't a very agreeable occurrence and all that, but——"

" But she said I neglected the patient. I *never* did. I wouldn't think of such a thing."

" Of course not. No. But, do you suppose that possibly getting engaged was an offence in itself ? Is Miss Whittaker engaged to anyone, by the way ? "

" No. You mean, was she jealous ? I'm sure Dr. Carr never gave the slightest, not the *slightest*——"

" Oh, *please*," cried Lord Peter, " please don't be ruffled. Such a nice word, ruffled—like a kitten, I always think—so furry and nice. But even without the least what-d'ye-call-it on Dr. Carr's side, he's a very prepossessin' person and all that. Don't you think there *might* be something in it?"

"I did think so once," admitted Miss Philliter, "but afterwards, when she got him into such awful trouble over the post-mortem, I gave up the idea."

"But she didn't object to the post-mortem?"

"She did not. But there's such a thing as putting yourself in the right in the eyes of your neighbours, Lord Peter, and then going off to tell people all about it at Vicarage tea-parties. I wasn't there, but you ask someone who was. I know those tea-parties."

"Well, it's not impossible. People can be very spiteful if they think they've been slighted."

"Perhaps you're right," said Nurse Philliter, thoughtfully. "But," she added suddenly, "that's no motive for murdering a perfectly innocent old lady."

"That's the second time you've used that word," said Wimsey, gravely. "There's no proof yet that it was murder."

"I know that."

"But you think it was?"

"I do."

"And you think she did it?"

"Yes."

Lord Peter walked across to the aspidistra in the bow-window and stroked its leaves thoughtfully. The silence was broken by a buxom nurse who, entering precipitately first and knocking afterwards, announced with a giggle :

"Excuse me, I'm sure, but you're in request this afternoon, Philliter. Here's Dr. Carr come for you."

Dr. Carr followed hard upon his name. The sight of Wimsey struck him speechless.

"I told you I'd be turnin' up again before long," said Lord Peter, cheerfully. "Sherlock is my name and Holmes is my nature. I'm delighted to see you, Dr. Carr. Your little matter is well in hand, and seein' I'm not required any longer I'll make a noise like a bee and buzz off."

" How did *he* get here? " demanded Dr. Carr, not altogether pleased.

" Didn't you send him? I think he's very nice," said Nurse Philliter.

" He's mad," said Dr. Carr.

" He's clever," said the red-haired nurse.

CHAPTER V

GOSSIP

" With vollies of eternal babble."

BUTLER : *Hudibras*

" So you are thinking of coming to live in Leahampton,"
said Miss Murgatroyd. " How *very* nice. I do hope you
will be settling down in the parish. We are *not* too well off
for week-day congregations—there is so much indifference
and so much *Protestantism* about. There ! I have dropped
a stitch. Provoking ! Perhaps it was meant as a little
reminder to me not to think uncharitably about Protestants.
All is well—I have retrieved it. Were you thinking of taking
a house, Miss Climpson ? "

" I am not quite sure," replied Miss Climpson. " Rents
are so very high nowadays, and I fear that to buy a house
would be almost beyond my means. I must look round very
carefully, and view the question from *all sides*. I should
certainly *prefer* to be in this parish—and close to the Church,
if possible. Perhaps the Vicar would know whether there
is likely to be anything suitable."

" Oh, yes, he would doubtless be able to suggest something. It is such a very nice, residential neighbourhood. I
am sure you would like it. Let me see—you are staying in
Nelson Avenue, I think Mrs. Tredgold said ? "

" Yes—with Mrs. Budge at Fairview."

" I am sure she makes you comfortable. Such a nice
woman, though I'm afraid she never stops talking. Hasn't
she got any ideas on the subject ? I'm sure if there's any
news going about, Mrs. Budge never fails to get hold of it."

" Well," said Miss Climpson, seizing the opening with a
swiftness which would have done credit to Napoleon, " she

did say something about a house in Wellington Avenue which she thought might be to let before long."

" Wellington Avenue? You surprise me! I thought I knew almost everybody there. Could it be the Parfitts— really moving at last! They have been talking about it for at least seven years, and I really had begun to think it was *all talk*. Mrs. Peasgood, do you hear that? Miss Climpson says the Parfitts are really leaving that house at last!"

" Bless me," cried Mrs. Peasgood, raising her rather prominent eyes from a piece of plain needlework and focusing them on Miss Climpson like a pair of opera-glasses. " Well, that *is* news. It must be that brother of hers who was staying with them last week. Possibly he is going to live with them permanently, and that would clinch the matter, of course, for they couldn't get on without another bedroom when the girls come home from school. A very sensible arrangement, I should think. I believe he is quite well off, you know, and it will be a very good thing for those children. I wonder where they will go. I expect it will be one of the new houses out on the Winchester Road, though of course that would mean keeping a car. Still, I expect he would want them to do that in any case. Most likely he will have it himself, and let them have the use of it."

" I don't think Parfitt was the name," broke in Miss Climpson hurriedly, " I'm sure it wasn't. It was a Miss somebody—a Miss Whittaker, I think, Mrs. Budge mentioned."

" Miss Whittaker? " cried both the ladies in chorus. " Oh, no! *surely* not? "

" I'm sure Miss Whittaker would have told me if she thought of giving up her house," pursued Miss Murgatroyd. " We are such great friends. I think Mrs. Budge must have run away with a wrong idea. People do build up such amazing stories out of nothing at all."

" I wouldn't go so far as that," put in Mrs. Peasgood, rebukingly. " There *may* be something in it. I know dear Miss Whittaker has sometimes spoken to me about wishing to take up chicken-farming. I daresay she has not mentioned the matter *generally*, but then she always confides in *me*. Depend upon it, that is what she intends to do."

" Mrs. Budge didn't actually say Miss Whittaker was moving," interposed Miss Climpson. " She said, I think, that Miss Whittaker had been left alone by some relation's death, and she wouldn't be surprised if she found the house lonely."

" Ah ! that's Mrs. Budge all over ! " said Mrs. Peasgood, nodding ominously. " A most excellent woman, but she sometimes gets hold of the wrong end of the stick. Not but what I've often thought the same thing myself. I said to poor Mary Whittaker only the other day, ' Don't you find it very lonely in that house, my dear, now that your poor dear Aunt is no more ? ' I'm sure it would be a very good thing if she did move, or got someone to live with her. It's not a natural life for a young woman, all alone like that, and so I told her. I'm one of those that believe in speaking their mind, you know, Miss Climpson."

" Well, now, so am I, Mrs. Peasgood," rejoined Miss Climpson promptly, " and that is what I said to Mrs. Budge at the time. I said, ' Do I understand that there was anything *odd* about the old lady's death ? '—because she had spoken of the *peculiar circumstances* of the case, and you know, I should not *at all like* to live in a house which could be called in any way *notorious*. I should really feel quite *uncomfortable* about it." In saying which, Miss Climpson no doubt spoke with perfect sincerity.

" But not at all—not at all," cried Miss Murgatroyd, so eagerly that Mrs. Peasgood, who had paused to purse up her face and assume an expression of portentous secrecy before replying, was completely crowded out and left at the post. " There never was a more wicked story. The death was natural—perfectly natural, and a most happy release, poor soul, I'm sure, for her sufferings at the last were truly terrible. It was all a scandalous story put about by that young Dr. Carr (whom I'm sure I never liked) simply to aggrandise himself. As though any doctor would pronounce so definitely upon what exact date it would please God to call a poor sufferer to Himself! Human pride and vanity make a most shocking exhibition, Miss Climpson, when they lead us to cast suspicion on innocent people, simply because we are wedded to our own presumptuous opinions. Poor Miss Whittaker! She went through a most terrible time. But it was proved—absolutely *proved*, that there was nothing in the story at all, and I hope that young man was properly ashamed of himself."

"There may be two opinions about that, Miss Murgatroyd," said Mrs. Peasgood. "I say what I think, Miss Climpson, and in my opinion there should have been an inquest. I try to be up-to-date, and I believe Dr. Carr to have been a very able young man, though of course, he was not the kind of old-fashioned family doctor that appeals to elderly people. It was a great pity that nice Nurse Philliter was sent away—that woman Forbes was no more use than a headache—to use my brother's rather vigorous expression. I don't think she knew her job, and that's a fact."

"Nurse Forbes was a charming person," snapped Miss Murgatroyd, pink with indignation at being called elderly.

"That may be," retorted Mrs. Peasgood, "but you can't get over the fact that she nearly killed herself one day by taking nine grains of calomel by mistake for three. She told me that herself, and what she did in one case she might do in another."

"But Miss Dawson wasn't given anything," said Miss Murgatroyd, "and at any rate, Nurse Forbes' mind was on her patient, and not on flirting with the doctor. I've always thought that Dr. Carr felt a spite against her for taking his young woman's place, and nothing would have pleased him better than to get her into trouble."

" You don't mean," said Miss Climpson, " that he would refuse a certificate and cause all that trouble, just to annoy the nurse. *Surely* no doctor would dare to do that."

" Of course not," said Mrs. Peasgood, " and nobody with a grain of sense would suppose it for a moment."

" Thank you very much, Mrs. Peasgood," cried Miss Murgatroyd, " thank you very much, I'm sure——"

" I say what I think," said Mrs. Peasgood.

" Then I'm glad I haven't such unchaïitable thoughts," said Miss Murgatroyd.

" I don't think your own observations are so remarkable for their charity," retorted Mrs. Peasgood.

Fortunately, at this moment Miss Murgatroyd, in her agitation, gave a vicious tweak to the wrong needle and dropped twenty-nine stitches at once. The Vicar's wife, scenting battle from afar, hurried over with a plate of scones, and helped to bring about a diversion. To her, Miss Climpson, doggedly sticking to her mission in life, broached the subject of the house in Wellington Avenue.

" Well, I don't know, I'm sure," replied Mrs. Tredgold, " but there's Miss Whittaker just arrived. Come over to my corner and I'll introduce her to you, and you can have a nice chat about it. You will like each other so much, she is such a keen worker. Oh ! and Mrs. Peasgood, my husband is so anxious to have a word with you about the choirboys' social. He is discussing it now with Mrs. Findlater. I wonder if you'd be so very good as to come and give him your opinion ? He values it so much."

Thus tactfully the good lady parted the disputants and, having deposited Mrs. Peasgood safely under the clerical wing, towed Miss Climpson away to an arm-chair near the tea-table.

" Dear Miss Whittaker, I so want you to know Miss Climpson. She is a near neighbour of yours—in Nelson

Avenue, and I hope we shall persuade her to make her home among us."

" That will be delightful," said Miss Whittaker.

The first impression which Miss Climpson got of Mary Whittaker was that she was totally out of place among the tea-tables of S. Onesimus. With her handsome, strongly-marked features and quiet air of authority, she was of the type that " does well " in City offices. She had a pleasant and self-possessed manner, and was beautifully tailored—not mannishly, and yet with a severe fineness of outline that negatived the appeal of a beautiful figure. With her long and melancholy experience of frustrated womanhood, observed in a dreary succession of cheap boarding-houses, Miss Climpson was able to dismiss one theory which had vaguely formed itself in her mind. This was no passionate nature, cramped by association with an old woman and eager to be free to mate before youth should depart. *That* look she knew well—she could diagnose it with dreadful accuracy at the first glance, in the tone of a voice saying, " How do you do ? " But meeting Mary Whittaker's clear, light eyes under their well-shaped brows, she was struck by a sudden sense of familiarity. She had seen that look before, though the where and the when escaped her. Chatting volubly about her arrival in Leahampton, her introduction to the Vicar and her approval of the Hampshire air and sandy soil, Miss Climpson racked her shrewd brain for a clue. But the memory remained obstinately somewhere at the back of her head. " It will come to me in the night," thought Miss Climpson, confidently, " and meanwhile I won't say anything about the house ; it would seem so pushing on a first acquaintance."

Whereupon, fate instantly intervened to overthrow this prudent resolve, and very nearly ruined the whole effect of Miss Climpson's diplomacy at one fell swoop.

The form which the avenging Errinyes assumed was that of the youngest Miss Findlater—the gushing one—

who came romping over to them, her hands filled with
baby-linen, and plumped down on the end of the sofa
beside Miss Whittaker.

"Mary my *dear*! Why didn't you tell me? You really
are going to start your chicken-farming scheme at once.
I'd no *idea* you'd got on so far with your plans. How *could*
you let me hear it first from somebody else? You promised
to tell me before anybody."

"But I didn't know it myself," replied Miss Whittaker,
coolly. "Who told you this wonderful story?"

"Why, Mrs. Peasgood said that she heard it from . . ."
Here Miss Findlater was in a difficulty. She had not yet
been introduced to Miss Climpson and hardly knew how
to refer to her before her face. "This lady" was what a
shop-girl would say; "Miss Climpson" would hardly
do, as she had, so to speak, no official cognisance of the
name; "Mrs. Budge's new lodger" was obviously impossible in the circumstances. She hesitated—then beamed
a bright appeal at Miss Climpson, and said: "Our new
helper—may I introduce myself? I do *so* detest formality,
don't you, and to belong to the Vicarage work-party is a
sort of introduction in itself, don't you think? Miss Climpson, I believe? How do you do? It is true, isn't it, Mary?
—that you are letting your house to Miss Climpson, and
starting a poultry-farm at Alford."

"Certainly not that I know of. Miss Climpson and I
have only just met one another." The tone of Miss
Whittaker's voice suggested that the first meeting might
very willingly be the last so far as she was concerned.

"Oh dear!" cried the youngest Miss Findlater, who was
fair and bobbed and rather coltish, "I believe I've dropped
a brick. I'm *sure* Mrs. Peasgood understood that it was all
settled." She appealed to Miss Climpson again.

"*Quite* a mistake!" said that lady, energetically, "what
must you be thinking of me, Miss Whittaker? *Of course*, I
could not *possibly* have said such a thing. I only happened

to mention—in the most *casual* way, that I was looking—
that is, *thinking* of looking about—for a house in the neighbourhood of the Church—so convenient you know, for
Early Services and *Saints' Days*—and it was suggested—
just *suggested*, I really forget by *whom*, that you *might*, just
possibly, at *some* time, consider letting your house. I assure
you, that was *all*." In saying which, Miss Climpson was
not wholly accurate or disingenuous, but excused herself
to her conscience on the rather jesuitical grounds that
where so much responsibility was floating about, it was
best to pin it down in the quarter which made for peace.
" Miss Murgatroyd," she added, " put me right at once,
for she said you were *certainly* not thinking of any such
thing, or you would have told her before anybody else."

Miss Whittaker laughed.

" But I shouldn't," she said, " I should have told my
house-agent. It's quite true, I did have it in mind, but I
certainly haven't taken any steps."

" You really are thinking of doing it, then ? " cried
Miss Findlater. " I do hope so—because, if you do, I mean
to apply for a job on the farm ! I'm simply longing to get
away from all these silly tennis-parties and things, and
live close to the Earth and the fundamental crudities. Do
you read Sheila Kaye-Smith ? "

Miss Climpson said no, but she was very fond of Thomas
Hardy.

" It really is terrible, living in a little town like this,"
went on Miss Findlater, " so full of aspidistras, you know,
and small gossip. You've no idea what a dreadfully gossipy
place Leahampton is, Miss Climpson. I'm sure, Mary dear,
you must have had more than enough of it, with that
tiresome Dr. Carr and the things people said. I don't
wonder you're thinking of getting rid of that house. I
shouldn't think you could ever feel comfortable in it
again."

" Why on earth not ? " said Miss Whittaker, lightly.

Too lightly? Miss Climpson was startled to recognise in eye and voice the curious quick defensiveness of the neglected spinster who cries out that she has no use for men.

" Oh well," said Miss Findlater, " I always think it's a little sad, living where people have died, you know. Dear Miss Dawson—though of course it really was merciful that she should be released—all the same——"

Evidently, thought Miss Climpson, she was turning the matter off. The atmosphere of suspicion surrounding the death had been in her mind, but she shied at referring to it.

" There are very few houses in which somebody hasn't died sometime or other," said Miss Whittaker. " I really can't see why people should worry about it. I suppose it's just a question of not realising. We are not sensitive to the past lives of people we don't know. Just as we are much less upset about epidemics and accidents that happen a long way off. Do you really suppose, by the way, Miss Climpson, that this Chinese business is coming to anything? Everybody seems to take it very casually. If all this rioting and Bolshevism was happening in Hyde Park, there'd be a lot more fuss made about it."

Miss Climpson made a suitable reply. That night she wrote to Lord Peter :

" Miss Whittaker has asked me to tea. She tells me that, *much as she would enjoy* an active, country life, with something definite to do, she has a *deep affection* for the house in Wellington Avenue, and *cannot tear herself away*. She seems *very anxious* to give this impression. Would it be *fair* for me to say ' The lady doth protest *too much*, methinks '? The *Prince of Denmark* might even add : ' Let the galled jade wince '— if one can use that expression of a *lady*. How wonderful Shakespeare is ! One can *always* find a phrase in his works for *any* situation ! "

CHAPTER VI

FOUND DEAD

" Blood, though it sleep a time, yet never dies."

CHAPMAN : *The Widow's Tears*

"YOU KNOW, WIMSEY, I think you've found a mare's nest," objected Mr. Parker. " I don't believe there's the slightest reason for supposing that there was anything odd about the Dawson woman's death. You've nothing to go on but a conceited young doctor's opinion and a lot of silly gossip."

" You've got an official mind, Charles," replied his friend. " Your official passion for evidence is gradually sapping your brilliant intellect and smothering your instincts. You're over-civilised, that's your trouble. Compared with you, I am a child of nature. I dwell among the untrodden ways beside the springs of Dove, a maid whom there are (I am shocked to say) few to praise, likewise very few to love, which is perhaps just as well. I *know* there is something wrong about this case."

" How ? "

" How ?—well, just as I know there is something wrong about that case of reputed Lafite '76 which that infernal fellow Pettigrew-Robinson had the nerve to try out on me the other night. It has a nasty flavour."

" Flavour be damned. There's no indication of violence or poison. There's no motive for doing away with the old girl. And there's no possibility of proving anything against anybody."

Lord Peter selected a Villar y Villar from his case, and lighted it with artistic care.

" Look here," he said, " will you take a bet about it ? I'll lay you ten to one that Agatha Dawson was murdered, twenty to one that Mary Whittaker did it, and fifty to one that I bring it home to her within the year. Are you on ? "

Parker laughed. " I'm a poor man, your Majesty," he temporised.

" There you are," said Lord Peter, triumphantly, " you're not comfortable about it yourself. If you were, you'd have said, ' It's taking your money, old chap,' and closed like a shot, in the happy assurance of a certainty."

" I've seen enough to know that nothing is a certainty," retorted the detective, " but I'll take you—in—half-crowns," he added, cautiously.

" Had you said ponies," replied Lord Peter, " I would have taken your alleged poverty into consideration and spared you, but seven-and-sixpence will neither make nor break you. Consequently, I shall proceed to make my statements good."

" And what step do you propose taking ? " inquired Parker, sarcastically. " Shall you apply for an exhumation order and search for poison, regardless of the analyst's report ? Or kidnap Miss Whittaker and apply the third-degree in the Gallic manner ? "

" Not at all. I am more modern. I shall use up-to-date psychological methods. Like the people in the Psalms, I lay traps ; I catch men. I shall let the alleged criminal convict herself."

" Go on ! You are a one, aren't you ? " said Parker, jeeringly.

" I am indeed. It is a well-established psychological fact that criminals cannot let well alone. They——"

" Revisit the place of the crime ? "

" Don't interrupt, blast you. They take unnecessary steps to cover the traces which they haven't left, and so invite, seriatim, Suspicion, Inquiry, Proof, Conviction and the

Gallows. Eminent legal writers—no, pax ! don't chuck that
S. Augustine about, it's valuable. Anyhow, not to cast the
jewels of my eloquence into the pig-bucket, I propose to
insert this advertisement in all the morning papers. Miss
Whittaker must read *some* product of our brilliant journ-
alistic age, I suppose. By this means, we shall kill two birds
with one stone."

" Start two hares at once, you mean," grumbled Parker.
" Hand it over."

" BERTHA and EVELYN GOTOBED, formerly in the service of Miss Agatha Dawson, of ' The Grove,' Wellington
Avenue, Leahampton, are requested to communicate
with J. Murbles, solicitor, of Staple Inn, when they will
hear of SOMETHING TO THEIR ADVANTAGE."

" Rather good, I think, don't you ? " said Wimsey. " Calculated to rouse suspicion in the most innocent mind. I bet
you Mary Whittaker will fall for that."

" In what way ? "

" I don't know. That's what's so interesting. I hope
nothing unpleasant will happen to dear old Murbles. I
should hate to lose him. He's such a perfect type of the
family solicitor. Still, a man in his profession must be prepared to take risks."

" Oh, bosh ! " said Parker. " But I agree that it might
be as well to get hold of the girls, if you really want to find
out about the Dawson household. Servants always know
everything."

" It isn't only that. Don't you remember that Nurse
Philliter said the girls were sacked shortly before she left
herself ? Now, passing over the odd circumstances of the
Nurse's own dismissal—the story about Miss Dawson's refusing to take food from her hands, which wasn't at all borne
out by the old lady's own attitude to her nurse—isn't it
worth considerin' that these girls should have been pushed

off on some excuse just about three weeks after one of those hysterical attacks of Miss Dawson's ? Doesn't it rather look as though everybody who was likely to remember anything about that particular episode had been got out of the way ? "

" Well, there was a good reason for getting rid of the girls."

" Crockery ?—well, nowadays it's not so easy to get good servants. Mistresses put up with a deal more carelessness than they did in the dear dead days beyond recall. Then, about that attack. Why did Miss Whittaker choose just the very moment when the highly-intelligent Nurse Philliter had gone for her walk, to bother Miss Dawson about signin' some tiresome old lease or other ? If business was liable to upset the old girl, why not have a capable person at hand to calm her down ? "

" Oh, but Miss Whittaker is a trained nurse. She was surely capable enough to see to her aunt herself."

" I'm perfectly sure she was a very capable woman indeed," said Wimsey, with emphasis.

" Oh, all right. You're prejudiced. But stick the ad. in by all means. It can't do any harm."

Lord Peter paused, in the very act of ringing the bell. His jaw slackened, giving his long, narrow face a faintly foolish and hesitant look, reminiscent of the heroes of Mr. P. G. Wodehouse.

" You don't think——" he began. " Oh ! rats ! " He pressed the button. " It *can't* do any harm, as you say. Bunter, see that this advertisement appears in the personal columns of all this list of papers, every day until further notice."

. . . .

The advertisement made its first appearance on the Tuesday morning. Nothing of any note happened during the week, except that Miss Climpson wrote in some distress

to say that the youngest Miss Findlater had at length succeeded in persuading Miss Whittaker to take definite steps
about the poultry farm. They had gone away together to
look at a business which they had seen advertised in the
Poultry News, and proposed to be away for some weeks.
Miss Climpson feared that under the circumstances she
would not be able to carry on any investigations of sufficient
importance to justify her *far too generous* salary. She had,
however, become friendly with Miss Findlater, who had
promised to tell her *all about* their doings. Lord Peter replied
in reassuring terms.

On the Tuesday following, Mr. Parker was just wrestling
in prayer with his charlady, who had a tiresome habit of
boiling his breakfast kippers till they resembled heavily
pickled loofahs, when the telephone whirred aggressively.

" Is that you, Charles ? " asked Lord Peter's voice. " I
say, Murbles has had a letter about that girl, Bertha
Gotobed. She disappeared from her lodgings last Thursday,
and her landlady, getting anxious, and having seen the
advertisement, is coming to tell us all she knows. Can you
come round to Staple Inn at eleven ? "

" Dunno," said Parker, a little irritably. " I've got a job
to see to. Surely you can tackle it by yourself."

" Oh, yes ! " The voice was peevish. " But I thought
you'd like to have some of the fun. What an ungrateful
devil you are. You aren't taking the faintest interest in this
case."

" Well—I don't believe in it, you know. All right—don't
use language like that—you'll frighten the girl at the
Exchange. I'll see what I can do. Eleven ?—right !—— Oh,
I say ! "

" Cluck ! " said the telephone.

" Rung off," said Parker, bitterly. " Bertha Gotobed.
H'm ! I could have sworn——"

He reached across to the breakfast-table for the *Daily
Yell*, which was propped against the marmalade jar, and

read with pursed lips a paragraph whose heavily leaded headlines had caught his eye, just before the interruption of the kipper episode.

"NIPPY" FOUND DEAD IN EPPING FOREST

——

£5 Note in Hand-bag.

——

He took up the receiver again and asked for Wimsey's number. The manservant answered him.

"His lordship is in his bath, sir. Shall I put you through?"

"Please," said Parker.

The telephone clucked again. Presently Lord Peter's voice came faintly, "Hullo!"

"Did the landlady mention where Bertha Gotobed was employed?"

"Yes—she was a waitress at the Corner House. Why this interest all of a sudden? You snub me in my bed, but you woo me in my bath. It sounds like a music-hall song of the less refined sort. Why, oh why?"

"Haven't you seen the papers?"

"No. I leave these follies till breakfast-time. What's up? Are we ordered to Shanghai? or have they taken sixpence off the income-tax?"

"Shut up, you fool, it's serious. You're too late."

"What for?"

"Bertha Gotobed was found dead in Epping Forest this morning."

"Good God! Dead? How? What of?"

"No idea. Poison or something. Or heart failure. No violence. No robbery. No clue. I'm going down to the Yard about it now."

" God forgive me, Charles. D'you know, I had a sort of awful feeling when you said that ad. could do no harm. Dead. Poor girl ! Charles, I feel like a murderer. Oh, damn ! and I'm all wet. It does make one feel so helpless. Look here, you spin down to the Yard and tell 'em what you know and I'll join you there in half a tick. Anyway, there's no doubt about it now."

" Oh, but, look here. It may be something quite different. Nothing to do with your ad."

" Pigs *may* fly. Use your common sense. Oh ! and Charles, does it mention the sister ? "

" Yes. There was a letter from her on the body, by which they identified it. She got married last month and went to Canada."

" That's saved her life. She'll be in absolutely horrible danger, if she comes back. We must get hold of her and warn her. And find out what she knows. Good-bye. I *must* get some clothes on. Oh, hell ! "

Cluck ! the line went dead again, and Mr. Parker, abandoning the kippers without regret, ran feverishly out of the house and down Lamb's Conduit Street to catch a diver tram to Westminster.

The Chief of Scotland Yard, Sir Andrew Mackenzie, was a very old friend of Lord Peter's. He received that agitated young man kindly and listened with attention to his slightly involved story of cancer, wills, mysterious solicitors and advertisements in the agony column.

" It's a curious coincidence," he said, indulgently, " and I can understand your feeling upset about it. But you may set your mind at rest. I have the police-surgeon's report, and he is quite convinced that the death was perfectly natural. No signs whatever of any assault. They will make an examination, of course, but I don't think there is the slightest reason to suspect foul play."

" But what was she doing in Epping Forest ? "

Sir Andrew shrugged gently.

" That must be inquired into, of course. Still—young people *do* wander about, you know. There's a fiancé somewhere. Something to do with the railway, I believe. Collins has gone down to interview him. Or she may have been with some other friend."

" But if the death was natural, no one would leave a sick or dying girl like that ? "

" *You* wouldn't. But say there had been some running about—some horse-play—and the girl fell dead, as these heart cases sometimes do. The companion may well have taken fright and cleared out. It's not unheard of."

Lord Peter looked unconvinced.

" How long has she been dead ? "

" About five or six days, our man thinks. It was quite by accident that she was found then at all ; it's quite an unfrequented part of the Forest. A party of young people were exploring with a couple of terriers, and one of the dogs nosed out the body."

" Was it out in the open ? "

" Not exactly. It lay among some bushes—the sort of place where a frolicsome young couple might go to play hide-and-seek."

" Or where a murderer might go to play hide and let the police seek," said Wimsey.

" Well, well. Have it your own way," said Sir Andrew, smiling. " If it was murder, it must have been a poisoning job, for, as I say, there was not the slightest sign of a wound or a struggle. I'll let you have the report of the autopsy. In the meanwhile, if you'd like to run down there with Inspector Parker, you can of course have any facilities you want. And if you discover anything, let me know."

Wimsey thanked him, and collecting Parker from an adjacent office, rushed him briskly down the corridor.

" I don't like it," he said, " that is, of course, it's very gratifying to know that our first steps in psychology have led to action, so to speak, but I wish to God it hadn't been quite such decisive action. We'd better trot down to Epping straight away, and see the landlady later. I've got a new car, by the way, which you'll like."

Mr. Parker took one look at the slim black monster, with its long rakish body and polished-copper twin exhausts, and decided there and then that the only hope of getting down to Epping without interference was to look as official as possible and wave his police authority under the eyes of every man in blue along the route. He shoe-horned himself into his seat without protest, and was more unnerved than relieved to find himself shoot suddenly ahead of the traffic —not with the bellowing roar of the ordinary racing engine, but in a smooth, uncanny silence.

" The new Daimler Twin-Six," said Lord Peter, skimming dexterously round a lorry without appearing to look at it. " With a racing body. Specially built . . . useful . . . gadgets . . . no row—hate row . . . like Edmund Sparkler . . . very anxious there should be no row . . . Little Dorrit . . . remember . . . call her Mrs. Merdle . . . for that reason . . . presently we'll see what she can do."

The promise was fulfilled before their arrival at the spot where the body had been found. Their arrival made a considerable sensation among the little crowd which business or curiosity had drawn to the spot. Lord Peter was instantly pounced upon by four reporters and a synod of Press photographers, whom his presence encouraged in the hope that the mystery might turn out to be a three-column splash after all. Parker, to his annoyance, was photographed in the undignified act of extricating himself from " Mrs. Merdle." Superintendent Walmisley came politely to his assistance, rebuked the onlookers, and led him to the scene of action.

The body had been already removed to the mortuary, but a depression in the moist ground showed clearly enough where it had lain. Lord Peter groaned faintly as he saw it.

" Damn this nasty warm spring weather," he said, with

feeling. " April showers—sun and water—couldn't be worse. Body much altered, Superintendent ? "

" Well, yes, rather, my lord, especially in the exposed parts. But there's no doubt about the identity."

" I didn't suppose there was. How was it lying ? "

" On the back, quite quiet and natural-like. No disarrangement of clothing, or anything. She must just have sat down when she felt herself bad and fallen back."

" M'm. The rain has spoilt any footprints or signs on the ground. And it's grassy. Beastly stuff, grass, eh, Charles ? "

" Yes. These twigs don't seem to have been broken at all, Superintendent."

" Oh, 'no," said the officer, " no signs of a struggle, as I pointed out in my report."

" No—but if she'd sat down here and fallen back as you suggest, don't you think her weight would have snapped some of these young shoots ? "

The Superintendent glanced sharply at the Scotland Yard man.

" You don't suppose she was brought and put here, do you, sir ? "

" I don't suppose anything," retorted Parker, " I merely drew attention to a point which I think you should consider. What are these wheel-marks ? "

" That's our car, sir. We backed it up here and took her up that way."

" And all this trampling is your men too, I suppose ? "

" Partly that, sir, and partly the party as found her."

" You noticed no other person's tracks, I suppose ? "

" No, sir. But it's rained considerably this last week. Besides, the rabbits have been all over the place, as you can see, and other creatures too, I fancy. Weasels, or something of that sort."

" Oh ! Well, I think you'd better take a look round. There might be traces of some kind a bit further away. Make a circle, and report anything you see. And you oughtn't to have let all that bunch of people get so near. Put a cordon round and tell 'em to move on. Have you seen all you want, Peter ? "

Wimsey had been poking his stick aimlessly into the bole of an oak-tree at a few yards' distance. Now he stooped and lifted out a package which had been stuffed into a cleft. The two policemen hurried forward with eager interest, which evaporated somewhat at sight of the find —a ham sandwich and an empty Bass bottle, roughly wrapped up in a greasy newspaper.

" Picnickers," said Walmisley, with a snort. " Nothing to do with the body, I daresay."

" I think you're mistaken," said Wimsey, placidly. " When did the girl disappear, exactly ? "

" Well, she went off duty at the Corner House at five a week ago to-morrow, that's Wednesday, 27th," said Parker.

" And this is the *Evening Views* of Wednesday, 27th," said Wimsey. " Late Final edition. Now that edition isn't on the streets till about 6 o'clock. So unless somebody brought it down and had supper here, it was probably brought by the girl herself or her companion. It's hardly likely anyone would come and picnic here afterwards, not with the body there. Not that bodies need necessarily interfere with one's enjoyment of one's food. À la guerre comme à la guerre. But for the moment there isn't a war on."

" That's true, sir. But you're assuming the death took place on the Wednesday or Thursday. She may have been somewhere else—living with someone in town or anywhere."

" Crushed again," said Wimsey. " Still, it's a curious coincidence."

" It is, my lord, and I'm very glad you found the things. Will you take charge of 'em, Mr. Parker, or shall I ? "

" Better take them along and put them with the other things," said Parker, extending his hand to take them from

Wimsey, whom they seemed to interest quite disproportionately. " I fancy his lordship's right and that the parcel
came here along with the girl. And that certainly looks
as if she didn't come alone. Possibly that young man of
hers was with her. Looks like the old, old story. Take care
of that bottle, old man, it may have finger-prints on it."

" You can have the bottle," said Wimsey. " May we
ne'er lack a friend or a bottle to give him, as Dick Swiveller
says. But I earnestly beg that before you caution your
respectable young railway clerk that anything he says may
be taken down and used against him, you will cast your
eye, and your nose, upon this ham sandwich."

" What's wrong with it ? " inquired Parker.

" Nothing. It appears to be in astonishingly good preservation, thanks to this admirable oak-tree. The stalwart
oak—for so many centuries Britain's bulwark against the
invader ! Heart of oak are our ships—not hearts, by the
way, as it is usually misquoted. But I am puzzled by
the incongruity between the sandwich and the rest of the
outfit."

" It's an ordinary ham sandwich, isn't it ? "

" Oh, gods of the wine-flask and the board, how long ?
how long ?—it is a ham sandwich, Goth, but not an ordinary one. Never did it see Lyons' kitchen, or the counter
of the multiple store or the delicatessen shop in the back
street. The pig that was sacrificed to make this dainty titbit fattened in no dull style, never knew the daily ration
of pig-wash or the not unmixed rapture of the domestic
garbage-pail. Observe the hard texture, the deep brownish
tint of the lean ; the rich fat, yellow as a Chinaman's cheek ;
the dark spot where the black treacle cure has soaked in,
to make a dish fit to lure Zeus from Olympus. And tell
me, man of no discrimination and worthy to be fed on
boiled cod all the year round, tell me how it comes that
your little waitress and her railway clerk come down to
Epping Forest to regale themselves on sandwiches made

from coal-black, treacle-cured Bradenham ham, which
long ago ran as a young wild boar about the woodlands,
till death translated it to an incorruptible and more glorious
body ? I may add that it costs about 3*s.* a pound uncooked
—an argument which you will allow to be weighty."

" That's odd, certainly," said Parker. " I imagine that
only rich people——"

" Only rich people or people who understand eating as
a fine art," said Wimsey. " The two classes are by no means
identical, though they occasionally overlap."

" It may be very important," said Parker, wrapping the
exhibits up carefully. " We'd better go along now and see
the body."

The examination was not a very pleasant matter, for
the weather had been damp and warm and there had
certainly been weasels. In fact, after a brief glance, Wimsey
left the two policemen to carry on alone, and devoted his
attention to the dead girl's handbag. He glanced through
the letter from Evelyn Gotobed—(now Evelyn Cropper)—
and noted down the Canadian address. He turned the cutting of his own advertisement out of an inner compartment,
and remained for some time in consideration of the £5
note which lay, folded up, side by side with a 10*s.* Treasury
note, 7*s.* 8*d.* in silver and copper, a latch-key and a powder
compacte.

" You're having this note traced, Walmisley, I suppose ? "

" Oh, yes, my lord, certainly."

" And the latch-key, I imagine, belongs to the girl's
lodgings."

" No doubt it does. We have asked her landlady to come
and identify the body. Not that there's any doubt about
it, but just as a matter of routine. She may give us some
help. Ah ! "—the Superintendent peered out of the mortuary door—" I think this must be the lady."

The stout and motherly woman who emerged from a

taxi in charge of a youthful policeman, identified the body
without difficulty, and amid many sobs, as that of Bertha
Gotobed. " Such a nice young lady," she mourned. " What
a terrible thing, oh, dear ! who would go to do a thing
like that ? I've been in such a state of worriment ever since
she didn't come home last Wednesday. I'm sure many's
the time I've said to myself I wished I'd had my tongue
cut out before I ever showed her that wicked advertisement. Ah, I see you've got it there, sir. A dreadful thing
it is that people should be luring young girls away with
stories about something to their advantage. A sinful old
devil—calling himself a lawyer, too ! When she didn't
come back and didn't come back I wrote to the wretch,
telling him I was on his track and was coming round to
have the law on him as sure as my name's Dorcas Gulliver.
He wouldn't have got round me—not that I'd be the bird
he was looking for, being sixty-one come Mid-Summer Day
—and so I told him."

Lord Peter's gravity was somewhat upset by this dia-
tribe against the highly respectable Mr. Murbles of Staple
Inn, whose own version of Mrs. Gulliver's communication
had been decently expurgated. " How shocked the old boy
must have been," he murmured to Parker. " I'm for it next
time I see him."

Mrs. Gulliver's voice moaned on and on.

" Such respectable girls, both of them, and Miss Evelyn
married to that nice young man from Canada. Deary me,
it will be a terrible upset for her. And there's poor John
Ironsides, was to have married Miss Bertha, the poor lamb,
this very Whitsuntide as ever is. A very steady, respectable
man—a clurk on the Southern, which he always used to
say, joking like, ' Slow but safe, like the Southern—that's
me, Mrs. G.' T'ch, t'ch—who'd a believed it ? And it's not
as if she was one of the flighty sort. I give her a latch-key
gladly, for she'd sometimes be on late duty, but never any
staying out after her time. That's why it worried me so,

her not coming back. There's many nowadays as would wash one's hands and glad to be rid of them, knowing what they might be up to. No. When the time passed and she didn't come back, I said, Mark my words, I said, she's bin kidnapped, I said, by that Murbles."

"Had she been long with you, Mrs. Gulliver?" asked Parker.

"Not above a fifteen month or so, she hadn't, but bless you, I don't have to know a young lady fifteen days to know if she's a good girl or not. You gets to know by the look of 'em almost, when you've 'ad my experience."

"Did she and her sister come to you together?"

"They did. They come to me when they was lookin' for work in London. And they could a' fallen into a deal worse hands I can tell you, two young things from the country, and them that fresh and pretty looking."

"They were uncommonly lucky, I'm sure, Mrs. Gulliver," said Lord Peter, "and they must have found it a great comfort to be able to confide in you and get your good advice."

"Well, I think they did," said Mrs. Gulliver, "not that young people nowadays seems to want much guidance from them as is older. Train up a child and away she go, as the Good Book says. But Miss Evelyn, that's now Mrs. Cropper—she'd had this London idea put into her head, and up they comes with the idea of bein' made ladies of, havin' only been in service before, though what's the difference between serving in one of them tea-shops at the beck of all the nasty tagrag and bobtail and serving in a lady's home, I *don't* see, except that you works harder and don't get your meals so comfortable. Still, Miss Evelyn, she was always the go-ahead one of the two, and she did very well for herself, I will say, meetin' Mr. Cropper as used to take his breakfast regular at the Corner House every morning and took a liking to the girl in the most honourable way."

" That was very fortunate. Have you any idea what gave them the notion of coming to town ? "

" Well, now, sir, it's funny you should ask that, because it was a thing I never could understand. The lady as they used to be in service with, down in the country, she put it into Miss Evelyn's head. Now, sir, wouldn't you think that with good service that 'ard to come by, she'd have done all she could to keep them with her ? But no ! There was a bit of trouble one day, it seems, over Bertha—this poor girl here, poor lamb—it do break one's 'eart to see her like that, don't it, sir ?—over Bertha 'avin' broke an old teapot—a very valuable one by all accounts, and the lady told 'er she couldn't put up with 'avin' her things broke no more. So she says : ' You'll 'ave to go,' she says, ' but,' she says, ' I'll give you a very good character and you'll soon get a good place. And I expect Evelyn 'll want to go with you,' she says, ' so I'll have to find someone else to do for me,' she says. ' But,' she says, ' why not go to London ? You'll do better there and have a much more interesting life than what you would at home,' she says. And the end of it was, she filled 'em up so with stories of how fine a place London was and how grand situations was to be had for the asking, that they was mad to go, and she give them a present of money and behaved very handsome, take it all round."

" H'm," said Wimsey, " she seems to have been very particular about her teapot. Was Bertha a great crockery-breaker ? "

" Well, sir, she never broke nothing of mine. But this Miss Whittaker—that was the name—she was one of these opiniated ladies, as will 'ave their own way in everythink. A fine temper she 'ad, or so poor Bertha said, though Miss Evelyn—her as is now Mrs. Cropper—*she* always 'ad an idea as there was somethink at the back of it. Miss Evelyn was always the sharp one, as you might say. But there, sir, we all 'as our peculiarities, don't we ? It's my own belief as the lady had somebody of her own choice as she wanted to put in the place of Bertha—that's this one—and Evelyn—as is now Mrs. Cropper, you understand me—and she jest trampled up an excuse, as they say, to get rid of 'em."

"Very possibly," said Wimsey. "I suppose, Inspector, Evelyn Gotobed——"

"Now Mrs. Cropper," put in Mrs. Gulliver with a sob.

"Mrs. Cropper, I should say—has been communicated with?"

"Oh, yes, my lord. We cabled her at once."

"Good. I wish you'd let me know when you hear from her."

"We shall be in touch with Inspector Parker, my lord, of course."

"Of course. Well, Charles, I'm going to leave you to it. I've got a telegram to send. Or will you come with me?"

"Thanks, no," said Parker. "To be frank, I don't like your methods of driving. Being in the Force, I prefer to keep on the windy side of the law."

"Windy is the word for you," said Peter, "I'll see you in Town, then."

CHAPTER VII

HAM AND BRANDY

" Tell me what you eat and I will tell you what you are."
                                        BRILLAT-SAVARIN

" WELL," said Wimsey, as Parker was ushered in that same evening by Bunter, " have you got anything fresh ? "

" Yes, I've got a new theory of the crime, which knocks yours into a cocked hat. I've got evidence to support it, too."

" Which crime, by the way ? "

" Oh, the Epping Forest business. I don't believe the old Dawson person was murdered at all. That's just an idea of yours."

" I see. And you're now going to tell me that Bertha Gotobed was got hold of by the White Slave people."

" How did you know ? " asked Parker, a little peevishly.

" Because Scotland Yard have two maggots which crop up whenever anything happens to a young woman. Either it's White Slavery or Dope Dens—sometimes both. You are going to say it's both."

" Well, I was, as a matter of fact. It so often is, you know. We've traced the £5 note."

" That's important, anyhow."

" Yes. It seems to me to be the clue to the whole thing. It is one of a series paid out to a Mrs. Forrest, living in South Audley Street. I've been round to make some inquiries."

" Did you see the lady ? "

" No, she was out. She usually is, I'm told. In fact, her habits seem to be expensive, irregular and mysterious. She has an elegantly furnished flat over a flower-shop."

" A service flat ? "

" No. One of the quiet kind, with a lift you work yourself. She only turns up occasionally, mostly in the evenings,
spends a night or two and departs. Food ordered in from
Fortnum & Mason's. Bills paid promptly by note or cheque.
Cleaning done by an elderly female who comes in about
eleven, by which time Mrs. Forrest has usually gone out."

" Doesn't anybody ever see her ? "

" Oh dear, yes ! The people in the flat below and the
girl at the flower-shop were able to give me quite a good
description of her. Tall, over-dressed, musquash and those
abbreviated sort of shoes with jewelled heels and hardly
any uppers—you know the sort of thing. Heavily peroxided;
strong aroma of orifan wafted out upon the passer-by ;
powder too white for the fashion and mouth heavily
obscured with sealing-wax red ; eyebrows painted black
to startle, not deceive ; finger-nails a monument to Kraska
—the pink variety."

" I'd no idea you studied the Woman's Page to such good
purpose, Charles."

" Drives a Renault Four-seater, dark green with tapestry
doings. Garages just round the corner. I've seen the man,
and he says the car was out on the night of the 27th. Went
out at 11.30. Returned about 8 the next morning."

" How much petrol had been used ? "

" We worked that out. Just about enough for a run to
Epping and back. What's more, the charwoman says that
there had been supper for two in the flat that night, and
three bottles of champagne drunk. Also, there is a ham in
the flat."

" A Bradenham ham ? "

" How do you expect the charwoman to know that ?
But I think it probably is, as I find from Fortnum &
Mason's that a Bradenham ham was delivered to Mrs.
Forrest's address about a fortnight ago."

" That sounds conclusive. I take it you think Bertha

Gotobed was inveigled there for some undesirable purpose by Mrs. Forrest, and had supper with her——"

" No ; I should think there was a man."

" Yes, of course. Mrs. F. brings the parties together and leaves them to it. The poor girl is made thoroughly drunk —and then something untoward happens."

" Yes—shock, perhaps, or a shot of dope."

" And they bustle her off and get rid of her. It's quite possible. The post-mortem may tell us something about it. Yes, Bunter, what is it ? "

" The telephone, my lord, for Mr. Parker."

" Excuse me," said Parker, " I asked the people at the flower-shop to ring me up here, if Mrs. Forrest came in. If she's there, would you like to come round with me ? "

" Very much."

Parker returned from the telephone with an air of subdued triumph.

" She's just gone up to her flat. Come along. We'll take a taxi—not that death-rattle of yours. Hurry up, I don't want to miss her."

The door of the flat in South Audley Street was opened by Mrs. Forrest in person. Wimsey recognised her instantly from the description. On seeing Parker's card, she made no objection whatever to letting them in, and led the way into a pink and mauve sitting-room, obviously furnished by contract from a Regent Street establishment.

" Please sit down. Will you smoke ? And your friend ? "

" My colleague, Mr. Templeton," said Parker, promptly.

Mrs. Forrest's rather hard eyes appeared to sum up in a practised manner the difference between Parker's seven-guinea " fashionable lounge suiting, tailored in our own workrooms, fits like a made-to-measure suit," and his " colleague's " Savile Row outlines, but beyond a slight additional defensiveness of manner she showed no disturbance. Parker noted the glance. " She's summing us up professionally," was his mental comment, " and she's not quite sure whether Wimsey's an outraged brother or husband or what. Never mind. Let her wonder. We may get her rattled."

"We are engaged, Madam," he began, with formal severity, "on an inquiry relative to certain events connected with the 26th of last month. I think you were in town at that time?"

Mrs. Forrest frowned slightly in the effort to recollect. Wimsey made a mental note that she was not as young as her bouffant apple-green frock made her appear. She was certainly nearing the thirties, and her eyes were mature and aware.

"Yes, I think I was. Yes, certainly. I was in town for several days about that time. How can I help you?"

"It is a question of a certain bank-note which has been traced to your possession," said Parker, "a £5 note numbered x/y58929. It was issued to you by Lloyds Bank in payment of a cheque on the 19th."

"Very likely. I can't say I remember the number, but I think I cashed a cheque about that time. I can tell in a moment by my cheque-book."

"I don't think it's necessary. But it would help us very much if you can recollect to whom you paid it."

"Oh, I see. Well, that's rather difficult. I paid my dressmaker's about that time—no, that was by cheque. I paid cash to the garage, I know, and I think there was a £5 note in that. Then I dined at Verry's with a woman friend —that took the second £5 note, I remember, but there was a third. I drew out £25—three fives and ten ones. Where did the third note go? Oh, of course, how stupid of me! I put it on a horse."

"Through a Commission Agent?"

"No. I had nothing much to do one day, so I went down to Newmarket. I put the £5 on some creature called Brighteye or Attaboy or some name like that, at 50 to 1. Of course the wretched animal didn't win, they never do.

A man in the train gave me the tip and wrote the name down for me. I handed it to the nearest bookie I saw—a funny little grey-haired man with a hoarse voice—and that was the last I saw of it."

" Could you remember which day it was ? "

" I think it was Saturday. Yes, I'm sure it was."

" Thank you very much, Mrs. Forrest. It will be a great help if we can trace those notes. One of them has turned up since in—other circumstances."

" May I know what the circumstances are, or is it an official secret ? "

Parker hesitated. He rather wished, now, that he had demanded point-blank at the start how Mrs. Forrest's £5 note had come to be found on the dead body of the waitress at Epping. Taken by surprise, the woman might have got flustered. Now, he had let her entrench herself securely behind this horse story. Impossible to follow up the history of a bank-note handed to an unknown bookie at a race-meeting. Before he could speak, Wimsey broke in for the first time, in a high, petulant voice which quite took his friend aback.

" You're not getting anywhere with all this," he complained. " I don't care a continental curse about the beastly note, and I'm sure Sylvia doesn't."

" Who is Sylvia ? " demanded Mrs. Forrest with considerable amazement.

" Who is Sylvia ? What is she ? " gabbled Wimsey, irrepressibly. " Shakespeare always has the right word, hasn't he ? But, God bless my soul, it's no laughing matter. It's very serious and you've no business to laugh at it. Sylvia is very much upset, and the doctor is afraid it may have an effect on her heart. You may not know it, Mrs. Forrest, but Sylvia Lyndhurst is my cousin. And what she wants to know, and what we all want to know—don't interrupt me, Inspector, all this shilly-shallying doesn't get us anywhere—I want to know, Mrs. Forrest, who was it dining here with you on the night of April 26th. Who was it ? Who was it ? Can you tell me that ? "

This time, Mrs. Forrest was visibly taken aback. Even under the thick coat of powder they could see the red flush up into her cheeks and ebb away, while her eyes took on an expression of something more than alarm—a kind of vicious fury, such as one may see in those of a cornered cat.

" On the 26th ? " she faltered. " I can't——"

" I knew it ! " cried Wimsey. " And that girl Evelyn was sure of it too. Who was it, Mrs. Forrest ? Answer me that ! "

" There—there was no one," said Mrs. Forrest, with a thick gasp.

" Oh, come, Mrs. Forrest, think again," said Parker, taking his cue promptly, " you aren't going to tell us that you accounted by yourself for three bottles of Veuve Clicquot and two people's dinners."

" Not forgetting the ham," put in Wimsey, with fussy self-importance, " the Bradenham ham specially cooked and sent up by Fortnum & Mason. Now, Mrs. Forrest——"

" Wait a moment. Just a moment. I'll tell you everything."

The woman's hands clutched at the pink silk cushions, making little hot, tight creases. " I—would you mind getting me something to drink ? In the dining-room, through there—on the sideboard."

Wimsey got up quickly and disappeared into the next room. He took rather a long time, Parker thought. Mrs. Forrest was lying back in a collapsed attitude, but her breathing was more controlled, and she was, he thought, recovering her wits. " Making up a story," he muttered savagely to himself. However, he could not, without brutality, press her at the moment.

Lord Peter, behind the folding doors, was making a good

deal of noise, chinking the glasses and fumbling about. However, before very long, he was back.

" 'Scuse my taking such a time," he apologised, handing Mrs. Forrest a glass of brandy and soda. " Couldn't find the syphon. Always was a bit wool-gathering, y'know. All my friends say so. Starin' me in the face all the time, what ? And then I sloshed a lot of soda on the sideboard. Hand shakin'. Nerves all to pieces and so on. Feelin' better ? That's right. Put it down. That's the stuff to pull you together. How about another little one, what ? Oh, rot, it can't hurt you. Mind if I have one myself ? I'm feelin' a bit flustered. Upsettin', delicate business and all that. Just another spot. That's the idea."

He trotted out again, glass in hand, while Parker fidgeted. The presence of amateur detectives was sometimes an embarrassment. Wimsey clattered in again, this time, with more common sense, bringing decanter, syphon and three glasses, bodily, on a tray.

" Now, now," said Wimsey, " now we're feeling better, do you think you can answer our question, Mrs. Forrest ? "

" May I know, first of all, what right you have to ask it ? "

Parker shot an exasperated glance at his friend. This came of giving people time to think.

" Right ? " burst in Wimsey. " Right ? Of course, we've a right. The police have a right to ask questions when anything's the matter. Here's murder the matter ! Right, indeed ? "

" Murder ? "

A curious intent look came into her eyes. Parker could not place it, but Wimsey recognised it instantly. He had seen it last on the face of a great financier as he took up his pen to sign a contract. Wimsey had been called to witness the signature, and had refused. It was a contract that ruined thousands of people. Incidentally, the financier had been murdered soon after, and Wimsey had declined

to investigate the matter, with a sentence from Dumas :
" Let pass the justice of God."

" I'm afraid," Mrs. Forrest was saying, " that in that
case I can't help you. I *did* have a friend dining with me on
the 26th, but he has not, so far as I know, been murdered,
nor has he murdered anybody."

" It was a man, then ? " said Parker.

Mrs. Forrest bowed her head with a kind of mocking
ruefulness. " I live apart from my husband," she murmured.

" I am sorry," said Parker, " to have to press for this
gentleman's name and address."

" Isn't that asking rather much ? Perhaps if you would
give me further details—— ? "

" Well, you see," cut in Wimsey again, " if we could just
know for certain it wasn't Lyndhurst. My cousin is so frightfully upset, as I said, and that Evelyn girl is making trouble.
In fact—of course one doesn't want it to go any further—
but actually Sylvia lost her head very completely. She made
a savage attack on poor old Lyndhurst—with a revolver,
in fact, only fortunately she is a shocking bad shot. It went
over his shoulder and broke a vase—most distressin' thing—
a Famille Rose jar, worth thousands—and of course it was
smashed to atoms. Sylvia is really hardly responsible when
she's in a temper. And, we thought, as Lyndhurst was
actually traced to this block of flats—if you could give us
definite proof it wasn't him, it might calm her down and
prevent murder being done, don't you know. Because,
though they might call it Guilty but Insane, still, it would
be awfully awkward havin' one's cousin in Broadmoor—
a first cousin, and really a very nice woman, when she's not
irritated."

Mrs. Forrest gradually softened into a faint smile.

" I think I understand the position, Mr. Templeton,"
she said, " and if I give you a name, it will be in strict confidence, I presume ? "

" Of course, of course," said Wimsey. " Dear me, I'm sure it's uncommonly kind of you."

" You'll swear you aren't spies of my husband's ? " she said, quickly. " I am trying to divorce him. How do I know this isn't a trap ? "

" Madam," said Wimsey, with intense gravity, " I swear to you on my honour as a gentleman that I have not the slightest connection with your husband. I have never even heard of him before."

Mrs. Forrest shook her head.

" I don't think, after all," she said, " it would be much good my giving you the name. In any case, if you asked him whether he'd been here, he would say no, wouldn't he ? And if you've been sent by my husband, you've got all the evidence you want already. But I give you my solemn assurance, Mr. Templeton, that I know nothing about your friend, Mr. Lyndhurst——"

" Major Lyndhurst," put in Wimsey, plaintively.

" And if Mrs. Lyndhurst is not satisfied, and likes to come round and see me, I will do my best to satisfy her of the fact. Will that do ? "

" Thank you very much," said Wimsey. " I'm sure it's as much as any one could expect. You'll forgive my abruptness, won't you ? I'm rather—er—nervously constituted, and the whole business is exceedingly upsetting. *Good* afternoon. Come on, Inspector, it's quite all right—you see it's quite all right. I'm really very much obliged—uncommonly so. Please don't trouble to see us out."

He teetered nervously down the narrow hall-way, in his imbecile and well-bred way, Parker following with a police-man-like stiffness. No sooner, however, had the flat-door closed behind them than Wimsey seized his friend by the arm and bundled him helter-skelter into the lift.

" I thought we should never get away," he panted. " Now, quick—how do we get round to the back of these flats ? "

" What do you want with the back ? " demanded Parker, annoyed. " And I wish you wouldn't stampede me like this. I've no business to let you come with me on a job at all, and if I do, you might have the decency to keep quiet."

" Right you are," said Wimsey, cheerfully, " just let's do this little bit and you can get all the virtuous indignation off your chest later on. Round here, I fancy, up this back alley. Step lively and mind the dust-bin. One, two, three, four—here we are ! Just keep a look-out for the passing stranger, will you ? "

Selecting a back window which he judged to belong to Mrs. Forrest's flat, Wimsey promptly grasped a drain-pipe and began to swarm up it with the agility of a cat-burglar. About fifteen feet from the ground he paused, reached up, appeared to detach something with a quick jerk, and then slid very gingerly to the ground again, holding his right hand at a cautious distance from his body, as though it were breakable.

And indeed, to his amazement, Parker observed that Wimsey now held a long-stemmed glass in his fingers, similar to those from which they had drunk in Mrs. Forrest's sitting-room.

" What on earth—— ? " said Parker.

" Hush ! I'm Hawkshaw the detective—gathering finger-prints. Here we come a-wassailing and gathering prints in May. That's why I took the glass back. I brought a different one in the second time. Sorry I had to do this athletic stunt, but the only cotton-reel I could find hadn't much on it. When I changed the glass, I tip-toed into the bathroom and hung it out of the window. Hope she hasn't been in there since. Just brush my bags down, will you, old man ? Gently—don't touch the glass."

" What the devil do you want finger-prints for ? "

" You're a grateful sort of person. Why, for all you know, Mrs. Forrest is someone the Yard has been looking for for years. And anyway, you could compare the prints with those on the Bass bottle, if any. Besides, you never know when finger-prints mayn't come in handy. They're excellent things to have about the house. Coast clear ? Right. Hail a taxi, will you ? I can't wave my hand with this glass in it. Look so silly, don't you know. I say ! "

" Well ? "

" I saw something else. The first time I went out for the drinks, I had a peep into her bedroom."

" Yes ? "

" What do you think I found in the wash-stand drawer ? "

" What ? "

" A hypodermic syringe ! "

" Really ? "

" Oh, yes, and an innocent little box of ampullæ, with a doctor's prescription headed ' The injection, Mrs. Forrest. One to be injected when the pain is very severe.' What do you think of that ? "

" Tell you when we've got the results of that post-mortem," said Parker, really impressed. " You didn't bring the prescription, I suppose ? "

" No, and I didn't inform the lady who we were or what we were after or ask her permission to carry away the family crystal. But I made a note of the chemist's address."

" Did you ? " ejaculated Parker. " Occasionally, my lad, you have some glimmerings of sound detective sense."

CHAPTER VIII

CONCERNING CRIME

" Society is at the mercy of a murderer who is remorseless, who takes no
accomplices and who keeps his head."

EDMUND PEARSON : *Murder at Smutty Nose*

*Letter from Miss Alexandra Katherine Climpson to Lord Peter
Wimsey.*

> " ' Fair View,'
> " Nelson Avenue,
> " Leahampton.
> " 12 May, 1927.

" MY DEAR LORD PETER,

" I have not *yet* been able to get ALL the information
you ask for, as Miss Whittaker has been away for some
weeks, inspecting *chicken-farms* ! ! With a view to purchase, I mean, of course, and not in any *sanitary capacity* (!).
I *really think* she means to set up farming *with Miss
Findlater*, though what Miss Whittaker can see in that
very gushing and really *silly* young woman I cannot
think. However, Miss Findlater has evidently quite a
' pash ' (as we used to call it at school) for Miss Whittaker, and I am afraid none of us are above being
flattered by such outspoken admiration. I must say, I
think it rather *unhealthy*—you may remember Miss
Clemence Dane's *very clever book* on the subject ?—I have
seen so *much* of that kind of thing in my rather WOMAN-
RIDDEN existence ! It has such a bad effect, as a rule,
upon the *weaker character* of the two—— But I must not
take up your time with my TWADDLE ! !

" Miss Murgatroyd, who was quite a friend of old *Miss*

Dawson, however, has been able to tell me a *little* about her past life.

" It seems that, until five years ago, Miss Dawson lived in Warwickshire with her cousin, a Miss Clara Whittaker, Mary Whittaker's great-aunt on the *father's* side. This Miss Clara was evidently rather a ' character,' as my dear father used to call it. In her day she was considered very ' advanced ' and *not quite nice* (!) because she *refused* several *good offers*, cut her hair SHORT (! !) and set up in business for herself as a HORSE-BREEDER ! ! ! Of course, nowadays, nobody would think anything of it, but *then* the old lady—or *young* lady as she was when she embarked on this *revolutionary* proceeding, was quite a PIONEER.

" Agatha Dawson was a school-fellow of hers, and *deeply attached* to her. And as a result of this friendship, Agatha's *sister*, HARRIET, married Clara Whittaker's *brother* JAMES'! But *Agatha* did not care about marriage, any more than *Clara*, and the two ladies lived together in a big old house, with immense stables, in a village in War-wickshire—Crofton, I think the name was. Clara Whit-taker turned out to be a remarkably *good business woman*, and worked up a big ' connection ' among the *hunting folk* in those parts. Her hunters became quite *famous*, and from a capital of a few thousand pounds with which she started she made quite a *fortune*, and was a *very rich woman* before her death ! Agatha Dawson never had anything to do with the *horsey* part of the business. She was the ' domestic ' partner, and looked after the *house* and the *servants*.

" When Clara Whittaker died, she left *all her money* to AGATHA, passing over her *own family*, with whom she was *not on very good terms*—owing to the narrow-minded atti-tude they had taken up about her horse-dealing ! ! Her nephew, Charles Whittaker, who was a clergyman, and the father of *our* Miss Whittaker, resented very much not getting the money, though, as he had kept up the feud in a very *un-Christian* manner, he had really *no right* to complain, especially as Clara had built up her fortune *entirely* by her own exertions. But, of course, he inherited the *bad, old-fashioned* idea that women *ought not* to be their own mistresses, or make money for themselves, or do what they liked with their own !

" He and his family were the only surviving Whittaker relations, and when *he and his wife* were killed in a motor-car accident, Miss Dawson asked Mary to leave her work as a nurse and make her home with her. So that, you see, Clara Whittaker's money was destined to *come back* to James Whittaker's daughter in the end ! ! Miss Dawson made it *quite* CLEAR that this was her intention, provided Mary would come and *cheer the declining days* of a lonely old lady !

" Mary accepted, and as her aunt—or, to speak more *exactly*, her great-aunt—had given up the big old Warwickshire house after Clara's death, they lived in London for a short time and then moved to Leahampton. As you know, poor old Miss Dawson was then already suffering from the *terrible disease* of which she died, so that Mary did not have to wait very long for Clara Whittaker's money ! !

" I hope this information will be of some *use* to you. Miss Murgatroyd did not, of course, know anything about the rest of the family, but she always understood that there were *no other* surviving relatives, either on the Whittaker or the Dawson side.

" When Miss Whittaker returns, I hope to *see more* of her. I enclose my *account* for expenses up to date. I do *trust* you will not consider it *extravagant*. How are your money-lenders progressing? I was sorry not to see more of those *poor women* whose cases I investigated—their stories were *so* PATHETIC !

> " I am,
> " Very sincerely yours,
> " ALEXANDRA K. CLIMPSON."

" P.S.—I *forgot* to say that Miss Whittaker has a little motor-car. I do not, of course, know anything about these matters, but Mrs. Budge's maid tells me that Miss Whittaker's maid says it is an Austen 7 (is this right ?). It is grey, and the number is XX9917."

Mr. Parker was announced, just as Lord Peter finished reading this document, and sank rather wearily in a corner of the chesterfield.

" What luck ? " inquired his lordship, tossing the letter over to him. " Do you know, I'm beginning to think you were right about the Bertha Gotobed business, and I'm rather relieved. I don't believe one word of Mrs. Forrest's story, for reasons of my own, and I'm now hoping that the wiping out of Bertha was a pure coincidence and nothing to do with my advertisement."

" Are you ? " said Parker, bitterly, helping himself to whisky and soda. " Well, I hope you'll be cheered to learn that the analysis of the body has been made, and that there is not the slightest sign of foul play. There is no trace of violence or of poisoning. There was a heart weakness of fairly long standing, and the verdict is syncope after a heavy meal."

" That doesn't worry me," said Wimsey. " We suggested shock, you know. Amiable gentleman met at flat of friendly lady suddenly turns funny after dinner and makes undesirable overtures. Virtuous young woman is horribly shocked. Weak heart gives way. Collapse. Exit. Agitation of amiable gentleman and friendly lady, left with corpse on their hands. Happy thought : motor-car ; Epping Forest ; *exeunt omnes*, singing and washing their hands. Where's the difficulty ? "

" Proving it is the difficulty, that's all. By the way, there were no finger-marks on the bottle—only smears."

" Gloves, I suppose. Which looks like camouflage, anyhow. An ordinary picnicking couple wouldn't put on gloves to handle a bottle of Bass."

" I know. But we can't arrest all the people who wear gloves."

" I weep for you, the Walrus said, I deeply sympathise. I see the difficulty, but it's early days yet. How about those injections ? "

" Perfectly O.K. We've interrogated the chemist and interviewed the doctor. Mrs. Forrest suffers from violent neuralgic pains, and the injections were duly prescribed. Nothing wrong there, and no history of doping or anything. The prescription is a very mild one, and couldn't possibly be fatal to anybody. Besides, haven't I told you that there was no trace of morphia or any other kind of poison in the body ? "

" Oh, well ! " said Wimsey. He sat for a few minutes looking thoughtfully at the fire.

" I see the case has more or less died out of the papers," he resumed, suddenly.

" Yes. The analysis has been sent to them, and there will be a paragraph to-morrow and a verdict of natural death, and that will be the end of it."

" Good. The less fuss there is about it the better. Has anything been heard of the sister in Canada ? "

" Oh, I forgot. Yes. We had a cable three days ago. She's coming over."

" Is she ? By Jove ! What boat ? "

" The *Star of Quebec*—due in next Friday."

" H'm ! We'll have to get hold of her. Are you meeting the boat ? "

" Good heavens, no ! Why should I ? "

" I think someone ought to. I'm reassured—but not altogether happy. I think I'll go myself, if you don't mind. I want to get that Dawson story—and this time I want to make sure the young woman doesn't have a heart attack before I interview her."

" I really think you're exaggerating, Peter."

" Better safe than sorry," said his lordship. " Have

another peg, won't you ? Meanwhile, what do you think of Miss Climpson's latest ? "

" I don't see much in it."

" No ? "

" It's a bit confusing, but it all seems quite straight-forward."

" Yes. The only thing we know now is that Mary Whit-taker's father was annoyed about Miss Dawson's getting his aunt's money and thought it ought to have come to him."

" Well, you don't suspect *him* of having murdered Miss Dawson, do you ? He died before her, and the daughter's got the money, anyhow."

" Yes, I know. But suppose Miss Dawson had changed her mind ? She might have quarrelled with Mary Whittaker and wanted to leave her money elsewhere."

" Oh, I see—and been put out of the way before she could make a will ? "

" Isn't it possible ? "

" Yes, certainly. Except that all the evidence we have goes to show that will-making was about the last job any-body could persuade her to do."

" True—while she was on good terms with Mary. But how about that morning Nurse Philliter mentioned, when she said people were trying to kill her before her time ? Mary may really have been impatient with her for being such an unconscionable time a-dying. If Miss Dawson became aware of that, she would certainly have resented it and may very well have expressed an intention of making her will in someone else's favour—as a kind of insurance against premature decease ! "

" Then why didn't she send for her solicitor ? "

" She may have tried to. But after all, she was bed-ridden and helpless. Mary may have prevented the message from being sent."

" That sounds quite plausible."

" Doesn't it ? That's why I want Evelyn Cropper's evidence. I'm perfectly certain those girls were packed off because they had heard more than they should. Or why such enthusiasm over sending them to London ? "

" Yes. I thought that part of Mrs. Gulliver's story was a bit odd. I say, how about the other nurse ? "

" Nurse Forbes ? That's a good idea. I was forgetting her. Think you can trace her ? "

" Of course, if you really think it important."

" I do. I think it's damned important. Look here, Charles, you don't seem very enthusiastic about this case."

" Well, you know, I'm not so certain it is a case at all. What makes you so fearfully keen about it ? You seem dead set on making it a murder, with practically nothing to go upon. Why ? "

Lord Peter got up and paced the room. The light from the solitary reading-lamp threw his lean shadow, diffused and monstrously elongated, up to the ceiling. He walked over to a book-shelf, and the shadow shrank, blackened, settled down. He stretched his hand, and the hand's shadow flew with it, hovering over the gilded titles of the books and blotting them out one by one.

" Why ? " repeated Wimsey. " Because I believe this is the case I have always been looking for. The case of cases. The murder without discernible means, or motive or clue. The norm. All these "—he swept his extended hand across the book-shelf, and the shadow outlined a vaster and more menacing gesture—"all these books on this side of the room are books about crimes. But they only deal with the abnormal crimes."

" What do you mean by abnormal crimes ? "

" The failures. The crimes that have been found out. What proportion do you suppose they bear to the successful crimes—the ones we hear nothing about ? "

" In this country," said Parker, rather stiffly, " we manage to trace and convict the majority of criminals——"

" My good man, I know that where a crime is known to have been committed, you people manage to catch the perpetrator in at least sixty per cent of the cases. But the moment a crime is even suspected, it falls, *ipso facto*, into the category of failures. After that, the thing is merely a question of greater or less efficiency on the part of the police. But how about the crimes which are never even suspected ? "

Parker shrugged his shoulders.

" How can anybody answer that ? "

" Well—one may guess. Read any newspaper to-day. Read the *News of the World*. Or, now that the Press has been muzzled, read the divorce court lists. Wouldn't they give you the idea that marriage is a failure ? Isn't the sillier sort of journalism packed with articles to the same effect ? And yet, looking round among the marriages you know of personally, aren't the majority of them a success, in a hum-drum, undemonstrative sort of way ? Only you don't hear of them. People don't bother to come into court and explain that they dodder along very comfortably on the whole, thank you. Similarly, if you read all the books on this shelf, you'd come to the conclusion that murder was a failure. But bless you, it's always the failures that make the noise. Successful murderers don't write to the papers about it. They don't even join in imbecile symposia to tell an inquisitive world ' What Murder means to me,' or ' How I became a Successful Poisoner.' Happy murderers, like happy wives, keep quiet tongues. And they probably bear just about the same proportion to the failures as the divorced couples do to the happily mated."

" Aren't you putting it rather high ? "

" I don't know. Nor does anybody. That's the devil of it. But you ask any doctor, when you've got him in an unbuttoned, well-lubricated frame of mind, if he hasn't often had grisly suspicions which he could not and dared not take steps to verify. You see by our friend Carr what happens when one doctor is a trifle more courageous than the rest."

" Well, he couldn't prove anything."

" I know. But that doesn't mean there's nothing to be proved. Look at the scores and scores of murders that have gone unproved and unsuspected till the fool of a murderer went too far and did something silly which blew up the whole show. Palmer, for instance. His wife and brother and mother-in-law and various illegitimate children, all peacefully put away—till he made the mistake of polishing Cook off in that spectacular manner. Look at George Joseph Smith. Nobody'd have thought of bothering any more about those first two wives he drowned. It was only when he did it the third time that he aroused suspicion. Armstrong, too, is supposed to have got away with many more crimes than he was tried for—it was being clumsy over Martin and the chocolates that stirred up the hornets' nest in the end. Burke and Hare were convicted of murdering an old woman, and then brightly confessed that they'd put away sixteen people in two months and no one a penny the wiser."

" But they *were* caught."

" Because they were fools. If you murder someone in a brutal, messy way, or poison someone who has previously enjoyed rollicking health, or choose the very day after a will's been made in your favour to extinguish the testator, or go on killing everyone you meet till people begin to think you're first cousin to a upas tree, naturally you're found out in the end. But choose somebody old and ill, in circumstances where the benefit to yourself isn't too apparent, and use a sensible method that looks like natural death or accident, and don't repeat your effects too often, and you're safe. I swear all the heart-diseases and gastric enteritis and influenzas that get certified are not nature's unaided work. Murder's so easy, Charles, so damned easy—even without special training."

Parker looked troubled.

" There's something in what you say. I've heard some funny tales myself. We all do, I suppose. But Miss Dawson——"

" Miss Dawson fascinates me, Charles. Such a beautiful subject. So old and ill. So likely to die soon. Bound to die before long. No near relations to make inquiries. No connections or old friends in the neighbourhood. And so rich. Upon my soul, Charles, I lie in bed licking my lips over ways and means of murdering Miss Dawson."

" Well, anyhow, till you can think of one that defies analysis and doesn't seem to need a motive, you haven't found the right one," said Parker, practically, rather revolted by this ghoulish conversation.

" I admit that," replied Lord Peter, " but that only shows that as yet I'm merely a third-rate murderer. Wait till I've perfected my method and then I'll show you— perhaps. Some wise old buffer has said that each of us holds the life of one other person between his hands—but only one, Charles, only one."

CHAPTER IX

THE WILL

" Our wills are ours to make them thine."

TENNYSON : *In Memoriam*

"HULLO! hullo—ullo! oh, operator, shall I call thee bird or but a wandering voice?... Not at all, I had no intention of being rude, my child, that was a quotation from the poetry of Mr. Wordsworth... well, ring him again... thank you, is that Dr. Carr?... Lord Peter Wimsey speaking... oh, yes... yes... aha!... not a bit of it.... We are about to vindicate you and lead you home, decorated with triumphal wreaths of cinnamon and senna-pods.... No, really... we've come to the conclusion that the thing is serious.... Yes.... I want Nurse Forbes' address.... Right, I'll hold on.... Luton?... oh, Tooting, yes, I've got that.... Certainly, I've no doubt she's a tartar, but I'm the Grand Panjandrum with the little round button a-top.... Thanks awfully... cheer-frightfully-ho!—oh! I say!—hullo!—I say, she doesn't do Maternity work, does she? Maternity work?—M for Mother-in-law—Maternity?—No—You're sure?... It would be simply awful if she did and came along.... I couldn't possibly produce a baby for her.... As long as you're quite sure.... Right—right—yes—not for the world—nothing to do with you at all. Good-bye, old thing, good-bye."

Lord Peter hung up, whistling cheerfully, and called for Bunter.

"My lord?"

"What is the proper suit to put on, Bunter, when one is an expectant father?"

" I regret, my lord, to have seen no recent fashions in paternity wear. I should say, my lord, whichever suit your lordship fancies will induce a calm and cheerful frame of mind in the lady."

" Unfortunately I don't know the lady. She is, in fact, only the figment of an over-teeming brain. But I think the garments should express bright hope, self-congratulation, and a tinge of tender anxiety."

" A newly married situation, my lord, I take it. Then I would suggest the lounge suit in pale grey—the willow-pussy cloth, my lord—with a dull amethyst tie and socks and a soft hat. I would not recommend a bowler, my lord. The anxiety expressed in a bowler hat would be rather of the financial kind."

" No doubt you are right, Bunter. And I will wear those gloves that got so unfortunately soiled yesterday at Charing Cross. I am too agitated to worry about a clean pair."

" Very good, my lord."

" No stick, perhaps."

" Subject to your lordship's better judgment, I should suggest that a stick may be suitably handled to express emotion."

" You are always right, Bunter. Call me a taxi, and tell the man to drive to Tooting."

·　·　·　·　·　·　·　·

Nurse Forbes regretted very much. She would have liked to oblige Mr. Simms-Gaythorpe, but she never undertook maternity work. She wondered who could have misled Mr. Simms-Gaythorpe by giving him her name.

" Well, y'know, I can't say I was misled," said Mr. Simms-Gaythorpe, dropping his walking-stick and retrieving it with an ingenuous laugh. " Miss Murgatroyd—you know Miss Murgatroyd of Leahampton, I think—yes—she —that is, I heard about you through her " (this was a fact), " and she said what a charming person—excuse my repeatin' these personal remarks, won't you?—what a charmin' person you were and all that, and how nice it would be if we could persuade you to come, don't you see. But she said she was afraid perhaps you *didn't* do maternity work. Still, y'know, I thought it was worth tryin', what? Bein' so anxious, what?—about my wife, that is, you see. So necessary to have someone young and cheery at these—er—critical times, don't you know. Maternity nurses often such ancient and ponderous sort of people—if you don't mind my sayin' so. My wife's highly nervous—naturally—first effort and all that—doesn't like middle-aged people tramplin' round—you see the idea?"

Nurse Forbes, who was a bony woman of about forty, saw the point perfectly, and was very sorry she really could not see her way to undertaking the work.

"It was very kind of Miss Murgatroyd," she said. "Do you know her well? Such a delightful woman, is she not?"

The expectant father agreed.

"Miss Murgatroyd was so very much impressed by your sympathetic way—don't you know—of nursin' that poor old lady, Miss Dawson, y'know. Distant connection of my own, as a matter of fact—er, yes—somewhere about fifteenth cousin twelve times removed. So nervous, wasn't she? A little bit eccentric, like the rest of the family, but a charming old lady, don't you think?"

"I became very much attached to her," said Nurse Forbes. "When she was in full possession of her faculties, she was a most pleasant and thoughtful patient. Of course, she was in great pain, and we had to keep her under morphia a great part of the time."

"Ah, yes! poor old soul! I sometimes think, Nurse, it's a great pity we aren't allowed just to help people off, y'know, when they're so far gone. After all, they're practically dead already, as you might say. What's the point of keepin' them sufferin' on like that?"

Nurse Forbes looked rather sharply at him.

" I'm afraid that wouldn't do," she said, " though one understands the lay person's point of view, of course. Dr. Carr was not of your opinion," she added, a little acidly.

" I think all that fuss was simply shockin'," said the gentleman warmly. " Poor old soul ! I said to my wife at the time, why couldn't they let the poor old thing rest. Fancy cuttin' her about, when obviously she'd just mercifully gone off in a natural way ! My wife quite agreed with me. She was quite upset about it, don't you know."

" It was very distressing to everybody concerned," said Nurse Forbes, " and of course, it put me in a very awkward position. I ought not to talk about it, but as you are one of the family, you will quite understand."

" Just so. Did it ever occur to you, Nurse "—Mr. Simms-Gaythorpe leaned forward, crushing his soft hat between his hands in a nervous manner—" that there might be something behind all that ? "

Nurse Forbes primmed up her lips.

" You know," said Mr. Simms-Gaythorpe, " there *have* been cases of doctors tryin' to get rich old ladies to make wills in their favour. You don't think—eh ? "

Nurse Forbes intimated that it was not her business to think things.

" No, of course not, certainly not. But as man to man— I mean, between you and me, what ?—wasn't there a little —er—friction, perhaps, about sending for the solicitor-johnnie, don't you know ? Of course, my Cousin Mary— I call her cousin, so to speak, but it's no relation at all, really—of course, I mean, she's an awfully nice girl and all that sort of thing, but I'd got a sort of idea perhaps she wasn't altogether keen on having the will-making wallah sent for, what ? "

" Oh, Mr. Simms-Gaythorpe, I'm sure you're quite wrong there. Miss Whittaker was most anxious that her aunt should have every facility in that way. In fact—I don't think I'm betraying any confidence in telling you this—she said to me, 'If at any time Miss Dawson should express a wish to see a lawyer, be sure you send for him at once.' And so, of course, I did."

" You did ? And didn't he come, then ? "

" Certainly he came. There was no difficulty about it at all."

" There ! That just shows, doesn't it ? how wrong some of these gossipy females can be ! Excuse me, but y'know, I'd got absolutely the wrong impression about the thing. I'm quite *sure* Mrs. Peasgood said that no lawyer had been sent for."

" I don't know what Mrs. Peasgood could have known about it," said Nurse Forbes with a sniff, " her permission was not asked in the matter."

" Certainly not—but you know how these ideas get about. But, I say—if there was a will, why wasn't it produced ? "

" I didn't say that, Mr. Simms-Gaythorpe. There was no will. The lawyer came to draw up a power of attorney, so that Miss Whittaker could sign cheques and so on for her aunt. That was very necessary, you know, on account of the old lady's failing powers."

" Yes—I suppose she was pretty woolly towards the end."

" Well, she was quite sensible when I took over from Nurse Philliter in September, except, of course, for that fancy she had about poisoning."

" She really was afraid of that ? "

" She said once or twice, ' I'm not going to die to please anybody, Nurse.' She had great confidence in me. She got on better with me than with Miss Whittaker, to tell you the truth, Mr. Simms-Gaythorpe. But during October, her mind began to give way altogether, and she rambled a lot. She used to wake up sometimes all in a fright and say, ' Have they passed it yet, Nurse ? '—just like that. I'd say, ' No, they haven't got that far yet,' and that would quiet her. Thinking of her hunting days, I expect she was. They often go back like that, you know, when they're being kept under drugs. Dreaming, like, they are, half the time."

" Then in the last month or so, I suppose she could hardly have made a will, even if she had wanted to."

" No, I don't think she could have managed it then."

" But earlier on, when the lawyer was there, she could have done so if she had liked ? "

" Certainly she could."

" But she didn't ? "

" Oh no. I was there with her all the time, at her particular request."

" I see. Just you and Miss Whittaker."

" Not even Miss Whittaker most of the time. I see what you mean, Mr. Simms-Gaythorpe, but indeed you should clear your mind of any unkind suspicions of Miss Whittaker. The lawyer and Miss Dawson and myself were alone together for nearly an hour, while the clerk drew up the necessary papers in the next room. It was all done then, you see, because we thought that a second visit would be too much for Miss Dawson. Miss Whittaker only came in quite at the end. If Miss Dawson had wished to make a will, she had ample opportunity to do so."

" Well, I'm glad to hear that," said Mr. Simms-Gaythorpe, rising to go. " These little doubts are so apt to make unpleasantness in families, don't you know. Well, I must be toddlin' now. I'm frightfully sorry you can't come to us, Nurse—my wife will be so disappointed. I must try to find somebody else equally charmin' if possible. Good-bye."

Lord Peter removed his hat in the taxi and scratched his head thoughtfully.

" Another good theory gone wrong," he murmured. " Well, there's another string to the jolly old bow yet. Cropper first and then Crofton—that's the line to take, I fancy."

PART II

THE LEGAL PROBLEM

" The gladsome light of jurisprudence."
SIR EDWARD COKE

NOTE—A genealogical table is printed
at the end of the book

CHAPTER X

THE WILL AGAIN

"The will! the will! We will hear Cæsar's will!"

JULIUS CÆSAR

"Oh, Miss Evelyn, my dear, oh, poor dear!"
The tall girl in black started, and looked round.

"Why, Mrs. Gulliver—how very, very kind of you to
come and meet me!"

"And glad I am to have the chance, my dear, all owing
to these kind gentlemen," cried the landlady, flinging her
arms round the girl and clinging to her to the great annoyance of the other passengers pouring off the gangway.
The elder of the two gentlemen referred to gently put his
hand on her arm, and drew them out of the stream of
traffic.

"Poor lamb!" mourned Mrs. Gulliver, "coming all
this way by your lonesome, and poor dear Miss Bertha
in her grave and such terrible things said, and her such
a good girl always."

"It's poor mother I'm thinking about," said the girl.
"I couldn't rest. I said to my husband, 'I must go,' I said,
and he said, 'My honey, if I could come with you I would,
but I can't leave the farm, but if you feel you ought to go,
you shall,' he said."

"Dear Mr. Cropper—he was always that good and
kind," said Mrs. Gulliver, "but here I am, forgittin' all
about the good gentlemen as brought me all this way to
see you. This is Lord Peter Wimsey, and this is Mr. Murbles,
as put in that unfortnit advertisement, as I truly believes
was the beginnin' of it all. 'Ow I wish I'd never showed
it to your poor sister, not but wot I believe the gentleman

acted with the best intentions, 'avin' now seen 'im, which at first I thought 'e was a wrong 'un."

"Pleased to meet you," said Mrs. Cropper, turning with the ready address derived from service in a big restaurant. "Just before I sailed I got a letter from poor Bertha enclosing your ad. I couldn't make anything of it, but I'd be glad to know anything which can clear up this shocking business. What have they said it is—murder?"

"There was a verdict of natural death at the inquiry," said Mr. Murbles, "but we feel that the case presents some inconsistencies, and shall be exceedingly grateful for your co-operation in looking into the matter, and also in connection with another matter which may or may not have some bearing upon it."

"Righto," said Mrs. Cropper. "I'm sure you're proper gentlemen, if Mrs. Gulliver answers for you, for I've never known her mistaken in a person yet, have I, Mrs. G? I'll tell you anything I know, which isn't much, for it's all a horrible mystery to me. Only I don't want you to delay me, for I've got to go straight on down to Mother. She'll be in a dreadful way, so fond as she was of Bertha, and she's all alone except for the young girl that looks after her, and that's not much comfort when you've lost your daughter so sudden."

"We shall not detain you a moment, Mrs. Cropper," said Mr. Murbles. "We propose, if you will allow us, to accompany you to London, and to ask you a few questions on the way, and then—again with your permission—we should like to see you safely home to Mrs. Gotobed's house, wherever that may be."

"Christchurch, near Bournemouth," said Lord Peter. "I'll run you down straight away, if you like. It will save time."

"I say, you know all about it, don't you?" exclaimed Mrs. Cropper with some admiration. "Well, hadn't we better get a move on, or we'll miss this train?"

" Quite right," said Mr. Murbles. " Allow me to offer you my arm."

Mrs. Cropper approving of this arrangement, the party made its way to the station, after the usual disembarkation formalities. As they passed the barrier on to the platform Mrs. Cropper gave a little exclamation and leaned forward as though something had caught her eye.

" What is it, Mrs. Cropper? " said Lord Peter's voice in her ear. " Did you think you recognised somebody? "

" You're a noticing one, aren't you? " said Mrs. Cropper. " Make a good waiter—you would—not meaning any offence, sir, that's a real compliment from one who knows. Yes, I did think I saw someone, but it couldn't be, because the minute she caught my eye she went away."

" Who did you think it was? "

" Why, I thought it looked like Miss Whittaker, as Bertha and me used to work for."

" Where was she? "

" Just down by that pillar there, a tall dark lady in a crimson hat and grey fur. But she's gone now."

" Excuse me."

Lord Peter unhitched Mrs. Gulliver from his arm, hitched her smartly on to the unoccupied arm of Mr. Murbles, and plunged into the crowd. Mr. Murbles, quite unperturbed by this eccentric behaviour, shepherded the two women into an empty first-class carriage which, Mrs. Cropper noted, bore a large label, " Reserved for Lord Peter Wimsey and party." Mrs. Cropper made some protesting observation about her ticket, but Mr. Murbles merely replied that everything was provided for, and that privacy could be more conveniently secured in this way.

" Your friend's going to be left behind," said Mrs. Cropper as the train moved out.

" That would be very unlike him," replied Mr. Murbles, calmly unfolding a couple of rugs and exchanging his old-fashioned top-hat for a curious kind of travelling cap with flaps to it. Mrs. Cropper, in the midst of her anxiety, could not help wondering where in the world he had contrived to purchase this Victorian relic. As a matter of fact, Mr. Murbles' caps were specially made to his own design by an exceedingly expensive West End hatter, who held Mr. Murbles in deep respect as a real gentleman of the old school.

Nothing, however, was seen of Lord Peter for something like a quarter of an hour, when he suddenly put his head in with an amiable smile and said :

" One red-haired woman in a crimson hat ; three dark women in black hats ; several nondescript women in those pull-on sort of dust-coloured hats ; old women with grey hair, various ; sixteen flappers without hats—hats on rack, I mean, but none of 'em crimson ; two obvious brides in blue hats ; innumerable fair women in hats of all colours ; one ash-blonde dressed as a nurse, none of 'em our friend as far as I know. Thought I'd best just toddle along the train to make sure. There's just one dark sort of female whose hat I can't see because it's tucked down beside her. Wonder if Mrs. Cropper would mind doin' a little stagger down the corridor to take a squint at her."

Mrs. Cropper, with some surprise, consented to do so.

" Right you are. 'Splain later. About four carriages along. Now, look here, Mrs. Cropper, if it *should* be anybody you know, I'd rather on the whole she didn't spot you watching her. I want you to walk along behind me, just glancin' into the compartments but keepin' your collar turned up. When we come to the party I have in mind, I'll make a screen for you, what ? "

These manœuvres were successfully accomplished, Lord Peter lighting a cigarette opposite the suspected compartment, while Mrs. Cropper viewed the hatless lady under cover of his raised elbows. But the result was disappointing. Mrs. Cropper had never seen the lady before, and a further

promenade from end to end of the train produced no better
results.

" We must leave it to Bunter, then," said his lordship,
cheerfully, as they returned to their seats. " I put him on
the trail as soon as you gave me the good word. Now, Mrs.
Cropper, we really get down to business. First of all, we
should be glad of any suggestions you may have to make
about your sister's death. We don't want to distress you,
but we have got an idea that there might, just possibly, be
something behind it."

" There's just one thing, sir—your lordship, I suppose I
should say. Bertha was a real good girl—I can answer
for that absolutely. There wouldn't have been any carryings-
on with her young man—nothing of that. I know people
have been saying all sorts of things, and perhaps, with lots
of girls as they are, it isn't to be wondered at. But, believe
me, Bertha wouldn't go for to do anything that wasn't
right. Perhaps you'd like to see this last letter she wrote me.
I'm sure nothing could be nicer and properer from a girl
just looking forward to a happy marriage. Now, a girl as
wrote like that wouldn't be going larking about, sir, would
she? I couldn't rest, thinking they was saying that about her."

Lord Peter took the letter, glanced through it, and
handed it reverently to Mr. Murbles.

" We're not thinking that at all, Mrs. Cropper, though of
course we're very glad to have your point of view, don't you
see. Now, do you think it possible your sister might have
been—what shall I say?—got hold of by some woman with
a plausible story and all that, and—well—pushed into some
position which shocked her very much? Was she cautious
and up to the tricks of London people and all that? "

And he outlined Parker's theory of the engaging Mrs.
Forrest and the supposed dinner in the flat.

" Well, my lord, I wouldn't say Bertha was a very quick
girl—not as quick as me, you know. She'd always be ready
to believe what she was told and give people credit for the

best. Took more after her father, like. I'm mother's girl, they always said, and I don't trust anybody further than I can see them. But I'd warned her very careful against taking up with women as talks to a girl in the street, and she did ought to have been on her guard."

" Of course," said Peter, " it may have been somebody she'd got to know quite well—say, at the restaurant, and she thought she was a nice lady and there'd be no harm in going to see her. Or the lady might have suggested taking her into good service. One never knows."

" I think she'd have mentioned it in her letters if she'd talked to the lady much, my lord. It's wonderful what a lot of things she'd find to tell me about the customers. And I don't think she'd be for going into service again. We got real fed up with service, down in Leahampton."

" Ah, yes. Now that brings us to quite a different point —the thing we wanted to ask you or your sister about before this sad accident took place. You were in service with this Miss Whittaker whom you mentioned just now. I wonder if you'd mind telling us just exactly why you left. It was a good place, I suppose ? "

" Yes, my lord, quite a good place as places go, though of course a girl doesn't get her freedom the way she does in a restaurant. And naturally there was a good deal of waiting on the old lady. Not as we minded that, for she was a very kind, good lady, and generous too."

" But when she became so ill, I suppose Miss Whittaker managed everything, what ? "

" Yes, my lord ; but it wasn't a hard place—lots of the girls envied us. Only Miss Whittaker was very particular."

" Especially about the china, what ? "

" Ah, they told you about that, then ? "

" I told 'em, dearie," put in Mrs. Gulliver, " I told 'em all about how you come to leave your place and go to London."

" And it struck us," put in Mr. Murbles, " that it was,

shall we say, somewhat rash of Miss Whittaker to dismiss so competent and, if I may put it so, so well-spoken and personable a pair of maids on so trivial a pretext."

"You're right there, sir. Bertha—I told you she was the trusting one—she was quite ready to believe as she done wrong, and thought how good it was of Miss Whittaker to forgive her breaking the china, and take so much interest in sending us to London, but I always thought there was something more than met the eye. Didn't I, Mrs. Gulliver?"

"That you did, dear ; something more than meets the eye, that's what you says to me, and what I agrees with."

"And did you, in your own mind," pursued Mr. Murbles, "connect this sudden dismissal with anything which had taken place ? "

"Well, I did then," replied Mrs. Cropper, with some spirit. " I said to Bertha—but she would hear nothing of it, taking after her father as I tell you—I said, ' Mark my words,' I said, ' Miss Whittaker don't care to have us in the house after the row she had with the old lady.' "

"And what row was that ? " inquired Mr. Murbles.

"Well, I don't know as I ought rightly to tell you about it, seeing it's all over now and we promised to say nothing about it."

"That, of course," said Mr. Murbles, checking Lord Peter, who was about to burst in impetuously, " depends upon your own conscience. But, if it will be of any help to you in making up your mind, I think I may say, in the strictest confidence, that this information may be of the utmost importance to us—in a roundabout way which I won't trouble you with—in investigating a very singular set of circumstances which have been brought to our notice. And it is just barely possible—again in a very roundabout way—that it may assist us in throwing some light on the melancholy tragedy of your sister's decease. Further than that I cannot go at the moment."

"Well, now," said Mrs. Cropper, " if that's so—though,

mind you, I don't see what connection there could be—but if you think that's so, I reckon I'd better come across with it, as my husband would say. After all, I only promised I wouldn't mention about it to the people in Leahampton, as might have made mischief out of it—and a gossipy lot they is, and no mistake."

" We've nothing to do with the Leahampton crowd," said his lordship, " and it won't be passed along unless it turns out to be necessary."

" Righto. Well, I'll tell you. One morning early in September Miss Whittaker comes along to Bertha and I, and says, ' I want you girls to be just handy on the landing outside Miss Dawson's bedroom,' she says, ' because I may want you to come in and witness her signature to a document. We shall want two witnesses,' she says, ' and you'll have to see her sign ; but I don't want to flurry her with a lot of people in the room, so when I give you the tip, I want you to come just inside the door without making a noise, so that you can see her write her name, and then I'll bring it straight across to you and you can write your names where I show you. It's quite easy,' she says, ' nothing to do but just put your names opposite where you see the word Witnesses.'

" Bertha was always a bit the timid sort—afraid of documents and that sort of thing, and she tried to get out of it. ' Couldn't Nurse sign instead of me ? ' she says. That was Nurse Philliter, you know, the red-haired one as was the doctor's fiancée. She was a very nice woman, and we liked her quite a lot. ' Nurse has gone out for her walk,' says Miss Whittaker, rather sharp, ' I want you and Evelyn to do it,' meaning me, of course. Well, we said we didn't mind, and Miss Whittaker goes upstairs to Miss Dawson with a whole heap of papers, and Bertha and I followed and waited on the landing, like she said."

" One moment," said Mr. Murbles, " did Miss Dawson often have documents to sign ? "

" Yes, sir, I believe so, quite frequently, but they was usually witnessed by Miss Whittaker or the nurse. There was some leases and things of that sort, or so I heard. Miss Dawson had a little house-property. And then there'd be the cheques for the housekeeping, and some papers as used to come from the Bank and be put away in the safe."

" Share coupons and so on, I suppose," said Mr. Murbles.

" Very likely, sir, I don't know much about those business matters. I did have to witness a signature once, I remember, a long time back, but that was different. The paper was brought down to me with the signature ready wrote. There wasn't any of this to-do about it."

" The old lady was capable of dealing with her own affairs, I understand ? "

" Up till then, sir. Afterwards, as I understood, she made it all over to Miss Whittaker—that was just before she got feeble-like, and was kept under drugs. Miss Whittaker signed the cheques then."

" The power of attorney," said Mr. Murbles, with a nod. " Well now, did you sign this mysterious paper ? "

" No, sir, I'll tell you how that was. When me and Bertha had been waiting a little time, Miss Whittaker comes to the door and makes us a sign to come in quiet. So we comes and stands just inside the door. There was a screen by the head of the bed, so we couldn't see Miss Dawson nor she us, but we could see her reflection quite well in a big looking-glass she had on the left side of the bed."

Mr. Murbles exchanged a significant glance with Lord Peter.

" Now be sure you tell us every detail," said Wimsey, " no matter how small and silly it may sound. I believe this is goin' to be very excitin'."

" Yes, my lord. Well, there wasn't much else, except that just inside the door, on the left-hand side as you went in, there was a little table, where Nurse mostly used to set down trays and things that had to go down, and it was cleared, and a piece of blotting-paper on it and an inkstand and pen, all ready for us to sign with."

" Could Miss Dawson see that ? " asked Mr. Murbles.

" No, sir, because of the screen."

" But it was inside the room."

" Yes, sir."

" We want to be quite clear about this. Do you think you could draw—quite roughly—a little plan of the room, showing where the bed was and the screen and the mirror, and so on ? "

" I'm not much of a hand at drawing," said Mrs. Cropper dubiously, " but I'll try."

Mr. Murbles produced a notebook and fountain pen, and after a few false starts, the following rough sketch was produced. (*See next page.*)

" Thank you, that is very clear indeed. You notice, Lord Peter, the careful arrangements to have the document signed in presence of the witnesses, and witnessed by them in the presence of Miss Dawson and of each other. I needn't tell you for what kind of document that arrangement is indispensable."

" Was that it, sir ? We couldn't understand why it was all arranged like that."

" It might have happened," explained Mr. Murbles, " that in case of some dispute about this document, you and your sister would have had to come into court and give evidence about it. And if so, you would have been asked whether you actually saw Miss Dawson write her signature, and whether you and your sister and Miss Dawson were all in the same room together when you signed your names as witnesses. And if that had happened, you could have said yes, couldn't you, and sworn to it ? "

" Oh, yes."

" And yet, actually, Miss Dawson would have known nothing about your being there."

'No, sir."

" That was it, you see."

" I see now, sir, but at the time Bertha and me couldn't make nothing of it."

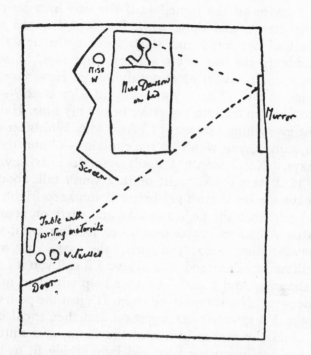

" But the document, you say, was never signed."

" No, sir. At any rate, we never witnessed anything. We saw Miss Dawson write her name—at least, I suppose it was her name—to one or two papers, and then Miss Whittaker puts another lot in front of her and says, ' Here's another little lot, auntie, some more of those income-tax forms.' So the old lady says, ' What are they exactly, dear, let me see ? ' So Miss Whittaker says, " Oh, only the usual things.' And Miss Dawson says, ' Dear, dear, what a lot of them. How complicated they do make these things to be sure.' And we could see that Miss Whittaker was giving her several papers, all laid on top of one another, with

just the places for the signatures left showing. So Miss
Dawson signs the top one, and then lifts up the paper and
looks underneath at the next one, and Miss Whittaker
says, ' They're all the same,' as if she was in a hurry to
get them signed and done with. But Miss Dawson takes
them out of her hand and starts looking through them,
and suddenly she lets out a screech, and says, ' I won't
have it, I won't have it ! I'm not dying yet. How dare you,
you wicked girl ! Can't you wait till I'm dead ?—You
want to frighten me into my grave before my time. Haven't
you got everything you want ? ' And Miss Whittaker says,
' Hush, auntie, you won't let me explain——' and the old
lady says, ' No, I won't, I don't want to hear anything
about it. I hate the thought of it. I won't talk about it.
You leave me be. I can't get better if you keep frightening
me so.' And then she begins to take and carry on dreadful,
and Miss Whittaker comes over to us looking awful white
and says, ' Run along, you girls,' she says, ' my aunt's
taken ill and can't attend to business. I'll call you if I want
you,' she says. And I said, ' Can we help with her, miss ? '
and she says, ' No, it's quite all right. It's just the pain come
on again. I'll give her her injection and then she'll be all
right.' And she pushes us out of the room, and shuts the
door, and we heard the poor old lady crying fit to break
anybody's heart. So we went downstairs and met Nurse
just coming in, and we told her Miss Dawson was took worse
again, and she runs up quick without taking her things off.
So we was in the kitchen, just saying it seemed rather funny-
like, when Miss Whittaker comes down again and says,
' It's all right now, and Auntie's sleeping quite peaceful,
only we'll have to put off business till another day.' And
she says, ' Better not say anything about this to anybody,
because when the pain comes on Aunt gets frightened and
talks a bit wild. She don't mean what she says, but if people
was to hear about it they might think it odd.' So I up and
says, ' Miss Whittaker,' I says, ' me and Bertha was never

ones to talk ' ; rather stiff, I said it, because I don't hold by gossip and never did. And Miss Whittaker says, ' That's quite all right,' and goes away. And the next day she gives us an afternoon off and a present—ten shillings each, it was, because it was her aunt's birthday, and the old lady wanted us to have a little treat in her honour."

" A very clear account indeed, Mrs. Cropper, and I only wish all witnesses were as sensible and observant as you are. There's just one thing. Did you by any chance get a sight of this paper that upset Miss Dawson so much ? "

" No, sir—only from a distance, that is, and in the looking-glass. But I think it was quite short—just a few lines of type-writing."

" I see. Was there a typewriter in the house, by the way ? "

" Oh, yes, sir. Miss Whittaker used one quite often for business letters and so on. It used to stand in the sitting-room."

" Quite so. By the way, do you remember Miss Dawson's solicitor calling shortly after this ? "

" No, sir. It was only a little time later Bertha broke the teapot and we left. Miss Whittaker gave her her month's warning, but I said no. If she could come down on a girl like that for a little thing, and her such a good worker, Bertha should go at once and me with her. Miss Whittaker said, ' Just as you like,' she said—she never was one to stand any back-chat. So we went that afternoon. But afterwards I think she was sorry, and came over to see us at Christchurch, and suggested why shouldn't we try for a better job in London. Bertha was a bit afraid to go so far —taking after Father, as I mentioned, but Mother, as was always the ambitious one, she says, ' If the lady's kind enough to give you a good start, why not go ? There's more chances for a girl in Town.' And I said to Bertha, private-like, afterwards, I says, ' Depend on it, Miss Whittaker wants to see the back of us. She's afraid we'll

get talking about the things Miss Dawson said that morning.
But, I says, if she's willing to pay us to go, why not go, I
says. A girl's got to look out for herself these days, and if
we go off to London she'll give us a better character than
what she would if we stayed. And anyway, I said, if we
don't like it we can always come home again.' So the long
and short was, we came to Town, and after a bit we got
good jobs with Lyons, what with the good character Miss
Whittaker gave us, and I met my husband there and
Bertha met her Jim. So we never regretted having taken
the chance—not till this dreadful thing happened to
Bertha."

The passionate interest with which her hearers had
received this recital must have gratified Mrs. Cropper's
sense of the dramatic. Mr. Murbles was very slowly
rotating his hands over one another with a dry, rustling
sound—like an old snake, gliding through the long grass
in search of prey.

" A little scene after your own heart, Murbles," said
Lord Peter, with a glint under his dropped eyelids. He
turned again to Mrs. Cropper.

" This is the first time you've told this story ? "

" Yes—and I wouldn't have said anything if it hadn't
been——"

" I know. Now, if you'll take my advice, Mrs. Cropper,
you won't tell it again. Stories like that have a nasty way
of bein' dangerous. Will you consider it an impertinence
if I ask you what your plans are for the next week or
two ? "

" I'm going to see Mother and get her to come back to
Canada with me. I wanted her to come when I got married,
but she didn't like going so far away from Bertha. She
was always Mother's favourite—taking so much after
Father, you see. Mother and me was always too much alike
to get on. But now she's got nobody else, and it isn't right
for her to be all alone, so I think she'll come with me. It's

a long journey for an ailing old woman, but I reckon blood's thicker than water. My husband said, ' Bring her back first-class, my girl, and I'll find the money.' He's a good sort, is my husband."

" You couldn't do better," said Wimsey, " and if you'll allow me, I'll send a friend to look after you both on the train journey and see you safe on to the boat. And don't stop long in England. Excuse me buttin' in on your affairs like this, but honestly I think you'd be safer elsewhere."

" You don't think that Bertha—— ? "

Her eyes widened with alarm.

" I don't like to say quite what I think, because I don't know. But I'll see you and your mother are safe, whatever happens."

" And Bertha ? Can I do anything about that ? "

" Well, you'll have to come and see my friends at Scotland Yard, I think, and tell them what you've told me. They'll be interested."

" And will something be done about it ? "

" I'm sure, if we can prove there's been any foul play, the police won't rest till it's been tracked down to the right person. But the difficulty is, you see, to prove that the death wasn't natural."

" I observe in to-day's paper," said Mr. Murbles, " that the local superintendent is now satisfied that Miss Gotobed came down alone for a quiet picnic and died of a heart attack."

" That man would say anything," said Wimsey. " We know from the post-mortem that she had recently had a heavy meal—forgive these distressin' details, Mrs. Cropper —so why the picnic ? "

" I suppose they had the sandwiches and the beer-bottle in mind," said Mr. Murbles, mildly.

" I see. I suppose she went down to Epping alone with a bottle of Bass and took out the cork with her fingers. Ever tried doing it, Murbles ? No ? Well, when they find the

corkscrew I'll believe she went there alone. In the meantime, I hope the papers will publish a few more theories
like that. Nothin' like inspiring criminals with confidence,
Murbles—it goes to their heads, you know."

CHAPTER XI

CROSS-ROADS

" Patience—and shuffle the cards."

DON QUIXOTE

LORD PETER took Mrs. Cropper down to Christchurch and returned to town to have a conference with Mr. Parker. The latter had just listened to his recital of Mrs. Cropper's story, when the discreet opening and closing of the flat door announced the return of Bunter.

" Any luck ? " inquired Wimsey.

" I regret exceedingly to have to inform your lordship that I lost track of the lady. In fact, if your lordship will kindly excuse the expression, I was completely done in the eye."

" Thank God, Bunter, you're human after all. I didn't know anybody could do you. Have a drink."

" I am much obliged to your lordship. According to instructions, I searched the platform for a lady in a crimson hat and a grey fur, and at length was fortunate enough to observe her making her way out by the station entrance towards the big bookstall. She was some way ahead of me, but the hat was very conspicuous, and, in the words of the poet, if I may so express myself, I followed the gleam."

" Stout fellow."

" Thank you, my lord. The lady walked into the Station Hotel, which, as you know, has two entrances, one upon the platform, and the other upon the street. I hurried after her for fear she should give me the slip, and made my way through the revolving doors just in time to see her back disappearing into the Ladies' Retiring Room."

" Whither, as a modest man, you could not follow her. I quite understand."

" Quite so, my lord. I took a seat in the entrance hall, in a position from which I could watch the door without appearing to do so."

" And discovered too late that the place had two exits, I suppose. Unusual and distressin'."

" No, my lord. That was not the trouble. I sat watching for three quarters of an hour, but the crimson hat did not reappear. Your lordship will bear in mind that I had never seen the lady's face."

Lord Peter groaned.

" I foresee the end of this story, Bunter. Not your fault. Proceed."

" At the end of this time, my lord, I felt bound to conclude either that the lady had been taken ill or that something untoward had occurred. I summoned a female attendant who happened to cross the hall and informed her that I had been entrusted with a message for a lady whose dress I described. I begged her to ascertain from the attendant in the Ladies' Room whether the lady in question was still there. The girl went away and presently returned to say that the lady had changed her costume in the cloakroom and had gone out half an hour previously."

" Oh, Bunter, Bunter. Didn't you spot the suitcase or whatever it was when she came out again ? "

" Excuse me, my lord. The lady had come in earlier in the day and had left an attaché-case in charge of the attendant. On returning, she had transferred her hat and fur to the attaché-case and put on a small black felt hat and a light-weight raincoat which she had packed there in readiness. So that her dress was concealed when she emerged and she was carrying the attaché-case, whereas, when I first saw her, she had been empty-handed."

" Everything foreseen. What a woman ! "

" I made immediate inquiries, my lord, in the region of

the hotel and the station, but without result. The black hat and raincoat were entirely inconspicuous, and no one remembered having seen her. I went to the Central Station to discover if she had travelled by any train. Several women answering to the description had taken tickets for various destinations, but I could get no definite information. I also visited all the garages in Liverpool, with the same lack of success. I am greatly distressed to have failed your lordship."

" Can't be helped. You did everything you could do. Cheer up. Never say die. And you must be tired to death. Take the day off and go to bed."

" I thank your lordship, but I slept excellently in the train on the way up."

" Just as you like, Bunter. But I did hope you sometimes got tired like other people."

Bunter smiled discreetly and withdrew.

" Well, we've gained this much, anyhow," said Parker. " We know now that this Miss Whittaker has something to conceal, since she takes such precautions to avoid being followed."

" We know more than that. We know that she was desperately anxious to get hold of the Cropper woman before anybody else could see her, no doubt to stop her mouth by bribery or by worse means. By the way, how did she know she was coming by that boat ? "

" Mrs. Cropper sent a cable, which was read at the inquest."

" Damn these inquests. They give away all the information one wants kept quiet, and produce no evidence worth having."

" Hear, hear," said Parker, with emphasis, " not to mention that we had to sit through a lot of moral punk by the Coroner, about the prevalence of jazz and the immoral behaviour of modern girls in going off alone with young men to Epping Forest."

" It's a pity these busy-bodies can't be had up for libel. Never mind. We'll get the Whittaker woman yet."

" Always provided it was the Whittaker woman. After all, Mrs. Cropper may have been mistaken. Lots of people do change their hats in cloak-rooms without any criminal intention."

" Oh, of course. Miss Whittaker's supposed to be in the country with Miss Findlater, isn't she ? We'll get the invaluable Miss Climpson to pump the girl when they turn up again. Meanwhile, what do you think of Mrs. Cropper's story ? "

" There's no doubt about what happened there. Miss Whittaker was trying to get the old lady to sign a will without knowing it. She gave it to her all mixed up with the income-tax papers, hoping she'd put her name to it without reading it. It must have been a will, I think, because that's the only document I know of which is invalid unless it's witnessed by two persons in the presence of the testatrix and of each other."

" Exactly. And since Miss Whittaker couldn't be one of the witnesses herself, but had to get the two maids to sign, the will must have been in Miss Whittaker's favour."

" Obviously. She wouldn't go to all that trouble to disinherit herself."

" But that brings us to another difficulty. Miss Whittaker, as next of kin, would have taken all the old lady had to leave in any case. As a matter of fact, she did. Why bother about a will ? "

" Perhaps, as we said before, she was afraid Miss Dawson would change her mind, and wanted to get a will made out before—no, that won't work."

" No—because, anyhow, any will made later would invalidate the first will. Besides, the old lady sent for her solicitor some time later, and Miss Whittaker put no obstacle of any kind in her way."

" According to Nurse Forbes, she was particularly anxious that every facility should be given."

" Seeing how Miss Dawson distrusted her niece, it's a bit surprising, really, that she didn't will the money away. Then it would have been to Miss Whittaker's advantage to keep her alive as long as possible."

" I don't suppose she really distrusted her—not to the extent of expecting to be made away with. She was excited and said more than she meant—we often do."

" Yes, but she evidently thought there'd be other attempts to get a will signed."

" How do you make that out ? "

" Don't you remember the power of attorney ? The old girl evidently thought that out and decided to give Miss Whittaker authority to sign everything for her so that there couldn't possibly be any jiggery-pokery about papers in future."

" Of course. Cute old lady. How very irritating for Miss Whittaker. And after that very hopeful visit of the solicitor, too. So disappointing. Instead of the expected will, a very carefully planted spoke in her wheel."

" Yes. But we're still brought up against the problem, why a will at all ? "

" So we are."

The two men pulled at their pipes for some time in silence.

" The aunt evidently intended the money to go to Mary Whittaker all right," remarked Parker at last. " She promised it so often—besides, I daresay she was a just-minded old thing, and remembered that it was really Whittaker money which had come to her over the head of the Rev. Charles, or whatever his name was."

" That's so. Well, there's only one thing that could prevent that happening, and that's—oh, lord ! old son. Do you know what it works out at ?—The old, old story, beloved of novelists—the missing heir ! "

" Good lord, yes, you're right. Damn it all, what fools we were not to think of it before. Mary Whittaker possibly found out that there was some nearer relative left, who would scoop the lot. Maybe she was afraid that if Miss Dawson got to know about it, she'd divide the money or disinherit Mary altogether. Or perhaps she just despaired of hammering the story into the old lady's head, and so hit on the idea of getting her to make the will unbeknownst to herself in Mary's favour."

" What a brain you've got, Charles. Or, see here, Miss Dawson may have known all about it, sly old thing, and determined to pay Miss Whittaker out for her indecent urgency in the matter of will-makin' by just dyin' intestate in the other chappie's favour."

" If she did, she deserved anything she got," said Parker, rather viciously. " After taking the poor girl away from her job under promise of leaving her the dibs."

" Teach the young woman not to be so mercenary," retorted Wimsey, with the cheerful brutality of the man who has never in his life been short of money.

" If this bright idea is correct," said Parker, " it rather messes up your murder theory, doesn't it ? Because Mary would obviously take the line of keeping her aunt alive as long as possible, in hopes she might make a will after all."

" That's true. Curse you, Charles, I see that bet of mine going west. What a blow for friend Carr, too. I did hope I was going to vindicate him and have him played home by the village band under a triumphal arch with ' Welcome, Champion of Truth ! ' picked out in red-white-and-blue electric bulbs. Never mind. It's better to lose a wager and see the light than walk in ignorance bloated with gold. —Or stop !—why shouldn't Carr be right after all ? Perhaps it's just my choice of a murderer that's wrong. Aha ! I see a new and even more sinister villain step upon the scene. The new claimant, warned by his minions——"

" What minions ? "

" Oh, don't be so pernickety, Charles. Nurse Forbes, probably. I shouldn't wonder if she's in his pay. Where was I ? I wish you wouldn't interrupt."

" Warned by his minions——" prompted Parker.

" Oh, yes—warned by his minions that Miss Dawson is hob-nobbing with solicitors and being tempted into making wills and things, gets the said minions to polish her off before she can do any mischief."

" Yes, but how ? "

" Oh, by one of those native poisons which slay in a split second and defy the skill of the analyst. They are familiar to the meanest writer of mystery stories. I'm not going to let a trifle like that stand in my way."

" And why hasn't this hypothetical gentleman brought forward any claim to the property so far ? "

" He's biding his time. The fuss about the death scared him, and he's lying low till it's all blown over."

" He'll find it much more awkward to dispossess Miss Whittaker now she's taken possession. Possession is nine points of the law, you know."

" I know, but he's going to pretend he wasn't anywhere near at the time of Miss Dawson's death. He only read about it a few weeks ago in a sheet of newspaper wrapped round a salmon-tin, and now he's rushing home from his distant farm in thing-ma-jig to proclaim himself as the long-lost Cousin Tom. . . . Great Scott ! that reminds me."

He plunged his hand into his pocket and pulled out a letter.

" This came this morning just as I was going out, and I met Freddy Arbuthnot on the doorstep and shoved it into my pocket before I'd read it properly. But I do believe there was something in it about a Cousin Somebody from some god-forsaken spot. Let's see."

He unfolded the letter, which was written in Miss Climpson's old-fashioned flowing hand, and ornamented with

such a variety of underlinings and exclamation marks as
to look like an exercise in musical notation.

" Oh, lord ! " said Parker.

" Yes, it's worse than usual, isn't it ?—it must be of
desperate importance. Luckily it's comparatively short."

" MY DEAR LORD PETER,

" I heard something this morning which MAY be of
use, so I HASTEN to communicate it ! ! You remember
I *mentioned before* that Mrs. Budge's *maid* is the SISTER of
the *present* maid at Miss *Whittaker's* ? WELL ! ! ! The AUNT
of these two girls came to *pay a visit* to Mrs. Budge's girl
this afternoon, and was *introduced* to *me*—of course, as
boarder at Mrs. Budge's I am naturally an *object of local
interest*—and, bearing *your instructions* in mind, I *encourage*
this to an extent I should not otherwise do ! !

" It appears that this *aunt* was well acquainted with
a *former housekeeper* of Miss Dawson's—*before* the time of
the Gotobed girls, I mean. The *aunt* is a highly *respectable* person of FORBIDDING ASPECT !—with a *bonnet* (!),
and to my mind, a most *disagreeable* CENSORIOUS woman.
However !—We got to speaking of Miss Dawson's death,
and this aunt—her name is Timmins—*primmed* up her
mouth and said : ' No unpleasant scandal would surprise
me about *that* family, Miss Climpson. They were *most*
UNDESIRABLY connected ! You recollect, Mrs. Budge,
that I felt *obliged to leave* after the appearance of that
most EXTRAORDINARY person who announced himself as
Miss Dawson's cousin.' Naturally, I asked *who* this *might
be*, not having heard of any *other relations* ! She said that
this person, whom she described as a *nasty*, DIRTY
NIGGER (! ! !) arrived one morning, dressed up as a
CLERGYMAN ! ! !—and sent her—Miss Timmins—to announce him to Miss Dawson as her COUSIN HALLE-
LUJAH ! ! ! Miss Timmins showed him up, *much against
her will*, she said, into the *nice*, CLEAN, drawing-room !

Miss Dawson, she said, actually *came down* to see this 'creature' instead of sending him about his 'black business' (!), and as a *crowning scandal*, asked him to *stay to lunch* !—'with her niece there, too,' Miss Timmins said, 'and this horrible *blackamoor* ROLLING his dreadful eyes at her.' Miss Timmins said that it 'regularly turned her stomach'—that was her phrase, and I trust you will excuse it—I understand that these *parts of the body* are frequently referred to in polite (!) society nowadays. In fact, it appears she *refused to cook the lunch* for the poor black man—(after all, even *blacks* are *God's creatures* and we might *all* be *black* OURSELVES if He had not in His infinite kindness seen fit to *favour us* with *white* skins ! !)—and walked straight out of the house ! ! ! So that unfortunately she cannot tell us anything *further* about this *remarkable* incident ! She is *certain*, however, that the 'nigger' had a *visiting-card*, with the name 'Rev. H. Dawson' upon it, and an address in foreign parts. It does seem *strange*, does it not, but I believe many of these *native preachers* are called to do *splendid work* among their own people, and no doubt a MINISTER is entitled to have a *visiting-card*, even when black ! ! !

        " In great haste,

          " Sincerely yours,

             " A. K. CLIMPSON."

" God bless my soul," said Lord Peter, when he had disentangled this screed—" here's our claimant ready made."

" With a hide as black as his heart, apparently," replied Parker. " I wonder where the Rev. Hallelujah has got to —and where he came from. He—er—he wouldn't be in ' Crockford,' I suppose."

" He would be, probably, if he's Church of England," said Lord Peter, dubiously, going in search of that valuable work of reference. " Dawson—Rev. George, Rev.

Gordon, Rev. Gurney, Rev. Habbakuk, Rev. Hadrian, Rev. Hammond—no, there's no Rev. Hallelujah. I was afraid the name hadn't altogether an established sound. It would be easier if we had an idea what part of the world the gentleman came from. 'Nigger,' to a Miss Timmins, may mean anything from a high-caste Brahmin to Sambo and Rastus at the Coliseum—it may even, at a pinch, be an Argentine or an Esquimaux."

"I suppose other religious bodies have their Crockfords," suggested Parker, a little hopelessly.

"Yes, no doubt—except perhaps the more exclusive sects—like the Agapemonites and those people who gather together to say OM. Was it Voltaire who said that the English had three hundred and sixty-five religions and only one sauce?"

"Judging from the War Tribunals," said Parker, "I should say that was an under-statement. And then there's America—a country, I understand, remarkably well supplied with religions."

"Too true. Hunting for a single dog-collar in the States must be like the proverbial needle. Still, we could make a few discreet inquiries, and meanwhile I'm going to totter up to Crofton with the jolly old 'bus."

"Crofton?"

"Where Miss Clara Whittaker and Miss Dawson used to live. I'm going to look for the man with the little black bag—the strange, suspicious solicitor, you remember, who came to see Miss Dawson two years ago, and was so anxious that she should make a will. I fancy he knows all there is to know about the Rev. Hallelujah and his claim. Will you come too?"

"Can't—not without special permission. I'm not officially on this case, you know."

"You're on the Gotobed business. Tell the Chief you think they're connected. I shall need your restraining presence. No less ignoble pressure than that of the regular

police force will induce a smoke-dried family lawyer to
spill the beans."

"Well, I'll try—if you'll promise to drive with reasonable precaution."

"Be thou as chaste as ice and have a licence as pure as
snow, thou shalt not escape calumny. I am *not* a dangerous
driver. Buck up and get your leave. The snow-white horse-
power foams and frets and the blue bonnet—black in this
case—is already, in a manner of speaking, over the border."

"You'll drive me over the border one of these days,"
grumbled Parker, and went to the 'phone to call up Sir
Andrew Mackenzie at Scotland Yard.

. . . .

Crofton is a delightful little old-world village, tucked
away amid the maze of criss-cross country roads which
fills the triangle of which Coventry, Warwick and Birmingham mark the angles. Through the falling night, " Mrs.
Merdle " purred her away delicately round hedge-blinded
corners and down devious lanes, her quest made no easier
by the fact that the Warwick County Council had pitched
upon that particular week for a grand repainting of sign-
posts and had reached the preliminary stage of laying a
couple of thick coats of gleaming white paint over all the
lettering. At intervals the patient Bunter unpacked himself
from the back seat and climbed one of these uncommuni-
cative guides to peer at its blank surface with a torch—a
process which reminded Parker of Alan Quartermaine trying to trace the features of the departed Kings of the
Kukuanas under their calcareous shrouds of stalactite. One
of the posts turned out to be in the wet-paint stage, which
added to the depression of the party. Finally, after several
misdirections, blind alleys and reversings back to the main
road, they came to a fourways. The signpost here must
have been in extra need of repairs, for its arms had been
removed bodily ; it stood, stark and ghastly—a long,

livid finger erected in wild protest to the unsympathetic heavens.

" It's starting to rain," observed Parker, conversationally.

" Look here, Charles, if you're going to bear up cheerfully and be the life and soul of the expedition, say so and have done with it. I've got a good, heavy spanner handy under the seat, and Bunter can help to bury the body."

" I think this must be Brushwood Cross," resumed Parker, who had the map on his knee. " If so, and if it's not Covert Corner, which I thought we passed half an hour ago, one of these roads leads directly to Crofton."

" That would be highly encouraging if we only knew which road we were on."

" We can always try them in turn, and come back if we find we're going wrong.".

" They bury *suicides* at cross-roads," replied Wimsey, dangerously.

" There's a man sitting under that tree," pursued Parker. " We can ask him."

" He's lost his way too, or he wouldn't be sitting there," retorted the other. " People don't sit about in the rain for fun."

At this moment the man observed their approach and, rising, advanced to meet them with raised, arresting hand.

Wimsey brought the car to a standstill.

" Excuse me," said the stranger, who turned out to be a youth in motor-cycling kit, " but could you give me a hand with my 'bus ? "

" What's the matter with her ? "

" Well, she won't go."

" I guessed as much," said Wimsey. " Though why she should wish to linger in a place like this beats me." He got out of the car, and the youth, diving into the hedge, produced the patient for inspection.

" Did you tumble there or put her there ? " inquired Wimsey, eyeing the machine distastefully.

" I put her there. I've been kicking the starter for hours but nothing happened, so I thought I'd wait till somebody came along."

" I see. What is the matter, exactly ? "

" I don't know. She was going beautifully and then she conked out suddenly."

" Have you run out of petrol ? "

" Oh, no. I'm sure there's plenty in."

" Plug all right ? "

" I don't know." The youth looked unhappy. " It's only my second time out, you see."

" Oh ! well—there can't be much wrong. We'll just make sure about the petrol first," said Wimsey, more cheerfully. He unscrewed the filler-cap and turned his torch upon the interior of the tank. " Seems all right." He bent over again, whistling, and replaced the cap. " Let's give her another kick for luck and then we'll look at the plug."

The young man, thus urged, grasped the handle-bars, and with the energy of despair delivered a kick which would have done credit to an army mule. The engine roared into life in a fury of vibration, racing heart-rendingly.

" Good God ! " said the youth, " it's a miracle."

Lord Peter laid a gentle hand on the throttle-lever and the shattering bellow calmed into a grateful purr.

" What did you do to it ? " demanded the cyclist.

" Blew through the filler-cap," said his lordship with a grin. " Air-lock in the feed, old son, that's all."

" I'm frightfully grateful."

" That's all right. Look here, can you tell us the way to Crofton ? "

" Sure. Straight down here. I'm going there, as a matter of fact."

" Thank Heaven. Lead and I follow, as Sir Galahad says. How far ? "

" Five miles."

" Decent inn ? "

" My governor keeps the ' Fox-and-Hounds.' Would that do ? We'd give you awfully decent grub."

" Sorrow vanquished, labour ended, Jordan passed. Buzz off, my lad. No, Charles, I will *not* wait while you put on a Burberry. Back and side go bare, go bare, hand and foot go cold, so belly-god send us good ale enough, whether it be new or old."

The starter hummed—the youth mounted his machine and led off down the lane after one alarming wobble—Wimsey slipped in the clutch and followed in his wake.

The " Fox-and-Hounds " turned out to be one of those pleasant, old-fashioned inns where everything is upholstered in horse-hair and it is never too late to obtain a good meal of cold roast sirloin and home-grown salad. The landlady, Mrs. Piggin, served the travellers herself. She wore a decent black satin dress and a front of curls of the fashion favoured by the Royal Family. Her round, cheerful face glowed in the firelight, seeming to reflect the radiance of the scarlet-coated huntsmen who galloped and leapt and fell on every wall through a series of sporting prints. Lord Peter's mood softened under the influence of the atmosphere and the house's excellent ale, and by a series of inquiries directed to the hunting-season, just concluded, the neighbouring families and the price of horseflesh, he dexterously led the conversation round to the subject of the late Miss Clara Whittaker.

" Oh, dear, yes," said Mrs. Piggin, " to be sure, we knew Miss Whittaker. Everybody knew her in these parts. A wonderful old lady she was. There's a many of her horses still in the country. Mr. Cleveland, he bought the best part of the stock, and is doin' well with them. Fine honest stock she bred, and they all used to say she was a woman of wonderful judgment with a horse—or a man either. Nobody ever got the better of her twice, and very few, once."

" Ah ! " said Lord Peter, sagaciously.

" I remember her well, riding to hounds when she was well over sixty," went on Mrs. Piggin, " and she wasn't one to wait for a gap, neither. Now Miss Dawson—that was her friend as lived with her—over at the Manor beyond the stone bridge—she was more timid-like. She'd go by the gates, and we often used to say she'd never be riding at all, but for bein' that fond of Miss Whittaker and not wanting to let her out of her sight. But there, we can't all be alike, can we, sir ?—and Miss Whittaker was altogether out of the way. They don't make them like that nowadays. Not but what these modern girls are good goers, many of them, and does a lot of things as would have been thought very fast in the old days, but Miss Whittaker had the knowledge as well. Bought her own horses and physicked 'em and bred 'em, and needed no advice from anybody."

" She sounds a wonderful old girl," said Wimsey, heartily. " I'd have liked to know her. I've got some friends who knew Miss Dawson quite well—when she was living in Hampshire, you know."

" Indeed, sir ? Well, that's strange, isn't it ? She was a very kind, nice lady. We heard she'd died, too. Of this cancer, was it ? That's a terrible thing, poor soul. And fancy you being connected with her, so to speak. I expect you'd be interested in some of our photographs of the Crofton Hunt. Jim ? "

" Hullo ! "

" Show these gentlemen the photographs of Miss Whittaker and Miss Dawson. They're acquainted with some friends of Miss Dawson down in Hampshire. Step this way —if you're sure you won't take anything more, sir."

Mrs. Piggin led the way into a cosy little private bar, where a number of hunting-looking gentlemen were enjoying a final glass before closing-time. Mr. Piggin, stout and genial as his wife, moved forward to do the honours.

" What'll you have, gentlemen ?—Joe, two pints of the winter ale. And fancy you knowing our Miss Dawson. Dear

me, the world's a very small place, as I often says to my wife.
Here's the last group as was ever took of them, when the
meet was held at the Manor in 1918. Of course, you'll
understand, it wasn't a regular meet, like, owing to the
War and the gentlemen being away and the horses too—
we couldn't keep things up regular like in the old days.
But what with the foxes gettin' so terrible many, and the
packs all going to the dogs—ha ! ha !—that's what I often
used to say in this bar—the 'ounds is going to the dogs, I
says. Very good, they used to think it. There's many a
gentleman has laughed at me sayin' that—the 'ounds, I
says, is goin' to the dogs—well, as I was sayin', Colonel
Fletcher and some of the older gentlemen, they says, we
must carry on somehow, they says, and so they 'ad one or
two scratch meets as you might say, just to keep the pack
from fallin' to pieces, as you might say. And Miss Whittaker,
she says, ' 'Ave the meet at the Manor, Colonel,' she says,
' it's the last meet I'll ever see, perhaps,' she says. And so
it was, poor lady, for she 'ad a stroke in the New Year.
She died in 1922. That's 'er, sitting in the pony-carriage and
Miss Dawson beside 'er. Of course, Miss Whittaker 'ad 'ad
to give up riding to 'ounds some years before. She was
gettin' on, but she always followed in the trap, up to the
very last. 'Andsome old lady, ain't she, sir ? ''

Lord Peter and Parker looked with considerable interest
at the rather grim old woman sitting so uncompromisingly
upright with the reins in her hand. A dour, weather-beaten
old face, but certainly handsome still, with its large nose
and straight, heavy eyebrows. And beside her, smaller,
plumper and more feminine, was the Agatha Dawson
whose curious death had led them to this quiet country
place. She had a sweet, smiling face—less dominating than
that of her redoubtable friend, but full of spirit and character. Without doubt they had been a remarkable pair of
old ladies.

Lord Peter asked a question or two about the family.

" Well, sir, I can't say as I knows much about that. We always understood as Miss Whittaker had quarrelled with her people on account of comin' here and settin' up for herself. It wasn't usual in them days for girls to leave home the way it is now. But if you're particularly interested, sir, there's an old gentleman here as can tell you all about the Whittakers and the Dawsons too, and that's Ben Cobling. He was Miss Whittaker's groom for forty years, and he married Miss Dawson's maid as come with her from Norfolk. Eighty-six 'e was, last birthday, but a grand old fellow still. We thinks a lot of Ben Cobling in these parts. 'Im and his wife lives in the little cottage what Miss Whittaker left them when she died. If you'd like to go round and see them to-morrow, sir, you'll find Ben's memory as good as ever it was. Excuse me, sir, but it's time. I must get 'em out of the bar.—Time, gentlemen, please ! Three and eightpence, sir, thank you, sir. Hurry up, gentlemen, please. Now then, Joe, look sharp."

" Great place, Crofton," said Lord Peter, when he and Parker were left alone in a great, low-ceilinged bedroom, where the sheets smelt of lavender. " Ben Cobling's sure to know all about Cousin Hallelujah. I'm looking forward to Ben Cobling."

CHAPTER XII

A TALE OF TWO SPINSTERS

" The power of perpetuating our property in our families is one of the
most valuable and interesting circumstances belonging to it."

BURKE : *Reflections on the Revolution*

THE RAINY NIGHT was followed by a sun-streaked morning. Lord Peter, having wrapped himself affectionately
round an abnormal quantity of bacon and eggs, strolled
out to bask at the door of the " Fox-and-Hounds." He filled
a pipe slowly and meditated. Within, a cheerful bustle in the
bar announced the near arrival of opening time. Eight
ducks crossed the road in Indian file. A cat sprang up upon
the bench, stretched herself, tucked her hind legs under
her and coiled her tail tightly round them as though to
prevent them from accidentally working loose. A groom
passed, riding a tall bay horse and leading a chestnut
with a hogged mane ; a spaniel followed them, running
ridiculously, with one ear flopped inside-out over his
foolish head.

Lord Peter said, " Hah ! "

The inn-door was set hospitably open by the barman, who
said, " Good morning, sir ; fine morning, sir," and vanished
within again.

Lord Peter said, " Umph." He uncrossed his right foot
from over his left and straddled happily across the threshold.

Round the corner by the church-yard wall a little bent
figure hove into sight—an aged man with a wrinkled face
and legs incredibly bowed, his spare shanks enclosed in
leather gaiters. He advanced at a kind of brisk totter
and civilly bared his ancient head before lowering himself
with an audible creak on to the bench beside the cat.

" Good morning, sir," said he.

" Good morning," said Lord Peter. " A beautiful day."

" That it be, sir, that it be," said the old man, heartily. " When I sees a beautiful May day like this, I pray the Lord He'll spare me to live in this wonderful world of His a few years longer. I do indeed."

" You look uncommonly fit," said his lordship, " I should think there was every chance of it."

" I'm still very hearty, sir, thank you, though I'm eighty-seven next Michaelmas."

Lord Peter expressed a proper astonishment.

" Yes, sir, eighty-seven, and if it wasn't for the rheumatics I'd have nothin' to complain on. I'm stronger maybe than what I look. I knows I'm a bit bent, sir, but that's the 'osses, sir, more than age. Regular brought up with 'osses I've been all my life. Worked with 'em, slept with 'em—lived in a stable, you might say, sir."

" You couldn't have better company," said Lord Peter.

" That's right, sir, you couldn't. My wife always used to say she was jealous of the 'osses. Said I preferred their conversation to hers. Well, maybe she was right, sir. A 'oss never talks no foolishness, I says to her, and that's more than you can always say of women, ain't it, sir ? "

" It is indeed," said Wimsey. " What are you going to have ? "

" Thank you, sir, I'll have my usual pint of bitter. Jim knows. Jim ! Always start the day with a pint of bitter, sir. It's 'olesomer than tea to my mind and don't fret the coats of the stomach."

" I dare say you're right," said Wimsey. " Now you mention it, there is something fretful about tea. Mr. Piggin, two pints of bitter, please, and will you join us ? "

" Thank you, my lord," said the landlord. " Joe ! Two large bitters and a Guinness. Beautiful morning, my lord

—'morning, Mr. Cobling—I see you've made each other's acquaintance already."

" By Jove ! so this is Mr. Cobling. I'm delighted to see you. I wanted particularly to have a chat with you."

" Indeed, sir ? "

" I was telling this gentleman—Lord Peter Wimsey his name is—as you could tell him all about Miss Whittaker and Miss Dawson. He knows friends of Miss Dawson's."

" Indeed ? Ah ! There ain't much I *couldn't* tell you about them ladies. And proud I'd be to do it. Fifty years I was with Miss Whittaker. I come to her as under-groom in old Johnny Blackthorne's time, and stayed on as head-groom after he died. A rare young lady she was in them days. Deary me. Straight as a switch, with a fine, high colour in her cheeks and shiny black hair—just like a beautiful two-year-old filly she was. And very sperrited. Wonnerful sperrited. There was a many gentlemen as would have been glad to hitch up with her, but she was never broke to harness. Like dirt, she treated 'em. Wouldn't look at 'em, except it might be the grooms and stable-hands in a matter of 'osses. And in the way of business, of course. Well, there is some creatures like that. I 'ad a terrier-bitch that way. Great ratter she was. But a business woman—nothin' else. I tried 'er with all the dogs I could lay 'and to, but it weren't no good. Bloodshed there was an' sich a row—you never 'eard. The Lord makes a few on 'em that way to suit 'Is own purposes, I suppose. There ain't no arguin' with females."

Lord Peter said " Ah ! "

The ale went down in silence.

Mr. Piggin roused himself presently from contemplation to tell a story of Miss Whittaker in the hunting-field. Mr. Cobling capped this by another. Lord Peter said " Ah ! " Parker then emerged and was introduced, and Mr. Cobling begged the privilege of standing a round of drinks. This ritual accomplished, Mr. Piggin begged the company would be his guests for a third round, and then excused himself on the plea of customers to attend to.

He went in, and Lord Peter, by skilful and maddeningly slow degrees, began to work his way back to the history of the Dawson family. Parker—educated at Barrow-in-Furness grammar school and with his wits further sharpened in the London police service—endeavoured now and again to get matters along faster by a brisk question. The result, every time, was to make Mr. Cobling lose the thread of his remarks and start him off into a series of interminable side-tracks. Wimsey kicked his friend viciously on the ankle-bone to keep him quiet, and with endless patience worked the conversation back to the main road again.

At the end of an hour or so, Mr. Cobling explained that his wife could tell them a great deal more about Miss Dawson than what he could, and invited them to visit his cottage. This invitation being accepted with alacrity, the party started off, Mr. Cobling explaining to Parker that he was eighty-seven come next Michaelmas, and hearty still, indeed, stronger than he appeared, bar the rheumatics that troubled him. " I'm not saying as I'm not bent," said Mr. Cobling, " but that's more the work of the 'osses. Regular lived with 'osses all my life——"

" Don't look so fretful, Charles," murmured Wimsey in his ear, " it must be the tea at breakfast—it frets the coats of the stomach."

Mrs. Cobling turned out to be a delightful old lady, exactly like a dried-up pippin and only two years younger than her husband. She was entranced at getting an opportunity to talk about her darling Miss Agatha. Parker, thinking it necessary to put forward some reason for the inquiry, started on an involved explanation, and was kicked again. To Mrs. Cobling, nothing could be more natural than that all the world should be interested in the Dawsons, and she prattled gaily on without prompting.

She had been in the Dawson family service as a girl—

almost born in it as you might say. Hadn't her mother been housekeeper to Mr. Henry Dawson, Miss Agatha's papa, and to his father before him? She herself had gone to the big house as stillroom maid when she wasn't but fifteen. That was when Miss Harriet was only three years old—her as afterwards married Mr. James Whittaker. Yes, and she'd been there when the rest of the family was born. Mr. Stephen—him as should have been the heir —ah, dear! only the trouble came and that killed his poor father and there was nothing left. Yes, a sad business that was. Poor Mr. Henry speculated with something— Mrs. Cobling wasn't clear what, but it was all very wicked and happened in London where there were so many wicked people—and the long and the short was, he lost it all, poor gentleman, and never held up his head again. Only fifty-four he was when he died; such a fine upright gentleman with a pleasant word for everybody. And his wife didn't live long after him, poor lamb. She was a Frenchwoman and a sweet lady, but she was very lonely in England, having no family and her two sisters walled up alive in one of them dreadful Romish Convents.

"And what did Mr. Stephen do when the money went?" asked Wimsey.

"Him? Oh, he went into business—a strange thing that did seem, though I have heard tell as old Barnabas Dawson, Mr. Henry's grandfather that was, was nought but a grocer or something of that—and they do say, don't they, that from shirtsleeves to shirtsleeves is three genera-tions? Still, it was very hard on Mr. Stephen, as had always been brought up to have everything of the best. And engaged to be married to a beautiful lady, too, and a very rich heiress. But it was all for the best, for when she heard Mr. Stephen was a poor man after all, she threw him over, and that showed she had no heart in her at all. Mr. Stephen never married till he was over forty, and then it was a lady with no family at all—not lawful, that

is, though she was a dear, sweet girl and made Mr. Stephen
a most splendid wife—she did indeed. And Mr. John, he
was their only son. They thought the world of him. It
was a terrible day when the news came that he was killed
in the War. A cruel business that was, sir, wasn't it?—
and nobody the better for it as I can see, but all these
shocking hard taxes, and the price of everything gone up
so, and so many out of work."

" So he was killed? That must have been a terrible
grief to his parents."

" Yes, sir, terrible. Oh, it was an awful thing altogether,
sir, for poor Mr. Stephen, as had had so much trouble
all his life, he went out of his poor mind and shot hisself.
Out of his mind he must have been, sir, to do it—and
what was more dreadful still, he shot his dear lady as
well. You may remember it, sir. There was pieces in the
paper about it."

" I seem to have some vague recollection of it," said
Peter, quite untruthfully, but anxious not to seem to
belittle the local tragedy. " And young John—he wasn't
married, I suppose."

" No, sir. That was very sad, too. He was engaged to a
young lady—a nurse in one of the English hospitals, as
we understood, and he was hoping to get back and be
married to her on his next leave. Everything did seem to
go all wrong together them terrible years."

The old lady sighed, and wiped her eyes.

" Mr. Stephen was the only son, then? "

" Well, not exactly, sir. There was the darling twins.
Such pretty children, but they only lived two days. They
come four years after Miss Harriet—her as married Mr.
James Whittaker."

" Yes, of course. That was how the families became
connected."

" Yes, sir. Miss Agatha and Miss Harriet and Miss
Clara Whittaker was all at the same school together, and

Mrs. Whittaker asked the two young ladies to go and spend their holidays with Miss Clara, and that was when Mr. James fell in love with Miss Harriet. She wasn't as pretty as Miss Agatha, to my thinking, but she was livelier and quicker—and then, of course, Miss Agatha was never one for flirting and foolishness. Often she used to say to me, ' Betty,' she said, ' I mean to be an old maid and so does Miss Clara, and we're going to live together and be ever so happy, without any stupid, tiresome gentlemen.' And so it turned out, sir, as you know, for Miss Agatha, for all she was so quiet, was very determined. Once she'd said a thing, you couldn't turn her from it—not with reasons, nor with threats, nor with coaxings—nothing ! Many's the time I've tried when she was a child—for I used to give a little help in the nursery sometimes, sir. You might drive her into a temper or into the sulks, but you couldn't make her change her little mind, even then."

There came to Wimsey's mind the picture of the stricken, helpless old woman, holding to her own way in spite of her lawyer's reasoning and her niece's subterfuge. A remarkable old lady, certainly, in her way.

" I suppose the Dawson family has practically died out, then," he said.

" Oh, yes, sir. There's only Miss Mary now—and she's a Whittaker, of course. She is Miss Harriet's grand-daughter, Mr. Charles Whittaker's only child. She was left all alone, too, when she went to live with Miss Dawson. Mr. Charles and his wife was killed in one of these dreadful motors—dear, dear—it seemed we was fated to have nothing but one tragedy after another. Just to think of Ben and me outliving them all."

" Cheer up, Mother," said Ben, laying his hand on hers. " The Lord have been wonderful good to us."

" That He have. Three sons we have, sir, and two daughters, and fourteen grandchildren and three great-grandchildren. Maybe you'd like to see their pictures, sir."

Lord Peter said he should like to very much, and Parker made confirmatory noises. The life-histories of all the children and descendants were detailed at suitable length. Whenever a pause seemed discernible, Parker would mutter hopefully in Wimsey's ear, " How about Cousin Halle- lujah ? " but before a question could be put, the intermin- able family chronicle was resumed.

" And for God's sake, Charles," whispered Peter, savagely, when Mrs. Cobling had risen to hunt for the shawl which Grandson William had sent home from the Dardanelles, " don't keep saying Hallelujah at me ! I'm not a revival meeting."

The shawl being duly admired, the conversation turned upon foreign parts, natives and black people generally, following on which, Lord Peter added carelessly :

" By the way, hasn't the Dawson family got some sort of connections in those foreign countries, somewhere ? "

Well, yes, said Mrs. Cobling, in rather a shocked tone. There had been Mr. Paul, Mr. Henry's brother. But he was not mentioned much. He had been a terrible shock to his family. In fact—a gasp here, and a lowering of the voice—he had *turned Papist* and become—a monk ! (Had he become a murderer, apparently, he could hardly have done worse.) Mr. Henry had always blamed himself very much in the matter.

" How was it his fault ? "

" Well, or course, Mr. Henry's wife—my dear mistress, you see, sir—she was French, as I told you, and of course, *she* was a Papist. Being brought up that way, she wouldn't know any better, naturally, and she was very young when she was married. But Mr. Henry soon taught her to be a Christian, and she put away her idolatrous ideas and went to the parish church. But Mr. Paul, *he* fell in love with one of her sisters, and the sister had been vowed to religion, as they called it, and had shut herself up in a nunnery." And then Mr. Paul had broken his heart and " gone

over " to the Scarlet Woman and—again the pause and
the hush—become a monk. A terrible to-do it made. And
he'd lived to be a very old man, and for all Mrs. Cobling
knew was living yet, still in the error of his ways.

" If he's alive," murmured Parker, " he's probably the
real heir. He'd be Agatha Dawson's uncle and her nearest
relation."

Wimsey frowned and returned to the charge.

" Well, it couldn't have been Mr. Paul I had in mind,"
he said, " because this sort of relation of Miss Agatha
Dawson's that I heard about was a real foreigner—in fact,
a very dark-complexioned man—almost a black man, or
so I was told."

" Black ? " cried the old lady—" oh, no, sir—that couldn't
be. Unless—dear Lord a' mercy, it couldn't be that, surely!
Ben, do you think it could be that?—Old Simon, you
know ? "

Ben shook his head. " I never heard tell much about
him."

" Nor nobody did," replied Mrs. Cobling, energetically.
" He was a long way back, but they had tales of him in the
family. ' Wicked Simon,' they called him. He sailed away to
the Indies, many years ago, and nobody knew what became
of him. Wouldn't it be a queer thing, like, if he was to have
married a black wife out in them parts, and this was his—
oh, dear—his grandson it 'ud have to be, if not his great-
grandson, for he was Mr. Henry's uncle, and that's a long
time ago."

This was disappointing. A grandson of " old Simon's "
would surely be too distant a relative to dispute Mary
Whittaker's title. However :

" That's very interesting," said Wimsey. " Was it the
East Indies or the West Indies he went to, I wonder ? "

Mrs. Cobling didn't know, but she believed it was
something to do with America.

" It's a pity as Mr. Probyn ain't in England any longer.

He could have told you more about the family than what
I can. But he retired last year and went away to Italy or
some such place."

" Who was he ? "

" He was Miss Whittaker's solicitor," said Ben, "and he
managed all Miss Dawson's business, too. A nice gentleman
he was, but uncommon sharp—ha, ha ! Never gave nothing
away. But that's lawyers all the world over," added he,
shrewdly, " take all and give nothing."

" Did he live in Crofton ? "

" No, sir, in Croftover Magna, twelve miles from here.
Pointer & Winkin have his business now, but they're young
men, and I don't know much about them."

Having by this time heard all the Coblings had to tell,
Wimsey and Parker gradually disentangled themselves and
took their leave.

" Well, Cousin Hallelujah's a wash-out," said Parker.

" Possibly—possibly not. There may be some connection.
Still, I certainly think the disgraceful and papistical Mr.
Paul is more promising. Obviously Mr. Probyn is the bird
to get hold of. You realise who he is ? "

" He's the mysterious solicitor, I suppose."

" Of course he is. He knows why Miss Dawson ought to
have made her will. And we're going straight off to Croftover Magna to look up Messrs. Pointer & Winkin, and see
what they have to say about it."

Unhappily, Messrs. Pointer & Winkin had nothing to
say whatever. Miss Dawson had withdrawn her affairs from
Mr. Probyn's hands and had lodged all the papers with her
new solicitor. Messrs. Pointer & Winkin had never had any
connection with the Dawson family. They had no objection,
however, to furnishing Mr. Probyn's address—Villa Bianca,
Fiesole. They regretted that they could be of no further
assistance to Lord Peter Wimsey and Mr. Parker. Good
morning.

" Short and sour," was his lordship's comment. " Well,

well—we'll have a spot of lunch and write a letter to Mr. Probyn and another to my good friend Bishop Lambert of the Orinoco Mission to get a line on Cousin Hallelujah. Smile, smile, smile. As Ingoldsby says : ' The breezes are blowing a race, a race ! The breezes are blowing—we near the chase ! ' Do ye ken John Peel ? Likewise, know'st thou the land where blooms the citron-flower ? Well, never mind if you don't—you can always look forward to going there for your honeymoon."

CHAPTER XIII

HALLELUJAH

*" Our ancestors are very good kind of folks, but they are the last people
I should choose to have a visiting acquaintance with."*

SHERIDAN : *The Rivals*

THAT EXCELLENT PRELATE, Bishop Lambert of the
Orinoco Mission, proved to be a practical and kind man.
He did not personally know the Rev. Hallelujah Dawson,
but thought he might belong to the Tabernacle Mission—
a Nonconformist body which was doing a very valuable
work in those parts. He would himself communicate with
the London Headquarters of this community and let Lord
Peter know the result. Two hours later, Bishop Lambert's
secretary had duly rung up the Tabernacle Mission and
received the very satisfactory information that the Rev.
Hallelujah Dawson was in England, and, indeed, available
at their Mission House in Stepney. He was an elderly
minister, living in very reduced circumstances—in fact,
the Bishop rather gathered that the story was a sad one.—
Oh, not at all, pray, no thanks. The Bishop's poor miserable
slave of a secretary did all the work. Very glad to hear from
Lord Peter, and was he being good ? Ha, ha ! and when
was he coming to dine with the Bishop ?

Lord Peter promptly gathered up Parker and swooped
down with him upon the Tabernacle Mission, before whose
dim and grim frontage Mrs. Merdle's long black bonnet and
sweeping copper exhaust made an immense impression. The
small fry of the neighbourhood had clustered about her
and were practising horn solos almost before Wimsey
had rung the bell. On Parker's threatening them with
punishment and casually informing them that he was a

police-officer, they burst into ecstasies of delight, and joining hands, formed a ring-o'-roses round him, under the guidance of a sprightly young woman of twelve years old or thereabouts. Parker made a few harassed darts at them, but the ring only broke up, shrieking with laughter, and reformed, singing. The Mission door opened at the moment, displaying this undignified exhibition to the eyes of a lank young man in spectacles, who shook a long finger disapprovingly and said, " Now, you children," without the slightest effect and apparently without the faintest expectation of producing any.

Lord Peter explained his errand.

" Oh, come in, please," said the young man, who had one finger in a book of theology. " I'm afraid your friend—er—this is rather a noisy district."

Parker shook himself free from his tormentors, and advanced, breathing threatenings and slaughter, to which the enemy responded by a derisive blast of the horn.

" They'll run those batteries down," said Wimsey.

" You can't do anything with the little devils," growled Parker.

" Why don't you treat them as human beings ? " retorted Wimsey. " Children are creatures of like passions with politicians and financiers. Here, Esmeralda ! " he added, beckoning to the ringleader.

The young woman put her tongue out and made a rude gesture, but observing the glint of coin in the outstretched hand, suddenly approached and stood challengingly before them.

" Look here," said Wimsey, " here's half a crown—thirty pennies, you know. Any use to you ? "

The child promptly proved her kinship with humanity. She became abashed in the presence of wealth, and was silent, rubbing one dusty shoe upon the calf of her stocking.

" You appear," pursued Lord Peter, " to be able to keep your young friends in order if you choose. I take you, in

fact, for a woman of character. Very well, if you keep them
from touching my car while I'm in the house, you get this
half-crown, see? But if you let 'em blow the horn, I shall
hear it. Every time the horn goes, you lose a penny, got
that? If the horn blows six times, you only get two bob.
If I hear it thirty times, you don't get anything. And I
shall look out from time to time, and if I see anybody
mauling the car about or sitting in it, *then* you don't get
anything. Do I make myself clear? "

" I takes care o' yer car fer 'arf a crahn. An' ef the 'orn
goes, you docks a copper 'orf of it."

" That's right."

" Right you are, mister. I'll see none on 'em touches it."

" Good girl. Now, sir."

The spectacled young man led them into a gloomy little
waiting-room, suggestive of a railway station and hung with
Old Testament prints.

" I'll tell Mr. Dawson you're here," said he, and vanished,
with the volume of theology still clutched in his hand.

Presently a shuffling step was heard on the coconut
matting, and Wimsey and Parker braced themselves to
confront the villainous claimant.

The door, however, opened to admit an elderly West
Indian, of so humble and inoffensive an appearance that
the hearts of the two detectives sank into their boots. Anything less murderous could scarcely be imagined, as he stood
blinking nervously at them from behind a pair of steel-
rimmed spectacles, the frames of which had at one time
been broken and bound with twine.

The Rev. Hallelujah Dawson was undoubtedly a man of
colour. He had the pleasant, slightly aquiline features and
brown-olive skin of the Polynesian. His hair was scanty and
greyish—not woolly, but closely curled. His stooping
shoulders were clad in a threadbare clerical coat. His
black eyes, yellow about the whites and slightly protruding,
rolled amiably at them, and his smile was open and frank.

" You asked to see me ? " he began, in perfect English,
but with the soft native intonation. " I think I have not the
pleasure—— ? "

" How do you do, Mr. Dawson ? Yes. We are—er—
makin' certain inquiries—er—in connection with the family
of the Dawsons of Crofton in Warwickshire, and it has been
suggested that you might be able to enlighten us, what ? as
to their West Indian connections—if you would be so
good."

" Ah, yes ! " The old man drew himself up slightly.
" I am myself—in a way—a descendant of the family.
Won't you sit down ? "

" Thank you. We thought you might be."

" You do not come from Miss Whittaker ? "

There was something eager, yet defensive in the tone.
Wimsey, not quite knowing what was behind it, chose the
discreeter part.

" Oh, no. We are—preparin' a work on County Families,
don't you know. Tombstones and genealogies and that sort
of thing."

" Oh !—yes—I hoped perhaps—— " The mild tones died
away in a sigh. " But I shall be very happy to help you in
any way."

" Well, the question now is, what became of Simon
Dawson ? We know that he left his family and sailed for the
West Indies in—ah !—in seventeen—— "

" Eighteen hundred and ten," said the old man, with surprising quickness. " Yes. He got into trouble when he was a
lad of sixteen. He took up with bad men older than himself,
and became involved in a very terrible affair. It had to do
with gaming, and a man was killed. Not in a duel—in those
days that would not have been considered disgraceful—
though violence is always displeasing to the Lord—but the
man was foully murdered and Simon Dawson and his
friends fled from justice. Simon fell in with the press-gang
and was carried off to sea. He served fifteen years and was

then taken by a French privateer. Later on he escaped and
—to cut a long story short—got away to Trinidad under
another name. Some English people there were kind to him
and gave him work on their sugar plantation. He did well
there and eventually became owner of a small plantation of
his own."

" What was the name he went by ? "

" Harkaway. I suppose he was afraid that they would
get hold of him as a deserter from the Navy if he went by his
own name. No doubt he should have reported his escape.
Anyway, he liked plantation life and was quite satisfied to
stay where he was. I don't suppose he would have cared
to go home, even to claim his inheritance. And then, there
was always the matter of the murder, you know—though
I dare say they would not have brought that trouble up
against him, seeing he was so young when it happened and
it was not his hand that did the awful deed."

" His inheritance ? Was he the eldest son, then ? "

" No. Barnabas was the eldest, but he was killed at Waterloo and left no family. Then there was a second son, Roger,
but he died of smallpox as a child. Simon was the third son."

" Then it was the fourth son who took the estate ? "

" Yes, Frederick. He was Henry Dawson's father. They
tried, of course, to find out what became of Simon, but in
those days it was very difficult, you understand, to get
information from foreign places, and Simon had quite
disappeared. So they had to pass him over."

" And what happened to Simon's children ? " asked
Parker. " Did he have any ? "

The clergyman nodded, and a deep, dusky flush showed
under his dark skin.

" I am his grandson," he said, simply. " That is why I
came over to England. When the Lord called me to feed His
lambs among my own people, I was in quite good circumstances. I had the little sugar plantation which had come
down to me through my father, and I married and was very

happy. But we fell on bad times—the sugar crop failed, and our little flock became smaller and poorer and could not give so much support to their minister. Besides, I was getting too old and frail to do my work—and I have a sick wife, too, and God has blessed us with many daughters, who needed our care. I was in great straits. And then I came upon some old family papers belonging to my grandfather, Simon, and learned that his name was not Harkaway but Dawson, and I thought, maybe I had a family in England and that God would yet raise up a table in the wilderness. Accordingly, when the time came to send a representative home to our London Headquarters, I asked permission to resign my ministry out there and come over to England."

" Did you get into touch with anybody ? "

" Yes. I went to Crofton—which was mentioned in my grandfather's letters—and saw a lawyer in the town there—a Mr. Probyn of Croftover. You know him ? "

" I've heard of him."

" Yes. He was very kind, and very much interested to see me. He showed me the genealogy of the family, and how my grandfather should have been the heir to the property."

" But the property had been lost by that time, had it not ? "

" Yes. And, unfortunately—when I showed him my grandmother's marriage certificate, he—he told me that it was no certificate at all. I fear that Simon Dawson was a sad sinner. He took my grandmother to live with him, as many of the planters did take women of colour, and he gave her a document which was supposed to be a certificate of marriage signed by the Governor of the country. But when Mr. Probyn inquired into it, he found that it was all a sham, and no such governor had ever existed. It was distressing to my feelings as a Christian, of course—but since there was no property, it didn't make any actual difference to us."

" That was bad luck," said Peter, sympathetically.

" I called resignation to my aid," said the old Indian, with a dignified little bow. " Mr. Probyn was also good enough to send me with a letter of introduction to Miss Agatha Dawson, the only surviving member of our family."

" Yes, she lived at Leahampton."

" She received me in the most charming way, and when I told her who I was—acknowledging, of course, that I had not the slightest claim upon her—she was good enough to make me an allowance of £100 a year, which she continued till her death."

" Was that the only time you saw her ? "

" Oh, yes. I would not intrude upon her. It could not be agreeable to her to have a relative of my complexion continually at her house," said the Rev. Hallelujah, with a kind of proud humility. " But she gave me lunch, and spoke very kindly."

" And—forgive my askin'—hope it isn't impertinent— but does Miss Whittaker keep up the allowance ? "

" Well, no—I—perhaps I should not expect it, but it would have made a great difference to our circumstances. And Miss Dawson rather led me to hope that it might be continued. She told me that she did not like the idea of making a will, but, she said, ' It is not necessary at all, Cousin Hallelujah, Mary will have all my money when I am gone, and she can continue the allowance on my behalf.' But perhaps Miss Whittaker did not get the money after all ? "

" Oh, yes, she did. It is very odd. She may have forgotten about it."

" I took the liberty of writing her a few words of spiritual comfort when her aunt died. Perhaps that did not please her. Of course, I did not write again. Yet I am loath to believe that she has hardened her heart against the unfortunate. No doubt there is some explanation."

" No doubt," said Lord Peter. " Well, I'm very grateful
to you for your kindness. That has quite cleared up the
little matter of Simon and his descendants. I'll just make
a note of the names and dates, if I may."

" Certainly. I will bring you the paper which Mr.
Probyn kindly made out for me, showing the whole of the
family. Excuse me."

He was not gone long, and soon reappeared with a
genealogy, neatly typed out on a legal-looking sheet of
blue paper.

Wimsey began to note down the particulars concerning
Simon Dawson and his son, Bosun, and his grandson,
Hallelujah. Suddenly he put his finger on an entry further
along.

" Look here, Charles," he said. " Here is our Father Paul
—the bad boy who turned R.C. and became a monk."

" So he is. But—he's dead, Peter—died in 1922, three
years after Agatha Dawson."

" Yes. We must wash him out. Well, these little setbacks
will occur."

They finished their notes, bade farewell to the Rev.
Hallelujah, and emerged to find Esmeralda valiantly
defending Mrs. Merdle against all-comers. Lord Peter
handed over the half-crown and took delivery of the car.

" The more I hear of Mary Whittaker," he said, " the
less I like her. She might at least have given poor old
Cousin Hallelujah his hundred quid."

" She's a rapacious female," agreed Parker. " Well,
anyway, Father Paul's safely dead, and Cousin Hallelujah
is illegitimately descended. So there's an end of the long-
lost claimant from overseas."

" Damn it all ! " cried Wimsey, taking both hands from
the steering-wheel and scratching his head, to Parker's
extreme alarm, " that strikes a familiar chord. Now where
in thunder have I heard those words before ? "

CHAPTER XIV

SHARP QUILLETS OF THE LAW

" Things done without example—in their issue
Are to be feared."

Henry VIII, 1, 2

"MURBLES is coming round to dinner to-night, Charles,"
said Wimsey. "I wish you'd stop and have grub with us too.
I want to put all this family history business before him."

" Where are you dining ? "

" Oh, at the flat. I'm sick of restaurant meals. Bunter
does a wonderful bloody steak and there are new peas and
potatoes and genuine English grass. Gerald sent it up from
Denver specially. You can't buy it. Come along. Ye olde
English fare, don't you know, and a bottle of what Pepys
calls Ho Bryon. Do you good."

Parker accepted. But he noticed that, even when speaking
on his beloved subject of food, Wimsey was vague and abstracted. Something seemed to be worrying at the back of
his mind, and even when Mr. Murbles appeared, full of
mild legal humour, Wimsey listened to him with extreme
courtesy indeed, but with only half his attention.

They were partly through dinner when, a propos of
nothing, Wimsey suddenly brought his fist down on the
mahogany with a crash that startled even Bunter, causing
him to jerk a great crimson splash of the Haut Brion over
the edge of the glass upon the tablecloth.

" Got it ! " said Lord Peter.

Bunter in a low shocked voice begged his lordship's
pardon.

" Murbles," said· Wimsey, without heeding him, " isn't
there a new Property Act ? "

" Why, yes," said Mr. Murbles, in some surprise. He had been in the middle of a story about a young barrister and a Jewish pawnbroker when the interruption occurred, and was a little put out.

" I knew I'd read that sentence somewhere—you know, Charles—about doing away with the long-lost claimant from overseas. It was in some paper or other about a couple of years ago, and it had to do with the new Act. Of course, it said what a blow it would be to romantic novelists. Doesn't the Act wash out the claims of distant relatives, Murbles ? "

" In a sense, it does," replied the solicitor. " Not, of course, in the case of entailed property, which has its own rules. But I understand you to refer to ordinary personal property or real estate not entailed."

" Yes—what happens to that, now, if the owner of the property dies without making a will ? "

" It is rather a complicated matter," began Mr. Murbles.

" Well, look here, first of all—before the jolly old Act was passed, the next-of-kin got it all, didn't he—no matter if he was only a seventh cousin fifteen times removed ? "

" In a general way, that is correct. If there was a husband or wife——"

" Wash out the husband and wife. Suppose the person is unmarried and has no near relations living. It would have gone——"

" To the next-of-kin, whoever that was, if he or she could be traced."

" Even if you had to burrow back to William the Conqueror to get at the relationship ? "

" Always supposing you could get a clear record back to so very early a date," replied Mr. Murbles. " It is, of course, in the highest degree improbable——"

" Yes, yes, I know, sir. But what happens now in such a case ? "

" The new Act makes inheritance on intestacy very

much simpler," said Mr. Murbles, setting his knife and fork together, placing both elbows on the table and laying the index-finger of his right hand against his left thumb in a gesture of tabulation.

" I bet it does," interpolated Wimsey. " I know what an Act to make things simpler means. It means that the people who drew it up don't understand it themselves and that every one of its clauses needs a law-suit to disentangle it. But do go on."

" Under the new Act," pursued Mr. Murbles, " one half of the property goes to the husband and wife, if living, and subject to his or her life-interest, then all to the children equally. But if there be no spouse and no children, then it goes to the father or mother of the deceased. If the father and mother are both dead, then everything goes to the brothers and sisters of the whole blood who are living at the time, but if any brother or sister dies before the intestate, then to his or her issue. In case there are no brothers or sisters of the——"

" Stop, stop ! you needn't go any further. You're absolutely sure of that ? It goes to the brothers' or sisters' issue ? "

" Yes. That is to say, if it were you that died intestate and your brother Gerald and your sister Mary were already dead, your money would be equally divided among your nieces and nephews."

" Yes, but suppose they were already dead too—suppose I'd gone tediously living on till I'd nothing left but great-nephews and great-nieces—would they inherit ? "

" Why—why, yes, I suppose they would," said Mr. Murbles, with less certainty, however. " Oh, yes, I think they would."

" Clearly they would," said Parker, a little impatiently, "if it says to the issue of the deceased's brothers and sisters."

" Ah ! but we must not be precipitate," said Mr. Murbles, rounding upon him. " To the lay mind, doubtless, the word 'issue' appears a simple one. But in law "—(Mr. Murbles, who up till this point had held the index-finger of the right-hand poised against the ring-finger of the left, in recognition of the claims of the brothers and sisters of the half-blood, now placed his left palm upon the table and wagged his right index-finger admonishingly in Parker's direction)—" in *law* the word may bear one of two, or indeed several interpretations, according to the nature of the document in which it occurs and the date of that document."

" But in the new Act——" urged Lord Peter.

" I am not, particularly," said Mr. Murbles, " a specialist in the law concerning property, and I should not like to give a decided opinion as to its interpretation, all the more as, up to the present, no case has come before the Courts bearing on the present issue—no pun intended, ha, ha, ha ! But my immediate and entirely tentative opinion—which, however, I should advise you not to accept without the support of some weightier authority—would be, I *think*, that issue in this case means issue *ad infinitum*, and that therefore the great-nephews and great-nieces would be entitled to inherit."

" But there might be another opinion ? "

" Yes—the question is a complicated one——"

" What did I tell you ? " groaned Peter. " I *knew* this simplifying Act would cause a shockin' lot of muddle."

" May I ask," said Mr. Murbles, " exactly why you want to know all this ? "

" Why, sir," said Wimsey, taking from his pocket-book the genealogy of the Dawson family which he had received from the Rev. Hallelujah Dawson, " here is the point. We have always talked about Mary Whittaker as Agatha Dawson's niece ; she was always called so and she speaks of the old lady as her aunt. But if you look at this, you will see that actually she was no nearer to her than great-niece : she was the grand-daughter of Agatha's sister Harriet."

"Quite true," said Mr. Murbles, "but still, she was apparently the nearest surviving relative, and since Agatha Dawson died in 1925, the money passed without any question to Mary Whittaker under the old Property Act. There's no ambiguity there."

"No," said Wimsey, "none whatever, that's the point. But——"

"Good God!" broke in Parker, "I see what you're driving at. When did the new Act come into force, sir?"

"In January, 1926," replied Mr. Murbles.

"And Miss Dawson died, rather unexpectedly, as we know, in November, 1925," went on Peter. "But supposing she had lived, as the doctor fully expected her to do, till February or March, 1926—are you absolutely positive, sir, that Mary Whittaker would have inherited then?"

Mr. Murbles opened his mouth to speak—and shut it again. He rubbed his hands very slowly the one over the other. He removed his eyeglasses and resettled them more firmly on his nose. Then:

"You are quite right, Lord Peter," he said in a grave tone, "this is a very serious and important point. Much too serious for me to give an opinion on. If I understand you rightly, you are suggesting that any ambiguity in the interpretation of the new Act might provide an interested party with a very good and sufficient motive for hastening the death of Agatha Dawson."

"I do mean exactly that. Of course, if the great-niece inherits anyhow, the old lady might as well die under the new Act as under the old. But if there was any doubt about it—how tempting, don't you see, to give her a little push over the edge, so as to make her die in 1925. Especially as she couldn't live long anyhow, and there were no other relatives to be defrauded."

"That reminds me," put in Parker, "suppose the great-niece is excluded from the inheritance, where does the money go?"

" It goes to the Duchy of Lancaster—or in other words, to the Crown."

" In fact," said Wimsey, " to no one in particular. Upon my soul, I really can't see that it's very much of a crime to bump a poor old thing off a bit previously when she's sufferin' horribly, just to get the money she intends you to have. Why the devil should the Duchy of Lancaster have it ? Who cares about the Duchy of Lancaster ? It's like defrauding the Income Tax."

" Ethically," observed Mr. Murbles, " there may be much to be said for your point of view. Legally, I am afraid, murder is murder, however frail the victim or convenient the result."

" And Agatha Dawson didn't want to die," added Parker, " she said so."

" No," said Wimsey, thoughtfully, " and I suppose she had a right to an opinion."

" I think," said Mr. Murbles, " that before we go any further, we ought to consult a specialist in this branch of the law. I wonder whether Towkington is at home. He is quite the ablest authority I could name. Greatly as I dislike that modern invention, the telephone, I think it might be advisable to ring him up."

Mr. Towkington proved to be at home and at liberty. The case of the great-niece was put to him over the 'phone. Mr. Towkington, taken at a disadvantage without his authorities, and hazarding an opinion on the spur of the moment, thought that in all probability the great-niece would be excluded from the succession under the new Act. But it was an interesting point, and he would be glad of an opportunity to verify his references. Would not Mr. Murbles come round and talk it over with him ? Mr. Murbles explained that he was at that moment dining with two friends who were interested in the question. In that case, would not the two friends also come round and see Mr. Towkington ?

"Towkington has some very excellent port," said Mr. Murbles, in a cautious aside, and clapping his hand over the mouthpiece of the telephone.

"Then why not go and try it?" said Wimsey, cheerfully.

"It's only as far as Gray's Inn," continued Mr. Murbles.

"All the better," said Lord Peter.

Mr. Murbles released the telephone and thanked Mr. Towkington. The party would start at once for Gray's Inn. Mr. Towkington was heard to say, "Good, good," in a hearty manner before ringing off.

On their arrival at Mr. Towkington's chambers the oak was found to be hospitably unsported, and almost before they could knock, Mr. Towkington himself flung open the door and greeted them in a loud and cheerful tone. He was a large, square man with a florid face and a harsh voice. In court, he was famous for a way of saying, "Come now," as a preface to tying recalcitrant witnesses into tight knots, which he would then proceed to slash open with a brilliant confutation. He knew Wimsey by sight, expressed himself delighted to meet Inspector Parker, and bustled his guests into the room with jovial shouts.

"I've been going into this little matter while you were coming along," he said. "Awkward, eh? ha! Astonishing thing that people can't say what they mean when they draw Acts, eh? ha! Why do you suppose it is, Lord Peter, eh? ha! Come now!"

"I suspect it's because Acts are drawn up by lawyers," said Wimsey with a grin.

"To make work for themselves, eh? I daresay you're right. Even lawyers must live, eh? ha! Very good. Well now, Murbles, let's just have this case again, in greater detail, d'you mind?"

Mr. Murbles explained the matter again, displaying the genealogical table and putting forward the point as regards a possible motive for murder.

" Eh, ha ! " exclaimed Mr. Towkington, much delighted, " that's good—very good—your idea, Lord Peter ? Very ingenious. Too ingenious. The dock at the Old Bailey is peopled by gentlemen who are too ingenious. Ha ! Come to a bad end one of these days, young man. Eh ? Yes— well, now, Murbles, the question here turns on the inter- pretation of the word ' issue '—you grasp that, eh, ha ! Yes. Well, *you* seem to think it means issue *ad infinitum*. How do you make that out, come now ? "

" I didn't say I thought it did ; I said I thought it might," remonstrated Mr. Murbles, mildly. " The general intention of the Act appears to be to exclude any remote kin where the common ancestor is further back than the grandparents —not to cut off the descendants of the brothers and sisters."

" Intention ? " snapped Mr. Towkington. " I'm aston- ished at you, Murbles ! The law has nothing to do with good intentions. What does the Act *say* ? It says, ' To the brothers and sisters of the whole blood and their issue.' Now, in the absence of any new definition, I should say that the word is here to be construed as before the Act it was construed on intestacy—in so far, at any rate, as it refers to personal property, which I understand the pro- perty in question to be, eh ? "

" Yes," said Mr. Murbles.

" Then I don't see that you and your great-niece have a leg to stand on—come now ! "

" Excuse me," said Wimsey, " but d'you mind—I know lay people are awful ignorant nuisances—but if you *would* be so good as to explain what the beastly word did or does mean, it would be frightfully helpful, don't you know."

" Ha ! Well, it's like this," said Mr. Towkington, graciously. " Before 1837——"

" Queen Victoria, I know," said Peter, intelligently.

" Quite so. At the time when Queen Victoria came to the throne, the word ' issue ' had no legal meaning—no legal meaning at all."

" You surprise me ! "

" You are too easily surprised," said Mr. Towkington.
" Many words have no legal meaning. Others have a legal
meaning very unlike their ordinary meaning. For example,
the word ' daffy-down-dilly.' It is a criminal libel to call
a lawyer a daffy-down-dilly. Ha ! Yes, I advise you never
to do such a thing. No, I certainly advise you *never* to do
it. Then again, words which are quite meaningless in your
ordinary conversation may have a meaning in law. For
instance, I might say to a young man like yourself, ' You
wish to leave such-and-such property to so-and-so.' And
you would very likely reply, ' Oh, yes, absolutely '—meaning nothing in particular by that. But if you were to write
in your will, ' I leave such-and-such property to so-and-
so *absolutely*,' then that word would bear a definite legal
meaning, and would condition your bequest in a certain
manner, and might even prove an embarrassment and
produce results very far from your actual intentions. Eh,
ha ! You see ? "

" Quite."

" Very well. Prior to 1837, the word ' issue ' meant
nothing. A grant ' to A. and his issue' merely gave A. a life
estate. Ha ! But this was altered by the Wills Act of 1837."

" As far as a will was concerned," put in Mr. Murbles.

" Precisely. After 1837, in a will, ' issue ' means ' heirs
of the body '—that is to say, ' issue *ad infinitum*.' In a
deed, on the other hand, ' issue ' retained its old meaning
—or lack of meaning, eh, ha ! You follow ? "

" Yes," said Mr. Murbles, " and on intestacy of personal
property——"

" I am coming to that," said Mr. Towkington.

" ——the word ' issue ' continued to mean ' heirs of the
body,' and that held good till 1926."

" Stop ! " said Mr. Towkington, " issue of the child or
children of the deceased certainly meant ' issue *ad infinitum* '—*but*—issue of any person *not* a child of the deceased

only meant the child of that person and did not include other descendants. And that undoubtedly held good till 1926. And since the new Act contains no statement to the contrary, I think we must presume that it continues to hold good. Ha ! Come now ! In the case before us, you observe that the claimant is *not* the child of the deceased nor issue of the child of the deceased ; nor is she the child of the deceased's sister. She is merely the grandchild of the deceased sister of the deceased. Accordingly, I think she is debarred from inheriting under the new Act, eh ? ha ! "

" I see your point," said Mr. Murbles.

" And moreover," went on Mr. Towkington, " after 1925, ' issue ' in a will or deed does *not* mean ' issue *ad infinitum.*' That at least is clearly stated, and the Wills Act of 1837 is revoked on that point. Not that that has any direct bearing on the question. But it may be an indication of the tendency of modern interpretation, and might possibly affect the mind of the court in deciding how the word ' issue ' was to be construed for the purposes of the new Act."

" Well," said Mr. Murbles, " I bow to your superior knowledge."

" In any case," broke in Parker, " any uncertainty in the matter would provide as good a motive for murder as the certainty of exclusion from inheritance. If Mary Whittaker only *thought* she might lose the money in the event of her great-aunt's surviving into 1926, she might quite well be tempted to polish her off a little earlier, and make sure."

" That's true enough," said Mr. Murbles.

" Shrewd, very shrewd, ha ! " added Mr. Towkington. " But you realise that all this theory of yours depends on Mary Whittaker's having known about the new Act and its probable consequences as early as October, 1925, eh, ha ! "

" There's no reason why she shouldn't," said Wimsey.
" I remember reading an article in the *Evening Banner*, I
think it was, some months earlier—about the time when
the Act was having its second reading. That's what put
the thing into my head—I was trying to remember all
evening where I'd seen that thing about washing out the
long-lost heir, you know. Mary Whittaker may easily have
seen it too."

" Well, she'd probably have taken advice about it if
she did," said Mr. Murbles. " Who is her usual man of
affairs ? "

Wimsey shook his head.

" I don't think she'd have asked him," he objected.
" Not if she was wise, that is. You see, if she did, and he
said she probably wouldn't get anything unless Miss Dawson either made a will or died before January, 1926, and
if after that the old lady did unexpectedly pop off in
October, 1925, wouldn't the solicitor-johnnie feel inclined
to ask questions ? It wouldn't be safe, don't y'know. I 'xpect
she went to some stranger and asked a few innocent little
questions under another name, what ? "

" Probably," said Mr. Towkington. " You show a remarkable disposition for crime, don't you, eh ? "

" Well, if I did go in for it, I'd take reasonable precautions," retorted Wimsey. " 'S wonderful, of course, the
tom-fool things murderers *do* do. But I have the highest
opinion of Miss Whittaker's brains. I bet she covered her
tracks pretty well."

" You don't think Mr. Probyn mentioned the matter,"
suggested Parker, " the time he went down and tried to
get Miss Dawson to make her will."

" I *don't*," said Wimsey, with energy, " but I'm pretty
certain he tried to explain matters to the old lady, only
she was so terrified of the very idea of a will she wouldn't
let him get a word in. But I fancy old Probyn was too
downy a bird to tell the heir that her only chance of gettin'

the dollars was to see that her great-aunt died off before the Act went through. Would *you* tell anybody that, Mr. Towkington ? "

" Not if I knew it," said that gentleman, grinning.

" It would be highly undesirable," agreed Mr. Murbles.

" Anyway," said Wimsey, " we can easily find out. Probyn's in Italy—I was going to write to him, but perhaps you'd better do it, Murbles. And, in the meanwhile, Charles and I will think up a way to find whoever it was that did give Miss Whittaker an opinion on the matter."

" You're not forgetting, I suppose," said Parker, rather dryly, " that before pinning down a murder to any particular motive, it is usual to ascertain that a murder has been committed ? So far, all we know is that, after a careful post-mortem analysis, two qualified doctors have agreed that Miss Dawson died a natural death."

" I wish you wouldn't keep on saying the same thing, Charles. It bores me so. It's like the Raven never flitting which, as the poet observes, still is sitting, still is sitting, inviting one to heave the pallid bust of Pallas at him and have done with it. You wait till I publish my epoch-making work : *The Murderer's Vade-Mecum, or* 101 *Ways of Causing Sudden Death*. That'll show you I'm not a man to be trifled with."

" Oh, well ! " said Parker.

But he saw the Chief Commissioner next morning and reported that he was at last disposed to take the Dawson case seriously.

CHAPTER XV

TEMPTATION OF ST. PETER

PIERROT : " Scaramel, I am tempted."
SCARAMEL : " Always yield to temptation."

L. HOUSMAN : *Prunella*

As PARKER came out from the Chief Commissioner's room, he was caught by an officer.

" There's been a lady on the 'phone to you," he said. " I told her to ring up at 10.30. It's about that now."

" What name ? "

" A Mrs. Forrest. She wouldn't say what she wanted."

" Odd," thought Parker. His researches in the matter had been so unfruitful that he had practically eliminated Mrs. Forrest from the Gotobed mystery—merely keeping her filed, as it were, in the back of his mind for future reference. It occurred to him, whimsically, that she had at length discovered the absence of one of her wine-glasses and was ringing him up in a professional capacity. His conjectures were interrupted by his being called to the telephone to answer Mrs. Forrest's call.

" Is that Detective-Inspector Parker ?—I'm so sorry to trouble you, but could you possibly give me Mr. Templeton's address ? "

" Templeton ? " said Parker, momentarily puzzled.

" Wasn't it Templeton—the gentleman who came with you to see me ? "

" Oh, yes, of course—I beg your pardon—I—the matter had slipped my memory. Er—you want his address ? "

" I have some information which I think he will be glad to hear."

" Oh, yes. You can speak quite freely to me, you know, Mrs. Forrest."

" Not *quite* freely," purred the voice at the other end of the wire, " you are rather official, you know. I should prefer just to write to Mr. Templeton privately, and leave it to him to take up with you."

" I see." Parker's brain worked briskly. It might be inconvenient to have Mrs. Forrest writing to Mr. Templeton at 110A, Piccadilly. The letter might not be delivered. Or, if the lady were to take it into her head to call and discovered that Mr. Templeton was not known to the porter, she might take alarm and bottle up her valuable information.

" I think," said Parker, " I ought not, perhaps, to give you Mr. Templeton's address without consulting him. But you could 'phone him——"

" Oh, yes, that would do. Is he in the book ? "

" No—but I can give you his private number."

" Thank you very much. You'll forgive my bothering you."

" No trouble at all." And he named Lord Peter's number.

Having rung off, he waited a moment and then called the number himself.

" Look here, Wimsey," he said, " I've had a call from Mrs. Forrest. She wants to write to you. I wouldn't give the address, but I've given her your number, so if she calls and asks for Mr. Templeton, you will remember who you are, won't you ? "

" Righty-ho ! Wonder what the fair lady wants."

" It's probably occurred to her that she might have told a better story, and she wants to work off a few additions and improvements on you."

" Then she'll probably give herself away. The rough sketch is frequently so much more convincing than the worked-up canvas."

" Quite so. I couldn't get anything out of her myself."

" No. I expect she's thought it over and decided that it's rather unusual to employ Scotland Yard to ferret out the whereabouts of errant husbands. She fancies there's something up, and that I'm a nice soft-headed imbecile whom she can easily pump in the absence of the official Cerberus."

" Probably. Well, you'll deal with the matter. I'm going to make a search for that solicitor."

" Rather a vague sort of search, isn't it ? "

" Well, I've got an idea which may work out. I'll let you know if I get any results."

.   .   .   .

Mrs. Forrest's call duly came through in about twenty minutes' time. Mrs. Forrest had changed her mind. Would Mr. Templeton come round and see her that evening— about 9 o'clock, if that was convenient ? She had thought the matter over and preferred not to put her information on paper.

Mr. Templeton would be very happy to come round. He had no other engagement. It was no inconvenience at all. He begged Mrs. Forrest not to mention it.

Would Mr. Templeton be so very good as not to tell any-body about his visit ? Mr. Forrest and his sleuths were con-tinually on the watch to get Mrs. Forrest into trouble, and the decree absolute was due to come up in a month's time. Any trouble with the King's Proctor would be positively disastrous. It would be better if Mr. Templeton would come by Underground to Bond Street, and proceed to the flats on foot, so as not to leave a car standing outside the door or put a taxi-driver into a position to give testimony against Mrs. Forrest.

Mr. Templeton chivalrously promised to obey these directions.

Mrs. Forrest was greatly obliged, and would expect him at nine o'clock.

" Bunter ! "

" My lord."

" I am going out to-night. I've been asked not to say where, so I won't. On the other hand, I've got a kind of feelin' that it's unwise to disappear from mortal ken, so to speak. Anything might happen. One might have a stroke, don't you know. So I'm going to leave the address in a sealed envelope. If I don't turn up before to-morrow mornin', I shall consider myself absolved from all promises, what ? "

" Very good, my lord."

" And if I'm not to be found at that address, there wouldn't be any harm in tryin'—say Epping Forest, or Wimbledon Common."

" Quite so, my lord."

" By the way, you made the photographs of those finger-prints I brought you some time ago ? "

" Oh, yes, my lord."

" Because possibly Mr. Parker may be wanting them presently for some inquiries he will be making."

" I quite understand, my lord."

" Nothing whatever to do with my excursion to-night, you understand."

" Certainly not, my lord."

" And now you might bring me Christie's catalogue. I shall be attending a sale there and lunching at the club."

And, detaching his mind from crime, Lord Peter bent his intellectual and financial powers to outbidding and breaking a ring of dealers, an exercise very congenial to his mischievous spirit.

.   .   .   .

Lord Peter duly fulfilled the conditions imposed upon him, and arrived on foot at the block of flats in South Audley Street. Mrs. Forrest, as before, opened the door to him herself. It was surprising, he considered, that, situated as she was, she appeared to have neither maid nor companion. But then, he supposed, a chaperon, however disarming of suspicion in the eyes of the world, might prove venal. On the whole, Mrs. Forrest's principle was a sound one : no accomplices. Many transgressors, he reflected, had

> " *died because they never knew*
> *These simple little rules and few.*"

Mrs. Forrest apologised prettily for the inconvenience to which she was putting Mr. Templeton.

" But I never know when I am not spied upon," she said. " It is sheer spite, you know. Considering how my husband has behaved to me, I think it is monstrous—don't you ? "

Her guest agreed that Mr. Forrest must be a monster, jesuitically, however, reserving the opinion that the monster might be a fabulous one.

" And now you will be wondering why I have brought you here," went on the lady. " Do come and sit on the sofa. Will you have whisky or coffee ? "

" Coffee, please."

" The fact is," said Mrs. Forrest, " that I've had an idea since I saw you. I—you know, having been much in the same position myself " (with a slight laugh) " I felt *so much* for your friend's wife."

" Sylvia," put in Lord Peter with commendable promptitude. " Oh, yes. Shocking temper and so on, but possibly some provocation. Yes, yes, quite. Poor woman. Feels things—extra sensitive—highly-strung and all that, don't you know."

" Quite so." Mrs. Forest nodded her fantastically turbanned head. Swathed to the eyebrows in gold tissue, with only two flat crescents of yellow hair plastered over her cheek-bones, she looked, in an exotic smoking-suit of embroidered tissue, like a young prince out of the Arabian

Nights. Her heavily ringed hands busied themselves with the coffee-cups.

"Well—I felt that your inquiries were really serious, you know, and though, as I told you, it had nothing to do with me, I was interested and mentioned the matter in a letter to—to my friend, you see, who was with me that night."

"Just so," said Wimsey, taking the cup from her, "yes—er—that was very—er—it was kind of you to be interested."

"He—my friend—is abroad at the moment. My letter had to follow him, and I only got his reply to-day."

Mrs. Forrest took a sip or two of coffee as though to clear her recollection.

"His letter rather surprised me. He reminded me that after dinner he had felt the room rather close, and had opened the sitting-room window—that window, there—which overlooks South Audley Street. He noticed a car standing there—a small closed one, black or dark blue or some such colour. And while he was looking idly at it—the way one does, you know—he saw a man and woman come out of this block of flats—not this door, but one or two along to the left—and get in and drive off. The man was in evening dress and he thought it might have been your friend."

Lord Peter, with his coffee-cup at his lips, paused and listened with great attention.

"Was the girl in evening dress, too?"

"No—that struck my friend particularly. She was in just a plain little dark suit, with a hat on."

Lord Peter recalled to mind as nearly as possible Bertha Gotobed's costume. Was this going to be real evidence at last?

"Th—that's very interesting," he stammered. "I suppose your friend couldn't give any more exact details of the dress?"

"No," replied Mrs. Forrest, regretfully, "but he said the man's arm was round the girl as though she was feeling

tired or unwell, and he heard him say, ' That's right—the
fresh air will do you good.' But you're not drinking your
coffee."

" I beg your pardon——" Wimsey recalled himself with
a start. " I was dreamin'—puttin' two and two together, as
you might say. So he *was* along here all the time—the artful
beggar. Oh, the coffee. D'you mind if I put this away and
have some without sugar ? "

" I'm *so* sorry. Men always seem to take sugar in black
coffee. Give it to me—I'll empty it away."

" Allow me." There was no slop-basin on the little table,
but Wimsey quickly got up and poured the coffee into the
window-box outside. " That's all right. How about another
cup for you ? "

" Thank you—I oughtn't to take it really, it keeps me
awake."

" Just a drop."

" Oh, well, if you like." She filled both cups and sat
sipping quietly. " Well—that's all, really, but I thought
perhaps I ought to let you know."

" It was very good of you," said Wimsey.

They sat talking a little longer—about plays in Town
(" I go out very little, you know, it's better to keep oneself
out of the limelight on these occasions "), and books (" I
adore Michael Arlen "). Had she read *Young Men in Love*
yet ? No—she had ordered it from the library. Wouldn't
Mr. Templeton have something to eat or drink ? Really ?
A brandy ? A liqueur ?

No, thank you. And Mr. Templeton felt he really ought
to be slippin' along now.

"No—don't go yet—I get so lonely, these long evenings."

There was a desperate kind of appeal in her voice. Lord
Peter sat down again.

She began a rambling and rather confused story about
her " friend." She had given up so much for the friend.
And now that her divorce was really coming off, she had a

terrible feeling that perhaps the friend was not as affectionate as he used to be. It was very difficult for a woman, and life was very hard.

And so on.

As the minutes passed, Lord Peter became uncomfortably aware that she was watching him. The words tumbled out—hurriedly, yet lifelesssly, like a set task, but her eyes were the eyes of a person who expects something. Something alarming, he decided, yet something she was determinded to have. It reminded him of a man waiting for an operation—keyed up to it—knowing that it will do him good—yet shrinking from it with all his senses.

He kept up his end of the fatuous conversation. Behind a barrage of small-talk, his mind ran quickly to and fro, analysing the position, getting the range . . .

Suddenly he became aware that she was trying—clumsily, stupidly and as though in spite of herself—to get him to make love to her.

The fact itself did not strike Wimsey as odd. He was rich enough, well-bred enough, attractive enough and man of the world enough to have received similar invitations fairly often in his thirty-seven years of life. And not always from experienced women. There had been those who sought experience as well as those qualified to bestow it. But so awkward an approach by a woman who admitted to already possessing a husband and a lover was a phenomenon outside his previous knowledge.

Moreover, he felt that the thing would be a nuisance. Mrs. Forrest was handsome enough, but she had not a particle of attraction for him. For all her make-up and her somewhat outspoken costume, she struck him as spinsterish—even epicene. That was the thing which puzzled him during their previous interview. Parker—a young man of rigid virtue and limited worldly knowledge—was not sensitive to these emanations. But Wimsey had felt her as something essentially sexless, even then. And he felt it even more strongly now. Never had he met a woman in whom " the great It," eloquently hymned by Mrs. Elinor Glyn, was so completely lacking.

Her bare shoulder was against him now, marking his broadcloth with white patches of powder.

Blackmail was the first explanation that occurred to him. The next move would be for the fabulous Mr. Forrest, or someone representing him, to appear suddenly in the doorway, aglow with virtuous wrath and outraged sensibilities.

" A very pretty little trap," thought Wimsey, adding aloud, " Well, I really must be getting along."

She caught him by the arm.

" Don't go."

There was no caress in the touch—only a kind of desperation.

He thought, " If she really made a practice of this, she would do it better."

" Truly," he said, " I oughtn't to stay longer. It wouldn't be safe for you."

" I'll risk it," she said.

A passionate woman might have said it passionately. Or with a brave gaiety. Or challengingly. Or alluringly. Or mysteriously.

She said it grimly. Her fingers dug at his arm.

" Well, damn it all, *I'll* risk it," thought Wimsey. " I must and will know what it's all about."

" Poor little woman." He coaxed into his voice the throaty, fatuous tone of the man who is preparing to make an amorous fool of himself.

He felt her body stiffen as he slipped his arm round her, but she gave a little sigh of relief.

He pulled her suddenly and violently to him, and kissed her mouth with a practised exaggeration of passion.

He knew then. No one who has ever encountered it can ever again mistake that awful shrinking, that uncontrollable revulsion of the flesh against a caress that is nauseous. He thought for a moment that she was going to be actually sick.

He released her gently, and stood up—his mind in a whirl, but somehow triumphant. His first instinct had been right, after all.

" That was very naughty of me," he said, lightly. " You made me forget myself. You will forgive me, won't you ? "

She nodded, shaken.

" And I really must toddle. It's gettin' frightfully late and all that. Where's my hat ? Ah, yes, in the hall. Now, good-bye, Mrs. Forrest, an' take care of yourself. An' thank you ever so much for telling me about what your friend saw."

" You are really going ? "

She spoke as though she had lost all hope.

" In God's name," thought Wimsey, " what does she want ? Does she suspect that Mr. Templeton is not every-thing that he seems ? Does she want me to stay the night so that she can get a look at the laundry-mark on my shirt ? Should I suddenly save the situation for her by offering her Lord Peter Wimsey's visiting-card ? "

His brain toyed freakishly with the thought as he babbled his way to the door. She let him go without further words.

As he stepped into the hall he turned and looked at her. She stood in the middle of the room, watching him, and on her face was such a fury of fear and rage as turned his blood to water.

CHAPTER XVI

A CAST-IRON ALIBI

" Oh, Sammy, Sammy, why vorn't there an alleybi ? "
Pickwick Papers

MISS WHITTAKER and the youngest Miss Findlater
had returned from their expedition. Miss Climpson, most
faithful of sleuths, and carrying Lord Peter's letter of
instructions in the pocket of her skirt like a talisman, had
asked the youngest Miss Findlater to tea.

As a matter of fact, Miss Climpson had become genuinely
interested in the girl. Silly affectation and gush, and a
parrot-repetition of the shibboleths of the modern school
were symptoms that the experienced spinster well understood. They indicated, she thought, a real unhappiness, a
real dissatisfaction with the narrowness of life in a country
town. And besides this, Miss Climpson felt sure that Vera
Findlater was being " preyed upon," as she expressed it
to herself, by the handsome Mary Whittaker. " It would
be a mercy for the girl," thought Miss Climpson, " if she
could form a genuine attachment to a young man. It is
natural for a schoolgirl to be *schwärmerisch*—in a young
woman of twenty-two it is thoroughly undesirable. That
Whittaker woman encourages it—she would, of course.
She likes to have someone to admire her and run her
errands. And she prefers it to be a stupid person, who will
not compete with her. If Mary Whittaker were to marry,
she would marry a rabbit." (Miss Climpson's active mind
quickly conjured up a picture of the rabbit—fair-haired
and a little paunchy, with a habit of saying, " I'll ask
the wife." Miss Climpson wondered why Providence saw

fit to create such men. For Miss Climpson, men were intended to be masterful, even though wicked or foolish. She was a spinster made and not born—a perfectly womanly woman.)

"But," thought Miss Climpson, " Mary Whittaker is not of the marrying sort. She is a professional woman by nature. She has a profession, by the way, but she does not intend to go back to it. Probably nursing demands too much sympathy—and one is under the authority of the doctors. Mary Whittaker prefers to control the lives of chicken. ' Better to reign in hell than serve in heaven.' Dear me ! I wonder if it is uncharitable to compare a fellow-being to Satan. Only in poetry, of course—I daresay that makes it not so bad. At any rate, I am certain that Mary Whittaker is doing Vera Findlater no good."

Miss Climpson's guest was very ready to tell about their month in the country. They had toured round at first for a few days, and then they had heard of a delightful poultry farm which was for sale, near Orpington in Kent. So they had gone down to have a look at it, and found that it was to be sold in about a fortnight's time. It wouldn't have been wise, of course, to take it over without some inquiries, and by the greatest good fortune they found a dear little cottage to let, furnished, quite close by. So they had taken it for a few weeks, while Miss Whittaker " looked round " and found out about the state of the poultry business in that district, and so on. They *had* enjoyed it so, and it was delightful keeping house together, right away from all the silly people at home.

"Of course, I don't mean you, Miss Climpson. You come from London and are so much more broadminded. But I simply can't stick the Leahampton lot, nor can Mary."

"It is very delightful," said Miss Climpson, " to be *free* from the conventions, I'm sure—especially if one is in company with a *kindred spirit*."

" Yes—of course Mary and I are tremendous friends, though she is so much cleverer than I am. It's absolutely settled that we're to take the farm and run it together. Won't it be wonderful ? "

" Won't you find it rather dull and lonely—just you two girls together ? You mustn't forget that you've been accustomed to see quite a lot of young people in Lea-hampton. Shan't you miss the tennis-parties, and the young men, and so on ? "

" Oh, no ! If you only knew what a stupid lot they are ! Anyway, I've no use for men ! " Miss Findlater tossed her head. " They haven't got any ideas. And they always look on women as sort of pets or playthings. As if a woman like Mary wasn't worth fifty of them ! You should have heard that Markham man the other day—talking politics to Mr. Tredgold, so that nobody could get a word in edgeways, and then saying, ' I'm afraid this is a very dull subject of conversation for you, Miss Whittaker,' in his condescending way. Mary said in that quiet way of hers, ' Oh, I think the *subject* is anything but dull, Mr. Markham.' But he was so stupid, he couldn't even grasp that and said, ' One doesn't expect ladies to be interested in politics, you know. But perhaps you are one of the modern young ladies who want the flapper's vote.' Ladies, indeed ! Why are men so insufferable when they talk about ladies ? "

" I think men are apt to be *jealous* of women," replied Miss Climpson, thoughtfully, " and jealousy *does* make people rather *peevish* and *ill-mannered*. I suppose that when one would *like* to despise a set of people and yet has a horrid suspicion that one *can't* genuinely despise them, it makes one *exaggerate* one's contempt for them in conversa-tion. That is why, my dear, I am always *very* careful not to speak sneeringly about men—even though they *often deserve* it, you know. But if I did, everybody would think I was an *envious old maid*, wouldn't they ? "

" Well, I mean to be an old maid, anyhow," retorted

Miss Findlater. " Mary and I have quite decided that.
We're interested in things, not in men."

" You've made a good start at finding out how it's going
to work," said Miss Climpson. " Living with a person for
a month is an *excellent* test. I suppose you had somebody
to do the housework for you."

" Not a soul. We did every bit of it, and it was great
fun. I'm ever so good at scrubbing floors and laying fires
and things, and Mary's a simply marvellous cook. It was
such a change from having the servants always bothering
round like they do at home. Of course, it was quite a
modern, labour-saving cottage—it belongs to some
theatrical people, I think."

" And what did you do when you weren't inquiring
into the poultry business ? "

" Oh, we ran round in the car and saw places and
attended markets. Markets are frightfully amusing, with
all the funny old farmers and people. Of course, I'd often
been to markets before, but Mary made it all so interesting
—and then, too, we were picking up hints all the time for
our own marketing later on."

" Did you run up to Town at all ? "

" No."

" I should have thought you'd have taken the opportunity for a little jaunt."

" Mary hates Town."

" I thought *you* rather enjoyed a run up now and then."

" I'm not keen. Not now. I used to think I was, but I
expect that was only the sort of spiritual restlessness one
gets when one hasn't an object in life. There's nothing
in it."

Miss Findlater spoke with the air of a disillusioned rake,
who has sucked life's orange and found it dead sea fruit.
Miss Climpson did not smile. She was accustomed to the
rôle of confidante.

" So you were together—just you two—all the time ? "

" Every minute of it. And we weren't bored with one
another a bit."

" I hope your experiment will prove very successful,"
said Miss Climpson. " But when you really start on your
life together, don't you think it would be wise to arrange
for a few *breaks* in it ? A little *change of companionship* is good
for *everybody*. I've known so many *happy friendships* spoilt
by people seeing *too much* of one another."

" They couldn't have been *real* friendships, then,"
asserted the girl, dogmatically. " Mary and I are *absolutely*
happy together."

" Still," said Miss Climpson, " if you don't mind an
old woman giving you a word of warning, I should be
inclined not to keep the bow *always* bent. Suppose Miss
Whittaker, for instance, wanted to go off and have a day
in Town on her own, say—or go to stay with friends—you
would have to learn not to mind that."

" Of course I shouldn't mind. Why——" she checked
herself. " I mean, I'm quite sure that Mary would be
every bit as loyal to me as I am to her."

" That's right," said Miss Climpson. " The longer I live,
my dear, the more *certain* I become that *jealousy* is the most
fatal of feelings. The Bible calls it ' cruel as the grave,' and
I'm sure that is so. *Absolute* loyalty, without jealousy, is
the essential thing."

" Yes. Though naturally one would hate to think that
the person one was really friends with was putting another
person in one's place . . . Miss Climpson, you do believe,
don't you, that a friendship ought to be ' fifty-fifty ' ? "

" That is the ideal friendship, I suppose," said Miss
Climpson, thoughtfully, " but I think it is a *very rare thing*.
Among women, that is. I doubt very much if I've ever
seen an example of it. *Men*, I believe, find it easier to give
and take in that way—probably because they have so
many outside interests."

" Men's friendships—oh yes ! I know one hears a lot

about them. But half the time, I don't believe they're *real* friendships at all. Men can go off for years and forget all about their friends. And they don't really confide in one another. Mary and I tell each other all our thoughts and feelings. Men seem just content to think each other good sorts without ever bothering about their inmost selves."

"Probably that's why their friendships last so well," replied Miss Climpson. "They don't make such demands on one another."

"But a great friendship does make demands," cried Miss Findlater eagerly. "It's got to be just everything to one. It's wonderful the way it seems to colour all one's thoughts. Instead of being centred in oneself, one's centred in the other person. That's what Christian love means—one's ready to die for the other person."

"Well, I don't know," said Miss Climpson. "I once heard a sermon about that from a most *splendid* priest— and he said that that kind of love might become *idolatry* if one wasn't very careful. He said that Milton's remark about Eve—you know, ' he for God only, she for God in him '—was not congruous with Catholic doctrine. One must get the *proportions* right, and it was *out of proportion* to see everything through the eyes of another fellow-creature."

"One must put God first, of course," said Miss Findlater, a little formally. "But if the friendship is mutual—that was the point—quite unselfish on both sides, it *must* be a good thing."

"Love is always good, when it's the *right kind*," agreed Miss Climpson, "but I don't think it ought to be too *possessive*. One has to *train* oneself——" she hesitated, and went on courageously—"and in any case, my dear, I cannot help feeling that it is more natural—more proper, in a sense—for a man and woman to be all in all to one another than for two persons of the same sex. Er—after all, it is a—a *fruitful* affection," said Miss Climpson, boggling a trifle at this idea, "and—and all that, you know, and I am sure that when the *right* MAN comes along for you——"

" Bother the right man ! " cried Miss Findlater, crossly. " I do hate that kind of talk. It makes one feel dreadful—like a prize cow or something. Surely, we have got beyond that point of view in these days."

Miss Climpson perceived that she had let her honest zeal outrun her detective discretion. She had lost the goodwill of her informant, and it was better to change the conversation. However, she could assure Lord Peter now of one thing. Whoever the woman was that Mrs. Cropper had seen at Liverpool, it was not Miss Whittaker. The attached Miss Findlater, who had never left her friend's side, was sufficient guarantee of that.

CHAPTER XVII

THE COUNTRY LAWYER'S STORY

" And he that gives us in these days new lords may give us new laws."

WITHER : *Contented Man's Morrice*

Letter from Mr. Probyn, retired Solicitor, of Villa Bianca, Fiesole, to Mr. Murbles, Solicitor, of Staple Inn.

" *Private and confidential.*

" DEAR SIR,

" I was much interested in your letter relative to the death of Miss Agatha Dawson, late of Leahampton, and will do my best to answer your inquiries as briefly as possible, always, of course, on the understanding that all information as to the affairs of my late client will be treated as strictly confidential. I make an exception, of course, in favour of the police officer you mention in connection with the matter.

" You wish to know (1) whether Miss Agatha Dawson was aware that it might possibly prove necessary, under the provisions of the new Act, for her to make a testamentary disposition, in order to ensure that her greatniece, Miss Mary Whittaker, should inherit her personal property. (2) Whether I ever urged her to make this testamentary disposition and what her reply was. (3) Whether I had made Miss Mary Whittaker aware of the situation in which she might be placed, supposing her great-aunt to die intestate later than December 31, 1925.

" In the course of the Spring of 1925, my attention was called by a learned friend to the ambiguity of the wording of certain clauses in the Act, especially in respect of the failure to define the precise interpretation to be placed on the word ' Issue.' I immediately passed in review the affairs of my various clients, with a view to satisfying myself that the proper dispositions had been made in each case to avoid misunderstanding and litigation in case of intestacy. I at once realised that Miss Whittaker's inheritance of Miss Dawson's property entirely depended on the interpretation given to the clauses in question. I was aware that Miss Dawson was extremely averse from making a will, owing to that superstitious dread of decease which we meet with so frequently in our profession. However, I thought it my duty to make her understand the question and to do my utmost to get a will signed. Accordingly, I went down to Leahampton and laid the matter before her. This was on March the 14th, or thereabouts—I am not certain to the precise day.

" Unhappily, I encountered Miss Dawson at a moment when her opposition to the obnoxious idea of making a will was at its strongest. Her doctor had informed her that a further operation would become necessary in the course of the next few weeks, and I could have selected no more unfortunate occasion for intruding the subject of death upon her mind. She resented any such suggestion —there was a conspiracy, she declared, to frighten her into dying under the operation. It appears that that very tactless practitioner of hers had frightened her with a similar suggestion before her previous operation. But she had come through that and she meant to come through this, if only people would not anger and alarm her.

" Of course, if she *had* died under the operation, the whole question would have settled itself and there would have been no need of any will. I pointed out that the very reason why I was anxious for the will to be made was

that I fully expected her to live on into the following
year, and I explained the provisions of the Act once
more, as clearly as I could. She retorted that in that case
I had no business to come and trouble her about the
question at all. It would be time enough when the Act
was passed.

" Naturally, the fool of a doctor had insisted that she
was not to be told what her disease was—they always do—
and she was convinced that the next operation would
make all right and that she would live for years. When I
ventured to insist—giving as my reason that we men of
law always preferred to be on the safe and cautious side,
she became exceedingly angry with me, and practically
ordered me out of the house. A few days afterwards I
received a letter from her, complaining of my impertinence, and saying that she could no longer feel any
confidence in a person who treated her with such inconsiderate rudeness. At her request, I forwarded all her
private papers in my possession to Mr. Hodgson, of
Leahampton, and I have not held any communication
with any member of the family since that date.

" This answers your first and second questions. With
regard to the third : I certainly did not think it proper
to inform Miss Whittaker that her inheritance might
depend upon her great-aunt's either making a will or
else dying before December 31, 1925. While I know
nothing to the young lady's disadvantage, I have always
held it inadvisable that persons should know too exactly
how much they stand to gain by the unexpected decease
of other persons. In case of any unforeseen accident, the
heirs may find themselves in an equivocal position, where
the fact of their possessing such knowledge might—if
made public—be highly prejudicial to their interests.
The most that I thought it proper to say was that if at
any time Miss Dawson should express a wish to see me,
I should like to be sent for without delay. Of course, the

withdrawal of Miss Dawson's affairs from my hands put it out of my power to interfere any further.

"In October, 1925, feeling that my health was not what it had been, I retired from business and came to Italy. In this country the English papers do not always arrive regularly, and I missed the announcement of Miss Dawson's death. That it should have occurred so suddenly and under circumstances somewhat mysterious, is certainly interesting.

"You say further that you would be glad of my opinion on Miss Agatha Dawson's mental condition at the time when I last saw her. It was perfectly clear and competent —in so far as she was ever competent to deal with business. She was in no way gifted to grapple with legal problems, and I had extreme difficulty in getting her to understand what the trouble was with regard to the new Property Act. Having been brought up all her life to the idea that property went of right to the next of kin, she found it inconceivable that this state of things should ever alter. She assured me that the law would never permit the Government to pass such an Act. When I had reluctantly persuaded her that it would, she was quite sure that no court would be wicked enough to interpret the Act so as to give the money to anybody but Miss Whittaker, when she was clearly the proper person to have it. ' Why should the Duchy of Lancaster have any right to it ? ' she kept on saying. ' I don't even know the Duke of Lancaster.' She was not a particularly sensible woman, and in the end I was not at all sure that I had made her comprehend the situation—quite apart from the dislike she had of pursuing the subject. However, there is no doubt that she was then quite *compos mentis*. My reason for urging her to make the will before her final operation was, of course, that I feared she might subsequently lose the use of her faculties, or—which comes to the same thing from a business point of view—

might have to be kept continually under the influence of opiates.

"Trusting that you will find here the information you require,

"I remain,
"Yours faithfully,
"THOS. PROBYN."

Mr. Murbles read this letter through twice, very thoughtfully. To even his cautious mind, the thing began to look like the makings of a case. In his neat, elderly hand, he wrote a little note to Detective-Inspector Parker, begging him to call at Staple Inn at his earliest convenience.

Mr. Parker, however, was experiencing nothing at that moment but inconvenience. He had been calling on solicitors for two whole days, and his soul sickened at the sight of a brass plate. He glanced at the long list in his hand, and distastefully counted up the scores of names that still remained unticked.

Parker was one of those methodical, painstaking people whom the world could so ill spare. When he worked with Wimsey on a case, it was an understood thing that anything lengthy, intricate, tedious and soul-destroying was done by Parker. He sometimes felt that it was irritating of Wimsey to take this so much for granted. He felt so now. It was a hot day. The pavements were dusty. Pieces of paper blew about the streets. Buses were grilling outside and stuffy inside. The Express Dairy, where Parker was eating a hurried lunch, seemed full of the odours of fried plaice and boiling tea-urns. Wimsey, he knew, was lunching at his club, before running down with Freddy Arbuthnot to see the New Zealanders at somewhere or other. He had seen him—a vision of exquisite pale grey, ambling gently along Pall Mall. Damn Wimsey! Why couldn't he have let Miss Dawson rest quietly in her grave? There she was, doing no harm to anybody—and Wimsey must insist on prying into her affairs and bringing the inquiry to such a point that Parker simply had to take official notice of it. Oh well ! he supposed he must go on with these infernal solicitors.

He was proceeding on a system of his own, which might or might not prove fruitful. He had reviewed the subject of the new Property Act, and decided that if and when Miss Whittaker had become aware of its possible effect on her own expectations, she would at once consider taking legal advice.

Her first thought would no doubt be to consult a solicitor in Leahampton, and unless she already had the idea of foul play in her mind, there was nothing to deter her from doing so. Accordingly, Parker's first move had been to run down to Leahampton and interview the three firms of solicitors there. All three were able to reply quite positively that they had never received such an inquiry from Miss Whittaker, or from anybody, during the year 1925. One solicitor, indeed —the senior partner of Hodgson & Hodgson, to whom Miss Dawson had entrusted her affairs after her quarrel with Mr. Probyn—looked a little oddly at Parker when he heard the question.

" I assure you, Inspector," he said, " that if the point had been brought to my notice in such a way, I should certainly have remembered it, in the light of subsequent events."

" The matter never crossed your mind, I suppose," said Parker, " when the question arose of winding up the estate and proving Miss Whittaker's claim to inherit ? "

" I can't say it did. Had there been any question of searching for next-of-kin it might—I don't say it would— have occurred to me. But I had a very clear history of the family connections from Mr. Probyn, the death took place nearly two months before the Act came into force, and the formalities all went through more or less automatically. In fact, I never thought about the Act one way or another in that connection."

Parker said he was not surprised to hear it, and favoured Mr. Hodgson with Mr. Towkington's learned opinion on the subject, which interested Mr. Hodgson very much. And that was all he got at Leahampton, except that he fluttered Miss Climpson very much by calling upon her and hearing all about her interview with Vera Findlater. Miss Climpson walked to the station with him, in the hope that they might meet Miss Whittaker—" I am sure you would be *interested* to *see* her "—but they were unlucky. On the whole, thought Parker, it might be just as well. After all, though he would like to see Miss Whittaker, he was not particularly keen on her seeing him, especially in Miss Climpson's company. " By the way," he said to Miss Climpson, " you had better explain me in some way to Mrs. Budge, or she may be a bit inquisitive."

" But I *have*," replied Miss Climpson, with an engaging giggle, " when Mrs. Budge said there was a Mr. Parker to see me, of course I realised at *once* that she mustn't know *who* you were, so I said, quite quickly, ' Mr. Parker ! Oh, that must be my nephew Adolphus.' You don't mind being Adolphus, do you ? It's funny, but that was the *only* name that came into my mind at the moment. I can't *think* why, for I've never known an Adolphus."

" Miss Climpson," said Parker, solemnly, " you are a marvellous woman, and I wouldn't mind even if you'd called me Marmaduke."

So here he was, working out his second line of inquiry. If Miss Whittaker did not go to a Leahampton solicitor, to whom would she go ? There was Mr. Probyn, of course, but he did not think she would have selected him. She would not have known him at Crofton, of course—she had never actually lived with her great-aunts. She had met him the day he came down to Leahampton to see Miss Dawson. He had not then taken her into his confidence about the object of his visit, but she must have known from what her aunt said that it had to do with the making of a will. In the light of her new knowledge, she would guess that Mr. Probyn had then had the Act in his mind, and had not thought fit to trust her with the facts. If she asked him now, he would probably reply that Miss Dawson's affairs were no longer in his hands, and refer her to Mr. Hodgson. And besides, if she asked the question and anything were to happen—Mr. Probyn might remember it. No, she would not have approached Mr. Probyn.

What then ?

To the person who has anything to conceal—to the person who wants to lose his identity as one leaf among the leaves of a forest—to the person who asks no more than to pass by and be forgotten, there is one name above others which promises a haven of safety and oblivion. London. Where no one knows his neighbour. Where shops do not know their customers. Where physicians are suddenly called to unknown patients whom they never see again. Where you may lie dead in your house for months together unmissed and unnoticed till the gas-inspector comes to look at the meter. Where strangers are friendly and friends are casual. London, whose rather untidy and grubby bosom is the repository of so many odd secrets. Discreet, incurious and all-enfolding London.

Not that Parker put it that way to himself. He merely thought, " Ten to one she'd try London. They mostly think they're safer there."

Miss Whittaker knew London, of course. She had trained at the Royal Free. That meant she would know Bloomsbury better than any other district. For nobody knew better than Parker how rarely Londoners move out of their own particular little orbit. Unless, of course, she had at some time during her time at the hospital been recommended to a solicitor in another quarter, the chances were that she would have gone to a solicitor in the Bloomsbury or Holborn district.

Unfortunately for Parker, this is a quarter which swarms

with solicitors. Gray's Inn Road, Gray's Inn itself, Bedford Row, Holborn, Lincoln's Inn—the brass plates grow all about as thick as blackberries.

Which was why Parker was feeling so hot, tired and fed-up that June afternoon.

With an impatient grunt he pushed away his eggy plate, paid-at-the-desk-please, and crossed the road towards Bedford Row, which he had marked down as his portion for the afternoon.

He started at the first solicitor's he came to, which happened to be the office of one J. F. Trigg. He was lucky. The youth in the outer office informed him that Mr. Trigg had just returned from lunch, was disengaged, and would see him. Would he walk in ?

Mr. Trigg was a pleasant, fresh-faced man in his early forties. He begged Mr. Parker to be seated and asked what he could do for him.

For the thirty-seventh time, Parker started on the opening gambit which he had devised to suit his purpose.

" I am only temporarily in London, Mr. Trigg, and finding I needed legal advice I was recommended to you by a man I met in a restaurant. He did give me his name, but it has escaped me, and anyway, it's of no great importance, is it ? The point is this. My wife and I have come up to Town to see her great-aunt, who is in a very bad way. In fact, she isn't expected to live.

" Well, now, the old lady has always been very fond of my wife, don't you see, and it has always been an understood thing that Mrs. Parker was to come into her money when she died. It's quite a tidy bit, and we have been—I won't say looking forward to it, but in a kind of mild way counting on it as something for us to retire upon later on. You understand. There aren't any other relations at all, so, though the old lady has often talked about making a will, we didn't worry much, one way or the other, because we took it for granted my wife would come in for anything there was.

But we were talking about it to a friend yesterday, and he took us rather aback by saying that there was a new law or something, and that if my wife's great-aunt hadn't made a will we shouldn't get anything at all. I think he said it would all go to the Crown. I didn't think that could be right and told him so, but my wife is a bit nervous—there are the children to be considered, you see—and she urged me to get legal advice, because her great-aunt may go off at any minute, and we don't know whether there is a will or not. Now, how does a great-niece stand under the new arrangements ? "

" The point has not been made very clear," said Mr. Trigg, " but my advice to you is, to find out whether a will has been made and if not, to get one made without delay if the testatrix is capable of making one. Otherwise I think there is a very real danger of your wife's losing her inheritance."

" You seem quite familiar with the question," said Parker, with a smile ; " I suppose you are always being asked it since this new Act came in ? "

" I wouldn't say ' always.' It is comparatively rare for a great-niece to be left as sole next-of-kin."

" Is it ? Well, yes, I should think it must be. Do you remember being asked that question in the summer of 1925, Mr. Trigg ? "

A most curious expression came over the solicitor's face —it looked almost like alarm.

" What makes you ask that ? "

" You need have no hesitation in answering," said Parker, taking out his official card. " I am a police officer and have a good reason for asking. I put the legal point to you first as a problem of my own, because I was anxious to have your professional opinion first."

" I see. Well, Inspector, in that case I suppose I am justified in telling you all about it. I *was* asked that question in June, 1925."

" Do you remember the circumstances ? "

" Clearly. I am not likely to forget them—or rather, the sequel to them."

" That sounds interesting. Will you tell the story in your own way and with all the details you can remember ? "

" Certainly. Just a moment." Mr. Trigg put his head out into the outer office. " Badcock, I am engaged with Mr. Parker and can't see anybody. Now, Mr. Parker, I am at your service. Won't you smoke ? "

Parker accepted the invitation and lit up his well-worn briar, while Mr. Trigg, rapidly smoking cigarette after cigarette, unfolded his remarkable story.

CHAPTER XVIII

THE LONDON LAWYER'S STORY

" I who am given to novel-reading, how often have I gone out with the doctor when the stranger has summoned him to visit the unknown patient in the lonely house. . . . This Strange Adventure may lead, in a later chapter, to the revealing of a mysterious crime."

The Londoner

"I THINK," said Mr. Trigg, "that it was on the 15th, or 16th June, 1925, that a lady called to ask almost exactly the same question that you have done—only that she represented herself as inquiring on behalf of a friend whose name she did not mention. Yes—I think I can describe her pretty well. She was tall and handsome, with a very clear skin, dark hair and blue eyes—an attractive girl. I remember that she had very fine brows, rather straight, and not much colour in her face, and she was dressed in something summery but very neat. I should think it would be called an embroidered linen dress—I am not an expert on those things—and a shady white hat of panama straw."

"Your recollection seems very clear," said Parker.

"It is ; I have rather a good memory ; besides, I saw her on other occasions, as you shall hear.

"At this first visit she told me—much as you did—that she was only temporarily in Town, and had been casually recommended to me. I told her that I should not like to answer her question off-hand. The Act, you may remember, had only recently passed its Final Reading, and I was by no means up in it. Besides, from just skimming through it, I had convinced myself that various important questions were bound to crop up.

"I told the lady—Miss Grant was the name she gave, by the way—that I should like to take counsel's opinion before giving her any advice, and asked if she could call again the following day. She said she could, rose and thanked me, offering me her hand. In taking it, I happened to notice rather an odd scar, running across the backs of all the fingers—rather as though a chisel or something had slipped at some time. I noticed it quite idly, of course, but it was lucky for me I did.

" Miss Grant duly turned up the next day. I had looked up a very learned friend in the interval, and gave her the same opinion that I gave you just now. She looked rather concerned about it—in fact, almost more annoyed than concerned.

" ' It seems rather unfair,' she said, ' that people's family money should go away to the Crown like that. After all, a great-niece is quite a near relation, really.'

" I replied that, provided the great-niece could call witnesses to prove that the deceased had always had the intention of leaving her the money, the Crown would, in all probability, allot the estate, or a suitable proportion of it, in accordance with the wishes of the deceased. It would, how-ever, lie entirely within the discretion of the court to do so or not, and, of course, if there had been any quarrel or dispute about the matter at any time, the judge might take an unfavourable view of the great-niece's application.

" ' In any case,' I added, ' I don't *know* that the great-niece is excluded under the Act—I only understand that she *may* be. In any case, there are still six months before the Act comes into force, and many things may happen before then.'

" ' You mean that Auntie may die,' she said, ' but she's not really dangerously ill—only mental, as Nurse calls it.'

" Anyhow, she went away then after paying my fee, and I noticed that the ' friend's great-aunt ' had suddenly be-come ' Auntie,' and decided that my client felt a certain personal interest in the matter."

" I fancy she had," said Parker. " When did you see her again ? "

" Oddly enough, I ran across her in the following December. I was having a quick and early dinner in Soho, before going on to a show. The little place I usually patronise was very full, and I had to sit at a table where a woman was already seated. As I muttered the usual formula about ' Was anybody sitting there,' she looked up, and I promptly recognised my client.

" ' Why, how do you do, Miss Grant ? ' I said.

" ' I beg your pardon,' she replied, rather stiffly. ' I think you are mistaken.'

" ' I beg *your* pardon,' said I, stiffer still, ' my name is Trigg, and you came to consult me in Bedford Row last June. But if I am intruding, I apologise and withdraw.'

" She smiled then, and said, ' I'm sorry, I did not recognise you for the moment.'

" I obtained permission to sit at her table.

" By way of starting a conversation, I asked whether she had taken any further advice in the matter of the inheritance. She said no, she had been quite content with what I had told her. Still to make conversation, I inquired whether the great-aunt had made a will after all. She replied, rather briefly, that it had not been necessary ; the old lady had died. I noticed that she was dressed in black, and was confirmed in my opinion that she herself was the great-niece concerned.

" We talked for some time, Inspector, and I will not conceal from you that I found Miss Grant a very interesting personality. She had an almost masculine understanding. I may say I am not the sort of man who prefers women to be brainless. No, I am rather modern in that respect. If ever I was to take a wife, Inspector, I should wish her to be an intelligent companion."

Parker said Mr. Trigg's attitude did him great credit. He also made the mental observation that Mr. Trigg would

probably not object to marrying a young woman who had
inherited money and was unencumbered with relations.

" It is rare," went on Mr. Trigg, " to find a woman with a
legal mind. Miss Grant was unusual in that respect. She
took a great interest in some case or other that was prominent in the newspapers at the time—I forget now what it was
—and asked me some remarkably sensible and intelligent
questions. I must say that I quite enjoyed our conversation.
Before dinner was over, we had got on to more personal
topics, in the course of which I happened to mention that
I lived in Golder's Green."

" Did she give you her own address ? "

" She said she was staying at the Peveril Hotel in Bloomsbury, and that she was looking for a house in Town. I said
that I might possibly hear of something out Hampstead
way, and offered my professional services in case she should
require them. After dinner I accompanied her back to her
hotel, and bade her good-bye in the lounge."

" She was really staying there, then ? "

" Apparently. However, about a fortnight later, I happened to hear of a house in Golder's Green that had fallen
vacant suddenly. It belonged, as a matter of fact, to a client
of mine. In pursuance of my promise, I wrote to Miss Grant
at the Peveril. Receiving no reply, I made inquiries there,
and found that she had left the hotel the day after our
meeting, leaving no address. In the hotel register, she
had merely given her address as Manchester. I was
somewhat disappointed, but thought no more about the
matter.

" About a month later—on January 26th, to be exact, I
was sitting at home reading a book, preparatory to retiring
to bed. I should say that I occupy a flat, or rather maison-
ette, in a small house which has been divided to make two
establishments. The people on the ground floor were away
at that time, so that I was quite alone in the house. My
housekeeper only comes in by the day. The telephone rang

—I noticed the time. It was a quarter to eleven. I answered it, and a woman's voice spoke, begging me to come instantly to a certain house on Hampstead Heath, to make a will for someone who was at the point of death."

" Did you recognise the voice ? "

" No. It sounded like a servant's voice. At any rate, it had a strong cockney accent. I asked whether to-morrow would not be time enough, but the voice urged me to hurry or it might be too late. Rather annoyed, I put my things on and went out. It was a most unpleasant night, cold and foggy. I was lucky enough to find a taxi on the nearest rank. We drove to the address, which we had great difficulty in finding, as everything was pitch-black. It turned out to be a small house in a very isolated position on the Heath—in fact, there was no proper approach to it. I left the taxi on the road, about a couple of hundred yards off, and asked the man to wait for me, as I was very doubtful of ever finding another taxi in that spot at that time of night. He grumbled a good deal, but consented to wait if I promised not to be very long.

" I made my way to the house. At first I thought it was quite dark, but presently I saw a faint glimmer in a ground-floor room. I rang the bell. No answer, though I could hear it trilling loudly. I rang again and knocked. Still no answer. It was bitterly cold. I struck a match to be sure I had come to the right house, and then I noticed that the front door was ajar.

" I thought that perhaps the servant who had called me was so much occupied with her sick mistress as to be unable to leave her to come to the door. Thinking that in that case I might be of assistance to her, I pushed the door open and went in. The hall was perfectly dark, and I bumped against an umbrella-stand in entering. I thought I heard a faint voice calling or moaning, and when my eyes had become accustomed to the darkness, I stumbled forward, and saw a dim light coming from a door on the left."

" Was that the room which you had seen to be illumined from outside ? "

" I think so. I called out, ' May I come in ? ' and a very low, weak voice replied, ' Yes, please.' I pushed the door open and entered a room furnished as a sitting-room. In one corner there was a couch, on which some bed-clothes appeared to have been hurriedly thrown to enable it to be used as a bed. On the couch lay a woman, all alone.

" I could only dimly make her out. There was no light in the room except a small oil-lamp, with a green shade so tilted as to keep the light from the sick woman's eyes. There was a fire in the grate, but it had burnt low. I could see, however, that the woman's head and face were swathed in white bandages. I put out my hand and felt for the electric switch, but she called out :

" ' No light, please—it hurts me.' "

" How did she see you put your hand to the switch ? "

" Well," said Mr. Trigg, " that was an odd thing. She didn't speak, as a matter of fact, till I had actually clicked the switch down. But nothing happened. The light didn't come on."

" Really ? "

" No. I supposed that the bulb had been taken away or had gone phut. However, I said nothing, and came up to the bed. She said in a sort of half-whisper, ' Is that the lawyer ? '

" I said, ' Yes,' and asked what I could do for her.

" She said, ' I have had a terrible accident. I can't live. I want to make my will quickly.' I asked whether there was nobody with her. ' Yes, yes,' she said in a hurried way, ' my servant will be back in a moment. She has gone to look for a doctor.' ' But,' I said, ' couldn't she have rung up ? You are not fit to be left alone.' ' We couldn't get through to one,' she replied, ' it's all right. She will be here soon. Don't waste time. I must make my will.' She spoke in a dreadful, gasping way, and I felt that the best thing would be to do what she wanted, for fear of agitating her. I drew a chair to the table where the lamp was, got out my fountain pen and a printed will-form with which I had provided myself, and expressed myself ready to receive her instructions.

" Before beginning, she asked me to give her a little brandy and water from a decanter which stood on the table. I did so, and she took a small sip, which seemed to revive her. I placed the glass near her hand, and at her suggestion mixed another glass for myself. I was very glad of it, for, as I said, it was a beast of a night, and the room was cold. I looked round for some extra coals to put on the fire, but could see none."

" That," said Parker, " is extremely interesting and suggestive."

" I thought it queer at the time. But the whole thing was queer. Anyway, I then said I was ready to begin. She said, ' You may think I am a little mad, because my head has been so hurt. But I am quite sane. But he shan't have a penny of the money.' I asked her if someone had attacked her. She replied, ' My husband. He thinks he has killed me. But I am going to live long enough to will the money away.' She then said that her name was Mrs. Marion Mead, and proceeded to make a will, leaving her estate, which amounted to about £10,000, among various legatees, including a daughter and three or four sisters. It was rather a complicated will, as it included various devices for tying up the daughter's money in a trust, so as to prevent her from ever handing over any of it to the father."

" Did you make a note of the names and addresses of the people involved ? "

" I did, but, as you will see later on, I could make no use of them. The testatrix was certainly clear-headed enough about the provisions of the will, though she seemed terribly weak, and her voice never rose above a whisper after that one time when she had called to me not to turn on the light.

"At length I finished my notes of the will, and started to draft it out on to the proper form. There were no signs of the servant's return, and I began to be really anxious. Also the extreme cold—or something else—added to the fact that it was now long past my bed-time, was making me appallingly sleepy. I poured out another stiff little dose of the brandy to warm me up, and went on writing out the will.

"When I had finished I said :

"'How about signing this ? We need another witness to make it legal.'

"She said, ' My servant must be here in a minute or two. I can't think what has happened to her.'

"'I expect she has missed her way in the fog,' I said. ' However, I will wait a little longer. I can't go and leave you like this.'

"She thanked me feebly, and we sat for some time in silence. As time went on, I began to feel the situation to be increasingly uncanny. The sick woman breathed heavily, and moaned from time to time. The desire for sleep overpowered me more and more. I could not understand it.

"Presently it occurred to me, stupefied though I felt, that the most sensible thing would be to get the taxi-man —if he was still there—to come in and witness the will with me, and then to go myself to find a doctor. I sat, sleepily revolving this in my mind, and trying to summon energy to speak. I felt as though a great weight of inertia was pressing down upon me. Exertion of any kind seemed almost beyond my powers.

"Suddenly something happened which brought me back to myself. Mrs. Mead turned a little over upon the couch and peered at me intently, as it seemed, in the lamp-light. To support herself, she put both her hands on the

edge of the table. I noticed, with a vague sense of something unexpected, that the left hand bore no wedding-ring.
And then I noticed something else.

" Across the back of the fingers of the right hand went
a curious scar—as though a chisel or some such thing had
slipped and cut them."

Parker sat upright in his chair.

" Yes," said Mr. Trigg, " that interests you. It startled
me. Or rather, startled isn't quite the word. In my oppressed state, it affected me like some kind of nightmare.
I struggled upright in my chair, and the woman sank back
upon her pillows.

" At that moment there came a violent ring at the
bell."

" The servant ? "

" No—thank Heaven it was my taxi-driver, who had
become tired of waiting. I thought—I don't quite know
what I thought—but I was alarmed. I gave some kind of
shout or groan, and the man came straight in. Happily,
I had left the door open as I had found it.

" I pulled myself together sufficiently to ask him to witness the will. I must have looked queer and spoken in a
strange way, for I remember how he looked from me to
the brandy-bottle. However, he signed the paper after
Mrs. Mead, who wrote her name in a weak, straggling
hand as she lay on her back.

" ' Wot next, guv'nor ? ' asked the man, when this was
done.

" I was feeling dreadfully ill by now. I could only say,
' Take me home.'

" He looked at Mrs. Mead and then at me, and said,
' Ain't there nobody to see to the lady, sir ? '

" I said, ' Fetch a doctor. But take me home first.'

" I stumbled out of the house on his arm. I heard him
muttering something about its being a rum start. I don't
remember the drive home. When I came back to life, I

was in my own bed, and one of the local doctors was standing over me.

" I'm afraid this story is getting very long and tedious. To cut matters short, it seems the taxi-driver, who was a very decent, intelligent fellow, had found me completely insensible at the end of the drive. He didn't know who I was, but he hunted in my pocket and found my visiting-card and my latch-key. He took me home, got me upstairs and, deciding that if I was drunk, I was a worse drunk than he had ever encountered in his experience, humanely went round and fetched a doctor.

" The doctor's opinion was that I had been heavily drugged with veronal or something of that kind. Fortunately, if the idea was to murder me, the dose had been very much under-estimated. We went into the matter thoroughly, and the upshot was that I must have taken about 30 grains of the stuff. It appears that it is a difficult drug to trace by analysis, but that was the conclusion the doctor came to, looking at the matter all round. Undoubtedly the brandy had been doped.

" Of course, we went round to look at the house next day. It was all shut up, and the local milkman informed us that the occupiers had been away for a week and were not expected home for another ten days. We got into communication with them, but they appeared to be perfectly genuine, ordinary people, and they declared they knew nothing whatever about it. They were accustomed to go away every so often, just shutting the house and not bothering about a caretaker or anything. The man came along at once, naturally, to investigate matters, but couldn't find that anything had been stolen or disturbed, except that a pair of sheets and some pillows showed signs of use, and a scuttle of coal had been used in the sitting-room. The coal-cellar, which also contained the electric meter, had been left locked and the meter turned off before the family left—they apparently had a few grains of sense—which accounts for the chill darkness of the house when I entered it. The visitor had apparently slipped back the catch of the pantry window—one of the usual gimcrack affairs— with a knife or something, and had brought her own lamp, siphon and brandy. Daring, but not really difficult.

" No Mrs. Mead or Miss Grant was to be heard of any-where, as I needn't tell you. The tenants of the house were not keen to start expensive inquiries—after all, they'd lost nothing but a shilling's worth of coals—and on considera-tion, and seeing that I hadn't actually been murdered or anything, I thought it best to let the matter slide. It was a most unpleasant adventure."

" I'm sure it was. Did you ever hear from Miss Grant again ? "

" Why, yes. She rang me up twice—once, after three months, and again only a fortnight ago, asking for an appointment. You may think me cowardly, Mr. Parker, but each time I put her off. I didn't quite know what might happen. As a matter of fact, the opinion I formed in my own mind was that I had been entrapped into that house with the idea of making me spend the night there and afterwards blackmailing me. That was the only ex-planation I could think of which would account for the sleeping-draught. I thought discretion was the better part of valour, and gave my clerks and my housekeeper in-structions that if Miss Grant should call at any time I was out and not expected back."

" H'm. Do you suppose she knew you had recognised the scar on her hand ? "

" I'm sure she didn't. Otherwise she would hardly have made advances to me in her own name again."

" No. I think you are right. Well, Mr. Trigg, I am much obliged to you for this information, which may turn out to be very valuable. And if Miss Grant should ring you up again—where did she call from, by the way ? "

" From call-boxes, each time. I know that, because the

operator always tells one when the call is from a public box. I didn't have the calls traced."

"No, of course not. Well, if she does it again, will you please make an appointment with her, and then let me know about it at once? A call to Scotland Yard will always find me."

Mr. Trigg promised that he would do this, and Parker took his leave.

"And now we know," thought Parker as he returned home, "that somebody—an odd unscrupulous somebody —was making inquiries about great-nieces in 1925. A word to Miss Climpson, I fancy, is indicated—just to find out whether Mary Whittaker has a scar on her right hand, or whether I've got to hunt up any more solicitors."

The hot streets seemed less oppressively oven-like than before. In fact, Parker was so cheered by his interview that he actually bestowed a cigarette-card upon the next urchin who accosted him.

PART III

THE MEDICO-LEGAL PROBLEM

" There's not a crime
But takes its proper change out still in crime
If once rung on the counter of this world."

E. B. BROWNING : *Aurora Leigh*

CHAPTER XIX

GONE AWAY

" There is nothing good or evil save in the will."

EPICTETUS

"You will not, I imagine, deny," observed Lord Peter, " that very odd things seem to happen to the people who are in a position to give information about the last days of Agatha Dawson. Bertha Gotobed dies suddenly, under suspicious circumstances ; her sister thinks she sees Miss Whittaker lying in wait for her at Liverpool docks ; Mr. Trigg is inveigled into a house of mystery and is semi-poisoned. I wonder what would have happened to Mr. Probyn, if he had been careless enough to remain in England."

" I deny nothing," replied Parker. " I will only point out to you that during the month in which these disasters occurred to the Gotobed family, the object of your suspicions was in Kent with Miss Vera Findlater, who never left her side."

" As against that undoubted snag," rejoined Wimsey, " I bring forward a letter from Miss Climpson, in which— amid a lot of rigmarole with which I will not trouble you —she informs me that upon Miss Whittaker's right hand there is a scar, precisely similar to the one which Mr. Trigg describes."

" Is there ? That does seem to connect Miss Whittaker pretty definitely with the Trigg business. But is it your theory that she is trying to polish off all the people who know anything about Miss Dawson ? Rather a big job, don't you think, for a single-handed female ? And if so, why is Dr. Carr spared ? and Nurse Philliter ? and Nurse

Forbes ? And the other doctor chappie ? And the rest of the population of Leahampton, if it comes to that ? "

" That's an interesting point which had already occurred to me. I think I know why. Up to the present, the Dawson case has presented two different problems, one legal and one medical—the motive and the means, if you like that better. As far as opportunity goes, only two people figure as possibles—Miss Whittaker and Nurse Forbes. The Forbes woman had nothing to gain by killin' a good patient, so for the moment we can wash her out.

" Well now, as to the medical problem—the means. I must say that up to now that appears completely insoluble. I am baffled, Watson (said he, his hawk-like eyes gleaming angrily from under the half-closed lids). Even I am baffled. But not for long ! (he cried, with a magnificent burst of self-confidence). My Honour (capital H) is concerned to track this Human Fiend (capitals) to its hidden source, and nail the whited sepulchre to the mast even though it crush me in the attempt ! Loud applause. His chin sank broodingly upon his dressing-gown, and he breathed a few guttural notes into the bass saxophone which was the cherished companion of his solitary hours in the bathroom."

Parker ostentatiously took up the book which he had laid aside on Wimsey's entrance.

" Tell me when you've finished," he said, caustically.

" I've hardly begun. The means, I repeat, seems insoluble—and so the criminal evidently thinks. There has been no exaggerated mortality among the doctors and nurses. On that side of the business the lady feels herself safe. No. The motive is the weak point—hence the hurry to stop the mouths of the people who knew about the legal part of the problem."

" Yes, I see. Mrs. Cropper had started back to Canada, by the way. She doesn't seem to have been molested at all."

" No—and that's why I still think there was somebody on the watch in Liverpool. Mrs. Cropper was only worth silencing so long as she had told nobody her story. That is why I was careful to meet her and accompany her ostentatiously to Town."

" Oh, rot, Peter ! Even if Miss Whittaker had been there —which we know she couldn't have been—how was she to know that you were going to ask about the Dawson business ? She doesn't know you from Adam."

" She might have found out who Murbles was. The advertisement which started the whole business was in his name, you know."

" In that case, why hasn't she attacked Murbles or you ? "

" Murbles is a wise old bird. In vain are nets spread in his sight. He is seeing no female clients, answering no invitations, and never goes out without an escort."

" I didn't know he took it so seriously."

" Oh, yes. Murbles is old enough to have learnt the value of his own skin. As for me—have you noticed the remarkable similarity in some ways between Mr. Trigg's adventure and my own little adventurelet, as you might say, in South Audley Street ? "

" What, with Mrs. Forrest ? "

" Yes. The secret appointment. The drink. The endeavour to get one to stay the night at all costs. I'm positive there was something in that sugar, Charles, that no sugar should contain—see Public Health (Adulteration of Food) Acts, various."

" You think Mrs. Forrest is an accomplice ? "

" I do. I don't know what she has to gain by it—probably money. But I feel sure there is some connection. Partly because of Bertha Gotobed's £5 note ; partly because Mrs. Forrest's story was a palpable fake—I'm certain the woman's never had a lover, let alone a husband—you can't mistake real inexperience ; and chiefly because of the similarity of method. Criminals always tend to repeat their effects. Look at George Joseph Smith and his brides. Look at Neill Cream. Look at Armstrong and his tea-parties."

" Well, if there's an accomplice, all the better. Accomplices generally end by giving the show away."

" True. And we are in a good position because up till now I don't think they know that we suspect any connection between them."

" But I still think, you know, we ought to get some evidence that actual crimes have been committed. Call me finicking, if you like. If you *could* suggest a means of doing away with these people so as to leave no trace, I should feel happier about it."

" The means, eh ?—Well, we do know something about it."

" As what ? "

" Well—take the two victims——"

" Alleged."

" All right, old particular. The two alleged victims and the two (alleged) intended victims. Miss Dawson was ill and helpless ; Bertha Gotobed possibly stupefied by a heavy meal and an unaccustomed quantity of wine ; Trigg was given a sufficient dose of veronal to send him to sleep, and I was offered something of probably the same kind—I wish I could have kept the remains of that coffee. So we deduce from that, what ? "

" I suppose that it was a means of death which could only be used on somebody more or less helpless or unconscious."

" Exactly. As for instance, a hypodermic injection—only nothing appears to have been injected. Or a delicate operation of some kind—if we could only think of one to fit the case. Or the inhalation of something—such as chloroform—only we could find no traces of suffocation."

" Yes. That doesn't get us very far, though."

" It's something. Then, again, it may very well be something that a trained nurse would have learnt or heard about. Miss Whittaker was trained, you know—which, by the way, was what made it so easy for her to bandage up her own head and provide a pitiful and unrecognisable spectacle for the stupid Mr. Trigg."

" It wouldn't have to be anything very out of the way—nothing, I mean, that only a trained surgeon could do, or that required very specialised knowledge."

" Oh, no. Probably something picked up in conversation with a doctor or the other nurses. I say, how about getting hold of Dr. Carr again ? Or, no—if he'd got any ideas on the subject he'd have trotted 'em out before now. I know ! I'll ask Lubbock, the analyst. He'll do. I'll get in touch with him to-morrow."

" And meanwhile," said Parker, " I suppose we just sit round and wait for somebody else to be murdered."

" It's beastly, isn't it ? I still feel poor Bertha Gotobed's blood on my head, so to speak. I say ! "

" Yes ? "

" We've practically got clear proof on the Trigg business. Couldn't you put the lady in quod on a charge of burglary while we think out the rest of the dope ? It's often done. It *was* a burglary, you know. She broke into a house after dark and appropriated a scuttleful of coal to her own use. Trigg could identify her—he seems to have paid the lady particular attention on more than one occasion—and we could rake up his taxi-man for corroborative detail."

Parker pulled at his pipe for a few minutes.

" There's something in that," he said finally. " I think perhaps it's worth while putting it before the authorities. But we mustn't be in too much of a hurry, you know. I wish we were further ahead with our other proofs. There's such a thing as Habeas Corpus—you can't hold on to people indefinitely just on a charge of stealing coal——"

" There's the breaking and entering, don't forget that.

It's burglary, after all. You can get penal servitude for
life for burglary."

" But it all depends on the view the law takes of the coal.
It might decide that there was no original intention of
stealing coal, and treat the thing as a mere misdemeanour
or civil trespass. Anyhow, we don't really *want* a conviction
for stealing coal. But I'll see what they think about it at
our place, and meanwhile I'll get hold of Trigg again and
try and find the taxi-driver. And Trigg's doctor. We might
get it as an attempt to murder Trigg, or at least to inflict
grievous bodily harm. But I should like some more evidence about——"

" Cuckoo ! So should I. But I can't manufacture evidence
out of nothing. Dash it all, be reasonable. I've built you
up a case out of nothing. Isn't that handsome enough ?
Base ingratitude—that's what's the matter with you."

.   .   .   .

Parker's inquiries took some time, and June lingered
into its longest days.

Chamberlin and Levine flew the Atlantic, and Segrave
bade farewell to Brooklands. The *Daily Yell* wrote anti-Red
leaders and discovered a plot, somebody laid claim to a
marquisate, and a Czecho-Slovakian pretended to swim
the Channel. Hammond out-graced Grace, there was an
outburst of murder at Moscow, Foxlaw won the Gold Cup
and the earth opened at Oxhey and swallowed up somebody's front garden. Oxford decided that women were
dangerous, and the electric hare consented to run at the
White City. England's supremacy was challenged at
Wimbledon, and the House of Lords made the gesture of
stooping to conquer.

Meanwhile, Lord Peter's projected *magnum opus* on a-
hundred-and-one ways of causing sudden death had
advanced by the accumulation of a mass of notes which
flowed all over the library at the flat, and threatened to

engulf Bunter, whose task it was to file and cross-reference and generally to produce order from chaos. Oriental scholars and explorers were button-holed in clubs and strenuously pumped on the subject of abstruse native poisons ; horrid experiments performed in German laboratories were communicated in unreadable documents ; and the life of Sir James Lubbock, who had the misfortune to be a particular friend of Lord Peter's, was made a burden to him with daily inquiries as to the post-mortem detection of such varying substances as chloroform, curare, hydrocyanic acid gas and diethylsulphonmethylethylmethane.

" But surely there *must* be something which kills without leaving a trace," pleaded Lord Peter, when at length informed that the persecution must cease. " A thing in such universal demand—surely it is not beyond the wit of scientists to invent it. It must exist. Why isn't it properly advertised ? There ought to be a company to exploit it. It's simply ridiculous. Why, it's a thing one might be wantin' one's self any day."

" You don't understand," said Sir James Lubbock. " Plenty of poisons leave no particular post-mortem appearances. And plenty of them—especially the vegetable ones—are difficult to find by analysis, unless you know what you are looking for. For instance, if you're testing for arsenic, that test won't tell you whether strychnine is present or not. And if you're testing for strychnine, you won't find morphia. You've got to try one test after another till you hit the right one. And of course there are certain poisons for which no recognised tests exist."

" I know all that," said Wimsey. " I've tested things myself. But these poisons with no recognised test—how do you set about proving that they're there ? "

" Well, of course, you'd take the symptoms into account, and so on. You would look at the history of the case."

" Yes—but I want a poison that doesn't produce any

symptoms. Except death, of course—if you call that a symptom. Isn't there a poison with no symptoms and no test? Something that just makes you go off, Pouf! like that?"

"Certainly not," said the analyst, rather annoyed—for your medical analyst lives by symptoms and tests, and nobody likes suggestions that undermine the very foundations of his profession—"not even old age or mental decay. There are always symptoms."

Fortunately, before the symptoms of mental decay could become too pronounced in Lord Peter, Parker sounded the call to action.

"I'm going down to Leahampton with a warrant," he said. "I may not use it, but the chief thinks it might be worth while to make an inquiry. What with the Battersea mystery and the Daniels business, and Bertha Gotobed, there seems to be a feeling that there have been too many unexplained tragedies this year, and the Press have begun yelping again, blast them! There's an article in *John Citizen* this week, with a poster: 'Ninety-six Murderers at Large,' and the *Evening Views* is starting its reports with 'Six weeks have now passed, and the police are no nearer the solution——' you know the kind of thing. We'll simply have to get some sort of move on. Do you want to come?"

"Certainly—a breath of country air would do me good, I fancy. Blow away the cobwebs, don't you know. It might even inspire me to invent a good way of murderin' people. 'O Inspiration, solitary child, warbling thy native woodnotes wild——' Did somebody write that, or did I invent it? It sounds reminiscent, somehow."

Parker, who was out of temper, replied rather shortly, and intimated that the police car would be starting for Leahampton in an hour's time.

"I will be there," said Wimsey, "though, mind you, I hate being driven by another fellow. It feels so unsafe.

Never mind. I will be bloody, bold and resolute, as Queen
Victoria said to the Archbishop of Canterbury."

.　　.　　.　　.　　.　　.　　.

They reached Leahampton without any incident to
justify Lord Peter's fears. Parker had brought another
officer with him, and on the way they picked up the Chief
Constable of the County, who appeared very dubiously
disposed towards their errand. Lord Peter, observing their
array of five strong men, going out to seize upon one young
woman, was reminded of the Marquise de Brinvilliers—
("What! all that water for a little person like me?")—
but this led him back to the subject of poison, and he
remained steeped in thought and gloom till the car drew
up before the house in Wellington Avenue.

Parker got out, and went up the path with the Chief
Constable. The door was opened to them by a frightened-
looking maid, who gave a little shriek at sight of them.

"Oh, sir! have you come to say something's happened
to Miss Whittaker?"

"Isn't Miss Whittaker at home, then?"

"No, sir. She went out in the car with Miss Vera Findlater on Monday—that's four days back, sir, and she hasn't
come home, nor Miss Findlater neither, and I'm frightened
something's happened to them. When I see you, sir, I
thought you was the police come to say there had been
an accident. I didn't know what to do, sir."

"Skipped, by God!" was Parker's instant thought,
but he controlled his annoyance, and asked:

"Do you know where they were going?"

"Crow's Beach, Miss Whittaker said, sir."

"That's a good fifty miles," said the Chief Constable.
"Probably they've just decided to stay there a day or
two."

"More likely gone in the opposite direction," thought
Parker.

" They didn't take no things for the night, sir. They went off about ten in the morning. They said they was going to have lunch there and come home in the evening. And Miss Whittaker hasn't written nor nothing. And her always so particular. Cook and me, we didn't know what——"

" Oh, well, I expect it's all right," said the Chief Constable. " It's a pity, as we particularly wanted to see Miss Whittaker. When you hear from her, you might say Sir Charles Pillington called with a friend."

" Yes, sir. But please, sir, what ought we to do, sir ? "

" Nothing. Don't worry. I'll have inquiries made. I'm the Chief Constable, you know, and I can soon find out whether there's been an accident or anything. But if there had been, depend upon it we should have heard about it. Come, my girl, pull yourself together, there's nothing to cry about. We'll let you know as soon as we hear anything."

But Sir Charles looked disturbed. Coming on top of Parker's arrival in the district, the thing had an unpleasant look about it.

Lord Peter received the news cheerfully.

" Good," said he, " joggle 'em up. Keep 'em moving. That's the spirit. Always like it when somethin' happens. My worst suspicions are goin' to be justified. That always makes one feel so important and virtuous, don't you think ? Wonder why she took the girl with her, though. By the way, we'd better look up the Findlaters. They may have heard something."

This obvious suggestion was acted upon at once. But at the Findlaters' house they drew blank. The family were at the seaside, with the exception of Miss Vera, who was staying in Wellington Avenue with Miss Whittaker. No anxiety was expressed by the parlour-maid and none, apparently, felt. The investigators took care not to arouse any alarm, and, leaving a trivial and polite message from Sir Charles, withdrew for a consultation.

" There's nothing for it, so far as I can see," said Parker,
" but an all-stations call to look out for the car and the
ladies. And we must put inquiries through to all the ports,
of course. With four days' start, they may be anywhere by
now. I wish to Heaven I'd risked a bit and started earlier,
approval or no approval. What's this Findlater girl like ?
I'd better go back to the house and get photographs of
her and the Whittaker woman. And, Wimsey, I wish you'd
look in on Miss Climpson and see if she has any information."

" And you might tell 'em at the Yard to keep an eye
on Mrs. Forrest's place," said Wimsey. " When anything
sensational happens to a criminal it's a good tip to watch
the accomplice."

" I feel sure you are both quite mistaken about this,"
urged Sir Charles Pillington. " Criminal—accomplice—
bless me ! I have had considerable experience in the course
of a long life—longer than either of yours—and I really
feel convinced that Miss Whittaker, whom I know quite
well, is as good and nice a girl as you could wish to find.
But there has undoubtedly been an accident of some kind,
and it is our duty to make the fullest investigation. I will
get on to Crow's Beach police immediately, as soon as I
know the description of the car."

" It's an Austin Seven and the number is XX9917,"
said Wimsey, much to the Chief Constable's surprise.
" But I doubt very much whether you'll find it at Crow's
Beach, or anywhere near it."

" Well, we'd better get a move on," snapped Parker.
" We'd better separate. How about a spot of lunch in an
hour's time at the George ? "

Wimsey was unlucky. Miss Climpson was not to be found.
She had had her lunch early and gone out, saying she felt
that a long country walk would do her good. Mrs. Budge
was rather afraid she had had some bad news—she had
seemed so upset and worried since yesterday evening.

" But indeed, sir," she added, " if you was quick, you might find her up at the church. She often drops in there to say her prayers like. Not a respectful way to approach a place of worship to my mind, do you think so yourself, sir ? Popping in and out on a week-day, the same as if it was a friend's house. And coming home from Communion as cheerful as anything and ready to laugh and make jokes. I don't see as how we was meant to make an ordinary thing of religion that way—so disrespectful and nothing uplifting to the 'art about it. But there ! we all 'as our failings, and Miss Climpson is a nice lady and that I must say, even if she is a Roaming Catholic or next door to one."

Lord Peter thought that Roaming Catholic was rather an appropriate name for the more ultramontane section of the High Church party. At the moment, however, he felt he could not afford time for religious discussion, and set off for the church in quest of Miss Climpson.

The doors of S. Onesimus were hospitably open, and the red Sanctuary lamp made a little spot of welcoming brightness in the rather dark building. Coming in from the June sunshine, Wimsey blinked a little before he could distinguish anything else. Presently he was able to make out a dark, bowed figure kneeling before the lamp. For a moment he hoped it was Miss Climpson, but presently saw to his disappointment that it was merely a Sister in a black habit, presumably taking her turn to watch before the Host. The only other occupant of the church was a priest in a cassock, who was busy with the ornaments on the High Altar. It was the Feast of S. John, Wimsey remembered suddenly. He walked up the aisle, hoping to find his quarry hidden in some obscure corner. His shoes squeaked. This annoyed him. It was a thing which Bunter never permitted. He was seized with a fancy that the squeak was produced by diabolic possession—a protest against a religious atmosphere on the part of his own particular besetting devil. Pleased with this thought, he moved forward more confidently.

The priest's attention was attracted by the squeak. He turned and came down towards the intruder. No doubt, thought Wimsey, to offer his professional services to exorcise the evil spirit.

"Were you looking for anybody?" inquired the priest, courteously.

"Well, I was looking for a lady," began Wimsey. Then it struck him that this sounded a little odd under the circumstances, and he hastened to explain more fully, in the stifled tones considered appropriate to consecrated surroundings.

"Oh, yes," said the priest, quite unperturbed, "Miss Climpson was here a little time ago, but I fancy she has gone. Not that I usually keep tabs on my flock," he added, with a laugh, "but she spoke to me before she went. Was it urgent? What a pity you should have missed her. Can I give any kind of message or help you in any way?"

"No, thanks," said Wimsey. "Sorry to bother you. Unseemly to come and try to haul people out of church, but—yes, it was rather important. I'll leave a message at the house. Thanks frightfully."

He turned away; then stopped and came back.

"I say," he said, "you give advice on moral problems and all that sort of thing, don't you?"

"Well, we're supposed to try," said the priest. "Is anything bothering you in particular?"

"Ye-es," said Wimsey, "nothing religious, I don't mean—nothing about infallibility or the Virgin Mary or anything of that sort. Just something I'm not comfortable about."

The priest—who was, in fact, the vicar, Mr. Tredgold—indicated that he was quite at Lord Peter's service.

"It's very good of you. Could we come somewhere where I didn't have to whisper so much. I never can explain things in a whisper. Sort of paralyses one, don't you know."

" Let's go outside," said Mr. Tredgold.

So they went out and sat on a flat tombstone.

" It's like this," said Wimsey. " Hypothetical case, you see, and so on. S'posin' one knows somebody who's very, very ill and can't last long anyhow. And they're in awful pain and all that, and kept under morphia—practically dead to the world, you know. And suppose that by dyin' straight away they could make something happen which they really wanted to happen and which couldn't happen if they lived on a little longer (I can't explain exactly how, because I don't want to give personal details and so on)—you get the idea ? Well, supposin' somebody who knew all that was just to give 'em a little push off so to speak—hurry matters on—why should that be a very dreadful crime ? "

" The law——" began Mr. Tredgold.

" Oh, the law says it's a crime, fast enough," said Wimsey. " But do you honestly think it's very bad ? I know you'd call it a sin, of course, but why is it so very dreadful ? It doesn't do the person any harm, does it ? "

" We can't answer that," said Mr. Tredgold, " without knowing the ways of God with the soul. In those last weeks or hours of pain and unconsciousness, the soul may be undergoing some necessary part of its pilgrimage on earth. It isn't our business to cut it short. Who are we to take life and death into our hands ? "

" Well, we do it all day, one way and another. Juries—soldiers—doctors—all that. And yet I do feel, somehow, that it isn't a right thing in this case. And yet, by interfering —finding things out and so on—one may do far worse harm. Start all kinds of things."

" I think," said Mr. Tredgold, " that the sin—I won't use that word—the damage to Society, the wrongness of the thing lies much more in the harm it does the killer than in anything it can do to the person who is killed.

Especially, of course, if the killing is to the killer's own advantage. The consequence you mention—this thing which the sick person wants done—does the other person stand to benefit by it, may I ask ? "

" Yes. That's just it. He—she—they do."

" That puts it at once on a different plane from just hastening a person's death out of pity. Sin is in the intention, not the deed. That is the difference between divine law and human law. It is bad for a human being to get to feel that he has any right whatever to dispose of another person's life to his own advantage. It leads him on to think himself above all laws—Society is never safe from the man who has deliberately committed murder with impunity. That is why—or one reason why—God forbids private vengeance."

" You mean that one murder leads to another."

" Very often. In any case it leads to a readiness to commit others."

" It has. That's the trouble. But it wouldn't have if I hadn't started trying to find things out. Ought I to have left it alone ? "

" I 'see. That is very difficult. Terrible, too, for you. You feel responsible."

" Yes."

" You yourself are not serving a private vengeance ? "

" Oh, no. Nothing really to do with me. Started in like a fool to help somebody who'd got into trouble about the thing through having suspicions himself. And my beastly interference started the crimes all over again."

" I shouldn't be too troubled. Probably the murderer's own guilty fears would have led him into fresh crimes even without your interference."

" That's true," said Wimsey, remembering Mr. Trigg.

" My advice to you is to do what you think is right, according to the laws which we have been brought up to respect. Leave the consequences to God. And try to think charitably, even of wicked people. You know what I mean. Bring the offender to justice, but remember that if we all got justice, you and I wouldn't escape either."

" I know. Knock the man down but don't dance on the body. Quite. Forgive my troublin' you—and excuse my bargin' off, because I've got a date with a friend. Thanks so much. I don't feel quite so rotten about it now. But I was gettin' worried."

Mr. Tredgold watched him as he trotted away between the graves. " Dear, dear," he said, " how nice they are. So kindly and scrupulous and so vague outside their public-school code. And much more nervous and sensitive than people think. A very difficult class to reach. I must make a special intention for him at Mass to-morrow."

Being a practical man, Mr. Tredgold made a knot in his handkerchief to remind himself of this pious resolve.

" The problem—to interfere or not to interfere—God's law and Cæsar's. Policemen, now—it's no problem to them. But for the ordinary man—how hard to disentangle his own motives. I wonder what brought him here. Could it possibly be—No ! " said the vicar, checking himself, " I have no right to speculate." He drew out his handker-chief again and made another mnemonic knot as a re-minder against his next confession that he had fallen into the sin of inquisitiveness.

CHAPTER XX

MURDER

SIEGFRIED : " What does this mean ? "
ISBRAND : " A pretty piece of kidnapping, that's all."
BEDDOES : *Death's Jest-Book*

PARKER, too, had spent a disappointing half-hour. It appeared that Miss Whittaker not only disliked having her photograph taken, but had actually destroyed all the existing portraits she could lay hands on, shortly after Miss Dawson's death. Of course, many of Miss Whittaker's friends might be in possession of one—notably, of course, Miss Findlater. But Parker was not sure that he wanted to start a local hue-and-cry at the moment. Miss Climpson might be able to get one, of course. He went round to Nelson Avenue. Miss Climpson was out ; there had been another gentleman asking for her. Mrs. Budge's eyes were beginning to bulge with curiosity—evidently she was becoming dubious about Miss Climpson's " nephew " and his friends. Parker then went to the local photographers. There were five. From two of them he extracted a number of local groups, containing unrecognisable portraits of Miss Whittaker at church bazaars and private theatricals. She had never had a studio portrait made in Leahampton.

Of Miss Findlater, on the other hand, he got several excellent likenesses—a slight, fair girl, with a rather sentimental look—plump and prettyish. All these he despatched to Town, with directions that they should be broadcast to the police, together with a description of the girl's dress when last seen.

The only really cheerful member of the party at the " George " were the second policeman, who had been having a pleasant gossip with various garage-proprietors and publicans, with a view to picking up information, and the Chief Constable, who was vindicated and triumphant. He had been telephoning to various country police-stations, and had discovered that XX9917 had actually been observed on the previous Monday by an A.A. scout on the road to Crow's Beach. Having maintained all along that the Crow's Beach excursion was a genuine one, he was inclined to exult over the Scotland Yard man. Wimsey and Parker dispiritedly agreed that they had better go down and make inquiries at Crow's Beach.

Meanwhile, one of the photographers, whose cousin was on the staff of the *Leahampton Mercury*, had put a call through to the office of that up-to-date paper, which was just going to press. A stop-press announcement was followed by a special edition ; somebody rang up the London *Evening Views* which burst out into a front-page scoop ; the fat was in the fire, and the *Daily Yell*, *Daily Views*, *Daily Wire* and *Daily Tidings*, who were all suffering from lack of excitement, came brightly out next morning with bold headlines about disappearing young women.

Crow's Beach, indeed, that pleasant and respectable watering-place, knew nothing of Miss Whittaker, Miss Findlater, or car XX9917. No hotel had received them ; no garage had refuelled or repaired them ; no policeman had observed them. The Chief Constable held to his theory of an accident, and scouting parties were sent out. Wires arrived at Scotland Yard from all over the place. They had been seen at Dover, at Newcastle, at Sheffield, at Winchester, at Rugby. Two young women had had tea in a suspicious manner at Folkestone ; a car had passed noisily through Dorchester at a late hour on Monday night ; a dark-haired girl in an " agitated condition " had entered a public-house in New Alresford just before closing-time and asked the way to Hazelmere. Among all these reports, Parker selected that of a boy-scout, who reported on the

Saturday morning that he had noticed two ladies with a car having a picnic on the downs on the previous Monday, not far from Shelly Head. The car was an Austin Seven—he knew that, because he was keen on motors (an unanswerable reason for accuracy in a boy of his age), and he had noticed that it was a London number, though he couldn't say positively what the number was.

Shelly Head lies about ten miles along the coast from Crow's Beach, and is curiously lonely, considering how near it lies to the watering-place. Under the cliffs is a long stretch of clear sandy beach, never visited, and overlooked by no houses. The cliffs themselves are chalk, and covered with short turf, running back into a wide expanse of downs, covered with gorse and heather. Then comes a belt of pine-trees, beyond which is a steep, narrow and rutty road, leading at length into the tarmac high-road between Ramborough and Ryders Heath. The downs are by no means frequented, though there are plenty of rough tracks which a car can follow, if you are not particular about comfort or fussy over your springs.

Under the leadership of the boy-scout, the police-car bumped uncomfortably over these disagreeable roads. It was hopeless to look for any previous car-tracks, for the chalk was dry and hard, and the grass and heath retained no marks. Everywhere, little dells and hollows presented themselves—all exactly alike, and many of them capable of hiding a small car, not to speak of the mere signs and remains of a recent picnic. Having arrived at what their guide thought to be approximately the right place, they pulled up and got out. Parker quartered the ground between the five of them and they set off.

Wimsey took a dislike to gorse-bushes that day. There were so many of them and so thick. Any of them might hold a cigarette package or a sandwich paper or a scrap of cloth or a clue of some kind. He trudged along unhappily, back bent and eyes on the ground, over one ridge and down i nto the hollow—then circling to right and to left, taking his bearings by the police-car ; over the next ridge and down into the next hollow ; over the next ridge——

Yes. There was something in the hollow.

He saw it first sticking out round the edge of a gorse-bush. It was light in colour, and pointed, rather like a foot.

He felt a little sick.

" Somebody has gone to sleep here," he said aloud.

Then he thought :

" Funny—it's always the feet they leave showing."

He scrambled down among the bushes, slipping on the short turf and nearly rolling to the bottom. He swore irritably.

The person was sleeping oddly. The flies must be a nuisance all over her head like that.

It occurred to him that it was rather early in the year for flies. There had been an advertising rhyme in the papers. Something about " Each fly you swat now means, remember, Three hundred fewer next September." Or was it a thousand fewer ? He couldn't get the metre quite right.

Then he pulled himself together and went forward. The flies rose up in a little cloud.

It must have been a pretty heavy blow, he thought, to smash the back of the skull in like that. The shingled hair was blonde. The face lay between the bare arms.

He turned the body on its back.

Of course, without the photograph, he could not—he need not—be certain that this was Vera Findlater.

All this had taken him perhaps thirty seconds.

He scrambled up to the rim of the hollow and shouted.

A small black figure at some distance stopped and turned. He saw its face as a white spot with no expression on it. He shouted again, and waved his arms in wide gestures of explanation. The figure came running ; it lurched slowly and awkwardly over the heathy ground. It was the policeman—a heavy man, not built for running in the heat. Wimsey shouted again, and the policeman shouted too.

Wimsey saw the others closing in upon him. The grotesque
figure of the boy-scout topped a ridge, waving its staff—
then disappeared again. The policeman was quite near
now. His bowler hat was thrust back on his head, and
there was something on his watch-chain that glinted in the
sun as he ran. Wimsey found himself running to meet him
and calling—explaining at great length. It was too far off
to make himself heard, but he explained, wordily, with
emphasis, pointing, indicating. He was quite breathless
when the policeman and he came together. They were
both breathless. They wagged their heads and gasped. It
was ludicrous. He started running again, with the man
at his heels. Presently they were all there, pointing,
measuring, taking notes, grubbing under the gorse-bushes.
Wimsey sat down. He was dreadfully tired.

" Peter," said Parker's voice, " come and look at this."
He got up wearily.

There were the remains of a picnic lunch a little farther
down the hollow. The policeman had a little bag in his
hand—he had taken it from under the body, and was now
turning over the trifles it contained. On the ground, close
to the dead girl's head, was a thick, heavy spanner—un-
pleasantly discoloured and with a few fair hairs sticking
to its jaws. But what Parker was calling his attention to
was none of these, but a man's mauve-grey cap.

" Where did you find that ? " asked Wimsey.

" Alf here picked it up at the top of the hollow," said
Parker.

" Tumbled off into the gorse it was," corroborated the
scout, " just up here, lying upside down just as if it had
fallen off somebody's head."

" Any footmarks ? "

" Not likely. But there's a place where the bushes are all
trodden and broken. Looks as if there'd been some sort of
struggle. What's become of the Austin ? Hi ! don't touch
that spanner, my lad. There may be finger-prints on it.

This looks like an attack by some gang or other. Any money in that purse? Ten-shilling note, sixpence and a few coppers—oh! Well, the other woman may have had more on her. She's very well off, you know. Held up for ransom, I shouldn't wonder." Parker bent down and very gingerly enfolded the spanner in a silk handkerchief, carrying it slung by the four corners. " Well, we'd better spread about and have a look for the car. Better try that belt of trees over there. Looks a likely spot. And, Hopkins—I think you'd better run back with our car to Crow's Beach and let 'em know at the station, and come back with a photographer. And take this wire and send it to the Chief Commissioner at Scotland Yard, and find a doctor and bring him along with you. And you'd better hire another car while you're about it, in case we don't find the Austin—we shall be too many to get away in this one. Take Alf back with you if you're not sure of finding the place again. Oh! and Hopkins, fetch us along something to eat and drink, will you, we may be at it a long time. Here's some money—that enough?"

" Yes, thank you, sir."

The constable went off, taking Alf, who was torn between a desire to stay and do some more detecting, and the pride and glory of being first back with the news. Parker gave a few words of praise for his valuable assistance which filled him with delight, and then turned to the Chief Constable.

" They obviously went off in this direction. Would you bear away to the left, sir, and enter the trees from that end, and Peter, will you bear to the right and work through from the other end, while I go straight up the middle? "

The Chief Constable, who seemed a good deal shaken by the discovery of the body, obeyed without a word. Wimsey caught Parker by the arm.

" I say," he said, " have you looked at the wound? Something funny, isn't there? There ought to be more mess, somehow. What do you think? "

" I'm not thinking anything for the moment," said

Parker, a little grimly. " We'll wait for the doctor's report.
Come on, Steve ! We want to dig out that car."

" Let's have a look at the cap. H'm. Sold by a gentleman
of the Jewish persuasion, resident in Stepney. Almost new.
Smells strongly of Californian Poppy—rather a swell sort of
gangsman, apparently. Quite one of the lads of the village."

" Yes—we ought to be able to trace that. Thank Heaven,
they always overlook something. Well, we'd better get along."

The search for the car presented no difficulties. Parker
stumbled upon it almost as soon as he got in under the trees.
There was a clearing, with a little rivulet of water running
through it, beside which stood the missing Austin. There
were other trees here, mingled with the pines, and the water
made an elbow and spread into a shallow pool, with a kind
of muddy beach.

The hood of the car was up, and Parker approached with
an uncomfortable feeling that there might be something
disagreeable inside, but it was empty. He tried the gears.
They were in neutral and the handbrake was on. On the
seat was a handkerchief—a large linen handkerchief, very
grubby and with no initials or laundry-mark. Parker
grunted a little over the criminal's careless habit of strewing his belongings about. He came round in front of the car
and received immediate further proof of carelessness. For
on the mud there were footmarks—two men's and a
woman's, it seemed.

The woman had got out of the car first—he could see
where the left heel had sunk heavily in as she extricated
herself from the low seat. Then the right foot—less heavily—
then she had staggered a little and started to run. But one
of the men had been there to catch her. He had stepped out
of the bracken in shoes with new rubbers on them, and there
were some scuffling marks as though he had held her and she
had tried to break away. Finally, the second man, who
seemed to possess rather narrow feet and to wear the long-
toed boots affected by Jew boys of the louder sort—had

come after her from the car—the marks of his feet were clear, crossing and half-obliterating hers. All three had stood together for a little. Then the tracks moved away, with those of the woman in the middle, and led up to where the mark of a Michelin balloon tyre showed clearly. The tyres on the Austin were ordinary Dunlops—besides, this was obviously a bigger car. It had apparently stood there for some little time, for a little pool of engine-oil had dripped from the crank-case. Then the bigger car had moved off, down a sort of ride that led away through the trees. Parker followed it for a little distance, but the tracks soon became lost in a thick carpet of pine-needles. Still, there was no other road for a car to take. He turned to the Austin to investigate further. Presently shouts told him that the other two were converging upon the centre of the wood. He called back and before long Wimsey and Sir Charles Pillington came crashing towards him through the bracken which fringed the pines.

" Well," said Wimsey, " I imagine we may put down this elegant bit of purple headgear to the gentleman in the slim boots. Bright yellow, I fancy, with buttons. He must be lamenting his beautiful cap. The woman's footprints belong to Mary Whittaker, I take it."

" I suppose so. I don't see how they can be the Findlater girl's. This woman went or was taken off in the car."

" They are certainly not Vera Findlater's—there was no mud on her shoes when we found her."

" Oh ! you were taking notice, then. I thought you were feeling a bit dead to the world."

" So I was, old dear, but I can't help noticin' things, though moribund. Hullo ! what's this ? "

He put his hand down behind the cushions of the car and pulled out an American magazine—that monthly collection of mystery and sensational fiction published under the name of *The Black Mask.*

" Light reading for the masses," said Parker.

" Brought by the gentleman in the yellow boots, perhaps," suggested the Chief Constable.

" More likely by Miss Findlater," said Wimsey.

" Hardly a lady's choice," said Sir Charles, in a pained tone.

" Oh, I dunno. From all I hear, Miss Whittaker was dead against sentimentality and roses round the porch, and the other poor girl copied her in everything. They might have a boyish taste in fiction."

" Well, it's not very important," said Parker.

" Wait a bit. Look at this. Somebody's been making marks on it."

Wimsey held out the cover for inspection. A thick pencil-mark had been drawn under the first two words of the title.

" Do you think it's some sort of message ? Perhaps the book was on the seat, and she contrived to make the marks unnoticed and shove it away here before they transferred her to the other car."

" Ingenious," said Sir Charles, " but what does it mean ? The Black. It makes no sense."

" Perhaps the long-toed gentleman was a nigger," suggested Parker. " Nigger taste runs rather to boots and hair-oil. Or possibly a Hindu or Parsee of sorts."

" God bless my soul," said Sir Charles, horrified, " an English girl in the hands of a nigger. How abominable ! "

" Well, we'll hope it isn't so. Shall we follow the road out or wait for the doctor to arrive ? "

" Better go back to the body, I think," said Parker. " They've got a long start of us, and half an hour more or less in following them up won't make much odds."

They turned from the translucent cool greenness of the little wood back on to the downs. The streamlet clacked merrily away over the pebbles, running out to the south-west on its way to the river and the sea.

" It's all very well your chattering," said Wimsey to the water. " Why can't you say what you've seen ? "

CHAPTER XXI

BY WHAT MEANS?

" Death hath so many doors to let out life."
BEAUMONT AND FLETCHER : *Custom of the Countr*

THE DOCTOR turned out to be a plumpish, fussy man
—and what Wimsey impatiently called a " Tutster." He
tutted over the mangled head of poor Vera Findlater as
though it was an attack of measles after a party or a self-
provoked fit of the gout.

" Tst, tst, tst. A terrible blow. How did we come by that,
I wonder ? Tst, tst. Life extinct ? Oh, for several days, you
know. Tst, tst—which makes it so much more painful, of
course. Dear me, how shocking for her poor parents. And
her sisters. They are very agreeable girls ; you know them,
of course, Sir Charles. Yes. Tst, tst."

" There is no doubt, I suppose," said Parker, " that it is
Miss Findlater."

" None whatever," said Sir Charles.

" Well, as you can identify her, it may be possible to
spare the relatives the shock of seeing her like this. Just a
moment, doctor—the photographer wants to record the
position of the body before you move anything. Now, Mr.
—Andrews ?—yes—have you ever done any photographs
of this kind before ? No ?—well, you mustn't be upset by it !
I know it's rather unpleasant. One from here, please, to
show the position of the body—now from the top of the
bank—that's right—now one of the wound itself—a close-up
view, please. Yes. Thank you. Now, doctor, you can turn
her over, please—I'm sorry, Mr. Andrews—I know
exactly how you are feeling, but these things have to be

done. Hullo ! look how her arms are all scratched about. Looks as if she'd put up a bit of a fight. The right wrist and left elbow—as though someone had been trying to hold her down. We must have a photograph of the marks, Mr. Andrews—they may be important. I say, doctor, what do you make of this on the face ? "

The doctor looked as though he would have preferred not to make so much as an examination of the face. However, with many tuts he worked himself up to giving an opinion.

" As far as one can tell, with all these post-mortem changes," he ventured, " it looks as though the face had been roughened or burnt about the nose and lips. Yet there is no appearance of the kind on the bridge of the nose, neck or forehead. Tst, tst—otherwise I should have put it down to severe sunburn."

" How about chloroform burns ? " suggested Parker.

" Tst, tst," said the doctor, annoyed at not having thought of this himself—" I wish you gentlemen of the police force would not be quite so abrupt. You want everything decided in too great a hurry. I was about to remark— if you had not anticipated me—that since I could *not* put the appearance down to sunburn, there remains some such possibility as you suggest. I can't possibly say that it *is* the result of chloroform—medical pronouncements of that kind cannot be hastily made without cautious investigation—but I was about to remark that it *might* be."

" In that case," put in Wimsey, " could she have died from the effects of the chloroform ? Supposing she was given too much or that her heart was weak ? "

" My good sir," said the doctor, deeply offended this time, " look at that blow upon the head, and ask yourself whether it is necessary to suggest any other cause of death. Moreover, if she had died of the chloroform, where would be the necessity for the blow ? "

" That is exactly what I was wondering," said Wimsey.

" I suppose," went on the doctor, " you will hardly dispute my medical knowledge ? "

" Certainly not," said Wimsey, " but as you say, it is unwise to make any medical pronouncement without cautious investigation."

" And this is not the place for it," put in Parker, hastily. " I think we have done all there is to do here. Will you go with the body to the mortuary, doctor. Mr. Andrews, I shall be obliged if you will come and take a few photographs of some footmarks and so on up in the wood. The light is bad, I'm afraid, but we must do our best."

He took Wimsey by the arm.

" The man is a fool, of course," he said, " but we can get a second opinion. In the meantime, we had better let it be supposed that we accept the surface explanation of all this."

" What is the difficulty ? " asked Sir Charles, curiously.

" Oh, nothing much," replied Parker. " All the appearances are in favour of the girls having been attacked by a couple of ruffians, who have carried Miss Whittaker off with a view to ransom, after brutally knocking Miss Findlater on the head when she offered resistance. Probably that is the true explanation. Any minor discrepancies will doubtless clear themselves up in time. We shall know better when we have had a proper medical examination."

They returned to the wood, where photographs were taken and careful measurements made of the footprints. The Chief Constable followed these activities with intense interest, looking over Parker's shoulder as he entered the particulars in his notebook.

" I say," he said, suddenly, " isn't it rather odd——"

" Here's somebody coming," broke in Parker.

The sound of a motor-cycle being urged in second gear over the rough ground proved to be the herald of a young man armed with a camera.

" Oh, God ! " groaned Parker. " The damned Press already."

He received the journalist courteously enough, showing him the wheel-tracks and the footprints, and outlining the kidnapping theory as they walked back to the place where the body was found.

" Can you give us any idea, Inspector, of the appearance of the two wanted men ? "

" Well," said Parker, " one of them appears to be something of a dandy ; he wears a loathsome mauve cap and narrow pointed shoes, and, if those marks on the magazine cover mean anything, one or other of the men may possibly be a coloured man of some kind. Of the second man, all we can definitely say is that he wears number 10 shoes, with rubber heels."

" I was going to say," said Pillington, " that, à propos de bottes, it is rather remarkable——"

" And this is where we found the body of Miss Findlater," went on Parker, ruthlessly. He described the injuries and the position of the body, and the journalist gratefully occupied himself with taking photographs, including a group of Wimsey, Parker and the Chief Constable standing among the gorse-bushes, while the latter majestically indicated the fatal spot with his walking-stick.

" And now you've got what you want, old son," said Parker, benevolently, " buzz off, won't you, and tell the rest of the boys. You've got all we can tell you, and we've got other things to do beyond granting special interviews."

The reporter asked no better. This was tantamount to making his information exclusive, and no Victorian matron could have a more delicate appreciation of the virtues of exclusiveness than a modern newspaper man.

" Well now, Sir Charles," said Parker, when the man had happily chugged and popped himself away, " what were you about to say in the matter of the footprints ? "

But Sir Charles was offended. The Scotland Yard man had snubbed him and thrown doubt on his discretion.

" Nothing," he replied. " I feel sure that my conclusions would appear very elementary to you."

And he preserved a dignified silence throughout the return journey.

.   .   .   .

The Whittaker case had begun almost imperceptibly, in the overhearing of a casual remark dropped in a Soho restaurant ; it ended amid a roar of publicity that shook England from end to end and crowded even Wimbledon into the second place. The bare facts of the murder and kidnapping appeared exclusively that night in a Late Extra edition of the *Evening Views*. Next morning it sprawled over the Sunday papers with photographs and full details, actual and imaginary. The idea of two English girls—the one brutally killed, the other carried off for some end unthinkably sinister, by a black man—aroused all the passion of horror and indignation of which the English temperament is capable. Reporters swarmed down upon Crow's Beach like locusts—the downs near Shelly Head were like a fair with motors, bicycles and parties on foot, rushing out to spend a happy week-end amid surroundings of mystery and bloodshed. Parker, who with Wimsey had taken rooms at the Green Lion, sat answering the telephone and receiving the letters and wires which descended upon him from all sides, with a stalwart policeman posted at the end of the passage to keep out all intruders.

Wimsey fidgeted about the room, smoking cigarette after cigarette in his excitement.

" This time we've got them," he said. " They've overreached themselves, thank God ! "

" Yes. But have a little patience, old man. We can't lose them—but we must have all the facts first."

" You're sure those fellows have got Mrs. Forrest safe ? "

" Oh, yes. She came back to the flat on Monday night—
or so the garage man says. Our men are shadowing her
continually and will let us know the moment anybody comes
to the flat."

" Monday night ! "

" Yes. But that's no proof in itself. Monday night is quite
a usual time for week-enders to return to Town. Besides,
I don't want to frighten her till we know whether she's the
principal or merely the accomplice. Look here, Peter, I've
had a message from another of our men. He's been looking
into the finances of Miss Whittaker and Mrs. Forrest. Miss
Whittaker has been drawing out big sums, ever since last
December year in cheques to Self, and these correspond
almost exactly, amount for amount, with sums which Mrs.
Forrest has been paying into her own account. That woman
has had a big hold over Miss Whittaker, ever since old Miss
Dawson died. She's in it up to the neck, Peter."

" I knew it. She's been doing the jobs while the Whittaker
woman held down her alibi in Kent. For God's sake,
Charles, make no mistake. Nobody's life is safe for a second
while either of them is at large."

" When a woman is wicked and unscrupulous," said
Parker, sententiously, " she is the most ruthless criminal in
the world—fifty times worse than a man, because she is
always so much more single-minded about it."

" They're not troubled with sentimentality, that's why,"
said Wimsey, " and we poor mutts of men stuff ourselves up
with the idea that they're romantic and emotional. All
punk, my son. Damn that 'phone ! "

Parker snatched up the receiver.

" Yes—yes—speaking. Good God, you don't say so. All
right. Yes. Yes, of course you must detain him. I think
myself it's a plant, but he must be held and questioned.
And see that all the papers have it. Tell 'em you're sure
he's the man. See ? Soak it well into 'em that that's the
official view. And—wait a moment—I want photographs

of the cheque and of any finger-prints on it. Send 'em down immediately by a special messenger. It's genuine, I suppose? The Bank people say it is? Good! What's his story? . . . Oh ! . . . any envelope?—Destroyed?—Silly devil. Right. Right. Good-bye."

He turned to Wimsey with some excitement.

" Hallelujah Dawson walked into Lloyds Bank in Stepney yesterday morning and presented Mary Whittaker's cheque for £10,000, drawn on their Leahampton branch to Bearer, and dated Friday 24th. As the sum was such a large one and the story of the disappearance was in Friday night's paper, they asked him to call again. Meanwhile, they communicated with Leahampton. When the news of the murder came out yesterday evening, the Leahampton manager remembered about it and 'phoned the Yard, with the result that they sent round this morning and had Hallelujah up for a few inquiries. His story is that the cheque arrived on Saturday morning, all by itself in an envelope, without a word of explanation. Of course the old juggins chucked the envelope away, so that we can't verify his tale or get a line on the post-mark. Our people thought the whole thing looked a bit fishy, so Hallelujah is detained pending investigation—in other words, arrested for murder and conspiracy ! "

" Poor old Hallelujah ! Charles, this is simply devilish ! That innocent, decent old creature, who couldn't harm a fly."

" I know. Well, he's in for it and will have to go through with it. It's all the better for us. Hell's bells, there's somebody at the door. Come in."

" It's Dr. Faulkner to see you, sir," said the constable, putting his head in.

" Oh, good. Come in, doctor. Have you made your examination ? "

" I have, Inspector. Very interesting. You were quite right. I'll tell you that much straight away."

" I'm glad to hear that. Sit down and tell us all about it."

" I'll be as brief as possible," said the doctor. He was a London man, sent down by Scotland Yard, and accustomed to police work—a lean, grey badger of a man, business-like and keen-eyed, the direct opposite of the " tutster " who had annoyed Parker the evening before.

" Well, first of all, the blow on the head had, of course, nothing whatever to do with the death. You saw yourself that there had been next to no bleeding. The wound was inflicted some time after death—no doubt to create the impression of an attack by a gang. Similarly with the cuts and scratches on the arms. They are the merest camouflage."

" Exactly. Your colleague——"

" My colleague, as you call him, is a fool," snorted the doctor. " If that's a specimen of his diagnosis, I should think there would be a high death-rate in Crow's Beach. That's by the way. You want the cause of death ? "

" Chloroform ? "

" Possibly. I opened the body but found no special symptoms suggestive of poisoning or anything. I have removed the necessary organs and sent them to Sir James Lubbock for analysis at your suggestion, but candidly I expect nothing from that. There was no odour of chloroform on opening the thorax. Either the time elapsed since the death was too long, as is very possible, seeing how volatile the stuff is, or the dose was too small. I found no indications of any heart weakness, so that, to produce death in a healthy young girl, chloroform would have had to be administered over a considerable time."

" Do you think it was administered at all ? "

" Yes, I think it was. The burns on the face certainly suggest it."

" That would also account for the handkerchief found in the car," said Wimsey.

" I suppose," pursued Parker, " that it would require

considerable strength and determination to administer chloroform to a strong young woman. She would probably resist strenuously."

"She would," said the doctor, grimly, "but the odd thing is, she didn't. As I said before, all the marks of violence were inflicted post-mortem."

"Suppose she had been asleep at the time," suggested Wimsey, "couldn't it have been done quietly then?"

"Oh, yes—easily. After a few long breaths of the stuff she would become semi-conscious and then could be more firmly dealt with. It is quite possible, I suppose, that she fell asleep in the sunshine, while her companion wandered off and was kidnapped, and that the kidnappers then came along and got rid of Miss Findlater."

"That seems a little unnecessary," said Parker. "Why come back to her at all?"

"Do you suggest that they both fell asleep and were both set on and chloroformed at the same time? It sounds rather unlikely."

"I don't. Listen, doctor—only keep this to yourself."

He outlined the history of their suspicions about Mary Whittaker, to which the doctor listened in horrified amazement.

"What happened," said Parker, "as we think, is this. We think that for some reason Miss Whittaker had determined to get rid of this poor girl who was so devoted to her. She arranged that they should go off for a picnic and that it should be known where they were going to. Then, when Vera Findlater was dozing in the sunshine, our theory is that she murdered her—either with chloroform or—more likely, I fancy—by the same method that she used upon her other victims, whatever that was. Then she struck her on the head and produced the other appearances suggestive of a struggle, and left on the bushes a cap which she had previously purchased and stained with brilliantine. I am, of course, having the cap traced. Miss Whittaker is a tall, powerful woman—I don't think it would be beyond her strength to inflict that blow on an unresisting body."

" But how about these footmarks in the wood ? "

" I'm coming to that. There are one or two very odd things about them. To begin with, if this was the work of a secret gang, why should they go out of their way to pick out the one damp, muddy spot in twenty miles of country to leave their footprints in, when almost anywhere else they could have come and gone without leaving any recognisable traces at all ? "

" Good point," said the doctor. " And I add to that, that they must have noticed they'd left a cap behind. Why not come back and remove it ? "

" Exactly. Then again. Both pairs of shoes left prints entirely free from the marks left by wear and tear. I mean that there were no signs of the heels or soles being worn at all, while the rubbers on the larger pair were obviously just out of the shop. We shall have the photographs here in a moment, and you will see. Of course, it's not impossible that both men should be wearing brand new shoes, but on the whole it's unlikely."

" It is," agreed the doctor.

" And now we come to the most suggestive thing of all. One of the supposed men had very much bigger feet than the other, from which you would expect a taller and possibly heavier man with a longer stride. But on measuring the footprints, what do we find ? In all three cases—the big man, the little man and the woman—we have exactly the same length of stride. Not only that, but the footprints have sunk into the ground to precisely the same depth, indicating that all three people were of the same weight. Now, the other discrepancies might pass, but that is absolutely beyond the reach of coincidence."

Dr. Faulkner considered this for a moment.

" You've proved your point," he said at length. " I consider that absolutely convincing."

" It struck even Sir Charles Pillington, who is none too bright," said Parker. " I had the greatest difficulty in preventing him from blurting out the extraordinary agreement of the measurements to that *Evening Views* man."

" You think, then, that Miss Whittaker had come provided with these shoes and produced the tracks herself."

" Yes, returning each time through the bracken. Cleverly done. She had made no mistake about superimposing the footprints. It was all worked out to a nicety—each set over and under the two others, to produce the impression that three people had been there at the same time. Intensive study of the works of Mr. Austin Freeman, I should say."

" And what next ? "

" Well, I think we shall find that this Mrs. Forrest, who we think has been her accomplice all along, had brought her car down—the big car, that is—and was waiting there for her. Possibly she did the making of the footprints while Mary Whittaker was staging the assault. Anyhow, she probably arrived there after Mary Whittaker and Vera Findlater had left the Austin and departed to the hollow on the downs. When Mary Whittaker had finished her part of the job, they put the handkerchief and the magazine called *The Black Mask* into the Austin and drove off in Mrs. Forrest's car. I'm having the movements of the car investigated, naturally. It's a dark blue Renault four-seater, with Michelin balloon-tyres, and the number is XO4247. We know that it returned to Mrs. Forrest's garage on the Monday night with Mrs. Forrest in it."

" But where is Miss Whittaker ? "

" In hiding somewhere. We shall get her all right. She can't get money from her own bank—they're warned. If Mrs. Forrest tries to get money for her, she will be followed. So if the worst comes to the worst, we can starve her out in time with any luck. But we've got another clue. There has been a most determined attempt to throw suspicion on an unfortunate relative of Miss Whittaker's—a black

Nonconformis. parson, with the remarkable name of Hallelujah Dawson. He has certain pecuniary claims on Miss Whittaker—not legal claims, but claims which any decent and humane person should have respected. She didn't respect them, and the poor old man might very well have been expected to nurse a grudge against her. Yesterday morning he tried to cash a Bearer cheque of hers for £10,000, with a lame-sounding story to the effect that it had arrived by the first post, without explanation, in an envelope. So, of course, he's had to be detained as one of the kidnappers."

" But that is very clumsy, surely. He's almost certain to have an alibi."

" I fancy the story will be that he hired some gangsters to do the job for him. He belongs to a Mission in Stepney—where that mauve cap came from—and no doubt there are plenty of tough lads in his neighbourhood. Of course we shall make close inquiries and publish details broadcast in all the papers."

" And then ? "

" Well then, I fancy, the idea is that Miss Whittaker will turn up somewhere in an agitated condition with a story of assault and holding to ransom made to fit the case. If Cousin Hallelujah has not produced a satisfactory alibi, we shall learn that he was on the spot directing the murderers. If he has definitely shown that he wasn't there, his name will have been mentioned, or he will have turned up at some time which the poor dear girl couldn't exactly ascertain, in some dreadful den to which she was taken in a place which she won't be able to identify."

" What a devilish plot."

" Yes. Miss Whittaker is a charming young woman. If there's anything she'd stop at, I don't know what it is. And the amiable Mrs. Forrest appears to be another of the same kidney. Of course, doctor, we're taking you into our confidence. You understand that our catching Mary

Whittaker depends on her believing that we've swallowed all these false clues of hers."

" I'm not a talker," said the doctor. " Gang you call it, and gang it is, as far as I'm concerned. And Miss Findlater was hit on the head and died of it. I only hope my colleague and the Chief Constable will be equally discreet. I warned them, naturally, after what you said last night."

" It's all very well," said Wimsey, " but what positive evidence have we, after all, against this woman ? A clever defending counsel would tear the whole thing to rags. The only thing we can absolutely *prove* her to have done is the burgling that house on Hampstead Heath and stealing the coal. The other deaths were returned natural deaths at the inquest. And as for Miss Findlater—even if we show it to be chloroform—well, chloroform isn't difficult stuff to get hold of—it's not arsenic or cyanide. And even if there were finger-prints on the spanner——"

" There were not," said Parker, gloomily. " This girl knows what she's about."

" What did she want to kill Vera Findlater for, anyway ? " asked the doctor, suddenly. " According to you, the girl was the most valuable bit of evidence she had. She was the one witness who could prove that Miss Whittaker had an alibi for the other crimes—if they were crimes."

" She may have found out too much about the connection between Miss Whittaker and Mrs. Forrest. My impression is that she had served her turn and become dangerous. What we're hoping to surprise now is some communication between Forrest and Whittaker. Once we've got that——"

" Humph ! " said Dr. Faulkner. He had strolled to the window. " I don't want to worry you unduly, but I perceive Sir Charles Pillington in conference with the Special Correspondent of the *Wire*. The *Yell* came out with the gang story all over the front page this morning, and a patriotic leader about the danger of encouraging coloured aliens. I needn't remind you that the *Wire* would be ready to corrupt the Archangel Gabriel in order to kill the *Yell's* story."

" Oh, hell ! " said Parker, rushing to the window.

" Too late," said the doctor. " The *Wire* man has vanished into the post office. Of course, you can 'phone up and try to stop it."

Parker did so, and was courteously assured by the editor of the *Wire* that the story had not reached him, and that if it did, he would bear Inspector Parker's instructions in mind.

The editor of the *Wire* was speaking the exact truth. The story had been received by the editor of the *Evening Banner*, sister paper to the *Wire*. In times of crisis, it is sometimes convenient that the left hand should not know what the right hand does. After all, it was an exclusive story.

CHAPTER XXII

A CASE OF CONSCIENCE

" I know thou art religious,
And hast a thing within thee called conscience,
With twenty popish tricks and ceremonies
Which I have seen thee careful to observe."

Titus Andronicus

THURSDAY, June 23rd, was the Eve of S. John. The
sober green workaday dress in which the church settles
down to her daily duties after the bridal raptures of Pente-
cost, had been put away, and the altar was white and
shining once again. Vespers were over in the Lady Chapel
at S. Onesimus—a faint reek of incense hung cloudily
under the dim beams of the roof. A very short acolyte with
a very long brass extinguisher snuffed out the candles,
adding the faintly unpleasant yet sanctified odour of hot
wax. The small congregation of elderly ladies rose up
lingeringly from their devotions and slipped away in a
series of deep genuflections. Miss Climpson gathered up a
quantity of little manuals, and groped for her gloves. In
doing so, she dropped her office-book. It fell, annoyingly,
behind the long kneeler, scattering as it went a small
pentecostal shower of Easter cards, book-markers, sacred
pictures, dried palms and Ave Marias into the dark corner
behind the confessional.

Miss Climpson gave a little exclamation of wrath as she
dived after them—and immediately repented this improper
outburst of anger in a sacred place. " Discipline," she
murmured, retrieving the last lost sheep from under a
hassock, " discipline. I must learn self-control." She
crammed the papers back into the office-book, grasped her

gloves and handbag, bowed to the Sanctuary, dropped her bag, picked it up this time in a kind of glow of martyrdom, bustled down the aisle and across the church to the south door, where the sacristan stood, key in hand, waiting to let her out. As she went, she glanced up at the High Altar, unlit and lonely, with the tall candles like faint ghosts in the twilight of the apse. It had a grim and awful look she thought, suddenly.

" Good night, Mr. Stanniforth," she said, quickly.

" Good night, Miss Climpson, good night."

She was glad to come out of the shadowy porch into the green glow of the June evening. She had felt a menace. Was it the thought of the stern Baptist, with his call to repentance ? the prayer for grace to speak the truth and boldly rebuke vice ? Miss Climpson decided that she would hurry home and read the Epistle and Gospel—curiously tender and comfortable for the festival of that harsh and uncompromising Saint. " And I can tidy up these cards at the same time," she thought.

Mrs. Budge's first-floor front seemed stuffy after the scented loveliness of the walk home. Miss Climpson flung the window open and sat down by it to rearrange her sanctified oddments. The card of the Last Supper went in at the Prayer of Consecration ; the Fra Angelico Annunciation had strayed out of the office for March 25th and was wandering among the Sundays after Trinity ; the Sacred Heart with its French text belonged to Corpus Christi ; the . . . " Dear me ! " said Miss Climpson, " I must have picked this up in church."

Certainly the little sheet of paper was not in her writing. Somebody must have dropped it. It was natural to look and see whether it was anything of importance.

Miss Climpson was one of those people who say : " I am not the kind of person who reads other people's postcards." This is clear notice to all and sundry that they are, precisely, that kind of person. They are not untruthful ;

the delusion is real to them. It is merely that Providence
has provided them with a warning rattle, like that of the
rattle-snake. After that, if you are so foolish as to leave
your correspondence in their way, it is your own affair.

Miss Climpson perused the paper.

In the manuals for self-examination issued to the
Catholic-minded, there is often included an unwise little
paragraph which speaks volumes for the innocent un-
worldliness of the compilers. You are advised, when preparing for confession, to make a little list of your misdeeds,
lest one or two peccadilloes should slip your mind. It is
true that you are cautioned against writing down the
names of other people or showing your list to your friends,
or leaving it about. But accidents may happen—and it
may be that this recording of sins is contrary to the mind
of the church, who bids you whisper them with fleeting
breath into the ear of a priest and bids him, in the same
moment that he absolves, forget them as though they had
never been spoken.

At any rate, somebody had been recently shriven of the
sins set forth upon the paper—probably the previous Saturday—and the document had fluttered down unnoticed
between the confession-box and the hassock, escaping the eye
of the cleaner. And here it was—the tale that should have
been told to none but God—lying open upon Mrs. Budge's
round mahogany table under the eye of a fellow-mortal.

To do Miss Climpson justice, she would probably have
destroyed it instantly unread, if one sentence had not caught
her eye :

" The lies I told for M. W.'s sake."

At the same moment she realised that this was Vera
Findlater's handwriting, and it " came over her like a
flash "—as she explained afterwards, exactly what the
implication of the words was.

For a full half-hour Miss Climpson sat alone, struggling
with her conscience. Her natural inquisitiveness said

"Read"; her religious training said, "You must not read"; her sense of duty to Wimsey, who employed her, said, "Find out"; her own sense of decency said, "Do no such thing"; a dreadful, harsh voice muttered gratingly, "Murder is the question. Are you going to be the accomplice of Murder?" She felt like Lancelot Gobbo between conscience and the fiend—but which was the fiend and which was conscience?

"To speak the truth and boldly rebuke vice."

Murder.

There was a real possibility now.

But *was* it a possibility? Perhaps she had read into the sentence more than it would bear.

In that case, was it not—almost—a duty to read further and free her mind from this horrible suspicion?

She would have liked to go to Mr. Tredgold and ask his advice. Probably he would tell her to burn the paper promptly and drive suspicion out of her mind with prayer and fasting.

She got up and began searching for the match-box. It would be better to get rid of the thing quickly.

What, exactly, was she about to do?—To destroy the clue to the discovery of a Murder?

Whenever she thought of the word, it wrote itself upon her brain in large capitals, heavily underlined. MURDER —like a police-bill.

Then she had an idea. Parker was a policeman—and probably also he had no particular feelings about the sacred secrecy of the Confessional. He had a Protestant appearance—or possibly he thought nothing of religion one way or the other. In any case, he would put his professional duty before everything. Why not send him the paper, without reading it, briefly explaining how she had come upon it? Then the responsibility would be his.

On consideration, however, Miss Climpson's innate honesty scouted this scheme as jesuitical. Secrecy was violated by this open publication as much as if she had read the thing—or more so. The old Adam, too, raised his head at this point, suggesting that if anybody was going to see the confession, she might just as well satisfy her own reasonable curiosity. Besides—suppose she was quite mistaken. After all, the "lies" might have nothing whatever to do with Mary Whittaker's alibi. In that case, she would have betrayed another person's secret wantonly, and to no purpose. If she *did* decide to show it, she was bound to read it first—in justice to all parties concerned.

Perhaps—if she just glanced at another word or two, she would see that it had nothing to do with—MURDER —and then she could destroy it and forget it. She knew that if she destroyed it unread she never would forget it, to the end of her life. She would always carry with her that grim suspicion. She would think of Mary Whittaker as—perhaps—a Murderess. When she looked into those hard blue eyes, she would be wondering what sort of expression they had when the soul behind them was plotting —MURDER. Of course, the suspicions had been there before, planted by Wimsey, but now they were her own suspicions. They crystallised—became real to her.

" What shall I do ? "

She gave a quick, shamefaced glance at the paper again. This time she saw the word " London."

Miss Climpson gave a kind of little gasp, like a person stepping under a cold shower-bath.

" Well," said Miss Climpson, " if this is a sin I am going to do it, and may I be forgiven."

With a red flush creeping over her cheeks as though she were stripping something naked, she turned her attention to the paper.

The jottings were brief and ambiguous. Parker might not have made much of them, but to Miss Climpson, trained in this kind of devotional shorthand, the story was clear as print.

" Jealousy "—the word was written large and underlined. Then there was a reference to a quarrel, to wicked
accusations and angry words and to a pre-occupation
coming between the penitent's soul and God. " Idol "—
and a long dash.

From these few fossil bones, Miss Climpson had little
difficulty in reconstructing one of those hateful and passionate " scenes " of slighted jealousy with which a woman-
ridden life had made her only too familiar. " I do everything for you—you don't care a bit for me—you treat me
cruelly—you're simply sick of me, that's what it is ! " And
" Don't be so ridiculous. Really, I can't stand this. Oh,
stop it, Vera ! I hate being slobbered over." Humiliating,
degrading, exhausting, beastly scenes. Girls' school,
boarding-house, Bloomsbury-flat scenes. Damnable selfish-
ness wearying of its victim. Silly *schwärmerei* swamping all
decent self-respect. Barren quarrels ending in shame and
hatred.

" Beastly, blood-sucking woman," said Miss Climpson,
viciously. " It's too bad. She's only making use of the
girl."

But the self-examiner was now troubled with a more
difficult problem. Piecing the hints together, Miss Climpson sorted it out with practised ease. Lies had been told
—that was wrong, even though done to help a friend. Bad
confessions had been made, suppressing those lies. This
ought to be confessed and put right. But (the girl asked
herself) had she come to this conclusion out of hatred of
the lies or out of spite against the friend ? Difficult, this
searching of the heart. And ought she, not content with
confessing the lies to the priest, also to tell the truth to the
world ?

Miss Climpson had here no doubt what the priest's ruling would be. " You need not go out of your way to betray your friend's confidence. Keep silent if you can, but
if you speak you must speak the truth. You must tell your

friend that she is not to expect any more lying from you. She is entitled to ask for secrecy—no more."

So far, so good. But there was a further problem.

"Ought I to connive at her doing what is wrong?"—and then a sort of explanatory aside—"the man in South Audley Street."

This was a little mysterious. . . . No!—on the contrary, it explained the whole mystery, jealousy, quarrel and all.

In those weeks of April and May, when Mary Whittaker had been supposed to be all the time in Kent with Vera Findlater, she had been going up to London. And Vera had promised to say that Mary was with her the whole time. And the visits to London had to do with a man in South Audley Street, and there was something sinful about it. That probably meant a love-affair. Miss Climpson pursed her lips virtuously, but she was more surprised than shocked. Mary Whittaker! she would never have suspected it of her, somehow. But it so explained the jealousy and the quarrel—the sense of desertion. But how had Vera found out? Had Mary Whittaker confided in her?—No; that sentence again, under the heading "Jealousy"—what was it—"following M. W. to London." She had followed then, and seen. And then, at some moment, she had burst out with her knowledge—reproached her friend. Yet this expedition to London must have happened before her own conversation with Vera Findlater, and the girl had then seemed so sure of Mary's affection. Or had it been that she was trying to persuade herself, with determined self-deception, that there was "nothing in" this business about the man? Probably. And probably some brutality of Mary's had brought all the miserable suspicions boiling to the surface, vocal, reproachful and furious. And so they had gone on to the row and the break.

"Queer," thought Miss Climpson, "that Vera has

never come and told me about her trouble. But perhaps she is ashamed, poor child. I haven't seen her for nearly a week. I think I'll call and see her and perhaps she'll tell me all about it. In which case "—cried Miss Climpson's conscience, suddenly emerging with a bright and beaming smile from under the buffets of the enemy—" in which case I shall know the whole history of it legitimately and can *quite honourably* tell Lord Peter about it."

The next day—which was the Friday—she woke, however, with an unpleasant ache in the conscience. The paper —still tucked into the office-book—worried her. She went round early to Vera Findlater's house, only to hear that she was staying with Miss Whittaker. " Then I suppose they've made it up," she said. She did not want to see Mary Whittaker, whether her secret was murder or mere immorality ; but she was tormented by the desire to clear up the matter of the alibi for Lord Peter.

In Wellington Avenue she was told that the two girls had gone away on the Monday and had not yet returned. She tried to reassure the maid, but her own heart misgave her. Without any real reason, she was uneasy. She went round to the church and said her prayers, but her mind was not on what she was saying. On an impulse, she caught Mr. Tredgold as he pottered in and out of the Sacristy, and asked if she might come the next evening to lay a case of conscience before him. So far, so good, and she felt that a " good walk " might help to clear the cob-webs from her brain.

So she started off, missing Lord Peter by a quarter of an hour, and took the train to Guildford and then walked and had lunch in a wayside tea-shop and walked back into Guildford and so came home, where she learnt that " Mr. Parker and ever so many gentlemen had been ask-ing for her all day, and what a dreadful thing, miss, here was Miss Whittaker and Miss Findlater disappeared and the police out looking for them, and them motor-cars was such dangerous things, miss, wasn't they? It was to be hoped there wasn't an accident."

And into Miss Climpson's mind there came, like an inspiration, the words, " South Audley Street."

Miss Climpson did not, of course, know that Wimsey was at Crow's Beach. She hoped to find him in Town. For she was seized with a desire, which she could hardly have explained even to herself, to go and look at South Audley Street. What she was to do when she got there she did not know, but go there she must. It was the old reluctance to make open use of that confession paper. Vera Findlater's story at first hand—that was the idea to which she obscurely clung. So she took the first train to Waterloo, leaving behind her, in case Wimsey or Parker should call again, a letter so obscure and mysterious and so lavishly underlined and interlined that it was perhaps fortunate for their reason that they were never faced with it.

In Piccadilly she saw Bunter, and learned that his lordship was at Crow's Beach with Mr. Parker, where he, Bunter, was just off to join him. Miss Climpson promptly charged him with a message to his employer slightly more involved and mysterious than her letter, and departed for South Audley Street. It was only when she was walking up it that she realised how vague her quest was and how little investigation one can do by merely walking along a street. Also, it suddenly occurred to her that if Miss Whittaker was carrying on anything of a secret nature in South Audley Street, the sight of an acquaintance patrolling the pavement would put her on her guard. Much struck by this reflection, Miss Climpson plunged abruptly into a chemist's shop and bought a toothbrush, by way of concealing her movements and gaining time. One can while away many minutes comparing the shapes, sizes and bristles of toothbrushes, and sometimes chemists will be nice and gossipy.

Looking round the shop for inspiration, Miss Climpson

observed a tin of nasal snuff labelled with the chemist's own name.

" I will take a tin of that, too, please," she said. " What *excellent* stuff it is—quite *wonderful*. I have used it for *years* and am really *delighted* with it. I recommend it to all my friends, particularly for *hay fever*. In fact, there's a friend of mine who often passes your shop, who told me only *yesterday* what a *martyr* she was to that complaint. ' My dear,' I said to her, ' you have only to get a tin of this *splendid* stuff and you will be *quite* all right *all* summer.' She was so *grateful* to me for telling her about it. Has she been in for it yet?" And she described Mary Whittaker closely.

It will be noticed, by the way, that in the struggle between Miss Climpson's conscience and what Wilkie Collins calls " detective fever," conscience was getting the worst of it and was winking at an amount of deliberate untruth which a little time earlier would have staggered it.

The chemist, however, had seen nothing of Miss Climpson's friend. Nothing, therefore, was to be done but to retire from the field and think what was next to be done. Miss Climpson left, but before leaving she neatly dropped her latchkey into a large basket full of sponges standing at her elbow. She felt she might like to have an excuse to visit South Audley Street again.

Conscience sighed deeply, and her guardian angel dropped a tear among the sponges.

Retiring into the nearest tea-shop she came to, Miss Climpson ordered a cup of coffee and started to think out a plan for honey-combing South Audley Street. She needed an excuse—and a disguise. An adventurous spirit was welling up in her elderly bosom, and her first dozen or so ideas were more lurid than practical.

At length a really brilliant notion occurred to her. She was (she did not attempt to hide it from herself) precisely the type and build of person one associates with the collection of subscriptions. Moreover, she had a perfectly good and genuine cause ready to hand. The church which she attended in London ran a slum mission, which was badly in need of funds, and she possessed a number of collecting cards, bearing full authority to receive subscriptions on its behalf. What more natural than that she should try a little house-to-house visiting in a wealthy quarter?

The question of disguise, also, was less formidable than it might appear. Miss Whittaker had only known her well-dressed and affluent in appearance. Ugly, clumping shoes, a hat of virtuous ugliness, a shapeless coat and a pair of tinted glasses would disguise her sufficiently at a distance. At close quarters, it would not matter if she was recognised, for if once she got to close quarters with Mary Whittaker, her job was done and she had found the house she wanted.

Miss Climpson rose from the table, paid her bill and hurried out to buy the glasses, remembering that it was Saturday. Having secured a pair which hid her eyes effectively without looking exaggeratedly mysterious, she made for her rooms in St. George's Square, to choose suitable clothing for her adventure. She realised, of course, that she could hardly start work till Monday—Saturday afternoon and Sunday are hopeless from the collector's point of view.

The choice of clothes and accessories occupied her for the better part of the afternoon. When she was at last satisfied she went downstairs to ask her landlady for some tea.

" Certainly, miss," said the good woman. " Ain't it awful, miss, about this murder? "

" What murder? " asked Miss Climpson, vaguely.

She took the *Evening Views* from her landlady's hand, and read the story of Vera Findlater's death.

    •   •   •   •   •   •   •   •

Sunday was the most awful day Miss Climpson had ever spent. An active woman, she was condemned to inactivity,

and she had time to brood over the tragedy. Not having
Wimsey's or Parker's inside knowledge, she took the
kidnapping story at its face value. In a sense, she found
it comforting, for she was able to acquit Mary Whittaker
of any share in this or the previous murders. She put them
down—except, of course, in the case of Miss Dawson,
and that might never have been a murder after all—to the
mysterious man in South Audley Street. She formed a
nightmare image of him in her mind—blood-boltered,
sinister, and—most horrible of all—an associate and
employer of debauched and brutal black assassins. To Miss
Climpson's credit be it said that she never for one moment
faltered in her determination to track the monster to his
lurking-place.

She wrote a long letter to Lord Peter, detailing her plans.
Bunter, she knew, had left 110A Piccadilly, so, after considerable thought, she addressed it to Lord Peter Wimsey,
c/o Inspector Parker, The Police-Station, Crow's Beach.
There was, of course, no Sunday post from Town. However,
it would go with the midnight collection.

On the Monday morning she set out early, in her old
clothes and her spectacles, for South Audley Street. Never
had her natural inquisitiveness and her hard training in
third-rate boarding-houses stood her in better stead. She
had learned to ask questions without heeding rebuffs—
to be persistent, insensitive and observant. In every flat
she visited she acted her natural self, with so much sincerity
and such limpet-like obstinacy that she seldom came away
without a subscription and almost never without some
information about the flat and its inmates.

By tea-time, she had done one side of the street and
nearly half the other, without result. She was just thinking
of going to get some food, when she caught sight of a
woman, about a hundred yards ahead, walking briskly
in the same direction as herself.

Now it is easy to be mistaken in faces, but almost

impossible not to recognise a back. Miss Climpson's heart
gave a bound. "Mary Whittaker!" she said to herself,
and started to follow.

The woman stopped to look into a shop window. Miss
Climpson hesitated to come closer. If Mary Whittaker was
at large, then—why then the kidnapping had been done
with her own consent. Puzzled, Miss Climpson determined
to play a waiting game. The woman went into the shop.
The friendly chemist's was almost opposite. Miss Climpson
decided that this was the moment to reclaim her latchkey.
She went in and asked for it. It had been put aside for her
and the assistant produced it at once. The woman was
still in the shop over the way. Miss Climpson embarked
upon a long string of apologies and circumstantial details
about her carelessness. The woman came out. Miss Climpson gave her a longish start, brought the conversation
to a close, and fussed out again, replacing the glasses
which she had removed for the chemist's benefit.

The woman walked on without stopping, but she looked
into the shop windows from time to time. A man with a
fruiterer's barrow removed his cap as she passed and scratched
his head. Almost at once, the woman turned quickly and
came back. The fruiterer picked up the handles of his
barrow and trundled it away into a side street. The woman
came straight on, and Miss Climpson was obliged to dive
into a doorway and pretend to be tying a bootlace, to avoid
a face to face encounter.

Apparently the woman had only forgotten to buy
cigarettes. She went into a tobacconist's and emerged again
in a minute or two, passing Miss Climpson again. That
lady had dropped her bag and was agitatedly sorting its
contents. The woman passed her without a glance and went
on. Miss Climpson, flushed from stooping, followed again.
The woman turned in at the entrance to a block of flats
next door to a florist's. Miss Climpson was hard on her
heels now, for she was afraid of losing her.

Mary Whittaker—if it was Mary Whittaker—went straight through the hall to the lift, which was one of the kind worked by the passenger. She stepped in and shot up. Miss Climpson—gazing at the orchids and roses in the florist's window—watched the lift out of sight. Then, with her subscription card prominently in her hand, she too entered the flats.

There was a porter on duty in a little glass case. He at once spotted Miss Climpson as a stranger and asked politely if he could do anything for her. Miss Climpson, selecting a name at random from the list of occupants in the entrance, asked which was Mrs. Forrest's flat. The man replied that that it was on the fourth floor, and stepped forward to bring the lift down for her. A man, to whom he had been chatting, moved quietly from the glass case and took up a position in the doorway. As the lift ascended, Miss Climpson noticed that the fruiterer had returned. His barrow now stood just outside.

The porter had come up with her, and pointed out the door of Mrs. Forrest's flat. His presence was reassuring. She wished he would stay within call till she had concluded her search of the building. However, having asked for Mrs. Forrest, she must begin there. She pressed the bell.

At first she thought the flat was empty, but after ringing a second time she heard footsteps. The door opened, and a heavily over-dressed and peroxided lady made her appearance, whom Lord Peter would at once—and embarrassingly —have recognised.

" I have come," said Miss Climpson, wedging herself briskly in at the doorway with the skill of the practised canvasser, " to try if I can enlist your help for our Mission Settlement. May I come in ? I am sure you——"

" No thanks," said Mrs. Forrest, shortly, and in a hurried, breathless tone, as if there was somebody behind her who she was anxious should not overhear her, " I'm not interested in Missions."

She tried to shut the door. But Miss Climpson had seen and heard enough.

" Good gracious ! " she cried, staring, " why, it's——"

" Come in." Mrs. Forrest caught her by the arm almost roughly and pulled her over the threshold, slamming the door behind them.

" How extraordinary ! " said Miss Climpson, " I hardly recognised you, Miss Whittaker, with your hair like that."

" You ! " said Mary Whittaker. " You—of all people ! " They sat facing one another in the sitting-room with its tawdry pink silk cushions. " I knew you were a meddler. How did you get here ? Is there anyone with you ? "

" No—yes—I just happened," began Miss Climpson vaguely. One thought was uppermost in her mind. " How did you get free ? What happened ? Who killed Vera ? " She knew she was asking her questions crudely and stupidly. " Why are you disguised like that ? "

" Who sent you ? " reiterated Mary Whittaker.

" Who is the man with you ? " pursued Miss Climpson. " Is he here ? Did he do the murder ? "

" What man ? "

" The man Vera saw leaving your flat. Did he——? "

" So that's it. Vera told you. The liar. I thought I had been quick enough."

Suddenly, something which had been troubling Miss Climpson for weeks crystallised and became plain to her. The expression in Mary Whittaker's eyes. A long time ago, Miss Climpson had assisted a relative to run a board-ing-house, and there had been a young man who paid his bill by cheque. She had had to make a certain amount of unpleasantness about the bill, and he had written the cheque unwillingly, sitting, with her eye upon him, at the little plush-covered table in the drawing-room. Then he had gone away—slinking out with his bag when no one was about. And the cheque had come back, like the bad penny that it was. A forgery. Miss Climpson had had to give evidence. She remembered now the odd, defiant look with which the young man had taken up his pen for his first plunge into crime. And to-day she was seeing it again—an unattractive mingling of recklessness and calculation. It was with the look which had once warned Wimsey and should have warned her. She breathed more quickly.

" Who was the man? "

" The man? " Mary Whittaker laughed suddenly. " A man called Templeton—no friend of mine. It's really funny that you should think he was a friend of mine. I would have killed him if I could."

" But where is he? What are you doing? Don't you know that everybody is looking for you? Why don't you——? "

" That's why! "

Mary Whittaker flung her ten o'clock edition of the *Evening Banner*, which was lying on the sofa. Miss Climpson read the glaring headlines :

" AMAZING NEW DEVELOPMENTS
IN CROW'S BEACH CRIME.

———

" WOUNDS ON BODY INFLICTED AFTER DEATH.

———

" FAKED FOOTPRINTS."

———

Miss Climpson gasped with amazement, and bent over the smaller type. " How extraordinary ! " she said, looking up quickly.

Not quite quickly enough. The heavy brass lamp missed her head indeed, but fell numbingly on her shoulder. She sprang to her feet with a loud shriek, just as Mary Whittaker's strong white hands closed upon her throat.

CHAPTER XXIII

—AND SMOTE HIM, THUS

" 'Tis not so deep as a well, nor so wide as a church-door ; but 'tis
enough, 'twill serve."

Romeo and Juliet

LORD PETER missed both Miss Climpson's communications. Absorbed in the police inquiry, he never thought to go back to Leahampton. Bunter had duly arrived with " Mrs. Merdle " on the Saturday evening. Immense police activity was displayed in the neighbourhood of the downs, and at Southampton and Portsmouth, in order to foster the idea that the authorities supposed the " gang " to be lurking in those districts. Nothing, as a matter of fact, was farther from Parker's thoughts. " Let her think she is safe," he said, " and she'll come back. It's the cat-and-mouse act for us, old man," Wimsey fretted. He wanted the analysis of the body to be complete and loathed the thought of the long days he had to wait. And he had small hope of the result.

" It's all very well sitting round with your large disguised policemen outside Mrs. Forrest's flat," he said irritably, over the bacon and eggs on Monday morning, " but you do realise, don't you, that we've still got no proof of murder. Not in one single case."

" That's so," replied Parker, placidly.

" Well, doesn't it make your blood boil ? " said Wimsey.

" Hardly," said Parker. " This kind of thing happens too often. If my blood boiled every time there was a delay in getting evidence, I should be in a perpetual fever. Why worry ? It may be that perfect crime you're so fond of talking about—the one that leaves no trace. You ought to be charmed with it."

" Oh, I daresay. O Turpitude, where are the charms that sages have seen in thy face ? Time's called at the Criminals' Arms, and there isn't a drink in the place. Wimsey's Standard Poets, with emendations by Thingummy. As a matter of fact, I'm not at all sure that Miss Dawson's death *wasn't* the perfect crime—if only the Whittaker girl had stopped at that and not tried to cover it up. If you notice, the deaths are becoming more and more violent, elaborate and unlikely in appearance. Telephone again. If the Post Office accounts don't show a handsome profit on telephones this year it won't be your fault."

" It's the cap and shoes," said Parker, mildly. " They've traced them. They were ordered from an outfitter's in Stepney, to be sent to the Rev. H. Dawson, Peveril Hotel, Bloomsbury, to await arrival."

" The Peveril again ! '

" Yes. I recognise the hand of Mr. Trigg's mysterious charmer. The Rev. Hallelujah Dawson's card, with message ' Please give parcel to bearer,' was presented by a District Messenger next day, with a verbal explanation that the gentleman found he could not get up to town after all. The messenger, obeying instructions received by telephone, took the parcel to a lady in a nurse's dress on the platform at Charing Cross. Asked to describe the lady, he said she was tall and wore blue glasses and the usual cloak and bonnet. So that's that."

" How were the goods paid for ? "

" Postal order, purchased at the West Central office at the busiest moment of the day."

" And when did all this happen ? "

" That's the most interesting part of the business. Last month, shortly before Miss Whittaker and Miss Findlater returned from Kent. This plot was well thought out beforehand."

" Yes. Well, that's something more for you to pin on to Mrs. Forrest. It looks like proof of conspiracy, but whether it's proof of murder——"

" It's *meant* to look like a conspiracy of Cousin Hallelujah's, I suppose. Oh, well, we shall have to trace the letters and the typewriter that wrote them and interrogate all these people, I suppose. God ! what a grind ! Hullo ! Come in ! Oh, it's you, doctor ? "

" Excuse my interrupting your breakfast," said Dr. Faulkner, " but early this morning, while lying awake, I was visited with a bright idea. So I had to come and work it off on you while it was fresh. About the blow on the head and the marks on the arms, you know. Do you suppose they served a double purpose ? Besides making it look like the work of a gang, could they be hiding some other, smaller mark ? Poison, for instance, could be injected, and the mark covered up by scratches and cuts inflicted after death."

" Frankly," said Parker, " I wish I could think it. It's a very sound idea and may be the right one. Our trouble is, that in the two previous deaths which we have been investigating, and which we are inclined to think form a part of the same series as this one, there have been no signs or traces of poison discoverable in the bodies at all by any examination or analysis that skill can devise. In fact, not only no proof of poison, but no proof of anything but natural death."

And he related the cases in fuller detail.

" Odd," said the doctor. " And you think this may turn out the same way. Still, in this case the death can't very well have been natural—or why these elaborate efforts to cover it up ? "

" It wasn't," said Parker ; " the proof being that—as we now know—the plot was laid nearly two months ago."

" But the method ! " cried Wimsey, " the method ! Hang it all—here are all we people with our brilliant brains and our professional reputations—and this half-trained girl out of a hospital can beat the lot of us. How was it done ? "

" It's probably something so simple and obvious that it's never occurred to us," said Parker. " The sort of principle you learn when you're in the fourth form and never apply to anything. Rudimentary. Like that motor-cycling imbecile we met up at Crofton, who sat in the rain and prayed for help because he'd never heard of an air-lock in his feed. Now I daresay that boy had learnt—— What's the matter with you ? "

" My God ! " cried Wimsey. He smashed his hand down among the breakfast things, upsetting his cup. " My God ! But that's it ! You've got it—you've done it—— Obvious ? God Almighty—it doesn't need a doctor. A garage hand could have told you. People die of it every day. Of course, it was an air-lock in the feed."

" Bear up, doctor," said Parker, " he's always like this when he gets an idea. It wears off in time. D'you mind explaining yourself, old thing ? "

Wimsey's pallid face was flushed. He turned on the doctor.

" Look here," he said, " the body's a pumping engine, isn't it ? The jolly old heart pumps the blood round the arteries and back through the veins and so on, doesn't it ? That's what keeps things working, what ? Round and home again in two minutes—that sort of thing ? "

" Certainly."

" Little valve to let the blood out ; 'nother little valve to let it in—just like an internal combustion engine, which it is ? "

" Of course."

" And s'posin' that stops ? "

" You die."

" Yes. Now, look here. S'posin' you take a good big hypodermic, empty, and dig it into one of the big arteries and push the handle—what would happen ? What would happen, doctor ? You'd be pumpin' a big air-bubble into your engine feed, wouldn't you ? What would become of your circulation, then ? "

" It would stop it," said the doctor, without hesitation. " That is why nurses have to be particular to fill the syringe properly, especially when doing an intra-venous injection."

" I *knew* it was the kind of thing you learnt in the fourth form. Well, go on. Your circulation would stop—it would be like an embolism in its effect, wouldn't it ? "

" Only if it was in a main artery, of course. In a small vein the blood would find a way round. That is why " (this seemed to be the doctor's favourite opening) " that is why it is so important that embolisms—blood-clots—should be dispersed as soon as possible and not left to wander about the system."

" Yes—yes—but the air-bubble, doctor—in a main artery—say the femoral or the big vein in the bend of the elbow—that would stop the circulation, wouldn't it ? How soon ? "

" Why, at once. The heart would stop beating."

" And then ? "

" You would die."

" With what symptoms ? "

" None to speak of. Just a gasp or two. The lungs would make a desperate effort to keep things going. Then you'd just stop. Like heart failure. It would *be* heart failure."

" How well I know it. . . . That sneeze in the carburettor —a gasping, as you say. And what would be the post-mortem symptoms ? "

" None. Just the appearances of heart failure. And, of course, the little mark of the needle, if you happened to be looking for it."

" You're sure of all this, doctor ? " said Parker.

" Well, it's simple, isn't it ? A plain problem in mechanics. Of course that would happen. It must happen."

" Could it be proved ? " insisted Parker.

" That's more difficult."

" We must try," said Parker. " It's ingenious, and it explains a lot of things. Doctor, will you go down to the mortuary again and see if you can find any puncture mark on the body. I really think you've got the explanation of the whole thing, Peter. Oh, dear ! Who's on the 'phone now ? . . . What ?—*what* ?—oh, hell !—— Well, that's torn it. She'll never come back now. Warn all the ports—send out an all-stations call—watch the railways and go through Bloomsbury with a toothcomb—that's the part she knows best. I'm coming straight up to Town now—yes, immediately. Right you are." He hung up the receiver with a few brief, choice expressions.

" That adjectival imbecile, Pillington, has let out all he knows. The whole story is in the early editions of the *Banner*. We're doing no good here. Mary Whittaker will know the game's up, and she'll be out of the country in two twos, if she isn't already. Coming back to Town, Wimsey ? "

" Naturally. Take you up in the car. Lose no time. Ring the bell for Bunter, would you ? Oh, Bunter, we're going up to Town. How soon can we start ? "

" At once, my lord. I have been holding your lordship's and Mr. Parker's things ready packed from hour to hour, in case a hurried adjournment should be necessary."

" Good man."

" And there is a letter for you, Mr. Parker, sir."

" Oh, thanks. Ah, yes. The finger-prints off the cheque. H'm. Two sets only—besides those of the cashier, of course —Cousin Hallelujah's and a female set, presumably those of Mary Whittaker. Yes, obviously—here are the four fingers of the left hand, just as one would place them to hold the cheque flat while signing."

" Pardon me, sir—but might I look at that photograph ? "

" Certainly. Take a copy for yourself. I know it interests you as a photographer. Well, cheerio, doctor. See you in Town some time. Come on, Peter."

Lord Peter came on. And that, as Dr. Faulkner would say, was why Miss Climpson's second letter was brought up from the police-station too late to catch him.

.   .   .   .

They reached Town at twelve—owing to Wimsey's brisk work at the wheel—and went straight to Scotland Yard, dropping Bunter, at his own request, as he was anxious to return to the flat. They found the Chief Commissioner in rather a brusque mood—angry with the *Banner* and annoyed with Parker for having failed to muzzle Pillington.

" God knows where she will be found next. She's probably got a disguise and a get-away all ready."

" Probably gone already," said Wimsey. " She could easily have left England on the Monday or Tuesday and nobody a penny the wiser. If the coast had seemed clear, she'd have come back and taken possession of her goods again. Now she'll stay abroad. That's all."

" I'm very much afraid you're right," agreed Parker, gloomily.

" Meanwhile, what is Mrs. Forrest doing ? "

" Behaving quite normally. She's been carefully shadowed, of course, but not interfered with in any way. We've got three men out there now—one as a coster—one as a dear friend of the hall-porter's who drops in every so often with racing tips, and an odd-job man doing a spot of work in the back-yard. They report that she has been in and out, shopping and so on, but mostly having her meals at home. No one has called. The men deputed to shadow her away from the flat have watched carefully to see if she speaks to anyone or slips money to anyone. We're pretty sure the two haven't met yet."

" Excuse me, sir." An officer put his head in at the door. " Here's Lord Peter Wimsey's man, sir, with an urgent message."

Bunter entered, trimly correct in bearing, but with a

glitter in his eye. He laid down two photographs on the table.

" Excuse me, my lord and gentlemen, but would you be so good as to cast your eyes on these two photographs ? "

" Finger-prints ? " said the Chief, interrogatively.

" One of them is our own official photograph of the prints on the £10,000 cheque," said Parker. " The other—where did you get this, Bunter ? It looks like the same set of prints, but it's not one of ours."

" They appeared similar, sir, to my uninstructed eye. I thought it better to place the matter before you."

" Send Dewsby here," said the Chief Commissioner.

Dewsby was the head of the finger-print department, and he had no hesitation at all.

" They are undoubtedly the same prints," he said.

A light was slowly breaking in on Wimsey.

" Bunter—did these come off that wine-glass ? "

" Yes, my lord."

" But they are Mrs. Forrest's ! "

" So I understood you to say, my lord, and I have filed them under that name."

" Then, if the signature on the cheque is genuine——"

" We haven't far to look for our bird," said Parker, brutally. " A double identity ; damn the woman, she's made us waste a lot of time. Well, I think we shall get her now, on the Findlater murder at least, and possibly on the Gotobed business."

" But I understood there was an alibi for that," said the Chief.

" There was," said Parker, grimly, " but the witness was the girl that's just been murdered. Looks as though she had made up her mind to split and was got rid of."

" Looks as though several people had had a near squeak of it," said Wimsey.

" Including you. That yellow hair was a wig, then."

" Probably. It never looked natural, you know. When I

was there that night she had on one of those close turban affairs—she might have been bald for all one could see."

" Did you notice the scar on the fingers of the right hand ? "

" I did not—for the very good reason that her fingers were stiff with rings to the knuckles. There was pretty good sense behind her ugly bad taste. I suppose I was to be drugged—or, failing that, caressed into slumber and then—shall we say, put out of circulation ! Highly distressin' incident. Amorous clubman dies in a flat. Relations very anxious to hush matter up. I was selected, I suppose, because I was seen with Evelyn Cropper at Liverpool. Bertha Gotobed got the same sort of dose, too, I take it. Met by old employer, accidentally, on leaving work—£5 note and nice little dinner—lashings of champagne—poor kid as drunk as a blind fiddler—bundled into the car— finished off there and trundled out to Epping in company with a ham sandwich and a bottle of Bass. Easy, ain't it— when you know how ? "

" That being so," said the Chief Commissioner, " the sooner we get hold of her the better. You'd better go at once, Inspector ; take a warrant for Whittaker or Forrest —and any help you may require."

" May I come ? " asked Wimsey, when they were outside the building.

" Why not ? You may be useful. With the men we've got there already we shan't need any extra help."

The car whizzed swiftly through Pall Mall, up St. James's Street and along Piccadilly. Half-way up South Audley Street they passed the fruit-seller, with whom Parker exchanged an almost imperceptible signal. A few doors below the entrance to the flats they got out and were almost immediately joined by the hall-porter's sporting friend.

" I was just going out to call you up," said the latter. " She's arrived."

" What, the Whittaker woman ? "

" Yes. Went up about two minutes ago."

" Is Forrest there too ? "

" Yes. She came in just before the other woman."

" Queer," said Parker. " Another good theory gone west. Are you sure it's Whittaker ? "

" Well, she's made up with old-fashioned clothes and greyish hair and so on. But she's the right height and general appearance. And she's running the old blue-spectacle stunt again. I think it's the right one—though of course I didn't get close to her, remembering your instructions."

" Well, we'll have a look, anyhow. Come along."

The coster had joined them now, and they all entered together.

" Did the old girl go up to Forrest's flat all right ? " asked the third detective of the porter.

" That's right. Went straight to the door and started something about a subscription. Then Mrs. Forrest pulled her in quick and slammed the door. Nobody's come down since."

" Right. We'll take ourselves up—and mind you don't let anybody give us the slip by the staircase. Now then, Wimsey, she knows you as Templeton, but she may still not know for certain that you're working with us. Ring the bell, and when the door's opened, stick your foot inside. We'll stand just round the corner here and be ready to rush."

This manœuvre was executed. They heard the bell trill loudly.

Nobody came to answer it, however. Wimsey rang again, and then bent his ear to the door.

" Charles," he cried suddenly, " there's something going on here." His face was white. " Be quick ! I couldn't stand *another*—— ! "

Parker hastened up and listened. Then he caught Peter's

stick and hammered on the door, so that the hollow lift-shaft echoed with the clamour.

" Come on there—open the door—this is the police."

And all the time, a horrid, stealthy thumping and gurgling sounded inside—dragging of something heavy and a scuffling noise. Then a loud crash, as though a piece of furniture had been flung to the floor—and then a loud hoarse scream, cut brutally off in the middle.

" Break in the door," said Wimsey, the sweat pouring down his face.

Parker signalled to the heavier of the two policemen. He came along, shoulder first, lunging. The door shook and cracked. Parker added his weight, thrusting Wimsey's slight body into the corner. They stamped and panted in the narrow space.

The door gave way, and they tumbled into the hall. Everything was ominously quiet.

" Oh, quick ! " sobbed Peter.

A door on the right stood open. A glance assured them that there was nothing there. They sprang to the sitting-room door and pushed it. It opened about a foot. Something bulky impeded its progress. They shoved violently and the obstacle gave. Wimsey leapt over it—it was a tall cabinet, fallen, with broken china strewing the floor. The room bore signs of a violent struggle—tables flung down, a broken chair, a smashed lamp. He dashed for the bed-room, with Parker hard at his heels.

The body of a woman lay limply on the bed. Her long, grizzled hair hung in a dank rope over the pillow and blood was on her head and throat. But the blood was running freely, and Wimsey could have shouted for joy at the sight. Dead men do not bleed.

Parker gave only one glance at the injured woman. He made promptly for the dressing-room beyond. A shot sang past his head—there was a snarl and a shriek—and the episode was over. The constable stood shaking his

bitten hand, while Parker put the come-along-o'-me grip
on the quarry. He recognised her readily, though the
peroxide wig had fallen awry and the blue eyes were
bleared with terror and fury.

" That'll do," said Parker, quietly, " the game's up. It's
not a bit of use. Come, be reasonable. You don't want us
to put the bracelets on, do you ? Mary Whittaker, alias
Forrest, I arrest you on the charge——" he hesitated for
a moment and she saw it.

" On what charge ? What have you got against
me ? "

" Of attempting to murder this lady, for a start," said
Parker.

" The old fool ! " she said, contemptuously, " she forced
her way in here and attacked me. Is that all ? "

" Very probably not," said Parker, " I warn you that
anything you say may be taken down and used in evidence
at your trial."

Indeed, the third officer had already produced a notebook and was imperturbably writing down : " When told
the charge, the prisoner said ' Is that all ? ' " The remark
evidently struck him as an injudicious one, for he licked his
pencil with an air of satisfaction.

" Is the lady all right—who is it ? " asked Parker,
coming back to a survey of the situation.

" It's Miss Climpson—God knows how she got here. I
think she's all right, but she's had a rough time."

He was anxiously sponging her head as he spoke, and at
that moment her eyes opened.

" Help ! " said Miss Climpson, confusedly. " The syringe
—you shan't—oh ! " She struggled feebly, and then
recognised Wimsey's anxious face. " Oh, dear ! " she
exclaimed, " Lord Peter. Such an upset. Did you get my
letter ? Is it all right ? . . . Oh, dear ! What a state I'm in.
I—that woman——"

" Now, don't worry, Miss Climpson," said Wimsey,

much relieved, " everything's quite all right and you mustn't talk. You must tell us about it later."

" What was that about a syringe ? " said Parker, intent on his case.

" She'd got a syringe in her hand," panted Miss Climpson, trying to sit up, and fumbling with her hands over the bed. " I fainted, I think—such a struggle—and something hit me on the head. And I saw her coming at me with the thing. And I knocked it out of her hand and I can't remember what happened afterwards. But I have *remarkable* vitality," said Miss Climpson, cheerfully. " My dear father always used to say ' Climpsons take a lot of killing ' ! "

Parker was groping on the floor.

" Here you are," said he. In his hand was a hypodermic syringe.

" She's mental, that's what she is," said the prisoner. " That's only the hypodermic I use for my injections when I get neuralgia. There's nothing in that."

" That is quite correct," said Parker, with a significant nod at Wimsey. " There is—nothing in it."

.   .   .   .

On the Tuesday night, when the prisoner had been committed for trial on the charges of murdering Bertha Gotobed and Vera Findlater, and attempting to murder Alexandra Climpson, Wimsey dined with Parker. The former was depressed and nervous.

" The whole thing's been beastly," he grumbled. They had sat up discussing the case into the small hours.

" Interesting," said Parker, " interesting. I owe you seven and six, by the way. We ought to have seen through that Forrest business earlier, but there seemed no real reason to suspect the Findlater girl's word as to the alibi. These mistaken loyalties make a lot of trouble.

" I think the thing that put us off was that it all started so early. There seemed no reason for it, but looking back on Trigg's story it's as plain as a pike-staff. She took a big risk with that empty house, and she couldn't always expect to find empty houses handy to do away with people in. The idea was, I suppose, to build up a double identity, so that, if Mary Whittaker was ever suspected of anything, she could quietly disappear and become the frail but otherwise innocent Mrs. Forrest. The real slip-up was forgetting to take back that £5 note from Bertha Gotobed. If it hadn't been for that, we might never have known anything about Mrs. Forrest. It must have rattled her horribly when we turned up there. After that, she was known to the police in both her characters. The Findlater business was a desperate attempt to cover up her tracks— and it was bound to fail, because it was so complicated."

"Yes. But the Dawson murder was beautiful in its ease and simplicity."

"If she had stuck to that and left well alone, we could never have proved anything. We can't prove it now, which is why I left it off the charge-sheet. I don't think I've ever met a more greedy and heartless murderer. She probably really thought that anyone who inconvenienced her had no right to exist."

"Greedy and malicious. Fancy tryin' to shove the blame on poor old Hallelujah. I suppose he'd committed the unforgivable sin of askin' her for money."

"Well, he'll get it, that's one good thing. The pit digged for Cousin Hallelujah has turned into a gold-mine. That £10,000 cheque has been honoured. I saw to that first thing, before Whittaker could remember to try and stop it. Probably she couldn't have stopped it anyway, as it was duly presented last Saturday."

"Is the money legally hers?"

"Of course it is. We know it was gained by a crime, but we haven't charged her with the crime, so that legally no such crime was committed. I've not said anything to Cousin Hallelujah, of course, or he mightn't like to take it. He thinks it was sent him in a burst of contrition, poor old dear."

"So Cousin Hallelujah and all the little Hallelujahs will be rich. That's splendid. How about the rest of the money? Will the Crown get it after all?"

"No. Unless she wills it to someone, it will go to the Whittaker next-of-kin—a first cousin, I believe, called Allcock. A very decent fellow, living in Birmingham. That is," he added, assailed by sudden doubt, "if first cousins *do* inherit under this confounded Act."

"Oh, I think first cousins are safe," said Wimsey, "though nothing seems safe nowadays. Still, dash it all, some relations must still be allowed a look-in, or what becomes of the sanctity of family life? If so, that's the most cheering thing about the beastly business. Do you know, when I rang up that man Carr and told him all about it, he wasn't a bit interested or grateful. Said he'd always suspected something like that, and he hoped we weren't going to rake it all up again, because he'd come into that money he told us about and was setting up for himself in Harley Street, so he didn't want any more scandals."

"I never did like that man. I'm sorry for Nurse Philliter."

"You needn't be. I put my foot in it again over that. Carr's too grand to marry a nurse now—at least, I fancy that's what it is. Anyway, the engagement's off. And I was so pleased at the idea of playing Providence to two deserving young people," added Wimsey, pathetically.

"Dear, dear! Well, the girl's well out of it. Hullo! there's the 'phone. Who on earth——? Some damned thing at the Yard, I suppose. At three ack emma! Who'd be a policeman?—Yes?—Oh!—right, I'll come round. The case has gone west, Peter."

"How?"

"Suicide. Strangled herself with a sheet. I'd better go round, I suppose."

"I'll come with you."

" An evil woman, if ever there was one," said Parker, softly, as they looked at the rigid body, with its swollen face and the deep, red ring about the throat.

Wimsey said nothing. He felt cold and sick. While Parker and the Governor of the prison made the necessary arrangements and discussed the case, he sat hunched unhappily upon his chair. Their voices went on and on interminably. Six o'clock had struck some time before they rose to go. It reminded him of the eight strokes of the clock which announce the running-up of the black and hideous flag.

As the gate clanged open to let them out, they stepped into a wan and awful darkness. The June day had risen long ago, but only a pale and yellowish gleam lit the half-deserted streets. And it was bitterly cold and raining.

" What is the matter with the day ? " said Wimsey. " Is the world coming to an end ? "

" No," said Parker, " it is the eclipse."

GENEALOGICAL TABLE FOLLOWS

Roger Dawson
b 1710 - Blacksmith of unknown family. M.1749 Susan Pethick, with £500 after her seduction by Lord Hatherford, and had by her

Barnabas Dawson
Grocer. b 1760; d. 1840   ▬

Barnabas Dawson
b. 1786. Killed at Waterloo, 1815
No Issue

Roger Dawson
b 1789; d. of the Small-pox 1801
No Issue

John Whittaker
b 1824, m. 1849 & had issue

N B DESCENDANTS OF AUNT SOPHIE DESMOULINS STILL LIVING, BEING KIN OF 6TH DEGREE

Henry Dawson
b. 1830; m. 1852, Sophie Desmoulins, one of 3 sisters (of whom the other 2 entered a convent and died unmarried) d 1884

2 Daughters
d. In infancy

Clara Whittaker
b.1850; d. 1922; unmarried
No Issue

James Whittaker
b.1852; m. 1873; d 1913   ═

Harriet Dawson
b.1854; m.1873; d.1910

Twin Sons
b. 1858, Survived only 2 days

·⋮·
N.B. ALBERTA ALLCOCK LEFT AS SOLE KIN AN ORPHAN NEPHEW, FIRST COUSIN TO MARY WHITTAKER AND HER SOLE HEIR

Rev. Charles Whittaker ·⋮·
b.1875; m. Alberta Allcock 1896; killed with his wife while motoring 1924

Mary Whittaker
b. 1898
Only surviving kin of 4 th. degree

Rupert Danby
Yeoman; only survivor of 4 brothers, of whom the remainder were killed or fled the country after the '45, leaving no heirs.

Henrietta Danby
b 1752; m. 1785; d 1822

Elizabeth Danby
b.1754 – m. 1779 Stephen Armstrong; descendants of the 4th generation still living. (Kin of 8th. degree)

Agatha Dawson
b. 1791; d. of the Small-pox 1801
No Issue

Frederick Dawson
b.1798; m. Lucy, daughter of Geo. Marston, orphan without kin. Killed by falling from his horse 1833.

Simon Dawson
b.1794. Sailed to the West Indies. No legitimate issue

Bosun Dawson
Natural son of Simon by a W. Indian woman. b.1842 m. 1887, Gloria, a woman of his mother's nationality.

Mary Ann Dawson
b.1831; d. of a decline 1848, unmarried
No Issue

Paul Dawson
b.1832. Turned R.C. & entered a monastery d. 1922
No Issue

Agatha Dawson
b. 1852; d. unmarried 1925.
No Issue

Stephen Dawson
b.1859; m. 1891; Rose, natural daughter of J. Fairbanks d. 1917.

Rev. Hallelujah Dawson
b. 1869.

John Dawson
b. 1893. Killed in the Great War, 1916 unmarried.

Clouds
of
Witness

THE SOLUTION OF

THE RIDDLESDALE MYSTERY

WITH

A REPORT

OF THE TRIAL OF

THE DUKE OF DENVER

BEFORE THE HOUSE OF LORDS

FOR

MURDER

———

The inimitable stories of Tong-king never have any real ending, and this one, being in his most elevated style, has even less end than most of them. But the whole narrative is permeated with the odour of joss-sticks and honourable high-mindedness, and the two characters are both of noble birth.

—*The Wallet of Kai-Lung.*

CONTENTS

CONTENTS

CHAPTER I

" OF HIS MALICE AFORETHOUGHT "

O, who hath done this deed?
—Othello.

LORD PETER WIMSEY stretched himself luxuriously between the sheets provided by the Hôtel Meurice. After his exertions in the unravelling of the Battersea Mystery, he had followed Sir Julian Freke's advice and taken a holiday. He had felt suddenly weary of breakfasting every morning before his view over the Green Park ; he had realised that the picking up of first editions at sales afforded insufficient exercise for a man of thirty-three ; the very crimes of London were over-sophisticated. He had abandoned his flat and his friends and fled to the wilds of Corsica. For the last three months he had forsworn letters, newspapers, and telegrams. He had tramped about the mountains, admiring from a cautious distance the wild beauty of Corsican peasant-women, and studying the vendetta in its natural haunt. In such conditions murder seemed not only reasonable, but lovable. Bunter, his confidential man and assistant sleuth, had nobly sacrificed his civilised habits, had let his master go dirty and even unshaven, and had turned his faithful camera from the recording of finger-prints to that of craggy scenery. It had been very refreshing.

Now, however, the call of the blood was upon Lord Peter. They had returned late last night in a vile train to Paris, and had picked up their luggage. The autumn light, filtering through the curtains, touched caressingly the silver-topped bottles on the dressing-table, outlined an electric lamp-shade and the shape of the telephone. A noise of running water near by proclaimed that Bunter had turned on the bath (h. & c.) and was laying out scented soap, bath-salts, the huge bath-sponge, for which there had been no scope in Corsica, and the delightful flesh-brush with the long handle, which rasped you so agreeably all down the spine. "Contrast," philosophised Lord Peter sleepily, "is life. Corsica—Paris—then London. . . . Good morning, Bunter."

"Good morning, my lord. Fine morning, my lord. Your lordship's bath-water is ready."

"Thanks," said Lord Peter. He blinked at the sunlight.

It was a glorious bath. He wondered, as he soaked in it, how he could have existed in Corsica. He wallowed happily and sang a few bars of a song. In a soporific interval he heard the valet de chambre bringing in coffee and rolls. Coffee and rolls! He heaved himself out with a splash, towelled himself luxuriously, enveloped his long-mortified body in a silken bath-robe, and wandered back.

To his immense surprise he perceived Mr. Bunter calmly replacing all the fittings in his dressing-case. Another astonished glance showed him the bags—scarcely opened the previous night—repacked, relabelled, and standing ready for a journey.

"I say, Bunter, what's up?" said his lordship. "We're stayin' here a fortnight y'know."

"Excuse me, my lord," said Mr. Bunter, deferentially, "but, having seen *The Times* (delivered here every morning by air, my lord ; and very expeditious I'm sure, all things considered), I made no doubt your lordship would be wishing to go to Riddlesdale at once."

"Riddlesdale !" exclaimed Peter. "What's the matter ? Anything wrong with my brother ?"

For answer Mr. Bunter handed him the paper, folded open at the heading :

RIDDLESDALE INQUEST.

DUKE OF DENVER ARRESTED

ON MURDER CHARGE.

Lord Peter stared as if hypnotised.

" I thought your lordship wouldn't wish to miss anything," said Mr. Bunter, " so I took the liberty——"

Lord Peter pulled himself together.

" When's the next train ? " he asked.

" I beg your lordship's pardon—I thought your lordship would wish to take the quickest route. I took it on myself to book two seats in the aeroplane *Victoria*. She starts at 11.30."

Lord Peter looked at his watch.

" Ten o'clock," he said. " Very well. You did quite right. Dear me ! Poor old Gerald arrested for murder. Uncommonly worryin' for him, poor chap. Always hated my bein' mixed up with police-courts. Now he's there himself. Lord Peter Wimsey in the witness-box—very distressin' to feelin's of a brother. Duke of Denver in the dock—worse still. Dear me ! Well, I suppose one must have breakfast."

" Yes, my lord. Full account of the inquest in the paper, my lord."

" Yes. Who's on the case, by the way ? "

" Mr. Parker, my lord."

" Parker ? That's good. Splendid old Parker ! Wonder how he managed to get put on to it. How do things look, Bunter ? "

" If I may say so, my lord, I fancy the investigations will prove very interesting. There are several extremely suggestive points in the evidence, my lord."

" From a criminological point of view I daresay it is interesting," replied his lordship, sitting down cheerfully to his *café au lait*, " but it's deuced awkward for my

11

brother, all the same, havin' no turn for criminology, what ? ”

“ Ah, well ! ” said Mr. Bunter, “ they say, my lord, there's nothing like having a personal interest.”

. . . . .

“ The inquest was held to-day at Riddlesdale, in the North Riding of Yorkshire, on the body of Captain Denis Cathcart, which was found at three o'clock on Thursday morning lying just outside the conservatory door of the Duke of Denver's shooting-box, Riddlesdale Lodge. Evidence was given to show that deceased had quarrelled with the Duke of Denver on the preceding evening, and was subsequently shot in a small thicket adjoining the house. A pistol belonging to the Duke was found near the scene of the crime. A verdict of murder was returned against the Duke of Denver. Lady Mary Wimsey, sister of the Duke, who was engaged to be married to the deceased, collapsed after giving evidence, and is now lying seriously ill at the Lodge. The Duchess of Denver hastened from town yesterday and was present at the inquest. Full report on p. 12.”

“ Poor old Gerald ! ” thought Lord Peter, as he turned to page 12 ; “ and poor old Mary ! I wonder if she really was fond of the fellow. Mother always said not, but Mary never would let on about herself.”

The full report began by describing the little village of Riddlesdale, where the Duke of Denver had recently taken a small shooting-box for the season. When the tragedy occurred the Duke had been staying there with a party of guests. In the Duchess's absence Lady Mary Wimsey had acted as hostess. The other guests were Colonel and Mrs. Marchbanks, the Hon. Frederick Arbuthnot, Mr. and Mrs. Pettigrew-Robinson, and the dead man, Denis Cathcart.

The first witness was the Duke of Denver, who claimed to have discovered the body. He gave evidence that he was coming into the house by the conservatory door at three o'clock in the morning of Thursday, October 14th, when his foot struck against something. He had switched on his electric torch and seen the body of Denis Cathcart at his feet. He had at once turned it over, and seen that Cathcart had been shot in the chest. He was quite dead. As Denver was bending over the body, he heard a cry in the conservatory, and, looking up, saw Lady Mary Wimsey gazing out horror-struck. She came out by the conservatory door, and exclaimed at once, " O God, Gerald, you've killed him ! " (Sensation.)*

The Coroner : " Were you surprised by that remark?"

Duke of D. : " Well, I was so shocked and surprised at the whole thing. I think I said to her, ' Don't look,' and she said, ' Oh, it's Denis ! Whatever can have happened ? Has there been an accident ? ' I stayed with the body, and sent her up to rouse the house."

The Coroner : " Did you expect to see Lady Mary Wimsey in the conservatory ? "

Duke of D. : " Really, as I say, I was so astonished all round, don't you know, I didn't think about it."

The Coroner : " Do you remember how she was dressed ? "

Duke of D. : " I don't think she was in her pyjamas." (Laughter.) " I think she had a coat on."

The Coroner : " I understand that Lady Mary Wimsey was engaged to be married to the deceased ? '

Duke of D. : " Yes."

The Coroner : " He was well known to you ? "

Duke of D. : " He was the son of an old friend of my father's ; his parents are dead. I believe he lived chiefly abroad. I ran across him during the war, and in 1919

---

*This report, though substantially the same as that read by Lord Peter in *The Times*, has been corrected, amplified and annotated from the shorthand report made at the time by Mr. Parker.

he came to stay at Denver. He became engaged to my sister at the beginning of this year."

The Coroner : " With your consent, and with that of the family ? "

Duke of D. : " Oh, yes, certainly."

The Coroner : " What kind of man was Captain Cathcart ? "

Duke of D. : " Well—he was a Sahib and all that. I don't know what he did before he joined in 1914. I think he lived on his income ; his father was well off. Crack shot, good at games, and so on. I never heard anything against him—till that evening."

The Coroner : " What was that ? "

Duke of D. : " Well—the fact is—it was deuced queer. He—— If anybody but Tommy Freeborn had said it I should never have believed it." (Sensation.)

The Coroner : " I'm afraid I must ask your grace of what exactly you had to accuse the deceased."

Duke of D. : " Well, I didn't—I don't—exactly accuse him. An old friend of mine made a suggestion. Of course I thought it must be all a mistake, so I went to Cathcart, and, to my amazement, he practically admitted it ! Then we both got angry, and he told me to go to the devil, and rushed out of the house." (Renewed sensation.)

The Coroner : " When did this quarrel occur ? "

Duke of D. : " On Wednesday night. That was the last I saw of him." (Unparalleled sensation.)

The Coroner : " Please, please, we cannot have this disturbance. Now, will your grace kindly give me, as far as you can remember it, the exact history of this quarrel ? "

Duke of D. : " Well, it was like this. We'd had a long day on the moors and had dinner early, and about half-past nine we began to feel like turning in. My sister and Mrs. Pettigrew-Robinson toddled on up, and we were havin' a last peg in the billiard-room when Fleming—that's my man—came in with the letters. They come

14

rather any old time in the evening, you know, we being two and a half miles from the village. No—I wasn't in the billiard-room at the time—I was lockin' up the gun-room. The letter was from an old friend of mine I hadn't seen for years—Tom Freeborn—used to know him at the House——"

The Coroner : " Whose house ? "

Duke of D. : " Oh, Christ Church, Oxford. He wrote to say he'd seen the announcement of my sister's engagement in Egypt."

The Coroner : " In Egypt ? "

Duke of D. : " I mean, *he* was in Egypt—Tom Freeborn, you see—that's why he hadn't written before. He engineers. He went out there after the war was over, you see, and, bein' somewhere up near the sources of the Nile, he doesn't get the papers regularly. He said, would I 'scuse him for interferin' in a very delicate matter, and all that, but did I know who Cathcart was ? Said he'd met him in Paris during the war, and he lived by cheatin' at cards—said he could swear to it, with details of a row there'd been in some French place or other. Said he knew I'd want to chaw his head off—Freeborn's, I mean—for buttin' in, but he'd seen the man's photo in the paper, an' he thought I ought to know."

The Coroner : " Did this letter surprise you ? "

Duke of D. : " Couldn't believe it at first. If it hadn't been old Tom Freeborn I'd have put the thing in the fire straight off, and, even as it was, I didn't quite know what to think. I mean, it wasn't as if it had happened in England, you know. I mean to say, Frenchmen get so excited about nothing. Only there was Freeborn, and he isn't the kind of man that makes mistakes."

The Coroner : " What did you do ? "

Duke of D. : " Well, the more I looked at it the less I liked it, you know. Still, I couldn't quite leave it like that, so I thought the best way was to go straight to Cathcart. They'd all gone up while I was sittin' thinkin'

15

about it, so I went up and knocked at Cathcart's door. He said, 'What's that ? ' or ' Who the devil's that ? ' or somethin' of the sort, and I went in. ' Look here,' I said, ' can I just have a word with you ? ' ' Well, cut it short, then,' he said. I was surprised—he wasn't usually rude. ' Well,' I said, ' fact is, I've had a letter I don't much like the look of, and I thought the best thing to do was to bring it straight away to you an' have the whole thing cleared up. It's from a man—a very decent sort—old college friend, who says he's met you in Paris.' ' Paris ! ' he said, in a most uncommonly unpieasant way. ' Paris ! What the hell do you want to come talkin' to me about Paris for ? ' ' Well,' I said, ' don't talk like that, because it's misleadin' under the circumstances.' ' What are you drivin' at ? ' says Cathcart. ' Spit it out and go to bed, for God's sake.' I said, ' Right oh ! I will. It's a man called Freeborn, who says he knew you in Paris and that you made money cheatin' at cards.' I thought he'd break out at that, but all he said was, ' What about it ? ' ' What about it ? ' I said. ' Well, of course, it's not the sort of thing I'm goin' to believe like that, right bang-slap off, without any proofs.' Then he said a funny thing. He said, ' Beliefs don't matter—it's what one *knows* about people.' ' Do you mean to say you don't deny it ? ' I said. ' It's no good my denying it,' he said ; ' you must make up your own mind. Nobody could *dis*-prove it.' And then he suddenly jumped up, nearly knocking the table over, and said, ' I don't care what you think or what you do, if you'll only get out. For God's sake leave me alone ! ' ' Look here,' I said, ' you needn't take it that way. I don't say I do believe it—in fact,' I said, ' I'm sure there must be some mistake ; only, you bein' engaged to Mary,' I said, ' I couldn't just let it go at that without looking into it, could I ? ' ' Oh ! ' says Cathcart, ' if that's what's worrying you, it needn't. That's off.' I said, ' What ? ' He said, 'Our engagement.' ' Off ? ' I said. ' But I was talking to Mary about it only yesterday.' ' I haven't told her yet,' he said. 'Well,' I said, 'I think that's damned cool. Who the hell do you think you are, to come here and jilt my sister?' Well, I said quite a lot, first and last. 'You can get out,' I said ; 'I've no use for swine like you.' 'I will,' he said, and he pushed past me an' slammed downstairs and out of the front door, an' banged it after him."

The Coroner : "What did you do?"

Duke of D. : "I ran into my bedroom, which has a window over the conservatory, and shouted out to him not to be a silly fool. It was pourin' with rain and beastly cold. He didn't come back, so I told Fleming to leave the conservatory door open—in case he thought better of it—and went to bed."

The Coroner : "What explanation can you suggest for Cathcart's behaviour?"

Duke of D. : "None. I was simply staggered. But I think he must somehow have got wind of the letter, and knew the game was up."

The Coroner : "Did you mention the matter to anybody else?"

Duke of D. : "No. It wasn't pleasant, and I thought I'd better leave it till the morning."

The Coroner : "So you did nothing further in the matter?"

Duke of D. : "No. I didn't want to go out huntin' for the fellow. I was too angry. Besides, I thought he'd change his mind before long—it was a brute of a night and he'd only a dinner-jacket."

The Coroner : "Then you just went quietly to bed and never saw deceased again?"

Duke of D. : "Not till I fell over him outside the conservatory at three in the morning."

The Coroner : "Ah yes. Now can you tell us how you came to be out of doors at that time?"

Duke of D. (hesitating) : "I didn't sleep well. I went out for a stroll."

The Coroner : "At three o'clock in the morning?"

17

Duke of D. : " Yes." With sudden inspiration :
" You see, my wife's away." (Laughter and some
remarks from the back of the room.)

The Coroner : "" Silence, please. . . . You mean to
say that you got up at that hour of an October night to
take a walk in the garden in the pouring rain ? "

Duke of D. : " Yes, just a stroll." (Laughter.)

The Coroner : " At what time did you leave your
bedroom ? "

Duke of D. : " Oh—oh, about half-past two, I should
think."

The Coroner : " Which way did you go out ? "

Duke of D. : " By the conservatory door."

The Coroner : " The body was not there when you
went out ? "

Duke of D. : " Oh, no ! "

The Coroner : " Or you would have seen it ? "

Duke of D. : " Lord, yes ! I'd have had to walk over
it."

The Coroner : " Exactly where did you go ? "

Duke of D. (vaguely) : " Oh, just round about."

The Coroner : " You heard no shot ? "

Duke of D. : " No."

The Coroner : " Did you go far away from the conservatory door and the shrubbery ? "

Duke of D. : " Well—I was some way away. Perhaps
that's why I didn't hear anything. It must have been."

The Coroner : " Were you as much as a quarter of a
mile away ? "

Duke of D. : " I should think I was—oh, yes, quite! "

The Coroner : " More than a quarter of a mile
away ? "

Duke of D. : " Possibly. I walked about briskly
because it was cold."

The Coroner : " In which direction ? "

Duke of D. (with visible hesitation) : " Round at
the back of the house. Towards the bowling-green."

The Coroner : " The bowling-green ? "

Duke of D. (more confidently) : " Yes."

The Coroner : " But if you were more than a quarter of a mile away, you must have left the grounds ? "

Duke of D. : " I—oh, yes—I think I did. Yes, I walked about on the moor a bit, you know."

The Coroner : " Can you show us the letter you had from Mr. Freeborn ? "

Duke of D. : " Oh, certainly—if I can find it. I thought I put it in my pocket, but I couldn't find it for that Scotland Yard fellow."

The Coroner : " Can you have accidentally destroyed it ? "

Duke of D. : " No—I'm sure I remember putting it—— Oh "—here the witness paused in very patent confusion, and grew red—" I remember now. I destroyed it."

The Coroner : " That is unfortunate. How was that ? "

Duke of D. : " I had forgotten ; it has come back to me now. I'm afraid it has gone for good."

The Coroner : " Perhaps you kept the envelope ? "

Witness shook his head.

The Coroner : " Then you can show the jury no proof of having received it ? "

Duke of D. : " Not unless Fleming remembers it."

The Coroner : " Ah, yes ! No doubt we can check it that way. Thank you, your grace. Call Lady Mary Wimsey."

The noble lady, who was, until the tragic morning of October 14th, the fiancée of the deceased, aroused a murmur of sympathy on her appearance. Fair and slender, her naturally rose-pink cheeks ashy pale, she seemed overwhelmed with grief. She was dressed entirely in black, and gave her evidence in a very low tone which was at times almost inaudible.*

After expressing his sympathy, the coroner asked, " How long had you been engaged to the deceased ? "

* From the newspaper report—*not* Mr. Parker.

19

Witness : " About eight months."

The Coroner : " Where did you first meet him ? "

Witness : " At my sister-in-law's house in London."

The Coroner : " When was that ? "

Witness : " I think it was June last year."

The Coroner : " You were quite happy in your engagement ? "

Witness : " Quite."

The Coroner : " You naturally saw a good deal of Captain Cathcart. Did he tell you much about his previous life ? "

Witness : " Not very much. We were not given to mutual confidences. We usually discussed subjects of common interest."

The Coroner : " You had many such subjects ? "

Witness : " Oh, yes."

The Coroner : " You never gathered at any time that Captain Cathcart had anything on his mind ? "

Witness : " Not particularly. He had seemed a little anxious the last few days."

The Coroner : " Did he speak of his life in Paris ? "

Witness : " He spoke of theatres and amusements there. He knew Paris very well. I was staying in Paris with some friends last February, when he was there, and he took us about. That was shortly after our engagement."

The Coroner : " Did he ever speak of playing cards in Paris ? "

Witness : " I don't remember."

The Coroner : " With regard to your marriage—had any money settlements been gone into ? "

Witness : " I don't think so. The date of the marriage was not in any way fixed."

The Coroner : " He always appeared to have plenty of money ? "

Witness : " I suppose so ; I didn't think about it."

The Coroner : " You never heard him complain of being hard up ? "

Witness : " Everybody complains of that, don't they ? "

The Coroner : " Was he a man of cheerful disposition ? "

Witness : " He was very moody, never the same two days together."

The Coroner : " You have heard what your brother says about the deceased wishing to break off the engagement. Had you any idea of this ? "

Witness : " Not the slightest."

The Coroner : " Can you think of any explanation now ? "

Witness : " Absolutely none."

The Coroner : " There had been no quarrel ? "

Witness : " No."

The Coroner : " So far as you knew, on the Wednesday evening, you were still engaged to deceased with every prospect of being married to him shortly ? "

Witness : " Ye-es. Yes, certainly, of course."

The Coroner : " He was not—forgive me this very painful question—the sort of man who would have been likely to lay violent hands on himself ? "

Witness : " Oh, I never thought—well, I don't know— I suppose he might have done. That would explain it, wouldn't it ? "

The Coroner : " Now, Lady Mary—please don't distress yourself, take your own time—will you tell us exactly what you heard and saw on Wednesday night and Thursday morning."

Witness : " I went up to bed with Mrs. Marchbanks and Mrs. Pettigrew-Robinson at about half-past nine, leaving all the men downstairs. I said good night to Denis, who seemed quite as usual. I was not downstairs when the post came. I went to my room at once. My room is at the back of the house. I heard Mr. Pettigrew-Robinson come up at about ten. The Pettigrew-Robinsons sleep next door to me. Some of the other men came up with him. I did not hear my

21

brother come upstairs. At about a quarter past ten I heard two men talking loudly in the passage, and then I heard someone run downstairs and bang the front door. Afterwards I heard rapid steps in the passage, and finally I heard my brother shut his door. Then I went to bed."

The Coroner : " You did not inquire the cause of the disturbance ? "

Witness (indifferently) : " I thought it was probably something about the dogs."

The Coroner : " What happened next ? "

Witness : " I woke up at three o'clock."

The Coroner : " What wakened you ? "

Witness : " I heard a shot."

The Coroner : " You were not awake before you heard it ? "

Witness : " I may have been partly awake. I heard it very distinctly. I was sure it was a shot. I listened for a few minutes, and then went down to see if anything was wrong."

The Coroner : " Why did you not call your brother or some other gentleman? "

Witness (scornfully) : " Why should I ? I thought it was probably only poachers, and I didn't want to make an unnecessary fuss at that unearthly hour."

The Coroner : " Did the shot sound close to the house ? "

Witness : "Fairly, I think—it is hard to tell when one is wakened by a noise—it always sounds so extra loud."

The Coroner : " It did not seem to be in the house or in the conservatory ? "

Witness : " No it was outside."

The Coroner : " So you went downstairs by yourself. That was very plucky of you, Lady Mary. Did you go immediately ? "

Witness : " Not quite immediately. I thought it over for a few minutes ; then I put on walking-shoes over bare feet, a heavy covert-coat, and a woolly cap.

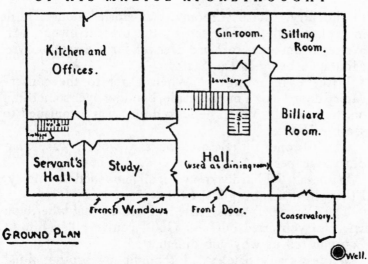

GROUND PLAN

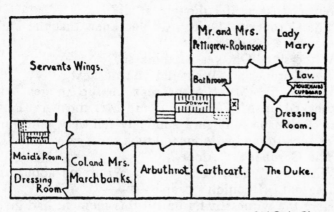

x.– Old Oak Chest.

It may have been five minutes after hearing the shot that I left my bedroom. I went downstairs and through the billiard-room to the conservatory."

The Coroner : " Why did you go out that way ? "

Witness : " Because it was quicker than unbolting either the front door or the back door."

At this point a plan of Riddlesdale Lodge was handed

to the jury. It is a roomy, two-storied house, built in a plain style, and leased by the present owner, Mr. Walter Montague, to Lord Denver for the season, Mr. Montague being in the States.

Witness (resuming) : " When I got to the conservatory door I saw a man outside, bending over something on the ground. When he looked up I was astonished to see my brother."

The Coroner : " Before you saw who it was, what did you expect ? "

Witness : " I hardly know—it all happened so quickly. I thought it was burglars, I think."

The Coroner : " His grace has told us that when you saw him you cried out, ' O God ! you've killed him ! ' Can you tell us why you did that ? "

Witness (very pale) : " I thought my brother must have come upon the burglar and fired at him in self-defence—that is, if I thought at all."

The Coroner : " Quite so. You knew that the Duke possessed a revolver ? "

Witness : " Oh, yes—I think so."

The Coroner : " What did you do next ? "

Witness : " My brother sent me up to get help. I knocked up Mr. Arbuthnot and Mr. and Mrs. Pettigrew-Robinson. Then I suddenly felt very faint, and went back to my bedroom and took some sal volatile."

The Coroner : " Alone ? "

Witness : " Yes, everybody was running about and calling out. I couldn't bear it—I——"

Here the witness, who up till this moment had given her evidence every collectedly, though in a low voice, collapsed suddenly, and had to be assisted from the room.

The next witness called was James Fleming, the man-servant. He remembered having brought the letters from Riddlesdale at 9.45 on Wednesday evening. He had taken three or four letters to the Duke in the gun-room. He could not remember at all whether one of them had had an Egyptian stamp. He did not collect stamps ; his hobby was autographs.

The Hon. Frederick Arbuthnot then gave evidence. He had gone up to bed with the rest at a little before ten. He had heard Denver come up by himself some time later—couldn't say how much later—he was brushing his teeth at the time. (Laughter.) Had certainly heard loud voices and a row going on next door and in the passage. Had heard somebody go for the stairs hell-for-leather. Had stuck his head out and seen Denver in the passage. Had said," Hello, Denver, what's the row ? " The Duke's reply had been inaudible. Denver had bolted into his bedroom and shouted out of the window, " Don't be an ass, man ! " He had seemed very angry indeed, but the Hon. Freddy attached no importance to that. One was always getting across Denver, but it never came to anything. More dust than kick in his opinion. Hadn't known Cathcart long— always found him all right—no, he didn't *like* Cathcart, but he was all right, you know, nothing wrong about him that he knew of. Good lord, no, he'd never heard it suggested he cheated at cards ! Well, no, of course, he didn't go about looking out for people cheating at cards —it wasn't a thing one expected. He'd been had that way in a club at Monte once—he'd had no hand in bringing it to light—hadn't noticed anything till the fun began. Had not noticed anything particular in Cathcart's manner to Lady Mary, or hers to him. Didn't suppose he ever would notice anything ; did not consider himself an observing sort of man. Was not interfering by nature ; had thought Wednesday evening's dust-up none of his business. Had gone to bed and to sleep.

The Coroner : " Did you hear anything further that night ? "

Hon. Frederick : " Not till poor little Mary knocked me up. Then I toddled down and found Denver in the conservatory, bathing Cathcart's head. We thought we ought to clean the gravel and mud off his face, you know."

The Coroner : " You heard no shot ? "

Hon. Frederick : " Not a sound. But I sleep pretty heavily."

Colonel and Mrs. Marchbanks slept in the room over what was called the study—more a sort of smoking-room really. They both gave the same account of a conversation which they had had at 11.30. Mrs. Marchbanks had sat up to write some letters after the Colonel was in bed. They had heard voices and someone running about, but had paid no attention. It was not unusual for members of the party to shout and run about. At last the Colonel had said, " Come to bed, my dear, it's half-past eleven, and we're making an early start to-morrow. You won't be fit for anything." He said this because Mrs. Marchbanks was a keen sportswoman and always carried her gun with the rest. She replied, " I'm just coming." The Colonel said, " You're the only sinner burning the midnight oil—everybody's turned in." Mrs. Marchbanks replied, " No, the Duke's still up ; I can hear him moving about in the study." Colonel Marchbanks listened and heard it too. Neither of them heard the Duke come up again. They had heard no noise of any kind in the night.

Mr. Pettigrew-Robinson appeared to give evidence with extreme reluctance. He and his wife had gone to bed at ten. They had heard the quarrel with Cathcart. Mr. Pettigrew-Robinson, fearing that something might be going to happen, opened his door in time to hear the Duke say, " If you dare to speak to my sister again I'll break every bone in your body," or words to that effect. Cathcart had rushed downstairs. The Duke was scarlet in the face. He had not seen Mr. Pettigrew-Robinson, but had spoken a few words to Mr. Arbuthnot, and rushed into his own bedroom. Mr. Pettigrew-Robinson had run out, and said to Mr. Arbuthnot, " I say, Arbuthnot," and Mr. Arbuthnot had very rudely slammed the door in his face. He had then gone to the Duke's door and said, " I say, Denver." The Duke had come out, pushing past him, without even noticing him, and gone to the head of the stairs. He had heard him tell Fleming to leave the conservatory door open, as Mr. Cathcart had gone out. The Duke had then returned. Mr. Pettigrew-Robinson had tried to catch him as he passed, and had said again, " I say, Denver, what's up?" The Duke had said nothing, and had shut his bedroom door with great decision. Later on, however, at 11.30 to be precise, Mr. Pettigrew-Robinson had heard the Duke's door open, and stealthy feet moving about the passage. He could not hear whether they had gone downstairs. The bathroom and lavatory were at his end of the passage, and, if anybody had entered either of them, he thought he should have heard. He had not heard the footsteps return. He had heard his travelling clock strike twelve before falling asleep. There was no mistaking the Duke's bedroom door, as the hinge creaked in a peculiar manner.

Mrs. Pettigrew-Robinson confirmed her husband's evidence. She had fallen asleep before midnight, and had slept heavily. She was a heavy sleeper at the beginning of the night, but slept lightly in the early morning. She had been annoyed by all the disturbance in the house that evening, as it had prevented her from getting off. In fact, she had dropped off about 10.30, and Mr. Pettigrew-Robinson had had to wake her an hour after to tell her about the footsteps. What with one thing and another she only got a couple of hours' good sleep. She woke up again at two, and remained broad awake till the alarm was given by Lady Mary. She could swear positively that she heard no shot in the night. Her window was next to Lady Mary's, on the opposite side from the conservatory. She had always been accustomed from a child to sleep with her window open. In reply to a question from the Coroner, Mrs. Pettigrew-Robinson said she had never felt there was a real, true affection between Lady Mary Wimsey and deceased. They seemed very off-hand, but that sort of thing was the fashion nowadays. She had never heard of any disagreement.

Miss Lydia Cathcart, who had been hurriedly summoned from town, then gave evidence about the deceased man. She told the Coroner that she was the Captain's aunt and his only surviving relative. She had seen very little of him since he came into possession of his father's money. He had always lived with his own friends in Paris, and they were such as she could not approve of.

" My brother and I never got on very well," said Miss Cathcart, " and he had my nephew educated abroad till he was eighteen. I fear Denis's notions were always quite French. After my brother's death Denis went to Cambridge, by his father's desire. I was left executrix of the will, and guardian till Denis came of age. I do not know why, after neglecting me all his life, my brother should have chosen to put such a responsibility upon me at his death, but I did not care to refuse. My house was open to Denis during his holidays from college, but he preferred, as a rule, to go and stay with his rich friends. I cannot now recall any of their names. When Denis was twenty-one he came into £10,000 a year. I believe it was in some kind of foreign property. I inherited a certain amount under the will as executrix, but I converted it all, at once, into good, sound, British securities. I cannot say what Denis did with his. It would not surprise me at all to hear that he had been cheating at cards. I have heard that the persons he consorted with in Paris were most undesirable. I never met any of them. I have never been in France."

John Hardraw, the gamekeeper, was next called. He and his wife inhabit a small cottage just inside the gate of Riddlesdale Lodge. The grounds, which measure twenty acres or so, are surrounded at this point by a strong paling ; the gate is locked at night. Hardraw stated that he had heard a shot fired at about ten minutes to twelve on Wednesday night, close to the cottage, as it seemed to him. Behind the cottage are ten acres of preserved plantation. He supposed that there were poachers about; they occasionally came in after hares. He went out with his gun in that direction, but saw nobody. He returned home at one o'clock by his watch.

The Coroner: "Did you fire your gun at any time?"

Witness: "No."

The Coroner: "You did not go out again?"

Witness: "I did not."

The Coroner: "Nor hear any other shots?"

Witness: "Only that one; but I fell asleep after I got back, and was wakened up by the chauffeur going out for the doctor. That would be at about a quarter past three."

The Coroner: "Is it not unusual for poachers to shoot so very near the cottage?"

Witness: "Yes, rather. If poachers do come, it is usually on the other side of the preserve, towards the moor."

Dr. Thorpe gave evidence of having been called to see deceased. He lived in Stapley, nearly fourteen miles from Riddlesdale. There was no medical man in Riddlesdale. The chauffeur had knocked him up at 3.45 a.m., and he had dressed quickly and come with him at once. They were at Riddlesdale Lodge at half-past four. Deceased, when he saw him, he judged to have been dead three or four hours. The lungs had been pierced by a bullet, and death had resulted from loss of blood, and suffocation. Death would not have resulted immediately—deceased might have lingered some time. He had made a post-mortem investigation, and found that the bullet had been deflected from a rib. There was nothing to show whether the wound had been self-inflicted or fired from another hand, at close quarters. There were no other marks of violence.

Inspector Craikes from Stapley had been brought

back in the car with Dr. Thorpe. He had seen the body. It was then lying on its back, between the door of the conservatory and the covered well just outside. As soon as it became light, Inspector Craikes had examined the house and grounds. He had found bloody marks all along the path leading to the conservatory, and signs as though a body had been dragged along. This path ran into the main path leading from the gate to the front door. (Plan produced.) Where the two paths joined, a shrubbery began, and ran down on both sides of the path to the gate and the gamekeeper's cottage. The blood-tracks had led to a little clearing in the middle of the shrubbery, about half-way between the house and the gate. Here the inspector found a great pool of blood, a handkerchief soaked in blood, and a revolver. The handkerchief bore the initials D. C., and the revolver was a small weapon of American pattern, and bore no mark. The conservatory door was open when the Inspector arrived, and the key was inside.

Deceased, when he saw him, was in dinner-jacket and pumps, without hat or overcoat. He was wet through, and his clothes, besides being much blood-stained, were very muddy and greatly disordered through the dragging of the body. The pocket contained a cigar-case and a small, flat pocket-knife. Deceased's bedroom had been searched for papers, etc., but so far nothing had been found to shed very much light on his circumstances.

The Duke of Denver was then recalled.

The Coroner : " I should like to ask your grace whether you ever saw deceased in possession of a revolver ? "

Duke of D. : " Not since the war."

The Coroner : " You do not know if he carried one about with him ? "

Duke of D. : " I have no idea."

The Coroner : " You can make no guess, I suppose, to whom this revolver belongs ? "

Duke of D. (in great surprise) : " That's my revolver

—out of the study table drawer. How did you get hold of that ? "—(Sensation.)

The Coroner : " You are certain ? "

Duke of D. : " Positive. I saw it there only the other day, when I was hunting out some photos of Mary for Cathcart, and I remember saying then that it was getting rusty lying about. There's the speck of rust."

The Coroner : " Did you keep it loaded ? "

Duke of D. : " Lord, no ! I really don't know why it was there. I fancy I turned it out one day with some old Army stuff, and found it among my shooting things when I was up at Riddlesdale in August. I think the cartridges were with it."

The Coroner : " Was the drawer locked ? "

Duke of D. : " Yes ; but the key was in the lock. My wife tells me I'm careless."

The Coroner : " Did anybody else know the revolver was there ? "

Duke of D. : " Fleming did, I think. I don't know of anybody else."

Detective-Inspector Parker of Scotland Yard, having only arrived on Friday, had been unable as yet to make any very close investigation. Certain indications led him to think that some person or persons had been on the scene of the tragedy in addition to those who had taken part in the discovery. He preferred to say nothing more at present.

The Coroner then reconstructed the evidence in chronological order. At, or a little after, ten o'clock there had been a quarrel between deceased and the Duke of Denver, after which deceased had left the house never to be seen alive again. They had the evidence of Mr. Pettigrew-Robinson that the Duke had gone down-stairs at 11.30, and that of Colonel Marchbanks that he had been heard immediately afterwards moving about in the study, the room in which the revolver produced in evidence was usually kept. Against this they had the

31

Duke's own sworn statement that he had not left his bedroom till half-past two in the morning. The jury would have to consider what weight was to be attached to those conflicting statements. Then, as to the shots heard in the night ; the gamekeeper had said he heard a shot at ten minutes to twelve, but he had supposed it to be fired by poachers. It was, in fact, quite possible that there had been poachers about. On the other hand, Lady Mary's statement that she had heard the shot at about three a.m. did not fit in very well with the doctor's evidence that when he arrived at Riddlesdale at 4.30 deceased had been already three or four hours dead. They would remember also that, in Dr. Thorpe's opinion, death had not immediately followed the wound. If they believed this evidence, therefore, they would have to put back the moment of death to between eleven p.m. and midnight, and this might very well have been the shot which the gamekeeper heard. In that case they had still to ask themselves about the shot which had awakened Lady Mary Wimsey. Of course, if they liked to put that down to poachers, there was no inherent impossibility.

They next came to the body of deceased, which had been discovered by the Duke of Denver at three a.m. lying outside the door of the small conservatory, near the covered well. There seemed little doubt, from the medical evidence, that the shot which killed deceased had been fired in the shrubbery, about seven minutes' distance from the house, and that the body of deceased had been dragged from that place to the house. Deceased had undoubtedly died as the result of being shot in the lungs. The jury would have to decide whether that shot was fired by his own hand or by the hand of another ; and, if the latter, whether by accident, in self-defence, or by malice aforethought with intent to murder. As regards suicide, they must consider what they knew of deceased's character and circumstances. Deceased was a young man in the prime of his strength, and apparently of considerable fortune. He had had a meritorious military career, and was liked by his friends. The Duke of Denver had thought sufficiently well of him to consent to his own sister's engagement to deceased. There was evidence to show that the fiancés, though perhaps not demonstrative, were on excellent terms. The Duke affirmed that on the Wednesday night deceased had announced his intention of breaking off the engagement. Did they believe that deceased, without even communicating with the lady, or writing a word of explanation or farewell, would thereupon rush out and shoot himself? Again, the jury must consider the accusation which the Duke of Denver said he had brought against deceased. He had accused him of cheating at cards. In the kind of society to which the persons involved in this inquiry belonged, such a misdemeanour as cheating at cards was regarded as far more shameful than such sins as murder and adultery. Possibly the mere suggestion of such a thing, whether well-founded or not, might well cause a gentleman of sensitive honour to make away with himself. But was deceased honourable? Deceased had been educated in France, and French notions of the honest thing were very different from British ones. The Coroner himself had had business relations with French persons in his capacity as a solicitor, and could assure such of the jury as had never been in France that they ought to allow for these different standards. Unhappily, the alleged letter giving details of the accusation had not been produced to them. Next, they might ask themselves whether it was not more usual for a suicide to shoot himself in the head. They should ask themselves how deceased came by the revolver. And, finally, they must consider, in that case, who had dragged the body towards the house, and why the person had chosen to do so, with great labour to himself and at the risk of extinguishing any lingering remnant of the vital spark,* instead of arousing the household and fetching help.

* Verbatim.

33

If they excluded suicide, there remained accident, manslaughter, or murder. As to the first, if they thought it likely that deceased or any other person had taken out the Duke of Denver's revolver that night for any purpose, and that, in looking at, cleaning, shooting with, or otherwise handling the weapon, it had gone off and killed deceased accidentally, then they would return a verdict of death by misadventure accordingly. In that case, how did they explain the conduct of the person, whoever it was, who had dragged the body to the door?

The Coroner then passed on to speak of the law concerning manslaughter. He reminded them that no mere words, however insulting or threatening, can be an efficient excuse for killing anybody, and that the conflict must be sudden and unpremeditated. Did they think, for example, that the Duke had gone out, wishing to induce his guest to return and sleep in the house, and that deceased had retorted upon him with blows or menaces of assault? If so, and the Duke, having a weapon in his hand, had shot deceased in self-defence, that was only manslaughter. But, in that case, they must ask themselves how the Duke came to go out to deceased with a lethal weapon in his hand? And this suggestion was in direct conflict with the Duke's own evidence.

Lastly, they must consider whether there was sufficient evidence of malice to justify a verdict of murder. They must consider whether any person had a motive, means, and opportunity for killing deceased; and whether they could reasonably account for that person's conduct on any other hypothesis. And, if they thought there *was* such a person, and that his conduct was in any way suspicious or secretive, or that he had wilfully suppressed evidence which might have had a bearing on the case, or (here the Coroner spoke with great emphasis, staring over the Duke's head) fabricated other evidence with intent to mislead—then all these circumstances might be sufficient to amount to a violent presumption of guilt against some party, in which case they

34

were in duty bound to bring in a verdict of wilful murder against that party. And, in considering this aspect of the question, the Coroner added, they would have to decide in their own minds whether the person who had dragged deceased towards the conservatory door had done so with the object of obtaining assistance or of thrusting the body down the garden well, which, as they had heard from Inspector Craikes, was situate close by the spot where the body had been found. If the jury were satisfied that deceased had been murdered, but were not prepared to accuse any particular person on the evidence, they might bring in a verdict of murder against an unknown person, or persons; but, if they felt justified in laying the killing at any person's door, then they must allow no respect of persons to prevent them from doing their duty.

Guided by these extremely plain hints, the jury, without very long consultation, returned a verdict of wilful murder against Gerald, Duke of Denver.

CHAPTER II

THE GREEN-EYED CAT

And here's to the hound
With his nose unto the ground——
　　　　　　　—Drink, Puppy, Drink.

S O M E people hold that breakfast is the best meal of the day. Others, less robust, hold that it is the worst, and that, of all breakfasts in the week, Sunday morning breakfast is incomparably the worst.

The party gathered about the breakfast-table at Riddlesdale Lodge held, if one might judge from their faces, no brief for that day miscalled of sweet refection and holy love. The only member of it who seemed neither angry nor embarrassed was the Hon. Freddy Arbuthnot, and he was silent, engaged in trying to take the whole skeleton out of a bloater at once. The very presence of that undistinguished fish upon the Duchess's breakfast-table indicated a disorganised household.

The Duchess of Denver was pouring out coffee. This was one of her uncomfortable habits. Persons arriving late for breakfast were thereby made painfully aware of their sloth. She was a long-necked, long-backed woman, who disciplined her hair and her children. She was never embarrassed, and her anger, though never permitted to be visible, made itself felt the more.

Colonel and Mrs. Marchbanks sat side by side. They had nothing beautiful about them but a stolid mutual affection. Mrs. Marchbanks was not angry, but she was embarrassed in the presence of the Duchess, because she could not feel sorry for her. When you felt sorry

36

for people you called them " poor old dear " or " poor
dear old man." Since, obviously, you could not call the
Duchess poor old dear, you were not being properly
sorry for her. This distressed Mrs. Marchbanks. The
Colonel was both embarrassed and angry—embarrassed
because, 'pon my soul, it was very difficult to know what
to talk about in a house where your host had been
arrested for murder ; angry in a dim way, like an injured
animal, because unpleasant things like this had no
business to break in on the shooting-season.

Mrs. Pettigrew-Robinson was not only angry, she was
outraged. As a girl she had adopted the motto stamped
upon the school notepaper : *Quæcunque honesta*. She
had always thought it *wrong* to let your mind *dwell* on
anything that was not really nice. In middle life she
still made a point of ignoring those newspaper paragraphs
which bore such headlines as : "ASSAULT UPON A SCHOOL-
TEACHER AT CRICKLEWOOD " ; " DEATH IN A PINT OF
STOUT " ; " £75 FOR A KISS " ; or " SHE CALLED HIM
HUBBYKINS." She said she could not see what *good* it
did you to know about such things. She regretted having consented to visit Riddlesdale Lodge in the absence
of the Duchess. She had never liked Lady Mary ; she
considered her a very objectionable specimen of the
modern independent young woman ; besides, there had
been that very undignified incident connected with a
Bolshevist while Lady Mary was nursing in London
during the war. Nor had Mrs. Pettigrew-Robinson at
all cared for Captain Denis Cathcart. She did not like
a young man to be handsome in that obvious kind of way.
But, of course, since Mr. Pettigrew-Robinson had
wanted to come to Riddlesdale, it was her place to be with
him. She was not to blame for the unfortunate result.

Mr. Pettigrew-Robinson was angry, quite simply, because the detective from Scotland Yard had not accepted
his help in searching the house and grounds for footprints. As an older man of some experience in these
matters (Mr. Pettigrew-Robinson was a county magis-

trate) he had gone out of his way to place himself at the man's disposal. Not only had the man been short with him, but he had rudely ordered him out of the conservatory, where he (Mr. Pettigrew-Robinson) had been reconstructing the affair from the point of view of Lady Mary.

All these angers and embarrassments might have caused less pain to the company had they not been aggravated by the presence of the detective himself, a quiet young man in a tweed suit, eating curry at one end of the table next to Mr. Murbles, the solicitor. This person had arrived from London on Friday, had corrected the local police, and strongly dissented from the opinion of Inspector Craikes. He had suppressed at the inquest information which, if openly given, might have precluded the arrest of the Duke. He had officiously detained the whole unhappy party, on the grounds that he wanted to re-examine everybody, and was thus keeping them miserably cooped up together over a horrible Sunday ; and he had put the coping-stone on his offences by turning out to be an intimate friend of Lord Peter Wimsey's, and having, in consequence, to be accommodated with a bed in the game-keeper's cottage and breakfast at the Lodge.

Mr. Murbles, who was elderly and had a delicate digestion, had travelled up in a hurry on Thursday night. He had found the inquest very improperly conducted and his client altogether impracticable. He had spent all his time trying to get hold of Sir Impey Biggs, K.C., who had vanished for the week-end, leaving no address. He was eating a little dry toast, and was inclined to like the detective, who called him " Sir," and passed him the butter.

" Is anybody thinking of going to church ? " asked the Duchess.

" Theodore and I should like to go," said Mrs. Pettigrew-Robinson, " if it is not too much trouble ; or we could walk. It is not so *very* far."

" It's two and a half miles, good," said Colonel March-banks.

Mr. Pettigrew-Robinson looked at him gratefully.

" Of course you will come in the car," said the Duchess. " I am going myself."

" Are you, though ? " said the Hon. Freddy. " I say, won't you get a bit stared at, what ? "

" Really, Freddy," said the Duchess, " does that matter ? "

" Well," said the Hon. Freddy, " I mean to say, these bounders about here are all Socialists and Metho-dists. . . ."

" If they are Methodists," said Mrs. Pettigrew-Robin-son, " they will not be at church."

" Won't they ? " retorted the Hon. Freddy. " You bet they will if there's anything to see. Why, it'll be better'n a funeral to 'em."

" Surely," said Mrs. Pettigrew-Robinson, " one has a *duty* in the matter, whatever our private feelings may be—especially at the present day, when people are so terribly *slack*."

She glanced at the Hon. Freddy.

" Oh, don't you mind me, Mrs. P.," said that youth amiably. " All *I* say is, if these blighters make things unpleasant, don't blame me."

" Whoever thought of blaming you, Freddy ? " said the Duchess.

" Manner of speaking," said the Hon. Freddy.

" What do you think, Mr. Murbles ? " inquired her ladyship.

" I feel," said the lawyer, carefully stirring his coffee, " that, while your intention is a very admirable one, and does you very great credit, my dear lady, yet Mr. Ar-buthnot is right in saying it may involve you in some—er—unpleasant publicity. Er—I have always been a sincere Christian myself, but I cannot feel that our religion demands that we should make ourselves con-spicuous—er—in such very painful circumstances."

Mr. Parker reminded himself of a dictum of Lord Melbourne.

" Well, after all," said Mrs. Marchbanks, " as Helen so rightly says, does it matter ? Nobody's really got anything to be ashamed of. There has been a stupid mistake, of course, but I don't see why anybody who wants to shouldn't go to church."

" Certainly not, certainly not, my dear," said the Colonel heartily. " We might look in ourselves, eh, dear ? Take a walk that way I mean, and come out before the sermon. I think it's a good thing. Shows *we* don't believe old Denver's done anything wrong, anyhow."

" You forget, dear," said his wife, " I've promised to stay at home with Mary, poor girl."

" Of course, of course—stupid of me," said the Colonel. " How is she ? "

" She was very restless last night, poor child," said the Duchess. " Perhaps she will get a little sleep this morning. It has been a shock to her."

" One which may prove a blessing in disguise," said Mrs. Pettigrew-Robinson.

" My dear ! " said her husband.

" Wonder when we shall hear from Sir Impey," said Colonel Marchbanks hurriedly.

" Yes, indeed," moaned Mr. Murbles. " I am counting on his influence with the Duke."

" Of course," said Mrs. Pettigrew-Robinson, " he must speak out—for everybody's sake. He must say what he was doing out of doors at that time. Or, if he does not, it must be discovered. Dear me ! That's what these detectives are for, aren't they ? "

" That is their ungrateful task," said Mr. Parker suddenly. He had said nothing for a long time, and everybody jumped.

" There," said Mrs. Marchbanks, " I expect you'll clear it all up in no time, Mr. Parker. Perhaps you've got the real mur—the culprit up your sleeve all the time."

" Not quite," said Mr. Parker, " but I'll do my best to get him. Besides," he added, with a grin, " I'll probably have some help on the job."

" From whom ? " inquired Mr. Pettigrew-Robinson.

" Her grace's brother-in-law."

" Peter ? " said the Duchess. " Mr. Parker must be amused at the family amateur," she added.

" Not at all," said Parker. " Wimsey would be one of the finest detectives in England if he wasn't lazy. Only we can't get hold of him."

" I've wired to Ajaccio—poste restante," said Mr. Murbles, " but I don't know when he's likely to call there. He said nothing about when he was coming back to England."

" He's a rummy old bird," said the Hon. Freddy tact-lessly, " but he oughter be here, what ? What I mean to say is, if anything happens to old Denver, don't you see, he's the head of the family, ain't he—till little Pickled Gherkins comes of age."

In the frightful silence which followed this remark, the sound of a walking-stick being clattered into an um-brella-stand was distinctly audible.

" Who's that, I wonder," said the Duchess.

The door waltzed open.

" Mornin', dear old things," said the newcomer cheer-fully. " How are you all ? Hullo, Helen ! Colonel, you owe me half a crown since last September year. Mornin', Mrs. Marchbanks, Mornin', Mrs. P. Well, Mr. Murbles, how d'you like this bili-beastly weather ? Don't trouble to get up, Freddy ; I'd simply hate to in-convenience you. Parker, old man, what a damned re-liable old bird you are ! Always on the spot, like that patent ointment thing. I say, have you all finished ? I meant to get up earlier, but I was snorin' so Bunter hadn't the heart to wake me. I nearly blew in last night, only we didn't arrive till 2 a.m. and I thought you wouldn't half bless me if I did. Eh, what, Colonel ? Aeroplane *Victoria* from Paris to London—North-

Eastern to Northallerton—damn bad roads the rest of the way, and a puncture just below Riddlesdale. Damn bad bed at the ' Lord in Glory ' ; thought I'd blow in for the last sausage here, if I was lucky. What ? Sunday morning in an English family and no sausages ? God bless my soul, what's the world coming to, eh, Colonel ? I say, Helen, old Gerald's been an' gone an' done it this time, what ? You've no business to leave him on his own, you know ; he always gets into mischief. What's that ? Curry ? Thanks, old man. Here, I say, you needn't be so stingy about it ; I've been travelling for three days on end. Freddy, pass the toast. Beg pardon, Mrs. Marchbanks ? Oh, rather, yes ; Corsica was per-fectly amazin'—all black-eyed fellows with knives in their belts and jolly fine-looking girls. Old Bunter had a regular affair with the inn-keeper's daughter in one place. D'you know, he's an awfully susceptible old beggar. You'd never think it, would you ? Jove ! I am hungry. I say, Helen, I meant to get you some fetchin' crêpe-de-Chine undies from Paris, but I saw that old Parker was gettin' ahead of me over the bloodstains, so we packed up our things and buzzed off."

Mrs. Pettigrew-Robinson rose.

" Theodore," she said, "I think we ought to be getting ready for church."

" I will order the car," said the Duchess. " Peter, of course I'm exceedingly glad to see you. Your leaving no address was most inconvenient. Ring for anything you want. It is a pity you didn't arrive in time to see Gerald."

" Oh, that's all right," said Lord Peter cheerfully ; " I'll look him up in quod. Y'know, it's rather a good idea to keep one's crimes in the family ; one has so many more facilities. I'm sorry for poor old Polly, though. How is she ? "

" She must not be disturbed to-day," said the Duchess with decision.

" Not a bit of it," said Lord Peter ; " she'll keep. To-day Parker and I hold high revel. To-day he shows me all the bloody footprints—it's all right, Helen, that's not swearin', that's an adjective of quality. I hope they aren't all washed away, are they, old thing?"

"No," said Parker, "I've got most of them under flower-pots."

"Then pass the bread and squish," said Lord Peter, "and tell me all about it."

The departure of the church-going element had induced a more humanitarian atmosphere. Mrs. Marchbanks stumped off upstairs to tell Mary that Peter had come, and the Colonel lit a large cigar. The Hon. Freddy rose, stretched himself, pulled a leather armchair to the fireside, and sat down with his feet on the brass fender, while Parker marched round and poured himself out another cup of coffee.

"I suppose you've seen the papers," he said.

"Oh, yes, I read up the inquest," said Lord Peter. "Y'know, if you'll excuse my saying so, I think you rather mucked it between you."

"It was disgraceful," said Mr. Murbles, "disgraceful. The Coroner behaved most improperly. He had no business to give such a summing-up. With a jury of ignorant country fellows, what could one expect? And the details that were allowed to come out! If I could have got here earlier——"

"I'm afraid that was partly my fault, Wimsey," said Parker penitently. "Craikes rather resents me. The Superintendent at Stapley sent to us over his head, and when the message came through I ran along to the Chief and asked for the job, because I thought if there should be any misconception or difficulty, you see, you'd just as soon I tackled it as anybody else. I had a few little arrangements to make about a forgery I've been looking into, and, what with one thing and another, I didn't get off till the night express. By the time I turned up on Friday, Craikes and the Coroner were already as thick as thieves, had fixed the inquest for that morning—which

43

was ridiculous—and arranged to produce their blessed evidence as dramatically as possible. I only had time to skim over the ground (disfigured, I'm sorry to say, by the prints of Craikes and his local ruffians), and really had nothing for the jury."

" Cheer up," said Wimsey. " I'm not blaming you. Besides, it all lends excitement to the chase."

" Fact is," said the Hon Freddy, " that we ain't popular with respectable Coroners. Giddy aristocrats and immoral Frenchmen. I say, Peter, sorry you've missed Miss Lydia Cathcart. You'd have loved her. She's gone back to Golders Green and taken the body with her."

" Oh, well," said Wimsey. " I don't suppose there was anything abstruse about the body."

" No," said Parker, " the medical evidence was all right as far as it went. He was shot through the lungs, and that's all."

" Though, mind you," said the Hon. Freddy, " he didn't shoot himself. I didn't say anything, not wishin' to upset old Denver's story, but, you know, all that stuff about his bein' so upset and go-to-blazes in his manner was all my whiskers."

" How do you know ? " said Peter.

" Why, my dear man, Cathcart'n I toddled up to bed together. I was rather fed up, havin' dropped a lot on some shares, besides missin' everything I shot at in the mornin', an' lost a bet I made with the Colonel about the number of toes on the kitchen cat, an' I said to Cathcart it was a hell of a damn-fool world, or words to that effect. ' Not a bit of it,' he said ; ' it's a damn good world. I'm goin' to ask Mary for a date to-morrow, an' then we'll go and live in Paris, where they understand sex.' I said somethin' or other vague, and he went off whistlin'."

Parker looked grave. Colonel Marchbanks cleared his throat.

" Well, well," he said, " there's no accounting for a man like Cathcart, no accounting at all. Brought up

in France, you know. Not at all like a straightforward
Englishman. Always up and down, up and down ! Very
sad, poor fellow. Well, well, Peter, hope you and Mr.
Parker will find out something about it. We mustn't
have poor old Denver cooped up in gaol like this, you
know. Awfully unpleasant for him, poor chap, and with
the birds so good this year. Well, I expect you'll be
making a tour of inspection, eh, Mr. Parker ? What do
you say to shoving the balls about a bit, Freddy ? "

" Right you are," said the Hon. Freddy ; " you'll have
to give me a hundred, though, Colonel."

" Nonsense, nonsense," said that veteran, in high good
humour ; " you play an excellent game."

Mr. Murbles having withdrawn, Wimsey and Parker
faced each other over the remains of the breakfast.

" Peter," said the detective, " I don't know if I've
done the right thing by coming. If you feel——"

" Look here, old man," said his friend earnestly, "let's
cut out the considerations of delicacy. We're goin' to
work this case like any other. If anything unpleasant
turns up, I'd rather you saw it than anybody else. It's
an uncommonly pretty little case, on its merits, and I'm
goin' to put some damn good work into it."

" If you're sure it's all right——"

" My dear man, if you hadn't been here I'd have
sent for you. Now let's get to business. Of course,
I'm settin' off with the assumption that old Gerald didn't
do it."

" I'm sure he didn't," agreed Parker.

" No, no," said Wimsey, " that isn't your line.
Nothing rash about you—nothing trustful. You are
expected to throw cold water on my hopes and doubt
all my conclusions."

" Right ho ! " said Parker. " Where would you like
to begin ? "

Peter considered. " I think we'll start from Cathcart's bedroom," he said.

. . . .

The bedroom was of moderate size, with a single window overlooking the front door. The bed was on the right-hand side, the dressing-table before the window. On the left was the fireplace, with an arm-chair before it, and a small writing-table.

" Everything's as it was," said Parker. " Craikes had that much sense."

" Yes," said Lord Peter. " Very well. Gerald says that when he charged Cathcart with bein' a scamp, Cathcart jumped up, nearly knockin' the table over. That's the writin'-table, then, so Cathcart was sittin' in the armchair. Yes, he was—and he pushed it back violently and rumpled up the carpet. See ! So far, so good. Now what was he doin' there ? He wasn't readin', because there's no book about, and we know that he rushed straight out of the room and never came back. Very good. Was he writin' ? No ; virgin sheet of blottin'-paper——"

" He might have been writing in pencil," suggested Parker.

" That's true, old Kill-Joy, so he might. Well, if he was he shoved the paper into his pocket when Gerald came in, because it isn't here ; but he didn't, because it wasn't found on his body ; so he wasn't writing."

" Unless he threw the paper away somewhere else," said Parker. " I haven't been all over the grounds, you know, and at the smallest computation—if we accept the shot heard by Hardraw at 11.50 as *the* shot—there's an hour and a half unaccounted for."

" Very well. Let's say there is nothing to show he was writing. Will that do ? Well, then——"

Lord Peter drew out a lens and scrutinised the surface of the armchair carefully before sitting down in it.

" Nothing helpful there," he said. " To proceed, Cathcart sat where I am sitting. He wasn't writing ; he—you're sure this room hasn't been touched ? "

" Certain."

" Then he wasn't smoking."

46

" Why not ? He might have chucked the stub of a cigar or cigarette into the fire when Denver came in."

" Not a cigarette," said Peter, " or we should find traces somewhere—on the floor or in the grate. That light ash blows about so. But a cigar—well, he might have smoked a cigar without leaving a sign, I suppose. But I hope he didn't."

" Why ? "

" Because, old son, I'd rather Gerald's account had some element of truth in it. A nervy man doesn't sit down to the delicate enjoyment of a cigar before bed, and cherish the ash with such scrupulous care. On the other hand, if Freddy's right, and Cathcart was feelin' unusually sleek and pleased with life, that's just the sort of thing he would do."

" Do you think Mr. Arbuthnot would have invented all that, as a matter of fact ? " said Parker thoughtfully. " He doesn't strike me that way. He'd have to be imaginative and spiteful to make it up, and I really don't think he's either."

" I know," said Lord Peter. " I've known old Freddy all my life, and he wouldn't hurt a fly. Besides, he simply hasn't the wits to make up any sort of a story. But what bothers me is that Gerald most certainly hasn't the wits either to invent that Adelphi drama between him and Cathcart."

" On the other hand," said Parker, " if we allow for a moment that he shot Cathcart, he had an incentive to invent it. He would be trying to get his head out of the—I mean, when anything important is at stake it's wonderful how it sharpens one's wits. And the story being so far-fetched does rather suggest an unpractised story-teller."

" True, O King. Well, you've sat on all my discoveries so far. Never mind. My head is bloody but unbowed. Cathcart was sitting here——"

" So your brother said."

" Curse you, I say he was ; at least, somebody was ;

47

he's left the impression of his sit-me-down-upon on the cushion."

" That might have been earlier in the day."

" Rot. They were out all day. You needn't overdo this Sadducee attitude, Charles. I say Cathcart was sitting here, and—hullo ! hullo ! "

He leaned forward and stared into the grate.

" There's some burnt paper here, Charles."

" I know. I was frightfully excited about that yesterday, but I found it was just the same in several of the rooms. They often let the bedroom fires go out when everybody's out during the day, and relight them about an hour before dinner. There's only the cook, housemaid, and Fleming here, you see, and they've got a lot to do with such a large party."

Lord Peter was picking the charred fragments over.

" I can find nothing to contradict your suggestion," he sadly said, " and this fragment of the *Morning Post* rather confirms it. Then we can only suppose that Cathcart sat here in a brown study, doing nothing at all. That doesn't get us much further, I'm afraid." He got up and went to the dressing-table.

" I like these tortoiseshell sets," he said, " and the perfume is ' *Baiser du Soir* '—very nice too. New to me. I must draw Bunter's attention to it. A charming manicure set, isn't it ? You know, I like being clean and neat and all that, but Cathcart was the kind of man who always impressed you as bein' just a little *too* well turned out. Poor devil ! And he'll be buried at Golders Green after all. I only saw him once or twice, you know. He impressed me as knowin' about everything there was to know. I was rather surprised at Mary takin' to him, but, then, I know really awfully little about Mary. You see, she's five years younger than me. When the war broke out she'd just left school and gone to a place in Paris, and I joined up, and she came back and did nursing and social work, so I only saw her occasionally. At that time she was rather taken up with new schemes for puttin' the world to rights and hadn't a lot to say to me. And she got hold of some pacifist fellow who was a bit of a stumer, I fancy. Then I was ill, you know, and then I got the chuck from Barbara and didn't feel much like botherin' about other people's heart-to-hearts, and then I got mixed up in the Attenbury diamond case—and the result is I know uncommonly little about my own sister. But it looks as though her taste in men had altered. I know my mother said Cathcart had charm ; that means he was attractive to women, I suppose. No man can see what makes that in another man, but mother is usually right. What's become of this fellow's papers?"

"He left very little here," replied Parker. "There's a cheque-book on Cox's Charing Cross branch, but it's a new one and not very helpful. Apparently he only kept a small current account with them for convenience when he was in England. The cheques are mostly to self, with an occasional hotel or tailor."

"Any pass-book ? "

"I think all his important papers are in Paris. He has a flat there, near the river somewhere. We're in communication with the Paris police. He had a room at the Albany. I've told them to lock it up till I get there. I thought of running up to town to-morrow."

"Yes, you'd better. Any pocket-book ? "

"Yes ; here you are. About £30 in various notes, a wine-merchant's card, and a bill for a pair of riding-breeches."

"No correspondence ? "

"Not a line."

"No," said Wimsey, "he was the kind, I imagine, that didn't keep letters. Much too good an instinct of self-preservation."

"Yes. I asked the servants about his letters, as a matter of fact. They said he got a good number, but never left them about. They couldn't tell me much about the ones he wrote, because all the outgoing letters are dropped into the post-bag, which is carried down to the post-office as it is and opened there, or handed over to the postman when—or if—he calls. The general impression was that he didn't write much. The house-maid said she never found anything to speak of in the waste-paper basket."

"Well, that's uncommonly helpful. Wait a moment. Here's his fountain-pen. Very handsome—Onoto with complete gold casing. Dear me ! entirely empty. Well, I don't know that one can deduce anything from that, exactly. I don't see any pencil about, by the way. I'm inclined to think you're wrong in supposing that he was writing letters."

"I didn't suppose anything," said Parker mildly. "I daresay you're right."

Lord Peter left the dressing-table, looked through the contents of the wardrobe, and turned over the two or three books on the pedestal beside the bed.

"*La Rôtisserie de la Reine Pédauque*, *L'Anneau d'-Améthyste*, *South Wind* (our young friend works out very true to type), *Chronique d'un Cadet de Coutras* (tut-tut, Charles !), *Manon Lescaut*. H'm ! Is there anything else in this room I ought to look at ? "

"I don't think so. Where'd you like to go now ? "

"We'll follow 'em down. Wait a jiff. Who are in the other rooms ? Oh, yes. Here's Gerald's room. Helen's at church. In we go. Of course, this has been dusted and cleaned up, and generally ruined for purposes of observation ? "

"I'm afraid so. I could hardly keep the Duchess out of her bedroom."

"No. Here's the window Gerald shouted out of. H'm ! Nothing in the grate here, naturally—the fire's been lit since. I say, I wonder where Gerald did put that letter to—Freeborn's, I mean."

"Nobody's been able to get a word out of him about it," said Parker. "Old Mr. Murbles had a fearful time with him. The Duke insists simply that he destroyed it. Mr. Murbles says that's absurd. So it is. If he was

going to bring that sort of accusation against his sister's
fiancé he'd want *some* evidence of a method in his mad-
ness, wouldn't he ? Or was he one of those Roman
brothers who say simply : ' As the head of the family I
forbid the banns and that's enough ' ? "

" Gerald," said Wimsey, " is a good, clean, decent,
thoroughbred public schoolboy, and a shocking ass.
But I don't think he's so mediaeval as that."

" But if he has the letter, why not produce it ? "

" Why, indeed ? Letters from old college friends in
Egypt aren't, as a rule, compromising."

" You don't suppose," suggested Parker tentatively,
" that this Mr. Freeborn referred in his letter to any
old—er—entanglement which your brother wouldn't
wish the Duchess to know about ? "

Lord Peter paused, while absently examining a row of
boots.

" That's an idea," he said. " There were occasions
—mild ones, but Helen would make the most of them."
He whistled thoughtfully. " Still, when it comes to the
gallows——"

" Do you suppose, Wimsey, that your brother really
contemplates the gallows ? " asked Parker.

" I think Murbles put it to him pretty straight," said
Lord Peter.

" Quite so. But does he actually realise—imagin-
atively—that it is possible to hang an English peer for
murder on circumstantial evidence ? "

Lord Peter considered this.

" Imagination isn't Gerald's strong point," he admitted. " I suppose they *do* hang peers ? They can't
be beheaded on Tower Hill or anything ? "

" I'll look it up," said Parker ; " but they certainly
hanged Earl Ferrers in 1760."

" Did they, though ? " said Lord Peter. " Ah, well,
as the old pagan said of the Gospels, after all, it was a long
time ago, and we'll hope it wasn't true."

" It's true enough," said Parker ; " and he was dissected and anatomised afterwards. But that part of the treatment is obsolete."

"We'll tell Gerald about it," said Lord Peter, "and persuade him to take the matter seriously. Which are the boots he wore Wednesday night?"

"These," said Parker, "but the fool's cleaned them."

"Yes," said Lord Peter bitterly. "M'm! a good heavy lace-up boot—the sort that sends the blood to the head."

"He wore leggings, too," said Parker; "these."

"Rather elaborate preparations for a stroll in the garden. But, as you were just going to say, the night was wet. I must ask Helen if Gerald ever suffered from insomnia."

"I did. She said she thought not as a rule, but that he occasionally had toothache, which made him restless."

"It wouldn't send one out of doors on a cold night, though. Well, let's get downstairs."

They passed through the billiard-room, where the Colonel was making a sensational break, and into the small conservatory which led from it.

Lord Peter looked gloomily round at the chrysanthemums and boxes of bulbs.

"These damned flowers look jolly healthy," he said. "Do you mean you've been letting the gardener swarm in here every day to water 'em?"

"Yes," said Parker apologetically, "I did. But he's had strict orders only to walk on these mats."

"Good," said Lord Peter. "Take 'em up, then, and let's get to work."

With his lens to his eye he crawled cautiously over the floor.

"They all came through this way, I suppose," he said.

"Yes," said Parker. "I've identified most of the marks. People went in and out. Here's the Duke. He comes in from outside. He trips over the body." (Parker had opened the outer door and lifted some matting, to show a trampled patch of gravel, discolo ed with blood.) " He kneels by the body. Here are his knees and toes. Afterwards he goes into the house, through the conservatory, leaving a good impression in black mud and gravel just inside the door."

Lord Peter squatted carefully over the marks.

" It's lucky the gravel's so soft here," he said.

" Yes. It's just a patch. The gardener tells me it gets very trampled and messy just here owing to his coming to fill cans from the water-trough. They fill the trough up from the well every so often, and then carry the water away in cans. It got extra bad this year, and they put down fresh gravel a few weeks ago."

" Pity they didn't extend their labours all down the path while they were about it," grunted Lord Peter, who was balancing himself precariously on a small piece of sacking. " Well, that bears out old Gerald so far. Here's an elephant been over this bit of box border. Who's that ? "

" Oh, that's a constable. I put him at eighteen stone. He's nothing. And this rubber sole with a patch on it is Craikes. He's all over the place. This squelchy-looking thing is Mr. Arbuthnot in bedroom slippers, and the goloshes are Mr. Pettigrew-Robinson. We can dismiss all those. But now here, just coming over the threshold, is a woman's foot in a strong shoe. I make that out to be Lady Mary's. Here it is again, just at the edge of the well. She came out to examine the body."

" Quite so," said Peter ; " and then she came in again, with a few grains of red gravel on her shoes. Well, that's all right. Hullo ! "

On the outer side of the conservatory were some shelves for small plants, and, beneath these, a damp and dismal bed of earth, occupied, in a sprawling and lacka-daisical fashion, by stringy cactus plants and a sporadic growth of maidenhair fern, and masked by a row of large chrysanthemums in pots.

" What've you got ? " inquired Parker, seeing his friend peering into this green retreat.

Lord Peter withdrew his long nose from between two pots and said : " Who put what down here ? "

Parker hastened to the place. There, among the cacti, was certainly the clear mark of some oblong object, with corners, that had been stood out of sight on the earth behind the pots.

" It's a good thing Gerald's gardener ain't one of those conscientious blighters that can't even let a cactus alone for the winter," said Lord Peter, " or he'd've tenderly lifted these little drooping heads—oh ! damn and blast the beastly plant for a crimson porcupine ! *You* measure it."

Parker measured it.

" Two and a half feet by six inches," he said. " And fairly heavy, for it's sunk in and broken the plants about. Was it a bar of anything ? "

" I fancy not," said Lord Peter. " The impression is deeper on the farther side. I think it was something bulky set up on edge, and leaned against the glass. If you asked for my private opinion I should guess that it was a suit-case."

" A suit-case ! " exclaimed Parker. " Why a suit-case ? "

" Why indeed ? I think we may assume that it didn't stay here very long. It would have been exceedingly visible in the daytime. But somebody might very well have shoved it in here if they were caught with it—say at three o'clock in the morning—and didn't want it to be seen."

" Then when did they take it away ? "

" Almost immediately, I should say. Before daylight, anyhow, or even Inspector Craikes could hardly have failed to see it."

" It's not the doctor's bag, I suppose ? "

" No—unless the doctor's a fool. Why put a bag inconveniently in a damp and dirty place out of the way when every law of sense and convenience would urge him to pop it down handy by the body ? No. Unless

Craikes or the gardener has been leaving things about, it was thrust away there on Wednesday night by Gerald, by Cathcart—or, I suppose, by Mary. Nobody else could be supposed to have anything to hide."

" Yes," said Parker, " one person."

" Who's that ? "

" The Person Unknown."

" Who's he ? "

For answer Mr. Parker proudly stepped to a row of wooden frames, carefully covered with matting. Stripping this away, with the air of a bishop unveiling a memorial, he disclosed a V-shaped line of footprints.

" These," said Parker, " belong to nobody—to nobody I've ever seen or heard of, I mean."

" Hurray ! " said Peter.

> "Then downwards from the steep hill's edge
> They tracked the footmarks small

(only they're largish)."

" No such luck," said Parker. " It's more a case of :

> They followed from the earthy bank
> Those footsteps one by one,
> Into the middle of the plank ;
> And farther there were none ! "

" Great poet, Wordsworth," said Lord Peter ; " how often I've had that feeling. Now let's see. These footmarks—a man's No. 10 with worn-down heels and a patch on the left inner side—advance from the hard bit of the path which shows no footmarks ; they come to the body—here, where that pool of blood is. I say, that's rather odd, don't you think ? No ? Perhaps not. There are no footmarks under the body ? Can't say, it's such a mess. Well, the Unknown gets so far—here's a footmark deeply pressed in. Was he just going to throw Cathcart into the well ? He hears a sound ; he starts ; he turns ; he runs on tiptoe—into the shrubbery, by Jove ! "

55

" Yes," said Parker, " and the tracks come out on one of the grass paths in the wood, and there's an end of them."

" H'm ! Well, we'll follow them later. Now where did they come from ? "

Together the two friends followed the path away from the house. The gravel, except for the little patch before the conservatory, was old and hard, and afforded but little trace, particularly as the last few days had been rainy. Parker, however, was able to assure Wimsey that there had been definite traces of dragging and blood-stains.

" What sort of bloodstains ? Smears ? "

" Yes, smears mostly. There were pebbles displaced, too, all the way—and now here is something odd."

It was the clear impression of the palm of a man's hand heavily pressed into the earth of a herbaceous border, the fingers pointing towards the house. On the path the gravel had been scraped up in two long furrows. There was blood on the grass border between the path and the bed, and the edge of the grass was broken and trampled.

" I don't like that," said Lord Peter.

" Ugly, isn't it ? " agreed Parker.

" Poor devil ! " said Peter. " He made a determined effort to hang on here. That explains the blood by the conservatory door. But what kind of a devil drags a corpse that isn't quite dead ? "

A few yards farther the path ran into the main drive. This was bordered with trees, widening into a thicket. At the point of intersection of the two paths were some further indistinct marks, and in another twenty yards or so they turned aside into the thicket. A large tree had fallen at some time and made a little clearing, in the midst of which a tarpaulin had been carefully spread out and pegged down. The air was heavy with the smell of fungus and fallen leaves.

" Scene of the tragedy," said Parker briefly, rolling back the tarpaulin.

Lord Peter gazed down sadly. Muffled in an overcoat and a thick grey scarf, he looked, with his long, narrow face, like a melancholy adjutant stork. The writhing body of the fallen man had scraped up the dead leaves and left a depression in the sodden ground. At one place the darker earth showed where a great pool of blood had soaked into it, and the yellow leaves of a Spanish poplar were rusted with no autumnal stain.

" That's where they found the handkerchief and revolver," said Parker. " I looked for finger-marks, but the rain and mud had messed everything up."

Wimsey took out his lens, lay down, and conducted a personal tour of the whole space slowly on his stomach, Parker moving mutely after him.

" He paced up and down for some time," said Lord Peter. " He wasn't smoking. He was turning something over in his mind, or waiting for somebody. What's this ? Aha ! Here's our No. 10 foot again, coming in through the trees on the farther side. No signs of a struggle. That's odd ! Cathcart was shot close up, wasn't he ? "

" Yes ; it singed his shirt-front."

" Quite so. Why did he stand still to be shot at ? "

" I imagine," said Parker, " that if he had an appointment with No. 10 Boots it was somebody he knew, who could get close to him without arousing suspicion."

" Then the interview was a friendly one—on Cathcart's side, anyhow. But the revolver's a difficulty. How did No. 10 get hold of Gerald's revolver ? "

" The conservatory door was open," said Parker dubiously.

" Nobody knew about that except Gerald and Fleming," retorted Lord Peter. " Besides, do you mean to tell me that No. 10 walked in here, went to the study, fetched the revolver, walked back here, and shot Cathcart ? It seems a clumsy method. If he wanted to do any shooting, why didn't he come armed in the first place ? "

" It seems more probable that Cathcart brought the revolver," said Parker.

" Then why no signs of a struggle ? "

" Perhaps Cathcart shot himself," said Parker.

" Then why should No. 10 drag him into a conspicuous position and then run away ? "

" Wait a minute," said Parker. " How's this ? No. 10 has an appointment with Cathcart—to blackmail him, let's say. He somehow gets word of his intention to him between 9.45 and 10.15. That would account for the alteration in Cathcart's manner, and allow both Mr. Arbuthnot and the Duke to be telling the truth. Cathcart rushes violently out after his row with your brother. He comes down here to keep his appointment. He paces up and down waiting for No. 10. No. 10 arrives and parleys with Cathcart. Cathcart offers him money. No. 10 stands out for more. Cathcart says he really hasn't got it. No. 10 says in that case he blows the gaff. Cathcart retorts, ' In that case you can go to the devil. I'm going there myself.' Cathcart, who has previously got hold of the revolver, shoots himself. No. 10 is seized with remorse. He sees that Cathcart isn't quite dead. He picks him up and part drags, part carries him to the house. He is smaller than Cathcart and not very strong, and finds it a hard job. They have just got to the conservatory door when Cathcart has a final hœmorrhage and gives up the ghost. No. 10 suddenly becomes aware that his position in somebody else's grounds, alone with a corpse at 3 a.m., wants some explaining. He drops Cathcart—and bolts. Enter the Duke of Denver and falls over the body. Tableau."

" That's good," said Lord Peter ; " that's very good. But when do you suppose it happened ? Gerald found the body at 3 a.m. ; the doctor was here at 4.30, and said Cathcart had been dead several hours. Very well. Now, how about that shot my sister heard at three o'clock ? "

" Look here, old man," said Parker, " I don't want to appear rude to your sister. May I put it like this ? I suggest that that shot at 3 a.m. was poachers."

" Poachers by all means," said Lord Peter. " Well, really, Parker, I think that hangs together. Let's adopt that explanation provisionally. The first thing to do is now to find No. 10, since he can bear witness that Cathcart committed suicide ; and that, as far as my brother is concerned, is the only thing that matters a rap. But for the satisfaction of my own curiosity I'd like to know: What was No. 10 blackmailing Cathcart about ? Who hid a suit-case in the conservatory ? And what was Gerald doing in the garden at 3 a.m. ? "

" Well," said Parker, " suppose we begin by tracing where No. 10 came from."

" Hi, hi ! " cried Wimsey, as they returned to the trail. " Here's something—here's real treasure-trove, Parker ! "

From amid the mud and the fallen leaves he retrieved a tiny, glittering object—a flash of white and green between his finger-tips.

It was a little charm such as women hang upon a bracelet—a diminutive diamond cat with eyes of bright emerald.

CHAPTER III

MUDSTAINS AND BLOODSTAINS

*Other things are all very well in their way, but give me
Blood . . . We say, " There it is ! that's Blood ! " It is
an actual matter of fact. We point it out. It admits of no
doubt. . . . We must have Blood, you know.*—David
Copperfield.

" H I T H E R T O , " said Lord Peter, as they picked
their painful way through the little wood on the trail of
Gent's No. 10's, " I have always maintained that those
obliging criminals who strew their tracks with little
articles of personal adornment—here he is, on a squashed
fungus—were an invention of detective fiction for the
benefit of the author. I see that I have still something
to learn about my job."

" Well, you haven't been at it very long, have you ?"
said Parker. " Besides, we don't know that the diamond
cat is the criminal's. It may belong to a member of your
own family, and have been lying here for days. It may
belong to Mr. What's-his-name in the States, or to the
last tenant but one, and have been lying here for years.
This broken branch may be our friend—I think it is."

" I'll ask the family," said Lord Peter, " and we
could find out in the village if anyone's ever inquired
for a lost cat. They're pukka stones. It ain't the sort
of thing one would drop without making a fuss about—
I've lost him altogether."

" It's all right—I've got him. He's tripped over a
root."

" Serve him glad," said Lord Peter viciously, straight-

ening his back. " I say, I don't think the human frame
is very thoughtfully constructed for this sleuth-hound
business. If one could go on all-fours, or had eyes in
one's knees, it would be a lot more practical."

" There are many difficulties inherent in a teleological
view of creation," said Parker placidly. " Ah ! here
we are at the park palings."

" And here's where he got over," said Lord Peter,
pointing to a place where the *chevaux de frise* on the top
was broken away. " Here's the dent where his heels
came down, and here's where he fell forward on hands
and knees. Hum ! Give us a back, old man, would
you ? Thanks. An old break, I see. Mr. Montague-
now-in-the-States should keep his palings in better
order. No. 10 tore his coat on the spikes all the same ;
he left a fragment of Burberry behind him. What luck !
Here's a deep, damp ditch on the other side, which I
shall now proceed to fall into."

A slithering crash proclaimed that he had carried out
his intention. Parker, thus callously abandoned, looked
round, and, seeing that they were only a hundred yards
or so from the gate, ran along and was let out, decorously,
by Hardraw, the gamekeeper, who happened to be coming out of the lodge.

" By the way," said Parker to him, " did you ever
find any signs of any poachers on Wednesday night
after all ? "

" Nay," said the man, " not so much as a dead rabbit.
I reckon t'lady wor mistaken, an 'twore the shot I heard
as killed t'Captain."

" Possibly," said Parker. " Do you know how long
the spikes have been broken off the palings over there ? "

" A moonth or two, happen. They should 'a' bin
put right, but the man's sick."

" The gate's locked at night, I suppose ? "

" Aye."

" Anybody wishing to get in would have to waken
you ? "

" Aye, that he would."

" You didn't see any suspicious character loitering about outside these palings last Wednesday, I suppose ? "

" Nay, sir, but my wife may ha' done. Hey, lass ! "

Mrs. Hardraw, thus summoned, appeared at the door with a small boy clinging to her skirts.

" Wednesday ? " said she. " Nay, I saw no loiterin' folks. I keep a look-out for tramps and such, as it be such a lonely place. Wednesday. Eh, now, John, that wad be t'day t'young mon called wi' t'motor-bike."

" Young man with a motor-bike ? "

" I reckon 'twas. He said he'd had a puncture and asked for a bucket o' watter."

" Was that all the asking he did ? "

" He asked what were t'name o' t'place and whose house it were."

" Did you tell him the Duke of Denver was living here ? "

" Aye, sir, and he said he supposed a many gentlemen came up for t'shooting."

" Did he say where he was going ? "

" He said he'd coom oop fra' Weirdale an' were makin' a trip into Coomberland."

" How long was he here ? "

" Happen half an hour. An' then he tried to get his machine started, an' I see him hop-hoppitin' away towards King's Fenton."

She pointed away to the right, where Lord Peter might be seen gesticulating in the middle of the road.

" What sort of a man was he ? "

Like most people, Mrs. Hardraw was poor at definition. She thought he was youngish and tallish, neither dark nor fair, in such a long coat as motor-bicyclists use, with a belt round it.

" Was he a gentleman ? "

Mrs. Hardraw hesitated, and Mr. Parker mentally classed the stranger as " Not quite quite."

" You didn't happen to notice the number of the bicycle ? "

Mrs. Hardraw had not. " But it had a side-car," she added.

Lord Peter's gesticulations were becoming quite violent, and Mr. Parker hastened to rejoin him.

" Come on, gossiping old thing," said Lord Peter unreasonably. " This is a beautiful ditch.

> From such a ditch as this,
> When the soft wind did gently kiss the trees
> And they did make no noise, from such a ditch
> Our friend, methinks, mounted the Troyan walls,
> And wiped his soles upon the greasy mud.

Look at my trousers ! "

" It's a bit of a climb from this side," said Parker.

" It is. He stood here in the ditch, and put one foot into this place where the paling's broken away and one hand on the top, and hauled himself up. No. 10 must have been a man of exceptional height, strength, and agility. I couldn't get my foot up, let alone reaching the top with my hand. I'm five foot nine. Could you ? "

Parker was six foot, and could just touch the top of the wall with his hand.

" I *might* do it—on one of my best days," he said, " for an adequate object, or after adequate stimulant."

" Just so," said Lord Peter. " Hence we deduce No. 10's exceptional height and strength."

" Yes," said Parker. " It's a bit unfortunate that we had to deduce his exceptional shortness and weakness just now, isn't it ? "

" Oh ! " said Peter. " Well—well, as you so rightly say, that *is* a bit unfortunate."

" Well, it may clear up presently. He didn't have a confederate to give him a back or a leg, I suppose ? "

" Not unless the confederate was a being without feet or any visible means of support," said Lord Peter, indicating the solitary print of a pair of patched 10's. " By the way, how did he make straight in the dark for the place where the spikes were missing ? Looks as though he belonged to the neighbourhood, or had reconnoitred previously."

" Arising out of that reply," said Parker, " I will now relate to you the entertaining ' gossip ' I have had with Mrs. Hardraw."

" Humph ! " said Wimsey at the end of it. " That's interesting. We'd better make inquiries at Riddlesdale and King's Fenton. Meanwhile we know where No. 10 came from ; now where did he go after leaving Cathcart's body by the well ? "

" The footsteps went into the preserve," said Parker. " I lost them there. There is a regular carpet of dead leaves and bracken."

" Well, but we needn't go through all that sleuth grind again," objected his friend. " The fellow went in, and, as he presumably is not there still, he came out again. He didn't come out through the gate or Hardraw would have seen him ; he didn't come out the same way he went in or he would have left some traces. Therefore he came out elsewhere. Let's walk round the wall."

" Then we'll turn to the left," said Parker, " since that's the side of the preserve, and he apparently went through there."

" True, O King ; and as this isn't a church, there's no harm in going round it widdershins. Talking of church, there's Helen coming back. Get a move on, old thing."

They crossed the drive, passed the cottage, and then, leaving the road, followed the paling across some open grass fields. It was not long before they found what they sought. From one of the iron spikes above them dangled forlornly a strip of material. With Parker's assistance Wimsey scrambled up in a state of almost lyric excitement.

" Here we are," he cried. " The belt of a Burberry ! No sort of precaution here. Here are the toe-prints of a fellow sprinting for his life. He tore off his Burberry ;

64

he made desperate leaps—one, two, three—at the palings. At the third leap he hooked it on to the spikes. He scrambled up, scoring long, scrabbling marks on the paling. He reached the top. Oh, here's a bloodstain run into this crack. He tore his hands. He dropped off. He wrenched the coat away, leaving the belt dangling——"

" I wish you'd drop off," grumbled Parker. " You're breaking my collar-bone."

Lord Peter dropped off obediently, and stood there holding the belt between his fingers. His narrow grey eyes wandered restlessly over the field. Suddenly he seized Parker's arm and marched briskly in the direction of the wall on the farther side—a low erection of unmortared stone in the fashion of the country. Here he hunted along like a terrier, nose foremost, the tip of his tongue caught absurdly between his teeth, then jumped over, and, turning to Parker, said :

" Did you ever read *The Lay of the Last Minstrel?* "

" I learnt a good deal of it at school," said Parker. " Why ? "

" Because there was a goblin page-boy in it," said Lord Peter, " who was always yelling ' Found ! Found! Found ! ' at the most unnecessary moments. I always thought him a terrible nuisance, but now I know how he felt. See here."

Close under the wall, and sunk heavily into the narrow and muddy lane which ran up here at right angles to the main road, was the track of a side-car combination.

" Very nice too," said Mr. Parker approvingly. " New Dunlop tyre on the front wheel. Old tyre on the back. Gaiter on the side-car tyre. Nothing could be better. Tracks come in from the road and go back to the road. Fellow shoved the machine in here in case anybody of an inquisitive turn of mind should pass on the road and make off with it, or take its number. Then he went round on shank's mare to the gap he'd spotted in the daytime and got over. After the Cathcart affair he took fright, bolted into the preserve, and took the shortest way to his bus, regardless. Well, now."

He sat down on the wall, and, drawing out his notebook, began to jot down a description of the man from the data already known.

" Things begin to look a bit more comfortable for old Jerry," said Lord Peter. He leaned on the wall and began whistling softly, but with great accuracy, that elaborate passage of Bach which begins " Let Zion's children."

.   .   .   .

" I wonder," said the Hon. Freddy Arbuthnot, "what damn silly fool invented Sunday afternoon."

He shovelled coals on to the library fire with a vicious clatter, waking Colonel Marchbanks, who said, " Eh ? Yes, quite right," and fell asleep again instantly.

" Don't *you* grumble, Freddy," said Lord Peter, who had been occupied for some time in opening and shutting all the drawers of the writing-table in a thoroughly irritating manner, and idly snapping to and fro the catch of the French window. " Think how dull old Jerry must feel. 'Spose I'd better write him a line."

He returned to the table and took a sheet of paper. " Do people use this room much to write letters in, do you know ? "

" No idea," said the Hon. Freddy. " Never write 'em myself. Where's the point of writin' when you can wire? Encourages people to write back, that's all. I think Denver writes here when he writes anywhere, and I saw the Colonel wrestlin' with pen and ink a day or two ago, didn't you, Colonel ? " (The Colonel grunted, answering to his name like a dog that wags its tail in its sleep.) " What's the matter ? Ain't there any ink ? "

" I only wondered," replied Peter placidly. He slipped a paper-knife under the top sheet of the blotting-pad and held it up to the light. " Quite right, old man. Give you full marks for observation. Here's Jerry's signature, and the Colonel's, and a big, sprawly hand, which I should judge to be feminine." He looked at the sheet again, shook his head, folded it up, and placed it in his pocket-book. " Doesn't seem to be anything there," he commented, " but you never know. ' Five something of fine something '—grouse, probably ; ' oe— is fou '—is found, I suppose. Well, it can't do any harm to keep it." He spread out his paper and began :

" DEAR JERRY,—Here I am, the family sleuth on the trail, and it's damned exciting——"

The Colonel snored.

Sunday afternoon. Parker had gone with the car to King's Fenton, with orders to look in at Riddlesdale on the way and inquire for a green-eyed cat, also for a young man with a side-car. The Duchess was lying down. Mrs. Pettigrew-Robinson had taken her husband for a brisk walk. Upstairs, somewhere, Mrs. March-banks enjoyed a perfect communion of thought with her husband.

Lord Peter's pen gritted gently over the paper, stopped, moved on again, stopped altogether. He leaned his long chin on his hands and stared out of the window, against which there came sudden little swishes of rain, and from time to time a soft, dead leaf. The Colonel snored ; the fire tinkled ; the Hon. Freddy began to hum and tap his fingers on the arms of his chair. The clock moved slothfully on to five o'clock, which brought teatime and the Duchess.

" How's Mary ? " asked Lord Peter, coming suddenly into the firelight.

" I'm really worried about her," said the Duchess. " She is giving way to her nerves in the strangest manner. It is so unlike her. She will hardly let anybody come near her. I have sent for Dr. Thorpe again."

" Don't you think she'd be better if she got up an' came downstairs a bit ? " suggested Wimsey. " Gets broodin' about things all by herself, I shouldn't wonder. Wants a bit of Freddy's intellectual conversation to cheer her up."

" You forget ; poor girl," said the Duchess, " she was engaged to Captain Cathcart. Everybody isn't as callous as you are."

" Any more letters, your grace ? " asked the footman, appearing with the post-bag.

" Oh, are you going down now ? " said Wimsey. " Yes, here you are—and there's one other, if you don't mind waitin' a minute while I write it. Wish I could write at the rate people do on the cinema," he added, scribbling rapidly as he spoke. " ' DEAR LILIAN,—Your father has killed Mr. William Snooks, and unless you send me £1,000 by bearer, I shall disclose all to your husband.—Sincerely, EARL OF DIGGLESBRAKE.' That's the style ; and all done in one scrape of the pen. Here you are, Fleming."

The letter was addressed to her grace the Dowager Duchess of Denver.

.   .   .   .

From the *Morning Post* of Monday, November—, 19— :

" ABANDONED MOTOR-CYCLE

" A singular discovery was made yesterday by a cattle-drover. He is accustomed to water his animals in a certain pond lying a little off the road about twelve miles south of Ripley. On this occasion he saw that one of them appeared to be in difficulties. On going to the rescue, he found the animal entangled in a motor-cycle, which had been driven into the pond and abandoned. With the assistance of a couple of workmen he extricated the machine. It is a Douglas, with dark-grey side-car. The number-plates and licence-holder have been carefully removed. The pond is a deep one, and the outfit was entirely submerged. It seems probable, however, that it could not have been there for more than a week, since the pond is much used on Sundays and Mondays for the watering of cattle. The police are. making search for the owner. The front tyre of the bicycle is a new Dunlop, and the side-car tyre has been repaired with a gaiter. The machine is a 1914 model, much worn."

" That seems to strike a chord," said Lord Peter musingly. He consulted a time-table for the time of the next train to Ripley, and ordered the car.

" And send Bunter to me," he added.

That gentleman arrived just as his master was struggling into an overcoat.

" What was that thing in last Thursday's paper about a number-plate, Bunter ? " inquired his lordship.

Mr. Bunter produced, apparently by legerdemain, a cutting from an evening paper :

" NUMBER-PLATE MYSTERY

" The Rev. Nathaniel Foulis, of St. Simon's, North Fellcote, was stopped at six o'clock this morning for riding a motor-cycle without number-plates. The reverend gentleman seemed thunderstruck when his attention was called to the matter. He explained that he had been sent for in great haste at 4 a.m. to administer the Sacrament to a dying parishioner six miles away. He hastened out on his motor-cycle, which he confidingly left by the roadside while executing his sacred duties. Mr. Foulis left the house at 5.30 without noticing that anything was wrong. Mr. Foulis is well known in North Fellcote and the surrounding country, and there seems little doubt that he has been the victim of a senseless practical joke. North Fellcote is a small village a couple of miles north of Ripley."

" I'm going to Ripley, Bunter," said Lord Peter.

" Yes, my lord. Does your lordship require me ? "

" No," said Lord Peter, " but—who has been lady's maiding my sister, Bunter ? "

" Ellen, my lord—the housemaid."

" Then I wish you'd exercise your powers of conversation on Ellen."

" Very good, my lord."

" Does she mend my sister's clothes, and brush her skirts, and all that ? "

" I believe so, my lord."

" Nothing she may think is of any importance, you know, Bunter."

" I wouldn't suggest such a thing to a woman, my lord. It goes to their heads, if I may say so."

" When did Mr. Parker leave for town ? "

" At six o'clock this morning, my lord."

   .   .   .   .

Circumstances favoured Mr. Bunter's inquiries. He bumped into Ellen as she was descending the back stairs with an armful of clothing. A pair of leather gauntlets was jerked from the top of the pile, and, picking them up, he apologetically followed the young woman into the servants' hall.

" There," said Ellen, flinging her burden on the table, " and the work I've had to get them, I'm sure. Tantrums, that's what I call it, pretending you've got such a headache you can't let a person into the room to take your things down to brush, and, as soon as they're out of the way, 'opping out of bed and trapesing all over the place. 'Tisn't what I call a headache, would you, now ? But there ! I daresay you don't get them like I do. Regular fit to split, my head is sometimes—couldn't keep on my feet, not if the house was burning down. I just have to lay down and keep laying—something cruel it is. And gives a person such wrinkles in one's forehead."

" I'm sure I don't see any wrinkles," said Mr. Bunter,

" but perhaps I haven't looked hard enough." An inter-
lude followed, during which Mr. Bunter looked hard
enough and close enough to distinguish wrinkles.
" No," said he, " wrinkles ? I don't believe I'd see any
if I was to take his lordship's big microscope he keeps up
in town."

" Lor' now, Mr. Bunter," said Ellen, fetching a
sponge and a bottle of benzene from the cupboard,
"what would his lordship be using a thing like that for,
now ? "

" Why, in our hobby, you see, Miss Ellen, which is
criminal investigation, we might want to see something
magnified extra big—as it might be handwriting in a
forgery case, to see if anything's been altered or rubbed
out, or if different kinds of ink have been used. Or we
might want to look at the roots of a lock of hair, to see if
it's been torn out or fallen out. Or take bloodstains, now;
we'd want to know if it was animals' blood or human
blood, or maybe only a glass of port."

" Now is it really true, Mr. Bunter," said Ellen, laying
a tweed skirt out upon the table and unstoppering the
benzene, " that you and Lord Peter can find out all
that ? "

" Of course, we aren't analytical chemists," Mr.
Bunter replied, " but his lordship's dabbled in a lot of
things—enough to know when anything looks suspicious,
and if we've any doubts we send to a very famous
scientific gentleman." (He gallantly intercepted Ellen's
hand as it approached the skirt with a benzene-soaked
sponge.) " For instance, now, here's a stain on the hem
of this skirt, just at the bottom of the side-seam. Now,
supposing it was a case of murder, we'll say, and the
person that had worn this skirt was suspected, I should
examine that stain." (Here Mr. Bunter whipped a lens
out of his pocket.) " Then I might try it at one edge
with a wet handkerchief." (He suited the action to the
word.) " And I should find, you see, that it came off
red. Then I should turn the skirt inside-out, I should

see that the stain went right through, and I should take my scissors " (Mr. Bunter produced a small, sharp pair) " and snip off a tiny bit of the inside edge of the seam, like this " (he did so) " and pop it into a little pill-box, so " (the pill-box appeared magically from an inner pocket), " and seal it up both sides with a wafer, and write on the top ' Lady Mary Wimsey's skirt,' and the date. Then I should send it straight off to the analytical gentleman in London, and he'd look through his microscope, and tell me right off that it was rabbit's blood, maybe, and how many days it had been there, and that would be the end of that," finished Mr. Bunter triumphantly, replacing his nail-scissors and thoughtlessly pocketing the pill-box with its contents.

" Well, he'd be wrong, then," said Ellen, with an engaging toss of the head, " because it's bird's blood, and not rabbit's at all, because her ladyship told me so ; and wouldn't it be quicker just to go and ask the person than get fiddling round with your silly old microscope and things ? "

" Well, I only mentioned rabbits for an example," said Mr. Bunter. " Funny she should have got a stain down there. Must have regularly knelt in it."

" Yes. Bled a lot, hasn't it, poor thing ? Somebody must 'a' been shootin' careless-like. 'Twasn't his grace, nor yet the Captain, poor man. Perhaps it was Mr. Arbuthnot. He shoots a bit wild sometimes. It's a nasty mess, anyway, and it's so hard to clean off, being left so long. I'm sure I wasn't thinking about cleaning nothing the day the poor Captain was killed ; and then the Coroner's inquest—'orrid, it was—and his grace being took off like that ! Well, there, it upset me. I suppose I'm a bit sensitive. Anyhow, we was all at sixes and sevens for a day or two, and then her ladyship shuts herself up in her room and won't let me go near the wardrobe. ' Ow ! ' she says, ' do leave that wardrobe door alone. Don't you know it squeaks, and my head's so bad and my nerves so bad I can't stand it,' she says. ' I was only going to brush your skirts, my lady,' I says. ' Bother my skirts,' says her ladyship, ' and do go away, Ellen. I shall scream if I see you fidgeting about there. You get on my nerves,' she says. Well, I didn't see why I should go on, not after being spoken to like that. It's very nice to be a ladyship, and all your tempers coddled and called nervous prostration. I know I was dreadfully cut up about poor Bert, my young man what was killed in the war—nearly cried my eyes out, I did ; but, law ! Mr. Bunter, I'd be ashamed to go on so. Besides, between you and I and the gate-post, Lady Mary wasn't that fond of the Captain. Never appreciated him, that's what I said to cook at the time, and she agreed with me. He had a way with him, the Captain had. Always quite the gentleman, of course, and never said anything as wasn't his place—I don't mean that—but I mean as it was a pleasure to do anythink for him. Such a handsome man as he was, too, Mr. Bunter."

" Ah ! " said Mr. Bunter. " So on the whole her ladyship was a bit more upset than you expected her to be ? "

" Well, to tell you the truth, Mr. Bunter, I think it's just temper. She wanted to get married and away from home. Drat this stain ! It's regular dried in. She and his grace never could get on, and when she was away in London during the war she had a rare old time, nursing officers, and going about with all kinds of queer people his grace didn't approve of. Then she had some sort of a love-affair with some quite low-down sort of fellow, so cook says ; I think he was one of them dirty Russians as wants to blow us all to smithereens—as if there hadn't been enough people blown up in the war already ! Anyhow, his grace made a dreadful fuss, and stopped supplies, and sent for her ladyship home, and ever since then she's been just mad to be off with somebody. Full of notions, she is. Makes me tired, I can tell you. Now, I'm sorry for his grace. I can see what he thinks. Poor gentleman ! And then to be taken up for murder and put in gaol, just like one of them nasty tramps. Fancy ! "

Ellen, having exhausted her breath and finished cleaning off the bloodstains, paused and straightened her back.

" Hard work it is," she said, " rubbing; I quite ache."

" If you would allow me to help you," said Mr. Bunter, appropriating the hot water, the benzene bottle, and the sponge.

He turned up another breadth of the skirt.

" Have you got a brush handy," he asked, " to take this mud off ? "

" You're as blind as a bat, Mr. Bunter," said Ellen, giggling. " Can't you see it just in front of you ? "

" Ah, yes," said the valet. " But that's not as hard a one as I'd like. Just you run and get me a real hard one, there's a dear good girl, and I'll fix this for you."

" Cheek ! " said Ellen. " But," she added, relenting before the admiring gleam in Mr. Bunter's eye, " I'll get the clothes-brush out of the hall for you. That's as hard as a brick-bat, that is."

No sooner was she out of the room than Mr. Bunter produced a pocket-knife and two more pill-boxes. In a twinkling of an eye he had scraped the surface of the skirt in two places and written two fresh labels :

" Gravel from Lady Mary's skirt, about 6 in. from hem."

" Silver sand from hem of Lady Mary's skirt."

He added the date, and had hardly pocketed the boxes when Ellen returned with the clothes-brush. The cleaning process continued for some time, to the accompaniment of desultory conversation. A third stain on the skirt caused Mr. Bunter to stare critically.

" Hullo ! " he said. " Her ladyship's been trying her hand at cleaning this herself."

" What ? " cried Ellen. She peered closely at the mark, which at one edge was smeared and whitened, and had a slightly greasy appearance.

"Well, I never," she exclaimed, "so she has! Whatever's that for, I wonder? And her pretending to be so ill she couldn't raise her head off the pillow. She's a sly one, she is."

"Couldn't it have been done before?" suggested Mr. Bunter.

"Well, she might have been at it between the day the Captain was killed and the inquest," agreed Ellen, "though you wouldn't think that was a time to choose to begin learning domestic work. *She* ain't much hand at it, anyhow, for all her nursing. I never believed that came to anything."

"She's used soap," said Mr. Bunter, benzening away resolutely. "Can she boil water in her bedroom?"

"Now, whatever should she do that for, Mr. Bunter?" exclaimed Ellen, amazed. "You don't think she keeps a kettle? I bring up her morning tea. Ladyships don't want to boil water."

"No," said Mr. Bunter, "and why didn't she get it from the bathroom?" He scrutinised the stain more carefully still. "Very amateurish," he said; "distinctly amateurish. Interrupted, I fancy. An energetic young lady, but not ingenious."

The last remarks were addressed in confidence to the benzene bottle. Ellen had put her head out of the window to talk to the gamekeeper.

. . . .

The Police Superintendent at Ripley received Lord Peter at first frigidly, and later, when he found out who he was, with a mixture of the official attitude to private detectives and the official attitude to a Duke's son.

"I've come to you," said Wimsey, "because you can do this combin'-out business a sight better'n an amateur like myself. I suppose your fine organisation's hard at work already, what?"

"Naturally," said the Superintendent, "but it's not altogether easy to trace a motor-cycle without knowing the number. Look at the Bournemouth Murder." He shook his head regretfully and accepted a Villar y Villar.

" We didn't think at first of connecting him with the number-plate business," the Superintendent went on in a careless tone which somehow conveyed to Lord Peter that his own remarks within the last half-hour had established the connection in the official mind for the first time. " Of course, if he'd been seen going through Ripley *without* a number-plate he'd have been noticed and stopped, whereas with Mr. Foulis's he was as safe as —as the Bank of England," he concluded in a burst of originality.

" Obviously," said Wimsey. " Very agitatin' for the parson, poor chap. So early in the mornin', too. I suppose it was just taken to be a practical joke ? "

" Just that," agreed the Superintendent, " but, after hearing what you have to tell us, we shall use our best efforts to get the man. I expect his grace won't be any too sorry to hear he's found. You may rely on us, and if we find the man or the number-plates——"

" Lord bless us and save us, man," broke in Lord Peter with unexpected vivacity, " you're not goin' to waste your time lookin' for the number-plates. What d'you s'pose he'd pinch the curate's plates for if he wanted to advertise his own about the neighbourhood ? Once you drop on them you've got his name and address; s'long as they're in his trousers pocket you're up a gum-tree. Now, forgive me, Superintendent, for shovin' along with my opinion, but I simply can't bear to think of you takin' all that trouble for nothin'—draggin' ponds an' turnin' over rubbish-heaps to look for number-plates that ain't there. You just scour the railway-stations for a young man six foot one or two with a No. 10 shoe, and dressed in a Burberry that's lost its belt, and with a deep scratch on one of his hands. And look here, here's my address, and I'll be very grateful if you'll let me know anything that turns up. So awkward for my brother, y'know, all this. Sensitive man ; feels it keenly. By the way, I'm a very uncertain bird—always hoppin' about ; you might wire me any news in duplicate, to Riddlesdale and to town—110 Piccadilly. Always delighted to see you, by the way, if ever you're in town. You'll forgive me slopin' off now, won't you ? I've got a lot to do."

. . . .

Returning to Riddlesdale, Lord Peter found a new visitor seated at the tea-table. At Peter's entry he rose into towering height, and extended a shapely, expressive hand that would have made an actor's fortune. He was not an actor, but he found this hand useful, nevertheless, in the exploitation of dramatic moments. His magnificent build and the nobility of his head and mask were impressive ; his features were flawless ; his eyes ruthless. The Dowager Duchess had once remarked : " Sir Impey Biggs is the handsomest man in England, and no woman will ever care twopence for him." He was, in fact, thirty-eight, and a bachelor, and was celebrated for his rhetoric and his suave but pitiless dissection of hostile witnesses. The breeding of canaries was his unexpected hobby, and besides their song he could appreciate no music but revue airs. He answered Wimsey's greeting in his beautiful, resonant, and exquisitely controlled voice. Tragic irony, cutting contempt, or a savage indignation were the emotions by which Sir Impey Biggs swayed court and jury ; he prosecuted murderers of the innocent, defended in actions for criminal libel, and, moving others, was himself as stone. Wimsey expressed himself delighted to see him in a voice, by contrast, more husky and hesitant even than usual.

" You just come from Jerry ? " he asked. " Fresh toast, please Fleming. How is he ? Enjoyin' it ? I never knew a fellow like Jerry for gettin' the least possible out of any situation. I'd rather like the experience myself, you know ; only I'd hate bein' shut up and watchin' the other idiots bunglin' my case. No reflection on Murbles and you, Biggs. I mean myself—I mean the man who'd be me if I was Jerry. You follow me ? "

" I was just saying to Sir Impey," said the Duchess, " that he really must make Gerald say what he was doing in the garden at three in the morning. If only I'd been at Riddlesdale none of this would have happened. Of course, *we* all know that he wasn't doing any harm, but we can't expect the jurymen to understand that. The lower orders are so prejudiced. It is absurd of Gerald not to realise that he must speak out. He has *no* consideration."

" I am doing my very best to persuade him, Duchess," said Sir Impey, " but you must have patience. Lawyers enjoy a little mystery, you know. Why, if everybody came forward and told the truth, the whole truth, and nothing but the truth straight out, we should all retire to the workhouse."

" Captain Cathcart's death is very mysterious," said the Duchess, " though when I think of the things that have come out about him it really seems quite providential, as far as my sister-in-law is concerned."

" I s'pose you couldn't get 'em to bring it in ' Death by the Visitation of God,' could you, Biggs ? " suggested Lord Peter. " Sort of judgment for wantin' to marry into our family, what ? "

" I have known less reasonable verdicts," returned Biggs dryly.. " It's wonderful what you can suggest to a jury if you try. I remember once at the Liverpool Assizes——"

He steered skilfully away into a quiet channel of reminiscence. Lord Peter watched his statuesque profile against the fire ; it reminded him of the severe beauty of the charioteer of Delphi and was about as communicative.

. . . . .

It was not until after dinner that Sir Impey opened his mind to Wimsey. The Duchess had gone to bed, and the two men were alone in the library. Peter, scrupulously in evening dress, had been valeted by Bunter, and had been more than usually rambling and cheerful all evening. He now took a cigar, retired to the largest chair, and effaced himself in a complete silence.

Sir Impey Biggs walked up and down for some half-hour, smoking. Then he came across with determination, brutally switched on a reading-lamp right into Peter's face, sat down opposite to him, and said:

" Now, Wimsey, I want to know all you know."

" Do you, though ? " said Peter. He got up, disconnected the reading-lamp, and carried it away to a side-table.

" No bullying of the witness, though," he added, and grinned.

" I don't care so long as you wake up," said Biggs, unperturbed. " Now then."

Lord Peter removed his cigar from his mouth, considered it with his head on one side, turned it carefully over, decided that the ash could hang on to its parent leaf for another minute or two, smoked without speaking until collapse was inevitable, took the cigar out again, deposited the ash entire in the exact centre of the ash-tray, and began his statement, omitting only the matter of the suit-case and Bunter's information obtained from Ellen.

Sir Impey Biggs listened with what Peter irritably described as a cross-examining countenance, putting a sharp question every now and again. He made a few notes, and, when Wimsey had finished, sat tapping his note-book thoughtfully.

" I think we can make a case out of this," he said, " even if the police don't find your mysterious man. Denver's silence is an awkward complication, of course." He hooded his eyes for a moment. " Did you say you'd put the police on to find the fellow ? "

" Yes."

" Have you a very poor opinion of the police ? "

" Not for that kind of thing. That's in their line ;
they have all the facilities, and do it well."

" Ah ! You expect to find the man, do you ? "

" I hope to."

" Ah ! What do you think is going to happen to my
case if you *do* find him, Wimsey ? "

" What do I——"

" See here, Wimsey," said the barrister, "you are not
a fool, and it's no use trying to look like a country
policeman. You are really trying to find this man ? "

" Certainly."

" Just as you like, of course, but my hands are rather
tied already. Has it ever occurred to you that perhaps
he'd better not be found ? "

Wimsey stared at the lawyer with such honest astonishment as actually to disarm him.

" Remember this," said the latter earnestly, " that
if once the police get hold of a thing or a person it's no
use relying on my, or Murbles's, or anybody's professional discretion. Everything's raked out into the
light of common day, and very common it is. Here's
Denver accused of murder, and he refuses in the most
categorical way to give me the smallest assistance."

" Jerry's an ass. He doesn't realise——"

" Do you suppose," broke in Biggs, " I have not made
it my business to *make* him realise ? All he says is,
' They can't hang me ; I didn't kill the man, though
I think it's a jolly good thing he's dead. It's no business
of theirs what I was doing in the garden.' Now I ask
you, Wimsey, is that a reasonable attitude for a man in
Denver's position to take up ? "

Peter muttered something about " Never had any
sense."

" Had anybody told Denver about this other
man ? "

" Something vague was said about footsteps at the
inquest, I believe."

" That Scotland Yard man is your personal friend, I'm told ? "

" Yes."

" So much the better. He can hold his tongue."

" Look here, Biggs, this is all damned impressive and mysterious, but what are you gettin' at ? Why shouldn't I lay hold of the beggar if I can ? "

" I'll answer that question by another." Sir Impey leaned forward a little. " Why is Denver screening him ? "

Sir Impey Biggs was accustomed to boast that no witness could perjure himself in his presence undetected. As he put the question, he released the other's eyes from his, and glanced down with finest cunning at Wimsey's long, flexible mouth and nervous hands. When he glanced up again a second later he met the eyes passing, guarded and inscrutable, through all the changes expressive of surprised enlightenment ; but by that time it was too late ; he had seen a little line at the corner of the mouth fade out, and the fingers relax ever so slightly. The first movement had been one of relief.

" B'Jove ! " said Peter. " I never thought of that. What sleuths you lawyers are. If that's so, I'd better be careful, hadn't I ? Always was a bit rash. My mother says—— "

" You're a clever devil, Wimsey," said the barrister. " I may be wrong, then. Find your man by all means. There's just one other thing I'd like to ask. Whom are *you* screening ? "

" Look here, Biggs," said Wimsey, " you're not paid to ask that kind of question here, you know. You can jolly well wait till you get into court. It's your job to make the best of the stuff we serve up to you, not to give us the third degree. Suppose I murdered Cathcart myself—— "

" You didn't."

" I know I didn't, but if I did I'm not goin' to have you askin' questions and lookin' at me in that tone of

voice. However, just to oblige you, I don't mind sayin'
plainly that I don't know who did away with the fellow.
When I do I'll tell you."

" You will ? "

" Yes, I will, but not till I'm sure. You people can
make such a little circumstantial evidence go such a
damn long way, you might hang me while I was only
in the early stages of suspectin' myself."

" H'm ! " said Biggs. " Meanwhile, I tell you candidly, I am taking the line that they can't make out
a case."

" Not proven, eh ? Well, anyhow, Biggs, I swear my
brother shan't hang for lack of my evidence."

" Of course not," said Biggs, adding inwardly : " but
you hope it won't come to that."

A spurt of rain plashed down the wide chimney and
sizzled on the logs.

.   .   .   .

" Craven Hotel,
" Strand, W.C.,
" *Tuesday.*

" MY DEAR WIMSEY,—A line as I promised, to
report progress, but it's precious little. On the
journey up I sat next to Mrs. Pettigrew-Robinson,
and opened and shut the window for her and looked
after her parcels. She mentioned that when your
sister roused the household on Thursday morning she
went first to Mr. Arbuthnot's room—a circumstance
which the lady seemed to think odd, but which is
natural enough when you come to think of it, the room
being directly opposite the head of the staircase. It
was Mr. Arbuthnot who knocked up the Pettigrew-
Robinsons, and Mr. P. ran downstairs immediately.
Mrs. P. then saw that Lady Mary was looking very
faint, and tried to support her. Your sister threw her
off—rudely, Mrs. P. says—declined ' in a most savage
manner ' all offers of assistance, rushed to her own

82

room, and locked herself in. Mrs. Pettigrew-Robinson listened at the door ' to make sure,' as she says, ' that everything was all right,' but, hearing her moving about and slamming cupboards, she concluded that she would have more chance of poking her finger into the pie downstairs, and departed.

" If Mrs. Marchbanks had told me this, I admit I should have thought the episode worth looking into, but I feel strongly that if I were dying I should still lock the door between myself and Mrs. Pettigrew-Robinson. Mrs. P. was quite sure that at no time had Lady Mary anything in her hand. She was dressed as described at the inquest—a long coat over her pyjamas (sleeping suit was Mrs. P's expression), stout shoes, and a woolly cap, and she kept these garments on throughout the subsequent visit of the doctor. Another odd little circumstance is that Mrs. Pettigrew-Robinson (who was awake, you remember, from 2. a.m. onwards) is certain that just *before* Lady Mary knocked on Mr. Arbuthnot's door she heard a door slam somewhere in the passage. I don't know what to make of this—perhaps there's nothing in it, but I just mention it.

" I've had a rotten time in town. Your brother-in-law elect was a model of discretion. His room at the Albany is a desert from a detecting point of view ; no papers except a few English bills and receipts, and invitations. I looked up a few of his inviters, but they were mostly men who had met him at the club or knew him in the Army, and could tell me nothing about his private life. He is known at several night-clubs. I made the round of them last night—or, rather, this morning. General verdict : generous but impervious. By the way, poker seems to have been his great game. No suggestion of anything crooked. He won pretty consistently on the whole, but never very spectacularly.

"I think the information we want must be in Paris.

I have written to the Sûreté and the Crédit Lyonnais to produce his papers, especially his account and cheque-book.

" I'm pretty dead with yesterday's and to-day's work. Dancing all night on top of a journey is a jolly poor joke. Unless you want me, I'll wait here for the papers, or I may run over to Paris myself.

" Cathcart's books here consist of a few modern French novels of the usual kind, and another copy of *Manon* with what the catalogues call ' curious ' plates. He must have had a life somewhere, mustn't he ?

" The enclosed bill from a beauty specialist in Bond Street may interest you. I called on her. She says he came regularly every week when he was in England.

" I drew quite blank at King's Fenton on Sunday —oh, but I told you that. I don't think the fellow ever went there. I wonder if he slunk off up into the moor. Is it worth rummaging about, do you think ? Rather like looking for a needle in a bundle of hay, It's odd about that diamond cat. You've got nothing out of the household, I suppose ? It doesn't seem to fit No. 10, somehow—and yet you'd think somebody would have heard about it in the village if it had been lost. Well, so long,

" Yours ever,
" CH. PARKER."

CHAPTER IV

—AND HIS DAUGHTER, MUCH-AFRAID

The women also looked pale and wan.—
The Pilgrim's Progress.

MR. BUNTER brought Parker's letter up to Lord Peter in bed on the Wednesday morning. The house was almost deserted, everybody having gone to attend the police-court proceedings at Northallerton. The thing would be purely formal, of course, but it seemed only proper that the family should be fully represented. The Dowager Duchess, indeed, was there—she had promptly hastened to her son's side and was living heroically in furnished lodgings, but the younger Duchess thought her mother-in-law more energetic than dignified. There was no knowing what she might do if left to herself. She might even give an interview to a newspaper reporter. Besides, at these moments of crisis a wife's right place is at her husband's side. Lady Mary was ill, and nothing could be said about that, and if Peter chose to stay smoking cigarettes in his pyjamas while his only brother was undergoing public humiliation, that was only what might be expected. Peter took after his mother. How that eccentric strain had got into the family her grace could not imagine, for the Dowager came of a good Hampshire family ; there must have been some foreign blood somewhere. Her own duty was clear, and she would do it.

Lord Peter was awake, and looked rather fagged, as though he had been sleuthing in his sleep. Mr. Bunter wrapped him solicitously in a brilliant Oriental robe, and placed the tray on his knees.

"Bunter," said Lord Peter rather fretfully, "your *café au lait* is the one tolerable incident in this beastly place."

"Thank you, my lord. Very chilly again this morning, my lord, but not actually raining."

Lord Peter frowned over his letter.

"Anything in the paper, Bunter?"

"Nothing urgent, my lord. A sale next week at Northbury Hall—Mr. Fleetwhite's library, my lord—a Caxton *Confessio Amantis*——"

"What's the good of tellin' me that when we're stuck up here for God knows how long? I wish to heaven I'd stuck to books and never touched crime. Did you send those specimens up to Lubbock?"

"Yes, my lord," said Bunter gently. Dr. Lubbock was the "analytical gentleman."

"Must have facts," said Lord Peter, "facts. When I was a small boy I always hated facts. Thought of 'em as nasty, hard things, all knobs. Uncompromisin'."

"Yes, my lord. My old mother——"

"Your mother, Bunter? I didn't know you had one. I always imagined you were turned out ready-made, so to speak. 'Scuse me. Infernally rude of me. Beg your pardon, I'm sure."

"Not at all, my lord. My mother lives in Kent, my lord, near Maidstone. Seventy-five, my lord, and an extremely active woman for her years, if you'll excuse my mentioning it. I was one of seven."

"That is an invention, Bunter. I know better. You are unique. But I interrupted you. You were goin' to tell me about your mother."

"She always says, my lord, that facts are like cows. If you look them in the face hard enough they generally run away. She is a very courageous woman, my lord."

Lord Peter stretched out his hand impulsively, but Mr. Bunter was too well trained to see it. He had, indeed, already begun to strop a razor. Lord Peter suddenly bundled out of bed with a violent jerk and sped across the landing to the bathroom.

Here he revived sufficiently to lift up his voice in " Come unto these Yellow Sands." Thence, feeling in a Purcellish mood, he passed to " I attempt from Love's Fever to Fly," with such improvement of spirits that, against all custom, he ran several gallons of cold water into the bath and sponged himself vigorously. Wherefore, after a rough towelling, he burst explosively from the bathroom, and caught his shin somewhat violently against the lid of a large oak chest which stood at the head of the staircase—so violently, indeed, that the lid lifted with the shock and shut down with a protesting bang.

Lord Peter stopped to say something expressive and to caress his leg softly with the palm of his hand. Then a thought struck him. He set down his towels, soap, sponge, loofah, bath-brush, and other belongings, and quietly lifted the lid of the chest.

Whether, like the heroine of *Northanger Abbey*, he expected to find anything gruesome inside was not apparent. It is certain that, like her, he beheld nothing more startling than certain sheets and counterpanes neatly folded at the bottom. Unsatisfied, he lifted the top one of these gingerly and inspected it for a few moments in the light of the staircase window. He was just returning it to its place, whistling softly the while, when a little hiss of indrawn breath caused him to look up with a start.

His sister was at his elbow. He had not heard her come, but she stood there in her dressing-gown, her hands clutched together on her breast. Her blue eyes were dilated till they looked almost black, and her skin seemed nearly the colour of her ash-blonde hair. Wimsey stared at her over the sheet he held in his arms, and the terror in her face passed over into his, stamping them suddenly with the mysterious likeness of blood-relationship.

87

Peter's own impression was that he stared "like a stuck pig" for about a minute. He knew, as a matter of fact, that he had recovered himself in a fraction of a second. He dropped the sheet into the chest and stood up.

"Hullo, Polly, old thing," he said, "where've you been hidin' all this time? First time I've seen you. 'Fraid you've been havin' a pretty thin time of it."

He put his arm round her, and felt her shrink.

"What's the matter?" he demanded. "What's up, old girl? Look here, Mary, we've never seen enough of each other, but I am your brother. Are you in trouble? Can't I——"

"Trouble?" she said. "Why, you silly old Peter, of course I'm in trouble. Don't you know they've killed my man and put my brother in prison? Isn't that enough to be in trouble about?" She laughed, and Peter suddenly thought, "She's talking like somebody in a blood-and-thunder novel." She went on more naturally. "It's all right, Peter, truly—only my head's so bad. I really don't know what I'm doing. What are you after? You made such a noise, I came out. I thought it was a door banging."

"You'd better toddle back to bed," said Lord Peter. "You're gettin' all cold. Why do girls wear such mimsy little pyjimjams in this damn cold climate? There, don't you worry. I'll drop in on you later and we'll have a jolly old pow-wow, what?"

"Not to-day—not to-day, Peter. I'm going mad, I think." ("Sensation fiction again," thought Peter.) "Are they trying Gerald to-day?"

"Not exactly trying," said Peter, urging her gently along to her room. "It's just formal, y'know. The jolly old magistrate bird hears the charge read, and then old Murbles pops up and says please he wants only formal evidence given as he has to instruct counsel. That's Biggy, y'know. Then they hear the evidence of arrest, and Murbles says old Gerald reserves his defence.

That's all till the Assizes—evidence before the Grand Jury—a lot of bosh! That'll be early next month, I suppose. You'll have to buck up and be fit by then."

Mary shuddered.

" No—no ! Couldn't I get out of it ? I couldn't go through it all again. I should be sick. I'm feeling awful. No, don't come in. I don't want you. Ring the bell for Ellen. No, let go ; go away ! I don't want you, Peter ! "

Peter hesitated, a little alarmed.

" Much better not, my lord, if you'll excuse me," said Bunter's voice at his ear. " Only produce hysterics," he added, as he drew his master gently from the door. " Very distressing for both parties, and altogether unproductive of results. Better to wait for the return of her grace, the Dowager."

" Quite right," said Peter. He turned back to pick up his paraphernalia, but was dexterously forestalled. Once again he lifted the lid of the chest and looked in.

" What did you say you found on that skirt, Bunter ? "

" Gravel, my lord, and silver sand."

" Silver sand."

. . . .

Behind Riddlesdale Lodge the moor stretched starkly away and upward. The heather was brown and wet, and the little streams had no colour in them. It was six o'clock, but there was no sunset. Only a paleness had moved behind the thick sky from east to west all day. Lord Peter, tramping back after a long and fruitless search for tidings of the man with the motor-cycle, voiced the dull suffering of his gregarious spirit. " I wish old Parker was here," he muttered, and squelched down a sheep-track.

He was making, not directly for the Lodge, but for a farmhouse about two and a half miles distant from it, known as Grider's Hole. It lay almost due north of Riddlesdale village, a lonely outpost on the edge of the

89

moor, in a valley of fertile land between two wide swells of heather. The track wound down from the height called Whemmeling Fell, skirted a vile swamp, and crossed the little river Ridd about half a mile before reaching the farm. Peter had small hope of hearing any news at Grider's Hole, but he was filled with a sullen determination to leave no stone unturned. Privately, however, he felt convinced that the motor-cycle had come by the high road, Parker's investigations notwithstanding, and perhaps passed directly through King's Fenton without stopping or attracting attention. Still, he had said he would search the neighbourhood, and Grider's Hole was in the neighbourhood. He paused to relight his pipe, then squelched steadily on. The path was marked with stout white posts at regular intervals, and presently with hurdles. The reason for this was apparent as one came to the bottom of the valley, for only a few yards on the left began the stretch of rough, reedy tussocks, with slobbering black bog between them, in which anything heavier than a water-wagtail would speedily suffer change into a succession of little bubbles. Wimsey stooped for an empty sardine-tin which lay, horridly battered, at his feet, and slung it idly into the quag. It struck the surface with a noise like a wet kiss, and vanished instantly. With that instinct which prompts one, when depressed, to wallow in every circumstance of gloom, Peter leaned sadly upon the hurdles and abandoned himself to a variety of shallow considerations upon (1) The vanity of human wishes ; (2) Mutability ; (3) First love ; (4) The decay of idealism ; (5) The aftermath of the Great War ; (6) Birth-control ; and (7) The fallacy of free-will. This was his nadir, however. Realising that his feet were cold and his stomach empty, and that he had still some miles to go, he crossed the stream on a row of slippery stepping-stones and approached the gate of the farm, which was not an ordinary five-barred one, but solid and uncompromising. A man was leaning over it, sucking a straw. He made no attempt to move at Wimsey's approach. "Good evening," said that nobleman in a sprightly manner, laying his hand on the catch. "Chilly, ain't it?"

The man made no reply, but leaned more heavily, and breathed. He wore a rough coat and breeches, and his leggings were covered with manure.

"Seasonable, of course, what?" said Peter. "Good for the sheep, I daresay. Makes their wool curl, and so on."

The man removed the straw and spat in the direction of Peter's right boot.

"Do you lose many animals in the bog?" went on Peter, carelessly unlatching the gate, and leaning upon it in the opposite direction. "I see you have a good wall all round the house. Must be a bit dangerous in the dark, what, if you're thinkin' of takin' a little evenin' stroll with a friend?"

The man spat again, pulled his hat over his forehead, and said briefly:

"What doost 'a want?"

"Well," said Peter, "I thought of payin' a little friendly call on Mr.—on the owner of this farm, that is to say. Country neighbours, and all that. Lonely kind of country, don't you see. Is he in, d'ye think?"

The man grunted.

"I'm glad to hear it," said Peter; "it's so uncommonly jolly findin' all you Yorkshire people so kind and hospitable, what? Never mind who you are, always a seat at the fireside and that kind of thing. Excuse me, but do you know you're leanin' on the gate so as I can't open it? I'm sure it's a pure oversight, only you mayn't realise that just where you're standin' you get the maximum of leverage. What an awfully charmin' house this is, isn't it? All so jolly stark and grim and all the rest of it. No creepers or little rose-grown porches or anything suburban of that sort. Who lives in it?"

91

The man surveyed him up and down for some moments, and replied, " Mester Grimethorpe."

" No, does he now ? " said Lord Peter. " To think of that. Just the fellow I want to see. Model farmer, what ? Wherever I go throughout the length and breadth of the North Riding I hear of Mr. Grimethorpe. ' Grimethorpe's butter is the best ' ; ' Grimethorpe's fleeces Never go to pieces ' ; ' Grimethorpe's pork Melts on the fork '; ' For Irish stews Take Grimethorpe's ewes ' ; ' A tummy lined with Grimethorpe's beef, Never, never comes to grief.' It has been my life's ambition to see Mr. Grimethorpe in the flesh. And you no doubt are his sturdy henchman and right-hand man. You leap from bed before the breaking-day, To milk the kine amid the scented hay. You, when the shades of evening gather deep, Home from the mountain lead the mild-eyed sheep. You, by the ingle's red and welcoming blaze, Tell your sweet infants tales of olden days ! A wonderful life, though a trifle monotonous p'raps in the winter. Allow me to clasp your honest hand."

Whether the man was moved by this lyric outburst, or whether the failing light was not too dim to strike a pale sheen from the metal in Lord Peter's palm, at any rate he moved a trifle back from the gate.

" Thanks awfully, old bean," said Peter, stepping briskly past him. " I take it I shall find Mr. Grimethorpe in the house ? "

The man said nothing till Wimsey had proceeded about a dozen yards up the flagged path, then he hailed him, but without turning round.

" Mester ! "

" Yes, old thing ? " said Peter affably, returning.

" Happen he'll set dog on tha."

" You don't say so ? " said Peter. " The faithful hound welcomes the return of the prodigal. Scene of family rejoicing. ' My own long lost boy ! ' Sobs and speeches, beer all round for the delighted tenantry.

Glees by the old fireside, till the rafters ring and all the smoked hams tumble down to join in the revelry. Good night, sweet Prince, until the cows come home and the dogs eat Jezebel in the portion of Jezreel when the hounds of spring are on winter's traces. I suppose," he added to himself, " they will have finished tea."

As Lord Peter approached the door of the farm his spirits rose. He enjoyed paying this kind of visit. Although he had taken to detecting as he might, with another conscience or constitution, have taken to Indian hemp—for its exhilarating properties—at a moment when life seemed dust and ashes, he had not primarily the detective temperament. He expected next to nothing from inquiries at Grider's Hole, and, if he had, he might probably have extracted all the information he wanted by a judicious display of Treasury notes to the glum man at the gate. Parker would in all likelihood have done so ; he was paid to detect and to do nothing else, and neither his natural gifts nor his education (at Barrow-in-Furness Grammar School) prompted him to stray into side-tracks at the beck of an ill-regulated imagination. But to Lord Peter the world presented itself as an entertaining labyrinth of side-issues. He was a respectable scholar in five or six languages, a musician of some skill and more understanding, something of an expert in toxicology, a collector of rare editions, an entertaining man-about-town, and a common sensationalist. He had been seen at half-past twelve on a Sunday morning walking in Hyde Park in a top-hat and frock-coat, reading the *News of the World*. His passion for the unexplored led him to hunt up obscure pamphlets in the British Museum, to unravel the emotional history of income-tax collectors, and to find out where his own drains led to. In this case, the fascinating problem of a Yorkshire farmer who habitually set the dogs on casual visitors imperatively demanded investigation in a personal interview. The result was unexpected.

His first summons was unheeded, and he knocked

again. This time there was a movement, and a surly male voice called out :

" Well, let 'un in then, dang 'un—and dang *thee*," emphasised by the sound of something falling or thrown across the room.

The door was opened unexpectedly by a little girl of about seven, very dark and pretty, and rubbing her arm as though the missile had caught her there. She stood defensively, blocking the threshold, till the same voice growled impatiently :

" Well, who is it ? "

" Good evening," said Wimsey, removing his hat. " I hope you'll excuse me droppin' in like this. I'm livin' at Riddlesdale Lodge."

" What of it ? " demanded the voice. Above the child's head Wimsey saw the outline of a big, thick-set man smoking in the inglenook of an immense fireplace. There was no light but the firelight, for the window was small, and dusk had already fallen. It seemed to be a large room, but a high oak settle on the farther side of the chimney ran out across it, leaving a cavern of impenetrable blackness beyond.

" May I come in ? " said Wimsey.

" If tha must," said the man ungraciously. " Shoot door, lass ; what art starin' at ? Go to thi moother and bid her mend thi manners for thee."

This seemed a case of the pot lecturing the kettle on cleanliness, but the child vanished hurriedly into the blackness behind the settle, and Peter walked in.

" Are you Mr. Grimethorpe ? " he asked politely.

" What if I am ? " retorted the farmer. " *I've* no call to be ashamed o' my name."

" Rather not," said Lord Peter, " nor of your farm. Delightful place, what ? My name's Wimsey, by the way—Lord Peter Wimsey, in fact, the Duke of Denver's brother, y'know. I'm sure I hate interruptin' you—you must be busy with the sheep and all that —but I thought you wouldn't mind if I just ran over in a neighbourly.

way. Lonely sort of country, ain't it? I like to know the people next door, and all that sort of thing. I'm used to London, you see, where people live pretty thick on the ground. I suppose very few strangers ever pass this way?"

"None," said Mr. Grimethorpe, with decision.

"Well, perhaps it's as well," pursued Lord Peter. "Makes one appreciate one's home circle more, what? Often think one sees too many strangers in town. Nothing like one's family when all's said and done—cosy, don't you know. You a married man, Mr. Grimethorpe?"

"What the hell's that to you?" growled the farmer, rounding on him with such ferocity that Wimsey looked about quite nervously for the dogs before-mentioned.

"Oh, nothin'," he replied, "only I thought that charmin' little girl might be yours."

"And if I thought she weren't," said Mr. Grimethorpe, "I'd strangle the bitch and her mother together. What hast got to say to that?"

As a matter of fact, the remark, considered as a conversational formula, seemed to leave so much to be desired that Wimsey's natural loquacity suffered a severe check. He fell back, however, on the usual resource of the male, and offered Mr. Grimethorpe a cigar, thinking to himself as he did so:

"What a hell of a life the woman must lead."

The farmer declined the cigar with a single word, and was silent. Wimsey lit a cigarette for himself and became meditative, watching his companion. He was a man of about forty-five, apparently, rough, harsh, and weather-beaten, with great ridgy shoulders and short, thick thighs—a bull-terrier with a bad temper. Deciding that delicate hints would be wasted on such an organism, Wimsey adopted a franker method.

"To tell the truth, Mr. Grimethorpe," he said, "I didn't blow in without any excuse at all. Always best to provide oneself with an excuse for a call, what?

Though it's so perfectly delightful to see you—I mean, no excuse might appear necessary. But fact is, I'm looking for a young man—a—an acquaintance of mine—who said he'd be roamin' about this neighbourhood some time or other about now. Only I'm afraid I may have missed him. You see, I've only just got over from Corsica—interestin' country and all that, Mr. Grimethorpe, but a trifle out of the way—and from what my friend said I think he must have turned up here about a week ago and found me out. Just my luck. But he didn't leave his card, so I can't be quite sure, you see. You didn't happen to come across him by any chance? Tall fellow with big feet on a motor-cycle with a side-car. I thought he might have come rootin' about here. Hullo! d'you know him?"

The farmer's face had become swollen and almost black with rage.

"What day sayst tha?" he demanded thickly.

"I thould think last Wednesday night or Thursday morning," said Peter, with a hand on his heavy malacca cane.

"I knew it," growled Mr. Grimethorpe. "—— the slut, and all these dommed women wi' their dirty ways. Look here, mester. The tyke were a friend o' thine? Well, I wor at Stapley Wednesday and Thursday—tha knew that, didn't tha? And so did thi friend, didn't 'un? An' if I hadn't, it'd 'a' bin the worse for 'un. He'd 'a' been in Peter's Pot if I'd 'a' cot 'un, an' that's where tha'll be thesen in a minute, blast tha! And if I find 'un sneakin' here again, I'll blast every boon in a's body and send 'un to look for thee there."

And with these surprising words he made for Peter's throat like a bull-dog.

"That won't do," said Peter, disengaging himself with an ease which astonished his opponent, and catching his wrist in a grip of mysterious and excruciating agony. "'Tisn't wise, y'know—might murder a fellow like that. Nasty business, murder. Coroner's inquest and all

96

that sort of thing. Counsel for the Prosecution askin'
all sorts of inquisitive questions, and a feller puttin' a
string round your neck. Besides, your method's a bit
primitive. Stand still, you fool, or you'll break your
arm. Feelin' better? That's right. Sit down. You'll
get into trouble one of these days, behavin' like that
when you're asked a civil question."

" Get out o' t'house," said Mr. Grimethorpe sullenly.

" Certainly," said Peter. " I have to thank you for a
very entertainin' evenin', Mr. Grimethorpe. I'm sorry
you can give me no news of my friend——"

Mr. Grimethorpe sprang up with a blasphemous
ejaculation, and made for the door, shouting " Jabez!"
Lord Peter stared after him for a moment, and then
stared round the room.

" Something fishy here," he said. " Fellow knows
somethin'. Murderous sort of brute. I wonder——"

He peered round the settle, and came face to face
with a woman—a dim patch of whiteness in the thick
shadow.

" You? " she said, in a low, hoarse gasp. " You?
You are mad to come here. Quick, quick! He has
gone for the dogs."

She placed her two hands on his breast, thrusting
him urgently back. Then, as the firelight fell upon his
face, she uttered a stifled shriek and stood petrified—a
Medusa-head of terror.

Medusa was beautiful, says the tale, and so was this
woman; a broad white forehead under massed, dusky
hair, black eyes glowing under straight brows, a wide,
passionate mouth—a shape so wonderful that even in
that strenuous moment sixteen generations of feudal
privilege stirred in Lord Peter's blood. His hands closed
over hers instinctively, but she pulled herself hurriedly
away and shrank back.

" Madam," said Wimsey, recovering himself, " I don't
quite——"

A thousand questions surged up in his mind, but

before he could frame them a long yell, and another, and then another came from the back of the house.

" Run, run ! " she said. " The dogs ! My God, my God, what will become of me ? Go, if you don't want to see me killed. Go, go ! Have pity ! "

" Look here," said Peter, " can't I stay and protect——"

" You can stay and murder me," said the woman. " Go ! "

Peter cast Public School tradition to the winds, caught up his stick, and went. The brutes were at his heels as he fled. He struck the foremost with his stick, and it dropped back, snarling. The man was still leaning on the gate, and Grimethorpe's hoarse voice was heard shouting to him to seize the fugitive. Peter closed with him ; there was a scuffle of dogs and men, and suddenly Peter found himself thrown bodily over the gate. As he picked himself up and ran, he heard the farmer cursing the man and the man retorting that he couldn't help it ; then the woman's voice, uplifted in a frightened wail. He glanced over his shoulder. The man and the woman and a second man who had now joined the party, were beating the dogs back, and seemed to be persuading Grimethorpe not to let them through. Apparently their remonstrances had some effect, for the farmer turned moodily away, and the second man called the dogs off, with much whip-cracking and noise. The woman said something, and her husband turned furiously upon her and struck her to the ground.

Peter made a movement to go back, but a strong conviction that he could only make matters worse for her arrested him. He stood still, and waited till she had picked herself up and gone in, wiping the blood and dirt from her face with her shawl. The farmer looked round, shook his fist at him, and followed her into the house. Jabez collected the dogs and drove them back, and Peter's friend returned to lean over the gate.

Peter waited till the door had closed upon Mr. and Mrs. Grimethorpe ; then he pulled out his handkerchief and, in the half-darkness, signalled cautiously to the man, who slipped through the gate and came slowly down to him

" Thanks very much," said Wimsey, putting money into his hand. " I'm afraid I've done unintentional mischief."

The man looked at the money and at him.

" 'Tes t' master's way wi' them as cooms t'look at t'missus," he said. " Tha's best keep away if so be tha wutna' have her blood on tha heid."

" See here," said Peter, " did you by any chance meet a young man with a motor-cycle wanderin' round here last Wednesday or thereabouts ? "

" Naay. Wednesday ? T'wod be day t'mester went to Stapley, Ah reckon, after machines. Naay, Ah seed nowt."

" All right. If you find anybody who did, let me know. Here's my name, and I'm staying at Riddlesdale Lodge. Good night ; many thanks."

The man took the card from him and slouched back without a word of farewell.

.   .   .   .   .

Lord Peter walked slowly, his coat collar turned up and his hat pulled over his eyes. This cinematographic episode had troubled his logical faculty. With an effort he sorted out his ideas and arranged them in some kind of order.

" First item," said he, " Mr. Grimethorpe. A gentleman who will stick at nothing. Hefty. Unamiable. Inhospitable. Dominant characteristic—jealousy of his very astonishing wife. Was at Stapley last Wednesday and Thursday buying machinery. (Helpful gentleman at the gate corroborates this, by the way, so that at this stage of the proceedings one may allow it to be a sound alibi.) Did not, therefore, see our mysterious friend with the side-car, *if* he was there. But is disposed to think he *was* there, and has very little doubt about what he came for. Which raises an interestin' point. Why the side-car? Awkward thing to tour about with. Very good. But if our friend came after Mrs. G. he obviously didn't take her. Good again.

" Second item, Mrs. Grimethorpe. Very singular item. By Jove ! " He paused meditatively to reconstruct a thrilling moment. " Let us at once admit that if No. 10 came for the purpose suspected he had every excuse for it. Well ! Mrs. G. goes in terror of her husband, who thinks nothing of knocking her down on suspicion. I wish to God—but I'd only have made things worse. Only thing you can do for the wife of a brute like that is to keep away from her. Hope there won't be murder done. One's enough at a time. Where was I ? "

" Yes—well, Mrs. Grimethorpe knows something—and she knows somebody. She took me for somebody who had every reason for not coming to Grider's Hole. Where was she, I wonder, while I was talking to Grimethorpe ? She wasn't in the room. Perhaps the child warned her. No, that won't wash ; I told the child who I was. Aha ! wait a minute. Do I see light ? She looked out of the window and saw a bloke in an aged Burberry. No. 10 is a bloke in an aged Burberry. Now, let's suppose for a moment she takes me for No. 10. What does she do ? She sensibly keeps out of the way—can't think why I'm such a fool as to turn up. Then, when Grimethorpe runs out shoutin' for the kennel-man, she nips down with her life in her hands to warn her—her—shall we say boldly her lover ?—to get away. She finds it isn't her lover, but only a gaping ass of (I fear) a very comin'-on disposition. New compromisin' position. She tells the ass to save himself and herself by clearin' out. Ass clears—not too gracefully. The next instalment of this enthrallin' drama will be shown in this theatre—when ? I'd jolly well like to know."

He tramped on for some time.

" All the same," he retorted upon himself, " all this throws no light on what No. 10 was doing at Riddlesdale Lodge."

At the end of his walk he had reached no conclusion.

" Whatever happens," he said to himself, " and if it can be done without danger to her life, I must see Mrs. Grimethorpe again."

CHAPTER V

THE RUE ST. HONORÉ AND THE RUE DE LA PAIX

I think it was the cat.—H.M.S. Pinafore

MR. PARKER sat disconsolate in a small *appartement* in the Rue St. Honoré. It was three o'clock in the afternoon. Paris was full of a subdued but cheerful autumn sunlight, but the room faced north, and was depressing, with its plain, dark furniture and its deserted air. It was a man's room, well appointed after the manner of a discreet club ; a room that kept its dead owner's counsel imperturbably. Two large saddlebag chairs in crimson leather stood by the cold hearth. On the mantelpiece was a bronze clock, flanked by two polished German shells, a stone tobacco-jar, and an Oriental brass bowl containing a long-cold pipe. There were several excellent engravings in narrow pearwood frames, and the portrait in oils of a rather florid lady of the period of Charles II. The window-curtains were crimson, and the floor covered with a solid Turkey carpet. Opposite the fireplace stood a tall mahogany book-case with glass doors, containing a number of English and French classics, a large collection of books on history and international politics, various French novels, a number of works on military and sporting subjects, and a famous French edition of the *Decameron* with the additional plates. Under the window stood a large bureau.

Parker shook his head, took out a sheet of paper, and began to write a report. He had breakfasted on coffee and rolls at seven ; he had made an exhaustive search of the flat ; he had interviewed the concierge, the manager of the Crédit Lyonnais, and the Prefect of Police for the Quartier, and the result was very poor indeed.

Information obtained from Captain Cathcart's papers: Before the war Denis Cathcart had undoubtedly been a rich man. He had considerable investments in Russia and Germany and a large share in a prosperous vineyard in Champagne. After coming into his property at the age of twenty-one he had concluded his three years' residence at Cambridge, and had then travelled a good deal, visiting persons of importance in various countries, and apparently studying with a view to a diplomatic career. During the period from 1913 to 1918 the story told by the books became intensely interesting, baffling, and depressing. At the outbreak of war he had taken a commission in the 15th ——shires. With the help of the cheque-book, Parker reconstructed the whole economic life of a young British officer—clothes, horses, equipment, travelling, wine and dinners when on leave, bridge debts, rent of the flat in the Rue St. Honoré, club subscriptions, and what not. This outlay was strictly moderate and proportioned to his income. Receipted bills, neatly docketed, occupied one drawer of the bureau, and a careful comparison of these with the cheque-book and the returned cheques revealed no discrepancy. But, beyond these, there appeared to have been another heavy drain upon Cathcart's resources. Beginning in 1913, certain large cheques, payable to self, appeared regularly at every quarter, and sometimes at shorter intervals. As to the destination of these sums, the bureau preserved the closest discretion ; there were no receipts, no memoranda of their expenditure.

The great crash which in 1914 shook the credits of the world was mirrored in little in the pass-book. The credits from Russian and German sources stopped dead ; those from the French shares slumped to a quarter of the original amount, as the tide of war washed over the vineyards and carried the workers away. For the first

year or so there were substantial dividends from capital
invested in French *rentes* ; then came an ominous entry
of 20,000 francs on the credit side of the account, and,
six months after, another of 30,000 francs. After that
the landslide followed fast. Parker could picture those
curt notes from the Front, directing the sale of Government securities, as the savings of the past six years
whirled away in the maelstrom of rising prices and collapsing currencies. The dividends grew less and less and
ceased ; then, more ominous still, came a series of
debits representing the charges on renewal of pro-
missory notes.

About 1918 the situation had become acute, and
several entries showed a desperate attempt to put matters
straight by gambling in foreign exchanges. There were
purchases, through the bank, of German marks, Russian
roubles, and Roumanian lei. Mr. Parker sighed sympathetically, when he saw this, thinking of £12 worth of
these delusive specimens of the engraver's art laid up
in his own desk at home. He knew them to be waste-
paper, yet his tidy mind could not bear the thought of
destroying them. Evidently Cathcart had found marks
and roubles very broken reeds.

It was about this time that Cathcart's pass-book began
to reveal the paying in of various sums in cash, some
large, some small, at irregular dates and with no particular consistency. In December, 1919, there had been
one of these amounting to as much as 35,000 francs.
Parker at first supposed that these sums might represent dividends from some separate securities which
Cathcart was handling for himself without passing
them through the bank. He made a careful search of
the room in the hope of finding either the bonds themselves or at least some memorandum concerning them,
but the search was in vain, and he was forced to conclude either that Cathcart had deposited them in some
secret place or that the credits in question represented
some different source of income.

Cathcart had apparently contrived to be demobilised almost at once (owing, no doubt, to his previous frequentation of distinguished governmental personages), and to have taken a prolonged holiday upon the Riviera. Subsequently a visit to London coincided with the acquisition of £700, which, converted into francs at the then rate of exchange, made a very respectable item in the account. From that time on, the outgoings and receipts presented a similar aspect and were more or less evenly balanced, the cheques to self becoming rather larger and more frequent as time went on, while during 1921 the income from the vineyard began to show signs of recovery.

Mr. Parker noted down all this information in detail, and, leaning back in his chair, looked round the flat. He felt, not for the first time, a distaste for his profession, which cut him off from the great masculine community whose members take each other for granted and respect their privacy. He relighted his pipe, which had gone out, and proceeded with his report.

Information obtained from Monsieur Turgeot, the manager of the Crédit Lyonnais, confirmed the evidence of the pass-book in every particular. Monsieur Cathcart had recently made all his payments in notes, usually in notes of small denominations. Once or twice he had had an overdraft—never very large, and always made up within a few months. He had, of course, suffered a diminution of income, like everybody else, but the account had never given the bank any uneasiness. At the moment it was some 14,000 francs on the right side. Monsieur Cathcart was always very agreeable, but not communicative—*très correct*.

Information obtained from the concierge :
One did not see much of Monsieur Cathcart, but he was *très gentil*. He never failed to say, " *Bon jour, Bourgois,*" when he came in or out. He received visitors sometimes—gentlemen in evening dress. One made card-parties. Monsieur Bourgois had never directed

any ladies to his rooms ; except once, last February, when he had given a lunch-party to some ladies *très comme il faut* who brought with them his fiancée, *une jolie blonde*. Monsieur Cathcart used the flat as a *pied à terre*, and often he would shut it up and go away for several weeks or months. He was *un jeune homme très rangé*). He had never kept a valet. Madame Leblanc, the cousin of one's late wife, kept his *appartement* clean. Madame Leblanc was very respectable. But certainly monsieur might have Madame Leblanc's address.

Information obtained from Madame Leblanc :

Monsieur Cathcart was a charming young man, and very pleasant to work for. Very generous and took a great interest in the family. Madame Leblanc was desolated to hear that he was dead, and on the eve of his marriage to the daughter of the English milady. Madame Leblanc had seen Mademoiselle last year when she visited Monsieur Cathcart in Paris ; she considered the young lady very fortunate. Very few young men were as serious as Monsieur Cathcart, especially when they were so good-looking. Madame Leblanc had had experience of young men, and she could relate many histories if she were disposed, but none of Monsieur Cathcart. He would not always be using his rooms ; he had the habit of letting her know when he would be at home, and she then went round to put the flat in order. He kept his things very tidy ; he was not like English gentlemen in that respect. Madame Leblanc had known many of them, who kept their affairs *sens dessus dessous*. Monsieur Cathcart was always very well dressed ; he was particular about his bath ; he was like a woman for his toilet, the poor gentleman. And so he was dead. *Le pauvre garçon!* Really it had taken away Madame Leblanc's appetite.

Information obtained from Monsieur the Prefect of Police :

Absolutely nothing. Monsieur Cathcart had never caught the eye of the police in any way. With regard to the sums of money mentioned by Monsieur Parker, if monsieur would give him the numbers of some of the notes, efforts would be made to trace them.

Where had the money gone ? Parker could think only of two destinations—an irregular establishment or a blackmailer. Certainly a handsome man like Cathcart might very well have a woman or two in his life, even without the knowledge of the concierge. Certainly a man who habitually cheated at cards—if he did cheat at cards—might very well have got himself into the power of somebody who knew too much. It was noteworthy that his mysterious receipts in cash began just as his economies were exhausted ; it seemed likely that they represented irregular gains from gambling—in the casinos, on the exchange, or, if Denver's story had any truth in it, from crooked play. On the whole, Parker rather inclined to the blackmailing theory. It fitted in with the rest of the business, as he and Lord Peter had reconstructed it at Riddlesdale.

Two or three things, however, still puzzled Parker. Why should the blackmailer have been trailing about the Yorkshire moors with a cycle and side-car ? Whose was the green-eyed cat ? It was a valuable trinket. Had Cathcart offered it as part of his payment ? That seemed somehow foolish. One could only suppose that the blackmailer had tossed it away with contempt. The cat was in Parker's possession, and it occurred to him that it might be worth while to get a jeweller to estimate its value. But the side-car was a difficulty, the cat was a difficulty, and, more than all, Lady Mary was a difficulty.

Why had Lady Mary lied at the inquest ? For that she had lied, Parker had no manner of doubt. He disbelieved the whole story of the second shot which had awakened her. What had brought her to the conservatory door at three o'clock in the morning ? Whose was the suit-case—if it was a suit-case—that had lain concealed among the cactus-plants ? Why this prolonged nervous breakdown, with no particular symptoms, which prevented Lady Mary from giving evidence before the magistrate or answering her brother's inquiries ? Could Lady Mary have been present at the interview in the shrubbery ? If so, surely Wimsey and he would have found her footprints. Was she in league with the blackmailer ? That was an unpleasant thought. Was she endeavouring to help her fiancé ? She had an allowance of her own—a generous one, as Parker knew from the Duchess. Could she have tried to assist Cathcart with money ? But in that case, why not tell all she knew ? The worst about Cathcart—always supposing that card-sharping were the worst—was now matter of public knowledge, and the man himself was dead. If she knew the truth, why did she not come forward and save her brother ?

And at this point he was visited by a thought even more unpleasant. If, after all, it had not been Denver whom Mrs. Marchbanks had heard in the library, but someone else—someone who had likewise an appointment with the blackmailer—someone who was on his side as against Cathcart—who knew that there might be danger in the interview. Had he himself paid proper attention to the grass lawn between the house and the thicket ? Might Thursday morning perhaps have revealed here and there a trodden blade that rain and sap had since restored to uprightness ? Had Peter and he found *all* the footsteps in the wood ? Had some more trusted hand fired that shot at close quarters ? Once again—*whose was the green-eyed cat?*

Surmises and surmises, each uglier than the last, thronged into Parker's mind. He took up a photograph of Cathcart with which Wimsey had supplied him, and looked at it long and curiously. It was a dark, handsome face ; the hair was black, with a slight wave, the nose large and well shaped, the big, dark eyes at once pleasing and arrogant. The mouth was good, though a little thick, with a hint of sensuality in its close curves ; the chin showed a cleft. Frankly, Parker confessed to himself, it did not attract him; he would have been inclined to dismiss the man as a " Byronic blighter," but experience told him that this kind of face might be powerful with a woman, either for love or hatred.

Coincidences usually have the air of being practical jokes on the part of Providence. Mr. Parker was shortly to be favoured—if the term is a suitable one—with a special display of this Olympian humour. As a rule, that kind of thing did not happen to him; it was more in Wimsey's line. Parker had made his way from modest beginnings to a respectable appointment in the C.I.D. rather by a combination of hard work, shrewdness, and caution than by spectacular displays of happy guesswork or any knack for taking fortune's tide at the flood. This time, however, he was given a " leading " from above, and it was only part of the nature of things and men that he should have felt distinctly ungrateful for it.

He finished his report, replaced everything tidily in the desk and went round to the police-station to arrange with the Prefect about the keys and the fixing of the seals. It was still early evening and not too cold; he determined, therefore, to banish gloomy thoughts by a *café-cognac* in the Boul' Mich', followed by a stroll through the Paris of the shops. Being of a kindly, domestic nature, indeed, he turned over in his mind the idea of buying something Parisian for his elder sister, who was unmarried and lived a rather depressing life in Barrow-in-Furness. Parker knew that she would take pathetic delight in some filmy scrap of lace underwear which no one but herself would ever see. Mr. Parker was not the kind of man to be deterred by the difficulty of buying ladies' underwear in a foreign language; he was not very imaginative. He remembered that a learned judge had one day asked in court what a camisole was, and recollected that there had seemed to be nothing particularly embarrassing about the garment when explained. He determined that he would find a really Parisian shop, and ask for a camisole. That would give him a start, and then mademoiselle would show him other things without being asked further.

Accordingly, towards six o'clock, he was strolling along the Rue de la Paix with a little carton under his arm. He had spent rather more money than he intended, but he had acquired knowledge. He knew for certain what a camisole was, and he had grasped for the first time in his life that crêpe-de-Chine had no recognisable relation to crape, and was astonishingly expensive for its bulk. The young lady had been charmingly sympathetic, and, without actually insinuating anything, had contrived to make her customer feel just a little bit of a dog. He felt that his French accent was improving. The street was crowded with people, slowly sauntering past the brilliant shop-windows. Mr. Parker stopped and gazed nonchalantly over a gorgeous display of jewellery, as though hesitating between a pearl necklace valued at 80,000 francs and a pendant of diamonds and aquamarines set in platinum.

And there, balefully winking at him from under a label inscribed " *Bonne fortune* " hung a green-eyed cat.

The cat stared at Mr. Parker, and Mr. Parker stared at the cat. It was no ordinary cat. It was a cat with a personality. Its tiny arched body sparkled with diamonds, and its platinum paws, set close together, and its erect and glittering tail were instinct in every line with the sensuous delight of friction against some beloved object. Its head, cocked slightly to one side, seemed to demand a titillating finger under the jaw. It was a minute work of art, by no journeyman hand. Mr. Parker fished in his pocket-book. He looked from the cat in his hand to the cat in the window. They were alike. They were astonishingly alike. They were identical. Mr. Parker marched into the shop.

" I have here," said Mr. Parker to the young man at the counter, " a diamond cat which greatly resembles one which I perceive in your window. Could you have the obligingness to inform me what would be the value of such a cat ? "

The young man replied instantly :

" But certainly, monsieur. The price of the cat is 5,000 francs. It is, as you perceive, made of the finest materials. Moreover, it is the work of an artist ; it is worth more than the market value of the stones."

" It is, I suppose, a mascot ? "

" Yes, monsieur ; it brings great good luck, especially at cards. Many ladies buy these little objects. We have here other mascots, but all of this special design are of similar quality and price. Monsieur may rest assured that his cat is a cat of pedigree."

" I suppose that such cats are everywhere obtainable in Paris," said Mr. Parker nonchalantly.

" But no, monsieur. If you desire to match your cat I recommend you to do it quickly. Monsieur Briquet had only a score of these cats to begin with, and there are now only three left, including the one in the window. I believe that he will not make any more. To repeat a thing often is to vulgarise it. There will, of course, be other cats——"

" I don't want another cat," said Mr. Parker, suddenly interested. " Do I understand you to say that cats such as this are only sold by Monsieur Briquet ? That my cat originally came from this shop ? "

" Undoubtedly, monsieur, it is one of our cats. These little animals are made by a workman of ours—a genius who is responsible for many of our finest articles."

" It would, I imagine, be impossible to find out to whom this cat was originally sold ? "

" If it was sold over the counter for cash it would be difficult, but if it was entered in our books it might not be impossible to discover, if monsieur desired it."

" I do desire it very much," said Parker, producing his card. " I am an agent of the British police, and it is of great importance that I should know to whom this cat originally belonged."

" In that case," said the young man, "I shall do better to inform monsieur the proprietor."

He carried away the card into the back premises, and presently emerged with a stout gentleman, whom he introduced as Monsieur Briquet.

In Monsieur Briquet's private office the books of the establishment were brought out and laid on the desk.

" You will understand, monsieur," said Monsieur Briquet, " that I can only inform you of the names and addresses of such purchasers of these cats as have had an account sent them. It is, however, unlikely that an object of such value was paid for in cash. Still, with rich Anglo-Saxons, such an incident may occur. We need not go back further than the beginning of the year, when these cats were made." He ran a podgy finger down the pages of the ledger. " The first purchase was on January 19th."

Mr. Parker noted various names and addresses, and at the end of half an hour Monsieur Briquet said in a final manner :

" That is all, monsieur. How many names have you there ? "

" Thirteen," said Parker.

" And there are still three cats in stock—the original number was twenty—so that four must have been sold for cash. If monsieur wishes to verify the matter we can consult the day-book."

The search in the day-book was longer and more tiresome, but eventually four cats were duly found to have been sold ; one on January 31st, another on February 6th, the third on May 17th, and the last on August 9th.

Mr. Parker had risen, and embarked upon a long string of compliments and thanks, when a sudden association of ideas and dates prompted him to hand Cathcart's photograph to Monsieur Briquet and ask whether he recognised it.

Monsieur Briquet shook his head.

" I am sure he is not one of our regular customers,"
he said, " and I have a very good memory for faces.
I make a point of knowing anyone who has any considerable account with me. And this gentleman has not
everybody's face. But we will ask my assistants."

The majority of the staff failed to recognise the photograph, and Parker was on the point of putting it back in
his pocket-book when a young lady, who had just
finished selling an engagement-ring to an obese and
elderly Jew, arrived, and said, without any hesitation :
" *Mais oui, je l'ai vu, ce monseiur-là*. It is the Englishman who bought a diamond cat for the *jolie blonde*."

" Mademoiselle," said Parker eagerly, " I beseech
you to do me the favour to remember all about it."

" *Parfaitement*," said she. " It is not the face one
would forget, especially when one is a woman. The
gentleman bought a diamond cat and paid for it—no, I
am wrong. It was the lady who bought it, and I remember now to have been surprised that she should pay like
that at once in money, because ladies do not usually
carry such large sums. The gentleman bought too. He
bought a diamond and tortoiseshell comb for the lady
to wear, and then she said she must give him something
pour porter bonheur, and asked me for a mascot that was
good for cards. I showed her some jewels more suitable
for a gentleman, but she saw these cats and fell in love
with them, and said he should have a cat and nothing
else ; she was sure it would bring him good hands. She
asked me if it was not so, and I said, ' Undoubtedly, and
monsieur must be sure never to play without it,' and he
laughed very much, and promised always to have it upon
him when he was playing."

" And how was she, this lady ? "

" Blonde, monsieur, and very pretty ; rather tall and
svelte, and very well dressed. A big hat and dark blue
costume. *Quoi encore? Voyons*—yes, she was a
foreigner."

" English ? "

"I do not know. She spoke French very, very well, almost like a French person, but she had just the little suspicion of accent."

"What language did she speak with the gentleman?"

"French, monsieur. You see, we were speaking together, and they both appealed to me continually, and so all the talk was in French. The gentleman spoke French *à merveille*, it was only by his clothes and a *je ne sais quoi* in his appearance that I guessed he was English. The lady spoke equally fluently, but one remarked just the accent from time to time. Of course, I went away from them once or twice to get goods from the window, and they talked then; I do not know in what language."

"Now, mademoiselle, can you tell me how long ago this was?"

"*Ah, mon Dieu, ça c'est plus difficile. Monsieur sait que les jours se suivent et se ressemblent. Voyons.*"

"We can see by the day-book," put in Monsieur Briquet, "on what occasion a diamond comb was sold with a diamond cat."

"Of course," said Parker hastily. "Let us go back."

They went back and turned to the January volume, where they found no help. But on February 6th they read:

Peigne en écaille et diamants . . . f.7,500
Chat en diamants (Dessin C-5) . . f.5,000

"That settles it," said Parker gloomily.

"Monsieur does not appear content," suggested the jeweller.

"Monsieur," said Parker, "I am more grateful than I can say for your very great kindness, but I will frankly confess that, of all the twelve months in the year, I had rather it had been any other."

Parker found this whole episode so annoying to his feelings that he bought two comic papers and, carrying them away to Boudet's at the corner of the Rue Auguste Léopold, read them solemnly through over his dinner, by way of settling his mind. Then, returning to his modest hotel, he ordered a drink, and sat down to compose a letter to Lord Peter. It was a slow job, and he did not appear to relish it very much. His concluding paragraph was as follows :

" I have put all these things down for you without any comment. You will be able to draw your own inferences as well as I can—better, I hope, for my own are perplexing and worrying me no end. They may be all rubbish—I hope they are ; I daresay something will turn up at your end to put quite a different interpretation upon the facts. But I do feel that they must be cleared up. I would offer to hand over the job, but another man might jump at conclusions even faster than I do, and make a mess of it. But of course, if you say so, I will be taken suddenly ill at any moment. Let me know. If you think I'd better go on grubbing about over here, can you get hold of a photograph of Lady Mary Wimsey, and find out if possible about the diamond comb and the green-eyed cat—also at exactly what date Lady Mary was in Paris in February. Does she speak French as well as you do ? Let me know how you are getting on.

" Yours ever,
" CHARLES PARKER."

He re-read the letter and report carefully and sealed them up. Then he wrote to his sister, did up his parcel neatly, and rang for the valet de chambre.

" I want this letter sent off at once, registered," he said, " and the parcel is to go to-morrow as a *colis postal*."

After which he went to bed, and read himself to sleep with a commentary on the Epistle to the Hebrews.

.   .   .   .   .   .

Lord Peter's reply arrived by return :

" DEAR CHARLES,—Don't worry. I don't like the look of things myself frightfully, but I'd rather you tackled the business than anyone else. As you say, the ordinary police bloke doesn't mind whom he arrests, provided he arrests someone, and is altogether a most damnable fellow to have poking into one's affairs. I'm putting my mind to getting my brother cleared—that *is* the first consideration, after all, and really anything else would be better than having Jerry hanged for a crime he didn't commit. Whoever did it, it's better the right person should suffer than the wrong. So go ahead.

" I enclose two photographs—all I can lay hands on for the moment. The one in nursing-kit is rather rotten, and the other's all smothered up in a big hat.

" I had a damn' queer little adventure here on Wednesday, which I'll tell you about when we meet. I've found a woman who obviously knows more than she ought, and a most promising ruffian—only I'm afraid he's got an alibi. Also I've got a faint suggestion of a clue about No. 10. Nothing much happened at Northallerton, except that Jerry was of course committed for trial. My mother is here, thank God ! and I'm hoping she'll get some sense out of Mary, but she's been worse the last two days—Mary, I mean, not my mother—beastly sick and all that sort of thing. Dr. Thingummy—who is an ass—can't make it out. Mother says it's as clear as noonday, and she'll stop it if I have patience a day or two. I made her ask about the comb and the cat. M. denies the cat altogether, but admits to a diamond comb bought in Paris —says she bought it herself. It's in town—I'll get it and send it on. She says she can't remember where she bought it, has lost the bill, but it didn't cost anything like 7,500 francs. She was in Paris from February 2nd to February 20th. My chief business now is to see Lubbock and clear up a little matter concerning silver sand.

" The Assizes will be the first week in November—
in fact, the end of next week. This rushes things a
bit, but it doesn't matter, because they can't try him
there ; nothing will matter but the Grand Jury, who
are bound to find a true bill on the face of it. After
that we can hang matters up as long as we like. It's
going to be a deuce of a business, Parliament sitting
and all. Old Biggs is fearfully perturbed under that
marble outside of his. I hadn't really grasped what a
fuss it was to try peers. It's only happened about once
in every sixty years, and the procedure's about as old
as Queen Elizabeth. They have to appoint a Lord
High Steward for the occasion, and God knows what.
They have to make it frightfully clear in the Commission that it *is* only for the occasion, because, somewhere about Richard III's time, the L.H.S. was such a
terrifically big pot that he got to ruling the roost.
So when Henry IV came to the throne, and the office
came into the hands of the Crown, he jolly well kept
it there, and now they only appoint a man *pro tem.*
for the Coronation and shows like Jerry's. The King
always pretends not to know there isn't a L.H.S.
till the time comes, and is no end surprised at having
to think of somebody to take on the job. Did you
know all this ? I didn't. I got it out of Biggy.

" Cheer up. Pretend you don't know that any of
these people are relations of mine. My mother sends
you her kindest regards and what not, and hopes she'll
see you again soon. Bunter sends something correct
and respectful ; I forget what.

" Yours in the brotherhood of detection,
" P.W."

It may as well be said at once that the evidence from
the photographs was wholly inconclusive.

CHAPTER VI

MARY QUITE CONTRARY

I am striving to take into public life what any man gets from his mother.—Lady Astor.

ON the opening day of the York Assizes, the Grand Jury brought in a true bill, against Gerald, Duke of Denver, for murder. Gerald, Duke of Denver, being accordingly produced in the court, the Judge affected to discover—what, indeed, every newspaper in the country had been announcing to the world for the last fortnight—that he, being but a common or garden judge with a plebeian jury, was incompetent to try a peer of the realm. He added, however, that he would make it his business to inform the Lord Chancellor (who also, for the last fortnight, had been secretly calculating the accommodation in the Royal Gallery and choosing lords to form the Select Committee). Order being taken accordingly, the noble prisoner was led away.

· · · · · ·

A day or two later, in the gloom of a London afternoon, Mr. Charles Parker rang the bell of a second-floor flat at No. 110 Piccadilly. The door was opened by Bunter, who informed him with a gracious smile that Lord Peter had stepped out for a few minutes but was expecting him, and would he kindly come in and wait.

" We only came up this morning," added the valet, " and are not quite straight yet, sir, if you will excuse us. Would you feel inclined for a cup of tea ? "

Parker accepted the offer, and sank luxuriously into a corner of the Chesterfield. After the extraordinary discomfort of French furniture there was solace in the enervating springiness beneath him, the cushions behind his head, and Wimsey's excellent cigarettes. What Bunter had meant by saying that things were " not quite straight yet " he could not divine. A leaping wood fire was merrily reflected in the spotless surface of the black baby grand ; the mellow calf bindings of Lord Peter's rare editions glowed softly against the black and primrose walls ; the vases were filled with tawny chrysanthemums; the latest editions of all the papers were on the table— as though the owner had never been absent.

Over his tea Mr. Parker drew out the photographs of Lady Mary and Denis Cathcart from his breast pocket. He stood them up against the teapot and stared at them, looking from one to the other as if trying to force a meaning from their faintly smirking, self-conscious gaze. He referred again to his Paris notes, ticking off various points with a pencil. " Damn ! " said Mr. Parker, gazing at Lady Mary. " Damn—damn— damn——"

The train of thought he was pursuing was an extra-ordinarily interesting one. Image after image, each rich in suggestion, crowded into his mind. Of course, one couldn't think properly in Paris—it was so uncomfortable and the houses were central heated. Here, where so many problems had been unravelled, there was a good fire. Cathcart had been sitting before the fire. Of course, he wanted to think out a problem. When cats sat staring into the fire they were thinking out pro-blems. It was odd he should not have thought of that before. When the green-eyed cat sat before the fire one sank right down into a sort of rich, black, velvety sug-gestiveness which was most important. It was luxurious to be able to think so lucidly as this, because otherwise it would be a pity to exceed the speed limit—and the black moors were reeling by so fast. But now he had really got the formula he wouldn't forget it again. The connection was just there—close, thick, richly coherent.

119

"The glass-blower's cat is bompstable," said Mr. Parker aloud and distinctly.

"I'm charmed to hear it," replied Lord Peter, with a friendly grin. "Had a good nap, old man?"

"I—what?" said Mr. Parker. "Hullo! Watcher mean, nap? I had got hold of a most important train of thought, and you've put it out of my head. What was it? Cat—cat—cat——" He groped wildly.

"You *said* ' The glass-blower's cat is bompstable,' " retorted Lord Peter. "It's a perfectly rippin' word, but I don't know what you mean by it."

"Bompstable?" said Mr. Parker, blushing slightly. "Bomp—oh, well, perhaps you're right—I may have dozed off. But, you know, I thought I'd just got the clue to the whole thing. I attached the greatest importance to that phrase. Even now—— No, now I come to think of it, my train of thought doesn't seem quite to hold together. What a pity. I thought it was so lucid."

"Never mind," said Lord Peter. "Just back?"

"Crossed last night. Any news?"

"Lots."

"Good?"

"No."

Parker's eyes wandered to the photographs.

"I don't believe it," he said obstinately. "I'm damned if I'm going to believe a word of it."

"A word of what?"

"Of whatever it is."

"You'll have to believe it, Charles, as far as it goes," said his friend softly, filling his pipe with decided little digs of the fingers. "I don't say "—dig—" that Mary " —dig—" shot Cathcart "—dig, dig—" but she has lied " —dig—" again and again."—Dig, dig—" She knows who did it "—dig—" she was prepared for it "—dig— " she's malingering and lying to keep the fellow shielded" —dig—" and we shall have to make her speak." Here he struck a match and lit the pipe in a series of angry little puffs.

120

" If you can think," said Mr. Parker, with some heat, " that that woman "—he indicated the photographs—" had any hand in murdering Cathcart, I don't care what your evidence is, you—hang it all, Wimsey, she's your own sister."

" Gerald is my brother," said Wimsey quietly. " You don't suppose I'm exactly enjoying this business, do you? But I think we shall get along very much better if we try to keep our tempers."

" I'm awfully sorry," said Parker. " Can't think why I said that—rotten bad form—beg pardon, old man."

" The best thing we can do," said Wimsey, " is to look the evidence in the face, however ugly. And I don't mind admittin' that some of it's a positive gargoyle.

" My mother turned up at Riddlesdale on Friday. She marched upstairs at once and took possession of Mary, while I drooped about in the hall and teased the cat, and generally made a nuisance of myself. *You* know. Presently old Dr. Thorpe called. I went and sat on the chest on the landing. Presently the bell rings and Ellen comes upstairs. Mother and Thorpe popped out and caught her just outside Mary's room, and they jibber-jabbered a lot, and presently mother came barging down the passage to the bathroom with her heels tapping and her earrings simply dancing with irritation. I sneaked after 'em to the bathroom door, but I couldn't see anything, because they were blocking the doorway, but I heard mother say, ' There, now, what did I tell you '; and Ellen said, ' Lawks ! your grace, who'd 'a' thought it ? '; and my mother said, ' All I can say is, if I had to depend on you people to save me from being murdered with arsenic or that other stuff with the name like anemones*—you know what I mean—that that very attractive-looking man with the preposterous beard used to make away with his wife and mother-in-

---

* Antimony ? The Duchess appears to have had Dr. Pritchard's case in mind.

law (who was vastly the more attractive of the two, poor thing), I might be being cut up and analysed by Dr. Spilsbury now—such a horrid, distasteful job he must have of it, poor man, and the poor little rabbits, too.' " Wimsey paused for breath, and Parker laughed in spite of his anxiety.

" I won't vouch for the exact words," said Wimsey, " but it was to that effect—you know my mother's style. Old Thorpe tried to look dignified, but mother ruffled up like a little hen and said, looking beadily at him : ' In *my* day we called that kind of thing hysterics and naughtiness. *We* didn't let girls pull the wool over our eyes like that. I suppose *you* call it a neurosis, or a suppressed desire, or a reflex, and coddle it. You might have let that silly child make herself really ill. You are all perfectly ridiculous, and no more fit to take care of yourselves than a lot of babies—not but what there are plenty of poor little things in the slums that look after whole families and show more sense than the lot of you put together. I am very angry with Mary, advertising herself in this way, and she's not to be pitied.' You know," said Wimsey, " I think there's often a great deal in what one's mother says."

" I believe you," said Parker.

" Well, I got hold of mother afterwards and asked her what it was all about. She said Mary wouldn't tell her anything about herself or her illness ; just asked to be let alone. Then Thorpe came along and talked about nervous shock—said he couldn't understand these fits of sickness, or the way Mary's temperature hopped about. Mother listened, and told him to go and see what the temperature was now. Which he did, and in the middle mother called him away to the dressing-table. But, bein' a wily old bird, you see, she kept her eyes on the looking-glass, and nipped round just in time to catch Mary stimulatin' the thermometer to terrific leaps on the hot-water bottle."

" Well, I'm damned ! " said Parker.

" So was Thorpe. All mother said was, that if he wasn't too old a bird yet to be taken in by that hoary trick he'd no business to be gettin' himself up as a grey-haired family practitioner. So then she asked the girl about the sick fits—when they happened, and how often, and was it after meals or before, and so on, and at last she got out of them that it generally happened a bit after breakfast and occasionally at other times. Mother said she couldn't make it out at first, because she'd hunted all over the room for bottles and things, till at last she asked who made the bed, thinkin', you see, Mary might have hidden something under the mattress. So Ellen said she usually made it while Mary had her bath. ' When's that ? ' says mother. ' Just before her breakfast,' bleats the girl. ' God forgive you all for a set of nincompoops,' says my mother. ' Why didn't you say so before ? ' So away they all trailed to the bathroom, and there, sittin' up quietly on the bathroom shelf among the bath salts and the Elliman's embrocation and the Kruschen feelings and the toothbrushes and things, was the family bottle of ipecacuanha—three-quarters empty ! Mother said—well, I told you what she said. By the way, how do you spell ipecacuanha ? "

Mr. Parker spelt it.

" Damn you ! " said Lord Peter. " I *did* think I'd stumped you that time. I believe you went and looked it up beforehand. *No* decent-minded person would know how to spell ipecacuanha out of his own head. Anyway, as you were saying, it's easy to see which side of the family has the detective instinct."

" I didn't say so——"

" I know. Why didn't you ? I think my mother's talents deserve a little acknowledgment. I said so to her, as a matter of fact, and she replied in these memorable words : ' My dear child, you can give it a long name if you like, but I'm an old-fashioned woman and I call it mother-wit, and it's so rare for a man to have it that if he does you write a book about him and call him

Sherlock Holmes.' However, apart from all that, I said to mother (in private, of course), ' It's all very well, but I can't believe that Mary has been going to all this trouble to make herself horribly sick and frighten us all just to show off. Surely she isn't that sort.' Mother looked at me as steady as an owl, and quoted a whole lot of examples of hysteria, ending up with the servant-girl who threw paraffin about all over somebody's house to make them think it was haunted, and finished up—that if all these new-fangled doctors went out of their way to invent subconsciousness and kleptomania, and complexes and other fancy descriptions to explain away when people had done naughty things, she thought one might just as well take advantage of the fact."

" Wimsey," said Parker, much excited, " did she mean she suspected something ? "

" My dear old chap," replied Lord Peter, " whatever can be known about Mary by putting two and two together my mother knows. I told her all *we* knew up to that point, and she took it all in, in her funny way, you know, never answering anything directly, and then she put her head on one side and said : ' If Mary had listened to me, and done something useful instead of that V.A.D. work, which never came to much, if you ask me —not that I have anything against V.A.D.'s in a general way, but that silly woman Mary worked under was the most terrible snob on God's earth—and there were very much more sensible things which Mary might really have done well, only that she was so crazy to get to London—I shall always say it was the fault of that ridiculous club—what could you expect of a place where you ate such horrible food, all packed into an underground cellar painted pink and talking away at the tops of their voices, and never any evening dress—only Soviet jumpers and side-whiskers. Anyhow, I've told that silly old man what to say about it, and they'll never be able to think of a better explanation for themselves.' Indeed, you know," said Peter, " I think if any of them start getting inquisitive, they'll have mother down on them like a ton of bricks."

" What do you really think yourself ? " asked Parker.

" I haven't come yet to the unpleasantest bit of the lot," said Peter. " I've only just heard it, and it did give me a nasty jar, I'll admit. Yesterday I got a letter from Lubbock saying he would like to see me, so I trotted up here and dropped in on him this morning. You remember I sent him a stain off one of Mary's skirts which Bunter had cut out for me ? I had taken a squint at it myself, and didn't like the look of it, so I sent it up to Lubbock, *ex abundantia cautelæ ;* and I'm sorry to say he confirms me. It's human blood, Charles, and I'm afraid it's Cathcart's."

" But—I've lost the thread of this a bit."

" Well, the skirt must have got stained the day Cathcart—died, as that was the last day on which the party was out on the moors, and if it had been there earlier Ellen would have cleaned it off. Afterwards Mary strenuously resisted Ellen's efforts to take the skirt away, and made an amateurish effort to tidy it up herself with soap. So I think we may conclude that Mary knew the stains were there, and wanted to avoid discovery. She told Ellen that the blood was from a grouse—which must have been a deliberate untruth."

" Perhaps," said Parker, struggling against hope to make out a case for Lady Mary, " she only said, ' Oh ! one of the birds must have bled,' or something like that."

" I don't believe," said Peter, " that one could get a great patch of human blood on one's clothes like that and not know what it was. She must have knelt right in it. It was three or four inches across."

Parker shook his head dismally, and consoled himself by making a note.

" Well, now," went on Peter, " on Wednesday night everybody comes in and dines and goes to bed except Cathcart, who rushes out and stays out. At 11.50 the gamekeeper, Hardraw, hears a shot which may very well have been fired in the clearing where the—well, let's say the accident—took place. The time also agrees with the medical evidence about Cathcart having already been dead three or four hours when he was examined at 4.30. Very well. At 3 a.m. Jerry comes home from somewhere or other and finds the body. As he is bending over it, Mary arrives in the most apropos manner from the house in her coat and cap and walking shoes. Now what is her story ? She says that at three o'clock she was awakened by a shot. Now nobody else heard that shot, and we have the evidence of Mrs. Pettigrew-Robinson, who slept in the next room to Mary, with her window open according to her immemorial custom, that she lay broad awake from 2 a.m. till a little after 3 a.m., when the alarm was given, and heard no shot. According to Mary, the shot was loud enough to waken her on the other side of the building. It's odd, isn't it, that the person already awake should swear so positively that she heard nothing of a noise loud enough to waken a healthy young sleeper next door ? And, in any case, *if* that was the shot that killed Cathcart, he can barely have been dead when my brother found him—and again, in that case, how was there time for him to be carried up from the shrubbery to the conservatory ? "

" We've been over all this ground," said Parker, with an expression of distaste. " We agreed that we couldn't attach any importance to the story of the shot."

" I'm afraid we've got to attach a great deal of importance to it," said Lord Peter gravely. " Now, what does Mary do ? Either she thought the shot——"

" There was no shot."

" I know that. But I'm examining the discrepancies of her story. She said she did not give the alarm because she thought it was probably only poachers. But, if it was poachers, it would be absurd to go down and investigate. So she explains that she thought it might be burglars. Now how does she dress to go and look for

126

burglars ? What would you or I have done ? I think
we would have taken a dressing-gown, a stealthy kind
of pair of slippers, and perhaps a poker or a stout stick—
not a pair of walking shoes, a coat, and a cap, of all
things ! "

" It was a wet night," mumbled Parker.

" My dear chap, if it's burglars you're looking for you
don't expect to go and hunt them round the garden.
Your first thought is that they're getting into the house,
and your idea is to slip down quietly and survey them
from the staircase or behind the dining-room door. Anyhow, fancy a present-day girl, who rushes about bare-
headed in all weathers, stopping to embellish herself in
a cap for a burglar-hunt—damn it all, Charles, it won't
wash, you know ! And she walks straight off to the
conservatory and comes upon the corpse, exactly as if
she knew where to look for it beforehand."

Parker shook his head again.

" Well, now. She sees Gerald stooping over Cathcart's body. What does she say ? Does she ask what's
the matter ? Does she ask who it is ? She exclaims :
' O God ! Gerald, you've killed him,' and *then* she
says, as if on second thoughts, ' Oh, it's Denis ! What
has happened ? Has there been an accident ? ' Now,
does that strike you as natural ? "

" No. But it rather suggests to me that it wasn't
Cathcart she expected to see there, but somebody else."

" Does it ? It rather sounds to me as if she was
pretending not to know who it was. First she says,
' You've killed him ! ' and then, recollecting that she
isn't supposed to know who ' he ' is, she says, ' Why,
it's Denis ! ' "

" In any case, then, if her first exclamation was
genuine, she didn't expect to find the man dead."

" No—no—we must remember that. The death *was*
a surprise. Very well. Then Gerald sends Mary up
for help. And here's where a little bit of evidence comes
in that you picked up and sent along. Do you remember
127

what Mrs. Pettigrew-Robinson said to you in the train? "

" About the door slamming on the landing, do you mean ? "

" Yes. Now I'll tell you something that happened to me the other morning. I was burstin' out of the bathroom in my usual breezy way when I caught myself a hell of a whack on that old chest on the landin', and the lid lifted up and shut down, *plonk !* That gave me an idea, and I thought I'd have a squint inside. I'd got the lid up and was lookin' at some sheets and stuff that were folded up at the bottom, when I heard a sort of gasp, and there was Mary, starin' at me, as white as a ghost. She gave me a turn, by Jove, but nothin' like the turn I'd given her. Well, she wouldn't say anything to me, and got hysterical, and I hauled her back to her room. But I'd seen something on those sheets."

" What ? "

" Silver sand."

" Silver—— "

" D'you remember those cacti in the greenhouse, and the place where somebody'd put a suit-case or something down ? "

" Yes."

" Well, there was a lot of silver sand scattered about —the sort people stick round some kinds of bulbs and things."

" And that was inside the chest too ? "

" Yes. Wait a moment. After the noise Mrs. Pettigrew-Robinson heard, Mary woke up Freddy and then the Pettigrew-Robinsons—and then what ? "

" She locked herself into her room."

" Yes. And shortly afterwards she came down and joined the others in the conservatory, and it was at this point everybody remembered noticing that she was wearing a cap and coat and walking shoes over pyjamas and bare feet."

" You are suggesting," said Parker, " that Lady Mary

was already awake and dressed at three o'clock, that she went out by the conservatory door with her suit-case, expecting to meet the—the murderer of her—damn it, Wimsey ! "

" We needn't go so far as that," said Peter ; " we decided that she *didn't* expect to find Cathcart dead."

" No. Well, she went, presumably to meet somebody."

" Shall we say, *pro tem.*, she went to meet No. 10 ? " suggested Wimsey softly.

" I suppose we may as well say so. When she turned on the torch and saw the Duke stooping over Cathcart she thought—by Jove, Wimsey, I was right after all ! When she said, ' You've killed him ! ' she meant No. 10—she thought it was No. 10's body."

" Of course ! " cried Wimsey. " I'm a fool ! Yes. Then she said, ' It's Denis—what has happened ? ' That's quite clear. And, meanwhile, what did she do with the suit-case ? "

" I see it all now," cried Parker. " When she saw that the body wasn't the body of No. 10 she realised that No. 10 must be the murderer. So her game was to prevent anybody knowing that No. 10 had been there. So she shoved the suit-case behind the cacti. Then, when she went upstairs, she pulled it out again, and hid it in the oak chest on the landing. She couldn't take it to her room, of course, because if anybody'd heard her come upstairs it would seem odd that she should run to her room before calling the others. Then she knocked up Arbuthnot and the Pettigrew-Robinsons—she'd be in the dark, and they'd be flustered and wouldn't see exactly what she had on. Then she escaped from Mrs. P., ran into her room, took off the skirt in which she had knelt by Cathcart's side, and the rest of her clothes, and put on her pyjamas and the cap, which someone might have noticed, and the coat, which they *must* have noticed, and the shoes, which had probably left footmarks already. Then she could go down and show herself.

129

Meantime she'd concocted the burglar story for the Coroner's benefit."

" That's about it," said Peter. " I suppose she was so desperately anxious to throw us off the scent of No. 10 that it never occurred to her that her story was going to help implicate her brother."

" She realised it at the inquest," said Parker eagerly. " Don't you remember how hastily she grasped at the suicide theory ? "

" And when she found that she was simply saving her—well, No. 10—in order to hang her brother, she lost her head, took to her bed, and refused to give any evidence at all. Seems to me there's an extra allowance of fools in my family," said Peter gloomily.

" Well, what could she have done, poor girl ? " asked Parker. He had been growing almost cheerful again. " Anyway, she's cleared——"

" After a fashion," said Peter, " but we're not out of the wood yet by a long way. Why is she hand-in-glove with No. 10 who is at least a blackmailer if not a murderer ? How did Gerald's revolver come on the scene ? And the green-eyed cat ? How much did Mary know of that meeting between No. 10 and Denis Cathcart ? And if she was seeing and meeting the man she might have put the revolver into his hands any time."

" No, no," said Parker. " Wimsey, don't think such ugly things as that."

" Hell ! " cried Peter, exploding. " I'll have the truth of this beastly business if we all go to the gallows together ! "

At this moment Bunter entered with a telegram addressed to Wimsey. Lord Peter read as follows :

" Party traced London ; seen Marylebone Friday. Further information from Scotland Yard.—POLICE-SUPERINTENDENT GOSLING, Ripley."

" Good egg ! " cried Wimsey. " Now we're gettin'

down to it. Stay here, there's a good man, in case anything turns up. I'll run round to the Yard now. They'll
send you up dinner, and tell Bunter to give you a bottle
of the Chateau Yquem—it's rather decent. So long."

He leapt out of the flat, and a moment later his taxi
buzzed away up Piccadilly.

CHAPTER VII

THE CLUB AND THE BULLET

He is dead, and by my hand. It were better that I were dead myself, for the guilty wretch I am.—Adventures of Sexton Blake.

HOUR after hour Mr. Parker sat waiting for his friend's return. Again and again he went over the Riddlesdale Case, checking his notes here, amplifying them there, involving his tired brain in speculations of the most fantastic kind. He wandered about the room, taking down here and there a book from the shelves, strumming a few unskilful bars upon the piano, glancing through the weeklies, fidgeting restlessly. At length he selected a volume from the criminological section of the bookshelves, and forced himself to read with attention that most fascinating and dramatic of poison trials— the Seddon Case. Gradually the mystery gripped him, as it invariably did, and it was with a start of astonishment that he looked up at a long and vigorous whirring of the door-bell, to find that it was already long past midnight.

His first thought was that Wimsey must have left his latchkey behind, and he was preparing a facetious greeting when the door opened—exactly as in the beginning of a Sherlock Holmes story—to admit a tall and beautiful young woman, in an extreme state of nervous agitation, with halo of golden hair, violet-blue eyes, and disordered apparel all complete ; for as she threw back her heavy travelling-coat he observed that she wore evening dress, with light green silk stockings and heavy brogue shoes thickly covered with mud.

"His lordship has not yet returned, my lady," said Mr. Bunter, "but Mr. Parker is here waiting for him, and we are expecting him at any minute now. Will your ladyship take anything?"

"No, no," said the vision hastily, "nothing, thanks. I'll wait. Good evening, Mr. Parker. Where's Peter?"

"He has been called out, Lady Mary," said Parker. "I can't think why he isn't back yet. Do sit down."

"Where did he go?"

"To Scotland Yard—but that was about six o'clock. I can't imagine——"

Lady Mary made a gesture of despair.

"I knew it. Oh, Mr. Parker, what am I to do?"

Mr. Parker was speechless.

"I *must* see Peter," cried Lady Mary. "It's a matter of life and death. Can't you send for him?"

"But I don't know where he is," said Parker. "Please, Lady Mary——"

"He's doing something dreadful—he's all *wrong*," cried the young woman, wringing her hands with desperate vehemence. "I must see him—tell him—— Oh! did anybody ever get into such dreadful trouble! I—oh!——"

Here the lady laughed loudly and burst into tears.

"Lady Mary—I beg you—please don't," cried Mr. Parker anxiously, with a strong feeling that he was being incompetent and rather ridiculous. "Please sit down. Drink a glass of wine. You'll be ill if you cry like that. If it is crying," he added dubiously to himself. "It *sounds* like hiccups. Bunter!"

Mr. Bunter was not far off. In fact, he was just outside the door with a small tray. With a respectful "Allow me, sir," he stepped forward to the writhing Lady Mary and presented a small phial to her nose. The effect was startling. The patient gave two or three fearful whoops, and sat up, erect and furious.

"How *dare* you, Bunter!" said Lady Mary. "Go away at once!"

"Your ladyship had better take a drop of brandy," said Mr. Bunter, replacing the stopper in the smelling-bottle, but not before Parker had caught the pungent, reek of ammonia. "This is the 1800 Napoleon brandy my lady. Please don't snort so, if I may make the suggestion. His lordship would be greatly distressed to think that any of it should be wasted. Did your ladyship dine on the way up? No? Most unwise, my lady, to undertake a long journey on a vacant interior. I will take the liberty of sending in an omelette for your ladyship. Perhaps you would like a little snack of something yourself, sir, as it is getting late?"

"Anything you like," said Mr. Parker, waving him off hurriedly. "Now, Lady Mary, you're feeling better, aren't you? Let me help you off with your coat."

No more of an exciting nature was said until the omelette was disposed of, and Lady Mary comfortably settled on the Chesterfield. She had by now recovered her poise. Looking at her, Parker noticed how her recent illness (however produced) had left its mark upon her. Her complexion had nothing of the brilliance which he remembered; she looked strained and white, with purple hollows under her eyes.

"I am sorry I was so foolish just now, Mr. Parker," she said, looking into his eyes with a charming frankness and confidence, "but I was dreadfully distressed, and I came up from Riddlesdale so hurriedly."

"Not at all," said Parker meaninglessly. "Is there anything I can do in your brother's absence?"

"I suppose you and Peter do everything together?"

"I think I may say that neither of us knows anything about this investigation which he has not communicated to the other."

"If I tell you, it's the same thing?"

"Exactly the same thing. If you can bring yourself to honour me with your confidence——"

"Wait a minute, Mr. Parker. I'm in a difficult position. I don't quite know what I ought—— Can

134

you tell me just how far you've got—what you have discovered ? "

Mr. Parker was a little taken aback. Although the face of Lady Mary had been haunting his imagination ever since the inquest, and although the agitation of his feelings had risen to boiling-point during this romantic interview, the official instinct of caution had not wholly deserted him. Holding, as he did, proofs of Lady Mary's complicity in the crime, whatever it was, he was not so far gone as to fling all his cards on the table.

" I'm afraid," he said, " that I can't quite tell you that. You see, so much of what we've got is only suspicion as yet. I might accidentally do great mischief to an innocent person."

" Ah ! You definitely suspect somebody, then ? "

" *In*definitely would be a better word for it," said Mr. Parker with a smile. " But if you have anything to tell us which may throw light on the matter, I beg you to speak. We may be suspecting a totally wrong person."

" I shouldn't be surprised," said Lady Mary, with a sharp, nervous little laugh. Her hand strayed to the table and began pleating the orange envelope into folds. " What do you want to know ? " she asked suddenly, with a change of tone. Parker was conscious of a new hardness in her manner—a something braced and rigid.

He opened his note-book, and as he began his questioning his nervousness left him ; the official reasserted himself.

" You were in Paris last February ? "

Lady Mary assented.

" Do you recollect going with Captain Cathcart— oh ! by the way, you speak French, I presume ? "

" Yes, very fluently."

" As well as your brother—practically without accent ? "

" Quite as well. We always had French governesses as children, and mother was very particular about it."

" I see. Well, now, do you remember going with

135

Captain Cathcart on February 6th to a jeweller's in the Rue de la Paix and buying, or his buying for you, a tortoiseshell comb set with diamonds and a diamond and platinum cat with emerald eyes ? "

He saw a lurking awareness come into the girl's eyes.

" Is that the cat you have been making inquiries about in Riddlesdale ? " she demanded.

It being never worth while to deny the obvious, Parker replied " Yes."

" It was found in the shrubbery, wasn't it ? "

" Had you lost it ? Or was it Cathcart's ? "

" If I said it was his——"

" I should be ready to believe you. *Was* it his ? "

" No "—a long breath—" it was mine."

" When did you lose it ? "

" That night."

" Where ? "

" I suppose in the shrubbery. Wherever you found it. I didn't miss it till later."

" Is it the one you bought in Paris ? "

" Yes."

" Why did you say before that it was not yours ? "

" I was afraid."

" And now ? "

" I am going to speak the truth."

Parker looked at her again. She met his eye frankly, but there was a tenseness in her manner which showed that it had cost her something to make her mind up.

" Very well," said Parker, " we shall all be glad of that, for I think there were one or two points at the inquest on which you didn't tell the truth, weren't there ? "

" Yes."

" Do believe," said Parker, " that I am sorry to have to ask these questions. The terrible position in which your brother is placed——"

" In which I helped to place him."

" I don't say that."

136

" I do. I helped to put him in gaol. Don't say I didn't, because I did."

" Well," said Parker, " don't worry. There's plenty of time to put it all right again. Shall I go on ? "

" Yes."

" Well, now, Lady Mary, it wasn't true about hearing that shot at three o'clock, was it ? "

" No."

" Did you hear the shot at all ? "

" Yes."

" When ? "

" At 11.50."

" What was it, then, Lady Mary, you hid behind the plants in the conservatory ? "

" I hid nothing there."

" And in the oak chest on the landing ? "

" My skirt."

" You went out—why ?—to meet Cathcart ? "

" Yes."

" Who was the other man ? "

" What other man ? "

" The other man who was in the shrubbery. A tall, fair man dressed in a Burberry ? "

" There was no other man."

" Oh, pardon me, Lady Mary. We saw his foot-marks all the way up from the shrubbery to the conservatory."

" It must have been some tramp. I know nothing about him."

" But we have proof that he was there—of what he did, and how he escaped. For heaven's sake, and your brother's sake, Lady Mary, tell us the truth—for that man in the Burberry was the man who shot Cathcart."

" No," said the girl, with a white face, " that is impossible."

" Why impossible ? "

" I shot Denis Cathcart myself."

.   .   .   .

137

"So that's how the matter stands, you see, Lord Peter," said the Chief of Scotland Yard, rising from his desk with a friendly gesture of dismissal. "The man was undoubtedly seen at Marylebone on the Friday morning, and, though we have unfortunately lost him again for the moment, I have no doubt whatever that we shall lay hands on him before long. The delay has been due to the unfortunate illness of the porter Morrison, whose evidence has been so material. But we are wasting no time now."

"I'm sure I may leave it to you with every confidence, Sir Andrew," replied Wimsey, cordially shaking hands. "I'm diggin' away too; between us we ought to get somethin'—you in your small corner and I in mine, as the hymn says—or is it a hymn? I remember readin' it in a book about missionaries when I was small. Did you want to be a missionary in your youth? I did. I think most kids do some time or another, which is odd, seein' how unsatisfactory most of us turn out."

"Meanwhile," said Sir Andrew Mackenzie, "if you run across the man yourself, let us know. I would never deny your extraordinary good fortune, or it may be good judgment, in running across the criminals we may be wanting."

"If I catch the bloke," said Lord Peter, "I'll come and shriek under your windows till you let me in, if it's the middle of the night and you in your little night-shirt. And talking of night-shirts reminds me that we hope to see you down at Denver one of these days, as soon as this business is over. Mother sends kind regards, of course."

"Thanks very much," replied Sir Andrew. "I hope you feel that all is going well. I had Parker in here this morning to report, and he seemed a little dissatisfied."

"He's been doing a lot of ungrateful routine work," said Wimsey, "and being altogether the fine, sound man he always is. He's been a damn good friend to me, Sir

Andrew, and it's a real privilege to be allowed to work with him. Well, so long, Chief."

He found that his interview with Sir Andrew Mackenzie had taken up a couple of hours, and that it was nearly eight o'clock. He was just trying to make up his mind where to dine when he was accosted by a cheerful young woman with bobbed red hair, dressed in a short checked skirt, brilliant jumper, corduroy jacket, and a rakish green velvet tam-o'-shanter.

" Surely," said the young woman, extending a shapely, ungloved hand, " it's Lord Peter Wimsey. How're you ? And how's Mary ? "

" B'Jove ! " said Wimsey gallantly, "it's Miss Tarrant. How perfectly rippin' to see you again. Absolutely delightful. Thanks, Mary ain't as fit as she might be—worryin' about this murder business, y'know. You've heard that we're what the poor so kindly and tactfully call ' in trouble,' I expect, what ? "

" Yes, of course," replied Miss Tarrant eagerly, " and, of course, as a good Socialist, I can't help rejoicing rather when a peer gets taken up, because it does make him look so silly, you know, and the House of Lords is silly, isn't it ? But, really, I'd rather it was anybody else's brother. Mary and I were such great friends, you know, and, of course, *you* do investigate things, don't you, not just live on your estates in the country and shoot birds ? So I suppose that makes a difference."

" That's very kind of you," said Peter. " If you can prevail upon yourself to overlook the misfortune of my birth and my other deficiencies, p'raps you would honour me by comin' along and havin' a bit of dinner somewhere, what ? "

" Oh, I'd have *loved* to," cried Miss Tarrant, with enormous energy, " but I've promised to be at the club to-night. There's a meeting at nine. Mr. Coke —the Labour leader, you know—is going to make a speech about converting the Army and Navy to Communism. We expect to be raided, and there's going to be a grand hunt for spies before we begin. But look here, do come along and dine with me there, and, if you like, I'll try to smuggle you in to the meeting, and you'll be seized and turned out. I suppose I oughtn't to have told you anything about it, because you ought to be a deadly enemy, but I can't really believe you're dangerous."

" I'm just an ordinary capitalist, I expect," said Lord Peter, " highly obnoxious."

" Well, come to dinner, anyhow. I *do* so want to hear all the news."

Peter reflected that the dinner at the Soviet Club would be worse than execrable, and was just preparing an excuse when it occurred to him that Miss Tarrant might be able to tell him a good many of the things that he didn't know, and really ought to know, about his own sister. Accordingly, he altered his polite refusal into a polite acceptance, and, plunging after Miss Tarrant, was led at a reckless pace and by a series of grimy short cuts into Gerrard Street, where an orange door, flanked by windows with magenta curtains, sufficiently indicated the Soviet Club.

The Soviet Club, being founded to accommodate free thinking rather than high living, had that curious amateur air which pervades all worldly institutions planned by unworldly people. Exactly why it made Lord Peter instantly think of mission teas he could not say, unless it was that all the members looked as though they cherished a purpose in life, and that the staff seemed rather sketchily trained and strongly in evidence. Wimsey reminded himself that in so democratic an institution one could hardly expect the assistants to assume that air of superiority which marks the servants in a West End club. For one thing, they would not be such capitalists. In the dining-room below the resemblance to a mission tea was increased by the exceedingly heated atmosphere, the babel of conversation, and the curious inequalities of the cutlery. Miss Tarrant secured seats at a rather crumby table near the serving-hatch, and Peter wedged himself in with some difficulty next to a very large, curly-haired man in a velvet coat, who was earnestly conversing with a thin, eager young woman in a Russian blouse, Venetian beads, a Hungarian shawl and a Spanish comb, looking like a personification of the United Front of the " Internationale."

Lord Peter endeavoured to please his hostess by a question about the great Mr. Coke, but was checked by an agitated " Hush ! "

" *Please* don't shout about it," said Miss Tarrant, leaning across till her auburn mop positively tickled his eyebrows. " It's *so* secret."

" I'm awfully sorry," said Wimsey apologetically. " I say, d'you know you're dipping those jolly little beads of yours in the soup ? "

" Oh, am I ? " cried Miss Tarrant, withdrawing hastily. " Oh, thank you so much. Especially as the colour runs. I hope it isn't arsenic or anything." Then, leaning forward again, she whispered hoarsely :

" The girl next me is Erica Heath-Warburton— the writer, you know."

Wimsey looked with a new respect at the lady in the Russian blouse. Few books were capable of calling up a blush to his cheek, but he remembered that one of Miss Heath-Warburton's had done it. The authoress was just saying impressively to her companion :

" —ever know a sincere emotion to express itself in a subordinate clause ? "

" Joyce has freed us from the superstition of syntax," agreed the curly man.

" Scenes which make emotional history," said Miss Heath-Warburton, " should ideally be expressed in a series of animal squeals."

" The D. H. Lawrence formula," said the other.

" Or even Dada," said the authoress.

" We need a new notation," said the curly-haired

man, putting both elbows on the table and knocking Wimsey's bread on to the floor. "Have you heard Robert Snoates recite his own verse to the tom-tom and the penny whistle?"

Lord Peter with difficulty detached his attention from this fascinating discussion to find that Miss Tarrant was saying something about Mary.

"One misses your sister very much" she said. "Her wonderful enthusiasm. She spoke so well at meetings. She had such a *real* sympathy with the worker."

"It seems astonishing to me," said Wimsey, "seeing Mary's never had to do a stroke of work in her life."

"Oh," cried Miss Tarrant, "but she *did* work. She worked for us. Wonderfully! She was secretary to our Propaganda Society for nearly six months. And then she worked so hard for Mr. Goyles. To say nothing of her nursing in the war. Of course, I don't approve of England's attitude in the war, but nobody would say the work wasn't hard."

"Who is Mr. Goyles?"

"Oh, one of our leading speakers—quite young, but the Government are really afraid of him. I expect he'll be here to-night. He has been lecturing in the North, but I believe he's back now."

"I say, do look out," said Peter. "Your beads are in your plate again."

"Are they? Well, perhaps they'll flavour the mutton. I'm afraid the cooking isn't very good here, but the subscription's so small, you see. I wonder Mary never told you about Mr. Goyles. They were so *very* friendly, you know, some time ago. Everybody thought she was going to marry him—but it seemed to fall through. And then your sister left town. Do you know about it?"

"That was the fellow, was it? Yes—well, my people didn't altogether see it, you know. Thought Mr. Goyles wasn't quite the son-in-law they'd take to. Family row and so on. Wasn't there myself; besides, Mary'd never listen to *me*. Still, that's what I gathered."

" Another instance of the absurd, old-fashioned tyranny of parents," said Miss Tarrant warmly. " You wouldn't think it could still be possible—in post-war times."

" I don't know," said Wimsey, " that you could exactly call it that. Not parents exactly. My mother's a remarkable woman. I don't think she interfered. Fact, I fancy she wanted to ask Mr. Goyles to Denver. But my brother put his foot down."

" Oh, well, what can you expect ? " said Miss Tarrant scornfully. " But I don't see what business it was of his."

" Oh, none," agreed Wimsey. " Only, owin' to my late father's circumscribed ideas of what was owin' to women, my brother has the handlin' of Mary's money till she marries with his consent. I don't say it's a good plan—I think it's a rotten plan. But there it is."

" Monstrous ! " said Miss Tarrant, shaking her head so angrily that she looked like shock-headed Peter. " Barbarous ! Simply feudal, you know. But, after all, what's money ? "

" Nothing, of course," said Peter. " But if you've been brought up to havin' it it's a bit awkward to drop it suddenly. Like baths, you know."

" I can't understand how it could have made any difference to Mary," persisted Miss Tarrant mournfully. " She liked being a worker. We once tried living in a workman's cottage for eight weeks, five of us, on eightteen shillings a week. It was a *marvellous* experience —on the very *edge* of the New Forest."

" In the winter ? "

" Well, no—we thought we'd better not *begin* with winter. But we had nine wet days, and the kitchen chimney smoked all the time. You see, the wood came out of the forest, so it was all damp."

" I see. It must have been uncommonly interestin'."

" It was an experience I shall *never* forget," said Miss Tarrant. " One felt so *close* to the earth and the primitive things. If only we could abolish industrialism. I'm afraid, though, we shall never get it put right without a ' bloody revolution,' you know. It's very terrible, of course, but salutary and inevitable. Shall we have coffee ? We shall have to carry it upstairs ourselves, if you don't mind. The maids don't bring it up after dinner."

Miss Tarrant settled her bill and returned, thrusting a cup of coffee into his hand. It had already overflowed into the saucer, and as he groped his way round a screen and up a steep and twisted staircase it overflowed quite an amount more.

Emerging from the basement, they almost ran into a young man with fair hair who was hunting for letters in a dark little row of pigeon-holes. Finding nothing, he retreated into the lounge. Miss Tarrant uttered an exclamation of pleasure.

" Why, there *is* Mr. Goyles," she cried.

Wimsey glanced across, and at the sight of the tall, slightly stooping figure with the untidy fair hair and the gloved right hand he gave an irrepressible little gasp.

" Won't you introduce me ? " he said.

" I'll fetch him," said Miss Tarrant. She made off across the lounge and addressed the young agitator, who started, looked across at Wimsey, shook his head. appeared to apologise, gave a hurried glance at his watch, and darted out by the entrance. Wimsey sprang forward in pursuit.

" Extraordinary," cried Miss Tarrant, with a blank face. " He says he has an appointment—but he can't surely be missing the——"

" Excuse me," said Peter. He dashed out, in time to perceive a dark figure retreating across the street. He gave chase. The man took to his heels, and seemed to plunge into the dark little alley which leads into the Charing Cross Road. Hurrying in pursuit, Wimsey was almost blinded by a sudden flash and smoke nearly in his face. A crashing blow on the left shoulder and a deafening report whirled his surroundings away. He staggered violently, and collapsed on to a second-hand brass bedstead.

CHAPTER VIII

MR. PARKER TAKES NOTES

A man was taken to the Zoo and shown the giraffe. After gazing at it a little in silence : " I don't believe it," he said.

PARKER'S first impulse was to doubt his own sanity; his next, to doubt Lady Mary's. Then, as the clouds rolled away from his brain, he decided that she was merely not speaking the truth.

" Come, Lady Mary," he said encouragingly, but with an accent of reprimand as to an over-imaginative child, " you can't expect us to believe that, you know."

" But you must," said the girl gravely ; " it's a fact. I shot him. I did, really. I didn't exactly mean to do it ; it was a—well, a sort of accident."

Mr. Parker got up and paced about the room.

" You have put me in a terrible position, Lady Mary," he said. " You see, I'm a police-officer. I never imagined——"

" It doesn't matter," said Lady Mary. " Of course you'll have to arrest me, or detain me, or whatever you call it. That's what I came for. I'm quite ready to go quietly—that's the right expression, isn't it ? I'd like to explain about it, though, first. Of course I ought to have done it long ago, but I'm afraid I lost my head. I didn't realise that Gerald would get blamed. I hoped they'd bring it in suicide. Do I make a statement to you now ? Or do I do it at the police-station ? "

Parker groaned.

" They won't—they won't punish me so badly if
it was an accident, will they ? " There was a quiver
in the voice.

" No, of course not—of course not. But if only you
had spoken earlier ! No," said Parker, stopping suddenly short in his distracted pacing and sitting down
beside her. " It's impossible—absurd." He caught
the girl's hand suddenly in his own. " Nothing will
convince me," he said. " It's absurd. It's not like
you."

" But an accident——"

" I don't mean that—you know I don't mean that.
But that you should keep silence——"

" I was afraid. I'm telling you now."

" No, no, no," cried the detective. " You're lying
to me. Nobly, I know ; but it's not worth it. No
man could be worth it. Let him go, I implore you.
Tell the truth. Don't shield this man. If he murdered Denis Cathcart——"

" *No !* " The girl sprang to her feet, wrenching
her hand away. " There was no other man. How
dare you say it or think it ! I killed Denis Cathcart,
I tell you, and you *shall* believe it. I swear to you
that there was no other man."

Parker pulled himself together.

" Sit down, please. Lady Mary, you are determined
to make this statement ? "

" Yes."

" Knowing that I have no choice but to act upon it ? "

" If you will not hear it I shall go straight to the
police."

Parker pulled out his note-book. " Go on," he said.

With no other sign of emotion than a nervous fidgeting with her gloves, Lady Mary began her confession in
a clear, hard voice, as though she were reciting it by
heart.

" On the evening of Wednesday, October 13th, I

147

went upstairs at half-past nine. I sat up writing a letter. At a quarter past ten I heard my brother and Denis quarrelling in the passage. I heard my brother call Denis a cheat, and tell him that he was never to speak to me again. I heard Denis run out. I listened for some time, but did not hear him return. At half-past eleven I became alarmed. I changed my dress and went out to try and find Denis and bring him in. I feared he might do something desperate. After some time I found him in the shrubbery. I begged him to come in. He refused, and he told me about my brother's accusation and the quarrel. I was very much horrified, of course. He said where was the good of denying anything, as Gerald was determined to ruin him, and asked me to go away and marry him and live abroad. I said I was surprised that he should suggest such a thing in the circumstances. We both became very angry. I said ' Come in now. To-morrow you can leave by the first train.' He seemed almost crazy. He pulled out a pistol and said that he'd come to the end of things, that his life was ruined, that we were a lot of hypocrites, and that I had never cared for him, or I shouldn't have minded what he'd done. Anyway, he said, if I wouldn't come with him it was all over, and he might as well be hanged for a sheep as a lamb—he'd shoot me and himself. I think he was quite out of his mind. He pulled out a revolver ; I caught his hand ; we struggled ; I got the muzzle right up against his chest, and—either I pulled the trigger or it went off of itself—I'm not clear which. It was all in such a whirl."

She paused. Parker's pen took down the words, and his face showed growing concern. Lady Mary went on :

" He wasn't quite dead. I helped him up. We struggled back nearly to the house. He fell once——"

" Why," asked Parker, " did you not leave him and run into the house to fetch help ? "

Lady Mary hesitated.

" It didn't occur to me. It was a nightmare. I could only think of getting him along. I think—*I think I wanted him to die.*"

There was a dreadful pause.

" He did die. He died at the door. I went into the conservatory and sat down. I sat for hours and tried to think. I hated him for being a cheat and a scoundrel. I'd been taken in, you see—made a fool of by a common sharper. I was glad he was dead. I must have sat there for hours without a coherent thought. It wasn't till my brother came along that I realised what I'd done, and that I might be suspected of murdering him. I was simply terrified. I made up my mind all in a moment that I'd pretend I knew nothing—that I'd heard a shot and come down. You know what I did."

" Why, Lady Mary," said Parker, in a perfectly toneless voice, " why did you say to your brother ' Good God, Gerald, you've killed him ' ? "

Another hesitant pause.

" I never said that. I said, ' Good God, Gerald, he's killed, then.' I never meant to suggest anything but suicide."

" You admitted to those words at the inquest ? "

" Yes——" Her hands knotted the gloves into all manner of shapes. " By that time I had decided on a burglar story, you see."

The telephone bell rang, and Parker went to the instrument. A voice came thinly over the wire :

" Is that 110 Piccadilly ? This is Charing Cross Hospital. A man was brought in to-night who says he is Lord Peter Wimsey. He was shot in the shoulder, and struck his head in falling. He has only just recovered consciousness. He was brought in at 9.15. No, he will probably do very well now. Yes, come round by all means."

" Peter has been shot," said Parker. " Will you

come round with me to Charing Cross Hospital ? They
say he is in no danger ; still——"

" Oh, quick ! " cried Lady Mary.

Gathering up Mr. Bunter as they hurried through
the hall, detective and self-accused rushed hurriedly
out into Pall Mall, and, picking up a belated taxi at
Hyde Park Corner, drove madly away through the
deserted streets.

CHAPTER IX

GOYLES

" —and the moral of that is——" said the Duchess.
—Alice's Adventures in Wonderland.

A PARTY of four were assembled next morning at a
very late breakfast, or very early lunch, in Lord Peter's
flat. Its most cheerful member, despite a throbbing
shoulder and a splitting headache, was undoubtedly
Lord Peter himself, who lay upon the Chesterfield
surrounded with cushions and carousing upon tea and
toast. Having been brought home in an ambulance, he
had instantly fallen into a healing sleep, and had woken
at nine o'clock aggressively clear and active in mind. In
consequence, Mr. Parker had been dispatched in a hurry,
half-fed and burdened with the secret memory of last
night's disclosures, to Scotland Yard. Here he had set
in motion the proper machinery for catching Lord
Peter's assassin. " Only don't you say anything about
the attack on me," said his lordship. " Tell 'em he's to
be detained in connection with the Riddlesdale case.
That's good enough for them." It was now eleven, and
Mr. Parker had returned, gloomy and hungry, and was
consuming a belated omelette and a glass of claret.

Lady Mary Wimsey was hunched up in the window-
seat. Her bobbed golden hair made a little blur of light
about her in the pale autumn sunshine. She had made
an attempt to breakfast earlier, and now sat gazing out
into Piccadilly. Her first appearance that morning had
been made in Lord Peter's dressing-gown, but she now

151

wore a serge skirt and jade-green jumper, which had been brought to town for her by the fourth member of the party, now composedly eating a mixed grill and sharing the decanter with Parker.

This was a rather short, rather plump, very brisk elderly lady, with bright black eyes like a bird's, and very handsome white hair exquisitely dressed. Far from looking as though she had just taken a long night journey, she was easily the most composed and trim of the four. She was, however, annoyed, and said so at considerable length. This was the Dowager Duchess of Denver.

" It is not so much, Mary, that you went off so abruptly last night—just before dinner, too—inconveniencing and alarming us very much—indeed, poor Helen was totally unable to eat her dinner, which was extremely distressing to her feelings, because, you know, she always makes such a point of never being upset about anything—I really don't know why, for some of the greatest men have not minded showing their feelings, I don't mean Southerners necessarily, but, as Mr. Chesterton very rightly points out—Nelson, too, who was certainly English if he wasn't Irish or Scotch, I forget, but United Kingdom, anyway (if that means anything nowadays with a Free State—such a ridiculous title, especially as it always makes one think of the Orange Free State, and I'm sure they wouldn't care to be mixed up with that, being so very green themselves). And going off without even proper clothes, and taking the car, so that I had to wait till the 1.15 from Northallerton—a ridiculous time to start, and such a bad train, too, not getting up till 10.30. Besides, if you *must* run off to town, why do it in that unfinished manner ? If you had only looked up the trains before starting you would have seen you would have half an hour's wait at Northallerton, and you could quite easily have packed a bag. It's so much better to do things neatly and thoroughly—even stupid things. And it was very stupid of you indeed to dash off like that, to embarrass and bore poor Mr. Parker with a lot of twaddle—though I suppose it was Peter you meant to see. You know, Peter, if you will haunt low places full of Russians and sucking Socialists taking themselves seriously, you ought to know better than to encourage them by running after them, however futile, and given to drinking coffee and writing poems with no shape to them, and generally ruining their nerves. And, in any case, it makes not the slightest difference ; I could have told Peter all about it myself, if he doesn't know already, as he probably does."

Lady Mary turned very white at this and glanced at Parker, who replied rather to her than to the Dowager :

" No, Lord Peter and I haven't had time to discuss anything yet."

" Lest it should ruin my shattered nerves and bring a fever to my aching brow," added that nobleman amiably. " You're a kind, thoughtful soul, Charles, and I don't know what I should do without you. I wish that rotten old second-hand dealer had been a bit brisker about takin' in his stock-in-trade for the night, though. Perfectly 'straor'nary number of knobs there are on a brass bedstead. Saw it comin', y'know, an' couldn't stop myself. However, what's a mere brass bedstead ? The great detective, though at first stunned and dizzy from his brutal treatment by the fifteen veiled assassins all armed with meat-choppers, soon regained his senses, thanks to his sound constitution and healthy manner of life. Despite the severe gassing he had endured in the underground room—eh ? A telegram ? Oh, thanks, Bunter."

Lord Peter appeared to read the message with great inward satisfaction, for his long lips twitched at the corners, and he tucked the slip of paper away in his pocket-book with a little sigh of satisfaction. He called to Bunter to take away the breakfast-tray and to renew the cooling bandage about his brow. This done, Lord Peter leaned back among his cushions, and with an air of malicious enjoyment launched at Mr. Parker the inquiry :

" Well, now, how did you and Mary get on last night ? Polly, did you tell him you'd done the murder ? "

Few things are more irritating than to discover, after you have been at great pains to spare a person some painful intelligence, that he has known it all along and is not nearly so much affected by it as he properly should be. Mr. Parker quite simply and suddenly lost his temper. He bounded to his feet, and exclaimed, without the least reason : " Oh, it's perfectly hopeless trying to do anything ! "

Lady Mary sprang from the window-seat.

" Yes, I did," she said. " It's quite true. Your precious case is finished, Peter."

The Dowager said, without the least discomposure : " You must allow your brother to be the best judge of his own affairs, my dear."

" As a matter of fact," replied his lordship, " I rather fancy Polly's right. Hope so, I'm sure. Anyway, we've got the fellow, so now we shall know."

Lady Mary gave a sort of gasp, and stepped forward with her chin up and her hands tightly clenched. It caught at Parker's heart to see overwhelming catastrophe so bravely faced. The official side of him was thoroughly bewildered, but the human part ranged itself instantly in support of that gallant defiance.

" Whom have they got ? " he demanded, in a voice quite unlike his own.

" The Goyles person," said Lord Peter carelessly. " Uncommon quick work, what ? But since he'd no more original idea than to take the boat-train to Folkestone they didn't have much difficulty."

" It isn't true," said Lady Mary. She stamped. " It's a lie. He wasn't there. He's innocent. I killed Denis."

" Fine," thought Parker, " fine ! Damn Goyles, anyway, what's he done to deserve it ? "

Lord Peter said : " Mary, don't be an ass."

" Yes," said the Dowager placidly. " I was going to suggest to you, Peter, that this Mr. Goyles—such a terrible name, Mary dear, I can't say I ever cared for it, even if there had been nothing else against him —especially as he would sign himself Geo. Goyles— G. e. o. you know, Mr. Parker, for George, and I never *could* help reading it as Gargoyles—I very nearly wrote to you, my dear, mentioning Mr. Goyles, and asking if you could see him in town, because there was something, when I came to think of it, about that ipecacuanha business that made me feel he might have something to do with it."

" Yes," said Peter, with a grin, " you always did find him a bit sickenin', didn't you ? "

" How can you, Wimsey ? " growled Parker reproachfully, with his eyes on Mary's face.

" Never mind him," said the girl. " If you can't be a gentleman, Peter——"

" Damn it all ! " cried the invalid explosively. " Here's a fellow who, without the slightest provocation, plugs a bullet into my shoulder, breaks my collar-bone, brings me up head foremost on a knobbly second-hand brass bedstead and vamooses, and when, in what seems to me jolly mild, parliamentary language, I call him a sickenin' feller my own sister says I'm no gentleman. Look at me ! In my own house, forced to sit here with a perfectly beastly headache, and lap up toast and tea, while you people distend and bloat yourselves on mixed grills and omelettes and a damn good vintage claret——"

" Silly boy," said the Duchess, " don't get so excited. And it's time for your medicine. Mr. Parker, kindly touch the bell."

Mr. Parker obeyed in silence. Lady Mary came slowly across, and stood looking at her brother.

" Peter," she said, " what makes you say that *he* did it ? "

" Did what ? "

" Shot—you ? " The words were only a whisper.
The entrance of Mr. Bunter at this moment with a
cooling draught dissipated the tense atmosphere. Lord
Peter quaffed his potion, had his pillows re-arranged,
submitted to have his temperature taken and his pulse
counted, asked if he might not have an egg for his
lunch, and lit a cigarette. Mr. Bunter retired, people
distributed themselves into more comfortable chairs, and
felt happier.

" Now, Polly, old girl," said Peter, " cut out the sob-
stuff. I accidentally ran into this Goyles chap last night
at your Soviet Club. I asked that Miss Tarrant to introduce me, but the minute Goyles heard my name, he
made tracks. I rushed out after him, only meanin' to
have a word with him, when the idiot stopped at the
corner of Newport Court, potted me, and bunked.
Silly-ass thing to do. I knew who he was. He couldn't
help gettin' caught."

" Peter——" said Mary in a ghastly voice.

" Look here, Polly," said Wimsey. " I did think of
you. Honest injun, I did. I haven't had the man
arrested. I've made no charge at all—have I, Parker ?
What did you tell 'em to do when you were down at
the Yard this morning ? "

" To detain Goyles pending inquiries, because he
was wanted as a witness in the Riddlesdale case," said
Parker slowly.

" He knows nothing about it," said Mary, doggedly
now. " He wasn't anywhere near. He is innocent of
that ! "

" Do you think so ? " said Lord Peter gravely. " If
you know he is innocent, why tell all these lies to screen
him ? It won't do, Mary. You know he was there—
and you think he is guilty."

" No ! "

" Yes," said Wimsey, grasping her with his sound
hand as she shrank away. " Mary, have you thought
what you are doing ? You are perjuring yourself and

putting Gerald in peril of his life, in order to shield from justice a man whom you suspect of murdering your lover and who has most certainly tried to murder me."

" Oh," cried Parker, in an agony, " all this interrogation is horribly irregular."

" Never mind him," said Peter. " Do you really think you're doing the right thing, Mary ? "

The girl looked helplessly at her brother for a minute or two. Peter cocked up a whimsical, appealing eye from under his bandages. The defiance melted out of her face.

" I'll tell the truth," said Lady Mary.

" Good egg," said Peter, extending a hand. " I'm sorry. I know you like the fellow, and we appreciate your decision enormously. Truly, we do. Now, sail ahead, old thing, and you take it down, Parker."

" Well, it really all started years ago with George. You were at the Front then, Peter, but I suppose they told you about it—and put everything in the worst possible light."

" I wouldn't say that, dear," put in the Duchess. " I think I told Peter that your brother and I were not altogether pleased with what we had seen of the young man— which was not very much, if you remember. He invited himself down one week-end when the house was very full, and he seemed to make a point of consulting nobody's convenience but his own. And you know, dear, you even said yourself you thought he was unnecessarily rude to poor old Lord Mountweazle."

" He said what he thought," said Mary. " Of course, Lord Mountweazle, poor dear, doesn't understand that the present generation is accustomed to discuss things with its elders, not just kow-tow to them. When George gave his opinion, he thought he was just contradicting."

" To be sure," said the Dowager, " when you flatly deny everything a person says it does sound like contradiction to the uninitiated. But all I remember saying to Peter was that Mr. Goyles's manners seemed to me to lack polish, and that he showed a lack of independence in his opinions."

" A lack of independence ? " said Mary, wide-eyed.

" Well, dear, I thought so. What oft was thought and frequently much better expressed, as Pope says—or was it somebody else ? But the worse you express yourself these days the more profound people think you —though that's nothing new. Like Browning and those quaint metaphysical people, when you never know whether they really mean their mistress or the Established Church, so bridegroomy and biblical—to say nothing of dear S. Augustine—the Hippo man, I mean, not the one who missionised over here, though I daresay he was delightful too, and in those days I suppose they didn't have annual sales of work and tea in the parish room, so it doesn't seem quite like what we mean nowadays by missionaries—he knew all about it—you remember about that mandrake—or is that the thing you had to get a big black dog for ? Manichee, that's the word. What was his name ? Was it Faustus ? Or am I mixing him up with the old man in the opera ? "

" Well, anyway," said Mary, without stopping to disentangle the Duchess's sequence of ideas, " George was the only person I really cared about—he still is. Only it did seem so hopeless. Perhaps you didn't say much about him, mother, but Gerald said *lots*—dreadful things ! "

" Yes," said the Duchess, " he said what he thought. The present generation does, you know. To the uninitiated, I admit, dear, it does sound a little rude."

Peter grinned, but Mary went on unheeding.

" George had simply *no* money. He'd really given everything he had to the Labour Party one way and another, and he'd lost his job in the Ministry of Information : they found he had too much sympathy with the Socialists abroad. It was awfully unfair. Anyhow, one couldn't be a burden on him ; and Gerald was a beast, and said he'd absolutely stop my allowance if I didn't send George away. So I did, but of course it didn't make a bit of difference to the way we both felt. I will say for mother she was a bit more decent. She said she'd help us if George got a job ; but, as I pointed out, if George got a job we shouldn't *need* helping ! "

" But, my dear, I could hardly insult Mr. Goyles by suggesting that he should live on his mother-in-law," said the Dowager.

" Why not ? " said Mary. " George doesn't believe in those old-fashioned ideas about property. Besides, if you'd given it to me, it would be *my* money. We believe in men and women being equal. Why should the one always be the bread-winner more than the other ? "

" I can't imagine, dear," said the Dowager. " Still, I could hardly expect poor Mr. Goyles to live on unearned increment when he didn't believe in inherited property."

" That's a fallacy," said Mary, rather vaguely. " Anyhow," she added hastily, " that's what happened. Then, after the war, George went to Germany to study Socialism and Labour questions there, and nothing seemed any good. So when Denis Cathcart turned up, I said I'd marry him."

" Why ? " asked Peter. " He never sounded to me a bit the kind of bloke for you. I mean, as far as I could make out, he was Tory and diplomatic and —well, quite crusted old tawny, so to speak, I shouldn't have thought you had an idea in common."

" No ; but then he didn't care twopence whether I had any ideas or not. I made him promise he wouldn't bother me with diplomats and people, and he said no, I could do as I liked, provided I didn't compromise him. And we were to live in Paris and go our own ways and not bother. And anything was better than staying here, and marrying somebody in one's own set, and opening bazaars and watching polo and meeting the Prince of Wales. So I said I'd marry Denis, because I didn't care about him, and I'm pretty sure he didn't care a halfpenny about me, and we should have left each other alone. I did so want to be left alone ! "

" Was Jerry all right about your money ? " inquired Peter.

" Oh, yes. He said Denis was no great catch—I do wish Gerald wasn't so vulgar, in that flat, early-Victorian way—but he said that, after George, he could only thank his stars it wasn't worse."

" Make a note of that, Charles," said Wimsey.

" Well, it seemed all right at first, but, as things went on, I got more and more depressed. Do you know, there was something a little alarming about Denis. He was so extraordinarily reserved. I know I wanted to be left alone, but—well, it was uncanny ! He was correct. Even when he went off the deep end and was passionate—which didn't often happen—he was correct about it. Extraordinary. Like one of those odd French novels, you know, Peter : frightfully hot stuff, but absolutely impersonal."

" Charles, old man ! " said Lord Peter.

" M'm ? "

" That's important. You realise the bearing of that?"

" No."

" Never mind. Drive on, Polly."

" Aren't I making your head ache ? "

" Damnably ; but I like it. Do go on. I'm not sprouting a lily with anguish moist and fever-dew, or anything like that. I'm getting really thrilled. What you've just said is more illuminating than anything I've struck for a week."

" Really ! " Mary stared at Peter with every trace of hostility vanished. " I thought you'd never understand that part."

" Lord ! " said Peter. " Why not ? "

Mary shook her head. " Well, I'd been corresponding all the time with George, and suddenly he wrote to me at the beginning of this month to say he'd come back from Germany, and had got a job on the *Thunderclap*— the Socialist weekly, you know— at a beginning screw of £4 a week, and wouldn't I chuck these capitalists and so on, and come and be an honest working woman with him. He could get me a secretarial job on the paper. I was to type and so on for him, and help him get his articles together. And he thought between us we should make £6 or £7 a week, which would be heaps to live on. And I was getting more frightened of Denis every day. So I said I would. But I knew there'd be an awful row with Gerald. And really I was rather ashamed—the engagement had been announced and there'd be a ghastly lot of talk and people trying to persuade me. And Denis might have made things horribly uncomfortable for Gerald—he was rather that sort. So we decided the best thing to do would be just to run away and get married first, and escape the wrangling."

" Quite so," said Peter. " Besides, it would look rather well in the paper, wouldn't it ? ' Peer's Daughter Weds Socialist—Romantic Side-car Elopement—" £6 a week Plenty," says Her Ladyship.' "

" Pig ! " said Lady Mary.

" Very good," said Peter, " I get you ! So it was arranged that the romantic Goyles should fetch you away from Riddlesdale—why Riddlesdale ? It would be twice as easy from London or Denver."

" No. For one thing he had to be up North. And everybody knows one in town, and—anyhow, we didn't want to wait."

" Besides, one would miss the Young Lochinvar touch. Well, then, why at the unearthly hour of 3 a.m.?"

" He had a meeting on Wednesday night at Northallerton. He was going to come straight on and pick me up, and run me down to town to be married by special license. We allowed ample time. George had to be at the office next day."

" I see. Well, I'll go on now, and you stop me if I'm wrong. You went up at 9.30 on Wednesday night. You packed a suit-case. You—did you think of writing any sort of letter to comfort your sorrowing friends and relations ? "

" Yes, I wrote one. But I——"

" Of course. Then you went to bed, I fancy, or, at any rate, turned the clothes back and lay down."

" Yes. I lay down. It was a good thing I did, as it happened——"

" True, you wouldn't have had much time to make the bed look probable in the morning, and we should have heard about it. By the way, Parker, when Mary confessed her sins to you last night, did you make any notes ? "

" Yes," said Parker, " if you can read my shorthand."

" Quite so," said Peter. " Well, the rumpled bed disposes of your story about never having gone to bed at all, doesn't it ? "

" And I thought it was such a good story ! "

" Want of practice," replied her brother kindly. " You'll do better, next time. It's just as well, really that it's so hard to tell a long, consistent lie. *Did* you, as a matter of fact, hear Gerald go out at 11.30, as Pettigrew-Robinson (damn his ears !) said ? "

" I fancy I did hear somebody moving about," said Mary, " but I didn't think much about it."

" Quite right," said Peter, "when I hear people movin' about the house at night, I'm much too delicate-minded to think anything at all."

" Of course," interposed the Duchess, " particularly in England, where it is so oddly improper to think. I will say for Peter that, if he can put a continental interpretation on anything, he will—so considerate of you, dear, as soon as you took to doing it in silence and not

162

mentioning it, as you so intelligently did as a child. You were really a very observant little boy, dear."

" And still is," said Mary, smiling at Peter with surprising friendliness.

" Old bad habits die hard," said Wimsey. " To proceed. At three o'clock you went down to meet Goyles. Why did he come all the way up to the house ? It would have been safer to meet him in the lane."

" I knew I couldn't get out of the lodge-gate without waking Hardraw, and so I'd have to get over the palings somewhere. I might have managed alone, but not with a heavy suit-case. So, as George would have to climb over, anyhow, we thought he'd better come and help carry the suit-case. And then we couldn't miss each other by the conservatory door. I sent him a little plan of the path."

" Was Goyles there when you got downstairs ? "

" No—at least—no, I didn't see him. But there was poor Denis's body, and Gerald bending over it. My first idea was that Gerald had killed George. That's why I said, ' Oh, God ! you've killed him ! ' " (Peter glanced across at Parker and nodded.) " Then Gerald turned him over, and I saw it was Denis—and then I'm sure I heard something moving a long way off in the shrubbery—a noise like twigs snapping—and it suddenly came over me, where was George ? Oh, Peter, I saw everything then, so clearly. I saw that Denis must have come on George waiting there, and attacked him— I'm sure Denis must have attacked him. Probably he thought it was a burglar. Or he found out who he was and tried to drive him away. And in the struggle George must have shot him. It was awful ! "

Peter patted his sister on the shoulder. " Poor kid," he said.

" I didn't know what to do," went on the girl. " I'd so awfully little time, you see. My one idea was that nobody must suspect anybody had been there. So I had quickly to invent an excuse for being there myself.

I shoved my suit-case behind the cactus-plants to start with. Jerry was taken up with the body and didn't notice—you know, Jerry never *does* notice things till you shove them under his nose. But I knew if there'd been a shot Freddy and the Marchbankses must have heard it. So I pretended I'd heard it too, and rushed down to look for burglars. It was a bit lame, but the best thing I could think of. Gerald sent me up to alarm the house, and I had the story all ready by the time I reached the landing. Oh, and I was quite proud of myself for not forgetting the suit-case ! "

" You dumped it into the chest," said Peter.

" Yes. I had a horrible shock the other morning when I found you looking in."

" Nothing like the shock I had when I found the silver sand there."

" Silver sand ? "

" Out of the conservatory."

" Good gracious ! " said Mary.

" Well, go on. You knocked up Freddy and the Pettigrew-Robinsons. Then you had to bolt into your room to destroy your farewell letter and take your clothes off."

" Yes. I'm afraid I didn't do that very naturally. But I couldn't expect anybody to believe that I went burglar-hunting in a complete set of silk undies and a carefully knotted tie with a gold safety-pin."

" No. I see your difficulty."

" It turned out quite well, too, because they were all quite ready to believe that I wanted to escape from Mrs. Pettigrew-Robinson—except Mrs. P. herself, of course."

" Yes ; even Parker swallowed that, didn't you, old man ? "

" Oh, quite, quite so," said Parker gloomily.

" I made a dreadful mistake about that shot," resumed Lady Mary. " You see, I explained it all so elaborately —and then I found that nobody had heard a shot at all. And afterwards they discovered that it had all happened in the shrubbery—and the time wasn't right, either. Then at the inquest I *had* to stick to my story—and it got to look worse and worse—and then they put the blame on Gerald. In my wildest moments I'd never thought of that. Of course, I see now how my wretched evidence helped."

" Hence the ipecacuanha," said Peter.

" I'd got into such a frightful tangle," said poor Lady Mary, " I thought I had better shut up altogether for fear of making things still worse."

" And did you still think Goyles had done it ? "

" I—I didn't know what to think," said the girl. " I don't now. Peter, who else *could* have done it ? "

" Honestly, old thing," said his lordship, " if he didn't do it, I don't know who did."

" He ran away, you see," said Lady Mary.

" He seems rather good at shootin' and runnin' away," said Peter grimly.

" If he hadn't done that to you," said Mary slowly, " I'd never have told you. I'd have died first. But of course, with his revolutionary doctrines—and when you think of red Russia and all the blood spilt in riots and insurrections and things—I suppose it does teach a contempt for human life."

" My dear," said the Duchess, " it seems to me that Mr. Goyles shows no especial contempt for his own life. You must try to look at the thing fairly. Shooting people and running away is not very heroic— according to *our* standards."

" The thing I don't understand," struck in Wimsey hurriedly, " is how Gerald's revolver got into the shrubbery."

" The thing I should like to know about," said the Duchess, " is, was Denis really a card-sharper ? "

" The thing *I* should like to know about," said Parker, " is the green-eyed cat."

" Denis *never* gave me a cat," said Mary. " That was a tarradiddle."

" Were you ever in a jeweller's with him in the Rue de la Paix ? "

" Oh, yes ; heaps of times. And he gave me a diamond and tortoiseshell comb. But never a cat."

" Then we may disregard the whole of last night's elaborate confession," said Lord Peter, looking through Parker's notes, with a smile. " It's really not bad, Polly, not bad at all. You've quite a talent for romantic fiction —no, I mean it ! Just here and there you need more attention to detail. For instance, you *couldn't* have dragged that badly wounded man all up the path to the house without getting blood all over your coat, you know. By the way, did Goyles know Cathcart at all ? "

" Not to my knowledge."

" Because Parker and I had an alternative theory, which would clear Goyles from the worst part of the charge, anyhow. Tell her, old man ; it was your idea."

Thus urged, Parker outlined the blackmail and suicide theory.

" That sounds plausible," said Mary—" academically speaking, I mean ; but it isn't a bit like George—I mean, blackmail is so *beastly*, isn't it ? "

" Well," said Peter, " I think the best thing is to go and see Goyles. Whatever the key to Wednesday night's riddle is, he holds it. Parker, old man, we're nearing the end of the chase."

CHAPTER X

NOTHING ABIDES AT THE NOON

" *Alas !* " *said Hiya,* " *the sentiments which this person expressed with irreproachable honourableness, when the sun was high in the heavens and the probability of secretly leaving an undoubtedly well-appointed home was engagingly remote, seem to have an entirely different significance when recalled by night in a damp orchard, and on the eve of their fulfilment.*"—The Wallet of Kai-Lung.

And his short minute, after noon, is night.—Donne.

MR. GOYLES was interviewed the next day at the police-station. Mr. Murbles was present, and Mary insisted on coming. The young man began by blustering a little, but the solicitor's dry manner made its impression.

" Lord Peter Wimsey identifies you," said Mr. Murbles, " as the man who made a murderous attack upon him last night. With remarkable generosity, he has forborne to press the charge. Now we know further that you were present at Riddlesdale Lodge on the night when Captain Cathcart was shot. You will no doubt be called as a witness in the case. But you would greatly assist justice by making a statement to us now. This is a purely friendly and private interview, Mr. Goyles. As you see, no representative of the police is present. We simply ask for your help. I ought, however, to warn you that, whereas it is, of course, fully competent for you to refuse to answer any of our questions, a refusal might lay you open to the gravest imputations."

" In fact," said Goyles, " it's a threat. If I don't tell you, you'll have me arrested on suspicion of murder."

" Dear me, no, Mr. Goyles," returned the solicitor. " We should merely place what information we hold in the hands of the police, who would then act as they thought fit. God bless my soul, no—anything like a threat would be highly irregular. In the matter of the assault upon Lord Peter, his lordship will, of course, use his own discretion."

" Well," said Goyles sullenly, " it's a threat, call it what you like. However, I don't mind speaking— especially as you'll be jolly well disappointed. I suppose you gave me away, Mary."

Mary flushed indignantly.

" My sister has been extraordinarily loyal to you, Mr. Goyles," said Lord Peter. " I may tell you, indeed, that she put herself into a position of grave personal inconvenience—not to say danger—on your behalf. You were traced to London in consequence of your having left unequivocal traces in your exceedingly hasty retreat. When my sister accidentally opened a telegram addressed to me at Riddlesdale by my family name she hurried immediately to town, to shield you if she could, at any cost to herself. Fortunately I had already received a duplicate wire at my flat. Even then I was not certain of your identity when I accidentally ran across you at the Soviet Club. Your own energetic efforts, however, to avoid an interview gave me complete certainty, together with an excellent excuse for detaining you. In fact, I'm uncommonly obliged to you for your assistance."

Mr. Goyles looked resentful.

" I don't know how you could think, George——" said Mary.

" Never mind what I think," said the young man, roughly. " I gather you've told 'em all about it now, anyhow. Well, I'll tell you my story as shortly as I can, and you'll see I know damn all about it. If you don't believe me I can't help it. I came along at about a quarter to three, and parked the 'bus in the lane."

" Where were you at 11.50 ? "

" On the road from Northallerton. My meeting didn't finish till 10.45. I can bring a hundred witnesses to prove it."

Wimsey made a note of the address where the meeting had been held, and nodded to Goyles to proceed.

" I climbed over the wall and walked through the shrubbery."

" You saw no person, and no body ? "

" Nobody, alive or dead."

" Did you notice any blood or footprints on the path ? "

" No. I didn't like to use my torch, for fear of being seen from the house. There was just light enough to see the path. I came to the door of the conservatory just before three. As I came up I stumbled over something. I felt it, and it was like a body. I was alarmed. I thought it might be Mary—ill or fainted or something. I ventured to turn on my light. Then I saw it was Cathcart, dead."

" You are sure he was dead ? "

" Stone dead."

" One moment," interposed the solicitor. " You say you saw that it was Cathcart. Had you known Cathcart previously ? "

" No, never. I meant that I saw it was a dead man, and learnt afterwards that it was Cathcart."

" In fact, you do not, now, know of your own know-ledge, that it was Cathcart ? "

" Yes—at least, I recognised the photographs in the papers afterwards."

" It is very necessary to be accurate in making a statement, Mr. Goyles. A remark such as you made just now might give a most unfortunate impression to the police or to a jury."

So saying, Mr. Murbles blew his nose, and resettled his pince-nez.

" What next ? " inquired Peter.

" I fancied I heard somebody coming up the path. I did not think it wise to be found there with the corpse, so I cleared out."

" Oh," said Peter, with an indescribable expression, " that was a very simple solution. You left the girl you were going to marry to make for herself the unpleasant discovery that there was a dead man in the garden and that her gallant wooer had made tracks. What did you expect *her* to think ? "

" Well, I thought she'd keep quiet for her own sake. As a matter of fact, I didn't think very clearly about anything. I knew I'd broken in where I had no business, and that if I was found with a murdered man it might look jolly queer for me."

" In fact," said Mr. Murbles, " you lost your head, young man, and ran away in a very foolish and cowardly manner."

" You needn't put it that way," retorted Mr. Goyles. " I was in a very awkward and stupid situation to start with."

" Yes," said Lord Peter ironically, " and 3 a.m. is a nasty, chilly time of day. Next time you arrange an elopement, make it for six o'clock in the evening, or twelve o'clock at night. You seem better at framing conspiracies than carrying them out. A little thing upsets your nerves, Mr. Goyles. I don't really think, you know, that a person of your temperament should carry fire-arms. What in the world, you blitherin' young ass, made you loose off that pop-gun at me last night ? You *would* have been in a damned awkward situation then, if you'd accidentally hit me in the head or the heart or anywhere that mattered. If you're so frightened of a dead body, why go about shootin' at people ? Why, why, why ? That's what beats me. If you're tellin' the truth now, you never stood in the slightest danger. Lord ! and to think of the time and trouble we've had to waste catchin' you—you ass ! And

170

poor old Mary, workin' away and half killin' herself, because she thought at least you wouldn't have run away unless there was somethin' to run from ! "

" You must make allowance for a nervous temperament," said Mary in a hard voice.

" If you knew what it felt like to be shadowed and followed and badgered——" began Mr. Goyles.

" But I thought you Soviet Club people enjoyed being suspected of things," said Lord Peter. " Why, it ought to be the proudest moment of your life when you're really looked on as a dangerous fellow."

" It's the sneering of men like you," said Goyles passionately, " that does more to breed hatred between class and class——"

" Never mind about that," interposed Mr. Murbles. " The law's the law for everybody, and you have managed to put yourself in a very awkward position, young man." He touched a bell on the table, and Parker entered with a constable. " We shall be obliged to you," said Mr. Murbles, " if you will kindly have this young man kept under observation. We make no charge against him so long as he behaves himself, but he must not attempt to abscond before the Riddlesdale case comes up for trial."

" Certainly not, sir," said Mr. Parker.

" One moment," said Mary. " Mr. Goyles, here is the ring you gave me. Good-bye. When next you make a public speech calling for decisive action I will come and applaud it. You speak so well about that sort of thing. But otherwise, I think we had better not meet again."

" Of course," said the young man bitterly, " your people have forced me into this position, and you turn round and sneer at me too."

" I didn't mind thinking you were a murderer," said Lady Mary spitefully, " but I *do* mind your being such an ass."

Before Mr. Goyles could reply, Mr. Parker, be-

171

wildered but not wholly displeased, manœuvred his charge out of the room. Mary walked over to the window, and stood biting her lips.

Presently Lord Peter came across to her. " I say, Polly, old Murbles has asked us to lunch. Would you like to come ? Sir Impey Biggs will be there."

" I don't want to meet him to-day. It's very kind of Mr. Murbles——"

" Oh, come along, old thing. Biggs is some celebrity, you know, and perfectly toppin' to look at, in a marbly kind of way. He'll tell you all about his canaries——"

Mary giggled through her obstinate tears.

" It's perfectly sweet of you, Peter, to try and amuse the baby. But I can't. I'd make a fool of myself. I've been made enough of a fool of for one day."

" Bosh," said Peter. " Of course, Goyles didn't show up very well this morning, but, then, he was in an awfully difficult position. *Do* come."

" I hope Lady Mary consents to adorn my bachelor establishment," said the solicitor, coming up. " I shall esteem it a very great honour. I really do not think I have entertained a lady in my chambers for twenty years—dear me, twenty years indeed it must be."

" In that case," said Lady Mary, " I simply *can't* refuse."

Mr. Murbles inhabited a delightful old set of rooms in Staple Inn, with windows looking out upon the formal garden, with its odd little flower-beds and tinkling fountain. The chambers kept up to a miracle the old-fashioned law atmosphere which hung about his own prim person. His dining-room was furnished in mahogany, with a Turkey carpet and crimson curtains. On his sideboard stood some pieces of handsome Sheffield plate and a number of decanters with engraved silver labels round their necks. There was a bookcase full of large volumes bound in law calf, and an oil-painting of a harsh-featured judge over the mantelpiece.

Lady Mary felt a sudden gratitude for this discreet and solid Victorianism.

" I fear we may have to wait a few moments for Sir Impey," said Mr. Murbles, consulting his watch. " He is engaged in Quangle & Hamper v. *Truth*, but they expect to be through this morning—in fact, Sir Impey fancied that midday would see the end of it. Brilliant man, Sir Impey. He is defending *Truth*."

" Astonishin' position for a lawyer, what ? " said Peter.

" The newspaper," said Mr. Murbles, acknowledging the pleasantry with a slight unbending of the lips, " against these people who profess to cure fifty-nine different diseases with the same pill. Quangle & Hamper produced some of their patients in court to testify to the benefits they'd enjoyed from the cure. To hear Sir Impey handling them was an intellectual treat. His kindly manner goes a long way with old ladies. When he suggested that one of them should show her leg to the Bench the sensation in court was really phenomenal."

" And did she show it ? " inquired Lord Peter.

" Panting for the opportunity, my dear Lord Peter, panting for the opportunity."

" I wonder they had the nerve to call her."

" Nerve ? " said Mr. Murbles. " The nerve of men like Quangle & Hamper has not its fellow in the universe, to adopt the expression of the great Shakespeare. But Sir Impey is not the man to take liberties with. We are really extremely fortunate to have secured his help.— Ah, I think I hear him ! "

A hurried footstep on the stair indeed announced learned counsel, who burst in, still in wig and gown, and full of apology.

" Extremely sorry, Murbles," said Sir Impey. " We became excessively tedious at the end, I regret to say. I really did my best, but dear old Dowson is getting as deaf as a post, you know, and terribly fumbling in his movements.—And how are you, Wimsey ? You look

173

as if you'd been in the wars. Can we bring an action for assault against anybody ? "

" Much better than that," put in Mr. Murbles ; " attempted murder, if you please."

" Excellent, excellent," said Sir Impey.

" Ah, but we've decided not to prosecute," said Mr. Murbles, shaking his head.

" Really ! Oh, my dear Wimsey, this will never do. Lawyers have to live, you know. Your sister ? I hadn't the pleasure of meeting you at Riddlesdale, Lady Mary. I trust you are fully recovered."

" Entirely, thank you," said Mary with emphasis.

" Mr. Parker—of course your name is very familiar. Wimsey, here, can't do a thing without you, I know. Murbles, are these gentlemen full of valuable information ? I am immensely interested in this case."

" Not just this moment, though," put in the solicitor.

" Indeed, no. Nothing but that excellent saddle of mutton has the slightest attraction for me just now. Forgive my greed."

" Well, well," said Mr. Murbles, beaming mildly, " let's make a start. I fear, my dear young people, I am old-fashioned enough not to have adopted the modern practice of cocktail-drinking."

" Quite right too," said Wimsey emphatically. " Ruins the palate and spoils the digestion. Not an English custom—rank sacrilege in this old Inn. Came from America—result, prohibition. That's what happens to people, who don't understand how to drink. God bless me, sir, why, you're giving us the famous claret. It's a sin so much as to mention a cocktail in its presence."

" Yes," said Mr. Murbles, " yes, that's the Lafite '75. It's very seldom, very seldom, I bring it out for anybody under fifty years of age—but you, Lord Peter, have a discrimination which would do honour to one of twice your years."

" Thanks very much, sir ; that's a testimonial I deeply appreciate. May I circulate the bottle, sir ? "

"Do, do—we will wait on ourselves, Simpson, thank you. After lunch," continued Mr. Murbles, "I will ask you to try something really curious. An odd old client of mine died the other day, and left me a dozen of '47 port."

"Gad!" said Peter. "'47! It'll hardly be drinkable, will it, sir?"

"I very greatly fear," replied Mr. Murbles, "that it will not. A great pity. But I feel that some kind of homage should be paid to so notable an antiquity."

"It would be something to say that one had tasted it," said Peter. "Like goin' to see the divine Sarah, you know. Voice gone, bloom gone, savour gone—but still a classic."

"Ah," said Mr. Murbles. "I remember her in her great days. We old fellows have the compensation of some very wonderful memories."

"Quite right, sir," said Peter, "and you'll pile up plenty more yet. But what was this old gentleman doing to let a vintage like that get past its prime?"

"Mr. Featherstone was a very singular man," said Mr. Murbles. "And yet—I don't know. He may have been profoundly wise. He had the reputation for extreme avarice. Never bought a new suit, never took a holiday, never married, lived all his life in the same dark, narrow chambers he occupied as a briefless barrister. Yet he inherited a huge income from his father, all of which he left to accumulate. The port was laid down by the old man, who died in 1860, when my client was thirty-four. He—the son, I mean—was ninety-six when he deceased. He said no pleasure ever came up to the anticipation, and so he lived like a hermit—doing nothing, but planning all the things he might have done. He wrote an elaborate diary, containing, day by day, the record of this visionary existence which he had never dared put to the test of actuality. The diary described minutely a blissful wedded life with the woman of his dreams. Every Christmas and Easter Day a bottle of

175

the '47 was solemnly set upon his table and solemnly removed, unopened, at the close of his frugal meal. An earnest Christian, he anticipated great happiness after death, but, as you see, he put the pleasure off as long as possible. He died with the words, " He is faithful that promised '—feeling to the end the need of assurance. A very singular man, very singular indeed—far removed from the adventurous spirit of the present generation."

" How curious and pathetic," said Mary.

" Perhaps he had at some time set his heart on something unattainable," said Parker.

" Well, I don't know," said Mr. Murbles. " People used to say that the dream-lady had not always been a dream, but that he never could bring himself to propose."

" Ah," said Sir Impey briskly, " the more I see and hear in the courts the more I am inclined to feel that Mr. Featherstone chose the better part."

" And are determined to follow his example—in that respect at any rate ? Eh, Sir Impey ! " replied Mr. Murbles, with a mild chuckle.

Mr. Parker glanced towards the window. It was beginning to rain.

Truly enough the '47 port was a dead thing ; the merest ghost of its old flame and flavour hung about it. Lord Peter held his glass poised a moment.

" It is like the taste of a passion that has passed its noon and turned to weariness," he said, with sudden gravity. " The only thing to do is to recognise bravely that it is dead, and put it away." With a determined movement, he flung the remainder of the wine into the fire. The mocking smile came back to his face :

> " What I like about Clive
> Is that he is no longer alive—
> There is a great deal to be said
> For being dead.

What classic pith and brevity in those four lines !—

However, in the matter of this case, we've a good deal to tell you, sir."

With the assistance of Parker, he laid before the two men of law the whole train of the investigation up to date, Lady Mary coming loyally up to the scratch with her version of the night's proceedings.

" In fact, you see," said Peter, " this Mr. Goyles has lost a lot by *not* being a murderer. We feel he would have cut a fine, sinister figure as a midnight assassin. But things bein' as they are, you see, we must make what we can of him as a witness, what ? "

" Well, Lord Peter," said Mr. Murbles slowly, " I congratulate you and Mr. Parker on a great deal of industry and ingenuity in working the matter out."

" I think we may say we have made some progress," said Parker.

" If only negatively," added Peter.

" Exactly," said Sir Impey turning on him with staggering abruptness. " Very negatively indeed. And, having seriously hampered the case for the defence, what are you going to do next ? "

" That's a nice thing to say," cried Peter indignantly, " when we've cleared up such a lot of points for you ! "

" I daresay," said the barrister, " but they're the sorts of points which are much better left muffled up."

" Damn it all, we want to get at the truth ! "

" Do you ? " said Sir Impey drily. " I don't. I don't care twopence about the truth. I want a case. It doesn't matter to me who killed Cathcart, provided I can prove it wasn't Denver. It's really enough if I can throw reasonable doubt on its being Denver. Here's a client comes to me with a story of a quarrel, a suspicious revolver, a refusal to produce evidence of his statements, and a totally inadequate and idiotic alibi. I arrange to obfuscate the jury with mysterious footprints, a discrepancy as to time, a young woman with a secret, and a general vague suggestion of something between a burglary and a *crime passionel*. And here you

177

come explaining the footprints, exculpating the unknown man, abolishing the discrepancies, clearing up the motives of the young woman, and most carefully throwing back suspicion to where it rested in the first place. What *do* you expect ? "

" I've always said," growled Peter, " that the professional advocate was the most immoral fellow on the face of the earth, and now I know for certain."

" Well, well," said Mr. Murbles, " all this just means that we mustn't rest upon our oars. You must go on, my dear boy, and get more evidence of a positive kind. If this Mr. Goyles did not kill Cathcart we must be able to find the person who did."

" Anyhow," said Biggs, " there's one thing to be thankful for—and that is, that you were still too unwell to go before the Grand Jury last Thursday, Lady Mary"—Lady Mary blushed—" and the prosecution will be building their case on a shot fired at three a.m. Don't answer any questions if you can help it, and we'll spring it on 'em."

" But will they believe anything she says at the trial after that ? " asked Peter dubiously.

" All the better if they don't. She'll be their witness. You'll get a nasty heckling, Lady Mary, but you mustn't mind that. It's all in the game. Just stick to your story and we'll deliver the goods. See ! " Sir Impey wagged a menacing finger.

" I see," said Mary. " And I'll be heckled like anything. Just go on stubbornly saying, ' I am telling the truth now.' That's the idea, isn't it ? "

" Exactly so," said Biggs. " By the way, Denver still refuses to explain his movements, I suppose ? "

" Cat-e-gori-cally," replied the solicitor. " The Wimseys are a very determined family," he added, " and I fear that, for the present, it is useless to pursue that line of investigation. If we could discover the truth in some other way, and confront the Duke with it, he might then be persuaded to add his confirmation."

" Well, now," said Parker, " we have, as it seems to me, still three lines to go upon. First, we must try to establish the Duke's alibi from external sources. Secondly, we can examine the evidence afresh with a view to finding the real murderer. And thirdly, the Paris police may give us some light upon Cathcart's past history."

" And I fancy I know where to go next for information on the second point," said Wimsey suddenly. " Grider's Hole."

" Whew-w ! " Parker whistled. " I was forgetting that. That's where that bloodthirsty farmer fellow lives, isn't it, who set the dogs on you ? "

" With the remarkable wife. Yes. See here, how does this strike you ? This fellow is ferociously jealous of his wife, and inclined to suspect every man who comes near her. When I went up there that day, and mentioned that a friend of mine might have been hanging about there the previous week, he got frightfully excited and threatened to have the fellow's blood. Seemed to know who I was referrin' to. Now, of course, with my mind full of No. 10—Goyles, you know —I never thought but what he was the man. But supposin' it was Cathcart ? You see, we know now, Goyles hadn't even been in the neighbourhood till the Wednesday, so you wouldn't expect what's-his-name— Grimethorpe—to know about him, but Cathcart might have wandered over to Grider's Hole any day and been seen. And look here ! Here's another thing that fits in. When I went up there Mrs. Grimethorpe evidently mistook me for somebody she knew, and hurried down to warn me off. Well, of course, I've been thinkin' all the time she must have seen my old cap and Burberry from the window and mistaken me for Goyles, but, now I come to think of it, I told the kid who who came to the door that I was from Riddlesdale Lodge. If the child told her mother, she must have thought it was Cathcart."

" No, no, Wimsey, that won't do," put in Parker ;
" she must have known Cathcart was dead by that time."

" Oh, damn it ! Yes, I suppose she must. Unless
that surly old devil kept the news from her. By Jove !
that's just what he would do if he'd killed Cathcart
himself. He'd never say a word to her—and I don't
suppose he would let her look at a paper, even if they
take one in. It's a primitive sort of place."

" But didn't you say Grimethorpe had an alibi ? "

" Yes, but we didn't really test it."

" And how d'you suppose he knew Cathcart was
going to be in the thicket that night ? "

Peter considered.

" Perhaps he sent for him," suggested Mary.

" That's right, that's right," cried Peter eagerly.
" You remember we thought Cathcart must somehow
or other have heard from Goyles, making an appointment—but suppose the message was from Grimethorpe,
threatening to split on Cathcart to Jerry."

" You are suggesting, Lord Peter," said Mr. Murbles,
in a tone calculated to chill Peter's blithe impetuosity,
" that, at the very time Mr. Cathcart was betrothed
to your sister, he was carrying on a disgraceful intrigue
with a married woman very much his social inferior."

" I beg your pardon, Polly," said Wimsey.

" It's all right," said Mary, " I—as a matter of fact,
it wouldn't surprise me frightfully. Denis was always—
I mean, he had rather Continental ideas about marriage
and that sort of thing. I don't think he'd have thought
that mattered very much. He'd probably have said
there was a time and place for everything."

" One of those watertight compartment minds," said
Wimsey thoughtfully. Mr. Parker, despite his long
acquaintance with the seamy side of things in London,
had his brows set in a gloomy frown of as fierce a provincial disapproval as ever came from Barrow-in-Furness.

" If you can upset this Grimethorpe's alibi," said Sir
Impey, fitting his right-hand finger-tips neatly between

the fingers of his left hand, " we might make some sort
of a case of it. What do you think, Murbles ? "

" After all," said the solicitor, " Grimethorpe and
the servant both admit that he, Grimethorpe, was not
at Grider's Hole on Wednesday night. If he can't
prove he was at Stapley he may have been at Riddlesdale."

" By Jove ! " cried Wimsey ; " driven off alone,
stopped somewhere, left the gee, sneaked back, met
Cathcart, done him in, and toddled home next day
with a tale about machinery."

" Or he may even have been to Stapley," put in
Parker ; " left early or gone late, and put in the murder
on the way. We shall have to check the precise times
very carefully."

" Hurray ! " cried Wimsey. " I think I'll be gettin'
back to Riddlesdale."

" I'd better stay here," said Parker. " There may
be something from Paris."

" Right you are. Let me know the minute anything
comes through. I say, old thing ! "

" Yes ? "

" Does it occur to you that what's the matter with
this case is that there are too many clues ? Dozens
of people with secrets and elopements bargin' about
all over the place——"

" I hate you, Peter," said Lady Mary.

CHAPTER XI

MERIBAH

Oh-ho, my friend ! You are gotten into Lob's pond.—
Jack the Giant-killer.

L o r d Peter broke his journey north at York, whither
the Duke of Denver had been transferred after the
Assizes, owing to the imminent closing-down of Northallerton Gaol. By dint of judicious persuasion, Peter
contrived to obtain an interview with his brother. He
found him looking ill at ease, and pulled down by the
prison atmosphere, but still unquenchably defiant.

" Bad luck, old man," said Peter, " but you're keepin'
your tail up fine. Beastly slow business, all this legal
stuff, what ? But it gives us time, an' that's all to the
good."

" It's a confounded nuisance," said his grace. " And
I'd like to know what Murbles means. Comes down
and tries to bully me—damned impudence ! Anybody'd
think he suspected me."

" Look here, Jerry," said his brother earnestly, " why
can't you let up on that alibi of yours ? It'd help no
end, you know. After all, if a fellow won't say what
he's been doin'——"

" It ain't my business to prove anything," retorted
his grace, with dignity. " They've got to show I was
there, murderin' the fellow. I'm not bound to say
where I was. I'm presumed innocent, aren't I, till
they prove me guilty ? I call it a disgrace. Here's a
murder committed, and they aren't taking the slightest
trouble to find the real criminal. I give 'em my word

182

of honour, to say nothin' of an oath, that I didn't kill Cathcart—though, mind you, the swine deserved it—but they pay no attention. Meanwhile, the real man's escapin' at his confounded leisure. If I were only free, I'd make a fuss about it."

" Well, why the devil don't you cut it short, then ? " urged Peter. " I don't mean here and now to me "—with a glance at the warder, within earshot—" but to Murbles. Then we could get to work."

" I wish you'd jolly well keep out of it," grunted the Duke. " Isn't it all damnable enough for Helen, poor girl, and mother, and everyone, without you makin' it an opportunity to play Sherlock Holmes ? I'd have thought you'd have had the decency to keep quiet, for the family's sake. I may be in a damned rotten position, but I ain't makin' a public spectacle of myself, by Jove!"

" Hell ! " said Lord Peter, with such vehemence that the wooden-faced warder actually jumped. " It's you that's makin' the spectacle ! It need never have started, but for you. Do you think *I* like havin' my brother and sister dragged through the Courts, and reporters swarmin' over the place, and paragraphs and news-bills with your name starin' at me from every corner, and all this ghastly business, endin' up in a great show in the House of Lords, with a lot of people togged up in scarlet and ermine, and all the rest of the damn-fool jiggery-pokery? People are beginnin' to look oddly at me in the Club, and I can jolly well hear 'em whisperin' that ' Denver's attitude looks jolly fishy, b'gad ! ' Cut it out, Jerry."

" Well, we're in for it now," said his brother, " and thank heaven there are still a few decent fellows left in the peerage who'll know how to take a gentleman's word, even if my own brother can't see beyond his rotten legal evidence."

As they stared angrily at one another, that mysterious sympathy of the flesh which we call family likeness sprang out from its hiding-place, stamping their totally

dissimilar features with an elfish effect of mutual caricature. It was as though each saw himself in a distorting
mirror, while the voices might have been one voice with
its echo.

" Look here, old chap," said Peter, recovering himself, " I'm frightfully sorry. I didn't mean to let myself
go like that. If you won't say anything, you won't.
Anyhow, we're all working like blazes, and we're sure to
find the right man before very long."

" You'd better leave it to the police," said Denver.
" I know you like playin' at detectives, but I do think
you might draw the line somewhere."

" That's a nasty one," said Wimsey. " But I don't
look on this as a game, and I can't say I'll keep out of
it, because I know I'm doin' valuable work. Still,
I can—honestly, I can—see your point of view. I'm
jolly sorry you find me such an irritatin' sort of person.
I suppose it's hard for you to believe I feel anything.
But I do, and I'm goin' to get you out of this, if Bunter
and I both perish in the attempt. Well, so long—that
warder's just wakin' up to say, ' Time, gentlemen.'
Cheer-oh, old thing ! Good luck ! "

He rejoined Bunter outside.

" Bunter," he said, as they walked through the
streets of the old city, " is my manner *really* offensive,
when I don't mean it to be ? "

" It is possible, my lord, if your lordship will excuse
my saying so, that the liveliness of your lordship's
manner may be misleading to persons of limited——"

" Be careful, Bunter ! "

" Limited imagination, my lord."

" Well-bred English people never have imagination,
Bunter."

" Certainly not, my lord. I meant nothing dis-
paraging."

" Well, Bunter—oh, lord ! there's a reporter ! Hide
me, quick ! "

" In here, my lord."

184

Mr. Bunter whisked his master into the cool emptiness of the Cathedral.

" I venture to suggest, my lord," he urged in a hurried whisper, " that we adopt the attitude and external appearance of prayer, if your lordship will excuse me."

Peeping through his fingers, Lord Peter saw a verger hastening towards them, rebuke depicted on his face. At that moment, however, the reporter entered in headlong pursuit, tugging a note-book from his pocket. The verger leapt swiftly on this new prey.

" The winder h'under which we stand," he began in a reverential monotone, " is called the Seven Sisters of York. They say——"

Master and man stole quietly out.

.   .   .   .   .

For his visit to the market town of Stapley Lord Peter attired himself in an aged Norfolk suit, stockings with sober tops, an ancient hat turned down all round, stout shoes, and carried a heavy ashplant. It was with regret that he abandoned his favourite stick—a handsome malacca, marked off in inches for detective convenience, and concealing a sword in its belly and a compass in its head. He decided, however, that it would prejudice the natives against him, as having a town-bred, not to say supercilious, air about it. The sequel to this commendable devotion to his art forcibly illustrated the truth of Gertrude Rhead's observation, " All this self-sacrifice is a sad mistake."

The little town was sleepy enough as he drove into it in one of the Riddlesdale dog-carts, Bunter beside him, and the under-gardener on the back seat. For choice, he would have come on a market-day, in the hope of meeting Grimethorpe himself, but things were moving fast now, and he dared not lose a day. It was a raw, cold morning, inclined to rain.

" Which is the best inn to put up at, Wilkes ? "

" There's t' ' Bricklayers' Arms,' my lord—a fine,

185

well-thought-of place, or t' ' Bridge and Bottle,' i' t' square, or t' ' Rose and Crown,' t'other side o' square."

" Where do the folks usually put up on market-days ? "

" Mebbe ' Rose and Crown ' is most popular, so to say—Tim Watchett, t' landlord, is a rare gossip. Now Greg Smith ower t'way at ' Bridge and Bottle,' he's nobbut a grimly, surly man, but he keeps good drink."

" H'm—I fancy, Bunter, our man will be more attracted by surliness and good drink than by a genial host. The ' Bridge and Bottle ' for us, I fancy, and, if we draw blank there, we'll toddle over to the ' Rose and Crown,' and pump the garrulous Watchett."

Accordingly they turned into the yard of a large, stony-faced house, whose long-unpainted sign bore the dim outline of a " Bridge Embattled," which local etymology had (by a natural association of ideas) trans-mogrified into the " Bridge and Bottle." To the grumpy ostler who took the horse Peter, with his most com-panionable manner, addressed himself :

" Nasty raw morning, isn't it ? "

" Eea."

" Give him a good feed. I may be here some time."

" Ugh ! "

" Not many people about to-day, what ? "

" Ugh ! "

" But I expect you're busy enough market-days."

" Eea."

" People come in from a long way round, I suppose."

" Co-oop ! " said the ostler. The horse walked three steps forward.

" Wo ! " said the ostler. The horse stopped, with the shafts free of the tugs ; the man lowered the shafts, to grate viciously on the gravel.

" Coom on oop ! " said the ostler, and walked calmly off into the stable, leaving the affable Lord Peter as thoroughly snubbed as that young sprig of the nobility had ever found himself.

" I am more and more convinced," said his lordship,
" that this is Farmer Grimethorpe's usual house of
call. Let's try the bar. Wilkes, I shan't want you for
a bit. Get yourself lunch if necessary. I don't know
how long we shall be."

" Very good, my lord."

In the bar of the " Bridge and Bottle " they found
Mr. Greg Smith gloomily checking a long invoice.
Lord Peter ordered drinks for Bunter and himself.
The landlord appeared to resent this as a liberty, and
jerked his head towards the barmaid. It was only
right and proper that Bunter, after respectfully returning thanks to his master for his half-pint, should fall
into conversation with the girl, while Lord Peter paid
his respects to Mr. Smith.

" Ah ! " said his lordship, " good stuff, that, Mr.
Smith. I was told to come here for real good beer, and,
by Jove ! I've been sent to the right place."

" Ugh ! " said Mr. Smith, " 'tisn't what it was. Nowt's
good these times."

" Well, I don't want better. By the way, is Mr.
Grimethorpe here to-day ? "

" Eh ? "

" Is Mr. Grimethorpe in Stapley this morning, d'you
know ? "

" How'd I know ? "

" I thought he always put up here."

" Ah ! "

" Perhaps I mistook the name. But I fancied he'd
be the man to go where the best beer is."

" Ay ? "

" Oh, well, if you haven't seen him, I don't suppose
he's come over to-day."

" Coom where ? "

" Into Stapley."

" Doosn't 'e live here ? He can go and coom without
my knowing."

" Oh, of course ! " Wimsey staggered under the
187

shock, and then grasped the misunderstanding. " I
don't mean Mr. Grimethorpe of Stapley, but Mr.
Grimethorpe of Grider's Hole."

" Why didn't tha say so ? Oh, him ? Ay."

" He's here to-day ? "

" Nay, I knaw nowt about 'un."

" He comes in on market-days, I expect."

" Sometimes."

" It's a longish way. One can put up for the night,
I suppose ? "

" Doosta want t'stay t'night ? "

" Well, no, I don't think so. I was thinking about
my friend Mr. Grimethorpe. I daresay he often has
to stay the night."

" Happen a does."

" Doesn't he stay here, then ? "

" Naay."

" Oh ! " said Wimsey, and thought impatiently:
" If all these natives are as oyster-like I *shall* have to
stay the night. . . . Well, well," he added aloud, " next
time he drops in say I asked after him."

" And who mought tha be ? " inquired Mr. Smith in a
hostile manner.

" Oh, only Brooks of Sheffield," said Lord Peter,
with a happy grin. " Good morning. I won't forget
to recommend your beer."

Mr. Smith grunted. Lord Peter strolled slowly out,
and before long Mr. Bunter joined him, coming out
with a brisk step and the lingering remains of what, in
anyone else, might have been taken for a smirk.

" Well ? " inquired his lordship. " I hope the young
lady was more communicative than that fellow."

" I found the young person " (" Snubbed again,"
muttered Lord Peter) " perfectly amiable, my lord,
but unhappily ill-informed. Mr. Grimethorpe is not
unknown to her, but he does not stay here. She has
sometimes seen him in company with a man called
Zedekiah Bone."

" Well," said his lordship, " suppose you look for Bone, and come and report progress to me in a couple of hours' time. I'll try the ' Rose and Crown.' We'll meet at noon under that thing."

" That thing," was a tall erection in pink granite, neatly tooled to represent a craggy rock, and guarded by two petrified infantry-men in trench helmets. A thin stream of water gushed from a bronze knob half-way up, a roll of honour was engraved on the octagonal base, and four gas-lamps on cast-iron standards put the finishing touch to a very monument of incongruity. Mr. Bunter looked carefully at it, to be sure of recognising it again, and moved respectfully away. Lord Peter walked ten brisk steps in the direction of the " Rose and Crown," then a thought struck him.

" Bunter ! "

Mr. Bunter hurried back to his side.

" Oh, nothing ! " said his lordship. " Only I've just thought of a name for it."

" For—— "

" That memorial," said Lord Peter. " I choose to call it ' Meribah.' "

" Yes, my lord. The waters of strife. Exceedingly apt, my lord. Nothing harmonious about it, if I may say so. Will there be anything further, my lord ? "

" No, that's all."

. . . . .

Mr. Timothy Watchett of the " Rose and Crown " was certainly a contrast to Mr. Greg Smith. He was a small, spare, sharp-eyed man of about fifty-five, with so twinkling and humorous an eye and so alert a cock of the head that Lord Peter summed up his origin the moment he set eyes on him.

" Morning, landlord," said he genially, " and when did *you* last see Piccadilly Circus ? "

" 'Ard to say, sir. Gettin' on for thirty-five year, I

reckon. Many's the time I said to my wife, ' Liz, I'll tike you ter see the 'Olborn Empire afore I die.' But, with one thing and another, time slips aw'y. One day's so like another—blowed if I ever remember 'ow old I'm gettin', sir."

" Oh, well, you've lots of time yet," said Lord Peter.

" I 'ope so, sir. I ain't never wot you may call got used ter these Northerners. That slow, they are, sir— it fair giv' me the 'ump when I first come. And the w'y they speak—that took some gettin' used to. Call that English, I useter say, give me the Frenchies in the Chantycleer Restaurong, I ses. But there, sir, custom's everything. Blowed if I didn't ketch myself a-syin' ' yon side the square ' the other day. Me ! "

" I don't think there's much fear of your turning into a Yorkshire man," said Lord Peter, " didn't I know you the minute I set eyes on you ? In Mr Watchett's bar I said to myself, ' My foot is on my native paving-stones.' "

" That's raight, sir. And, bein' there, sir, what can I 'ave the pleasure of offerin' you ? . . . Excuse me, sir, but 'aven't I seen your fice somewhere ? "

" I don't think so," said Peter ; " but that reminds me. Do you know one, Mr. Grimethorpe ? "

" I know five Mr. Grimethorpes. W'ich of 'em was you meanin', sir ? "

" Mr. Grimethorpe of Grider's Hole."

The landlord's cheerful face darkened.

" Friend of yours, sir ? "

" Not exactly. An acquaintance."

" There naow ! " cried Mr. Watchett, smacking his hand down upon the counter. " I knowed as I knowed your fice ! Don't you live over at Riddlesdale, sir ? "

" I'm stayin' there."

" I knowed it," retorted Mr. Watchett triumphantly. He dived behind the counter and brought up a bundle of newspapers, turning over the sheets excitedly with a well-licked thumb. " There ! Riddlesdale ! That's it, of course."

He smacked open a *Daily Mirror* of a fortnight or so ago. The front page bore a heavy block headline : THE RIDDLESDALE MYSTERY. And beneath was a lifelike snapshot entitled, " *Lord Peter Wimsey, the Sherlock Holmes of the West End, who is devoting all his time and energies to proving the innocence of his brother, the Duke of Denver.*" Mr. Watchett gloated.

" You won't mind my syin' 'ow proud I am to 'ave you in my bar, my lord.—'Ere, Jem, you attend ter them gentlemen ; don't you see they're wytin' ?— Follered all yer caises I 'ave, my lord, in the pipers— jest like a book they are. An' ter think——"

" Look here, old thing," said Lord Peter, " d'you mind not talkin' quite so loud. Seein' dear old Felix is out of the bag, so to speak, do you think you could give me some information and keep your mouth shut, what ? "

" Come be'ind into the bar-parlour, my lord. No-body'll 'ear us there," said Mr. Watchett eagerly, lifting up the flap. " Jem, 'ere ! Bring a bottle of—what'll you 'ave, my lord ? "

" Well, I don't know how many places I may have to visit," said his lordship dubiously.

" Jem, bring a quart of the old ale.—It's special, that's wot it is, my lord. I ain't never found none like it, except it might be once at Oxford. Thanks, Jem. Naow you get along sharp and attend to the customers. Now, my lord."

Mr. Watchett's information amounted to this. That Mr. Grimethorpe used to come to the " Rose and Crown " pretty often, especially on market-days. About ten days previously he had come in lateish, very drunk and quarrelsome, with his wife, who seemed, as usual, terrified of him. Grimethorpe had demanded spirits, but Mr. Watchett had refused to serve him. There had been a row, and Mrs. Grimethorpe had endeavoured to get her husband away. Grimethorpe had promptly knocked her down, with epithets reflecting upon her virtue, and Mr. Watchett had at once called upon the potmen to turn Grimethorpe out, refusing to have him in the house again. He had heard it said on all sides that Grimethorpe's temper, always notoriously bad, had become positively diabolical of late.

"Could you hazard, so to speak, a calculation as to how long, or since when?"

"Well, my lord, come to think of it, especially since the middle of last month—p'r'aps a bit earlier."

"M'm!"

"Not that I'd go for to insinuate anythink, nor your lordship, neither, of course," said Mr. Watchett quickly.

"Certainly not," said Lord Peter. "What about?"

"Ah!" said Mr. Watchett, "there it is, wot abaht?"

"Tell me," said Lord Peter, "do you recollect Grimethorpe comin' into Stapley on October 13th—a Wednesday, it was."

"That would be the day of the—ah! to be sure! Yes, I do recollect it, for I remember thinking it was odd him comin' here except on a market-day. Said he 'ad ter look at some machinery—drills and such, that's raight. 'E was 'ere raight enough."

"Do you remember what time he came in?"

"Well, naow, I've a fancy 'e was 'ere ter lunch. The waitress'd know. 'Ere, Bet!" he called through the side door, "d'yer 'appen to recollect whether Mr. Grimethorpe lunched 'ere October the 13th—Wednesday it were, the d'y the pore gent was murdered over at Riddlesdale?"

"Grimethorpe o' Grider's Hole?" said the girl, a well-grown young Yorkshire woman. "Yes! 'E took loonch, and coom back to sleep. Ah'm not mistook, for ah waited on 'un, an' took up 'is watter i' t'morning, and 'e only gied me tuppence."

"Monstrous!" said Lord Peter. "Look here, Miss Elizabeth, you're sure it was the thirteenth? Because

192

I've got a bet on it with a friend, and I don't want to lose the money if I can help it. You're positive it was Wednesday night he slept here ? I could have sworn it was Thursday."

" Naay, sir, t'wor Wednesday for I remember hearing the men talking o' t'murder i' t'bar, an' telling Mester Grimethorpe next daay."

" Sounds conclusive. What did Mr. Grimethorpe say about it ? "

" There now," cried the young woman, " 'tis queer you should ask that ; everyone noticed how strange he acted. He turned all white like a sheet, and looked at both his hands, one after the other, and then he pushes 'es hair off 's forehead—dazed-like. We reckoned he hadn't got over the drink. He's more often drunk than not. Ah wouldn't be his wife for five hundred pounds."

" I should think not," said Peter ; " you can do a lot better than that. Well, I suppose I've lost my money, then. By the way, what time did Mr. Grimethorpe come in to bed ? "

" Close on two i' t'morning," said the girl, tossing her head. " He were locked oot, an' Jem had to go down and let 'un in."

" That so ? " said Peter. " Well, I might try to get out on a technicality, eh, Mr. Watchett ? Two o'clock is Thursday, isn't it ? I'll work that for all it's worth. Thanks frightfully. That's all I want to know."

Bet grinned and giggled herself away, comparing the generosity of the strange gentleman with the stinginess of Mr. Grimethorpe. Peter rose.

" I'm no end obliged, Mr. Watchett," he said. " I'll just have a word with Jem. Don't say anything, by the way."

" Not me," said Mr. Watchett ; " I knows wot's wot. Good luck, my lord."

Jem corroborated Bet. Grimethorpe had returned

193

at about 1.50 a.m. on October 14th, drunk, and plastered with mud. He had muttered something about having run up against a man called Watson.

The ostler was next interrogated. He did not think that anybody could get a horse and trap out of the stable at night without his knowing it. He knew Watson. He was a carrier by trade, and lived in Windon Street. Lord Peter rewarded his informant suitably, and set out for Windon Street.

But the recital of his quest would be tedious. At a quarter-past noon he joined Bunter at the Meribah memorial.

" Any luck ? "

" I have secured certain information, my lord, which I have duly noted. Total expenditure on beer for self and witnesses 7s. 2d., my lord."

Lord Peter paid the 7s. 2d. without a word, and they adjourned to the " Rose and Crown." Being accommodated in a private parlour, and having ordered lunch, they proceeded to draw up the following schedule :

GRIMETHORPE'S MOVEMENTS. *Wednesday, October 13th to Thursday, October 14th.*
October 13th :

12.30 p.m.	Arrives " Rose and Crown."
1.0 p.m.	Lunches.
3.0 p.m.	Orders two drills from man called Gooch in Trimmer's Lane.
4.30 p.m.	Drink with Gooch to clinch bargain.
5.0 p.m.	Calls at house of John Watson carrier, about delivering some dog-food. Watson absent. Mrs. Watson says W. expected back that night. G. says will call again.
5.30 p.m.	Calls on Mark Dolby, grocer, to complain about some tinned salmon.
5.45 p.m.	Calls on Mr. Hewitt, optician, to pay bill for spectacles and dispute the amount.
6.0 p.m.	Drinks with Zedekiah Bone at " Bridge and Bottle."
6.45 p.m.	Calls again on Mrs. Watson. Watson not yet home.
7.0 p.m.	Seen by Constable Z15 drinking with several men at " Pig and Whistle." Heard to use threatening language with regard to some person unknown.

194

7.20 p.m.	Seen to leave " Pig and Whistle " with two men (not yet identified).
October 14th :	
1.15 a.m.	Picked up by Watson, carrier, about a mile out on road to Riddlesdale, very dirty and ill-tempered, and not quite sober.
1.45 a.m.	Let into " Rose and Crown " by James Johnson, potman.
9.0 a.m.	Called by Elizabeth Dobbin.
9.30 a.m.	In Bar of " Rose and Crown." Hears of man murdered at Riddlesdale. Behaves suspiciously.
10.15 a.m.	Cashes cheque £129 17s. 8d. at Lloyds Bank.
10.30 a.m.	Pays Gooch for drills.
11.5 a.m.	Leaves " Rose and Crown " for Grider's Hole.

Lord Peter looked at this for a few minutes, and put his finger on the great gap of six hours after 7.20.

" How far to Riddlesdale, Bunter ? "

" About thirteen and three-quarter miles, my lord."

" And the shot was heard at 10.55. It couldn't be done on foot. Did Watson explain why he didn't get back from his round till two in the morning ? "

" Yes, my lord. He says he reckons to be back about eleven, but his horse cast a shoe between King's Fenton and Riddlesdale. He had to walk him quietly into Riddlesdale—about 3½ miles—getting there about ten, and knock up the blacksmith. He turned in to the ' Lord in Glory ' till closing time, and then went home with a friend and had a few more. At 12.40 he started off home, and picked Grimethorpe up a mile or so out, near the cross roads."

" Sounds circumstantial. The blacksmith and the friend ought to be able to substantiate it. But we simply must find those men at the ' Pig and Whistle.' "

" Yes, my lord. I will try again after lunch."

It was a good lunch. But that seemed to exhaust their luck for the day, for by three o'clock the men had not been identified, and the scent seemed cold.

Wilkes, the groom, however, had his own contribution to the inquiry. He had met a man from King's Fenton at lunch, and they had, naturally, got to talking over the mysterious murder at the Lodge, and the man

had said that he knew an old man living in a hut on
the Fell, who said that on the night of the murder
he'd seen a man walking over Whemmeling Fell in
the middle of the night. " And it coom to me, all of
a sooden, it mought be his grace," said Wilkes brightly.

Further inquiries elicited that the old man's name
was Groot, and that Wilkes could easily drop Lord
Peter and Bunter at the beginning of the sheep-path
which led up to his hut.

Now, had Lord Peter taken his brother's advice,
and paid more attention to English country sports
than to incunabula and criminals in London—or had
Bunter been brought up on the moors, rather than in
a Kentish village—or had Wilkes (who was a Yorkshire
man bred and born, and ought to have known better)
not been so outrageously puffed up with the sense of
his own importance in suggesting a clue, and with
impatience to have that clue followed up without delay—
or had any one of the three exercised common sense—
this preposterous suggestion would never have been
made, much less carried out, on a November day in the
North Riding. As it was, however, Lord Peter and
Bunter left the trap at the foot of the moor-path at
ten minutes to four, and, dismissing Wilkes, climbed
steadily up to the wee hut on the edge of the fell.

.   .   .   .   .

The old man was extremely deaf, and, after half an
hour of interrogation, his story did not amount to
much. On a night in October, which he thought
might be the night of the murder, he had been sitting
by his peat fire when—about midnight, as he guessed—
a tall man had loomed up out of the darkness. He
spoke like a Southerner, and said he had got lost on
the moor. Old Groot had come to his door and pointed
out the track down towards Riddlesdale. The stranger
had then vanished, leaving a shilling in his hand. He
could not describe the stranger's dress more particularly
than that he wore a soft hat and an overcoat, and,

he thought, leggings. He was pretty near sure it was the night of the murder, because afterwards he had turned it over in his mind and made out that it might have been one of yon folk at the Lodge—possibly the Duke. He had only arrived at this result by a slow process of thought, and had not " come forward," not knowing whom or where to come to.

With this the inquirers had to be content, and, presenting Groot with half a crown, they emerged upon the moor at something after five o'clock.

" Bunter," said Lord Peter through the dusk, " I am abso-bally-lutely positive that the answer to all this business is at Grider's Hole."

" Very possibly, my lord."

Lord Peter extended his finger in a south-easterly direction. " That is Grider's Hole," he said. " Let's go."

" Very good, my lord."

So, like two Cockney innocents, Lord Peter and Bunter set forth at a brisk pace down the narrow moor-track towards Grider's Hole, with never a glance behind them for the great white menace rolling silently down through the November dusk from the wide lone-liness of Whemmeling Fell.

· · · · ·

" Bunter ! "

" Here, my lord ! "

The voice was close at his ear.

" Thank God ! I thought you'd disappeared for good. I say, we ought to have known."

" Yes, my lord."

It had come on them from behind, in a single stride, thick, cold, choking—blotting each from the other, though they were only a yard or two apart.

" I'm a fool, Bunter," said Lord Peter.

" Not at all, my lord."

" Don't move ; go on speaking."

" Yes, my lord."

Peter groped to the right and clutched the other's sleeve.

" Ah ! Now what are we to do ? "

" I couldn't say, my lord, having no experience. Has the—er—phenomenon any habits, my lord ? "

" No regular habits, I believe. Sometimes it moves. Other times it stays in one place for days. We can wait all night, and see if it lifts at daybreak."

" Yes, my lord. It is unhappily somewhat damp."

" Somewhat—as you say," agreed his lordship, with a short laugh.

Bunter sneezed, and begged pardon politely.

" If we go on going south-east," said his lordship, " we shall get to Grider's Hole all right, and they'll jolly well *have* to put us up for the night—or give us an escort. I've got my torch in my pocket, and we can go by compass—oh, hell ! "

" My lord ? "

" I've got the wrong stick. This beastly ash ! No compass, Bunter—we're done in."

" Couldn't we keep on going downhill, my lord ? "

Lord Peter hesitated. Recollections of what he had heard and read surged up in his mind to tell him that uphill or downhill seems much the same thing in a fog. But man walks in a vain shadow. It is hard to believe that one is really helpless. The cold was icy. " We might try," he said weakly.

" I have heard it said, my lord, that in a fog one always walked round in a circle," said Mr. Bunter, seized with a tardy diffidence.

" Not on a slope, surely," said Lord Peter, beginning to feel bold out of sheer contrariness.

Bunter, being out of his element, had, for once, no good counsel to offer.

" Well, we can't be much worse off than we are," said Lord Peter. " We'll try it, and keep on shouting."

He grasped Bunter's hand, and they strode gingerly forward into the thick coldness of the fog.

How long that nightmare lasted neither could have said. The world might have died about them. Their own shouts terrified them ; when they stopped shouting the dead silence was more terrifying still. They stumbled over tufts of thick heather. It was amazing how, deprived of sight, they exaggerated the inequalities of the ground. It was with very little confidence that they could distinguish uphill from downhill. They were shrammed through with cold, yet the sweat was running from their faces with strain and terror.

Suddenly—from directly before them as it seemed, and only a few yards away—there rose a long, horrible shriek—and another—and another.

" My God ! What's that ? "

" It's a horse, my lord."

" Of course." They remembered having heard horses scream like that. There had been a burning stable near Poperinghe——

" Poor devil," said Peter. He started off impulsively in the direction of the sound, dropping Bunter's hand.

" Come back, my lord," cried the man in a sudden agony. And then, with a frightened burst of enlightenment :

" For God's sake stop, my lord—the bog ! "

A sharp shout in the utter blackness.

" Keep away there—don't move—it's got me ! "

And a dreadful sucking noise.

CHAPTER XII

THE ALIBI

When actually in the embrace of a voracious and power-ful wild animal, the desirability of leaving a limb is not a matter to be subjected to lengthy consideration.—The Wallet of Kai-Lung.

" I TRIPPED right into it," said Wimsey's voice steadily, out of the blackness. " One sinks very fast. You'd better not come near, or you'll go too. We'll yell a bit. I don't think we can be very far from Grider's Hole."

" If your lordship will keep shouting," returned Mr. Bunter, " I think—I can—get to you," he panted, un-tying with his teeth the hard knot of a coil of string.

" Oy ! " cried Lord Peter obediently. " Help ! Oy ! Oy ! "

Mr. Bunter groped towards the voice, feeling cauti-ously before him with his walking-stick.

" Wish you'd keep away, Bunter," said Lord Peter peevishly. " Where's the sense of both of us——? " He squelched and floundered again.

" Don't do that, my lord," cried the man entreat-ingly. " You'll sink farther in."

" I'm up to my thighs now," said Lord Peter.

" I'm coming," said Bunter. " Go on shouting. Ah, here's where it gets soggy."

He felt the ground carefully, selected a tussocky bit which seemed reasonably firm, and drove his stick well into it.

" Oy ! Hi ! Help ! " said Lord Peter, shouting lustily.

Mr. Bunter tied one end of the string to the walking-stick, belted his Burberry tightly about him, and, laying himself cautiously down upon his belly, advanced, clue in hand, like a very Gothic Theseus of a late and degenerate school.

The bog heaved horribly as he crawled over it, and slimy water squelched up into his face. He felt with his hands for tussocks of grass, and got support from them when he could.

" Call out again, my lord ! "

" Here ! " The voice was fainter and came from the right. Bunter had lost his line a little, hunting for tussocks. " I daren't come faster," he explained. He felt as though he had been crawling for years.

" Get out while there's time," said Peter. " I'm up to my waist. Lord ! this is rather a beastly way to peg out."

" You won't peg out," grunted Bunter. His voice was suddenly quite close. " Your hands now."

For a few agonising minutes two pairs of hands groped over the invisible slime. Then :

" Keep yours still," said Bunter. He made a slow, circling movement. It was hard work keeping his f ce out of the mud. His hands slithered over the slobbery surface—and suddenly closed on an arm.

" Thank God ! " said Bunter. " Hang on here, my lord."

He felt forward. The arms were perilously close to the sucking mud. The hands crawled clingingly up his arms and rested on his shoulders. He grasped Wimsey beneath the armpits and heaved. The exertion drove his own knees deep into the bog. He straightened himself hurriedly. Without using his knees he could get no purchase, but to use them meant certain death. They could only hang on desperately till help came—or till the strain became too great. He could not even shout ; it was almost more than he could do to keep his mouth free of water. The dragging strain on his

201

shoulders was intolerable; the mere effort to breathe meant an agonising crick in the neck.

"You must go on shouting, my lord."

Wimsey shouted. His voice was breaking and fading.

"Bunter, old thing," said Lord Peter, "I'm simply beastly sorry to have let you in for this."

"Don't mention it, my lord," said Bunter, with his mouth in the slime. A thought struck him.

"What became of your stick, my lord?"

"I dropped it. It should be somewhere near, if it hasn't sunk in."

Bunter cautiously released his left hand and felt about.

"Hi! Hi! Help!"

Bunter's hand closed over the stick, which, by a happy accident, had fallen across a stable tuft of grass. He pulled it over to him, and laid it across his arms, so that he could just rest his chin upon it. The relief to his neck was momentarily so enormous that his courage was renewed. He felt he could hang on for ever.

"Help!"

. . . . .

Minutes passed like hours.

. . . . .

"See that?"

A faint, flickering gleam somewhere away to the right. With desperate energy both shouted together.

"Help! Help! Oy! Oy! Help!"

An answering yell. The light swayed—came nearer— a spreading blur in the fog.

"We *must* keep it up," panted Wimsey. They yelled again.

"Where be?"

"Here!"

"Hello!" A pause. Then:

"Here be stick," said a voice, suddenly near.

"Follow the string!" yelled Bunter. They heard

two voices, apparently arguing. Then the string was twitched.

" Here ! Here ! Two of us ! Make haste ! "

More consultation.

" Hang on, canst a ? "

" Yes, if you're quick."

" Fetchin' hurdle. Two on 'ee, sayst a ? "

" Yes."

" Deep in ? "

" One of us."

" Aw reet. Jem's comin'."

A splattering noise marked the arrival of Jem with a hurdle. Then came an endless wait. Then another hurdle, the string twitching, and the blur of the lantern bobbing violently about. Then a third hurdle was flung down, and the light came suddenly out of the mist. A hand caught Bunter by the ankle.

" Where's t'other ? "

" Here—nearly up to his neck. Have you a rope ? "

" Aye, sure. Jem ! T'rope ! "

The rope came snaking out of the fog. Bunter grasped it, and passed it round his master's body.

" Now—coom tha back and heave."

Bunter crawled cautiously backwards upon the hurdle. All three set hands upon the rope. It was like trying to heave the earth out of her course.

" 'Fraid I'm rooted to Australia," panted Peter apologetically. Bunter sweated and sobbed.

" It's aw reet—he's coomin' ! "

With slow heavings the rope began to come towards them. Their muscles cracked.

Suddenly, with a great *plop !* the bog let go its hold. The three at the rope were hurled head over heels upon the hurdles. Something unrecognisable in slime lay flat, heaving helplessly. They dragged at him in a kind of frenzy, as though he might be snatched back from them again. The evil bog stench rose thickly round them. They crossed the first hurdle—the second

—the third—and rose staggeringly to their feet on firm ground.

" What a beastly place," said Lord Peter faintly. " 'Pologise, stupid of me to have forgotten—what'sy name ? "

" Well, tha's loocky," said one of their rescuers. " We thowt we heerd someun a-shouting. There be few folks as cooms oot o' Peter's Pot dead or alive, I reckon."

" Well, it was nearly potted Peter that time," said his lordship, and fainted.

. . . . .

To Lord Peter the memory of his entry that night into the farmhouse at Grider's Hole always brought with it a sensation of nightmare. The coils of fog rolled in with them as the door opened, and through them the firelight leapt steamily. A hanging lamp made a blur. The Medusa-head of Mrs. Grimethorpe, terribly white against her black hair, peered over him. A hairy paw caught her by the shoulder and wrenched her aside.

" Shameless ! A mon—ony mon—that's a' tha thinks on. Bide till tha's wanted. What's this ? "

Voices—voices—ever so many fierce faces peering down all round.

" Peter's Pot ? An' what were 'ee a-wanting on t'moor this time night ? No good. Nobbody but a fool or a thief 'ud coom oop 'ere i' t'fog."

One of the men, a farm labourer with wry shoulders and a thin, malicious face, suddenly burst into tuneless song :

" I been a-courtin' Mary Jane
On Ilkla' Moor bar t'at."

" Howd toong ! " yelled Grimethorpe, in a fury. " Doost want Ah should break ivery bwoan i' thi body ? " He turned on Bunter. " Tak thesen off, Ah tell tha. Tha'rt here for no good."

" But, William——" began his wife. He snapped round at her like a dog, and she shrank back.

" Naay now, naay now," said a man, whom Wimsey dimly recognised as the fellow who had befriended him on his previous visit, " tha mun' taak them in for t' night, racken, or there'll be trouble wi' t' folk down yonder at t' Lodge, lat aloan what police 'ull saay. Ef t' fellow 'm coom to do harm, 'ee's doon it already—to 'unself. Woan't do no more to-night—look at 'un. Bring 'un to fire, mon," he added to Bunter, and then, turning to the farmer again, " 'Tes tha'll be in Queer Street ef 'e wor to goo an' die on us wi' noomony or rhoomaticks."

This reasoning seemed partly to convince Grimethorpe. He made way, grumbling, and the two chilled and exhausted men were brought near the fire. Somebody brought two large, steaming tumblers of spirits. Wimsey's brain seemed to clear, then swim again drowsily, drunkenly.

. . . . .

Presently he became aware that he was being carried upstairs and put to bed. A big, old-fashioned room, with a fire on the hearth and a huge, grim four-poster. Bunter was helping him out of soaked clothes ; rubbing him. Another man appeared from time to time to help him. From below came the bellowing sound of Grimethorpe's voice, blasphemously uplifted. Then the harsh, brassy singing of the wry-shouldered man :

> " Then woorms will coom an' ate thee oop
> On Ilkla' Moor bar t'at . . . .
>
> Then doocks will coom an' ate oop woorms
> On Ilkla' Moor . . . ."

Lord Peter rolled into bed.

" Bunter—where—you all right ? Never said thank you—dunno what I'm doing—anywhere to sleep—what ? "

He drifted away into oblivion. The old song came up mockingly, and wound its horrible fancies into his dreams :

> " Then we shall coom an' ate oop doocks
> On Ilkla' Moor bar t'at . . . .
> An' that is how—an' that is how—is how . . . ."

.   .   .   .   .

When Wimsey next opened his eyes a pale November sun was struggling in at the window. It seemed that the fog had fulfilled its mission and departed. For some time he lay, vaguely unaware of how he came to be where he was ; then the outlines of recollection straightened themselves, the drifting outposts of dreams were called back, the burden of his preoccupation settled down as usual. He became aware of an extreme bodily lassitude, and of the dragging pain of wrenched shoulder muscles. Examining himself perfunctorily, he found a bruised and tender zone beneath the armpits and round his chest and back, where the rescuing rope had hauled at him. It was painful to move, so he lay back and closed his eyes once more.

Presently the door opened to admit Bunter, neatly clothed and bearing a tray from which rose a most excellent odour of ham and eggs.

" Hullo, Bunter ! "

" Good morning, my lord ! I trust your lordship has rested.'

" Feel as fit as a fiddle, thanks—come to think of it, why fiddle ?—except for a general feeling of havin' been violently massaged by some fellow with cast-iron fingers and knobbly joints. How about you ? "

" The arms are a trifle fatigued, thank you, my lord ; otherwise, I am happy to say, I feel no trace of the misadventure. Allow me, my lord."

He set the tray tenderly upon Lord Peter's ready knees.

" They must be jolly well dragged out of their

sockets," said his lordship, "holdin' me up all that ghastly long time. I'm so beastly deep in debt to you already, Bunter, it's not a bit of use tryin' to repay it. You know I won't forget, anyhow, don't you? All right, I won't be embarrassin' or anything—thanks awfully, anyhow. That's that. What? Did they give you anywhere decent to sleep? I didn't seem to be able to sit up an' take notice last night."

"I slept excellently, I thank your lordship." Mr. Bunter indicated a kind of truckle-bed in a corner of the room. "They would have given me another room, my lord, but in the circumstances, I preferred to remain with your lordship, trusting you would excuse the liberty. I told them that I feared the effects of prolonged immersion upon your lordship's health. I was uneasy, besides, about the intention of Grimethorpe. I feared he might not feel altogether hospitably disposed, and that he might be led into some hasty action if we were not together."

"I shouldn't wonder. Most murderous-lookin' fellow I ever set eyes on. I'll have to talk to him this morning— or to Mrs. Grimethorpe. I'd take my oath she could tell us something, what?"

"I should say there was very little doubt of it, my lord."

"Trouble is," pursued Wimsey, with his mouth full of egg, "I don't know how to get at her. That jolly husband of hers seems to cherish the most unpleasant suspicions of anything that comes this way in trousers. If he found out we'd been talkin' to her, what you may call privately, he might, as you say, be hurried by his feelin's into doin' something regrettable."

"Just so, my lord."

"Still, the fellow must go an' look after his bally old farm some time, and then, p'raps, we'll be able to tackle her. Queer sort of woman—damn fine one, what? Wonder what she made of Cathcart?" he added musingly.

Mr. Bunter volunteered no opinion on this delicate point.

" Well, Bunter, I think I'll get up. I don't suppose we're altogether welcome here. I didn't fancy the look in our host's eye last night."

" No, my lord. He made a deal of opposition about having your lordship conveyed to this room."

" Why, whose room is it ? "

" His own and Mrs. Grimethorpe's, my lord. It appeared most suitable, there being a fireplace, and the bed already made up. Mrs. Grimethorpe showed great kindness, my lord, and the man Jake pointed out to Grimethorpe that it would doubtless be to his pecuniary advantage to treat your lordship with consideration."

" H'm. Nice, graspin' character, ain't he ? Well, it's up and away for me. O Lord ! I *am* stiff. I say, Bunter, have I any clothes to put on ? "

" I have dried and brushed your lordship's suit to the best of my ability, my lord. It is not as I should wish to see it, but I think your lordship will be able to wear it to Riddlesdale."

" Well, I don't suppose the streets will be precisely crowded," retorted his lordship. " I *do* so want a hot bath. How about shavin' water ? "

" I can procure that from the kitchen, my lord."

Bunter padded away, and Lord Peter, having pulled on a shirt and trousers with many grunts and groans, roamed over to the window. As usual with hardy country dwellers, it was tightly shut, and a thick wedge of paper had been rammed in to keep the sash from rattling. He removed this and flung up the sash. The wind rollicked in, laden with peaty moor scents. He drank it in gladly. It was good to see the jolly old sun after all—he would have hated to die a sticky death in Peter's Pot. For a few minutes he stood there, returning thanks vaguely in his mind for the benefits of existence. Then he withdrew to finish dressing. The wad of paper was still in his hand, and he was about to fling it into the

208

fire, when a word caught his eye. He unrolled the paper. As he read it his eyebrows went up and his mouth pursed itself into an indescribable expression of whimsical enlightenment. Bunter, returning with the hot water, found his master transfixed, the paper in one hand, and his socks in the other, and whistling a complicated passage of Bach under his breath.

" Bunter," said his lordship, " I am, without exception, the biggest ass in Christendom. When a thing is close under my nose I can't see it. I get a telescope, and look for the explanation in Stapley. I deserve to be crucified upside-down, as a cure for anæmia of the brain. Jerry ! Jerry ! But, naturally, of course, you rotten ass, isn't it obvious ? Silly old blighter. Why couldn't he tell Murbles or me ? "

Mr. Bunter advanced, the picture of respectful inquiry.

" Look at it—look at it ! " said Wimsey, with a hysterical squeak of laughter. " O Lord ! O Lord ! Stuck into the window-frame for anybody to find. *Just* like Jerry. Signs his name to the business in letters a foot long, leaves it conspicuously about, and then goes away and is chivalrously silent."

Mr. Bunter put the jug down upon the washstand in case of accident, and took the paper.

It was the missing letter from Tommy Freeborn.

No doubt about it. There it was—the evidence which established the truth of Denver's evidence. More —which established his alibi for the night of the 13th.

Not Cathcart—Denver.

Denver suggesting that the shooting party should return in October to Riddlesdale, where they had opened the grouse season in August. Denver sneaking hurriedly out at 11.30 to walk two miles across the fields on a night when Farmer Grimethorpe had gone to buy machinery. Denver carelessly plugging a rattling sash on a stormy night with an important letter bearing his title on it for all to see. Denver padding back at three in the morning like a homing tom-cat, to fall over his guest's dead body by the conservatory. Denver, with his kind, stupid, English-gentleman ideas about honour, going obstinately off to prison, rather than tell his solicitor where he had been. Denver misleading them all into the wildest and most ingenious solutions of a mystery which now stood out clear as seven sunbeams. Denver, whose voice the woman had thought she recognised on the memorable day when she flung herself into the arms of his brother. Denver calmly setting in motion the enormous, creaking machinery of a trial by his noble peers in order to safeguard a woman's reputation.

This very day, probably, a Select Committee of lords was sitting " to inspect the Journals of this House upon former trials of peers in criminal cases, in order to bring the Duke of Denver to a speedy trial, and to report to the House what they should think proper thereupon." There they were : moving that an address be presented to His Majesty by the lords with white staves, to acquaint His Majesty of the date proposed for the trial ; arranging for fitting up the Royal Gallery at Westminster ; humbly requesting the attendance of a sufficient police force to keep clear the approaches leading to the House ; petitioning His Majesty graciously to appoint a Lord High Steward ; ordering, in sheeplike accordance with precedent, that all lords be summoned to attend in their robes ; that every lord, in giving judgment, disclose his opinion upon his honour, laying his right hand upon his heart ; that the Sergeant-at-Arms be within the House to make proclamations in the King's name for keeping silence—and so on, and on, unendingly. And there, jammed in the window-sash, was the dirty little bit of paper which, discovered earlier, would have made the whole monstrous ceremonial unnecessary.

Wimsey's adventure in the bog had unsettled his

210

nerves. He sat down on the bed and laughed, with the tears streaming down his face.

Mr. Bunter was speechless. Speechlessly he produced a razor—and to the end of his days Wimsey never knew how or from whom he had so adequately procured it—and began to strop it thoughtfully upon the palm of his hand.

Presently Wimsey pulled himself together and staggered to the window for a little cooling draught of moor air. As he did so, a loud hullabaloo smote his ear, and he perceived, in the courtyard below, Farmer Grimethorpe striding among his dogs ; when they howled he struck at them with a whip, and they howled again. Suddenly he glanced up at the window, with an expression of such livid hatred that Wimsey stepped hurriedly back as though struck.

While Bunter shaved him he was silent.

.   .   .   .   .

The interview before Lord Peter was a delicate one ; the situation, however one looked at it, unpleasant. He was under a considerable debt of gratitude to his hostess ; on the other hand, Denver's position was such that minor considerations really had to go to the wall. His lordship had, nevertheless, never felt quite such a cad as he did while descending the staircase at Grider's Hole.

In the big farm kitchen he found a stout countrywoman, stirring a pot of stew. He asked for Mr. Grimethorpe, and was told that he had gone out.

" Can I speak to Mrs. Grimethorpe, please ? "

The woman looked doubtfully at him, wiped her hands on her apron, and, going into the scullery, shouted, " Mrs. Grimethorpe ! " A voice replied from somewhere outside.

" Gentleman wants see tha."

" Where is Mrs. Grimethorpe ? " broke in Peter hurriedly.

" I' t'dairy, recken."

" I'll go to her there," said Wimsey, stepping briskly out. He passed through a stone-paved scullery, and across a yard, in time to see Mrs. Grimethorpe emerging from a dark doorway opposite.

Framed there, the cold sunlight just lighting upon her still, dead-white face and heavy, dark hair, she was more wonderful than ever. There was no trace of Yorkshire descent in the long, dark eyes and curled mouth. The curve of nose and cheekbones vouched for an origin immensely remote ; coming out of the darkness, she might have just risen from her far tomb in the Pyramids, dropping the dry and perfumed grave-bands from her fingers.

Lord Peter pulled himself together.

" Foreign," he said to himself matter-of-factly. " Touch of Jew perhaps, or Spanish, is it ? Remarkable type. Don't blame Jerry. Couldn't live with Helen myself. Now for it."

He advanced quickly.

" Good morning," she said, " are you better ? "

" Perfectly all right, thank you—thanks to your kindness, which I do not know how to repay."

" You will repay any kindness best by going at once," she answered in her remote voice. " My husband does not care for strangers, and 'twas unfortunate the way you met before."

" I will go directly. But I must first beg for the favour of a word with you." He peered past her into the dimness of the dairy. " In here, perhaps ? "

" What do you want with me ? "

She stepped back, however, and allowed him to follow her in.

" Mrs. Grimethorpe, I am placed in a most painful position. You know that my brother, the Duke of Denver, is in prison, awaiting his trial for a murder which took place on the night of October 13th ? "

Her face did not change. " I have heard so."

" He has, in the most decided manner, refused to

212

state where he was between eleven and three on that night. His refusal has brought him into great danger of his life."

She looked at him steadily.

" He feels bound in honour not to disclose his whereabouts, though I know that, if he chose to speak, he could bring a witness to clear him."

" He seems to be a very honourable man." The cold voice wavered a trifle, then steadied again.

" Yes. Undoubtedly, from his point of view, he is doing the right thing. You will understand, however, that, as his brother, I am naturally anxious to have the matter put in its proper light."

" I don't understand why you are telling me all this. I suppose, if the thing is disgraceful, he doesn't want it known."

" Obviously. But to us—to his wife and young son, and to his sister and myself—his life and safety are matters of the first importance."

" Of more importance than his honour ? "

" The secret is a disgraceful one in a sense, and will give pain to his family. But it would be an infinitely greater disgrace that he should be executed for murder. The stigma in that case would involve all those who bear his name. The shame of the truth will, I fear, in this very unjust society of ours, rest more upon the witness to his alibi than upon himself."

" Can you in that case expect the witness to come forward ? "

" To prevent the condemnation of an innocent man ? Yes, I think I may venture to expect even that."

" I repeat—why are you telling me all this ? "

" Because, Mrs. Grimethorpe, you know, even better than I, how innocent my brother is of this murder. Believe me, I am deeply distressed at having to say these things to you."

" I know nothing about your brother."

" Forgive me, that is not true."

213

" I know nothing. And surely, if the Duke will not speak, you should respect his reasons."

" I am not bound in any way."

" I am afraid I cannot help you. You are wasting time. If you cannot produce your missing witness, why do you not set about finding the real murderer ? If you do so you surely need not trouble about this alibi. Your brother's movements are his own business."

" I could wish," said Wimsey, " you had not taken up this attitude. Believe me, I would have done all I could to spare you. I have been working hard to find, as you say, the real murderer, but with no success. The trial will probably take place at the end of the month."

Her lips twitched a little at that, but she said nothing.

" I had hoped that with your help we might agree on some explanation—less than the truth, perhaps, but sufficient to clear my brother. As it is, I fear I shall have to produce the proof I hold, and let matters take their course."

That, at last, struck under her guard. A dull flush crept up her cheeks ; one hand tightened upon the handle of the churn, where she had rested it.

" What do you mean by proof ? "

" I can prove that on the night of the 13th my brother slept in the room I occupied last night," said Wimsey, with calculated brutality.

She winced. " It is a lie. You cannot prove it. He will deny it. I shall deny it."

" He was not there ? "

" No."

" Then how did this come to be wedged in the sash of the bedroom window ? "

At sight of the letter she broke down, crumpling up in a heap against the table. The set lines of her face distorted themselves into a mere caricature of terror.

" No, no, no ! It is a lie ! God help me ! "

" Hush ! " said Wimsey peremptorily. " Someone

will hear you." He dragged her to her feet. " Tell the truth, and we will see if we can find a way out. It is true—he was here that night ? "

" You know it."

" When did he come ? "

" At a quarter past twelve."

" Who let him in ? "

" He had the keys."

" When did he leave you ? "

" A little after two."

" Yes, that fits in all right. Three quarters of an hour to go and three quarters to come back. He stuck this into the window, I suppose, to keep it from rattling ? "

" There was a high wind—I was nervous. I thought every sound was my husband coming back."

" Where was your husband ? "

" At Stapley."

" Had he suspected this ? "

" Yes, for some time."

" Since my brother was here in August ? "

" Yes. But he could get no proof. If he had had proof he would have killed me. You have seen him. He is a devil."

" M'm."

Wimsey was silent. The woman glanced fearfully at his face and seemed to read some hope there, for she clutched him by the arm.

" It you call me to give evidence," she said, " he will know. He *will* kill me. For God's sake, have pity. That letter is my death-warrant. Oh, for the mother that bore you, have mercy upon me. My life is a hell, and when I die I shall go to hell for my sin. Find some other way—you can—you must."

Wimsey gently released himself.

" Don't do that, Mrs. Grimethorpe. We might be seen. I am deeply sorry for you, and, if I can get my brother out of this without bringing you in, I promise you I will. But you see the difficulty. Why don't you leave this man ? He is openly brutal to you."

She laughed.

" Do you think he'd leave me alive while the law was slowly releasing me ? Knowing him, do you think so ? "

Wimsey really did not think so.

" I will promise you this, Mrs. Grimethorpe. I will do all I can to avoid having to use your evidence. But if there should be no other way, I will see that you have police protection from the moment that the subpœna is served on you."

" And for the rest of my life ? "

" When you are once in London we will see about freeing you from this man."

" No. If you call upon me, I am a lost woman. But you will find another way ? "

" I will try, but I can promise nothing. I will do everything that is possible to protect you. If you care at all for my brother——"

" I don't know. I am so horribly afraid. He was kind and good to me. He was—so different. But I am afraid—I'm afraid."

Wimsey turned. Her terrified eyes had seen the shadow cross the threshold. Grimethorpe was at the door, glowering in upon them.

" Ah, Mr. Grimethorpe," exclaimed Wimsey cheerfully, " there you are. Awfully pleased to see you and thank you, don'tcherknow, for puttin' me up. I was just saying so to Mrs. Grimethorpe, an' asking her to say good-bye to you for me. Must be off now, I'm afraid. Bunter and I are ever so grateful to you both for all your kindness. Oh, and I say, could you find me the stout fellows who hauled us out of that Pot of yours last night—if it is yours. Nasty, damp thing to keep outside the front door, what ? I'd like to thank 'em."

" Dom good thing for unwelcome guests," said the

man ferociously. " An' tha'd better be off afore Ah throws thee out."

" I'm just off," said Peter. " Good-bye again, Mrs. Grimethorpe, and a thousand thanks."

He collected Bunter, rewarded his rescuers suitably, took an affectionate farewell of the enraged farmer, and departed, sore in body and desperately confused in mind.

CHAPTER XIII

MANON

" *That one word, my dear Watson, should have told me the whole story, had I been the ideal reasoner which you are so fond of depicting.*"—Memoirs of Sherlock Holmes.

" T H A N K God," said Parker. " Well, that settles it."

" It does—and yet again, it doesn't," retorted Lord Peter. He leaned back against the fat silk cushion in the sofa corner meditatively.

" Of course, it's disagreeable having to give this woman away," said Parker sensibly and pleasantly, " but these things have to be done."

" I know. It's all simply awfully nice and all that. And Jerry, who's got the poor woman into this mess, has to be considered first. I know. And if we don't restrain Grimethorpe quite successfully, and he cuts her throat for her, it'll be simply rippin' for Jerry to think of all his life. . . . . Jerry ! I say, you know, what frightful idiots we were not to see the truth right off ! I mean—of course, my sister-in-law is an awfully good woman, and all that, but Mrs. Grimethorpe— whew ! I told you about the time she mistook me for Jerry. One crowded, split second of glorious all-overishness. I ought to have known then. Our voices are alike, of course, and she couldn't see in that dark kitchen. I don't believe there's an ounce of any feeling left in the woman except sheer terror—but, ye gods ! what eyes and skin ! Well, never mind. Some undeserving fellows have all the luck. Have you got any really good stories ? No ? Well, I'll tell you some—enlarge your mind and all that. Do you know the rhyme about the young man at the War Office ? "

Mr. Parker endured five stories with commendable patience, and then suddenly broke down.

" Hurray ! said Wimsey. " Splendid man ! I love to see you melt into a refined snigger from time to time. I'll spare you the really outrageous one about the young housewife and the traveller in bicycle-pumps. You know, Charles, I really *should* like to know who did Cathcart in. Legally, it's enough to prove Jerry innocent, but, Mrs. Grimethorpe or no Mrs. Grimethorpe, it doesn't do us credit in a professional capacity. ' The father weakens, but the governor is firm ' ; that is, as a brother I am satisfied—I may say light-hearted—but as a sleuth I am cast down, humiliated, thrown back upon myself, a lodge in a garden of cucumbers. Besides, of all defences an alibi is the most awkward to establish, unless a number of independent and disinterested witnesses combine to make it thoroughly air-tight. If Jerry sticks to his denial, the most they can be sure of is that *either* he *or* Mrs. Grimethorpe is being chivalrous."

" But you've got the letter."

" Yes. But how are we going to prove that it came that evening ? The envelope is destroyed. Fleming remembers nothing about it. Jerry might have received it days earlier. Or it might be a complete fake. Who is to say that I didn t put it in the window myself and pretend to find it. After all, I'm hardly what you would call disinterested."

" Bunter saw you find it."

" He didn't, Charles. At that precise moment he was out of the room fetching shaving-water."

" Oh, was he ? "

" Moreover, only Mrs. Grimethorpe can swear to what is really the important point—the moment of Jerry's arrival and departure. Unless he was at Grider's Hole before 12.30 at least, it's immaterial whether he was there or not."

"Well," said Parker, "can't we keep Mrs. Grimethorpe up our sleeve, so to speak——"

"Sounds a bit abandoned," said Lord Peter, "but we will keep her with pleasure if you like."

"—and meanwhile," pursued Mr. Parker, unheeding, "do our best to find the actual criminal?"

"Oh, yes," said Lord Peter, "and that reminds me. I made a discovery at the Lodge—at least, I think so. Did you notice that somebody had been forcing one of the study windows?"

"No, really?"

"Yes; I found distinct marks. Of course, it was a long time after the murder, but there were scratches on the catch all right—the sort of thing a penknife would leave."

"What fools we were not to make an examination at the time!"

"Come to think of it, why should you have? Anyhow, I asked Fleming about it, and he said he did remember, now he came to think of it, that on the Thursday morning he'd found the window open, and couldn't account for it. And here's another thing. I've had a letter from my friend Tim Watchett. Here it is:

"MY LORD.—About our conversation. I have found a Man who was with the Party in question at the 'Pig and Whistle' on the night of the 13th ult. and he tells me that the Party borrowed his bicycle, and same was found afterwards in the ditch where Party was picked up with the Handlebars bent and wheels buckled.

"Trusting to the Continuance of your esteemed favour.

"TIMOTHY WATCHETT."

"What do you think of that?"

"Good enough to go on," said Parker. "At least, we are no longer hampered with horrible doubts."

" No. And, though she's my sister, I must say that of all the blithering she-asses Mary is the blitheringest. Taking up with that awful bounder to start with——"

" She was jolly fine about it," said Mr. Parker, getting rather red in the face. " It's just because she's your sister that you can't appreciate what a fine thing she did. How should a big, chivalrous nature like hers see through a man like that ? She's so sincere and thorough herself, she judges everyone by the same standard. She wouldn't believe anybody could be so thin and wobbly-minded as Goyles till it was *proved* to her. And even then she couldn't bring herself to think ill of him till he'd given himself away out of his own mouth. It was wonderful, the way she fought for him. Think what it must have meant to such a splendid, straightforward woman to——"

" All right, all right," cried Peter, who had been staring at his friend, transfixed with astonishment. " Don't get worked up. I believe you. Spare me. I'm only a brother. All brothers are fools. All lovers are lunatics—Shakespeare says so. Do you want Mary, old man ? You surprise me, but I believe brothers always are surprised. Bless you, dear children ! "

" Damn it all, Wimsey," said Parker, very angry, " you've no right to talk like that. I only said how greatly I admired your sister—everyone must admire such pluck and staunchness. You needn't be insulting. I know she's Lady Mary Wimsey and damnably rich, and I'm only a common police official with nothing a year and a pension to look forward to, but there's no need to sneer about it."

" I'm not sneering," retorted Peter indignantly. " I can't imagine why anybody should want to marry my sister, but you're a friend of mine and a damn good sort, and you've my good word for what it's worth. Besides —dash it all, man !—to put it on the lowest grounds, do look what it might have been ! A Socialist Conchy of neither bowels nor breeding, or a card-sharping dark

221

horse with a mysterious past ! Mother and Jerry must have got to the point when they'd welcome a decent, God-fearing plumber, let alone a policeman. Only thing I'm afraid of is that Mary, havin' such beastly bad taste in blokes, won't know how to appreciate a really decent fellow like you, old son."

Mr. Parker begged his friend's pardon for his unworthy suspicions, and they sat a little time in silence. Parker sipped his port, and saw unimaginable visions warmly glowing in its rosy depths. Wimsey pulled out his pocket-book, and began idly turning over its contents, throwing old letters into the fire, unfolding and refolding memoranda, and reviewing a miscellaneous series of other people's visiting-cards. He came at length to the slip of blotting-paper from the study at Riddlesdale, to whose fragmentary markings he had since given scarcely a thought.

Presently Mr. Parker, finishing his port and recalling his mind with an effort, remembered that he had been meaning to tell Peter something before the name of Lady Mary had driven all other thoughts out of his head. He turned to his host, open-mouthed for speech, but his remark never got beyond a preliminary click like that of a clock about to strike, for, even as he turned, Lord Peter brought his fist down on the little table with a bang that made the decanters ring, and cried out in the loud voice of complete and sudden enlightenment :

" *Manon Lescaut !* "

" Eh ? " said Mr. Parker.

" Boil my brains ! " said Lord Peter. " Boil 'em and mash 'em and serve 'em up with butter as a dish of turnips, for it's damn well all they're fit for ! Look at me ! " (Mr. Parker scarcely needed this exhortation.) " Here we've been worryin' over Jerry, an' worryin' over Mary, an' huntin' for Goyleses an' Grimethorpes and God knows who—and all the time I'd got this little bit of paper tucked away in my pocket. The blot upon the paper's rim a blotted paper was to him, and it was nothing more. But Manon, Manon! Charles, if I'd had the grey matter of a woodlouse that book ought to have told me the whole story. And think what we'd have been saved ! "

" I wish you wouldn't be so excited," said Parker. " I'm sure it's perfectly splendid for you to see your way so clearly, but I never read *Manon Lescaut*, and you haven't shown me the blotting-paper, and I haven't the foggiest idea what you've discovered."

Lord Peter passed the relic over without comment.

" I observe," said Parker, " that the paper is rather crumpled and dirty, and smells powerfully of tobacco and Russian leather, and deduce that you have been keeping it in your pocket-book."

" No ! " said Wimsey incredulously. " And when you actually saw me take it out ! Holmes, how do you do it ? "

" At one corner," pursued Parker, " I see two blots, one rather larger than the other. I think someone must have shaken a pen there. Is there anything sinister about the blot ? "

" I haven't noticed anything."

" Some way below the blots the Duke has signed his name two or three times—or, rather, his title. The inference is that his letters were not to intimates."

" The inference is justifiable, I fancy."

" Colonel Marchbanks has a neat signature."

" He can hardly mean mischief," said Peter. " He signs his name like an honest man ! Proceed."

" There's a sprawly message about five something of fine something. Do you see anything occult there ? "

" The number five may have a cabalistic meaning, but I admit I don't know what it is. There are five senses, five fingers, five great Chinese precepts, five books of Moses, to say nothing of the mysterious entities hymned in the Dilly Song—' Five are the flamboys under the pole.' I must admit that I have always

223

panted to know what the five flamboys were. But, not knowing, I get no help from it in this case."

"Well, that's all, except a fragment consisting of ' oe ' on one line, and ' is fou—' below it."

"What do you make of that ? "

" ' Is found,' I suppose."

"Do you ? "

"That seems the simplest interpretation. Or possibly ' his foul '—there seems to have been a sudden rush of ink to the pen just there. Do you think it is ' his foul ' ? Was the Duke writing about Cathcart's foul play ? Is that what you mean ? "

"No, I don't make that of it. Besides, I don't think it's Jerry's writing."

"Whose is it ? "

"I don't know, but I can guess."

"And it leads somewhere ? "

"It tells the whole story."

"Oh, cough it up, Wimsey. Even Dr. Watson would lose patience."

"Tut, tut ! Try the line above."

"Well, there's only ' oe.' "

"Yes, well ? "

"Well, I don't know. Poet, poem, manœuvre, Loeb edition, Citroen—it might be anything."

"Dunno about that. There aren't lashings of English words with ' oe ' in them—and it's written so close it almost looks like a diphthong at that."

"Perhaps it isn't an English word."

"Exactly ; perhaps it isn't."

"Oh ! Oh, I see. French ? "

"Ah, you're gettin' warm."

" *Sœur—œuvre—œuf—bœuf——* "

"No, no. You were nearer the first time."

" *Sœur—cœur !* "

" *Cœur.* Hold on a moment. Look at the scratch in front of that."

"Wait a bit—*er—cer——* "

" How about *percer* ? "

" I believe you're right. ' *Percer le cœur.*' "

" Yes. Or ' *perceras le cœur.*' "

" That's better. It seems to need another letter or two."

" And now your ' is found ' line."

" *Fou !* "

" Who ? "

" I didn't say ' who '; I said '*fou.*' "

" I know you did. I said who ? "

" Who ? "

" Who's *fou* ? "

" Oh, *is*. By Jove, ' *suis* ' ! ' *Je suis fou.*' "

" *A la bonne heure !* And I suggest that the next words are ' *de douleur*,' or something like it."

" They might be."

" Cautious beast ! I say they are."

" Well, and suppose they are ? "

" It tells us everything."

" Nothing ! "

" Everything, I say. Think. This was written on the day Cathcart died. Now who in the house would be likely to write these words, ' *perceras le cœur . . . je suis fou de douleur* ' ? Take everybody. I know it isn't Jerry's fist, and he wouldn't use those expressions. Colonel or Mrs. Marchbanks ? Not Pygmalion likely ! Freddy ? Couldn't write passionate letters in French to save his life."

" No, of course not. It would have to be either Cathcart or—Lady Mary."

" Rot ! It couldn't be Mary."

" Why not ? "

" Not unless she changed her sex, you know."

" Of course not. It would have to be ' *je suis folle.*' Then Cathcart——"

" Of course. He lived in France all his life. Consider his bank-book. Consider——"

" Lord ! Wimsey, we've been blind."

" Yes."

" And listen ! I was going to tell you. The Sûreté write me that they've traced one of Cathcart's bank-notes."

" Where to ? "

" To a Mr. François who owns a lot of house property near the Etoile."

" And lets it out in *appartements !* "

" No doubt."

" When's the next train ? Bunter ! "

" My lord ! "

Mr. Bunter hurried to the door at the call.

" The next boat-train for Paris ? "

" Eight-twenty, my lord, from Waterloo."

" We're going by it. How long ? "

" Twenty minutes, my lord."

" Pack my toothbrush and call a taxi."

" Certainly, my lord."

" But, Wimsey, what light does it throw on Cath-cart's murder ? Did this woman——"

" I've no time," said Wimsey hurriedly. " But I'll be back in a day or two. Meanwhile——"

He hunted hastily in the bookshelf.

" Read this."

He flung the book at his friend and plunged into his bedroom.

At eleven o'clock, as a gap of dirty water disfigured with oil and bits of paper widened between the *Nor-mannia* and the quay ; while hardened passengers for-tified their sea-stomachs with cold ham and pickles, and the more nervous studied the Boddy jackets in their cabins ; while the harbour lights winked and swam right and left, and Lord Peter scraped acquaintance with a second-rate cinema actor in the bar, Charles Parker sat, with a puzzled frown, before the fire at 110 Piccadilly, making his first acquaintance with the delicate master-piece of the Abbé Prévost.

CHAPTER XIV

THE EDGE OF THE AXE TOWARDS HIM

Scene i. *Westminster Hall. Enter as to the Parliament, Bolingbroke, Aumerle, Northumberland, Percy, Fitzwater, Surrey, the Bishop of Carlisle, the Abbot of Westminster, and another Lord, Herald, Officers, and Bagot.*

BOLINGBROKE : Call forth Bagot.
                  Now, Bagot, freely speak thy mind ;
                  What thou dost know of noble Glou-
                    cester's death ;
                  Who wrought it with the king, and who
                    performed
                  The bloody office of his timeless end.

BAGOT :   Then set before my face the Lord
                  Aumerle.
                                King Richard II.

T H E historic trial of the Duke of Denver for murder opened as soon as Parliament reassembled after the Christmas vacation. The papers had leaderettes on " Trial by his Peers," by a Woman Barrister, and " The Privilege of Peers : should it be abolished ? " by a Student of History. The *Evening Banner* got into trouble for contempt by publishing an article entitled " The Silken Rope " (by an Antiquarian), which was deemed to be prejudicial, and the *Daily Trumpet*—the Labour organ—inquired sarcastically why, when a peer

was tried, the fun of seeing the show should be reserved
to the few influential persons who could wangle tickets
for the Royal Gallery.

Mr. Murbles and Detective Inspector Parker, in close
consultation, went about with preoccupied faces, while
Sir Impey Biggs retired into a complete eclipse for three
days, revolved about by Mr. Glibbery, K.C., Mr.
Brownrigg-Fortescue, K.C., and a number of lesser
satellites. The schemes of the Defence were kept dark
indeed—the more so that they found themselves on the
eve of the struggle deprived of their principal witness,
and wholly ignorant whether or not he would be forthcoming with his testimony.

Lord Peter had returned from Paris at the end of
four days, and had burst in like a cyclone at Great
Ormond Street. " I've got it," he said, " but it's touch
and go. Listen ! "

For an hour Parker had listened, feverishly taking
notes.

" You can work on that," said Wimsey. " Tell
Murbles. I'm off."

His next appearance was at the American Embassy.
The Ambassador, however, was not there, having
received a royal mandate to dine. Wimsey damned the
dinner, abandoned the polite, horn-rimmed secretaries,
and leapt back into his taxi with a demand to be driven
to Buckingham Palace. Here a great deal of insistence
with scandalised officials produced first a higher
official, then a very high official, and, finally, the American Ambassador and a Royal Personage while the meat
was yet in their mouths.

" Oh, yes," said the Ambassador, " of course it can
be done——"

" Surely, surely," said the Personage genially, " we
mustn't have any delay. Might cause an international
misunderstanding, and a lot of paragraphs about Ellis
Island. Terrible nuisance to have to adjourn the trial—
dreadful fuss, isn't it ? Our secretaries are everlastingly

bringing things along to our place to sign about extra policemen and seating accommodation. Good luck to you, Wimsey! Come and have something while they get your papers through. When does your boat go?"

"To-morrow morning, sir. I'm catching the Liverpool train in an hour—if I can."

"You surely will," said the Ambassador cordially, signing a note. "And they say the English can't hustle."

So, with his papers all in order, his lordship set sail from Liverpool the next morning, leaving his legal representatives to draw up alternative schemes of defence.

. . . . .

"Then the peers, two by two, in their order, beginning with the youngest baron."

Garter King-of-Arms, very hot and bothered, fussed unhappily around the three hundred or so British peers who were sheepishly struggling into their robes, while the heralds did their best to line up the assembly and keep them from wandering away when once arranged.

"Of all the farces!" grumbled Lord Attenbury irritably. He was a very short, stout gentleman of a choleric countenance, and was annoyed to find himself next to the Earl of Strathgillan and Begg, an extremely tall, lean nobleman, with pronounced views on Prohibition and the Legitimation question.

"I say, Attenbury," said a kindly, brick-red peer, with five rows of ermine on his shoulder, "is it true that Wimsey hasn't come back? My daughter tells me she heard he'd gone to collect evidence in the States. Why the States?"

"Dunno," said Attenbury; "but Wimsey's a dashed clever fellow. When he found those emeralds of mine, you know, I said——"

"Your grace, your grace," cried Rouge Dragon desperately, diving in, "your grace is out of line again."

"Eh, what?" said the brick-faced peer. "Oh, damme! Must obey orders, I suppose, what?" And was towed away from the mere earls and pushed into position next to the Duke of Wiltshire, who was deaf, and a distant connection of Denver's on the distaff side.

The Royal Gallery was packed. In the seats reserved below the Bar for peeresses sat the Dowager Duchess of Denver, beautifully dressed and defiant. She suffered much from the adjacent presence of her daughter-in-law, whose misfortune it was to become disagreeable when she was unhappy—perhaps the heaviest curse that can be laid on man, who is born to sorrow.

Behind the imposing array of Counsel in full-bottomed wigs in the body of the hall were seats reserved for witnesses, and here Mr. Bunter was accommodated—to be called if the defence should find it necessary to establish the alibi—the majority of the witnesses being pent up in the King's Robing-Room, gnawing their fingers and glaring at one another. On either side, above the Bar, were the benches for the peers—each in his own right a judge both of fact and law—while on the high dais the great chair of state stood ready for the Lord High Steward.

The reporters at their little table were beginning to fidget and look at their watches. Muffled by the walls and the buzz of talk, Big Ben dropped eleven slow notes into the suspense. A door opened. The reporters started to their feet; counsel rose; everybody rose; the Dowager Duchess whispered irrepressibly to her neighbour that it reminded her of the Voice that breathed o'er Eden; and the procession streamed slowly in, lit by a shaft of wintry sunshine from the tall windows.

The proceedings were opened by a Proclamation of Silence from the Sergeant-at-Arms, after which the Clerk of the Crown in Chancery, kneeling at the foot of the throne, presented the Commission under the Great Seal to the Lord High Steward,* who, finding no use for it, returned it with great solemnity to the Clerk

---

* The Lord Chancellor held the appointment on this occasion as usual.

of the Crown. The latter accordingly proceeded to read it at dismal and wearisome length, affording the assembly an opportunity of judging just how bad the acoustics of the chamber were. The Sergeant-at-Arms retorted with great emphasis, " God Save the King," whereupon Garter King-of-Arms and the Gentleman Usher of the Black Rod, kneeling again, handed the Lord High Steward his staff of office. (" So picturesque, isn't it ? " said the Dowager—" quite High Church, you know.")

The Certiorari and Return followed in a long, sonorous rigmarole, which, starting with George the Fifth by the Grace of God, called upon all the Justices and Judges of the Old Bailey, enumerated the Lord Mayor of London, the Recorder, and a quantity of assorted aldermen and justices, skipped back to our Lord the King, roamed about the City of London, Counties of London and Middlesex, Essex, Kent, and Surrey, mentioned our late Sovereign Lord King William the Fourth, branched off to the Local Government Act one thousand eight hundred and eighty-eight, lost its way in a list of all treasons, murders, felonies, and misdemeanours by whomsoever and in what manner soever done, committed or perpetrated and by whom or to whom, when, how and after what manner and of all other articles and circumstances concerning the premises and every one of them and any of them in any manner whatsoever, and at last, triumphantly, after reciting the names of the whole Grand Jury, came to the presentation of the indictment with a sudden, brutal brevity.

" The Jurors for our Lord the King upon their oaths present that the most noble and puissant prince Gerald Christian Wimsey, Viscount St. George, Duke of Denver, a Peer of the United Kingdom of Great Britain and Ireland, on the thirteenth day of October in the year of Our Lord one thousand nine hundred and twenty—in the Parish of Riddlesdale in the County of Yorkshire did kill and murder Denis Cathcart."

231

"After which, Proclamation* was made by the Sergeant-at-Arms for the Gentleman Usher of the Black Rod to call in Gerald Christian Wimsey, Viscount St. George, Duke of Denver, to appear at the Bar to answer his indictment, who, being come to the Bar, kneeled until the Lord High Steward acquainted him that he might rise."

The Duke of Denver looked very small and pink and lonely in his blue serge suit, the only head uncovered among all his peers, but he was not without a certain dignity as he was conducted to the " Stool placed within the Bar," which is deemed appropriate to noble prisoners, and he listened to the Lord High Steward's rehearsal of the charge with a simple gravity which became him very well.

"Then the said Duke of Denver was arraigned by the Clerk of the Parliaments in the usual manner and asked whether he was Guilty or Not Guilty, to which he pleaded Not Guilty."

Whereupon Sir Wigmore Wrinching, the Attorney-General, rose to open the case for the Crown.

After the usual preliminaries to the effect that the case was a very painful one and the occasion a very solemn one, Sir Wigmore proceeded to unfold the story from the beginning : the quarrel, the shot at 3 a.m., the pistol, the finding of the body, the disappearance of the letter, and the rest of the familiar tale. He hinted, moreover, that evidence would be called to show that the quarrel between Denver and Cathcart had motives other than those alleged by the prisoner, and that the latter would turn out to have had " good reason to fear exposure at Cathcart's hands." At which point the accused was observed to glance uneasily at his solicitor. The exposition took only a short time, and Sir Wigmore proceeded to call witnesses.

The prosecution being unable to call the Duke of

* For Report of the procedure see House of Lords Journal for the dates in question.

Denver, the first important witness was Lady Mary Wimsey. After telling about her relations with the murdered man, and describing the quarrel, " At three o'clock," she proceeded, " I got up and went downstairs."

" In consequence of what did you do so ? " inquired Sir Wigmore, looking round the Court with the air of a man about to produce his great effect.

" In consequence of an appointment I had made to meet a friend."

All the reporters looked up suddenly, like dogs expecting a piece of biscuit, and Sir Wigmore started so violently that he knocked his brief over upon the head of the Clerk to the House of Lords sitting below him.

" Indeed ! Now, witness, remember you are on your oath, and be very careful. What was it caused you to wake at three o'clock ? "

" I was not asleep. I was waiting for my appointment."

" And while you were waiting did you hear anything ? "

" Nothing at all."

" Now, Lady Mary, I have here your deposition sworn before the Coroner. I will read it to you. Please listen very carefully. You say, ' At three o'clock I was wakened by a shot. I thought it might be poachers. It sounded very loud, close to the house. I went down to find out what it was.' Do you remember making that statement ? "

" Yes, but it was not true."

" Not true ? "

" No."

" In the face of that statement, you still say that you heard nothing at three o'clock ? "

" I heard nothing at all. I went down because I had an appointment."

" My lords," said Sir Wigmore, with a very red face.

" I must ask leave to treat this witness as a hostile witness."

Sir Wigmore's fiercest onslaught, however, produced no effect, except a reiteration of the statement that no shot had been heard at any time. With regard to the finding of the body, Lady Mary explained that when she said, " Oh, God ! Gerald, you've killed him," she was under the impression that the body was that of the friend who had made the appointment. Here a fierce wrangle ensued as to whether the story of the appointment was relevant. The Lords decided that on the whole it was relevant ; and the entire Goyles story came out, together with the intimation that Mr. Goyles was in court and could be produced. Eventually, with a loud snort, Sir Wigmore Wrinching gave up the witness to Sir Impey Biggs, who, rising suavely and looking extremely handsome, brought back the discussion to a point long previous.

" Forgive the nature of the question," said Sir Impey, bowing blandly, "but will you tell us whether, in your opinion, the late Captain Cathcart was deeply in love with you ? "

" No, I am sure he was not ; it was an arrangement for our mutual convenience."

" From your knowledge of his character, do you suppose he was capable of a very deep affection ? "

" I think he might have been, for the right woman. I should say he had a very passionate nature."

" Thank you. You have told us that you met Captain Cathcart several times when you were staying in Paris last February. Do you remember going with him to a jeweller's—Monsieur Briquet's in the Rue de la Paix ? "

" I may have done ; I cannot exactly remember."

" The date to which I should like to draw your attention is the sixth."

" I could not say."

" Do you recognise this trinket ? "

Here the green-eyed cat was handed to witness.

" No ; I have never seen it before."

" Did Captain Cathcart ever give you one like it ? "

" Never."

" Did you ever possess such a jewel ? "

" I am quite positive I never did."

" My lords, I put in this diamond and platinum cat. Thank you, Lady Mary."

James Fleming, being questioned closely as to the delivery of the post, continued to be vague and forgetful, leaving the Court, on the whole, with the impression that no letter had ever been delivered to the Duke. Sir Wigmore, whose opening speech had contained sinister allusions to an attempt to blacken the character of the victim, smiled disagreeably, and handed the witness over to Sir Impey. The latter contented himself with extracting an admission that witness could not swear positively one way or the other, and passed on immediately to another point.

" Do you recollect whether any letters came by the same post for any of the other members of the party ? "

" Yes ; I took three or four into the billiard-room."

" Can you say to whom they were addressed ? "

" There were several for Colonel Marchbanks and one for Captain Cathcart."

" Did Captain Cathcart open his letter there and then ? "

" I couldn't say, sir. I left the room immediately to take his grace's letters to the study."

" Now will you tell us how the letters are collected for the post in the morning at the Lodge ? "

" They are put into the post-bag, which is locked. His grace keeps one key and the post-office has the other. The letters are put in through a slit in the top."

" On the morning after Captain Cathcart's death were the letters taken to the post as usual ? "

" Yes, sir."

" By whom ? "

" I took the bag down myself, sir."

" Had you an opportunity of seeing what letters were in it ? "

" I saw there was two or three when the postmistress took 'em out of the bag, but I couldn't say who they was addressed to or anythink of that."

" Thank you."

Sir Wigmore Wrinching here bounced up like a very irritable jack-in-the-box.

" Is this the first time you have mentioned this letter which you say you delivered to Captain Cathcart on the night of his murder ? "

" My lords," cried Sir Impey. " I protest against this language. We have as yet had no proof that any murder was committed."

This was the first indication of the line of defence which Sir Impey proposed to take, and caused a little rustle of excitement.

" My lords," went on Counsel, replying to a question of the Lord High Steward, " I submit that so far there has been no attempt to prove murder, and that, until the prosecution have established the murder, such a word cannot properly be put into the mouth of a witness."

" Perhaps, Sir Wigmore, it would be better to use some other word."

" It makes no difference to our case, my lord ; I bow to your lordships' decision. Heaven knows that I would not seek, even by the lightest or most trivial word, to hamper the defence on so serious a charge."

" My lords," interjected Sir Impey, " if the learned Attorney-General considers the word murder to be a triviality, it would be interesting to know to what words he does attach importance."

" The learned Attorney-General has agreed to substitute another word," said the Lord High Steward soothingly, and nodding to Sir Wigmore to proceed.

Sir Impey, having achieved his purpose of robbing the Attorney-General's onslaught on the witness of some of its original impetus, sat down, and Sir Wigmore repeated his question.

"I mentioned it first to Mr. Murbles about three weeks ago."

"Mr. Murbles is the solicitor for the accused, I believe."

"Yes, sir."

"And how was it," inquired Sir Wigmore ferociously, settling his pince-nez on his rather prominent nose, and glowering at the witness, "that you did not mention this letter at the inquest or at the earlier proceedings in the case?"

"I wasn't asked about it, sir."

"What made you suddenly decide to go and tell Mr. Murbles about it?"

"He asked me, sir."

"Oh, he asked you; and you conveniently remembered it when it was suggested to you?"

"No, sir. I remembered it all the time. That is to say, I hadn't given any special thought to it, sir."

"Oh, you remembered it all the time, though you hadn't given any thought to it. Now I put it to you that you had not remembered about it at all till it was suggested to you by Mr. Murbles."

"Mr. Murbles didn't suggest nothing, sir. He asked me whether any other letters came by that post, and then I remembered it."

"Exactly. When it was suggested to you, you remembered it, and not before."

"No, sir. That is, if I'd been asked before I should have remembered it and mentioned it, but, not being asked, I didn't think it would be of any importance, sir."

"You didn't think it of any importance that this man received a letter a few hours before his—decease?"

"No, sir. I reckoned if it had been of any importance the police would have asked about it, sir."

"Now, James Fleming, I put it to you again that it never occurred to you that Captain Cathcart might

237

have received a letter the night he died till the idea was put into your head by the defence."

The witness, baffled by this interrogative negative, made a confused reply, and Sir Wigmore, glancing round the house as much as to say, " You see this shifty fellow," proceeded :

" I suppose it didn't occur to you either to mention to the police about the letters in the post-bag ? "

" No, sir."

" Why not ? "

" I didn't think it was my place, sir."

" Did you think about it at all ? "

" No, sir."

" Do you ever think ? "

" No, sir—I mean, yes, sir."

" Then will you please think what you are saying now."

" Yes, sir."

" You say that you took all these important letters out of the house without authority and without acquainting the police ? "

" I had my orders, sir."

" From whom ? "

" They was his grace's orders, sir."

" Ah ! His grace's orders. When did you get that order ? "

" It was part of my regular duty, sir, to take the bag to the post each morning."

" And did it not occur to you that in a case like this the proper information of the police might be more important than your orders ? "

" No, sir."

Sir Wigmore sat down with a disgusted look ; and Sir Impey took the witness in hand again.

" Did the thought of this letter delivered to Captain Cathcart never pass through your mind between the day of the death and the day when Mr. Murbles spoke to you about it ? "

" Well, it did pass through my mind, in a manner of speaking, sir."

" When was that ? "

" Before the Grand Jury, sir."

" And how was it you didn't speak about it then ? "

" The gentleman said I was to confine myself to the questions, and not say nothing on my own, sir."

" Who was this very peremptory gentleman ? "

" The lawyer that came down to ask questions for the Crown, sir."

" Thank you," said Sir Impey smoothly, sitting down, and leaning over to say something, apparently of an amusing nature, to Mr. Glibbery.

The question of the letter was further pursued in the examination of the Hon. Freddy. Sir Wigmore Wrinching laid great stress upon this witness's assertion that deceased had been in excellent health and spirits when retiring to bed on the Wednesday evening, and had spoken of his approaching marriage. " He seemed particularly cheerio, you know," said the Hon. Freddy.

" Particularly what ? " inquired the Lord High Steward.

" Cheerio, my lord," said Sir Wigmore, with a deprecatory bow.

" I do not know whether that is a dictionary word," said his lordship, entering it upon his notes with meticulous exactness, " but I take it to be synonymous with cheerful."

The Hon. Freddy, appealed to, said he thought he meant more than just cheerful, more merry and bright, you know.

" May we take it that he was in exceptionally lively spirits ? " suggested Counsel.

" Take it in any spirit you like," muttered the witness, adding, more happily, " Take a peg of John Begg."

" The deceased was particularly lively and merry when he went to bed," said Sir Wigmore, frowning horribly, " and looking forward to his marriage in the near future. Would that be a fair statement of his condition ? "

The Hon. Freddy agreed to this.

Sir Impey did not cross-examine as to witness's account of the quarrel, but went straight to his point.

" Do you recollect anything about the letters that were brought in the night of the death ? "

" Yes ; I had one from my aunt. The Colonel had some, I fancy, and there was one for Cathcart."

" Did Captain Cathcart read his letter there and then?"

" No, I'm sure he didn't. You see, I opened mine, and then I saw he was shoving his away in his pocket, and I thought——"

" Never mind what you thought," said Sir Impey. " What did you do ? "

" I said, ' Excuse me, you don't mind, do you ? ' And he said, ' Not at all ' ; but he didn't read his ; and I remember thinking——"

" We can't have that, you know," said the Lord High Steward.

" But that's why I'm so sure he didn't open it," said the Hon. Freddy, hurt. " You see, I said to myself at the time what a secretive fellow he was, and that's how I know."

Sir Wigmore, who had bounced up with his mouth open, sat down again.

" Thank you, Mr. Arbuthnot," said Sir Impey, smiling.

Colonel and Mrs. Marchbanks testified to having heard movements in the Duke's study at 11.30. They had heard no shot or other noise. There was no cross-examination.

Mr. Pettigrew-Robinson gave a vivid account of the quarrel, and asserted very positively that there could be no mistaking the sound of the Duke's bedroom door.

" We were then called up by Mr. Arbuthnot at a little after 3 a.m.," proceeded witness, " and went down to the conservatory, where I saw the accused and Mr. Arbuthnot washing the face of the deceased. I pointed out to them what an unwise thing it was to do this, as they might be destroying valuable evidence for the police. They paid no attention to me. There were a number of footmarks round about the door which I wanted to examine, because it was my theory that——"

"My lords," cried Sir Impey, "we really cannot have this witness's theory."

"Certainly not!" said the Lord High Steward. "Answer the questions, please, and don't add anything on your own account."

"Of course," said Mr. Pettigrew-Robinson. "I don't mean to imply that there was anything wrong about it, but I considered——"

"Never mind what you considered. Attend to me, please. When you first saw the body, how was it lying?"

"On its back, with Denver and Arbuthnot washing its face. It had evidently been turned over, because——"

"Sir Wigmore," interposed the Lord High Steward, "you really must control your witness."

"Kindly confine yourself to the evidence," said Sir Wigmore, rather heated. "We do not want your deductions from it. You say that when you saw the body it was lying on its back. Is that correct?"

"And Denver and Arbuthnot were washing it."

"Yes. Now I want to pass to another point. Do you remember an occasion when you lunched at the Royal Automobile Club?"

"I do. I lunched there one day in the middle of last August—I think it was about the sixteenth or seventeenth."

"Will you tell us what happened on that occasion?"

"I had gone into the smoke-room after lunch, and was reading in a high-backed armchair, when I saw the prisoner at the Bar come in with the late Captain Cathcart. That is to say, I saw them in the big mirror over the mantelpiece. They did not notice there was anyone there, or they would have been a little more careful what they said, I fancy. They sat down near me and started talking, and presently Cathcart leaned over and said something in a low tone which I couldn't catch. The prisoner leapt up with a horrified face, exclaiming, ' For God's sake, don't give me away, Cathcart—there'd be the devil to pay.' Cathcart said something reassuring—I didn't hear what, he had a furtive sort of voice—and the prisoner replied, " Well, don't, that's all. I couldn't afford to let anybody get hold of it.' The prisoner seemed greatly alarmed. Captain Cathcart was laughing. They dropped their voices again, and that was all I heard."

" Thank you."

Sir Impey took over the witness with a Belial-like politeness.

" You are gifted with very excellent powers of observation and deduction, Mr. Pettigrew-Robinson," he began, " and no doubt you like to exercise your sympathetic imagination in a scrutiny of people's motives and characters ? "

" I think I may call myself a student of human nature," replied Mr. Pettigrew-Robinson, much mollified.

" Doubtless, people are inclined to confide in you ? "

" Certainly. I may say I am a great repository of human documents."

" On the night of Captain Cathcart's death your wide knowledge of the world was doubtless of great comfort and assistance to the family ? "

" They did not avail themselves of my experience, sir," said Mr. Pettigrew-Robinson, exploding suddenly. " I was ignored completely. If only my advice had been taken at the time——"

" Thank you, thank you," said Sir Impey, cutting short an impatient exclamation from the Attorney-General, who thereupon rose and demanded :

" If Captain Cathcart had had any secret or trouble

of any kind in his life, you would have expected him to tell you about it ? "

"From any right-minded young man I might certainly have expected it," said Mr. Pettigrew-Robinson blusteringly ; " but Captain Cathcart was disagreeably secretive. On the only occasion when I showed a friendly interest in his affairs he was very rude indeed. He called me——"

" That'll do," interposed Sir Impey hastily, the answer to the question not having turned out as he expected. " What the deceased called you is immaterial."

Mr. Pettigrew-Robinson retired, leaving behind him the impression of a man with a grudge—an impression which seemed to please Mr. Glibbery and Mr. Brownrigg-Fortescue extremely, for they chuckled continuously through the evidence of the next two witnesses.

Mrs. Pettigrew-Robinson had little to add to her previous evidence at the inquest. Miss Cathcart was asked by Sir Impey about Cathcart's parentage, and explained, with deep disapproval in her voice, that her brother, when an all-too-experienced and middle-aged man of the world, had nevertheless " been entangled by " an Italian singer of nineteen, who had " contrived " to make him marry her. Eighteen years later both parents had died. " No wonder," said Miss Cathcart, " with the rackety life they led," and the boy had been left to her care. She explained how Denis had always chafed at her influence, gone about with men she disapproved of, and eventually gone to Paris to make a diplomatic career for himself, since which time she had hardly seen him.

An interesting point was raised in the cross-examination of Inspector Craikes. A penknife being shown him, he identified it as the one found on Cathcart's body.

By Mr. Glibbery : " Do you observe any marks on the blade ? "

" Yes, there is a slight notch near the handle."

" Might the mark have been caused by forcing back the catch of a window ? "

Inspector Craikes agreed that it might, but doubted whether so small a knife would have been adequate for such a purpose. The revolver was produced, and the question of ownership raised.

" My lords," put in Sir Impey, "we do not dispute the Duke's ownership of the revolver."

The Court looked surprised, and, after Hardraw the gamekeeper had given evidence of the shot heard at 11.30, the medical evidence was taken.

Sir Impey Biggs : " Could the wound have been self-inflicted ? "

" It could, certainly."

" Would it have been instantly fatal ? "

" No. From the amount of blood found upon the path it was obviously not immediately fatal."

" Are the marks found, in your opinion, consistent with deceased having crawled towards the house ? "

" Yes, quite. He might have had sufficient strength to do so."

" Would such a wound cause fever ? "

" It is quite possible. He might have lost consciousness for some time, and contracted a chill and fever by lying in the wet."

" Are the appearances consistent with his having lived for some hours after being wounded ? "

" They strongly suggest it."

Re-examining, Sir Wigmore Wrinching established that the wound and general appearance of the ground were equally consistent with the theory that deceased had been shot by another hand at very close quarters, and dragged to the house before life was extinct.

" In your experience is it more usual for a person committing suicide to shoot himself in the chest or in the head ? "

" In the head is perhaps more usual."

THE EDGE OF THE AXE

" So much as almost to create a presumption of murder when the wound is in the chest ? "

" I would not go so far as that."

" But, other things being equal, you would say that a wound in the head is more suggestive of suicide than a body-wound ? "

" That is so."

Sir Impey Biggs : " But suicide by shooting in the heart is not by any means impossible ? "

" Oh, dear, no."

" There have been such cases ? "

" Oh, certainly ; many such."

" There is nothing in the medical evidence before you to exclude the idea of suicide ? "

" Nothing whatever."

This closed the case for the Crown.

CHAPTER XV

BAR FALLING

Copyright by Reuter, Press Association Exchange Telegraph, and Central News.

W H E N Sir Impey Biggs rose to make his opening speech for the defence on the second day, it was observed that he looked somewhat worried—a thing very unusual in him. His remarks were very brief, yet in those few words he sent a thrill through the great assembly.

" My lords, in rising to open this defence I find myself in a more than usually anxious position. Not that I have any doubt of your lordships' verdict. Never perhaps has it been possible so clearly to prove the innocence of any accused person as in the case of my noble client. But I will explain to your lordships at once that I may be obliged to ask for an adjournment, since we are at present without an important witness and a decisive piece of evidence. My lords, I hold here in my hand a cablegram from this witness—I will tell you his name ; it is Lord Peter Wimsey, the brother of the accused. It was handed in yesterday at New York. I will read it to you. He says : ' Evidence secured. Leaving to-night with Air Pilot Grant. Sworn copy and depositions follow by S.S. *Lucarnia* in case accident. Hope arrive Thursday.' My lords, at this moment this all-important witness is cleaving the air high above the wide Atlantic. In this wintry weather he is braving a peril which would appal any heart but his own and that of the world-famous aviator whose help he has enlisted, so that no moment may be lost in freeing his noble brother from this terrible charge. My lords, the barometer is falling."

An immense hush, like the stillness of a black frost, had fallen over the glittering benches. The lords in their scarlet and ermine, the peeresses in their rich furs, counsel in their full-bottomed wigs and billowing gowns, the Lord High Steward upon his high seat, the ushers and the heralds and the gaudy kings-of arms, rested rigid in their places. Only the prisoner looked across at his counsel and back to the Lord High Steward in a kind of bewilderment, and the reporters scribbled wildly and desperately stop-press announcements—lurid headlines, picturesque epithets, and alarming weather predictions, to halt hurrying London on its way : " PEER'S SON FLIES ATLANTIC " ; " BROTHER'S DEVOTION " ; " WILL WIMSEY BE IN TIME ? " ; " RIDDLESDALE MURDER CHARGE : AMAZING DEVELOPMENT." This was news. A million tape-machines ticked it out in offices and clubs, where clerks and messenger-boys gloated over it and laid wagers on the result ; the thousands of monster printing-presses sucked it in, boiled it into lead, champed it into slugs, engulfed it in their huge maws, digested it to paper, and flapped it forth again with clutching talons ; and a blue-nosed, ragged veteran of Vimy Ridge, who had once assisted to dig Major Wimsey out of a shell-hole, muttered : "Gawd 'elp 'im, 'e's a real decent little blighter," as he tucked his newspapers into the iron grille of a tree in Kingsway and displayed his placard to the best advantage.

After a brief statement that he intended, not merely to prove his noble client's innocence but (as a work of supererogation) to make clear every detail of the tragedy, Sir Impey Biggs proceeded without further delay to call his witnesses.

Among the first was Mr. Goyles, who testified that he had found Cathcart already dead at 3 a.m., with his head close to the water-trough which stood near the well. Ellen, the maid-servant, next confirmed

James Fleming's evidence with regard to the post-bag, and explained how she changed the blotting-paper in the study every day.

The evidence of Detective-Inspector Parker aroused more interest and some bewilderment. His description of the discovery of the green-eyed cat was eagerly listened to. He also gave a minute account of the foot-prints and marks of dragging, especially the imprint of a hand in the flower-bed. The piece of blotting-paper was then produced, and photographs of it circulated among the peers. A long discussion ensued on both these points, Sir Impey Biggs endeavouring to show that the imprint on the flower-bed was such as would have been caused by a man endeavouring to lift himself from a prone position, Sir Wigmore Wrinching doing his best to force an admission that it might have been made by deceased in trying to prevent himself from being dragged along.

" The position of the fingers being towards the house appears, does it not, to negative the suggestion of dragging ? " suggested Sir Impey.

Sir Wigmore, however, put it to the witness that the wounded man might have been dragged head foremost.

" If, now," said Sir Wigmore. " I were to drag you by the coat-collar—my lords will grasp my conten-tion——"

" It appears," observed the Lord High Steward, " to be a case for *solvitur ambulando*." (Laughter.) " I suggest that when the House rises for lunch, some of us should make the experiment, choosing a member of similar height and weight to the deceased." (All the noble lords looked round at one another to see which unfortunate might be chosen for the part.)

Inspector Parker then mentioned the marks of forcing on the study window.

" In your opinion, could the catch have been forced back by the knife found on the body of the deceased ? "

" I know it could, for I made the experiment myself with a knife of exactly similar pattern."

After this the message on the blotting-paper was read backwards and forwards and interpreted in every possible way, the defence insisting that the language was French and the words " *Je suis fou de douleur*," the prosecution scouting the suggestion as far-fetched, and offering an English interpretation, such as " is found " or " his foul." A handwriting expert was then called, who compared the handwriting with that of an authentic letter of Cathcart's, and was subsequently severely handled by the prosecution.

These knotty points being left for the consideration of the noble lords, the defence then called a tedious series of witnesses : the manager of Cox's and Monsieur Turgeot of the Crédit Lyonnais, who went with much detail into Cathcart's financial affairs ; the concierge and Madame Leblanc from the Rue St. Honoré ; and the noble lords began to yawn, with the exception of a few of the soap and pickles lords, who suddenly started to make computations in their note-books, and exchanged looks of intelligence as from one financier to another.

Then came Monsieur Briquet, the jeweller from the Rue de la Paix, and the girl from his shop, who told the story of the tall, fair, foreign lady and the purchase of the green-eyed cat—whereat everybody woke up. After reminding the assembly that this incident took place in February, when Cathcart's fiancée was in Paris, Sir Impey invited the jeweller's assistant to look round the house and tell them if she saw the foreign lady. This proved a lengthy business, but the answer was finally in the negative.

" I do not want there to be any doubt about this," said Sir Impey, " and, with the learned Attorney-General's permission, I am now going to confront this witness with Lady Mary Wimsey."

Lady Mary was accordingly placed before the witness, who replied immediately and positively : " No, this is not the lady ; I have never seen this lady in my life. There is the resemblance of height and colour and the hair bobbed, but there is nothing else at all—not the least in the world. It is not the same type at all. Mademoiselle is a charming English lady, and the man who marries her will be very happy, but the other was *belle à se suicider*—a woman to kill, suicide one's self, or send all to the devil for, and believe me, gentlemen " (with a wide smile to her distinguished audience), " we have the opportunity to see them in my business."

There was a profound sensation as this witness took her departure, and Sir Impey scribbled a note and passed it down to Mr. Murbles. It contained the one word, " Magnificent ! " Mr. Murbles scribbled back : " Never said a word to her. Can you beat it ? " and leaned back in his seat smirking like a very neat little grotesque from a Gothic corbel.

The witness who followed was Professor Hébert, a distinguished exponent of international law, who described Cathcart's promising career as a rising young diplomat in Paris before the war. He was followed by a number of officers who testified to the excellent war record of the deceased. Then came a witness who gave the aristocratic name of du Bois-Gobey Houdin, who perfectly recollected a very uncomfortable dispute on a certain occasion when playing cards with le Capitaine Cathcart, and having subsequently mentioned the matter to Monsieur Thomas Freeborn, the distinguished English engineer. It was Parker's diligence that had unearthed this witness, and he looked across with an undisguised grin at the discomfited Sir Wigmore Wrinching. When Mr. Glibbery had dealt with all these the afternoon was well advanced, and the Lord High Steward accordingly asked the lords if it was their pleasure that the House be adjourned till the next day at 10.30 of the clock in the forenoon, and the lords replying " Aye " in a most exemplary chorus, the House was accordingly adjourned.

250

A scurry of swift black clouds with ragged edges was driving bleakly westward as they streamed out into Parliament Square, and the seagulls screeched and wheeled inwards from the river. Charles Parker wrapped his ancient Burberry closely about him as he scrambled on to a 'bus to get home to Great Ormond Street. It was only one more drop in his cup of discomfort that the conductor greeted him with " Outside only ! " and rang the bell before he could get off again. He climbed to the top and sat there holding his hat on. Mr. Bunter returned sadly to 110 Piccadilly, and wandered restlessly about the flat till seven o'clock, when he came into the sitting-room and switched on the loud speaker.

" London calling," said the unseen voice impartially. " 2LO calling. Here is the weather forecast. A deep depression is crossing the Atlantic, and a secondary is stationary over the British Isles. Storms, with heavy rain and sleet, will be prevalent, rising to a gale in the south and south-west. . . ."

" You never know," said Bunter. " I suppose I'd better light a fire in his bedroom."

" Further outlook similar."

CHAPTER XVI

THE SECOND STRING

O, whan he came to broken briggs
He bent his bow and swam,
And whan he came to the green grass growin'
He slacked his shoone and ran.

O, whan he came to Lord William's gates
He baed na to chap na ca',
But set his bent bow till his breast,
An' lightly lap the wa'.

—Ballad of Lady Maisry.

L O R D PETER peered out through the cold scurry of cloud. The thin struts of steel, incredibly fragile, swung slowly across the gleam and glint far below, where the wide country dizzied out and spread like a revolving map. In front the sleek leather back of his companion humped stubbornly, sheeted with rain. He hoped that Grant was feeling confident. The roar of the engine drowned the occasional shout he threw to his passenger as they lurched from gust to gust.

He withdrew his mind from present discomforts and went over that last, strange, hurried scene. Fragments of conversation spun through his head.

" Mademoiselle, I have scoured two continents in search of you."

" *Voyons*, then, it is urgent. But be quick for the big bear may come in and be grumpy, and I do not like *des histoires*."

There had been a lamp on a low table; he remembered the gleam through the haze of short gold hair. She was a tall girl, but slender, looking up at him from the huge black-and-gold cushions.

"Mademoiselle, it is incredible to me that you should ever—dine or dance—with a person called Van Humperdinck."

Now what had possessed him to say that—when there was so little time, and Jerry's affairs were of such importance?

"Monsieur van Humperdinck does not dance. Did you seek me through two continents to say that?"

"No, I am serious."

"*Eh bien*, sit down."

She had been quite frank about it.

"Yes, poor soul. But life was very expensive since the war. I refused several good things. But always *des histoires*. And so little money. You see, one must be sensible. There is one's old age. It is necessary to be provident, *hein*?"

"Assuredly." She had a little accent—very familiar. At first he could not place it. Then it came to him—Vienna before the war, that capital of incredible follies.

"Yes, yes, I wrote. I was very kind, very sensible. I said, '*Je ne suis pas femme à supporter de gros ennuis.' Cela se comprend, n'est-ce pas?*"

That was readily understood. The 'plane dived sickly into a sudden pocket, the propeller whirring helplessly in the void, then steadied and began to nose up the opposite spiral.

"I saw it in the papers—yes. Poor boy! Why should anybody have shot him?"

"Mademoiselle, it is for that I have come to you. My brother, whom I dearly love, is accused of the murder. He may be hanged."

"Brr!"

"For a murder he did not commit."

"*Mon pauvre enfant——*"

" Mademoiselle, I implore you to be serious. My brother is accused, and will be standing his trial——"

Once her attention had been caught she had been all sympathy. Her blue eyes had a curious and attractive trick—a full lower lid that shut them into glimmering slits.

" Mademoiselle, I implore you, try to remember what was in his letter."

' But, *mon pauvre ami*, how can I ? I did not read it. It was very long, very tedious, full of *histoires*. The thing was finished—I never bother about what cannot be helped, do you ? "

But his real agony at this failure had touched her.

" Listen, then ; all is perhaps not lost. It is possible the letter is still somewhere about. Or we will ask Adèle. She is my maid. She collects letters to blackmail people—oh, yes, I know ! But she is *habile comme tout pour la toilette*. Wait—we will look first."

Tossing out letters, trinkets, endless perfumed rubbish from the little gimcrack secretaire, from drawers full of lingerie (" I am so untidy—I am Adèle's despair") from bags—hundreds of bags—and at last Adèle, thin-lipped and wary-eyed, denying everything till her mistress suddenly slapped her face in a fury, and called her ugly little names in French and German.

" It is useless, then," said Lord Peter. " What a pity that Mademoiselle Adèle cannot find a thing so valuable to me."

The word " valuable " suggested an idea to Adèle. There was Mademoiselle's jewel-case which had not been searched. She would fetch it.

" *C'est cela que cherche monsieur ?* "

After that the sudden arrival of Mr. Cornelius van Humperdinck, very rich and stout and suspicious, and the rewarding of Adèle in a tactful, unobtrusive fashion by the elevator shaft.

Grant shouted, but the words flipped feebly away

into the blackness and were lost. "What ? " bawled
Wimsey in his ear. He shouted again, and this time the
word " juice " shot into sound and fluttered away.
But whether the news was good or bad Lord Peter
could not tell.

. . . . .

Mr. Murbles was aroused a little after midnight by
a thunderous knocking upon his door. Thrusting his
head out of the window in some alarm, he saw the porter
with his lantern steaming through the rain, and behind
him a shapeless figure which for the moment Mr.
Murbles could not make out.

" What's the matter ? " said the solicitor.

" Young lady askin' urgently for you, sir."

The shapeless figure looked up, and he caught the
spangle of gold hair in the lantern-light under the little
tight hat.

" Mr. Murbles, please come. Bunter rang me up.
There's a woman come to give evidence. Bunter doesn't
like to leave her—she's frightened—but he says it's
frightfully important, and Bunter's always right, you
know."

" Did he mention the name ? "

" A Mrs. Grimethorpe."

" God bless me! Just a moment, my dear young lady,
and I will let you in."

And, indeed, more quickly than might have been
expected, Mr. Murbles made his appearance in a Jaeger
dressing-gown at the front door.

" Come in, my dear. I will get dressed in a very few
minutes. It was quite right of you to come to me. I'm
very, very glad you did. What a terrible night ! Perkins,
would you kindly wake up Mr. Murphy and ask him
to oblige me with the use of his telephone ? "

Mr. Murphy—a noisy Irish barrister with a hearty
manner—needed no waking. He was entertaining a
party of friends, and was delighted to be of service.

" Is that you Biggs ? Murbles speaking. That alibi——"

" Yes ? "

" Has come along of its own accord."

" My God ! You don't say so ! "

" Can you come round to 110 Piccadilly ? "

" Straight away."

It was a strange little party gathered round Lord Peter's fire—the white-faced woman, who started at every sound ; the men of law, with their keen, disciplined faces ; Lady Mary ; Bunter, the efficient. Mrs. Grimethorpe's story was simple enough. She had suffered the torments of knowledge ever since Lord Peter had spoken to her. She had seized an hour when her husband was drunk in the " Lord in Glory," and had harnessed the horse and driven in to Stapley.

" I couldn't keep silence. It's better my man should kill me, for I'm unhappy enough, and maybe I couldn't be any worse off in the Lord's hand—rather than they should hang him for a thing he never done. He was kind, and I was desperate miserable, that's the truth, and I'm hoping his lady won't be hard on him when she knows it all."

" No, no," said Mr. Murbles, clearing his throat. " Excuse me a moment, madam. Sir Impey——"

The lawyers whispered together in the window-seat.

" You see," said Sir Impey, " she has burnt her boats pretty well now by coming at all. The great question for us is, Is it worth the risk ? After all, we don't know what Wimsey's evidence amounts to."

" No, that is why I feel inclined—in spite of the risk—to put this evidence in," said Mr. Murbles.

" I am ready to take the risk," interposed Mrs. Grimethorpe starkly.

" We quite appreciate that," replied Sir Impey. " It is the risk to our client we have to consider first of all."

" Risk ? " cried Mary. " But surely this clears him ! "

" Will you swear absolutely to the time when his grace of Denver arrived at Grider's Hole, Mrs. Grimethorpe ? " went on the lawyer, as though he had not heard her.

" It was a quarter past twelve by the kitchen clock— 'tis a very good clock."

" And he left you at——"

" About five minutes past two."

" And how long would it take a man, walking quickly, to get back to Riddlesdale Lodge ? "

" Oh, wellnigh an hour. It's rough walking, and a steep bank up and down to the beck."

" You mustn't let the other counsel upset you on those points, Mrs. Grimethorpe, because they will try to prove that he had time to kill Cathcart either before he started or after he returned, and by admitting that the Duke had something in his life that he wanted kept secret we shall be supplying the very thing the prosecution lack—*a motive for murdering anyone who might have found him out.*"

There was a stricken silence.

" If I may ask, madam," said Sir Impey, " has any person any suspicion ? "

" My husband guessed," she answered hoarsely. " I am sure of it. He has always known. But he couldn't prove it. That very night——"

" What night ? "

" The night of the murder—he laid a trap for me. He came back from Stapley in the night, hoping to catch us and do murder. But he drank too much before he started, and spent the night in the ditch, or it might be Gerald's death you'd be inquiring into, and mine, as well as the other."

It gave Mary an odd shock to hear her brother's name spoken like that, by that speaker and in that company. She asked suddenly, apropos of nothing, " Isn't Mr. Parker here ? "

" No, my dear," said Mr. Murbles reprovingly,
" this is not a police matter."

" The best thing we can do, I think," said Sir Impey,
" is to put in the evidence, and, if necessary, arrange
for some kind of protection for this lady. In the meantime——"

" She is coming round with me to mother," said Lady
Mary determinedly.

" My dear lady," expostulated Mr. Murbles, " that
would be very unsuitable in the circumstances. I think
you hardly grasp——"

" Mother said so," retorted her ladyship. "Bunter,
call a taxi."

Mr. Murbles waved his hands helplessly, but Sir
Impey was rather amused. " It's no good, Murbles,"
he said. " Time and trouble will tame an advanced
young woman, but an advanced old woman is uncontrollable by any earthly force."

So it was from the Dowager's town house that Lady
Mary rang up Mr. Charles Parker to tell him the news.

CHAPTER XVII

THE ELOQUENT DEAD

Je connaissais Manon : pourquoi m'affliger tant d'un malheur que j'avais dû prévoir.—Manon Lescaut.

T H E gale had blown itself out into a wonderful fresh day, with clear spaces of sky, and a high wind rolling boulders of cumulus down the blue slopes of air.

The prisoner had been wrangling for an hour with his advisers when finally they came into court, and even Sir Impey's classical face showed flushed between the wings of his wig.

" I'm not going to say anything," said the Duke obstinately. " Rotten thing to do. I suppose I can't prevent you callin' her if she insists on comin'—damn' good of her—makes me feel no end of a beast."

" Better leave it at that," said Mr. Murbles. " Makes a good impression, you know. Let him go into the box and behave like a perfect gentleman. They'll like it."

Sir Impey, who had sat through the small hours altering his speech, nodded.

The first witness that day came as something of a surprise. She gave her name and address as Eliza Briggs, known as Madame Brigette of New Bond Street, and her occupation as beauty specialist and perfumer. She had a large and aristocratic clientele of both sexes, and a branch in Paris.

Deceased had been a client of hers in both cities for several years. He had massage and manicure. After the war he had come to her about some slight scars caused by grazing with shrapnel. He was extremely

259

particular about his personal appearance, and, if you called that vanity in a man, you might certainly say he was vain. Thank you. Sir Wigmore Wrinching made no attempt to cross-examine the witness, and the noble lords wondered to one another what it was all about.

At this point Sir Impey Biggs leaned forward, and, tapping his brief impressively with his forefinger, began:

" My lords, so strong is our case that we had not thought it necessary to present an alibi——" when an officer of the court rushed up from a little whirlpool of commotion by the door and excitedly thrust a note into his hand. Sir Impey read, coloured, glanced down the hall, put down his brief, folded his hands over it, and said in a sudden, loud voice which penetrated even to the deaf ear of the Duke of Wiltshire :

" My lords, I am happy to say that our missing witness is here. I call Lord Peter Wimsey."

Every neck was at once craned, and every eye focused on the very grubby and oily figure that came amiably trotting up the long room. Sir Impey Biggs passed the note down to Mr. Murbles, and, turning to the witness, who was yawning frightfully in the intervals of grinning at all his acquaintances, demanded that he should be sworn.

The witness's story was as follows :

" I am Lord Peter Wimsey, brother of the accused. I live at 110 Piccadilly. In consequence of what I read on that bit of blotting-paper which I now identify, I went to Paris to look for a certain lady. The name óf the lady is Mademoiselle Simone Vonderaa. I found she had left Paris in company with a man named Van Humperdinck. I followed her, and at length came up with her in New York. I asked her to give me the letter Cathcart wrote on the night of his death. (Sensation). I produce that letter, with Mademoiselle Vonderaa's signature on the corner, so that it can be identified if Wiggy there tries to put it over you. (Joyous sensation, in which the indignant protests of prosecuting counsel were drowned.) And I'm sorry I've given you such short notice of this, old man, but I only got it the day before yesterday. We came as quick as we could, but we had to come down near Whitehaven with engine trouble, and if we had come down half a mile sooner I shouldn't be here now." (Applause, hurriedly checked by the Lord High Steward.)

" My lords," said Sir Impey, " your lordships are witnesses that I have never seen this letter in my life before. I have no idea of its contents ; yet so positive am I that it cannot but assist my noble client's case, that I am willing—nay, eager—to put in this document immediately, as it stands, without perusal, to stand or fall by the contents."

" The handwriting must be identified as that of the deceased," interposed the Lord High Steward.

The ravening pencils of the reporters tore along the paper. The lean young man who worked for the *Daily Trumpet* scented a scandal in high life and licked his lips, never knowing what a much bigger one had escaped him by a bare minute or so.

Miss Lydia Cathcart was recalled to identify the handwriting, and the letter was handed to the Lord High Steward, who announced :

" The letter is in French. We shall have to swear an interpreter."

" You will find," said the witness suddenly, " that those bits of words on the blotting-paper come out of the letter. You'll 'scuse my mentioning it."

" Is this person put forward as an expert witness ?" inquired Sir Wigmore witheringly.

" Right ho ! " said Lord Peter. " Only, you see, it has been rather sprung on Biggy as you might say.

" Biggy and Wiggy
Were two pretty men,
They went into court
When the clock——"

" Sir Impey, I must really ask you to keep your witness in order."

Lord Peter grinned, and a pause ensued while an interpreter was fetched and sworn. Then, at last, the letter was read, amid a breathless silence :

> " Riddlesdale Lodge,
> " Stapley,
> " N.E. Yorks.
> " *le* 13 *Octobre*, 192—

" SIMONE,—Je viens de recevoir ta lettre. Que dire ? Inutiles, les prières ou les reproches. Tu ne comprendras—tu ne liras même pas.

" N'ai-je pas toujours su, d'ailleurs, que tu devais infailliblement me trahir ? Depuis huit ans déjà je souffre tous les torments que puisse infliger la jalousie. Je comprends bien que tu n'as jamais voulu me faire de la peine. C'est tout justement cette insouciance, cette légèreté, cette façon séduisante d'être malhonnête, que j'adorais en toi. J'ai tout su, et je t'ai aimée.

" Ma foi, non, ma chère, jamais je n'ai eu la moindre illusion. Te rappelles-tu cette première rencontre, un soir au Casino ? Tu avais dix-sept ans, et tu étais jolie à ravir. Le lendemain tu fus à moi. Tu m'as dit, si gentiment, que tu m'aimais bien, et que j'étais, moi, le premier. Ma pauvre enfant, tu en as menti. Tu riais, toute seule, de ma naiveté—il y avait bien de quoi rire ! Dès notre premier baiser, j'ai prévu ce moment.

" Mais écoute, Simone. J'ai la faiblesse de vouloir te montrer exactement ce que tu as fait de moi. Tu regretteras peut-être en peu. Mais, non—si tu pouvais regretter quoi que ce fût, tu ne serais plus Simone.

" Il y a huit ans, la veille de la guerre, j'étais riche— moins riche que ton Américain, mais assez riche pour te donner l'éstablissement qu'il te fallait. Tu étais

moins exigeante avant la guerre, Simone—qui est-ce
qui, pendant mon absence, t'a enseigné le goût du
luxe ? Charmante discrétion de ma part de ne jamais
te le demander ! Eh bien, une grande partie de ma
fortune se trouvant placée en Russie et en Allemagne,
j'en ai perdu plus des trois-quarts. Ce que m'en
restait en France a beaucoup diminué en valeur. Il
est vrai que j'avais mon traitement de capitaine dans
l'armée britannique, mais c'est peu de chose, tu
sais. Avant même la fin de la guerre, tu m'avais
mangé toutes mes économies. C'était idiot, quoi ? Un
jeune homme qui a perdu les trois-quarts de ses rentes
ne se permet plus une maîtresse et un appartement
Avenue Kléber. Ou il congédie madame, ou bien il
lui demande quelques sacrifices. Je n'ai rien osé
demander. Si j'étais venu un jour te dire, ' Simone,
je suis pauvre '—que m'aurais-tu répondu ?

" Sais-tu ce que j'ai fait ? Non—tu n'as jamais
pensé à demander d'où venait cet argent. Qu'est-ce
que cela pouvait te faire que j'ai tout jeté—fortune,
honneur, bonheur—pour te posséder ? J'ai joué,
désespérément, éperdument—j'ai fait pis : j'ai triché
au jeu. Je te vois hausser les épaules—tu ris—tu
dis, ' Tiens, c'est malin, ça ! ' Oui, mais cela ne
se fait pas. On m'aurait chassé du régiment. Je
devenais le dernier des hommes.

" D'ailleurs, cela ne pouvait durer. Déjà un soir à
Paris on m'a fait une scène désagréable, bien qu'on
n'ait rien pu prouver. C'est alors que je me suis
fiancé avec cette demoiselle dont je t'ai parlé, la
fille du duc anglais. Le beau projet, quoi ! Entre-
tenir ma maîtresse avec l'argent de ma femme ! Et
je l'aurais fait—et je le ferais encore demain, si
c'était pour te reposséder.

" Mais tu me quittes. Cet Américain est riche—
archi-riche. Depuis longtemps tu me répètes que
ton appartement est trop petit et que tu t'ennuies
à mourir. Cet ' ami bienveillant ' t'offre les autos,

les diamants, les mille-et-une nuits, la lune ! Auprès de ces merveilles, évidemment, que valent l'amour et l'honneur ?

" Enfin, le bon duc est d'une stupidité très commode. Il laisse traîner son révolver dans le tiroir de son bureau. D'ailleurs, il vient de me demander une explication à propos de cette histoire de cartes. Tu vois qu'en tout cas la partie était finie. Pourquoi t'en vouloir ? On mettra sans doute mon suicide au compte de cet exposé. Tant mieux, je ne veux pas qu'on affiche mon histoire amoureuse dans les journaux.

" Adieu, ma bien-aimée—mon adorée, mon adorée, ma Simone. Sois heureuse avec ton nouvel amant. Ne pense plus à moi. Qu'est-ce tout cela peut bien te faire ? Mon Dieu, comme je t'ai aimée—comme je t'aime toujours, malgré moi. Mais c'en est fini. Jamais plus tu ne me perceras le cœur. Oh ! J'enrage —je suis fou de douleur ! Adieu.

" DENIS CATHCART."

TRANSLATION

" SIMONE,—I have just got your letter. What am I to say ? It is useless to entreat or reproach you. You would not understand, or even read the letter.

" Besides, I always knew you must betray me some day. I have suffered a hell of jealousy for the last eight years. I know perfectly well you never meant to hurt me. It was just your utter lightness and carelessness and your attractive way of being dishonest which was so adorable. I knew everything, and loved you all the same.

" Oh, no, my dear, I never had any illusions. You remember our first meeting that night at the Casino. You were seventeen, and heart-breakingly lovely. You came to me the very next day. You told me, very prettily, that you loved me and that I was the first. My poor little girl, that wasn't true. I expect, when you were alone, you laughed to think I was so easily taken in. But there was nothing to laugh at. From our very first kiss I foresaw this moment.

" I'm afraid I'm weak enough, though, to want to tell you just what you have done for me. You may be sorry. But no—if you could regret anything, you wouldn't be Simone any longer.

" Eight years ago, before the war, I was rich—not so rich as your new American, but rich enough to give you what you wanted. You didn't want quite so much before the war, Simone. Who taught you to be so extravagant while I was away ? I think it was very nice of me never to ask you. Well, most of my money was in Russian and German securities, and more than three-quarters of it went west. The remainder in France went down considerably in value. I had my captain's pay, of course, but that didn't amount to much. Even before the end of the war you had managed to get through all my savings. Of course, I was a fool. A young man whose income has been reduced by three-quarters can't afford an expensive mistress and a flat in the Avenue Kléber. He ought either to dismiss the lady or to demand a little self-sacrifice. But I didn't dare demand anything. Suppose I had come to you one day and said, ' Simone, I've lost my money '— what would you have said to me ?

" What do you think I did ? I don't suppose you ever thought about it at all. You didn't care if I was chucking away my money and my honour and my happiness to keep you. I gambled desperately. I did worse, I cheated at cards. I can see you shrug your shoulders and say, ' Good for you ! ' But it's a rotten thing to do—a rotter's game. If anybody had found out they'd have cashiered me.

" Besides, it couldn't go on for ever. There was one row in Paris, though they couldn't prove anything. So then I got engaged to the English girl I told you about—the duke's daughter. Pretty, wasn't it ? I actually brought myself to consider keeping my mistress on my wife's money ! But I'd have done it, and I'd do it again, to get you back.

" And now you've chucked me. This American is colossally rich. For a long time you've been dinning into my ears that the flat is too small and that you're bored to death. Your ' good friend ' can offer you cars, diamonds—Aladdin's palace—the moon ! I admit that love and honour look pretty small by comparison.

" Ah, well, the Duke is most obligingly stupid. He leaves his revolver about in his desk drawer. Besides, he's just been in to ask what about this card-sharping story. So you see the game's up, any-how. I don't blame you. I suppose they'll put my suicide down to fear of exposure. All the better. I don't want my love-affairs in the Sunday Press.

" Good-bye, my dear—oh, Simone, my darling, my darling, good-bye. Be happy with your new lover. Never mind me—what does it all matter ? My God—how I loved you, and how I still love you in spite of myself. It's all done with. You'll never break my heart again. I'm mad—mad with misery ! Good-bye."

CHAPTER XVIII

THE SPEECH FOR THE DEFENCE

" Nobody ; I myself ; farewell "—Othello.

A F T E R the reading of Cathcart's letter even the appearance of the prisoner in the witness-box came as an anti-climax. In the face of the Attorney-General's cross-examination he maintained stoutly that he had wandered on the moor for several hours without meeting anybody, though he was forced to admit that he had gone downstairs at 11.30, and not at 2.30, as he had stated at the inquest. Sir Wigmore Wrinching made a great point of this, and, in a spirited endeavour to suggest that Cathcart was blackmailing Denver, pressed his questions so hard that Sir Impey Biggs, Mr. Murbles, Lady Mary, and Bunter had a nervous feeling that learned counsel's eyes were boring through the walls to the side-room where, apart from the other witnesses, Mrs. Grimethorpe sat waiting. After lunch Sir Impey Biggs rose to make his plea for the defence.

" My lords,—Your lordships have now heard—and I, who have watched and pleaded here for these three anxious days, know with what eager interest and with what ready sympathy you have heard—the evidence brought by my noble client to defend him against this dreadful charge of murder. You have listened while as it were from his narrow grave, the dead man has lifted his voice to tell you the story of that fatal night of the thirteenth of October, and I feel sure you can have no doubt in your hearts that that story is the true one. As your lordships know, I was myself totally ignorant of the contents of that letter until I heard it read in Court just now, and, by the profound impression it made upon my own mind, I can judge how tremendously and how painfully it must have affected your lordships. In my long experience at the criminal bar, I think I have never met with a history more melancholy than that of the unhappy young man whom a fatal passion—for here indeed we may use that well-worn expression in all the fulness of its significance—whom a truly fatal passion thus urged into deep after deep of degradation, and finally to a violent death by his own hand.

" The noble peer at the Bar has been indicted before your lordships of the murder of this young man. That he is wholly innocent of the charge must, in the light of what we have heard, be so plain to your lordships that any words from me might seem altogether superfluous. In the majority of cases of this kind the evidence is confused, contradictory ; here, however, the course of events is so clear, so coherent, that had we ourselves been present to see the drama unrolled before us, as before the all-seeing eye of God, we could hardly have a more vivid or a more accurate vision of that night's adventures. Indeed, had the death of Denis Cathcart been the sole event of the night, I will venture to say that the truth could never have been one single moment in doubt. Since, however, by a series of unheard-of coincidences, the threads of Denis Cathcart's story became entangled with so many others, I will venture to tell it once again from the beginning, lest, in the confusion of so great a cloud of witnesses, any point should still remain obscure.

" Let me, then, go back to the beginning. You have heard how Denis Cathcart was born of mixed parentage —from the union of a young and lovely southern girl with an Englishman twenty years older than herself : imperious, passionate, and cynical. Till the age of 18 he lives on the Continent with his parents, travelling from place to place, seeing more of the world even than the average young Frenchman of his age, learning the code of love in a country where the *crime passionel* is understood and forgiven as it never can be over here.

" At the age of 18 a terrible loss befalls him. In a very short space of time he loses both his parents— his beautiful and adored mother and his father, who might, had he lived, have understood how to guide the impetuous nature which he had brought into the world. But the father dies, expressing two last wishes, both of which, natural as they were, turned out in the circumstances to be disastrously ill-advised. He left his son to the care of his sister, whom he had not seen for many years, with the direction that the boy should be sent to his own old University.

" My lords, you have seen Miss Lydia Cathcart, and heard her evidence. You will have realised how uprightly, how conscientiously, with what Christian disregard of self, she performed the duty entrusted to her, and yet how inevitably she failed to establish any real sympathy between herself and her young ward. He, poor lad, missing his parents at every turn, was plunged at Cambridge into the society of young men of totally different upbringing from himself. To a young man of his cosmopolitan experience the youth of Cambridge, with its sports and rags and naïve excursions into philosophy o' nights, must have seemed unbelievably childish. You all, from your own recollections of your Alma Mater, can reconstruct Denis Cathcart's life at Cambridge, its outward gaiety, its inner emptiness.

" Ambitious of embracing a diplomatic career, Cathcart made extensive acquaintances among the sons of rich and influential men. From a worldly point of view he was doing well, and his inheritance of a handsome fortune at the age of twenty-one seemed to open up the path to very great success. Shaking the academic dust of Cambridge from his feet as soon as his Tripos was passed, he went over to France, established himself in Paris, and began, in a quiet, determined kind of way, to carve out a little niche for himself in the world of international politics.

" But now comes into his life that terrible influence which was to rob him of fortune, honour, and life itself. He falls in love with a young woman of that exquisite, irresistible charm and beauty for which the Austrian capital is world-famous. He is enthralled body and soul, as utterly as any Chevalier des Grieux, by Simone Vonderaa.

" Mark that in this matter he follows the strict, continental code : complete devotion, complete discretion. You have heard how quietly he lived, how *rangé* he appeared to be. We have had in evidence his discreet banking-account, with its generous cheques drawn to self, and cashed in notes of moderate denominations, and with its regular accumulation of sufficient ' economies ' quarter by quarter. Life has expanded for Denis Cathcart. Rich, ambitious, possessed of a beautiful and complaisant mistress, the world is open before him.

" Then, my lords, across this promising career there falls the thunderbolt of the Great War—ruthlessly smashing through his safeguards, overthrowing the edifice of his ambition, destroying and devastating here, as everywhere, all that made life beautiful and desirable.

" You have heard the story of Denis Cathcart's distinguished army career. On that I need not dwell. Like thousands of other young men, he went gallantly through those five years of strain and disillusionment, to find himself left, in the end, with his life and health indeed, and, so far, happy beyond many of his comrades, but with his life in ruins about him.

" Of his great fortune—all of which had been invested in Russian and German securities—literally nothing is left to him. What, you say, did that matter to a young man so well equipped, with such excellent connections, with so many favourable openings, ready

269

to his hand ? He needed only to wait quietly for a few years, to reconstruct much of what he had lost. Alas ! my lords, he could not afford to wait. He stood in peril of losing something dearer to him than fortune or ambition ; he needed money in quantity, and at once.

" My lords, in that pathetic letter which we have heard read nothing is more touching and terrible than that confession : ' I knew you could not but be unfaithful to me.' All through that time of seeming happiness he knew—none better—that his house was built on sand. ' I was never deceived by you,' he says. From their earliest acquaintance she had lied to him, and he knew it, and that knowledge was yet powerless to loosen the bands of his fatal fascination. If any of you, my lords, have known the power of love exercised in this irresistible—I may say, this predestined manner—let your experience interpret the situation to you better than any poor words of mine can do. One great French poet and one great English poet have summed the matter up in a few words. Racine says of such a fascination :

C'est Vénus tout entière à sa proie attachée.

And Shakespeare has put the lover's despairing obstinacy into two piteous lines :

If my love swears that she is made of truth
I will believe her, though I know she lies.

My lords, Denis Cathcart is dead ; it is not our place to condemn him, but only to understand and pity him.

" My lords, I need not put before you in detail the shocking shifts to which this soldier and gentleman unhappily condescended. You have heard the story in all its cold, ugly details upon the lips of Monsieur du Bois-Gobey Houdin, and, accompanied by unavailing expressions of shame and remorse, in the last words of the deceased. You know how he gambled, at first honestly—then dishonestly. You know from whence he derived those large sums of money which came at irregular intervals, mysteriously and in cash, to bolster up a bank-account always perilously on the verge of depletion. We need not, my lords, judge too harshly of the woman. According to her own lights, she did not treat him unfairly. She had her interests to consider. While he could pay for her she could give him beauty and passion and good humour and a moderate faithfulness. When he could pay no longer she would find it only reasonable to take another position. This Cathcart understood. Money he must have, by hook or by crook. And so, by an inevitable descent, he found himself reduced to the final deep of dishonour.

" It is at this point, my lords, that Denis Cathcart and his miserable fortunes come into the life of my noble client and of his sister. From this point begin all those complications which led to the tragedy of October 14th, and which we are met in this solemn and historic assembly to unravel.

" About eighteen months ago Cathcart, desperately searching for a secure source of income, met the Duke of Denver, whose father had been a friend of Cathcart's father many years before. The acquaintance prospered, and Cathcart was introduced to Lady Mary Wimsey, at that time (as she has very frankly told us) ' at a loose end,' ' fed up,' and distressed by the dismissal of her fiancé, Mr. Goyles. Lady Mary felt the need of an establishment of her own, and accepted Denis Cathcart, with the proviso that she should be considered a free agent, living her own life in her own way, with the minimum of interference. As to Cathcart's object in all this, we have his own bitter comment, on which no words of mine could improve : ' I actually brought myself to consider keeping my mistress on my wife's money.'

" So matters go on until October of this year. Cathcart is now obliged to pass a good deal of his time in England with his fiancée, leaving Simone Vonderaa un-

271

guarded in the Avenue Kléber. He seems to have felt
fairly secure so far ; the only drawback was that Lady
Mary, with a natural reluctance to commit herself to
the hands of a man she could not really love, had so far
avoided fixing a definite date for the wedding. Money
is shorter than it used to be in the Avenue Kléber, and
the cost of robes and millinery, amusements and so
forth, has not diminished. And, meanwhile, Mr.
Cornelius van Humperdinck, the American millionaire,
has seen Simone in the Bois, at the races, at the opera, in
Denis Cathcart's flat.

"But Lady Mary is becoming more and more uneasy
about her engagement. And at this critical moment,
Mr. Goyles suddenly sees the prospect of a position,
modest but assured, which will enable him to maintain
a wife. Lady Mary makes her choice. She consents to
elope with Mr. Goyles, and by an extraordinary fatality
the day and hour selected are 3 a.m. on the morning
of October 14th.

"At about 9.30 on the night of Wednesday, October
13th, the party at Riddlesdale Lodge are just separating
to go to bed. The Duke of Denver was in the gun-
room, the other men were in the billiard-room, the
ladies had already retired, when the manservant, Fleming, came up from the village with the evening post. To
the Duke of Denver he brought a letter with news of a
startling and very unpleasant kind. To Denis Cathcart
he brought another letter—one which we shall never see,
but whose contents it is easy enough to guess.

"You have heard the evidence of Mr. Arbuthnot
that, before reading this letter, Cathcart had gone upstairs gay and hopeful, mentioning that he hoped soon
to get a date fixed for the marriage. At a little after ten,
when the Duke of Denver went up to see him, there was
a great change. Before his grace could broach the
matter in hand Cathcart spoke rudely and harshly, appearing to be all on edge, and entreating to be left alone.
Is it very difficult, my lords, in the face of what we have

heard to-day—in the face of our knowledge that Mademoiselle Vonderaa crossed to New York on the *Berengaria*
on October 15th—to guess what news had reached Denis
Cathcart in that interval to change his whole outlook
upon life ?

" At this unhappy moment, when Cathcart is brought
face to face with the stupefying knowledge that his
mistress has left him, comes the Duke of Denver with
a frightful accusation. He taxes Cathcart with the vile
truth—that this man, who has eaten his bread and
sheltered under his roof, and who is about to marry his
sister, is nothing more nor less than a card-sharper.
And when Cathcart refuses to deny the charge—when
he, most insolently, as it seems, declares that he is no
longer willing to wed the noble lady to whom he is
affianced—is it surprising that the Duke should turn
upon the impostor and forbid him ever to touch or
speak to Lady Mary Wimsey again ? I say, my lords,
that no man with a spark of honourable feeling would
have done otherwise. My client contents himself with
directing Cathcart to leave the house next day ; and
when Cathcart rushes madly out into the storm he calls
after him to return, and even takes the trouble to direct
the footman to leave open the conservatory door for
Cathcart's convenience. It is true that he called Cathcart a dirty scoundrel, and told him he should have been
kicked out of his regiment, but he was justified ; while
the words he shouted from the window—' Come back,
you fool,' or even, according to one witness, ' you b——
fool '—have almost an affectionate ring in them.
(Laughter.)

" And now I will direct your lordships' attention to
the extreme weakness of the case against my noble client
from the point of view of motive. It has been suggested that the cause of the quarrel between them was
not that mentioned by the Duke of Denver in his evidence, but something even more closely personal to
themselves. Of this contention not a jot or tittle, not

the slightest shadow of evidence, has been put forward except, indeed, that of the extraordinary witness, Robinson, who appears to bear a grudge against his whole acquaintance, and to have magnified some trifling allusion into a matter of vast importance. Your lordships have seen this person's demeanour in the box, and will judge for yourselves how much weight is to be attached to his observations. While we on our side have been able to show that the alleged cause of complaint was perfectly well founded in fact.

" So Cathcart rushes out into the garden. In the pelting rain he paces heedlessly about, envisaging a future stricken at once suddenly barren of love, wealth, and honour.

" And, meanwhile, a passage door opens, and a stealthy foot creeps down the stair. We know now whose it is—Mrs. Pettigrew-Robinson has not mistaken the creak of the door. It is the Duke of Denver.

" That is admitted. But from this point we join issue with my learned friend for the prosecution. It is suggested that the Duke, on thinking matters over, determines that Cathcart is a danger to society and better dead—or that his insult to the Denver family can only be washed out in blood. And we are invited to believe that the Duke creeps downstairs, fetches his revolver from the study table, and prowls out into the night to find Cathcart and make away with him in cold blood.

" My lords, is it necessary for me to point out the inherent absurdity of this suggestion ? What conceivable reason could the Duke of Denver have for killing, in this cold-blooded manner, a man of whom a single word has rid him already and for ever ? It has been suggested to you that the injury had grown greater in the Duke's mind by brooding—had assumed gigantic proportions. Of that suggestion, my lords, I can only say that a more flimsy pretext for fixing an impulse to murder upon the shoulders of an innocent man was never devised, even by the ingenuity of an advocate. I will not waste my time or insult you by arguing about it. Again it has been suggested that the cause of quarrel was not what it appeared, and the Duke had reason to fear some disastrous action on Cathcart's part. Of this contention I think we have already disposed ; it is an assumption constructed *in vacuo*, to meet a set of circumstances which my learned friend is at a loss to explain in conformity with the known facts. The very number and variety of motives suggested by the prosecution is proof that they are aware of the weakness of their own case. Frantically they cast about for any sort of explanation to give colour to this unreasonable indictment.

" And here I will direct your lordships' attention to the very important evidence of Inspector Parker in the matter of the study window. He has told you that it was forced from outside by the latch being slipped back with a knife. If it was the Duke of Denver, who was in the study at 11.30, what need had he to force the window ? He was already inside the house. When, in addition, we find that Cathcart had in his pocket a knife, and that there are scratches upon the blade such as might come from forcing back a metal catch, it surely becomes evident that not the Duke, but Cathcart himself forced the window and crept in for the pistol, not knowing that the conservatory door had been left open for him.

" But there is no need to labour this point—we *know* that Captain Cathcart was in the study at that time, for we have seen in evidence the sheet of blotting-paper on which he blotted his letter to Simone Vonderaa, and Lord Peter Wimsey has told us how he himself removed that sheet from the study blotting-pad a few days after Cathcart's death.

" And let me here draw your attention to the significance of one point in the evidence. The Duke of Denver has told us that he saw the revolver in his drawer a short time before the fatal 13th, when he and Cathcart were together."

The Lord High Steward : " One moment, Sir Impey, that is not quite as I have it in my notes."

Counsel : " I beg your lordship's pardon if I am wrong."

L.H.S. : " I will read what I have. ' I was hunting for an old photograph of Mary to give Cathcart, and that was how I came across it.' There is nothing about Cathcart being there."

Counsel : " If your lordship will read the next sentence——"

L.H.S. : " Certainly. The next sentence is : ' I remember saying at the time how rusty it was getting.' "

Counsel : " And the next ? "

L.H.S. : " ' To whom did you make that observation ? ' Answer : ' I really don't know, but I distinctly remember saying it.' "

Counsel : " I am much obliged to your lordship. When the noble peer made that remark he was looking out some photographs to give to Captain Cathcart. I think we may reasonably infer that the remark was made to the deceased."

L.H.S. (to the House) : " My lords, your lordships will, of course, use your own judgment as to the value of this suggestion."

Counsel : " If your lordships can accept that Denis Cathcart may have known of the existence of the revolver, it is immaterial at what exact moment he saw it. As you have heard, the table-drawer was always left with the key in it. He might have seen it himself at any time, when searching for an envelope or sealing-wax or what not. In any case, I contend that the movements heard by Colonel and Mrs. Marchbanks on Wednesday night were those of Denis Cathcart. While he was writing his farewell letter, perhaps with the pistol before him on the table—yes, at that very moment the Duke of Denver slipped down the stairs and out through the conservatory door. Here is the incredible part of this affair—that again and again we find two series of events, wholly unconnected between themselves, converging upon the same point of time, and causing endless confusion. I have used the word ' incredible '—not because any coincidence is incredible, for we see more remarkable examples every day of our lives than any writer of fiction would dare to invent—but merely in order to take it out of the mouth of the learned Attorney-General, who is preparing to make it return, boomerang-fashion, against me. (Laughter.)

" My lords, this is the first of these incredible—I am not afraid of the word—coincidences. At 11.30 the Duke goes downstairs and Cathcart enters the study. The learned Attorney-General, in his cross-examination of my noble client, very justifiably made what capital he could out of the discrepancy between witness's statement at the inquest—which was that he did not leave the house till 2.30—and his present statement—that he left it at half-past eleven. My lords, whatever interpretation you like to place upon the motives of the noble Duke in so doing, I must remind you once more that at the time when that first statement was made everybody supposed that the shot had been fired at three o'clock, and that the misstatement was then useless for the purpose of establishing an alibi.

" Great stress, too, has been laid on the noble Duke's inability to establish this alibi for the hours from 11.30 to 3 a.m. But, my lords, if he is telling the truth in saying that he walked all that time upon the moors without meeting anyone, what alibi could he establish ? He is not bound to supply a motive for all his minor actions during the twenty-four hours. No rebutting evidence has been brought to discredit his story. And it is perfectly reasonable that, unable to sleep after the scene with Cathcart, he should go for a walk to calm himself down.

" Meanwhile, Cathcart has finished his letter and tossed it into the post-bag. There is nothing more ironical in the whole of this case than that letter. While the body of a murdered man lay stark upon the threshold, and detectives and doctors searched everywhere for clues, the normal routine of an ordinary English household went, unquestioned, on. That letter, which contained the whole story, lay undisturbed in the post-bag, till it was taken away and put in the post as a matter of course, to be fetched back again, at enormous cost, delay, and risk of life, two months later in vindication of the great English motto : ' Business as usual.'

" Upstairs, Lady Mary Wimsey was packing her suitcase and writing a farewell letter to her people. At length Cathcart signs his name ; he takes up the revolver and hurries out into the shrubbery. Still he paces up and down, with what thoughts God alone knows—reviewing the past, no doubt, racked with vain remorse, most of all, bitter against the woman who has ruined him. He bethinks him of the little love-token, the platinum-and-diamond cat which his mistress gave him for good luck ! At any rate, he will not die with *that* pressing upon his heart. With a furious gesture he hurls it far from him. He puts the pistol to his head.

" But something arrests him. Not that ! Not that ! He sees in fancy his own hideously disfigured corpse—the shattered jaw—the burst eyeball—blood and brains horribly splashed about. No. Let the bullet go cleanly to the heart. Not even in death can he bear the thought of looking—*so !*

" He places the revolver against his breast and draws the trigger. With a little moan, he drops to the sodden ground. The weapon falls from his hand ; his fingers scrabble a little at his breast.

" The gamekeeper who heard the shot is puzzled that poachers should come so close. Why are they not on the moors ? He thinks of the hares in the plantation. He takes his lantern and searches in the thick drizzle. Nothing. Only soggy grass and dripping trees. He is human. He concludes his ears deceived him, and he returns to his warm bed. Midnight passes. One o'clock passes.

" The rain is less heavy now. Look ! In the shrubbery—what was that ? A movement. The shot man is moving—groaning a little—crawling to his feet. Chilled to the bone, weak from loss of blood, shaking with the fever of his wound, he but dimly remembers his purpose. His groping hands go to the wound in his breast. He pulls out a handkerchief and presses it upon the place. He drags himself up, slipping and stumbling. The handkerchief slides to the ground, and lies there beside the revolver among the fallen leaves.

" Something in his aching brain tells him to crawl back to the house. He is sick, in pain, hot and cold by turns, and horribly thirsty. There someone will take him in and be kind to him—give him things to drink. Swaying and starting, now falling on hands and knees, now reeling to and fro, he makes that terrible nightmare journey to the house. Now he walks, now he crawls, dragging his heavy limbs after him. At last, the conservatory door ! Here there will be help. And water for his fever in the trough by the well. He crawls up to it on hands and knees, and strains to lift himself. It is growing very difficult to breathe—a heavy weight seems to be bursting his chest. He lifts himself—a frightful hiccuping cough catches him—the blood rushes from his mouth. He drops down. It is indeed all over.

" Once more the hours pass. Three o'clock, the hour of rendezvous, draws on. Eagerly the young lover leaps the wall and comes hurrying through the shrubbery to greet his bride to be. It is cold and wet, but his happiness gives him no time to think of his surroundings. He passes through the shrubbery without a thought. He reaches the conservatory door, through which in a few moments love and happiness will come to him. And in that moment he stumbles across—the dead body of a man !

" Fear possesses him. He hears a distant footstep.

279

With but one idea—escape from this horror of horrors—he dashes into the shrubbery, just as, fatigued perhaps a little, but with a mind soothed by his little expedition, the Duke of Denver comes briskly up the path, to meet the eager bride over the body of her betrothed.

" My lords, the rest is clear. Lady Mary Wimsey, forced by a horrible appearance of things into suspecting her lover of murder, undertook—with what courage every man amongst you will realise—to conceal that George Goyles ever was upon the scene. Of this ill-considered action of hers came much mystery and perplexity. Yet, my lords, while chivalry holds its own, not one amongst us will breathe one word of blame against that gallant lady. As the old song says :

> God send each man at his end
> Such hawks, such hounds, and such a friend.

" I think, my lords, that there is nothing more for me to say. To you I leave the solemn and joyful task of freeing the noble peer, your companion, from this unjust charge. You are but human, my lords, and some among you will have grumbled, some will have mocked on assuming these mediaeval splendours of scarlet and ermine, so foreign to the taste and habit of a utilitarian age. You know well enough that

> 'Tis not the balm, the sceptre and the ball,
> The sword, the mace, the crown imperial,
> The intertissued robe of gold and pearl,
> The farcèd title, nor the tide of pomp
> That beats upon the high shores of the world

that can add any dignity to noble blood. And yet, to have beheld, day after day, the head of one of the oldest and noblest houses in England standing here, cut off from your fellowship, stripped of his historic honours, robed only in the justice of his cause—this cannot have failed to move your pity and indignation.

THE SPEECH FOR THE DEFENCE

" My lords, it is your happy privilege to restore to
his grace the Duke of Denver these traditional symbols
of his exalted rank. When the clerk of this House shall
address to you severally the solemn question : Do you
find Gerald, Duke of Denver, Viscount St. George,
guilty or not guilty of the dreadful crime of murder,
every one of you may, with a confidence unmarred by
any shadow of doubt, lay his hand upon his heart and
say, ' Not guilty, upon my honour.' "

CHAPTER XIX

WHO GOES HOME?

Drunk as a lord? As a class they are really very sober.
Judge Cluer, in court.

W H I L E the Attorney-General was engaged in the ungrateful task of trying to obscure what was not only plain,
but agreeable to everybody's feelings, Lord Peter
hauled Parker off to a Lyons over the way, and listened,
over an enormous dish of eggs and bacon, to a brief
account of Mrs. Grimethorpe's dash to town, and a long
one of Lady Mary's cross-examination.

"What are you grinning about?" snapped the
narrator.

"Just natural imbecility," said Lord Peter. "I say,
poor old Cathcart. She *was* a girl! For the matter of
that, I suppose she still is. I don't know why I should
talk as if she'd died away the moment I took my eyes
off her."

"Horribly self-centred, you are," grumbled Mr.
Parker.

"I know. I always was from a child. But what
worries me is that I seem to be gettin' so susceptible.
When Barbara turned me down——"

"You're cured," said his friend brutally. "As a
matter of fact, I've noticed it for some time."

Lord Peter sighed deeply. "I value your candour,
Charles," he said, "but I wish you hadn't such an unkind way of putting things. Besides—— I say, are
they coming out?"

282

The crowd in Parliament Square was beginning to stir and spread. Sparse streams of people began to drift across the street. A splash of scarlet appeared against the grey stone of St. Stephen's. Mr. Murbles's clerk dashed in suddenly at the door.

"All right, my lord—acquitted—unanimously—and will you please come across, my lord?"

They ran out. At sight of Lord Peter some excited bystanders raised a cheer. The great wind tore suddenly through the Square, bellying out the scarlet robes of the emerging peers. Lord Peter was bandied from one to the other, till he reached the centre of the group.

"Excuse me, your grace."

It was Bunter. Bunter, miraculously, with his arms full of scarlet and ermine, enveloping the shameful blue serge suit which had been a badge of disgrace.

"Allow me to offer my respectful congratulations, your grace."

"Bunter!" cried Lord Peter. "Great God, the man's gone mad! Damn you, man, take that thing away," he added, plunging at a tall photographer in a made-up tie.

"Too late, my lord," said the offender, jubilantly pushing in the slide.

"Peter," said the Duke. "Er—thanks, old man."

"All right," said his lordship. "Very jolly trip and all that. You're lookin' very fit. Oh, don't shake hands—there, I knew it! I heard that man's confounded shutter go."

They pushed their way through the surging mob to the cars. The two Duchesses got in, and the Duke was following, when a bullet crashed through the glass of the window, missing Denver's head by an inch, and ricocheting from the wind-screen among the crowd.

A rush and a yell. A big bearded man struggled for a moment with three constables; then came a succession of wild shots, and a fierce rush—the crowd parting, then closing in, like hounds on the fox, streaming past the Houses of Parliament, heading for Westminster Bridge.

" He's shot a woman—he's under that 'bus—no, he isn't—hi !—murder !—stop him ! " Shrill screams and yells—police whistles blowing—constables darting from every corner—swooping down in taxis—running.

The driver of a taxi spinning across the bridge saw the fierce face just ahead of his bonnet, and jammed on the brakes, as the madman's fingers closed for the last time on the trigger. Shot and tyre exploded almost simultaneously ; the taxi slewed giddily over to the right, scooping the fugitive with it, and crashed horribly into a tram standing vacant on the Embankment dead-end.

" I couldn't 'elp it," yelled the taxi-man, " 'e fired at me. Ow, Gawd, I couldn't 'elp it."

Lord Peter and Parker arrived together, panting.

" Here, constable," gasped his lordship ; " I know this man. He has an unfortunate grudge against my brother. In connection with a poaching matter—up in Yorkshire. Tell the coroner to come to me for information."

" Very good, my lord."

" Don't photograph *that*," said Lord Peter to the man with the reflex, whom he suddenly found at his elbow.

The photographer shook his head.

" They wouldn't like to see that, my lord. Only the scene of the crash and the ambulance-men. Bright, newsy pictures, you know. Nothing gruesome"— with an explanatory jerk of the head at the great dark splotches in the roadway—" it doesn't pay."

A red-haired reporter appeared from nowhere with a note-book.

" Here," said his lordship, " do you want the story ? I'll give it you now."

.   .   .   .   .

There was not, after all, the slightest trouble in the matter of Mrs. Grimethorpe. Seldom, perhaps, has a ducal escapade resolved itself with so little embarrassment. His grace, indeed, who was nothing if not a gentleman, braced himself gallantly for a regretful and sentimental interview. In all his rather stupid affairs he had never run away from a scene, or countered a storm of sobs with that maddening " Well, I'd better be going now " which has led to so many despairs and occasionally to cold shot. But, on this occasion, the whole business fell flat. The lady was not interested.

" I am free now," she said. " I am going back to my own people in Cornwall. I do not want anything, now that he is dead." The Duke's dutiful caress was a most uninteresting failure.

Lord Peter saw her home to a respectable little hotel in Bloomsbury. She liked the taxi, and the large, glittering shops, and the sky-signs. They stopped at Piccadilly Circus to see the Bonzo dog smoke his gasper and the Nestlé's baby consume his bottle of milk. She was amazed to find that the prices of the things in Swan & Edgar's window were, if anything, more reasonable than those current in Stapley.

" I should like one of those blue scarves," she said, " but I'm thinking 'twould not be fitting, and me a widow."

" You could buy it now, and wear it later on," suggested his lordship, " in Cornwall, you know."

" Yes." She glanced at her brown stuff gown. " Could I buy my blacks here ? I shall have to get some for the funeral. Just a dress and a hat—and a coat, maybe."

" I should think it would be a very good idea."

" Now ? "

" Why not ? "

" I have money," she said ; " I took it from his desk. It's mine now, I suppose. Not that I'd wish to be beholden to him. But I don't look at it that way."

" I shouldn't think twice about it, if I were you," said Lord Peter.

285

She walked before him into the shop—her own woman at last.

.   .   .   .   .

In the early hours of the morning Inspector Sugg, who happened to be passing Parliament Square, came upon a taxi-man apparently addressing a heated expostulation to the statue of Lord Palmerston. Indignant at this senseless proceeding, Mr. Sugg advanced, and then observed that the statesman was sharing his pedestal with a gentleman in evening dress, who clung precariously with one hand, while with the other he held an empty champagne-bottle to his eye, and surveyed the surrounding streets.

" Hi," said the policeman, " what are you doing there ? Come off of it ! "

" Hullo ! " said the gentleman, losing his balance quite suddenly, and coming down in a jumbled manner. " Have you seen my friend ? Very odd thing—damned odd. 'Spec you know where find him, what ? When in doubt—tasker pleeshman, what ? Friend of mine. Very dignified sort of man 'nopera-hat. Freddy—good ol' Freddy. Alwaysh answersh t'name—jush like jolly ol' bloodhound ! " He got to his feet and stood beaming on the officer.

" Why, if it ain't his lordship," said Inspector Sugg, who had met Lord Peter in other circumstances. " Better be gettin' home, my lord. Night air's chilly-like, ain't it ? You'll catch a cold or summat o' that. Here's your taxi—just you jump in now."

" No," said Lord Peter. " No. Couldn' do that. Not without frien'. Good ol' Freddy. Never—desert —friend ! Dear ol' Sugg. Wouldn't desert Freddy." He attempted an attitude, with one foot poised on the step of the taxi, but, miscalculating his distance, stepped heavily into the gutter, thus entering the vehicle unexpectedly, head first.

Mr. Sugg tried to tuck his legs in and shut him up, but

his lordship thwarted this movement with unlooked-for agility, and sat firmly on the step.

" Not my taxi," he explained solemnly. " Freddy's taxi. Not right—run away with frien's taxi. Very odd. Jush went roun' corner to fesh Fred'sh taxshi—Freddy jush went roun' corner fesh *my* taxi—fesh friend'sh taxshi—friendship sush a beautiful thing—don't you thing-so, Shugg ? Can't leave frien'. Beshides—there'sh dear ol' Parker."

" Mr. Parker ? " said the Inspector apprehensively. " Where ? "

" Hush ! " said his lordship. " Don' wake baby, theresh good shoul. Neshle'sh baby—jush shee 'm neshle, don't he neshle nishely ? "

Following his lordship's gaze, the horrified Sugg observed his official superior cosily tucked up on the far side of Palmerston and smiling a happy smile in his sleep. With an exclamation of alarm he bent over and shook the sleeper.

" Unkind ! " cried Lord Peter in a deep, reproachful tone. " Dishturb poor fellow—poor hardworkin' pleeshman. Never getsh up till alarm goes. . . . 'Stra'or'nary thing," he added, as though struck by a new idea, " why hashn't alarm gone off, Shugg ? " He pointed a wavering finger at Big Ben. " They've for-forgotten to wind it up. Dishgrayshful. I'll write to *The T-T-Timesh* about it."

Mr. Sugg wasted no words, but picked up the slumbering Parker and hoisted him into the taxi.

" Never—never—deshert——" began Lord Peter, resisting all efforts to dislodge him from the step, when a second taxi, advancing from Whitehall, drew up, with the Hon. Freddy Arbuthnot cheering loudly at the window.

" Look who's here ! " cried the Hon. Freddy. " Jolly, jolly, jolly ol' Sugg. Let'sh all go home together."

" That'sh *my* taxshi," interposed his lordship, with dignity, staggering across to it. The two whirled together for a moment ; then the Hon. Freddy was flung into Sugg's arms, while his lordship, with a satisfied air, cried " Home ! " to the new taxi-man, and instantly fell asleep in a corner of the vehicle.

Mr. Sugg scratched his head, gave Lord Peter's address, and watched the cab drive off. Then, supporting the Hon. Freddy on his ample bosom, he directed the other man to convey Mr. Parker to 12a Great Ormond Street.

" Take me home," cried the Hon. Freddy, bursting into tears, " they've all gone and left me ! "

" You leave it to me, sir," said the Inspector. He glanced over his shoulder at St. Stephen's, whence a group of Commons were just issuing from an all-night sitting.

" Mr. Parker an' all," said Inspector Sugg, adding devoutly, " Thank Gawd there weren't no witnesses."

The Unpleasantness at the Bellona Club

CONTENTS

Contents

CHAPTER I

Old Mossy-face

"WHAT IN THE WORLD, WIMSEY, ARE YOU DOING in this Morgue?" demanded Captain Fentiman, flinging aside the "Evening Banner" with the air of a man released from an irksome duty.

"Oh, I wouldn't call it that," retorted Wimsey, amiably. "Funeral Parlor at the very least. Look at the marble. Look at the furnishings. Look at the palms and the chaste bronze nude in the corner."

"Yes, and look at the corpses. Place always reminds me of that old thing in 'Punch,' you know— 'Waiter, take away Lord Whatsisname, he's been dead two days.' Look at Old Ormsby there, snoring like a hippopotamus. Look at my revered grandpa —dodders in here at ten every morning, collects the 'Morning Post' and the armchair by the fire, and becomes part of the furniture till the evening. Poor old devil. Suppose I'll be like that one of these days. I wish to God Jerry had put me out with the rest of 'em. What's the good of coming through for this sort of thing? What'll you have?"

"Dry martini," said Wimsey. "And you? Two

1

dry martinis, Fred, please. Cheer up. All this remembrance-day business gets on your nerves, don't it? It's my belief most of us would be only too pleased to chuck these community hysterics if the beastly newspapers didn't run it for all it's worth. However, it don't do to say so. They'd hoof me out of the Club if I raised my voice beyond a whisper."

"They'd do that anyway, whatever you were saying," said Fentiman, gloomily. "What *are* you doing here?"

"Waitin' for Colonel Marchbanks," said Wimsey. "Bung-ho!"

"Dining with him?"

"Yes."

Fentiman nodded quietly. He knew that young Marchbanks had been killed at Hill 60, and that the Colonel was wont to give a small, informal dinner on Armistice night to his son's intimate friends.

"I don't mind old Marchbanks," he said, after a pause. "He's a dear old boy."

Wimsey assented.

"And how are things going with you?" he asked.

"Oh, rotten as usual. Tummy all wrong and no money. What's the damn good of it, Wimsey? A man goes and fights for his country, gets his inside gassed out, and loses his job, and all they give him is the privilege of marching past the Cenotaph once a year and paying four shillings in the pound income-tax. Sheila's queer too—overwork, poor girl.

2

It's pretty damnable for a man to have to live on his wife's earnings, isn't it? I can't help it, Wimsey. I go sick and have to chuck jobs up. Money—I never thought of money before the War, but I swear nowadays I'd commit any damned crime to get hold of a decent income."

Fentiman's voice had risen in nervous excitement. A shocked veteran, till then invisible in a neighbouring armchair, poked out a lean head like a tortoise and said "Sh!" viperishly.

"Oh, I wouldn't do that," said Wimsey, lightly. "Crime's a skilled occupation, y' know. Even a comparative imbecile like myself can play the giddy sleuth on the amateur Moriarity. If you're thinkin' of puttin' on a false mustache and lammin' a millionaire on the head, don't do it. That disgustin' habit you have of smoking cigarettes down to the last millimeter would betray you anywhere. I'd only have to come on with a magnifyin' glass and a pair of callipers to say 'The criminal is my dear old friend George Fentiman. Arrest that man!' You might not think it, but I am ready to sacrifice my nearest and dearest in order to curry favour with the police and get a par. in the papers."

Fentiman laughed, and ground out the offending cigarette stub on the nearest ash-tray.

"I wonder anybody cares to know you," he said. The strain and bitterness had left his voice and he sounded merely amused.

"They wouldn't," said Wimsey, "only they think I'm too well-off to have any brains. It's like hearing that the Earl of Somewhere is taking a leading part in a play. Everybody takes it for granted he must act rottenly. I'll tell you my secret. All my criminological investigations are done for me by a 'ghost' at £3 a week, while I get the headlines and frivol with well-known journalists at the Savoy."

"I find you refreshing, Wimsey," said Fentiman, languidly. "You're not in the least witty, but you have a kind of obvious facetiousness which reminds me of the less exacting class of music-hall."

"It's the self-defense of the first-class mind against the superior person," said Wimsey. "But, look here, I'm sorry to hear about Sheila. I don't want to be offensive, old man, but why don't you let me——"

"Damned good of you," said Fentiman, "but I don't care to. There's honestly not the faintest chance I could ever pay you, and I haven't quite got to the point yet——"

"Here's Colonel Marchbanks," broke in Wimsey, "we'll talk about it another time. Good evening, Colonel."

"Evening, Peter. Evening, Fentiman. Beautiful day it's been. No—no cocktails, thanks, I'll stick to whisky. So sorry to keep you waiting like this, but I was having a yarn with poor old Grainger

4

upstairs. He's in a baddish way, I'm afraid. Between you and me, Penberthy doesn't think he'll last out the winter. Very sound man, Penberthy—wonderful, really, that he's kept the old man going so long with his lungs in that frail state. Ah, well! it's what we must all come to. Dear me, there's your grandfather, Fentiman. He's another of Penberthy's miracles. He must be ninety, if he's a day. Will you excuse me for a moment? I must just go and speak to him."

Wimsey's eyes followed the alert, elderly figure as it crossed the spacious smoking-room, pausing now and again to exchange greetings with a fellow-member of the Bellona Club. Drawn close to the huge fireplace stood a great chair with ears after the Victorian pattern. A pair of spindle shanks with neatly-buttoned shoes propped on a footstool were all that was visible of General Fentiman.

"Queer, isn't it," muttered his grandson, "to think that for Old Mossy-face there the Crimea is still *the* War, and the Boer business found him too old to go out. He was given his commission at seventeen, you know—was wounded at Majuba—"

He broke off. Wimsey was not paying attention. He was still watching Colonel Marchbanks.

The Colonel came back to them, walking very quietly and precisely. Wimsey rose and went to meet him.

"I say, Peter," said the Colonel, his kind face

5

gravely troubled, "just come over here a moment. I'm afraid something rather unpleasant has happened."

Fentiman looked round, and something in their manner made him get up and follow them over to the fire.

Wimsey bent down over General Fentiman and drew the "Morning Post" gently away from the gnarled old hands, which lay clasped over the thin chest. He touched the shoulder—put his hand under the white head huddled against the side of the chair. The Colonel watched him anxiously. Then, with a quick jerk, Wimsey lifted the quiet figure. It came up all of a piece, stiff as a wooden doll.

Fentiman laughed. Peal after hysterical peal shook his throat. All round the room, scandalized Bellonians creaked to their gouty feet, shocked by the unmannerly noise.

"Take him away!" said Fentiman, "take him away. He's been dead two days! So are you! So am I! We're all dead and we never noticed it!"

CHAPTER II

The Queen Is Out

IT IS DOUBTFUL WHICH OCCURRENCE WAS MORE disagreeable to the senior members of the Bellona Club—the grotesque death of General Fentiman in their midst or the indecent neurasthenia of his grandson. Only the younger men felt no sense of outrage; they knew too much. Dick Challoner—known to his intimates as Tin-Tummy Challoner, owing to the fact that he had been fitted with a spare part after the second battle of the Somme—took the gasping Fentiman away into the deserted library for a stiffener. The Club Secretary hurried in, in his dress-shirt and trousers, the half-dried lather still clinging to his jaws. After one glance he sent an agitated waiter to see if Dr. Penberthy was still in the Club. Colonel Marchbanks laid a large silk handkerchief reverently over the rigid face in the arm-chair and remained quietly standing. A little circle formed about the edge of the hearth-rug, not quiet certain what to do. From time to time it was swelled by fresh arrivals, whom the news had greeted in the hall as they wandered in. A little group appeared from the bar. "What? old

Fentiman?" they said. "Good God, you don't say so. Poor old blighter. Heart gone at last, I suppose"; and they extinguished cigars and cigarettes, and stood by, not liking to go away again.

Dr. Penberthy was just changing for dinner. He came down hurriedly, caught just as he was going out to an Armistice dinner, his silk hat tilted to the back of his head, his coat and muffler pushed loosely open. He was a thin, dark man with the abrupt manner which distinguishes the Army Surgeon from the West-end practitioner. The group by the fire made way for him, except Wimsey, who hung rather foolishly upon the big elbow-chair, gazing in a helpless way at the body.

Penberthy ran practised hands quickly over neck, wrists and knee-joints.

"Dead several hours," he pronounced, sharply. "Rigor well-established—beginning to pass off." He moved the dead man's left leg in illustration; it swung loose at the knee. "I've been expecting this. Heart very weak. Might happen any moment. Any one spoken to him to-day?"

He glanced round interrogatively.

"I saw him here after lunch," volunteered somebody. "I didn't speak."

"I thought he was asleep," said another.

Nobody remembered speaking to him. They were so used to old General Fentiman, slumbering by the fire.

8

"Ah, well," said the doctor. "What's the time? Seven?" He seemed to make a rapid calculation. "Say five hours for rigor to set in—must have taken place very rapidly—he probably came in at his usual time, sat down and died straight away."

"He always walked from Dover Street," put in an elderly man, "I told him it was too great an exertion at his age. You've heard me say so, Ormsby."

"Yes, yes, quite," said the purple-faced Ormsby. "Dear me, just so."

"Well, there's nothing to be done," said the doctor. "Died in his sleep. Is there an empty bedroom we can take him to, Culyer?"

"Yes, certainly," said the Secretary. "James, fetch the key of number sixteen from my office and tell them to put the bed in order. I suppose, eh, doctor?—when the rigor passes off we shall be able to—eh?"

"Oh, yes, you'll be able to do everything that's required. I'll send the proper people in to lay him out for you. Somebody had better let his people know—only they'd better not show up till we can get him more presentable."

"Captain Fentiman knows already," said Colonel Marchbanks. "And Major Fentiman is staying in the Club—he'll probably be in before long. Then there's a sister, I think."

"Yes, old Lady Dormer," said Penberthy, "she lives round in Portman Square. They haven't been on speaking terms for years. Still, she'll have to know."

"I'll ring them up," said the Colonel. "We can't leave it to Captain Fentiman, he's in no fit state to be worried, poor fellow. You'll have to have a look at him, doctor, when you've finished here. An attack of the old trouble—nerves, you know."

"All right. Ah! is the room ready, Culyer? Then we'll move him. Will somebody take his shoulders —no, not you, Culyer" (for the Secretary had only one sound arm), "Lord Peter, yes, thank you—lift carefully."

Wimsey put his long, strong hands under the stiff arms; the doctor gathered up the legs; they moved away. They looked like a dreadful little Guy Fawkes procession, with that humped and unreverend mannikin bobbing and swaying between them.

The door closed after them, and a tension seemed removed. The circle broke up into groups. Somebody lit a cigarette. The planet's tyrant, dotard Death, had held his gray mirror before them for a moment and shown them the image of things to come. But now it was taken away again. The unpleasantness had passed. Fortunate, indeed, that Penberthy was the old man's own doctor. He knew all about it. He could give a certificate. No inquest. Nothing undesirable. The members of the Bellona Club could go to dinner.

Colonel Marchbanks turned to go through the far door towards the library. In a narrow ante-room between the two rooms there was a convenient telephone-cabinet for the use of those members who did not wish to emerge into the semi-publicity of the entrance-hall.

"Hi, colonel! not that one. That instrument's out of order," said a man called Wetheridge, who saw him go. "Disgraceful, I call it. I wanted to use the 'phone this morning, and—oh! hullo! the notice has gone. I suppose it's all right again. They ought to let one know."

Colonel Marchbanks paid little attention to Wetheridge. He was the club grumbler, distinguished even in that fellowship of the dyspeptic and peremptory—always threatening to complain to the Committee, harassing the Secretary and constituting a perennial thorn in the sides of his fellow-members. He retired, murmuring, to his chair and the evening paper, and the Colonel stepped into the telephone-cabinet to call up Lady Dormer's house in Portman Square.

Presently he came out through the library into the entrance-hall, and met Penberthy and Wimsey just descending the staircase.

"Have you broken the news to Lady Dormer?" asked Wimsey.

"Lady Dormer is dead," said the Colonel. "Her maid tells me she passed quietly away at half-past ten this morning."

11

CHAPTER III

Hearts Count More Than Diamonds

ABOUT TEN DAYS AFTER THAT NOTABLE ARMISTICE Day, Lord Peter Wimsey was sitting in his library, reading a rare fourteenth century manuscript of Justinian. It gave him particular pleasure, being embellished with a large number of drawings in sepia, extremely delicate in workmanship, and not always equally so in subject. Beside him on a convenient table stood a long-necked decanter of priceless old port. From time to time he stimulated his interest with a few sips, pursing his lips thoughtfully, and slowly savouring the balmy after-taste.

A ring at the front-door of the flat caused him to exclaim "Oh, hell!" and cock an attentive ear for the intruder's voice. Apparently the result was satisfactory, for he closed the Justinian and had assumed a welcoming smile when the door opened.

"Mr. Murbles, my lord."

The little elderly gentleman who entered was so perfectly the family solicitor as really to have no distinguishing personality at all, beyond a great kindliness of heart and a weakness for soda-mint lozenges.

12

"I am not disturbing you, I trust, Lord Peter."

"Good lord, no, sir. Always delighted to see you. Bunter, a glass for Mr. Murbles. Very glad you've turned up, sir. The Cockburn '80 always tastes a lot better in company—discernin' company, that is. Once knew a fellow who polluted it with a Trichinopoly. He was not asked again. Eight months later, he committed suicide. I don't say it was on that account. But he was earmarked for a bad end, what?"

"You horrify me," said Mr. Murbles, gravely. "I have seen many men sent to the gallows for crimes with which I could feel much more sympathy. Thank-you, Bunter, thank-you. You are quite well, I trust?"

"I am in excellent health, I am obliged to you, sir."

"That's good. Been doing any photography lately?"

"A certain amount, sir. But merely of a pictorial description, if I may venture to call it so. Criminological material, sir, has been distressingly deficient of late."

"Perhaps Mr. Murbles has brought us something," suggested Wimsey.

"No," said Mr. Murbles, holding the Cockburn '80 beneath his nostrils and gently agitating the glass to release the ethers, "no, I can't say I have, precisely. I will not disguise that I have come in

13

the hope of deriving benefit from your trained habits of observation and deduction, but I fear—that is, I trust—in fact, I am confident—that nothing of an undesirable nature is involved. The fact is," he went on, as the door closed upon the retreating Bunter, "a curious question has arisen with regard to the sad death of General Fentiman at the Bellona Club, to which, I understand, you were a witness."

"If you understand that, Murbles," said his lordship, cryptically, "you understand a damn sight more than I do. I did not witness the death—I witnessed the discovery of the death—which is a very different thing, by a long chalk."

"By how long a chalk?" asked Mr. Murbles, eagerly. "That is just what I am trying to find out."

"That's very inquisitive of you," said Wimsey. "I think perhaps it would be better . . ." he lifted his glass and tilted it thoughtfully, watching the wine coil down in thin flower-petallings from rim to stem . . . "if you were to tell me exactly what you want to know . . . and why. After all . . . I'm a member of the Club . . . family associations chiefly, I suppose . . . but there it is."

Mr. Murbles looked up sharply, but Wimsey's attention seemed focussed upon the port.

"Quite so," said the solicitor. "Very well. The facts of the matter are these. General Fentiman

14

had, as you know, a sister Felicity, twelve years younger than himself. She was very beautiful and very wilful as a girl, and ought to have made a very fine match, but for the fact that the Fentimans, though extremely well-descended, were anything but well-off. As usual at that period, all the money there was went to educating the boy, buying him a commission in a crack regiment and supporting him there in the style which was considered indispensable for a Fentiman. Consequently there was nothing left to furnish a marriage-portion for Felicity, and that was rather disastrous for a young woman sixty years ago.

"Well, Felicity got tired of being dragged through the social round in her darned muslins and gloves that had been to the cleaners—and she had the spirit to resent her mother's perpetual strategies in the match-making line. There was a dreadful, decrepit old viscount, eaten up with diseases and dissipations, who would have been delighted to totter to the altar with a handsome young creature of eighteen, and I am sorry to say that the girl's father and mother did everything they could to force her into accepting this disgraceful proposal. In fact, the engagement was announced and the wedding-day fixed, when, to the extreme horror of her family, Felicity calmly informed them one morning that she had gone out before breakfast and actually got married, in the most indecent

secrecy and haste, to a middle-aged man called
Dormer, very honest and abundantly wealthy, and
—horrid to relate—a prosperous manufacturer.
Buttons, in fact—made of papier mâché or something, with a patent indestructible shank—were the
revolting antecedents to which this headstrong
young Victorian had allied herself.

"Naturally there was a terrible scandal, and the
parents did their best—seeing that Felicity was a
minor—to get the marriage annulled. However,
Felicity checkmated their plans pretty effectually
by escaping from her bedroom—I fear, indeed, that
she actually climbed down a tree in the back-
garden, crinoline and all—and running away with
her husband. After which, seeing that the worst
had happened—indeed, Dormer, a man of prompt
action, lost no time in putting his bride in the
family way—the old people put the best face they
could on it in the grand Victorian manner. That
is, they gave their consent to the marriage, forwarded their daughter's belongings to her new
home in Manchester, and forbade her to darken
their doors again."

"Highly proper," murmured Wimsey. "I'm determined never to be a parent. Modern manners
and the break-up of the fine old traditions have
simply ruined the business. I shall devote my life
and fortune to the endowment of research on the
best method of producin' human beings decorously

16

and unobtrusively from eggs. All parental responsibility to devolve upon the incubator."

"I hope not," said Mr. Murbles. "My own profession is largely supported by domestic entanglements. To proceed. Young Arthur Fentiman seems to have shared the family views. He was disgusted at having a brother-in-law in buttons, and the jests of his mess-mates did nothing to sweeten his feelings toward his sister. He became impenetrably military and professional, crusted over before his time, and refused to acknowledge the existence of anybody called Dormer. Mind you, the old boy was a fine soldier, and absolutely wrapped up in his Army associations. In due course he married—not well, for he had not the means to entitle him to a noble wife, and he would not demean himself by marrying money, like the unspeakable Felicity. He married a suitable gentlewoman with a few thousand pounds. She died (largely, I believe, owing to the military regularity with which her husband ordained that she should perform her maternal functions), leaving a numerous but feeble family of children. Of these, the only one to attain maturity was the father of the two Fentimans you know—Major Robert and Captain George Fentiman."

"I don't know Robert very well," interjected Wimsey. "I've met him. Frightfully hearty and all that—regular army type."

"Yes, he's of the old Fentiman stock. Poor George inherited a weakly strain from his grandmother, I'm afraid."

"Well, nervous, anyhow," said Wimsey, who knew better than the old solicitor the kind of mental and physical strain George Fentiman had undergone. The War pressed hardly upon imaginative men in responsible positions. "And then he was gassed and all that, you know," he added, apologetically.

"Just so," said Mr. Murbles. "Robert, you know, is unmarried and still in the Army. He's not particularly well-off, naturally, for none of the Fentimans ever had a bean, as I believe one says nowadays; but he does very well. George——"

"Poor old George! All right, sir, you needn't tell me about him. Usual story. Decentish job—imprudent marriage—chucks everything to join up in 1914—invalided out—job gone—health gone—no money—heroic wife keeping the home-fires burning—general fed-upness. Don't let's harrow our feelings. Take it as read."

"Yes, I needn't go into that. Their father is dead, of course, and up till ten days ago there were just two surviving Fentimans of the earlier generation. The old General lived on the small fixed income which came to him through his wife and his retired pension. He had a solitary little flat in Dover Street and an elderly man-servant, and he practically lived at the Bellona Club. And there was his sister, Felicity."

"How did she come to be Lady Dormer?"

"Why, that's where we come to the interesting part of the story. Henry Dormer——"

"The button-maker?"

"The button-maker. He became an exceedingly rich man indeed—so rich, in fact, that he was able to offer financial assistance to certain exalted persons who need not be mentioned and so, in time, and in consideration of valuable services to the nation not very clearly specified in the Honours List, he became Sir Henry Dormer, Bart. His only child—a girl—had died, and there was no prospect of any further family, so there was, of course, no reason why he should not be made a baronet for his trouble."

"Acid man you are," said Wimsey. "No reverence, no simple faith or anything of that kind. Do lawyers ever go to heaven?"

"I have no information on that point," said Mr. Murbles, dryly. "Lady Dormer——"

"Did the marriage turn out well otherwise?" inquired Wimsey.

"I believe it was perfectly happy," replied the lawyer, "an unfortunate circumstance in one way, since it entirely precluded the possibility of any reconciliation with her relatives. Lady Dormer, who was a fine, generous-hearted woman, frequently

19

made overtures of peace, but the General held sternly aloof. So did his son—partly out of respect for the old boy's wishes, but chiefly, I fancy, because he belonged to an Indian regiment and spent most of his time abroad. Robert Fentiman, however, showed the old lady a certain amount of attention, paying occasional visits and so forth, and so did George at one time. Of course they never let the General know a word about it, or he would have had a fit. After the War, George rather dropped his great-aunt—I don't know why."

"I can guess," said Wimsey. "No job—no money, y' know. Didn't want to look pointed. That sort of thing, what?"

"Possibly. Or there may have been some kind of quarrel. I don't know. Anyway, those are the facts. I hope I am not boring you, by the way?"

"I am bearing up," said Wimsey, "waiting for the point where the Money comes in. There's a steely legal glitter in your eye, sir, which suggests that the thrill is not far off."

"Quite correct," said Mr. Murbles. "I now come —thank-you, well, yes—I will take just one more glass. I thank Providence I am not of a gouty constitution. Yes. Ah!—We now come to the melancholy event of November 11th last, and I must ask you to follow me with the closest attention."

"By all means," said Wimsey, politely.

"Lady Dormer," pursued Mr. Murbles, leaning

20

earnestly forward, and punctuating every sentence with sharp little jabs of his gold-mounted eye-glasses, held in his right finger and thumb, "was an old woman, and had been ailing for a very long time. However, she was still the same headstrong and vivacious personality that she had been as a girl, and on the fifth of November she was suddenly seized with a fancy to go out at night and see a display of fireworks at the Crystal Palace or some such place—it may have been Hampstead Heath or the White City—I forget, and it is of no consequence. The important thing is, that it was a raw, cold evening. She insisted on undertaking her little expedition nevertheless, enjoyed the entertainment as heartily as the youngest child, imprudently exposed herself to the night air and caught a severe cold which, in two days' time, turned to pneumonia. On November 10th she was sinking fast, and scarcely expected to live out the night. Accordingly, the young lady who lived with her as her ward—a distant relative, Miss Ann Dorland —sent a message to General Fentiman that if he wished to see his sister alive, he should come immediately. For the sake of our common human nature, I am happy to say that this news broke down the barrier of pride and obstinacy that had kept the old gentleman away so long. He came, found Lady Dormer just conscious, though very feeble, stayed with her about half an hour and departed, still stiff as a ramrod, but visibly softened. This was about four o'clock in the afternoon. Shortly afterwards, Lady Dormer became unconscious, and, indeed, never moved or spoke again, passing peacefully away in her sleep at half-past ten the following morning.

"Presumably the shock and nervous strain of the interview with his long-estranged sister had been too much for the old General's feeble system, for, as you know, he died at the Bellona Club at some time—not yet clearly ascertained—on the same day, the eleventh of November.

"Now then, at last—and you have been very patient with my tedious way of explaining all this —we come to the point at which we want your help."

Mr. Murbles refreshed himself with a sip of port, and, looking a little anxiously at Wimsey, who had closed his eyes and appeared to be nearly asleep, he resumed.

"I have not mentioned, I think, how I come to be involved in this matter myself. My father was the Fentimans' family solicitor, a position to which I naturally succeeded when I took over the business at his death. General Fentiman, though he had little enough to leave, was not the sort of disorderly person who dies without making a proper testamentary disposition. His retired pension, of course, died with him, but his small private estate was

22

properly disposed by will. There was a small legacy
—fifty pounds—to his man-servant (a very attached and superior fellow); then one or two
trifling bequests to old military friends and the
servants at the Bellona Club (rings, medals,
weapons and small sums of a few pounds each).
Then came the bulk of his estate, about £2,000,
invested in sound securities, and bringing in
an income of slightly over £100 per annum.
These securities, specifically named and enumerated, were left to Captain George Fentiman, the
younger grandson, in a very proper clause, which
stated that the testator intended no slight in thus
passing over the elder one, Major Robert, but that,
as George stood in the greater need of monetary
help, being disabled, married, and so forth, whereas
his brother had his profession and was without ties,
George's greater necessity gave him the better claim
to such money as there was. Robert was finally
named as executor and residuary legate, thus suc-
ceeding to all such personal effects and monies as
were not specifically devised elsewhere. Is that
clear?"

"Clear as a bell. Was Robert satisfied with that
arrangement?"

"Oh dear, yes; perfectly. He knew all about the
will beforehand and had agreed that it was quite
fair and right."

"Nevertheless," said Wimsey, "it appears to be

such a small matter, on the face of it, that you must be concealing something perfectly devastating up your sleeve. Out with it, man, out with it! Whatever the shock may be, I am braced to bear it."

"The shock," said Mr. Murbles, "was inflicted on me, personally, last Friday by Lady Dormer's man of business—Mr. Pritchard of Lincoln's Inn. He wrote to me, asking if I could inform him of the exact hour and minute of General Fentiman's decease. I replied, of course, that, owing to the peculiar circumstances under which the event took place, I was unable to answer his question as precisely as I could have wished, but that I understood Dr. Penberthy to have given it as his opinion that the General had died some time in the forenoon of November 11th. Mr. Pritchard then asked if he might wait upon me without delay, as the matter he had to discuss was of the most urgent importance. Accordingly I appointed a time for the interview on Monday afternoon, and when Mr. Pritchard arrived he informed me of the following particulars.

"A good many years before her death, Lady Dormer—who, as I said before, was an eminently generous-minded woman—made a will. Her husband and her daughter were then dead. Henry Dormer had few relations, and all of them were fairly wealthy people. By his own will he had

24

sufficiently provided for these persons, and had left
the remainder of his property, amounting to something like seven hundred thousand pounds, to his
wife, with the express stipulation that she was to
consider it as her own, to do what she liked with,
without any restriction whatsoever. Accordingly,
Lady Dormer's will divided this very handsome fortune—apart from certain charitable and personal
bequests with which I need not trouble you—
between the people who, for one reason and another, had the greatest claims on her affection.
Twelve thousand pounds were to go to Miss Ann
Dorland. The whole of the remainder was to pass
to her brother, General Fentiman, if he was still
living at her death. If, on the other hand, he should
pre-decease her, the conditions were reversed. In
that case, the bulk of the money came to Miss
Dorland, and fifteen thousand pounds were to be
equally divided between Major Robert Fentiman
and his brother George."

Wimsey whistled softly.

"I quite agree with you," said Mr. Murbles. "It
is a most awkward situation. Lady Dormer died at
precisely 10:37 A. M. on November 11th. General
Fentiman died that same morning at some time,
presumably after 10 o'clock, which was his usual
hour for arriving at the Club, and certainly before
7 P. M. when his death was discovered. If he died
immediately on his arrival, or at any time up to

25

10:36, then Miss Dorland is an important heiress, and my clients the Fentimans get only seven thousand pounds or so apiece. If, on the other hand, his death occurred even a few seconds after 10:37, Miss Dorland receives only twelve thousand pounds, George Fentiman is left with the small pittance bequeathed to him under his father's will—while Robert Fentiman, the residuary legatee, inherits a very considerable fortune of well over half a million."

"And what," said Wimsey, "do you want me to do about it?"

"Why," replied the lawyer, with a slight cough, "it occurred to me that you, with your—if I may say so—remarkable powers of deduction and analysis might be able to solve the extremely difficult and delicate problem of the precise moment of General Fentiman's decease. You were in the Club when the death was discovered, you saw the body, you know the places and the persons involved, and you are, by your standing and personal character, exceptionally well fitted to carry out the necessary investigations without creating any—ahem!—public agitation or—er—scandal, or, in fact, notoriety, which would, I need hardly say, be extremely painful to all concerned."

"It's awkward," said Wimsey, "uncommonly awkward."

"It is indeed," said the lawyer with some warmth,

26

"for as we are now situated, it is impossible to execute either will or—or in short do anything at all. It is most unfortunate that the circumstances were not fully understood at the time, when the —um—the body of General Fentiman was available for inspection. Naturally, Mr. Pritchard was quite unaware of the anomalous situation, and as I knew nothing about Lady Dormer's will, I had no idea that anything beyond Dr. Penberthy's certificate was, or ever could become, necessary."

"Couldn't you get the parties to come to some agreement?" suggested Wimsey.

"If we are unable to reach any satisfactory conclusion about the time of the death, that will probably be the only way out of the difficulty. But at the moment there are certain obstacles——"

"Somebody's being greedy, eh?—You'd rather not say more definitely, I suppose? No? H'm, well! From a purely detached point of view it's a very pleasin' and pretty little problem, you know."

"You will undertake to solve it for us then, Lord Peter?"

Wimsey's fingers tapped out an intricate fugal passage on the arm of his chair.

"If I were you, Murbles, I'd try again to get a settlement."

"Do you mean," asked Mr. Murbles, "that you think my clients have a losing case?"

"No—I can't say that. By the way, Murbles, who is your client—Robert or George?"

"Well, the Fentiman family in general. I know, naturally, that Robert's gain is George's loss. But none of the parties wishes anything but that the actual facts of the case should be determined."

"I see. You'll put up with anything I happen to dig out?"

"Of course."

"However favourable or unfavourable it may be?"

"I should not lend myself to any other course," said Mr. Murbles, rather stiffly.

"I know that, sir. But—well!—I only mean that —Look here, sir! when you were a boy, did you ever go about pokin' sticks and things into peaceful, mysterious lookin' ponds, just to see what was at the bottom?"

"Frequently," replied Mr. Murbles. "I was extremely fond of natural history and had a quite remarkable collection (if I may say so at this distance of time) of pond fauna."

"Did you ever happen to stir up a deuce of a stink in the course of your researches?"

"My dear Lord Peter—you are making me positively uneasy."

"Oh, I don't know that you need be. I am only giving you a general warning, you know. Of course, if you wish it, I'll investigate this business like a shot."

"It's very good of you," said Mr. Murbles.

"Not at all. *I* shall enjoy it all right. If anything odd comes of it, that's your funeral. You never know, you know."

"If you decide that no satisfactory conclusion can be arrived at," said Mr. Murbles, "we can always fall back on the settlement. I am sure all parties wish to avoid litigation."

"In case the estate vanishes in costs? Very wise. I hope it may be feasible. Have you made any preliminary inquiries?"

"None to speak of. I would rather you undertook the whole investigation from the beginning."

"Very well. I'll start to-morrow and let you know how it gets on."

The lawyer thanked him and took his departure. Wimsey sat pondering for a short time—then rang the bell for his man-servant.

"A new notebook, please, Bunter. Head it 'Fentiman' and be ready to come round with me to the Bellona Club to-morrow, complete with camera and the rest of the outfit."

"Very good, my lord. I take it your lordship has a new inquiry in hand?"

"Yes, Bunter—quite new."

"May I venture to ask if it is a promising case, my lord?"

"It has its points. So has a porcupine. No matter. Begone, dull care! Be at great pains, Bunter, to cultivate a detached outlook on life. Take example by the bloodhound, who will follow up with equal and impartial zest the trail of a parricide or of a bottle of aniseed."

"I will bear it in mind, my lord."

Wimsey moved slowly across to the little black baby grand that stood in the corner of the library.

"Not Bach this evening," he murmured to himself. "Bach for to-morrow when the gray matter begins to revolve." A melody of Parry's formed itself crooningly under his fingers. 'For man worketh in a vain shadow . . . he heapeth up riches and cannot tell who shall gather them.' He laughed suddenly, and plunged into an odd, noisy, and painfully inharmonious study by a modern composer in the key of seven sharps.

CHAPTER IV

Lord Peter Leads A Club

"YOU ARE QUITE SURE THIS SUIT IS ALL RIGHT, Bunter?" said Lord Peter, anxiously.

It was an easy lounge suit, tweedy in texture, and a trifle more pronounced in colour and pattern than Wimsey usually permitted himself. While not unsuitable for town wear, it yet diffused a faint suggestion of hills and the sea.

"I want to look approachable," he went on, "but on no account loud. I can't help wondering whether that stripe of invisible green wouldn't have looked better if it had been a remote purple."

This suggestion seemed to disconcert Bunter. There was a pause while he visualized a remote purple stripe. At length, however, the palpitating balance of his mind seemed to settle definitely down.

"No, my lord," he said firmly, "I do *not* think purple would be an improvement. Interesting— yes; but, if I may so express myself, decidedly less affable."

"Thank goodness," said his lordship, "I'm sure you're right. You always are. And it would have

31

been a bore to get it changed now. You are sure you've removed all the newness, eh? Hate new clothes."

"Positive, my lord. I assure your lordship that the garments have every appearance of being several months old."

"Oh, all right. Well, give me the malacca with the foot-rule marked on it—and where's my lens?"

"Here, my lord." Bunter produced an innocent-looking monocle, which was, in reality, a powerful magnifier. "And the finger-print powder is in your lordship's right-hand coat-pocket."

"Thanks. Well, I think that's all. I'll go on now, and I want you to follow on with the doings in about an hour's time."

The Bellona Club is situated in Piccadilly, not many hundred yards west of Wimsey's own flat, which overlooks the Green Park. The commissionaire greeted him with a pleased smile.

"Mornin', Rogers, how are you?"

"Very well, my lord, I thank you."

"D'you know if Major Fentiman is in the Club, by the way?"

"No, my lord. Major Fentiman is not residing with us at present. I believe he is occupying the late General Fentiman's flat, my lord."

"Ah, yes—very sad business, that."

"Very melancholy, my lord. Not a pleasant thing to happen in the Club. Very shocking, my lord."

"Yes—still, he was a very old man. I suppose it had to be some day. Queer to think of 'em all sittin' round him there and never noticin', eh, what?"

"Yes, my lord. It gave Mrs. Rogers quite a turn when I told her about it."

"Seems almost unbelievable, don't it? Sittin' round all those hours—must have been several hours, I gather, from what the doctor says. I suppose the old boy came in at his usual time, eh?"

"Ah! regular as clock-work, the General was. Always on the stroke of ten. 'Good-morning, Rogers', he'd say, a bit stiff-like, but very friendly. And then, 'Fine morning,' he'd say, as like as not. And sometimes ask after Mrs. Rogers and the family. A fine old gentleman, my lord. We shall all miss him."

"Did you notice whether he seemed specially feeble or tired that morning at all?" inquired Wimsey, casually, tapping a cigarette on the back of his hand.

"Why, no, my lord. I beg your pardon, I fancied you knew. I wasn't on duty that day, my lord. I was kindly given permission to attend the ceremony at the Cenotaph. Very grand sight, it was, too, my lord. Mrs. Rogers was greatly moved."

"Oh, of course, Rogers—I was forgetting. Naturally, you would be there. So you didn't see the General to say good-bye, as it were. Still, it

33

wouldn't have done to miss the Cenotaph. Matthews took your duty over, I suppose."

"No, my lord. Matthews is laid up with 'flu, I am sorry to say. It was Weston was at the door all morning, my lord."

"Weston? Who's he?"

"He's new, my lord. Took the place of Briggs. You recollect Briggs—his uncle died and left him a fish-shop."

"Of course he did; just so. When does Weston come on parade? I must make his acquaintance."

"He'll be here at one o'clock, when I go to my lunch, my lord."

"Oh, right! I'll probably be about then. Hallo, Penberthy! You're just the man I want to see. Had your morning's inspiration? Or come in to look for it?"

"Just tracking it to its lair. Have it with me."

"Right you are, old chap—half a mo' while I deposit my outer husk. I'll follow you."

He glanced irresolutely at the hall-porter's desk, but seeing the man already engaged with two or three inquiries, plunged abruptly into the cloakroom, where the attendant, a bright cockney with a Sam Weller face and an artificial leg, was ready enough to talk about General Fentiman.

"Well, now, my lord, that's funny you should ask me that," he said, when Wimsey had dexterously worked in an inquiry as to the time of the

34

General's arrival at the Bellona. "Dr. Penberthy was askin' the same question. It's a fair puzzle, that is. I could count on the fingers of one 'and the mornings I've missed seein' the General come in. Wonderful regular, the General was, and him being such a very old gentleman, I'd make a point of being 'andy, to 'elp him off with his overcoat and such. But there! He must a' come in a bit late, that morning, for I never see him, and I thought at lunch-time, 'The General must be ill,' I thinks. And I goes round, and there I see his coat and 'at 'ung up on his usual peg. So I must 'a missed him. There was a lot of gentlemen in and out that morning, my lord, bein' Armistice Day. A number of members come up from the country and wanting their 'ats and boots attended to, my lord, so that's how I come not to notice, I suppose."

"Possibly. Well, he was in before lunch, at any rate."

"Oh, yes, my lord. 'Alf-past twelve I goes off, and his hat and coat were on the peg then, because I see 'em."

"That gives us a terminus ad quem at any rate," said Wimsey, half to himself.

"I beg your lordship's pardon?"

"I was saying, that shows he came in before half-past twelve—and later than ten o'clock, you think."

"Yes, my lord. I couldn't say to a fraction, but

I'm sure if 'e'd arrived before a quarter-past ten I should have seen 'im. But after that, I recollect I was very busy, and he must 'a slipped in without me noticing him."

"Ah, yes—poor old boy! Still, no doubt he'd have liked to pass out quietly like that. Not a bad way to go home, Williamson."

"Very good way, my lord. We've seen worse than that. And what's it all come to, after all? They're all sayin' as it's an unpleasant thing for the Club, but *I* say, where's the odds? There ain't many 'ouses what somebody ain't died in, some time or another. We don't think any the worse of the 'ouses, so why think the worse of the Club?"

"You're a philosopher, Williamson." Wimsey climbed the short flight of marble steps and turned into the bar. "It's narrowin' down," he muttered to himself. "Between ten-fifteen and twelve-thirty. Looks as if it was goin' to be a close run for the Dormer stakes. But—dash it all! Let's hear what Penberthy has to say."

The doctor was already standing at the bar with a whisky-and-soda before him. Wimsey demanded a Worthington and dived into his subject without more ado.

"Look here," he said, "I just wanted a word with you about old Fentiman. Frightfully confidential, and all that. But it seems the exact time of the poor old blighter's departure has become an im-

36

portant item. Question of succession. Get me? They don't want a row made. Asked me, as friend of the family and all that, don't y' know, to barge round and ask questions. Obviously, you're the first man to come to. What's your opinion? Medical opinion, apart from anything else?"

Penberthy raised his eyebrows.

"Oh? there's a question, is there? Thought there might be. That lawyer-fellow, what's-his-name, was here the other day, trying to pin me down. Seemed to think one can say to a minute when a man died by looking at his back teeth. I told him it wasn't possible. Once give these birds an opinion, and the next thing is, you find yourself in a witness-box, swearing to it."

"I know. But one gets a general idea."

"Oh, yes. Only you have to check up your ideas by other things—facts, and so on. You can't just theorize."

"Very dangerous things, theories. F'r instance—take this case—I've seen one or two stiff 'uns in my short life, and, if I'd started theorizin' about this business, just from the look of the body, d'you know what I'd have said?"

"God knows what a layman would say about a medical question," retorted the doctor, with a sour little grin.

"Hear, hear!—Well, I should have said he'd been dead a long time."

37

"That's pretty vague."

"You said yourself that rigour was well advanced. Give it, say, six hours to set in and—when did it pass off?"

"It was passing off then—I remarked upon it at the time."

"So you did. I thought rigour usually lasted twenty-four hours or so."

"It does, sometimes. Sometimes it goes off quickly. Quick come, quick go, as a rule. Still, I agree with you, that in the absence of other evidence, I should have put the death rather earlier than ten o'clock."

"You admit that?"

"I do. But we know he came in not earlier than a quarter past ten."

"You've seen Williamson, then?"

"Oh, yes. I thought it better to check up on the thing as far as possible. So I can only suppose that, what with the death being sudden, and what with the warmth of the room—he was very close to the fire, you know—the whole thing came on and worked itself off very quickly."

"H'm! Of course, you knew the old boy's constitution very well."

"Oh, rather. He was very frail. Heart gets a bit worn-out when you're over the four-score and ten, you know. I should never have been surprised at

38

his dropping down anywhere. And then, he'd had a bit of a shock, you see."

"What was that?"

"Seeing his sister the afternoon before. They told you about that, I imagine, since you seem to know all about the business. He came along to Harley Street afterwards and saw me. I told him to go to bed and keep quiet. Arteries very strained, and pulse erratic. He was excited—naturally. He ought to have taken a complete rest. As I see it, he must have insisted on getting up, in spite of feeling groggy, walked here—he *would* do it—and collapsed straight away."

"That's all right, Penberthy, but when—just when—did it happen?"

"Lord knows. I don't. Have another?"

"No, thanks; not for the moment. I say, I suppose you are perfectly satisfied about it all?"

"Satisfied?" The doctor stared at him. "Yes, of course. If you mean, satisfied as to what he died of—of course I'm satisfied. I shouldn't have given a certificate if I hadn't been satisfied."

"Nothing about the body struck you as queer?"

"What sort of thing?"

"You know what I mean as well as I do," said Wimsey, suddenly turning and looking the other straight in the face. The change in him was almost startling—it was as if a steel blade had whipped

39

suddenly out of its velvet scabbard. Penberthy met his eye, and nodded slowly.

"Yes, I do know what you mean. But not here. We'd better go up to the Library. There won't be anybody there."

CHAPTER V

—And Finds The Club Suit Blocked

THERE NEVER WAS ANYBODY IN THE LIBRARY AT the Bellona. It was a large, quiet, pleasant room, with the bookshelves arranged in bays; each of which contained a writing-table and three or four chairs. Occasionally some one would wander in to consult the Times Atlas, or a work on Strategy and Tactics, or to hunt up an ancient Army list, but for the most part it was deserted. Sitting in the farthest bay, immured by books and silence, confidential conversation could be carried on with all the privacy of the confessional.

"Well, now," said Wimsey, "what about it?"

"About—?" prompted the doctor, with professional caution.

"About that leg?"

"I wonder if anybody else noticed that?" said Penberthy.

"I doubt it. I did, of course. But then, I make that kind of thing my hobby. Not a popular one, perhaps—an ill-favoured thing, but mine own. In fact, I've got rather a turn for corpses. But not knowin' quite what it meant, and seein' you didn't seem to want to call attention to it, I didn't put myself forward."

"No—I wanted to think it over. You see, it suggested, at the first blush, something rather——"

"Unpleasant," said Wimsey. "If you knew how often I'd heard that word in the last two days! Well, let's face it. Let's admit, straight away, that, once rigor sets in, it stays in till it starts to pass off, and that, when it *does* start to go it usually begins with the face and jaw, and not suddenly in one knee-joint. Now Fentiman's jaw and neck were as rigid as wood—I felt 'em. But the left leg swung loose from the knee. Now how do you explain that?"

"It is extremely puzzling. As no doubt you are aware, the obvious explanation would be that the joint had been forcibly loosened by somebody or something, after rigor had set in. In that case of course, it wouldn't stiffen up again. It would remain loose until the whole body relaxed. But how it happened——"

"That's just it. Dead people don't go about jamming their legs into things and forcing their own joints. And surely, if anybody had found the body like that he would have mentioned it. I mean, can you imagine one of the waiter-johnnies, for instance, finding an old gentleman stiff as a poker in the best arm-chair and then just givin' him a dose of knee-jerks and leavin' him there?"

42

"The only thing I could think of," said Penberthy, "was that a waiter or somebody had found him, and tried to move him—and then got frightened and barged off without saying anything. It sounds absurd. But people do do odd things, especially if they're scared."

"But what was there to be scared of?"

"It might seem alarming to a man in a very nervous state. We have one or two shell-shock cases here that I wouldn't answer for in an emergency. It would be worth considering, perhaps, if any one had shown special signs of agitation or shock that day."

"That's an idea," said Wimsey, slowly. "Suppose—suppose, for instance, there was somebody connected in some way with the General, who was in an unnerved state of mind—and suppose he came suddenly on this stiff corpse. You think he might—possibly—lose his head?"

"It's certainly possible. I can imagine that he might behave hysterically, or even violently, and force the knee-joint back with some unbalanced idea of straightening the body out and making it look more seemly. And then, you know, he might just run away from the thing and pretend it hadn't happened. Mind you, I'm not saying it was so, but I can easily see it happening. And that being so, I thought it better to say nothing about it. It would be a very unpl—— distressing thing to bring to people's notice. And it might do untold harm to the nervous case to question him about it. I'd rather let sleeping dogs lie. There was nothing wrong about the death, that's definite. As for the rest— our duty is to the living; we can't help the dead."

"Quite. Tell you what, though, I'll have a shot at finding out whether—we may as well say what we mean—whether George Fentiman was alone in the smoking-room at any time during the day. One of the servants may have noticed. It seems the only possible explanation. Well, thanks very much for your help. Oh, by the way, you said at the time that the rigor was passing off when we found the body—was that just camouflage, or does it still hold good?"

"It was just beginning to pass off in the face and jaw as a matter of fact. It had passed away completely by midnight."

"Thanks. That's another fact, then. I like facts, and there are annoyin'ly few of them in this case. Won't you have another whisky?"

"No thanks. Due at my surgery. See you another time. Cheerio!"

Wimsey remained for a few moments after he had gone, smoking meditatively. Then he turned his chair to the table, took a sheet of paper from the rack and began to jot down a few notes of the case with his fountain-pen. He had not got far, however, before one of the Club servants entered, peering into all the bays in turn, looking for somebody.

"Want me, Fred?"

"Your lordship's man is here, my lord, and says you may wish to be advised of his arrival."

"Quite right. I'm just coming." Wimsey took up the blotting-pad to blot his notes. Then his face changed. The corner of a sheet of paper protruded slightly. On the principle that nothing is too small to be looked at, Wimsey poked an inquisitive finger between the leaves, and extracted the paper. It bore a few scrawls relating to sums of money, very carelessly and shakily written. Wimsey looked at it attentively for a moment or two, and shook the blotter to see if it held anything further. Then he folded the sheet, handling it with extreme care by the corners, put it in an envelope and filed it away in his note-case. Coming out of the library, he found Bunter waiting in the hall, camera and tripod in hand.

"Ah, here you are, Bunter. Just a minute, while I see the Secretary." He looked in at the office, and found Culyer immersed in some accounts.

"Oh, I say, Culyer—'mornin' and all that—yes, disgustingly healthy, thanks, always am—I say, you recollect old Fentiman poppin' off in that inconsiderate way a little time ago?"

"I'm not likely to forget it," said Culyer, with a wry face. "I've had three notes of complaint from

45

Wetheridge—one, because the servants didn't notice the matter earlier, set of inattentive rascals and all that; two, because the undertaker's men had to take the coffin past his door and disturbed him; three, because somebody's lawyer came along and asked him questions—together with distant allusions to the telephones being out of order and a shortage of soap in the bathroom. Who'd be a secretary?"

"Awfully sorry for you," said Wimsey with a grin. "I'm not here to make trouble. Au contraire, as the man said in the Bay of Biscay when they asked if he'd dined. Fact is, there's a bit of a muddle about the exact minute when the old boy passed out—mind you, this is in strict confidence—and I'm havin' a look into it. Don't want a fuss made, but I'd like a few photographs of the place, just to look at in absence and keep the lie of the land under my hawk-like optic, what? I've got my man here with a camera. D'you mind pretendin' he's the bloke from 'The Twaddler' or the 'Picture News,' or something, and givin' him your official blessin' while he totters round with the doings?"

"Mysterious idiot—of course, if you like. Though how photographs of the place to-day are going to give you a line on the time of a death which happened ten days ago, I don't pretend to understand. But, I say—it's all fair and above-board? We don't want any——"

"Of course not. That's the idea. Strictest confidence—any sum up to £50,000 on your note of hand alone, delivered in plain vans, no reference needed. Trust little Peter."

"Oh, right-ho! What d'you want done?"

"I don't want to go round with Bunter. Give the show away. May he be called in here?"

"Certainly."

A servant was sent to fetch Bunter, who came in looking imperturbably prim and point-device. Wimsey looked him over and shook his head.

"I'm sorry, Bunter, but you don't look in the least like the professional photographer from 'The Twaddler.' That dark-gray suit is all right, but you haven't got quite the air of devil-may-care seediness that marks the giants of Fleet Street. D'you mind stickin' all those dark-slides into one pocket and a few odd lenses and doodahs into the other, and rufflin' your manly locks a trifle? That's better. Why have you no pyro stains on the right thumb and forefinger?"

"I attribute it, my lord, principally to the circumstance that I prefer metol-quinol for the purpose of development."

"Well, you can't expect an outsider to grasp a thing like that. Wait a minute. Culyer, you seem to have a fairly juicy pipe there. Give us a cleaner."

Wimsey thrust the instrument energetically

through the stem of the pipe, bringing out a revolting collection of brown, oily matter.

"Nicotine poisoning, Culyer—that's what you'll
die of if you aren't jolly careful. Here you are,
Bunter. Judiciously smeared upon the finger tips,
that should give quite the right effect. Now, look
here, Mr. Culyer here will take you round. I want
a shot of the smoking-room from the entrance,
a close up of the fireplace, showing General Fentiman's usual chair, and another shot from the door
of the ante-room that leads into the library. Another shot through the ante-room into the library,
and some careful studies of the far bay of the
library from all points of view. After that, I want
two or three views of the hall, and a shot of the
cloak-room; get the attendant there to show you
which was General Fentiman's customary peg, and
take care that that gets into the picture. That's
all for the moment, but you can take anything
else that seems necessary for purposes of camouflage. And I want all the detail you can possibly
get in, so stop down to whatever it is and take as
long as you like. You'll find me knocking about
somewhere when you've finished, and you'd better
get some more plates in, because we're going on to
another place."

"Very good, my lord."

"Oh, and, Culyer, by the way. Dr. Penberthy
sent a female in to lay the General out, didn't

he? D'you happen to remember when she arrived?"

"About nine o'clock the next morning, I think."

"Have you got her name, by any chance?"

"I don't think so. But I know she came from Merritt's, the undertakers—round Shepherd's Market way. They'd probably put you on to her."

"Thanks frightfully, Culyer. I'll make myself scarce now. Carry on, Bunter."

Wimsey thought for a moment; then strolled across to the smoking-room, exchanged a mute greeting with one or two of the assembled veterans, picked up the "Morning Post," and looked round for a seat. The great arm-chair with ears still stood before the fire, but some dim feeling of respect for the dead had left it vacant. Wimsey sauntered over to it, and dropped lazily into its well-sprung depths. A veteran close at hand looked angrily at him and rustled the "Times" loudly. Wimsey ignored these signals, barricading himself behind his paper. The veteran sank back again, muttering something about "young men" and "no decency." Wimsey sat on unmoved, and paid no attention, even when a man from "The Twaddler" came in, escorted by the Secretary, to take photographs of the smoking-room. A few sensitives retired before this attack. Wetheridge waddled away with a grumbling protest into the library. It gave Wimsey considerable

49

satisfaction to see the relentless camera pursue him into that stronghold.

It was half-past twelve before a waiter approached Lord Peter to say that Mr. Culyer would be glad to speak to him for a moment. In the office, Bunter reported his job done, and was despatched to get some lunch and a fresh supply of plates. Wimsey presently went down to the dining-room, where he found Wetheridge already established, getting the first cut off the saddle of mutton, and grumbling at the wine. Wimsey went deliberately over, greeted him heartily, and sat down at the same table.

Wetheridge said it was beastly weather. Wimsey agreed amiably. Wetheridge said it was scandalous, seeing what one paid for one's food in this place, that one couldn't get anything fit to eat. Wimsey, who was adored by chef and waiters alike for his appreciation of good food, and had been sent the choicest cut without having to ask for it, sympathized with this sentiment too. Wetheridge said he had been chased all over the Club that morning by an infernal photographer fellow, and that one got no peace these days with all this confounded publicity. Wimsey said it was all done for advertisement, and that advertisement was the curse of the age. Look at the papers—nothing but advertisements from cover to cover. Wetheridge said that in his time, by gad, a respectable Club would

have scorned advertisements, and that he could remember the time when newspapers were run by
gentlemen for gentlemen. Wimsey said that nothing was what it had been; the thought it must be
due to the War.

"Infernal slackness, that's what it is," said
Wetheridge. "The service in this place is a disgrace.
That fellow Culyer doesn't know his job. This
week it's the soap. Would you believe it, there was
none—actually none—in the bathroom yesterday.
Had to ring for it. Made me late for dinner. Last
week it was the telephone. Wanted to get through
to a man down in Norfolk. Brother was a friend of
mine—killed on the last day of the War, half an
hour before the guns stopped firing—damnable
shame—always ring up on Armistice Day, say a
few words, don't you know—hr'rm!"

Wetheridge, having unexpectedly displayed this
softer side of his character, relapsed into a snorting
silence.

"Couldn't you get through, sir?" inquired Wimsey, with feeling. Anything that had happened at
the Bellona Club on Armistice Day was of interest
to him.

"I got *through* all right," said Wetheridge, mo-
rosely. "But, confound it all, I had to go down to
the cloak-room to get a call from one of the boxes
there. Didn't want to hang about the entrance.
Too many imbeciles coming in and out. Exchanging

silly anecdotes. Why a solemn national occasion should be an excuse for all these fools meeting and talking rot, I don't know."

"Beastly annoyin'. But why didn't you tell 'em to put the call through to the box by the library?"

"Aren't I telling you? The damned thing was out of order. Damned great notice stuck across it as cool as you please—'Instrument out of order.' Just like that. No apology. Nothing. Sickening, I call it. I told the fellow at the switch-board it was a disgrace. And all he said was, he hadn't put the notice up, but he'd draw attention to the matter."

"It was all right in the evening," said Wimsey, "because I saw Colonel Marchbanks using it."

"I know it was. And then, dashed if we didn't get the fool thing ringing, ringing at intervals all the next morning. Infuriating noise. When I told Fred to stop it, he just said it was the Telephone Company testing the line. They've no business to make a row like that. Why can't they test it quietly, that's what I want to know?"

Wimsey said telephones were an invention of the devil. Wetheridge grumbled his way through to the end of lunch, and departed. Wimsey returned to the entrance-hall, where he found the assistant commissionaire on duty, and introduced himself.

Weston, however, was of no assistance. He had not noticed General Fentiman's arrival on the eleventh. He was not acquainted with many of the

52

members, having only just taken over his new duties. He thought it odd that he should not have noticed so very venerable a gentleman, but the fact remained that he had not. He regretted it extremely. Wimsey gathered that Weston was annoyed at having lost a chance of reflected celebrity. He had missed his scoop, as the reporters say.

Nor was the hall-porter any more helpful. The morning of November 11th had been a busy one. He had been in and out of his little glass pigeon-hole continually, shepherding guests into various rooms to find the members they wanted, distributing letters and chatting to country members who visited the Bellona seldom and liked to "have a chat with Piper" when they did. He could not recollect seeing the General. Wimsey began to feel that there must have been a conspiracy to overlook the old gentleman on the last morning of his life.

"You don't think he never was here at all, do you, Bunter?" he suggested. "Walkin' about invisible and tryin' hard to communicate, like the unfortunate ghost in that story of somebody or other's?"

Bunter was inclined to reject the psychic view of the case. "The General must have been here in the body, my lord, because there *was* the body."

"That's true," said Wimsey. "I'm afraid we can't explain away the body. S'pose that means I'll have to question every member of this beastly Club separately. But just at the moment I think we'd better go round to the General's flat and hunt up Robert Fentiman. Weston, get me a taxi, please."

CHAPTER VI

A Card of Re-Entry

THE DOOR OF THE LITTLE FLAT IN DOVER STREET was opened by an elderly man-servant, whose anxious face bore signs of his grief at his master's death. He informed them that Major Fentiman was at home and would be happy to receive Lord Peter Wimsey. As he spoke, a tall, soldierly man of about forty-five came out from one of the rooms and hailed his visitor cheerily.

"That you, Wimsey? Murbles told me to expect you. Come in. Haven't seen you for a long time. Hear you're turning into a regular Sherlock. Smart bit of work that was you put in over your brother's little trouble. What's all this? Camera? Bless me, you're going to do our little job in the professional manner, eh? Woodward, see that Lord Peter's man has everything he wants. Have you had lunch? Well, you'll have a spot of something, I take it, before you start measuring up the footprints. Come along. We're a bit at sixes and sevens here, but you won't mind."

He led the way into the small, austerely-furnished sitting room.

"Thought I might as well camp here for a bit, while I get the old man's belongings settled up. It's going to be a deuce of a job, though, with all this fuss about the will. However, I'm his executor, so all this part of it falls to me in any case. It's very decent of you to lend us a hand. Queer old girl, Great-aunt Dormer. Meant well, you know, but made it damned awkward for everybody. How are you getting along?"

Wimsey explained the failure of his researches at the Bellona.

"Thought I'd better get a line on it at this end," he added. "If we know exactly what time he left here in the morning, we ought to be able to get an idea of the time he got to the Club."

Fentiman screwed his mouth into a whistle.

"But, my dear old egg, didn't Murbles tell you the snag?"

"He told me nothing. Left me to get on with it. What *is* the snag?"

"Why, don't you see, the old boy never came home that night."

"Never came home?—Where was he, then?"

"Dunno. That's the puzzle. All we know is . . . wait a minute, this is Woodward's story; he'd better tell you himself. Woodward!"

"Yes, sir."

"Tell Lord Peter Wimsey the story you told me —about that telephone-call, you know."

"Yes, sir. About nine o'clock . . ."

"Just a moment," said Wimsey, "I do like a story to begin at the beginning. Let's start with the morning—the mornin' of November 10th. Was the General all right that morning? Usual health and spirits and all that?"

"Entirely so, my lord. General Fentiman was accustomed to rise early, my lord, being a light sleeper, as was natural at his great age. He had his breakfast in bed at a quarter to eight—tea and buttered toast, with a hegg lightly boiled, as he did every day in the year. Then he got up, and I helped him to dress—that would be about half-past eight to nine, my lord. Then he took a little rest, after the exertion of dressing, and at a quarter to ten I fetched his hat, overcoat, muffler and stick, and saw him start off to walk to the Club. That was his daily routine. He seemed in very good spirits—and in his usual health. Of course, his heart was always frail, my lord, but he seemed no different from ordinary."

"I see. And in the ordinary way he'd just sit at the Club all day and come home—when, exactly?"

"I was accustomed to have his evening meal ready for him at half-past seven precisely, my lord."

"Did he always turn up to time?"

"Invariably so, my lord. Everything as regular as on parade. That was the General's way. About

57

three o'clock in the afternoon, there was a ring on the telephone. We had the telephone put in, my lord, on account of the General's heart, so that we could always call up a medical man in case of emergency."

"Very right, too," put in Robert Fentiman.

"Yes, sir. General Fentiman was good enough to say, sir, he did not wish me to have the heavy responsibility of looking after him alone in case of illness. He was a very kind, thoughtful gentleman." The man's voice faltered.

"Just so," said Wimsey. "I'm sure you must be very sorry to lose him, Woodward. Still, one couldn't expect otherwise, you know. I'm sure you looked after him splendidly. What was it happened about three o'clock?"

"Why, my lord, they rang up from Lady Dormer's to say as how her ladyship was very ill, and would General Fentiman please come at once if he wanted to see her alive. So I went down to the Club myself. I didn't like to telephone, you see, because General Fentiman was a little hard of hearing—though he had his faculties wonderful well for a gentleman of his age—and he never liked the telephone. Besides, I was afraid of the shock it might be to him, seeing his heart was so weak—which, of course, at his age you couldn't hardly expect otherwise—so that was why I went myself."

"That was very considerate of you."

"Thank you, my lord. Well, I see General Fentiman, and I give him the message—careful-like, and breaking it gently as you might say. I could see he was took aback a bit, but he just sits thinking for a few minutes, and then he says, 'Very well, Woodward, I will go. It is certainly my duty to go.' So I wraps him up careful, and gets him a taxi, and he says, 'You needn't come with me, Woodward. I don't quite know how long I shall stay there. They will see that I get home quite safely.' So I told the man where to take him and came back to the flat. And that, my lord, was the last time I see him."

Wimsey made a sympathetic clucking sound.

"Yes, my lord. When General Fentiman didn't return at his usual time, I thought he was maybe staying to dine at Lady Dormer's, and took no notice of it. However, at half-past eight, I began to be afraid of the night-air for him; it was very cold that day, my lord, if you remember. At nine o'clock, I was just thinking of calling up the household at Lady Dormer's to ask when he was to be expected home, when the 'phone rang."

"At nine exactly?"

"About nine. It might have been a little later, but not more than a quarter-past at latest. It was a gentleman spoke to me. He said: 'Is that General Fentiman's flat?' I said, 'Yes, who is it, please?' And he said, 'Is that Woodward?' giving my name, just like that. And I said 'Yes.' And he said, 'Oh, Woodward, General Fentiman wishes me to tell you not to wait up for him, as he is spending the night with me.' So I said, 'Excuse me, sir, who is it speaking, please?' And he said, 'Mr. Oliver.' So I asked him to repeat the name, not having heard it before, and he said 'Oliver'— it came over very plain, 'Mr. Oliver,' he said, 'I'm an old friend of General Fentiman's, and he is staying to-night with me, as we have some business to talk over.' So I said, 'Does the General require anything, sir?'—thinking, you know, my lord, as he might wish to have his sleeping-suit and his tooth-brush or somethink of that, but the gentleman said no, he had got everything necessary and I was not to trouble myself. Well, of course, my lord, as I explained to Major Fentiman, I didn't like to take upon myself to ask questions, being only in service, my lord; it might seem taking a liberty. But I was very much afraid of the excitement and staying up late being too much for the General, so I went so far as to say I hoped General Fentiman was in good health and not tiring of himself, and Mr. Oliver laughed and said he would take very good care of him and send him to bed straight away. And I was just about to make so bold as to ask him where he lived, when he rang off. And that was all I knew till I heard next day of the General being dead, my lord."

"There now," said Robert Fentiman. "What do you think of that?"

"Odd," said Wimsey, "and most unfortunate as it turns out. Did the General often stay out at night, Woodward?"

"Never, my lord. I don't recollect such a thing happening once in five or six years. In the old days, perhaps, he'd visit friends occasionally, but not of late."

"And you'd never heard of this Mr. Oliver?"

"No, my lord."

"His voice wasn't familiar?"

"I couldn't say but what I might have heard it before, my lord, but I find it very difficult to recognize voices on the telephone. But I thought at the time it might be one of the gentlemen from the Club."

"Do *you* know anything about the man, Fentiman?"

"Oh, yes—I've met him. At least, I suppose it's the same man. But I know nothing about him. I fancy I ran across him once in some frightful crush or other, a public dinner, or something of that kind, and he said he knew my grandfather. And I've seen him lunching at Gatti's and that sort of thing. But I haven't the remotest idea where he lives or what he does."

"Army man?"

"No—something in the engineering line, I fancy."

"What's he like?"

"Oh, tall, thin, gray hair and spectacles. About sixty-five to look at. He may be older—must be, if he's an old friend of grandfather's. I gathered he was retired from whatever it is he did, and lived in some suburb, but I'm hanged if I can remember which."

"Not very helpful," said Wimsey. "D'you know, occasionally I think there's quite a lot to be said for women."

"What's that got to do with it?"

"Well, I mean, all this easy, uninquisitive way men have of makin' casual acquaintances is very fine and admirable and all that—but look how inconvenient it is! Here you are. You admit you've met this bloke two or three times, and all you know about him is that he is tall and thin and retired into some unspecified suburb. A woman, with the same opportunities, would have found out his address and occupation, whether he was married, how many children he had, with their names and what they did for a living, what his favourite author was, what food he liked best, the name of his tailor, dentist and bootmaker, when he knew your grandfather and what he thought of him—screeds of useful stuff!"

"So she would," said Fentiman, with a grin. "That's why I've never married."

"I quite agree," said Wimsey, "but the fact remains that as a source of information you're simply a wash-out. Do, for goodness' sake, pull yourself together and try to remember something a bit more definite about the fellow. It may mean half a million to you to know what time grand-pa set off in the morning from Tooting Bec or Finchley or wherever it was. If it was a distant suburb, it would account for his arriving rather late at the Club—which is rather in your favour, by the way."

"I suppose it is. I'll do my best to remember. But I'm not sure that I ever knew."

"It's awkward," said Wimsey. "No doubt the police could find the man for us, but it's not a police case. And I don't suppose you particularly want to advertise."

"Well—it may come to that. But naturally, we're not keen on publicity if we can avoid it. If only I could remember exactly what work he said he'd been connected with."

"Yes—or the public dinner or whatever it was where you first met him. One might get hold of a list of the guests."

"My dear Wimsey—that was two or three years ago!"

"Or maybe they know the blighter at Gatti's."

"That's an idea. I've met him there several times. Tell you what, I'll go along there and make inquiries, and if they don't know him, I'll make a point of lunching there pretty regularly. He's almost bound to turn up again."

"Right. You do that. And meanwhile, do you mind if I have a look round the flat?"

"Rather not. D'you want me? Or would you rather have Woodward? He really knows a lot more about things."

"Thanks. I'll have Woodward. Don't mind me. I shall just be fussing about."

"Carry on by all means. I've got one or two drawers full of papers to go through. If I come across anything bearing on the Oliver bloke I'll yell out to you."

"Right."

Wimsey went out, leaving him to it, and joined Woodward and Bunter, who were conversing in the next room. A glance told Wimsey that this was the General's bedroom.

On a table beside the narrow iron bedstead was an old-fashioned writing-desk. Wimsey took it up, weighed it in his hands a moment and then took it to Robert Fentiman in the other room. "Have you opened this?" he asked.

"Yes—only old letters and things."

"You didn't come across Oliver's address, I suppose?"

64

"No. Of course I looked for that."

"Looked anywhere else? Any drawers? Cup-boards? That sort of thing?"

"Not so far," said Fentiman, rather shortly.

"No telephone memorandum or anything—you've tried the telephone-book, I suppose?"

"Well, no—I can't very well ring up perfect strangers and—"

"And sing 'em the Froth-Blowers' Anthem? Good God, man, anybody'd think you were chasing a lost umbrella, not half a million of money. The man rang you up, so he may very well be on the 'phone himself. Better let Bunter tackle the job. He has an excellent manner on the line; people find it a positive pleasure to be tr-r-roubled by him."

Robert Fentiman greeted this feeble pleasantry with an indulgent grin, and produced the telephone directory, to which Bunter immediately applied himself. Finding two-and-a-half columns of Olivers, he removed the receiver and started to work steadily through them in rotation. Wimsey returned to the bedroom. It was in apple-pie order—the bed neatly made, the wash-hand apparatus set in order, as though the occupant might return at any moment, every speck of dust removed—a tribute to Woodward's reverent affection, but a depressing sight for an investigator. Wimsey sat down, and let his eye rove slowly from the hanging wardrobe, with its polished doors, over the orderly line of boots and shoes arranged on their trees on a small shelf, the dressing table, the washstand, the bed and the chest of drawers which, with the small bedside table and a couple of chairs, comprised the furniture.

"Did the General shave himself, Woodward?"

"No, my lord; not latterly. That was my duty, my lord."

"Did he brush his own teeth, or dental plate, or whatever it was?"

"Oh, yes, my lord. Gneral Fentiman had an excellent set of teeth for his age."

Wimsey fixed his powerful monocle into his eye, and carried the tooth-brush over to the window. The result of the scrutiny was unsatisfactory. He looked round again.

"Is that his walking-stick?"

"Yes, my lord."

"May I see it?"

Woodward brought it across, carrying it, after the manner of a well-trained servant, by the middle. Lord Peter took it from him in the same manner, suppressing a slight, excited smile. The stick was a heavy malacca, with a thick crutch-handle of polished ivory, suitable for sustaining the feeble steps of old age. The monocle came into play again, and this time its owner gave a chuckle of pleasure.

"I shall want to take a photograph of this stick presently, Woodward. Will you be very careful to see that it is not touched by anybody beforehand?"

"Certainly, my lord."

Wimsey stood the stick carefully in its corner again, and then, as though it had put a new train of ideas into his mind, walked across to the shoe-shelf.

"Which were the shoes General Fentiman was wearing at the time of his death?"

"These, my lord."

"Have they been cleaned since?"

Woodward looked a trifle stricken.

"Not to say cleaned, my lord. I just wiped them over with a duster. They were not very dirty, and somehow—I hadn't the heart—if you'll excuse me, my lord."

"That's very fortunate."

Wimsey turned them over and examined the soles very carefully, both with the lens and with the naked eye. With a small pair of tweezers, taken from his pocket, he delicately removed a small fragment of pile—apparently from a thick carpet —which was clinging to a projecting brad, and stored it carefully away in an envelope. Then, putting the right shoe aside, he subjected the left to a prolonged scrutiny, especially about the inner edge of the sole. Finally he asked for a sheet of paper, and wrapped the shoe up as tenderly as

67

though it had been a piece of priceless Waterford glass.

"I should like to see all the clothes General Fentiman was wearing that day—the outer garments, I mean—hat, suit, overcoat and so on."

The garments were produced, and Wimsey went over every inch of them with the same care and patience, watched by Woodward with flattering attention.

"Have they been brushed?"

"No, my lord—only shaken out." This time Woodward offered no apology, having grasped dimly that polishing and brushing were not acts which called for approval under these unusual circumstances.

"You see," said Wimsey, pausing for a moment to note an infinitesimally small ruffling of the threads on the left-hand trouser leg, "we might be able to get some sort of a clew from the dust on the clothes, if any—to show us where the General spent the night. If—to take a rather unlikely example—we were to find a lot of sawdust, for instance, we might suppose that he had been visiting a carpenter. Or a dead leaf might suggest a garden or a common, or something of that sort. While a cobweb might mean a wine-cellar, or—or a potting-shed—and so on. You see?"

"Yes, my lord" (rather doubtfully).

"You don't happen to remember noticing that

68

little tear—well, it's hardly a tear—just a little roughness. It might have caught on a nail."

"I can't say I recollect it, my lord. But I might have overlooked it."

"Of course. It's probably of no importance. Well—lock the things up carefully. It's just possible I might have to have the dust extracted and analyzed. Just a moment—Has anything been removed from these clothes? The pockets were emptied, I suppose?"

"Yes, my lord."

"There was nothing unusual in them?"

"No, my lord. Nothing but what the General always took out with him. Just his handkerchief, keys, money and cigar-case."

"H'm. How about the money?"

"Well, my lord—I couldn't say exactly as to that. Major Fentiman has got it all. There was two pound notes in his note-case, I remember. I believe he had two pounds ten when he went out, and some loose silver in the trouser pocket. He'd have paid his taxi-fare and his lunch at the Club out of the ten-shilling note."

"That shows he didn't pay for anything unusual, then, in the way of train or taxis backwards and forwards, or dinner, or drinks."

"No, my lord."

"But naturally, this Oliver fellow would see to all that. Did the General have a fountain pen?"

"No, my lord. He did very little writing, my lord. I was accustomed to write any necessary letters to tradesmen, and so on."

"What sort of nib did he use, when he did write?"

"A J pen, my lord. You will find it in the sitting-room. But mostly I believe he wrote his letters at the Club. He had a very small private correspondence—it might be a letter or so to the Bank or to his man of business, my lord."

"I see. Have you his check-book?"

"Major Fentiman has it, my lord."

"Do you remember whether the General had it with him when he last went out?"

"No, my lord. It was kept in his writing desk as a rule. He would write the checks for the household here, my lord, and give them to me. Or occasionally he might take the book down to the Club with him."

"Ah! well, it doesn't look as though the mysterious Mr. Oliver was one of those undesirable blokes who demand money. Right you are, Woodward. You're perfectly certain that you removed nothing whatever from those clothes except what was in the pockets?"

"I am quite positive of that, my lord."

"That's very odd," said Wimsey, half to himself. "I'm not sure that it isn't the oddest thing about the case."

"Indeed, my lord? Might I ask why?"

"Why," said Wimsey, "I should have expected—" he checked himself. Major Fentiman was looking in at the door.

"What's odd, Wimsey?"

"Oh, just a little thing struck me," said Wimsey, vaguely. "I expected to find something among those clothes which isn't there. That's all."

"Impenetrable sleuth," said the major, laughing. "What are you driving at?"

"Work it out for yourself, my dear Watson," said his lordship, grinning like a dog. "You have all the data. Work it out for yourself, and let me know the answer."

Woodward, a trifle pained by this levity, gathered up the garments and put them away in the wardrobe.

"How's Bunter getting on with those calls?"

"No luck, at present."

"Oh!—well, he'd better come in now and do some photographs. We can finish the telephoning at home. Bunter!—Oh, and, I say, Woodward—d'you mind if we take your finger-prints?"

"Finger-prints, my lord?"

"Good God, you're not trying to fasten anything on Woodward?"

"Fasten what?"

"Well—I mean, I thought it was only burglars and people who had finger-prints taken."

"Not exactly. No—I want the General's finger-prints, really, to compare them with some others I got at the Club. There's a very fine set on that walking-stick of his, and I want Woodward's, just to make sure I'm not getting the two sets mixed up. I'd better take yours, too. It's just possible you might have handled the stick without noticing."

"Oh, I get you, Steve. I don't think I've touched the thing, but it's as well to make sure, as you say. Funny sort of business, what? Quite the Scotland Yard touch. How d'you do it?"

"Bunter will show you."

Bunter immediately produced a small inking-pad and roller, and a number of sheets of smooth, white paper. The fingers of the two candidates were carefully wiped with a clean cloth, and pressed first on the pad and then on the paper. The impressions thus obtained were labeled and put away in envelopes, after which the handle of the walking-stick was lightly dusted with gray powder, bringing to light an excellent set of prints of a right-hand set of fingers, super-imposed here and there, but quite identifiable. Fentiman and Woodward gazed fascinated at this entertaining miracle.

"Are they all right?"

"Perfectly so, sir; they are quite unlike either of the other two specimens."

"Then presumably they're the General's. Hurry up and get a negative."

Bunter set up the camera and focussed it.

"Unless," observed Major Fentiman, "they are Mr. Oliver's. That would be a good joke, wouldn't it?"

"It would, indeed," said Wimsey, a little taken aback. "A very good joke—on somebody. And for the moment, Fentiman, I'm not sure which of us would do the laughing."

CHAPTER VII

The Curse of Scotland

WHAT WITH TELEPHONE CALLS AND THE DEVELopment of photographs, it appeared obvious that Bunter was booked for a busy afternoon. His master, therefore, considerately left him in possession of the flat in Piccadilly, and walked abroad to divert himself in his own peculiar way.

His first visit was to one of those offices which undertake to distribute advertisements to the press. Here he drew up an advertisement addressed to taxi-drivers and arranged for it to appear, at the earliest possible date, in all the papers which men of that profession might be expected to read. Three drivers were requested to communicate with Mr. J. Murbles, Solicitor, of Staple Inn, who would recompense them amply for their time and trouble. First: any driver who remembered taking up an aged gentleman from Lady Dormer's house in Portman Square or the near vicinity on the afternoon of November 10th. Secondly: any driver who recollected taking up an aged gentleman at or near Dr. Penberthy's house in Harley Street at some

74

time in the afternoon or evening of November 10th. And thirdly: any driver who had deposited a similarly aged gentleman at the door of the Bellona Club between 10 and 12.30 in the morning of November 11th.

"Though probably," thought Wimsey, as he footed the bill for the insertions, to run for three days unless cancelled, "Oliver had a car and ran the old boy up himself. Still, it's just worth trying."

He had a parcel under his arm, and his next proceeding was to hail a cab and drive to the residence of Sir James Lubbock, the well-known analyst. Sir James was fortunately at home and delighted to see Lord Peter. He was a square-built man, with a reddish face and strongly-curling gray hair, and received his visitor in his laboratory, where he was occupied in superintending a Marsh's test for arsenic.

"D'ye mind just taking a pew for a moment, while I finish this off?"

Wimsey took the pew and watched, interested, the flame from the Bunsen burner playing steadily upon the glass tube, and the dark brown deposit slowly forming and deepening at the narrow end. From time to time, the analyst poured down the thistle-funnel a small quantity of a highly disagreeable-looking liquid from a stoppered phial; once his assistant came forward to add a few more drops of what Wimsey knew must be hydrochloric acid. Presently, the disagreeable liquid having all been transferred to the flask, and the deposit having deepened almost to black at its densest part, the tube was detached and taken away, and the burner extinguished, and Sir James Lubbock, after writing and signing a brief note, turned round and greeted Wimsey cordially.

"Sure I am not interrupting you, Lubbock?"

"Not a scrap. We've just finished. That was the last mirror. We shall be ready in good time for our appearance in Court. Not that there's much doubt about it. Enough of the stuff to kill an elephant. Considering the obliging care we take in criminal prosecutions to inform the public at large that two or three grains of arsenic will successfully account for an unpopular individual, however tough, it's surprising how wasteful people are with their drugs. You can't teach 'em. An office-boy who was as incompetent as the average murderer would be sacked with a kick in the bottom. Well, now! and what's your little trouble?"

"A small matter," said Wimsey, unrolling his parcel and producing General Fentiman's left boot, "it's cheek to come to you about it. But I want very much to know what this is, and as it's strictly a private matter, I took the liberty of bargin' round to you in a friendly way. Just along the inside of the sole, there—on the edge."

76

"Blood?" suggested the analyst, grinning.

"Well, no—sorry to disappoint you. More like paint, I fancy."

Sir James looked closely at the deposit with a powerful lens.

"Yes; some sort of brown varnish. Might be off a floor or a piece of furniture. Do you want an analysis?"

"If it's not too much trouble."

"Not at all. I think we'll get Saunders to do it; he has made rather a specialty of this kind of thing. Saunders, would you scrape this off carefully and see what it is? Get a slide of it, and make an analysis of the rest, if you can. How soon is it wanted?"

"Well, I'd like it as soon as possible. I don't mean within the next five minutes."

"Well, stay and have a spot of tea with us, and I dare say we can get something ready for you by then. It doesn't look anything out of the way. Knowing your tastes, I'm still surprised it isn't blood. Have you no blood in prospect?"

"Not that I know of. I'll stay to tea with pleasure, if you're certain I'm not being a bore."

"Never that. Besides, while you're here, you might give me your opinion on those old medical books of mine. I don't suppose they're particularly valuable, but they're quaint. Come along."

Wimsey passed a couple of hours agreeably with

Lady Lubbock and crumpets and a dozen or so antiquated anatomical treatises. Presently Saunders returned with his report. The deposit was nothing more nor less than an ordinary brown paint and varnish of a kind well known to joiners and furniture-makers. It was a modern preparation, with nothing unusual about it; one might find it anywhere. It was not a floor-varnish—one would expect to meet it on a door or partition or something of that sort. The chemical formula followed.

"Not very helpful, I'm afraid," said Sir James.

"You never know your luck," replied Wimsey. "Would you be good enough to label the slide and sign your name to it, and to the analysis, and keep them both by you for reference in case they're wanted?"

"Sure thing. How do you want 'em labeled?"

"Well—put down 'Varnish from General Fentiman's left boot,' and 'Analysis of varnish from General Fentiman's left boot,' and the date, and I'll sign it, and you and Saunders can sign it, and then I think we shall be all right."

"Fentiman? Was that the old boy who died suddenly the other day?"

"It was. But it's no use looking at me with that child-like air of intelligent taking-notice, because I haven't got any gory yarn to spin. It's only a question of where the old man spent the night, if you *must* know."

"Curiouser and curiouser. Never mind, it's nothing to do with me. Perhaps when it's all over, you'll tell me what it's about. Meanwhile the labels shall go on. You, I take it, are ready to witness to the identity of the boot, and I can witness to having seen the varnish on the boot, and Saunders can witness that he removed the varnish from the boot and analyzed it and that this is the varnish he analyzed. All according to Cocker. Here you are. Sign here and here, and that will be eight-and-sixpence, please."

"It might be cheap at eight-and-sixpence," said Wimsey. "It might even turn out to be cheap at eight hundred and sixty quid—or eight thousand and sixty."

Sir James Lubbock looked properly thrilled.

"You're only doing it to annoy, because you know it teases. Well, if you must be sphinx-like, you must. I'll keep these things under lock and key for you. Do you want the boot back?"

"I don't suppose the executor will worry. And a fellow looks such a fool carrying a boot about. Put it away with the other things till called for, there's a good man."

So the boot was put away in a cupboard, and Lord Peter was free to carry on with his afternoon's entertainment.

His first idea was to go on up to Finsbury Park, to see the George Fentimans. He remembered in time, however, that Sheila would not yet be home from her work—she was employed as cashier in a fashionable tea-shop—and further (with a forethought rare in the well-to-do) that if he arrived too early he would have to be asked to supper, and that there would be very little supper and that Sheila would be worried about it and George annoyed. So he turned in to one of his numerous Clubs, and had a Sole Colbert very well cooked, with a bottle of Liebfraumilch; an Apple Charlotte and light savoury to follow, and black coffee and a rare old brandy to top up with—a simple and satisfactory meal which left him in the best of tempers.

The George Fentimans lived in two ground-floor rooms with use of kitchen and bathroom in a semi-detached house with a blue and yellow fanlight over the door and Madras muslin over the windows. They were really furnished apartments, but the landlady always referred to them as a flat, because that meant that tenants had to do their own work and provide their own service. The house felt stuffy as Lord Peter entered it, because somebody was frying fish in oil at no great distance, and a slight unpleasantness was caused at the start by the fact that he had rung only once, thus bringing up the person in the basement, whereas a better-instructed caller would have rung twice, to indicate that he wanted the ground floor.

80

Hearing explanations in the hall, George put his head out of the dining-room and said, "Oh! hullo!"

"Hullo," said Wimsey, trying to find room for his belongings on an overladen hat-stand, and eventually disposing of them on the handle of a perambulator. "Thought I'd just come and look you up. Hope I'm not in the way."

"Of course not. Jolly good of you to penetrate to .this ghastly hole. Come in. Everything's in a beastly muddle as usual, but when you're poor you have to live like pigs. Sheila, here's Lord Peter Wimsey—you have met, haven't you?"

"Yes, of course, How nice of you to come round. Have you had dinner?"

"Yes, thanks."

"Coffee?"

"No, thanks, really—I've only just had some."

"Well," said George, "there's only whisky to offer you."

"Later on, perhaps, thanks, old man. Not just now. I've had a brandy. Never mix grape and grain."

"Wise man," said George, his brow clearing, since as a matter of fact, there was no whisky nearer than the public-house, and acceptance would have meant six-and-six, at least, besides the exertion of fetching it.

Sheila Fentiman drew an armchair forward, and

herself sat down on a low pouffe. She was a woman of thirty-five or so, and would have been very good-looking but for an appearance of worry and ill-health that made her look older than her age.

"It's a miserable fire," said George, gloomily, "is this all the coal there is?"

"I'm sorry," said Sheila, "she didn't fill it up properly this morning."

"Well, why can't you see that she does? It's always happening. If the scuttle isn't absolutely empty she seems to think she needn't bother about filling it up."

"I'll get some."

"No, it's all right. I'll go. But you ought to tell her about it."

"I will—I'm always telling her."

"The woman's no more sense than a hen. No—don't you go, Sheila—I won't have you carrying coal."

"Nonsense," said his wife, rather acidly. "What a hypocrite you are, George. It's only because there's somebody here that you're so chivalrous all at once."

"Here, let me," said Wimsey, desperately, "I like fetching coal. Always loved coal as a kid. Anything grubby or noisy. Where is it? Lead me to it!"

Mrs. Fentiman released the scuttle, for which George and Wimsey politely struggled. In the end they all went out together to the inconvenient bin in the back yard, Wimsey quarrying the coal, George receiving it in the scuttle and the lady lighting them with a long candle, insecurely fixed in an enamel candle-stick several sizes too large.

"And tell Mrs. Crickett," said George, irritably sticking to his grievance, "that she must fill that scuttle up properly every day."

"I'll try. But she hates being spoken to. I'm always afraid she'll give warning."

"Well, there are other charwomen, I suppose?"

"Mrs. Crickett is very honest."

"I know; but that's not everything. You could easily find one if you took the trouble."

"Well, I'll see about it. But why don't *you* speak to Mrs. Crickett? I'm generally out before she gets here."

"Oh, yes, I know. You needn't keep on rubbing it in about your having to go out to work. You don't suppose I *enjoy* it, do you? Wimsey can tell you how I feel about it."

"Don't be so silly, George. Why is it, Lord Peter, that men are so cowardly about speaking to servants?"

"It's the woman's job to speak to servants," said George, "no business of mine."

"All right—I'll speak, and you'll have to put up with the consequences."

"There won't *be* any consequences, my dear, if

you do it tactfully. I can't think why you want to make all this fuss."

"Right-oh, I'll be as tactful as I can. You don't suffer from charladies, I suppose, Lord Peter?"

"Good lord, no!" interrupted George. "Wimsey lives decently. They don't know the dignified joys of hard-upness in Piccadilly."

"I'm rather lucky," said Wimsey, with that apologetic air which seems forced on anybody accused of too much wealth. "I have an extraordinarily faithful and intelligent man who looks after me like a mother."

"Daresay he knows when he's well off," said George, disagreeably.

"I dunno. I believe Bunter would stick to me whatever happened. He was my N.C.O. during part of the War, and we went through some roughish bits together, and after the whole thing was over I hunted him up and took him on. He was in service before that, of course, but his former master was killed and the family broken up, so he was quite pleased to come along. I don't know what I should do without Bunter now."

"Is that the man who takes the photographs for you when you are on a crime-hunt?" suggested Sheila, hurriedly seizing on this, as she hoped, non-irritant topic.

"Yes. He's a great hand with a camera. Only drawback is that he's occasionally immured in the dark-room and I'm left to forage for myself. I've got a telephone extension through to him. 'Bunter?'—'Yes, my lord!'—'Where are my dress studs?'—'In the middle section of the third small right-hand drawer of the dressing-cabinet, my lord.'—'Bunter!'—'Yes, my lord.'—'Where have I put my cigarette case?'—'I fancy I observed it last on the piano, my lord.'—'Bunter!'—'Yes, my lord!' —'I've got into a muddle with my white tie.'— 'Indeed, my lord?'—'Well, can't you do anything about it?'—'Excuse me, my lord, I am engaged in the development of a plate.'—'To hell with the plate!'—'Very good, my lord.'—'Bunter—stop— don't be precipitate—finish the plate and then come and tie my tie.'—'Certainly, my lord.' And then I have to sit about miserably till the infernal plate is fixed, or whatever it is. Perfect slave in my own house—that's what I am."

Sheila laughed.

"You look a very happy and well-treated slave. Are you investigating anything just now?"

"Yes. In fact—there you are again—Bunter has retired into photographic life for the evening. I haven't a roof to cover me. I have been wandering round like the what d'you call it bird, which has no feet——"

"I'm sorry you were driven to such desperation as to seek asylum in our poverty-stricken hovel," said George, with a sour laugh.

Wimsey began to wish he had not come. Mrs. Fentiman looked vexed.

"You needn't answer that," she said, with an effort to be light, "there *is* no answer."

"I'll send it to Aunt Judith of 'Rosie's Weekly Bits,'" said Wimsey. "A makes a remark to which there is no answer. What is B to do?"

"Sorry," said George, "my conversation doesn't seem to be up to standard. I'm forgetting all my civilized habits. You'd better go on and pay no attention to me."

"What's the mystery on hand now?" asked Sheila, taking her husband at his word.

"Well, actually it's about this funny business of the old General's will," said Wimsey. "Murbles suggested I should have a look into the question of the survivorship."

"Oh, do you think you can really get it settled?"

"I hope so very much. But it's a very fine-drawn business—may resolve itself into a matter of seconds. By the way, Fentiman, were you in the Bellona smoking-room at all during the morning of Armistice Day?"

"So *that's* what you've come about. Why didn't you say so? No, I wasn't. And what's more, I don't know anything at all about it. And why that infuriating old hag of a Dormer woman couldn't make a decent, sensible will while she was about it, I don't know. Where was the sense of leaving all

86

those wads of money to the old man, when she knew perfectly well he was liable to peg out at any moment. And then, if he did die, handing the whole lot over to the Dorland girl, who hasn't an atom of claim on it? She might have had the decency to think about Robert and us a bit."

"Considering how rude you were to her and Miss Dorland, George, I wonder she even left you the seven thousand."

"What's seven thousand to her? Like a five-pound note to any ordinary person. An insult, I call it. I daresay I was rude to her, but I jolly well wasn't going to have her think I was sucking up to her for her money."

"How inconsistent you are, George. If you didn't want the money, why grumble about not getting it?"

"You're always putting me in the wrong. You know I don't mean that. I *didn't* want the money —but the Dorland girl was always hinting that I did, and I ticked her off. I didn't know anything about the confounded legacy, and I didn't want to. All I mean is, that if she did want to leave anything to Robert and me, she might have made it more than a rotten seven thousand apiece."

"Well! don't grumble at it. It would be uncommonly handy at the moment."

"I know—isn't that exactly what I'm saying? And now the old fool makes such a silly will that

I don't know whether I'm to get it or not. I can't even lay hands on the old Governor's two thousand. I've got to sit here and twiddle my thumbs while Wimsey goes round with a tape measure and a tame photographer to see whether I'm entitled to my own grandfather's money!"

"I know it's frightfully trying, darling. But I expect it'll all come right soon. It wouldn't matter if it weren't for Dougal MacStewart."

"Who's Dougal MacStewart?" inquired Wimsey, suddenly alert. "One of our old Scottish families, by the name. I fancy I have heard of him. Isn't he an obliging, helpful kind of chap, with a wealthy friend in the City?"

"Frightfully obliging," said Sheila, grimly. "He simply forces his acquaintances on one. He——"

"Shut up, Sheila," interrupted her husband, rudely. "Lord Peter doesn't want to know all the sordid details of our private affairs."

"Knowing Dougal," said Wimsey, "I daresay I could give a guess at them. Some time ago you had a kind offer of assistance from our friend Mac-Stewart. You accepted it to the mild tune of—what was it?"

"Five hundred," said Sheila.

"Five hundred. Which turned out to be three-fifty in cash and the rest represented by a little honorarium to his friend in the City who advanced

the money in so trustful a manner without security. When was that?"

"Three years ago—when I started that tea-shop
in Kensington."

"Ah, yes. And when you couldn't quite manage
that sixty per cent per month or whatever it was,
owing to trade depression, the friend in the City
was obliging enough to add the interest to the
principal, at great inconvenience to himself—and
so forth. The MacStewart way is familiar to me.
What's the demd total now, Fentiman, just out of
curiosity?"

"Fifteen hundred by the thirtieth," growled
George, "if you must know."

"I warned George—" began Sheila, unwisely.

"Oh, you always know what's best! Anyhow, it
was your tea business. I told you there was no
money in it, but women always think they can
run things on their own nowadays."

"I know, George. But it was MacStewart's interest that swallowed up the profits. You know I
wanted you to borrow the money from Lady
Dormer."

"Well, I wasn't going to, and that's flat. I told
you so at the time."

"Well, but look here," said Wimsey, "you're
perfectly all right about MacStewart's fifteen hundred, anyway, whichever way the thing goes. If
General Fentiman died before his sister, you get

seven thousand; if he died after her, you're certain of his two thousand, by the will. Besides, your brother will no doubt make a reasonable arrangement about sharing the money he gets as residuary legatee. Why worry?"

"Why? Because here's this infernal legal rigamarole tying the thing up and hanging it out till God knows when, and I can't touch anything."

"I know, I know," said Wimsey, patiently, "but all you've got to do is to go to Murbles and get him to advance you the money on your expectations. You can't get away with less than two thousand, whatever happens, so he'll be perfectly ready to do it. In fact, he's more or less bound to settle your just debts for you, if he's asked."

"That's just what I've been telling you, George," said Mrs. Fentiman, eagerly.

"Of course, you *would* be always telling me things. You never make mistakes, do you? And suppose the thing goes into Court and we get let in for thousands of pounds in fees and things, Mrs. Clever, eh?"

"I should leave it to your brother to go into Court, if necessary," said Wimsey, sensibly. "If he wins, he'll have plenty of cash for fees, and if he loses, you'll still have your seven thousand. You go to Murbles—he'll fix you up. Or, tell you what! ——I'll get hold of friend MacStewart and see if I can't arrange to get the debt transferred to me.

He won't consent, of course, if he knows it's me, but I can probably do it through Murbles. Then we'll threaten to fight him on the ground of extortionate interest and so on. We'll have some fun with it."

"Dashed good of you, but I'd rather not, thanks."

"Just as you like. But anyway, go to Murbles. He'll get it squared up for you. Anyhow, I don't think there will be any litigation about the will. If we can't get to the bottom of the survivorship question, I should think you and Miss Dorland would be far better advised to come to a settlement out of Court. It would probably be the fairest way in any case. Why don't you?"

"Why? Because the Dorland female wants her pound of flesh. That's why!"

"Does she? What kind of woman is she?"

"One of these modern, Chelsea women. Ugly as sin and hard as nails. Paints things—ugly, skinny prostitutes with green bodies and no clothes on. I suppose she thinks if she can't be a success as a woman she'll be a half-baked intellectual. No wonder a man can't get a decent job these days with these hard-mouthed, cigarette-smoking females all over the place, pretending they're geniuses and business women and all the rest of it."

"Oh, come, George! Miss Dorland isn't doing anybody out of a job; she couldn't just sit there all day being Lady Dormer's companion. What's the harm in her painting things?"

"Why couldn't she be a companion? In the old days, heaps of unmarried women were companions, and let me tell you, my dear girl, they had a much better time than they have now, with all this jazzing and short skirts and pretending to have careers. The modern girl hasn't a scrap of decent feeling or sentiment about her. Money—money and notoriety, that's all she's after. That's what we fought the war for—and that's what we've come back to!"

"George, do keep to the point. Miss Dorland doesn't jazz—"

"I am keeping to the point. I'm talking about modern women. I don't say Miss Dorland in particular. But you *will* go taking everything personally. That's just like a woman. You can't argue about things in general—you always have to bring it down to some one little personal instance. You will side-track."

"I wasn't side-tracking. We started to talk about Miss Dorland."

"You said a person couldn't just be somebody's companion, and I said that in the old days plenty of nice women were companions and had a jolly good time——"

"I don't know about that."

"Well, I do. They did. And they learned to be

decent companions to their husbands, too. Not always flying off to offices and clubs and parties like they are now. And if you think men like that sort of thing, I can tell you candidly, my girl, they don't. They hate it."

"Does it matter? I mean, one doesn't have to bother so much about husband-hunting to-day."

"Oh, no! Husbands don't matter at all, I suppose, to you advanced women. Any man will do, as long as he's got money——"

"Why do you say 'you' advanced women? I didn't say *I* felt that way about it. I don't *want* to go out to work——"

"There you go. Taking everything to yourself. I *know* you don't want to work. I know it's only because of the damned rotten position I'm in. You needn't keep on about it. I know I'm a failure. Thank your stars, Wimsey, that when you marry you'll be able to support your wife."

"George, you've no business to speak like that. I didn't mean that at all. You said——"

"I know what I said, but you took it all the wrong way. You always do. It's no good arguing with a woman. No—that's enough. For God's sake don't start all over again. I want a drink. Wimsey, you'll have a drink. Sheila, tell that girl of Mrs. Munns's to go round for half a bottle of Johnny Walker."

"Couldn't you get it yourself, dear? Mrs. Munns

doesn't like us sending her girl. She was frightfully disagreeable last time."

"How can I go? I've taken my boots off. You do make such a fuss about nothing. What does it matter if old Mother Munns does kick up a shindy? She can't eat you."

"No," put in Wimsey. "But think of the corrupting influence of the jug-and-bottle department on Mrs. Munns's girl. I approve of Mrs. Munns. She has a motherly heart. I myself will be the St. George to rescue Mrs. Munns's girl from the Blue Dragon. Nothing shall stop me. No, don't bother to show me the way. I have a peculiar instinct about pubs. I can find one blindfold in a pea-souper with both hands tied behind me."

Mrs. Fentiman followed him to the front door. "You mustn't mind what George says to-night. His tummy is feeling rotten and it makes him irritable. And it has been so worrying about this wretched money business."

"That's all right," said Wimsey. "I know exactly. You should see me when my tummy's upset. Took a young woman out the other night— lobster mayonnaise, meringues and sweet champagne—her choice—oh, lord!"

He made an eloquent grimace and departed in the direction of the public house.

When he returned, George Fentiman was standing on the doorstep.

"I say, Wimsey—I do apologize for being so bloody rude. It's my filthy temper. Rotten bad form. Sheila's gone up to bed in tears, poor kid. All my fault. If you knew how this damnable situation gets on my nerves—though I know there's no excuse . . ."

" 'S quite all right," said Wimsey. "Cheer up. It'll all come out in the wash."

"My wife—" began George again.

"She's damned fine, old man. But what it is, you both want a holiday."

"We do, badly. Well, never say die. I'll see Murbles, as you suggest, Wimsey."

Bunter received his master that evening with a prim smirk of satisfaction.

"Had a good day, Bunter?"

"Very gratifying indeed, I thank your lordship. The prints on the walking-stick are indubitably identical with those on the sheet of paper you gave me."

"They are, are they? That's something. I'll look at 'em to-morrow, Bunter—I've had a tiring evening."

CHAPTER VIII

Lord Peter Leads Through Strength

AT ELEVEN O'CLOCK THE NEXT MORNING, LORD
Peter Wimsey, unobtrusively attired in a navy-blue
suit and dark gray tie, suitable for a house of
mourning, presented himself at the late Lady
Dormer's house in Portman Square.

"Is Miss Dorland at home?"

"I will inquire, sir."

"Kindly give her my card and ask if she can
spare me a few moments."

"Certainly, my lord. Will your lordship be good
enough to take a seat?"

The man departed, leaving his lordship to cool
his heels in a tall, forbidding room, with long
crimson curtains, a dark red carpet and mahogany
furniture of repellent appearance. After an interval of nearly fifteen minutes, he reappeared, bearing a note upon a salver. It was briefly worded:

"Miss Dorland presents her compliments to Lord
Peter Wimsey, and regrets that she is not able to
grant him an interview. If, as she supposes, Lord
Peter has come to see her as the representative of

96

Major and Captain Fentiman, Miss Dorland requests that he will address himself to Mr. Pritchard, solicitor, of Lincoln's Inn, who is dealing, on her behalf, with all matters connected with the will of the late Lady Dormer."

"Dear me," said Wimsey to himself, "this looks almost like a snub. Very good for me, no doubt. Now I wonder—" He read the note again. "Murbles must have been rather talkative. I suppose he told Pritchard he was putting me on to it. Very indiscreet of Murbles and not like him."

The servant still stood mutely by, with an air of almost violently disassociating himself from all commentary.

"Thank you," said Wimsey. "Would you be good enough to say to Miss Dorland that I am greatly obliged to her for this information."

"Very good, my lord."

"And perhaps you would kindly call me a taxi."

"Certainly, my lord."

Wimsey entered the taxi with all the dignity he could summon, and was taken to Lincoln's Inn.

Mr. Pritchard was nearly as remote and snubbing in his manner as Miss Dorland. He kept Lord Peter waiting for twenty minutes and received him glacially, in the presence of a beady-eyed clerk.

"Oh, good morning," said Wimsey, affably. "Excuse my callin' on you like this. More regular to do it through Murbles, I s'pose—nice old boy,

Murbles, isn't he? But I always believe in goin' as direct to the point as may be. Saves time, what?"

Mr. Pritchard bowed his head and asked how he might have the pleasure of serving his lordship.

"Well, it's about this Fentiman business. Survivorship and all that. Nearly said survival. Appropriate, what? You might call the old General a survival, eh?"

Mr. Pritchard waited without moving.

"I take it Murbles told you I was lookin' into the business, what? Tryin' to check up on the timetable and all that?"

Mr. Pritchard said neither yea nor nay, but placed his fingers together and sat patiently.

"It's a bit of a problem, you know. Mind if I smoke? Have one yourself?"

"I am obliged to you, I never smoke in business hours."

"Very proper. Much more impressive. Puts the wind up the clients, what? Well, now, I just thought I'd let you know that it's likely to be a close-ish thing. Very difficult to tell to a minute or so, don't you know. May turn out one way— may turn out the other—may turn completely bafflin' and all that. You get me?"

"Indeed?"

"Oh, yes, absolutely. P'raps you'd like to hear how far I've got." And Wimsey recounted the history of his researches at the Bellona, in so far as the

98

evidence of the commissionaires and the hall-porter were concerned. He said nothing of his interview with Penberthy, nor of the odd circumstances connected with the unknown Oliver, confining himself to stressing the narrowness of the time-limits between which the General must be presumed to have arrived at the Club. Mr. Pritchard listened without comment. Then he said:

"And what, precisely, have you come to suggest?"

"Well, what I mean to say is, don't you know, wouldn't it be rather a good thing if the parties could be got to come to terms? Give and take, you see—split the doings and share the proceeds? After all, half a million's a goodish bit of money— quite enough for three people to live on in a quiet way, don't you think? And it would save an awful lot of trouble and—ahem—lawyers' fees and things."

"Ah!" said Mr. Pritchard. "I may say that I have been expecting this. A similar suggestion was made to me earlier by Mr. Murbles, and I then told him that my client preferred not to entertain the idea. You will permit me to add, Lord Peter, that the reiteration of this proposal by you, after your employment to investigate the facts of the case in the interests of the other party, has a highly suggestive appearance. You will excuse me, perhaps, if I warn you further that your whole course of conduct in this matter seems to me open to a very undesirable construction."

Wimsey flushed.

"You will perhaps permit *me*, Mr. Pritchard, to inform you that I am not 'employed' by anybody. I have been requested by Mr. Murbles to ascertain the facts. They are rather difficult to ascertain, but I have learned one very important thing from you this afternoon. I am obliged to you for your assistance. Good morning."

The beady-eyed clerk opened the door with immense politeness.

"Good morning," said Mr. Pritchard.

"Employed, indeed," muttered his lordship, wrathfully. "Undesirable construction. I'll construct him. That old brute knows something, and if he knows something, that shows there's something to be known. Perhaps he knows Oliver; I shouldn't wonder. Wish I'd thought to spring the name on him and see what he said. Too late now. Never mind, we'll get Oliver. Bunter didn't have any luck with those 'phone calls, apparently. I think I'd better get hold of Charles."

He turned into the nearest telephone-booth and gave the number of Scotland Yard. Presently an official voice replied, of which Whimsey inquired whether Detective-Inspector Parker was available. A series of clicks proclaimed that he was being put through to Mr. Parker, who presently said: "Hullo!"

"Hullo, Charles. This is Peter Wimsey. Look here, I want you to do something for me. It isn't a criminal job, but it's important. A man calling himself Oliver rang up a number in Mayfair at a little after nine on the night of November 10th. Do you think you could get that call traced for me?"

"Probably. What was the number?"

Wimsey gave it.

"Right you are, old chap. I'll have it looked up and let you know. How goes it? Anything doing?"

"Yes—rather a cozy little problem—nothing for you people—as far as I know, that is. Come round one evening and I'll tell you about it, unofficially."

"Thanks very much. Not for a day or two, though. We're run off our feet with this crate business."

"Oh, I know—the gentleman who was sent from Sheffield to Euston in a crate, disguised as York hams. Splendid. Work hard and you will be happy. No, thanks, my child, I don't want another twopenn'orth—I'm spending the money on sweets. Cheerio, Charles!"

The rest of the day Wimsey was obliged to pass in idleness, so far as the Bellona Club affair was concerned. On the following morning he was rung up by Parker.

"I say—that 'phone-call you asked me to trace."

"Yes?"

"It was put through at 9.13 p.m. from a public call-box at Charing Cross Underground Station."

"Oh, hell!—the operator didn't happen to notice the bloke, I suppose?"

"There isn't an operator. It's one of those automatic boxes."

"Oh!—may the fellow who invented them fry in oil. Thanks frightfully, all the same. It gives us a line on the direction, anyhow."

"Sorry I couldn't do better for you. Cheerio!"

"Oh, cheer-damnably-ho!" retorted Wimsey, crossly, slamming the receiver down. "What is it, Bunter?"

"A district messenger, with a note, my lord."

"Ah,—from Mr. Murbles. Good. This may be something. Yes. Tell the boy to wait, there's an answer." He scribbled quickly. "Mr. Murbles has got an answer to that cabman advertisement, Bunter. There are two men turning up at six o'clock, and I'm arranging to go down and interview them."

"Very good, my lord."

"Let's hope that means we get a move on. Get me my hat and coat—I'm running round to Dover Street for a moment."

Robert Fentiman was there when Wimsey called, and welcomed him heartily.

"Any progress?"

"Possibly a little this evening. I've got a line on those cabmen. I just came round to ask if you could let me have a specimen of old Fentiman's fist."

"Certainly. Pick what you like. He hasn't left much about. Not exactly the pen of a ready writer. There are a few interesting notes of his early campaigns, but they're rather antiques by this time."

"I'd rather have something quite recent."

"There's a bundle of cancelled cheques here, if that would do."

"It would do particularly well—I want something with figures in it if possible. Many thanks. I'll take these."

"How on earth is his handwriting going to tell you when he pegged out?"

"That's my secret, dash it all! Have you been down to Gatti's?"

"Yes. They seem to know Oliver fairly well by sight, but that's all. He lunched there fairly often, say once a week or so, but they don't remember seeing him since the eleventh. Perhaps he's keeping under cover. However, I'll haunt the place a bit and see if he turns up."

"I wish you would. His call came from a public box, so that line of inquiry peters out."

"Oh, bad luck!"

"You've found no mention of him in any of the General's papers?"

"Not a thing, and I've gone through every bit and scrap of writing in the place. By the way, have you seen George lately?"

"Night before last. Why?"

"He seems to me to be in rather a queer state. I went round last night and he complained of being spied on or something."

"Spied on?"

"Followed about. Watched. Like the blighters in the 'tec stories. Afraid all this business is getting on his nerves. I hope he doesn't go off his rocker or anything. It's bad enough for Sheila as it is. Decent little woman."

"Thoroughly decent," agreed Wimsey, "and very fond of him."

"Yes. Works like billy-oh to keep the home together and all that. Tell you the truth, I don't know how she puts up with George. Of course, married couples are always sparring and so on, but he ought to behave before other people. Dashed bad form, being rude to your wife in public. I'd like to give him a piece of my mind."

"He's in a beastly galling position," said Wimsey. "She's his wife and she's got to keep him, and I know he feels it very much."

"Do you think so? Seems to me he takes it rather as a matter of course. And whenever the poor little woman reminds him of it, he thinks she's rubbing it in."

"Naturally, he hates being reminded of it. And I've heard Mrs. Fentiman say one or two sharp things to him."

"I daresay. Trouble with George is, he can't control himself. He never could. A fellow ought to pull himself together and show a bit of gratitude. He seems to think that because Sheila has to work like a man she doesn't want the courtesy and—you know, tenderness and so on—that a woman ought to get."

"It always gives me the pip," said Wimsey, "to see how rude people are when they're married. I suppose it's inevitable. Women are funny. They don't seem to care half so much about a man's being honest and faithful—and I'm sure your brother's all that—as for their opening doors and saying thank-you. I've noticed it lots of times."

"A man ought to be just as courteous after marriage as he was before," declared Robert Fentiman, virtuously.

"So he ought, but he never is. Possibly there's some reason we don't know about," said Wimsey. "I've asked people, you know—my usual inquisitiveness—and they generally just grunt and say that their wives are sensible and take their affection for granted. But I don't believe women ever get sensible, not even through prolonged association with their husbands."

The two bachelors wagged their heads, solemnly.

"Well, I think George is behaving like a sweep," said Robert, "but perhaps I'm hard on him. We never did get on very well. And anyhow, I don't pretend to understand women. Still, this persecution-mania, or whatever it is, is another thing. He ought to see a doctor."

"He certainly ought. We must keep an eye on him. If I see him at the Bellona I'll have a talk to him and try and get out of him what it's all about."

"You won't find him at the Bellona. He's avoided it since all this unpleasantness started. I think he's out hunting for jobs. He said something about one of those motor people in Great Portland Street wanting a salesman. He can handle a car pretty well, you know."

"I hope he gets it. Even if it doesn't pay very well it would do him a world of good to have something to do with himself. Well, I'd better be amblin' off. Many thanks, and let me know if you get hold of Oliver."

"Oh, rather!"

Wimsey considered a few moments on the doorstep, and then drove straight down to New Scotland Yard, where he was soon ushered in to Detective-Inspector Parker's office.

Parker, a square-built man in the late thirties, with the nondescript features which lend themselves so excellently to detective purposes, was possibly Lord Peter's most intimate—in some ways his only intimate friend. The two men had worked out many cases together and each respected the other's qualities, though no two characters could have been more widely different. Wimsey was the Roland of the combination—quick, impulsive, careless and an artistic jack-of-all-trades. Parker was the Oliver—cautious, solid, painstaking, his mind a blank to art and literature and exercising itself, in spare moments, with Evangelical theology. He was the one person who was never irritated by Wimsey's mannerisms, and Wimsey repaid him with a genuine affection foreign to his usually detached nature.

"Well, how goes it?"

"Not so bad. I want you to do something for me."

"Not really?"

"Yes, really, blast your eyes. Did you ever know me when I didn't? I want you to get hold of one of your handwriting experts to tell me if these two fists are the same."

He put on the table, on the one hand the bundle of used cheques, and on the other the sheet of paper he had taken from the library at the Bellona Club.

Parker raised his eyebrows.

"That's a very pretty set of finger-prints you've been pulling up there. What is it? Forgery?"

"No nothing of that sort. I just want to know

whether the same bloke who wrote these cheques made the notes too."

Parker rang a bell, and requested the attendance of Mr. Collins.

"Nice fat sums involved, from the looks of it," he went on, scanning the sheet of notes appreciatively. "£150,000 to R., £300,000 to G.—lucky G.—who's G? £20,000 here and £50,000 there. Who's your rich friend, Peter?"

"It's that long story I was going to tell you about when you'd finished your crate problem."

"Oh, is it? Then I'll make a point of solving the crate without delay. As a matter of fact, I'm rather expecting to hear something about it before long. That's why I'm here, dancing attendance on the 'phone. Oh, Collins, this is Lord Peter Wimsey, who wants very much to know whether these two handwritings are the same."

The expert took up the paper and the cheques and looked them over attentively.

"Not a doubt about it, I should say, unless the forgery has been astonishingly well done. Some of the figures, especially, are highly characteristic. The fives, for instance and the threes, and the fours, made all of a piece with the two little loops. It's a very old-fashioned handwriting, and made by a very old man, in not too-good health, especially this sheet of notes. Is that the old Fentiman who died the other day?"

"Well, it is, but you needn't shout about it. It's just a private matter."

"Just so. Well, I should say you need have no doubt about the authenticity of that bit of paper, if that's what you are thinking of."

"Thanks. That's precisely what I do want to know. I don't think there's the slightest question of forgery or anything. In fact, it was just whether we could look on these rough notes as a guide to his wishes. Nothing more."

"Oh, yes, if you rule out forgery, I'd answer for it any day that the same person wrote all these cheques and the notes."

"That's fine. That checks up the results of the finger-print test too. I don't mind telling you, Charles," he added, when Collins had departed, "that this case is getting damned interesting."

At this point the telephone rang, and Parker, after listening for some time, ejaculated "Good work!" and then, turning to Wimsey,

"That's our man. They've got him. Excuse me if I rush off. Between you and me, we've pulled this off rather well. It may mean rather a big thing for me. Sure we can't do anything else for you? Because I've got to get to Sheffield. See you to-morrow or next day."

He caught up his coat and hat and was gone. Wimsey made his own way out and sat for a long time at home, with Bunter's photographs of the Bellona Club before him, thinking.

At six o'clock, he presented himself at Mr. Murbles' Chambers in Staple Inn. The two taxi-drivers had already arrived and were seated, well on the edges of their chairs, politely taking old sherry with the solicitor.

"Ah!" said Mr. Murbles, "this is a gentleman who is interested in the inquiry we are making. Perhaps you would have the goodness to repeat to him what you have already told me. I have ascertained enough," he added, turning to Wimsey, "to feel sure that these are the right drivers, but I should like you to put any questions you wish yourself. This gentleman's name is Swain, and his story should come first, I think."

"Well, sir," said Mr. Swain, a stout man of the older type of driver, "you was wanting to know if anybody picked up an old gent in Portman Square the day before Armistice Day rahnd abaht the afternoon. Well, sir, I was goin' slow through the Square at 'arf-past four, or it might be a quarter to five on that 'ere day, when a footman comes out of a 'ouse—I couldn't say the number for certain, but it was on the east side of the Square as might be abaht the middle—and 'e makes a sign for me to stop. So I draws up, and presently a very old gent comes out. Very thin, 'e was, an' muffled up, but I see 'is legs and they was very thin and 'e

110

looked abaht a 'undred an' two by 'is face, and
walked with a stick. 'E was upright, for such a very
old gent, but 'e moved slow and rather feeble. An
old milingtary gent, I thought 'e might be—'e 'ad
that way of speakin', if you understand me, sir.
So the footman tells me to drive 'im to a number
in 'Arley Street."

"Do you remember it?"

Swain mentioned a number which Wimsey
recognized as Penberthy's.

"So I drives 'im there. And 'e asks me to ring the
bell for 'im, and when the young man comes to the
door to ask if the doctor could please see General
Fenton, or Fennimore or some such name, sir."

"Was it Fentiman, do you think?"

"Well, yes, it might 'ave been Fentiman. I think
it was. So the young man comes back and says,
yes, certingly, so I 'elps the old gent aht. Very
faint, 'e seemed, and a very bad colour, sir, breathin'
'eavy and blue-like abaht the lips. Pore old b . . .,
I thinks, beggin' yer pardon, sir, 'e won't be 'ere
long, I thinks. So we 'elps him up the steps into the
'ouse and 'e gives me my fare and a shilling for
myself, and that's the last I see of 'im, sir."

"That fits in all right with what Penberthy said,"
agreed Wimsey. "The General felt the strain of his
interview with his sister and went straight round
to see him. Right. Now how about this other part
of the business?"

111

"Well," said Mr. Murbles, "I think this gentleman, whose name is—let me see—Hinkins—yes. I think Mr. Hinkins picked up the General when he left Harley Street."

"Yes, sir," agreed the other driver, a smartish-looking man with a keen profile and a sharp eye. "A very old gentleman, like what we've 'eard described, took my taxi at this same number in 'Arley Street at 'alf past five. I remember the day very well, sir; November 10th it was, and I remember it because, after I done taking him where I'm telling you, my magneto started to give trouble, and I didn't 'ave the use of the 'bus on Armistice Day, which was a great loss to me, because that's a good day as a rule. Well, this old military gentleman gets in, with his stick and all, just as Swain says, only I didn't notice him looking particular ill, though I see he was pretty old. Maybe the doctor would have given him something to make him better."

"Very likely," said Mr. Murbles.

"Yes, sir. Well, he gets in, and he says, 'Take me to Dover Street,' he says, but if you was to ask me the number, sir, I'm afraid I don't rightly remember, because, you see, we never went there after all."

"Never went there?" cried Wimsey.

"No, sir. Just as we was comin' out into Cavendish Square, the old gentleman puts his head out

112

and says, 'Stop!' So I stops, and I see him wavin' his hand to a gentleman on the pavement. So this other one comes up, and they has a few words together and then the old——"

"One moment. What was this other man like?"

"Dark and thin, sir, and looked about forty. He had on a gray suit and overcoat and a soft hat, with a dark handkerchief round his throat. Oh, yes, and he had a small black mustache. So the old gentleman says, 'Cabman,' he says, just like that, 'cabman, go back up to Regent's Park and drive round till I tell you to stop.' So the other gentleman gets in with him, and I goes back and drives round the Park, quiet-like, because I guessed they wanted to 'ave a bit of a talk. So I goes twice round, and as we was going round the third time, the younger gentleman sticks 'is 'ed out and says, 'Put me down at Gloucester Gate.' So I puts him down there, and the old gentleman says, 'Good-bye, George, bear in mind what I have said.' So the gentleman says, 'I will, sir,' and I see him cross the road, like as if he might be going up Park Street."

Mr. Murbles and Wimsey exchanged glances.

"And then where did you go?"

"Then, sir, the fare says to me, 'Do you know the Bellona Club in Piccadilly?' he says. So I says, 'Yes, sir.' "

"The Bellona Club?"

"Yes, sir."

113

"What time was that?"

"It might be getting on for half-past six, sir. I'd been driving very slow, as I tells you, sir. So I takes him to the Club, like he said, and in he goes, and that's the last I see of him, sir."

"Thanks very much," said Wimsey. "Did he seem to be at all upset or agitated when he was talking to the man he called George?"

"No, sir, I couldn't say that. But I thought he spoke a bit sharp-like. What you might call telling him off, sir."

"I see. What time did you get to the Bellona?"

"I should reckon it was about twenty minutes to seven, sir, or just a little bit more. There was a tidy bit of traffic about. Between twenty and ten to seven, as near as I can recollect."

"Excellent. Well, you have both been very helpful. That will be all to-day, but I'd like you to leave your names and addresses with Mr. Murbles, in case we might want some sort of a statement from either of you later on. And—er——"

A couple of Treasury notes crackled. Mr. Swain and Mr. Hinkins made suitable acknowledgment and departed, leaving their addresses behind them.

"So he went back to the Bellona Club. I wonder what for?"

"I think I know," said Wimsey. "He was accustomed to do any writing or business there, and I fancy he went back to put down some notes as to

114

what he meant to do with the money his sister was leaving him. Look at this sheet of paper, sir. That's the General's handwriting, as I've proved this after-noon, and those are his finger-prints. And the initials R and G probably stand for Robert and George, and these figures for the various sums he meant to leave them."

"That appears quite probable. Where did you find this?"

"In the end bay of the library at the Bellona, sir, tucked inside the blotting-paper."

"The writing is very weak and straggly."

"Yes—quite tails off, doesn't it. As though he had come over faint and couldn't go on. Or perhaps he was only tired. I must go down and find out if anybody saw him there that evening. But Oliver, curse him! is the man who knows. If only we could get hold of Oliver."

"We've had no answer to our third question in the advertisement. I've had letters from several drivers who took old gentlemen to the Bellona that morning, but none of them corresponds with the General. Some had check overcoats, and some had whiskers and some had bowler hats or beards —whereas the General was never seen without his silk hat and had, of course, his old-fashioned long military mustache."

"I wasn't hoping for very much from that. We might put in another ad. in case anybody picked him up from the Bellona on the evening or night of the 10th, but I've got a feeling that this infernal Oliver probably took him away in his own car. If all else fails, we'll have to get Scotland Yard on to Oliver."

"Make careful inquiries at the Club, Lord Peter. It now becomes more than possible that somebody saw Oliver there and noticed them leaving together."

"Of course. I'll go along there at once. And I'll put the advertisement in as well. I don't think we'll rope in the B.B.C. It is so confoundedly public."

"That," said Mr. Murbles, with a look of horror, "would be *most* undesirable."

Wimsey rose to go. The solicitor caught him at the door.

"Another thing we ought really to know," he said, "is what General Fentiman was saying to Captain George."

"I've not forgotten that," said Wimsey, a little uneasily. "We shall have—oh, yes—certainly—of course, we shall have to know that."

CHAPTER IX

Knave High

"LOOK HERE, WIMSEY," SAID CAPTAIN CULYER OF
the Bellona Club, "aren't you ever going to get
finished with this investigation or whatever it is?
The members are complaining, really they are, and
I can't blame them. They find your everlasting
questions an intolerable nuisance, old boy, and I
can't stop them from thinking there must be something behind it. People complain that they can't get
attention from the porters or the waiters because
you're everlastingly there chatting, and if you're
not there, you're hanging round the bar, eaves-
dropping. If this is your way of conducting an
inquiry tactfully, I wish you'd do it tactlessly. It's
becoming thoroughly unpleasant. And no sooner
do you stop it, than the other fellow begins."

"What other fellow?"

"That nasty little skulking bloke who's always
turning up at the service door and questioning the
staff."

"I don't know anything about *him*," replied
Wimsey, "I never heard of him. I'm sorry I'm being

a bore and all that, though I swear I couldn't be worse than some of your other choice specimens in that line, but I've hit a snag. This business—quite in your ear, old bean—isn't as straightforward as it looks on the surface. That fellow Oliver whom I mentioned to you——"

"He's not known here, Wimsey."

"No, but he may have been here."

"If nobody saw him, he can't have been here."

"Well, then, where did General Fentiman go to when he left. And when did he leave. That's what I want to know. Dash it all, Culyer, the old boy's a landmark. We know he came back here on the evening of the 10th—the driver brought him to the door, Rogers saw him come in and two members noticed him in the smoking room just before seven. I have a certain amount of evidence that he went into the library. And he can't have stayed long, because he had his outdoor things with him. Somebody *must* have seen him leave. It's ridiculous. The servants aren't all blind. I don't like to say it, Culyer, but I can't help thinking that somebody has been bribed to hold his tongue . . . Of course, I knew that would annoy you, but how can you account for it? Who's this fellow you say has been hangin' round the kitchen?"

"I came across him one morning when I'd been down to see about the wine. By the way, there's a case of Margaux come in which I'd like your

118

opinion on some day. The fellow was talking to Babcock, the wine steward, and I asked him pretty sharply what he wanted. He thanked me, and said he had come from the railway to enquire after a packing-case that had gone astray, but Babcock, who is a very decent fellow, told me afterwards that he had been working the pump-handle about old Fentiman, and I gathered he had been pretty liberal with his cash. I thought you were up to your tricks again."

"Is the fellow a sahib?"

"Good God, no. Looks like an attorney's clerk or something. A nasty little tout."

"Glad you told me. I shouldn't wonder if he's the snag I'm up against. Probably Oliver coverin' his tracks."

"Do you suspect this Oliver of something wrong?"

"Well—I rather think so. But I'm damned if I know quite what. I think he knows something about old Fentiman that we don't. And of course he knows how he spent the night, and that's what I'm after."

"What the devil does it matter how he spent the night? He can't have been very riotous, at his age."

"It might throw some light on the time he arrived in the morning, mightn't it?"

"Oh—Well, all I can say is, I hope to God you'll hurry up and finish with it. This Club's becoming a perfect bear-garden. I'd almost rather have the police in."

"Keep hopin'. You may get 'em yet."

"You don't mean that, seriously?"

"I'm never serious. That's what my friends dislike about me. Honestly, I'll try and make as little row as I can. But if Oliver is sending his minions to corrupt your staff and play old harry with my investigations, it's going to make it damned awkward. I wish you'd let me know if the fellow turns up again. I'd like to cast my eye over him."

"All right, I will. And do clear out now, there's a good fellow."

"I go," said Wimsey, "my tail well tucked down between my legs and a flea in each ear. Oh! by the way——"

"*Well?*" (in an exasperated tone).

"When did you last see George Fentiman?"

"Not for donkey's years. Not since it happened."

"I thought not. Oh, and by the way——"

"*Yes?*"

"Robert Fentiman was actually staying in the Club at the time, wasn't he?"

"Which time?"

"The time it happened, you ass."

"Yes, he was. But he's living at the old man's place now."

"I know, thanks. But I wondered whether— Where does he live when he isn't in town?"

120

"Out at Richmond, I think. In rooms, or something."

"Oh, does he? Thanks very much. Yes, I really will go. In fact, I've practically gone."

He went. He never stopped going till he came to Finsbury Park. George was out, and so, of course, was Mrs. Fentiman, but the charwoman said she had heard the Captain mention he was going down to Great Portland Street. Wimsey went in pursuit. A couple of hours spent lounging round show-rooms and talking to car-demonstrators, nearly all of whom were, in one manner or another, his dear old pals, resulted in the discovery that George Fentiman was being taken on by the Walmisley-Hubbard outfit for a few weeks to show what he could do.

"Oh, he'll do you all right," said Wimsey, "he's a damn fine driver. Oh, lord, yes! *He's* all right."

"He looks a bit nervy," said the particular dear old pal attached to the Walmisley-Hubbard show. "Wants bucking up, what? That reminds me. What about a quick one?"

Wimsey submitted to a mild quick one and then wandered back to look at a new type of clutch. He spun out this interesting interview till one of the Walmisley-Hubbard "shop 'buses" came in with Fentiman at the wheel.

"Hullo!" said Wimsey, "trying her out?"

"Yes. I've got the hang of her all right."

121

"Think you could sell her?" asked the old pal.

"Oh, yes. Soon learn to show her off. She's a jolly decent 'bus."

"That's good. Well, I expect you're about ready for a quick one. How about it, Wimsey?"

They had a quick one together. After this, the dear old pal remembered that he must buzz off because he'd promised to hunt up a customer.

"You'll turn up to-morrow, then?" he said to George. "There's an old bird down at Malden wants to have a trial trip. I can't go, so you can have a shot at him. All right?"

"Perfectly."

"Righty-ho! I'll have the 'bus ready for you at eleven. Cheer-most-frightfully-ho! So long."

"Little sunbeam about the house, isn't he?" said Wimsey.

"Rather. Have another?"

"I was thinking, how about lunch? Come along with me if you have nothing better to do."

George accepted and put forward the names of one or two restaurants.

"No," said Wimsey, "I've got a fancy to go to Gatti's to-day, if you don't mind."

"Not at all, that will do splendidly. I've seen Murbles, by the bye, and he's prepared to deal with the MacStewart man. He thinks he can hold him off till it's all settled up—if it ever *is* settled."

"That's good," said Wimsey, rather absently.

"And I'm damned glad about this chance of a job," went on George. "If it turns out any good, it'll make things a lot easier—in more than one way."

Wimsey said heartily that he was sure it would, and then relapsed into a silence unusual with him, which lasted all the way to the Strand.

At Gatti's he left George in a corner while he went to have a chat with the head-waiter, emerging from the interview with a puzzled expression which aroused even George's curiosity, full as he was of his own concerns.

"What's up? Isn't there anything you can bear to eat?"

"It's all right. I was just wondering whether to have *moules marinières* or not."

"Good idea."

Wimsey's face cleared, and for some time they absorbed mussels from the shell with speechless, though not altogether silent, satisfaction.

"By the way," said Wimsey, suddenly, "you never told me that you had seen your grandfather the afternoon before he died."

George flushed. He was struggling with a particularly elastic mussel, firmly rooted to the shell, and could not answer for a moment.

"How on earth?—confound it all, Wimsey, are *you* behind this infernal watch that's being kept on me?"

123

"Watch?"

"Yes, I said watch. I call it a damn rotten thing to do. I never thought for a moment you had anything to do with it."

"I haven't. Who's keeping a watch on you?"

"There's a fellow following me about. A spy. I'm always seeing him. I don't know whether he's a detective or what. He looks like a criminal. He came down in the 'bus with me from Finsbury Park this morning. He was after me all day yesterday. He's probably about now. I won't have it. If I catch sight of him again I shall knock his dirty little head off. Why should I be followed and spied on? I haven't done anything. And now *you* begin."

"I swear I've nothing to do with anybody following you about. Honestly, I haven't. I wouldn't employ a man, anyway, who'd let a bloke see that he was being followed. No. When I start huntin' you, I shall be as silent and stealthy as a gas-leak. What's this incompetent blood-hound like to look at?"

"Looks like a tout. Small, thin, with his hat pulled down over his eyes and an old rain-coat with the collar turned up. And a very blue chin."

"Sounds like a stage detective. He's a silly ass anyway."

"He gets on my nerves."

"Oh, all right. Next time you see him, punch his head."

124

"But what does he want?"

"How should I know? What have you been doing?"

"Nothing, of course. I tell you, Wimsey, I believe there's some sort of conspiracy going on to get me into trouble, or do away with me, or something. I can't stand it. It's simply damnable. Suppose this fellow starts hanging round the Walmisley-Hubbard place. Look nice, won't it, for their salesman to have a 'tec on his heels all the time? Just as I hoped things were coming right——"

"Bosh!" said Wimsey. "Don't let yourself get rattled. It's probably all imagination, or just a coincidence."

"It isn't. I wouldn't mind betting he's outside in the street now."

"Well, then, we'll settle his hash when we get outside. Give him in charge for annoying you. Look here, forget him for a bit. Tell me about the old General. How did he seem, that last time you saw him?"

"Oh, he seemed fit enough. Crusty, as usual."

"Crusty, was he? What about?"

"Private matters," said George, sullenly.

Wimsey cursed himself for having started his questions tactlessly. The only thing now was to retrieve the situation as far as possible.

"I'm not at all sure," he said, "that relations shouldn't all be painlessly put away after three-score and ten. Or at any rate segregated. Or have their tongues sterilized, so that they can't be poisonously interferin'."

"I wish they were," growled George. "The old man—damn it all, I know he was in the Crimea, but he's no idea what a real war's like. He thinks things can go on just as they did half a century ago. I daresay he never did behave as I do. Anyway, I know he never had to go to his wife for his pocket-money, let alone having the inside gassed out of him. Coming preaching to me—and I couldn't say anything, because he was so confoundedly old, you know."

"Very trying," murmured Wimsey, sympathetically.

"It's all so damned unfair," said George. "Do you know," he burst out, the sense of grievance suddenly overpowering his wounded vanity, "the old devil actually threatened to cut me out of the miserable little bit of money he had to leave me if I didn't 'reform my domestic behaviour.' That's the way he talked. Just as if I was carrying on with another woman or something. I know I did have an awful row with Sheila one day, but of course I didn't mean half I said. She knows that, but the old man took it all seriously."

"Half a moment," broke in Wimsey, "did he say all this to you in the taxi that day?"

"Yes, he did. A long lecture, all about the purity

126

and courage of a good woman, driving round and round Regent's Park. I had to promise to turn over a new leaf and all that. Like being back at one's prep. school."

"But didn't he mention anything about the money Lady Dormer was leaving to him?"

"Not a word. I don't suppose he knew about it."

"I think he did. He'd just come from seeing her, you know, and I've a very good idea she explained matters to him then."

"Did she? Well, that rather explains it. I thought he was being very pompous and stiff about it. He said what a responsibility money was, you know, and how he would like to feel that anything he left to me was being properly used and all that. And he rubbed it in about my not having been able to make good for myself—that was what got my goat—and about Sheila. Said I ought to appreciate a good woman's love more, my boy, and cherish her and so on. As if I needed him to tell me that. But of course, if he knew he was in the running for this half-million, it makes rather a difference. By jove, yes! I expect he would feel a bit anxious at the idea of leaving it all to a fellow he looked on as a waster."

"I wonder he didn't mention it."

"You didn't know grandfather. I bet he was thinking over in his mind whether it wouldn't be better to give my share to Sheila, and he was sounding me, to see what sort of disposition I'd got. The old fox! Well, I did my best to put myself in a good light, of course, because just at the moment I didn't want to lose my chance of his two thousand. But I don't think he found me satisfactory. I say," went on George, with rather a sheepish laugh, "perhaps it's just as well he popped off when he did. He might have cut me off with a shilling, eh?"

"Your brother would have seen you through in any case."

"I suppose he would. Robert's quite a decent sort, really, though he does get on one's nerves so."

"Does he?"

"He's so thick-skinned; the regular unimaginative Briton. I believe Robert would cheerfully go through another five years of war and think it all a very good rag. Robert was proverbial, you know, for never turning a hair. I remember Robert, at that ghastly hole at Carency, where the whole ground was rotten with corpses—ugh!—potting those swollen great rats for a penny a time, and laughing at them. Rats. Alive and putrid with what they'd been feeding on. Oh, yes. Robert was thought a damn good soldier."

"Very fortunate for him," said Wimsey.

"Yes. He's the same sort as grandfather. They liked each other. Still, grandfather was very decent about me. A beast, as the schoolboy said, but a just beast. And Sheila was a great favourite of his."

128

"Nobody could help liking her," said Wimsey, politely.

Lunch ended on a more cheerful note than it had begun. As they came out into the street, however, George Fentiman glanced round uneasily. A small man in a buttoned-up overcoat and with a soft hat pulled down over his eyes, was gazing into the window of a shop near at hand.

George strode up to him.

"Look here, you!" he said. 'What the devil do you mean by following me about? You clear off, d'you hear?"

"I think you are mistaken, sir," said the man, quietly enough. "I have never seen you before."

"Haven't you, by jove? Well, *I've* seen *you* hanging about, and if you do it any more, I'll give you something to remember me by. D'you hear?"

"Hullo!" said Wimsey, who had stopped to speak to the commissionaire, "what's up?—Here, you, wait a moment!"

But at sight of Wimsey, the man had slipped like an eel among the roaring Strand traffic, and was lost to view.

George Fentiman turned to his companion triumphantly.

"Did you see that? That lousy little beggar! Made off like a shot when I threatened him. That's the fellow who's been dogging me about for three days."

"I'm sorry," said Wimsey, "but it was not your prowess, Fentiman. It was my awful aspect that drove him away. What is it about me? Have I a front like Jove to threaten and command? Or am I wearing a repulsive tie?"

"He's gone, anyway."

"I wish I'd had a better squint at him. Because I've got a sort of idea that I've seen those lovely features before, and not so long ago, either. Was this the face that launched a thousand ships? No, I don't think it was that."

"All I can say is," said George, "that if I see him again, I'll put such a face on him that his mother won't know him."

"Don't do that. You might destroy a clue. I— wait a minute—I've got an idea. I believe it must be the same man who's been haunting the Bellona and asking questions. Oh, hades! and we've let him go. And I'd put him down in my mind as Oliver's minion. If ever you see him again, Fentiman, freeze on to him like grim death. I want to talk to him."

CHAPTER X

Lord Peter Forces A Card

"HULLO!"

"Is that you, Wimsey? Hullo! I say, is that Lord Peter Wimsey. Hullo! I must speak to Lord Peter Wimsey. Hullo!"

"All right. I've said hullo. Who're you? And what's the excitement?"

"It's me. Major Fentiman. I say—*is* that Wimsey?"

"Yes. Wimsey speaking. What's up?"

"I can't hear you."

"Of course you can't if you keep on shouting. This is Wimsey. Good morning. Stand three inches from the mouthpiece and speak in an ordinary voice. Do not say hullo! To recall the operator, depress the receiver *gently* two or three times."

"Oh, shut up! don't be an ass. I've seen Oliver."

"Have you, where?"

"Getting into a train at Charing Cross."

"Did you speak to him?"

"No—it's maddening. I was just getting my ticket when I saw him passing the barrier. I tore down after him. Some people got in my way, curse

131

them. There was a Circle train standing at the platform. He bolted in and they clanged the doors. I rushed on, waving and shouting, but the train went out. I cursed like anything."

"I bet you did. How very sickening."

"Yes, wasn't it? I took the next train——"

"What for?"

"Oh, I don't know. I thought I might spot him on a platform somewhere."

"What a hope! You didn't think to ask where he'd booked for?"

"No. Besides, he probably got the ticket from an automatic."

"Probably. Well, it can't be helped, that's all. He'll probably turn up again. You're sure it was he?"

"Oh, dear, yes. I couldn't be mistaken. I'd know him anywhere. I thought I'd just let you know."

"Thanks awfully. It encourages me extremely. Charing Cross seems to be a haunt of his. He 'phoned from there on the evening of the tenth, you know."

"So he did."

"I'll tell you what we'd better do, Fentiman. The thing is getting rather serious. I propose that you should go and keep an eye on Charing Cross station. I'll get hold of a detective——"

"A police detective?"

"Not necessarily. A private one would do. You

132

and he can go along and keep watch on the station for, say a week. You must describe Oliver to the detective as best you can, and you can watch turn and turn about."

"Hang it all, Wimsey—it'll take a lot of time. I've gone back to my rooms at Richmond. And besides, I've got my own duties to do."

"Yes, well, while you're on duty the detective must keep watch."

"It's a dreadful grind, Wimsey." Fentiman's voice sounded dissatisfied.

"It's half a million of money. Of course, if you're not keen——"

"I *am* keen. But I don't believe anything will come of it."

"Probably not; but it's worth trying. And in the meantime, I'll have another watch kept at Gatti's."

"At Gatti's?"

"Yes. They know him there. I'll send a man down——"

"But he never comes there now."

"Oh, but he may come again. There's no reason why he shouldn't. We know now that he's in town, and not gone out of the country or anything. I'll tell the management that he's wanted for an urgent business matter, so as not to make unpleasantness."

"They won't like it."

"Then they'll have to lump it."

"Well, all right. But, look here—*I'll* do Gatti's."

"That won't do. We want you to identify him at Charing Cross. The waiter or somebody can do the identifying at Gatti's. You say they know him."

"Yes, of course they do. But——"

"But what?—By the way, which waiter is it you spoke to. I had a talk with the head man there yesterday, and he didn't seem to know anything about it."

"No—it wasn't the head waiter. One of the others. The plump, dark one."

"All right. I'll find the right one. Now, will you see to the Charing Cross end?"

"Of course—if you really think it's any good."

"Yes, I do. Right you are. I'll get hold of the 'tec and send him along to you, and you can arrange with him."

"Very well."

"Cheerio!"

Lord Peter rang off and sat for a few moments, grinning to himself. Then he turned to Bunter.

"I don't often prophesy, Bunter, but I'm going to do it now. Your fortune told by hand or cards. Beware of the dark stranger. That sort of thing."

"Indeed, my lord?"

"Cross the gipsy's palm with silver. I see Mr. Oliver. I see him taking a journey in which he will cross water. I see trouble. I see the ace of spaces—upside-down, Bunter."

"And what then, my lord?"

"Nothing. I look into the future and I see a blank. The gipsy has spoken."

"I will bear it in mind, my lord."

"Do. If my prediction is not fulfilled, I will give you a new camera. And now I'm going round to see that fellow who calls himself Sleuths Incorporated, and get him to put a good man on to keep watch at Charing Cross. And after that, I'm going down to Chelsea and I don't quite know when I shall be back. You'd better take the afternoon off. Put me out some sandwiches or something, and don't wait up if I'm late."

Wimsey disposed quickly of his business with Sleuths Incorporated, and then made his way to a pleasant little studio overlooking the river at Chelsea. The door, which bore a neat label "Miss Marjorie Phelps," was opened by a pleasant-looking young woman with curly hair and a blue overall heavily smudged with clay.

"Lord Peter! How nice of you. Do come in."

"Shan't I be in the way?"

"Not a scrap. You don't mind if I go on working."

"Rather not."

"You could put the kettle on and find some food if you liked to be really helpful. I just want to finish up this figure."

"That's fine. I took the liberty of bringing a pot of Hybla honey with me."

"What sweet ideas you have! I really think you are one of the nicest people I know. You don't talk rubbish about art, and you don't want your hand held, and your mind always turns on eating and drinking."

"Don't speak too soon. I don't want my hand held, but I did come here with an object."

"Very sensible of you. Most people come without any."

"And stay interminably."

"They do."

Miss Phelps cocked her head on one side and looked critically at the little dancing lady she was modeling. She had made a line of her own in pottery figurines, which sold well and were worth the money.

"That's rather attractive," said Wimsey.

"Rather pretty-pretty. But it's a special order, and one can't afford to be particular. I've done a Christmas present for you, by the way. You'd better have a look at it, and if you think it offensive we'll smash it together. It's in that cupboard."

Wimsey opened the cupboard and extracted a little figure about nine inches high. It represented a young man in a flowing dressing-gown, absorbed in the study of a huge volume held on his knee. The portrait was life-like. He chuckled.

"It's damned good, Marjorie. A very fine bit of modeling. I'd love to have it. You aren't multiplying it too often, I hope? I mean, it won't be on sale at Selfridges?"

"I'll spare you that. I thought of giving one to your mother."

"That'll please her no end. Thanks ever so. I shall look forward to Christmas, for once. Shall I make some toast?"

"Rather!"

Wimsey squatted happily down before the gas-fire, while the modeler went on with her work. Tea and figurine were ready almost at the same moment, and Miss Phelps, flinging off her overall, threw herself luxuriously into a battered arm-chair by the hearth.

"And what can I do for you?"

"You can tell me all you know about Miss Ann Dorland."

"Ann Dorland? Great heavens! You haven't fallen for Ann Dorland, have you? I've heard she's coming into a lot of money."

"You have a perfectly disgusting mind, Miss Phelps. Have some more toast. Excuse me licking my fingers. I have not fallen for the lady. If I had, I'd manage my affairs without assistance. I haven't even seen her. What's she like?"

"To look at?"

"Among other things."

"Well, she's rather plain. She has dark, straight hair, cut in a bang across the forehead and bobbed

—like a Flemish page. Her forehead is broad and she has a square sort of face and a straight nose— quite good. Also, her eyes are good—gray, with nice heavy eyebrows, not fashionable a bit. But she has a bad skin and rather sticky-out teeth. And she's dumpy."

"She's a painter, isn't she?"

"M'm—well! she paints."

"I see. A well-off amateur with a studio."

"Yes. I will say that old Lady Dormer was very decent to her. Ann Dorland, you know, is some sort of far-away distant cousin on the female side of the Fentiman family, and when Lady Dormer first got to hear of her she was an orphan and incredibly poverty-stricken. The old lady liked to have a bit of young life about the house, so she took charge of her, and the wonderful thing is that she didn't try to monopolize her. She let her have a big place for a studio and bring in any friends she liked and go about as she chose—in reason, of course."

"Lady Dormer suffered a good deal from oppressive relations in her own youth," said Wimsey.

"I know, but most old people seem to forget that. I'm sure Lady Dormer had time enough. She must have been rather unusual. Mind you, I didn't know her very well, and I don't really know a great deal about Ann Dorland. I've been there, of course. She gave parties—rather incompetently. And she comes round to some of our studios from time to time. But she isn't really one of us."

"Probably one has to be really poor and hard-working to be that."

"No. You, for instance, fit in quite well on the rare occasions when we have the pleasure. And it doesn't matter not being able to paint. Look at Bobby Hobart and his ghastly daubs—he's a perfect dear and everybody loves him. I think Ann Dorland must have a complex of some kind. Complexes explain so much, like the blessed word hippopotamus."

Wimsey helped himself lavishly to honey and looked receptive.

"I think really," went on Miss Phelps, "that Ann ought to have been something in the City. She has brains, you know. She'd run anything awfully well. But she isn't creative. And then, of course, so many of our little lot seem to be running love-affairs. And a continual atmosphere of hectic passion is very trying if you haven't got any of your own."

"Has Miss Dorland a mind above hectic passion?"

"Well, no. I daresay she would quite have liked —but nothing ever came of it. Why are you interested in having Ann Dorland analyzed?"

"I'll tell you some day. It isn't just vulgar curiosity."

"No, you're very decent as a rule, or I wouldn't

be telling you all this. I think, really, Ann has a sort of fixed idea that she couldn't ever possibly attract any one, and so she's either sentimental and tiresome, or rude and snubbing, and our crowd does hate sentimentality and simply can't bear to be snubbed. Ann's rather pathetic, really. As a matter of fact, I think she's gone off art a bit. Last time I heard about her, she had been telling some one she was going in for social service, or sick-nursing, or something of that kind. I think it's very sensible. She'd probably get along much better with the people who do that sort of thing. They're so much more solid and polite."

"I see. Look here, suppose I ever wanted to run across Miss Dorland accidentally on purpose—where should I be likely to find her?"

"You *do* seem thrilled about her! I think I should try the Rushworths. They go in rather for science and improving the submerged tenth and things like that. Of course, I suppose Ann's in mourning now, but I don't think that would necessarily keep her away from the Rushworths'. Their gatherings aren't precisely frivolous."

"Thanks very much. You're a mine of valuable information. And, for a woman, you don't ask many questions."

"Thank you for those few kind words, Lord Peter."

"I am now free to devote my invaluable attention to *your* concerns. What is the news? And who is in love with whom?"

"Oh, life is a perfect desert. Nobody is in love with me, and the Schlitzers have had a worse row than usual and separated."

"No!"

"Yes. Only, owing to financial considerations, they've got to go on sharing the same studio—you know, that big room over the mews. It must be very awkward having to eat and sleep and work in the same room with somebody you're being separated from. They don't even speak, and it's very awkward when you call on one of them and the other has to pretend not to be able to see or hear you."

"I shouldn't think one could keep it up under those circumstances."

"It's difficult. I'd have had Olga here, only she is so dreadfully bad-tempered. Besides, neither of them will give up the studio to the other."

"I see. But isn't there any third party in the case?"

"Yes—Ulric Fiennes, the sculptor, you know. But he can't have her at his place because his wife's there, and he's really dependent on his wife, because his sculping doesn't pay. And besides, he's at work on that colossal group for the Exhibition and he can't move it; it weighs about twenty tons. And if he went off and took Olga away, his wife would lock

141

him out of the place. It's very inconvenient being a sculptor. It's like playing the double-bass; one's so handicapped by one's baggage."

"True. Whereas, when you run away with me, we'll be able to put all the pottery shepherds and shepherdesses in a handbag."

"Of course. What fun it will be. Where shall we run to?"

"How about starting to-night and getting as far as Oddenino's and going on to a show—if you're not doing anything?"

"You are a loveable man, and I shall call you Peter. Shall we see 'Betwixt and Between?' "

"The thing they had such a job to get past the censor? Yes, if you like. Is it particularly obscene?"

"No, epicene, I fancy."

"Oh, I see. Well, I'm quite agreeable. Only I warn you that I shall make a point of asking you the meaning of all the risky bits in a very audible voice."

"That's your idea of amusement, is it?"

"Yes. It does make them so wild. People say 'Hush!' and giggle, and if I'm lucky I end up with a gorgeous row in the bar."

"Then I won't risk it. No. I'll tell you what I'd really love. We'll go and see 'George Barnwell' at the Elephant and have a fish-and-chips supper afterwards."

This was agreed upon, and was voted in retro-

142

spect a most profitable evening. It finished up with grilled kippers at a friend's studio in the early hours. Lord Peter returned home to find a note upon the hall-table.

"My lord,

The person from Sleuths Incorporated rang up to-day that he was inclined to acquiesce in your lordship's opinion, but that he was keeping his eye upon the party and would report further to-morrow. The sandwiches are on the dining-room table, if your lordship should require refreshment.

"Yours obediently,

"M. BUNTER."

"Cross the gipsy's palm with silver," said his lordship, happily, and rolled into bed.

CHAPTER XI

Lord Peter Clears Trumps

"SLEUTH'S INCORPORATED'S" REPORT, WHEN IT came, might be summed up as "Nothing doing and Major Fentiman convinced that there never will be anything doing; opinion shared by Sleuths Incorporated." Lord Peter's reply was: "Keep on watching and something will happen before the week is out."

His lordship was justified. On the fourth evening, "Sleuths Incorporated" reported again by telephone. The particular sleuth in charge of the case had been duly relieved by Major Fentiman at 6 P.M. and had gone to get his dinner. On returning to his post an hour later, he had been presented with a note left for him with the ticket-collector at the stair-head. It ran: "Just seen Oliver getting into taxi. Am following. Will communicate to refreshment-room. Fentiman." The sleuth had perforce to return to the refreshment room and hang about waiting for a further message. "But all the while, my lord, the second man I put on as instructed by you, my lord, was a-following the

Major unbeknownst." Presently a call was put through from Waterloo. "Oliver is on the Southampton train. I am following." The sleuth hurried down to Waterloo, found the train gone and followed on by the next. At Southampton he made inquiries and learned that a gentleman answering to Fentiman's description had made a violent disturbance as the Havre boat was just starting, and had been summarily ejected at the instance of an elderly man whom he appeared to have annoyed or attacked in some way. Further investigation among the Port authorities made it clear that Fentiman had followed this person down, made himself offensive on the train and been warned off by the guard, collared his prey again on the gangway and tried to prevent him from going aboard. The gentleman had produced his passport and pièces d'identité, showing him to be a retired manufacturer of the name of Postlethwaite, living at Kew. Fentiman had insisted that he was, on the contrary, a man called Oliver, address and circumstances unknown, whose testimony was wanted in some family matter. As Fentiman was unprovided with a passport and appeared to have no official authority for stopping and questioning travelers, and as his story seemed vague and his manner agitated, the local police had decided to detain Fentiman. Postlethwaite was allowed to proceed on his way, after leaving his address in England and his destination, which, as he contended, and as he produced papers and correspondence to prove, was Venice.

The sleuth went round to the police-station, where he found Fentiman, apoplectic with fury, threatening proceedings for false imprisonment. He was able to get him released, however, on bearing witness to Fentiman's identity and good faith, and after persuading him to give a promise to keep the peace. He had then reminded Fentiman that private persons were not entitled to assault or arrest peaceable people against whom no charge could be made, pointing out to him that his proper course, when Oliver denied being Oliver, would have been to follow on quietly and keep a watch on him, while communicating with Wimsey or Mr. Murbles or Sleuths Incorporated. He added that he was himself now waiting at Southampton for further instructions from Lord Peter. Should he follow to Venice, or send his subordinate, or should he return to London? In view of the frank behaviour of Mr. Postlethwaite, it seemed probable that a genuine mistake had been made as to identity, but Fentiman insisted that he was not mistaken.

Lord Peter, holding the trunk line, considered for a moment. Then he laughed.

"Where is Major Fentiman?" he asked.

"Returning to town, my lord. I have represented to him that I have now all the necessary information to go upon, and that his presence in Venice would only hamper my movements, now that he has made himself known to the party."

"Quite so. Well, I think you might as well send your man on to Venice, just in case it's a true bill. And listen" . . . He gave some further instructions, ending with: "And ask Major Fentiman to come and see me as soon as he arrives."

"Certainly, my lord."

"What price the gipsy's warning now?" said Lord Peter, as he communicated this piece of intelligence to Bunter.

Major Fentiman came round to the flat that afternoon, in a whirl of apology and indignation.

"I'm sorry, old man. It was damned stupid of me, but I lost my temper. To hear that fellow calmly denying that he had ever seen me or poor old grandfather, and coming out with his bits of evidence so pat, put my bristles up. Of course, I see now that I made a mistake. I quite realize that I ought to have followed him up quietly. But how was I to know that he wouldn't answer to his name?"

"But you ought to have guessed when he didn't, that either you had made a mistake or that he had some very good motive for trying to get away," said Wimsey.

"I wasn't accusing him of anything."

"Of course not, but he seems to have thought you were."

147

"But why?—I mean, when I first spoke to him, I just said, 'Mr. Oliver, I think?' And he said, 'You are mistaken.' And I said, 'Surely not. My name's Fentiman, and you knew my grandfather, old General Fentiman.' And he said he hadn't the pleasure. So I explained that we wanted to know where the old boy had spent the night before he died, and he looked at me as if I was a lunatic. That annoyed me, and I said I knew he was Oliver, and then he complained to the guard. And when I saw him just trying to hop off like that, without giving us any help, and when I thought about that half-million, it made me so mad I just collared him. 'Oh, no, you don't,' I said—and that was how the fun began, don't you see."

"I see perfectly," said Wimsey. "But don't *you* see, that if he really *is* Oliver and has gone off in that elaborate manner, with false passports and everything, he must have something important to conceal."

Fentiman's jaw dropped.

"You don't mean—you don't mean there's anything funny about the death? Oh! surely not."

"There must be something funny about Oliver, anyway, mustn't there? On your own showing?"

"Well, if you look at it that way, I suppose there must. I tell you what, he's probably got into some bother or other and is clearing out. Debt, or a

148

woman, or something. Of course that must be it. And I was beastly inconvenient popping up like that. So he pushed me off. I see it all now. Well, in that case, we'd better let him rip. We can't get him back, and I daresay he won't be able to tell us anything after all."

"That's possible, of course. But when you bear in mind that he seems to have disappeared from Gatti's, where you used to see him, almost immediately after the General's death, doesn't it look rather as though he was afraid of being connected up with that particular incident?"

Fentiman wriggled uncomfortably.

"Oh, but, hang it all! What could he have to do with the old man's death?"

"I don't know. But I think we might try to find out."

"How?"

"Well, we might apply for an exhumation order."

"Dig him up!" cried Fentiman, scandalized.

"Yes. There was no post-mortem, you know."

"No, but Penberthy knew all about it and gave the certificate."

"Yes; but at that time there was no reason to suppose that anything was wrong."

"And there isn't now."

"There are a number of peculiar circumstances, to say the least."

"There's only Oliver—and I may have been mistaken about him."

"But I thought you were so sure?"

"So I was. But—this is preposterous, Wimsey! Besides, think what a scandal it would make!"

"Why should it? You are the executor. You can make a private application and the whole thing can be done quite privately."

"Yes, but surely the Home Office would never consent, on such flimsy grounds."

"I'll see that they do. They'll know I wouldn't be keen on anything flimsy. Little bits of fluff were never in my line."

"Oh, do be serious. What reason can we give?"

"Quite apart from Oliver, we can give a very good one. We can say that we want to examine the contents of the viscera to see how soon the General died after taking his last meal. That might be of great assistance in solving the question of the survivorship. And the law, generally speaking, is nuts on what they call the orderly devolution of property."

"Hold on! D'you mean to say you can tell when a bloke died just by looking inside his tummy?"

"Not exactly, of course. But one might get an idea. If we found, that is, that he'd only that moment swallowed his brekker, it would show that he'd died not very long after arriving at the Club."

"Good lord!—that would be a poor look-out for me."

"It might be the other way, you know."

"I don't like it, Wimsey. It's very unpleasant. I wish to goodness we could compromise on it."

"But the lady in the case won't compromise. You know that. We've got to get at the facts somehow. I shall certainly get Murbles to suggest the exhumation to Pritchard."

"Oh, lord! What'll *he* do?"

"Pritchard? If he's an honest man and his client's an honest woman, they'll support the application. If they don't, I shall fancy they've something to conceal."

"I wouldn't put it past them. They're a low-down lot. But they can't do anything without my consent, can they?"

"Not exactly—at least, not without a lot of trouble and publicity. But if *you're* an honest man, you'll give your consent. *You've* nothing to conceal, I suppose?"

"Of course not. Still, it seems rather——"

"They suspect us already of some kind of dirty work," persisted Wimsey. "That brute Pritchard as good as told me so. I'm expecting every day to hear that he has suggested exhumation off his own bat. I'd rather we got in first with it."

"If that's the case, I suppose we must do it. But I can't believe it'll do a bit of good, and it's sure to get round and make an upheaval. Isn't there some other way—you're so darned clever——"

"Look here, Fentiman. Do you want to get at the facts? Or are you out to collar the cash by hook or by crook? You may as well tell me frankly which it is."

"Of course I want to get at the facts."

"Very well; I've told you the next step to take."

"Damn it all," said Fentiman, discontentedly; "I suppose it'll have to be done, then. But I don't know whom to apply to or how to do it."

"Sit down, then, and I'll dictate the letter for you."

From this there was no escape, and Robert Fentiman did as he was told, grumbling.

"There's George. I ought to consult him."

"It doesn't concern George, except indirectly. That's right. Now write to Murbles, telling him what you're doing and instructing him to let the other party know."

"Oughtn't we to consult about the whole thing with Murbles first?"

"I've already consulted Murbles, and he agrees it's the thing to do."

"These fellows would agree to anything that means fees and trouble."

"Just so. Still, solicitors are necessary evils. Is that finished?"

"Yes."

"Give the letters to me; I'll see they're posted. Now you needn't worry any more about it. Murbles and I will see to it all, and the detective-wallah is looking after Oliver all right, so you can run away and play."

"You——"

"I'm sure you're going to say how good it is of me to take all this trouble. Delighted, I'm sure. It's of no consequence. A pleasure, in fact. Have a drink."

The disconcerted major refused the drink rather shortly and prepared to depart.

"You mustn't think I'm not grateful, Wimsey, and all that. But it is rather unseemly."

"With all your experience," said Wimsey, "you oughtn't to be so sensitive about corpses. We've seen many things much unseemlier than a nice, quiet little resurrection in a respectable cemetery."

"Oh, I don't care twopence about the corpse," retorted the Major, "but the thing doesn't look well. That's all."

"Think of the money," grinned Wimsey, shutting the door of the flat upon him.

He returned to the library, balancing the two letters in his hand. "There's many a man now walking the streets of London," said he, "through not clearing trumps. Take these letters to the post, Bunter. And Mr. Parker will be dining here with me this evening. We will have a *perdrix aux choux*

153

and a savoury to follow, and you can bring up two bottles of the *Chambertin*."

"Very good, my lord."

Wimsey's next proceeding was to write a little confidential note to an official whom he knew very well at the Home Office. This done, he returned to the telephone and asked for Penberthy's number.

"That you, Penberthy? . . . Wimsey speaking. . . . Look here, old man, you know that Fentiman business? . . . Yes, well, we're applying for an exhumation."

"For a *what?*"

"An exhumation. Nothing to do with your certificate. We know *that's* all right. It's just by way of getting a bit more information about when the beggar died."

He outlined his suggestion.

"Think there's something in it?"

"There might be, of course."

"Glad to hear you say that. I'm a layman in these matters, but it occurred to me as a good idea."

"Very ingenious."

"I always was a bright lad. You'll have to be present, of course."

"Am I to do the autopsy?"

"If you like. Lubbock will do the analysis."

"Analysis of what?"

"Contents of the doings. Whether he had kidneys on toast or eggs and bacon and all that."

154

"Oh, I see. I doubt if you'll get much from that, after all this time."

"Possibly not, but Lubbock had better have a squint at it."

"Yes, certainly. As I gave the certificate, it's better that my findings should be checked by somebody."

"Exactly. I knew you'd feel that way. You quite understand about it?"

"Perfectly. Of course, if we'd had any idea there was going to be all this uncertainty, I'd have made a post-mortem at the time."

"Naturally you would. Well, it can't be helped. All in the day's work. I'll let you know when it's to be. I suppose the Home Office will send somebody along. I thought I ought just to let you know about it."

"Very good of you. Yes. I'm glad to know. Hope nothing unpleasant will come out."

"Thinking of your certificate?"

"Oh, well—no—I'm not worrying much about that. Though you never know, of course. I was thinking of that rigour, you know. Seen Captain Fentiman lately?"

"Yes. I didn't mention—"

"No. Better not, unless it becomes absolutely necessary. Well, I'll hear from you later, then?"

"That's the idea. Good-bye."

That day was a day of incident.

About four o'clock a messenger arrived, panting, from Mr. Murbles. (Mr. Murbles refused to have his chambers desecrated by a telephone.) Mr. Murbles' compliments, and would Lord Peter be good enough to read this note and let Mr. Murbles have an immediate answer.

The note ran:

"Dear Lord Peter,

In re Fentiman deceased. Mr. Pritchard has called. He informs me that his client is now willing to compromise on a division of the money if the Court will permit. Before I consult my client, Major Fentiman, I should be greatly obliged by your opinion as to how the investigation stands at present.

Yours faithfully,
Jno. Murbles."

Lord Peter replied as follows:

"Dear Mr. Murbles,

Re Fentiman deceased. Too late to compromise now, unless you are willing to be party to a fraud. I warned you, you know. Robert has applied for exhumation. Can you dine with me at 8?

P. W."

Having sent this off, his lordship rang for Bunter.

"Bunter, as you know, I seldom drink champagne. But I am inclined to do so now. Bring a glass for youself as well."

The cork popped merrily, and Lord Peter rose to his feet.

"Bunter," said he, "I give you a toast. The triumph of Instinct over Reason!"

CHAPTER XII

Lord Peter Turns A Trick

DETECTIVE-INSPECTOR PARKER CAME TO DINNER encircled in a comfortable little halo of glory. The Crate Mystery had turned out well and the Chief Commissioner had used expressions suggestive of promotion in the immediate future. Parker did justice to his meal and, when the party had adjourned to the library, gave his attention to Lord Peter's account of the Bellona affair with the cheerful appreciation of a connoisseur sampling a vintage port. Mr. Murbles, on the other hand, grew more and more depressed as the story was unfolded.

"And what do you think of it?" inquired Wimsey.

Parker opened his mouth to reply, but Mr. Murbles was beforehand with him.

"This Oliver appears to be a very elusive person," said he.

"Isn't he?" agreed Wimsey, dryly. "Almost as elusive as the famous Mrs. Harris. Would it altogether surprise you to learn that when I asked a few discreet questions at Gatti's, I discovered not only that nobody there had the slightest recollection of Oliver, but that no inquiries about him had ever been made by Major Fentiman?"

"Oh, dear me!" said Mr. Murbles.

"You forced Fentiman's hand very ingeniously by sending him down with your private sleuth to Charing Cross," remarked Parker, approvingly.

"Well, you see, I had a feeling that unless we did something pretty definite, Oliver would keep vanishing and reappearing like the Cheshire Cat, whenever our investigations seemed to be taking an awkward turn."

"You are intimating, if I understand you rightly," said Mr. Murbles, "that this Oliver has no real existence."

"Oliver was the carrot on the donkey's nose," said Peter, "my noble self being cast for the part of the donkey. Not caring for the rôle, I concocted a carrot of my own, in the person of Sleuths Incorporated. No sooner did my trusting sleuth depart to his lunch than, lo and behold! the hue and cry is off again after Oliver. Away goes friend Fentiman—and away goes Sleuth Number Two, who was there all the time, neatly camouflaged, to keep his eye on Fentiman. Why Fentiman should have gone to the length of assaulting a perfect stranger and accuse him of being Oliver, I don't know. I fancy his passion for thoroughness made him over-reach himself a bit there."

159

"But what exactly has Major Fentiman been doing?" asked Mr. Murbles. "This is a very painful business, Lord Peter. It distresses me beyond words. Do you suspect him of—er—?"

"Well," said Wimsey, "I knew *something* odd had happened, you know, as soon as I saw the General's body—when I pulled the *Morning Post* away so easily from his hands. If he had really died clutching it, the rigour would have made his clutch so tight that one would have had to pry the fingers open to release it. And then, that knee-joint!"

"I didn't quite follow about that."

"Well, you know that when a man dies, rigour begins to set in after a period of some hours, varying according to the cause of death, temperature of the room and a lot of other conditions. It starts in the face and jaw and extends gradually over the body. Usually it lasts about twenty-four hours and then passes off again in the same order in which it started. But if, during the period of rigidity, you loosen one of the joints by main force, then it doesn't stiffen again, but remains loose. Which is why, in a hospital, if the nurses have carelessly let a patient die and stiffen with his knees up, they call in the largest and fattest person on the staff to sit on the corpse's knees and break the joints loose again."

Mr. Murbles shuddered distastefully.

"So that, taking the loose knee-joint and the

160

general condition of the body together, it was obvious from the start that somebody had been tampering with the General. Penberthy knew that too, of course, only, being a doctor, he wasn't going to make any indiscreet uproar if he could avoid it. It doesn't pay, you know."

"I suppose not."

"Well, then, you came round to me, sir, and insisted on making the uproar. I warned you, you know, to let sleeping dogs lie."

"I wish you had spoken more openly."

"If I had, would you have cared to hush the matter up?"

"Well, well," said Mr. Murbles, polishing his eyeglasses.

"Just so. The next step was to try and find out what had actually happened to the General on the night of the 10th, and morning of the 11th. And the moment I got round to his flat I was faced with two entirely contradictory pieces of evidence. First, there was the story about Oliver, which appeared more or less remarkable upon the face of it. And secondly, there was Woodward's evidence about the clothes."

"What about them?"

"I asked him, you remember, whether anything at all had been removed from the clothes after he had fetched them away from the cloak-room at the Bellona, and he said, nothing. His memory as to

161

other points seemed pretty reliable, and I felt sure that he was honest and straightforward. So I was forced to the conclusion that, wherever the General had spent the night, he had certainly never set foot in the street the next morning."

"Why?" asked Mr. Murbles. "What did you expect to find on the clothes?"

"My dear sir, consider what day it was. November 11th. Is it conceivable that, if the old man had been walking in the streets as a free agent on Armistice Day, he would have gone into the Club without his Flanders poppy? A patriotic, military old bird like that? It was really unthinkable."

"Then where was he? And how did he get into the Club? He was there, you know."

"True; he *was* there—in a state of advanced rigour. In fact, according to Penberthy's account, which, by the way, I had checked by the woman who laid out the body later, the rigour was even then beginning to pass off. Making every possible allowance for the warmth of the room and so on, he must have been dead long before ten in the morning, which was his usual time for going to the Club."

"But, my dear lad, bless my soul, that's impossible. He couldn't have been carried in there dead. Somebody would have noticed it."

"So they would. And the odd thing is that nobody ever saw him arrive at all. What is more,

162

nobody saw him leave for the last time on the previous evening. General Fentiman—one of the best-known figures in the Club! And he seems to have become suddenly invisible. That won't do, you know."

"What is your idea, then? That he slept the night in the Club?"

"I think he slept a very peaceful and untroubled sleep that night—in the Club."

"You shock me inexpressibly," said Mr. Murbles. "I understand you to suggest that he died—"

"Some time the previous evening. Yes."

"But he couldn't have sat there all night in the smoking-room. The servants would have been bound to—er—notice him."

"Of course. But it was to somebody's interest to see that they didn't notice. Somebody who wanted it thought that he hadn't died till the following day, after the death of Lady Dormer."

"Robert Fentiman."

"Precisely."

"But how did Robert know about Lady Dormer?"

"Ah! That is a point I'm not altogether happy about. George had an interview with General Fentiman after the old man's visit to his sister. George denies that the General mentioned anything to him about the will, but then, if George was in the plot he naturally would deny it. I am rather concerned about George."

"What had he to gain?"

"Well, if George's information was going to make a difference of half a million to Robert, he would naturally expect to be given a share of the boodle, don't you think?"

Mr. Murbles groaned.

"Look here," broke in Parker, "this is a very pretty theory, Peter, but, allowing that the General died, as you say, on the evening of the tenth, where was the body? As Mr. Murbles says, it would have been a trifle noticeable if left about."

"No, no," said Mr. Murbles, seized with an idea. "Repellent as the whole notion is to me, I see no difficulty about that. Robert Fentiman was at that time living in the Club. No doubt the General died in Robert's bedroom and was concealed there till the next morning!"

Wimsey shook his head. "That won't work. I think the General's hat and coat and things were in Robert's bedroom, but the corpse couldn't have been. Think, sir. Here is a photograph of the entrance-hall, with the big staircase running up in full view of the front door and the desk and the bar-entrance. Would you risk carrying a corpse downstairs in the middle of the morning, with servants and members passing in and out continually? And the service stairs would be even worse.

164

They are right round the other side of the building, with continual kitchen traffic going on all the time. No. The body wasn't in Robert's bedroom."

"Where, then?"

"Yes, where? After all, Peter, we've got to make this story hold water."

Wimsey spread the rest of the photographs out upon the table.

"Look for yourselves," he said. "Here is the end bay of the library, where the General was sitting making notes about the money he was to inherit. A very nice, retired spot, invisible from the doorway, supplied with ink, blotter, writing-paper and every modern convenience, including the works of Charles Dickens elegantly bound in morocco. Here is a shot of the library taken from the smoking-room, clean through the ante-room and down the gangway—again a tribute to the convenience of the Bellona Club. Observe how handily the telephone cabinet is situated, in case—"

"The telephone cabinet?"

"Which, you will remember, was so annoyingly labeled 'Out of Order' when Wetheridge wanted to telephone. I can't find anybody who remembers putting up that notice, by the way."

"Good God, Wimsey. Impossible. Think of the risk."

"What risk? If anybody opened the door, there was old General Fentiman, who had gone in, not seeing the notice, and died of fury at not being able to get his call. Agitation acting on a weak heart and all that. Not *very* risky, really. Unless somebody was to think to inquire about the notice, and probably it wouldn't occur to any one in the excitement of the moment."

"You're an ingenious beast, Wimsey."

"Aren't I? But we can prove it. We're going down to the Bellona Club to prove it now. Half-past eleven. A nice, quiet time. Shall I tell you what we are going to find inside that cabinet?"

"Finger-prints?" suggested Mr. Murbles, eagerly.

"Afraid that's too much to hope for after all this time. What do you say, Charles?"

"I say we shall find a long scratch on the paint," said Parker, "where the foot of the corpse rested and stiffened in that position."

"Holed it in one, Charles. And that, you see, was when the leg had to be bent with violence in order to drag the corpse out."

"And as the body was in a sitting position," pursued Parker, "we shall, of course, find a seat inside the cabinet."

"Yes, and, with luck, we *may* find a projecting nail or something which caught the General's trouser-leg when the body was removed."

"And possibly a bit of carpet."

"To match the fragment of thread I got off the corpse's right boot? I hope so."

"Bless my soul," said Mr. Murbles. "Let us go at once. Really, this is most exciting. That is, I am profoundly grieved. I hope it is not as you say."

They hastened downstairs and stood for a few moments waiting for a taxi to pass. Suddenly Wimsey made a dive into a dark corner by the porch. There was a scuffle, and out into the light came a small man, heavily muffled in an overcoat, with his hat thrust down to his eyebrows in the manner of a stage detective. Wimsey unbonneted him with the air of a conjuror producing a rabbit from a hat.

"So it's you, is it? I thought I knew your face. What the devil do you mean by following people about like this?"

The man ceased struggling and glanced sharply up at him with a pair of dark, beady eyes.

"Do you think it wise, my lord, to use violence?"

"Who is it?" asked Parker.

"Pritchard's clerk. He's been hanging round George Fentiman for days. Now he's hanging round me. He's probably the fellow that's been hanging round the Bellona. If you go on like this, my man, you'll find yourself hanging somewhere else one of these days. Now, see here. Do you want me to give you in charge?"

"That is entirely as your lordship pleases," said the clerk, with a cunning sneer. "There is a police-

167

man just round the corner, if you wish to attract publicity."

Wimsey looked at him for a moment, and then began to laugh.

"When did you last see Mr. Pritchard? Come on, out with it! Yesterday? This morning? Have you seen him since lunch time?"

A shadow of indecision crossed the man's face.

"You haven't? I'm sure you haven't! Have you?"

"And why not, my lord?"

"You go back to Mr. Pritchard," said Wimsey, impressively, and shaking his captive gently by the coat-collar to add force to his words, "and if he doesn't countermand your instructions and call you off this sleuthing business (which, by the way, you do very amateurishly), I'll give you a fiver. See? Now, hop it. I know where to find you and you know where to find me. Good-night and may Morpheus hover over your couch and bless your slumbers. Here's our taxi."

CHAPTER XIII

Spades Are Trumps

IT WAS CLOSE ON ONE O'CLOCK WHEN THE THREE men emerged from the solemn portals of the Bellona Club. Mr. Murbles was very much subdued. Wimsey and Parker displayed the sober elation of men whose calculations have proved satisfactory. They had found the scratches. They had found the nail in the seat of the chair. They had even found the carpet. Moreover, they had found the origin of Oliver. Reconstructing the crime, they had sat in the end bay of the library, as Robert Fentiman might have sat, casting his eyes around him while he considered how he could best hide and cover up this extremely inopportune decease. They had noticed how the gilt lettering on the back of a volume caught the gleam from the shaded reading lamp. "Oliver Twist." The name, not consciously noted at the time, had yet suggested itself an hour or so later to Fentiman, when, calling up from Charing Cross, he had been obliged to invent a surname on the spur of the moment.

And, finally, placing the light, spare form of the

169

unwilling Mr. Murbles in the telephone cabinet, Parker had demonstrated that a fairly tall and strong man could have extricated the body from the box, carried it into the smoking-room and arranged it in the armchair by the fire, all in something under four minutes.

Mr. Murbles made one last effort on behalf of his client.

"There were people in the smoking-room all morning, my dear Lord Peter. If it were as you suggest, how could Fentiman have made sure of four, or even three minutes secure from observation while he brought the body in?"

"Were people there *all* morning, sir? Are you sure? Wasn't there just one period when one could be certain that everybody would be either out in the street or upstairs on the big balcony that runs along in front of the first-floor windows, looking out—and listening? It was Armistice Day, remember."

Mr. Murbles was horror-struck.

"The two-minutes' silence?—God bless my soul! How abominable! How—how blasphemous! Really, I cannot find words. This is the most disgraceful thing I ever heard of. At the moment when all our thoughts should be concentrated on the brave fellows who laid down their lives for us —to be engaged in perpetrating a fraud—an irreverent crime—"

"Half a million is a good bit of money," said Parker, thoughtfully.

"Horrible!" said Mr. Murbles.

"Meanwhile," said Wimsey, "what do you propose to do about it?"

"Do?" spluttered the old solicitor, indignantly. "Do?—Robert Fentiman will have to confess to this disgraceful plot immediately. Bless my soul! To think that I should be mixed up in a thing like this! He will have to find another man of business in future. We shall have to explain matters to Pritchard and apologize. I really hardly know how to tell him such a thing."

"I rather gather he suspects a good deal of it already," said Parker, mildly. "Else why should he have sent that clerk of his to spy on you and George Fentiman? I daresay he has been keeping tabs on Robert, too."

"I shouldn't wonder," said Wimsey. "He certainly treated me like a conspirator when I called on him. The only thing that puzzles me now is why he should have suddenly offered to compromise."

"Probably Miss Dorland lost patience, or they despaired of proving anything," said Parker. "While Robert stuck to that Oliver story, it would be very hard to prove anything."

"Exactly," said Wimsey. "That is why I had to hang on so long, and press Robert so hard about

171

it. I might suspect Oliver to be non-existent, but one can't prove a negative."

"And suppose he still sticks to the story now?"

"Oh! I think we can put the wind up him all right," said Wimsey. "By the time we've displayed our proofs and told him exactly what he was doing with himself on November 10th and 11th, he'll have no more spirit in him than the Queen of Sheba."

"It must be done at once," said Mr. Murbles. "And of course this exhumation business will have to be stopped. I will go round and see Robert Fentiman to-morrow—this morning, that is."

"Better tell him to trot round to your place," said Wimsey. "I'll bring all the evidence round there, and I'll have the varnish on the cabinet analyzed and shown to correspond with the sample I took from the General's boots. Make it for two o'clock, and then we can all go round and interview Pritchard afterwards."

Parker supported this suggestion. Mr. Murbles was so wrought up that he would gladly have rushed away to confront Robert Fentiman immediately. It being, however, pointed out to him that Fentiman was in Richmond, that an alarm at this ungodly hour might drive him to do something desperate, and also that all three investigators needed repose, the old gentleman gave way and permitted himself to be taken home to Staple Inn.

172

Wimsey went round to Parker's flat in Great Ormond Street to have a drink before turning in, and the session was prolonged till the small hours had begun to grow into big hours and the early workman was abroad.

. . . .

Lord Peter, having set the springe for his woodcock, slept the sleep of the just until close upon eleven o'clock the next morning. He was aroused by voices without, and presently his bedroom door was flung open to admit Mr. Murbles, of all people, in a high state of agitation, followed by Bunter, protesting.

"Hullo, sir!" said his lordship, much amazed. "What's up?"

"We have been outwitted," cried Mr. Murbles, waving his umbrella, "we have been forestalled! We should have gone to Major Fentiman last night. I wished to do so, but permitted myself to be persuaded against my better judgment. It will be a lesson to me."

He sat down, panting a little.

"My dear Mr. Murbles," said Wimsey, pleasantly, "your method of recalling one to the dull business of the day is as delightful as it is unexpected. Anything better calculated to dispel that sluggish feeling I can scarcely imagine. But pardon me—you are somewhat out of breath. Bunter! a whisky-and-soda for Mr. Murbles."

"Indeed no!" ejaculated the solicitor, hurriedly. "I couldn't touch it. Lord Peter—"

"A glass of sherry?" suggested his lordship, helpfully.

"No, no—nothing, thanks. A shocking thing has occurred. We are left—"

"Better and better. A shock is exactly what I feel to need. My *café-au-lait*, Bunter—and you may turn the bath on. Now, sir—out with it. I am fortified against anything."

"Robert Fentiman," announced Mr. Murbles, impressively, "has disappeared."

He thumped his umbrella.

"Good God!" said Wimsey.

"He has gone," repeated the solicitor. "At ten o'clock this morning I attended in person at his rooms in Richmond—in *person*—in order to bring him the more effectually to a sense of his situation. I rang the bell. I asked for him. The maid told me he had left the night before. I asked where he had gone. She said she did not know. He had taken a suit-case with him. I interviewed the landlady. She told me that Major Fentiman had received an urgent message during the evening and had informed her that he was called away. He had not mentioned where he was going nor how soon he would return. I left a note addressed to him, and hastened back to Dover Street. The flat there was

174

shut up and untenanted. The man Woodward was nowhere to be found. I then came immediately to you. And I find you—"

Mr. Murbles waved an expressive hand at Wimsey, who was just taking from Bunter's hands a chaste silver tray, containing a Queen Anne coffee-pot and milk-jug, a plate of buttered toast, a delicate china coffee-cup and a small pile of correspondence.

"So you do," said Wimsey. "A depraved sight, I am afraid. H'm! It looks very much as though Robert had got wind of trouble and didn't like to face the music."

He sipped his *café-au-lait* delicately, his rather bird-like face cocked sideways. "But why worry? He can't have got very far."

"He may have gone abroad."

"Possibly. All the better. The other party won't want to take proceedings against him over there. Too much bother—however spiteful they may feel. Hallo! Here's a writing I seem to recognize. Yes. It is my sleuth from Sleuths Incorporated. Wonder what *he* wants. I told him to go home and send the bill in.—Whew!"

"What is it?"

"This is the bloke who chased Fentiman to Southampton. Not the one who went on to Venice after the innocent Mr. Postlethwaite; the other. He's writing from Paris. He says:

'My lord,

While making a few inquiries at Southampton pursuant to the investigation with which your lordship entrusted me' (what marvelous English those fellows write, don't they? Nearly as good as the regular police), 'I came, almost accidentally' ('almost' is good) 'upon a trifling clue which led me to suppose that the party whom I was instructed by your lordship to keep under observation had been less in error than we were led to suppose, and had merely been misled by a confusion of identity natural in a gentleman not scientifically instructed in the art of following up suspected persons. In short' (thank God for that!) 'in short, I believe that I have myself come upon the track of O.' (These fellows are amazingly cautious; he might just as well write Oliver and have done with it), 'and have followed the individual in question to this place. I have telegraphed to the gentleman your friend' (I presume that means Fentiman) 'to join me immediately with a view to identifying the party. I will of course duly acquaint your lordship with any further developments in the case, and believe me'—and so forth.

"Well, I'm damned!"

"The man must be mistaken, Lord Peter."

"I jolly well hope so," said Wimsey, rather red in the face. "It'll be a bit galling to have Oliver turning up, just when we've proved so conclusively that he doesn't exist. Paris! I suppose he means that Fentiman spotted the right man at Waterloo and lost him on the train or in the rush for the boat. And got hold of Postlethwaite instead. Funny. Meanwhile, Fentiman's off to France. Probably taken the 10.30 boat from Folkestone. I don't know how we're to get hold of him."

"How very extraordinary," said Mr. Murbles. "Where does that detective person write from?"

"Just 'Paris,'" said Wimsey. "Bad paper and worse ink. And a small stain of *vin ordinaire*. Probably written in some little café yesterday afternoon. Not much hope there. But he's certain to let me know where they get to."

"We must send some one to Paris immediately in search of them," declared Mr. Murbles.

"Why?"

"To fetch Major Fentiman back."

"Yes, but look here, sir. If there really is an Oliver after all, it rather upsets our calculations, doesn't it?"

Mr. Murbles considered this.

"I cannot see that it affects our conclusions as to the hour of the General's death," he said.

"Perhaps not, but it considerably alters our position with regard to Robert Fentiman."

"Ye—es. Yes, that is so. Though," said Mr. Murbles, severely, "I still consider that the story requires close investigation."

"Agreed. Well, look here. I'll run over to Paris myself and see what I can do. And you had better temporize with Pritchard. Tell him you think there will be no need to compromise and that we hope soon to be in possession of the precise facts. That'll show him we don't mean to have any truck with anythin' fishy. I'll learn him to cast nasturtiums at me!"

"And—oh, dear! there's another thing. We must try and get hold of Major Fentiman to stop this exhumation."

"Oh, lord!—Yes. That's a bit awkward. Can't you stop it by yourself?"

"I hardly think I can. Major Fentiman has applied for it as executor, and I cannot quite see what I can do in the matter without his signature. The Home Office would hardly—"

"Yes. I quite see that you can't mess about with the Home Office. Well, though, that's easy. Robert never was keen on the resurrection idea. Once we've got his address, he'll be only too happy to send you a chit to call the whole thing off. You leave it to me. After all, even if we don't find Robert for a few days and the old boy has to be dug up after all, it won't make things any worse. Will it?"

Mr. Murbles agreed, dubiously.

"Then I'll pull the old carcass together," said Wimsey, brightly, flinging the bedclothes aside and leaping to his feet, "and toddle off to the City of Light. Will you excuse me for a few moments, sir? The bath awaits me. Bunter, put a few things into a suit-case and be ready to come with me to Paris."

. . . .

On second thoughts, Wimsey waited till the next day, hoping, as he explained, to hear from the detective. As nothing reached him, however, he started in pursuit, instructing the head office of Sleuths Incorporated to wire any information received to him at the Hôtel Meurice. The next news that arrived from him was a card to Mr. Murbles written on a P.L.M. express, which said simply, "Quarry gone on to Rome. Hard on trail. P.W." The next day came a foreign telegram: "Making for Sicily. Faint but pursuing. P.W."

In reply to this, Mr. Murbles wired: "Exhumation fixed for day after to-morrow. Please make haste."

To which Wimsey replied: "Returning for exhumation. P.W."

He returned alone.

"Where is Robert Fentiman?" demanded Mr. Murbles, agitatedly.

Wimsey, his hair matted damply and his face white from traveling day and night, grinned feebly.

179

"I rather fancy," he said, in a wan voice, "that Oliver is at his old tricks again."

"Again?" cried Mr. Murbles, aghast. "But the letter from your detective was genuine."

"Oh, yes—that was genuine enough. But even detectives can be bribed. Anyhow, we haven't seen hide or hair of our friends. They've been always a little ahead. Like the Holy Grail, you know. Fainter by day but always in the night blood-red, and sliding down the blackened marsh, blood-red—perfectly bloody, in fact. Well, here we are. When does the ceremony take place? Quietly, I take it? No flowers?"

.   .   .   .

The "ceremony" took place, as such ceremonies do, under the discreet cover of darkness. George Fentiman, who, in Robert's absence, attended to represent the family, was nervous and depressed. It is trying enough to go to the funeral of one's friends and relations, amid the grotesque pomps of glass hearses, and black horses, and wreaths, and appropriate hymns "beautifully" rendered by well-paid choristers, but, as George irritably remarked, the people who grumble over funerals don't realize their luck. However depressing the thud of earth on the coffin-lid may be, it is music compared to the rattle of gravel and thump of spades which herald a premature and unreverend resurrection,

180

enveloped in clouds of formalin and without benefit of clergy.

Dr. Penberthy also appeared abstracted. and
anxious to get the business over. He made the
journey to the cemetery ensconced in the farthest
corner of the big limousine, and discussed thyroid
abnormalities with Dr. Horner, Sir James Lubbock's assistant, who had come to help with the
autopsy. Mr. Murbles was, naturally, steeped in
gloom. Wimsey devoted himself to his accumu-
lated correspondence, out of which one letter only
had any bearing on the Fentiman case. It was from
Marjorie Phelps, and ran:

"If you want to meet Ann Dorland, would you
care to come along to a 'do' at the Rushworths'
Wednesday week? It will be very deadly, because
Naomi Rushworth's new young man is going to
read a paper on ductless glands which nobody
knows anything about. However, it appears that
ductless glands will be 'news' in next to no time—
ever so much more up-to-date than vitamins—so
the Rushworths are all over glands—in the social
sense, I mean. Ann D. is certain to be there, because as I told you, she is taking to this healthy
bodies for all stunt, or whatever it is, so you'd better
come. It will be company for me!—and I've got
to go, anyway, as I'm supposed to be a friend of
Naomi's. Besides, they say that if one paints or
sculps or models, one ought to know all about

181

glands, because of the way they enlarge your jaw and alter your face, or something. Do come, because if you don't I shall be fastened on by some deadly bore or other—and I shall have to hear all Naomi's raptures about the man, which will be too awful."

Wimsey made a note to be present at this enlivening party, and looking round, saw that they were arriving at the Necropolis—so vast, so glittering with crystal-globed wreaths, so towering with sky-scraping monuments, that no lesser name would serve it. At the gate they were met by Mr. Pritchard in person (acidulated in his manner and elaborately polite to Mr. Murbles), and by the Home Office representative (suave and bland and disposed to see reporters lurking behind every tombstone.) A third person, coming up, proved to be an official from the Cemetery Company, who took charge of the party and guided them along the neat graveled walks to where digging operations were already in process.

The coffin, being at length produced and identified by its brass plate, was then carefully borne to a small outbuilding close at hand, which appeared to be a potting-shed in ordinary life, converted by a board and a couple of trestles into a temporary mortuary. Here a slight halt and confusion was caused by the doctors, demanding in aggressively cheerful and matter-of-fact tones more light and space to work in. The coffin was placed on a bench; somebody produced a mackintosh sheet and spread it on the trestle table; lamps were brought and suitably grouped. After which, the workmen advanced, a little reluctantly, to unscrew the coffin lid, preceded by Dr. Penberthy, scattering formalin from a spray, rather like an infernal thurifer at some particularly unwholesome sacrifice.

"Ah! very nice indeed," said Dr. Horner, appreciatively, as the corpse was disengaged from the coffin and transferred to the table. "Excellent. Not much difficulty over this job. That's the best of getting on to it at once. How long has he been buried, did you say? Three or four weeks? He doesn't look it. Will you make the autopsy or shall I? Just as you like. Very well. Where did I put my bag? Ah! thank you, Mr.—er—er—" (An unpleasantly-occupied pause, during which George Fentiman escaped, murmuring that he thought he'd have a smoke outside). "Undoubted heart trouble, of course, I don't see any unusual appearances, do you? . . . I suppose we'd better secure the stomach as it stands . . . pass me the gut, would you? Thanks. D'you mind holding while I get this ligature on? Ta." (Snip, snip.) "The jars are just behind you. Thanks. Look out! You'll have it over. Ha! ha! that was a near thing. Reminds me of Palmer, you know—and Cook's stomach—

183

always think that a very funny story, ha, ha!—I won't take all the liver—just a sample—it's only a matter of form—and sections of the rest—yes—better have a look at the brain while we are about it, I suppose. Have you got the large saw?"

"How callous these medical men seem," murmured Mr. Murbles.

"It's nothing to them," said Wimsey. "Horner does this kind of job several times a week."

"Yes, but he need not be so noisy. Dr. Penberthy behaves with decorum."

"Penberthy runs a practice," said Wimsey with a faint grin. "He has to exercise a little restraint over himself. Besides, he knew old Fentiman, and Horner didn't."

At length the relevant portions of General Fentiman's anatomy having been collected into suitable jars and bottles, the body was returned to the coffin and screwed down. Penberthy came across to Wimsey and took his arm.

"We ought to be able to get a pretty good idea of what you want to know," he said. "Decomposition is very little advanced, owing to an exceptionally well-made coffin. By the way" (he dropped his voice) "that leg, you know—did it ever occur to you—or rather, did you ever discover any explanation of that?"

"I *did* have an idea about it," admitted Wimsey, "but I don't yet know whether it was the right

one. I shall probably know for certain in a day
or two."

"You think the body was interfered with?" said
Penberthy, looking him steadily in the face.

"Yes, and so do you," replied Wimsey, returning the gaze.

"I've had my suspicions all the time, of course.
I told you so, you know. I wonder whether—you
don't think I was wrong to give the certificate,
do you?"

"Not unless you suspected anything wrong with
the death itself," said Wimsey. "Have you and
Horner noticed anything queer?"

"No. But—oh, well! having patients dug up
always makes me worried, you know. It's easy to
make a mistake and one looks an awful fool in
court. I'd hate being made to look a fool just at
present," added the doctor with a nervous laugh.
"I'm thinking of—great Scott, man! how you
startled me!"

Dr. Horner had brought a large, bony hand
down on his shoulder. He was a red-faced, jovial
man, and he smiled as he held up his bag before
them.

"All packed up and ready," he announced. "Got
to be getting back now, aha! Got to be getting
back."

"Have the witnesses signed the labels?" asked
Penberthy, rather shortly.

185

"Yes, yes, quite all right. Both the solicitor johnnies, so they can't quarrel about *that* in the witness-box," replied Horner. "Come along, please —I've got to get off."

They found George Fentiman outside, seated on a tombstone, and sucking at an empty pipe.

"Is it all over?"

"Yes."

"Have they found anything?"

"Haven't looked yet," broke in Horner, genially. "Not at the part which interests *you*, that is. Leave that for my colleague Lubbock, you know. Soon give you an answer—say, in a week's time."

George passed his handkerchief over his forehead, which was beaded with little drops of sweat.

"I don't like it," he said. "But I suppose it had to be done. What was that? I thought—I'd swear I saw something moving over there."

"A cat, probably," said Penberthy, "there's nothing to be alarmed at."

"No," said George, "but sitting about here, one—fancies things." He hunched his shoulders, squinting round at them with the whites of his eyeballs showing.

"Things," he said, "people—going to and fro . . . and walking up and down. Following one."

CHAPTER XIV

Grand Slam In Spades

ON THE SEVENTH MORNING AFTER THE EXHUMA-
tion—which happened to be a Tuesday—Lord
Peter walked briskly into Mr. Murbles' chambers
in Staple Inn, with Detective-Inspector Parker at
his heels.

"Good morning," said Mr. Murbles, surprised.

"Good morning," said Wimsey. "Hark! hark!
the lark at heaven's gate sings. He is coming, my
own, my sweet, were it ever so airy a tread. He
will be here in a quarter of an hour."

"Who will?" demanded Mr. Murbles, somewhat
severely.

"Robert Fentiman."

Mr. Murbles gave a little ejaculation of surprise.

"I had almost given up hope in that direction,"
he said.

"So had not I. I said to myself, he is not lost but
gone before. And it was so. Charles, we will lay
out the *pièces de conviction* on the table. The
boots. The photographs. The microscopic slides
showing the various specimens. The paper of notes

187

from the library. The outer garments of the
deceased. Just so. And 'Oliver Twist.' Beautiful.
Now, as Sherlock Holmes says, we shall look imposing enough to strike terror into the guilty breast,
though armed in triple steel."

"Did Fentiman return of his own accord?"

"Not altogether. He was, if I may so express
myself, led. Almost, in fact, led on. O'er moor and
fen, o'er crag and torrent till, don't you know.
What is that noise in the outer room? It is, it is
the cannon's opening roar."

It was, indeed, the voice of Robert Fentiman,
not in the best of tempers. In a few seconds he
was shown in. He nodded curtly to Mr. Murbles,
who replied with a stiff bow, and then turned
violently upon Wimsey.

"Look here, what's the meaning of all this?
Here's that damned detective fellow of yours leading me a devil of a dance all over Europe and home
again, and then this morning he suddenly turns
round and tells me that you want to see me here
with news about Oliver. What the devil do you
know about Oliver?"

"Oliver?" said Wimsey. "Oh, yes—he's an elusive personality. Almost as elusive in Rome as he
was in London. Wasn't it odd, Fentiman, the way
he always seemed to bob up directly your back was
turned? Wasn't it funny, the way he managed to
disappear from places the moment you set foot in

188

'em? Almost like the way he used to hang about Gatti's and then give you and me the slip. Did you have a jolly time abroad, old man? I suppose you didn't like to tell your companion that he and you were chasing a will o' the wisp?"

Robert Fentiman's face was passing through phases ranging from fury to bewilderment and back again. Mr. Murbles interrupted.

"Has this detective vouchsafed any explanation of his extraordinary behaviour, in keeping us in the dark for nearly a fortnight as to his movements?"

"I'm afraid I owe you the explanation," said Wimsey, airily. "You see, I thought it was time the carrot was dangled before the other donkey. I knew that if we pretended to find Oliver in Paris, Fentiman would be in honour bound to chase after him. In fact, he was probably only too pleased to get away—weren't you, Fentiman?"

"Do you mean to say that you invented all this story about Oliver, Lord Peter?"

"I did. Not the original Oliver, of course, but the Paris Oliver. I told the sleuth to send a wire from Paris to summon our friend away and keep him away."

"But why?"

"I'll explain that later. And of course you had to go, hadn't you, old man? Because you couldn't very well refuse to go without confessing that there was no such person as Oliver?"

189

"Damnation!" burst out Fentiman, and then suddenly began to laugh. "You cunning little devil! I began to think there was something fishy about it, you know. When that first wire came, I was delighted. Thought the sleuth-hound fellow had made a perfectly providential floater, don't you know. And the longer we kept tootin' round Europe the better I was pleased. But when the hare started to double back to England, home and beauty, I began to get the idea that somebody was pullin' my leg. By the way, was that why I was able to get all my visas with that uncanny facility at an unearthly hour overnight?"

"It was," said Wimsey, modestly.

"I might have known there was something wrong about it. You devil! Well—what now?— If you've exploded Oliver, I suppose you've spilled all the rest of the beans, eh?"

"If you mean by that expression," said Mr. Murbles, "that we are aware of your fraudulent and disgraceful attempt to conceal the true time of General Fentiman's decease, the answer is, Yes— we do know it. And I may say that it has come as a most painful shock to my feelings."

Fentiman flung himself into a chair, slapping his thigh and roaring with laughter.

"I might have known you'd be on to it," he gasped, "but it was a damn good joke, wasn't it? Good lord! I couldn't help chuckling to myself,

190

you know. To think of all those refrigerated old imbeciles at the Club sittin' solemnly round there, and comin' in and noddin' to the old guv'nor like so many mandarins, when he was as dead as a door-nail all the time. That leg of his was a bit of a slip-up, of course, but that was an accident. Did you ever find out where he was all the time?"

"Oh, yes—pretty conclusively. You left your marks on the cabinet, you know."

"No, did we? Hell!"

"Yes—and when you stuck the old boy's overcoat back in the cloak-room, you forgot to stick a poppy in it."

"Oh, lord! that *was* a bloomer. D'you know, I never thought of that. Oh, well! I suppose I couldn't hope to carry it off with a confounded bloodhound like you on the trail. But it was fun while it lasted. Even now, the thought of old Bunter solemnly callin' up two and a half columns of Olivers makes me shout with joy. It's almost as good as getting the half-million."

"That reminds me," said Wimsey. "The one thing I don't know is how you knew about the half-million. Did Lady Dormer tell you about her will? Or did you hear of it from George?"

"George? Great scott, no! George knew nothing about it. The old boy told me himself."

"General Fentiman?"

"Of course. When he came back to the Club that night, he came straight up to see me."

"And we never thought of that," said Wimsey, crushed. "Too obvious, I suppose."

"You can't be expected to think of everything," said Robert, condescendingly. "I think you did very well, take it all round. Yes—the old boy toddled up to me and told me all about it. He said I wasn't to tell George, because he wasn't quite satisfied with George—about Sheila, you know—and he wanted to think it over and see what was best to be done, in the way of making a new will, you see."

"Just so. And he went down to the library to do it."

"That's right; and I went down and had some grub. Well then, afterwards I thought perhaps I hadn't said quite enough on behalf of old George. I mean, the guv'nor needed to have it pointed out to him that George's queerness was caused a great deal by bein' dependent on Sheila and all that, and if he had some tin of his own he'd be much better-tempered—you get me? So I hopped through to the library to find the guv'—and there he was—dead!"

"What time was that?"

"Somewhere round about eightish, I should think. Well, I was staggered. Of course, my first idea was to call for help, but it wasn't any go.

192

He was quite dead. And then it jolly well came over me all at once how perfectly damnably we had missed the train. Just to think of that awful Dorland woman walking into all those thousands— I tell you, it made me so bally wild, I could have exploded and blown the place up! . . . And then, you know, I began to get a sort of creepy feeling, alone there with the body and nobody in the library at all. We seemed cut off from the world, as the writing fellows say. And then it just seemed to take hold of my mind, why should he have died like that?—I did have a passing hope that the old girl might have pegged out first, and I was just going along to the telephone to find out, when— thinking of the telephone cabinet, you see—the whole thing popped into my head ready-made, as you might say. In three minutes I'd lugged him along and stuck him up on the seat, and then I hopped back to write a label for the door. I say, I thought I was jolly smart to remember not to blot that label on the library blotting-paper."

"Believe me," said Wimsey, "I appreciated that point."

"Good. I'm glad you did. Well, it was pretty plain sailing after that. I got the guv'nor's togs from the cloak-room and took 'em up to my room, and then I thought about old Woodward sittin' up waitin' for him. So I trundled out and went down to Charing Cross—how do you think?"

"By bus?"

"Not quite as bad as that. By Underground. I did realize it wouldn't work to call a taxi."

"You show quite a disposition for fraud, Fentiman."

"Yes, don't I?—Well, all that was easy. I must say, I didn't pass a frightfully good night."

"You'll take it more calmly another time."

"Yes—it was my maiden effort in crime, of course. The next morning——"

"Young man," said Mr. Murbles, in an awful voice, "we will draw a veil over the next morning. I have listened to your shameless statement with a disgust which words cannot express. But I cannot, and I will not sit here and listen while you congratulate yourself, with a cynicism at which you should blush, on having employed those sacred moments when every thought should have been consecrated——"

"Oh, punk!" interrupted Robert, rudely. "My old pals are none the worse because I did a little bit of self-help. I know fraud isn't altogether the clean potato, but, dash it all! surely we have a better right to the old boy's money than that girl. I bet *she* never did anything in the Great War, Daddy. Well, it's all gone bust—but it was a darn good stunt while it lasted."

"I perceive," replied Mr. Murbles, icily, "that any appeal to your better feelings would be waste of time. I imagine, however, you realize that fraud is a penal offence."

"Yes—that's a nuisance, isn't it? What are we going to do about it? Do I have to go and eat humble pie to old Pritchard? Or does Wimsey pretend to have discovered something frightfully abstruse from looking at the body?—Oh, good lord, by the way—what's happened about that confounded exhumation stunt? I never thought a word more about it. I say, Wimsey, was that the idea? Did you know then that I'd been trying to work this stunt and was it your notion you could get me out of it?"

"Partly."

"Damned decent of you. You know, I did tumble to it that you'd got a line on me when you sent me down with that detective fellow to Charing Cross. And, I say, you nearly had me there! I'd made up my mind to pretend to go after Oliver—you know—and then I spotted that second bloodhound of yours on the train with me. That gave me gooseflesh all over. The only thing I could think of—short of chucking up the whole show—was to accuse some harmless old bird of being Oliver—as a proof of good faith, don't you see."

"That was it, was it? I thought you must have some reason."

"Yes—and then, when I got that summons to

Paris, I thought I must, somehow, have diddled the lot of you. But I suppose that was all arranged for. I say, Wimsey, why? Did you just want to get your own back, or what? Why did you want me out of England?"

"Yes, indeed, Lord Peter," said Mr. Murbles, gravely. "I think you owe *me* at least some explanation on that point."

"Don't you see," said Wimsey, "Fentiman was his grandfather's executor. If I got him out of the way, you couldn't stop the exhumation."

"Ghoul!" said Robert. "I believe you batten on corpses."

Wimsey laughed, rather excitedly.

"Fentiman," he said, "what would you give at this moment for your chance of that half-million?"

"Chance?" cried Fentiman. "There's no chance at all. What do you mean?"

Wimsey slowly drew a paper from his pocket.

"This came last night," he said. "And, by jove, my lad, it's lucky for you that you had a good bit to lose by the old man's death. This is from Lubbock—

'Dear Lord Peter,

I am sending you a line in advance to let you know the result of the autopsy on General Fentiman. As regards the ostensible reason for the investigation, I may say that there was no food in

196

the stomach and that the last meal had been taken several hours previously. The important point, however, is that, following your own rather obscurely-expressed suggestion, I tested the viscera for poison and discovered traces of a powerful dose of digitalin, swallowed not very long previous to decease. As you know, with a subject whose heart was already in a weak state, the result of such a dose could not but be fatal. The symptoms would be a slowing-down of the heart's action and collapse—practically indistinguishable from a violent heart-attack.

I do not, of course, know what your attitude in this business is, though I congratulate you on the perspicacity which prompted you to suggest an analysis. In the meanwhile, of course, you will realize that I am obliged to communicate the result of the autopsy to the public prosecutor.' "

Mr. Murbles sat petrified.

"My God!" cried Fentiman. And then again, "My God!—Wimsey—if I'd known—if I'd had the faintest idea—I wouldn't have touched the body for twenty millions. Poison! Poor old blighter! What a damned shame! I remember now his saying that night he felt a bit sickish, but I never thought—I say, Wimsey—you do believe, don't you, that I hadn't the foggiest? I say—that awful female—I knew she was a wrong 'un. But poison! that is too thick. Good lord!"

Parker, who had hitherto preserved the detached expression of a friendly spectator, now beamed. "Damn good, old man!" he cried, and smote Peter on the back. Professional enthusiasm overcame him. "It's a real case," he said, "and you've handled it finely, Peter. I didn't know you had it in you to hang on so patiently. Forcing the exhumation on 'em through putting pressure on Major Fentiman was simply masterly! Pretty work! Pretty work!"

"Thank you, Charles," said Wimsey, dryly. "I'm glad somebody appreciates me. Anyhow," he added, viciously, "I bet that's wiped old Pritchard's eye."

And at this remark, even Mr. Murbles showed signs of returning animation.

CHAPTER XV

Shuffle The Cards And Deal Again

A HASTY CONSULTATION WITH THE POWERS that be at Scotland Yard put Detective-Inspector Parker in charge of the Fentiman case, and he promptly went into consultation with Wimsey.

"What put you on to this poison business?" he asked.

"Aristotle, chiefly," replied Wimsey. "He says, you know, that one should always prefer the probable impossible to the improbable possible. It was possible, of course, that the General should have died off in that neat way at the most confusing moment. But how much nicer and more probable that the whole thing had been stage-managed. Even if it had seemed much more impossible I should have been dead nuts on murder. And there really was nothing impossible about it. Then there was Pritchard and the Dorland woman. Why should they have been so dead against compromise and so suspicious about things unless they had inside information from somewhere. After all, they hadn't seen the body as Penberthy and I did."

"That leads on to the question of who did it. Miss Dorland is the obvious suspect, naturally."

"She's got the biggest motive."

"Yes. Well, let's be methodical. Old Fentiman was apparently as right as rain up till about half past three when he started off for Portman Square, so that the drug must have been given him between then and eightish, when Robert Fentiman found him dead. Now who saw him between those two times?"

"Wait a sec. That's not absolutely accurate. He must have *taken* the stuff between those two times, but it might have been *given* him earlier. Suppose, for instance, somebody had dropped a poisoned pill into his usual bottle of soda-mints or whatever he used to take. That could have been worked at any time."

"Well—not too early on, Peter. Suppose he had died a lot too soon and Lady Dormer had heard about it."

"It wouldn't have made any difference. She wouldn't need to alter her will, or anything. The bequest to Miss Dorland would just stand as before."

"Quite right. I was being stupid. Well, then, we'd better find out if he did take anything of that kind regularly. If he did, who would have had the opportunity to drop the pill in?"

"Penberthy, for one."

"The doctor?—yes, we must stick his name down as a possible, though he wouldn't have had the slightest motive. Still, we'll put him in the column headed Opportunity."

"That's right, Charles. I do like your methodical ways."

"Attraction of opposites," said Parker, ruling a notebook into three columns. "Opportunity. Number 1, Dr. Penberthy. If the tablets or globules or whatever they were, were Penberthy's own prescription, he would have a specially good opportunity. Not so good, though, if they were the kind of things you get ready-made from the chemist in sealed bottles."

"Oh, bosh! he could always have asked to have a squint at 'em to see if they were the right kind. I insist on having Penberthy in. Besides, he was one of the people who saw the General between the critical hours—during what we may call the administration period, so he had an extra amount of opportunity."

"So he had. Well, I've put him down. Though there seems no reason for him——"

"I'm not going to be put off by a trifling objection like that. He had the opportunity, so down he goes. Well, then, Miss Dorland comes next."

"Yes. She goes down under opportunity and also under motive. She certainly had a big interest in polishing off the old man, she saw him during the

201

period of administration and she very likely gave him something to eat or drink while he was in the house. So she is a very likely subject. The only difficulty with her is the difficulty of getting hold of the drug. You can't get digitalin just by asking for it, you know."

"N—no. At least, not by itself. You can get it mixed up with other drugs quite easily. I saw an ad. in the *Daily Views* only this morning, offering a pill with half a grain of digitalin in it."

"Did you? where?—oh, that! Yes, but it's got nux vomica in it too, which is supposed to be an antidote. At any rate, it bucks the heart up by stimulating the nerves, so as to counteract the slowing-down action of the digitalin."

"H'm. Well, put down Miss Dorland under Means with a query-mark. Oh, of course, Penberthy has to go down under Means too. He is the one person who could get the stuff without any bother."

"Right. Means: No. 1, Dr. Penberthy. Opportunity: No. 1, Dr. Penberthy, No. 2, Miss Dorland. We'll have to put in the servants at Lady Dormer's too, shan't we? Any of them who brought him food or drink, at any rate."

"Put 'em in, by all means. They might have been in collusion with Miss Dorland. And how about Lady Dormer herself?"

202

"Oh, come, Peter. There wouldn't be any sense in that."

"Why not? She may have been planning revenge on her brother all these years, camouflaging her feelings under a pretense of generosity. It would be rather fun to leave a terrific legacy to somebody you loathed, and then, just when he was feelin' nice and grateful and all over coals of fire, poison him to make sure he didn't get it. We simply must have Lady Dormer. Stick her down under Opportunity and under Motive."

"I refuse to do more than Opportunity and Motive (query?)."

"Have it your own way. Well, now—there are our friends the two taxi-drivers."

"I don't think you can be allowed those. It would be awfully hard work poisoning a fare, you know."

"I'm afraid it would. I say! I've just got a rippin' idea for poisoning a taxi-man, though. You give him a dud half-crown, and when he bites it——"

"He dies of lead poisoning. That one's got whiskers on it."

"Juggins. You poison the half-crown with Prussic acid."

"Splendid! And he falls down foaming at the mouth. That's frightfully brilliant. Do you mind giving your attention to the matter in hand?"

203

"You think we can leave out the taxi-drivers, then?"

"I think so."

"Right-oh! I'll let you have them. That brings us, I'm sorry to say, to George Fentiman."

"You've got rather a weakness for George Fentiman, haven't you?"

"Yes—I like old George. He's an awful pig in some ways, but I quite like him."

"Well, I don't know George, so I shall firmly put him down. Opportunity No. 3, he is."

"He'll have to go down under Motive, too, then."

"Why? What did he stand to gain by Miss Dorland's getting the legacy?"

"Nothing—if he knew about it. But Robert says emphatically that he didn't know. So does George. And if he didn't, don't you see, the General's death meant that he would immediately step into that two thousand quid which Dougal McStewart was being so pressing about."

"McStewart?—oh, yes—the money-lender. That's one up to you, Peter; I'd forgotten him. That certainly does put George on the list of the possibles. He was pretty sore about things too, wasn't he?"

"Very. And I remember his saying one rather unguarded thing at least down at the Club on the very day the murder—or rather, the death—was discovered."

"That's in his favour, if anything," said Parker, cheerfully, "unless he's very reckless indeed."

"It won't be in his favour with the police," grumbled Wimsey.

"My dear man!"

"I beg your pardon. I was forgetting for the moment. I'm afraid you are getting a little above your job, Charles. So much intelligence will spell either a Chief-Commissionership or ostracism if you aren't careful."

"I'll chance that. Come on—get on with it. Who else is there?"

"There's Woodward. Nobody could have a better opportunity of tampering with the General's pill-boxes."

"And I suppose his little legacy might have been a motive."

"Or he may have been in the enemy's pay. Sinister men-servants so often are, you know. Look what a boom there has been lately in criminal butlers and thefts by perfect servants."

"That's a fact. And now, how about the people at the Bellona?"

"There's Wetheridge. He's a disagreeable devil. And he has always cast covetous eyes at the General's chair by the fire. I've seen him."

"Be serious, Peter."

"I'm perfectly serious. I don't like Wetheridge. He annoys me. And then we mustn't forget to put down Robert."

"Robert? Why, he's the one person we can definitely cross off. He knew it was to his interest to keep the old man alive. Look at the pains he took to cover up the death."

"Exactly. He is the Most Unlikely Person, and that is why Sherlock Holmes would suspect him at once. He was, by his own admission, the last person to see General Fentiman alive. Suppose he had a row with the old man and killed him, and then discovered, afterwards, about the legacy."

"You're scintillating with good plots to-day, Peter. If they'd quarreled, he might possibly have knocked his grandfather down—though I don't think he'd do such a rotten and unsportsmanlike thing—but he surely wouldn't have poisoned him."

Wimsey sighed.

"There's something in what you say," he admitted. "Still, you never know. Now then, is there any name we've thought of which appears in all three columns of our list?"

"No, not one. But several appear in two."

"We'd better start on those, then. Miss Dorland is the most obvious, naturally, and after her, George, don't you think?"

"Yes. I'll have a round-up among all the chemists who may possibly have supplied her with the digitalin. Who's her family doctor?"

"Dunno. That's your pigeon. By the way, I'm supposed to be meeting the girl at a cocoa-party or something of the sort to-morow. Don't pinch her before then if you can help it."

"No; but it looks to me as though we might need to put a few questions. And I'd like to have a look round Lady Dormer's house."

"For heaven's sake, don't be flat-footed about it, Charles. Use tact."

"You can trust your father. And, I say, you might take me down to the Bellona in a tact-ful way. I'd like to ask a question or two there."

Wimsey groaned.

"I shall be asked to resign if this goes on. Not that it's much loss. But it would please Wetheridge so much to see the back of me. Never mind. I'll make a Martha of myself. Come on."

The entrance of the Bellona Club was filled with an unseemly confusion. Culyer was arguing heat-edly with a number of men and three or four members of the committee stood beside him with brows as black as thunder. As Wimsey entered, one of the intruders caught sight of him with a yelp of joy.

"Wimsey—Wimsey, old man! Here, be a sport and get us in on this. We've got to have the story some day. You probably know all about it, you old blighter."

It was Salcombe Hardy of the *Daily Yell*, large and untidy and slightly drunk as usual. He gazed at Wimsey with child-like blue eyes. Barton of the *Banner*, red-haired and pugnacious, faced round promptly.

"Ah, Wimsey, that's fine. Give us a line on this, can't you? Do explain that if we get a story we'll be good and go."

"Good lord," said Wimsey, "how do these things get into the papers?"

"I think it's rather obvious," said Culyer, acidly.

"It wasn't me," said Wimsey.

"No, no," put in Hardy. "You mustn't think that. It was my stunt. In fact, I saw the whole show up at the Necropolis. I was on a family vault, pretending to be a recording angel."

"You would be," said Wimsey. "Just a moment, Culyer." He drew the secretary aside. "See here, I'm damned annoyed about this, but it can't be helped. You can't stop these boys when they're after a story. And anyway, it's all got to come out. It's a police affair now. This is Detective-Inspector Parker of Scotland Yard."

"But what's the matter?" demanded Culyer.

"Murder's the matter, I'm afraid."

"Oh, hell!"

"Sorry and all that. But you'd better grin and

bear it. Charles, give these fellows as much story as you think they ought to have and get on with it. And, Salcombe, if you'll call off your tripe-hounds, we'll let you have an interview and a set of photographs."

"That's the stuff," said Hardy.

"I'm sure," agreed Parker, pleasantly, "that you lads don't want to get in the way, and I'll tell you all that's advisable. Show us a room, Captain Culyer, and I'll send out a statement and then you'll let us get to work."

This was agreed, and, a suitable paragraph having been provided by Parker, the Fleet Street gang departed, bearing Wimsey away with them like a captured Sabine maiden to drink in the nearest bar, in the hope of acquiring picturesque detail.

"But I wish you'd kept out of it, Sally," mourned Peter.

"Oh, God," said Salcombe, "nobody loves us. It's a forsaken thing to be a poor bloody reporter." He tossed a lank black lock of hair back from his forehead and wept.

· · · · · · · ·

Parker's first and most obvious move was to interview Penberthy, whom he caught at Harley Street, after surgery hours.

"Now I'm not going to worry you about that certificate, doctor," he began, pleasantly. "We're all liable to make mistakes, and I understand that a death resulting from an over-dose of digitalin would look very like a death from heart-failure."

"It would *be* a death from heart-failure," corrected the doctor, patiently. Doctors are weary of explaining that heart-failure is not a specific disease, like mumps or housemaid's knee. It is this incompatibility of outlook between the medical and the lay mind which involves counsel and medical witnesses in a fog of misunderstanding and mutual irritation.

"Just so," said Parker. "Now, General Fentiman had got heart disease already, hadn't he? Is digitalin a thing one takes for heart disease?"

"Yes; in certain forms of heart disease, digitalin is a very valuable stimulant."

"Stimulant? I thought it was a depressant."

"It acts as a stimulant at first; in later stages it depresses the heart's action."

"Oh, I see." Parker did not see very well, since, like most people, he had a vague idea that each drug has one simple effect appropriate to it, and is, specifically, a cure for something or the other. "It first speeds up the heart and then slows it down."

"Not exactly. It strengthens the heart's action by retarding the beat, so that the cavities can be more completely emptied and the pressure is relieved. We give it in certain cases of valvular disease—under proper safeguards, of course."

210

"Were you giving it to General Fentiman?"

"I had given it him from time to time."

"On the afternoon of November 10th,—you remember that he came to you in consequence of a heart attack. Did you give him digitalin then?"

Dr. Penberthy appeared to hesitate painfully for a moment. Then he turned to his desk and extracted a large book.

"I had better be perfectly frank with you," he said. "I did. When he came to me, the feebleness of the heart's action and the extreme difficulty in breathing suggested the urgent necessity of a cardiac stimulant. I gave him a prescription containing a small quantity of digitalin to relieve this condition. Here is the prescription. I will write it out for you."

"A small quantity?" repeated Parker.

"Quite small, combined with other drugs to counteract the depressing after-effects."

"It was not as large as the dose afterwards found in the body?"

"Good heavens, no—nothing like. In a case like General Fentiman's, digitalin is a drug to be administered with the greatest caution."

"It would not be possible, I suppose, for you to have made a mistake in dispensing? To have given an overdose by error?"

"That possibility occurred to me at once, but as soon as I heard Sir James Lubbock's figures, I

211

realized that it was quite out of the question. The dose given was enormous; nearly two grains. But, to make quite certain, I have had my supply of the drug carefully checked, and it is all accounted for."

"Who did that for you?"

"My trained nurse. I will let you have the books and chemists' receipts."

"Thank you. Did your nurse make up the dose for General Fentiman?"

"Oh, no; it is a prescription I always keep by me, ready made up. If you'd like to see her, she will show it to you."

"Thanks very much. Now, when General Fentiman came to see you, he had just had an attack. Could that have been caused by digitalin?"

"You mean, had he been poisoned before he came to me? Well, of course, digitalin is rather an uncertain drug."

"How long would a big dose like that take to act?"

"I should expect it to take effect fairly quickly. In the ordinary way it would cause sickness and vertigo. But with a powerful cardiac stimulant like digitalin, the chief danger is that any sudden movement, such as springing suddenly to one's feet from a position of repose, is liable to cause sudden syncope and death. I should say that this was what occurred in General Fentiman's case."

212

"And that might have happened at any time after the administration of the dose?"

"Just so."

"Well, I'm very much obliged to you, Dr. Penberthy. I will just see your nurse and take copies of the entries in your books, if I may."

This done, Parker made his way to Portman Square, still a little hazy in his mind as to the habits of the common foxglove when applied internally —a haziness which was in no way improved by a subsequent consultation of the Materia Medica, the Pharmacopœia, Dixon Mann, Taylor, Glaister, and others of those writers who have so kindly and helpfully published their conclusions on toxicology.

CHAPTER XVI

Quadrille

"MRS. RUSHWORTH, THIS IS LORD PETER WIMSEY. Naomi, this is Lord Peter. He's fearfully keen on glands and things, so I've brought him along. And Naomi, do tell me all about your news. Who is it? Do I know him?"

Mrs. Rushworth was a long, untidy woman, with long, untidy hair wound into bell-pushes over her ears. She beamed short-sightedly at Peter.

"So glad to see you. So very wonderful about glands, isn't it? Dr. Voronoff, you know, and those marvelous old sheep. Such a hope for all of us. Not that dear Walter is specially interested in rejuvenation. Perhaps life is long and difficult enough as it is, don't you think—so full of problems of one kind and another. And the insurance companies have quite set their faces against it, or so I understand. That's natural, isn't it, when you come to think of it. But the effect on character is so interesting, you know. Are you devoted to young criminals by any chance?"

Wimsey said that they presented a very perplexing problem.

"How very true. So perplexing. And just to think that we have been quite wrong about them all these thousands of years. Flogging and bread-and-water, you know, and Holy Communion, when what they really needed was a little bit of rabbit-gland or something to make them just as good as gold. Quite terrible, isn't it? And all those poor freaks in sideshows, too—dwarfs and giants, you know—all pineal or pituitary, and they come right again. Though I daresay they make a great deal more money as they are, which throws such a distressing light on unemployment, does it not?"

Wimsey said that everything had the defects of its qualities.

"Yes, indeed," agreed Mrs. Rushworth. "But I think it is so infinitely more heartening to look at it from the opposite point of view. Everything has the qualities of its defects, too, has it not? It is so important to see these things in their true light. It will be such a joy for Naomi to be able to help dear Walter in this great work. I hope you will feel eager to subscribe to the establishment of the new Clinic."

Wimsey asked, what new Clinic.

"Oh! hasn't Marjorie told you about it? The new Clinic to make everybody good by glands. That is what dear Walter is going to speak about. He is so keen and so is Naomi. It was such a joy to me when Naomi told me that they were really engaged, you

215

know. Not that her old mother hadn't suspected something, of course," added Mrs. Rushworth, archly. "But young people are so odd nowadays and keep their affairs so much to themselves."

Wimsey said that he thought both parties were heartily to be congratulated. And indeed, from what he had seen of Naomi Rushworth, he felt that she at least deserved congratulation, for she was a singularly plain girl, with a face like a weasel.

"You will excuse me if I run off and speak to some of these other people, won't you?" went on Mrs. Rushworth. "I'm sure you will be able to amuse yourself. No doubt you have many friends in my little gathering."

Wimsey glanced round and was about to felicitate himself on knowing nobody, when a familiar face caught his eye.

"Why," said he, "there is Dr. Penberthy."

"Dear Walter!" cried Mrs. Rushworth, turning hurriedly in the direction indicated. "I declare, so he is. Ah, well—now we shall be able to begin. He should have been here before, but a doctor's time is never his own."

"Penberthy?" said Wimsey, half aloud, "good lord!"

"Very sound man," said a voice beside him. "Don't think the worse of his work from seeing him in this crowd. Beggars in a good cause can't be choosers, as we parsons know too well."

Wimsey turned to face a tall, lean man, with a handsome, humourous face, whom he recognized as a well-known slum padre.

"Father Whittington, isn't it?"

"The same. You're Lord Peter Wimsey, I know. We've got an interest in crime in common, haven't we? I'm interested in this glandular theory. It may throw a great light on some of our heart-breaking problems."

"Glad to see there's no antagonism between religion and science," said Wimsey.

"Of course not. Why should there be? We are all searching for Truth."

"And all these?" asked Wimsey, indicating the curious crowd with a wave of the hand.

"In their way. They mean well. They do what they can, like the woman in the Gospels, and they are surprisingly generous. Here's Penberthy, looking for you, I fancy. Well, Dr. Penberthy, I've come, you see, to hear you make mincemeat of original sin."

"That's very open-minded of you," said Penberthy, with a rather strained smile. "I hope you are not hostile. We've no quarrel with the Church, you know, if she'll stick to her business and leave us to ours."

"My dear man, if you can cure sin with an injection, I shall be only too pleased. Only be sure you don't pump in something worse in the process. You

217

know the parable of the swept and garnished house."

"I'll be as careful as I can," said Penberthy. "Excuse me one moment. I say, Wimsey, you've heard all about Lubbock's analysis, I suppose."

"Yes. Bit of a startler, isn't it?"

"It's going to make things damnably awkward for me, Wimsey. I wish to God you'd given me a hint at the time. Such a thing never once occurred to me."

"Why should it? You were expecting the old boy to pop off from heart, and he did pop off from heart. Nobody could possibly blame you."

"Couldn't they? That's all you know about juries. I wouldn't have had this happen, just at this moment, for a fortune. It couldn't have chosen a more unfortunate time."

"It'll blow over, Penberthy. That sort of mistake happens a hundred times a week. By the way, I gather I'm to congratulate you. When did this get settled? You've been very quiet about it."

"I was starting to tell you up at that infernal exhumation business, only somebody barged in. Yes. Thanks very much. We fixed it up—oh! about a fortnight or three weeks ago. You have met Naomi?"

"Only for a moment this evening. My friend Miss Phelps carried her off to hear all about you."

"Oh, yes. Well, you must come along and talk

218

to her. She's a sweet girl, and very intelligent. The old lady's a bit of a trial, I don't mind saying, but her heart's in the right place. And there's no doubt she gets hold of people whom it's very useful to meet."

"I didn't know you were such an authority on glands."

"I only wish I could afford to be. I've done a certain amount of experimental work under Professor Sligo. It's the Science of the Future, as they say in the press. There really isn't any doubt about that. It puts biology in quite a new light. We're on the verge of some really interesting discoveries, no doubt about it. Only what with the anti-vivisectors and the parsons and the other old women, one doesn't make the progress one ought. Oh, lord— they're waiting for me to begin. See you later."

"Half a jiff. I really came here—no, dash it, that's rude! But I'd no idea you were the lecturer till I spotted you. I originally came here (that sounds better) to get a look at Miss Dorland of Fentiman fame. But my trusty guide has abandoned me. Do you know Miss Dorland? Can you tell me which she is?"

"I know her to speak to. I haven't seen her this evening. She may not turn up, you know."

"I thought she was very keen on—on glands and things."

"I believe she is—or thinks she is. Anything does

219

for these women, as long as it's new—especially if it's sexual. By the way, I don't intend to be sexual."

"Bless you for that. Well, possibly Miss Dorland will show up later."

"Perhaps. But—I say, Wimsey. She's in rather a queer position, isn't she? She may not feel inclined to face it. It's all in the papers, you know."

"Dash it, don't I know it? That inspired tippler, Salcombe Hardy, got hold of it somehow. I think he bribes the cemetery officials to give him advance news of exhumations. He's worth his weight in pound notes to the *Yell.* Cheerio! Speak your bit nicely. You don't mind if I'm not in the front row, do you? I always take up a strategic position near the door that leads to the grub."

. . . .

Penberthy's paper struck Wimsey as being original and well-delivered. The subject was not altogether unfamiliar to him, for Wimsey had a number of distinguished scientific friends who found him a good listener, but some of the experiments mentioned were new and the conclusions suggestive. True to his principles, Wimsey made a bolt for the supper-room, while polite hands were still applauding. He was not the first, however. A large figure in a hard-worked looking dress-suit was already engaged with a pile of savoury sandwiches and a whisky-and-soda. It turned at his approach and beamed at him from its liquid and innocent blue eyes. Sally Hardy—never quite drunk and never quite sober—was on the job, as usual. He held out the sandwich-plate invitingly.

"Damn good, these are," he said. "What are you doing here?"

"What are you, if it comes to that?" asked Wimsey.

Hardy laid a fat hand on his sleeve.

"Two birds with one stone," he said, impressively. "Smart fellow, that Penberthy. Glands are news, you know. He knows it. He'll be one of these fashionable practitioners"—Sally repeated this phrase once or twice, as it seemed to have got mixed up with the soda—"before long. Doing us poor bloody journalists out of a job like . . . and . . ." (He mentioned two gentlemen whose signed contributions to popular dailies were a continual source of annoyance to the G.M.C.)

"Provided he doesn't damage his reputation over this Fentiman affair," rejoined Wimsey, in a refined shriek which did duty for a whisper amid the noisy stampede which had followed them up to the refreshment-table.

"Ah! there you are," said Hardy. "Penberthy's news in himself. He's a story, don't you see. We'll have to sit on the fence a bit, of course, till we see which way the cat jumps. I'll have a par. about it at the end, mentioning that he attended old Fentiman. Presently we'll be able to work up a little

221

thing on the magazine page about the advisability of a p.m. in all cases of sudden death. You know—even experienced doctors may be deceived. If he comes off very badly in cross-examination, there can be something about specialists not always being trustworthy—a kind word for the poor down-trodden G.P. and all that. Anyhow, he's worth a story. It doesn't matter what you say about him, provided you say something. You couldn't do us a little thing—about eight hundred words, could you —about rigor mortis or something? Only make it snappy."

"I could not," said Wimsey. "I haven't time and I don't want the money. Why should I? I'm not a dean or an actress."

"No, but you're news. You can give me the money, if you're so beastly flush. Look here, have you got a line on this case at all? That police friend of yours won't give anything away. I want to get something in before there's an arrest, because after that it's contempt. I suppose it's the girl you're after, isn't it? Can you tell me anything about her?"

"No—I came here to-night to get a look at her, but she hasn't turned up. I wish you could dig up her hideous past for me. The Rushworths must know something about her, I should think. She used to paint or something. Can't you get on to that?"

Hardy's face lighted up.

"Waffles Newton will probably know something," he said. "I'll see what I can dig out. Thanks very much, old man. That's given me an idea. We might get one of her pictures on the back pages. The old lady seems to have been a queer old soul. Odd will, wasn't it?"

"Oh, I can tell you all about that," said Wimsey. "I thought you probably knew."

He gave Hardy the history of Lady Dormer as he had heard it from Mr. Murbles. The journalist was enthralled.

"Great stuff!" he said. "That'll get 'em. Romance there! This'll be a scoop for the *Yell*. Excuse me. I want to 'phone it through to 'em before somebody else gets it. Don't hand it out to any of the other fellows."

"They can get it from Robert or George Fentiman," warned Wimsey.

"Not much, they won't," said Salcombe Hardy, feelingly. "Robert Fentiman gave old Barton of the *Banner* such a clip under the ear this morning that he had to go and see a dentist. And George has gone down to the Bellona, and they won't let anybody in. I'm all right on this. If there's anything I can do for you, I will, you bet. So long."

He faded away. A hand was laid on Peter's arm.

"You're neglecting me shockingly," said Marjorie Phelps. "And I'm frightfully hungry. I've been doing my best to find things out for you."

"That's top-hole of you. Look here. Come and sit out in the hall; it's quieter. I'll scrounge some grub and bring it along."

He secured a quantity of curious little stuffed buns, four *petits-fours,* some dubious claret-cup and some coffee and brought them with him on a tray, snatched while the waitress's back was turned.

"Thanks," said Marjorie, "I deserve all I can get for having talked to Naomi Rushworth. I cannot like that girl. She hints things."

"What, particularly?"

"Well, I started to ask about Ann Dorland. So she said she wasn't coming. So I said, 'Oh, why?' and she said, 'She *said* she wasn't well.' "

"Who said?"

"Naomi Rushworth said Ann Dorland said she couldn't come because she wasn't well. But she said that was only an excuse, of course."

"Who said?"

"Naomi said. So I said, was it? And she said yes, she didn't suppose she felt like facing people very much. So I said, 'I thought you were such friends.' So she said, 'Well, we are, but of course Ann always was a little abnormal, you see.' So I said that was the first I had heard of it. And she gave me one of her catty looks and said, 'Well, there was Ambrose Ledbury, wasn't there? But of course you had other

224

things to think of then, hadn't you?' The little beast. She meant Komski. And after all, everybody knows how obvious she's made herself over this man Penberthy."

"I'm sorry, I've got mixed."

"Well, I was rather fond of Komski. And I did almost promise to live with him, till I found that his last three women had all got fed up with him and left him, and I felt there must be something wrong with a man who continually got left, and I've discovered since that he was a dreadful bully when he dropped that touching lost-dog manner of his. So I was well out of it. Still, seeing that Naomi had been going about for the last year nearly, looking at Dr. Penberthy like a female spaniel that thinks it's going to be whipped, I can't see why she need throw Komski in my face. And as for Ambrose Ledbury, anybody might have been mistaken in him."

"Who was Ambrose Ledbury?"

"Oh, he was the man who had that studio over Boulter's Mews. Powerfulness was his strong suit, and being above worldly considerations. He was rugged and wore homespun and painted craggy people in bedrooms, but his colour was amazing. He really could paint and so we could excuse a lot, but he was a professional heart-breaker. He used to gather people up hungrily in his great arms, you know—that's always rather irresistible. But he had no discrimination. It was just a habit, and his affairs never lasted long. But Ann Dorland was really rather overcome, you know. She tried the craggy style herself, but it wasn't at all her line—she hasn't any colour-sense, so there was nothing to make up for the bad drawing."

"I thought you said she didn't have any affairs."

"It wasn't an affair. I expect Ledbury gathered her up at some time or other when there wasn't anybody else handy, but he did demand good looks for anything serious. He went off to Poland a year ago with a woman called Natasha somebody. After that, Ann Dorland began to chuck painting. The trouble was, she took things seriously. A few little passions would have put her right, but she isn't the sort of person a man can enjoy flirting with. Heavy-handed. I don't think she would have gone on worrying about Ledbury if he hadn't happened to be the one and only episode. Because, as I say, she did make a few efforts, but she couldn't bring 'em off."

"I see."

"But that's no reason why Naomi should turn round like that. The fact is, the little brute's so proud of having landed a man—*and* an engagement ring—for herself, that she's out to patronize everybody else."

"Oh?"

"Yes; besides, everything is looked at from dear

Walter's point of view now, and naturally Walter isn't feeling very loving towards Ann Dorland."

"Why not?"

"My dear man, you're being very discreet, aren't you? Naturally, everybody's saying that she did it."

"Are they?"

"Who else could they think did it?"

Wimsey realized, indeed, that everybody must be thinking it. He was exceedingly inclined to think it himself.

"Probably that's why she didn't turn up."

"Of course it is. She's not a fool. She must know."

"That's true. Look here, will you do something for me? Something more, I mean?"

"What?"

"From what you say, it looks as though Miss Dorland might find herself rather short of friends in the near future. If she comes to you . . ."

"I'm not going to spy on her. Not if she had poisoned fifty old generals."

"I don't want you to. But I want you to keep an open mind, and tell me what you think. Because I don't want to make a mistake over this. And I'm prejudiced. I want Miss Dorland to be guilty. So I'm very likely to persuade myself she is when she isn't. See?"

"Why do you want her to be guilty?"

"I oughtn't to have mentioned that. Of course, I don't want her found guilty if she isn't really."

"All right. I won't ask questions. And I'll try and see Ann. But I won't try to worm anything out of her. That's definite. I'm standing by Ann."

"My dear girl," said Wimsey, "you're not keeping an open mind. You think she did it."

Marjorie Phelps flushed.

"I don't. Why do you think that?"

"Because you're so anxious not to worm anything out of her. Worming couldn't hurt an innocent person."

"Peter Wimsey! You sit there, looking a perfectly well-bred imbecile, and then in the most underhand way you twist people into doing things they ought to blush for. No wonder you detect things. I will *not* do your worming for you!"

"Well, if you don't, I shall know your opinion, shan't I?"

The girl was silent for a moment. Then she said: "It's all so beastly."

"Poisoning is a beastly crime, don't you think?" said Wimsey.

He got up quickly. Father Whittington was approaching, with Penberthy.

"Well," said Lord Peter, "have the altars reeled?"

"Dr. Penberthy has just informed me that they haven't a leg to stand on," replied the priest, smiling. "We have been spending a pleasant quarter of

228

an hour abolishing good and evil. Unhappily, I understand his dogma as little as he understands mine. But I exercised myself in Christian humility. I said I was willing to learn."

Penberthy laughed.

"You don't object, then, to my casting out devils with a syringe," he said, "when they have proved obdurate to prayer and fasting?"

"Not at all. Why should I? So long as they *are* cast out. And provided you are certain of your diagnosis."

Penberthy crimsoned and turned away sharply.

"Oh, lord!" said Wimsey. "That was a nasty one. From a Christian priest, too!"

"What have I said?" cried Father Whittington, much disconcerted.

"You have reminded Science," said Wimsey, "that only the Pope is infallible."

CHAPTER XVII

Parker Plays A Hand

"NOW, MRS. MITCHAM," SAID INSPECTOR PARKER,
affably. He was always saying "Now, Mrs. Somebody," and he always remembered to say it affably.
It was part of the routine.

The late Lady Dormer's housekeeper bowed
frigidly, to indicate that she would submit to
questioning.

"We want just to get the exact details of every
little thing that happened to General Fentiman the
day before he was found dead. I am sure you will
help us. Do you recollect exactly what time he got
here?"

"It would be round about a quarter to four—
not later; I am sure I could not say exactly to the
minute."

"Who let him in?"

"The footman."

"Did you see him then?"

"Yes; he was shown into the drawing-room, and
I came down to him and brought him upstairs to
her ladyship's bedroom."

"Miss Dorland did not see him then?"

"No; she was sitting with her ladyship. She sent her excuses by me, and begged General Fentiman to come up."

"Did the General seem quite well when you saw him?"

"So far as I could say he seemed well—always bearing in mind that he was a very old gentleman and had heard bad news."

"He was not bluish about the lips, or breathing very heavily, or anything of that kind?"

"Well, going up the stairs tried him rather."

"Yes, of course it would."

"He stood still on the landing for a few minutes to get his breath. I asked him whether he would like to take something, but he said no, he was all right."

"Ah! I daresay it would have been a good thing if he had accepted your very wise suggestion, Mrs. Mitcham."

"No doubt he knew best," replied the house-keeper, primly. She considered that in making ob-servations the policeman was stepping out of his sphere.

"And then you showed him in. Did you witness the meeting between himself and Lady Dormer?"

"I did not" (emphatically). "Miss Dorland got up and said 'How do you do, General Fentiman?' and shook hands with him, and then I left the room, as it was my place to do."

231

"Just so. Was Miss Dorland alone with Lady Dormer when General Fentiman was announced?"

"Oh, no—the nurse was there."

"The nurse—yes, of course. Did Miss Dorland and the nurse stay in the room all the time that the General was there?"

"No. Miss Dorland came out again in about five minutes and came downstairs. She came to me in the housekeeper's room, and she looked rather sad. She. said, 'Poor old dears,'—just like that."

"Did she say any more?"

"She said: 'They quarrelled, Mrs. Mitcham, ages and ages ago, when they were quite young, and they've never seen each other since.' Of course, I was aware of that, having been with her ladyship all these years, and so was Miss Dorland."

"I expect it would seem very pitiful to a young lady like Miss Dorland?"

"No doubt; she is a young lady with feelings; not like some of those you see nowadays."

Parker wagged his head sympathetically.

"And then?"

"Then Miss Dorland went away again, after a little talk with me, and presently Nellie came in— that's the housemaid."

"How long after was that?"

"Oh, some time. I had just finished my cup of tea which I have at four o'clock. It would be about half past. She came to ask for some brandy for the

General, as he was feeling badly. The spirits are kept in my room, you see, and I have the key."

Parker showed nothing of his special interest in this piece of news.

"Did you see the General when you took the brandy?"

"I did not take it." Mrs. Mitcham's tone implied that fetching and carrying was not part of her duty. "I sent it by Nellie."

"I see. So you did not see the General again before he left?"

"No. Miss Dorland informed me later that he had had a heart attack."

"I am very much obliged to you, Mrs. Mitcham. Now I should like just to ask Nellie a few questions."

Mrs. Mitcham touched a bell. A fresh-faced pleasant-looking girl appeared in answer.

"Nellie, this police-officer wants you to give him some information about that time General Fentiman came here. You must tell him what he wants to know, but remember he is busy and don't start your chattering. You can speak to Nellie here, officer."

And she sailed out.

"A bit stiff, isn't she?" murmured Parker, in an awestruck whisper.

"She's one of the old-fashioned sort, I don't mind saying," agreed Nellie with a laugh.

233

"She put the wind up me. Now, Nellie—" he took up the old formula, "I hear you were sent to get some brandy for the old gentleman. Who told you about it?"

"Why, it was like this. After the General had been with Lady Dormer getting on for an hour, the bell rang in her ladyship's room. It was my business to answer that, so I went up, and Nurse Armstrong put her head out and said, 'Get me a drop of brandy, Nellie, quick, and ask Miss Dorland to come here. General Fentiman's rather unwell.' So I went for the brandy to Mrs. Mitcham, and on the way up with it, I knocked at the studio door where Miss Dorland was."

"Where's that, Nellie?"

"It's a big room on the first floor—built over the kitchen. It used to be a billiard-room in the old days, with a glass roof. That's where Miss Dorland does her painting and messing about with bottles and things, and she uses it as a sitting-room, too."

"Messing about with bottles?"

"Well, chemists' stuff and things. Ladies have to have their hobbies, you know, not having any work to do. It makes a lot to clear up."

"I'm sure it does. Well, go on, Nellie—I didn't mean to interrupt."

"Well, I gave Nurse Armstrong's message, and Miss Dorland said, 'Oh, dear, Nellie,' she said, 'poor old gentleman. It's been too much for him. Give me

234

the brandy, I'll take it along. And run along and get Dr. Penberthy on the telephone.' So I gave her the brandy and she took it upstairs."

"Half a moment. Did you see her take it upstairs?"

"Well, no, I don't think I actually saw her go up—but I thought she did. But I was going down to the telephone, so I didn't exactly notice."

"No—why should you?"

"I had to look Dr. Penberthy's number up in the book, of course. There was two numbers, and when I got his private house, they told me he was in Harley Street. While I was trying to get the second number Miss Dorland called over the stairs to me. She said 'Have you got the doctor, Nellie?' And I said, 'No, miss, not yet. The doctor's round in Harley Street.' And she said, 'Oh! well, when you get him, say General Fentiman's had a bad turn and he's coming round to see him at once.' So I said, 'Isn't the doctor to come here, miss?' And she said, 'No; the General's better now and he says he would rather go round there. Tell William to get a taxi.' So she went back, and just then I got through to the surgery and said to Dr. Penberthy's man to expect General Fentiman at once. And then he came downstairs with Miss Dorland and Nurse Armstrong holding on to him, and he looked mortal bad, poor old gentleman. William—the footman, you know, came in then and said he'd got the taxi, and he put General Fentiman into it, and then Miss Dorland and Nurse went upstairs again, and that was the end of it."

"I see. How long have you been here, Nellie?"

"Three years—sir." The "sir" was a concession to Parker's nice manners and educated way of speech. "Quite the gentleman," as Nellie remarked afterwards to Mrs. Mitcham, who replied, "No, Nellie—gentlemanlike I will not deny, but a policeman is a person, and I will trouble you to remember it."

"Three years? That's a long time as things go nowadays. Is it a comfortable place?"

"Not bad. There's Mrs. Mitcham, of course, but I know how to keep the right side of her. And the old lady—well, she was a real lady in every way."

"And Miss Dorland?"

"Oh, she gives no trouble, except clearing up after her. But she always speaks nicely and says please and thank you. I haven't any complaints."

"Modified rapture," thought Parker. Apparently Ann Dorland had not the knack of inspiring passionate devotion. "Not a very lively house, is it, for a young girl like yourself?"

"Dull as ditchwater," agreed Nellie, frankly. "Miss Dorland would have what they called studio parties sometimes, but not at all smart and nearly all young ladies—artists and such-like."

"And naturally it's been quieter still since Lady

236

Dormer died. Was Miss Dorland very much distressed at her death?"

Nellie hesitated.

"She was very sorry, of course; her ladyship was the only one she had in the world. And then she was worried with all this lawyer's business—something about the will, I expect you know, sir?"

"Yes, I know about that. Worried, was she?"

"Yes, and that angry—you wouldn't believe. There was one day Mr. Pritchard came, I remember particular, because I happened to be dusting the hall at the time, you see, and she was speaking that quick and loud I couldn't help hearing. 'I'll fight it for all I'm worth,' that was what she said and 'a . . . something—to defraud'—what would that be, now?"

"Plot?" suggested Parker.

"No—a—a conspiracy, that's it. A conspiracy to defraud. And then I didn't hear any more till Mr. Pritchard came out, and he said to her, 'Very well, Miss Dorland, we will make an independent inquiry.' And Miss Dorland looked so eager and angry, I was surprised. But it all seemed to wear off, like. She hasn't been the same person the last week or so."

"How do you mean?"

"Well, don't you notice it yourself, sir? She seems so quiet and almost frightened-like. As if she'd had a shock. And she cries a dreadful lot. She didn't do that at first."

"How long has she been so upset?"

"Well, I think it was when all this dreadful business came out about the poor old gentleman being murdered. It is awful, sir, isn't it? Do you think you'll catch the one as did it?"

"Oh, I expect so," said Parker, cheerfully. "That came as a shock to Miss Dorland, did it?"

"Well, I should say so. There was a little bit in the paper, you know, sir, about Sir James Lubbock having found out about the poisoning, and when I called Miss Dorland in the morning I took leave to point it out. I said, 'That's a funny thing, miss, isn't it, about General Fentiman being poisoned,' just like that, I said. And she said, 'Poisoned, Nellie? you must be mistaken'. So I showed her the bit in the paper and she looked just dreadful."

"Well, well," said Parker, "it's a very horrid thing to hear about a person one knows. Anybody would be upset."

"Yes, sir; me and Mrs. Mitcham was quite overcome. 'Poor old gentleman,' I said, 'whatever should anybody want to do him in for? He must have gone off his head and made away with himself,' I said. Do you think that was it, sir?"

"It's quite possible, of course," said Parker, genially.

"Cut up about his sister dying like that, don't

you think? That's what I said to Mrs. Mitcham.
But she said a gentleman like General Fentiman
wouldn't make away with himself and leave his
affairs in confusion like he did. So I said, 'Was his
affairs in confusion then?' and she said, 'They're
not your affairs, Nellie, so you needn't be discussing them.' What do you think yourself, sir?"

"I don't think anything yet," said Parker, "but
you have been very helpful. Now, would you
kindly run and ask Miss Dorland if she could spare
me a few minutes?"

Ann Dorland received him in the back drawing-
room. He thought what an unattractive girl she
was, with her sullen manner and gracelessness of
form and movement. She sat huddled on one end
of the sofa, in a black dress which made the worst
of her sallow, blotched complexion. She had certainly been crying Parker thought, and when she
spoke to him, it was curtly, in a voice roughened
and hoarse and curiously lifeless.

"I am sorry to trouble you again," said Parker,
politely.

"You can't help yourself, I suppose." She avoided
his eye, and lit a fresh cigarette from the stump of
the last.

"I just want to have any details you can give me
about General Fentiman's visit to his sister. Mrs.
Mitcham brought him up to her bedroom, I understand."

239

She gave a sulky nod.

"You were there?"

She made no answer.

"Were you with Lady Dormer?" he insisted, rather more sharply.

"Yes."

"And the nurse was there too?"

"Yes."

She would not help him at all.

"What happened?"

"Nothing happened. I took him up to the bed and said, 'Auntie, here's General Fentiman.'"

"Lady Dormer was conscious, then?"

"Yes."

"Very weak, of course?'

"Yes."

"Did she say anything?"

"She said 'Arthur!' that's all. And he said, 'Felicity!' And I said, 'You'd like to be alone,' and went out."

"Leaving the nurse there?"

"I couldn't dictate to the nurse. She had to look after her patient."

"Quite so. Did she stay there throughout the interview?"

"I haven't the least idea."

"Well," said Parker, patiently, "you can tell me this. When you went in with the brandy, the nurse was in the bedroom then?"

240

"Yes, she was."

"Now, about the brandy. Nellie brought that up to you in the studio, she tells me."

"Yes."

"Did she come into the studio?"

"I don't understand."

"Did she come right into the room, or did she knock at the door and did you come out to her on the landing?"

This roused the girl a little. "Decent servants don't knock at doors," she said, with a contemptuous rudeness; "she came in, of course."

"I beg your pardon," retorted Parker, stung. "I thought she might have knocked at the door of your private room."

"No."

"What did she say to you?"

"Can't you ask *her* all these questions?"

"I have done so. But servants are not always accurate; I should like your corroboration." Parker had himself in hand again now, and spoke pleasantly.

"She said that Nurse Armstrong had sent her for some brandy, because General Fentiman was feeling faint, and told her to call me. So I said she had better go and telephone Dr. Penberthy while I took the brandy."

All this was muttered hurriedly, and in such a

241

low tone that the detective could hardly catch the words.

"And then did you take the brandy straight upstairs?"

"Yes, of course."

"Taking it straight out of Nellie's hands? Or did she put it down on the table or anywhere?"

"How the hell should I remember?"

Parker disliked a swearing woman, but he tried hard not to let this prejudice him.

"You can't remember—at any rate, you know you went straight on up with it? You didn't wait to do anything else?"

She seemed to pull herself together and make an effort to remember.

"If it's so important as that, I think I stopped to turn down something that was boiling."

"Boiling? On the fire?"

"On the gas-ring," she said, impatiently.

"What sort of thing."

"Oh, nothing—some stuff."

"Tea or cocoa, or something like that, do you mean?"

"No—some chemical things," she said, letting the words go reluctantly.

"Were you making chemical experiments?"

"Yes—I did a bit—just for fun—a hobby, you know—I don't do anything at it now. I took up the brandy——"

242

Her anxiety to shelve the subject of chemistry seemed to be conquering her reluctance to get on with the story.

"You were making chemical experiments— although Lady Dormer was so ill?" said Parker, severely.

"It was just to occupy my mind," she muttered.

"What was the experiment?"

"I don't remember."

"You can't remember at all?"

"NO!" she almost shouted at him.

"Never mind. You took the brandy upstairs?"

"Yes—at least, it isn't really upstairs. It's all on the same landing, only there are six steps up to Auntie's room. Nurse Armstrong met me at the door, and said 'He's better now,' and I went in and saw General Fentiman sitting in a chair, looking very queer and gray. He was behind a screen where Auntie couldn't see him, or it would have been a great shock to her. Nurse said, 'I've given him his drops and I think a little brandy will put him right again.' So we gave him the brandy—only a small dose, and after a bit, he got less deathly-looking and seemed to be breathing better. I told him we were sending for the doctor, and he said he'd rather go round to Harley Street. I thought it was rash, but Nurse Armstrong said he seemed really better, and it would be a mistake to worry him into doing what he didn't want. So I told Nellie to warn the doctor and send William for a taxi. General Fentiman seemed stronger then, so we helped him downstairs and he went off in the taxi."

Out of this spate of words, Parker fixed on the one thing he had not heard before.

"What drops were those the Nurse gave him?"

"His own. He had them in his pocket."

"Do you think she could possibly have given him too much? Was the quantity marked on the bottle?"

"I haven't the remotest idea. You'd better ask her."

"Yes, I shall want to see her, if you will kindly tell me where to find her."

"I've got the address upstairs. Is that all·you want?"

"I should just like, if I may, to see Lady Dormer's room and the studio."

"What for?"

"It's just a matter of routine. We are under orders to see everything there is to see," replied Parker, reassuringly.

They went upstairs. A door on the first-floor landing immediately opposite the head of the staircase led into a pleasant, lofty room, with old-fashioned bedroom furniture in it.

"This is my aunt's room. She wasn't really my aunt, of course, but I called her so."

"Quite. Where does that second door lead to?"

244

"That's the dressing-room. Nurse Armstrong slept there while Auntie was ill."

Parker glanced in to the dressing-room, took in the arrangement of the bedroom and expressed himself satisfied.

She walked past him without acknowledgment while he held the door open. She was a sturdily-built girl, but moved with a languor distressing to watch—slouching, almost aggressively unalluring.

"You want to see the studio?"

"Please."

She led the way down the six steps and along a short passage to the room which, as Parker already knew, was built out at the back over the kitchen premises. He mentally calculated the distance as he went.

The studio was large and well-lit by its glass roof. One end was furnished like a sitting-room; the other was left bare, and devoted to what Nellie called "mess." A very ugly picture (in Parker's opinion) stood on an easel. Other canvases were stacked round the walls. In one corner was a table covered with American cloth, on which stood a gas-ring, protected by a tin plate, and a Bunsen burner.

"I'll look up that address," said Miss Dorland, indifferently, "I've got it here somewhere."

She began to rummage in an untidy desk. Parker

strolled up to the business end of the room, and explored it with eyes, nose and fingers.

The ugly picture on the easel was newly-painted; the smell told him that, and the dabs of paint on the palette were still soft and sticky. Work had been done there within the last two days, he was sure. The brushes had been stuck at random into a small pot of turpentine. He lifted them out; they were still clogged with paint. The picture itself was a landscape, he thought, roughly drawn and hot and restless in colour. Parker was no judge of art; he would have liked to get Wimsey's opinion. He explored further. The table with the Bunsen burner was bare, but in a cupboard close by he discovered a quantity of chemical apparatus of the kind he remembered using at school. Everything had been tidily washed and stacked away. Nellie's job, he imagined. There were a number of simple and familiar chemical substances in jars and packages, occupying a couple of shelves. They would probably have to be analyzed, he thought, to see if they were all they seemed. And what useless nonsense it all was, he thought to himself; anything suspicious would obviously have been destroyed weeks before. Still, there it was. A book in several volumes on the top shelf caught his attention: it was Quain's Dictionary of Medicine. He took down a volume in which he noticed a paper mark. Opening it at the marked place, his eye fell upon the

words: "Rigor mortis," and, a little later on—
"action of certain poisons." He was about to read
more, when he heard Miss Dorland's voice just
behind him.

"That's all nothing," she said, "I don't do any of
that muck now. It was just a passing craze. I paint,
really. What do you think of this?" She indicated
the unpleasant landscape.

Parker said it was very good.

"Are these your work, too?" he asked, indicating
the other canvases.

"Yes," she said.

He turned a few of them to the light, noticing
at the same time how dusty they were. Nellie had
scamped this bit of the work—or perhaps had been
told not to touch. Miss Dorland showed a trifle
more animation than she had done hitherto, while
displaying her works. Landscape seemed to be
rather a new departure; most of the canvases were
figure-studies. Mr. Parker thought that, on the
whole, the artist had done wisely to turn to landscape. He was not well acquainted with the modern
school of thought in painting, and had difficulty in
expressing his opinion of these curious figures,
with their faces like eggs and their limbs like rubber.

"That is the Judgment of Paris," said Miss Dorland.

"Oh, yes," said Parker. "And this?"

247

"Oh, just a study of a woman dressing. It's not very good. I think this portrait of Mrs. Mitcham is rather decent, though."

Parker stared aghast; it might possibly be a symbolic representation of Mrs. Mitcham's character, for it was very hard and spiky; but it looked more like a Dutch doll, with its triangular nose, like a sharp-edged block of wood, and its eyes mere dots in an expanse of liver-coloured cheek.

"It's not very like her," he said, doubtfully.

"It's not meant to be."

"This seems better—I mean, I like this better," said Parker, turning the next picture up hurriedly.

"Oh, that's nothing—just a fancy head."

Evidently this picture—the head of a rather cadaverous man, with a sinister smile and a slight cast in the eye—was despised—a Philistine backsliding, almost like a human being. It was put away, and Parker tried to concentrate his attention on a "Madonna and Child" which, to Parker's simple evangelical mind, seemed an abominable blasphemy.

Happily, Miss Dorland soon wearied, even of her paintings, and flung them all back into the corner.

"D'you want anything else?" she demanded abruptly. "Here's that address."

Parker took it.

"Just one more question," he said, looking her hard in the eyes. "Before Lady Dormer died—

before General Fentiman came to see her—did you know what provision she had made for you and for him in her will?"

The girl stared back at him, and he saw panic come into her eyes. It seemed to flow all over her like a wave. She clenched her hands at her sides, and her miserable eyes dropped beneath his gaze, shifting as though looking for a way out.

"Well?" said Parker.

"No!" she said. "No! of course not. Why should I?" Then, surprisingly, a dull crimson flush flooded her sallow cheeks and ebbed away, leaving her looking like death.

"Go away," she said, furiously, "you make me sick."

CHAPTER XVIII

Picture-cards

"SO I'VE PUT A MAN IN AND HAD ALL THE THINGS in that cupboard taken away for examination," said Parker.

Lord Peter shook his head.

"I wish I had been there," he said, "I should have liked to see those paintings. However——"

"They might have conveyed something to you," said Parker, "you're artistic. You can come along and look at them any time, of course. But it's the time factor that's worrying me, you know. Supposing she gave the old boy digitalin in his B and S, why should it wait all that time before working? According to the books, it ought to have popped him off in about an hour's time. It was a biggish dose, according to Lubbock."

"I know. I think you're up against a snag there. That's why I should have liked to see the pictures."

Parker considered this apparent *non sequitur* for a few moments and gave it up.

"George Fentiman——" he began.

"Yes," said Wimsey, "George Fentiman. I must be getting emotional in my old age, Charles, for I

250

have an unconquerable dislike to examining the question of George Fentiman's opportunities."

"Bar Robert," pursued Parker, ruthlessly, "he was the last interested person to see General Fentiman."

"Yes—by the way, we have only Robert's unsupported word for what happened in that last interview between him and the old man."

"Come, Wimsey—you're not going to pretend that Robert had any interest in his grandfather's dying before Lady Dormer. On the contrary."

"No—but he might have had some interest in his dying before he made a will. Those notes on that bit of paper. The larger share was to go to George. That doesn't entirely agree with what Robert said. And if there was no will, Robert stood to get everything."

"So he did. But by killing the General then, he made sure of getting nothing at all."

"That's the awkwardness. Unless he thought Lady Dormer was already dead. But I don't see how he could have thought that. Or unless——"

"Well?"

"Unless he gave his grandfather a pill or something to be taken at some future time, and the old boy took it too soon by mistake."

"That idea of a delayed-action pill is the most tiresome thing about this case. It makes almost anything possible."

251

"Including, of course, the theory of its being given to him by Miss Dorland."

"That's what I'm going to interview the nurse about, the minute I can get hold of her. But we've got away from George."

"You're right. Let's face George. I don't want to, though. Like the lady in Maeterlinck who's running round the table while her husband tries to polish her off with a hatchet, I am not gay. George is the nearest in point of time. In fact he fits very well in point of time. He parted from General Fentiman at about half-past six, and Robert found Fentiman dead at about eight o'clock. So allowing that the stuff was given in a pill——"

"Which it would have to be, in a taxi," interjected Parker.

"As you say—in a pill, which would take a bit longer to get working than the same stuff taken in solution—why then the General might quite well have been able to get to the Bellona and see Robert before collapsing."

"Very nice. But how did George get the drug?"

"And how did he happen to have it on him just at that time? He couldn't possibly have known that General Fentiman would run across him just at that moment. Even if he'd known of his being at Lady Dormer's, he couldn't be expecting him to go from there to Harley Street."

"He might have been carrying the stuff about with him, waiting for a good opportunity to use it. And when the old man called him up and started jawing him about his conduct and all that, he thought he'd better do the job quick, before he was cut out of the will."

"Um!—but why should George be such a fool, then, as to admit he'd never heard about Lady Dormer's will? If he had heard of it, we couldn't possibly suspect him. He'd only to say the General told him about it in the taxi."

"I suppose it hadn't struck him in that light."

"Then George is a bigger ass than I took him for."

"Possibly he is," said Parker, dryly. "At any rate, I have put a man on to make inquiries at his home."

"Oh! have you? I say, do you know, I wish I'd left this case alone. What the deuce did it matter if old Fentiman was pushed painlessly off a bit before his time? He was simply indecently ancient."

"We'll see if you say that in sixty years' time," said Parker.

"By that time we shall, I hope, be moving in different circles. I shall be in the one devoted to murderers and you in the much lower and hotter one devoted for those who tempt others to murder them. I wash my hands of this case, Charles. There's nothing for me to do now you have come into it.

253

It bores and annoys me. Let's talk about something else."

Wimsey might wash his hands, but, like Pontius Pilate, he found society irrationally determined to connect him with an irritating and unsatisfactory case.

At midnight, the telephone bell rang.

He had just gone to bed, and cursed it.

"Tell them I'm out," he shouted to Bunter, and cursed again on hearing the man assure the unknown caller that he would see whether his lordship had returned. Disobedience in Bunter spelt urgent necessity.

"Well?"

"It is Mrs. George Fentiman, my lord; she appears to be in great distress. If your lordship wasn't in I was to beg you to communicate with her as soon as you arrived."

"Punk! they're not on the 'phone."

"No, my lord."

"Did she say what the matter was?"

"She began by asking if Mr. George Fentiman was here, my lord."

"Oh, hades!"

Bunter advanced gently with his master's dressing-gown and slippers. Wimsey thrust himself into them savagely and padded away to the telephone.

"Hullo!"

"Is that Lord Peter?—Oh, *good!*" The line

sighed with relief—a harsh sound, like a death-rattle. "Do you know where George is?"

"No idea. Hasn't he come home?"

"No—and I'm frightened. Some people were here this morning . . ."

"The police."

"Yes . . . George . . . they found something . . . I can't say it all over the 'phone . . . but George went off to Walmisley-Hubbard's with the car . . . and they say he never came back there . . . and . . . you remember that time he was so funny before . . . and got lost . . ."

"Your six minutes are up," boomed the voice of the Exchange, "will you have another call?"

"Yes, please . . . oh, don't cut us off . . . wait . . . oh! I haven't any more pennies . . . Lord Peter . . ."

"I'll come round at once," said Wimsey, with a groan.

"Oh, thank you—thank you so much!"

"I say—where's Robert?"

"Your six minutes are up," said the voice, finally, and the line went dead with a metallic crash.

"Get me my clothes," said Wimsey, bitterly—"give me those loathsome and despicable rags which I hoped to have put off forever. Get me a taxi. Get me a drink. Macbeth has murdered sleep. Oh! and get me Robert Fentiman, first."

Major Fentiman was not in town, said Woodward. He had gone back to Richmond again. Wimsey tried to get through to Richmond. After a long time, a female voice, choked with sleep and fury, replied. Major Fentiman had not come home. Major Fentiman kept very late hours. Would she give Major Fentiman a message when he did come in? Indeed she would not. She had other things to do than to stay up all night answering telephone calls and giving messages to Major Fentiman. This was the second time that night, and she had told the other party that she could not be responsible for telling Major Fentiman this, that and the other. Would she leave a note for Major Fentiman, asking him to go round to his brother's house at once? Well now, was it reasonable to expect her to sit up on a bitter cold night writing letters? Of course not, but this was a case of urgent illness. It would be a very great kindness. Just that—to go round to his brother's house and say the call came from Lord Peter Wimsey.

"Who?"

"Lord Peter Wimsey."

"Very well, sir. I beg your pardon if I was a bit short, but really——"

"You weren't, you snobby old cat, you were infernally long," breathed his lordship inaudibly. He thanked her, and rang off.

Sheila Fentiman was anxiously waiting for him on the doorstep, so that he was saved the embarrass-

ment of trying to remember which was the right
number of rings to give. She clasped his hand
eagerly as she drew him in.

"Oh! it is good of you. I'm so worried. I say,
don't make a noise, will you? They complain, you
know." She spoke in a harassed whisper.

"Blast them, let them complain," said Wimsey,
cheerfully. "Why shouldn't you make a row when
George is upset? Besides, if we whisper, they'll
think we're no better than we ought to be. Now,
my child, what's all this? You're as cold as a *pêche
Melba*. That won't do. Fire half out—where's the
whisky?"

"Hush! I'm all right, really. George——"

"You're not all right. Nor am I. As George
Robey says, this getting up from my warm bed and
going into the cold night air doesn't suit me." He
flung a generous shovelful of coals on the fire and
thrust the poker between the bars. "And you've had
no grub. No wonder you're feeling awful."

Two places were set at the table—untouched—
waiting for George. Wimsey plunged into the
kitchen premises, followed by Sheila uttering agitated remonstrances. He found some disagreeable
remnants—a watery stew, cold and sodden; a basin
half-full of some kind of tinned soup; a chill suet
pudding put away on a shelf.

"Does your woman cook for you? I suppose she
does, as you're both out all day. Well, she can't

cook, my child. No matter, here's some Bovril—
she can't have hurt that. You go and sit down and
I'll make you some."

"Mrs. Munns——"

"Blow Mrs. Munns!"

"But I must tell you about George."

He looked at her, and decided that she really
must tell him about George.

"I'm sorry. I didn't mean to bully. One has an
ancestral idea that women must be treated like
imbeciles in a crisis. Centuries of the 'women-and-
children-first' idea, I suppose. Poor devils!"

"Who, the women?"

"Yes. No wonder they sometimes lose their
heads. Pushed into corners, told nothing of what's
happening and made to sit quiet and do nothing.
Strong men would go dotty in the circs. I suppose
that's why we've always grabbed the privilege of
rushing about and doing the heroic bits."

"That's quite true. Give me the kettle."

"No, no, I'll do that. You sit down and—I mean,
sorry, *take* the kettle. Fill it, light the gas, put it
on. And tell me about George."

The trouble, it seemed, had begun at breakfast.
Ever since the story of the murder had come out,
George had been very nervy and jumpy, and, to
Sheila's horror, had "started muttering again."
"Muttering," Wimsey remembered, had formerly
been the prelude to one of George's "queer fits."

258

These had been a form of shell-shock, and they had generally ended in his going off and wandering about in a distraught manner for several days, sometimes with partial and occasionally with complete temporary loss of memory. There was the time when he had been found dancing naked in a field among a flock of sheep, and singing to them. It had been the more ludicrously painful in that George was altogether tone-deaf, so that his singing, though loud, was like a hoarse and rumbling wind in the chimney. Then there was a dreadful time when George had deliberately walked into a bonfire. That was when they had been staying down in the country. George had been badly burnt, and the shock of the pain had brought him round. He never remembered afterwards why he had tried to do these things, and had only the faintest recollection of having done them at all. The next vagary might be even more disconcerting.

At any rate, George had been "muttering."

They were at breakfast that morning, when they saw two men coming up the path. Sheila, who sat opposite the window, saw them first, and said carelessly: "Hullo! who are these? They look like plain-clothes policemen." George took one look, jumped up and rushed out of the room. She called to him to know what was the matter, but he did not answer, and she heard him "rummaging" in the back room, which was the bedroom. She was going to him, when she heard Mr. Munns open the door to the policemen and then heard them inquiring for George. Mr. Munns ushered them into the front room with a grim face on which "police" seemed written in capital letters. George——

At this point the kettle boiled. Sheila was taking it off the stove to make the Bovril, when Wimsey became aware of a hand on his coat-collar. He looked round into the face of a gentleman who appeared not to have shaved for several days.

"Now then," said this apparition, "what's the meaning of this?"

"Which," added an indignant voice from the door, "I thought as there was something behind all this talk of the Captain being missing. You didn't expect him to be missing, I suppose, ma'am. Oh, dear no! Nor your gentleman friend, neither, sneaking up in a taxi and you waiting at the door so's Munns and me shouldn't hear. But I'd have you know this is a respectable house, Lord Knows Who or whatever you call yourself—more likely one of these low-down confidence fellers, I expect, if the truth was known. With a monocle too, like that man we was reading about in the News of the World. And in my kitchen too, and drinking my Bovril in the middle of the night, the impudence! Not to speak of the goings-in-and-out all day, banging the front door, and that was the police come here this morning, you think I didn't know?

260

Up to something, that's what they've been, the pair of them, and the captain as he says he is but that's as may be, I daresay he had his reasons for clearing off, and the sooner you goes after him my fine madam, the better I'll be pleased, I can tell you."

"That's right," said Mr. Munns—"ow!"

Lord Peter had removed the intrusive hand from his collar with a sharp jerk which appeared to cause anguish out of all proportion to the force used.

"I'm glad you've come along," he said. "In fact, I was just going to give you a call. Have you anything to drink in the house, by the way?"

"Drink?" cried Mrs. Munns on a high note, "the impudence! And if I see you, Joe, giving drinks to thieves and worse in the middle of the night in my kitchen, you'll get a piece of my mind. Coming in here as bold as brass, and the captain run away, and asking for drink——"

"Because," said Wimsey, fingering his note-case, "the public houses in this law-abiding neighbourhood are of course closed. Otherwise a bottle of Scotch——"

Mr. Munns appeared to hesitate.

"Call yourself a man!" said Mrs. Munns.

"Of course," said Mr. Munns, "if I was to go in a friendly manner to Jimmy Rowe at the Dragon, and ask him to give me a bottle of Johnny Walker as a friend to a friend, and provided no money was to pass between him and me, that is——"

"A good idea," said Wimsey, cordially.

Mrs. Munns gave a loud shriek.

"The ladies," said Mr. Munns, "gets nervous at times." He shrugged his shoulders.

"I daresay a drop of Scotch wouldn't do Mrs. Munns's nerves any harm," said Wimsey.

"If you dare, Joe Munns," said the landlady, "if you dare to go out at this time of night, hob-nobbing with Jimmy Rowe and making a fool of yourself with burglars and such——"

Mr. Munns executed a sudden volte-face.

"You shut up!" he shouted. "Always sticking your face in where you aren't wanted."

"Are you speaking to me?"

"Yes. Shut up!"

Mrs. Munns sat down suddenly on a kitchen chair and began to sniff.

"I'll just hop round to the Dragon now, sir," said Mr. Munns, "before old Jimmy goes to bed. And then we'll go into this here."

He departed. Possibly he forgot what he had said about no money passing, for he certainly took the note which Wimsey absent-mindedly held out to him.

"Your drink's getting cold," said Wimsey to Sheila.

She came across to him.

"Can't we get rid of these people?"

"In half a jiff. It's no good having a row with

them. I'd do it like a shot, only, you see, you've got to stay on here for a bit, in case George comes back."

"Of course. I'm sorry for all this upset, Mrs. Munns," she added, a little stiffly, "but I'm so worried about my husband."

"Husband?" snorted Mrs. Munns. "A lot husbands are to worry about. Look at that Joe. Off he goes to the Dragon, never mind what I say to him. They're dirt, that's what husbands are, the whole pack of them. And I don't care what anybody says."

"Are they?" said Wimsey. "Well, I'm not one—yet—so you needn't mind what you say to me."

"It's the same thing," said the lady, viciously, "husbands and parricides, there's not a halfpenny to choose between them. Only parricides aren't respectable—but then, they're easier got rid of."

"Oh!" replied Wimsey, "but I'm not a parricide either—not Mrs. Fentiman's parricide at any rate, I assure you. Hullo! here's Joe. Did you get the doings, old man? You did? Good work. Now, Mrs. Munns, have just a spot with us. You'll feel all the better for it. And why shouldn't we go into the sitting-room where it's warmer?"

Mrs. Munns complied. "Oh, well," she said, "here's friends all round. But you'll allow it all looked a bit queer, now, didn't it? And the police this morning, asking all those questions, and emptying the dust-bin all over the backyard."

"Whatever did they want with the dust-bin?"

"Lord knows; and that Cummins woman looking on all the time over the wall. I can tell you, I was vexed. 'Why, Mrs. Munns,' she said, 'have you been poisoning people?' she said. 'I always told you,' she said, 'your cooking 'ud do for somebody one of these days.' The nasty cat."

"What a rotten thing to say," said Wimsey, sympathetically. "Just jealousy, I expect. But what did the police find in the dust-bin?"

"Find? Them find anything? I should like to see them finding things in my dust-bin. The less I see of their interfering ways the better I'm pleased. I told them so. I said, 'If you want to come upsetting my dust-bin,' I said, 'you'll have to come with a search-warrant,' I said. That's the law and they couldn't deny it. They said Mrs. Fentiman had given them leave to look, so I told them Mrs Fentiman had no leave to give them. It was my dust-bin, I told them, not hers. So they went off with a flea in their ear."

"That's the stuff to give 'em, Mrs. Munns."

"Not but what I'm respectable. If the police come to me in a right and lawful manner, I'll gladly give them any help they want. I don't want to get into trouble, not for any number of captains. But interference with a free-born woman

264

and no search-warrant I will *not* stand. And they can either come to me in a fitting way or they can go and whistle for their bottle."

"What bottle?" asked Wimsey, quickly.

"The bottle they were looking for in my dust-bin, what the captain put there after breakfast." Sheila gave a faint cry.

"What bottle was that, Mrs. Munns?"

"One of them little tablet bottles," said Mrs. Munns, "same as you have standing on the wash-hand stand, Mrs. Fentiman. When I saw the Captain smashing it up in the yard with a poker——"

"There now, Primrose," said Mr. Munns, "can't you see as Mrs. Fentiman ain't well?"

"I'm quite all right," said Sheila, hastily, pushing away the hair which clung damply to her forehead. "What was my husband doing?"

"I saw him," said Mrs. Munns, "run out into the back yard—just after your breakfast it was, because I recollect Munns was letting the officers into the house at the time. Not that I knew then who it was, for, if you will excuse me mentioning of it, I was in the outside lavatory, and that was how I come to see the Captain. Which ordinarily, you can't see the dust-bin from the house, my lord I should say, I suppose, if you really are one, but you meet so many bad characters nowadays that one can't be too careful—on account of the lavatory standing out as you may say and hiding it."

265

"Just so," said Wimsey.

"So when I saw the captain breaking the bottle as I said, and throwing the bits into the dust-bin, 'Hullo!' I said, 'that's funny,' and I went to see what it was and I put it in an envelope, thinking, you see, as it might be something poisonous, and the cat such a dreadful thief as he is, I never can keep him out of that dust-bin. And when I came in, I found the police here. So after a bit, I found them poking about in the yard and I asked them what they were doing there. Such a mess as they'd made, you never would believe. So they showed me a little cap they'd found, same as it might be off that tablet bottle. 'Did I know where the rest of it was?' they said. And I said, what business had they got with the dust-bin at all. So they said——"

"Yes, I know," said Wimsey. "I think you acted very sensibly, Mrs. Munns. And what did you do with the envelope and things?"

"I kept it," replied Mrs. Munns, nodding her head, "I kept it. Because, you see, if they *did* return *with* a warrant and I'd destroyed that bottle, where should *I* be?"

"Quite right," said Wimsey, with his eye on Sheila.

"Always keep on the right side of the law," agreed Mr. Munns, "and nobody can't interfere with you. That's what I say. I'm a Conservative, I

266

am. I don't hold with these Socialist games. Have another."

"Not just now," said Wimsey. "And we really must not keep you and Mrs. Munns up any longer. But, look here! You see, Captain Fentiman had shell-shock after the War, and he is liable to do these little odd things at times—break things up, I mean, and lose his memory and go wandering about. So Mrs. Fentiman is naturally anxious about his not having turned up this evening."

"Ay," said Mr. Munns, with relish, "I knew a fellow like that. Went clean off his rocker he did one night. Smashed up his family with a beetle—a paviour he was by profession, and that's how he came to have a beetle in the house—pounded 'em to a jelly, he did, his wife and five little children, and went off and drownded himself in the Regent's Canal. And, what's more, when they got him out, he didn't remember a word about it, not one word. So they sent him to—what's that place? Dartmoor? no, Broadmoor, that's it, where Ronnie True went to with his little toys and all."

"Shut up, you fool," said Wimsey, savagely.

"Haven't you got feelings?" demanded his wife.

Sheila got up, and made a blind effort in the direction of the door.

"Come and lie down," said Wimsey, "you're worn out. Hullo! there's Robert, I expect. I left a message for him to come round as soon as he got home."

Mr. Munns went to answer the bell.

"We'd better get her to bed as quick as possible," said Wimsey to the landlady. "Have you got such a thing as a hot-water bottle?"

Mrs. Munns departed to fetch one, and Sheila caught Wimsey's hand.

"Can't you get hold of that bottle? Make her give it you. You can. You can do anything. Make her."

"Better not," said Wimsey. "Look suspicious. Look here, Sheila, what *is* the bottle?"

"My heart medicine. I missed it. It's something to do with digitalin."

"Oh, lord," said Wimsey, as Robert came in.

.   .   .   .

"It's all pretty damnable," said Robert.

He thumped the fire gloomily; it was burning badly, the lower bars were choked with the ashes of a day and night.

"I've been having a talk with Frobisher," he added. "All this talk in the Club—and the papers— naturally he couldn't overlook it."

"Was he decent?"

"Very decent. But of course I couldn't explain the thing. I'm sending in my papers."

Wimsey nodded. Colonel Frobisher could scarcely

overlook an attempted fraud—not after things had been said in the papers.

"If I'd only let the old man alone. Too late now. He'd have been buried. Nobody would have asked questions."

"I didn't *want* to interfere," said Wimsey, defending himself against the unspoken reproach.

"Oh, I know. I'm not blaming you. People . . . money oughtn't to depend on people's deaths . . . old people, with no use for their lives . . . it's a devil of a temptation. Look here, Wimsey, what are we to do about this woman?"

"The Munns female?"

"Yes. It's the devil and all she should have got hold of the stuff. If they find out what it's supposed to be, we shall be blackmailed for the rest of our lives."

"No," said Wimsey, "I'm sorry, old man, but the police have got to know about it."

Robert sprang to his feet.

"My God!—you wouldn't——"

"Sit down, Fentiman. Yes, I must. Don't you see I must? We can't suppress things. It always means trouble. It's not even as though they hadn't got their eye on us already. They're suspicious——"

"Yes, and why?" burst out Robert, violently. "Who put it into their heads? . . . For God's sake don't start talking about law and justice! Law and justice! You'd sell your best friend for the sake of making a sensational appearance in the witness-box, you infernal little police spy!"

"Chuck that, Fentiman!"

"I'll not chuck it! You'd go and give away a man to the police—when you know perfectly well he isn't responsible—just because you can't afford to be mixed up in anything unpleasant. I know you. Nothing's too dirty for you to meddle in, provided you can pose as the pious little friend of justice. You make me sick!"

"I tried to keep out of this——"

"You tried!—don't be a blasted hypocrite! You get out of it now, and stay out—do you hear?"

"Yes, but listen a moment——"

"Get out!" said Robert.

Wimsey stood up.

"I know how you feel, Fentiman——"

"Don't stand there being righteous and fore-bearing, you sickening prig. For the last time—are you going to shut up, or are you going to trot round to your policeman friend and earn the thanks of a grateful country for splitting on George? Get on! Which is it to be?"

"You won't do George any good——"

"Never mind that. Are you going to hold your tongue?"

"Be reasonable, Fentiman."

"Reasonable be damned. Are you going to the police? No shuffling. Yes or no?"

"Yes."

"You dirty little squirt," said Robert, striking out passionately. Wimsey's return blow caught him neatly on the chin and landed him in the waste-paper basket.

"And now, look here," said Wimsey, standing over him, hat and stick in hand. "It's no odds to me what you do or say. You think your brother murdered your grandfather. I don't know whether he did or not. But the worst thing you can do for him is to try and destroy evidence. And the worst thing you can possibly do for his wife is to make her a party to anything of the sort. And next time you try to smash anybody's face in, remember to cover up your chin. That's all. I can let myself out. Good-bye."

· · · · · · · ·

He went round to 12 Great Ormond Street and routed Parker out of bed.

Parker listened thoughtfully to what he had to say.

"I wish we'd stopped Fentiman before he bolted," he said.

"Yes; why didn't you?"

"Well, Dykes seems to have muffed it rather. I wasn't there myself. But everything seemed all right. Fentiman looked a bit nervy, but many people do when they're interviewed by the police—think of their hideous pasts, I suppose, and won-

271

der what's coming next. Or else it's just stage-fright. He stuck to the same tale he told you— said he was quite sure the old General hadn't taken any pills or anything in the taxi—didn't attempt to pretend he knew anything about Lady Dormer's will. There was nothing to detain him for. He said he had to get to his job in Great Portland Street. So they let him go. Dykes sent a man to follow him up, and he went along to Hubbard-Walmisley's all right. Dykes said, might he just have a look round the place before he went, and Mrs. Fentiman said certainly. He didn't expect to find anything, really. Just happened to step into the back-yard, and saw a bit of broken glass. He then had a look round, and there was the cap of the tablet-bottle in the dust-bin. Well, then, of course, he started to get interested, and was just having a hunt through for the rest of it, when old mother Munns appeared and said the dust-bin was her property. So they had to clear out. But Dykes oughtn't to have let Fentiman go till they'd finished going over the place. He 'phoned through to Hubbard-Walmisley's at once, and heard that Fentiman had arrived and immediately gone out with the car, to visit a prospective customer in Herts. The fellow who was supposed to be trailing Fentiman got carburetor trouble just beyond St. Albans, and by the time he was fixed, he'd lost Fenti-man."

272

"Did Fentiman go to the customer's house?"

"Not he. Disappeared completely. We shall find the car, of course—it's only a matter of time."

"Yes," said Wimsey. His voice sounded tired and constrained.

"This alters the look of things a bit," said Parker, "doesn't it?"

"Yes."

"What have you done to your face, old man?"

Wimsey glanced at the looking-glass, and saw that an angry red flush had come up on the cheek-bone.

"Had a bit of a dust-up with Robert," he said.

"Oh!"

Parker was aware of a thin veil of hostility, drawn between himself and the friend he valued. He knew that for the first time, Wimsey was seeing him as the police. Wimsey was ashamed and his shame made Parker ashamed too.

"You'd better have some breakfast," said Parker. His voice sounded awkward to himself.

"No—no thanks, old man. I'll go home and get a bath and shave."

"Oh, right-oh!"

There was a pause.

"Well, I'd better be going," said Wimsey.

"Oh, yes," said Parker again. "Right-oh!"

"Er—cheerio!" said Wimsey at the door.

"Cheerio!" said Parker.

273

The bedroom door shut. The flat-door shut. The front-door shut.

Parker pulled the telephone towards him and called up Scotland Yard.

. . . .

The atmosphere of his own office was bracing to Parker when he got down there. For one thing, he was taken aside by a friend and congratulated in conspiratorial whispers.

"Your promotion's gone through," said the friend. "Dead certainty. The Chief's no end pleased. Between you and me, of course. But you've got your Chief-Inspectorship all right. Damn good."

Then, at ten o'clock, the news came through that the missing Walmisley-Hubbard had turned up. It had been abandoned in a remote Hertford-shire lane. It was in perfectly good order, the gear-lever in neutral and the tank full of petrol. Evi-dently, Fentiman had left it and wandered away somewhere, but he could not be far off. Parker made the necessary arrangements for combing out the neighbourhood. The bustle and occupation soothed his mind. Guilty or insane or both, George Fentiman had to be found; it was just a job to be done.

The man who had been sent to interview Mrs. Munns (armed this time with a warrant) returned with the fragments of the bottle and tablets.

Parker duly passed these along to the police analyst. One of the detectives who was shadowing Miss Dorland rang up to announce that a young woman had come to see her, and that the two had then come out carrying a suit-case and driven away in a taxi. Maddison, the other detective, was following them. Parker said, "All right; stay where you are for the present," and considered this new development. The telephone rang again. He thought it would be Maddison, but it was Wimsey—a determinedly brisk and cheerful Wimsey this time.

"I say, Charles. I want something."

"What?"

"I want to go and see Miss Dorland."

"You can't. She's gone off somewhere. My man hasn't reported yet."

"Oh! Well, never mind her. What I really want to see is her studio."

"Yes? Well, there's no reason why you shouldn't."

"Will they let me in?"

"Probably not. I'll meet you there and take you in with me. I was going out any way. I've got to interview the nurse. We've just got hold of her."

"Thanks awfully. Sure you can spare the time?"

"Yes. I'd like your opinion."

"I'm glad somebody wants it. I'm beginning to feel like a pelican in the wilderness."

"Rot! I'll be round in ten minutes."

"Of course," explained Parker, as he ushered Wimsey into the studio, "we've taken away all the chemicals and things. There's not much to look at, really."

"Well, you can deal best with all that. It's the books and paintings I want to look at. H'm! Books, you know, Charles, are like lobster-shells. We surround ourselves with 'em, and then we grow out of 'em and leave 'em behind, as evidences of our earlier stages of development."

"That's a fact," said Parker. "I've got rows of school-boy stuff at home—never touch it now, of course. And W. J. Locke—read everything he wrote once upon a time. And Le Queux, and Conan Doyle, and all that stuff."

"And now you read theology. And what else?"

"Well, I read Hardy a good bit. And when I'm not too tired, I have a go at Henry James."

"The refined self-examinations of the infinitely-sophisticated. 'M-m. Well now. Let's start with the shelves by the fireplace. Dorothy Richardson—Virginia Woolf—E. B. C. Jones—May Sinclair—Katherine Mansfield—the modern female writers are well represented, aren't they? Galsworthy. Yes. No J. D. Beresford—no Wells—no Bennett. Dear me, quite a row of D. H. Lawrence. I wonder if she reads him very often."

He pulled down "Women in Love" at random, and slapped the pages open and shut.

"Not kept very well dusted, are they? But they have been read. Compton Mackenzie—Storm Jameson—yes—I see."

"The medical stuff is over here."

"Oh!—a few text-books—first steps in chemistry. What's that tumbled down at the back of the book-case? Louis Berman, eh? *The Personal Equation*. And here's *Why We Behave Like Human Beings*. And Julian Huxley's essays. A determined effort at self-education here, what?"

"Girls seem to go in for that sort of thing nowadays."

"Yes—hardly nice, is it? Hullo!"

"What?"

"Over here by the couch. This represents the latest of our lobster-shells, I fancy. Austin Freeman, Austin Freeman, Austin Freeman—bless me! she must have ordered him in wholesale. *Through the Wall*—that's a good 'tec story, Charles—all about the third degree—Isabel Ostrander—three Edgar Wallaces—the girl's been indulging in an orgy of crime!"

"I shouldn't wonder," said Parker, with emphasis. "That fellow Freeman is full of plots about poisonings and wills and survivorship, isn't he?"

"Yes"—Wimsey balanced *A Silent Witness* gently in his hand, and laid it down again. "This one, for instance, is all about a bloke who murdered somebody and kept him in cold storage till

277

he was ready to dispose of him. It would suit Robert Fentiman."

Parker grinned.

"A bit elaborate for the ordinary criminal. But I daresay people do get ideas out of these books. Like to look at the pictures? They're pretty awful."

"Don't try to break it gently. Show us the worst at once. . . . Oh, lord!"

"Well, it gives *me* a pain," said Parker. "But I thought perhaps that was my lack of artistic education."

"It was your natural good taste. What vile colour, and viler drawing."

"But nobody cares about drawing nowadays, do they?"

"Ah! but there's a difference between the man who can draw and won't draw, and the man who can't draw at all. Go on. Let's see the rest."

Parker produced them, one after the other. Wimsey glanced quickly at each. He had picked up the brush and palette and was fingering them as he talked.

"These," he said, "are the paintings of a completely untalented person, who is, moreover, trying to copy the mannerisms of a very advanced school. By the way, you have noticed, of course, that she has been painting within the last few days, but chucked it in sudden disgust. She has left the paints on the palette, and the brushes are still stuck

278

in the turps, turning their ends up and generally ruining themselves. Suggestive, I fancy. The—stop a minute! Let's look at that again."

Parker had brought forward the head of the sallow, squinting man which he had mentioned to Wimsey before.

"Put that up on the easel. That's very interesting. The others, you see, are all an effort to imitate other people's art, but this—this is an effort to imitate nature. Why?—it's very bad, but it's meant for somebody. And it's been worked on a lot. Now what was it made her do that?"

"Well, it wasn't for his beauty, I should think."

"No?—but there must have been a reason. Dante, you may remember, once painted an angel. Do you know the limerick about the old man of Khartoum?"

"What did he do?"

"He kept two black sheep in his room. They remind me (he said) Of two friends who are dead, But I cannot remember of whom."

"If that reminds you of anybody you know, I don't care much for your friends. I never saw an uglier mug."

"He's not beautiful. But I think the sinister squint is chiefly due to bad drawing. It's very difficult to get eyes looking the same way, when you can't draw. Cover up one eye, Charles—not yours, the portrait's."

Parker did so.

Wimsey looked again, and shook his head.

"It escapes me for the moment," he said. "Probably it's nobody I know after all. But, whoever it is, surely this room tells you something."

"It suggests to me," said Parker, "that the girl's been taking more interest in crimes and chemistry stuff than is altogether healthy in the circumstances."

Wimsey looked at him for a moment.

"I wish I could think as you do."

"What *do* you think?" demanded Parker, impatiently.

"No," said Wimsey. "I told you about that George business this morning, because glass bottles are facts, and one mustn't conceal facts. But I'm not obliged to tell you what I think."

"You don't think, then, that Ann Dorland did the murder?"

"I don't know about that, Charles. I came here hoping that this room would tell me the same thing that it told you. But it hasn't. It's told me different. It's told me what I thought all along."

"A penny for your thoughts, then," said Parker, trying desperately to keep the conversation on a jocular footing.

"Not even thirty pieces of silver," replied Wimsey, mournfully.

Parker stacked the canvasses away without another word.

CHAPTER XIX

Lord Peter Plays Dummy

"DO YOU WANT TO COME WITH ME TO THE Armstrong woman?"

"May as well," said Wimsey, "you never know."

Nurse Armstrong belonged to an expensive nursing home in Great Wimpole Street. She had not been interviewed before, having only returned the previous evening from escorting an invalid lady to Italy. She was a large, good-looking, imperturbable woman, rather like the Venus of Milo, and she answered Parker's questions in a cheerful, matter-of-fact tone, as though they had been about bandages or temperatures.

"Oh, yes, constable; I remember the poor old gentleman being brought in, perfectly."

Parker had a natural dislike to being called constable. However, a detective must not let little things like that irritate him.

"Was Miss Dorland present at the interview between your patient and her brother?"

"Only for a few moments. She said good afternoon to the old gentleman and led him up to the bed, and then, when she saw them comfortable together, she went out."

"How do you mean, comfortable together?"

"Well, the patient called the old gentleman by his name, and he answered, and then he took her hand and said, 'I'm sorry, Felicity; forgive me,' or something of that sort, and she said, 'There's nothing to forgive; don't distress yourself, Arthur,'— crying, he was, the poor old man. So he sat down on the chair by the bed, and Miss Dorland went out."

"Nothing was said about the will?"

"Not while Miss Dorland was in the room, if that's what you mean."

"Suppose anybody had listened at the door afterwards—could they have heard what was said?"

"Oh, no! The patient was very weak and spoke very low. I couldn't hear myself half she said."

"Where were you?"

"Well, I went away, because I thought they'd like to be alone. But I was in my own room with the door open between, and I was looking in most of the time. She was so ill, you see, and the old gentleman looked so frail, I didn't like to go out of earshot. In our work, you see, we often have to see and hear a lot that we don't say anything about."

"Of course, Nurse—I am sure you did quite

282

right. Now when Miss Dorland brought the brandy up—the General was feeling very ill?"

"Yes—he had a nasty turn. I put him in the big chair and bent him over till the spasm went off. He asked for his own medicine, and I gave it to him—no, it wasn't drops—it was amyl nitrate; you inhale it. Then I rang the bell and sent the girl for the brandy."

"Amyl nitrate—you're sure that's all he had?"

"Positive; there wasn't anything else. Lady Dormer had been having strychnine injections to keep her heart going, of course, and we'd tried oxygen; but we shouldn't give him those, you know."

She smiled, competently, condescendingly.

"Now, you say Lady Dormer had been having this, that and the other. Were there any medicines lying about that General Fentiman might have accidentally taken up and swallowed?"

"Oh, dear no."

"No drops or tabloids or anything of that kind?"

"Certainly not; the medicines were kept in my room."

"Nothing on the bedside table or the mantel-piece?"

"There was a cup of diluted Listerine by the bed, for washing out the patient's mouth from time to time, that was all."

"And there's no digitalin in Listerine—no, of course not. Well now, who brought up the brandy-and-water?"

"The housemaid went to Mrs. Mitcham for it. I should have had some upstairs, as a matter of fact, but the patient couldn't keep it down. Some of them can't, you know."

"Did the girl bring it straight up to you?"

"No—she stopped to call Miss Dorland on the way. Of course, she ought to have brought the brandy at once and gone to Miss Dorland afterwards—but it's anything to save trouble with these girls, as I daresay you know."

"Did Miss Dorland bring it straight up—?" began Parker. Nurse Armstrong broke in upon him.

"If you're thinking, did she put the digitalin into the brandy, you can dismiss that from your mind, constable. If he'd had as big a dose as that in solution at half past four, he'd have been taken ill ever so much earlier than he was."

"You seem to be well up in the case, Nurse."

"Oh, I am. Naturally I was interested, Lady Dormer being my patient and all."

"Of course. But all the same, *did* Miss Dorland bring the brandy straight along to you?"

"I think so. I heard Nellie go along the passage on the half landing, and looked out to call to her, but by the time I'd got the door open, I saw Miss

284

Dorland coming out of the studio with the brandy in her hand."

"And where was Nellie then?"

"Just got back to the end of the passage and starting downstairs to the telephone."

"At that rate, Miss Dorland couldn't have been more than ten seconds alone with the brandy," said Peter, thoughtfully. "And who gave it to General Fentiman?"

"I did. I took it out of Miss Dorland's hand at the door and gave it to him at once. He seemed better then, and only took a little of it."

"Did you leave him again?"

"I did not. Miss Dorland went out on to the landing presently to see if the taxi was coming."

"She was never alone with him?"

"Not for a moment."

"Did you like Miss Dorland, Nurse? Is she a nice girl, I mean?" Wimsey had not spoken for so long that Parker quite started.

"She was always very pleasant to me," said Nurse Armstrong. "I shouldn't call her an attractive girl, not to my mind."

"Did she ever mention Lady Dormer's testamentary arrangements in your hearing?" asked Parker, picking up what he conceived to be Wimsey's train of thought.

"Well—not exactly. But I remember her once talking about her painting, and saying she did it for a hobby, as her aunt would see she always had enough to live on."

"That's true enough," said Parker. "At the worst, she would get fifteen thousand pounds, which carefully invested, might mean six or seven hundred a year. She didn't say she expected to be very rich?"

"No."

"Nor anything about the General?"

"Not a word."

"Was she happy?" asked Wimsey.

"She was upset, naturally, with her aunt being so ill."

"I don't mean that. You are the sort of person who observes a lot—nurses are awfully quick about that kind of thing, I've noticed. Did she strike you as a person who—who felt right with life, as you might say?"

"She was one of the quiet ones. But—yes—I should say she was satisfied with things all right."

"Did she sleep well?"

"Oh, she was a very sound sleeper. It was a job to wake her if anything was wanted in the night."

"Did she cry much?"

"She cried over the old lady's death; she had very nice feelings."

"Some natural tears she shed, and all that. She didn't lie about and have awful howling fits or anything like that?"

"Good gracious, no!"

"How did she walk?"

"Walk?"

"Yes, walk. Was she what you'd call droopy?"

"Oh, no—quick and brisk."

"What was her voice like?"

"Well, now, that was one of the nice things about her. Rather deep for a woman, but with what I might call a tune in it. Melodious," said Nurse Armstrong, with a faint giggle, "that's what they call it in novels."

Parker opened his mouth and shut it again.

"How long did you stay on at the house after Lady Dormer died?" pursued Wimsey.

"I waited on till after the funeral, just in case Miss Dorland should need anybody."

"Before you left, did you hear anything of this trouble about the lawyers and the wills?"

"They were talking about it downstairs. Miss Dorland said nothing to me herself."

"Did she seem worried?"

"Not to notice."

"Had she any friends with her at the time?"

"Not staying in the house. She went out to see some friends one evening, I think—the evening before I left. She didn't say who they were."

"I see. Thank you, Nurse."

Parker had no more questions to put, and they took their leave.

"Well," said Parker, "how anybody could admire that girl's voice——"

"You noticed that! My theory is coming out right, Charles. I wish it wasn't. I'd *rather* be wrong. I should like to have you look pitifully at me and say, 'I told you so.' I can't speak more strongly than that."

"Hang your theories!" said Parker. "It looks to me as if we shall have to wash out the idea that General Fentiman got his dose in Portman Square. By the way, didn't you say you'd met the Dorland girl at the Rushworths?"

"No. I said I went hoping to meet her, but she wasn't there."

"Oh, I see. Well, that'll do for the moment. How about a spot of lunch?"

At which point they turned the corner and ran slap into Salcombe Hardy, emerging from Harley Street. Wimsey clutched Parker's arm suddenly. "I've remembered," he said.

"What?"

"Who that portrait reminds me of. Tell you later."

Sally, it appeared, was also thinking of grub. He was, in fact, due to meet Waffles Newton at the Falstaff. It ended in their all going to the Falstaff.

"And how's it all going?" demanded Sally, ordering boiled beef and carrots.

288

He looked limpidly at Parker, who shook his head.

"Discreet man, your friend," said Sally to Peter. "I suppose the police are engaged in following up a clew—or have we reached the point when they are completely baffled? Or do we say that an arrest is imminent, eh?"

"Tell us your own version, Sally. Your opinion's as good as anybody's."

"Oh, mine!—Same as yours—same as everybody's. The girl was in league with the doctor, of course. Pretty obvious, isn't it?"

"Maybe," said Parker, cautiously. "But that's a hard thing to prove. We know, of course, that they both sometimes went to Mrs. Rushworth's house, but there's no evidence that they knew each other well."

"But, you ass, she—" Wimsey blurted out. He shut his mouth again with a snap. "No, I won't. Fish it out for yourselves."

Illumination was flooding in on him in great waves. Each point of light touched off a myriad others. Now a date was lit up, and now a sentence. The relief in his mind would have been overwhelming, had it not been for that nagging central uncertainty. It was the portrait that worried him most. Painted as a record, painted to recall beloved features—thrust face to the wall and covered with dust.

289

Sally and Parker were talking.

". . . moral certainty is not the same thing as proof."

"Unless we can show that she knew the terms of the will. . . ."

". . . why wait till the last minute? It could have been done safely any time. . . ."

"They probably thought it wasn't necessary. The old lady looked like seeing him into his grave easily. If it hadn't been for the pneumonia."

"Even so, they had five days."

"Yes—well, say she didn't know till the very day of Lady Dormer's death. . . ."

"She might have told her then. Explained . . . seeing the thing had become a probability. . . ."

"And the Dorland girl arranged for the visit to Harley Street. . . ."

". . . plain as the nose on your face."

Hardy chuckled.

"They must have got a thundering shock when the body turned up the next morning at the Bellona. I suppose you gave Penberthy a good grueling about that rigor."

"Pretty fair. He fell back on professional caution, naturally."

"It's coming to him in the witness-box. Does he admit knowing the girl?"

"He says he just knows her to speak to. But one's got to find somebody who has seen them together.

290

You remember the Thompson case. It was the interview in the tea-shop that clinched it."

"What I want to know," said Wimsey, "is why——"

"Why what?"

"Why didn't they compromise?" It was not what he had been going to say, but he felt defeated, and those words would end the sentence as well as any others.

"What's that?" asked Hardy, quickly.

Peter explained.

"When the question of survivorship came up, the Fentimans were ready to compromise and split the money. Why didn't Miss Dorland agree? If your idea is the right one, it was much the safest way. But it was she who insisted on an inquiry."

"I didn't know that," said Hardy. He was annoyed. All kinds of "stories" were coming his way to-day, and to-morrow there would probably be an arrest, and he wouldn't be able to use them.

"They *did* agree to compromise in the end," said Parker. "When was that?"

"After I told Penberthy there was going to be an exhumation," said Wimsey, as though in spite of himself.

"There you are! They saw it was getting too dangerous."

"Do you remember how nervous Penberthy was at the exhumation?" said Parker. "That man——

291

what's his name's—joke about Palmer, and knocking over the jar?"

"What was that?" demanded Hardy again. Parker told him, and he listened, grinding his teeth. Another good story gone west. But it would all come out at the trial, and would be worth a headline.

"Robert Fentiman ought to be given a medal," said Hardy. "If he hadn't gone butting in——"

"Robert Fentiman?" inquired Parker, distantly. Hardy grinned.

"If he didn't fix up the old boy's body, who did? Give us credit for a little intelligence."

"One admits nothing," said Parker, "but——"

"But everybody says he did it. Leave it at that. Somebody did it. If Somebody hadn't butted in, it would have been jam for the Dorland."

"Well, yes. Old Fentiman would just have gone home and pegged out quietly—and Penberthy would have given the certificate."

"I'd like to know how many inconvenient people are polished off that way. Damn it—it's so easy."

"I wonder how Penberthy's share of the boodle was to be transferred to him."

"I don't," said Hardy. "Look here—here's this girl. Calls herself an artist. Paints bad pictures. Right. Then she meets this doctor fellow. He's mad on glands. Shrewd man—knows there's money in glands. *She* starts taking up glands. Why?"

"That was a year ago."

"Precisely. Penberthy isn't a rich man. Retired Army surgeon, with a brass plate and a consulting-room in Harley Street—shares the house with two other hard-up brass-platers. Lives on a few old dodderers down at the Bellona. Has an idea, if only he could start one of these clinics for rejuvenating people, he could be a millionaire. All these giddy old goats who want their gay time over again—why, they're a perfect fortune to the man with a bit of capital and a hell of a lot of cheek. Then this girl comes along—rich old woman's heiress—and he goes after her. It's all fixed up. He's to accommodate her by removing the obstacle to the fortune, and she obligingly responds by putting the money into his clinic. In order not to make it too obvious, she has to pretend to get a dickens of an interest in glands. So she drops painting and takes to medicine. What could be clearer?"

"But that means," put in Wimsey, "that she must have known all about the will at least a year ago."

"Why not?"

"Well that brings us back to the old question: Why the delay?"

"And it gives us the answer," said Parker. "They waited till the interest in the glands and things was so firmly established and recognized by everybody

293

that nobody would connect it with the General's death."

"Of course," said Wimsey. He felt that matters were rushing past him at a bewildering rate. But George was safe, anyhow.

"How soon do you think you'll be able to take action?" asked Hardy. "I suppose you'll want a bit more solid proof before you actually arrest them."

"I'd have to be certain that they don't wriggle out of it," said Parker, slowly. "It's not enough to prove that they were acquainted. There may be letters, of course, when we go over the girl's things. Or Penberthy's—though he's hardly the man to leave compromising documents lying about."

"You haven't detained Miss Dorland?"

"No; we've let her loose—on a string. I don't mind telling you one thing. There's been no communication of any kind with Penberthy."

"Of course there hasn't," said Wimsey. "They've quarreled."

The others stared at him.

"How do you know that?" demanded Parker, annoyed.

"Oh, well—it doesn't matter—I *think* so, that's all. And any way, they would take jolly good care not to communicate, once the alarm was given."

"Hullo!" broke in Hardy, "here's Waffles. Late again. Waffles!—what *have* you been doing, old boy?"

294

"Interviewing the Rushworths," said Waffles, edging his way into a chair by Hardy. He was a thin, sandy person, with a tired manner. Hardy introduced him to Wimsey and Parker.

"Got your story in?"

"Oh, yes. Awful lot of cats these women are. Ma Rushworth—she's the sloppy sort of woman with her head in the clouds all the time, who never sees anything till it's stuck right under her nose—she pretends, of course, that she always thought Ann Dorland was an unwholesome kind of girl. I nearly asked why, in that case, she had her about the house; but I didn't. Anyway, Mrs. Rushworth said, they didn't know her very intimately. They wouldn't, of course. Wonderful how these soulful people sheer off at the least suggestion of unpleasantness."

"Did you get anything about Penberthy?"

"Oh, yes—I got something."

"Good?"

"Oh, yes."

Hardy, with Fleet Street's delicate reticence towards the man with an exclusive story, did not press the question. The talk turned back and went over the old ground. Waffles Newton agreed with Salcombe Hardy's theory.

"The Rushworths must surely know something. Not the mother, perhaps—but the girl. If she's engaged to Penberthy, she'll have noticed any other woman who seemed to have an understanding with him. Women see these things."

"You don't suppose that they're going to confess that dear Dr. Penberthy ever had an understanding with anybody but dear Naomi," retorted Newton. "Besides, they aren't such fools as not to know that Penberthy's connection with the Dorland girl must be smothered up at all costs. They know she did it, all right, but they aren't going to compromise him."

"Of course not," said Parker, rather shortly. "The mother probably knows nothing, anyway. It's a different matter if we get the girl in the witness-box——"

"You won't," said Waffles Newton. "At least, you'll have to be jolly quick."

"Why?"

Newton waved an apologetic hand.

"They're being married to-morrow," he said, "special license. I say, that's not to go further, Sally."

"That's all right, old man."

"Married?" said Parker. "Good lord! that forces our hand a bit. Perhaps I'd better pop off. So long —and thanks very much for the tip, old man."

Wimsey followed him into the street.

"We'll have to put the stopper on this marriage business, quick," said Parker, madly waving to a taxi, which swooped past and ignored him. "I didn't want to move just at present, because I wasn't ready, but it'll be the devil and all if the Rushworth girl gets hitched up to Penberthy and we can't take her evidence. Devil of it is, if she's determined to go on with it, we can't stop it without arresting Penberthy. Very dangerous, when there's no real proof. I think we'd better have him down to the Yard for interrogation and detain him."

"Yes," said Wimsey. "But—look here, Charles."

A taxi drew up.

"What?" said Parker, sharply, with his foot on the step. "I can't wait, old man. What is it?"

"I—look here, Charles—this is all wrong," pleaded Wimsey. "You may have got the right solution, but the working of the sum's all wrong. Same as mine used to be at school, when I'd looked up the answer in the crib and had to fudge in the middle part. I've been a fool. I ought to have known about Penberthy. But I don't believe this story about bribing and corrupting him, and getting him to do the murder. It doesn't fit."

"Doesn't fit what?"

"Doesn't fit the portrait. Or the books. Or the way Nurse Armstrong described Ann Dorland. Or your description of her. It's a mechanically perfect explanation, but I swear it's all wrong."

"If it's mechanically perfect," said Parker, "that's good enough. It's far more than most explanations are. You've got that portrait on the brain. It's because you're artistic, I suppose."

For some reason, the word "artistic" produces the most alarming reactions in people who know anything about art.

"Artistic be damned!" said Wimsey, spluttering with fury, "it's because I'm an ordinary person, and have met women, and talked to them lik. ordinary human beings——"

"You and your women," said Parker, rudely.

"Well—I and my women, what about it? One learns something. You're on the wrong tack about this girl."

"I've met her and you haven't," objected Parker. "Unless you're suppressing something. You keep on hinting things. Anyhow, I've met the girl, and she impressed me as being guilty."

"And I haven't met her, and I'll swear she isn't guilty."

"You must know, of course."

"I do happen to know about this."

"I'm afraid your unsupported opinion will hardly be sufficient to refute the weight of evidence."

"You haven't any real evidence, if it comes to that. You don't know that they were ever alone together; you don't know that Ann Dorland knew about the will; you can't prove that Penberthy administered the poison——"

"I don't despair of getting all the evidence necessary," said Parker, coldly, "provided you don't
keep me here *all* day." He slammed the taxi-door.

"What a beast of a case this is," thought Wimsey.
"That makes two silly, sordid rows to-day. Well,
what next?" He considered a moment.

"My spirit needs soothing," he decided. "Femi-
nine society is indicated. Virtuous feminine society.
No emotions. I'll go and have tea with Marjorie
Phelps."

CHAPTER XX

Ann Dorland Goes Misere

THE STUDIO DOOR WAS OPENED BY A GIRL HE DID not know. She was not tall, but compactly and generously built. He noticed the wide shoulders and the strong swing of the thighs before he had taken in her face. The uncurtained window behind her threw her features into shadow, he was only aware of thick black hair, cut in a square bob, with a bang across the forehead.

"Miss Phelps is out."

"Oh!—will she be long?"

"Don't know. She'll be in to supper."

"Do you think I might come in and wait?"

"I expect so, if you're a friend of hers."

The girl fell back from the doorway and let him pass. He laid his hat and stick on the table and turned to her. She took no notice of him, but walked over to the fireplace and stood with one hand on the mantelpiece. Unable to sit down, since she was still standing, Wimsey moved to the modeling-board, and raised the wet cloth that covered the little mound of clay.

300

He was gazing with an assumption of great interest at the half-modeled figure of an old flower-seller, when the girl said:

"I say!"

She had taken up Marjorie Phelps' figurine of himself, and was twisting it over in her fingers.

"Is this you?"

"Yes—rather good of me, don't you think?"

"What do you want?"

"Want?"

"You've come here to have a look at me, haven't you?"

"I came to see Miss Phelps."

"I suppose the policeman at the corner comes to see Miss Phelps too."

Wimsey glanced out of the window. There *was* a man at the corner—an elaborately indifferent lounger.

"I am sorry," said Wimsey, with sudden enlightenment. "I'm really awfully sorry to seem so stupid, and so intrusive. But honestly, I had no idea who you were till this moment."

"Hadn't you? Oh, well, it doesn't matter."

"Shall I go?"

"You can please yourself."

"If you really mean that, Miss Dorland, I should like to stay. I've been wanting to meet you, you know."

"That was nice of you," she mocked. "First you

wanted to defraud me, and now you're trying
to——"

"To what?"

She shrugged her wide shoulders.

"Yours is not a pleasant hobby, Lord Peter
Wimsey."

"Will you believe me," said Wimsey, "when I
assure you that I was never a party to the fraud.
In fact, I showed it up. I did, really."

"Oh, well. It doesn't matter now."

"But do please believe that."

"Very well. If you say so, I must believe it."

She threw herself on the couch near the fire.

"That's better," said Wimsey. "Napoleon or
somebody said that you could always turn a tragedy into a comedy, by sittin' down. Perfectly true,
isn't it? Let's talk 'about something ordinary till
Miss Phelps comes in. Shall we?"

"What do you want to talk about?"

"Oh, well—that's rather embarrassin'. Books."
He waved a vague hand. "What have you been
readin' lately?"

"Nothing much."

"Don't know what I should do without books.
Fact, I always wonder what people did in the old
days. Just think of it. All sorts of bothers goin'
on—matrimonial rows and love-affairs—prodigal
sons and servants and worries—and no books to
turn to."

302

"People worked with their hands instead."

"Yes—that's frightfully jolly for the people who can do it. I envy them myself. You paint, don't you?"

"I try to."

"Portraits?"

"Oh, no—figure and landscape chiefly."

"Oh! . . . A friend of mine—well, it's no use disguising it—he's a detective—you've met him, I think . . ."

"That man? Oh, yes. Quite a polite sort of detective."

"He told me he'd seen some stuff of yours. It rather surprised him, I think. He's not exactly a modernist. He seemed to think your portraits were your best work."

"There weren't many portraits. A few figure-studies . . ."

"They worried him a bit." Wimsey laughed. "The only thing he understood, he said, was a man's head in oils. . . ."

"Oh, that!—just an experiment—a fancy thing. My best stuff is some sketches I did of the Wiltshire Downs a year or two ago. Direct painting, without any preliminary sketch."

She described a number of these works.

"They sound ever so jolly," said Wimsey. "Great stuff. I wish I could do something of that kind. As

I say, I have to fall back on books for my escape. Reading *is* an escape to me. Is it to you?"

"How do you mean?"

"Well—it is to most people, I think. Servants and factory hands read about beautiful girls loved by dark, handsome men, all covered over with jewels and moving in scenes of gilded splendour. And passionate spinsters read Ethel M. Dell. And dull men in offices read detective stories. They wouldn't, if murder and police entered into their lives."

"I don't know," she said. "When Crippen and Le Neve were taken on the steamer, they were reading Edgar Wallace." Her voice was losing its dull harshness; she sounded almost interested.

"Le Neve was reading it," said Wimsey, "but I've never believed she knew about the murder. I think she was fighting desperately to know nothing about it—reading horrors, and persuading herself that nothing of that kind had happened, or could happen, to her. I think one might do that, don't you?"

"I don't know," said Ann Dorland. "Of course, a detective story keeps your brain occupied. Rather like chess. Do you play chess?"

"No good at it. I like it—but I keep on thinking about the history of the various pieces, and the picturesqueness of the moves. So I get beaten. I'm not a player."

304

"Nor am I. I wish I were."

"Yes—that would keep one's mind off things with a vengeance. Draughts or dominoes or patience would be even better. No connection with anything. I remember," added Wimsey, "one time when something perfectly grinding and hateful had happened to me. I played patience all day. I was in a nursing home—with shell-shock—and other things. I only played one game, the very simplest . . . the demon . . . a silly game with no ideas in it at all. I just went on laying it out and gathering it up . . . hundred times in an evening . . . so as to stop thinking."

"Then you too . . ."

Wimsey waited; but she did not finish the sentence.

"It's a kind of drug, of course. That's an awfully trite thing to say, but it's quite true."

"Yes, quite."

"I read detective stories too. They were about the only thing I could read. All the others had the war in them—or love . . . or some damn thing I didn't want to think about."

She moved restlessly.

"You've been through it, haven't you?" said Wimsey, gently.

"Me? . . . well . . . all this . . . it isn't pleasant, you know . . . the police . . . and . . . and everything."

305

"You're not really worried about the police, are you?"

She had cause to be, if she only knew it, but he buried this knowledge at the bottom of his mind, defying it to show itself.

"Everything's pretty hateful, isn't it?"

"Something's hurt you . . . all right . . . don't talk about it if you don't want to . . . a man?"

"It usually is a man, isn't it?"

Her eyes were turned away from him, and she answered with a kind of shamefaced defiance.

"Practically always," said Wimsey. "Fortunately, one gets over it."

"Depends what it is."

"One gets over everything," repeated Wimsey, firmly. "Particularly if one tells somebody about it."

"One can't always tell things."

"I can't imagine anything really untellable."

"Some things are so beastly."

"Oh, yes—quite a lot of things. Birth is beastly—and death—and digestion, if it comes to that. Sometimes when I think of what's happening inside me to a beautiful *suprème de sole,* with the caviare in boats, and the *croûtons* and the jolly little twists of potato and all the gadgets—I could cry. But there it is, don't you know."

Ann Dorland suddenly laughed.

"That's better," said Wimsey. "Look here, you've

306

been brooding over this and you're seeing it all out of proportion. Let's be practical and frightfully ordinary. Is it a baby?"

"Oh, no!"

"Well—that's rather a good thing, because babies, though no doubt excellent in their way, take a long time and come expensive. Is it blackmail?"

"Good heavens, no!"

"Good. Because blackmail is even longer and more expensive than babies. Is it Freudian, or sadistic, or any of those popular modern amusements?"

"I don't believe you'd turn a hair if it was."

"Why should I?—I can't think of anything worse to suggest, except what Rose Macaulay refers to as 'nameless orgies.' Or diseases, of course. It's not leprosy or anything?"

"What a mind you've got," she said, beginning to laugh. "No, it isn't leprosy."

"Well, what *did* the blighter do?"

Ann Dorland smiled faintly: "It's nothing, really."

"If only Heaven prevents Marjorie Phelps from coming in," thought Wimsey, "I'm going to get it now . . . It must have been something, to upset you like this," he pursued aloud, "you're not the kind of woman to be upset about nothing."

"You don't think I am?" She got up and faced

him squarely. "He said . . . he said . . . I imagined things . . . he said . . . he said I had a mania about sex. I suppose you would call it Freudian, really," she added hastily, flushing an ugly crimson.

"Is that all?" said Wimsey. "I know plenty of people who would take that as a compliment . . . But obviously you don't. What exact form of mania did he suggest . . .?"

"Oh, the gibbering sort that hangs round church doors for curates," she broke out, fiercely. "It's a lie. He did—he *did*—pretend to—want me and all that. The beast! . . . I can't tell you the things he said . . . and I'd made such a fool of myself. . . ."

She was back on the couch, crying, with large, ugly, streaming tears, and snorting into the cushions. Wimsey sat down beside her.

"Poor kid," he said. This, then, was at the back of Marjorie's mysterious hints, and those scratch-cat sneers of Naomi Rushworth's. The girl had wanted love-affairs, that was certain; imagined them perhaps. There had been Ambrose Ledbury. Between the normal and the abnormal, the gulf is deep, but so narrow that misrepresentation is made easy.

"Look here." He put a comforting arm round Ann's heaving shoulders. "This fellow—was it Penberthy, by the way?"

"How did you know?"

"Oh!—the portrait, and lots of things. The things you liked once, and then wanted to hide away and forget. He's a rotter, anyway, for saying that kind of thing—even if it was true, which it isn't. You got to know him at the Rushworth's, I take it—when?"

"Nearly two years ago."

"Were you keen on him then?"

"No. I—well, I was keen on somebody else. Only that was a mistake too. He—he was one of those people, you know."

"They can't help themselves," said Wimsey, soothingly. "When did the change-over happen?"

"The other man went away. And later on, Dr. Penberthy—oh! I don't know! He walked home with me once or twice, and then he asked me to dine with him—in Soho."

"Had you at that time told any one about this comic will of Lady Dormer's?"

"Of course not. How could I? I never knew anything about it till after she died."

Her surprise sounded genuine enough.

"What did you think? Did you think the money would come to you?"

"I knew that some of it would; Auntie told me she would see me provided for."

"There were the grandsons, of course."

"Yes; I thought she would leave most of it to

them. It's a pity she didn't, poor dear. Then there wouldn't have been all this dreadful bother."

"People so often seem to lose their heads when they make wills. So you were a sort of dark horse at that time. H'm. Did this precious Penberthy ask you to marry him?"

"I thought he did. But he says he didn't. We talked about founding his clinic; I was to help him."

"And that was when you chucked painting for books about medicine and first-aid classes. Did your aunt know about the engagement?"

"He didn't want her told. It was to be our secret, till he got a better position. He was afraid she might think he was after the money."

"I daresay he was."

"He made out he was fond of me," she said, miserably.

"Of course, my dear child; your case is not unique. Didn't you tell any of your friends?"

"No." Wimsey reflected that the Ledbury episode had probably left a scar. Besides—did women tell things to other women? He had long doubted it.

"You were still engaged when Lady Dormer died, I take it?"

"As engaged as we ever were. Of course, he told me that there was something funny about the body. He said you and the Fentimans were trying to defraud me of the money. I shouldn't have minded for myself—it was more money than I should have known what to do with. But it would have meant the clinic, you see."

"Yes, you could start a pretty decent clinic with half a million. So that was why you shot me out of the house."

He grinned—and then reflected a few moments.

"Look here," he said, "I'm going to give you a bit of a shock, but it'll have to come sooner or later. Has it ever occurred to you that it was Penberthy who murdered General Fentiman?"

"I—wondered," she said, slowly. "I couldn't think—who else—But you know they suspect *me?*"

"Oh, well—*cui bono* and all that—they couldn't overlook you. They have to suspect every possible person, you know."

"I don't blame them at all. But I didn't, you know."

"Of course not. It was Penberthy. I look at it like this. Penberthy wanted money; he was sick of being poor, and he knew you would be certain to get *some* of Lady Dormer's money. He'd probably heard about the family quarrel with the General, and expected it would be the lot. So he started to make your acquaintance. But he was careful. He asked you to keep it quiet—just in case, you see. The money might be so tied up that you couldn't

311

give it him, or you might lose it if you married, or it might only be quite a small annuity, in which case he'd want to look for somebody richer."

"We considered those points when we talked it over about the clinic."

"Yes. Well, then, Lady Dormer fell ill. The General went round and heard about the legacy that was coming to him. And then he toddled along to Penberthy, feeling very groggy, and promptly told him all about it. You can imagine him saying: 'You've got to patch me up long enough to get the money.' That must have been a nasty jar for Penberthy."

"It was. You see, he didn't even hear about my twelve thousand."

"Oh?"

"No. Apparently what the General said was, 'If only I last out poor Felicity, all the money comes to me. Otherwise it goes to the girl and my boys only get seven thousand apiece.' That was why——"

"Just a moment. When did Penberthy tell you about that?"

"Why, later—when he said I was to compromise with the Fentimans."

"That explains it. I wondered why you gave in so suddenly. I thought, then, that you—Well, anyhow, Penberthy hears this, and gets the brilliant idea of putting General Fentiman out of the way. So he gives him a slow-working kind of a pill——"

"Probably a powder in a very tough capsule that would take a long time to digest."

"Good idea. Yes, very likely. And then the General, instead of heading straight for home, as he expected, goes off to the Club and dies there. And then Robert——"

He explained in detail what Robert had done, and resumed.

"Well, now—Penberthy was in a bad fix. If he drew attention at the time to the peculiar appearance of the corpse, he couldn't reasonably give a certificate. In which case there would be a post-mortem and an analysis, and the digitalin would be found. If he kept quiet, the money might be lost and all his trouble would be wasted. Maddenin' for him, wasn't it? So he did what he could. He put the time of the death as early as he dared, and hoped for the best."

"He told me he thought there would be some attempt to make it seem later than it really was. I thought it was *you* who were trying to hush everything up. And I was so furious that of course I told Mr. Pritchard to have a proper inquiry made and on no account to compromise."

"Thank God you did," said Wimsey.

"Why?"

"I'll tell you presently. But Penberthy now—I

can't think why *he* didn't persuade you to compromise. That would have made him absolutely safe."

"But he did! That's what started our first quarrel. As soon as he heard about it, he said I was a fool not to compromise. I couldn't understand his saying that, since he himself had said there was something wrong. We had a fearful row. That was the time I mentioned the twelve thousand that was coming to me anyway."

"What did he say?"

" 'I didn't know that.' Just like that. And then he apologized and said that the law was so uncertain, it would be best to agree to divide the money anyhow. So I rang up Mr. Pritchard and told him not to make any more fuss. And we were friends again."

"Was it the day after that, that Penberthy—er—said things to you?"

"Yes."

"Right. Then I can tell you one thing: he would never have been so brutal if he hadn't been in fear of his life. Do you know what had happened in between?"

She shook her head.

"I had been on the 'phone to him, and told him there was going to be an autopsy."

"Oh!"

"Yes—listen—you needn't worry any more

about it. He knew that the poison would be discovered, and that if he was known to be engaged to you, he was absolutely bound to be suspected. So he hurried to cut the connection with you—purely in self-defense."

"But why do it in that brutal way?"

"Because, my dear, he knew that that particular accusation would be the very last thing a girl of your sort would tell people about. He made it absolutely impossible for you to claim him publicly. And he bolstered it up by engaging himself to the Rushworth female."

"He didn't care how *I* suffered."

"He was in a beast of a hole," said Wimsey, apologetically. "Mind you, it was a perfectly diabolical thing to do. I daresay he's feeling pretty rotten about it."

Ann Dorland clenched her hands.

"I've been so horribly ashamed——"

"Well, you aren't any more, are you?"

"No—but——" A thought seemed to strike her. "Lord Peter—I can't *prove* a word of this. Everybody will think I was in league with him. And they'll think that our quarrel and his getting engaged to Naomi was just a put-up job between us to get us both out of a difficulty."

"You've got brains," said Wimsey, admiringly. "*Now* you see why I thanked God you'd been so keen on an inquiry at first. Pritchard can make it

315

pretty certain that you weren't an accessory before the fact, anyhow."

"Of course—so he can. Oh, I'm so glad! I *am* so glad." She burst into excited sobs and clutched Wimsey's hand. "I wrote him a letter—right at the beginning—saying I'd read about a case in which they'd proved the time of somebody's death by looking into his stomach, and asking if General Fentiman couldn't be dug up."

"Did you? Splendid girl! You *have* got a head on your shoulders! . . . No, I observe that it's on my shoulders. Go on. Have a real, good howl—I feel rather like howling myself. I've been quite worried about it all. But it's all right now, isn't it?"

"I am a fool . . . but I'm so thankful you came."

"So am I. Here, have a hanky. Poor old dear! . . . Hullo! there's Marjorie."

He released her and went out to meet Marjorie Phelps at the door.

"Lord Peter! Good lord!"

"Thank you, Marjorie," said Wimsey, gravely.

"No, but listen! Have you seen Ann?—I took her away. She's frightfully queer—and there's a policeman outside. But whatever she's done, I couldn't leave her alone in that awful house. You haven't come to—to——"

"Marjorie!" said Wimsey, "don't you ever talk to me again about feminine intuition. You've been

316

thinking all this time that that girl was suffering from guilty conscience. Well, she wasn't. It was a man, my child—a MAN!"

"How do you know?"

"My experienced eye told me as much at the first glance. It's all right now. Sorrow and sighing have fled away. I am going to take your young friend out to dinner."

"But why didn't she tell me what it was all about?"

"Because," said Wimsey, mincingly, "it wasn't the kind of thing one woman tells another."

CHAPTER XXI

Lord Peter Calls A Bluff

"IT IS NEW TO ME," SAID LORD PETER, GLANCING
from the back window of the taxi at the other taxi
which was following them, "to be shadowed by
the police, but it amuses them and doesn't hurt us."

He was revolving ways and means of proof in his
mind. Unhappily, all the evidence in favour of
Ann Dorland was evidence against her as well—
except, indeed, the letter to Pritchard. Damn Penberthy. The best that could be hoped for now was
that the girl should escape from public inquiry
with a verdict of 'Not proven.' Even if acquitted
—even if never charged with the murder—she
would always be suspect. The question was not one
which could be conveniently settled by a brilliant
flash of deductive logic, or the discovery of a blood-
stained thumb-mark. It was a case for lawyers to
argue—for a weighing of the emotional situation
by twelve good and lawful persons. Presumably the
association could be proved—the couple had met
and dined together; probably the quarrel could be
proved—but what next? Would a jury believe in

the cause of the quarrel? Would they think it a pre-arranged blind, or perhaps—or mistake it for the falling-out of rogues among themselves? What would they think of this plain, sulky, inarticulate girl, who had never had any real friends, and whose clumsy and tentative graspings after passion had been so obscure, so disastrous?

Penberthy, too—but Penberthy was easier to understand. Penberthy, cynical and bored with poverty, found himself in contact with this girl, who might be so well-off some day. And Penberthy, the physician, would not mistake the need for passion that made the girl such easy stuff to work on. So he carried on—bored with the girl, of course—keeping it all secret, till he saw which way the cat was going to jump. Then the old man—the truth about the will—the opportunity. And then, upsettingly, Robert . . . Would the jury see it like that?

Wimsey leaned out of the cab window and told the driver to go to the Savoy. When they arrived, he handed the girl over to the cloak-room attendant. "I am going up to change," he added, and turning, had the pleasure of seeing his sleuth arguing with the porter in the entrance-hall.

Bunter, previously summoned by telephone, was already in attendance with his master's dress clothes. Having changed, Wimsey passed through the hall again. The sleuth was there, quietly wait-

319

ing. Wimsey grinned at him, and offered him a
drink.

"I can't help it, my lord," said the detective.

"Of course not; you've sent for a bloke in a
boiled shirt to take your place, I suppose?"

"Yes, my lord."

"More power to his elbow. So long."

He rejoined his charge and they went into the
dining-room. Dressed in a green which did not
suit her, she was undoubtedly plain. But she had
character; he was not ashamed of her. He offered
her the menu.

"What shall it be?" he asked. "Lobster and
champagne?"

She laughed at him.

"Marjorie says you are an authority on food. I
don't believe authorities on food ever take lobster
and champagne. Anyway, I don't like lobster,
much. Surely there's something they do best here,
isn't there? Let's have that."

"You show the right spirit," said Wimsey. "I
will compose a dinner for you."

He called the head waiter, and went into the
question scientifically.

"*Huîtres Musgrave*—I am opposed on principle
to the cooking of oysters—but it is a dish so excellent that one may depart from the rules in its
favour. Fried in their shells, Miss Dorland, with
little strips of bacon. Shall we try it?—The soup

320

must be *Tortue Vraie,* of course. The fish—
oh! just a *Filet de Sole,* the merest mouthful, a
hyphen between the prologue and the main
theme."

"That all sounds delightful. And what is the
main theme to be?"

"I think a *Faisan Rôti* with *Pommes Byron.* And
a salad to promote digestion. And, waiter—be sure
the salad is dry and perfectly crisp. A *Soufflé
Glace* to finish up with. And bring me the wine-
list."

They talked. When she was not on the defensive,
the girl was pleasant enough in manner; a trifle
downright and aggressive, perhaps, in her opinions,
but needing only mellowing.

"What do you think of the *Romanée Conti?*"
he asked, suddenly.

"I don't know much about wine. It's good. Not
sweet, like Sauterne. It's a little—well—harsh. But
it's harsh without being thin—quite different from
that horrid Chianti people always seem to drink
at Chelsea parties."

"You're right; it's rather unfinished, but it has
plenty of body—it'll be a grand wine in ten years'
time. It's 1915. Now, you see. Waiter, take this
away and bring me a bottle of the 1908."

He leaned towards his companion.

"Miss Dorland—may I be impertinent?"

"How? Why?"

"Not an artist, not a bohemian, and not a professional man;—a man of the world."

"What *do* you mean by those cryptic words?"

"For you. That is the kind of man who is going to like you very much. Look! that wine I've sent away—it's no good for champagne-and-lobster sort of person, nor for very young people—it's too big and rough. But it's got the essential guts. So have you. It takes a fairly experienced palate to appreciate it. But you and it will come into your own one day. Get me?"

"Do you think so?"

"Yes. But your man won't be at all the sort of person you're expecting. You have always thought of being dominated by somebody, haven't you?"

"Well——"

"But you'll find that yours will be the leading brain of the two. He will take great pride in the fact. And you will find the man reliable and kind, and it will turn out quite well."

"I didn't know you were a prophet."

"I am, though."

Wimsey took the bottle of 1908 from the waiter and glanced over the girl's head at the door. A man in a boiled shirt was making his way in, accompanied by the manager.

"I am a prophet," said Wimsey. "Listen. Something tiresome is going to happen—now, this minute. But don't worry. Drink your wine, and trust."

The manager had brought the man to their table. It was Parker.

"Ah!" said Wimsey, brightly. "You'll forgive our starting without you, old man. Sit down. I think you know Miss Dorland."

Parker bowed and sat down.

"Have you come to arrest me?" asked Ann.

"Just to ask you to come down to the Yard with me," said Parker, smiling pleasantly and unfolding his napkin.

Ann looked palely at Wimsey, and took a gulp of the wine.

"Right," said Wimsey. "Miss Dorland has quite a lot to tell you. After dinner will suit us charmingly. What will you have?"

Parker, who was not imaginative, demanded a grilled steak.

"Shall we find any other friends at the Yard?" pursued Wimsey.

"Possibly," said Parker.

"Well, cheer up! You put me off my food, looking so grim. Hullo! Yes, waiter, what is it?"

"Excuse me, my lord; is this gentleman Detective-Inspector Parker?"

"Yes, yes," said Parker, "what's the matter?"

"You're wanted on the 'phone, sir."

Parker departed.

"It's all right," said Wimsey to the girl. "I know you're straight, and I'll damn well see you through."

"What am I do to?"

"Tell the truth."

"It sounds so silly."

"They've heard lots of very much sillier stories than that."

"But—I don't want to—to be the one to——"

"You're still fond of him, then?"

"*No!*—but I'd rather it wasn't me."

"I'll be frank with you. I think it's going to be between you and him that suspicion will lie."

"In that case"—she set her teeth—"he can have what's coming to him."

"Thank the lord! I thought you were going to be noble and self-sacrificing and tiresome. You know. Like the people whose noble motives are misunderstood in chapter one and who get dozens of people tangled up in their miserable affairs till the family lawyer solves everything on the last page but two."

Parker had come back from the telephone.

"Just a moment!" He spoke in Peter's ear.

"Hullo?"

"Look here; this is awkward. George Fentiman——"

"Yes?"

"He's been found in Clerkenwell."

"Clerkenwell?"

"Yes; must have wandered back by 'bus or something. He's at the police-station; in fact he's given himself up."

"Good lord!"

"For the murder of his grandfather."

"The devil he has!"

"It's a nuisance; of course it must be looked into. I think perhaps I'd better put off interrogating Dorland and Penberthy. What are you doing with the girl, by the way?"

"I'll explain later. Look here—I'll take Miss Dorland back to Marjorie Phelps' place, and then come along and join you. The girl won't run away; I know that. And anyhow, you've got a man looking after her."

"Yes, I rather wish you would come with me; Fentiman is pretty queer, by all accounts. We've sent for his wife."

"Right. You buzz off, and I'll join you in—say in three quarters of an hour. What address? Oh, yes, righty-ho! Sorry you're missing your dinner."

"It's all in the day's work," growled Parker, and took his leave.

. . . .

George Fentiman greeted them with a tired white smile.

"Hush!" he said. "I've told them all about it. *He's* asleep; don't wake him."

"Who's asleep, dearest?" said Sheila.

"I mustn't say the name," said George, cunningly. "He'd hear it—even in his sleep—even if you whispered it. But he's tired, and he nodded off. So I ran in here and told them all about it while he snored."

The police superintendent tapped his forehead significantly behind Sheila's back.

"Has he made any statement?" asked Parker.

"Yes, he insisted on writing it himself. Here it is. Of course . . ." the Superintendent shrugged his shoulders.

"That's all right," said George. "I'm getting sleepy myself. I've been watching him for a day and a night, you know. I'm going to bed. Sheila— it's time to go to bed."

"Yes, dear."

"We'll have to keep him here to-night, I suppose," muttered Parker. "Has the doctor seem him?"

"We've sent for him, sir."

"Well, Mrs. Fentiman, I think if you'd take your husband into the room the officer will show you, that would be the best way. And we'll send the doctor in to you when he arrives. Perhaps it would be as well that he should see his own medical man too. Whom would you like us to send for?"

"Dr. Penberthy has vetted him from time to

time, I think," put in Wimsey, suddenly. "Why not send for him?"

Parker gasped involuntarily.

"He might be able to throw some light on the symptoms," said Wimsey, in a rigid voice.

Parker nodded.

"A good idea," he agreed. He moved to the telephone. George smiled as his wife put her arm about his shoulder.

"Tired," he said, "very tired. Off to bed, old girl."

A police-constable opened the door to them, and they started through it together; George leaned heavily on Sheila; his feet dragged.

"Let's have a look at his statement," said Parker.

It was written in a staggering handwriting, much blotted and erased, with words left out and repeated here and there.

"I am making this statement quickly while he is asleep, because if I wait he may wake up and stop me. You will say I was moved and seduced by instigation of but what they will not understand is that he is me and I am him. I killed my grandfather by giving him digitalin. I did not remember it till I saw the name on the bottle, but they have been looking for me ever since, so I know that he must have done it. That is why they began following me about, but he is very clever and misleads them. When he is awake. We were dancing all last night

and that is why he is tired. He told me to smash
the bottle so that you shouldn't find out, but they
know I was the last person to see him. He is very
cunning, but if you creep on him quickly now
that he is asleep you will be able to bind him in
chains and cast him into the pit and then I shall
be able to sleep.

George Fentiman."

"Off his head, poor devil," said Parker. "We
can't pay much attention to this. What did he say
to you, superintendent?"

"He just came in, sir, and said 'I'm George
Fentiman and I've come to tell you about how I
killed my grandfather.' So I questioned him, and he
rambled a good bit and then he asked for a pen
and paper to make his statement. I thought he
ought to be detained, and I rang up the Yard, sir."

"Quite right," said Parker.

The door opened and Sheila came out.

"He's fallen asleep," she said. "It's the old trouble
come back again. He thinks he's the devil, you
know. He's been like that twice before," she added,
simply. "I'll go back to him till the doctors come."

The police-surgeon arrived first and went in;
then, after a wait of a quarter of an hour, Penberthy came. He looked worried, and greeted
Wimsey abruptly. Then he, too, went into the
inner room. The others stood vaguely about, and

328

were presently joined by Robert Fentiman, whom an urgent summons had traced to a friend's house.

Presently the two doctors came out again.

"Nervous shock with well-marked delusions," said the police-surgeon, briefly. "Probably be all right to-morrow. Sleeping it off now. Been this way before, I understand. Just so. A hundred years ago they'd have called it diabolic possession, but *we* know better."

"Yes," said Parker, "but do you think he is under a delusion in saying he murdered his grandfather? Or did he actually murder him under the influence of this diabolical delusion? That's the point."

"Can't say just at present. Might be the one—might be the other. Much better wait till the attack passes off. You'll be able to find out better then."

"You don't think he's permanently—insane, then?" demanded Robert, with brusque anxiety.

"No—I don't. I think it's what you'd call a nerve-storm. That is your opinion, too, I believe?" he added, turning to Penberthy.

"Yes; that is my opinion."

"And what do you think about this delusion, Dr. Penberthy?" went on Parker. "Did he do this insane act?"

"He certainly thinks he did it," said Penberthy; "I couldn't possibly say for certain whether he has any foundation for the belief. From time to time he undoubtedly gets these fits of thinking that the

329

devil has taken hold of him, and of course it's hard to say what a man might or might not do under the influence of such a delusion."

He avoided Robert's distressed eyes, and addressed himself exclusively to Parker.

"It seems to me," said Wimsey, "if you'll excuse me pushin' my opinion forward and all that—it seems to me that's a question of fact that can be settled without reference to Fentiman and his delusions. There's only the one occasion on which the pill could have been administered—would it have produced the effect that was produced at that particular time, or wouldn't it? If it couldn't take effect at 8 o'clock, then it couldn't, and there's an end of it."

He kept his eyes fixed on Penberthy, and saw him pass his tongue over his dry lips before speaking.

"I can't answer that off-hand," he said.

"The pill might have been introduced into General Fentiman's stock of pills at some other time," suggested Parker.

"So it might," agreed Penberthy.

"Had it the same shape and appearance as his ordinary pills?" demanded Wimsey, again fixing his eyes on Penberthy.

"Not having seen the pill in question, I can't say," said the latter.

"In any case," said Wimsey, "the pill in question, which was one of Mrs. Fentiman's, I understand, had strychnine in it as well as digitalin. The analysis of the stomach would no doubt have revealed strychnine if present. That can be looked into."

"Of course," said the police-surgeon. "Well, gentlemen, I don't think we can do much more to-night. I have written out a prescription for the patient, with Dr. Penberthy's entire agreement"—he bowed; Penberthy bowed—"I will have it made up, and you will no doubt see that it is given to him. I shall be here in the morning."

He looked interrogatively at Parker, who nodded.

"Thank you, doctor; we will ask you for a further report to-morrow morning. You'll see that Mrs. Fentiman is properly looked after, Superintendent. If you wish to stay here and look after your brother and Mrs. Fentiman, Major, of course you may, and the Superintendent will make you as comfortable as he can."

Wimsey took Penberthy by the arm.

"Come round to the Club with me for a moment, Penberthy," he said. "I want to have a word with you."

CHAPTER XXII

The Cards On The Table

THERE WAS NOBODY IN THE LIBRARY AT THE Bellona Club; there never is. Wimsey led Penberthy into the farthest bay and sent a waiter for two double whiskies.

"Here's luck!" he said.

"Good luck," replied Penberthy. "What is it?"

"Look here," said Wimsey. "You've been a soldier. I think you're a decent fellow. You've seen George Fentiman. It's a pity, isn't it?"

"What about it?"

"If George Fentiman hadn't turned up with that delusion of his," said Wimsey, "you would have been arrested for the murder this evening. Now the point is this. When you are arrested, nothing, as things are, can prevent Miss Dorland's being arrested on the same charge. She's quite a decent girl, and you haven't treated her any too well, have you? Don't you think you might make things right for her by telling the truth straight away?"

Penberthy sat with a white face and said nothing.

"You see," went on Wimsey, "if once they get

332

her into the dock, she'll always be a suspected person. Even if the jury believe her story—and they may not, because juries are often rather stupid—people will always think there was 'something in it.' They'll say she was a very lucky woman to get off. That's damning for a girl, isn't it? They might even bring her in guilty. You and I know she isn't—but—you don't want the girl hanged, Penberthy, do you?"

Penberthy drummed on the table.

"What do you want me to do?" he said at last.

"Write a clear account of what actually happened," said Wimsey. "Make a clean job of it for these other people. Make it clear that Miss Dorland had nothing to do with it."

"And then?"

"Then do as you like. In your place I know what I should do."

Penberthy propped his chin on his hands and sat for some minutes staring at the works of Dickens in the leather-and-gold binding.

"Very well," he said at last. "You're quite right. I ought to have done it before. But—damn it!—if ever a man had rotten luck . . .

"If only Robert Fentiman hadn't been a rogue. It's funny, isn't it? That's your wonderful poetic justice, isn't it? If Robert Fentiman had been an honest man, I should have got my half-million, and Ann Dorland would have got a perfectly good husband, and the world would have gained a fine clinic, incidentally. But as Robert was a rogue—here we are . . .

"I didn't intend to be such a sweep to the Dorland girl. I'd have been decent to her if I'd married her. Mind you, she did sicken me a bit. Always wanting to be sentimental. It's true, what I said—she's a bit cracked about sex. Lots of 'em are. Naomi Rushworth, for instance. That's why I asked her to marry me. I had to be engaged to somebody, and I knew she'd take any one who asked her . . .

"It was so hideously easy, you see . . . that was the devil of it. The old man came along and put himself into my hands. Told me with one breath that I hadn't a dog's chance of the money, and in the next, asked me for a dose. I just had to put the stuff into a couple of capsules and tell him to take them at 7 o'clock. He put them in his spectacle-case, to make sure he wouldn't forget them. Not even a bit of paper to give me away. And the next day I'd only to get a fresh supply of the stuff and fill up the bottle. I'll give you the address of the chemist who sold it. Easy?—it was laughable . . . people put such power in our hands. . . .

"I never meant to get led into all this rotten way of doing things—it was just self-defense. I still don't care a damn about having killed the old man. I could have made better use of the money than

Robert Fentiman. He hasn't got two ideas in his head, and he's perfectly happy where he is. Though I suppose he'll be leaving the Army now . . . As for Ann, she ought to be grateful to me in a way. I've secured her the money, anyhow."

"Not unless you make it clear that she had no part in the crime," Wimsey reminded him.

"That's true. All right. I'll put it all on paper for you. Give me half an hour, will you?"

"Right you are," said Wimsey.

He left the library and wandered into the smoking-room. Colonel Marchbanks was there, and greeted him with a friendly smile.

"Glad you're here, Colonel. Mind if I come and chat to you for a moment?"

"By all means, my dear boy. I'm in no hurry to get home. My wife's away. What can I do for you?"

Wimsey told him, in a lowered voice. The Colonel was distressed.

"Ah, well," he said, "you've done the best thing, to my mind. I look at these matters from a soldier's point of view, of course. Much better to make a clean job of it all. Dear, dear! Sometimes, Lord Peter, I think that the War has had a bad effect on some of our young men. But then, of course, all are not soldiers by training, and that makes a great difference. I certainly notice a less fine sense of honour in these days than we had when I was a boy. There were not so many excuses made then for people; there were things that were done and things that were not done. Nowadays men—and, I am sorry to say, women too—let themselves go in a way that is to me quite incomprehensible. I can understand a man's committing murder in hot blood—but poisoning—and then putting a good, ladylike girl into such an equivocal position—no! I fail to understand it. Still, as you say, the right course is being taken at last."

"Yes," said Wimsey.

"Excuse me for a moment," said the Colonel, and went out.

When he returned, he went with Wimsey into the library. Penberthy had finished writing and was reading his statement through.

"Will that do?" he asked.

Wimsey read it, Colonel Marchbanks looking over the pages with him.

"That is quite all right," he said. "Colonel Marchbanks will witness it with me."

This was done. Wimsey gathered the sheets together and put them in his breast-pocket. Then he turned silently to the Colonel, as though passing the word to him.

"Dr. Penberthy," said the old man, "now that that paper is in Lord Peter Wimsey's hands, you understand that he can only take the course of communicating with the police. But as that would cause a great deal of unpleasantness to yourself and to other people, you may wish to take another way out of the situation. As a doctor, you will perhaps prefer to make your own arrangements. If not——"

He drew out from his jacket-pocket the thing which he had fetched.

"If not, I happen to have brought this with me from my private locker. I am placing it here, in the table-drawer, preparatory to taking it down into the country to-morrow. It is loaded."

"Thank you," said Penberthy.

The Colonel closed the drawer slowly, stepped back a couple of paces and bowed gravely. Wimsey put his hand on Penberthy's shoulder for a moment, then took the Colonel's arm. Their shadows moved, lengthened, shortened, doubled and crossed as they passed the seven lights in the seven bays of the library. The door shut after them.

"How about a drink, Colonel?" said Wimsey.

They went into the bar, which was just preparing to close for the night. Several other men were there, talking over their plans for Christmas.

"I'm getting away south," said Tin-Tummy Challoner. "I'm fed up with this climate and this country."

"I wish you'd look us up, Wimsey," said another man. "We could give you some very decent shooting. We're having a sort of house-party; my wife,

337

you know—must have all these young people round
—awful crowd of women. But I'm getting one or
two men who can play bridge and handle a gun,
and it would be a positive charity to see me through.
Deadly season, Christmas. Can't think why they
invented it."

"It's all right if you've got kids," interrupted a
large, red-faced man with a bald head. "The little
beggars enjoy it. You ought to start a family,
Anstruther."

"All very well," said Anstruther, "you're cut out
by nature to dress up as Father Christmas. I tell
you, what with one thing and another, entertaining and going about, and the servants we have to
keep in a place like ours, it's a job to keep things
going. If you know of a good thing, I wish you'd
put me on to it. It's not as though——"

"Hullo!" said Challoner, "what was that?"

"Motor-bike, probably," said Anstruther. "As I
was saying, it's not as though——"

"Something's happened," broke in the red-faced
man, setting down his glass.

There were voices, and the running to and fro of
feet. The door was flung open. Startled faces turned
towards it. Wetheridge burst in, pale and angry.

"I say, you fellows," he cried, "here's another
unpleasantness. Penberthy's shot himself in the
library. People ought to have more consideration
for the members. Where's Culyer?"

338

Wimsey pushed his way out into the entrance-hall. There, as he had expected, he found the plain-clothes detective who had been told off to shadow Penberthy.

"Send for Inspector Parker," he said. "I have a paper to give him. Your job's over; it's the end of the case."

Post-Mortem

"AND GEORGE IS ALL RIGHT AGAIN NOW?"

"Thank heaven, yes—getting on splendidly. The doctor says he worked himself into it, just out of worry lest he should be suspected. It never occurred to me—but then George is very quick at putting two and two together."

"Of course he knew he was one of the last people to see his grandfather."

"Yes, and seeing the name on the bottle—and the police coming——"

"That did it. And you're sure he's all right?"

"Oh, rather. The minute he knew that it was all cleared up, he seemed to come out from under a blanket. He sent you all sorts of messages, by the way."

"Well, as soon as he's fit you must come and dine with me . . ."

. . . .

". . . A simple case, of course, as soon as you had disentangled the Robert part of it."

"A damned unsatisfactory case, Charles. Not the kind I like. No real proof."

"Nothing in it for us, of course. Just as well it

340

never came to trial, though. With juries you never know."

"No; they might have let Penberthy off; or convicted them both."

"Exactly. If you ask me, I think Ann Dorland is a very lucky young woman."

"Oh, God!—you *would* say that . . ."

. . . .

". . . Yes, of course, I'm sorry for Naomi Rushworth. But she needn't be so spiteful. She goes about hinting that of course dear Walter was got over by that Dorland girl and sacrificed himself to save her."

"Well, that's natural, I suppose. You thought Miss Dorland had done it yourself at one time, you know, Marjorie."

"I didn't know then about her being engaged to Penberthy. And I think he deserved all he got . . . Well, I know he's dead, but it was a rotten way to treat a girl, and Ann's far too good for that kind of thing. People have a perfect right to want love-affairs. You men always think . . ."

"Not me, Marjorie. I don't think."

"Oh, you! You're almost human. I'd almost take you on myself if you asked me. You don't feel inclined that way, I suppose?"

"My dear—if a great liking and friendship were enough, I would—like a shot. But that wouldn't satisfy you, would it?"

341

"It wouldn't satisfy *you*, Peter. I'm sorry. Forget it."

"I won't forget it. It's the biggest compliment I've ever had paid me. Great Scott! I only wish . . ."

"There! that's all right, you needn't make a speech. And you won't go away tactfully forever, will you?"

"Not if you don't want me to."

"And you won't be embarrassed?"

"No, I won't be embarrassed. Portrait of a young man poking the fire to bits to indicate complete freedom from embarrassment. Let's go and feed somewhere, shall we? . . ."

. . . .

". . . Well, and how did you get on with the heiress and the lawyers and all that lot?"

"Oh! there was a long argument. Miss Dorland insisted on dividing the money, and I said no, I couldn't think of it. She said it was only hers as the result of a crime, and Pritchard and Murbles said she wasn't responsible for other people's crimes. And I said it would look like my profiting by my own attempt at fraud, and she said, not at all, and we went on and on, don't you know. That's a damned decent girl, Wimsey."

"Yes, I know. The moment I found she preferred burgundy to champagne I had the highest opinion of her."

342

"No, really—there's something very fine and straightforward about her."

"Oh, yes—not a bad girl at all; though I shouldn't have said she was quite your sort."

"Why not?"

"Well—arty and all that. And her looks aren't her strong point."

"You needn't be offensive, Wimsey. Surely I may be allowed to appreciate a woman of intelligence and character. I may not be highbrow, but I have *some* ideas beyond the front row of the chorus. And what that girl went through with that blighter Penberthy makes my blood boil."

"Oh, you've heard all about that?"

"I have. She told me, and I respected her for it. I thought it most courageous of her. It's about time somebody brought a little brightness into that poor girl's life. You don't realize how desperately lonely she has been. She had to take up that art business to give her an interest, poor child, but she's really cut out for an ordinary, sensible, feminine life. You may not understand that, with your ideas, but she has really a very sweet nature."

"Sorry, Fentiman."

"She made me ashamed, the way she took the whole thing. When I think of the trouble I got her into, owing to my damned dishonest tinkering about with—you know——"

"My dear man, you were perfectly providential.

343

If you hadn't tinkered about, as you say, she'd be married to Penberthy by now."

"That's true—and that makes it so amazing of her to forgive me. She *loved* that blighter, Wimsey. You don't know. It's absolutely pathetic."

"Well, you'll have to do your best to make her forget it."

"I look on that as a duty, Wimsey."

"Just so. Doing anything to-night? Care to come and look at a show?"

"Sorry—I'm booked. Taking Miss Dorland to the new thing at the Palladium, in fact. Thought it'd do her good—buck her up and so on."

"Oh?—good work!—Here's luck to it . . ."

.   .   .   .

". . . and the cooking is getting perfectly disgraceful. I spoke to Culyer about it only yesterday. But he won't do anything. I don't know what's the good of the committee. This club isn't half what it used to be. In fact, Wimsey, I'm thinking of resigning."

"Oh, don't do that, Wetheridge. It wouldn't be the same place without you."

"Look at all the disturbance there has been lately. Police and reporters—and then Penberthy blowing his brains out in the library. And the coal's all slate. Only yesterday something exploded like a shell—I assure you, exactly like a shell—in the card-room; and as nearly as possible got me in the eye. I said

344

to Culyer, 'This must *not* occur again.' You may laugh, but I knew a man who was blinded by a thing popping out suddenly like that. These things never happened before the War, and—great heavens! William! Look at this wine! Smell it! *Taste* it! Corked? Yes, I should think it *was* corked! My God! I don't know what's come to this Club."

The Five Red Herrings

CONTENTS

FOREWORD

To my friend Joe Dignam,
kindliest of landlords

DEAR JOE,—

Here at last is your book about Gatehouse and Kirkcudbright. All the places are real places and all the trains are real trains, and all the landscapes are correct, except that I have run up a few new houses here and there. But you know better than anybody that none of the people are in the least like the real people, and that no Galloway artist would ever think of getting intoxicated or running away from his wife or bashing a fellow-citizen over the head. All that is just put in for fun and to make it more exciting.

If I have accidentally given any real person's name to a nasty character, please convey my apologies to that person, and assure him or her that it was entirely unintentional. Even bad characters have to be called something. And please tell Provost Laurie that though this story is laid in the petrol-gas period, I have not forgotten that Gatehouse will now have its electric light by which to read this book.

And if you should meet Mr. Millar of the Ellangowan Hotel, or the station-master at Gatehouse, or the booking-clerks at Kirkcudbright, or any of the hundred-and-one kindly people who so patiently answered my questions about railway-tickets and omnibuses and the old mines over at Creetown, give them my very best thanks for their assistance and my apologies for having bothered them so.

Give my love to everybody, not forgetting Felix, and tell Mrs. Dignam that we shall come back next summer to eat some more potato-scones at the Anwoth.

DOROTHY L. SAYERS.

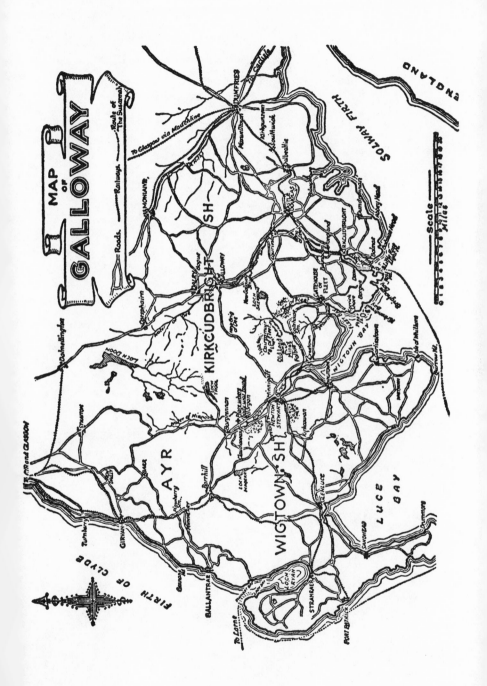

CAMPBELL QUICK

IF ONE lives in Galloway, one either fishes or paints. "Either" is perhaps misleading, for most of the painters are fishers also in their spare time. To be neither of these things is considered odd and almost eccentric. Fish is the standard topic of conversation in the pub and the post-office, in the garage and the street, with every sort of person, from the man who arrives for the season with three Hardy rods and a Rolls-Royce, to the man who leads a curious, contemplative life, watching the salmon-nets on the Dee. Weather, which in other parts of the Kingdom is gauged by the standards of the farmer, the gardener, and the week-ender, is considered in Galloway in terms of fish and paint. The fisherman-painter has the best of the bargain as far as the weather goes, for the weather that is too bright for the trout deluges his hills and his sea with floods of radiant colours; the rain that interrupts picture-making puts water into the rivers and the lochs and sends him hopefully forth with rod and creel; while on cold dull days, when there is neither purple on the hills nor fly on the river, he can join a friendly party in a cosy bar and exchange information about Cardinals and March Browns, and practise making intricate knots in gut.

The artistic centre of Galloway is Kirkcudbright, where the painters form a scattered constellation, whose nucleus is in the High Street, and whose outer stars twinkle in remote hillside cottages, radiating brightness as far as Gatehouse-of-Fleet. There are large and stately studios, panelled and high, in strong stone houses filled with gleaming brass and polished oak. There are workaday studios—summer perching-places rather than settled homes—where a good north light and a litter of brushes and canvas form the whole of the artistic stock-in-trade. There are little homely studios, gay with blue and red and yellow curtains and odd scraps of pottery, tucked away down narrow closes and adorned with gardens, where old-fashioned flowers riot in the rich

1

and friendly soil. There are studios that are simply and solely barns, made beautiful by ample proportions and high-pitched rafters, and habitable by the addition of a tortoise stove and a gas-ring. There are artists who have large families and keep domestics in cap and apron; artists who engage rooms, and are taken care of by landladies; artists who live in couples or alone, with a woman who comes in to clean; artists who live hermit-like and do their own charing. There are painters in oils, painters in water-colour, painters in pastel, etchers and illustrators, workers in metal; artists of every variety, having this one thing in common—that they take their work seriously and have no time for amateurs.

Into this fishing and painting community, Lord Peter Wimsey was received on friendly and even affectionate terms. He could make a respectable cast, and he did not pretend to paint, and therefore, though English and an "incomer," gave no cause of offence. The Southron is tolerated in Scotland on the understanding that he does not throw his weight about, and from this peculiarly English vice Lord Peter was laudably free. True, his accent was affected and his behaviour undignified to a degree, but he had been weighed in the balance over many seasons and pronounced harmless, and when he indulged in any startling eccentricity, the matter was dismissed with a shrug and a tolerant, "Christ, it's only his lordship."

Wimsey was in the bar of the McClellan Arms on the evening that the unfortunate dispute broke out between Campbell and Waters. Campbell, the landscape painter, had had maybe one or two more wee ones than was absolutely necessary, especially for a man with red hair, and their effect had been to make him even more militantly Scottish than usual. He embarked on a long eulogy on what the Jocks had done in the Great War, only interrupting his tale to inform Waters in parenthesis that all the English were of mongrel ancestry and unable even to pronounce their own bluidy language.

Waters was an Englishman of good yeoman stock, and, like all Englishmen, was ready enough to admire and praise all foreigners, but, like all Englishmen, he did not like to hear them praise themselves. To boast loudly in public of one's own country seemed to him indecent—like enlarging on the physical perfections of one's own wife in a smoking-room. He listened with that tolerant, petrified smile which the foreigner takes and indeed quite correctly takes, to indicate a self-satisfaction so impervious that it will not even trouble to justify itself.

Campbell pointed out that all the big administrative posts in London were held by Scotsmen, that England had never succeeded in conquering Scotland, that if Scotland wanted Home Rule, by God, she would take it, that when certain specified English regiments had gone to pieces they had had to send for Scottish officers to control them, and that when any section of the front line had found itself in a tight place, its mind was at once relieved by knowing that the Jocks were on its left. "You ask anybody who was in the War, my lad," he added, acquiring in this way an unfair advantage over Waters, who had only just reached fighting age when the War ended, "they'll tell you what they thought of the Jocks."

"Yes," said Waters, with a disagreeable sneer, "I know what they said. 'They skite too much.'"

Being naturally polite and in a minority, he did not add the remainder of that offensive quotation, but Campbell was able to supply it for himself. He burst into an angry retort, which was not merely nationally, but also personally abusive.

"The trouble with you Scotch," said Waters, when Campbell paused to take breath, "is that you have an inferiority complex."

He emptied his glass in a don't-careish manner and smiled at Wimsey.

It was probably the smile even more than the sneer which put the final touch to Campbell's irritation. He used a few brief and regrettable expressions, and transferred the better part of the contents of his glass to Waters' countenance.

"Och, noo, Mr. Campbell," protested Wullie Murdoch. He did not like these disturbances in his bar.

But Waters by this time was using even more regrettable language than Campbell as they wrestled together among the broken glass and sawdust.

"I'll break your qualified neck for this," he said savagely, "you dirty Highland tyke."

"Here, chuck it, Waters," said Wimsey, collaring him, "don't be a fool. The fellow's drunk."

"Come away, man, said McAdam, the fisherman, enveloping Campbell in a pair of brawny arms. "This is no way to behave. Be quiet."

The combatants fell apart, panting.

"This won't do," said Wimsey, "this isn't the League of Nations. A plague on both your houses! Have a bit of sense."

"He called me a ——," muttered Waters, wiping the whiskey from his face. "I'm damned if I'll stand it. He'd better keep out of my way, that's all." He glared furiously at Campbell.

"You'll find me if you want me," retorted Campbell. "*I* shan't run away."

"Now, now, gentlemen," said Murdoch.

"He comes here," said Campbell, "with his damned sneering ways——"

"Nay, Mr. Campbell," said the landlord, "but ye shuldna ha' said thae things to him."

"I'll say what I damn well like to him," insisted Campbell.

"Not in my bar," replied Murdoch, firmly.

"I'll say them in any damned bar I choose," said Campbell, "and I'll say it again—he's a——."

"Hut!" said McAdam, "ye'll be thinkin' better of it in the morning. Come away now—I'll give ye a lift back to Gatehouse."

"You be damned," said Campbell, "I've got my own car and I can drive it. And I don't want to see any of the whole blasted lot of ye again."

He plunged out, and there was a pause.

"Dear, dear," said Wimsey.

"I think I'd best be off out of it too," said Waters, sullenly.

Wimsey and McAdam exchanged glances.

"Bide a bit," said the latter. "There's no need to be in sic a hurry. Campbell's a hasty man, and when there's a wee bit drink in him he says mair nor he means."

"Ay," said Murdoch, "but he had no call to be layin' them names to Mr. Waters, none at all. It's a verra great pity—a verra great pity indeed."

"I'm sorry if I was rude to the Scotch," said Waters, "I didn't mean to be, but I can't stand that fellow at any price."

"Och, that's a' richt," said McAdam. "Ye meant no harm, Mr. Waters. What'll ye have?"

"Oh, a double Scotch," replied Waters, with rather a shame-faced grin.

"That's right," said Wimsey, "drown remembrance of the insult in the wine of the country."

A man named McGeoch, who had held aloof from the disturbance, rose up and came to the bar.

"Another Worthington," he said briefly. "Campbell will be getting into trouble one of these days, I shouldn't wonder. The manners of him are past all bearing. You heard what he said to Strachan up at the golf-course the other day. Making himself out the boss of the whole place. Strachan told him if he saw him on the course again, he'd wring his neck."

The others nodded silently. The row between Campbell and the golf-club secretary at Gatehouse had indeed become local history.

"And I would not blame Strachan, neither," went on McGeoch. "Here's Campbell only lived two seasons in Gatehouse, and he's setting the whole place by the ears. He's a devil when he's drunk and a lout when he's sober. It's a great shame. Our little artistic community has always got on well together, without giving offence to anybody. And now there are nothing·but rows and bickerings—all through this fellow Campbell."

"Och," said Murdoch, "he'll settle down in time. The man's no a native o' these parts and he doesna verra weel understand his place. Forbye, for all his havers, he's no a Scotsman at a', for everybody knows he's fra' Glasgow, and his mother was an Ulsterwoman, by the name of Flanagan."

"That's the sort that talks loodest," put in Murray, the banker, who was a native of Kirkwall, and had a deep and not always silent contempt for anybody born south of Wick. "But it's best to pay no attention to him. If he gets what is coming to him, I'm thinking it'll no be from anybody here."

He nodded meaningly.

"Ye'll be thinking of Hugh Farren?" suggested McAdam.

"I'll be naming no names," said Murray, "but it's well known that he has made trouble for himself with a certain lady."

"It's no fault of the lady's," said McGeoch, emphatically.

"I'm not saying it is. But there's some gets into trouble without others to help them to it."

"I shouldn't have fancied Campbell in the rôle of a homebreaker," said Wimsey, pleasantly.

"I shouldn't fancy him at all," growled Waters, "but he fancies himself quite enough, and one of these days——"

"There, there," said Murdoch, hastily. "It's true he's no a verra popular man, is Campbell, but it's best to be patient and tak' no notice of him."

"That's all very well," said Waters.

"And wasn't there some sort of row about fishing?" interrupted Wimsey. If the talk had to be about Campbell, it was better to steer it away from Waters at all costs.

"Och, ay," said McAdam. "Him and Mr. Jock Graham is juist at daggers drawn aboot it. Mr. Graham will be fishing the pool below Campbell's hoose. Not but there's plenty pools in the Fleet wi'out disturbin' Campbell, if the man wad juist be peaceable aboot it. But it's no his pool when a's said and dune—the river's free— and it's no to be expectit that Mr. Graham will pay ony heed to his claims, him that pays nae heed to onybody."

"Particularly," said McGeoch, "after Campbell had tried to duck him in the Fleet."

"Did he though, by Jove?" said Wimsey, interested.

"Ay, but he got weel duckit himsel'," said Murdoch, savouring the reminiscence. "And Graham's been fushin' there every nicht since then, wi' yin or twa of the lads. He'll be there the nicht, I wadna wonder."

"Then if Campbell's spoiling for a row, he'll know where to go for it," said Wimsey. "Come on, Waters, we'd better make tracks."

Waters, still sulky, rose and followed him. Wimsey steered him home to his lodgings, prattling cheerfully, and tucked him into bed.

"And I shouldn't let Campbell get on your nerves," he said, interrupting a long grumble, "he's not worth it. Go to sleep and forget it, or you'll do no work to-morrow. That's pretty decent, by the way," he added, pausing before a landscape which was propped on the chest of drawers. "You're a good hand with the knife, aren't you, old man?"

"Who, me?" said Waters. "You don't know what you're talking about. Campbell's the only man who can handle a knife in this place—according to him. He's even had the blasted cheek to say Gowan is an out-of-date old blunderer."

"That's high treason, isn't it?"

"I should think so. Gowan's a real painter—my God, it makes

me hot when I think of it. He actually said it at the Arts Club in Edinburgh, before a whole lot of people, friends of Gowan's."

"And what did Gowan say?"

"Oh, various things. They're not on speaking terms now. Damn the fellow. He's not fit to live. You heard what he said to me?"

"Yes, but I don't want to hear it again. Let the fellow dree his own weird. He's not worth bothering with."

"No, that's a fact. And his work's not so wonderful as to excuse his beastly personality."

"Can't he paint?"

"Oh, he can paint—after a fashion. He's what Gowan calls him —a commercial traveller. His stuff's damned impressive at first sight, but it's all tricks. Anybody could do it, given the formula. I could do a perfectly good Campbell in half an hour. Wait a moment, I'll show you."

He thrust out a leg from the bed. Wimsey pushed him firmly back again.

"Show me some other time. When I've seen his stuff. I can't tell if the imitation's good till I've seen the original, can I?"

"No. Well, you go and look at his things and then I'll show you. Oh, Lord, my head's fuzzy like nothing on earth."

"Go to sleep," said Wimsey. "Shall I tell Mrs. McLeod to let you sleep in, as they say? And call you with a couple of aspirins on toast?"

"No; I've got to be up early, worse luck. But I shall be all right in the morning."

"Well, cheerio, then, and sweet dreams," said Wimsey.

He shut the door after him carefully and wandered thoughtfully back to his own habitation.

. . . .

Campbell, chugging fitfully homewards across the hill which separates Kirkcudbright from Gatehouse-of-Fleet, recapitulated his grievances to himself in a sour monotone, as he mishandled his gears. That damned, sneering, smirking swine Waters! He'd managed to jolt him out of his pose of superiority, anyhow. Only he wished it hadn't happened before McGeoch. McGeoch would tell Strachan, and Strachan would redouble his own good opinion of himself. "You see," he would say, "I turned the man off the golf-course and look how right I was to do it. He's just a fellow that gets drunk and quarrels in public-houses." Curse Strachan, with his perpetual sergeant-major's air of having you on the mat. Strachan, with his domesticity and his precision and his local influence, was at the base of all the trouble, if one came to think of it. He pretended to say nothing, and all the time he was spreading rumours and scandal and setting the whole place against one. Strachan was a friend of that fellow Farren too. Farren would hear about it, and would jump at the excuse to make himself still more obnoxious. There would have been no silly row that night at all if it hadn't been for Farren. That disgusting scene before dinner! That was what had driven him, Campbell, to the McClellan Arms. His hand hesitated on the wheel. Why not go back straight away and have the thing out with Farren?

After all, what did it matter? He stopped the car and lit a cigarette, smoking fast and savagely. If the whole place *was* against him, he hated the place anyhow. There was only one decent person in it, and she was tied up to that brute Farren. The worst of it was, she was devoted to Farren. She didn't care twopence for anybody else, if Farren would only see it. And he, Campbell, knew it as well as anybody. He wanted nothing wrong. He only wanted, when he was tired and fretted, and sick of his own lonely, uncomfortable shack of a place, to go and sit among the cool greens and blues of Gilda Farren's sitting-room and be soothed by her slim beauty and comforting voice. And Farren, with no more sense or imagination than a bull, must come blundering in, breaking the spell, putting his own foul interpretation on the thing, trampling the lilies in Campbell's garden of refuge. No wonder Farren's landscapes looked as if they were painted with an axe. The man had no delicacy. His reds and blues hurt your eyes, and he saw life in reds and blues. If Farren were to die, now, if one could take his bull-neck in one's hands and squeeze it till his great staring blue eyes popped out like—he laughed—like bull's-eyes—that was a damned funny joke. He'd like to tell Farren that and see how he took it.

Farren was a devil, a beast, a bully, with his artistic temperament, which was nothing but inartistic temper. There was no peace with Farren about. There was no peace anywhere. If he went back to Gatehouse, he knew what he would find there. He had only to look out of his bedroom window to see Jock Graham whipping the water just under the wall of the house—doing it on purpose to annoy him. Why couldn't Graham leave him alone? There was better fishing up by the dams. The whole thing was sheer persecution. It wasn't any good, either, to go to bed and take no notice. They would wake him up in the small hours, banging at his window and bawling out the number of their catch—they might even leave a contemptuous offering of trout on his window-sill, wretched little fish like minnows, which ought to have been thrown back again. He only hoped Graham would slip up on the stones one night and fill his waders and be drowned among his infernal fish. The thing that riled him most of all was that this nightly comedy was played out under the delighted eye of his neighbour, Ferguson. Since that fuss about the garden-wall, Ferguson had become absolutely intolerable.

It was perfectly true, of course, that he had backed his car into Ferguson's wall and knocked down a stone or two, but if Ferguson had left his wall in decent repair it wouldn't have done any damage. That great tree of Ferguson's had sent its roots right under the wall and broken up the foundations, and what was more, it threw up huge suckers in Campbell's garden. He was perpetually rooting the beastly things up. A man had no right to grow trees under a wall so that it tumbled down at the slightest little push, and then demand extravagant payments for repairs. He would not repair Ferguson's wall. He would see Ferguson damned first.

He gritted his teeth. He wanted to get out of this stifle of petty quarrels and have one good, big, blazing row with somebody. If only he could have smashed Water's face to pulp—let himself go— had the thing out, he would have felt better. Even now he could go back—or forward—it didn't matter which, and have the whole blasted thing right out with somebody.

He had been brooding so deeply that he never noticed the hum of a car in the distance and the lights flickering out and disappearing as the road dipped and wound. The first thing he heard was a violent squealing of brakes and an angry voice demanding:

"What the bloody hell are you doing, you fool, sitting out like that in the damn middle of the road right on the bend?" And then, as he turned, blinking in the glare of the headlights, to grapple with this new attack, he heard the voice say, with a kind of exasperated triumph:

"Campbell. Of course. I might have known it couldn't be anybody else."

CHAPTER II

CAMPBELL DEAD

"DID ye hear aboot Mr. Campbell?" said Mr. Murdoch of the McClellan Arms, polishing a glass carefully as a preparation for filling it with beer.

"Why, what further trouble has he managed to get into since last night?" asked Wimsey. He leaned an elbow on the bar and prepared to relish anything that might be offered to him.

"He's deid," said Mr. Murdoch.

"Deid?" said Wimsey, startled into unconscious mimicry.

Mr. Murdoch nodded.

"Och, ay; McAdams juist brocht the news in from Gatehouse. They found the body at 2 o'clock up in the hills by Newton-Stewart.

"Good heavens!" said Wimsey ."But what did he die of?"

"Juist tummled intae the burn," replied Mr. Murdoch, "an' drooned himself, by what they say. The pollis'll be up there now tae bring him doon."

"An accident, I suppose."

"Ay, imph'm. The folk at the Borgan seed him pentin' there shortly after 10 this morning on the wee bit high ground by the brig, and Major Dougal gaed by at 2 o'clock wi' his rod an' spied the body liggin' in the burn. It's slippery there and fou o' broken rocks. I'm thinkin' he'll ha' climbed doon tae fetch some watter for his pentin', mebbe, and slippit on the stanes."

"He wouldn't want water for oil-paints," said Wimsey, thoughtfully, "but he might have wanted to mix mustard for his sandwiches or fill a kettle or get a drop for his whiskey. I say, Murdoch, I think I'll just toddle over there in the car and have a look at him. Corpses are rather in my line, you know. Where is this place exactly?"

"Ye maun tak' the coast-road through Creetown to Newton-Stewart," said Mr. Murdoch, "and turn to the richt over the brig and then to the richt again at the sign-post along the road to Bar-

grennan and juist follow the road till ye turn over a wee brig on
the richt-hand side over the Cree and then tak' the richt-hand road."

"In fact," said Wimsey, "you keep on turning to the right. I think
I know the place. There's a bridge and another gate, and a burn
with salmon in it."

"Ay, the Minnoch, whaur Mr. Dennison caught the big fish last
year. Well, it'll be juist afore ye come to the gate, away to your
left abune the brig."

Wimsey nodded.

"I'll be off then," he said, "I don't want to miss the fun. See you
later, old boy. I say—I don't mind betting this is the most popular
thing Campbell ever did. Nothing in life became him like the leaving it, eh, what?"

.   .   .   .

It was a marvellous day in late August, and Wimsey's soul
purred within him as he pushed the car along. The road from
Kirkcudbright to Newton-Stewart is of a varied loveliness hard to
surpass, and with a sky full of bright sun and rolling cloud-banks,
hedges filled with flowers, a well-made road, a lively engine and
the prospect of a good corpse at the end of it, Lord Peter's cup of
happiness was full. He was a man who loved simple pleasures.

He passed through Gatehouse, waving a cheerful hand to the
proprietor of the Anwoth Hotel, climbed up beneath the grim
blackness of Cardoness Castle, drank in for the thousandth time the
strange, Japanese beauty of Mossyard Farm, set like a red jewel
under its tufted trees on the blue sea's rim, and the Italian loveliness
of Kirkdale, with its fringe of thin and twisted trees and the blue
Wigtownshire coast gleaming across the bay. Then the old Border
keep of Barholm, surrounded by white-washed farm buildings; then
a sudden gleam of bright grass, like a lawn in Avalon, under the
shade of heavy trees. The wild garlic was over now, but the scent
of it seemed still to hang about the place in memory, filling it with
the shudder of vampire wings and memories of the darker side of
Border history. Then the old granite crushing mill on its white jetty,
surrounded by great clouds of stone-dust, with a derrick sprawled
across the sky and a tug riding at anchor. Then the salmon-nets and
the wide semi-circular sweep of the bay, rosy every summer with
sea-pinks, purple-brown with the mud of the estuary, majestic with

the huge hump of Cairnsmuir rising darkly over Creetown. Then the open road again, dipping and turning—the white lodge on the left, the cloud-shadows rolling, the cottages with their roses and asters clustered against white and yellow walls; then Newton-Stewart, all grey roofs huddling down to the stony bed of the Cree, its thin spires striking the sky-line. Over the bridge and away to the right by the kirkyard, and then the Bargrennan road, curling like the road to Roundabout, with the curves of the Cree glittering through the tree-stems and the tall blossoms and bracken golden by the wayside. Then the lodge and the long avenue of rhododendrons —then a wood of silver birch, mounting, mounting to shut out the sunlight. Then a cluster of stone cottages—then the bridge and the gate, and the stony hillroad, winding between mounds round as the hill of the King of Elf-land, green with grass and purple with heather and various with sweeping shadows.

Wimsey pulled up as he came to the second bridge and the rusty gate, and drew the car on to the grass. There were other cars there, and glancing along to the left he saw a little group of men gathered on the edge of the burn forty or fifty yards from the road. He approached by way of a little sheep-track, and found himself standing on the edge of a scarp of granite that shelved steeply down to the noisy waters of the Minnoch. Beside him, close to the edge of the rock, stood a sketching easel, with a stool and a palette. Down below, at the edge of a clear brown pool, fringed with knotted hawthorns, lay something humped and dismal, over which two or three people were bending.

A man, who might have been a crofter, greeted Wimsey with a kind of cautious excitement.

"He's doon there, sir. Ay, he'll juist ha' slippit over the edge. Yon's Sergeant Dalziel and Constable Ross, mekkin' their investigation the noo."

There seemed little doubt how the accident had happened. On the easel was a painting, half, or more than half finished, the paint still wet and shining. Wimsey could imagine the artist getting up, standing away to view what he had done—stepping farther back towards the treacherous granite slope. Then the scrape of a heel on the smooth stone, the desperate effort to recover, the slither of leather on the baked short grass, the stagger, the fall, and the bump,

bump, bump of the tumbling body, sheer down the stone face of the ravine to where the pointed rocks grinned like teeth among the chuckling water.

"I know the man," said Wimsey. "It's a very nasty thing, isn't it? I think I'll go down and have a look."

"Ye'll mind your footing," said the crofter.

"I certainly will," said Wimsey, clambering crablike among the stones and bracken. "I don't want to make another police-exhibit."

The Sergeant looked up at the sound of Wimsey's scrambling approach. They had met already, and Dalziel was prepared for Wimsey's interest in corpses, however commonplace the circumstances.

"Hech, my lord," said he, cheerfully. "I dooted ye'd be here before verra long. Ye'll know Dr. Cameron, maybe?"

Wimsey shook hands with the doctor—a lanky man with a noncommittal face—and asked how they were getting on with the business.

"Och, well, I've examined him," said the doctor. "He's dead beyond a doubt—been dead some hours, too. The rigor, ye see, is well developed."

"Was he drowned?"

"I cannot be certain about that. But my opinion—mind ye, it is only my opinion—is that he was not. The bones of the temple are fractured, and I would be inclined to say he got his death in falling or in striking the stones in the burn. But I cannot make a definite pronouncement, you understand, till I have had an autopsy and seen if there is any water in his lungs."

"Quite so," said Wimsey. "The bump on the head might only have made him unconscious, and the actual cause of death might be drowning."

"That is so. When we first saw him, he was lying with his mouth under water, but that might very well come from washing about in the scour of the burn. There are certain abrasions on the hands and head, some of which are—again in my opinion—post-mortem injuries. See here—and here."

The doctor turned the corpse over, to point out the marks in question. It moved all of a piece, crouched and bundled together, as though it had stiffened in the act of hiding its face from the brutal teeth of the rocks.

"But here's where he got the big dunt," added the doctor. He guided Wimsey's fingers to Campbell's left temple, and Wimsey felt the bone give under his light pressure.

"Nature has left the brain ill-provided in those parts," remarked Dr. Cameron. "The skull there is remarkably thin, and a comparatively trifling blow will crush it like an egg-shell."

Wimsey nodded. His fine, long fingers were gently exploring head and limbs. The doctor watched him with grave approval.

"Man," he said, "ye'd make a fine surgeon. Providence has given ye the hands for it."

"But not the head," said Wimsey, laughing. "Yes, he's got knocked about a bit. I don't wonder coming down that bank full tilt."

"Ay, it's a dangerous place," said the Sergeant. "Weel, noo, doctor, I'm thinkin' we've seen a' that's to be seen doon here. We would better be getting the body up to the car."

"I'll go back and have a look at the painting," said Wimsey, "unless I can help you with the lifting. I don't want to be in the way."

"Nay, nay," said the Sergeant. "Thank you for the offer, my lord, but we can manage fine by oorsel's."

The Sergeant and a constable bent over and seized the body. Wimsey waited to see that they required no assistance, and then scrambled up to the top of the bank again.

He gave his first attention to the picture. It was blocked in with a free and swift hand, and lacked the finishing touches, but it was even so a striking piece of work, bold in its masses and chiaroscuro, and strongly laid on with the knife. It showed a morning lighting— he remembered that Campbell had been seen painting a little after 10 o'clock. The grey stone bridge lay cool in the golden light, and the berries of a rowan-tree, good against witchcraft, hung yellow and red against it, casting splashes of red reflection upon the brown and white of the tumbling water beneath. Up on the left, the hills soared away in veil on veil of misty blue to meet the hazy sky. And splashed against the blue stood the great gold splendour of the bracken, flung in by spadefuls of pure reds and yellows.

Idly, Wimsey picked up the palette and painting-knife which lay upon the stool. He noticed that Campbell used a simple palette of few colours, and this pleased him, for he liked to see economy of means allied with richness of result. On the ground was an aged satchel, which had evidently seen long service. Rather from habit than with any eye to deduction, he made an inventory of its contents.

In the main compartment he found a small flask of whiskey, half-full, a thick tumbler and a packet of bread and cheese, eight brushes, tied together with a dejected piece of linen which had once been a handkerchief but was now dragging out a dishonoured existence as a paint-rag, a dozen loose brushes, two more painting-knives and a scraper. Cheek by jowl with these were a number of tubes of paint. Wimsey laid them out side by side on the granite, like a row of little corpses.

There was a half-pound tube of vermilion spectrum, new, clean and almost unused, a studio-size tube of ultramarine No. 2, half-full, another of chrome yellow, nearly full, and another of the same, practically empty. Then came a half-pound tube of viridian, half-full, a studio-size cobalt three-quarters empty, and then an extremely dirty tube, with its label gone, which seemed to have survived much wear and tear without losing much of its contents. Wimsey removed the cap and diagnosed it as crimson lake. Finally, there was an almost empty studio-size tube of rose madder and a half-pound lemon yellow, partly used and very dirty.

Wimsey considered this collection for a moment, and then dived confidently into the satchel again. The large compartment, however, yielded nothing further except some dried heather, a few shreds of tobacco and a quantity of crumbs, and he turned his attention to the two smaller compartments.

In the first of these was, first, a small screw of grease-proof paper on which brushes had been wiped; next, a repellent little tin, very sticky about the screw-cap, containing copal medium; and, thirdly, a battered dipper, matching the one attached to the palette.

The third and last compartment of the satchel offered a more varied bag. There was a Swan vesta box, filled with charcoal, a cigarette-tin, also containing charcoal and a number of sticks of red chalk, a small sketch-book, heavily stained with oil, three or four canvas-separators, on which Wimsey promptly pricked his fingers, some wine-corks and a packet of Gold Flakes.

Wimsey's air of idleness had left him. His long and inquisitive nose seemed to twitch like a rabbit's as he turned the satchel upside down and shook it, in the vain hope of extracting something more from its depths. He rose, and searched the easel and the ground about the stool very carefully.

A wide cloak of a disagreeable check pattern lay beside the easel. He picked it up and went deliberately through the pockets. He found a pen-knife, with one blade broken, half a biscuit, another packet of cigarettes, a box of matches, a handkerchief, two trout-casts in a transparent envelope, and a piece of string.

He shook his head. None of these was what he wanted. He searched the ground again, casting like a hound on the trail, and then, still dissatisfied, began to lower himself gingerly down the smooth face of the rock. There were crannies here into which something might have fallen, clumps of bracken and heather, prickly roots of gorse. He hunted and felt about in every corner, stabbing his fingers again at every move and swearing savagely. Small fragments of gorse worked their way up his trouser-legs and into his shoes. The heat was stifling. Close to the bottom he slipped, and did the last yard or so on his hinderparts, which irritated him. At a shout from the top of the bank he looked up. The Sergeant was grinning down at him.

"Reconstructing the accident, my lord?"

"Not exactly," said Wimsey. "Here, wait just a moment, will you?"

He scrambled up again. The corpse was now laid as decently as possible on a stretcher, awaiting removal.

"Have you searched his pockets?" panted Wimsey.

"Not yet, my lord. Time enough for that at the station. It's purely a formality, ye ken."

"No, it's not," said Wimsey. He pushed his hat back and wiped the sweat from his forehead. "There's something funny about this, Dalziel. That is, there may be. Do you mind if I go over his belongings now?"

"Not at all, not at all," said Dalziel, heartily. "There's no sic a great hurry. We may as weel dew 't first as last."

Wimsey sat down on the ground beside the stretcher, and the Sergeant stood by with a notebook to chronicle the finds.

The right-hand coat pocket contained another handkerchief, a Hardy catalogue, two crumpled bills and an object which caused the Sergeant to exclaim laughingly, "What's this, lip-stick?"

"Nothing so suggestive," said Wimsey, sadly, "it's a holder for lead-pencil—made in Germany, to boot. Still, if that's there, there might be something else."

The left-hand pocket, however, produced nothing more exciting than a corkscrew and some dirt; the breast-pocket, only an Ingersoll watch, a pocket comb and a half-used book of stamps; and Wimsey turned, without much hope, to the trouser-pockets, for the dead man wore no waistcoat.

Here, on the right, they found a quantity of loose cash, the notes and coins jumbled carelessly together, and a bunch of keys on a ring. On the left, an empty match-box and a pair of folding nail-scissors. In the hip-pocket, a number of dilapidated letters, some newspaper cuttings and a small notebook with nothing in it.

Wimsey sat up and stared at the Sergeant.

"It's not here," he said, "and I don't like the look of it at all, Dalziel. Look here, there's just one possibility. It may have rolled down into the water. For God's sake get your people together and hunt for it—now. Don't lose a minute."

Dalziel gazed at this excitable Southerner in some astonishment, and the constable pushed back his cap and scratched his head.

"What would we be lookin' for?" he demanded, reasonably.

(Here Lord Peter Wimsey told the Sergeant what he was to look for and why, but as the intelligent reader will readily supply these details for himself, they are omitted from this page.)

"It'll be important, then, to your way o' thinking," said Dalziel, with the air of a man hopefully catching, through a forest of obscurity, the first, far-off glimmer of the obvious.

"Important?" said Wimsey. "Of course it's important. Incredibly, urgently, desperately important. Do you think I should be sliding all over your infernal granite making a blasted pincushion of myself if it wasn't important?"

This argument seemed to impress the Sergeant. He called his forces together and set them to search the path, the bank and the burn for the missing object. Wimsey, meanwhile, strolled over to a shabby old four-seater Morris, which stood drawn well up on the grass at the beginning of the sheep-track.

"Ay," said Constable Ross, straightening his back and sucking his fingers, preliminary to a further hunt among the prickles, "yon's his car. Maybe ye'll find what ye're wantin' in it, after all."

"Don't you believe it, laddies," said Wimsey. Nevertheless, he subjected the car to a careful scrutiny, concentrated for the most part upon the tonneau. A tarry smear on the back cushions seemed to interest him particularly. He examined it carefully with a lens, whistling gently the while. Then he searched further and discovered another on the edge of the body, close to the angle behind the driver's seat. On the floor of the car lay a rug, folded up. He shook it out and looked it over from corner to corner. Another patch of grit and tar rewarded him.

Wimsey pulled out a pipe and lit it thoughtfully. Then he hunted in the pockets of the car till he found an ordnance map of the district. He climbed into the driver's seat, spread out the map on the wheel, and plunged into meditation.

Presently the Sergeant came back, very hot and red in the face, in his shirt-sleeves.

"We've searched high and low," he said, stooping to wring the water from his trouser-legs, "but we canna find it. Maybe ye'll be tellin' us now why the thing is so important."

"Oh?" said Wimsey. "You look rather warm, Dalziel. I've cooled off nicely, sitting here. It's not there, then?"

"It is not," said the Sergeant, with emphasis.

"In that case," said Wimsey, "you had better go to the coroner —no, of course, you don't keep coroners in these parts. The Procurator-Fiscal is the lad. You'd better go to the Fiscal and tell him the man's been murdered."

"Murdered?" said the Sergeant.

"Yes," said Wimsey, "och, ay; and likewise hoots! Murrrderrrt is the word."

"Eh!" said the Sergeant. "Here, Ross!"

The constable came up to them at a slow gallop.

"Here's his lordship," said the Sergeant, "is of opeenion the man's been murdered."

"Is he indeed?" said Ross. "Ay, imph'm. And what would bring his lordship to that conclusion?"

"The rigidity of the corpse," said Wimsey, "the fact that you can't find what you're looking for, these smears of tar on the Morris, and the character of the deceased. He was a man anybody might have felt proud to murder."

"The rigidity of the corpse, now," said Dalziel. "That'll be a matter for Dr. Cameron."

"I confess," said the doctor, who had now joined them, "that has been puzzling me. If the man had not been seen alive just after 10 o'clock this morning, I would have said he had been nearer twelve hours dead."

"So should I," said Wimsey. "On the other hand, you'll notice that that painting, which was put on with a quick-drying copal medium, is still comparatively wet, in spite of the hot sun and the dry air."

"Ay," said the doctor. "So I am forced to the conclusion that the chill of the water produced early rigor."

"I do not submit to force," said Wimsey. "I prefer to believe that the man was killed about midnight. I do not believe in that painting. I do not think it is telling the truth. I know that it is absolutely impossible for Campbell to have been working here on that painting this morning."

"Why so?" inquired the Sergeant.

"For the reasons I gave you before," said Wimsey. "And there's another small point—not very much in itself, but supporting the same conclusion. The whole thing looks—and is meant to look—as though Campbell had got up from his painting, stepped back to get a better view of his canvas, missed his footing and fallen down.

But his palette and painting-knife were laid down on his stool. Now it's far more likely that, if he were doing that, he would have kept his palette on his thumb and his knife or brush in his hand, ready to make any little extra touch that was required. I don't say he might not have laid them down. I only say it would have looked more natural if we had found the palette beside the body and the knife half-way down the slope."

"Ay," said Ross. "I've seen 'em dew that. Steppin' back wi' their eyes half-shut and then hoppin' forward wi' the brush as if they was throwin' darts."

Wimsey nodded.

"It's my theory," he said, "that the murderer brought the body here this morning in Campbell's own car. He was wearing Campbell's soft hat and that foul plaid cloak of his so that anybody passing by might mistake him for Campbell. He had the body on the floor of the tonneau and on top of it he had a push-cycle, which has left tarry marks on the cushions. Tucked in over the whole lot he had this rug, which has tar-marks on it too. Then I think he dragged out the corpse, carried it up the sheep-track on his shoulders and tumbled it into the burn. Or possibly he left it lying on the top of the bank, covered with the rug. Then, still wearing Campbell's hat and cloak, he sat down and faked the picture. When he had done enough to create the impression that Campbell had been here painting, he took off the cloak and hat, left the palette and knife on the seat and went away on his push-bike. It's a lonely spot, here. A man might easily commit a dozen murders, if he chose his time well."

"That's a verra interesting theory," said Dalziel.

"You can test it," said Wimsey. "If anybody saw Campbell this morning to speak to, or close enough to recognise his face, then, of course, it's a wash-out. But if they only saw the hat and cloak, and especially if they noticed anything bulky in the back of the car with a rug over it, then the theory stands. Mind you, I don't say the bicycle is absolutely necessary to the theory, but it's what I should have used in the murderer's place. And if you'll look at this smear of tar under the lens, I think you'll see traces of the tread of a tyre."

"I'll no say ye're no richt," said Dalziel.

"Very well," said Wimsey. "Now let's see what our murderer

has to do next." He flapped the map impressively, and the two policemen bent their heads over it with him.

"Here he is," said Wimsey, "with only a bicycle to help or hinder him, and he's got to establish some sort of an alibi. He may not have bothered about anything very complicated, but he'd make haste to dissociate himself from this place as quickly as possible. And I don't fancy he'd be anxious to show himself in Newton-Stewart or Creetown. There's nowhere much for him to go northward—it only takes him up into the hills round Larg and the Rhinns of Kells. He could go up to Glen Trool, but there's not much point in that; he'd only have to come back the same way. He might, of course, follow the Cree back on the eastern bank as far as Minniegaff, avoiding Newton-Stewart, and strike across country to New Galloway, but it's a long road and keeps him hanging about much too close to the scene of the crime. In my opinion, his best way would be to come back to the road and go northwest by Bargrennan, Cairnderry, Creeside and Drumbain, and strike the railway at Barrhill. That's about nine or ten miles by road. He could do it, going briskly, in an hour, or, as it's a rough road, say an hour and a half. Say he finished the painting at 11 o'clock, that brings him to Barrhill at 12.30. From there he could get a train to Stranraer and Port Patrick, or even to Glasgow, or, of course, if he dumped the bicycle, he might take a motor-bus to somewhere. If I were you, I'd have a hunt in that direction."

The Sergeant glanced at his colleagues and read approval in their eyes.

"And whae d'ye think, my lord, wad be the likeliest pairson to hae committed the crime?" he inquired.

"Well," said Wimsey, "I can think of half a dozen people with perfectly good motives. But the murderer's got to be an artist, and a clever one, for that painting would have to pass muster as Campbell's work. He must know how to drive a car, and he must possess, or have access to, a bicycle. He must be fairly hefty, to have carried the body up here on his back, for I see no signs of dragging. He must have been in contact with Campbell after 9.15 last night, when I saw him leave the McClellan Arms alive and kicking. He must know the country and the people pretty well, for he obviously knew that Campbell lived alone with only a charwoman coming in, so that his early morning departure would surprise nobody. He either lives in the same way himself, or else had a very good excuse for being up and out before breakfast this morning. If you find a man who fulfils all these conditions, he's probably the right one. His rail-way-ticket, if he took one, ought to be traceable. Or it's quite possible I may be able to put my finger on him myself, working on different lines and with rather less exertion."

"Och, weel," said the Sergeant, "if ye find him, ye'll let us know."

"I will," said Wimsey, "though it will be rather unpleasant, because ten to one he'll be some bloke I know and like much better than Campbell. Still, it doesn't do to murder people, however offensive they may be. I'll do my best to bring him in captive to my bow and spear—if he doesn't slay me first."

CHAPTER III

FERGUSON

ON HIS way back to Kirkcudbright, it occurred to Wimsey that it was more than time for tea, and further, that it would be a good idea to visit Campbell's cottage. He accordingly pulled up at the Anwoth Hotel, and, while voraciously filling himself up with potato-scones and ginger-cake, made out a rough list of possible suspects.

At the end of the meal, the list stood as follows:

Living in Kirkcudbright:—

1. Michael Waters—28—5 foot 10 inches—unmarried—living in lodgings· with private latch-key—landscape painter—boasts of being able to counterfeit Campbell's style—quarrelled with Campbell previous night and threatened to break his neck.

2. Hugh Farren—35—5 foot 9 inches—figure and landscape painter—particularly broad in the shoulder—married—known to be jealous of Campbell—lives alone with a wife who is apparently much attached to him.

3. Matthew Gowan—46—6 foot 1 inch—figure and landscape painter, also etcher—unmarried—house with servants—wealthy—known to have been publicly insulted by Campbell—refuses to speak to him.

Living in Gatehouse-of-Fleet:—

4. Jock Graham—36—5 foot 11 inches—unmarried—staying at Anwoth Hotel—portrait painter—keen fisherman—reckless—known to be carrying on a feud with Campbell and to have ducked him in the Fleet after being assaulted by him.

5. Henry Strachan—38—6 foot 2 inches—married—one child, one servant—portrait painter and illustrator—secretary of golf-club —known to have quarrelled with Campbell and turned him off the golf-course.

The list had reached this stage when the landlord of the hotel came in. Wimsey gave him the latest news of the Campbell affair, without, however, referring to the murder theory, and remarked that he thought of running along to Campbell's house, to see if anything was known there about his movements.

"I doot ye'll no be hearin' much there," said the landlord. "Mrs. Green that does his work is away home, but she knows juist naething at a', except that when she arrived this mornin' at 8 o'clock to put the place in order, he had went oot. And Mr. Ferguson that lives next him was away to Glasgow by the first train."

"Ferguson?" said Wimsey. "I think I've met him. Didn't he do those mural paintings for the town hall at some place or other?"

"Ay, he's a verra gude penter. Ye'll have seen him gaun aboot in his wee Austin. He has the stujo next to Campbell's every summer."

"Is he married?"

"Ay, but his wife's away the noo, visitin' wi' friends in Edinbro'. I believe they du not get on so verra weel tegither."

"Who, Ferguson and Campbell?"

"No, no, Ferguson and Mrs. Ferguson. But the ither's true, too. He and Campbell had an awfu' quarrel aboot a bit wall of Ferguson's that Campbell knocked down wi' his car."

"I wonder if there is a single person in the Strewarty that Campbell didn't have a row with," thought Wimsey, and made an addition to his list:—

6. John Ferguson—about 36—about 5 foot 10 inches—grass-widower—landscape and figures—row about a wall.

"By the way," he went on, "is Jock Graham anywhere about?"

"Och, Jock—he's away oot. He didna come hame last nicht at a'. He said he might be fishin' up at Loch Trool."

"Oho!" said Wimsey. "Up at Loch Trool, is he? How did he go?"

"I couldna say. I think the factor had invitit him. He'll ha' spent last nicht in Newton-Stewart, maybe, and went up wi' the factor in the mornin'. Or he will ha' been fishin' the loch all nicht."

"Will he, though?" said Wimsey. This put a new complexion on the matter. An active man might have driven the body up to the

Minnoch and walked back to Newton-Stewart in time to keep his
appointment, if that appointment was not an early one. But it would
have to be, of course, for a day's fishing, and Jock Graham liked
to work by night.

"Will he be back to-night, Joe?"

"I couldna say at all," said the landlord, scattering his hopes at
a blow. "They'll maybe tak' twae nichts if the fishin's gude."

"H'm!" said Wimsey. "And very nice, too. Well, I'll be getting
on."

He paid his bill and came downstairs, accompanied by the landlord.

"How's Andy?" he asked, casually.

"Qch, fine," said the other. "He's in a great way, though, to-day.
Some fellow's pinched his push-bike. An' the worst is, he had juist
fitted it wi' new tyres on both wheels."

Wimsey, with his thumb on the self-starter, paused, electrified.
"How's that?"

"It's his ain fault. He will go leavin' it aboot the place. It'll be
some o' these trampin' fellows that sells carpets, verra like. There's
naebody in Gatehouse wad du sic a thing."

"When did he miss it?"

"This mornin', when he was aff to schule. It's a gude thing it
wasna the motor-bike he's always after me to be givin' him."

"I daresay somebody's just borrowed it," said Wimsey.

"That's so. It may turn up yet. Well, gude day to your lordship."

Wimsey did not cross the bridge, but turned up the road to the
railway station. He passed the turning on the left leading past Anwoth Old Kirk to the Creetown road, and followed the course of
the Fleet till he came to a small lane on the right. At the end
of this stood two little detached cottages, side by side, looking over
a deep pool—in fact, the famous disputed pool in which Jock Graham
had ducked the deceased Campbell.

Under normal circumstances, Wimsey would have expected to
find both doors confidingly on the latch, but to-day the lower cottage, which was Campbell's, had been locked—probably by the police. Wimsey peered in through all the ground-floor windows in
turn. Everything seemed peaceful and in order as the charwoman
had left it that morning. There was a sitting-room of bachelor ap-

pearance in front and a kitchen behind—the usual but and ben with a bedroom over. In addition, a glass-roofed studio had been built out beyond the kitchen. At the right-hand side, the shed that had housed the Morris stood empty, a fresh set of tyre-tracks in the dust showing where the car had been taken out that morning. Just beyond, a wooden gate led into an untidy little garden. From the end of the studio a party-wall of rough stone ran down, separating the yard and garden from those belonging to the other cottage, and Wimsey noticed a breach in the wall and the pile of débris which marked where Campbell had backed injudiciously while turning into the garage, and given cause for so much unneighbourly feeling.

Ferguson's cottage was the mirror-image of Campbell's, but his garden was neatly cared-for, and his garage was brand-new and built, regrettably, of corrugated iron. Wimsey pushed open the door and was confronted by a new and shining two-seater of a popular type.

This surprised him for a moment. Ferguson had taken the early train to Glasgow, and Gatehouse Station is six and a half miles from the town. Why had Ferguson not taken the car? He could easily have left it at the station till his return. It appeared to be a new toy; perhaps he had not cared to leave it in strange hands? Or perhaps he meant to be away a long time? Or perhaps——?

Wimsey lifted the bonnet thoughtfully. Yes, that was the explanation. A gap and some loose connections showed that the magneto had been taken away. Quite probably Ferguson had carried it off with him to Glasgow for repairs. How, then, had Ferguson got to the station? A friendly lift? The 'bus? Or a bicycle? The simplest way was to go and ask. At a small country station no passenger goes unnoticed, and one might as well make sure that Ferguson really had travelled by that train.

Wimsey closed the bonnet and shut the garage-door carefully after him. The house-door was open and he walked in and glanced round. It was as neat and non-committal as any house could be. Everything had been swept, dusted and tidied up by Mrs. Green, including the contents of the studio; for when the artist is away the charwoman will always play among the paint-pots, and no amount of remonstrance will prevent it. Wimsey glanced at some figure-studies piled against the wall, squinnied up his eyes at an elaborate and mannered piece of decorative landscape on the easel, noted casually that Ferguson got his painting materials from Roberson's, glanced along a row of detective novels on the sitting-room bookshelf, and tried the lid of the writing-bureau. It was unlocked, and disclosed an orderly row of pigeon-holes, with everything in its place. Wimsey put down Ferguson as a man of an almost morbidly exact mentality. There was nothing here to throw any light on Campbell's death, but he became all the more anxious to get hold of Ferguson. The way in which the cottages were built, detached and sharing one common entrance yard, ensured that everything which was done in the one could be overlooked from the other. If anything unusual had happened to Campbell the previous night, Ferguson could scarcely have failed to see something of it. And, on the other hand, if Ferguson had not seen it, then nobody had, for the two little houses stood remote from all other neighbours, hidden at the bottom of the rough, leafy lane, with the Water of Fleet lipping by at the bottom of the gardens. If Jock Graham, indeed, had been fishing Standing-Stone Pool that night—but no! He was supposed to have gone to Loch Trool. Ferguson was the man. It would be advisable to get quickly upon the track of Ferguson.

Wimsey went back to his car and started away up the long hill road to Gatehouse Station, which lies at the edge of the Galloway hill-country, looking away over the Fleet Valley and the viaduct and frowned on by the lofty scarp of the Clints of Dromore.

．　　．　　．　　．　　．　　．　　．

The railway-station at Gatehouse is approached by one of those gates so numerous in the Border Country, which provide some slight restraint upon straying cattle but to the impatient motorist appear an unmitigated nuisance. As usual, however, at this point, an obliging old gentleman emerged from the little group of cottages by the wayside and let Wimsey through.

Immediately beyond the gate, the road branches right and left into a rough, stony track, of which the left-hand side goes deviously down to Creetown, while the right-hand side wanders away to Dromore and ends abruptly at the railway viaduct. Wimsey crossed this road and kept straight on down a steep little approach, heavily masked by rhododendrons, which brought him to the station.

The line from Castle-Douglas to Stranraer is a single one, but boasts of two sets of rails at Gatehouse Station, for the better convenience of passengers and to allow of the passing of trains. Wimsey approached the station-master, who was profiting by a slack period between two trains to study the *Glasgow Bulletin* in his office.

"I've been trying to find Mr. Ferguson," said Wimsey, after the usual greetings, "to fix up a fishing-party at Loch Skerrow, but I'm told he went away this morning by the 9.8. Is that so?"

"Ay, that is so. I saw him mysel'."

"I wonder when he'll be back. Was he going to Glasgow, do you know, or only to Dumfries?"

"He mentioned he was gaun to Glasgow," said the station-master, "but he'll maybe be back the nicht. Angus here will be able to tell ye if he took a return ticket."

The booking-clerk, who shared the station-master's office, remembered Mr. Ferguson very well, because he had taken a first-class return to Glasgow, an extravagance somewhat unusual among the artist community.

"But of course," said Wimsey, "the ticket is available for three months. He's not bound to return to-day. Did he leave his car here, I wonder?"

"He didna come by car," said the clerk. "He tell't me the magneto was broken down, and he was obliged to take the train from here, instead o' drivin' to Dumfries."

"Oh, then he bicycled up, I suppose," said Wimsey, carelessly.

"Nay," said the station-master, "he'll have come with Campbell's 'bus. He arrived aboot that time, did he no, Angus?"

"He did that. He was talkin' with Rabbie McHardy when he came in. He'll maybe have told him how long he thocht to be stayin' in Glasgow."

"Thanks," said Wimsey. "I'll have a word with Rabbie. I wanted to charter a boat for to-morrow, but if Ferguson isn't going to be back, it's not much use, is it?"

He chatted for a few minutes more, giving them a suitably censored account of the Campbell affair, and then took his leave. He had not got very much farther, except that he seemed to have more or less eliminated Ferguson from his list of suspects. He would have to check him up, of course, and see that he really had arrived in Glasgow. This might present a little difficulty, but it was merely routine-work for Dalziel and his myrmidons.

Wimsey looked at his watch. Jock Graham was at present the most promising candidate for criminal honours, but since he had disappeared, there was nothing to be done about him for the present. There was, however, still time to go and interview Strachan, and so round off his inquiries in Gatehouse.

CHAPTER IV

STRACHAN

STRACHAN lived in a pleasant, middle-sized house handily situated for him a little way out of Gatehouse on the road that goes up to the golf-course. The neat maid who came to the door smiled kindly upon the visitor and said that the master was at home and would his lordship please step in.

His lordship stepped accordingly into the sitting-room, where he found Mrs. Strachan seated by the window instructing her small daughter Myra in the art of plain knitting.

Wimsey apologised for calling just before dinner, and explained that he wanted to fix up with Strachan about a foursome.

"Well, I don't quite know," said Mrs. Strachan, a trifle doubtfully. "I don't think Harry is likely to be playing for a day or two. He's had rather a tiresome—oh, well! I really don't know. Myra, dear, run and tell Daddy Lord Peter Wimsey is here and wants to talk to him. You know, I never like to make any sort of arrangements for Harry—I *always* manage to put my foot in it."

She giggled—she was rather a giggly woman at the best of times. Nervousness, Wimsey supposed. Strachan had an abrupt manner which tended to make people nervous, and Wimsey more than suspected him of being a bit of a domestic tyrant.

He said something vague about not wanting to be a nuisance.

"Of *course* not," said Mrs. Strachan, keeping an uneasy eye on the door, "how *could* you be a nuisance? We're always so *delighted* to see you. And what have you been doing with yourself this beautiful day?"

"I've been up to the Minnoch to see the body," said Wimsey, cheerfully.

"The body?" cried Mrs. Strachan, with a little squeal. "How dreadful that sounds! What *do* you mean? A salmon, or something?"

"No, no," said Wimsey. "Campbell—Sandy Campbell—haven't you heard?"

32

"No, what?" Mrs. Strachan opened her large baby-blue eyes very wide indeed. "Has anything happened to Mr. Campbell?"

"Good Lord," said Wimsey, "I thought everybody knew. He's dead. He tumbled into the Minnoch and got killed."

Mrs. Strachan gave a shrill shriek of horror.

"Killed? How perfectly dreadful! Was he drowned?"

"I don't quite know," said Wimsey. "I think he bashed his head in, but he may have been drowned as well."

Mrs. Strachan shrieked again.

"When did it happen?"

"Well," said Wimsey, cautiously, "they found him about lunch-time."

"Good gracious! And we never knew anything about it. Oh, Harry"—as the door opened—"what *do* you think? Lord Peter says poor Mr. Campbell has been killed up at the Minnoch!"

"Killed?" said Strachan. "What do you mean, Milly? Who killed him?"

Mrs. Strachan shrieked a third time, more loudly.

"Of course I don't mean that, Harry. How absurd and how horrible! He fell down and cut his head open and got drowned."

Strachan came forward rather slowly and greeted Wimsey with a nod.

"What's all this about, Wimsey?"

"It's perfectly true," said Wimsey. "They found Campbell's dead body in the Minnoch at 2 o'clock. Apparently he had been painting and slipped over the edge of the granite and cracked his skull on the stones."

He spoke a little absently. It was surely not his fancy that his host looked exceedingly pale and upset, and now, as Strachan turned his face round into the full light of the window, it was obvious that he was suffering from a black eye—a very handsome and well-developed black eye, rich in colour and full in contour.

"Oh!" said Strachan. "Well, I'm not surprised, you know. That's a very dangerous spot. I told him so on Sunday, and he called me a fool for my pains."

"Why, was he up there on Sunday?" said Wimsey.

"Yes, making a sketch or something. You remember, Milly, just on the other side of the burn from where we were picnicking."

"Goodness!" exclaimed Mrs. Strachan, "was *that* the place? Oo!

how perfectly horrid! I'll never go there again, never. You may say what you like. Wild horses wouldn't drag me."

"Don't be ridiculous, Milly. Of course you needn't go there if you don't want to."

"I should always be afraid of Myra falling in and being killed," said Mrs. Strachan.

"Very well, then," said her husband, impatiently. "Don't go there. That settles that. How did all this happen, Wimsey?"

Lord Peter told the story again, with such detail as he thought desirable.

"That's exactly like Campbell," said Strachan. "He walks about —that is, he used to walk about—with his eyes on his canvas and his head in the air, never looking in the least where he was going. I shouted out to him on Sunday to be careful—he couldn't hear what I said, or pretended he couldn't, and I actually took the trouble to fag round to the other side of the stream and warn him what a slippery place it was. However, he was merely rude to me, so I left it at that. Well, he's done it once too often, that's all."

"Oh, don't speak in that unfeeling tone," exclaimed Mrs. Strachan. "The poor man's dead, and though he wasn't a very nice man, one can't help feeling sorry about it."

Strachan had the grace to mutter that he *was* sorry, and that he never wished any harm to the fellow. He leaned his forehead on his hand, as if his head was aching badly.

"You seem to have been in the wars a bit yourself," remarked Wimsey.

Strachan laughed.

"Yes," he said, "most ridiculous thing. I was up on the golf-course after breakfast when some putrid fool sliced a ball about a thousand miles off the fairway and got me slap-bang in the eye."

Mrs. Strachan gave another small squeak of surprise.

"Oh!" she said, and then subsided swiftly as Strachan turned his parti-coloured eyes warningly upon her.

"How tiresome," said Wimsey. "Who was the blighter?"

"Haven't the faintest idea," replied Strachan, carelessly. "I was completely knocked out for the moment, and when I pulled myself together again and went to spy out the land, I only saw a party of men making off in the distance. I felt too rotten to bother about it. I simply made tracks for the club-house and a drink. I've got the ball, though—a Silver King. If anybody comes to claim it I shall tell him where he gets off."

"It's a nasty knock," said Wimsey, sympathetically. "A beautiful specimen of its kind, but uncommonly painful, I expect. It's come up nicely, hasn't it? When exactly did you get it?"

"Oh, quite early," said Strachan. "About 9 o'clock, I should think. I went and lay down in my room at the club-house all morning, I felt so rotten. Then I came straight home, so that's why I hadn't heard about Campbell. Dash it all, this means a funeral, I suppose. It's a bit awkward. In the ordinary way we should send a wreath from the Club, but I don't quite know what to do under the circumstances, because last time he was here I told him to send in his resignation."

"It's a nice little problem," said Wimsey. "But I think I should send one, all the same. Shows a forgiving spirit and all that. Keep your vindictiveness for the person who damaged your face. Whom were you playing with, by the way? Couldn't he have identified the assassin?"

Strachan shook his head.

"I was just having a practice round against bogey," he said. "I caddied for myself, so there were no witnesses."

"Oh, I see. Your hands look a bit knocked about, too. You seem to have spent a good bit of your time in the rough. Well, I really came in to ask you to make up a foursome to-morrow with Waters and Bill Murray and me, but I don't suppose you'll, so to speak, feel that your eye is in just yet awhile?"

"Hardly," said Strachan, with a grim smile.

"Then I'll be popping off," said Wimsey, rising. "Cheerio, Mrs. Strachan. Cheerio, old man. Don't bother to see me off the premises. I know my way out."

Strachan, however, insisted on accompanying him as far as the gate.

At the corner of the road Wimsey overtook Miss Myra Strachan and her nurse taking an evening stroll. He stopped the car and asked if they would like a little run.

Myra accepted gleefully, and her attendant made no objection. Wimsey took the child up beside him, packed the nurse into the back seat and urged the Daimler Double-Six to show off her best paces.

Myra was delighted.

"Daddy never goes as fast as this," she said, as they topped the tree-hung rise by Cally Lodge and sailed like an aeroplane into the open country.

Wimsey glanced at the speedometer-needle, which was flickering about the 85 mark, and took the corner on a spectacular skid.

"That's a fine black eye your Dad's got," he remarked.

"Yes, isn't it? I asked him if he'd been fighting, and he told me not to be impertinent. I like fighting. Bobby Craig gave *me* a black eye once. But I made his nose bleed, and they had to send his suit to the cleaners."

"Young women oughtn't to fight," said Wimsey, reprovingly, "not even modern young women."

"Why not? I like fighting. Oo! look at the cows!"

Wimsey trod hastily on the brake and reduced the Daimler to a ladylike crawl.

"All the same, I believe he *was* fighting," said Myra. "He never came home last night, and Mummy was ever so frightened. She's afraid of our car, you know, because it goes so fast, but it doesn't go as fast as yours. Does that cow want to toss us?"

"Yes," said Wimsey. "It probably mistakes us for a pancake."

"Silly! Cows don't eat pancakes, they eat oil-cake. I ate some once, but it was very nasty, and I was sick."

"Serve you right," said Wimsey. "I'd better put you down here, or you won't be back by bedtime. Perhaps I'd better run you part of the way home."

"Oh, please do," said Myra. "Then we can drive the cows and make them run like anything."

"That would be very naughty," said Wimsey. "It isn't good for cows to run fast. You are an impertinent, blood-thirsty, greedy and unkind young person, and one of these days you'll be a menace to society."

"How lovely! I could have a pistol and a beautiful evening dress, and lure people to opium-dens and stick them up. I think I'd better marry you, because you've got such a fast car. That would be useful, you see."

"Very," said Wimsey, gravely. "I'll bear the idea in mind. But you might not want to marry me later on, you know."

CHAPTER V

WATERS

IT AMUSED Lord Peter to lead the simple life at Kirkcudbright. Greatly to the regret of the hotel-keepers, he had this year chosen to rent a small studio at the end of a narrow cobbled close, whose brilliant blue gate proclaimed it to the High Street as an abode of the artistically-minded. His explanation of this eccentric conduct was that it entertained him to watch his extremely correct personal man gutting trout and washing potatoes under an outside tap, and receiving the casual visitor with West End ceremony.

As he clattered down the close, picking his way past the conglomeration of bicycles which almost blocked the entrance, Wimsey perceived this efficient person waiting upon the doorstep with an expression which, though strictly controlled, might almost have been called eager.

"Hullo, Bunter!" said his lordship, cheerfully. "What's for dinner? I'm feeling uncommonly ready for it. There's a beautiful corpse up at Creetown."

"I apprehended, my lord, that your lordship would be engaged in investigation. Not being certain of the exact hour of your lordship's return, I thought it wiser, my lord, to prepare a dish of stewed beef with thick gravy and vegetables, which could, in case of necessity, be kept hot without deterioration."

"Excellent," said his lordship.

"Thank you, my lord. I understand from the butcher that the portion of the animal which I have been accustomed to call shin of beef is termed in these parts the—er—hough."

"I believe you are right, Bunter."

"I did not take the man's word for it," said Bunter, with melancholy dignity. "I inspected the carcase and ascertained that the correct cut was removed from it."

"You are always so thorough," said Wimsey, appreciatively.

"I do my best, my lord. Would your lordship desire me to refer to the comestible as—er—hough—during our residence in this country?"

"It would be a graceful concession to national feeling, Bunter, if you can bring yourself to do it."

"Very good, my lord. I presume that the leg of mutton will again pass under the appellation of jiggot, as on the occasion of your lordship's previous visit?"

"Certainly, Bunter."

"Yes, my lord." Bunter sighed deeply. "Whatever is correct I will endeavour to do to your lordship's satisfaction."

"Thank you, Bunter. We must try to be correct under all circumstances."

"Yes, my lord. Dinner will be served in twenty minutes, as soon as the potatoes are ready."

"Right-ho!" said his lordship. "I'll just run across the close and have a chin-wag with Miss Selby till dinner-time."

"Pardon me, my lord. I understand that the ladies have gone away."

"Gone away?" said Wimsey, rather taken aback.

"Yes, my lord. I was informed by the young person who attends upon them that they had gone away to Glasgow."

"Oh!" said Wimsey, "they're away to Glasgow. But that probably only means that they are out for the day. It does not necessarily imply, as it does down South, that they have packed up bag and baggage and departed on a long visit. Well, I'll go and hunt up Mr. Waters. I rather want to see him. I may bring him back to dinner."

"Very good, my lord."

Wimsey crossed the High Street and knocked upon the door of Waters' lodgings. The landlady answered his knock and in reply to his inquiry observed that "Mr. Waters was away just now."

"When will he be back?"

"I couldna say, my lord, but I'm thinkin' he'll be stayin' the nicht in Glasgow."

"Everybody seems to have gone to Glasgow," said Wimsey.

"Och, ay. They'll all have went tae the Exhibition. Mr. Waters was away by the first train."

"What! the 8.45?" said Wimsey, incredulously. From what he had seen of Waters the previous night he had hardly expected such energy.

"Ay," said the landlady, placidly. "He had his breakfast at 8 o'clock and was away with Miss Selby and Miss Cochran."

Wimsey felt rather relieved. He had been afraid for the moment that this early activity might have something a little sinister about it. But, chaperoned by Miss Selby and Miss Cochran, Waters could scarcely have got into mischief. One more of his six suspects seemed to be safely eliminated. He left a message that he would like to see Mr. Waters as soon as he got back and returned to Blue Gate Close.

He had finished his savoury stew, and was enjoying an admirable cheese soufflé, when there was a sound of two pairs of heavy boots labouring over the cobbles, followed by that of a voice inquiring for his lordship.

"Hullo!" said Wimsey, "is that you, Dalziel?"

"Yes, my lord." The Sergeant shouldered his way through the narrow doorway and stood aside to allow his companion to pass. "I've been reportin' this matter to Sir Maxwell Jamieson, the Chief Constable, an' he has been gude enough to come round wi' me for a word wi' your lordship."

"Splendid!" said Wimsey, heartily. "Delighted to see you both. We haven't met before, Sir Maxwell, but that's not to say I don't know you well by reputation, as, I fancy, you know me. There was a trifling complaint of speeding last year, I believe, in which justice was rather more than tempered with mercy. Have a drink."

"Well," said Dalziel, when Wimsey's proffered hospitality had been accepted, with suitable signs of appreciation, "I've been makin' inquiries along the line in accordance wi' the theory, but I'm no sae verra weel satisfied t'ane way or t'ither. But first of a', I'd have ye ken I've interviewed the folk at Borgan, and they tell me young Jock saw Campbell pentin' there at ten minutes past ten when he gaed oot tae tak' a message to a wumman at Clauchaneasy, and he was still sittin' there when Jock returned at five minutes past eleven. Sae ye see, he couldna ha' left the place till a few minutes past eleven at the airliest."

"When you say he saw Campbell, do you mean that he knew it was Campbell or that he only thought it was?"

"Nay, he disna ken Campbell, but he saw a man in a big black hat and a plaid cloak, like Campbell was wearin'. An' he thinks there was a big plaid or rug liggin' by the side of him."

"Then it may have been the murderer."

"Ay, so it may, but it's the time o' day I wad dra' your attention to. Ye'll admit that, murderer or no murderer, he couldn'a ha' left yon place till past eleven?"

"That seems clear enough."

"Well, then, we come tae the investigation consairnin' the railway. There's no sae mony trains in the day between Stranraer and Girvan stops at Pinwherry or Barrhill."

The Sergeant pulled an L.M.S. time-table from his pocket and smacked it out upon the table.

"Let's tak' the trains tae Stranraer first. The murderer micht verra likely be thinkin' o' escapin' by the boat fra' Stranraer, ye ken, and if so, it's in Ireland we'll have to be lookin' for him."

He pulled out a thick pencil and jotted the times down on a sheet of paper.

	a.m.	p.m.
Girvan	10.45	2.16
Pinmore	11.1	2.31
Pinwherry	11.8	2.39
Barrhill	11.18	2.50
Glenwhilly	11.33	3.6
New Luce	11.41	3.13
Dunragit	11.52	3.26
Castle Kennedy	12 noon	3.33
Stranraer	12.7	3.39

Wimsey shook his head.

"He couldn't catch the first train—not on a bicycle, at any rate. Barrhill is his nearest point, and, if you give him only five minutes to pack his traps and get started, that leaves a bare eight minutes for ten miles or so. It's just conceivable that he might do it by car if he blinded like hell and the train happened to be late, but how could he have got the spare car along? Of course he could have hung about somewhere in the hills and taken the 2.50, or he could have ridden farther and picked the same train up at another station, but that would give him a very poor alibi."

"That's so, my lord," said Dalziel. "I hadna overlookit the

possibeelity. Noo, there's a report come in fra' the station-master at Pinwherry that there was a gentleman tuk the 2.39 at Pinwherry. He paid particular attention to him because he was a stranger and appeared out of the ordinar' nairvous and excited."

"Where did he book to?"

"That's juist the interesting part of the matter. He tuk his teecket to Stranraer——"

"Why, of course," said Wimsey, with his eye on the time-table. "That explains why he waited for that train. That's the one that makes the connection with the boat to Larne. It's a rotten connection at that—over three hours to wait in Stranraer—but it's apparently the only one there is."

"I was aboot to tell ye," said the Sergeant, "the gentleman inquired maist anxiously about the connection and seemed sair disappointit to lairn that there was no boat before 7 o'clock."

"That fits in all right," said Wimsey, "though it's queer he didn't find out about the boats earlier, while he was thinking this crime out so carefully. What was this fellow like?"

"Juist a youngish body in a grey suit and soft hat, they tell me, an' carryin' a wee attaché-case. Rather tall than short, wi' a sma' dark moustache. The station-master wad ken him agin."

"Did he give any particular account of himself?"

"He said somethin' o' havin' misread the time-table and thocht there was a boat at 3.50."

"Well, that's perfectly possible," said Wimsey. "You see there are three lines at the bottom of the page showing the steamer connections from Stranraer Pier to Larne and Belfast, and just above them, three lines showing the train-connection between Stranraer, Colfin and Port Patrick. It's easy to mistake the one for the other. But look here, Dalziel, if there was no boat for him before 7, you must have been in time to catch him."

"That's a fact, my lord, and so soon as I had the report I telephoned through tae the pollis at Stranraer to have a sairch made; but I got their answer juist before comin' over here, and it was tae the effect that there was no sic a pairson on the boat."

"Damn it!" said Wimsey.

"They are conducting an inquiry in Stranraer, in case he should be in hidin' there, and are stoppin' all cars enterin' and leavin'

the toon, and naiturally they will keep a strict eye on to-morrow's
boat. But it is no unthinkable that the felly isna mekkin' for Larne
at a'. That may ha' been juist a blind."

"Did he actually go to Stranraer?"

"It seems so. The teeckets ha' been checkit, and the third-class
teecket issued at Pinwherry was duly given up at Stranraer. Unfortunately, the porter whae collectit it is no an obsairvin' body
and canna say what like the mon was that handit it tae him."

"Well, you seem to have done pretty well on that part of the
business," said Wimsey, "considering the shortness of the time. And
it looks as though we really had got on to something. By the way,
did the station-master at Pinwherry mention whether the passenger
had a bicycle?"

"Nay, he hadna a bicycle. I askit him how he came there, but
naebody had noticed him come. It seems he juist walkit intae the
station."

"Well, of course, if he was taking the Irish boat, he would probably get rid of the bicycle first. He had plenty of time to hide it
up in the hills. Well—that looks rather hopeful. Still, we mustn't
rely on it too much. How about the trains in the other direction—
the ones going to Glasgow?"

Dalziel turned over a couple of pages, licked the thick pencil
and produced a new list.

Stranraer.	a.m. dep. 11.35	p.m. 12.30 (from Stranraer Pier)	p.m. 4.5
Castle Kennedy	11.42	..	4.12
Dunragit	11.52	12.42	4.20
New Luce	12.7 p.m.	..	4.33
Glenwhilly	12.19	..	4.45
Barrhill	12.35	..	5.0
Pinwherry	12.43	..	5.8
Pinmore	12.56	..	5.18
Girvan { arr.	1.6	1.37	5.28
{ dep.	1.11	1.42	5.36

"There are opportunities there, too," said Wimsey. "How about the 12.35? He could catch that easily and go on to Glasgow, and from there he could get anywhere."

"Ay, that's so. That was what I thocht masel'. I telephoned tae the station-master at Barrhill, but there was only four passengers by thet train, an' he knowed them a' pairsonally."

"Oh!" said Wimsey. "I see. That rather puts the lid on that, then."

"Ay. But there's anither thing. I didna rest satisfied wi' that. I pursued my inquiries at the ither stations along the line an' I found there was a gentleman wi' a bicycle tuk the 1.11 train at Girvan."

"Was there, by Jove!" Wimsey pulled out his map of the district and studied it intently.

"It could be done, Dalziel, it could be done! Barrhill is nine miles from the scene of the crime and Girvan is, say, twelve miles further on—call it twenty-one miles altogether. If he started at 11.10 that would give him two hours, which means just over ten miles an hour—easy enough for a good cyclist. Was the train punctual, by the way?"

"It was. Ay, he could ha' done it."

"Did the station-master give any description of him?"

"He said that accordin' tae the porter he was juist an ordinary gentleman of thirty or forty years of age, in a grey suit and a check cap pu'd weel doon. Clean-shaven, or nearly so, and of middling size, and he was wearin' big glasses wi' they tinted lenses."

"That's suspicious," said Wimsey. "Would the porter be able to identify him, do you think?"

"Ay, I'm thinkin' he wad. He said the gentleman spoke like an Englishman."

"Did he?" Wimsey considered his six suspects. Waters was a Londoner and spoke standard public-school English. Strachan, though a Scot, habitually spoke with an English accent, having been educated at Harrow and Cambridge. He, however, was a noticeably tall man. It could hardly be he. Gowan was double-tongued; he spoke English with Wimsey and the broadest Scots with the natives —but then, Gowan's grand silky beard which had never known a razor was pointed out to visitors as one of the local sights of Kirkcudbright. Graham was completely Londonised, and his English would pass muster at Oxford. His astonishing blue eyes were his one really memorable feature—was this the explanation of the tinted glasses? Farren—his Scots tongue was unmistakable; nobody, surely, could mistake him for an Englishman. His whole person was noticeable, too—the wide, ridgy shoulders, tumbling fair hair and queer, light eyes, temperish, pouted mouth and heavy jaw. Ferguson, too, was Scottish in accent, though not in idiom, and in feature might be almost anything.

"Did the gentleman give any particular account of himself?" asked Wimsey, coming rather suddenly out of his abstraction.

"No, he only got tae the station as the train was standin' at the platform, but he said something about startin' late fra' Ballantrae. He tuk his ticket for Ayr and the machine was labelled according."

"We may be able to trace that," said Wimsey.

"Ay, that's so. I hae sent an inquiry to Ayr and to Glesga'. They'll maybe remember 't."

"And, maybe not," said Wimsey. "Well, now, Dalziel, I also, as the lady said, have not been idle."

He produced his list of suspects.

"Mind you," he said, warningly, "this list may not be complete. But we know the man we are looking for is a painter, which narrows the field considerably. And all these six people are known to have had it in for Campbell in one way or another, though some of the motives may seem pretty inadequate."

The Sergeant peered thoughtfully at the list, and so did Sir Maxwell. The latter's jurisdiction extended over both Kirkcudbrightshire and Wigtownshire, and he knew all the artists more or less well, though not with any great intimacy, his own interests being military and sporting.

"Now," said Wimsey, "two of these people have alibis. Ferguson was duly seen on to the 9.8 from Gatehouse. He had no bicycle with him, and he booked to Glasgow. There's a picture exhibition on there, and no doubt that's what he was making for. Waters also departed for Glasgow by the 8.45 from Kirkcudbright, in company with Miss Selby and Miss Cochran. If they all met at the show they will prove each other's alibis all right. Strachan was out all night and came home at lunch-time with a black eye, and what is more, he is telling lies about it." He gave a brief summary of his conversations with Strachan and Myra.

"That looks bad," said Dalziel.

"Yes; we mustn't pin all our faith to the cyclist at Girvan, or even to the mysterious passenger at Pinwherry; they may both be perfectly genuine travellers. Strachan might quite well have been painting up at the Minnoch at 11 o'clock and ridden back to Gatehouse by lunch-time. It's only twenty-seven miles. It would be dangerous, because he might be recognised, but people who commit murders must take a few risks. Besides, he might have hidden his car somewhere on the road the day before, and picked it up on his way back, bringing the bicycle with him. Did I mention to you, by the way, that there's a bicycle disappeared from the Anworth Hotel at Gatehouse?"

Dalziel shook his head.

"It's a case wi' a great number of possibeelities," he said. "Always supposin' that it *is* a case. We havena got the doctor's opeenion yet."

"That'll come to-morrow, I suppose?"

"Ay. The maitter has been laid before the Fiscal, and there will be a post-morten examination. There's Campbell's sister expectit the nicht—it seems she's his only relation—an' they'll maybe wait till she has seen the corpse, forbye the licht will be better for the doctor in the mornin'."

.   .   .   .

After the Sergeant and his companion had gone, Wimsey remained smoking thoughtfully for some time. He was worried about Waters. He had left him the night before in a dangerous mood. The last train from Glasgow got in to Kirkcudbright at 9.00. If Waters had really gone to see the Exhibition, it was not reasonable to expect him back that night. He would only have got in to Glasgow at 2.16, and would have had to leave again at 5.30. Nobody would go all that way in order to spend a bare three hours in the town. Except, possibly, to establish an alibi. Could one establish an alibi that way?

Wimsey turned to the time-table again. Kirkcudbright depart 8.45. That was capable of proof by witnesses. Tarff 8.53, Brig-of-Dee 9.2—nothing to be done from there, except by car. Castle-Douglas 9.7. That was different. Castle-Douglas was a junction. From there one might turn back in the direction of Newton-Stewart. Yes. There was a train. This was ridiculous, of course, because Waters had travelled with the two women, but there was no harm in working it out. Castle-Douglas 9.14, Newton-Stewart

10.22. Wimsey breathed a sigh of relief. If the murderer had been seen painting at 10 o'clock, that let out Waters. He could not have got even so far as Newton-Stewart by that time.

But all this depended on the doctor's report. If both Wimsey and he had been mistaken about the rigor—then it was possible that Campbell himself had been painting at the Minnoch till five minutes past eleven. In which case—Wimsey thumbed the time-table again.

In which case a train reaching Newton-Stewart at 10.22 might prove very handy to an intending murderer—supposing the murderer knew already that Campbell meant to paint that day at the Minnoch. A car from Newton-Stewart would bring him to the scene of the crime in twenty minutes—time enough and to spare. And though Waters had no car, such things can be hired. There would be a risk, certainly, for in country districts people know one another, and indeed, who would hire out a driverless car to a man he did not know, without making careful inquiries? Yet, if the deposit were big enough, he might take the risk. It would not do to cross Waters off the list too promptly.

At this point Wimsey cursed himself for a fool. It was as certain as anything could be that Waters had travelled peacefully to Glasgow under the eyes of his friends, and would return peacefully with them the next day.

He looked at his watch. It was not possible, of course, that Waters had returned by the 9 o'clock train. Still, it would do no harm to go and see.

He walked along the High Street. There was no light either in Waters' sitting-room or in his bedroom, both of which faced upon the street. The landlady would think him daft if he made any more inquiries. There was Waters' studio—a big converted barn up a turning off the Tongland Road. If he had come back, he certainly would not be working there at this hour. Still, when one is restless, any excuse will serve to take a little walk.

Wimsey made his way past the Castle, up the little flight of steps and over the green by the harbour. The tide was dropping, and the long mud-flats of the estuary glimmered faintly in the pale midsummer night. The yacht that had come in that morning still lay close against the harbour wall, her spars and rigging making a bold foreground of interlaced verticals and horizontals against the galumphing curves of the ugly concrete bridge. Wimsey crossed the open space where the 'buses congregate by day, plunged down the little alley by the gasworks and came out past the station on to the Tongland Road.

Crossing the street, he turned off again to the right and found himself in a happy backwater, with an ancient over-shot water-mill, a few cottages and a wide open space, grassy and forlorn, surrounded by sheds and derelict outbuildings.

Waters' studio was approached by a little winding path among overgrown bushes and lush grass. He pushed open the gate and tried the door. It was locked, and there was no sign of life about the place. The silence was intense. He heard some small animal move in the grass, the plop, plopping from the wooden trough over the paddles of the mill-wheel; far off, somewhere in the town, a dog barked hoarsely.

Wimsey turned to go. As he went, the stony path creaking under his feet, the door of one of the cottages was flung suddenly open, letting a long bar of light stream suddenly across the ground. Framed in the door he saw the silhouette of a woman peering out anxiously into the silvery darkness.

It occurred to Wimsey suddenly that this was Farren's house, and he paused, half-decided to stop and speak. But as he hesitated, somebody laid a hand on the woman's shoulder and drew her in, shutting the door. There had been something quick and stealthy about the action that banished Wimsey's plan, half-formed. The second figure had been a man's, but it was taller and bigger than Farren's. He felt sure that it was not Farren, and that, if he knocked, the door would not open to his knocking.

CHAPTER VI

FARREN

SIR MAXWELL JAMIESON was not a man to rush into precipitate action. Sound and cautious, with a reputation for taciturnity, he preferred to know exactly where he stood before committing himself to stirring up scandal by vexatious inquiries. He was not over-pleased to find Wimsey palpitating on his doorstep the next morning, shortly after breakfast, when he himself had barely had time to read the paper.

He was too wise to ignore Wimsey and his theories. He knew that Lord Peter had an uncanny nose for a crime, and that his help was valuable, but he did not care for this English habit of rushing into situations on a high tide of chatter and excitement. It was true that Wimsey had shown a certain amount of tact in coming to him. There was no telephone in Blue Gate Close, and if Wimsey must have the latest intelligence piping hot, it was better that he should apply for it in private than interrogate Sergeant Dalziel over the line in a hotel bar.

But Sir Maxwell was not yet perfectly convinced that there was any murder to be investigated. All this talk about missing objects and bicycles was well enough, but it was a small basis on which to rear so threatening a structure of accusation. Doubtless, if the things were more carefully searched for, they would be found, and the whole murder theory would collapse. Certainly, there was that awkward point about the rigor, but Sir Maxwell, turning over the pages of Taylor and Glaister, felt convinced that it was not possible to lay down any very exact or reliable laws about the onset of rigor.

He frowned over Wimsey's list of suspects—a disagreeable document, he thought, and savouring strongly of the libellous. All these people were highly respected citizens. Take Gowan, for instance —a leading inhabitant of Kirkcudbright for over fifteen years, well known and well liked, in spite of his small vanities and somewhat overbearing manner. He was wealthy, kept a good house, with an English butler and housekeeper, and owned two cars, with a chauffeur to drive them when required. Was it likely that he would be found knocking his fellow-artists on the head and tumbling them into salmon-rivers in the neighbouring county? What possible motive could he have for it? There had been talk of some disagreement about a picture, but, in Sir Maxwell's experience, artists frequently disagreed about pictures, with no more consequences than a little cold-shouldering or the formation of a clique. Waters, again—a pleasant young man enough, though inclined to irritate his neighbours by his South-country mannerisms. It was unfortunate that he should have fallen out with Campbell, but surely he was not the man to harbour murderous resentment for a hasty word spoken over a drink. And Farren——

Sir Maxwell paused there, in justice to Wimsey. Where women were concerned, you never knew. Campbell had been rather a frequent visitor at the cottage by the old mill. It was said—there had been talk—threats had been uttered. If there was anything in it, there might be some difficulty in getting at the truth here. Farren's suspicions had probably been quite unfounded, for one could hardly look at Mrs. Farren and believe evil of her. Still, wives will tell lies and provide alibis, even for the most unreasonable of husbands, and indeed, the more virtuous the wife, the more obstinate the liar, under such conditions. With considerable discomfort, Sir Maxwell admitted to himself that he could not undertake to say that the Farrens were, in the nature of things, clear of all suspicion.

Then of course there were those people over at Gatehouse. Jock Graham—a harum-scarum, word-and-a-blow fellow if ever there was one. Clever, too. If it came to picking the man with the brains to plan an ingenious crime and the coolness to carry it through, then Graham was the man for his money, every time. Graham had had plenty of practice in the execution of practical jokes, and he could tell a circumstantial lie, looking you square in the eyes with the face of an angel. Ferguson was notoriously on bad terms with his wife. Sir Maxwell knew nothing else to his disadvantage, but he noted it, in his upright Presbyterian mind, as a discreditable fact. Strachan—well, Strachan was secretary of the golf-club and weel-respectit. Surely Strachan, like Gowan, could be ruled out.

The telephone rang. Wimsey pricked up his ears. Sir Maxwell raised the receiver with irritating deliberation. He spoke, then turned to Wimsey.

"It's Dalziel. You had better listen in on the extension."

"Is't you, Sir Maxwell? . . . Ay, we have the doctor's report.
. . . Ay, it supports the theory of murder richt eneugh. There
was nae water in the lungs at a'. The mon was deid before he got
intae the burn. 'Twas the scart on the heid that did it. The bone
is a' crushed intae the brain. Och, ay, the wound was made before
death, and he must ha' died almost immediately. There's a wheen
mair blows to the heid an' body, but the doctor thinks some o'
them will ha' been made after death, wi' the body pitchin' doon
the burnside an' washin' aboot amang the stanes."

"What about the time of the death?"

"Ay, Sir Maxwell, I was juist comin' to that. The doctor says
Campbell will ha' been deid at least six hours when he first saw
the body, an' mair likely twelve or thirteen. That'll pit the time
o' the murder in the late nicht or the airly mornin'—at ony rate
between midnicht and nine o'clock. And a verra suspeecious an'
corroboratin' circumstance is that the man had nae food in his
wame at a'. He was kilt before he had ta'en ony breakfast."

"But," said Wimsey, cutting in on the conversation, "if he had
had his breakfast early, it might have passed out of the stomach
before lunch-time."

"Ay, that's so. But it wadna ha' passed oot o' him a'tegither. The
doctor says his interior was as toom as a drum, an' he will stake
his professional credit he hadna eaten onything sin' the previous
nicht."

"Well, he ought to know," said Wimsey.

"Ay, that's so. That's his lordship speakin', is't no? Your lordship will be gratified by this support for our theory."

"It may be gratifying," said Jamieson, "but I wish very much
it hadn't happened."

"That's so, Sir Maxwell. Still, there's little doot it has happened and we maun du the best we can by it. There is another
remarkable circumstance, an' that is that we can find no recognisable finger-prints upon the artistic paraphernalia, and it has the.
appearance as if the user of them had been doin' his pentin' in gloves.
An' the steerin'-wheel o' the car is wiped as clean as a whistle. Ay,
I'm thinking the case is weel substantiated. Is it your opeenion, Sir
Maxwell, that we should mak' the fact o' the murder public?"

"I hardly know, Sergeant. What do you think yourself? Have you consulted with Inspector Macpherson?"

"Weel, sir, he thinks we maun gie some gude reason for makin' our inquiries. . . . Ay, we'll best gae cannily aboot it, but there's folk talkin' a'ready aboot the quarrel wi' Waters . . . ay, an' wi' Farren . . . ay . . . ay . . . an' there's a story about Strachan bein' over in Creetown the nicht of the crime speirin' after Farren. . . . I doot we'll no be able to keep the thing hushed up."

"I see. Well, perhaps we had better let it be known that there is a possibility of foul play—that we are not quite satisfied, and so on. But you'd better not tell anybody what the doctor says about the time of death. I'll be over presently and have a word with the Fiscal. And meanwhile I'll get the Kirkcudbright police on to making a few inquiries."

"Ay, sir, 'twill be best for them to sort it their end. I've a report here fra' Stranraer I'll hae to deal wi' masel'. They've detained a young fellow that was boardin' the Larne boat . . . ay, weel, I'll ring ye again later, Sir Maxwell."

The Chief Constable hung up the receiver, and confronted Wimsey with a dour smile.

"It certainly looks as though you were right," he admitted reluctantly. "But," he added, more cheerfully, "now that they've traced the man at Stranraer, it will probably all be cleared up this morning."

"Maybe," said Wimsey, "but I rather doubt whether the man who fixed that accident up so cleverly would be fool enough to give himself away by making a belated bolt to Ireland. Don't you?"

"That's a fact," said Jamieson. "If he'd wanted to escape he could have taken yesterday morning's boat. And if he wanted to play the innocent, he could do it better at home."

"H'm!" said Wimsey. "I think, you know, the time has come to talk of many things with Farren and Gowan and Waters—only he's disappeared—and, in fact, with all the good people of Kirkcudbright. A little tactful gossip, Sir Maxwell, by a cheerful, friendly, inquisitive bloke like myself, may do wonders in a crisis. Nothing unusual in my making my morning rounds of the studios, is there? Nobody minds me. Why, bless you, I've got some of 'em so tame, they'll let me sit round and watch 'em paint. An official personage like you might embarrass them, don't you know, but there's no dignity about me. I'm probably the least awe-inspiring man in Kirkcudbright. I was born looking foolish and every day in every way I am getting foolisher and foolisher. Why, even you, Chief, let me come here and sit round on your official chairs and smoke a pipe and look on me as nothing more than an amiable nuisance—don't you?"

"There may be something in what you say," agreed Jamieson, "but you'll be discreet, mind. There's no need to mention the word murder."

"None whatever," said Wimsey. "I'll let them mention it first. Well, toodle-oo!"

Wimsey may not have been an awe-inspiring person to look at, but his reception at Farren's house did not altogether justify his boast that "nobody marked him." The door was opened by Mrs. Farren who, at sight of him, fell back against the wall with a gasp which might have been merely of surprise but sounded more like alarm.

"Hullo!" said Wimsey, breezing cheerily over the threshold, "how are you, Mrs. Farren? Haven't seen you for an age—well, since Friday night at Bobbie's, but it seems like an age. Is everything bright and blooming? Where's Farren?"

Mrs. Farren, looking like a ghost painted by Burne-Jones in one of his most pre-Raphaelite moments, extended a chill hand.

"I'm very well, thank you. Hugh's out. Er—won't you come in?"

Wimsey, who was already in, received this invitation in his heartiest manner.

"Well—that's very good of you. Sure I'm not in the way? I expect you're cooking or something, aren't you?"

Mrs. Farren shook her head and led the way into the little sitting-room with the sea-green and blue draperies and the bowls of orange marigolds.

"Or is it scarves this morning?" Mrs. Farren wove hand-spun wool in rather attractive patterns. "I envy you that job, you know. Sort of Lady of Shalott touch about it. The curse is come upon me, and all that sort of thing. You promised one day to let me have a twirl at the wheel."

"I'm afraid I'm being lazy to-day," said Mrs. Farren, with a faint smile. "I was just—I was only—excuse me one moment."

She went out, and Wimsey heard her speaking to somebody at the back of the house—the girl, no doubt, who came in to do the rough work. He glanced round the room, and his quick eye noted its curiously forlorn appearance. It was not untidy, exactly; it told no open tale of tumult; but the cushions were crushed, a flower or two here and there was wilted; there was a slight film of dust on the window-sill and on the polished table. In the houses of some of his friends this might have meant mere carelessness and a mind above trifles like dust and disorder, but with Mrs. Farren it was a phenomenon full of meaning. To her, the beauty of an ordered life was more than a mere phrase; it was a dogma to be preached, a cult to be practised with passion and concentration. Wimsey, who was imaginative, saw in those faint traces the witness to a night of suspense, a morning of terror; he remembered the anxious figure at the door, and the man—yes. There had been a man there, too. And Farren was away. And Mrs. Farren was a very beautiful woman, if you liked that style of thing, with her oval face and large grey eyes and those thick masses of copper-coloured hair, parted in the middle and rolled in a great knot on the nape of the neck.

A step passed the window—Jeanie, with a basket on her arm. Mrs. Farren came back and sat down in a high, narrow-backed chair, looking out and past him like a distressed beggar-maid beginning to wonder whether Cophetua was not something of a trial in family life.

"And where," said Wimsey, with obtuse tactlessness, "has Farren disappeared to?"

The large eyes shadowed suddenly with fear or pain.

"He's gone out—somewhere."

"The gay dog," said Wimsey. "Or is he working?"

"I—don't quite know." Mrs. Farren laughed. "You know what this place is. People go off, saying they'll be back to dinner, and then they meet a man, or somebody says the fish are rising somewhere, and that's the last you see of them."

"I know—it's shameful," said Wimsey, sympathetically. "Do you mean he didn't even come home to his grub?"

"Oh—I was only speaking generally. He was home to dinner all right."

"And then barged out afterwards, saying he wanted some Gold

Flakes and would be back in ten minutes, I suppose. It's disheartening, isn't it, the way we behave. I'm a shocking offender myself, though my conscience is fairly easy. After all, Bunter is paid to put up with me. It's not as though I had a devoted wife warming my slippers and looking out of the front-door every five minutes to see if I'm going to turn up."

Mrs. Farren drew in her breath sharply.

"Yes, it's terrible, isn't it?"

"Terrible. No, I mean it. I do think it's unfair. After all, one never knows what may happen to people. Look at poor Campbell."

This time there was no doubt about it. Mrs. Farren gave a gasp of terror that was almost a cry; but she recovered herself immediately.

"Oh, Lord Peter, do tell me, what really *has* happened? Jeanie came in with some dreadful story about his being killed. But she gets so excited, and talks such broad Scotch that I really couldn't make it out."

"It's a fact, I'm afraid," said Wimsey, soberly. "They found him lying in the Minnoch yesterday afternoon, with his head bashed in."

"With his head bashed in? You don't mean——"

"Well, it's difficult to say quite how it happened. The river is full of rocks just there, you see——"

"Did he fall in?"

"It looks like it. He was in the water. But he wasn't drowned, the doctor says. It was the blow on the head that did it."

"How dreadful!"

"I wonder you hadn't heard about it before," said Wimsey. "He was a great friend of yours, wasn't he?"

"Well—yes—we knew him very well." She stopped, and Wimsey thought she was going to faint. He sprang up.

"Look here—I'm afraid this has been too much of a shock for you. Let me get some water."

"No—no——" She flung out a hand to restrain him, but he had already darted across the passage into the studio, where he remembered to have seen a tap and a sink. The first thing he noticed there was Farren's sketching-box, standing open on the table, the paints scattered about and the palette flung down higgedly-piggledy among them. An old painting-coat hung behind the door, and Wimsey inspected it inside and out with some care, but seemed to find nothing in it worthy of attention. He filled a cup at the tap, with his eyes roving about the room. The studio-easel stood in its place with a half-finished canvas upon it. The small sketching-easel was propped against the sink, strapped up. Farren had not gone out to paint, evidently.

The water, splashing on his hand, reminded him of what he was supposed to be there for. He wiped the cup and turned to leave the studio. As he did so, he caught sight of Farren's fishing-tackle standing in the corner behind the door. Two trout-rods, a salmon-rod, net, gaff, creel and waders. Well, there might be a fourth rod, of course, and one can fish without creel or waders. But, standing there so quietly, the things had a look of settled complete-ness.

He returned to the sitting-room. Mrs. Farren waved the cup impatiently aside.

"Thank you—I don't need it. I told you I didn't. I'm quite all right." Her worried and sleepless eyes belied her. Wimsey felt that he was being a brute, but somebody would be asking questions soon enough. As well he as the police, he thought.

"Your husband ought to be here soon," he said. "The news will be all over the country by now. It's surprising, really, he hasn't got back already. You don't know at all where he is?"

"I haven't the faintest idea."

"I mean, I'd gladly take a message or do anything of that sort."

"Why should you? Thank you all the same. But really, Lord Peter, you talk as though the death were in my family. We knew Mr. Campbell very well, of course, but after all, there's no reason for me to be so prostrated as all that. . . . I'm afraid I may sound callous——"

"Not at all. I only thought you looked a bit upset. I'm very glad you're not. Perhaps I misunderstood——"

"Perhaps you did," she said in an exhausted voice. Then she seemed to gather up her spirits a little, and turned upon him almost eagerly.

"I was sorry for Mr. Campbell. He was a bitterly unpopular man, and he felt that more than people ever realised. He had a perpetual grudge against everybody. That's unattractive. And the more you hate everybody for hating you, the more unattractive you grow and the more they go on hating you. I understood that. I didn't like the man. One couldn't. But I tried to be fair. I daresay people did misunderstand. But one can't stop doing what's right because people misunderstand, can one?"

"No," said Wimsey. "If you and your husband——"

"Oh," she said, "Hugh and I understood one another."

Wimsey nodded. She was lying, he thought. Farren's objections to Campbell had been notorious. But she was the kind of woman who, if once she set out to radiate sweetness and light, would be obstinate in her mission. He studied the rather full, sulky mouth and narrow, determined forehead. It was the face of a woman who would see only what she wished to see—who would think that one could abolish evils from the world by pretending that they were not there. Such things, for instance, as jealousy or criticism of herself. A dangerous woman, because a stupid woman. Stupid and dangerous, like Desdemona.

"Well, well," he said lightly. "Let's hope the truant will turn up soon. He promised to show me some of his stuff. I'm very keen to have a look at it. I daresay I shall meet him as I buzz about the country. On his bike, as usual, I suppose?"

"Oh, yes, he's got his bicycle with him."

"I think there are more bicycles per head of the population in Kirkcudbright than in any town I ever struck," said Wimsey.

"That's because we're all so hardworking and poor."

"Just so. Nothing is so virtuous as a bicycle. You can't imagine a bicyclist committing a crime, can you?—except of course, murder or attempted murder."

"Why murder?"

"Well, the way they rush about in gangs on the wrong side of the road and never have any brakes or bells or lights. I, call it murder, when they nearly have you into the ditch. Or suicide."

He jumped to his feet with an exclamation of concern. This time Mrs. Farren had really fainted.

CHAPTER VII

GRAHAM

LORD PETER WIMSEY, having rendered first aid to Mrs. Farren, left her comfortably reclining on the couch in the sitting-room and went in search of Jeanie. He discovered her in the fishmonger's and dispatched her home with the tidings that her mistress was unwell.

"Ay," said Jeanie, philosophically, "I'm no surprised. She's troubled in her mind aboot Mr. Farren. And nae wonder, wi' him mekkin' a' that disturbance and gaein' aff that gate an' never comin' back for twa nichts."

"Two nights?" said Wimsey.

"Ay. Nicht before last it was he went aff on his bicycle, swearin' somethin' awfu' an' nae ward tae say whaur he was gaein' nor what he was gaein' to du."

"Then he wasn't at home last night for dinner?"

"Him? Hame for's denner? 'Deed no, nor ony time o' the day. Monday nicht it was he come back an' fund Campbell i' the hoose an' sent him packin', an' after that there was sic a collie-shangie it nigh frighted my brither's wife into a fit an' her verra near her time, tu. An' oot he gaes and away, wi' Mistress Farren runnin' oot o' the door after him wi' the tears fallin' doon her cheeks. I dinna ken for why she takes on so aboot the man. I'd let him gae an' be daumed tae him, wi' his jealousies an' his tempers."

Wimsey began to see why Jeanie had been sent out on an errand in such a hurry. It was foolish, though, for nobody could expect the girl to hold her tongue over so fine a piece of gossip. Sooner or later, the tale would have come out to somebody. Even now he observed that curious glances were following them down the street.

He asked a few more questions. No, Jeanie's brother's wife could not say exactly what the quarrel was about, but she had witnessed it from her bedroom window. Mr. Campbell had been in about 6 o'clock, and then Mr. Farren had come in and Mr. Campbell had gone away almost immediately. She could not say there had

57

been any dispute between Farren and Campbell. But then Mr. and
Mrs. Farren had talked about an hour in the sitting-room and Mr.
Farren had walked about the room and waved his hands a great
deal, and Mrs. Farren had cried. Then there had been a shouting
and a kind of a skelloch, and Mr. Farren had run out of the
door cramming his hat over his eyes, and had snatched up his bicycle.
And Mrs. Farren had run out to stop him and he had shaken her
roughly off and ridden away. Nor had he been home syne, for
Jeanie's brother's wife had kept a look-out for him, being interested to see what might happen.

That was Monday and this was Wednesday; and on the Tuesday, Campbell had been found dead up at the Minnoch.

Wimsey said good-bye to Jeanie, with a caution against talking
too much about her employers' affairs, and turned in the direction
of the police-station. Then he changed his mind. No need to make
trouble before it was wanted. There might be other developments.
It would not be a bad idea to run over to Gatehouse. There was
a question he wanted to ask Mrs. Green who did the charring for
Campbell. Also, something might have been found at Campbell's
house—letters, papers or what-not. In any case, a wee run in the
car would do him no harm.

Passing over the bridge at Gatehouse, with these intentions, he
was arrested by the sight of a tall man standing outside the Anwoth
Hotel in conference with the local constable. The man, who was
very shabbily dressed in an ancient burberry, dilapidated plus-four,
disreputable boots and leggings and a knapsack, waved a hand in
violent greeting. Wimsey pulled up with reckless haste, nearly slay-
ing the hotel cat, and waived violently back.

"Hullo—ullo—ullo!" he cried. "Where d'you spring from, you
old ruffian?"

"That's just what everybody seems anxious to know," said the
untidy man, extending a large, raw-boned hand. "I don't seem to
be allowed to go away on a little private matter without a hue and
cry. What's it all about?"

Wimsey glanced at the constable, who shook his head mysteriously.

"Having received orders," he began, "to make an inquiry——"

"But you haven't received orders to make a mystery, have you?"
said the untidy man. "What's the matter? Am I supposed to have
committed a crime? What is it? Drunk and disorderly, eh? or

riding a push-bike without a tail-light? or driving to the public danger, or what?"

"Weel, now, Mr. Graham, sir—in the matter of the bicycle, I wad be glad to know——"

"Not guilty this time," said Mr. Graham, promptly. "And in any case borrowing isn't stealing, you know."

"Have you been borrowing push-bikes?" asked Wimsey, with interest. "You shouldn't. It's a bad habit. Push-bikes are the curse of this country. Their centre of gravity is too high, for one thing, and their brakes are never in order."

"I know," said Mr. Graham, "it's shameful. Every bicycle I borrow is worse than the last. I often have to speak quite firmly about it. I nearly broke my neck the other day on young Andy's."

"Oh," said the landlord, who had come up during this conversation, "it's ye, is't, Mr. Graham, that's got the lad's bicycle? Ye're welcome eneugh tae't, I'm no sayin' the contrary, but the lad's been a bit put out, not knowin' whaur it had disappeared tae."

"It's gone again, has it?" said Mr. Graham. "Well, I tell you it's not me this time. You can tell Andy I'll never borrow his miserable machine again till he has the decency to put it in order. And whoever did take it, God help him, that's all I can say, for he'll probably be found dead in a ditch."

"That may be, Mr. Graham," said the constable, "but I'd be glad if ye wad tell me——"

"Damn it!" said Jock Graham. "No, I will not tell you where I've been. Why should I?"

"Well, it's like this, old dear," said Wimsey. "You may possibly have heard in your mysterious retreat, that Campbell was found dead in a river yesterday afternoon."

"Campbell? Good Lord! No, I hadn't heard. Well, well, well. I hope his sins are forgiven him. What had he done? Taken too many wee halves and walked over the dock at Kirkcudbright?"

"Well, no. Apparently he had been painting and slipped on the stones and bashed his head in."

"Bashed his head in? Not drowned, then?"

"No, not drowned."

"Oh! Well, I always told him he was born to be hanged, but apparently he's got out of it another way. Still, I was right about his not being drowned. Well, poor devil, there's an end of him. I think

we'd better go in and have one on the strength of it, don't you?
Just a little one to the repose of his soul. He wasn't a man I liked,
but I'm sorry in a way to think I'll never pull his leg again. You'll
join us, officer?"

"Thank you, sir, but if ye'd kindly——"

"Leave it to me," murmured Wimsey, jogging the constable's
elbow and following Graham into the bar.

"How have you managed not to hear about it, Jock?" he went
on, when the drinks had been served. "Where have you been hiding
the last two days?"

"That's telling. You're as inquisitive as our friend here. I've been
living a retired life—no scandal—no newspapers. But do tell me
about Campbell. When did all this happen?"

"They found the body about 2 o'clock," said Wimsey. "He
seems to have been seen alive and painting at five past eleven."

"They didn't lose much time about it, then. You know, I've
often thought that one might have an accident up in the hills
about here and be lost for weeks. Still, it's a fairly well-frequented
spot up there at the Minnoch—in the fishing season, at any rate.
I don't suppose——"

"And how did ye ken, might I ask, sir, that the accident took
place up at the Minnoch?"

Jock Graham stared at the constable's excited face.

"How did I——? Oh-ho! To quote an extremely respectable
and primly-dressed woman I once happened to overhear conversing
with a friend in Theobald's Road, there's bloody more in it than
meets the bloody eye. This anxiety about my whereabouts and this
bash on Campbell's head—do I understand, constable, that I am
suspected of having bashed the good gentleman and tumbled him
into the stream like the outlandish knight in the ballad?"

"Well, not exactly, sir, but as a matter of routine——"

"I see."

"Och, now!" exclaimed the landlord, on whom a light had been
slowly breaking. "Ye're not meanin' tae tell as the puir man was
murdered?"

"That's as may be," said the constable.

"He does mean it," said Graham. "I read it in his expressive eye.
Here's a nice thing to happen in a quiet country spot."

"It's a terrible thing," said the landlord.

"Come now, Jock," said Wimsey. "Put us out of our misery. You can see the suspense is telling on us. How *did* you know Campbell was up at the Minnoch?"

"Telepathy," said Graham, with a wide grin. "I look into your minds and the picture comes before me—the burn full of sharp stones—the steep slope of granite leading down to it—the brig— the trees and the dark pool under them—and I say, 'The Minnoch, by Jove!' Perfectly simple, Watson."

"I didn't know you were a thought-reader."

"It's a suspicious circumstance, isn't it? As a matter of fact, I'm not. I knew Campbell was going to be up at the Minnoch yesterday because he told me so."

"He told you so?"

"Told me so. Yes, why not? I did sometimes speak to Campbell without throwing boots at him, you know. He told me on Monday that he was going up the next day to paint the bridge. Sketched it out for me, grunting all the time—you know his way."

Graham pulled a piece of chalk from his pocket and set to work on the bar counter, his face screwed up into a life-like imitation of Campbell's heavy jowl and puffed lips, and his hand roughing in outlines with Campbell's quick, tricky touch. The picture came up before their eyes with the conjuring quickness of a lightning-sketch at the cinema—the burn, the trees, the bridge and a mass of bulging white cloud, so like the actual canvas Wimsey had seen on the easel that he was thoroughly startled.

"You ought to be making a living by impersonations, Jock."

"That's my trouble. Too versatile. Paint in everybody's style except my own. Worries the critics. 'Mr. Graham is still fumbling for an individual style'—that kind of thing. But it's fun. Look, here's Gowan."

He rubbed out the sketch and substituted a vivid chalk impression of one of Gowan's characteristic compositions—a grim border-keep, a wide sweep of coast, a boat in the foreground, with muscular fishermen bending over their nets.

"Here's Ferguson—one tree with decorative roots, one reflection of same in water—dim blue distance; in fact, general blues all over—one heap of stones to hold the composition up. Here's Farren—view of the roofs of Kirkcudbright complete with Tolbooth, looking like Noah's Ark built out of nursery bricks—ver-

milion, Naples yellow, ultramarine—sophisticated *naïveté* and no
cast shadows. Waters—'none of these charlatans take the trouble to
draw'—bird's-eye view of a stone-quarry with every bump identifiable—horse and cart violently foreshortened at the bottom, to show
that he can do it. Bless you"—he slopped some beer on the counter
and wiped the mess away with a ragged sleeve—"the whole bunch
of them have only got one gift between them that I lack, and that's
the single eye, more's the pity. They're perfectly sincere, I'm not
—that's what makes the difference. I tell you, Wimsey, half those
damned portraits people pay me for are caricatures—only the fools
don't know it. If they did, they'd rather die than sign the cheques."

Wimsey laughed. If Graham was playing for time, he was doing
it well. If he was trying to avert suspicion from his dangerous gift
of imitation, his air of careless frankness could not possibly be better
done. And his explanation was plausible enough—why, indeed,
should Campbell not have mentioned where he was going—to
Graham or to anyone?

The constable was registering impatience.

"As a matter of routine," he murmured.

"Oh," said Mr. Graham. "This lad's one of the bulldog breed."

"Obviously," said Wimsey, "like St. Gengulphus. They cried out,
'Good gracious! How very tenacious!' It's no good, old man. He
means to have his answer."

"Poor fellow!" said Graham. "Want must be his master, as
nurses said in the good old days before Montessori was heard of.
I was not up at the Minnoch. But where I was is my affair."

"Weel, sir," said the constable, nonplussed. Between the Judges'
Rules, the Royal Commission, his natural disinclination to believe
anything wrong about Mr. Graham, and his anxiety to pull off a
coup, he felt his position to be a difficult one.

"Run along, laddies," said Graham, kindly. "You're only wasting your time. You've only to look at me to know that I wouldn't
hurt a fly. For all you know, the murderer's escaping while you
and I exchange merry quips over a pint of bitter."

"I understand," said the constable, "that ye refuse cateegoorically
tae state whaur ye were on last Monday nicht."

"Got it at last!" cried Graham. "We're slow but sure in this
country, Wimsey. That's right. I refuse categorically, absolutely,
in toto and entirely. Make a note of it in case you forget it."

The constable did so with great solemnity.

"Ah, weel," he said, "I'll hae tae be reportin' this tae the authorities."

"Right," said Graham. "I'll have a word with them."

The constable shook his head doubtfully and departed with slow reluctance.

"Poor devil!" said Graham. "It's a shame to tease him. Have another, Wimsey?"

Wimsey declined, and Graham took himself off rather abruptly, saying that he must go down and see to things at his studio.

The landlord of the Anwoth followed him with his eyes.

"What's behind that?" said Wimsey, carelessly.

"Och, it will be some tale or anither," replied the landlord. "He's a perfect gentleman, is Graham, and a great lad for the leddies."

"Quite so," said Wimsey. "And that reminds me, Rob, I've got a new limerick for you."

"Have ye noo?" said the landlord, and carefully closed the door between the inn-parlour and the bar.

Having delivered himself of his limerick and taken his leave, Wimsey turned his attention again to business. Mrs. Green, the charwoman, lived in a small cottage at no great distance. She was making bannocks when Wimsey arrived, but having dusted the flour from her hands and transferred the bannocks to the girdle, was willing enough to talk about the sudden death of her gentleman.

Her Scots was broad and her manner excitable, but after putting his questions two or three times, Wimsey succeeded in understanding her replies.

"Did Mr. Campbell take any breakfast before he went out on Monday morning?"

Yes, he did. There had been the remains of some bacon and eggs on the table and a used teapot and cup. Forbye, the loaf and butter had diminished, by comparison with the previous night, and there had been slices cut from the ham.

"Was that Mr. Campbell's usual breakfast?"

Ay, fried eggs and bacon were his breakfast, as regular as clockwork. Two eggs and two rashers, and that was what he had taken that morning, for Mrs. Green had counted.

"Did Mr. Ferguson eat his breakfast that morning also?"

Yes, Mr. Ferguson had taken a kipper with a cup of coffee. Mrs. Green had herself brought in a pair of kippers for him on Saturday, and he had had the one on Sunday morning and the other on Monday morning. There had been nothing unusual about either cottage, that she could see, and so she had told the policeman when he called upon her.

Wimsey turned these matters over in his mind as he ran back to Kirkcudbright. The doctor's report made those two eggs and rashers a suspicious circumstance. Somebody had breakfasted in Campbell's cottage, and the person who could do that most easily was Ferguson. Alternatively, if it was not Ferguson, Ferguson might have seen whoever it was. Tiresome of Ferguson to have gone off to Glasgow like that.

As for Graham, apparently he had not been at Glen Trool. His silence might have half a dozen different explanations. "The leddies" was the most obvious; it would be well, in Graham's own interests, to discover whether he had any local attachment. Or he might merely have discovered some remote river, rich in trout, which he wished to keep to himself. Or he might just be doing it to annoy. One could not tell. Beneath all his surface eccentricity, Graham was a man who kept his wits about him. Still, in a country place, where everybody knows everybody, it is impossible to keep one's movements altogether secret. Somebody would have seen Graham—that is, if somebody chose to speak. But that was as doubtful as everything else about the case, for your country-dweller is a master of pregnant silences.

Wimsey called at Sir Maxwell Jamieson's to make his report about the eggs and bacon, which was received with an "Ay, imph'm" of the driest kind. There had been no further news from Dalziel, and he went home, first calling across the way, only to ascertain that Waters had not yet returned.

Bunter received him with respectful welcome, but appeared to have something preying on his mind. On inquiry, however, this turned out to be merely the discovery that the Scotch were so lost to all sense of propriety as to call a dish an "ashet"—obviously with the deliberate intention of confusing foreigners and making them feel like bulls in china-shops.

Wimsey sympathised and, to take Bunter's mind off this mortifying experience, mentioned his meeting with Jock Graham.

"Indeed, my lord? I was already apprised of Mr. Graham's re-appearance. I understand, my lord, that he was in Creetown on Monday night."

"Was he, by Jove? How do you know?"

Bunter coughed.

"After the interview with the young person at the china-shop, my lord, I stepped for a few moments into the McClellan Arms. Not into the public bar, my lord, but into the bar-parlour adjacent. While there, I accidentally overheard some persons mention the circumstance in the bar."

"What sort of persons?"

"Roughly dressed persons, my lord. I apprehend that they might have been engaged in the fishing-trade."

"Was that all they said?"

"Yes, my lord. One of them unfortunately glanced into the bar-parlour and discovered my presence, and after that they said nothing further about the matter."

"Who were they, do you know?"

"I endeavoured to ascertain from the landlord, but he said no more than that they were a bunch of lads from the harbour."

"Oh! And that's all you ever will hear, I expect. H'm. Did you manage to see any of them?"

"Only the one who looked in at the door, and him only for a brief interval. The rest had their backs to the bar door when I emerged, my lord, and I did not care to appear inquisitive."

"No. Well—Creetown is on the way to Newton-Stewart, but it's a far cry from there to the Minnoch. Did they mention the time at which they saw Mr. Graham?"

"No, my lord, but, from the circumstance that they alluded to the number of drinks he consumed, I apprehend that it would be before closing-time."

"Ah!" said Wimsey. "An inquiry among the Creetown pubs might settle that. Very well, Bunter. I think I shall go out and clear my wits with a round of golf this afternoon. And I'll have a grilled steak and chips at 7.30."

"Very good, my lord."

．　　．　　．　　．　　．　　．　　．

Wimsey had his round of golf with the Provost, but without

much satisfaction beyond that of beating him five up and three to play. He deduced from this victory that the Provost was not altogether easy in his mind, but he failed altogether to draw him on the subject of Campbell. It was "an unfortunate occurrence," and the Provost thought that "it might be a wee while before they got to the bottom of it"—and after that the conversation was firmly led away to the quoiting match at Gatehouse, the recent regatta at Kirkcudbright, the shortage of salmon and depredations of poachers in the estuary, and the problems of sewage-distribution in tidal waters.

At half-past nine, when Wimsey had absorbed his grilled steak and a rhubarb-tart, and was dreaming over some old numbers of *The Gallovidian,* he was aroused by a clatter of feet upon the cobblestones of the close. He was just rising to look out of the window, when there was a knock upon the door, and a cheerful female voice called: "May we come in?"

Miss Selby and Miss Cochran occupied adjacent cottages and were continually to be found taking tea in each other's living-rooms or bathing together on the sands at the Doon. Miss Selby was tall, dark, rather angular, rather handsome in an uncompromising kind of way and painted rather good, strong, angular and handsome figure-studies in oils. Miss Cochran was round, cheerful, humorous and grey-haired; she illustrated magazine stories in line and wash. Wimsey liked them both, because they had no nonsense about them, and they liked him for the same reason, and also because they found Bunter extremely amusing. Bunter was always distressed to see them cooking their own dinners and putting up their own curtains. He would step reproachfully to their assistance, and take the hammer and nails from their hands, with a respectful, "Allow me, miss"; and would obligingly offer to look after stews and casseroles during their absence. They rewarded him with gifts of vegetables and flowers from their garden—gifts which Bunter would receive with a respectful, "Thank you, miss. His lordship will be greatly obliged." While Wimsey was greeting his visitors, Bunter now advanced unobtrusively and inquired, as soon as there was a pause in the conversation, whether the ladies would take supper after their journey.

The ladies replied that they were quite well-fed, but a little investigation showed that they had indeed had nothing since tea-time except a few sandwiches on the train. Wimsey promptly ordered omelettes, a bottle of claret and the remains of the rhubarb-tart to be brought forward, and, when Bunter had withdrawn to prepare the feast, said:

"Well, you've missed all the excitement."

"So they told us at the station," said Miss Cochran. "What is it all about? Is it true that Mr. Campbell is dead?"

"Quite true. He was found in the river——"

"And now they're saying he's been murdered," put in Miss Selby.

"Oh, they're saying that, are they? Well, that's true, too."

"Good gracious!" said Miss Selby.

"And who is it they're saying has done it?" demanded Miss Cochran.

"They don't know yet," said Wimsey, "but there's a kind of an idea that it was a premeditated job."

"Oh, why?" asked Miss Cochran, bluntly.

"Oh, well, because the symptoms point that way, you know, and there doesn't seem to have been any robbery from the person, or anything—and—in fact, several things."

"And in fact you know more than you think you ought to tell us. Well, it's fortunate we've got an alibi, isn't it, Margaret? We've been in Glasgow ever since yesterday morning. It was on Tuesday it happened, wasn't it?"

"It seems so," said Wimsey, "but just to make sure, they are checking up everybody's whereabouts from Monday night onwards."

"Who's everybody?"

"Well—the people who knew Campbell best, and so on."

"I see. Well, you know we were here on Monday night, because we said good-night to you when you came in, and we went off by the 8.45 yesterday morning and we've got any amount of witnesses to show that we were in Glasgow between then and now, so I imagine we're all right. Besides it would have taken more powerful people than Mary or me to tackle Mr. Campbell. What a relief to know that we can't possibly be suspected!"

"No—you two and Waters are out of the running all right, I fancy."

"Oh? Where was Mr. Waters?"

"Wasn't he with you?"

"With us?"

They stared at one another. Wimsey apologised.

"I'm sorry. Mrs. Doings—his landlady, what's her name?—told me Waters had gone with you two to Glasgow."

"She must have got hold of the wrong end of the stick. He said on Sunday evening at Bob Anderson's that he might possibly turn up, but he didn't, so we thought he'd changed his mind. Anyhow, we didn't really expect him, did we, Mary?"

"No. But isn't he here, then, Lord Peter?"

"Well, as a matter of fact, he's not," said Wimsey, aghast.

"Oh, well, he must be somewhere," said Miss Cochran, comfortably.

"Naturally," said Wimsey, "but he certainly went off at about 8.30 yesterday morning, saying he was going to Glasgow. Or at least, he seems to have left that impression behind him."

"Well, he certainly never came to the station," said Miss Selby, decidedly. "And he wasn't at the show either day, that I could see. But of course he may have had other fish to fry."

Wimsey scratched his head.

"I must interview that woman again," he said. "I must have misunderstood her. But it's exceedingly odd. Why should he get up and go out early if he wasn't going to Glasgow? Especially——"

"Especially what?" said Miss Cochran.

"Well, I shouldn't have expected it," said Wimsey. "He was a bit lit-up the night before, and as a rule it takes a lot to get Waters out of bed at the best of times. It's rather unfortunate. Still, we can't do much till he turns up."

"We?" said Miss Selby.

"The police, I mean," said Wimsey, blushing a little.

"You'll be helping the police, I expect," said Miss Cochran. "I was forgetting that you had such a reputation as a Sherlock. I'm sorry we don't seem able to help. You'd better ask Mr. Ferguson. He may have run across Mr. Waters somewhere in Glasgow."

"Oh, Ferguson was there, was he?"

Wimsey put his question carelessly, but not so carelessly as to deceive Miss Cochran, who darted a shrewd glance at him.

"Yes, he was there. I believe we can give ye the precise time we saw him." (As Miss Cochran became more emphatic, she became more Scottish in her accent. She planted her plump feet squarely on the ground and leaned forward with a hand on each knee, like an argumentative workman in a tram.) "That train of ours gets in at 2.16—it's a bad train, stops at every station, and we'd have done better to wait and take the 1.46 at Dumfries, only we wanted to meet Margaret's sister Kathleen and her husband and they were away to England by the 4 o'clock train. They came to the station to meet us, and we went into the hotel and had a bit of lunch, for we hadn't had anything since 8 o'clock—there's none served on that train—and the hotel was as good a place as any to have our bit of talk in. We saw them off at 4 o'clock, and then we had a wee argument whether we would go straight on to my cousin's where we were staying, or look in at the Gallery first. I said it was too late to do anything, but Margaret said it would be a good idea just to go down and see where they'd hung the different things, and then to come back next day and have our proper look at them; and I agreed that was a sensible notion. So we took the tram and we got into the Exhibition just about half-past four, or a few minutes earlier, and in the first room, whom should we see but Mr. Ferguson, just coming away. So of course we spoke to him and he said he'd been through the rooms pretty thoroughly once and was coming back next day. However, he went round once again with us."

Wimsey, who had been trying to hold the whole local time-table in his head and was hurriedly calculating arrivals and departures, broke in at this point.

"I suppose he really *had* been through the place already?"

"Oh, yes. He told us beforehand where everything was, and mentioned the ones he liked. He'd come in on the same train as we did—only I suppose he would go straight up to the Exhibition."

"On your train—the 2.16. Yes, of course, he would join it at Dumfries. It leaves there at 11.22, doesn't it? Yes, that's right. Did you see him at Dumfries?"

"No, but that doesn't mean he wasn't there. He'd travel smoking, anyway, and we made for a nice, old-fashioned Ladies' Compartment, not being great smokers in confined spaces. Anyhow, he saw us at Glasgow if we didn't see him, because the first thing he said when we met him was, 'I saw you at the station, but you didn't see me. Was that Kathleen and her good man with you?' And then he mentioned that he had been in the same train."

"Pretty good," said Wimsey. "Well, as you say, we'll have to see Ferguson—I mean, the police will have to see him."

Miss Cochran shook her head.

"You can't deceive me," she said. "You're in it up to the eyes. If the truth were told, I dare say you did it yourself."

"No," said Wimsey. "This is about the only murder I couldn't possibly have committed. I haven't the technical skill."

CHAPTER VIII

GOWAN

INSPECTOR MACPHERSON of Kirkcudbright was one of those painstaking and unimaginative people for whom no hypothesis is too far-fetched to be investigated. He liked material clues. He paid no attention to such a trivial consideration as psychological improbability. The Chief Constable had put before him the ascertained facts about Campbell's death, and he saw that they pointed to the guilt of some artist or other. He liked them. The medical evidence was what he liked best; good, solid, meaty stuff about rigor and the alimentary canal. The business about trains and time-tables pleased him too; it lent itself to being set out in tabular form and verified. The bit about the picture was less satisfactory: it depended on technical matters which he did not personally understand, but he was open-minded enough to accept expert opinion on such matters. He would, for instance, have taken his Cousin Tom's advice on electricity or his sister Alison's opinion about ladies' underwear, and he was not unprepared to admit that a gentleman like Wimsey might know more than he did about artists and their paraphernalia.

Accordingly, he perceived that all artists were, for his purpose, suspect, no matter how rich, respectable or mild-mannered they might be, and whether they were known to have quarrelled with Campbell or not. Kirkcudbright was his district, and his job was to collect alibis and information from every artist in Kirkcudbright, young or old, male or female, virtuous or wicked, indiscriminately. He went about the thing in a conscientious manner, not omitting Marcus McDonald, who was bedridden, or Mrs. Helen Chambers, who had only just settled in Kirkcudbright, or old John Peterson, who was ninety-two, or Walter Flanagan who had returned from the Great War with an artificial leg. He noted the absence of Waters and Farren, though he did not get as much out of Mrs. Farren as Lord Peter had done; and during the afternoon he presented himself at Mr. Gowan's front-door, notebook in hand and rectitude upon his brow. He had left Gowan to the last, because

71

it was well-known that Mr. Gowan worked in the mornings and resented interruptions before lunch, and Inspector Macpherson had no notion of making difficulties for himself.

The English butler opened the door, and in reply to the Inspector's inquiry, remarked briefly:

"Mr. Gowan is not at home."

The Inspector explained that his business was official, and again requested an interview with Mr. Gowan.

The butler replied loftily:

"Mr. Gowan is h'out."

The Inspector begged to know when Mr. Gowan would be in again.

The butler condescended to explain further.

"Mr. Gowan is away."

To the Scottish mind, this expression has not the same finality that it has to the English mind. The Inspector asked whether Mr. Gowan would be back that evening.

The butler, driven to be explicit, announced imperturbably:

"Mr. Gowan has gone to London."

"Is that so?" said the Inspector, annoyed with himself for having put off his visit so long. "When did he go?"

The butler appeared to think this catechism ill-bred, but nevertheless replied:

"Mr. Gowan left for London on Monday night."

The Inspector was startled.

"At what time on Monday night?"

The butler appeared to undergo a severe internal struggle, but answered, with great self-control:

"Mr. Gowan took the h'eight forty-five train from Dumfries."

The Inspector thought for a moment. If this was true, it left Gowan out altogether. But it must, of course, be verified.

"I think," he said, "that I had best step in for a moment."

The butler appeared to hesitate, but, seeing that a number of inhabitants from the close opposite had come out to stare at the Inspector and himself, he graciously gave way and let Macpherson in to the handsome panelled entrance-hall.

"I am investigatin'," said the Inspector, "this maitter o' the death o' Mr. Campbell."

The butler bowed his head silently.

"I will tell ye, wi'oot circumlocution, that there is mair than a suspeecion that the puir gentleman was murdered."

"So," said the butler, "I h'understand."

"It is important, ye ken," went on Macpherson, "that we should get all possible information from those that saw Mr. Campbell of late."

"Quite so."

"And as a matter of routine, ye understand, that we should ken whaur everybody was at the time the calamity occurred."

"Exactly," said the butler.

"Nae doot," pursued the Inspector, "if Mr. Gowan were at hame, he wad be anxious tae gie us a' the assistance in his power."

The butler was sure that Mr. Gowan would be only too happy to do so.

The Inspector opened his notebook.

"Your name is Halcock, is't no?" he began.

The butler corrected him.

"H'alcock," he said, reprovingly.

"H, a, double-l?" suggested the Inspector.

"There is no h'aitch in the name, young man. H'ay is the first letter, and there is h'only one h'ell."

"I beg your pardon," said the Inspector.

"Granted," said Mr. Alcock.

"Weel, noo, Mr. Alcock, juist a pure formality, ye understand, whit time did Mr. Gowan leave Kirkcudbright on Monday nicht?"

"It would be shortly after h'eight."

"Whae drove him?"

"Hammond, the chauffeur."

"Ammond?" said the Inspector.

"Hammond," said the butler, with dignity. "H'albert Hammond is his name—with a h'aitch."

"I beg your pardon," said the Inspector.

"Granted," said Mr. Alcock. "Perhaps you would wish to speak to Hammond?"

"Presently," said the Inspector. "Can ye tell me whether Mr. Gowan had seen Mr. Campbell at a' on the Monday?"

"I could not undertake to say."

"Mr. Gowan was friendly with Mr. Campbell?"

"I could not undertake to say."

"Has Mr. Campbell visited at the house recently?"

"Mr. Campbell has never visited at this house to my knowledge."

"Indeed? Imph'm." The Inspector knew as well as Mr. Alcock that Gowan held himself very much aloof from the rest of the artistic population, and seldom invited anybody except for a stately bridge-party now and again, but he felt it his duty to put these questions officially. He ploughed on conscientiously.

"Noo, I'm only juist checkin' up on this maitter, ye ken, wi' a' Mr. Campbell's acquaintances. Can ye tell me what Mr. Gowan did on the Monday?"

"Mr. Gowan rose at 9 o'clock according to custom and breakfasted at 9.30. He then took a turn in the garden and retired to his studio in the customary manner. He partook of luncheon at the usual time, 1.30. H'after luncheon, he was again engaged on his h'artistic pursuits till 4 o'clock, when tea was served in the library."

The butler paused.

"Ay?" said the Inspector, encouragingly.

"H'after tea," went on the butler, more slowly, "he went out for a run in the two-seater."

"Did Hammond drive him?"

"No. When Mr. Gowan takes the two-seater, he is accustomed to drive himself."

"Ah? Ay. Whaur did he go?"

"I could not undertake to say."

"Weel, when did he return?"

"At about 7 o'clock."

"And then?"

"Mr. Gowan then made the h'observation that he had decided to go to town that night."

"Had he said anything aboot that airlier?"

"No. Mr. Gowan is in the habit of making occasional journeys to town."

"Without previous notice?"

The butler bowed.

"It didna strike ye as unusual in any way?"

"Certainly not."

"Ay, imph'm. Did he dine before leaving?"

"No. I understood Mr. Gowan to say that he would be dining on the train."

"On the train? Ye say he took the 8.45 from Dumfries?"

"So I was given to understand."

"But, man, are ye no aware that the 8.45 disna mak' ony connection wi' London? It arrives in Carlisle at 9.59, which is verra late tae get dinner, and after that there's nae train tae London till five meenuts past twelve. Wherefore did he no tak' his dinner here an' catch the 11.8 at Dumfries?"

"I could not undertake to say. Mr. Gowan did not h'inform me. Possibly Mr. Gowan had some business to transact at Carlisle."

The Inspector gazed at Mr. Alcock's large, white, imperturbable face, and said:

"Ay, that may be. Did Mr. Gowan say how long he would be away?"

"Mr. Gowan mentioned that he might be h'absent for a week or ten days."

"Did he give you any address?"

"He desired that letters should be forwarded to his club."

"And that is?"

"The Mahlstick, in Piccadilly."

The Inspector made a note of the address, and added:

"Have ye heard from Mr. Gowan since his departure?"

The butler raised his eyebrows.

"No." He paused, and then went on less frigidly. "Mr. Gowan would not write unless he had occasion to mention any special h'instructions."

"Ay, that's so. Then so far as ye ken, Mr. Gowan is at this moment in London."

"For all I know to the contrary, he is."

"Imph'm. Weel, noo—I wad like tae speak a word wi' Hammond."

"Very good." Mr. Alcock rang the bell, which was answered by a young and rather pretty maid.

"Betty," said Mr. Alcock. "h'inform Hammond that his presence is required by the H'Inspector."

"Juist a moment," said Macpherson. "Betty, ma lass, whit time did Mr. Gowan leave here o' Monday nicht?"

"Aboot 8 o'clock, sir," said the girl, quickly, with a little glance at the butler.

"Did he dine before he went?"

"I—I cannot juist charge ma memory, sir."

"Come, my girl," said Mr. Alcock, magisterially, "surely you can remember that. There's nothing to be frightened about."

"N-n-no, Mr. Alcock."

"No," said Mr. Alcock. "You are quite sure about that. Mr. Gowan did not dine at home on Monday?"

"No."

Mr. Alcock nodded.

"Then run and give Hammond my message—unless the Inspector wants to ask you anything further?"

"No," said Macpherson.

"Has onything happened?" asked Betty, tremulously.

"Nothing whatever, nothing whatever," replied the butler. "The Inspector is just making some routine inquiries, as I understand. And, Betty, just you give that message to Hammond and come straight back. No stopping and chattering. The Inspector has his work to get through, same as you and me."

"Yes—I mean, no, Mr. Alcock."

"A good girl," said the butler, as Betty ran out, "but slow in the uptake, if you understand me."

"Imph'm," said Inspector Macpherson.

Hammond, the chauffeur, was a small, perky man, mongrel in speech, but betraying a strong streak of the fundamental cockney. The Inspector reeled off his preliminary speech about routine inquiries, and then came to the point.

"Did ye drive Mr. Gowan onywhere on Monday last?"

"That's right. Drove 'im ter Dumfries."

"What time?"

"Eight o'clock for the 8.45."

"In the two-seater?"

"Naow, in the saloon."

"What time did Mr. Gowan come in wi' the two-seater?"

"'Baht a quarter past seven, might be earlier, might be later. I was 'avin' me supper at 'alf-past seven, and the Riley was in the garridge w'en I come back there."

"Did Mr. Gowan tak' ony luggage wi' him?"

"Bit of a bag, like. One 'er they 'tashy cases—'baht so long."

He indicated a spread of about two feet.

"Ay, imph'm. Did ye see him get into the train?"

"Naow. 'E walked into the station and told me ter cut along 'ome."

"What time was that?"

"Eight thirty-five as near as makes no difference."

"And ye cam' straight back tae Kirkcudbright?"

Sure thing. Naow. Wait a mo. I brought a parcel o' stuff back with me."

"Ay? An' whit stuff wad that be?"

"Two pictures of Mr. Gowan's, what belonged to a gentleman in Dumfries. The boss didn't want 'em sent by train, so I picked 'em up at the house. They was all done up waitin' to be collected."

"Ye went tae this hoose after ye had left Mr. Gowan at the station?"

"That's right. Gentleman name of Phillips. Want 'is address?"

"Ay—ye may as weel gie't me."

The chauffeur gave it.

"Did Mr. Gowan mek ony mention o' whaur he was gaein'?"

" 'E only said 'e wanted ter catch the train for Carlisle."

"Carlisle?"

"That's right."

"He didna say for London?"

"Not ter me. Train for Carlisle, 'e says."

"Ay—and when did he first gi' ye the order?"

"Mr. Alcock comes down w'en I was 'avin' me supper, and says Mr. Gowan wanted the saloon round at 8 o'clock ter tike 'im ter Dumfries. And I says, 'Right-oh!' I says, 'an' I can pick up them there pitchers at the same time.' That's what I says and that's what I done."

"Ay, verra guid. That's quite clear. Thank you, Mr. Hammond. This is naething at a', ye understand, but juist a simple formality."

"Thet's all right. Finni?"

"What's that?"

"I says, finni? meaning, is that O.K.? complete? 'ave yer done?"

"Oo, ay, there's nae mair I'll be wantin' from ye at the moment."

"Well, cheerio, then," said the chauffeur.

"Did you wish to see Mrs. Alcock?" inquired the butler, politely, but with the air of one prepared to endure all things.

"Och, no—I'm thinkin' it'll no be necessary. Thank ye verra much, Mr. Alcock."

"Don't mention it," said the butler. "I trust that you will soon have the miscreant by the heels. Very happy to have been of use, I am sure. There are two steps h'up to the front door. A beautiful h'evening, is it not? Reelly, the sky is quite a poem. Good h'evening, Inspector."

"A' the same," said the Inspector to himself, "it'll no be amiss tae make inquiries at Dumfries. They'll no have forgotten Gowan, wi' his big black beard. It's a queer thing he should suddenly be wantin' tae spend twa-three hours in Carlisle waitin' for a train tae London. He micht verra weel ha' hired anither car tae fetch him hame."

He considered a little, as he wandered thoughtfully towards the police-station.

"Forbye," he continued, "yon lassie didna seem juist sae ready wi' her replies as they twa."

He pushed back his cap and scratched his head.

"Nae maitter," said he, cheerfully, "I'll sort it yet."

CHAPTER IX

MRS. McLEOD

THINGS were lively in the close that night. Wimsey had escorted his visitors to their doors, and was thinking of turning in, when the sudden opening of the blue gate and the cries of a fellow-creature entangled and in pain urged him to go to the assistance of the Chief Constable, who had become involved with the bicycles in the narrow passage.

"I don't mind telling you," said Sir Maxwell, when at length he was safely seated in Wimsey's armchair and comforted with Scotch, "that I am greatly disturbed about all this business. If I could see any clear line to follow up, it would be more satisfactory. Even supposing that your list of suspects comprises the whole of the possibilities (which at present, mark you, I am not disposed to grant) —even then, I simply do not know where to start an inquiry. That one or two of them should have no good alibis is only what one might expect—but that practically all of them should be open to suspicion really bewilders me."

"Dear me!" said Wimsey.

"Graham and Strachan," went on the Chief Constable, "were both out all night, as you know, and have no explanations. Ferguson appears, from what you say, to be all right, but he has not been interrogated yet, and really, after to-day's experiences, I am beginning to doubt whether anybody's movements will bear investigation. Farren's disappearance is so suspicious that, if it were not for the extraordinary behaviour of the rest, I should get out a warrant for him straight away. Gowan——"

"Surely not Gowan, too?"

"Gowan has gone to England, and there are points in Inspector Macpherson's report——"

"I haven't heard that yet."

"No." The Chief Constable gave the gist of the Inspector's interview with the servants, and resumed:

"There are undoubtedly points there that need looking into. And now comes a most infernal business about Waters."

"Unbosom yourself," said Wimsey. "Trouble shared is trouble halved."

"Well," said Sir Maxwell, "when Waters didn't turn up to-day with the ladies yonder. Inspector Macpherson made a few further inquiries of Mrs. McLeod, who seems to have misled you—though, I think and hope, unintentionally. And these inquiries brought to light a very remarkable circumstance.

"Apparently Waters did ask to be called early on the Tuesday morning and did make the remark that he rather thought of going to Glasgow. On the Monday night, Mrs. McLeod heard him come in with you and go up to bed. Then you went out again. She puts this at about 10.30. Is that right?"

"Meaning, did I leave about 10.30? Yes, that's near enough."

"Well, then, some time between 11 and midnight, Mrs. MeLeod heard somebody throwing pebbles at Waters' bedroom window. Her room is next but one to his, and they both look out on the High Street. She looked out, and saw a man down below. She couldn't make him out very well, but he seemed to be shortish and broad, well wrapped up in an overcoat and muffler. She was just going to shout down and tell him to shut up, when Waters' window opened, and she heard Waters say angrily:

" 'What the devil do you want?' "

"The man in the street said something which she did not catch, and then Waters said:

" 'Well, don't make that blasted row. I'm coming down.' "

"She then leaned out a little further and saw a four-seater car standing a few yards down the street. Waters came down presently in some sort of outdoor togs—a sweater and trousers, she thinks— and he and the man went into Waters' sitting-room. They talked there for a bit, and Mrs. McLeod went back to bed. Presently she heard somebody run up to Waters' bedroom and down again, and the front door was opened and shut. Mrs. McLeod looked out once more, and saw both men climb into the car and move off. In about three-quarters of an hour—being thoroughly wakened up by that time—she heard the door open softly again, and footsteps tiptoeing up the stairs into Waters' bedroom.

"Nothing more happened after that, and at 7.30 she knocked on Waters' door as arranged, with his shaving water, and at 8 o'clock she put his breakfast in the sitting-room. She then went out to the back of the house to do some household work, and at 8.20 when she came in again, Waters had eaten a sketchy sort of breakfast and gone.

"Now, there are two more interesting points. First of all, Waters went—ostensibly to see an exhibition in Glasgow—in an old sweater, a pair of grey flannel bags, tennis-shoes and an old burberry. And secondly, he took his bicycle with him."

"What?" cried Wimsey.

"He took his bicycle with him. Or rather, to be accurate, his bicycle, which stands just inside the front door, was there on the Monday night and was gone at 8.20. The presumption is that Waters took it."

"Good Lord!"

"What do you make of that?" demanded the Chief Constable.

"What you want me to make of it," said Wimsey, slowly, "is that the man in the street was Campbell, come back to finish out his row with Waters. That they went off together to fight it out. That in the row, Campbell got his head bashed in. That Waters then concealed the body somewhere. That he came home, in order to look as ordinary as possible. That he then thought out a plan of concealment, and that next morning he went off at the time previously appointed, put the body and the bicycle in Campbell's car, and hared off to the Minnoch to fake the accident."

"Can you make anything else of it?"

"I *might* make fifty things," said Wimsey, "but—not to practice any mean concealment, I will admit that the circumstances seem to fit the crime. Except, perhaps, for one point."

"Yes, I thought of that. What did he do with the body between midnight and 8 a.m.?"

"No," said Wimsey. "No—I see no difficulty about that. All he had to do was to put the body in the car and run it along to his studio. There is plenty of open space there where people often stand cars and carts, and nobody would take any notice of an old car with junk in it, covered with a rug. It's not as if he'd left it in Piccadilly Circus. People leave cars in the street all night in this place, and nobody bothers. No, that's not what's puzzling me."

"Well?"

"Well! if all that is true, where is Waters? He ought to have been here yesterday, blatantly establishing his entire innocence.

What's the good of concocting an elaborate fake like that, and then drawing suspicion on yourself by running away?"

"Perhaps he got cold feet when he'd done it. Anyhow, your objection applies to them all, except Strachan and possibly Ferguson."

"That's true. Well, Chief, I think you'll have to send out the hue and cry after Waters."

"I suppose I shall. Will this mean Scotland Yard, do you suppose?"

"Well, you'll have to get help in tracing these people all over the country. They may be anywhere. But I'm still inclined to think that it's a case where local knowledge can make the running best. But I'm not in a position to pronounce, don't you know."

"Of course, I'd rather we could work it ourselves. Macpherson is a good man and so is Dalziel."

"That reminds me," said Wimsey, "how about the young man they detained at Stranraer?"

Sir Maxwell groaned.

"A wash-out. He turns out to be a perfectly respectable stranger employed in a linen manufactory at Larne. Apparently he had leave to visit his family, who live in some obscure farm near Pinwherry. He was given a long week-end, finishing up on Monday night. It seems there was some kind of a jollification on the Monday night, and the lad was over-persuaded to stay on for it. On Tuesday, as soon as he had recovered his senses, he bolted off to the station, thinking he could get back that afternoon, but mistook the time-table, and then found he could get no boat before 7 o'clock that evening."

"Having, of course, missed the morning boat."

"Exactly. That was what he originally intended to catch, of course, but owing to the jollification, he didn't. Well, having got to Stranraer, he decided that there was no point in returning that night, and that he might as well stay over and take the 6.10 boat on Wednesday morning. Consequently, Dalziel's message to the Stranraer police caught him as he was boarding this morning's boat. Dalziel has been working like a nigger all day, getting him identified by his family and by the station-master at Pinwherry and by the people at Larne, and the upshot of it is that his story is perfectly straight, and that he's guilty of nothing worse than being too drunk to go back to work on Monday night. Confound the fellow! He's wasted a whole day of our best man's time, and left us exactly where we were before. I hope he's sacked, that's all."

"Oh, don't be vindictive," said Wimsey. "He couldn't know how inconvenient he was going to be. He 'maun ha' gotten a rare fricht,' as the man in Ian Hay's book said about the lice in his blanket.

The Chief Constable grunted.

"Any more news of the man with the bicycle who took the train at Girvan?"

"No, except that they've checked the tickets and decided that he went to Ayr all right."

"How about the bicycle?"

"The bicycle-ticket appears to have been given up too, though we can't trace any ticket-collector who remembers anything about it. It would be much easier if we knew what kind of bicycle we were looking for."

"M'm. Yes. It wouldn't be a bad idea to get hold of some exact descriptions Mrs. McLeod ought to know what Waters' bike looked like. I bet Andy could tell you every scratch and scrape on his old crock. It's got new tyres on, by the way. That ought to be a help."

"And then there's Farren's bicycle."

"So there is. And there's a very fine selection of bicycles, male and female, up our close. Anybody who urgently wanted to borrow one in Gatehouse or Kirkcudbright wouldn't have very great difficulty. And they all look much alike—honest, hard-working bicycles, half as old as time. For all we know, the murderer's bicycle, if he was a murderer, and used one, may have come peacefully back home by this time."

"That's a fact," said the Chief Constable. "But we'll circulate those descriptions all the same."

CHAPTER X

SERGEANT DALZIEL

ON THE Thursday morning, Sergeant Dalziel woke unrefreshed and irritable. He had rather counted upon the young man at Stanraer. To have a murder reported at lunch-time on Tuesday, and to catch the murderer at 6.30 the next morning would, he felt, have been a smart piece of work. Now he had to start all over again. The voluminous, contradictory and confusing reports from Kirkcudbright worried him. Also he felt dissatisfied about the bicyclist at Girvan. Surely it must be possible to trace him and his bicycle. These inquiries by telephone were never satisfactory. There was nothing for it, he supposed, but to go himself. With a grunt of annoyance, he tucked himself into his shabby car, collected Police Constable Ross to act as his aide-de-camp, and set out to collect descriptions.

He began with the Anwoth Hotel. Here he had the advantage of interviewing the outraged owner of the missing bicycle. Information was forthcoming in abundance. He had to look for a six-year-old Raleigh, with two new Dunlop tyres. The frame was painted black; one of the handle-bar grips was slightly broken; the bell was missing and the brakes defective. There was a tool-bag containing a repair outfit; a pump on the cross-bar, and a carrier at the back. The Sergeant wrote down all the particulars, promised his best attention and passed on his way.

At Waters' lodgings, his task was more difficult. Mrs. McLeod had seen the bicycle week after week standing in her front passage, but, like most people of her type and sex, had only the very vaguest idea of its appearance. It was "an auld yin," it was of "the ordinar' colour," she "couldna charge her memory" as to its fittings, though she thought there was, or had been, a lamp on it, because she had once had occasion to complain of drips on her floor. As for the maker's name, it had not occurred to her to look for it.

Her small son, however, proved more observant. He declared that it was a very old Humber, very rusty, and that it had neither bell nor lamp nor pump. "But there's Mr. Waters' name on a wee luggage label," he added, pleased to supply so helpful a clue.

"Ay, but I doot it'll no be there the noo," said the Sergeant.

He passed on to Mrs. Farren's. Here he at first drew a complete blank. Mrs. Farren "had not the faintest idea" what was the make of her husband's bicycle. She apologised for being so unpractical, and gave the Sergeant the impression that such details were beneath an artist's notice.

"I'm sure," she added, "I couldn't even tell you what make my own is."

"H'm," said the Sergeant, struck by an idea, "could ye let me have a look at your own bicycle, ma'am?"

"Oh, certainly." She led the way to an outhouse, and indicated a clean, well-kept Sunbeam, not new, but well-oiled, and with all its parts in good condition.

"Ye keep it verra nice," said Dalziel, approvingly.

"I like to have everything orderly and clean," said Mrs. Farren. "There is a real beauty in cleanliness and decency. Even inanimate things may breathe out a kind of loveliness if they are well cared-for. Do not you think so?"

"Nae doot, Mistress Farren, nae doot, ma'am. Wad this machine and your husband's have been bought at the same time?"

"Oh, no—his is newer than this."

"Ah!" said Dalziel, disappointed. "Imph'm. Aweel, nae doot, Mr. Farren'll be returnin' home before verra long. Ye ha' heard naething from him, I suppose?"

"No. But that's not really surprising. He does go off like this sometimes, for days together. You know what men are—especially artists and fishers."

"Och, ay," said Dalziel, comfortably. "Weel, if we should meet wi' him onywhere, we'll tell him he's expectit hame. Could I speak a bit word wi' the lassie? She'll maybe ken what kind o' bicycle it is."

"Jeanie? Oh, certainly—though I doubt if she'll know much about it. I am always telling her she should be more observant—though I'm afraid I'm a bad example to follow. By the way, Sergeant, do you mind telling me why——"

She stopped and laid her hand on her throat as if the words were difficult to say, or as though, while feeling bound to ask the question, she were reluctant to hear the answer.

"Why, what were ye aboot tae say?"

"Why all this fuss about my husband's bicycle?"

The Sergeant looked hard at her for a moment, then turned his eyes away and answered pleasantly:

"Och, 'tis naething. But there's several bicycles missin' lately, and we've found a dealer at Castle-Douglas wi' twa-three machines he disna seem able tae gie a verra gude account on. Sae we're juist mekkin' a sort o' round-up throughout the district, tae see if we can identify ony o' them. However, ye're quite sure Mr. Farren has his bicycle wi' him?"

"So far as I know. Why not? He—went away on it. But—I don't know of course—he may have left it somewhere—how should I know? He might have had it stolen since Monday, anywhere, by anybody. I—have you found it anywhere?"

Under Dalziel's steadfast eye, she was fumbling and stammering.

"I'll tak' ma aith," said Dalziel to himself, "she kens fine there is some importance tae be attached tae the bicycle, and she disna ken whether tae say her man had it or no. Whae could ha' tell't her? It's no that Lord Peter, for he's clever, wi' a' his bletherin' talk. And it's no Macpherson, he'd never let oot a word. There's some yin is expectin' yon bicycle tae be found in a queer place, I reckon."

Jeanie proved, indeed, to know as little about the bicycle as was to be expected, and produced no information beyond the fact that Mr. Farren was accustomed to clean both machines himself, and took "a wheen o' trouble" over them. A man who cared for his tools, evidently, and particular .in certain matters, though he was an artist.

A bicycle-shop in the town was more helpful. The machine was a Raleigh, not new, but in very good condition, black, with plated handle-bars. The shop had fitted a new Dunlop tyre to the back wheel a few weeks previously; the front tyre was of the same make and about six months old. Bell, brakes, lamps, and brackets were all in good order.

Armed with these particulars, the Sergeant made his way to Girvan Station. Here he found the porter concerned, a middle-aged man named McSkimming, who repeated to him, in rather more detail, the account he had already given to the station-master.

The train from Stranraer was due in at 1.6, and on the Tuesday it had come in well up to time. It had just entered the station, when a gentleman had come in hurriedly, wheeling a bicycle. He had called to McSkimming, and the man had noticed the high, affected English voice, with its "Heah, portah!" The gentleman had told him to label the bicycle for Ayr, quick, and the porter had wheeled the machine along to the little case containing luggage-labels. While he was labelling it, the gentleman was undoing a strap which held a small leather case to the carrier, saying that he would take it in the carriage with him. As time was short, he had pulled out a note-case from his pocket and sent McSkimming off to buy him a third-class ticket and bicycle-ticket for Ayr. Running back with these, the man had seen his passenger standing at the door of a third-class Smoker. He had handed over the tickets and received his tip, and had then placed the bicycle in the rear van. The train had moved out almost immediately afterwards.

No, he had not noticed the gentleman's face particularly. He was wearing a grey flannel suit and a check cap, and he had passed his handkerchief over his face from time to time, as though he were very hot with bicycling in the sun. As he gave the tip he had said something about being glad he had caught the train, and that it was a stiff pull from Ballantrae. He wore slightly tinted spectacles—the sort that is used to shield the eyes from sun-glare. He might have been clean-shaven, or he might have had a small moustache. McSkimming had had no time to notice details, forbye he had been feeling very unwell at the time with an awful pain to his stomach. If anything, he was feeling still worse to-day, and dooted that handling heavy luggage on a hot day did a man no good.

Dalziel sympathised and asked whether he thought he would be able to identify the man or the bicycle if he saw them again.

The porter did not know—he thought not. The bicycle had been old and dusty. He had not noticed the make. It was not his business. His business was to label it for Ayr, and he had so labelled it and put it in the van, and there was an end of it.

So far, so good. The bicycle had had a carrier, but then, many bicycles had that. It had looked old, and therefore was not very likely to have been Farren's, but it might have been either of the other two. There seemed to be no doubt that passenger and bicycle, whoever and whatever they might be, had travelled safely by the 1.11 to Ayr.

Dalziel thanked and rewarded the porter and returned to his car.

Consulting the time-table, he saw that the train stopped only once before Ayr, and that was at Maybole. It would be worth while to call and see if, by any chance, the passenger had left the train there, instead of going on to Ayr.

At Maybole he interviewed the station-master, and learned that only two passengers had alighted from the Stranraer train on the Tuesday. Both were women, and neither had a bicycle. This was only what he might have expected. The station-master added that the tickets of all passengers for Ayr by the train in question would be collected at Maybole. Eight third-class tickets had been given up —as was proved by a reference to the booking-clerk's returns—including a third-class ticket from Girvan. Any discrepancy between the number of tickets issued and collected would be checked at the Audit Office at Glasgow and reported within three days, so that if there was anything wrong about these tickets, they might expect to hear about it by the next day. The bicycle-ticket of a passenger travelling to Ayr would not be collected at Maybole; it would be retained by him until he claimed the machine at Ayr.

Dalziel left instructions that any query arising about tickets should be at once reported to him, and the two policemen then made their way to Ayr.

Ayr is a good-sized station, acting as a junction for several lines of traffic. The main line from Stranraer to Glasgow runs straight through the station. On the east side of the main line is the principal platform, containing the booking-hall, bookstall and station entrance, with a number of bays for branch lines.

Here Dalziel directed his first inquiries to the question of the bicycle ticket. A reference to the records showed that a ticket issued from Girvan to cover a twenty-five mile journey had been duly given up at Ayr. The next question was, to whom had the ticket been handed? Since the passenger-tickets had all been collected at Maybole, there would have been no collector at the barrier on that particular occasion. Therefore, presumably, the ticket would have been given up to the porter who removed the bicycle from the van.

Dalziel and Ross interviewed the porters in turn, but all were quite positive that they had not taken any bicycle out of the Stranraer train on the Tuesday. One of them, however, recollected something about the ticket. After seeing a number of passengers out of the train, he had gone back to the rear brake to deal with the luggage. The guard had then handed him a bicycle ticket, saying that it belonged to a gentleman who had taken his bicycle out himself and wheeled it away. The porter had considered this a shabby trick to avoid giving a tip, but he supposed that the traveller had been in a hurry, since the guard had seen him briskly wheeling the machine away in the direction of the exit. By that time the passenger would, of course, have left the station. People were often mean about tips, bicyclists especially. With times so hard and money so tight you didn't get twopence nowadays where once you would have got sixpence or a shilling. Call this a Socialist Government. Things were harder than ever for a working man, and as for Jimmy Thomas, he had sold himself, lock, stock and barrel, to the capitalists. If he (the porter) had had the right treatment, he would have been something better than an ordinary porter long before this, but with everybody getting at you all at once——

Dalziel cut short this jeremiad by asking whether the same guard would be travelling on the train that afternoon. The porter said, Yes, he would, and Dalziel determined to wait and interview him when he arrived. In the meantime he thought he and Ross might as well get some lunch, after which they would have to find somebody who had seen the bicyclist leave the station.

Over a hasty meal in the refreshment-room, the two officers discussed their campaign. It might take some time to trace the movements of their quarry after leaving Ayr Station, and it was necessary that Dalziel should be back at Newton-Stewart as early as possible, to keep in touch with Macpherson. There were a number of routine inquiries to be made at Glasgow, and it would, he felt, be advisable to get hold of photographs of all the persons at present under suspicion, in order that the bicyclist might be identified, if possible. Since all the men were well-known artists, it seemed likely that an inquiry among the leading Glasgow news-agencies would produce the photographs, and this would be a far better plan than asking for them directly at Gatehouse and Kirkcudbright, which would have the effect of putting the suspects on their guard. It was therefore decided that Dalziel should board the train from Stranraer when it came in, and proceed to Glasgow, interviewing the guard on the way. Ross should keep the car and pursue his investigations as and how he could, reporting to Newton-Stewart from time to time. If he got on the bicyclist's track, he was to follow where it led and, if necessary, detain the man when he found him.

At 1.48, the train came in, and Dalziel got into it, after ascertaining that the guard was, in fact, the same man who had been in charge on the Tuesday. As it drew away from Ayr, he observed Ross engaged in conversation with the bookstall clerk. Ross was an energetic and enthusiastic man, and the Sergeant felt sure that he would not be slack in his investigations. He rather wished that he had felt justified in himself taking over the more adventurous and entertaining side of the inquiry, but he reflected that there was, after all, no certainty that the elusive bicyclist had anything to do with the crime, and that it would not do for him, in his position, to lose himself indefinitely on what might prove to be a wild-goose chase. He made his way along the train to the guard's van.

The guard perfectly remembered the incident of the bicycle. The train had scarcely drawn up at the station before a passenger—a youngish man in a check cap and grey flannel suit and wearing Crookes' glasses—had come running along the platform to the van. He had addressed the guard, saying that he wanted his bicycle got out immediately, as he had no time to lose. The porters were all up in front, and the guard had himself opened the van and handed out the bicycle, first glancing at the label to make sure that it was the right one. It was labelled to Ayr correctly enough, and he remembered its being put in at Girvan. The gentleman thrust the ticket into his hand, together with a shilling tip, and immediately walked away with the bicycle in the direction of the exit. The guard further recollected that the passenger had been carrying a small attaché-case. He had not seen him actually leave the station, because he had had to see to the coupling of the Pullman Restaurant Car, which was put on at Ayr. Before leaving the station, he had handed the bicycle-ticket over to a porter to be sent to headquarters in the usual way.

Dalziel asked next for a personal description of the traveller. This was not so easy to get. The guard had only seen him for about half a minute. He thought he would be between thirty and forty, of middle height, and either clean-shaven or wearing a small, fair moustache. Not a dark moustache—the guard felt sure he would have noticed that. His hair was almost invisible beneath his cap, but the guard's general impression was of a fairish man with a fresh complexion. He might perhaps have been mouse-coloured or sandy. His eyes, beneath the glasses, were at any rate not noticeably dark—blue, grey or hazel, possibly. The guard, like the porter at Girvan, had particularly noticed the high, affected English voice. He thought he might recognise a photograph of the man if he saw it, but he really could not be sure. Everything about the man, with the exception of the voice and the glasses, might be called nondescript. The bicycle was an old and shabby one. The guard had not observed the make, but he had noticed that the tyres were comparatively new.

Dalziel nodded. He knew better than to expect a recognisable description of a man in a cap and glasses, seen only for a few seconds by a busy official at a railway-station. He went back to his compartment and passed the time making notes of the case until the train, after only a brief halt at Paisley, Gilmour Street, drew in to St. Enoch Station.

Here there was nothing for him to do except to inquire whether all tickets collected on the Tuesday had already been forwarded to the Audit Office. Being assured that this was so, he betook himself thither and was soon closeted with the head official there.

His business here was purely routine matter of checking the tickets issued and collected on the Tuesday between Gatehouse and St. Enoch and Kirkcudbright and St. Enoch respectively. He found that these had already been made up and found to agree perfectly with the returns sent in by the issuing clerks. Wimsey's vague suggestion that Waters might have started from Kirkcudbright with a Glasgow ticket and disappeared *en route* was evidently incorrect. If, unseen by either the officials or by Miss Selby and Miss Cochran, he had indeed taken the 8.45 from Kirkcudbright, he must have booked to some intermediate station. But there seemed no reason at all to suppose that he had ever started by that train at all. Waters had simply disappeared and taken his bicycle with him. Was this, or was it not, the bicycle which had travelled to Ayr? The Sergeant, remembering that young Andrew had fitted new tyres not long before, was more inclined to think that this might be the Anwoth Hotel bicycle, but then he had no evidence about the condition of Waters' tyres.

He inquired for Ferguson's ticket, which was readily identified, being the only first-class ticket issued from Gatehouse to Glasgow that day. It had been duly punched at Maxwelltown, between Gatehouse and Dumfries, and again at Hurlford and Mauchline, between Dumfries and St. Enoch, thus affording definite proof that Ferguson had made the whole journey as he had purported to do.

Not satisfied with this, Dalziel demanded a check of all tickets issued on Tuesday on all lines within a fifty-mile radius of Newton-Stewart, in case some interesting discrepancy of some sort should turn up somewhere, and then departed for the Central Police Station at Glasgow.

Here he set on foot inquiries for a bicyclist seen travelling over the road between Bargrennan and Girvan between 11 a.m. and 1.11 p.m. on Tuesday morning, as also for any bicyclist seen in the neighbourhood of Ayr on the Tuesday afternoon, or traveling on any line out of Ayr or any of the neighbouring stations on Tuesday afternoon or Wednesday. For it readily occurred to him that the bicyclist might have ridden from Ayr to some near-by station and re-booked there, after, perhaps, disguising his appearance in some way. He then remembered that the compromising bicycle might have been abandoned in some convenient spot, and sent out a further call to search station-cloakrooms for unclaimed bicycles and report any bicycle left derelict by the roadside round about Ayr and the neighbourhood. He gave a general description of the three missing bicycles, asking, however, that reports should not be confined to these two makes, but extended to include any bicycle found abandoned during the prescribed period.

Having put the machinery of the law in motion, he turned his attention to the matter of the photographs. He had little difficulty in collecting what he needed among the newspaper offices of the city, and finished up at 6 o'clock with a fine collection of portraits of all six artists. He then discovered that he had missed the last train to Newton-Stewart, and that his only hope of getting back that night was to go to Girvan or Lockerbie and drive home.

His own car was, of course, at Ayr. Wearily, the Sergeant went to the 'phone and rang up the Ayr police to discover if Constable Ross was still in the town. But luck was against him. Ross had been in and left a message that he was following up a clue in the direction of Kilmarnock and would report again.

Cursing his fate—though somewhat cheered by the thought of a clue—Dalziel then rang up Kirkcudbright. Inspector Macpherson answered him. Yes, a great deal of new evidence had come in. Yes, the Inspector thought Dalziel had better get back that night if he

could. What a pity he had now just missed the 6.20 to Girvan.
(Sergeant Dalziel gritted his teeth.) Well, it couldna be helped.
Let him take the 7.30, getting in at 9.51, and a car would be sent
to meet him.

The Sergeant replied, with a certain grim satisfaction, that the
9.51 only ran on Saturdays and the 9.56 only on Wednesdays,
and that, this being a Thursday, they would have to meet him at
8.55 at Ayr. The Inspector retorted that in that case he had better
hire a car at Ayr. Finding that there was no help for it, Sergeant
Dalziel abandoned all hopes of a comfortable night of dinner, talkie
and bed at Glasgow, and reluctantly retired to the refreshment-
room for an early supper before catching the 7.30.

CHAPTER XI

INSPECTOR MACPHERSON

AT HEADQUARTERS, meanwhile, the market in evidence was looking up. At least, as Wimsey observed to the Chief Constable, it was not looking up so much as looking about in all directions.

The first piece of excitement' was provided by a young farmer, who presented himself rather diffidently at Kirkcudbright police-station and asked to see Inspector Macpherson.

It appeared that he had been having a drink at the Murray Arms in Gatehouse at about 9 o'clock on the Monday night, when Mr. Farren had come suddenly into the bar, looking very wild and queer, and had asked in a loud, peremptory tone, "Where's that b—— Campbell?" On perceiving that Campbell was not anywhere in the house, he had calmed down a little, and ordered two or three whiskeys in quick succession. The witness had tried to find out what the trouble was about, but had extracted nothing from Farren but a few vague threats. Presently, Farren had again started asking where Campbell was. Witness, who had lately come in from Kirkcudbright, and knew for a fact that Campbell was in the McClellan Arms, formed the opinion that Farren was in a dangerous mood and, in order to avert an encounter, had said, untruthfully, that he fancied he had seen Mr. Campbell in his car taking the road to Creetown. Farren had then muttered something about "getting him yet," adding a number of abusive epithets, from which witness gathered that the quarrel had something to do with Mrs. Farren. He (Farren) had then hurried out of the bar and witness had seen him ride off, not, however, in the direction of Creetown, but towards Kirkcudbright. Witness had not felt satisfied and had run out after him. When, however, Farren had got as far as the War Memorial, he had turned off to the left along the road to the golf-links. Witness had then shrugged his shoulders and dismissed the matter from his mind.

On Wednesday, however, when it became clear, through the activities of the police, that Campbell was considered to have been murdered, the incident presented itself in a more sinister light. He (witness) had consulted with the barman at the Murray Arms and with one or two men who had been in the bar with him during Farren's visit, and they had decided that the police ought to be told. Witness had been chosen as spokesman, and here he was. Witness had been reluctant to get Mr. Farren into trouble, but murder was murder and there you were.

Macpherson thanked the farmer and immediately put an inquiry through to Creetown, to find out whether Farren had, after all, followed the false trail in that direction. It was puzzling that he should have turned off by the golf-links. He had left Campbell in Kirkcudbright some three hours previously, and it was likely enough, that failing to find him in Gatehouse, he should have gone back to search for him on the Kirkcudbright road. But why the golf-links? Unless——

Unless he had gone to visit Strachan. Strachan and Farren were well known to be particularly friendly. Had there been some sort of complicity here? Had Strachan been at home between 9 and 10 on Monday night? That was comparatively easy to ascertain. The Inspector telephoned to Gatehouse for information and waited.

Then came the second excitement of the day—much more definite and encouraging. It presented itself in the shape of a small and very timid child of about ten, haled along by a determined mother, who incited her offspring to speech by alternately shaking her and offering to "skelp her ower the lug" if she did not do as she was told.

"I kenned fine," said the mother, "as she'd been up tae some mischief an' I wadna rest while I'd got it oot o' her. (Blow your nose an' speak civil to the policeman, or he'll hae ye locked up.) She's a bad girl, stravaiguin' aboot the country wi' the laddies, when she should be in her bed. But they'll no listen tae their mithers these days. Ye canna do onything wi' them."

The Inspector expressed his sympathy, and asked the lady's name.

"Mrs. McGregor, I am, an' we have our cottage between Gatehoose an' Kirkcudbright—ye'll ken the place—near by Auchenhaye. Me an' my man was away tae Kirkcudbright last Monday nicht, an' Helen was alone at hame. An' no sooner are we away than she's away oot, leavin' the door open behind her as like as not for onybody tae come in——"

"Jist a moment," said the Inspector. "This wee lassie will be Helen, I'm thinkin'."

"Ay, that's Helen. I thought it best tae bring her, seein' as this puir Mr. Campbell has been pit oot o' the way, so the postman says. An' I says tae George, if Mr. Campbell was fightin' on the road Monday night, then the pollis ought tae know it. An' George says——"

The Inspector interrupted again.

"If your wee Helen can tell us onything aboot Mr. Campbell, we wad like fine tae hear it. Now, Mistress McGregor, will ye jist let the lassie tell us her ain tale fra' the beginning. Come along, Helen, dinna be frightened, now. Speak up."

Helen, thus encouraged, began her story, which, between her own agitation and her mother's interruptions, was rather a tangled one. However, by dint of coaxing and the gift of a bag of sweeties which a constable was sent out to procure, the Inspector eventually succeeded in getting the tangle straightened out.

Mr. and Mrs. McGregor had gone over to Kirkcudbright on the Monday evening in a neighbour's car, to visit some friends, leaving Helen with strict instructions to lock the cottage door and put herself to bed. Instead of this, the abandoned child had gone out to play with some little boys belonging to a neighbouring farm. They had strayed down the road to some fields about half a mile away, where the boys were going to set some highly illegal rabbit-snares.

The Inspector shook his head slightly at this, but gave his promise that nothing dreadful should be done to the marauders, and Helen, who seemed to have been more troubled by this thought than by her mother's threats of punishment, went on more coherently with her story.

The place where they were looking for rabbits was about half-way between Gatehouse and Kirkcudbright, at a point where the road makes a very sharp and dangerous S-bend between two stone walls. It was a fine night, not dark, but dusk, and with a slight ground-mist lying in streaks on the hills. The boys had wandered well away into the fields and were intending to stay out much later, but at about a quarter to ten Helen, remembering that her parents would soon be home, had left them and started to go back by the road. She knew it was a quarter to ten, because one of the boys had a new watch which his grandfather had given him.

She crossed the fields and was just about to climb over the wall into the road, when she noticed a man in a car, drawn up stationary by the roadside and headed towards Gatehouse. The engine was running, and at that very moment, the driver pulled the car out across the road as though he was about to turn. At the same time, she heard another car approaching fast from the direction of Gatehouse.

She described the spot very exactly. It was not the sharpest and most dangerous part of the bend, where the walls are high on either side, but was what might be described as the lower bend of the S— the bend nearer Kirkcudbright. Here the turn is shallower and wider, and the wall on the side where she stood is a sunk wall, with gorse bushes and brambles beneath it. The approaching car came very quickly round the upper bend, just as the first car turned across the road, blocking the way. There was a sharp squeal of brakes, and the second car stopped, slewing violently to the right and avoiding a crash by a miracle. The driver had shouted out something and the first man had replied, and then the driver of the second car had said in a loud and angry tone, "Campbell! Of course! It would be Campbell"—or words to that effect.

Then there had been a sharp exchange of abuse, and Campbell had stopped his engine and got out. She had seen him jump on the other man's running-board. There was some sort of struggle and then, all in a moment, both men were out on the road, fighting and struggling. There were blows and a great deal of foul language. She could not see exactly what was going on, because the men were on the far side of the two cars. They had fallen to the ground and seemed to be rolling over one another. Nor could she say what the cars were like, except that Campbell's was a four-seater and the other a large two-seater with very bright lights.

When the struggle had gone on for some little time, she got a bad fright. A big spanner was flung suddenly into the air. It just missed her head and fell close beside her. She cowered down again under the wall, afraid to stay where she was and yet anxious to find out what was happening. She heard horrid sounds as though somebody was being thumped and throttled. After a little time she peeped up again and saw something which frightened her still more. A man was getting up from the roadside, and over his shoulders he had got the body of another man. From the limp way in which it hung she thought the man must be dead. She didn't scream, because she was afraid if she did that the terrible man would hear her and kill her too. He carried the body over to the two-seater car and slumped it into the passenger's seat. This was the car which stood nearest to Gatehouse. She didn't see the face of the living man, because it was all bent down under the burden he was carrying, but as he passed in front of the lights of the four-seater to get to the other car she caught a glimpse of the dead man's face and it looked very dreadful and white. She couldn't describe it, except that she thought it was clean-shaven and the eyes were shut. The terrible man then got into the driver's seat and backed the two-seater away round the bend in the direction of Gatehouse. She heard the engine change its note, and the lights moved backwards and forwards as though the car were turning round. Then she heard it move off again, and the noise of the engine gradually died away.

When it had gone, she climbed over the wall, and thought she would have a look at the four-seater car, which was still standing half-across the road. It was headed towards Gatehouse, and its lights were turned towards the off-side of the road. Before she could examine it, however, she heard footsteps coming along from the direction of Gatehouse. She hoped it was somebody who would look after her and take her home, and then, suddenly, for no reason, it came over her that this was the bad man coming back to kill her. She was dreadfully alarmed, and started to run home as fast as she could. Then she heard an engine started up and hid herself in the bushes, thinking that the bad man was pursuing her in the car. Nothing came, however, and after a time she ventured out again and hurried home. Just as she got inside her own gate, a car flashed past at a furious pace towards Kirkcudbright. She got into the cottage just as the kitchen clock was striking ten. She rushed into the bedroom and jumped into bed, just as she was, and pulled the clothes over her head.

Mrs. McGregor then took up the tale. She and her husband had got home at 10.30, and found the child shivering and crying in bed with all her clothes on. She was so terrified that they could get nothing out of her. All they could do was to scold her soundly, undress her and put her to bed properly, give her a hot drink and stand by till she fell asleep from sheer exhaustion. All next day she refused to tell them anything, but the next night she had woken them up three times by crying out in her sleep that the bad man was coming to kill her. On Wednesday evening, her father, who made a great pet of the child, succeeded in getting the story out of her, and when they heard the name of Campbell mentioned, they decided that the police ought to be told. In answer to a question of the Inspector's, Mrs. McGregor said that their kitchen clock was five or six minutes slow.

The Inspector thanked them both very much—and felt that he had indeed good reason to be grateful. He told Helen that she was a brave lassie, begged her mother not to punish her, in view of the great importance of her story, and ended the interview with a strongly-worded caution against passing the story on to anybody else.

When they had gone, he sat back to think it out. The times agreed fairly well with the doctor's report, except that he was now obliged to place the actual moment of the murder rather earlier than he had expected. As he interpreted it, Campbell and the other man had met and quarrelled, and Campbell had been killed in the struggle. The murderer must then have pushed Campbell's body into the two-seater car and concealed it somewhere at the side of the road. Then he had come back, fetched Campbell's car, and driven it back to Gatehouse, where it would, of course, be wanted to stage the fake accident. At some later time, he must have come back, collected his own car with the body in it, and—well, what? Driven it back to Gatehouse?

The Inspector grunted. There were difficulties here. Why in the world had not the murderer put Campbell's body straight away into Campbell's Morris and driven off with it there and then? Why court discovery by leaving the body by the roadside for anyone to find during the time it would take him to drive the Morris back to Gatehouse and return on his bicycle? For he must have come back on a bicycle or on foot, if he was going to take his own car away. A bicycle was the obvious thing for him to use, and he might quite well have brought it back in the dickey of the two-seater. But the difficulty remained: why had he left the corpse behind him?

It was possible, thought Macpherson—indeed, it was more than possible—that the murderer had not at that time thought out the

scheme of the alibi and the faked accident. Perhaps that explained
it. He meant simply to drive away as though nothing had happened,
and it was only afterwards that, having worked out his elaborate
plan, he had returned to collect the corpse. But no! that would not
work. It was Campbell's car that he had driven away with. The
only explanation of that was that he had already planned the faked
accident in his own mind. But that seemed simply incredible. Taking the child's account as reliable, which it appeared to be, it seemed
obvious that the encounter between Campbell and the other man
was fortuitous. Surely, in those few brief moments after the struggle,
it would hardly have been possible for the murderer to work out
his elaborate plan of escape.

And yet—*had* the meeting been, after all, fortuitous? Campbell's
behavior, if you came to think of it, suggested the exact contrary.
He had planted his car in the road at the exact point where it was
most difficult for two vehicles to pass, and when he had heard the
other car coming, he had actually drawn out so as to block the
way still further. A crazy thing to do, since it was more likely to
provoke a fatal accident than any other kind of encounter. Still, it
was known that Campbell was drunk at the time, and this might
have blinded him to the risk of a collision.

But, if the witness was to be trusted (and, after all, he could
not pick and choose, believing one bit of evidence and rejecting
another to suit his own theories), then it was clear that, whoever had
expected the meeting, it was not the murderer. And if the murderer
had not foreseen the meeting, he could not have premeditated the
crime, and so could not have prepared the faked alibi beforehand.

"Ay," said the Inspector to himself, "but that doesna follow, by
no manner of means. He might weel ha' premeditated the alibi, in-
tendin' tae commit the murder at some ither place or time. Then,
meetin' wi' Campbell in that verra convenient manner, he may ha'
cairrrit oot his nefarious design forthwith."

There still remained the difficulty about the car. And there was
the account of the man who had driven so furiously along towards
Kirkcudbright a short time after the encounter. Was he the murderer? Impossible, if the murderer was taking Campbell's car to
Gatehouse. If he was somebody else, who was he? He must have
passed the murderer on the road. He would have to be found. After
a little further thought, the Inspector gave up this part of the prob-

lem as insoluble for the moment, and turned to another aspect of the matter.

How did his story fit in, if at all, with the evidence about Farren? And here, suddenly, the Inspector gave a great smack with his hand upon the table. Of course! the times fitted perfectly, and here was the explanation of why Farren had turned up the road to the golf-links. Evidently he had seen through the young farmer's well-meant lie about Creetown. He had searched Gatehouse for Campbell and, failing to find him there, had come to the conclusion that he must be still in Kirkcudbright. He had then hurried off to see Strachan, obviously for the purpose of borrowing Strachan's car. Whether or not Strachan was an accomplice was not quite plain. Probably not. No. Again, the Inspector smacked the table with enlightenment. This explained the whole thing—the taking of the wrong car, the leaving the body and everything. Farren's original idea had been to put the guilt of the murder on Strachan. The body was to have been found in Strachan's car and the inference was to have been that Strachan had decoyed Campbell away and murdered him.

A very poor plan, of course. Strachan would immediately tell the story of how he had lent the car to Farren. Probably he would be able to produce witnesses of the transaction. Moreover, the thing would in itself have a very unlikely appearance. What man would be fool enough to leave his own car lying about with a murdered body in it? This was, in fact, the very point which had immediately struck the Inspector himself, and Farren, when he thought over what he had done, could not fail to see how unreasonable his first idea was. But while driving Campbell's car back to Gatehouse, he would have time to think matters over. A better idea would occur to him —the idea of faking the accident at the Minnoch. What then? What would he do?

He would first, of course, take Campbell's car back and put it in the garage. Then he would have to go and collect his own bicycle from Strachan's house. At that time of night it would be easy enough to do so without being seen, supposing, as was possible, that he had left the machine somewhere handy—say, just inside the garden gate.

With considerable excitement, the Inspector drew a pad of paper towards him, and began to jot down a schedule of times, heading the document boldly: "The Case against Hugh Farren."

Monday.

6 p.m.	Farren returns home and finds Campbell there. Turns him out of the house. (Jeanie's sister's evidence.)
7 p.m.	After a quarrel with his wife, during which she presumably makes some damaging admission about Campbell, Farren departs on his bicycle.
9 p.m.	Farren enters the Murray Arms, looking for Campbell. (The farmer's evidence.)
9.15 p.m.	(about). Farren goes to Strachan's house and borrows car.
9.45 p.m.	(about). Meeting with Campbell on the Kirkcudbright road. Murder of Campbell. (Helen McGregor's evidence.)
9.55 p.m.	Farren plants the body in Strachan's car.
10 p.m.	(or thereabouts). Farren starts back in Campbell's car.
10.10 p.m.	Farren arrives in Gatehouse (say five miles) and garages Campbell's car.
10.30 p.m.	Farren arrives on foot at Strachan's house to fetch bicycle.
11 p.m.	Farren arrives on bicycle at the scene of the crime.
11.10 p.m.	Farren is back with the body at Campbell's house. Hides the body in the house or garage.
11.20 p.m.	Farren returns car to Strachan's house.
11.40 p.m.	Farren is back at Campbell's house to prepare evidence of Campbell's having spent the night and breakfasted there.

The Inspector gazed with some complacency upon this schedule. Some of the times were, of course, only approximate, but the essential points corresponded well enough, and, making every allowance for Farren's being a slow walker, or bungling parts of his procedure, he had ample time to carry out all these manœuvres before Tuesday morning.

Encouraged by this, the Inspector proceeded, rather more tentatively, with the rest of his theory.

According to the evidence of "young Jock" at Borgan, the spurious Campbell had been seen sitting by the Minnoch at 10.10 on the Tuesday morning. This, therefore, gave the latest possible moment for Farren's arrival there. Actually, the Inspector thought it would probably have been earlier. Farren would certainly not have risked hanging about in Campbell's cottage very late in the morning. He would have been up and away well before 8 a.m., when Mrs. Green was due to arrive. On the other hand, he would not have started ridiculously early, because of Ferguson. It would be necessary that Ferguson, if he happened to hear Campbell's car go out, should be able to swear that it left at a reasonable hour in the morning. Accordingly, the Inspector put down at a venture—

7.30   Farren leaves Campbell's house, wearing Campbell's hat and cloak, with the body tucked away on the floor of the car and the bicycle on top, all covered by the rug.

8.35   (say). Farren arrives at the Minnoch, hides the corpse and starts on his painting.

10.10 Farren (disguised as Campbell) seen by Jock for first time.

11.05 Farren seen by Jock for the second time.

Here the Inspector paused uncertainly. Was two-and-a-half hours too long to allow for the painting of that picture? He knew very little about artists, and the thing had seemed to him a rough and sketchy affair. He must ask somebody who knew.

But there! What a thick-headed fool he was! Of course, Farren could not begin to paint till the light was good. He mightn't know much, but he did know that. He thoughtfully shook a few blots from his fountain-pen and continued.

It now seemed very probable that Farren was the passenger at Girvan. The schedule would therefore run on:—

Tuesday.

11.10 a.m.   Farren throws body into the river, puts on cap and overcoat and starts for Girvan on his bicycle.

1.07 p.m.   Arrives at Girvan. Has bicycle labelled for Ayr.

1.11 p.m.   Takes train for Ayr.

1.48 p.m.   Arrives Ayr.

Here, for the moment, the Inspector's deductions came to an end. Dalziel, he knew, was following up the trail of the bicycle.

It would be better to wait for his report before carrying the schedule any further. But he had not done so badly. He had at last succeeded in fixing the crime definitely upon one person, and in producing a plausible time-scheme to which to work. Fortunately, also, it was one that was susceptible of confirmation at several points.

He glanced over his paper again.

If Farren had been searching for Campbell in Gatehouse between 8 o'clock and 9.15, there ought to be evidence of other calls besides that at the Murray Arms. Inquiries would have to be made at the Angel and the Anwoth. But surely, before asking at public-houses, Farren would have tried Campbell's house. If so, it was almost impossible that he should not have been seen. For one thing, he would have had to cross the bridge twice, and there is no hour of the day at which the bridge at Gatehouse is not occupied by at least one idler. The bridge is the common club and gathering-place of the Gatehouse population, who meet there for the exchange of gossip, the counting of passing cars and rising trout, and the discussion of local politics. Even if, by a miracle, the bridge should have been clear on both occasions, there was the long bench outside the Anwoth Hotel, on which fishermen sit to tie knots, pat Bounce the dog and inquire of Felix the cat how many rats he has killed during the day. Lastly, supposing Farren to have escaped notice at both these points, there was always the possibility that Ferguson had been at home and had seen him come to the cottage.

Then, if Strachan's car had been taken out, surely somebody would know of it. Strachan himself might refuse information or lie stoutly in defence of his friend, but there still remained Mrs. Strachan, the child and the maid. They could not possibly all be in the plot. According to the theory, Farren had called three times at Strachans' —at about 9.15, to borrow the car; at about 10.40, to fetch the bicycle; at about 11.30, to return the car. The first and last of these visits at any rate ought to have left traces behind them.

Next, there were the three night visits to Campbell's house—the first, to garage Campbell's car; the second to bring in the body; the third, on foot, to fake the evidence. No, that was not necessarily correct. There might have been only two visits. It was more likely that on the first occasion the car had been left somewhere to be picked up on the final visit. That would reduce the risk very considerably. In fact, the body might have been transferred to Campbell's car at some quiet spot, thus doing away with the necessity of entering Campbell's place twice in two different cars—a proceeding bound to arouse suspicion. The transfer could not, naturally, have taken place in Gatehouse itself—that would have been the act of a madman. But it might have been done anywhere between Kirkcudbright and Gatehouse, or on the unfrequented piece of road between the War Memorial and Strachan's house. Or, if Strachan was indeed involved, it might have been done still more quietly and safely at Strachan's house itself.

The Inspector made an alteration or two in his time-table to correspond with this new theory, and made a note to advertise for any passer-by who might have seen a Morris car with Campbell's number-plates stationary at any point on the route.

Finally, the Tuesday morning's journey could now be corroborated. If his calculations were exact, Campbell's car must have passed through Gatehouse a little after 7.30; through Creetown about 8 o'clock; and through Newton-Stewart at about 8.15. Somebody must undoubtedly have seen it. The Newton-Stewart police were, in fact, already investigating this point, but now that he could give them the approximate times, his task would be easier.

Inspector Macpherson put a call through to Newton-Stewart and another to Gatehouse, and then turned back with renewed appetite for a fresh bite at his problem.

And now he suddenly realised, what he had momentarily overlooked in working out his times, that he had one piece of hugely important evidence lying ready to his hand. With any luck at all, he had the weapon!

That heavy spanner, which had hurtled through the air and nearly laid out the unfortunate little Helen—what else could it be but the blunt instrument which had crashed in Campbell's skull? It was perhaps odd that it should have drawn no blood, but much depended on the kind of spanner it was. Anyway, the great thing was to get hold of it. The doctor would tell him if it was a suitable weapon to have inflicted the blow. How fortunate that the corpse was still above ground! It was to be buried next day. He must get hold of that spanner instantly. The Inspector was simmering with suppressed excitement as he pulled on his cap and hastened out to his car.

CHAPTER XII

FERGUSON'S STORY

ON THE same Thursday morning that took Sergeant Dalziel and Constable Ross to Ayr and set Inspector Macpherson to work at time-schedules, Lord Peter Wimsey presented himself at the farther of the two cottages at Standing Stone Pool.

The door was opened by Mr. Ferguson in person, palette in hand, and dressed in a pair of aged flannel bags, an open shirt and a shapeless and bulging jacket. He seemed a little disconcerted at the sight of an early visitor. Wimsey hastened to explain himself.

"I don't know if you remember me. My name's Wimsey. I fancy we met once at Bob Anderson's."

"Yes, of course. Come in. When I heard you knock I thought you were going to be a pound of sausages or the man from the greengrocer's. I'm afraid the place is in rather a mess. I've been away for a couple of days, and Mrs. Green seized the opportunity to tidy up, with the result that I've had to spend a couple of hours untidying it again." He waved his hand towards a litter of canvases, rags, dippers, bottles and other paraphernalia. "I never can find anything I want in a tidy studio."

"And now I've come bargin' in and interrupting you just as you were settling down to work."

"Not a bit. It doesn't worry me. Have a drink?"

"No, thanks, I've just had one. You carry on and don't mind me."

Wimsey cleared a number of books and papers from a chair and sat down, while Ferguson returned to the contemplation of a large canvas, in which Wimsey recognized the typical Ferguson of Graham's malicious description—the tree with twisted roots, the reflection, the lump of granite and the blue distance and the general air of decorative unreality.

"Been in Glasgow, haven't you?"

"Yes. Ran up to look at the show."

"Is it a good one?"

106

"Not bad." Ferguson squeezed out some green paint on to his palette. "Craig's got some fine studies, and there's a good thing of Donaldson's. The usual allowance of duds, of course. I really went to see the Farquharsons."

He added a blob of scarlet vermilion to the semi-circle of colours, and appeared to think that his palette was made up, for he took up a bunch of brushes and began to mix two or three paints together.

Wimsey asked a few more questions about the Exhibition, and then remarked carelessly:

"So you've lost your next-door neighbour."

"Yes. I don't care to think too much about that. Campbell and I were not exactly on the best of terms, but—I wish he could have departed some other way."

"It's all rather queer," said Wimsey. "I suppose you've had the police round, asking the usual questions."

"Oh, yes. Apparently it's just as well I had an alibi. I say, Wimsey—you know all about this kind of thing—I suppose it's a fact that he was—that it wasn't an accident?"

"That does seem to be the case, I'm afraid."

"What makes them think so?"

"Oh, well, I'm an outsider, you know, and of course the police aren't giving their game away. But I think it was something to do with his being dead before he got into the river and all that kind of guff, don't you know."

"I see. I heard something about a bash on the head. What's the idea? That somebody snooped up behind and did him for his money?"

"Something like that, I daresay. Though, naturally, the police can't tell if he was robbed till they know how much he had on him. They're making inquiries at the bank and all that, I expect."

"Funny sort of place for a tramp to hang around, isn't it?"

"Oh, I dunno. There might have been some fellow sleepin' up there in the hills."

"H'm. Why couldn't he just have hit his head on the stones in falling?"

Wimsey groaned within himself. This perpetual parrying of pertinent questions was growing wearisome. One after another, everybody wanted to know the same thing. He replied, vacuously:

"Couldn't say. Seems on the whole the likeliest idea, don't it? If I were you, I'd ask the doctor johnnie."

"He wouldn't say, any more than you."

Ferguson went on for a few minutes dabbing paint on to his canvas in silence. Wimsey noticed that he seemed to be working at random, and was not surprised when he suddenly threw the palette on to the table and, turning round, demanded suddenly:

"Look here, Wimsey. Tell me one thing. It's no good your pretending you don't know, because you do. Is there any doubt at all that Campbell died the same morning that he was found?"

Wimsey felt as though he had suddenly received a jolt on the solar plexus. Whatever made the man ask that—if it was not the self-betrayal of a guilty conscience? Not being very sure how to answer, he asked, quite simply, the question he had just asked himself.

"What ever makes you ask that?"

"And why ever can't you give me a straightforward answer?"

"Well," said Wimsey, "it seems such a damn funny question. I mean—oh, well, of course—perhaps they didn't tell you about the picture?"

"What picture?"

"The picture Campbell had been painting. The paint was still wet on it. So he must have been alive that morning, or he couldn't have painted it, could he?"

"Ah!" Ferguson let out a long breath, as though his mind were relieved of some anxiety. He picked his palette up again. "No, they didn't tell me about that. That settles it, of course."

He stepped back a couple of paces and regarded his canvas with head cocked and eyes half-shut.

"But what made you ask?"

"Well," said Ferguson. He took up a palette-knife and began scraping off all the paint he had just put on. "Well—the police have been asking questions. I wondered—— See here"—his face was close to the painting and he went on scraping without looking at Wimsey—"perhaps you can tell me what I ought to do about it."

"About what?" said Wimsey.

"About the police. The first thing they did was to go into my movements, starting from Monday night. That was simple enough, as far as Tuesday went, because I took the 9.8 to Glasgow and was there all day. But I had to admit that I was here all Monday night, and they became—damnably inquisitive."

"Did they? Well, I'm blessed."

"That was why I wanted to know, don't you see? It's extremely unpleasant if—well, if there's any doubt about Campbell having been alive on the Tuesday morning."

"Yes, I see your point. Well, so far as I know—mind, I don't pretend to know everything—but so far as I know, anybody who has a complete alibi for Tuesday morning is perfectly safe."

"I'm glad of that. Not so much for my own sake, though naturally one isn't keen on being suspected of things. But—the fact is, Wimsey, I didn't quite know what to say to those fellows."

"Oh?" said Wimsey, his eyes all over the place. "I say, I like that thing over there, with the white cottages and the heather in the foreground. It sits very nicely up against the slope of the hill."

"Yes, it isn't so bad. I'll tell you what, Wimsey, after what you've said, I don't so much mind—that is, when those fellows were here, I thought there might possibly be something in it, so I—reserved judgment, so to speak. But perhaps I'd better spill the beans to you, and then you can say whether I ought to mention it. I'm not particularly anxious to make trouble. On the other hand, you know, I don't want to be an accessory to anything."

"If my opinion is worth anything," said Wimsey, "I'd say, cough it up. After all, if anybody did do the poor devil in, it's rather up to one to get it detected, and so on."

"I suppose it is, though one can't bring people to life again, unfortunately. If one could, of course, one wouldn't hesitate. Still——"

"Besides," said Wimsey, "you never know which way evidence is going to work. People sometimes hang on to information with the bright idea of shieldin' their husbands or sons or best girl, and give the police a hell of a time, and when it does come out, it proves to be the one thing in the world that was wanted to save their necks —the husbands' and sons' and best girls' necks I mean, of course."

Ferguson looked dissatisfied.

"If I only knew why they wanted to know about Monday night," he said, slowly.

"They want to find the last person who saw the man alive," said Wimsey, promptly. "It's always done. It's part of the regular show. You get it in all the mystery stories. Of course, the last person to see him never commits the crime. That would make it too easy. One of these days I shall write a book in which two men are seen to walk down a cul-de-sac, and there is a shot and one man is found murdered and the other runs away with a gun in his hand, and after twenty chapters stinking with red herrings, it turns out that the man with the gun did it after all."

"Well, nine times out of ten he has done it—in real life, that is —hasn't he? Well, I don't know."

"What *have* you told the police, anyhow?" asked Wimsey, losing patience a little, and fiddling with a tube of white paint.

"I said I'd been at home all evening, and they asked if I had seen or heard anything suspicious next door. I said I hadn't, and I can't say exactly that I did, you know. They asked if I'd seen Campbell come home and I said I hadn't seen him, but I'd heard the car come in. That was a little after 10. I heard it strike, and thought it was about time I pottered off to bed, as I had to catch a train next morning. I'd had a last drink and tidied up and picked out a book to read and had just toddled upstairs when I heard him."

"Was that the last you heard of him?"

"Ye—es. Except that I had a hazy kind of idea that I heard the door open and shut again shortly afterwards, as if he had gone out again. But I can't say for certain. He must have come back again later, if he did go out, because I saw him go out again in his car in the morning."

"Well, that's valuable. What time was that?"

"Some time between 7.30 and 7.45—I can't say to the moment. I was just finishing dressing. I had to get my own breakfast, you see, so as to catch the 'bus for the 9.8. It's six and a half miles to that bally station."

"You actually saw Campbell in the car?"

"Oh, yes, I saw him all right. At least, I suppose if I had to go into the witness-box, I could only swear to his clothes and general appearance. I didn't see his face. But there was no doubt it was Campbell all right."

"I see." Wimsey's heart, which had missed a beat, calmed down again. He had seen the handcuffs closing on Ferguson. If he had sworn to seeing Campbell alive at an hour when Wimsey knew him to have been dead——! But things were not made as easy as all that for detectives.

"What had he got on?"

"Oh, that hideous check coat and the famous hat. There's no mistaking them."

"No. Well, what is it you didn't let up about?"

"One or two other things. First of all—though I don't see that that can have had anything to do with it—there was a sort of hullabaloo about 8 o'clock on Monday evening."

"Was there? I say, Ferguson, I'm so sorry, I've burst a perfectly good Winsor & Newton tube. It's my beastly habit of fidgeting. It's all bulged out at the end."

"Has it? Oh, it doesn't matter. Roll it up. Here's a rag. Did you get it on your coat?"

"No, thanks, it's all right. What sort of hullabaloo?"

"Fellow came round banging on Campbell's door and using language. Campbell was out—rather fortunately, because I gathered there was a perfectly good shindy brewing."

"Who was the fellow?"

Ferguson glanced at Wimsey, then back at his canvas, and said in a low tone:

"As a matter of fact, I'm afraid it was Farren."

Wimsey whistled.

"Yes, I stuck my head out and told him not to make such a filthy row and he asked me where the something-or-other that what-d'ye-call it Campbell was. I said I hadn't seen him all day and advised Farren to remove himself. So then he started some rigmarole about always finding the so-and-so hanging round his place and he wanted to have it out with him, and if once he laid hands on Campbell he would do all kinds of nasty things to him, inside and out. Of course, I paid no attention to it. Farren's always going off the deep end, but he's like the Queen of Hearts—never executes nobody, you know. I told Farren to forget about it, and he told me to go and do this and that to myself, and by that time I'd got fed up, so I retorted that he could go away and hang himself, and he said that was exactly what he was going to do, only he must slay Campbell first. So I said, Right-ho! but not to disturb hard-working people. So he hung about a bit and then took himself off."

"On his two legs?"

"No, on a bicycle."

"Oh, yes, of course. He could hardly have walked from Kirk-cudbright. I say, Ferguson, how much is there in that business about Mrs. Farren?"

"Damn all, if you ask me. I think Campbell was fond of her in his way, but she's much too high-minded to get herself into trouble. She likes to do the motherly business—inspiration, you know, and influence of a pure woman. Do good, and never mind what the rude world says. Sweetness and beautiful lives and all that rot. Dash it! What have I done with the cobalt? Can't stick the woman, you know, never could. Oh! I've got it in my pocket, as usual. Yes. As you may know, my wife and I don't live together, and Gilda Farren takes it upon herself to lecture me. At least, I've choked her off now, but she once had the impertinence to try and 'bring us together.' Blast her cheek! She created a damned embarrassing situation. Not that it matters now. But I can't stick those interfering, well-meaning bitches. Now, whenever she meets me, she looks mournfully and forgivingly in my eyes. I can't stand that kind of muck."

"Beastly," agreed Wimsey. "Like the people who offer to pray for you. Did Farren depart altogether, or did he by any chance come back?"

"I don't know. That's just the point. *Somebody* came later on."

"When was that?"

"Just after midnight, but I didn't get up to see who it was. Somebody knocked at the door and presently whoever it was went in, but I didn't bother to get up and look. And then I went off to sleep."

"And didn't hear the person go?"

"No. I've no idea how long he—or she—stayed."

"She?"

"I say he or she, because I really haven't the least idea which it was. I don't think it was Farren, though, because I fancy I heard a car. You might give me that rag, if you've finished with it. I'm really frightfully vague about the whole business. To tell the truth, I thought it was Jock Graham up to his games again."

"That's quite likely. H'm. If I were you, Ferguson, I think I'd mention it."

"What? Just that midnight visitor, do you mean? Or Farren as well?"

"Farren too. But particularly the midnight person. After all, he apparently *was* the last to see Campbell alive."

"What do you mean? I saw him in the morning."

"Saw him to speak to," said Wimsey. "He might be able to give the police valuable help, if they could get hold of him."

"Why hasn't he come forward, then?"

"Oh, Lord! a hundred reasons. He may have been selling illicit salmon, or, as you say, he may have been she. One never knows."

"True. All right. I'll come clean, as they say. I'd better do it at once, or they'll think I know more than I do."

"Yes," said Wimsey. "I shouldn't waste any time."

He wasted none himself, but drove straight back to Kirkcudbright, where he met Inspector Macpherson just stepping into his car.

CHAPTER XIII

LORD PETER WIMSEY

"HULLO—ULLO—ULLO!" cried Wimsey. "Where are you off to? I've got something for you."

The Inspector clambered out of the car again and greeted Wimsey cordially.

"Weel, noo," said he, "I had something tae show ye, too. Wull ye step intae the station a wee while?"

The Inspector was in no way sorry to get someone to admire his time-schedule, and Wimsey applauded generously. "What's more," said he, "I can fill up a blank or two for you."

He unfolded his budget, while the Inspector sat licking his lips.

"Ay," said the latter, " 'tis a' clear as daylight. Puir Farren—he must ha' been in a rare way tae go and do such a thing. Peety we ha' lost sae much time. It's a hundred to one he's oot o' the country by noo."

"Out of the country or out of the world," suggested Wimsey.

"Ay, that's a fact. He said he wad hae'd oot wi' Campbell an' then mak' away wi' himsel'. They often says it an' doesna do't, but whiles they do't a' the same."

"Yes," said Wimsey.

"I'm thinking," pursued Macpherson, "we'll no be far wrang if we send a search-party up into them hills beyond Creetown. Ye'll mind the sad affair there was a year or two ago, with the puir woman as threw hersel' doon one o' the auld lead-mines. Where there's been trouble once there may be again. It wad be a terrible thing if the puir man's body was to be lyin' up yonder and us not tae find it. Ay. D'ye ken, my lord, I'm thinkin' this'll juist be the verra thing that Mistress Farren's fearin', though she disna like tae say so."

"I absolutely agree," said Wimsey. "I think she believes her husband's killed himself, and daren't say so because she suspects he may have done the murder. You'd better get your sleuth-hounds out at once, Inspector, and then we'll pop along and have a hunt for this spanner."

"There's a terrible deal of work tae be done," said Macpherson. "I'll doot we'll no have men enough for a' these investigations."

"Cheer up," said Wimsey. "You've pretty well narrowed it down now, haven't you?"

"Ay," replied the Inspector, cautiously, "but I'm no countin' upon it. There's mony a slip, an' I'm no losin' sight o' ony o' my suspectit pairsons, juist yet awhile."

Wee Helen had described the site of Campbell's encounter with the man in the car so exactly that there was no necessity to take her along with them to point it out. "We'll be mair comfortable and private-like on our own," observed Macpherson, and heaved himself with a sigh of contentment into the front seat of Wimsey's huge Daimler. Six or seven minutes brought them to the bend. Here Wimsey deposited the Inspector, and here, after stowing the car out of the way of other travellers, he joined him in his search.

According to Helen's story, she had taken up her position beneath the sunk wall, on the left-hand side of the road going towards Gatehouse. Wimsey and Macpherson therefore started, one at either end of the bend, searching within a couple of yards from the wall and working gradually towards one another. It was back-breaking exercise, for the grass was rather long, and as he groped, Wimsey found himself versifying after the manner of the old man sitting on a gate.

> *"But I was scheming to devise*
> *A wheeze to catch the spanner,*
> *With magnets of uncommon size,*
> *And sell it for a tanner,*
>
> *Or train a pack of skilful hounds*
> *To scent it like a rabbit,*
> *And something, something, something—ounds*
> *And something, something habit."*

He paused and straightened his spine.

"Not very lively," he mused; "better, I think, for a Heath Robinson picture.

Or purchase half a ton of flints
And hurl them in the dark
And something or the other ending in the glints,
And a last line ending in see the spark.

I ought to have brought Bunter. This is menial toil. It's really beneath the dignity of any human being, unless one is like the army of Napoleon which is popularly reputed to have marched on its belly. Hullo! hullo! hullo!"

His walking-stick—which he carried with him everywhere, even in the car, for fear that by some accident he might be obliged to stagger a few steps when he got to places—struck against something which gave out a metallic noise. He stooped, looked, and let out a loud yell.

The Inspector came galloping up.

"Here you are," said Wimsey, with conscious pride.

It was a big King Dick spanner, slightly rusty with the dew, lying within a couple of feet of the wall.

"Ye've no touched it?" asked the Inspector, anxiously.

"What do you take me for?" retorted Wimsey, hurt.

Macpherson knelt down, drew out a tape-measure and solemnly measured the distance of the spanner from the wall. He then peered over the wall into the road and, drawing out his notebook, made a careful plan of the exact position. After that, he took out a large jack-knife and thrust it in among the stones of the wall, by way of making the indication still more precise, and only after performing these rites did he very gingerly lift the spanner, covering his fingers with a large white handkerchief and wrapping the folds of the linen tenderly about it.

"There might be finger-prints, ye ken," said he.

"Ay, there might," agreed Wimsey, in the language of the country.

"And then we've only tae get the prints of Farren and compare them. How will we do that now?"

"Razor," said Wimsey, "palette-knife, picture-frames, pots—anything in his studio. Studios are never dusted. I suppose the actual riot took place on the other side of the road. There won't be much trace of it now, I'm afraid."

The Inspector shook his head.

"It's no likely, wi' cars and cattle passin' up and doon. There was no bloodshed, an' this dry grass takes no marks, mair's the pity. But we'll tak' a look round."

The tarmac itself betrayed nothing, and the indications in the grass were so vague that nothing could be made of them. Presently, however, Wimsey, beating about among a tuft of bramble and bracken, uttered a small astonished noise.

"What's that?" asked Macpherson.

"What indeed?" said Wimsey. "It's one of these problems, Inspector, that's what it is. Did you ever hear of the Kilkenny cats that fought till only their tails were left behind them? Now here are two gentlemen having a fight, and both of them spirited away, leaving only a tuft of hair. And what's more, it's the wrong colour. What do you make of that?"

He held up in his hand a tuft of curly blackness suggestive of an Assyrian wall-painting.

"That's a queer thing," said Macpherson.

"Cut off, not torn out," said Wimsey. He pulled a lens from his pocket and examined the trophy carefully. "It's soft and silky, and it's never been trimmed at the distal end; it might come from one of those sweet old-fashioned, long-haired girls, but the texture's a bit on the coarse side. It's a job for an expert, really, to say where it does come from."

The Inspector handled it carefully and peered through the lens with as much intelligence as he could assume on the spur of the moment.

"What makes ye say it's never been trimmed?" he inquired.

"See how the points taper. Is there a female in the country with hair so black and so curly, that's never been shingled or bingled? Were our blokes wrestling for a love-token, Inspector? But whose? Not Mrs. Farren's, unless she's turned from a Burne-Jones to a Rossetti in the night. But if it isn't Mrs. Farren's, Inspector, where's our theory?"

"Hoots!" said the Inspector. "Maybe it has naething tae do wi' the case at a'."

"How sensible you are," said Wimsey, "and how imperturbable. Calm without something or other, without o'erflowing, full. Talking of that, how soon will the pubs be open? Hullo! here's another bunch of hair. Some love-token! I say, let's trot home with this and interview Bunter. I've a notion it may interest him."

"Ye think so?" said Macpherson. "Weel, that's no a bad idea, neither. But I'm thinkin' we'll better be away tae Newton-Stewart first. We'll have tae find the doctor and get the undertaker tae open the coffin. I've a great fancy tae see how this spanner fits yon wound in the heid."

"Very good," said Wimsey, "so have I. But just a minute. We'd better have a look first and see if we can find out what happened to the body. The murderer stuck it into his car and drove off towards Gatehouse with it. He can't have gone far, because he very soon came back for Campbell's Morris, so there ought to be a gate about here somewhere. In fact, I fancy I remember seeing one."

The search did not take long. About fifty yards farther along the bend they came to a rusty iron gate on the right-hand side. This led into a grassy lane which, after about thirty yards, turned abruptly to the left and was hidden behind some bushes.

"Here's the place," said Wimsey. "There's been a car up here lately. You can see where the wing scraped the post. The gate has a hook and chain—easy enough to undo. He must have backed it in up to the bend. Then, if he turned the lights off, it would be absolutely invisible from the road. There's no difficulty about that, and there's no other possible hiding-place for a mile or so, I'm certain of that. Well, that's uncommonly satisfactory. I gloat, as Stalky says. Back we go to the car, Inspector. Spit on your hands and grasp the coachwork firmly. I'm feeling sprightly, and I'm going to break all records between here and Newton-Stewart."

.   .   .   .

Dr. Cameron was greatly interested in the spanner, and experienced so much difficulty in keeping his hands off it, that it was thought best to have it tested for finger-prints before anything else was done. By the combined exertions of the police-staff, the local photographer and Wimsey, this was done. A magnificent thumb-print made its appearance after a dusting with mercury powder, and a perfectly good negative was "secured," to use the journalist's pet phrase.

In the meantime, a constable had rounded up the undertaker, who arrived in great excitement, swallowing the last fragments of

his tea. A slight further delay was caused by its occurring to somebody that the Fiscal should be notified. The Fiscal, fortunately
enough, happened to be in the town, and joined the party, explaining to Wimsey as they drove along to the mortuary that this was
the most painful case he had handled in the whole of his experience,
and that he had been much struck by the superiority of the Scots
law to the English in these matters. "For," said he, "the publicity
of a coroner's inquest is bound to give much unnecessary pain to
the relations, which is avoided by our method of private investigation."

"That is very true," said Wimsey, politely, "but think of all the
extra fun we get from the Sunday newspapers. Inquests are jam to
them."

"We then proceeded," ran Inspector Macpherson's official notes
on this occasion, "to the mortuary, where the coffin was unscrewed
in the presence of the Fiscal, Dr. Cameron, James McWhan (the
undertaker), Lord Peter Wimsey and myself, and the body of
Campbell extracted. On comparison of the spanner formerly mentioned with the wounds upon the head of the corpse, Dr. Cameron
gave it as his opinion that a contused area upon the left cheek-bone
agreed exactly in contour with the head of the said spanner and
had in all probability been inflicted by that or by a similar instrument. With regard to the larger contused area upon the temple,
which had occasioned death, Dr. Cameron could not speak with
certainty, but said that its appearance was consistent with the use
of the said spanner."

After this triumphant entry, which bears the marks of considerable
literary effort, appears another.

"Acting upon the suggestion of Lord Peter Wimsey" (the Inspector was a just man, giving honour where it was due, regardless
of his own lacerated feelings), "the fingerprints of the corpse were
then taken." (This last phrase is erased, and a better locution substituted), "a record was then secured of the finger-prints of the
corpse. On comparison of this record with the thumb-print found
upon the spanner, these were both found to be identical. Acting
upon instructions, I dispatched both records to Glasgow for expert
scrutiny."

In this stately paragraph, nothing is said of the bitter disappointment experienced by the Inspector. It had seemed to him, with that

finger-print in his hands, as though his case were concluded, and now, suddenly, he was taken up and cast down into the old outer darkness of uncertainty and gnashing of teeth. But his behaviour was handsome to the last degree.

"It's a great maircy," said he to Wimsey, "that your lordship should ha' taken the notion tae have that done. It wad never have entered my heid. We might have eliminated a' six suspects on the strength o' that deceivin' finger-print. It was a gran' notion of yours, my lord, a gran' notion."

He sighed deeply.

"Cheer up," said Wimsey. "It's all the luck of the game. Come and have a spot of dinner with me at the Galloway Arms."

Now that was an unlucky suggestion.

.   .   .   .

The gathering in Bob Anderson's studio was well attended that night. Bob was an artist, the geniality of whose temperament is best vouched for by the fact that it had never for one moment occurred to anybody engaged on the case that he could by any chance have hated Campbell, damaged Campbell, or been mixed up for a single moment in the Campbell mystery. He had lived in Kirkcudbright for nearly as many years as Gowan, and was extremely popular, not only with all the artists, but also with the local inhabitants, particularly with the fishermen and the men employed about the harbour. He seldom visited anybody, preferring to be at home every evening in the week, and all the news of the town was bound to filter through Bob's studio in time.

When Wimsey poked his long nose round the door on that Thursday evening, he found a full house already assembled. Miss Cochran and Miss Selby were there, of course, and Jock Graham (in a remarkable costume, comprising a fisherman's jersey, a luggage strap, riding-breeches and rope-soled deck-shoes), and Ferguson (rather surprisingly, for he did not as a rule go out of an evening), the Harbour-master, the doctor, Strachan (his black eye almost faded out), a Mrs. Terrington, who worked in metal, a long, thin, silent man, called Temple, of whom Wimsey knew nothing except that his handicap was five at St. Andrews, and finally, Mrs., Miss and young Mr. Anderson. The babble of conversation was terrific.

Wimsey's entrance was greeted by a welcoming shout.

"Here he is! Here he is! Come away in! Here's the man to tell us all about it!"

"All about what?" said Wimsey, knowing only too well. "What to back for the Leger?"

"Leger be damned. All about this business of poor Campbell. It's terrible the way the police come running in and out of one's house. One doesn't feel safe for a moment. Luckily I've got a cast-iron alibi, or I'd begin to feel I was a criminal myself."

"No, Bob, not you," said Wimsey.

"Oh, ye never know these days. But very fortunately I was at dinner with the Provost Monday night and didn't get home till midnight, and on Tuesday morning I was showing myself up and down St. Cuthbert's Street. But tell us, Wimsey, you that's hand in glove with the police——"

"I'm not allowed to tell anything," said Wimsey, plaintively. "You mustn't tempt me. It's not fair. I could not love thee, Bob, so much, loved I not honour more. Besides, I'm supposed to be finding things out, not giving information away."

"Well, you're welcome to all we know," said Miss Selby.

"Am I?" said Wimsey. "Tell me, then, how many hundred people in the country, besides Jock, knew that Campbell meant to go up to the Minnoch on Tuesday?"

"You had better ask who did not?" said the doctor. "He said so here on the Sunday night. He'd been making a preliminary sketch that afternoon. Monday he was going to fish in some wonderful place he wouldn't tell anybody about——"

"I know where it was, all the same," put in Graham.

"You would. And Tuesday he was going to paint the Minnoch if the weather held. You heard him say so, Sally."

"I did," said Miss Cochran.

"I was here, too," said Ferguson, "and I remember it perfectly. I fancy I said something about it to Farren on the Monday morning, because he had a tea-party or something fixed up for Brighouse Bay on Tuesday and said he hoped they wouldn't run into Campbell."

"I knew, too," said Strachan. "My wife and I met him up there on Sunday, as I think I mentioned to Wimsey."

Wimsey nodded. "Campbell seems to have been more communicative than usual," he remarked.

"Och," said Bob, "Campbell was not such a bad fellow if you took him the right way. He had an aggressive manner, but I believe it was mostly due to a feeling that he was out of everything. He used to have awful arguments with people——"

"He was an opinionated man," said the Harbour-master.

"Yes, but that made it all the more amusing. One couldn't take Campbell seriously."

"No, one couldn't," said Graham.

"Gowan did, for one," said the doctor.

"Ah, but Gowan takes everything very seriously, and himself most of all."

"All the same," said Mrs. Anderson, "Campbell ought not to have spoken of Gowan as he did."

"Gowan's away, isn't he? They told me he had gone to London. By the way, Wimsey, what's happened to Waters?"

"I haven't the foggiest. As far as I can make out, he's supposed to be in Glasgow. Did you see anything of him, Ferguson?"

"No. The police asked me that. Do I take it that Waters is suspected of anything?"

"Waters was here on Sunday night," observed the doctor, "but he didn't stay very long after Campbell came in."

"You're a great man for facts, doctor. But if Waters was in Glasgow he couldn't have been up at the Minnoch."

"The odd thing," said Miss Selby, "is that nobody saw him in Glasgow. He was supposed to be going by our train, but he didn't, did he, Mr. Ferguson?"

"I didn't see him. But I wasn't looking out for him particularly. I saw you two get in at Dumfries, and I saw you again with your party at St. Enoch Station. But I went off in rather a hurry. I had some shopping to do before I got down to the show. As a matter of fact, the whole thing was very irritating. Something went wrong with my magneto, otherwise I should have got up early and run over to catch the 7.30 express from Dumfries, instead of waiting for that ghastly 11.22, which stops at every station."

"Rather than travel by a confirmed stopper," said Wimsey, "I'd have waited a little longer and gone by the 1.46."

"Taking the 10.56 from Gatehouse, you mean?"

"Or the 11 o'clock 'bus. It gets you in to Dumfries at 12.25."

"No, it doesn't," said Strachan. "That's the Sunday 'bus. The week-day 'bus goes at 10."

"Well, anyway, I couldn't," said Ferguson, "because I'd made an appointment to meet a man at the show at 3.15, and the 1.46 doesn't get in to Glasgow till 3.34. So I had to make a martyr of myself. And the sickening thing was that my man never turned up after all. I found a note at my hotel, saying he'd been called to see a sick relative."

"Sick relatives ought to be forbidden by law," said Wimsey.

"Yes; I was damned fed-up. However, I took my mag. along to Sparkes & Crisp, and it's still there, confound it. Something obscure in the armature winding, as far as I could make out—I don't think they knew themselves. And it's practically a new car, too; only done a few thousand. I'm claiming under guarantee."

"Oh, well," said Wimsey, consolingly, "Sparkes & Crisp will provide a nice little alibi for you."

"Yes; I don't know exactly when I got there, but they'll be able to say. I took a tram up. I should think I got to their place about 3 o'clock. The train was a quarter of an hour late, of course; it always is."

"It was nearer twenty minutes late," said Miss Selby, severely. "We were very much annoyed about it. It cut down our time with Kathleen."

"Local trains always are late," said Wimsey. "It's one of the rules. It's done so that the guard and the engine-driver can step out and admire the station-master's garden at every stop. You know those gardening competitions they have in railway magazines. Well, that's how they're run. The guard gets off at Kirkgunzeon or Brig o' Dee with a yard measure in his hand and measures the prize marrow and says: 'Twa fut four inches—that'll no dew, Mr. McGeoch. They've got one at Dalbeattie that beats ye by twa inches. Here, George, come and look at this.' So the engine-driver strolls over and says, 'Och, ay, imph'm, ye'll dew weel tae gie't a mulch o' liquid guano and aspidistra tonic.' And then they go back to Dalbeattie and tell them that the marrow at Kirkgunzeon is hauling up on them hand over fist. It's no good laughing. I know they do it. If not, what on earth do they do, hanging everlastingly about at these three-by-four stations?"

"You ought to be ashamed of yourselves," said Miss Anderson, "talking such nonsense, with poor Mr. Campbell lying dead."

"They're burying him to-morrow, aren't they?" said Jock Graham, suddenly and tactlessly. "At Gatehouse. Does one go? I haven't any wedding-garments."

"Oh, dear," said Bob. "Never thought of that. We must go, I suppose. Look odd if we didn't. Besides, I'd like to show respect to the poor fellow. Surely we can go as we are."

"You can't go in those terrific tweeds, Bob," said Miss Selby.

"Why not?" demanded Bob. "I can feel just as sorry in a check suit as in a frock-coat smelling of moth-balls. I shall go in my ordinary working-clothes—with a black tie, naturally. Can you see me in a top-hat?"

"Dad, you are dreadful," said Miss Anderson.

"My God!" said Wimsey. "I hope Bunter has remembered to order a wreath. I expect he has. He remembers everything. Did you decide to send one from the Club, Strachan?"

"Oh, yes," said Strachan. "We all agreed it was the right thing to do."

"The trouble with Campbell," said the five-handicap man unexpectedly, "was that he was a bad loser. A slice off the tee or a foozled approach-shot would put him off his game for the afternoon."

Having unburdened his mind of this criticism, he retired in obscurity again and spoke no more.

"He was having a one-man show in London this autumn, wasn't he?" said Ferguson.

"I expect his sister will carry on with that," said the doctor. "It will probably be a great success."

"I never know what the doctor means by those remarks," said young Anderson. "What's the sister like, by the way? Has anybody seen her?"

"She called here yesterday," said Mrs. Anderson. "A nice, quiet girl. I liked her."

"What did she think about it all?"

"Well, Jock, what could she think? She seemed very much distressed, as you would expect."

"No idea of who might have done it, I suppose?" suggested Wimsey.

"No—I gathered that she hadn't seen anything of her brother for some years. She's married to an engineer in Edinburgh, and, though she didn't say much, I rather fancy the two men didn't hit it off very well."

"It's all very unpleasant and mysterious," said Mrs. Anderson. "I hope very much it'll all turn out to be a mare's nest. I can't really believe that anybody about here could have committed a murder. I think the police are just anxious to make a sensation. Probably it was only an accident, after all."

The doctor opened his mouth, but caught Wimsey's eye, and shut it again. Wimsey guessed that his colleague at Newton-Stewart must have said something, and hastened to lead the conversation away on lines which would at the same time convey a warning and possibly also elicit useful information.

"A great deal," he said, "depends on how long Campbell actually spent at the Minnoch on Tuesday. We know—at least, Ferguson knows—that he started out about 7.30. It's about twenty-seven miles—say he got up there between 8.30 and 8.45. How long would it take him to do his sketch?"

"Starting from scratch?"

"That's just what one can't be sure of. But say he set out with a blank canvas."

"Which he probably did," said Strachan. "He showed me his rough sketch in his sketch-book on Sunday, and on Monday he didn't go up."

"So far as we know," said Ferguson.

"Exactly. So far as we know."

"Well, then?" said Wimsey.

"We haven't seen the picture," said Bob. "So how can we tell?"

"Look here," said Wimsey. "I know how we could get a rough idea. Supposing all you fellows were each to start off with a panel that size and a rough charcoal outline—could you kind of fudge something up, imitating Campbell's style as much as possible, while I stood over you with a stop-watch? We could take the average of your speeds and get a sort of line on the thing that way."

"Reconstruct the crime?" said young Anderson, laughing.

"In a sense."

"But Wimsey, that's all very well. No two men paint at the same rate, and if I, for instance, tried to paint like Campbell, with a palette-knife, I should make an awful muck of it, and get no-where."

"Possibly—but then your styles are so very unlike, Ferguson. But Jock can imitate anybody, I know, and Waters said it would be easy to fake a perfectly plausible Campbell. And Bob here is an expert with the knife."

"I'll be sporting, Lord Peter," said Miss Selby, surprisingly. "If it's really going to do any good, I don't mind making a fool of myself."

"That's the spirit," said Graham. "I'm on, Peter."

"I don't mind having a dash at it," said Strachan.

"All right, then," said Bob. "We all will. Have we got to go up to the scene of the tragedy, old man?"

"Starting at 7.30?" said Miss Selby.

"It's no good getting there too early," objected Strachan, "because of the light."

"That's one of the things we've got to prove," said Wimsey. "How soon he could have got going on it."

"Ugh!" said Bob Anderson. "It's against my principles to get up in the small hours."

"Never mind," said Wimsey. "Think how helpful it may be."

"Oh, well—is it to-morrow morning you're thinking of?"

"The sooner the better."

"Will you convey us there?"

"In the utmost luxury. And Bunter shall provide hot coffee and sandwiches."

"Be sporting," said Miss Selby.

"If we must——" said Bob.

"I think it's monstrous," said Ferguson. "Going over in car-loads like that and having a picnic. What will people take us for?"

"What does it matter what they take us for?" retorted Graham. "I think you're absolutely right, Wimsey. Damn it all, we *ought* to do what we can. I'll be there. Come on, Ferguson, don't you let us down."

"I'll come if you like," said Ferguson, "but I do think it's rather disgusting, all the same."

"Miss Selby, Bob, Strachan, Ferguson, Graham, and me as timekeeper. Coffee and palette-knives for six. Strachan, you'd better run Ferguson and Graham up, and I'll take the Kirkcudbright contingent. I'll get a police witness as well. That's fine."

"I believe you enjoy it, Lord Peter," said Mrs. Terrington. "I suppose you get carried away by these investigations."

"They are always interesting," admitted Wimsey. "Every man is thrilled by his own job. Isn't that so, Mr. Doulton?" he added, addressing the Harbour-master.

"That's so, my lord. I remember having tae du much the same thing, mony years since, in an inquest upon a sailing-vessel that ran aground in the estuary and got broken up by bumping herself to bits in a gale. The insurance folk thocht that the accident wasna a'tegither straightforward. We tuk it upon oorsels tae demonstrate that wi' the wind and tide settin' as they did, the boat should ha' been well away fra' the shore, if they had started at the hour they claimed to ha' done. We lost the case, but I've never altered my opeenion."

"That estuary can be awkward if you don't know the channels," said Bob.

"Ay, that's true. But a man of experience, as this skipper was, should no ha' made such a mistake, unless indeed he was drunk at the time."

"That's a thing that might happen to anybody," said Wimsey. "Who were those fellows that were kicking up such a row in the town over the week-end?"

"Och, they were juist a couple a' English gentlemen fra' the wee yacht that was anchored up by the Doon," said the Harbour-master, placidly. "There was nae harm in them at a'. Verra decent, hospitable fellows, father and son, and knew how tae handle a boat. They were aff on Tuesday mornin', makin' their way up the west coast to Skye, they tell't me."

"Well, they've got fine weather for it," said the doctor.

"Ay, imph'm. But I'm thinkin' there'll be a bit of a change the nicht. The wind's shiftin', and there's one o' they depressions coming over fra' Iceland."

"I wish they'd keep their depressions at home," grumbled Wimsey, thinking of his experiment.

* * * * * * * *

The meeting did not break up till 11 o'clock. Stepping out into the street, Wimsey became immediately aware of the change in the weather. A soft dampness beat on his cheek, and the sky was overcast with a close veil of drifting cloud.

He was about to turn into Blue Gate Close, when he saw, far away at the end of the street, the red tail-lamp of a car. It was difficult to judge distances in the close blackness, but his instinct seemed to tell him that the car was standing before Gowan's house. Possessed by curiosity, he strolled down the street towards it. Presently, straining eyes and ears, he seemed to hear a stir of low voices, and to see two muffled figures cross the pavement.

"Something's happening!" he said to himself, and started to run, noiselessly, on rubber soles. Now he heard distinctly enough the starting of the engine. He redoubled his speed.

Something tripped him—he stumbled and sprawled headlong, bruising himself painfully. When he picked himself up, the red tail-light was vanishing round the corner.

The Harbour-master appeared suddenly at his elbow, assisting him to rise.

"It's a fair scandal," said the Harbour-master, "the way they doorsteps is built right oot tae the edge o' the pavement. Are ye hurt, my lord? The Council should du something aboot it. I remember, when I was a young man——"

"Excuse me," said Wimsey. He rubbed his knees and elbows. "No harm done. Forgive me, won't you? I have an appointment."

He dashed off in the direction of the police-station, leaving the Harbour-master to stare after him in surprise.

CHAPTER XIV

CONSTABLE ROSS

THE next day dawned wild and stormy, with heavy rain and violent squalls of southwest wind. Wimsey's sketching-party was perforce postponed. Nevertheless, the day was not wholly lacking in incident.

The first thing that happened was the sudden return of Constable Roos from Ayr, with a remarkable story.

He had gone out on the previous night to Kilmarnock, to investigate the history of a bicyclist in a burberry, who had been seen to leave Ayr station shortly after 1.48. This trail, however, had petered out. He found the man without the least difficulty. He proved to be a perfectly innocent and respectable young farmer who had come to the station to inquire about some goods lost in transit.

Ross had then made further inquiries in and about the town, with the following result.

"The bookstall clerk had seen the passenger in grey pass his bookstall at 1.49, in the direction of the exit. He had not seen him actually leave the station, because of the corner of the bookstall, which cut off his view of the exit.

A taxi-driver, standing just outside the station exit, had seen a young man in a burberry come out with a bicycle. (This was the farmer whom Ross subsequently interviewed.) He also saw a youngish man in a cap and a grey flannel suit come out, carrying a small attaché-case, but without a bicycle. A fare had then hailed him and he had driven away, but he fancied he had seen the man in grey turn into a small side-street. This would be about two minutes after the Stranraer train came in—say, at 1.50.

At about 2.20, a porter who was taking along a truck of luggage to the 2.25 for Carlisle, noticed a man's bicycle standing against a board which displayed time-tables and railway posters, just above the bays on the booking-hall side of the platform. He examined it and found that it had an L.M.S. label for Euston.

He knew nothing about it, except that he had a dim impression that it had been there for some little time. Supposing that it was in charge of one of his colleagues and possibly belonged to some passenger who was breaking his journey at Carlisle, he left it where it was. At 5 o'clock, however, he noticed that it was still there, and asked the other porters about it. None of them remembered handling it or labelling it, but since it was there, with its label all in order, he did his duty by it and put it into the 5.20 express for Euston. If the passenger to whom it belonged had travelled by the 2.25, the bicycle would arrive in Euston by the same train as himself, for the 2.25 does not run to Euston, and London passengers would have to change at Carlisle and wait two-and-a-quarter hours till the 5.20 came in to take them on.

This porter, having had his attention particularly directed to the bicycle, had examined it fairly closely. It was a Raleigh, not new and not in very good condition, but with good tyres front and back.

Ross jumped when he heard this description, and eagerly examined all the porters. He completely failed, however, to discover the man who had affixed the Euston label to it, or to get any information about its owner.

The booking-clerk had issued ten tickets to Carlisle by the 2.25 —five third singles, three singles to returns, a first single and a first return—and two third singles to Euston. He had issued no long-distance bicycle-ticket by that train or by the 5.20, which had carried eight passengers from Ayr. A porter, not the same man who had put the bicycle into the 5.20, remembered a gentleman in a grey suit who had travelled to Carlisle on the 2.25 without luggage; he had asked him some question about the route, which was via Mauchline. This person did not wear glasses and had said nothing at all about any bicycle, nor had any passenger by the 5.20 mentioned a bicycle.

Constable Ross next endeavoured to trace the man in the grey suit who had vanished down the side-street, but without success. It was a small alley, rather than a street, containing nothing but the back-entrances of some warehouses and a public convenience.

The bookstall clerk, interrogated again, thought he remembered seeing a man in a soft felt hat and a burberry pass the bookstall with a bicycle at about 1.53 from the direction of the booking-hall, but had not paid much attention to him. Nobody else had noticed this person at all, as the Stranraer train was just due out again to Glasgow and there was a considerable number of passengers hurrying to catch it.

Two porters, who had seen the last of the luggage into the Glasgow train at 1.54, swore definitely that there was no bicycle in either of the vans.

Constable Ross hardly knew what to make of all this. The description of the bicycle coincided almost exactly with that of the machine taken from the Anwoth Hotel and, rather less closely, with that of Farren's bicycle. But how had it come to bear a Euston label? The bicycle put in at Girvan had been labelled for Ayr by the porter, and this point was verified by the guard who put it out at Ayr. It was quite impossible that it could have been re-labelled at Ayr, during the train's six minutes' wait at that station, for throughout that period one porter or another had been continually on duty beside the case containing labels, and all were prepared to swear that the bicycle had not passed through their hands.

The only possibility was that the bicycle had somehow been re-labelled after the Glasgow train had gone; but it was not labelled by a porter, for none of them remembered it.

What had become of the man in the grey suit?

If he was the same person as the man in the burberry who had been seen by the bookstall clerk wheeling a bicycle at 1.53, he must have put on the burberry somewhere outside (in the public convenience?) and returned via the booking-hall. What, then, had become of him? Had he hung about the station till 2.55? If so, where? He had not gone into the refreshment-room, for the girl there was positive that she had seen nobody of the sort. He had not been seen in the waiting-rooms or on the platform. Presumably he had left the bicycle by the hoarding and then gone out again, or taken some other train.

But which train?

He had not gone on to Glasgow by the 1.54, because it was quite certain that the bicycle could not have been re-labelled before the train left.

There remained the 1.56 to Muirkirk, the 2.12 and the 2.23 to Glasgow, the 2.30 to Dalmellington, the 2.35 to Kilmarnock and the 2.45 to Stranraer, besides, of course, the 2.25 itself.

Of these seven possibilities, Ross was able to eliminate the 1.56, the 2.30 and the 2.35. Nobody in the least corresponding to the description had travelled by any of them. The 2.45 to Stranraer he thought he could also dismiss. It had the advantage of bringing the murderer (if it was the murderer) back on his tracks—and Ross bore in mind Wimsey's remark that the murderer would probably wish to reappear at home as soon and as plausibly as possible—but it seemed almost inconceivable that anybody should take the trouble to go all the way to Ayr to get rid of a bicycle which could have been dumped so much more readily and easily at some point nearer home.

There remained the two Glasgow trains and the 2.25. The 2.12 to Glasgow was a comparatively slow train, getting in at 3.30; the 2.23 was the Stranraer boat-train, getting in at 3.29. The former had the advantage of getting the traveller away from the station earlier. He made inquiries about both trains, and received, in each case, vague descriptions of men in burberries and grey suits. It depressed him that this style of dress should be so common. He played a little with the idea that the wanted man might have changed his clothes before leaving Ayr, but dismissed the idea. He could not have carried a second suit of clothes as well as a burberry in the little attaché-case, and he could hardly have gone out, bought a suit in the town and taken a room to change in. At least, he *could* have done so, but it would have been unnecessarily risky. In that case he would have had to go by a much later train, and the more time he wasted at Ayr, the more worthless his alibi would be. And if he had not wanted to establish an alibi, what was the meaning of the elaborate proceedings at the Minnoch? If, then, he had gone on to Glasgow, he could not have arrived there before 3.29 at the earliest, and in all probability would not have travelled later.

There remained the 2.55. He might have been the grey-suited traveller who had travelled to Euston. But if so, why take the bicycle with him, acknowledged or unacknowledged? He might just as well have left it on the platform at Ayr.

But no! Perhaps the best thing he could have done was to take it with him. He would know that it might be inquired for—as a stolen bicycle at least, if not as a piece of evidence in a murder plot. Euston was larger and farther from the site of the crime than Ayr. A bicycle could be lost very conveniently in London, and so long as he had not been seen to travel with it, he could deny all knowledge of it.

Constable Ross was not entirely satisfied with any of these explanations. It was perfectly possible that the man had not travelled by any train at all. He might still be walking about Ayr. He might have taken a car or a 'bus to anywhere. He felt that the thing was becoming too complicated to tackle single-handed. Accordingly he decided to return to Newton-Stewart with his report and get further instructions.

The first necessity was obviously to find out what had happened to the bicycle if and when it had got to London. Dalziel put an inquiry through to Euston. The reply came back in an hour's time. A bicycle answering to the description had duly arrived on the 5 a.m. train on Wednesday morning. As it had not been claimed, it had been placed in the left-luggage office to await its owner. It was a Raleigh corresponding to the description issued.

The police scratched their heads about this, and instructed the railway authorities to hold the machine until someone could come and identify it. In the meantime, if anybody called for it, he was to be detained. A call was put through to the London police requesting assistance in this part of the business, though it seemed likely that, if the bicycle was indeed the one which had been stolen, anybody who called for it would be foolish indeed.

"He couldna get it if he did call for 't," said Constable Ross. "They'd no gie 't up wi'oot a ticket."

"Wad they no?" said Sergeant Dalziel. "An' if the fellow had got oot o' the train an' purchased a ticket at some other station? At Carlisle or Crewe or Rugby, maybe?"

"That's a fact," said Ross. "But had he done so, he'd have called for 't earlier. The later he leaves it the mair risky it wad be for him."

"Ay, we'll be thankful it isna away already," said Dalziel.

"Imph'm," said Ross, pleased with himself.

Inspector Macpherson was pleased, too. He had driven over early to Newton-Stewart to lay his time-table before Sergeant Dalziel, and he preened himself.

"It a' fits in fine wi' my theory," said he. "If yon's no Farren's bicycle, I'll eat my hat."

•   •   •   •   •   •   •   •   •

In the meantime, however, a shock was being prepared for Sergeant Dalziel. Full of pride in his own swift efficiency, he had, on his way back from Ayr the previous night, left a set of photographs at Girvan police-station, with instructions that they were to be shown to the porter McSkimming, as soon as he arrived in the morning, to see if he could identify the man in the grey suit. Now the Girvan police rang through to say that the porter had been carried off to hospital during the night, the "awfu' pain in his stomach" having suddenly developed into acute appendicitis. A call to the hospital brought the news that the man was being operated upon at that very moment, and would certainly be able to make no statement for some time. Disquieting details were added about "perforation," "threatenings of peritonitis" and "condition of the heart unsatisfactory." Dalziel swore, and instantly packed Ross off again with a set of photographs to show to the station officials at Ayr.

The next blow was directed at Inspector Macpherson, and caught him right on the midriff.

"If yon's no Farren's bicycle," he had said, "I will eat my hat."

The words were scarcely out of his mouth before the telephone bell rang.

"This is the Creetown police speaking," said a voice. "We've found yon bicycle o' Mr. Farren's lyin' abandoned in the hills by Falbae. There's nae doot it's his all right, for his name is written on a label tied to the handle-bars."

.   .   .   .

It will be remembered that on the previous evening, the Inspector had dispatched a party to search the neighbourhood of certain disused lead-mines, the scene of an unfortunate disaster a year or two before. These mines consisted of half a dozen or more narrow shafts cut in the hill-granite a few miles east of Creetown. They were reached by following the road to a farm called Falbae. From there a sheep-track or two led to the mines, which were surface-workings only, from thirty to forty feet deep at most. Some of the supporting beams of the cages were still in position, though all the tackle had long since disappeared. The mines had a bad name, particularly since an unhappy girl had thrown herself down one of them, and nobody went near them, except an occasional shepherd. The people of the farm had little occasion to visit the place, and the road ended at the farm. Though the mines were comparatively close to civilisation, they were, for all practical purposes, as lonely and desolate as though they had been in the middle of a desert.

It was in this ill-omened spot that Farren's bicycle had been found. Macpherson, hastily driving over to investigate, found the Creetown policeman and a number of volunteer assistants clustered round the head of one of the pits. A man was fitting a rope about his waist preparatory to descending.

The bicycle was lying where it had been found—a few hundred yards beyond the farm, and half a mile or so from the nearest pit. It was in good order, though the plated parts were slightly rusty from lying four nights among the bracken. There were no signs of accident or violence. It seemed simply to have been flung down and left when the track became too rough and steep for bicycling.

"Ye've no found the body?" said Macpherson.

No, they had found no body or clothing, but it seemed only too probable that the unfortunate Farren might be lying at the foot of one of the pits. They were intending—subject to instructions—to explore all the shafts in turn. It might be an awkward job, for one or two of them had water at the bottom. Macpherson told them to carry on and report the moment anything turned up. Then, deeply disappointed and chagrined, he made his mournful way back to Kirkcudbright.

To the Chief Constable fell the unpleasant task of telling Mrs. Farren about the fears they entertained about her husband. She was smiling when she met him at the door, and looked more cheerful than she had been for some days, and Sir Maxwell found it hard to enter upon his story. She took it well, on the whole. He laid stress on the fact that nothing as yet definitely pointed to suicide and that the search was only a matter of precaution.

"I quite understand," said Mrs. Farren, "and it is most good of you. You are very kind. I can't really believe that Hugh would do such a dreadful thing. I'm sure it's all a mistake. He is rather eccentric, you know, and I think it's much more likely that he has just wandered off somewhere. But of course you must search the mines. I quite see that."

The Chief Constable made a few other inquiries, as tactfully as he could.

"Well, yes—if you know that already—I must admit that he was rather in a temper when he went away. Hugh is excitable, and he was upset by something that happened about the dinner. Oh, dear, no—nothing whatever to do with Mr. Campbell. What a ridiculous idea!"

Sir Maxwell felt he could not let this pass. He explained, as kindly as possible, that Farren had been heard to make some very unfortunate observations that same evening with reference to Mr. Campbell.

Mrs. Farren then admitted that her husband had, indeed, objected to Campbell's repeated visits to the house.

"But as soon as he came to think it over," she said, "he would realise that he was doing me an injustice. He would never go so far as to lay violent hands on himself—or on anybody else. Sir Maxwell, you *must* believe me. I *know* my husband. He's impulsive, but with him everything blows over very quickly. I am as certain as I stand here that he is alive and well, and that he has done nothing rash. Even if—even if you should find his dead body, nothing will persuade me but that he has met with an accident. Anything else is unthinkable—and before long you will come back and tell me that I am right."

She spoke with so much conviction that Jamieson was shaken in his belief. He said that he very much trusted that events would prove Mrs. Farren right, and took his leave. As he went, Strachan's car passed him at the turn of the lane, and glancing over his shoulder, he saw it stop at Mrs. Farren's door.

"Whatever it is about Farren," he said, "Strachan is in it, up to the hilt."

He hesitated for a moment, and then turned back. He remembered that Macpherson had so far received no reply to his inquiry at Gatehouse about Strachan's whereabouts at 9.15 on Monday night.

"Oh, Mr. Strachan!" he said.

"Oh, good morning, Sir Maxwell."

"I just wanted to ask you something. I don't know if you've heard this—er—this rather disquieting news about Farren?"

"No. What about him?"

Sir Maxwell explained about the discovery of the bicycle.

"Oh!" said Strachan. "Yes—h'm—well—that does look rather

bad, doesn't it? Farren's a temperamental beggar, you know. I hope there's nothing in it. Does Mrs. Farren know?"

"Yes; I thought it better she should be prepared—just in case——"

"M'm. Is she upset?"

"No; she's being very brave. By the way, my people were trying to get hold of you yesterday evening."

"Were they? I'm so sorry. We'd all gone down to Sand Green and the girl had her night out. What did you want me for?"

"Just to ask if you happened to be at home on Monday night at a quarter past nine."

"Monday night? Let me see. No, I wasn't. No. I went up to fish at Tongland. Why?"

"Farren was seen going up the Laurieston Road, and we thought he might have been calling at your place."

"Not that I know of," said Strachan. "But I'll ask my wife. She'll know, or the girl will, if she doesn't. But they never said anything about it, so I don't think he can have called. Poor devil! I should never forgive myself if I thought that he was looking for me and that I might have prevented him from—— But we don't know yet that anything has happened to him."

"Of course not," said the Chief Constable. "We'll hope for the best, anyway."

He turned away homewards.

"Poker-faced man, that," he muttered to himself. "I don't trust him. But of course Farren may have nothing to do with all this. This extraordinary story of Wimsey's——"

For Wimsey had, an hour or so earlier, given him a shock beside which all other shocks were a gentle tickling.

CHAPTER XV

BUNTER

THE shock was a staggerer of the first water, and lost nothing of its force by being conveyed in terms of the most melancholy reproach. With bent head Wimsey bowed to the storm, and at the end had so little spirit left in him that he meekly allowed himself to be stripped of his grey flannel suit and sent to attend Campbell's funeral in a black morning-coat, top-hat and black kid gloves, to the consternation of his friends and the immense admiration of Mr. McWhan.

The trouble was this. On the Thursday morning, Bunter had asked for and received leave of absence in order to attend the cinema. Owing to Wimsey's having dinner with Inspector Macpherson at Newton-Stewart and then gone straight on to Bob Anderson's, he had not seen Bunter again until he returned between midnight and one o'clock in the morning after his visit to the police-station.

Then his first words were:

"Bunter! Something's going on at Mr. Gowan's house."

To which Bunter replied:

"I was about, my lord, to make a similar communication to your lordship."

"Somebody's just made a moonlight flitting," said Wimsey. "I've been round to tell the police. At least," he corrected himself, "not moonlight, because there is no moon; in fact, it's beastly dark and I fell over some confounded steps, but the principle is the same and have you got any arnica?"

Bunter's reply was memorable:

"My lord, I have already taken upon me, in your lordship's absence, to acquaint Sir Maxwell Jamieson with Mr. Gowan's project of escape. I have every reason to anticipate that he will be detained at Dumfries or Carlisle. If your lordship will kindly remove your garments, I will apply suitable remedies to the contusions."

"For God's sake, Bunter," said Lord Peter, flinging himself into a chair, "explain yourself."

"When," said Bunter, "your lordship was good enough to acquaint me with the result of Inspector Macpherson's inquiry at Mr. Gowan's house, it came into my mind that possibly a greater amount of information might be elicited from Mr. Gowan's domestic staff by a gentleman's personal attendant than by an officer of the law. With this object in view, my lord, I desired permission to attend the cinematograph performance to-night. There is"—Bunter coughed slightly—"a young person employed in Mr. Gowan's household by the name of Elizabeth, from whom, in the course of a casual conversation yesterday, I obtained the information that she was to receive permission to spend this evening out. I invited her to attend the cinematograph entertainment in my company. The film was one which I had already seen in London, but to her it was a novelty and she accepted with apparent pleasure."

"No doubt," said Wimsey.

"During the course of the performance I contrived to render our relations somewhat more confidential."

"Bunter! Bunter!"

"Your lordship need be under no apprehension. In short, the young person confessed to me that she had some cause for dissatisfaction with her present situation. Mr. Gowan was kind, and Mrs. Alcock was kind and so was Mr. Alcock, but during the last few days certain circumstances had arisen which had put her into a state of considerable trepidation. I naturally inquired what these circumstances might be. In reply she gave me to understand that her alarm was occasioned by the presence of a mysterious stranger in the house."

"You paralyse me!"

"Thank you, my lord. I pressed the young woman for further particulars, but she appeared apprehensive of being overheard in so public a place. I accordingly waited until the close of the performance, which took place at 10 o'clock, and invited her to take a stroll in the environs of the town.

"Not to trouble you with a long story, my lord, I succeeded at length in eliciting from her the following particulars. The mysterious occurrences of which she complained had commenced to eventuate on Monday last, on which day she had received permission to spend the evening with a sick relative. On returning to the house at half-past 10, she was informed that Mr. Gowan had been suddenly called away to London and had departed by the 8.45 train for Carlisle. She alleges that she would have thought nothing of this circumstance, had not the butler and the housekeeper taken such excessive pains to impress it upon her mind.

"The next day she was further surprised by being expressly forbidden by Mrs. Alcock to enter a certain corridor at the top of the house. This was a corridor leading to some disused rooms and one which, under ordinary circumstances, it would never have occurred to her to enter. Being, however, of the female sex, the prohibition immediately aroused in her a strong spirit of inquiry, and, on the first possible occasion, when she had reason to suppose the rest of the staff occupied downstairs, she went into the forbidden corridor and listened. She heard nothing, but to her alarm detected a faint odour of disinfectant—an odour which immediately connected itself in her mind with the idea of death. Which reminds me, my lord, to suggest that your lordship's injuries——"

"Never mind my injuries. Carry on."

"The young woman, alarmed as she was, was still more frightened by hearing footsteps ascending the stairs. Not wishing to be caught in an act of disobedience, she hastened to conceal herself inside a small broom-cupboard at the head of the staircase. Peeping through the crack, she observed Alcock, carrying a jug of hot water and a safety-razor, pass along the corridor and enter a room at the end. Convinced that there was a corpse in the house, and that Alcock was on his way to wash and shave it in preparation for burial, she rushed downstairs and indulged in hysterics in the pantry. Fortunately Mrs. Alcock was not at hand, and in time she contrived to control her feelings and go about her duties in the accustomed manner.

"Immediately after lunch she was sent out upon an errand in the town, but she was afraid to communicate her suspicions to anybody. On returning, she was kept fully occupied by various tasks, and was never out of sight of one or the other of her fellow-domestics until bedtime. She spent the night in a condition of nervous apprehension, trying but failing to summon up courage to investigate the mysterious corridor again.

"Early in the morning she began to feel that even the most disagreeable certainty was preferable to agitating suspicions. She got up, crept cautiously past the bedroom of the two Alcocks and went up to the top of the house again. She ventured a little way down the corridor, when she was rooted to the spot by the sound of a hollow groan."

"Really, Bunter," said Wimsey, "your narrative style would do credit to the *Castle of Otranto*."

"Thank you, my lord. I am only acquainted by repute with the work you mention, but I understand that it enjoyed a considerable vogue in its day. The girl Elizabeth was hesitating whether to shriek or to run away, when she happened to tread upon a loose board, which made a loud noise. Thinking that the sound would awaken the Alcocks, she was preparing to retreat once more to the shelter of the broom-cupboard, when the door at the end of the passage was opened in a stealthy manner and a terrible face looked out at her."

Bunter appeared to be enjoying the sensation he was producing, and paused.

"A terrible face," said Wimsey. "Very well, I've got that. A terrible face. Next, please!"

"The face, as I understand," pursued Bunter, "was enveloped in grave-clothes. The jaws were closely bound up, the features were hideous and the lips writhed away from the protruding teeth and the apparition was of a ghastly pallor."

"Look here, Bunter," said Wimsey, "could you not cut out some of the fancy adjectives and say plainly what the face was like?"

"I had not myself the opportunity of observing the face," said Bunter, reprovingly, "but the impression produced on me by the young woman's observations was that of a dark-haired, clean-shaven man with protruding teeth under the affliction of some form of physical suffering."

"Oh, it was a man, then?"

"That was Elizabeth's opinion. A lock of hair was visible beneath the bandages. The eyes appeared to be shut, or partly shut, for, although she was standing in full view, the man said in a muffled tone, 'Is that you, Alcock?' She did not reply, and presently the apparition retired into the room and shut the door. She then heard a bell ring violently. She rushed down the passage in blind alarm, encountering Alcock as he issued from his bedroom. Too terrified to think what she was doing, she gasped out: 'Oh, what is it? What is it?' Alcock replied: 'It must be those dratted mice playing with the bell-wires. Go back to bed, Betty.' She then remembered that she deserved rebuke for having gone into the upstairs corridor and retired to her own room to hide her head in the bedclothes."

"The best thing she could do," said Wimsey.

"Precisely, my lord. Thinking the matter over during the forenoon, she came to the very reasonable conclusion that the person she had seen might, after all, not be a living corpse but merely a sick man. She was, however, quite sure that she had never seen the person's face in her life. She now noticed that food was disappearing at every meal in excess of that consumed by herself and the Alcocks, and this she found encouraging, because, as she observed, dead folks do not eat."

"True," replied Wimsey. "As G. K. C. says, 'I'd rather be alive than not.'"

"Quite so, my lord. I spoke as encouragingly as possible to the young woman and offered to accompany her back to Mr. Gowan's house. She informed me, however, that she had received permission to spend the night at her mother's."

"Indeed?" said Wimsey.

"Precisely. I therefore took her home and returned to the High Street, where I observed Mr. Gowan's saloon car standing before the door. It was then five minutes to eleven. It was borne in upon me, my lord, that some person was about to take a surreptitious departure from Mr. Gowan's residence, and that Elizabeth had been given a night's leave of absence in order that she might not be a witness of the proceedings."

"I think the inference is justifiable, Bunter."

"Yes, my lord. I took the liberty of concealing myself at the corner of the street contiguous to Mr. Gowan's house where the little flight of steps leads down to the river. Presently a tall figure, closely muffled in a scarf and overcoat with the hat pulled well down to conceal the features, emerged from the doorway. I could not see the features at all, but I am confident that the form was that of a male person. A few words were exchanged in a low tone with the chauffeur, and the impression produced upon my mind was that the speaker was Mr. Gowan himself."

"Gowan? Then who was the mysterious stranger?"

"I could not say, my lord. The car moved away, and, on consulting my watch, I found that the time was three minutes past eleven."

"H'm," said Wimsey.

"I formed the opinion, my lord, that Mr. Gowan had, after all, not departed from Kirkcudbright on the Monday evening as Alcock had stated, but that he had remained concealed in his own house in attendance upon the sick person observed by Elizabeth."

"Curiouser and curiouser," said Wimsey.

"I returned here," pursued Bunter, "and consulted the local time-table. I found that there was a train leaving Dumfries for Carlisle and the South at two minutes past midnight. It appeared conceivable that Mr. Gowan was intending to catch it either at Dumfries or at Castle-Douglas."

"Did you see any luggage taken out?"

"No, my lord; but it might have been previously placed in the car."

"Of course it might. Did you inform the police?"

"I thought it best, my lord, in view of the delicacy of the circumstances, to communicate directly with Sir Maxwell Jamieson. I hastened to the Selkirk Arms and put in a call from there."

"You must have passed me," said Wimsey. "I had just hared across to the police-station, but Inspector Macpherson wasn't there."

"I regret extremely that I should have missed your lordship. I informed Sir Maxwell of the circumstances, and I understood him to say that he would immediately telephone to Castle-Douglas and Dumfries, with a view to intercepting Mr. Gowan if he should make his appearance at either of those points, and that he would also circulate a description of the car and its driver."

"Well, well, well," said Wimsey. "For a quiet country place, Kirkcudbright seems to boast a bright lot of inhabitants. They appear and disappear like Cheshire cats. I give it up. Bring forward the arnica and a whiskey-and-soda, and let's get to bed. All I know is, that it's perfectly useless for me to try and detect things. You're always off the mark before me."

The real sting of this episode lay in its tail. Inspector Macpherson came in next day after lunch in an irritable frame of mind. Not only had his rest been broken the previous night by an alarm of burglars at a house on the outskirts of the town, which turned out to be purely fictitious, not only had he thereby missed the scoop about

Gowan, but the Chief Constable had bungled matters somehow. Though he had (or so he said) immediately telephoned descriptions of the car and its occupants to Castle-Douglas, Dumfries, Carlisle and all the intermediate stations up to Euston, nothing whatever had been seen of any of them. Inquiries in the Stranraer direction had proved equally useless.

"It's fair rideeculous," said the Inspector. "It's pairfectly feasible that the car shuld ha' stopped on the outskirts of Castle-Douglas or Dumfries tae let Gowan tak' the train on his ain feet, but that they should ha' missed Gowan is no thinkable—and him so conspicuous wi' his big black beard an' a'."

Wimsey suddenly uttered a loud yelp.

"Oh, Inspector, Inspector! He's done it on us! What dolts and ninnies we are! And now I suppose that damned photograph has been circulated all over the country. Show Bunter the specimen, Inspector. I told you we ought to have done that before we did anything else. This will be the death of us. We shall never hold up our heads again. The specimen, Inspector, the specimen!"

"By God!" said the Inspector, "I believe your lordship's right. Tae think o' that, noo. An' me sae sairtain that it was Farren!"

He drew out his notebook and handed the bunch of curly black hair to Bunter.

"My lord," said the latter, reproachfully, "it is most regrettable that I did not see this before. Without presuming to speak as an expert, I may say that on several occasions I had the opportunity of examining the beard of a person belonging to the Mohammedan persuasion. You are doubtless aware, my lord, that the strict followers of this sect consider it unlawful to trim the hair of the face, with the consequence that the beard is extremely silky in texture, each hair preserving the natural tapering point."

Wimsey, without a word, handed Bunter his lens.

"Your lordship has doubtless observed," pursued Bunter, "that this specimen conforms in every particular to this description, and having seen Mr. Gowan's beard, I do not hesitate to give it as my personal opinion—subject to expert correction—that Mr. Gowan will now be found to be deprived, in whole or in part, of that facial adornment."

"I'm afraid you're right, Bunter," said Wimsey, sadly. "Now we know who the mysterious stranger was, and what he was suffering from. You'll have to revise your time-scheme, Inspector, and put Gowan in the leading rôle."

"I must go and send off a corrected description at once," said the Inspector.

"Just so," said Wimsey. "But have you the slightest idea what Gowan looks like without his beard? Inspector, I venture to prophesy that it will be a shock to you. When a man grows a jungle of face-fungus up to his cheek-bones and half-way down his chest, he had generally something to hide. I have known revelations——" he sighed. "Do you realise, my dear man, that you have never seen *anything* of Gowan, except his eyes and a somewhat exaggerated nose?"

"We'll catch him by his nose," said the Inspector, without the slightest humorous intention. He bustled away.

"Bunter," said Wimsey, "this case resembles the plot of a Wilkie Collins novel, in which everything happens just too late to prevent the story from coming to a premature happy ending."

"Yes, my lord."

"The trouble about this, Bunter, is that it completely destroys our theory, and apparently lets out Farren."

"Quite so, my lord."

"And unless your friend Betty is lying, it lets out Gowan too."

"That appears to be the case, my lord."

"Because, if he was hiding at home all Monday night and Tuesday morning, suffering from an accident, he couldn't have been painting pictures beyond Newton-Stewart."

"I quite see that, my lord."

"But is Betty telling the truth?"

"She appeared to me to be an honest young woman, my lord. But you will recollect that it was not until after lunchtime on the Tuesday that she saw Alcock enter the Bluebeard's Chamber, if I may use so fanciful an expression, and that the sick man was not seen by her in person until early on Wednesday morning."

"True," said Wimsey, thoughtfully. "We have no evidence that he was there on Tuesday at all. Alcock will have to be interrogated. And in my opinion, Alcock is a man of considerable resource and sagacity."

"Exactly so, my lord. And, what is more, Alcock has disappeared also."

CHAPTER XVI

CHIEF INSPECTOR PARKER

THE mystery of the car turned out to have a perfectly simple explanation. It was reported from a small hotel at Brig of Dee, a village a few miles out on the Kirkcudbright side of Castle-Douglas. A visit by the police discovered Messrs. Alcock and Hammond calmly seated at lunch. Their story was a straightforward one. Mr. Gowan had written from London, suggesting that, in his absence, they should take a holiday, and giving them his permission to use the car. They had decided on a little fishing excursion, and here they were. They had started late, on account of some small repairs which Hammond had had to make to the engine. The muffled-up person who had got in was Alcock himself. Certainly the Inspector could see Mr. Gowan's letter. Here it was, written from Mr. Gowan's club, the Mahlstick, on the club's own paper, and posted in London on the Wednesday.

As for Bunter's story, Alcock denied it altogether. The girl Betty was a foolish and hysterical young person, who imagined a great deal of nonsense. It was perfectly true that Mrs. Alcock had forbidden her to go into the disused part of the house. Betty was a great deal too fond of wasting her time. There were a lot of old magazines kept up there in a box-room, and the girl was always sneaking in there to read them when she ought to be engaged on household duties. Mrs. Alcock had had occasion to speak to her about it before. As regards the Tuesday, it was a fact that he (Alcock) had gone up there with hot water. One of the dogs had been hurt in a rabbit snare. He had made it a bed in the disused room and washed the wounds out with disinfectant. Mrs. Alcock would show the dog to the police if they cared to call. As for the alleged apparition on Wednesday morning, it was quite obvious that the girl had merely been suffering from nightmare, due to her own ridiculous fancies about corpses. There was no sick person there and never had been. Mr. Gowan had left Kirkcudbright, as previously stated, by car on Monday evening to catch the 8.45. The person whom Bunter had seen entering the car on the Thursday night had been Alcock. Hammond and Mrs. Alcock could confirm all this.

They could, and did, confirm it. The injured dog was produced and found to be actually suffering from a nasty sore in the leg, and Betty, when closely questioned, admitted that she had frequently got into trouble through reading magazines in the box-room.

As against this, there was the evidence of a garage proprietor at Castle-Douglas that a gentleman, giving his name as Rogers, had telephoned the previous evening for a fast car to catch the 12.2 express at Dumfries. He had got ready a 14 h.p. Talbot, which was a new and speedy car, and at about twenty minutes past eleven, the gentleman had walked into the garage. He was tall and had dark eyes and what the proprietor described as a "rabbity" face. The proprietor had himself driven Mr. Rogers to Dumfries and set him down at the station at four minutes to twelve precisely.

The booking-clerk at Dumfries confirmed this up to a point. He remembered selling a first-class ticket for Euston to a gentleman who had come in just before midnight. He did not remember the gentleman very distinctly—he was much like other gentlemen, but he agreed that he had rather a big nose and stick-out teeth.

The ticket-collector on the train was not helpful. Gentlemen on night-trains tended to be sleepy and muffled-up. Several first-class gentlemen had joined the 12.2 at Dumfries. Certainly he had seen nobody remotely resembling the photograph of Gowan. Was there anybody at all like what Gowan would be if clean-shaven? Well, there now, that was asking something, that was. Had the Inspector any idea what a 'edge-'og would look like without its spikes? No, nor he didn't suppose nobody had, neither. He was a ticket-collector, not a puzzle-picture expert. The booking-clerk at Dumfries expressed a similar opinion, still more forcibly.

Inspector Macpherson, whom this dreary investigation had carried as far as Euston, then turned his attention to the club from which Gowan was supposed to have written. Here the news was a little more cheering. Mr. Gowan had certainly not been staying there. One or two letters had arrived for him, which had been collected by a gentleman presenting Mr. Gowan's card. The gentleman had signed a receipt for them. Might the Inspector see the receipt? Certainly he might. The signature was J. Brown. The Inspector wondered how many J. Browns there might be among Lon-

don's four million, and turned his weary steps towards Scotland
Yard.

Here he asked for Chief Inspector Parker, who received him with
more than official cordiality. Any friend of Wimsey's was entitled
to Parker's best attention, and the complicated story of Gowan
and the spanner, Farren, Strachan and the two bicycles, was sympathetically listened to.

"We'll find Gowan for you all right," said Parker, encouragingly. "With the very precise details you have produced for us it
ought not to take long. What do you want done with him when
we've got him?"

"Weel, noo, Mr. Parker," said the Inspector, deferentially, "do
ye think we have enough evidence tae arrest him?"

Parker turned this over carefully.

"I take it," he said, "that your idea is that Gowan met this man
Campbell in the road between Gatehouse and Kirkcudbright and
killed him in a quarrel. Then he got frightened and decided to fake
up the accident. His first step was to cut off his own very conspicuous
beard, in the hope, I suppose, of getting through the Gatehouse end
of the business unrecognised. It must have been an awkward bit of
barbering. Still, he might have managed to produce a fairly good
imitation of a man who hadn't shaved for a fortnight. Then he went
through all the movements which you originally ascribed to Farren. He hid the body up the side-lane and drove Campbell's own
car back to Gatehouse. Now, why should he have done that?"

"There!" said the Inspector, "yon's the great deeficulty. Wherefore did he no tak' the corp back wi' him? It was verra weel under-
standable when we supposed that the murderer was Farren in Strachan's car, because we had the theory that he meant at first tae pit
the blame on Strachan, but what for should Gowan du sic a fulish
thing?"

"Well, let's see," said Parker. "He had to get Campbell's car
back somehow. Ferguson might have noticed if the wrong car came
in. But he didn't take the body with him on that journey, because,
again, Ferguson or somebody might have spotted him with it.
Gowan's car was a two-seater. Perhaps the dickey wasn't big enough
to hide the corpse properly. He decides that it's better to risk leaving
the corpse and his own car in the lane than to drive openly back
to Gatehouse with a dead man upright in the seat beside him. Very

well. Now he's got to get back to the scene of the crime. How? On foot?—No, this, I take it, is the point at which the bicycle was pinched from the what-d'ye-call-it hotel."

"Verra like," said the Inspector.

"You may have to alter your times a trifle here, but you've still got ample margin. You had 10.20 as the time for Campbell's car to arrive at Standing Stone Pool. Now then. Your man has still got to do the journey back on a bicycle. But he hasn't got to waste time going on foot to Strachan's house. So, if anything, he will get to the scene of the crime a trifle earlier than we supposed. He picks up his own car, puts the bike in the dickey—we've got to allow that—however, it would be pretty dark by that time and probably no one would notice. By the way, I see that this fellow Ferguson says that Campbell's car came in a little after 10 o'clock. Well, that fits your first time-table all right. It means that the murderer brought the car straight away in after the crime. But I see you've made an alteration here."

"Ay," said Macpherson. "We thocht he wad ha' lodged Campbell's car somewhere on the road an' transferred the body tae 't on his second journey. It wad be suspicious like for a second car tae come in tae Campbell's place."

"True; but if Ferguson is right about his times, that can't be the case. Is Ferguson an exact man?"

"Ay; they tell me he has a gran' memory for details."

"Then the murderer *must* have come in a second time with the body in his own car. It's odd that Ferguson shouldn't have heard the second car either come or go."

"Ay, that's a fact."

"The second car—when would it have got in? Between five and six miles on a push-bike—say half-an-hour. That brings it to 10.50. The bicycle put into the dickey and five or six miles back in a fast car—say fifteen minutes at the outside. That gives us 11.5 for the second time of arrival. Ferguson says he went to bed shortly after 10. He must have been asleep, that's all. And still asleep when the car went out again—the murderer's car, I mean. No, that won't do. How and when did Gowan—if he was the murderer—get his car back to Kirkcudbright? He had to be on the spot in Gatehouse to look after the body and prepare his fake for the next morning. I suppose he *could* have driven his car home to Kirkcudbright during the small hours and then walked or push-cycled back to Gatehouse."

"Ay, there's nae doot he cud ha' done it. But it wadna be necessary. The chauffeur Hammond cud ha' driven him over again."

"So he could. That makes Hammond rather definitely an accomplice. But there's no reason why he shouldn't be. If Gowan committed the murder, all his servants, except possibly Betty, are obviously lying like Ananias, and one degree of guilt more or less makes no difference. Well, that explains that all right, and we've only got to suppose that Gowan carried out the rest of the scheme according to plan, changed over into the London train at Ayr and is now lurking in London till his beard's grown again. And that explains—what would otherwise seem rather odd—why, having faked the murder, he didn't disarm suspicion by showing himself openly in Kirkcudbright."

"Ay," said Macpherson, excitedly, "but dinna ye see it explains naething at a'? It disna fit the description o' the man in the grey suit that tuk the bicycle tae Ayr. Nor it disna explain Betty's tale to Bunter, nor the muffled-up man escapin' fra' Gowan's hoose at deid o' nicht, nor the rabbity-faced fellow in the train fra' Castle-Douglas tae Euston. An' hoo aboot yon man that came knockin' on Campbell's door o' Monday midnicht?"

Parker rubbed his jaw thoughtfully.

"It's funny about the description of the man," he said. "Perhaps Gowan contrived to disguise himself in some way, with a false fair moustache, or something. And the girl's story may, as Alcock suggests, be partly imagination. Gowan may have returned to Kirkcudbright on Tuesday afternoon instead of going straight through to London, though I can't think why he should, and the letter sent from the Mahlstick certainly suggests that he was in London on the Wednesday. And the rabbity man may be somebody different altogether. And I'm inclined to think that the man who knocked at midnight *was* somebody different altogether."

"But," said the Inspector, "if that man gaed into the hoose and found Campbell dead and Gowan there, why hasna he come forward tae say so?"

"Possibly he was after no good," suggested Parker. "He may, as you previously remarked, have been a lady. Still, I admit that there are awkward gaps in the story. I think we'd better get on the tracks of Gowan and the rabbity man separately, and try to find out definitely which way Gowan really went. And when we do catch Gowan, I think perhaps we'd better not arrest him, but merely detain him on the ground that he can give information. After all, Inspector, we don't even know for an absolute certainty that it was he who met Campbell on the road. There may be other people with black beards."

"There's nae ither *artist* wi' a black beard like yon," said Macpherson, stubbornly. "Not in a' the district."

"Hell! yes," said Parker. "He's got to be an artist, of course. Well, anyhow, we'll detain Gowan."

Inspector Macpherson thanked him.

"And now there's this man Farren," went on Parker. "Do you want him too? Supposing he's not down a mine."

"I'm thinkin' he did ought tae be found," said the Inspector. "He was heard tae utter threats—an' forbye, he's disappeared, which in itself is distressin' tae his family an' friends."

"True. Well, we'll make inquiries for him as a lost, stolen or strayed. That will do no harm. But I daresay you've got him up your end somewhere. Who else is there? The Englishman—what's his name?—Waters. How about him?"

"I'd forgot Waters," replied Macpherson, frankly. "I canna see how he comes intae 't at a'."

"Nor do I," said Parker. "Well, we'll leave him out. And of course we're watching that bike at Euston to see if anybody's fool enough to come for it. And you'd better send somebody down to identify it, because it may not be the right one at all. Is that all? Suppose now we go and have a drink after all this talking? Oh, by the way, can you tell me what school Gowan went to? No? Oh, well, it doesn't matter. He's probably in the reference-books."

The Inspector still seemed a little unhappy.

"What is it?" said Parker.

"Ye havena——" he began. And then added, impulsively, "if we canna find somethin' sune, I'm thinkin' ye'll be hearin' officially fra' the Chief Constable."

"Oh!" said Parker. "But I don't see any need for that. You have lost no time, and you seem to me to be doing very well. We have to give you help at this end, of course—just as you would help me if one of my pet-lambs escaped to Scotland—but surely there's no call for us to take over the management of the case. It seems to be a matter in which the local man has all the advantages on his side."

"Ay," said the Inspector, "but it's an awfu' big job."

He sighed heavily.

CHAPTER XVII

LORD PETER WIMSEY

"STRACHAN!" said Lord Peter Wimsey.

Mr. Strachan started so violently that he nearly pitched himself and his canvas into a rock-pool. He was perched rather uneasily on a lump of granite on the Carrick shore, and was industriously painting the Isles of Fleet. There was a strong wind and the menace of heavy storm, which together were producing some curious cloud effects over a rather fretful-looking sea.

"Oh, hullo, Wimsey!" he said. "How on earth did you get here?"

"Drove here," said Wimsey. "Fresh air and that kind of thing." He sat down on a convenient knob of rock, settled his hat more firmly on his head and pulled out a pipe, with the air of a man who has at last found an abiding-place.

Strachan frowned. He did not much care for spectators when he was painting, but Wimsey was working away in a leisurely manner with his tobacco-pouch, and appeared impervious to nods and winks.

"Very windy, isn't it?" said Strachan, when the silence had lasted some time.

"Very," said Wimsey.

"But it's not raining," pursued Strachan.

"Not yet," said Wimsey.

"Better than yesterday," said Strachan, and realised at once that he had said a foolish thing. Wimsey turned his head instantly and said brightly:

"Tons better. Really, you know, you'd think they'd turned on the water-works yesterday on purpose to spoil my sketching-party."

"Oh, well," said Strachan.

"Well, perhaps it was rather a wild idea," said Wimsey, "but it appealed to me rather. That's rather nice," he added, "how long have you been on that?"

"About an hour," said Strachan.

153

"You use very big brushes. Broad, sweepin' style and all that. Campbell used the knife a lot, didn't he?"

"Yes."

"Is it quick work with a knife?"

"Yes, generally speaking, it is."

"Do you work as fast as Campbell?"

"I shouldn't work quite as fast as he would with a knife, if you mean that, because I should fumble it a bit, unless I had practice with it first. But using my own methods, I could probably produce a finished sketch nearly as fast as he could."

"I see. What do you call an ordinary time for a finished sketch?"

"Oh—well, what size of sketch?"

"About the size you're working on now."

"I shall have done everything I want to this in another half-hour—or perhaps a little bit longer. Provided the whole show doesn't carry away first," he added, as a fresh gust came drumming off the sea, making the easel vibrate and rock, in spite of the heavy stone slung between its legs.

"Oh, you're well ballasted. But I wonder you don't use a sketching-box on days like this."

"Yes; I don't know why I don't, except that I never have done and am not used to it. One gets into habits."

"I suppose one does."

"I'm rather methodical, really," said Strachan. "I could lay my hands on any of my tools in the dark. Some people seem to like muddle, and all their stuff chucked into a satchel anyhow. I lay everything out before I begin—tubes of colour in the same order on my tray, dipper just here, spare brushes hung on there—even my palette is always made up in the same order, though not always with the same colours, of course. But, roughly speaking, it follows the order of the spectrum."

"I see," said Wimsey. "I'm not methodical myself, but I do admire method. My man, Bunter, is a marvel in that way. It is such a grief to him to find all kinds of odds and ends bulging my pockets or chucked helter-skelter into the collar-drawer."

"Oh, I'm terrible about drawers, too," said Strachan. "My tidiness begins and ends with my painting. It's just habit, as I said before. I haven't a tidy mind."

"Haven't you? Aren't you good at dates and figures and time-tables and all that sort of thing?"

"Not the least. Hopelessly unobservant. I haven't even got a good visual memory. Some people can come back from a place and make a picture of it with every house and tree in its place, but I have to see things before I can draw them. It's a drawback in a way."

"Oh, I could do that," said Wimsey. "If I could draw, I mean, F'r instance—take the road between Gatehouse and Kirkcudbright. I could make a plan of that, here and now, with every corner, every house, practically every tree and gate on the road marked. Or if you drove me along it blindfold, I could recite to you exactly what we were passing at every moment."

"I couldn't do that," said Strachan. "I've been over it hundreds of times, of course, but I'm always seeing things I hadn't noticed before. Of course I get the fun of having perpetual surprises."

"Yes; you're safeguarded against boredom. But sometimes an eye for detail is a good thing. If you want to tell a good, plausible circumstantial lie, for example."

"Oh!" said Strachan. "Yes, I suppose it would be—under those circumstances."

"Your little story of the golf-ball on the links, for example," said Wimsey. "How much better it would have been if surrounded and supported by stout, upstanding, well-thought-out details. It wasn't a fearfully good lie to start with, of course, because it really left rather *too* much time unaccounted for. But since you stood committed to it, you should have made more of it."

"I don't know what you mean," said Strachan, stiffly. "If you doubt my word——"

"Of course I doubt it. I don't believe it for a moment. Nor would anybody. For one thing, you didn't tell your wife the same story you told me. That was careless. If you're going to tell a lie, it should always be the same lie. Then you omitted to mention what hole you were playing when it happened. There never was a man telling a golfing story who didn't buttress it about with every kind of geographical and historical detail. That was poor psychology on your part. Thirdly, you said you were up at the golf-course all morning, quite forgetting that there might be plenty of witnesses to say you'd never been near the place, and that, as a matter of fact, you'd instructed Tom Clark to roll the greens that morning. He was on the ninth, as a matter of fact, between 10 and 11 o'clock, and can swear that you didn't come in, and if you'd gone up later, you'd hardly have called it 'after breakfast.' Besides——"

"Look here," said Strachan, with a lowering brow, "what the devil do you mean by talking to me like this?"

"I'm just wondering," said Wimsey, "whether you cared to suggest any other explanation for that black eye of yours. I mean, if you liked to give it to me now, and it happens to be—well, say, anything in the nature of a domestic fracas, or anything, I—er—I might not need to pass it on, you see."

"I don't see at all," said Strachan. "I think it's damned impertinence."

"Don't say that," pleaded Wimsey. "Look here, old man, your midnight revels are nothing to me. If you were out on the tiles, or anything——"

"If you take that tone to me, I'll break your neck."

"For God's sake," cried Wimsey, "don't use any *more* threats."

Strachan looked at him, and slowly flushed a deep crimson from brow to throat.

"Are you accusing me," he demanded, thickly, "of having anything to do with murdering Campbell?"

"I'm not accusing anybody," said Wimsey, lightly, "of murdering him—yet." He suddenly scrambled to his feet, and stood poised on the rock, looking out away from Strachan over the sea. The clouds had blown together into one threatening mass, and the waves were lipping along cold and yellow, showing snarling little teeth of foam. "But I do accuse you," he said, turning suddenly and leaning back against the wind to keep his balance, "I do accuse you of knowing a good deal more about it than you have told the police. Wait! Don't be violent. You fool! *It's dangerous to be violent.*"

He caught Strachan's wrist as the blow glanced past his ear.

"Listen, Strachan, listen, man. I know I look tempting, standing here like this. Damn it, that's what I did it for. I'm a smaller man than you are, but I could chuck you into eternity with a turn of the wrist. Stand still. That's better. Don't you *ever* think two minutes ahead? Do you really suppose you can settle everything by brute force in this blundering way? Suppose you *had* knocked me down. Suppose I had split my head open, like Campbell. What would you have done then? Would you be better off, or worse off? What would you have done with the body, Strachan?"

The painter looked at him, and put the back of his hand up against his forehead with a sort of desperation in the gesture.

"My God, Wimsey," he said, "you deadly devil!" He stepped back and sat down on his camp-stool, shaking. "I meant to kill you then. I've got such a hell of a temper. What made you do that?"

"I wanted to see what sort of a temper you had got," said Wimsey, coolly. "And you know," he added, "as a matter of fact, if you had killed me, you would have run very little risk. You had only to go away and leave me, hadn't you? My car would have been here. Everybody would have thought I'd just been blown off my feet and cracked my skull—like Campbell. What evidence would there have been against you?"

"None, I suppose," said Strachan.

"You think that?" said Wimsey. "Do you know, Strachan, I almost wish I had let you knock me over—just to see what you would do. Well, never mind. It's starting to rain. We'd better pack up and go home."

"Yes," said the other. He was still very white, but he started meekly to put his painting materials together. Wimsey noticed that, in spite of his obvious agitation, he worked swiftly and neatly, evidently following out some habitual order of working. He secured the wet canvas in a carrier, mechanically putting in the canvas-pins and pulling the straps tightly, transferred the brushes to a tin case and the palette to a box and then collected the tubes of paint from the ledge of the easel.

"Hullo!" he said, suddenly.

"What's up?" said Wimsey.

"The cobalt's not here," said Strachan, dully, "it must have rolled off."

Wimsey stooped.

"Here it is," he said, extracting it from a clump of heather. "Is that the lot?"

"That's the lot," said Strachan. He laid the tubes in their box, folded up and strapped the easel and stood, as though waiting for orders.

"Then we'd better make tracks," said Wimsey, turning up his coat-collar, for the rain had started to come down heavily.

"Look here," said Strachan, still motionless in the downpour, "what are you going to do?"

"Go home," said Wimsey. "Unless"—he looked hard at Strachan—"unless there's anything you want to tell me."

"I'll tell you this," said Strachan. "One of these days you'll go too far, and somebody *will* murder you."

"I shouldn't be in the least surprised," said Lord Peter, pleasantly.

CHAPTER XVIII

MRS. SMITH-LEMESURIER

ALL this time there was a gentleman who was feeling rather hurt and neglected, and that was the young constable who had so signally failed in interviewing Mr. Jock Graham. This young man, whose name was Duncan, was keen about his profession, and he was acutely aware that he was not being given a proper chance. Graham had laughed at him; Sergeant Dalziel, importantly rushing about after bicycles and railway-tickets, had callously ignored his suggestions and left him to deal with drunks and motoring offences. Nobody took P. C. Duncan into his confidence. No matter. P. C. Duncan would pursue a line of his own. Perhaps, when he had shown them what he could do, they would be sorry.

There was not doubt at all in Duncan's mind that Jock Graham's movements required investigating. There were rumours. Hints were dropped in bars. Fishermen had been seen to nudge one another and fall suddenly silent when Graham's name was mentioned. Unfortunately, it is hardly possible for a local policeman in a country place to snoop about, wheedling information out of the inhabitants after the manner of Sherlock Holmes. His features are known. He is a marked man. Duncan played a little with the idea of getting himself up (when off duty) as an aged clergyman or a Breton onion-seller, but a glance in the mirror at his stalwart frame and round, ruddy cheeks was enough to rob him of his self-confidence. He envied the Scotland Yard detective who, lost among a multitudinous population and backed by a powerful force, can go about, impenetrable and unknown, hobnobbing with thieves in the East End or with dukes and millionaires in Mayfair night-clubs. Alas! in Creetown and Newton-Stewart he had only to poke his nose round the door to be known and avoided.

He made persistent inquiries, cajoling and even threatening one or two people who appeared to know more than they should. Unhappily, the Scottish peasant has a remarkable talent for silence when he likes and, unhappily also, Jock Graham was a popular man. After several days of this kind of thing, Duncan did, however, contrive to unearth one piece of definite information. A farmer who was passing along in a cart towards Bargrennan at 11.30 on the Tuesday morning, had seen a man walking along the farther side of the Cree as though coming from the scene of the crime. The man had immediately ducked down as though to escape observation, but not before the farmer had definitely recognised him as Graham. But further than this, Duncan succeeded only in hearing and raising rumours. A journalist on the *Glasgow Clarion*, to whom he had rather rashly said more than he ought, came out with an unfortunate article, and P. C. Duncan received a severe rebuke from his harassed superiors.

"An' if Graham was as guilty as sin," said Sergeant Dalziel angrily —this occurred on the same day that the porter at Girvan developed appendicitis, and the Sergeant was quite ready to take it out of somebody—"what for wad ye be tellin' him that he's suspectit, an' givin' him the chance to make up an alibi? Wull ye look at this, noo?" He flapped the *Clarion* before Duncan's unhappy eyes. " 'Reason tae suppose that the crime was committit by an airtist.' Isna yon precisely the fact that we was wishfu' tae conceal frae the suspecks? 'Weel-known airtist interviewed by oor correspondent.' Whae tell't ye tae send yon fellie speirin' round at Graham's place? If ye canna lairn discretion, Charlie Duncan, ye wad du better tae fin' some ither profession."

However, this indiscretion had its consequences. On the Saturday morning, Sergeant Dalziel was seated in his office when a lady was ushered in, demurely dressed in a black costume and close-fitting hat. She smiled nervously at the Sergeant, and murmured that she desired to make a statement in connection with Campbell's murder.

Dalziel knew the lady well enough. She was Mrs. Smith-Lemesurier, an "in-comer" of some three years' standing in Newton-Stewart, and giving herself out to be the widow of an African civil servant. She lived, simply and inexpensively, in a small converted cottage, with a French maid. Her manner was plaintive and artless, her age rather more than it appeared, and young men who knew no better were apt to see in her a refreshing revelation of an unfashionable womanliness. Why she should have chosen to settle in this out-of-the-way spot was never explained. Mrs. Smith-Lemesurier herself was accustomed to say that the rents in Scotland were so low, and that she had to do the best she could with her poor little income. It did not matter where she lived, she would add, sadly; since her husband's death she was all alone in the world. Lord Peter Wimsey had been introduced to her the previous year at a small sale of work which was being held in connection with the Episcopalian Church. He had afterwards expressed the coarse opinion that the lady was "out for blood." This was ungrateful, since Mrs. Smith-Lemesurier had devoted herself to him very charmingly throughout what must have been to him a tedious afternoon, and had sold him a green silk sachet with "Pyjamas" embroidered upon it with her own hands. "I can't give money," said Mrs. Smith-Lemesurier, smiling shyly up at him, for she was a dainty little person, "but I can give my work, and it's the intention that counts, isn't it?"

Sergeant Dalziel placed a chair for his visitor, and softened his rugged tones as he inquired what he could do for her.

Mrs. Smith-Lemesurier hunted in her vanity-bag for some time, and eventually produced the cutting from the *Glasgow Clarion* which had brought P. C. Duncan so much trouble and reproof.

"I just wanted to ask," she said, raising her speedwell-blue eyes pleadingly to the policeman's face, "whether there is any foundation for—for the dreadful insinuations in this."

Sergeant Dalziel read the paragraph through as carefully as though he had never seen it before, and replied cautiously:

"Ay, imph'm. That's as may be."

"You see," said Mrs. Smith-Lemesurier, "it says that the m-m-murder must have been committed by an artist. Wh-what makes them say that?"

"Weel," said the Sergeant, "I'll no be sayin' that there mightna be some evidence tae point in that direction."

"Oh!" said the lady. "I hoped—I thought—I fancied perhaps this reporter was making it all up out of his own head. They are such terrible people, you know. Did he really get that idea from—from the police?"

"I couldna verra weel say," replied the Sergeant. "He'll maybe ha' caught it fra' some ither irresponsible pairson."

"But the police do think that?" she insisted.

"I'll no be sayin' so," said Sergeant Dalziel, "but seein' as the deceased was an airtist himsel' and that the most of his friends was airtists, there is always the possibeelity."

Mrs. Smith-Lemesurier fumbled with a clasp of her bag.

"And then," she said, "it goes on to mention Mr. Graham."

"Ay, it does so," said the Sergeant.

"Surely, surely"—the blue eyes again sought the Sergeant's—"it can't be that you—that you actually suspect Mr. Graham of this dreadful thing?"

Sergeant Dalziel cleared his throat.

"Och, weel noo," said he, "there is always some groonds for sus-peecion when a crime is committed an' a pairson willna state juist whaur he was at the time. I wadna say that there was what they ca' a violent presumption of guilt, but there's groonds for what we may ca' a general suspeecion."

"I see. Tell me, officer—supposing—supposing anybody were to clear your mind of this—general suspicion against Mr. Graham—it wouldn't be necessary to—to—to make the explanation public?"

"That depends," said Dalziel, eyeing his visitor rather more closely, "on the nature of the explanation. If it was such as tae re-move a' possibeelity of this gentleman's bein' consairned, an' if it was weel supportit by proofs, an' provided that the maitter never cam' tae trial, there wad be nae need tae mak' onything public at a'."

"Ah! then, in that case—oh, Mr. Dalziel, I can rely on your dis-cretion, can't I? It's such a dreadful thing to have to tell you—just consider—but I'm sure you will understand—in my sad, lonely posi-tion—I—oh! I don't know how to say it."

Mrs. Smith-Lemesurier dragged out a wispy handkerchief and temporarily veiled the light of the speedwell eyes.

"Come, noo," said the Sergeant, gently, "there's no call tae fash yoursel'. We hear an awfu' lot o' things, in oor profession, that we niver think twice on. Forbye," he added, helpfully, "I'm a mairrit man."

"I don't know that that doesn't make it worse," bleated Mrs. Smith-Lemesurier. "But I'm sure," she added, peeping hopefully up over the edge of the handkerchief, "you're a kind, understanding man, and wouldn't make it worse for me than you could help."

" 'Deed, no," said the Sergeant. "Dinna fash yoursel', Mrs. Smith-Lemesurier. Juist tell me a' aboot it, as if I micht be your feyther."

"I will, thank you, I will. Mr. Graham would never say anything, of course, he's too kind and too chivalrous. Mr. Dalziel—he couldn't tell you where he was on Monday night—because—he was —with me."

Mrs. Smith-Lemesurier paused with a little gasp. Sergeant Dalziel, for whom this revelation held by this time no element of surprise, nodded paternally.

"Ay, imph'm, is that so? That's a verra guid reason for him tae keep silence, a verra satisfactory reason indeed. Can ye tell me, Mrs. Smith-Lemesurier, at whit time Mr. Graham came tae your hoose and left ye again?"

The lady squeezed the filmy handkerchief between her small, plump hands.

"He came to dinner, at about 8 o'clock. And he left me again after breakfast. That would be a little after 9."

The Sergeant made a note on a slip of paper.

"And did naebody see him come or gae?"

"No. We were—very careful."

"Ay. How did he come?"

"I think he said a friend had given him a lift into Newton-Stewart."

"Whit friend wad that be?"

"I don't know—he didn't say. Oh, Mr. Dalziel, shall you have to find out? My maid can tell you when he arrived. Is it necessary to bring this other person into it?"

"Maybe no," said the Sergeant. "An' he went aff again after 9 o'clock? Your maid can witness that tu, I'm thinkin'."

"Yes, of course."

"An' he was in the hoose a' the time?"

"He—he was never out of my sight," moaned Mrs. Smith-Lemesurier, again overcome by the painfulness of this confession.

The Sergeant looked at her shaking shoulders and hardened his heart.

"An' whit makes ye think, ma'am, that this story provides Mr. Graham wi' an alibi for the murder o' Campbell, that was fund wi' his heid dunted in at 2 o'clock o' Tuesday afternoon?"

Mrs. Smith-Lemesurier gave a little shriek.

"Oh!" She stared at him wildly. "I didn't know. I thought—look at that horrid newspaper. It said Mr. Graham refused to state where he was the previous night. I don't understand. I imagined—oh! don't, don't say it doesn't clear him after all!"

"I'll no gae sae far as tae say that," said the Sergeant, "but ye'll see for yersel' that it disna cover a' the groond. Mr. Graham was twa days missin'. Ye dinna ken whaur he went after he left your hoose?"

"No—no—I've no idea. Oh, my God! Why did I ever come here? I made so certain that it was an alibi for the Monday night you wanted."

"Weel, that's a' tae the guid," said the Sergeant, comfortingly. "It's verra like, when he kens that the Monday nicht is accountit for, he'll tell us aboot the ither maitter. Noo, I'll juist rin ye back tae your hoose in my car and get a wee word fra' your maid, by way o' corroboration. Dry your eyes, ma'am. I'll no say a word mair than is necessary. It's verra courageous of ye tae ha' come tae me wi' your story, an' ye can coont upon ma' discretion."

The maid's story agreed word for word with that of the mistress —as, indeed, the Sergeant had expected it would. He did not care for the woman—a sly foreign creature, he thought her—but he could not shake her on any essential point.

The whole episode was disquieting. No sooner had that infernal paragraph appeared in the paper than he had expected an alibi to be produced. He had said as much to the unhappy Duncan. But why this particular alibi? The woman's story was not improbable in itself, given Jock Graham and given Mrs. Smith-Lemesurier, only—why the alibi for the Monday night only? He read the newspaper cutting again. "—Mr. J. Graham, the distinguished artist, who laughingly refused to state where he had been between Monday night and Wednesday morning." No; nobody could have deduced from that that Monday night was the crucial period. Wimsey must have been talking. God knew what he had been blurting out in the course of his unofficial inquiries. If it was not Wimsey——

If it was not Wimsey, then nothing but guilty knowledge could possibly account for that alibi, so neatly covering the time of Campbell's death. And if Jock Graham had guilty knowledge, then what became of the beautiful theory about Farren, and the hopeful imbroglio about the bicycle?

The Sergeant groaned aloud. He might have groaned still more deeply if he had known that Inspector Macpherson and Chief Inspector Parker of Scotland Yard were at that very moment engaged in destroying the beautiful Farren theory in favour of a Gowan theory.

His eye fell upon an object lying on his desk. It was a grey felt hat—the sole treasure-trove that the search-party had so far brought back from Falbae. It was not Farren's. Mrs. Farren and Jeanie had both repudiated it. It bore no name. It was just another puzzle. He turned it about in his hands discontentedly.

The telephone rang. Sergeant Dalziel lifted the receiver. The speaker was the police-superintendent at Glasgow.

"We've got a man here who says he is Mr. Waters of Kirkcudbright. Are you still wanting him? He was just boarding the Dumfries train."

"Whit account does he gie o' himsel'?"

"Says he's just off a yachting expedition. He made no attempt to deny his identity. What shall we do with him?"

"Detain him," said Sergeant Dalziel, desperately. "I'll be along on the next train."

"I'll tak' nae mair chances," he added to himself, as he hurriedly prepared for his journey. "I'll detain the whole bluidy lot o' them."

CHAPTER XIX

WATERS' STORY

TO HIS great surprise, the Sergeant found Wimsey at the Glasgow police-station before him. He was waiting placidly in the Superintendent's office, with his hands clasped over his walking-stick and his chin on his hands, and he greeted the Sergeant with exasperating cheerfulness.

"Hullo—ullo—ullo!" he said. "So here we are again."

"An' hoo did yew get here?" snapped Dalziel, his Galloway accent very pronounced and sharpening his u's almost to the point of menace.

"In a rather roundabout way," said Wimsey, "but, generally speaking, by train. I spent last night in Campbell's cottage. Arrived in Glasgow by the 2.16 to see Picture Exhibition. Distressed fellow-countryman wires to Kirkcudbright that he is in the hands of the children of Amalek and will I come and disentangle him. Faithful valet sends wire on to Picture Exhibition. Intelligent attendant at Exhibition identifies me and delivers wire. Like a mother-eagle I fly to the place where distressed fellow-countryman, like wounded eaglet, bleeds, metaphorically speaking. You know my friend, Superintendent Robertson?"

"Oh, yes," said the Superintendent, "Sergeant Dalziel has been over about this matter before. Well, now, Sergeant, you'd probably like to see this man Waters straight away. He's told his story to us, but you had best hear it from himself. Forbes, just bring Waters in here again."

After a few moments the door opened, to admit an exceedingly dishevelled and exceedingly angry Waters, dressed in a grubby waterproof and very grubby sweater and flannel trousers. His untidy hair was pushed up into a dissipated-looking comb by a linen bandage which half covered one eye, and gave him a rake-helly and piratical appearance.

"Good Lord, man!" exclaimed Wimsey, "what the devil have you been doing to yourself?"

"Doing to myself?" retorted Waters. "What the devil have all you people been doing? What's all this damned fuss about? What's all this tripe about Campbell? What in thunder do these damned idiots mean by arresting me? What the hell has it all got to do with me, anyhow?"

"My dear man," said Wimsey, breaking in before the Sergeant could speak, "your eloquence is extremely impressive, but not more so than your appearance, which is, if I may say so, picturesque in the extreme. Your absence from your usual haunts has been causing acute distress to your friends—a distress and anxiety which the manner of your return is doing nothing to allay. Before embarking on any discussion about Campbell or any other extraneous subject, will you so far relieve the agony of mind of a sympathising compatriot as to say where you have been, why you have not written and why you appear to have been indulging in a free fight, with extensive damage to your handsome façade?"

"I never knew such a lot of silly fuss about nothing," grumbled Waters. "I've been yachting with a bloke, that's all—old Tom Drewitt of Trinity, as a matter of fact. We were running up the west coast, and he was going to put me off at Gourock on Thursday, only we fell in with a bit of bad weather and had to run across and hang round the Irish coast for a couple of days while it blew itself out. I don't know if you fancy hugging a lee shore full of rocks in a sou'westerly gale. All I can say is, we didn't. I daresay I am a bit untidy—so'd you be, after five days in Tom's dirty little wind-jamming beast of a boat. I've no skin left on my hands, and it's not the fault of that young lout of Tom's that I'm still alive. He got the wind up—Tom ought to have stuck to the tiller himself. Boom came across and nearly cracked my head open. Tom wanted me to go on with him this morning up to Skye, but I wasn't having any. I told him he could damn well put me off at Gourock and if ever I sailed with him again it would be when that cub of his was drowned and out of harm's way."

"See here, noo," put in Sergeant Dalziel. "Let's get a' this story correct. Ye say ye started oot wi' this man Drewitt on his yacht. When did ye go aboard, sir?"

"Look here, why all this?" said Waters, appealing to Wimsey.

"Better tell him what he wants to know," said Wimsey. "I'll explain later."

"Oh, all right, if you say so. Well, I'll tell you exactly what happened. Last Monday night I was in bed and asleep, when I heard some fool chucking stones at my window. I went down, and there was Drewitt. You remember Drewitt, Wimsey? Or was he before your time?"

"I never knew any Trinity men," said Wimsey. "The Jews have no dealings with the Samaritans."

"Of course, you were at Balliol. Well, it doesn't matter. Anyway, I let Drewitt in and gave him a drink. It was about 11 o'clock at night, I think, and I was rather fed-up at being roused out, because I meant to go up to Glasgow by the 8.45, and I wanted my beauty-sleep. Besides, I felt rather bloody. You remember, Wimsey —I'd had that scrimmage with Campbell at the McClellan Arms. By the way, what is this story about Campbell?"

"Tell you later, old man. Carry on."

"Well, I told Drewitt I was going to Glasgow, and he said he'd got a better idea than that. Why not come with him? He was running up that way, and if I wasn't in a hurry I might just as well join him and do a bit of fishing and get the sea-air. It was lovely weather and his boat, *Susannah,* he calls her, could make the voyage in two or three days, or we could muck about a bit longer if we wanted to, and if the wind didn't hold, we could fall back on the auxiliary motor. Well, it sounded all right, and it didn't matter to me when I got to Glasgow, so I said I'd think about it. So then he said wouldn't I go with him anyhow and have a look at the *Susannah.* He'd got her lying off the Doon."

"That's right," said Wimsey to Dalziel. "There was a boat there on Monday night, and she went off Tuesday morning."

"You seem to know all about it," said Waters. "Well, I thought I might as well have the run. It seemed the best way of getting Drewitt out of the house, so I put on a coat and went up with him. He'd hired a car from somewhere or other and he ran me along. He wanted me to go aboard and meet his whelp, but I didn't want to do that. I hadn't made up my mind, you see. So he brought me back again and dropped me at the corner of the road where it turns off to Brogue. He'd have come all the way, only I wouldn't let him, because I knew I'd have to ask him in again and give him another drink, and I'd had quite as much as I wanted already. So I walked back into Kirkcudbright, and left it with him that I'd think it over, and if I wasn't on board at half-past 9, he wasn't to wait any longer, because I shouldn't be coming and he'd miss the tide.

"Well, I didn't really intend to go, but I turned in and had a good sleep and next morning when Mrs. McLeod called me, the weather looked damn good, and I thought why not, after all? So I had my breakfast and got my bike out and pushed off."

"Ye didna tell Mrs. McLeod whaur ye were gaein'."

"No, there wasn't any need. She knew I was going to Glasgow and might be away some days, and it was no concern of hers how I went. As a matter of fact she was out at the back somewhere, and I didn't see her. I bicycled up to the Doon, signalled to Drewitt and he took me off."

"What did you do with your bicycle?" asked Wimsey.

"I just shoved it into a little shed-place there is up there, among the trees. I'd often put it there before when I was painting or bathing off the Doon, and it never came to any harm. Well, that was that. As I was saying, we had rather bad luck with the weather and one thing and another, and we didn't get to Gourock till this morning."

"Did ye no touch onywhere?"

"Yes—I can give you the itinerary if you want it. We dropped down the estuary with the morning tide, passing the Ross Light some time before 10. Then we held on across Wigtown Bay, passing Barrow Head fairly close in. We had a good southeasterly breeze and made the Mull about tea-time. Then we followed the coast northwards, passing Port Patrick at about 7 o'clock, and anchored for the night in Lady Bay, just outside Loch Ryan. I can't give you more details than that, as I'm no yachtsman. That was Tuesday. On Wednesday we lazed about and did a bit of fishing, and then, about lunch-time, the wind started to haul round to the southwest and Drewitt said he thought we'd better run across to Larne instead of carrying on up to Gourock as we intended. We put in at Larne for the night and took some beer and stuff aboard. On Thursday it was fine enough, but blowing rather a lot, so we sailed up to Ballycastle. It was a bally place, too. I began to think I was wasting my time. I was sick, too. Friday was a foul beast of a day, raining like hell and blowing. However, Tom Drewitt seemed to think it was the kind of day he liked to be out in. Said he didn't care how it blew, provided he had plenty of sea-room or words to that effect. We staggered across to Arran, and I was sick all the time. That was the day I got this crack on the head, curse it. I made Tom put in somewhere under the lee of the island, and in the night the wind dropped, thank God! This morning we got up to Gourock and I shook the dust of the beastly boat off my feet. No more sailing-boats for me, thank you. For complete boredom and physical misery, commend me to a small sailing-vessel in a gale of wind. Have you ever tried cooking fish on a dirty little oil-stove, with your knees above your head? Oh, well, perhaps you enjoy that sort of thing. I don't. Nothing but fish and corned beef for four days —that's not my idea of amusement. Go on up the coast, indeed! Not on your sweet life, I told him. I got off that damned old wherry as quick as I bloody well could, and went on by train to Glasgow and got a hot bath and a shave, and my God! I needed them. And I was just starting off to catch the 5.20 to Dumfries, when these police imbeciles came along and collared me. And now, *do* you mind telling me what it's all about?"

"Did ye no see a newspaper all those four days?"

"We saw a *Daily Mail* at Larne on Thursday morning and I got an *Express* in Glasgow this afternoon, but I can't say I read them very carefully; why?"

"The story tallies all right, what?" said Wimsey, nodding to the Sergeant.

"Ay, imph'm. It tallies well enough, only for the evidence of this man Drewitt."

"He'll have to be found, of course," said the Glasgow Superintendent. "Where will he be just now, Mr. Waters?"

"Oh, God knows!" said Waters, wearily. "Somewhere off Kintyre, I should imagine. Don't you believe what I'm telling you?"

"Of course; why not?" said the Superintendent. "But, you see, sir, it's our duty to obtain corroboration of your statement if possible. Did Mr. Drewitt carry a wireless set on board?"

"Wireless set? The filthy canoe hadn't so much as a spare frying-pan," said Waters, crossly. "Do you mind telling me what I'm accused of?"

"Ye're no accused of onything at all," said the Sergeant. "If I'd been accusin' ye of onything," he added, cannily, "I would ha' warned ye that ye'd no need tae be answerin' my questions."

"Wimsey, I can't make head or tail of all this. For God's sake, what is all this mystery?"

"Well," said Wimsey, consulting the Superintendent by a look, and receiving a nodded permission to speak, "you see, it's like this, old horse. Last Tuesday morning they found Campbell lying dead in the Minnoch with a nasty crack in his head, made with a blunt instrument. And as you had last been seen with your ten fingers on his throat, threatening to do him in, we rather wondered, you know, what had become of you and all that."

"My God!" said Waters.

. . . .

"Noo, that," remarked Sergeant Dalziel to Wimsey, some time later, when Waters had retired to write agitated letters and telegrams addressed to the *Susannah* at various possible and impossible ports, "that is a verra inconvenient piece of evidence. Naiturally, we'll be findin' this felly Drewitt, an' naiturally the baith o' them will be in the same story tegither. But even supposin' Waters went on board at the Doon as he said—an' whae's tae tell that?—he may ha' bin pit ashore again at any point."

"Wait a minute," said Wimsey. "How about the body? He couldn't very well have taken that on board with him."

"Ay, that's so. That's verra true. But supposin' Drewitt runs him up in the night tae the Minnoch——"

"No," said Wimsey. "You're forgetting. The man who threw stones at the window may have been Campbell or he may have been Drewitt. He can't have been both. And somebody came back to Waters' bedroom that night and ate his breakfast in the morning. He can't have been Campbell, and it's extremely unlikely that it was Drewitt, so it must have been Waters. He couldn't have got up to the Minnoch and back again in the time."

"But Drewitt might ha' cairrit the corpse away for him."

"That depends. He'd have had to know the country pretty well to find the right place in the dark. And when was all this planned? If the man at the window was Campbell, how did Waters get into communication with Drewitt? If Drewitt was the man at the window, when and where was Campbell murdered? Hang it all, Sergeant, you can't have it both ways. If Waters went on board when he said he did, he's got his alibi. Otherwise, I freely admit that there may be a flaw in the thing. It's perfectly possible that the *Susannah* may have picked him up at some point or other on the Tuesday night. Suppose, for example, that Waters knew beforehand that the boat would be at Lady Bay that night. He could have hired a car somewhere and picked the *Susannah* up there, and the rest of the tale could have been concocted between them. The point you've got to prove is that Waters went aboard the *Susannah* on the Tuesday morning. There are cottages down at the Doon. Surely to goodness somebody must have seen him."

"That's a fact," said the Sergeant.

"And the bicycle should be there, too."

"Aweel," said Dalziel, resignedly, "I can see there'll be no kirk for me the morn. It's awfu', the wark there is in a case the like o' this. An' there's no train back tae Newton-Stewart the nicht."

"No more there is," said Wimsey. "Life's just one damn thing after another."

"It is that," said Sergeant Dalziel.

CHAPTER XX

FARREN'S STORY

GILDA FARREN sat, upright as a lily-stalk, in the high-backed chair, spinning wool. Her dress was mediæval, with its close bodice and full, long skirt, just lifted from the ground by the foot that swayed placidly upon the treadle. It had a square neck and long, close-fitting sleeves, and it was made of a fine cream-coloured serge which gave her an air of stately purity. Besides, it had the advantage of not showing the fluff of white wool which settles all over the spinning-woman and tends to give her the appearance of a person who has slept in her clothes. Lord Peter Wimsey, seated rather closely beside her, to avoid the draught from the whirling wheel, noted this detail with sardonic appreciation.

"Well, Mrs. Farren," he said cheerfully, "we shall soon have the truant husband back now."

The long hands seemed to falter for a moment in feeding the flock to the spindle, and the thread ran fine and thickened again.

"What makes you think that?" asked Mrs. Farren, never turning her red-gold head.

"All-stations call," said Wimsey, lighting another cigarette. "Nothing agitating, you know. Anxious friends and relations, and all that."

"That," said Mrs. Farren, "is a very great impertinence."

"I admit," said Wimsey, "that you don't seem frightfully anxious. If it isn't rude to ask, why aren't you?"

"I think it is rather rude," said Mrs. Farren.

"Sorry," said Wimsey, "but the question remains. Why aren't you? Abandoned bicycle—dangerous old mine—indefatigable police with ropes and grappling-hooks—empty chair—deserted home—and a lady who sits spinning an even thread. It might be thought puzzling."

"I have already said," replied Mrs. Farren, "that I consider all that story about mines and suicide to be absurd. I am not responsible for the foolish ideas of country policemen. I resent this inquisitive-

173

ness about my private affairs extremely. The police I can forgive,
Lord Peter, but what business is it of yours?"

"None whatever," said Wimsey, cheerfully. "Only, if you cared
to tell me the facts, I might be able to quell the riot."

"What facts?"

· "You might tell me, for instance," said Wimsey, "where the
letter came from."

The right hand paused and fumbled in its task. The thread
whisked out of the left-hand thumb and finger and wound itself
up sharply on the spindle. Mrs. Farren uttered a little exclamation
of annoyance, stopped the wheel, and unwound the thread again.

"I beg your pardon," she said, when she had made the join in
the wool. She re-started the wheel with a light touch of the hand.
"What was that you said?"

"I said you might tell me where the letter came from."

"What letter?"

"The letter your husband wrote you on Thursday."

"If," said Mrs. Farren, "the police have been tampering with
my correspondence, they can probably give you all the information
you want—unless, of course, they also dislike interference."

Her breath was coming short and angrily.

"Well," replied Wimsey, "as a matter of fact they omitted that
simple precaution. But since you admit the existence of the letter——"

"I admit nothing of the sort."

"Come now," said Wimsey. "You are not one of Nature's gifted
liars, Mrs. Farren. Up to Thursday, you were genuinely frightened
and anxious about your husband. On Friday you were pretending
to be anxious, but you were not. To-day I suggest that you received
a letter from your husband on Friday morning, and you leap to
the conclusion that the police have been investigating your correspondence. Therefore you did receive a letter. Why deny it?"

"Why should I tell you anything about it?"

"Why indeed? I have only to wait a day or two and I shall
get the answer from Scotland Yard."

"What has Scotland Yard to do with it?"

"Surely, Mrs. Farren, you must know that your husband is, or
may be, a valuable witness in the Campbell case?"

"Why?"

"Well, you know, he went off from here looking for Campbell. He was last heard of inquiring for Campbell in Gatehouse. It would be interesting to know if he did meet Campbell—wouldn't it?"

"Lord Peter Wimsey!" Mrs. Farren stopped the wheel and turned indignantly to face him. "Have you ever thought how contemptible you are? We have received you here in Kirkcudbright as a friend. Everybody has shown you kindness. And you repay it by coming into the houses of your friends as a police-spy. If there is anything meaner than a man who tries to bully and trap a woman into betraying her husband, it is the wife who falls into the trap!"

"Mrs. Farren," said Wimsey, getting up, with a white face, "if it is a question of betrayal, then I beg your pardon. I shall say nothing to the police about the letter or about what you have just said. But in that case I can only say again—and this time as a warning—that they have sent out an all-stations call from London and that from to-day your correspondence *will* be watched. In telling you so, I am possibly betraying official secrets and making myself an accessory after the fact to a murder. However——"

"How dare you?"

"To be frank with you," said Wimsey, taking the question at its face-value, "I do not think I am running any very great risk. If I did, I might be more cautious."

"Do you dare to suggest that I believe my husband to be guilty of murder?"

"If I must answer that, then—I think you have thought so. I am not sure that you do not think so now. But I thought it possible that you believed him innocent, in which case, the sooner he returns to give an account of himself, the better for himself and for everybody."

He took up his hat and turned to go. He had his hand on the latch when she called him back.

"Lord Peter!"

"Think before you speak," he said hastily.

"You—you are quite mistaken. I am sure my husband is innocent. There is another reason——"

He looked at her.

"Ah!" he said. "Stupid of me. It is your own pride that you are sheltering now." He came back into the room, treading gently, and laid his hat on the table. "My dear Mrs. Farren, will you believe me when I say that all men—the best and the worst alike —have these moments of rebellion and distaste? It is nothing. It is a case for understanding and—if I may say so—response."

"I am ready," said Gilda Farren, "to forgive——"

"Never do that," said Wimsey. "Forgiveness is the one unpardonable sin. It is almost better to make a scene—though," he added, thoughtfully, "that depends on the bloke's temperament."

"I should certainly not make a scene," said Mrs. Farren.

"No," said Wimsey. "I see that."

"I shall not do anything," said Mrs. Farren. "To be insulted was enough. To be deserted as well——" Her eyes were hard and angry. "If he chooses to come back, I shall receive him, naturally. But it is nothing to me what he chooses to do with himself. There seems to be no end to what women have to endure. I should not say as much as this to you, if——"

"If I didn't know it already," put in Wimsey.

"I have tried to look as though nothing was the matter," said Mrs. Farren, "and to put a good face on it. I do not want to show my husband up before his friends."

"Quite so," said Wimsey. "Besides," he added, rather brutally, "it might look as though you yourself had failed in some way."

"I have always done my duty as his wife."

"Too true," said Wimsey. "He put you up on a pedestal, and you have sat on it ever since. What more could you do?"

"I have been faithful to him," said Mrs. Farren, with rising temper. "I have worked to keep the house beautiful and—and to make it a place of refreshment and inspiration. I have done all I could to further his ambitions. I have borne my share of the household expenses——" Here she seemed suddenly to become aware of a tinge of bathos and went on hurriedly, "You may think all this is nothing, but it means sacrifice and hard work."

"I know that," replied Wimsey, quietly.

"Is it my fault that—just because this house was always a peaceful and beautiful place—that unhappy man should have come to me to tell me his troubles? Is that any reason why I should be outraged by vile suspicions? Do *you* believe there was anything more than sympathy in my feelings for Sandy Campbell?"

"Not for a moment," said Wimsey.

"Then why couldn't my husband believe it?"

"Because he was in love with you."

"That is not the kind of love I recognise as love. If he loved me he should have trusted me."

"As a matter of fact," said Wimsey. "I quite agree with you. But everybody has his own ideas about love, and Hugh Farren is a decent man."

"Is it decent to believe vile things of other people?"

"Well—the two things often go together, I'm afraid. I mean, virtuous people are generally rather stupid about those things. That's why bad men always have devoted wives—they're not stupid. Same with bad women—they usually have their husbands on a lead. It oughtn't to be like that, but there it is."

"Do you consider yourself a decent man when you talk like that?"

"Oh dear no," said Wimsey. "But I'm not stupid. My wife won't have that to complain of."

"You seem to imagine that infidelity is a trifle, compared with——"

"With stupidity. I don't quite say that. But the one can cause quite as much upheaval as the other, and the trouble is that it's incurable. One of those things one has to put up with. I shan't necessarily be unfaithful to my wife, but I shall know enough about infidelity to know it when I see it, and not mistake other things for it. If I were married to you, for example, I should know that under no circumstances would you ever be unfaithful to me. For one thing, you haven't got the temperament. For another, you would never like to think less of yourself than you do. For a third, it would offend your æsthetic taste. And for a fourth, it would give other people a handle against you."

"Upon my word," said Mrs. Farren, "your reasons are more insulting than my husband's suspicions."

"You're quite right," said Wimsey. "They are."

"If Hugh were here," said Mrs. Farren, "he would throw you out of the window."

"Probably," said Wimsey. "In fact, now that I've put it to you in the right light, you can see that his attitude towards you is rather a compliment than otherwise."

"Go and see him," said Mrs. Farren, fiercely. "Tell him what you have been saying to me—if you dare—and see what he says to you."

"With pleasure," said Wimsey, "if you will give me his address."

"I don't know it," said Mrs. Farren, shortly. "But the postmark was Brough in Westmorland."

"Thank you," said Wimsey, "I will go and see him—and, by the way, I shall not mention this to the police."

.   .   .   .

At an early hour on Monday morning, a large black Daimler car, with an outsize bonnet and racing body, moved in leisurely silence down the main street of Brough. The driver, glancing carelessly from side to side through his monocle, appeared to be about to pull up at the principal hotel; then, suddenly changing his mind, he moved forward again, and eventually stopped the car before a smaller inn, distinguished by the effigy of a spirited bull, careering ferociously in an emerald green meadow beneath a bright summer sky.

He pushed open the door and strode in. The innkeeper was polishing glasses in the bar, and bade him a polite good morning.

"A fine morning," said the traveller.

"Ay, so 'tis," agreed the innkeeper.

"Can you give me a bit of breakfast?"

The innkeeper appeared to turn this suggestion over in his mind. "Hey, mother!" he bellowed at last, turning towards an inner door, "canst a' give breakfast to t' gentleman?"

His shout brought out a comely woman in the middle forties who, after looking the gentleman over and summing him up, reckoned that she could, if a dish of eggs and Cumberland ham would suit the gentleman.

Nothing could be better, in the gentleman's opinion. He was ushered into a parlour full of plush-covered chairs and stuffed birds, and invited to take a seat. After an interval, a sturdy young woman appeared to lay the table. After a further interval came a large and steaming tea-pot, a home-baked loaf, a plate of buns, a large pat of butter and two sorts of jam. Finally, the landlady reappeared, escorting the ham and eggs in person.

The motorist complimented her on the excellence of the food and fell to with an appetite, mentioning that he had just come down from Scotland. He made a few sensible observations on the curing of hams, and gave an intelligent account of the method used in Ayrshire. He also inquired particularly after a certain kind of cheese peculiar to the district. The landlady—in whom the monocle had at first raised some doubts—began to think that he was a more homely body than he appeared at first sight, and obligingly offered to send the girl round to the shop to procure a cheese for him.

"I can see you know the town, sir," she observed.

"Oh, yes—I've been through here lots of times, though I don't think I've ever pulled up here before. You're looking very smart and all that—got the old Bull repainted, I see."

"Ah, you noticed 'en, sir. Well, that was nobbut finished yesterday. 'Twas done by a painter gentleman. He came walking into t' bar Thursday and says to George, 'Landlord,' he says, 'the signboard would do wi' a bit paint. If I make 'ee a fine new bull for 'en, will 'ee let me have a room cheap?' George, he didn't know what to think, but t' gentleman says, 'Look here,' he says, 'I'll make 'ee a fair offer. Here's my money. Gie me my food and lodging and I'll do my best by t' bull, and if tha likes 'en when a's done, tha canst allow what tha likes for 'en on t' bill.' On walking-tour, a' said a' was, and a' had one of these little boxes full of paints wi' 'en, so that we could see a' was an artist."

"Funny," said the motorist. "Had he any luggage?"

"A little bag-like—nothing much. But anybody could see a' was a gentleman. Well, George didn't know what to think."

From what the traveller had seen of George, this seemed very probable. There was a kind of stolid dignity about George which suggested that he disliked being flurried.

Apparently, however, the mysterious artist had then and there, with a piece of black stuff, sketched on the back of an envelope, a bull so rampant, so fierce, so full of fire and vigour, as to appeal very strongly to George's agrarian instincts. After some discussion, the bargain was struck, the old bull taken down and the paints brought out. On Thursday the new bull had made his appearance on one side of the sign, head down and tail up, steam issuing from his nostrils, and the painter had explained that this represented the frame of mind of the hungry traveller bellowing for his food. On Friday, a second bull was drawn and coloured on the other side, sleek, handsome and contented, having fed well and received the best of treatment. On Saturday, the sign had been set out to dry in the wash-house. On Sunday, the painter had applied a coat of varnish on both sides and set the board back in the wash-house. On Sunday night, the varnish, though still a little tacky, seemed to be dry enough to allow of the sign's being put in place, and there it was. The painter had taken his departure on foot on Sunday afternoon. George had been so pleased with the bull that he had refused to take any money at all from the gentleman, and had given him an introduction to a friend of his in a neighbouring village, who also had a sign that needed renewal.

The motorist listened with great interest to this story and carelessly inquired the painter's name. The landlady produced her visitor's book.

" 'Tis wrote here," said she. "Mr. H. Ford of London, but by a's speech you'd ha' taken 'en for a Scotsman."

The motorist looked down at the book, with a slight smile twisting the corners of his long mouth. Then he pulled a fountain-pen from his pocket and wrote, beneath the signature of Mr. H. Ford:

"Peter Wimsey. Kurkcudbright. Good baiting at the Bull."

Then, getting up and buckling the belt of his leather coat, he observed, pleasantly:

"If any friends of mine should come inquiring for Mr. Ford, be sure you show them that book, and say I left my compliments for Mr. Parker of London."

"Mester Parker?" said the landlady, mystified, but impressed. "Well, to be sure, I'll tell 'en, sir."

Wimsey paid his bill and went out. As he drove away he saw her standing, book in hand, under the signboard, staring at the bull which capered so bravely on the bright green grass.

The village mentioned by the landlady was only about six miles from Brough, and was reached by a side-turning. It possessed only one inn, and that inn had no sign, only an empty iron bracket. Wimsey smiled again, stopped his car at the door and passed into the bar, where he ordered a tankard of beer.

"What's the name of your inn?" he asked, presently.

The landlord, a brisk Southerner, grinned widely.

"Dog and Gun, sir. The sign's took down to be repainted. Gen-

tleman a-workin' on it now in the back garden. One of these travelling painter chaps—gentleman, though. Comes from over the
Border by his way of talkin'. Old George Weatherby sent him on
here. Tells me he's made a good job o' the old Bull in Brough.
Working his way down to London, by what I can make out. Very
pleasant gentleman. Real artist—paints pictures for the London
shows, or so he tells me. My sign won't be any the worse for a
dab o' fresh paint—besides, it amuses the kids to watch him muckin'
about."

"Nothing I like better myself," said Wimsey, "than to hang
round while another fellow does a spot of work."

"No? Well, that's so, sir. If you like to step into the garden, sir,
you'll see him."

Wimsey laughed and wandered out, tankard in hand. He dodged
under a little archway, covered with a tangle of faded ramblers,
and there, sure enough, squatting on an upturned bucket with the
signboard of the Dog and Gun propped on a kitchen-chair before
him, was the missing Hugh Farren, whistling cheerfully, as he
squeezed out paint upon his palette.

Farren's back was turned towards Wimsey and he did not turn
his head. Three children watched, fascinated, as the thick blobs
of colour oozed out on to the board.

"What's that, mister?"

"That's the green for the gentleman's coat. No—don't pinch it,
or you'll get it all over you. Yes, you can put the cap on. Yes,
that's to keep it from drying up. Yes, put it back in the box. . . .
That's yellow. No, I know there isn't any yellow in the picture,
but I want it to mix with the green to make it brighter. You'll
see. Don't forget the cap. What? Oh, anywhere in the box. White
—yes, it's a big tube, isn't it? You see, you have to put a little
white into most of the colours—why? Well, they wouldn't come
right without it. You'll see when I do the sky. What's that? You
want the dog made white all over? No, I can't make it a picture of
Scruggs. Why not? Well, Scruggs isn't the right sort of dog to
take out shooting. Well, he's not, that's why. This has got to be
a retriever. All right, well, I'll put in a liver-and-white spaniel.
Oh, well, it's rather a pretty dog with long ears. Yes, I daresay
it is like Colonel Amery's. No, I don't know Colonel Amery. Did
you put the cap on that white paint? Dash it! if you go losing

things like that I'll send you back to Mother and she'll spank you. What? Well, the gentleman has a green coat because he's a gamekeeper. Possibly Colonel Amery's gamekeeper doesn't, but this one does. No, I don't know why gamekeepers wear green coats—to keep them warm, I expect. No, I haven't got any brown paint same as that tree-trunk. I get that by mixing other colours. No, I've got all the colours I want now. You can put 'em away and shut the box. Yes, I can tell pretty well how much I want before I start. That's called a palette knife. No, it isn't meant to be sharp. It's meant for cleaning your palette and so on. Some people use a knife to paint with. Yes, it's nice and wiggly, but it won't stand too much of that kind of treatment, my lad. Yes, of course you can paint with a knife if you want to. You can paint with your fingers if it comes to that. No, I shouldn't advise you to try. Yes, well, it makes a rougher kind of surface, all blobs and chunks of paint. All right, I'll show you presently. Yes, I'm going to begin with the sky. Why? Well, why do you think? Yes, because it's at the top. Yes, of course that blue's too dark, but I'm going to put some white in it. Yes, *and* some green. You didn't know there was any green in the sky? Well, there is. And sometimes there's purple and pink too. No, I'm not going to paint a purple and pink sky. The gentleman and the dogs have only just started out. It's morning in this picture. Yes, I know, on the other side they're coming home with a lot of birds and things. I'll put a pink and purple sunset into that if you're good and don't ask too many questions. No, be a good girl and don't joggle my arm. Oh, Lord!"

"Hullo, Farren!" said Wimsey. "Finding the young idea a bit too eager for information, eh?"

"My God!" said the painter. "Wimsey, by all that's holy! How did you get here? Don't say my wife sent you!"

"Not exactly," said Wimsey. "And yet, now you mention it, I believe she did do something of the sort."

Farren sighed.

"Come on," he said. "Spit it out and get it over. Run away to your mother, bairns. I've got to talk to this gentleman."

"Look here," said Wimsey, when they were alone. "I want to say, first of all, that I haven't the faintest right to ask questions. But I'd be damned glad if you'd tell me exactly what you've been up to since Monday night."

"I suppose my conduct is being harshly criticised at Kirkcudbright," said Farren. "Deserting the home, and all that?"

"Well, no," said Wimsey. "Your wife has stuck to it that there's nothing unusual in your disappearance. But—as a matter of fact—the police have been hunting for you everywhere."

"The police? Why in the world——?"

"I think I'll smoke a pipe," said Wimsey. "Well, the fact that you were talking rather wildly about suicide and other things, don't you know. And then your bicycle being found close to those old mines up beyond Creetown. It—suggested things, you see."

"Oh! I'd forgotten about the bicycle. Yes, but surely Gilda—I wrote to her."

"She isn't worried about that, now."

"I suppose she must have been rather anxious. I ought to have written earlier. But—damn it! I never thought about their finding that. And—by Jove! old Strachan will have been in a bit of a stew."

"Why Strachan, particularly?"

"Well, surely he told people—didn't he?"

"Look here, Farren, what the devil are you talking about?"

"About Monday night. Poor old Strachan! He must have thought I'd really gone and done it."

"When did you see Strachan, then?"

"Why, that night, up by the mines. Didn't you know?"

"I don't know anything," said Wimsey. "Suppose you tell me the story right end foremost."

"All right. I don't mind. I suppose you know that I had a bit of a row that night with Campbell. Oh! that reminds me, Wimsey. Didn't I see something funny in the paper about Campbell? Something about his being found dead?"

"He's been murdered," said Wimsey, abruptly.

"Murdered? That wasn't what I saw. But I haven't looked at a paper for days. I only saw—when was it?—Wednesday morning, I think—something about 'well-known Scottish painter found dead in a river.' "

"Oh, well, it hadn't got out then. But he was bumped off, as a matter of fact, some time on Monday night or Tuesday morning—up at the Minnoch."

"Was he? Serve the beggar right. Oh, by the way, I seem to

see something behind this. Am I supposed to have done it, Wimsey?"

"I don't know," said Wimsey, truthfully. "But there is a feeling that perhaps you ought to come forward and say something. You were looking for him, you know, on Monday night."

"Yes, I was. And if I'd met him, there *would* have been murder done. But as a matter of fact, I didn't meet him."

"You can prove that?"

"Well—I don't know that I can if it comes to that. This isn't serious, is it?"

"I don't know. Let's have the story, Farren."

"I see. Well. Well, I came home about six o'clock on Monday and found that blighter making love to my wife. I was fed up, Wimsey. I hoofed. him out and I daresay I made a bit of an ass of myself."

"Wait a minute. Did you actually see Campbell?"

"He was just making off when I came in. I told him to clear out, and then I went in and spoke my mind. I told Gilda I wouldn't have the fellow there. She stuck up for him, and that annoyed me. Mind you, Wimsey, I haven't a word against Gilda except that she can't and won't understand that Campbell is—was—a poisonous sort of hound and that she was making me a laughing-stock. She's got an idea about being kind and sympathetic, and she can't see that that sort of thing doesn't work with fellows like Campbell. Dash it all, I *know* the blighter was crazy about her. And when I tried, quite nicely, to point out that she was making a fool of herself, she got on her high horse and—— Damn it, Wimsey! I don't want to talk like a pig about my wife, but the fact is, she's too good and too full of ideals to understand what the ordinary man is like. You do see what I mean?"

"Perfectly," said Wimsey.

"Because my wife really is a wonderful woman. Only—well, I daresay I said a lot of silly things."

"I know exactly the sort of thing you said," observed Wimsey. "She didn't tell me, but I can imagine it. You stormed about, and she told you not to have coarse ideas, and you got hotter, and she got colder, and you said things you didn't mean in the hope of bringing her to your arms, so to speak, and then she said you were insulting and burst into tears, and then you worked yourself up into half-believing the accusations you'd only made to annoy her, and then you threatened murder and suicide and went out to get drunk. Bless your soul, you're not the first and won't be the last."

"Well, you've got it about right," said Farren. "Only I really did begin to believe it at the time. At least, I believed Campbell was out to do all the mischief he could. I did get drunk. I had one or two in the town, and then I barged off to Gatehouse to find Campbell."

"How did you miss him in Kirkcudbright? He was at the McClellan Arms all the time."

"I never thought of that. I just hared off to Gatehouse. He wasn't in his cottage, and Ferguson yelled out to me. I thought of having a row with Ferguson, but I wasn't as drunk as all that. Then I went and had a few more. Somebody told me they'd seen Campbell go out to Creetown, so I went after him."

"No, you didn't," said Wimsey. "You went up the road to the golf-links."

"Did I? Oh, yes, so I did. I went to find Strachan, but he was out. I left a note or a message for him, I think; to tell the truth, I'm not very clear about it. But I think I told him I was going to Creetown to do Campbell in and cut my own throat. Some rot or other. . . . I say, poor old Strachan! He must have had a time! Did he show that note to the police?"

"Not that I know of."

"Oh! no, I suppose he wouldn't. Strachan's a good sort. Well, I went over to Creetown. The pubs were shut when I got there, but I went in and got hold of a man there—by Jove! no, I suppose he wouldn't have come forward, either. Well, never mind the man—I don't want to get him into trouble. The point is that I raised a bottle of whiskey after closing-time."

"Yes?"

"Well, I'm a bit vague about the next part of it, but I know I remember going up into the hills, with some vague idea of chucking myself down one of the pits. I wandered round. I remember wheeling the damned bike over the rough stuff—and then, damn it all, I came to the mouth of one of the mines. Nearly fell into it. I sat down and moralised a bit on the brink, with the help of the whiskey. I must have been damned drunk. I don't know how long that lasted. Well, then, presently I heard somebody shouting and I shouted back. I felt like that. Somebody came up, and started talking. It was old Strachan. At least, my impression is that it was Strachan, but I freely admit that I may be mixing things up a bit. I know he talked and talked and tried to get hold of me, and I struggled and fought him. It was a lovely fight, I do know that. Then I knocked him down and started to run. I ran like hell. My God! it was fine. Drink takes me in the head, you know; my legs are always all right. I simply bounced over the heather, and the stars bounced along with me. Good God! I remember that now. I don't know how long it went on. And then I lost my footing and went rolling away down a slope somewhere. I suppose I fetched up all right at the bottom, because, when I woke it was well on in the morning, and I was lying in a sort of hollow among the bracken, quite snug and cosy and without so much as a headache.

"I didn't know where I was. But I didn't care. I just felt that nothing mattered at all. I didn't want to go home. I didn't care a hang about Campbell. I just felt as if all the cares of the world had tumbled off my back and left me alone in the sunshine. I walked straight ahead. I was getting damned hungry by that time, because I'd had no dinner the night before, but there wasn't so much as a shepherd's hut in sight. I walked and walked. The place was full of wee burns and I had plenty to drink. After hours and hours I struck a road and walked along, not meeting anybody. And then, some time about mid-day, I crossed a bridge and knew where I was. It was the place they call New Brig o' Dee, on the New Galloway Road. I hadn't really come so very far. I expect I must have made a bit of a circle, though I thought I was keeping the sun on my right all the time."

"The sun moves, you know," said Wimsey, "or appears to."

"Yes—I don't think I realised how long I'd been going. Anyhow, I got there, and started to walk towards New Galloway. I met some sheep and a few cows and carts, and at last a fellow with a lorry overtook me. He took me as far as New Galloway, and I got something to eat there."

"What time was that?" asked Wimsey, quickly.

"Oh, it must have been nearly three. Then I wondered what to do with myself. I'd got about ten pounds in my pocket and my one idea was that I didn't want to go back. I was finished. Done. I wanted to go gipsying. I didn't give a damn if I never saw the

Tollbooth spire again. I saw an empty lorry labelled with the name of a Glasgow firm on it, and I bargained with the man to take me to Dumfries. They were going that way."

"What was the name of the firm?"

"Eh? Oh, I don't know. There were two very decent fellows on it and we talked about fishing."

"Where did they put you off?"

"Just before we got to Dumfries. I wanted to think a bit, you see. It was a question whether I'd take the train there or put up in some pub or other. I was afraid of running into some of our crowd at the station. Besides, some of the railway people there would have known me. I often go to Dumfries. That was the trouble about the pub idea too. . . . I don't know if I can explain how I felt, Wimsey. It was as if I'd escaped from something and was afraid of being—well, bagged. I mean, if I had met anyone who knew me, I should have fudged up some tale about fishing or painting and made everything sound quite ordinary, and then I should have gone home. You see? It wouldn't have been the same if I'd had to make up an elaborate deception about it. You're not free when you have to tell lies to escape. It's not worth it. I can't possibly make you understand that."

"Why not?" said Wimsey. "It would be like buying a week-end wedding-ring."

"Yes—just as tedious as if it were 22-carat. And signing the hotel register and wondering if the reception-clerk believed you. Wimsey, you're rich and there's nothing to stop you from doing what you like. Why do you trouble to be respectable?"

"Just because there's nothing to stop me from doing what I like, probably. I get my fun out of it."

"I know you do," said Farren, looking at him in a puzzled way. "It's odd. You create an illusion of liberty. Is it money? Or is it being unmarried? But there are plenty of unmarried men who don't——"

"Aren't we wandering slightly from the matter in hand?" said Wimsey.

"Perhaps. Well—I went into a little inn—a one-horse little place—and had a drink in the four-ale bar. There was a young fellow there with a bike and side-car. He said he was going through to Carlisle. That gave me an idea. I asked him if he'd take me and he said he would. He was a decent bloke and didn't ask any questions."

"What was his name?"

"I didn't ask, nor did he. I said I was on a walking-tour and that my belongings were waiting for me in Carlisle. But he didn't seem to bother. I never met such a reasonable man."

"What was he?"

"I gathered that he had something to do with the second-hand motor trade and was taking the bike in part-exchange for something. I shouldn't have known that, only he apologised for its internals not being in perfect trim. In fact, something went wrong with them on the road and I had to hold an electric torch for him while he put it right. He didn't seem to have many ideas beyond plugs and things. He didn't talk. Said he'd been thirty-six hours on the road, but I needn't worry, because he could drive in his sleep."

Wimsey nodded. He knew the helots of the second-hand-motor trade. Grim, silent, cynical, abroad at all hours and in all weathers, they are men accustomed to disillusionment and disaster. To deliver their melancholy screws to their customers and depart before inconvenient discoveries are made; to scramble home with their surprise-packets of old iron before the patched radiator bursts or the clutch gives way—this is their sole preoccupation. Always dog-tired, dirty and prepared for the worst, habitually hard-up and morose, they are not likely to be inquisitive about stranded travellers who offer to pay for a lift.

"So you got to Carlisle?"

"Yes. I slept most of the time, except, of course, when I was holding the torch. I enjoyed the bits when I was awake. Not knowing who he was made it better. Do you know, I hadn't been in a side-car before. It's not like a car. Cars fascinate me, too, though the only two or three times I tried to drive one I didn't get much kick out of it. I like *being* driven—and this side-car business gets my imagination. The power is outside you, and you are pulled along —in tow, so to speak. Like being eloped with. You seem to notice the strength of the machine more than you do in a car. Why is that?"

Wimsey shook his head.

"Perhaps I was imagining things. Well, anyhow, we got to Carlisle in the morning and I had some grub in a sort of tea-shop place. Then, of course, I had to decide on something. I bought a clean shirt and some socks and a tooth-brush and so on, and a knapsack to shove them into. It was only then that I thought about money. I'd have to cash a cheque somewhere. But that meant telling people where I was. I mean, the bank people would have to ring up Kirkcudbright and all that. I thought it would be more fun to pay my way. I'd still got enough to buy paints with, so I went into an art-dealer's and got a box and a palette and some brushes and colours——"

"Winsor & Newton, I observe," said Wimsey.

"Yes. You can get them easily in most places, you know. I usually get my stuff from Paris, but Winsor & Newton are perfectly reliable. I thought I'd make my way down into the Lake Country and paint little pictures for tourists or something. It's fearfully easy. You can knock off two or three in a day—hills and water and mists, you know—and idiots will give you ten bob a time, if the stuff's sentimental enough. I knew a man who always paid for his holidays that way. Didn't sign 'em in his own name, naturally. It's a form of mass-production."

"Hence the idea of Mr. H. Ford?"

"Oh, you've been to the Bull at Brough? Yes—the idea rather tickled me. Well, after I'd bought the paints I had just about enough left to bribe another lorry-driver. But I didn't. I found a man with a Riley—Oxford fellow—a frightfully good sort. He was heading south and told me I could go as far as I liked with him and damn paying for it. He talked all right. His name was John Barrett and he was just fooling round amusing himself. Didn't know where he was going. Had just got the new car and wanted to see what she could do. Damn it, he did, too. I was never so frightened in my life."

"Where did he live?"

"Oh, London, somewhere. He told me the place, but I can't remember it now. He asked a lot of questions, too, but I just said I was a travelling artist and he thought it was a fearfully good wheeze. I didn't mind telling him that, because by that time it was true, you see. He asked what one could make out of it and all that, and I gave him all the stuff I'd had from my friend, and he asked me where I'd been last and I said in Galloway. It was just as easy as that. But when we got to Brough, I said I'd get off there. I felt I was too young to die—just as I was starting off on an adventure, too. He was a bit disappointed, but he wished me luck and all that. I went to the Bull, because it looked less grand than the other place, and that was where I got the idea about the sign. Good thing I did, too, because the weather turned nasty the next day, and I hadn't altogether reckoned with that when I made my plan about doing the hills and lakes and things. So that was that, and here I am."

Farren took up his brushes again and renewed his assault upon the Dog and Gun.

"Very jolly," said Wimsey. "But you know, it all boils down to this, that you can't produce a single witness to say where you were between Monday night and Tuesday afternoon at 3 o'clock."

"Oh! no—I'd forgotten about all that. But, I mean, all this isn't serious, really? And after all, I've got a perfectly natural, straightforward explanation."

"It sounds natural enough to me, perhaps," said Wimsey, "but whether the police will take that view——"

"Damn the police! I say, Wimsey——"

The shadow of something cold and deadly crept into the painter's eyes.

"Does this mean I've got to go back, Wimsey?"

"I'm afraid," said Wimsey, "I'm very much afraid——" He was looking back over Farren's shoulder at the back door of the inn, from which two squarely-built men in tweeds were emerging. Farren, catching the infection of uneasiness, turned his head.

"My God," he said. "It's all up. Bagged. Trapped. Prison."

"Yes," said Wimsey, almost inaudibly. "And you won't escape this time—ever."

CHAPTER XXI

STRACHAN'S STORY

"BICYCLES?" said Inspector Macpherson. "Dinna ye talk tae me o' bicycles. I'm fair fed up wi' the name o' them. Wad ye believe that there could be sic a stour aboot twa-three bicycles? Here's ane o' them at Euston and anither up at Creetoon, and as if that wasn't eneugh, here's Waters' bicycle vanished and naebody kens whether we should arrest Waters for murder or make a sairch for a bicycle-thief."

"It's very trying," said Wimsey. "And I suppose nobody saw Waters go aboard at the Doon?"

"An' if onybody had seen him," said the Inspector, wrathfully, "wad I be fashin' masel' the noo? There's a mon saw anither mon wadin' across the sand, but he was half a mile off, an' whae's tae say it was Waters?"

"I must say," said Wimsey, "that I never in all my life heard of such an unconvincing bunch of alibis. By the way, Inspector, did you check up that story of Ferguson's?"

"Ferguson?" said the Inspector, in the resentful accents of a schoolboy burdened with too much homework. "Oo, ay, we havena forgot Ferguson. I went tae Sparkes & Crisp an' interviewed the employees. There was twa of them remembered him weel eneugh. The lad doonstairs in the show-room couldna speak with sairtainty tae the time, but he recognised Ferguson from his photograph as havin' brocht in a magneto on the Monday afternoon. He said Mr. Saunders wad be the man tae see tae that, and pit a ca' through on the house telephone tae Mr. Sparkes, an' he had the young fellow in. Saunders is ane o' they bright lads. He picked the photograph at once oot o' the six I showed him an' turned up the entry o' the magneto in the day-book."

"Could he swear to the time Ferguson came in?"

"He wadna charge his memory wi' the precise minute, but he said he had juist come in fra' his lunch an' found Ferguson waitin' for him. His lunch-time is fra' 1.30 tae 2.30, but he was a bit

191

late that day, an' Ferguson had been waitin' on him a wee while.
He thinks it wad be aboot ten minutes tae three."

"That's just about what Ferguson made it."

"Near eneugh."

"H'm. That sounds all right. Was that all Saunders had to say?"

"Ay. Forbye that he said he couldna weel understand whit had
happened tae the magneto. He said it looked as though some yin
had been daein' it a wilfu' damage."

"That's funny. That would be the mechanic's report, of course.
Did you see the mechanic at all?"

The Inspector admitted that he had not done so, not seeing what
bearing it could have upon the case.

"Was you thinkin', maybe," he suggested, "that some felonious
body was interested in seein' that Ferguson didna' take oot his car
that mornin'?"

"Inspector," said Wimsey, "you are a mind-reader. I was thinking exactly that."

Farren had returned to Kirkcudbright. His dream of escape had
vanished. His wife had forgiven him. His absence was explained as
a trifling and whimsical eccentricity. Gilda Farren sat, upright and
serene, spinning the loose white flock into a strong thread that
wound itself ineluctably to smother the twirling spindle. The story
had been told to the police. Sir Maxwell Jamieson shook his head
over it. Short of arresting Farren, they must remain content with his
story or else disprove it. And they could not very well arrest Farren,
for they might want to arrest Waters or Gowan or Graham or even
Strachan, all of whose stories were equally odd and suspicious. It
would be preposterous to arrest five people for one crime.

The porter at Girvan was still desperately ill. He had—out of
pure perversity, no doubt—developed peritonitis. The Euston bicycle
had been duly identified as the property of young Andrew of the
Anwoth, but what evidence was there that it had any connection
with Campbell? If Farren were the murderer it had obviously no
connection with it at all, for Farren could not have taken the Ayr
train at Girvan and been in New Galloway at 3 o'clock. And that
part of Farren's story was true, anyway, for they had checked it.
No, Farren, like the rest, must have rope given him. So Farren
sat sulkily in his studio and Mrs. Farren span—not a rope, perhaps,

but fetters at any rate—in the sitting-room with the cool blue curtains.

The Chief Constable took upon himself the task of interviewing Strachan, who received him with politeness, but without enthusiasm.

"We have obtained a statement from Mr. Farren," said Sir Maxwell, "with reference to his movements on Monday night and Tuesday morning, which requires your corroboration."

"Indeed," said Strachan. "In what way?"

"Come," said the Chief Constable, "you know very well in what way. We know, from Mr. Farren's story, that you have not told us all the facts about your own movements at that time. Now that Mr. Farren has given his explanation, you have no longer any reason for reticence."

"I don't altogether understand this," said Strachan. "Mr. Farren, as I am told, went for a holiday trip to England and has returned. Why should I answer any questions about his private affairs? To what is the inquiry directed?"

"Mr. Strachan," said the Chief Constable, "I do most earnestly beg you not to take up this attitude. It can do no good and only creates difficulties and, if I may say so, suspicion. You are perfectly well aware that we are inquiring into the circumstances of Mr. Campbell's murder, and that it is absolutely necessary for us to obtain information about all the persons who saw Mr. Campbell shortly before his death. Mr. Farren saw him at 6 o'clock on Monday week, and he has given us an account of his movements since that time. This account requires your corroboration. If you can give it, where is the point of refusing?"

"The point is," said Strachan, "that Mr. Farren is going about at liberty, and that therefore, presumably, you have nothing against him. In that case, I am not bound to answer any impertinent queries about his behaviour or his personal affairs. If, on the other hand, you intend to accuse him or me of anything criminal, it is your duty to say so, and also to warn us that we are not obliged to answer your questions."

"Of course," said Sir Maxwell, smothering his annoyance, "you are not in any way bound to answer if you think that by so doing you will incriminate yourself. But you cannot prevent us from drawing the natural conclusion from your refusal."

"Is that a threat?"

"Certainly not. It is a warning."

"And if I thank you for the warning and still decline to make a statement?"

"In that case, well——"

"In that case your only alternative is to arrest me and charge me with murder, or with complicity. Are you prepared to go as far as that?"

The Chief Constable was not by any means prepared, but he replied, curtly:

"You will have to take your chance of that."

Strachan paused, tapping his fingers on the table. The clock on the mantelpiece ticked loudly, and the voice of Myra floated in from the garden, playing at tig with her mother and the nurse.

"Very well," said Strachan, at last. "What does Farren say that wants my corroboration?"

Sir Maxwell Jamieson was annoyed again at the obviousness of this trap.

"I am afraid that won't do, Mr. Strachan," he said, a little acidly. "It will be better, I think, that you should begin from the beginning and give me your own account of what happened."

"What do you call the beginning?"

"Begin by saying where you were on Monday afternoon."

"On Monday afternoon? I was out, painting."

"Whereabouts?"

"Up at Balmae. Would you like proof of that? I can show you the canvas, but of course that won't bear visible signs of having been painted on Monday. However, I daresay somebody saw the car. I stuck it in a field and walked down to the edge of the cliff. Subject of the painting, Ross Island. Price, when finished, 50 guineas."

"What time did you leave there?"

"About half-past seven."

"Did the light remain good as long as that?"

"Good heavens!" said Strachan. "Are the police going to display intelligence about art? No, it didn't, but I had taken my dinner out with me. The dinner consisted of cold meat sandwiches, baps, brown bread, cheese and tomatoes, with a bottle of Worthington. To entertain myself during the orgy I had a book—a very nice book, all about a murder committed in this part of the country. *Sir John Magill's Last Journey*, by one Mr. Crofts. You should read it. The police in that book called in Scotland Yard to solve their problems for them."

Sir Maxwell took this information without wincing, and merely demanded:

"Did you then return to Gatehouse?"

"I did not. I went on to Tongland."

"Passing through Kirkcudbright?"

"Not being in an aeroplane, obviously I had to pass through Kirkcudbright."

"I mean, at what time?"

"At about 8 o'clock."

"Did anybody see you?"

"I have no doubt they did. It is my experience that one never passes through Kirkcudbright or anywhere else without being seen by at least half a dozen people."

"You did not stop at all?"

"I did not."

"You went on to Tongland. And there?"

"I fished. Total bag, one trout, three-quarters of a pound, one ditto, seven ounces, and three that were too young to leave home."

"Did you see anybody there?"

"I don't know that I did. The keeper knows me, but he wasn't there. But I daresay some busybody or other noticed me."

"When did you leave Tongland?"

"Round about 11 o'clock, I think. The fish seemed to have lost enthusiasm, and so did I."

"And then?"

"Then I went home like a good little boy. I got back some time round about midnight."

"You could produce witnesses to that, of course?"

"Of course. My wife and my servant. But naturally they would swear to anything I told them to swear to."

"No doubt," said Sir Maxwell, unmoved by this sarcasm. "What then?"

"I went out again in the car."

"Why?"

"To look for Farren."

"What made you do that?"

"I found a note from him waiting for me."

"Have you still got that note?"

"No, I burnt it."

"What was in it?"

"He told me that he was going to commit suicide. I thought I ought to follow him and stop him."

"Did he say where he was going?"

"No, but I thought he would probably go up into the hills by Creetown. We had sometimes discussed the question of suicide, and the old mines up there seemed to have a kind of attraction for him."

"I see. You went straight over to Creetown?"

"Yes."

"Are you quite sure, Mr. Strachan?"

"Yes, of course."

Sir Maxwell was a cautious man, but there was something guarded in Strachan's tone which warned him that this was a lie, and a sudden illumination moved him to risk a bluff.

"Then you would be very much surprised if I told you that your car had been seen on the road between the Anwoth Hotel and Standing Stone Pool between midnight and 12.30?"

Strachan was obviously not prepared for this.

"Yes," he said, "I should be surprised."

"It is surprising," rejoined the Chief Constable, "but, as you say, there is always some busybody about. Anyway, now that you are reminded of it, you do recollect going in that direction?"

"Well, yes. I had forgotten about it for the moment; I went—I thought——"

"You went to Campbell's house, Mr. Strachan. As a matter of fact, you were seen there. Why did you go?"

"I thought possibly I might find Farren there."

"Why?"

"Oh, well—he didn't like Campbell very much, and I thought —it struck me as just possible that he might have had the idea of getting an explanation or something from Campbell."

"That was an odd thing for you to think, was it not?"

"Not very. After all, it's no good pretending that Campbell and he were on good terms. They had had a quarrel that evening——"

"Yes, but you didn't know that at the time, Mr. Strachan. You tell me that you went straight through from Balmae to Tongland without stopping or speaking to anybody in Kirkcudbright."

"No, that's true. But of course, if Farren wanted to commit suicide, I could put two and two together."

"I see. It was just a guess. There was nothing in Mr. Farren's note to suggest that he might be going to see Mr. Campbell?"

"Nothing whatever."

"Mr. Strachan, I must warn you that if you persist in concealing the truth, you may involve yourself in very serious trouble. We know the contents of the note."

"Oh!" Strachan shrugged his shoulders. "If you know, why ask me?"

"We are asking you for independent corroboration, Mr. Strachan, and I must say that you are making things very difficult for Mr. Farren and for us by this attitude."

"Well, if Farren has told you—— Very well, then, the note did mention Campbell, and I went along to see if Farren was there, and, if not, to warn Campbell."

"To warn him? You took Mr. Farren's threats very seriously, then?"

"Well, not very seriously. But they are both excitable men, and I thought that there might be a great deal of unpleasantness if they met in that mood, and possibly a really nasty row."

"Did you deliver the warning?"

"The house was empty. I knocked two or three times and then, as everything was dark, I went in."

"The door was open, then?"

"No, but I knew where to find the key."

"Was that a thing everybody knew?"

"How should I know? I only knew that I'd often seen Campbell hang it up, after locking the door, on a particular nail hidden behind the gutter-spout."

"I see. So you went in?"

"Yes. Everything was quite clean and tidy and it didn't look as though Campbell had been in. There were no supper-dishes or anything about, and he wasn't in bed, because I went upstairs to see. I left a note for him on the table and came away again, relocking the door and putting the key back where I found it."

Only by a great effort of self-control did the Chief Constable keep from showing the staggering effect of this piece of news. He succeeded in asking, in matter-of-fact tones:

"What exactly did you say in the note?" As Strachan seemed to hesitate, he added, with more assurance than he felt:

"Try to make your recollection more precise this time, Mr. Strachan. As you see, we are sometimes able to check these items."

"Yes," said Strachan, coolly. "As a matter of fact, I've been rather wondering why I haven't heard about the note before."

"Have you? Didn't you take it for granted that Campbell had received it and destroyed it?"

"I did at first," said Strachan, "and that was why I thought all this fuss about Monday night so unnecessary. If Campbell came in after I was there, then he was alive long after I saw him. He had his breakfast, didn't he? At least, I understood so—and I supposed he had seen the note then and got rid of it."

"But you don't think that now?"

"Well, if you got the note, he obviously didn't. And if you'd found it on his dead body, you'd surely have mentioned it before this."

"I did not say," said Sir Maxwell, patiently, "*when* the note had come into our possession."

For some reason, this remark appeared to unnerve Strachan, and he remained silent.

"Well now," said the Chief Constable, "do you mind telling me what was in the note? You have had plenty of time to think it over."

"To invent something, you mean? Well, I'm not going to invent, but I can't undertake to remember it word for word. I think I said something like this: 'Dear Campbell,—I am rather anxious about F. He is in a highly-wrought-up state and is threatening to do you some injury. However much he may have to complain of your behaviour—and you know best about this—I think it advisable to put you on your guard.' It was something like that, and I signed it with my initials."

"You thought it worth while to write that note about a friend of yours to a man you personally disliked—and you still say you did not take Farren's threats seriously?"

"Well, you never know. I was thinking more of Farren than of

Campbell. I didn't want him to get into trouble—an action for assault, or anything of that kind."

"It still seems to me a fairly strong step to take, Mr. Strachan. How often had Farren seriously threatened to harm Campbell?"

"He had occasionally expressed himself in rather a reckless manner."

"Had he ever attacked him?"

"N—no. There was a slight fuss once———"

"I seem to remember hearing something about a quarrel—about six months ago, was it?"

"About that. But it didn't amount to anything."

"In any case, you thought the matter of enough importance to write that note to a man as notoriously indiscreet and fiery-tempered as Campbell. That speaks for itself, doesn't it? What happened next?"

"I went up to Creetown in my car and turned off up the hill road. I left the car where the road ends just beyond Falbae, and went along on foot calling Farren as I went. There was no moon, but it was starlight and I had my torch with me. I know that road pretty well. At least, it isn't a road, but a sort of shepherd's path. When I got close to the old mines I began searching about carefully. Presently I thought I saw something move and I shouted again. Then I saw that there really was a man there. He ran away and I followed him and caught him up. I said, 'My God, Farren, is that you?' and he said, 'What the hell do you want?' So I caught hold of him."

"Was it Farren?"

Strachan seemed to hesitate again, but finally replied, "Yes, it was."

"Well?"

"Well, I argued with him for some time and tried to persuade him to come home. He absolutely refused and started to move off again. I took him by the arm, but he struggled with me and in the confusion he hit me in the face and knocked me down. By the time I had scrambled up again he had got away from me, and I could hear him scrambling over some stones in the distance. I ran after him. It was pretty dark, of course, but the sky was quite clear and one could see moving objects like lumps of grey shadow. I caught glimpses of him now and again when he came up on the sky-line. You know that place—all dips and hillocks. I was getting pretty well winded and I was thinking about him and didn't look where I was going. I tripped over a bunch of stuff and found myself falling head-first—over the edge of the world, it seemed to me. I bumped and banged against what felt like baulks of timber, and finally brought up against something. I was completely knocked out of course. Anyhow, when I came to my senses I found myself at the bottom of a pretty deep place with black darkness rising up all round me and a patch of starlight at the top. I felt round very cautiously and tried to get up, but the moment I was on my feet, I went all sick and giddy and lost consciousness again. I don't know how long that lasted. It must have been a good many hours, because when I came to myself again it was broad daylight, and I was able to see where I was."

"One of the old shafts, I suppose."

"Yes. Lord! it was a place! I don't suppose it was more than forty feet deep, but that looked quite enough to me, and it went sheer up like a chimney, with a little square of light twinkling away at the top; it seemed a mile off. It was narrow, fortunately. By spread-eagling myself I could get a grip on the sides and hoist myself painfully up by inches, but it was slow work, and my head was so swimmy and my legs so weak that I simply tumbled down again after the first two or three attempts. I yelled and yelled, hoping against hope that somebody might hear me, but the place was as silent as the grave. I was extraordinarily lucky not to have broken a leg or an arm. If I had, I suppose I should have been down there now."

"No," said the Chief Constable. "We should have brought you up on Friday or Saturday."

"Ah!—well, by that time I don't suppose I should have been in any condition to worry about it. Well, after resting a bit more I got my head and legs under better control, and gradually wormed my way up. It was a slow job, because the sides were smooth and didn't give much foothold or handhold, and sometimes I'd lose purchase and slip down a few feet. Fortunately there were horizontal beams across the sides at intervals, and I was able to catch on to them and give myself a bit of a breather from time to time. I kept on hoping that the people at the farm would find my car and come to look for me, but if they did see it, they probably thought I was fishing or picnicking somewhere and attached no importance to it. I clawed my way up—happily I'm on the tall and hefty side—and at last—God! it was a relief—I found myself at the top and hooked an arm out on to the blessed grass. There was an awful tussle with that last foot or so—I thought I should never heave myself over the edge, but I managed it somehow. I dragged my legs out after me, feeling as though they were made of solid lead, and then I just rolled over and lay gasping. Ugh!"

Strachan paused, and the Chief Constable congratulated him.

"Well, I lay there for a bit. It was a gorgeous day, very windy and sunny, and I tell you that the world looked good to me for a bit. I was quivering like a blanc-mange, and hungry and thirsty—ye gods!"

"What time do you think that was?"

"I couldn't be sure, because my watch had stopped. It's a wrist-watch, and must have got a bump in the fall. I rested a bit—half an hour, perhaps—and then I pulled myself together and tried to find out where I was. The mines are scattered about a good bit, and I couldn't recognize the place. However, presently I found a burn and had a drink and stuck my head in the water. After that I felt better, only I discovered that I'd collected a magnificent black eye when Farren punched me in the face, and of course I was wrenched and bruised from head to foot. The back of my head still has a lump on it like an egg; I suppose that was what knocked me out. The next thing was to find the car. I calculated that I must be nearly two miles from Falbae, and decided that if I followed the flow of the burn, I must be going in the right direction, so I set off downstream. It was damned hot, and I'd lost my hat. Did you find it, by the way?"

"Yes, but we didn't know what to make of it. It must have got knocked off in your rough-and-tumble with Farren, and at first we thought it was his, but Mrs. Farren said it wasn't, so we didn't know quite what to think."

"Well, now you know. The fact that you found it there ought to prove my story pretty well, don't you think?"

The Chief Constable had been thinking that very thing, but at the sharply triumphant note in Strachan's voice, a doubt shot through him. What would have been easier than to drop a hat at a suitable place, any time between Tuesday and Friday, as a foundation for this highly dramatic story?

"Never mind what I think, Mr. Strachan," said he. "Go on. What did you do next?"

"Well, I kept on down the burn, and after a time I came in sight of the road and the car. It was just where I had left it, and the dashboard clock made it a quarter past twelve."

"Didn't you see anybody on the way back?"

"Well, yes—I did see one man. But I—well, I lay doggo till he had passed."

"Why?"

Strachan looked rather uncomfortable.

"Because—well, because I wasn't exactly ready to answer questions. I didn't know what had become of Farren. I realised that it looked as though I'd been in the wars, and if Farren's body was going to be found down a hole or anything it might look rather queer for me."

"But surely——"

"Yes, I know just what you're going to say. But surely, if I thought that, I ought to have told somebody and got a search-party going. But don't you see, it was perfectly possible that Farren had come to his senses and gone quietly home. It would have been perfectly idiotic to start a rumpus and make a scandal all about nothing. It seemed to me that the best thing I could do was to get back quietly and find out what really had happened. I had a beast of a time starting up the car. I'd left the lights on the night before, with the idea of finding it again, and the batteries had run down. I had to swing her over with the starting-handle, and it was heavy work. Those Chrysler 70's have rather a big engine. Still, I managed to get her going after about a quarter of an hour——"

"Surely you could have got help from the farm."

Strachan made a gesture of impatience.

"Haven't I told you that I didn't want to attract attention? As a matter of fact, I was afraid all the time that somebody would hear me and come up to see what was happening. But they didn't. Probably they were all at their dinner. I had an old cap and a motoring coat in the car, so I tidied myself up as best I could, and got on to the back road—the one through Knockeans. It crosses the Skyre

Burn just beyond Glen and comes out by Anwoth Auld Kirk. I got back home about half-past one."

The Chief Constable nodded.

"Was your family alarmed by your being out all night?"

"No. I forgot to say that when I got Farren's note I ran up and told my wife that I'd been called away and that I didn't want anything said about it."

"I see. What did you do when you got home?"

"I rang up the McClellan Arms in Kirkcudbright and asked them kindly to send a message up to the Farrens to say, would Mr. Farren ring me up about a fishing appointment. The call came through in about half an hour's time, when I'd had a bath and felt rather better. Mrs. Farren had come down and said Hugh wasn't at home and could she take a message? I told her to say absolutely nothing to anybody for the moment, but that I would come over and see her after lunch, as I had something rather important to tell her. She gave a bit of a gasp, and I said, had Hugh come home last night, and to answer only yes or no. She said, No. And I said, Had there been any sort of trouble with Campbell? and she said, Yes. So I told her to say nothing about that either, and I would come over as soon as I could."

"How much did you tell your wife about all this?"

"Only that Farren had got himself into a state of mind and left home, and that she was on no account to say anything to anyone about it, or about my having come home so late and in such a pickle. When I'd made myself reasonably presentable, I had some lunch. I needed it by that time."

"I expect you did. Did you, in fact, go over to Kirkcudbright afterwards?"

"No, I didn't."

"Why not?"

There was something about the Chief Constable's dogged "Why?" and "Why not?" that was irritating as well as disquieting. Strachan shifted awkwardly in his seat.

"I changed my mind about it."

"Why?"

"I was going to go, of course." Strachan appeared to lose the scent for a moment and then went off on a fresh cast. "We dine in the middle of the day on account of my little girl. We had roast jiggot of mutton. It wasn't ready till past two o'clock. That was later than our usual time, of course, but they'd kept it back with the idea that I might turn up. I wanted that mutton, and I didn't want to appear unusual before the servant. So we took our time over dinner and hadn't finished till nearly three. About a quarter past three it would be before I was ready to start. I went down to open the gate for the car. I saw Tom Clark coming down from the golf-course. Just opposite my gate he met the Gatehouse policeman. They didn't see me, because of the hedge."

The Chief Constable made no comment. Strachan swallowed hard and continued.

"The constable said, 'Is the Provost up at the golf-course?' Clark said, 'Ay, he is that.' The constable said. 'He's wanted. Mr. Campbell's been found lying dead at Newton-Stewart.' After that they moved farther up the road, and I didn't hear any more. So I went back to the house to think about it."

"What did you think about it?"

"I couldn't make up my mind what to think about it. I couldn't see how it was going to affect me. But I didn't feel that it was quite the moment to go up to the Farrens'. It might cause comment. At any rate, I wanted time to consider."

"Was that the first you had heard about Campbell?"

"Of course it was. Why, the news had only just come through."

"Did it surprise you?"

"Naturally."

"But you didn't rush out as anybody else would have done and demand details?"

"No."

"Why?"

"What the devil do you mean, why? I didn't, that's all."

"I see. When Lord Peter Wimsey called later in the evening, you still hadn't been over to Kirkcudbright?"

"No."

"He brought the news of Campbell's death to your wife. Had she heard about it before?"

"No. I didn't know any particulars and I thought it better not to mention it."

"Did you tell Lord Peter that you knew about it already?"

"No."

"Why not?"

"I thought my wife would think it odd that I'd said nothing about it to her."

"Was anything said about your black eye?"

"Yes. I gave a—er—a fictitious explanation."

"Why?"

"I didn't see what business it was of Wimsey's."

"And what did your wife think of that explanation?"

"I don't see what business that is of yours."

"Were you at that time of the opinion that Farren had committed a murder?"

"There wasn't any question of murder at that time."

"Precisely, Mr. Strachan. That is what makes your behaviour appear so odd. You went over and saw Mrs. Farren late that night?"

"I did."

"What did you say to her?"

"I told her the events of the previous night."

"Was that all? You did not, for example, say that you expected a charge of murder to be preferred against Farren and that she was to be very careful what she said to the police?"

Strachan's eyes narrowed.

"Isn't that one of those questions which you are not supposed to ask, nor I to answer?"

"Have it your own way, Mr. Strachan." The Chief Constable got up. "You seem to be well acquainted with the law. You know, for example, that an accessory to murder after the fact is liable to the same punishment as the principal?"

"Certainly I do, Sir Maxwell. I also know that you are not allowed to use threats, either overt or implicit, in interrogating a witness. Is there anything further I can do for you?"

"Nothing, thank you," replied the Chief Constable, politely.

•   •   •   •   •   •   •   •

Indeed, he thought, as he drove back to Kirkcudbright, Strachan had done quite enough. If the story about the note left on Campbell's table were true—and he was inclined to believe it—then Strachan had shattered the whole elaborate theory that the police had been building up. For what it meant was clearly this. Either Campbell had been alive after Strachan's visit—in which case there had been no murder on the Gatehouse-Kirkcudbright road—or else some other person, hitherto unknown, had entered the cottage after midnight, and that person was undoubtedly the murderer.

There was, of course, the possibility that there never had been any note, and that Strachan had found Campbell at home and killed him. This agreed with Ferguson's evidence. But in that case, why invent the tale about the note at all, unless to throw suspicion on Farren? That was ridiculous, because the only reasonable explanation of Strachan's conduct otherwise was that he was either shielding Farren or in league with him.

Some other person—some other person. Who could that be? So far, Ferguson's story had been amply borne out. The first arrival of the car with the body, the second arrival of Strachan—if a third person had arrived, how unfortunate that Ferguson should not have heard him come! Ferguson——

Ferguson.

Yes, well, what about Ferguson?

He, of all people, could have entered Campbell's cottage unnoticed. He had only to walk round and open the door with that convenient key, which he must have seen Campbell hide a hundred times.

But then, that was absurd. Not only had Ferguson got an alibi— the Chief Constable did not set any undue value on alibis—but this theory left one huge question unanswered. *Where had Campbell been when Strachan came in?* If Strachan had found him there, why should he not have said so?

Suppose Strachan had found Campbell lying there dead—killed by Ferguson at some earlier moment. What then? Was Strachan in league with Ferguson?

Here was a real idea at last. All their difficulties had arisen from supposing that only one artist had been concerned in the crime. Ferguson could have committed the murder and established an alibi by going to Glasgow, while Strachan remained behind to concoct the faked accident and paint the picture.

All that story about fighting Farren and tumbling down a mine was very thin. Strachan had been up at Newton-Stewart all that time. His return by the by-road between Creetown and Anwoth Kirk could probably be proved, and agreed reasonably well with the time necessary for taking the body to the Minnoch, painting the picture and making his escape.

Only—why bring Farren into it? Could Strachan not have invented some better excuse for being out all night than one which involved his best friend? One, too, which was so suspicious in itself? It argued a degree of cold-blooded villainy that one would hardly expect from Strachan.

A clever fellow, though. One who saw the drift of your questions before you asked them. A keen, canny, cautious devil. A man who could think a plan like this out beforehand.

Clever, to think of taking that hat up to Falbae and leaving it there on the edge of the mine-shaft. But he had shown his triumph a bit too openly there.

The Chief Constable felt more satisfied than he had done for some time. He unbent so far as to go and look for Wimsey, to tell him all about it. But Wimsey was not at home.

CHAPTER XXII

GRAHAM'S STORY

"I DO wish Wimsey," said Waters, irritably, "you would get something to do. Why not go fishing, or take the car out for a run? I can't paint properly with you snooping round all the time. It puts me off my stroke."

"I'm sorry," said Wimsey. "It fascinates me. I think the most joyous thing in life is to loaf round and watch another bloke doing a job of work. Look how popular the men are who dig up London with electric drills. Duke's son, cook's son, son of a hundred kings —people will stand there for hours on end, with their ear-drums splitting—why? Simply for the pleasure of being idle while other people work."

"Very likely," said Waters. "But the row fortunately prevents them from hearing the workmen's comments on their behaviour. How would you like me to sit round and watch you detecting things?"

"That's different," said Wimsey. "The essence of detection is secrecy. It has no business to be spectacular. But you can watch me if you like."

"Right-ho! You run away and do some detecting, and I'll come and watch you when I've finished this panel."

"Don't disturb yourself," said Wimsey, pleasantly. "You can watch me now. There's no charge."

"Oh! are you detecting now?"

"Like anything. If you could take the top of my head off you would see the wheels whizzing round."

"I see. You're not detecting me, I hope."

"Everybody always hopes that."

Waters glanced at him sharply and uneasily, and laid his palette aside.

"Look here, Wimsey—you're not suggesting anything? I've told you all about my movements, and I suppose you believe me. The police may be excused for seeing nothing but the obvious, but I should have thought that you at least had commonsense. If I had been murdering Campbell, surely I should have taken care to provide myself·with a better alibi."

"It depends on how clever you are," replied Wimsey, coolly. "You remember Poe's bit about that in *The Purloined Letter*. A very stupid murderer doesn't bother about an alibi at all. A murderer one degree cleverer says, 'If I am to escape suspicion, I must have a good alibi.' But a murderer who was cleverer still might say to himself, 'Everyone will expect the murderer to provide a first-class alibi; therefore, the better my alibi, the more they will suspect me. I will go one better still; I will provide an alibi which is obviously imperfect. Then people will say that surely, if I had been guilty, I should have provided a better alibi.' If I were a murderer myself, that is what I should do."

"Then you would probably come to a sticky end."

"Very likely; because the police might be so stupid that they never got beyond the first step in the reasoning. It's a pity about that bicycle of yours, isn't it?"

Waters took up his palette again.

"I don't want to discuss this stupid business."

"Nor do I. Go on painting. What a lot of brushes you've got. Do you use them all?"

"Oh, no!" said Waters, sarcastically. "I keep them there for swank."

"Do you always keep everything in this satchel? It's just like a woman's vanity-bag, all higgledy-piggledy."

"I can always find things when I want them."

"Campbell used a satchel, too."

"Then that was a bond of union between us, wasn't it?" Waters snatched the satchel, rather impatiently, out of Wimsey's hands, ferreted out a tube of rose madder, dabbed some paint on his palette, screwed up the tube and tossed it back into the bag again.

"Do you use rose madder?" said Wimsey, inquisitively. "Some people say it's such an awkward colour."

"It's handy sometimes—if you know how to use it."

"Isn't it supposed to be rather fugitive?"

"Yes—I don't use much of it. Have you been taking an art course?"

"Something like it. Studying different methods and all that. It's very interesting. I'm sorry I never saw Campbell at work. He———"

"For God's sake, don't keep harping on Campbell!"

"No? But I so well remember your saying that you could do a perfectly good imitation of Campbell if you liked. That was just before he was bumped off—do you remember?"

"I don't remember anything about it."

"Well, you were a bit tight at the time, and I don't suppose you meant it. There's a bit about him in the *Sunday Chronicle* this week. I've got it somewhere. Oh, yes—it says he is a great loss to the artistic world. 'His inimitable style,' it says. Still, I suppose they have to say something. 'Highly individual technique'; that's a good phrase. 'Remarkable power of vision and unique colour-sense placed him at once in the first rank.' I notice that people who die suddenly generally seem to be in the first rank."

Waters snorted.

"I know that fellow who does the *Sunday Chronicle* stuff. One of the Hambledon gang. But Hambledon *is* a painter. Campbell took Hambledon's worst tricks and made a style out of them. I tell you———"

The door of the studio burst open and Jock Graham tumbled in, breathless.

"I say, is Wimsey here? Sorry, Waters, but I must speak to Wimsey. No, it's all right, I don't want to take him away. Wimsey, old man, I'm in the most ghastly hole. It's too awful. Have you heard about it? It's only just been sprung upon me."

"Go to, go to," said Wimsey, "you have heard what you should not. Put on your nightgown, look not so pale. I tell you yet again, Campbell's dead; 'a cannot come out on's grave."

"I wish he could."

"Wake Duncan with thy knocking? I would thou couldst."

"Oh, stop drivelling, Wimsey. This really is damnable."

"O horror, horror, horror," pursued Wimsey, staggering realistically into a corner, "tongue nor heart cannot conceive nor name it. Where got'st thou that goose-look?"

"Goose is right enough," said Graham. "That's exactly what I'm looking like just now."

"Geese are made to be plucked," said Wimsey, eyeing him shrewdly, "and so are you."

"Was that a lucky shot, or did you mean it?"

"What is all this about?" asked Waters, peevishly.

"I don't mind you knowing," said Graham. "It'll be all over the county in half a moment if something isn't done about it. My God!" He wiped his forehead and dropped heavily into the nearest chair.

"Well, well," said Wimsey.

"Listen! You know all this fuss there is about Campbell. That constable fellow, Duncan——"

"I told you Duncan came into it somewhere."

"Shut up! That fool came asking questions about where I'd been on Tuesday and so on. I never took the thing seriously, you know. I told him to run away and play. Then something got into the papers——"

"I know, I know," said Wimsey. "We can take that part as read."

"All right. Well—you know that female at Newton-Stewart— the Smith-Lemesurier woman?"

"I have met her."

"God! so have I. She got hold of me this morning——"

"Jock! Jock!"

"I couldn't make out what she was driving at first of all. She hinted and smiled and languished at me and said that whatever I had done wouldn't make any difference to her friendship, and talked about honour and sacrifice and God knows what, till finally I had almost to shake it out of her. Do you know what she's done?"

"Oh, yes," said Wimsey, cheerfully. "All is known. A lady's reputation has been sacrificed on the altar of affection. But, dear old boy, we do not blame you. We know that, rather than compromise a noble woman, you would have gone to the scaffold with your lips locked in a chivalrous silence. I do not know which is the nobler soul—the woman who without a thought of self—I seem to be dropping into blank verse."

"My dear Wimsey, don't say you ever thought for one moment that there was a word of truth in it."

"Frankly, I never did. I have known you do many rash things, but I gave you credit for seeing through Mrs. Smith-Lemesurier."

"I should hope so. But what on earth am I to do?"

"It's awkward," said Wimsey, "it's awkward. Short of admitting where you really were that night, there is nothing for it but to accept the sacrifice and with the sacrifice, the lady. And I greatly fear the lady means matrimony. Still, that's a thing that overtakes most of us, and most of us survive it."

"It's blackmail," groaned Graham. "And after all, what have I done to deserve it? I tell you that beyond a passing compliment or so I've never—dash it all!"

"Not so much as a squeeze of the hand?"

"Well, possibly a squeeze of the hand. I mean to say, hang it, one must be civil."

"Or a kiss or so—meaning no harm?"

"No, no, Wimsey. I never went as far as that. I may be a bad lad, but I have some instincts of self-protection. No, really."

"Well, never mind," said Wimsey, consolingly. "Perhaps the love will come after marriage. When you look at her over the coffee-pot and say to yourself, 'To this noble woman's pure affection I owe my life and freedom,' your heart will reproach you for your coldness."

"Life and freedom be damned! Don't be a fool. Just imagine how frightful it was. I had to be absolutely brutal before I could get away."

"Did you repulse the dear little woman?"

"Yes, I did. I told her not to be a damned idiot, and she burst into tears. It's appalling. What those people there will think——"

"What people where?"

"At the hotel. She walked in there and asked for me, and I left her howling on the drawing-room sofa. God knows what she's telling people! I ought to have seen her off the premises, but I—my God, Wimsey, she frightened me. I fled for my life. People ought to be had up for making scenes in public places. That old padre who's staying there barged in in the middle, just as the waterworks were in full play. I'll have to leave the place!"

"You don't seem to have played your cards very well."

"I shall have to go and make it right with the police, of course. But what's the good? Nobody will ever believe that there wasn't something in it."

"How true that is! What are you going to say to the police?"

"Oh, I shall have to tell them where I was. That part's O.K. But don't you see that the mere fact of that woman's having trotted out that tale will be proof enough that I'd given cause for it? She's absolutely got me taped, old man. Scotland isn't big enough to hold

both of us. I shall have to go to Italy or somewhere. The more I
prove that story to be a lie, the more obvious it will be that she
couldn't have told such a lie unless we were on terms of the most
damnable intimacy."

"Isn't life difficult?" said Wimsey. "It all shows how careful one
should be to tell the police everything at the first possible moment.
Had you only been frank with that zealous young constable, all this
would have been avoided."

"I know, but I didn't want to get anybody into trouble. You
see, Wimsey, the fact is, I was out poaching with Jimmy Fleeming,
up at Bargrennan. I thought it would be good fun. We were net-
ting the pool just below the fall."

"Oh, were you? That's the Earl of Galloway's water."

"Yes. We were out all Monday night. We had a damn good
time, only I had more whiskey than was good for me. But that's
by the way. There's a little sort of hut-place up there. It belongs
to one of the men on the estate. We camped there. I wasn't feeling
altogether so good on the Tuesday, so I stayed up there and on
Tuesday night we had another go at it, because Monday had produced more fun than fish. We did rather well on Tuesday. Some of
these fellows are damn good sorts. I get a lot more kick out of that
crowd than I do out of what's called our own class. Jimmy Fleeming has an amazing collection of good stories. And the side-lights
you get on the lives of respectable citizens! Besides, men like that
know a damn sight more than ordinary educated people. What they
don't know about fish, flesh and fowl isn't worth knowing. And
they're all damn good friends of mine. It makes me sick to think of
giving them away to the police."

"You are an ass, Graham," said Wimsey. "Why the hell didn't
you come and tell me about it in the first place?"

"You'd have had to tell the police."

"Oh, I know—but that could have been squared. Are these fellows prepared to give evidence now?"

"I haven't said anything to them. How could I? Dash it, I'm
not such a swine as to go and ask them. I've no doubt they'd back
me up, but I can't ask them to. It isn't done."

"The best thing you can do," said Wimsey, "is to go straight to
Sir Maxwell Jamieson and cough it all up. He's very decent, and I
bet he'll see that your friends don't suffer. By the way, you're

sure they can answer for you on Tuesday as well as Monday night?"

"Oh, yes, Jimmy and another bloke were hanging round most of Tuesday morning off and on. But that doesn't matter a damn. The thing I want to get clear is this business about Monday night."

"I know. But Tuesday morning is what's going to interest the police."

"Good Lord, Wimsey—this rot about Campbell isn't serious, really?"

"That's what I say," struck in Waters, grimly. "We seem to be in the same boat, Graham. I am supposed to have faked an alibi, suborned my friends and played merry hell generally. As far I can see, Wimsey, Graham is just as clever a murderer as I am. However, no doubt you are the super-detective who can see through both of us. We can't both be guilty, anyhow."

"Why not?" said Wimsey. "You may be accomplices for all I know. Of course, that makes you not quite so clever, because the best murderers don't have accomplices, but one can't always expect perfection."

"But really and truly, Wimsey, what is the evidence about the murder, if it is one? Everybody seems to be full of mysterious hints, but you can't get out of anybody why it is murder, or when it is supposed to have happened, or what it was done with or why, or anything about it—except, according to the papers, that it was done by an artist. What's the point? Did the assassin leave his fingerprints behind in paint, or what?"

"I can't tell you," said Wimsey. "But I don't mind saying this, that the whole thing turns upon how quickly Campbell could have got that sketch done. If I could have had that painting-party we planned——"

"By Jove, yes! We never did that stunt," said Graham.

"Look here, let's do it now," said Wimsey. "Both you and Waters claim to be able to imitate Campbell's style. Start off now and do something and I'll time you. Half a jiff! I'll run around to the police-station and borrow the sketch for you to copy. It won't be quite the same thing, but it will give us an idea."

.   .   .   .

Inspector Macpherson released the canvas without demur, but

without enthusiasm. He seemed, indeed, so much depressed that Wimsey paused to ask what was the matter with him.

"Maitter eneugh," said Macpherson. "We've found a mon that saw Campbell's car goin' up tae the Minnoch on Tuesday mornin', an' the time-table's a' went tae hell."

"No!" said Wimsey.

"Ay. There's yin o' the men as is workin' at the road-mendin' on the Newton-Stewart road, an' he saw the car wi' Campbell in 't— that'll be the pairson that was got up tae luik like Campbell—pass the New Galloway turnin' on the road betune Creetoon and New-ton-Stewart at five an' twenty meenuts tae ten. He disna ken Camp-bell, but he described the car an' the hat and cloak, an' he tuk parteecular notice o't because it was goin' fast an' nearly ran him doon as he was comin' away on his bicycle tae deliver a message for the foreman."

"Five-and-twenty to ten," said Wimsey, thoughtfully. "That's a bit on the late side."

"Ay. We was calculatin' on him startin' oot at 7.30 fra' Gate-house."

"Oh, I don't mind that," said Wimsey. "He must have cleared off before Mrs. Green came, and parked the body somehow, though why he should have taken such a risk I don't know. It's the other end of the business that's worrying me. At that rate he wouldn't be up at the Minnoch much before ten. We reckoned that to catch the train at Girvan, he'd have to start off again at about 11.10. He'd have to be pretty quick with his picture."

"That's so, he would that. But there's more to it. We've found a man that passed yon bicyclist on the way tae Girvan, an' it's juist impossible that he could have caught the train at all!"

"Don't be ridiculous," said Wimsey, "he must have caught it, be-cause he did catch it."

"That's so, but it must ha' been anither man a'tegither."

"Well, then," said Wimsey. "If it was another man altogether it wasn't our man at all. Do be logical."

The Inspector shook his head, just as a constable knocked at the door and, putting his head in, announced that Sergeant Dalziel was here with Mr. Clarence Gordon to see the Inspector.

"Here's the verra man," said Macpherson. "Ye'd better wait an' see what he has to say."

Mr. Clarence Gordon was a stout little gentleman with a pronounced facial angle, who pulled his hat off in a hurry at the sight
of Wimsey."

"Be covered, be covered," said that gentleman, graciously. "I
fancy you may be asked to make a sworn statement."

Mr. Gordon spread out his hands deprecatingly.

"I am thure," he said, pleasantly, "that I thall be only too willing
to athitht the polithe in any way and to thwear to vat ith nethethary.
But I athk you, gentlemen, to take into conthiderathon the interrup-
thon to my bithneth. I have come from Glathgow at conthiderable
inconvenienth——"

"Of course, of course, Mr. Gordon," said the Inspector. "It's
verra gude of ye."

Mr. Gordon sat down, and, spreading the four fat fingers of
his left hand upon his knee, so as to display to full advantage a
handsome ruby ring, raised his right hand, by way of adding emphasis to his statement and began:

"My name ith Clarenth Gordon. I am a commerthial traveller
for the firm of Moth & Gordon, Glathgow—ladieth' dretheth and
hothiery. Here ith my card. I travel thith dithtrict on alternate Mon-
dayth, thpending the night at Newton-Thtewart and returning on
Tuethday afternoonth by the Bargrennan road to Girvan and Ayr
where I have many good cuthomerth. Latht Tuethday week I
thtarted from Newton-Thtewart in my limouthine ath uthual after
an early lunth. I patht Barrhill at a little after half-patht twelve. I
remember theeing the train go out of the thtathion jutht before I got
there. That ith how I know the time. I had patht through the village
when I thaw a bithcyclitht in a grey thuit riding very fatht along
the road in front of me. I thay to mythelf: 'There ith a man in a
great hurry in the middle of the road—I mutht blow my horn
loudly.' He ith vobbling from thide to thide, you underthtand, with
hith head down. I thay to mythelf again, 'If he ith not careful, he
will have an acthident.' I blow very loud, and he hearth me, and
drawth to the thide of the road. I path him, and I thee hith fathe
very vite. That ith all. I do not thee him again, and he ith the only
bithyclitht I thee on all that road till I get to Girvan."

"Half-past twelve," said Wimsey. "No—later—the train leaves
Barrhill at 12.35. You're right, Inspector, that can't be our man.
It's twelve miles, good, from Barrhill to Girvan, and the man with

the grey suit—*our* man, I mean—was there at 1.7. I don't think he could possibly do it. Even a good bicyclist could hardly manage twenty-four miles an hour over twelve miles along that road—not on the Anwoth Hotel bicycle, anyhow. You would want a trained man on a racing machine. You are quite sure, Mr. Gordon, that you didn't pass another bicyclist further along the road?"

"Not a tholitary one," replied Mr. Gordon, earnestly, raising all his fingers protestingly and sawing the air, "not a thingle thoul on a bithcycle at all. I thould have notithed it, becauth I am a very careful driver, and I do not like puth-thyclithtth. No, I thee nobody. I take no notith of thith man at the time, of courthe. But on Thunday my vife tellth me, 'Clarentn, there wath a call come through on the vireleth for travellerth by the Bargrennan road to thay if they thaw a bithyclitht latht Tuethday week. Did you hear it?' I thay, 'No, I am travelling all the week and I cannot alwayth be lithening to the vireleth.' Vell, my vife tellth me what it ith, and I thay, 'Vell, when I have time I go to tell the polithe what I have theen. And here I'am. It ith very inconvenient and not good for bithneth, but it ith my duty ath a thitithen. I tell my firm —the both ith my brother—and he thay, 'Clarenth, you mutht tell the polithe. It cannot be helped.' Tho I came, and here I am and that ith all I know."

"Thank you verra much, Mr. Gordon; ye have given us some valuable information an' we're much obliged tae ye. Now, there's juist one other thing. Could ye tell us if the man ye saw is one o' these, sir?"

The Inspector spread the six photographs out on the table, and Mr. Clarence Gordon bent dubiously over them.

"I hardly thaw the man, you know," he said, "and he vore thpectacleth, and there ith no photo here with thpectacleth. I do not think it wath thith one, though." He set Strachan's photograph aside. "That man hath a military look, and I thould thay he vould be a big, heavy man. Thith wath not a very big man, the man I thaw. And he did not have a beard. Now *thith* man"—Mr. Gordon gazed at the photograph of Graham very intently—"thith man hath very remarkable eyeth, but with thpectacleth he might be anybody. You thee? Thpectacleth vould be a good dithguithe for him. Thith one it might be altho, but he hath a mouthtathe—I cannot remember if the man I thaw had one. It wath not a big one, if he had. Thith might be he and tho might thith or thith. No, I cannot tell."

"Never mind, Mr. Gordon, ye have done verra weel, an' we're greatly obliged to ye."

"I may go now? I have my bithneth to conthider."

The Inspector released him and turned to Wimsey.

"Not Strachan and not Gowan," he said. "Gowan's a verra big man."

"Not the murderer at all, apparently," said Wimsey. "Another red herring, Inspector."

"The place is fair lousy wi' red herrings," mourned Inspector Macpherson. "But it's a miracle to me that yon bicycle should ha' got itself tae Euston an' have no connection wi' the crime. It's no reasonable. Where did the Girvan man come from? And he had the grey suit and the spectacles an' a'. But—twelve miles in thirty minutes—I'm wonderin' could it no be done after all? If ony of our men was trained as an athlete——"

"Try *Who's Who*," suggested Wimsey—"it may throw some light on their hideous pasts. I must run away now. I've got two artists straining at the leash. Cry havoc! and let slip the dogs of war. It's curious how blank verse seems to come natural to me to-day. It just shows how blank my mind is, I suppose."

. . . .

On returning he found that Waters had supplied Graham with canvas, palette, knife and brushes and was arguing cheerfully with him about the rival merits of two different kinds of sketching easel.

Wimsey stood Campbell's sketch up on the table before them.

"Oh, that's the subject, is it?" said Graham. "H'm. Very characteristic. Almost ultra-characteristic, don't you think, Waters?"

"That's exactly what one expects from the Campbells of this world," said Waters. "The trick degenerates into a mannerism, and they paint caricatures of their own style. As a matter of fact, it's apt to happen to anybody. Even Corot, for instance. I went to a Corot exhibition once, and 'pon my soul, after seeing a hundred or so Corots gathered together, I began to have my doubts. And he *was* a master."

Graham picked the canvas up and carried it across to the light. He frowned and rubbed the surface with a thoughtful thumb.

"Funny," he said, "the handling isn't altogether . . . How many people have seen this, Wimsey?"

"Only myself and the police, so far. And the Fiscal, naturally."

"Ah!—well! Do you know, I should have said—if I didn't know what it was——"

"Well?"

"I should almost have thought I had done it myself. There's a slight flavour of pastiche about it. And there's a sort of—just look at those stones in the burn, Waters, and the shadow under the bridge. It's rather more cold and cobalty than Campbell's usual style." He held it away at arm's length. "Looks as though he'd been experimenting. There's a lack of freedom about it, somehow. Don't you think so?"

Waters came up and stared over his shoulder.

"Oh, I don't know, Graham. Yes, I see what you mean. It looks a bit fumbled here and there. No, not quite that. A little tentative. That's not the word, either. Insincere. But that's exactly what I complain of in all Campbell's stuff. It makes its effect all right, but when you come to look into it, it doesn't stand up to inspection. I call that a thoroughly Campbellish piece of work. A poor Campbell, if you like, but full of Campbellisms."

"I know," said Graham. "It reminds me of what the good lady said about *Hamlet*—that it was all quotations."

"G. K. Chesterton says," put in Wimsey, "that most people with a very well-defined style write at times what look like bad parodies of themselves. He mentions Swinburne, for instance—that bit about 'From the lilies and languors of virtue to the raptures and roses of vice.' I expect painters do the same. But of course I don't know a thing about it."

Graham looked at him, opened his mouth to speak, and shut it again.

"Well, chuck it here," said Waters. "If we've got to copy the beastly thing, we'd better start. Can you see all right there? I'll put the paints on the table here. And please don't throw them on the floor in your usual dirty way."

"I don't," said Graham, indignantly. "I collect them neatly in my hat, if I'm not wearing it, and if I am, I lay them handily in the grass. I'm not always fumbling about for them in a satchel among my sandwiches. It's a miracle to me that you don't eat your colours and put the bloater-paste on the canvas."

"I never keep sandwiches in my satchel," retorted Waters. "I put them in my pocket. The left-hand pocket. Always. You may think I'm not methodical, but I always know where to find everything. Ferguson puts tubes in his pockets, and that's why his handkerchiefs always look like paint-rags."

"That's better than going round with crumbs in your clothing," said Graham. "To say nothing of the time when Mrs. McLeod thought the drains were wrong, till she traced the stink to your old painting-coat. What was it? Liver-sausage?"

"That was an oversight. You don't expect me to go about like Gowan, carrying a sort of combined picnic-basket and sketching-box, with a partition for each colour and a portable kettle, do you?"

"Oh, Gowan? That's pure swank. Do you remember the day I pinched his box and filled all the partitions up with wee fush?"

"That was a good riot," said Waters, reminiscently. "He couldn't use the box for a week because of the fishy smell. And he had to stop painting, because it put him out to have his arrangements upset. Or so he said."

"Oh, Gowan's a man of method," said Graham. "I'm like a Waterman pen—I function in any position. But he has to have everything just so. Never mind. Here I am, like a fish out of water. I don't like your knife, I don't like your palette and I simply loathe your easel. But you don't imagine trifles like that are going to put me off. Not on your life. Have at it. Are you standing by with the stop-watch, Wimsey?"

"Yes. Are you ready? One, two, three—go!"

"By the way, I suppose we can't expect you to tell us whether the object of all this is to incriminate us? I mean, do we get hanged for being quick or for being slow?"

"I haven't worked it out yet," said Wimsey, "but I don't mind telling you that the less you dawdle the better I shall be pleased."

"It's not altogether a fair test," said Waters, mashing up his blue and white to the colour of a morning sky. "Copying a canvas isn't the same thing as painting direct. It's bound to be rather quicker."

"Slower," said Graham.

"Different, anyhow."

"It's the technique that's a nuisance," said Graham. "I don't feel handy with so much knife-work."

"I do," said Waters. "I use the knife myself quite a lot."

"I used to," said Graham, "but I've chucked it lately. I suppose we needn't follow every scratch and scrape exactly, Wimsey?"

"If you try to do that," said Waters, "it will certainly make you slower."

"I'll let you off that," said Wimsey. "I only want you to get somewhere about the same amount of paint on the canvas."

. . . .

The two men worked on in silence for some time, while Wimsey fidgeted restlessly about the studio, picking things up and putting them down and whistling tuneless fragments of Bach.

At the end of an hour, Graham was a little farther advanced than Waters, but the panel was still incomplete as compared with the model.

After another ten minutes Wimsey took up his stand behind the painters and watched them with a maddening kind of intentness. Waters fidgeted, scraped out something he had done, put it in again, cursed and said:

"I wish you'd go away."

"Nerves cracking up under the strain," commented Wimsey, dispassionately.

"What's the matter, Wimsey? Are we behind time?"

"Not quite," said Wimsey, "but very nearly."

"Well, you can reckon on another half-hour as far as I'm concerned," said Graham, "and if you flurry me it'll probably be longer still."

"Never mind, do the thing properly. Even if you upset my calculations, it doesn't matter. I shall probably be able to get round it somehow."

The half-hour dragged to an end. Graham, glancing from the model to the copy, said, "There, that's the best I can make of it," threw down his palette and stretched himself. Waters glanced across at his work and said, "You've beaten me on time," and painted on.

He put in another fifteen minutes or so and announced that he had finished. Wimsey strolled over and examined the results. Graham and Waters rose and did likewise.

"Not bad efforts, on the whole," suggested Graham, half-shutting his eyes and retiring suddenly on to Wimsey's toes.

"You've got that stuff on the bridge very well," said Waters. "Thoroughly Campbellian."

"Your burn is better than mine and better than Campbell's, if it comes to that," replied Graham. "However, I take it that intrinsic artistic merit is not important in this particular case."

"Not a bit," said Wimsey. He seemed to have suddenly grown more cheerful. "I'm frightfully obliged to you both. Come and have a drink. Several drinks. I rather want to celebrate."

"What?" said Waters, his face going very red and suddenly white again.

"Why?" said Graham. "Do you mean to say you've got your man? Is it one of us?"

"Yes," said Wimsey. "I mean, I think I've got the man. I ought to have known long ago. In fact, I never was in very much doubt. But now I know for certain."

CHAPTER XXIII

GOWAN'S STORY

"A CALL for you from London, sir," said the constable.

"Is that Inspector Macpherson of Kirk-kud-brite?" demanded London in ladylike tones.

"Ay," said Inspector Macpherson.

"*One* moment, please."

A pause. Then, "You're through," and an official voice: "Is that Kirkcudbright Police Station? Is that Inspector Macpherson speaking? This is Scotland Yard. *One* moment, please."

A shorter pause. Then:

"Is that Inspector Macpherson? Oh, good morning, Inspector. This is Parker—Chief Inspector Parker of Scotland Yard. How are you?"

"Fine, thank you, sir. An' hoo's yersel'?"

"Blooming, thanks. Well, Inspector, we've found your man for you. He's come across with quite an entertaining story, but it's not quite the story you want. It's certainly important. Will you come and have a look at him or shall we send him up to you, or shall we just send the story and keep an eye on him?"

"Well, what does he say?"

"He admits meeting Campbell on the road that night and fighting with him, but he says he didn't kill him."

"That's only tae be expectit. What does he say he did wi' him?"

A long chuckle rippled over the four hundred miles of wire.

"He says he didn't do anything with him. He says you've got it all wrong. He says *he* was the dead body in the car."

"What!"

"He says he was the body—Gowan was."

"Och, tae hell wi' 't!" exclaimed the Inspector, oblivious of etiquette. Parker chuckled again.

"He says Campbell knocked him out and left him there."

"Does he so, sir? Weel, I'm thinkin' it'll be best I should come an' see him. Can ye keep him till I come?"

"We'll do our best. You don't want him charged?"

"No, we'd better no charge him. The Chief Constable has thocht o' a new theory a'tegither. I'll be takin' the next train."

"Good. I don't think he'll object to waiting for you. As far as I can make out, there's only one thing he's really scared of, and that's being sent back to Kirkcudbright. Right; we'll expect you. How's Lord Peter Wimsey?"

"Och, he's jist awfu' busy wi' yin thing an' anither. He's a bright lad, yon."

"You can trust his judgment, though," said Parker.

"I ken that fine, sir. Will I bring him with me?"

"We're always glad to see him," said Parker. "He's a little ray of sunshine about the old place. Invite him by all means. I think he would like to see Gowan."

.   .   .   .

But Lord Peter Wimsey refused the invitation.

"I'd adore to come," he said, "but I feel it would be mere self-in-dulgence. I fancy I know what story he's going to tell." He grinned. "I shall be missing something. But I can really be more useful—if I'm useful at all, that is—this end. Give old Parker my love, will you, and tell him I've solved the problem."

"Ye've solved the problem?"

"Yes. The mystery is a mystery no longer."

"Wull ye no tell me what ye've made o't?"

"Not yet. I haven't proved anything. I'm only sure in my own mind."

"An' Gowan?"

"Oh, don't neglect Gowan. He's vitally important. And remember to take that spanner with you."

"Is't Gowan's spanner to your way of thinkin'?"

"It is."

"An' them marks on the corpse?"

"Oh, yes, that's all right. You can take it those marks come from the spanner."

"Gowan says——" began the Inspector.

Wimsey looked at his watch.

"Away with you and catch your train," he said, cheerfully. "There's a surprise waiting for you at the end of the journey."

.   .   .   .

When Inspector Macpherson was shown into Parker's room, there was a dejected-looking man seated on a chair in the corner. Parker, after greeting the Inspector warmly, turned to this person and said:

"Now, Mr. Gowan, you know Inspector Macpherson, of course. He's very anxious to hear your story from yourself."

The man raised a face like the face of a sulky rabbit, and Inspector Macpherson, wheeling suddenly round upon him, fell back with a startled snort.

"Him? Yon's no the man."

"Isn't he?" said Parker. "He says he is, anyhow."

"It's no Gowan," said Macpherson, "nor onything like him. I never saw yon ferrety-faced fellow in my life."

This was more than the gentleman in question could put up with.

"Don't be a fool, Macpherson," he said.

At the sound of his voice, the Inspector appeared to suffer a severe internal upheaval. The man got up and came forward into the light. Macpherson gazed in speechless bewilderment at the cropped black hair, the strong nose, the dark eyes, which gazed with an expression of blank astonishment from beneath a forehead denuded of eyebrows, the small, pinched mouth, with the upper teeth protruding over the lower lip, and the weak little chin which ran helplessly away to a long neck with a prominent Adam's-apple. The whole appearance of the apparition was not improved by a ten days' growth of black beard, which imparted a suggestion of seediness and neglect.

"It's Gowan's voice, right eneugh," admitted the Inspector.

"I think," said Parker, smothering his amusement, "that you find the removal of the beard and moustache a little misleading. Put on your hat, Mr. Gowan, and wrap your scarf about your chin. Then, perhaps——"

The Inspector gazed with a kind of horror, as this metamorphosis was accomplished.

"Ay," he said, "ay, ye're right, sir, an' I'm wrang. But losh!— I beg your pardon, sir, but I couldna ha' believed——"

He stared hard, and walked slowly round the captive as if still unable to credit his own eyes.

"If you've quite finished making an ass of yourself, Macpherson," said Mr. Gowan, coldly, "I'll tell you my story and get away. I've other things to do than fool around in police-stations."

"That's as may be," said the Inspector. He would not have spoken in that tone to the great Mr. Gowan of Kirkcudbright, but for this unkempt stranger he felt no sort of respect. "Ye have given us an awfu' deal o' trouble, Mr. Gowan, an' them servants o' yours will find theirsel's afore the Fiscal for obstructin' the pollis in the pairformance o' their duty. Noo I'm here tae tak' yer statement, and it is ma duty tae warn ye——"

Gowan waved an angry hand, and Parker said:

"He has been already cautioned, Inspector."

"Verra gude," said Macpherson, who by now had regained his native self-confidence. "Noo, Mr. Gowan, wull ye please tell me when an' where ye last saw Mr. Campbell that's deid, an' for why ye fled fra' Scotland in disguise?"

"I don't in the least mind telling you," said Gowan, impatiently, "except that I don't suppose you'll be able to hold your tongue about it. I'd been fishing up on the Fleet——"

"A moment, Mr. Gowan. Ye wull be speakin' o' the events of the Monday, I'm thinkin'."

"Of course. I'd been fishing up on the Fleet, and I was driving back from Gatehouse to Kirkcudbright at about a quarter to ten when I nearly ran into that damned fool Campbell at the S-bend just beyond the junction of the Kirkcudbright road with the main road from Castle-Douglas to Gatehouse. I don't know what the man thought he was doing, but he had got his car stuck right across the road. Fortunately it wasn't at the most dangerous bit of the bend, or there would probably have been a most unholy smash. It was on the second half, where the curve is less abrupt. There's a stone wall one side and a sunk wall the other."

Inspector Macpherson nodded.

"I told him to get out of the way and he refused. He was undoubtedly drunk and in a very nasty mood. I'm sorry, I know he's dead, but it doesn't alter the fact that he always was one of Nature's prize swine, and that night he was at his very worst. He got out of his car and came up to me, saying that he was just about ready for a row, and if I wanted one I could have one. He jumped on my running-board and used the foulest language. I don't know now what it was all about. I had done nothing to provoke him, except to tell him to take his cursed car out of the way."

Gowan hesitated for a moment.

"I want you to understand," he went on, "that the man was drunk, dangerous and—as I thought at the moment—half off his rocker. He was a great, broad-shouldered, hefty devil, and I was jammed up behind the steering-column. I had a heavy King Dick spanner beside me in the pocket of the car and I grabbed hold of it—purely in self-defence. In fact, I only meant to threaten him with it."

"Is this the spanner?" interjected Macpherson, producing the instrument from his coat pocket.

"Very likely," said Gowan. "I don't profess to know one spanner from another as a shepherd knows his sheep, but it was a similar spanner at any rate. Where did you find that?"

"Go on with your statement, please, Mr. Gowan."

"You're very cautious. Campbell had got the door of the car open, and I wasn't going to sit there to be hammered into a jelly without defending myself. I pushed out from behind the wheel into the passenger's seat and stood up, with the spanner in my hand. He aimed a blow at me and I landed him one with the spanner. It caught him on the cheek-bone but not very heavily, because he dodged it. I should think it must have marked him, though," added the speaker, with appreciation.

"It did that," said Macpherson, dourly.

"I can't pretend to be sorry to hear it. I jumped out at him, and he got me by the legs and we both rolled out into the road together. I hit out with the spanner for all I was worth, but he was about three times as strong as I was. He got his hands round my throat as we struggled, and I thought he was going to choke me. I couldn't shout and my only hope was that someone would come along. But by a damned bit of luck the road was absolutely deserted. He let go my throat just in time not to strangle me altogether and sat on my chest. I tried to get another one in with the spanner, but he snatched it out of my hand and threw it away. I was horribly impeded all this time by having my driving-gloves on."

"Ah!" said the Inspector.

"Ah, what?"

"That explains a lot, doesn't it?" said Parker.

"I don't follow you."

"Never mind, Mr. Gowan. Carry on."

"Well, after that——"

Gowan seemed now to have got to the most distasteful part of his story.

"I was in a pretty bad way by this time," he said, apologetically, "half-choked, you know. And whenever I tried to struggle, he lammed me in the face. Well, he—he got out a pair of nail-scissors —and he was calling me the most filthy names all this time—he got out his scissors——"

A twinkle—unsuppressible—gleamed in the Inspector's eye.

"I think we can guess at what happened then, Mr. Gowan," said he. "Forbye we found a nice wee hantle of black beard by the road-side."

"The damned brute!" said Gowan. "He didn't stop at the beard. He took off hair, eyebrows—everything. As a matter of fact. I didn't know that till later. His final blow knocked me out."

He felt his jaw-bone tenderly.

"When I came to," he went on, "I found myself in my own car in a sort of grass lane. I couldn't think where I was at first, but after a bit I made out that he'd run the car up a sort of cart-way just off the road. There's an iron gate that you go through. I daresay you know the place."

"Ay."

"Well—I was in a hell of a state. I felt frightfully ill. And besides—how on earth could I show myself in Kirkcudbright like that? I didn't know what to do, but I had to do something. I jammed my hat on, wound a scarf round the lower part of my face, and hared home like hell. It was lucky I didn't meet much on the road, because I was all to pieces—couldn't control the car. However, I got home—somewhere about a quarter past ten, I think.

"Alcock was a brick. Of course I had to tell him everything and he concocted all the plot. He got me up to bed without meeting his wife or the girl, and gave me first-aid for cuts and bruises and a hot bath, and then he suggested that I should pretend to have gone off to Carlisle. Our first idea was to say I was ill, but that would have meant visitors and fuss, and we should have had to have the doctor in, and square him. So that night we decided to pretend I'd gone to Carlisle by the 11.8 from Dumfries. Of course, we never supposed there'd be any inquiry, and we didn't think it worth while to send the car out specially. My housekeeper was roped into the conspiracy, but we thought it better not to trust the girl. She would be certain to talk. It was her night out, as it happened, so she wouldn't need to know when I came in, or anything, and the only person who'd know anything would be Campbell. He might talk, of course, but we had to risk that, and, after all, when he came to his senses, he might realise that he'd be letting himself in for a charge of assault if he wasn't careful. Anyway, anything was better than going about in Kirkcudbright and being commiserated."

Gowan wriggled on his chair.

"Quite so, quite so," said Parker, soothingly. He passed the back of his thumb carelessly down his own profile as he spoke. It was irregular, but the chin was reassuringly prominent. He was clean-shaven and could, he felt, stand it reasonably well.

"Next day," said Gowan, "we heard the news about Campbell's death. Naturally, we never thought but that it was an accident, but we did realise that it was just possible somebody might want to ask me whether I'd seen him the evening before. It was then that Alcock had his bright idea. Hammond had actually been over to Dumfries the evening before at about 8.45 to do an errand, and Alcock suggested that he should tell everybody that I'd taken the 8.45 to Carlisle. Hammond was quite game to back up the story, and as people would have seen the car go, it all looked quite plausible. Of course there was the chance that I'd been seen driving home later than that, but we thought we could bluff that out as mistaken identity. Apparently the question didn't crop up?"

"Oddly eneugh," said Macpherson, "it didna. At least, not while a gude bit later."

"No. Well, Alcock was marvellous. He suggested that I should send a letter off by Tuesday afternoon's post, addressed to a friend in London—you know, Chief Inspector, Major Aylwin, through whom you got on my track—enclosing a letter from me to Alcock with directions that it was to be posted immediately. The letter was written as from my club, telling Alcock that he and Hammond could take the saloon and go for a holiday, as I should be detained for some time in Town. The idea was that they should smuggle me away with them in the car and drop me just outside Castle-Douglas, in time to catch the train to Town. I knew that I should never be recognised there without my beard, though, of course, Hammond or the car might have been identified. The letter duly came back to Alcock by the second post on Thursday, and we carried out the rest of the plan that night. Did it work?"

"Not altogether," said Macpherson, drily. "We made oot that part o't pretty weel."

"Of course, all this time I hadn't the faintest idea that Campbell had been murdered. Alcock must have known, I suppose, and it would really have been better if he'd told me. But he knew, too, of course, that I couldn't have had anything to do with it, and I shouldn't think it ever occurred to him that I could be suspected. I had so obviously left Campbell in the rudest of health and spirits."

He made a wry face.

"There's not much else to say. I felt horribly groggy all Tuesday and Wednesday, and I had gravel-rash all over my face. The brute had rolled me on the rough ground, blast him! Alcock was a splendid nurse. He got the wounds clean and put healing stuff on them. Regular professional touch he had at it, the old scout. Wouldn't touch me without washing himself elaborately in Lysol —took my temperature three times a day and all that. I believe he rather enjoyed it. On Thursday night I'd practically healed up, and was perfectly fit to travel. I got to Town without any trouble, and have been living all this time with Major Aylwin, who has been extremely decent to me. I only hope I shan't be wanted in Kirkcudbright just at present. When Mr. Parker turned up this morning— by the way, Mr. Parker, how did you spot me?"

"Pretty easily," said Parker, "when we'd written to your old school and got a photograph of you without your beard. We found the porter who had taken your luggage at Euston, the taxi-driver who had taken you to Major Aylwin's flat and the porter of the flats, who all recognised you. After that, you know, we had only to ring the bell and walk in."

"Good God!" said Gowan. "I never thought about those old photographs."

"The men hesitated a bit at first," said Parker, "till we had the bright notion of painting out the eyebrows as well. That made the appearance so—pardon me—peculiar, that they identified you with little cries of satisfaction."

Gowan flushed.

"Well," he said, "that's my statement. Can I go home now?"

Parker consulted Macpherson by a look.

"We'll have the statement put in writing," he said, "and perhaps then you will sign it. After that, I see no reason why you shouldn't go back to Major Aylwin's, but we shall ask you to keep in touch with us and not to change your address without letting us know."

Gowan nodded, and later, when the statement had been typed out and signed, took his departure, still with the same startled look upon his eyebrowless face.

CHAPTER XXIV

FARREN : FERGUSON : STRACHAN

THE Procurator-Fiscal had called a council of war. Sir Maxwell Jamieson had brought Lord Peter with him. Inspector Macpherson was there by right of office and so was Sergeant Dalziel. Dr. Cameron was there, to see that nothing was suggested which would conflict with the medical evidence. In addition, Constable Ross and Constable Duncan were present by invitation. This was magnanimous on the part of their superiors, to whom Duncan had contrived to give a good deal of trouble, but there was a feeling that, in this confused and disconcerting case, even the opinion of a subordinate might be worth hearing.

The Fiscal opened the discussion by requesting the Chief Constable to state his views, but the latter demurred. He suggested that the police might, perhaps, put forward their theories with greater freedom if they were not previously biased by hearing his opinion. The result of this was a polite contest for second place between Macpherson and Dalziel, which was eventually won by Macpherson, on the ground that, as the body had actually been discovered in the Newton-Stewart district, Dalziel had, so to speak, the premier claim upon it.

Dalziel rather nervously cleared his throat.

"Weel noo, my lord, Mr. Fiscal, Sir Maxwell and gentlemen," he began, somewhat influenced in his opening by the recollection of the procedure at Football Club dinners, "it wad appear tae be uncontrovairtible that this puir gentleman met his death some time Monday night by the use of a blunt instrument, an' that his boady was conveyed tae the place whaur it was found. Forbye I'm thinkin' we're a' agreed that the pairson as kill't him wull ha' been an airtist, Lord Peter Wimsey havin' pointed oot that the verra handsome piece o' pentin' foond at the locus o' the crime must ha' been projuiced by the murderer himself. Owin' tae the careful inquiries o' Inspector Macpherson, we are able tae state that a' the airtists in this district can be accountit for durin' the period covered by the crime, forbye five, or maybe six, which is Mr. Farren, Mr. Gowan, Mr. Waters in Kirkcudbright, an' Mr. Strachan, Mr. Graham an' possibly Mr. Ferguson in Gatehouse. A' these six airtists had a motive for killin' the deceased, in so far as they had bin kent tae utter threats against him, and moreover, by a remairkable coincidence, no yin o' them possesses a satisfactory alibi for the haill period under consideration.

"A' six o' them hae made statements claimin' tae exonerate themsel's, an' if we agree that the guilt lies betune the six o' them, yin or mair o' them must be tellin' lees.

"Noo, takin' everything intae consideration, I am of the opeenion that oor inquiries should be directit tae the movements o' Mr. Farren, and for why? Because he had a much bigger motive for murder than the lave o' them. He seems tae ha' considered that the deceased was payin' too much attention tae Mistress Farren. I'm sayin' nae word against the leddy, but that was the idea this Farren had got intae his heid. I canna credit that ony gentleman wad murder anither for twa-three words about a bit picture, or for a wee difference of opeenion consairnin' a game o' gowf, or a couple troot or a quarrel aboot nationalities. But when it's a maitter o' a man's domestic happiness, there, tae my thinkin', ye have a gude cause for murder.

"We ken weel that Farren set oot fra' Kirkcudbright that night wi' the fixed intention o' findin' Campbell an' doin' him some damage. He gaed doon tae the cottage, where he was seen by Mr. Ferguson, an' he gaed up to Mr. Strachan's hoose, an' by his ain confession he left a letter tae say as he was away tae find Campbell an' hae't oot wi' him. After this, he disappears till we find him at 3 o'clock on the Tuesday afternoon on the New Galloway road.

"Noo, the Inspector and me thocht first of a' that Farren had murdered Campbell on the road betune Gatehoose and Kirkcudbright, an' we were puzzled how he cam' there and why he should ha' carried on that queer way wi' Campbell's car. We were obleeged tae bring Mr. Strachan intil't. But noo we see as there was no necessity far a' they whig-maleeries. We ken noo that 'twas Mr. Gowan as met Campbell on the road an' was assaulted by him, an' that Campbell gaed away hame in his ain car as was likely eneugh. We ken likewise, fra' Mr. Ferguson's and Mr. Strachan's evidence, that either Campbell was alive after midnight or that some ither pairson entered the cottage. It is my belief that yon ither pairson was Farren, as had been lyin' in wait for Campbell in the vicinity o' the cottage."

"Just a minute," put in Sir Maxwell. "I take it you accept Strachan's statement as far as the note and his subsequent visit to the cottage are concerned."

"Ay, sir, I do that. Bein' friendly wi' Mr. Farren, he wadna hae inventit sic a tale, an' it agrees fine wi' Farren's ain statement. I'll tell ye what I think wull ha' been the way o't. I've got it a' writ doon here on a bit paper."

The Sergeant wrestled with the pocket of his tunic and produced a fat notebook, from which he extracted a rather grubby sheet of paper, folded extremely small. He spread this out on the table, flattening it with the palm of a broad hand, and, having thus reduced it to order, passed it to the Fiscal, who, settling his glasses more firmly on his nose, read aloud as follows:—

Case against Farren

6 p. m. Farren at Kirkcudbright. Finds Campbell in the house. Quarrel with Mrs. Farren.

7 p. m. Farren proceeds by bicycle to Gatehouse.

8 p. m. Farren arrives at Standing Stone cottage asking for Campbell, and is seen by Ferguson.

8–9.15 p. m. Farren in various public-houses, using threats against Campbell.

9.15 p. m. Farren goes to Strachan's house and leaves note (on bicycle).

9.25 till after dark. Farren in hiding, probably somewhere on the Lauriston or Castramont Road.

9.45 p. m. Campbell meets Gowan when returning from Kirkcudbright.

10.20 p. m. Campbell returns to Standing Stone cottage with car. Heard by Ferguson.

10.20 p. m.–12 midnight. Some time during this period Farren proceeds to Campbell's cottage on bicycle. Lets himself in and kills Campbell. Hides body. (Note: Ferguson presumably asleep.) Farren goes out, locking door. Remains in hiding, perhaps in garage.

12 midnight. Strachan arrives in car (heard by Ferguson). Enters by means of key. Leaves note and departs.

Monday 12 midnight–Tuesday 7.30 a. m. Farren reenters cottage, destroys Strachan's note, puts body in car, matures plan of escape, puts bicycle and painting materials in car, prepares and eats Campbell's breakfast.

7.30 a. m. Farren, disguised as Campbell, starts out from Gatehouse in Campbell's car. Seen by Ferguson.

9.35 a. m. Farren in Campbell's car seen by workman passing turning to New Galloway road between Creetown and Newton-Stewart.

10 a. m. Farren arrives at Minnoch with body.

10–11.30 a. m. Farren paints picture.

11.30 a. m. Farren throws body into Minnoch and departs on bicycle, using the side road from Bargrennan to Minnigaff. (Note: conjectural; no witness as yet produced.) Eight or nine miles.

12.30 p. m. Farren arrives at Falbae. Leaves bicycle in vicinity of disused mine.

12.30–3 p. m. Farren walks by New Galloway road to Brig o' Dee; eleven miles; but he may easily have taken a lift from a passing motorist.

The rest of Farren's movements as per his statement.

"That," said the Fiscal, looking round over the tops of his glasses, "appears to me a very plausible and workmanlike conjecture."

"It's damned good," said Wimsey.

"Really," said Sir Maxwell, "it seems to cover almost everything, and almost shakes me in my own convictions. It is so beautifully simple."

"Is it no," said Macpherson, "a wee thing too simple? It disna tak' intae account the remairkable episode o' the bicycle that was sent fra' Ayr tae Euston."

Sergeant Dalziel, modestly elated by the applause of the three most distinguished persons in the company, was encouraged to dissent from his superior's view.

"I dinna see," said he, "why yon bicycle should be took intae account at a'. I see no necessity tae connect it wi' the maitter o' Campbell. If onybody was tae steal a bicycle fra' the Anwoth, and if, some gate, it was sent tae Lunnon by a mistake, that's yin thing, but what for should we suppose the murderer wad gae oot o' his way tae indulge in such antics, when there's anither explanation that's plain an' simple?"

"Yes," said the Fiscal, "but why should a man take the trouble to steal a bicycle from Gatehouse to go to Ayr, when he could easily have gone the whole way by train? I'll not deny there's something very mysterious about the story of the bicycle."

"Ay," said Macpherson, "an' how do ye account for the surprisin' length o' time ta'en to get fra' Gatehoose tae the New Galloway road? It's only seventeen mile by the high road when a's said an' dune."

Dalziel looked a little dashed at this, but Wimsey came to his assistance.

"Farren told me," he said, "that he had only driven a car two or three times in his life. He may have got into some difficulty or other. Suppose he ran out of petrol, or got a blocked feed or something. He would probably first of all have a shot at doing something himself—sit about pressing the self-starter or peering hopefully under the bonnet—before he could prevail on himself to ask anybody for help. Possibly he merely ran out of petrol, and had to shove the car down a side-road somewhere and walk to the nearest garage. Or suppose he went by the old road past Gatehouse Station and got into difficulties up there. An inexperienced driver might waste a lot of time."

"It's possible," said Macpherson, with a dissatisfied air. "It's possible. I wadna go farther than that."

"By the way," said the Chief Constable, "on your theory, Dalziel, how do you account for Strachan's hat and the tale he told about meeting Farren up at Falbae? Because, if your version is correct, that must have been pure invention."

"I account for't this way," said Dalziel. "I think it's a fact that Mr. Strachan searched for Farren at Falbae as he said, an' didna find hide nor hair on him. An' it may verra weel be that he tummel't intae the mine as he says he did. But I think that, no findin' him, he was feart Farren had been up tae mischief, an' when he heard o' the findin' o' Campbell's boady, he juist added a wee word or twa tae his story, tae gie Farren some kind of an alibi. 'Deed an' I'm thinkin' 'tis gude proof o' my theory that Strachan still evidently suspects Farren. Ye ken fine yersel', Sir Maxwell, that he was awfu' saircumspect in tellin' ye his tale and wadna ha' tell't ye a single word o' Farren's note if ye hadna persuadit him ye kenned the truth a'ready."

"Ay," said the Chief Constable, "but I had my own notion about that."

"Well, let's hear your notion, Sir Maxwell," said the Fiscal.

"I was wishful," said Sir Maxwell, "to let the police have their say first, but perhaps my idea does come in better at this point. Of course, the very first thing that struck me was the obvious collusion between Farren and Strachan to conceal something, but I looked at it in rather a different way. In my opinion, it was Strachan that had the guilty knowledge, and his difficulty was to protect himself without implicating Farren too much. Farren, by his behaviour and his threats and his disappearance, provided an almost perfect screen for Strachan, and it is, I think, very much to Strachan's credit that he was so unwilling to make use of it.

"Now, the weak point of your story, Dalziel, if I may say so, seems to me to occur at the moment of the murder itself. I simply cannot believe that, if it took place as you say at the cottage, between midnight and morning, it could have done so without disturbing Ferguson. Campbell was a powerful man, and, unless he was battered to death in his sleep, there would have been a noise and a struggle. Given the characters of all the people concerned, I cannot bring myself to believe that this was a case of a midnight assassin, creeping stealthily up to Campbell's bedroom and felling him with one blow, before he had time to cry out. It is, in particular, exceedingly unlike what one might expect from Farren. On the other hand, if there was a noisy fight, I cannot understand why Ferguson heard nothing of it. It was August, the windows would be wide open, and, in any case, besides the actual noise of the quarrel, there would be a great deal of going to and fro in the night, taking the corpse out to the car and so on, that Ferguson could scarcely have failed to hear.

"My theory is this. I think Farren's story is true. It is too absurd and whimsical a story not to be true, and all Farren's alleged actions are exactly the sort of daft thing Farren would do. I feel sure that Farren isn't the man to plan out an elaborate fake like the planting of the body and the painting of the picture. The man who did that was perfectly cool and unemotional, and he would have known a great deal better than to go and lose himself in that suspicious way immediately afterwards. No. Depend upon it, the man who committed the crime would take the very first opportunity of reappearing in his usual haunts.

"The way I see it is this. Strachan got that note from Farren and went down to the cottage as he said. When he got there, one of two things happened, and I am not perfectly sure which. I *think* Campbell opened the door to him and I think that he went in and had an interview with Campbell which ended in a violent quarrel and struggle. I think Ferguson was awakened by the noise, and came down just at the moment when Strachan had knocked Campbell down and killed him. Or possibly he arrived to find Strachan and Campbell fighting together, and then himself struck the blow which finished Campbell. There is the third possibility that the situation was reversed, and that Strachan came in to find Campbell already dead and Ferguson standing over him red-handed. I think that is rather less likely, for a reason I'll explain later.

"In any case, I'm sure we have this situation—the two men at the cottage with Campbell's dead body and one at least of them guilty of killing him. Now, what would they do next? It is quite conceivable that, if only one of them had a hand in it, the other should at first threaten to inform the police, but there might be difficulties about that. Both men were well known to have quarrelled previously with Campbell, and the accused man might very well threaten to bring a counter-accusation. In any case, I fancy they realised that they were both of them in an exceedingly awkward position, and decided to help each other out if possible.

"Which of the two had the idea of faking the accident I don't know, of course, but I should imagine it would be Strachan. He is a man of particularly quick and keen intellect—just the sort that can think well ahead and foresee the consequences of his actions. The first bold outline of the idea would probably be his, but Ferguson no doubt helped, with his remarkable memory for details.

"They would hope, naturally, that the whole thing would be accepted as pure accident, but they would remember that, if once a murder was suspected, they would need alibis to cover the whole period from midnight to the following midday. Obviously, they couldn't both have alibis for the whole period, but they might do equally well by dividing the time. Eventually they decided that Strachan was to establish the alibi for the night hours, while Ferguson did everything necessary in connection with the body, and that Ferguson would then establish his alibi for the next morning, while Strachan painted the picture."

The Chief Constable paused and looked round to see how his audience were taking this. Encouraged by a little hum of appreciative surprise, he took up his tale again.

"The reason why they worked it that way is, I think, that Ferguson had already announced his intention of going to Glasgow in the morning, and that any sudden change of plan might appear odd. They now had to think of some alibi which Strachan could reasonably put forward at that hour of the night, and the best thing they could think of was that he should carry out his original intention of going after Farren."

"But," interposed the Fiscal, "was not that a very difficult and uncertain plan on which to rely? It was a hundred to one against his meeting Farren. Would it not have been simpler to knock up some person with a suitable story? He could, for instance, have communicated to somebody his fears about Farren, and even taken that person with him as a witness to his alibi."

"I don't think so," said Sir Maxwell. "That point occurred to me also, but when I came to think the matter over, I saw that Strachan's plan was about the best he could have adopted in the circumstances. For one thing, I believe that it would have been very awkward for him to present himself in public at that moment. I think that he had already received that blow in the eye which he afterwards accounted for in another manner. That is why I said I felt pretty sure that Strachan took part in the struggle with Campbell, even though he may not have struck the fatal blow himself. Moreover, suppose he did knock somebody up to inquire about Farren, and suppose that somebody kindly offered to accompany him in his search? He would then, as the Fiscal truly says, have an unimpeachable witness to his alibi—certainly he would. But what if he could not get rid of the witness in time to do the very important job he had to do the next morning? What reason could he possibly give for abandoning his search for Farren and rushing away to Newton-Stewart? And how could he prevent people from knowing where he was going, if once he got a hue-and-cry started? Whatever happened, he had to get up to the Minnoch early the next morning, and he had to do it in secret.

"As a matter of fact, I don't think his plan turned out as he intended. Indeed, it went very near to miscarrying altogether. I feel sure his original intention was to find Farren and bring him home—either to Kirkcudbright or to his own house at Gatehouse. He could then have explained his black eye as being due to a fall sustained in his search at Falbae."

"But," objected Wimsey, who had been following all this argument with a keenness which his half-drooped eyelids scarcely veiled, "he'd still have to trundle off to the Minnoch next morning, wouldn't he, old thing?"

"Yes," said Sir Maxwell, "so he would. But if he had dropped Farren at Kirkcudbright, he could easily have driven straight away again from there. He would hardly be expected to stay and make a third in the conjugal reunion. Then he could have gone off where he liked—perhaps leaving some sort of reassuring message for Mrs. Strachan. Or similarly, if he had taken Farren to Gatehouse, he could then have gone off for the ostensible purpose of reassuring Mrs. Farren about her husband. When he was once away, he could always be detained somewhere, by engine-trouble or what not. I see no great difficulty about that."

"All right," said Wimsey. "I pass that. Roll on, thou deep and dark blue ocean, roll."

"Well then, Strachan drove off in search of Farren, leaving Ferguson to pack the body up and do all the necessary things about the house. And by the way, I may as well say at this point that I don't think any of you have paid sufficient attention to these things that were done about the house. The man who did them must have known a great deal about Campbell's manner of living. He must have known exactly when to expect Mrs. Green, for example, and the way Campbell behaved when at home—whether he was tidy or untidy, for instance, and what sort of breakfast he usually had, and all that kind of thing. Otherwise, Mrs. Green would have noticed that something out of the ordinary had happened. Now, how could Farren or Waters or Gowan or Graham be aware of all these domestic details? The man who would know them was Ferguson, who was his next-door neighbour and employed the same daily woman. He would be the one person who might habitually see Campbell having breakfast and puttering about the house; and what he didn't know from his own observation he'd be sure to get from Mrs. Green in the course of her daily gossip."

"That's a damned good point, Chief," said Wimsey, with the detached air of an Eton boy applauding a good stroke by a Harrow captain. "Damned good. Of course, Mrs. Green would be full of information. 'Och, Mr. Campbell's an awfu' mon wi' his pyjammers. Yesterday he was leavin' them in the coal-hole an' them only jist back fra' the laundry. An' to-day I'm findin' them in the stoojo an' him usin' them for a pentin'-rag.' One learns a lot about one's neighbours by listening to what is called kitchen-talk."

"Ay, that's so," said Macpherson, a little doubtfully.

Sir Maxwell smiled. "Yes," he said, "When I came to think the matter over, that struck me very forcibly. But to go on with Strachan. There's no doubt he did find Farren, and there, I admit, he was rather lucky, though perhaps the chances against his doing so were not quite a hundred to one. After all, he had an extremely good idea where Farren was likely to be found, and he knew the ground about Falbae pretty well."

"Ay, that's so," said Dalziel, "but whit wad he ha' done, sir, if Farren really had throwed himsel' doon the mine?"

"That would have been rather unfortunate for him, I admit," said the Chief Constable. "In that case, he would have had to forego his alibi for the early morning. All he could have done would be to leave some object or objects at Falbae to show that he had been there—his hat, for example, or his overcoat—and carry out his painting job at the Minnoch as early as possible, returning later to give the alarm and start the search for Farren. He could explain that he had been searching in some other place in the interim. It wouldn't have been so good, but it would have been fairly good, especially as the subsequent discovery of Farren's body would have been a very good witness to the truth of his story. However, he did find Farren, so we need not bother about that.

"Unhappily, however, the plan came rather unstuck at this point. Farren, instead of coming quietly, escaped, and Strachan tumbled into a mine. This very nearly prevented Strachan from carrying out his part of the plot at all. He did fall down, he did have a job to extricate himself—though it didn't take him quite as long as he said it did—and that was why he was so late in getting up to the Minnoch. If his plan had worked out properly, he no doubt hoped to be back with Farren at, say, 3 o'clock in the morning, and then go straight on to pick up the car and the body where Ferguson had left them ready for him."

"And where would that be?" asked the Fiscal.

"I can't say exactly, but the idea would be for Ferguson to drive Campbell's car up to some suitable spot—say by the old road through Gatehouse Station to Creetown—and leave it there to be picked up and taken on by Strachan. Ferguson would then return on a bicycle——"

"What bicycle?" said Wimsey.

"Any bicycle," retorted the Chief Constable, "except, of course, the Anwoth Hotel bicycle that we've heard so much about. It's not difficult to borrow bicycles in these parts, and he would have had plenty of time to bring it back and leave it where he found it. Ferguson would be back, say, at 7 o'clock, in good time to eat his own breakfast and catch the omnibus for Gatehouse Station."

"He must have been full of breakfast by that time," observed the Fiscal, "having already eaten Campbell's."

"My dear man," said the Chief Constable, rather irritably, "if you had committed a murder and were trying to get away with it, you wouldn't let a trifle like a second breakfast stand in your way."

"If I had committed a murder," replied the Fiscal, "I would feel no appetite even for one breakfast."

The Chief Constable restrained any expression of feeling at this frivolous comment. Macpherson, who had been jotting words and figures in his notebook, struck in at this point.

"Then I take it, sir, this'll be your time-table for the crime."

Case against Ferguson and Strachan

Monday.

    9.15 p. m. Farren leaves note at Strachan's house.

   10.20 p. m. Campbell returns home after encounter with Gowan.

   12 midnight or thereabouts. Strachan returns home and finds note.

Tuesday.

12.10 a. m. (say). Strachan goes to Campbell's cottage; is joined by Ferguson. Murder is committed.

12.10–12.45 (say). Plan of fake accident evolved. Strachan starts for Falbae, taking Campbell's hat and cloak, painting materials, etc., in car.

2–3 a. m. During this period Strachan and Farren meet and Farren escapes.

3.30 a. m. (say). Strachan falls down mine.

4 a. m. (say). Ferguson arrives at some spot on old road from Gatehouse Station to Creetown, with Campbell's car containing body and bicycle. Leaves car hidden.

5–6 a. m. Ferguson returns on bicycle to Gatehouse by old road.

9 a. m. Strachan extricates himself from mine and finds his car.

9.8 a. m. Ferguson takes the train to Dumfries.

9.20 a. m. Strachan arrives at rendezvous, transfers himself to Campbell's car. Hides own car. Disguises himself.

9.35 a. m. Strachan disguised as Campbell seen by workman passing turning to New Galloway.

10 a. m. Strachan arrives at Minnoch. Plants body and paints picture.

11.15 a. m. Strachan finishes picture.

Here Macpherson paused.

"How will Strachan get back tae his car, sir? 'Tis fourteen mile gude. He culdna du't on his twa feet?"

"Farren's bicycle," replied the Chief Constable, promptly. "You should have made him pick that up at Falbae. Of course, if his original plan hadn't gone wrong, he would either have borrowed another bicycle or had time to go on foot, but under the circumstances, with Farren's machine lying ready to hand, he would take advantage of it."

"Ay, sir; but ye have an answer tae everything." Macpherson shook his head soberly and returned to his time-table.

12.45 p. m. Strachan returns on Farren's bicycle to Creetown; abandons bicycle. Transfers to own car.

1.15 p. m. Strachan returns to Gatehouse by Skyre Burn road.

"That," said the Fiscal, who had been checking this time-table with the Chief Constable's report of his interview with Strachan, "agrees very well with Strachan's statement to you."

"It does," replied Sir Maxwell, "and, what is still more important, it agrees with the facts. We have found a man who distinctly remembers seeing Strachan passing along the Skyre Burn road between 1 o'clock and 1.20. Moreover, we have traced his telephone-call to the McClellan Arms, and it was put through at 1.18 precisely."

"You realise," said Wimsey, "that you've only allowed him an hour and a quarter for painting that picture. I had two of the slickest men in the district working on it, and the quicker painter of the two couldn't get the result under an hour and a half."

"That's true," said the Chief Constable, grimly, "but he wasn't painting for his life, you know."

"I wad like tae be sairtain o' that," said a voice. Everybody was surprised. P. C. Duncan had sat so silent that they had almost forgotten his existence.

"Is that so?" said the Chief Constable. "Well, Duncan, you're here to give us your opinion. Suppose we have it now."

The policeman shifted on his chair and glanced uneasily at Dalziel. He had an obscure idea that he was going to let himself in for a wigging, but he stuck manfully to his guns, and opened fire with a flourish.

CHAPTER XXV

GRAHAM : GOWAN : WATERS

"THEM twa theories," said P. C. Duncan, "is jist fine, an' I'm no sayin' the contrair', but, mon! they're jist awfu' complicated. It mak's ma heid spin only tae think o' them. I wadna wish tae be puttin' masel' forrit, but I wad like fine tae know how Sir Maxwell Jamieson thinks that yon plan could ha' been a' talked oot in three-quarters o' an hour."

"Well," replied Sir Maxwell, "those times are very elastic. Provided we get Strachan up to Falbae before it's too light for tumbling into mines, I don't mind how late you make him start."

"But no matter for that," put in the Fiscal, seeing that Duncan looked a little discouraged. "If you have a better and simpler idea to offer, by all means put it forward."

"I was jist thinkin', then," said Duncan, "and beggin' your pardon, Dr. Cameron, whether it was not, after all, possible that the man was kill't the same day he was found. Ye'll no be offended, doctor?"

"Not at all," said Dr. Cameron, heartily. "Speak out your mind, man. This business of speaking to the precise time of death is not so easy as ye'd think by reading detective novels. In my experience, the older a medical man gets, the less willing he is to make *ex cathedra* pronouncements, and the more he learns that Nature has her own ways of confounding self-confident prophets."

"Ay," said Duncan, "I've jist been readin' a wee buik aboot the subject. It's a gran' buik, an' it was gied me by my feyther for my last birthday. My feyther was an awfu' weel-eddicated mon for his station in life, an' he wad always be tellin' me that studyin' was the road tae success."

He laid a large, square, brown-paper parcel on the table as he spoke, and slowly untied the stout string with which it was secured.

"This here," said he, as the last knot yielded and the paper was turned back to disclose the "wee buik"—a formidable volume nine inches long by six inches across and thick in proportion—"this here is ca'ed *Forensic Medicine and Toxicology* by Dixon Mann, an' there's gran' readin' in it for a man in oor profession. Noo, there's a passage here as I'd like tae get your opinion on, doctor. I've pit a wee bit paper tae mark the place. Ay, here 'tis, page thirty-seven. This is aboot the death-stiffenin'."

. "*Rigor mortis*," said the doctor.

"Ay, that's what it is, only here it's ca'ed Cay-day-verric Rigeedity, but 'tis that same rigor he means. Yon's jist his difficult name fo't. Noo, here's whit this man says, an' he'll be a great authority, for my puir feyther paid a terrible deal o' money for the buik. 'Under ordinary circumstances the'—och, dear!—'the s-k-e-l-e-t-a-l, the skeeleetal muscles begin tae stiffen in fra' fower tae ten hours after death.' Fower tae ten hours. Noo, that'll gie us what ye might ca' a margin o' six hours' error in estimatin' the time o' death. Wull't no, doctor?"

"Other things being equal," said the doctor, "yes."

"Ay, an' here again: 'It is fully developed,' that is, the rigor, ye onnerstand, 'in fra' twa tae three hours.' That'll gie us anither hour's margin."

"Well, yes."

"Ay. 'This condition lasts for a period varyin' from a few hours tae six or eight days.' There's a terrible big difference there, doctor!"

"So there is," said Dr. Cameron, smiling slightly, "but there are other things to be taken into consideration besides *rigor mortis*. You'll not be suggesting the body was six or eight days old?"

"Not at all, doctor. But it gaes on tae say, 'Twenty-four tae forty-eight hours may be regarded as the average duration of cada——' that is, o' this rigor. Ye'll allow, maybe, that this great authority isna so varra preceese tae twa-three hours. Noo, then, doctor, when ye saw this corpse at 3 o'clock o' the afternoon, how stiff was he?"

"He was quite stiff," replied the doctor. "That is, to employ the stately language of your great authority, the cadaveric rigidity was fully established. This made it probable that the man had then been dead not less than six hours and probably—taking the appearance of the bruises, etc., into account—considerably longer. Taking Mr. Dixon Mann's pronouncement as the basis of a diagnosis, you will see that it would allow death to have taken place as much as thirteen hours earlier—ten hours to start the rigor and three to develop it fully. That is, the death might have taken place as late as 9 a. m. or as early as midnight, and the body would still have been stiff at 3 p. m., without its being necessary to presume anything abnormal in the onset or development of the rigor."

"Ay, but——" began Macpherson, hastily.

"Ay, that's jist what I——" began Duncan, at the same moment.

"One minute," said the doctor. "I know what ye're about to say, Inspector. I'm not fully allowing for the case that the rigor might have been completely established some time before I saw it. Supposing the rigor had come on slowly and had been fully developed, say, at 1 o'clock. That would make it possible that the death took place as early as 10 p. m. the day before. I told you before that that was not impossible."

Macpherson gave a satisfied grunt.

"Campbell was a man in vigorous health," went on the doctor, "and he died from a sudden blow. If you'll consult that authority of yours a bit farther on, Duncan, you'll see it says that, under those conditions, the onset of cadaveric rigidity is likely to be slow."

"Ay, doctor," persisted the policeman, "but ye'll see also that when the subject is exhausted an' depressed in his physical strength, the rigidity may come on verra quick. Noo, I was thinkin' that yon Campbell must ha' passed an awfu' exhaustin' nicht. He was fightin' wi' Mr. Waters at 9 o'clock or thereabouts, he was fightin' again wi' Mr. Gowan at 9.45, an' he had his inside fu' o' whuskey forbye, which is well known tae be depressin' in its effects—that is," he added hastily, catching a slight grin on Wimsey's face, "after the high speerits o' the moment is wore off. Then he's away oot airly in the mornin' wi'oot his breakfast, as was established by examination o' his insides, an' he drives his car twenty-seven mile. Wad he no be sufficiently exhausted wi' a' that tae stiffen up quick when he was killed?"

"You seem to have thought this out, Duncan," said the doctor. "I see I shall have to be careful, or I shall be caught tripping. I will only say this. The average duration of *rigor mortis* is from twenty-four to forty-eight hours. Campbell's body was rigid when I saw it on Tuesday afternoon at 3 o'clock, and it was still rigid on Wednesday night when it was put into its coffin. On Thursday evening, when I examined it in the presence of a number of you gentlemen, the rigidity had entirely passed off. That gives a fairly average duration for the rigor. In general, a quick onset is followed by a short duration, and a slow onset by a long duration. In this case, the duration appeared average to slow, and I conclude that the onset would also have been average to slow. That is why I finally gave it as my considered opinion that the most probable time of death was somewhere round about midnight, and this agreed with the general appearance of the body and the bruises."

"How about the contents of the stomach?" asked Sir Maxwell.

"The contents of the stomach was whiskey," said the doctor, drily, "but I'm not saying how late on Monday night the deceased would be drinking whiskey."

"But," said Duncan, "supposin' the murder didna take place till 9 o'clock or so on the Tuesday, that wad shorten the duration of the rigor."

"Well, of course," said the doctor. "If he didn't die till Tuesday morning, that might bring the duration of the rigor down to a little over thirty-six hours. I can only speak to the period between 3 p. m. on Tuesday and 7 p. m. on Wednesday, when I handed it over to the undertaker."

"Well, the point appears to be," said the Fiscal, "that, though the appearances suggest to you a death round about midnight, you may be in error to the extent of an hour or two either way."

"That is so."

"Could you be in error to the extent of eight or nine hours?"

"I would not like to think so," replied the doctor, cautiously, "but I would not say it was impossible. There's very few things impossible in Nature, and an error in diagnosis is not one of them."

"Weel," said Dalziel, eyeing his subordinate with some disfavour, "ye hear what the doctor says. He'll no say it is impossible, an' that's mair nor ye could ha' expectit, an' you tae be questionin' his great experience, with your *rigor mortis* an' your auld feyther, an' your wee buik an' a'. 'Tis tae be hoped ye can gie a gude reason for your presumption. Ye'll kindly excuse him, doctor. Duncan is a gude lad, but he's ower zealous."

Duncan, thus stimulated, began again, blushing hotly all over his face.

"Weel, sirs, the point I started from was this, that oot of a' six suspects there's not one that's been proved to ha' been nigh the place where the corpse was found, only Mr. Graham. But we've evidence that Graham was actually seen at Bargrennan the verra morning o' the murder. An', what's mair, he admits tae't himsel'."

"That's a fact," said the Fiscal. "You've got in here in your notes that this man Brown saw Graham walking along the banks of the Cree just below Bargrennan at half-past eleven on Tuesday morning. He says that Graham was going upstream, and that when he saw Brown approaching, he scrambled quickly down the bank as though to avoid observation. That certainly looks like a suspicious circumstance."

"Ay," said Duncan, excitedly. "An' when Graham is questioned, what does he say? First of a', he refuses tae state whaur he's been. An' that, mind you, before there's ony suspicion gi'en oot that Campbell's death was mair nor an accident. That's yin thing. Secondly, as sune as it's known through the papers that it may be a case o' murder, he comes forrit wi' a fause alibi for the Monday nicht only."

"Stop a moment, Duncan," said Sir Maxwell. "If, as you seem to suppose, Graham did not commit the murder till Tuesday morning, there would be no point in his bringing forward an alibi for Monday night. He'd know it would not cover him."

"Ay, that's so," said Duncan, screwing up his ingenuous face into an expression of the most concentrated cunning, "but it was the leddy brought forrit the alibi, an' why? Because it had been pit aboot —I'm no sayin' by whom—that the murder was maist probably committed o' the Monday nicht. Then the leddy—that kens fine Graham did the murder but isna sae weel informed as tae the time—fa's heid ower heels intae the trap. She says, 'He couldna ha' done't; he was wi' me.' Mr. Dalziel asks her sharp and sudden, 'How long was he wi' you?' She says, 'Till past 9 o'clock,' knowin' verra weel that if she was tae say till 12 o'clock or some such hour, the next question wad be, 'Did naebody see him leavin' the hoose?' —which, wi' a' the folks astir in the toon, is no verra probable. Verra gude. Then Graham hears on't an' says tae himsel', 'I maun du better than that. Likely enough I was recognised by that fellow up yonder. I'll say I was the haill of they two nichts and days up at Bargrennan poachin' wi' Jimmy Fleeming an' Jimmy'll bear me oot.' An' that's when he comes in wi' his second alibi."

"Jimmy Fleming does bear him out, as far as I can see," observed the Fiscal, turning over his papers.

"Och, ay," said Duncan, "Jimmy Fleeming's the biggest leear in the Stewartry. Forbye, Graham is weel likit by that poachin' lot. There's no a man among them that wadna swear to a wee lie or so tae protect Graham."

"That's true enough," said Macpherson. "An there's no need for them tae be tellin' sic a big lie, neither. They'd be up half the nicht wi' their poachin' an' sleepin' half the day. What's tae hinder Graham walking off an' committin' his murder—ay, an' pentin' his bit picture—wi'oot them knowin'? He wad say he's ta'en a wee walk, maybe. Or maybe they'd be sleepin' and never notice when he comed or gaed?"

"Your idea, Duncan, is that Campbell came up to the Minnoch—when, exactly?"

"That's clear enough," said Wimsey. "We've got to take Ferguson's times, because, on this assumption, there's no reason for doubting them. Starting at 7.30, and driving at an ordinary speed, he wouldn't be likely to do the twenty-seven miles in much under an hour. Say he arrives there at 8.30 and sits down and gets his painting things out. Graham, taking his morning walk, gets along there at, say, 8.45. They quarrel, and Campbell is knocked into the river and killed. At 9 o'clock, summer time, Graham might reasonably begin to do his painting. It takes him an hour and a half. We know that, because we've seen him do it—at least, I have. That brings us to half-past ten. But we know he was still there at five past eleven, so we'll have to give him till then. That's quite likely, because if, when I saw him, he was merely copying his own painting, he'd probably do it quicker than if it was his first effort. As soon as he's finished, and the road is free of inquisitive passers-by, he strolls back to his sleeping friends, who will subsequently be ready to swear that they never took their eyes off him the whole time. That's your theory, isn't it, Duncan?"

"Ay, that's it," said Duncan, gratified.

"It's not a bad one, either, as far as it goes," went on his lordship, with the air of a man sampling a glass of old port. "It has at least three snags, but I daresay they could be demolished with a little goodwill. First, the doctor has got to be all wrong in his calculations, but, as he doesn't seem to mind that, neither need we. Secondly, who ate Campbell's breakfast? Well, we can suppose that, having drunk rather deeply the night before, he nevertheless courageously cooked his egg and rasher and, having cooked them, didn't like the look of them and shot them into the fire. Or we can suppose—though I should hate to do so—that Mrs. Green ate them herself and said she hadn't. Or we can suppose that Campbell ate them, was promptly sick, and filled up the void with whiskey. Any one of those suppositions would account for the conditions as found, eh, doctor?

"Then there are the marks of tar on Campbell's Morris, which we put down to bicycle-tyres, but they might quite well have been due to something else. I pointed them out in the first place, but I wouldn't be bigoted about them on that account. They're not significant enough to wreck a theory on.

"The big snag in Duncan's ingenious reconstruction is the man who saw the car pass the New Galloway turning at 9.45. I'm afraid Duncan hasn't accounted for him at all. Still, we can say he was mistaken. If a doctor can be mistaken, so can an honest workman. He didn't see the number of the car, so it may have been another Morris."

"But the piled-up stuff under the rug at the back," said the Chief Constable, "and the driver's conspicuous cloak. You can't get away from them."

"Can't I?" said Wimsey. "You don't know me. I could get away from a galloping fire-engine. You'd been advertising for a Morris car driven by a man in a loud cloak, with a pile of luggage behind, hadn't you? Well, you know what happens when you advertise for things. A man sees something that corresponds to part of the description and imagines the rest. Probably twenty Morris cars drove over the main road from Castle-Douglas to Stranraer that morning and probably half of those had luggage in them. Several of them may have been driven by gentlemen whose dress was more noisy than discriminating. Your man had no very particular reason to notice the car at the time, except that he shot out on it unexpectedly. If the truth was known, he was probably riding carelessly himself. The car got in his way and annoyed him, and if he can persuade himself that he had an encounter with a desperado fleeing from justice, he's not going to stick at remembering a few things that weren't there. There are plenty of people who are always ready to remember more than they saw."

"That's awfu' tru," sighed Macpherson.

"I will tell you a thing I like about this theory of Duncan's," said the Fiscal. "It makes it appear likely that the crime was unpremeditated. It is more likely that Graham, coming suddenly upon Campbell like that, should quarrel with him and knock him down than that anybody should contrive a scheme to carry a dead body all those miles and plant it in so awkward a place."

"The place was more or less forced on the murderer, was it not, by Campbell's expressed intention of painting there that day?"

"But he might be supposed to have changed his mind, Sir Maxwell."

"To an innocent man," said Macpherson, acutely, "that supposition wad present no difficulty at all. But a murderer might weel be ower particular, even tae the point o' riskin' the miscarriage of his plans by an unnecessary verisimilitude."

"Well, Inspector," said the Chief Constable, "I can see that you are not altogether satisfied with any of our theories. Let us have yours."

The Inspector brightened. This was his moment. He felt convinced that he, and no other person, had the right sow by the ear, and was, indeed, extremely grateful to Dalziel, Sir Maxwell and Duncan for having produced such inferior animals and refrained from spoiling his market.

"The Sergeant said just noo," said he, "that Jimmy Fleeming was the biggest leear in the Stewartry. Weel, I ken three that's bigger leears than him, an' that's Gowan and his pack of English servants. An' ye'll mind that they three are the only pairsons that's proved oot o' their own mouths tae be leears, exceptin' Strachan an' his bit tale aboot a gowf-ball.

"I believe Gowan killed Campbell when they met on the road, an' I dinna credit one word o' that story aboot his beard.

"Noo, I've written doon the course o' events as I see them, an' I'll ask ye tae read it out for me, Mr. Fiscal, seein' as ye're better accustomed tae speakin' in public than I am."

With these words, the Inspector handed over a neatly-written manuscript which he produced from his breast-pocket, and leaned back with the shy smile of a poet attending a public reading of his own works.

The Fiscal adjusted his glasses and, in a clear voice, proceeded to do justice to—

The Case against Gowan

The evidence of the girl Helen Macgregor is that Campbell met with another motorist, since proved and admitted to be Gowan, on the Gatehouse-Kirkcudbright road at about 9.45 on Monday night. That there was a quarrel, and that one of the parties then placed the inanimate body of the other party in the two-seater car and drove off with it in the direction of Gatehouse. That she then became frightened and ran home. This story was subsequently substantiated by the finding of a spanner, bearing Campbell's fingerprints, close to the locus of the alleged assault, and by the discovery of car-tracks tending to show that a car had been driven into a grass lane, through a gate some fifty yards from the said locus.

In my opinion, the crime is to be reconstructed as follows.

Having killed Campbell in the struggle, Gowan's first consideration was to remove the corpse to a place where it would not be seen by a passer-by. This he effected by placing it in his own car, driving up to the gate, and dumping the body inside. He selected his own car for this purpose because it was the nearest to Gatehouse and could be more readily shifted by him. If he had put the body at once in Campbell's car, he would have had to move his own car first, to get the other past, and someone might have arrived while he was so doing. If such a person had found Campbell's car obstructing the road and had ascertained upon investigation that it contained a dead body it would have a very suspicious appearance.

He then brought up Campbell's car, drove it through the gate, placed the body in it and deposited it at some distance up the lane. He then proceeded on foot to his own car, turned it and returned in it to Kirkcudbright. He could accomplish this, driving *like hell* [the last two words were carefully ruled out] in a reckless manner in rather under five minutes. Say at 10.10. The girl Helen saw him when he passed her house.

He would find Hammond on duty and would urge him to return with him at once. On reaching the scene of the crime at, say,

10.20, he would proceed on foot to the Morris car and drive it out of the lane in the direction of Gatehouse, while Hammond would return with the two-seater to Kirkcudbright.

Gowan could be back with the Morris at Standing Stone cottage at, say, 10.30. (Note: Ferguson gives the time as 10.15, but he only says "about.")

Gowan then conceives the plan of simulating an accident to Campbell. Since his black beard would make it impossible to impersonate Campbell, he shaves this off with Campbell's razor, carefully cleaning the same, and destroying the hair in the fire, except a portion which he reserved for another purpose.

When Strachan arrived, Gowan was in hiding some place or other, probably in the garage. On Strachan's departure, he returned to the cottage in a stealthy manner, destroyed the note and proceeded with his preparations.

At 7.30 he would start out with the car, disguised in Campbell's clothes and carrying the corpse, the painting materials and the bicycle, which he would have taken from the Anwoth Hotel. Now we have to account for the long time taken by him to arrive at the New Galloway road, where he was seen by the workman. In my opinion he proceeded to some town or village not yet ascertained, and there instructed Hammond to meet him at some point with the two-seater. In my opinion this would be a locality in the neighbourhood of Pinwherry. Inquiries have been set on foot to trace this telephone message within an area of thirty miles round about Gatehouse.

At this point the Chief Constable interrupted the reading.

"Could not the call be readily traced at the Kirkcudbright end?" he inquired.

"No, no," said Wimsey, before Macpherson could speak. "Hammond would have been instructed to go somewhere else to get it. A desperate fellow like Gowan isn't going to take all this trouble only to trip up on a trifle like a telephone call, eh, Macpherson?"

"That's so," said the Inspector. "That's jist exactly what was in my mind."

"Then why did he not tell Hammond what to do when they were together, and avoid the telephone call altogether?" demanded Sir Maxwell.

"He hadn't made his plan then," said Wimsey. "How fretful you people are! Do give the man time to think. His first idea is, 'Let's get the body away off this road that I'm known to have driven along. I'll plant it somewhere. I don't know where. I'll think it out and 'phone you to-morrow at 8 o'clock. Go to Lauriston or Tywnholm (or Kamschatka or Timbuctoo or whatever was the handiest place) and I'll put the call through to you there.' After all, you've got to explain the delay on the road somehow. Ferguson is a liar, Strachan fell down a mine, Farren—let me see; oh, yes— Farren was a poor hand with a car and Gowan made a telephone call. Please go on with the reading, Fiscal."

Gowan then proceeded to the site on the Minnoch and painted his picture. This would occupy him till about 11.30. He then mounted the bicycle and rode along the road to Pinwherry and Girvan to the spot selected by him. It would be just as he had passed Barrhill that he was observed by Mr. Clarence Gordon. Mr. Gordon said that the bicyclist was not a very tall man, but Gowan would not look so tall if he was bent down over a bicycle and pedalling fast. Without his beard, Gowan would not be recognizable from his photograph. Hammond would meet him with the two-seater some place between Barrhill and Girvan, and he would be provided with any necessary tackle for securing the bicycle to the car. They would drive together to just this side of Girvan, where Hammond would alight, take the bicycle and proceed to Ayr, contriving whether by design or mischance to lose the bicycle in the station. It will be remembered that the person travelling with the bicycle was said to speak like an Englishman. Gowan then proceeded with the car to some point from which he could write and dispatch his letter to Major Aylwin. He would not wish to make his appearance in Kirkcudbright without his beard so that he probably did not return till that night. Efforts are being made to trace the movements of the car during this period.

With reference to the portions of beard discovered on the Gate-house-Kirkcudbright road. It would occur to Gowan and his confederates that the fact of murder might be suspected and his own movements investigated. In that case the shaving-off of his beard and his disappearance to London might present a suspicious appearance. They therefore concocted a story to fit the case, and planted the portions of hair by the roadside in order to support this invention. This was the story subsequently told by Gowan at Scotland Yard, which was very misleading, on account of containing so large a proportion of facts. The details of Gowan's escape from Kirkcudbright occurred exactly as related in his statement. This is the case against Gowan as presented by me.

(*Signed*) JOHN MACPHERSON,
Inspector of Police.

   •   •   •   •   •   •   •   •

"Ingeniouser and ingeniouser," said Wimsey. "There are a good many details that need verification, but the whole thing is very pretty indeed. What a shocking set of crooks these English servants are! Not even murder will turn them from their feudal devotion to the man who pays!"

The Inspector flushed.

"Ye're tryin' tae make a fool of me, my lord," he said, reproachfully.

"Indeed, no," replied his lordship. "One thing in your story pleases me particularly, and that is that you have bravely tackled the business of the bicycle at Euston, which everybody else has fought shy of."

At this point, Constable Ross cleared his throat in so pointed a manner that everyone turned to look at him.

"I perceive from your manner, Ross," said his lordship, "that to you also the word bicycle has not been devoid of significance. With the permission of these other gentlemen, I should greatly like to hear your version of the matter."

The constable looked. at the Chief Constable for his approval, and receiving a nod, embarked upon his theory.

"The thing that's in my mind," said he, "is this man Waters. Here's a man wi' a verra unsatisfactory alibi, which is no capable o' proof. We have not yet established communication wi' this man Drewitt an' his sailing-yacht——"

"Just a moment, Ross," broke in the Chief Constable. "We got a wire in from him this morning from Arisaig. We just missed him at Oban. He wires, 'Waters joined us at Doon 8.30 Tuesday morning. Left yacht Gourock Saturday. Writing.' He has also, I understand, made a confirmatory statement to the police."

"Ay," said Ross, not in the least disconcerted, "ay, imph'm. But we dinna ken what kind o' a man is this Drewitt. He'll be for backin' up Waters ony gait, tae my thinkin'. He may swear till he's black in the face Waters went aboard at the Doon, but the fact remains that naebody saw him to speak to, an' the bicycle has clean disappeared. In my opinion, yon bicycle is doon in the deep waters betune Arran an' Stranraer, an' ye'll never see it mair till it rises oot o' the sea tae bear witness at the great Day of Judgment. Wi'oot," he added, with some sacrifice of picturesqueness, "ye sairch for't wi' deep-sea tackle."

"What's your idea, then, Ross?"

"Well, Sir Maxwell, 'tis this, an' 'tis awfu' clear an' simple tae my thinkin'. Here's Campbell, fou' as a puggie an' lookin' for trouble. He has a row wi' Waters an' says it'll no end there. He's aff away to Gatehouse, an' he meets Gowan an' gets the better o' him. 'That's fine,' thinks he, 'it's my night the night.' He's away home an' he gets drinkin' again, and he thinks to himsel', 'What for wad I no drag that bastard Waters' (beggin' your pardon) 'oot o' his bed an' finish wi' him now?' He gets his car oot again an' starts away. Ferguson will be asleep an' no hearin' him. He admits himsel' he didna hear Strachan gae, an' what for wad he ha' heard Campbell? He drives ower tae Kirkcudbright an' chucks stones at Waters' window. Waters looks oot, sees him an' thinks, 'We'll no have a row in the street.' He lets him in an' they talk a bit, an' yin or 'tither o' them says, 'We'll away up tae the stoojo an' fight it oot.' They do so, an' Campbell's killt.

"Waters is in an awfu' pickle and doesna ken what tae do. He's comin' oot o' the stoojo in a distracted condition when he meets his friend Drewitt, that's visitin' there wi' his hired car. 'Drewitt,' says he, 'I'm in awfu' trouble. I've killt a man,' he says, 'an' I dinna ken what tae do. It was a fair fight,' he says, 'but they'll bring it in murder an' I'll be hangit.' Then they puts their heids tegither an' makes a plan. Drewitt's away tae Mrs. McLeod's for tae impairsonate Waters. An' ye'll mind," added Constable Ross, forcibly, "that Mrs. McLeod never set eyes on her lodger fra' the time he went oot a little after midnight. She *heard* him come upstairs, she heard him ca' oot when she brought up the water, an' when she came in fra' the back o' the hoose, he'd eaten his breakfast and away."

"Drewitt would be takin' an awfu' risk," said Macpherson.

"Ay, but murderers maun tak' risks," said Ross. "In the meantime, Waters is away wi' Campbell's car an' his bicycle at the same time that Drewitt entered the hoose. Then he does a' the same things as we've suggested for the other suspects. He's away wi' the body at 7.30. I'm thinkin' he'll ha' ta'en the auld road through Gatehouse Station an' he'll maybe have had engine trouble in that lonely place, or burst a tyre an' had tae change the wheel. The road's wicked wi' the ruts and the stones thereabouts. Ony gait, he passes the New Galloway turnin' at 9.35 an' arrives at the Minnoch at 10. He pents his picture, throws the body into the burn and makes off on his bicycle. He has plenty o' time, for he'll no be able tae carry oot the rest o' his plan before nightfall. He hides up in the hills, an' it's here he'll be cursin' himsel', for he'll ha' forgot tae bring wi' him the sandwiches that was found in Campbell's satchel. Ay, he'll be fine an' empty before night. When 'tis safe for him tae move, he rides his bicycle tae the appointed meetin'-place wi' Drewitt.

"Drewitt will ha' been workin' up the coast, like he said. It will ha' been Drewitt as was seen tae go aboard at the Doon, an' after that, the course o' the yacht will agree wi' Waters' statement. In the night, she'll make across fra' Lady Bay tae Finnart Bay, an' pick up Waters that's ridden doon by the high road fra' Pinwherry. They take the bicycle on board an' return tae lie up in Lady Bay. After that they hae only tae carry oot their original sailing plan, an' land Waters at Gourock on Saturday mornin', after sinkin' the bicycle some place where it'll no be easy found. Man! it's as plain as the nose on your face."

"But——" said the Chief Constable.

"But——" said the Inspector.

"But——" said the Sergeant.

"But——" said Constable Duncan.

"Imph'm," said the Fiscal. "All these theories are very interesting, gentlemen, but they are all conjectural. I congratulate you all extremely upon your ingenuity and hard work, but to say which theory is the most probable is a harder choice than that between Portia's caskets. It appears to me that all are worth being followed up, and that the next step is to prosecute inquiries which may tend to confirm either one or the other of them. The movements of all cars upon the roads in the district must be checked with the greatest possible care. The man Drewitt must be interviewed and closely questioned, and the persons living about Finnart Bay and Lady Bay must be asked whether they observed anything of the movements of the yacht. At least we can feel certain that one among the five theories presented to us must be the true one, and that is something. Do you not think so, Lord Peter?"

"Yes, Wimsey," said the Chief Constable. "You told the Inspector the other day that you had solved the problem. Are you in a position to give a casting vote? Which of our suspects is the murderer?"

CHAPTER XXVI

THE MURDERER

"THIS," said Lord Peter Wimsey, "is the proudest moment of my life. At last I really feel like Sherlock Holmes. A Chief Constable, a Police Inspector, a Police Sergeant and two constables have appealed to me to decide between their theories, and with my chest puffed like a pouter-pigeon, I can lean back in my chair and say, 'Gentlemen, you are all wrong.' "

"Damn it," said the Chief Constable, "we can't *all* be wrong."

"You remind me," said Wimsey, "of the steward who said to the Channel passenger, 'You can't be sick here.' You can all be wrong and you are."

"But we've suspected everybody," said Sir Maxwell. "See here, Wimsey, you're not going to turn round now and say that the crime was committed by Mrs. Green or the milkman, or somebody we've never heard of? That would be in the very worst tradition of the lowest style of detective fiction. Besides, you said yourself that the murderer was an artist, and you even picked out those six artists yourself. Are you going back on that now?"

"No," said Wimsey, "I wouldn't do anything quite so mean as that. I'll qualify my original statement. You are all wrong, but one of you is less wrong than the rest. Still none of you has got the right murderer, and none of you has got the whole of the method right, though some of you have got bits of it."

"Don't be portentous and tiresome, Wimsey," said Sir Maxwell. "There is a serious side to this matter. If you possess any information that we do not, you ought to let us have it. In fact, you ought to have let us have it at once, instead of wasting our time like this."

"I did let you have it at once," said Wimsey. "I let you have it on the day of the crime, only you keep on forgetting it. And I haven't really been holding anything up my sleeve. I had to wait till all the suspects were roped in before I could be certain of my theory, because at any moment something might have turned up to unsettle it. And I haven't actually proved it now, though I'll undertake to do it any time you like."

"Come, come," said the Fiscal, "please tell us what it is you're wanting to prove, and you shall be given every opportunity."

"Right-ho! I will be good. Now we'll have to go back to the discovery of the body. The crucial point of the whole problem was there, and I pointed it out to you, Dalziel, and that was the thing that made us sure from the start that Campbell's death was murder and no accident.

"You remember how we found the body. It was lying in the burn, cold and stiff, and on the easel up above there was a picture, half-finished, together with a palette, a satchel and a painting-knife. We went through all the belongings of the dead man, and I said to you, 'There's something missing, and if we can't find it, it means murder.' You remember that, Dalziel?"

"I mind it fine, Lord Peter."

"In Campbell's satchel we found nine tubes of oil colour—vermilion, ultramarine, two chrome yellows, viridian, cobalt, crimson lake, rose madder and lemon yellow. But there was no flake white. Now, as I explained to you at the time, it is absolutely impossible for a painter in oils to make a picture without using flake white. It is the fundamental medium which he uses to mix with his other colours to produce various shades of light and shadow. Even a man like Campbell, who used a great deal of pure colour, would as soon think of setting out to paint without flake white as you would set out to catch trout without a cast. And in any case, the proof that Campbell had been using flake white that morning was proved by the picture itself, which contained huge masses of white cloud, wet and fresh and just laid on.

"A glance at the palette confirmed this. It had seven blobs of colour on it, in this order: White, cobalt, viridian, vermilion, ultramarine, chrome yellow and rose madder.

"Well, you know how we searched for that missing tube of colour. We turned out Campbell's pockets, we scoured every inch of the ground and we lifted—or rather, you lifted, because I'd made tracks like a sensible man—every stone in that confounded stream, right down to the bridge. I told you the tube would probably be a big one, but that it might, of course, be nearly empty and therefore rather light. If it had been anywhere about, I think we may take it that you would have found it."

"Ay," said Dalziel, "ye may confidently assume that, my lord."

"Very well, then. There was, of course, the faint possibility that, after Campbell's death, someone had come up and removed the tube, but we felt that to be too fantastic for consideration. Why should anybody steal just that one thing and nothing else? And then, there was the condition of the body, which suggested that death had occurred a good deal earlier than the amount of work on the picture would lead one to suppose. And by the way, doctor, I may as well relieve your mind and say at once that, in spite of Duncan's able and ingenious special pleading, your estimate of the time of death was perfectly sound."

"I'm glad to hear it."

"Yes. Well, the question was, what had happened to the flake white? Taking all the appearances into consideration, I formed the opinion that (*a*) Campbell had been murdered, (*b*) the murderer had painted the picture, (*c*) he had for some reason taken the flake white away with him.

"Now, why should he take it away? It would be the silliest possible thing for him to do, since its absence would instantly arouse suspicion. He must have taken it by mistake, and that meant that he must have automatically put it in the place where he was accustomed to put tubes of colour while painting. He hadn't put it in any of the ordinary places—on the ground, or in a box, or in the satchel or on the tray attached to the easel. He must have bestowed it about his person somewhere, and a pocket was the likeliest place. So that from that moment I felt we ought to look about for a painter with the untidy habit of dropping paints into his pockets."

"You didn't mention that," said Dalziel, reproachfully.

"No, because I was afraid—forgive me—that if I had, you might possibly go and make inquiries about it, and if once the murderer had his attention drawn to this unfortunate habit of his, there would be an end of the habit and the inquiry. Besides, several painters might have the same habit. Or I might be entirely mistaken about the whole thing—it was a slender clue, and I might be straining it too far. I thought my best plan was to snoop about the studios and watch people at work and find out what their habits were. That was obviously a job which I, as a private person, could do better than any official. But I gave you the pointer, Dalziel, and you put it into your report. Anybody could have come to the same conclusion as I did. Why didn't anybody?"

"Never mind why we didn't, Wimsey," said Sir Maxwell. "Go on with your story."

"The next thing," said Wimsey, "was—why all this elaborate fake with the picture? Why should a murderer hang round the place of the crime painting pictures? Obviously, to disguise the fact that Campbell had been killed at—well, whatever time he was killed. Say the previous night. That meant that the murderer hadn't got a good alibi for the previous night or whenever it was. But if he wanted to make it look as though Campbell had been killed that morning, it meant that he must be preparing himself a cast-iron alibi for that particular morning. So I decided that I knew four things about the murderer already: (1). he was an artist, or he couldn't have painted the picture, (2) he had a habit of putting paints in his pocket, (3) he had a weak alibi for the actual time of death, (4) he would have a good alibi for Tuesday morning.

"Then came the discovery of the tar-marks on the car. That suggested that the alibi had somehow been worked out with the aid of a bicycle. But I couldn't get farther than that, because I didn't know when Campbell was killed, or when he was supposed to have started out for the Minnoch, or how long the picture would take to paint, or any details of that kind. But what I did know was that Campbell had been a quarrelsome kind of devil, and that at least six artists in the district had been going about shouting for his blood.

"Now the confusing thing about this case was that of these six artists, five had disappeared. Of course it isn't in the least unusual for five artists to be away from the district at the same time. There was the Exhibition at Glasgow, to which several people had gone, including Ferguson. There was fishing, which often takes people out at night—there were hundreds of perfectly legitimate things they might have been doing. But the fact remained that those five people were not available for inquiries. You can't sit round and watch a man painting when you don't know where he is. The only man I could get hold of at once was Strachan, and when I came to look into his case, it appeared that his alibi was anything but satisfactory, not only for the Monday night but for the Tuesday morning as well; to say nothing of his having a black eye and a generally dilapidated appearance.

"So that was how the case stood then. Graham, vanished; Farren vanished; Waters vanished; Gowan gone to London; Ferguson gone to Glasgow; Strachan, at home, but obviously telling lies.

"Strachan, I may say, I almost absolved at once, though I thought it possible that he had some guilty knowledge of some kind. I was looking for a murderer with a good alibi, and Strachan's was about as bad and clumsy as it could be. Graham, Farren and Waters had to wait; they might turn up with excellent alibis; I couldn't tell. Only I had expected something more obvious and immediate. The two most suspicious people, from my point of view, were Ferguson and Gowan, because they had alibis supported by outside people. But if Gowan's alibi was sound, it covered the night as well as the morning; therefore the man who best fulfilled all the conditions was Ferguson. He had an alibi of exactly the kind that I expected. It covered the morning only; it was watertight in every joint; and it was established by people like station-masters and bus-conductors, who could have no possible reason for lying about it. If Ferguson had really travelled by the 9.8 train from Gatehouse to Dumfries, he *could not* have painted the picture.

"Well, then the rest of the people began to filter along. Graham turned up with no explanation at all, and he gave me a bad jolt; because Graham is the one man of the six who has, not only imagination, but the same *kind* of imagination as my own. I could see Graham working out that train of thought about the alibi and saying to himself that any alibi would be suspect, and that the biggest proof of innocence would be to have none. I believe that at that point I suspected Graham more than anybody else. He said he could imitate Campbell's style of painting—went out of his way to demonstrate it, too. I had an awful feeling that we should never be able to pin Graham down to anything. His manner was perfect. He took exactly the right line about the thing. And he didn't mean to commit himself until he knew what he had got to meet.

"Then Ferguson came back, with plenty of witnesses to show that he had really been to Glasgow, and told us a story which gave us at last a few real times to go upon. I am sure that all the times he gave us were perfectly correct, by the way, and that he didn't fall asleep or miss anything. I barged in on him and studied his method of painting and all that, and got him settled in my mind.

"That was the day we began to get a line on that bicycle business at Ayr. Now, I don't want to be rude to anybody, but I do think that bicycle ought to have been taken into account in any explanation of the crime. The whole affair was so extremely odd that it could hardly be an accident or a coincidence. It didn't throw any light on the personality of the murderer, of course, because, though it was a Gatehouse bicycle, that merely meant that the crime had been worked from Gatehouse, which was overwhelmingly probable in any case. It was a great pity that the unfortunate porter at Girvan should have crocked up when he did. If he could have identified one of those photographs, he might have spared us a lot of trouble.

"Thursday—what did I do on Thursday? Of course, yes—we got the story of the row on the Gatehouse-Kirkcudbright road, and the spanner and the black hair. We rather tripped up on that, Macpherson. If we'd been a bit quicker, we could have caught Gowan before he eloped and saved several railway-fares to London. It was my fault, because I was taken up with my painting idea, and went round to Bob Anderson's to propose a sort of reconstruction up at the Minnoch. I was going to cart a lot of painters up there and set them to paint in Campbell's manner and see how long it took them. Graham and Strachan and Ferguson were there. They all agreed to try, except that Ferguson thought the idea wasn't in very good taste. But the weather spoilt that plan.

"What happened then? Oh, yes. I went over to the Carrick shore and watched Strachan painting, and he started to knock me into the sea, but thought better of it. By that time it was clear enough that he was either concealing something or shielding somebody, and the probability was that he was mixed up in Farren's disappearance. I'd seen him over at Mrs. Farren's, you know, on the Tuesday night, when I was inspecting Waters' studio and observing what a handy place the lane was for a car-park.

"Saturday, I didn't do much, but Waters came back and we got that remarkable story from Mrs. Smith-Lemesurier. I was still uncertain about Graham. It was far too stupid a story for him to put up, but, as Duncan pointed out, the lady might have lost her head and concocted it without reference to him.

"On Sunday I bullied Mrs. Farren into telling me where to find her husband. I ran him to earth on Monday and had a look at his painting methods, just before the official sleuths came along. So now I had only three more of my painters to inspect. After that, the

Chief Constable got Strachan's story, but I knew all I needed to know about Strachan by that time.

"My final job was to get hold of Graham and Waters and put them on to copying Campbell's painting. That killed four birds with one stone. It told me how they both used their colours, it gave me the time-factor I wanted to make my theory complete and, as it happened, they gave me, in conversation, the information I wanted about Gowan. That was why, Inspector, I told you that I didn't need to go and see Gowan.

"Now what you are all panting to know is—what did these six people do with their colours?

"Gowan, it appeared, was a fearfully spick and span fellow. He couldn't paint without having everything just so. He had a place for everything and everything in its place. He was the last person in the world to put paints in his pockets. And besides, to tell you the truth, I feel sure that he couldn't have produced that imitation of Campbell's style. He is too set in his methods. Nor do I think he would have the brains to carry out the fake from first to last. All the clever part of his little disappearance was planned and executed by Alcock, who has the makings of a very fine schemer indeed.

"Waters habitually chucks his paints into a satchel. Consequently, with Campbell's satchel handy, he would naturally have chucked them into it. And though he boasted of being able to imitate Campbell, he was slow at copying him, and his imitation was not extraordinarily good. But yet it wasn't bad enough to look like a deliberate attempt to do it badly. And neither he nor Graham looked in the least as though they had any unpleasant associations with the picture.

"Graham—well, Graham is a very clever man. *He* knew straight away that the painting wasn't Campbell's. He didn't exactly say so, in so many words, but he noticed differences in the style and remarked upon them. That might, of course, have been the culminating point in his scheme of overreaching me, but I was pretty sure it wasn't. He seemed genuinely puzzled and suspicious. He also said that when painting out of doors, he put his tubes either on the ground or in his hat, and Waters bore him out in this. Neither Graham nor Waters showed any tendency to drop paints into their pockets. I watched them for an hour and a half, without surprising so much as a half-checked movement.

"Farren uses a sketching-box and is particular about putting each tube back in its place immediately after use. I can't say what he would do when he hadn't a box handy, but while I was at Mrs. Farren's I inspected the pockets of his old painting-jacket, and found that they had no tubes in them and no marks of paint on the lining. Besides, I eliminated Farren the moment I found that he had no alibi for Tuesday morning. The whole point of the fake was to support an alibi. If it didn't do that, it wasn't worth doing.

"Strachan lays his colours out on the tray of his easel, always in the same order, and he makes up his palette in a uniform order, too—the order of the spectrum. Now Campbell's palette was not made up like that, and the tubes of paint were all in the satchel— except, of course, the flake white. While watching Strachan, I took the opportunity to abstract a tube of cobalt, but he missed it instantly when he came to pack up, though he was all of a dither at the time, on account of the things I'd been saying to him. *He* wasn't the man to go off with an incriminating tube of flake white in his pocket.

"And now we come to Ferguson. Ferguson always puts paints in his pocket; I saw him do it. Ferguson gets his colours from Robertson's, but he had a pound tube of Winsor & Newton on his table; I saw and handled it. It was Ferguson's mania for a particular kind of bluish shadow-tint that puzzled Jock Graham in the faked picture. Ferguson, and nobody else, faked that picture and established that alibi.

"Wait a minute. There are one or two other points about Ferguson that I want to make. He is the one man with the alibi that it was the aim and object of the murderer to establish by means of the fake. He is known to have a remarkable visual memory for details. It was Ferguson who objected to the painting expedition to the Minnoch. And I take off my hat to Sir Maxwell Jamieson for affirming, in the face of all probability, that Ferguson was the man with the special knowledge to produce all the right appearances at the cottage to deceive Mrs. Green."

There was a short silence when Wimsey had finished this long speech, which he delivered with an unaccustomed sobriety of style, and then Sir Maxwell said:

"That is all very well, Wimsey, and it sounds very convincing, but unless you can break down Ferguson's alibi, it goes for nothing at all. We know that he—or somebody—went from Gatehouse to Dumfries with the 9.8 and on to Glasgow. The ticket was clipped at three points on the journey, and given up at Glasgow. And besides, Ferguson was seen at Glasgow by those magneto people, and by Miss Selby and Miss Cochran. Are you suggesting that he had an accomplice to impersonate him, or what?"

"No. He hadn't an accomplice. But he was a student of detective literature. Now, I'll tell you what I propose to do with your permission. To-morrow is Tuesday again, and we shall find all the trains running as they did on the morning of the alibi. We will go down to the cottage to-night and reconstruct the whole course of events from beginning to end. I will undertake to show you exactly how the thing was worked. If I break down at any point, then my theory breaks down. But if I get through, I will not only prove that the thing is possible but also that it was done that way."

"Ye canna say fairer than that," said Inspector Macpherson.

"The only thing is," said Wimsey, "that we must get Ferguson out of the way. If he sees what we're doing, he'll bolt."

"Let him," said Macpherson, grimly. "If he bolts, we'll ken fine that he's guilty."

"Good idea," said Wimsey. "Now, look here, we shall want a smallish, heavyish man to be Campbell. All you police blokes are too big. I'm afraid it will have to be you, Sir Maxwell."

"I don't mind," said that stout soldier, gamely, "provided you stop short at throwing me into the burn."

"I won't do that, but you'll have to do some very uncomfortable motoring, I'm afraid. Then we shall want two observers, one to stay with the corpse and the other to keep an eye on me. They will get a lot of strenuous exercise. How about you, Fiscal?"

"No, no," said that gentleman, "I'm over old for traipsing about the country."

"Then it had better be Inspector Macpherson and the Sergeant. You can come as a passenger, Fiscal, if you like. Then we shall want a bicycle, since the real bicycle is still patiently sitting at Euston, waiting for somebody to be fool enough to claim it; eggs and bacon for everybody, and an extra car to carry the observers."

The Inspector undertook to procure all the necessary commodities.

"Ross and Duncan," he added, "can watch Ferguson. Ye understand. Whatever place he goes, ye'll shadow him, an' if he tries tae bolt, ye'll arrest him."

"That's the spirit," said Wimsey. "Sir Maxwell, you will start out from Kirkcudbright after the pubs close, and you'll be waiting at the S-bend at 9.45. You, Macpherson, can take the observation car and play Gowan's part in the business, but instead of returning to Kirkcudbright, you will follow the Chief Constable down to Gatehouse, so as to be ready to act Strachan's part when the time comes. You, Dalziel, will cling to me and watch me like a cat watching a mouse-hole. You, Fiscal, will do as you like. And we'll all start by having a very good dinner, for we've got a strenuous bit of work before us."

CHAPTER XXVII

LORD PETER WIMSEY

"HULLO!" said Ferguson.

"Hullo!" said Wimsey. "This is the Procurator-Fiscal and this is Sergeant Dalziel of Newton-Stewart, whom I fancy you've met before. We are making a little experiment in connection with Campbell's death and we want to use your house, if we may. It's a good place to observe from, don't you know."

"I trust we will not be putting you out, Mr. Ferguson," added the Fiscal, courteously.

"Not at all," said Ferguson. "Come in. What exactly do you want to do?"

"We are going to reconstruct the events of the Monday night," said Wimsey, "and we want you to tell us if we go wrong at any point."

"Oh, certainly, with pleasure. When does the show start?"

Wimsey looked at his watch.

"Eight o'clock. It ought to be starting now. Will you do Farren, Dalziel, or shall I? You'd better, because then I can stay here under the Fiscal's eye."

"Verra gude," said Dalziel, and departed.

"Where were you sitting, Ferguson, when Farren arrived?"

"Here," said Ferguson, indicating an arm-chair by the fire.

"Good; then will you sit there again and do whatever it was you did that night? The Fiscal shall take the opposite corner and I will sit here between you."

"Who are you supposed to be?" asked Ferguson, with polite interest.

"Nobody just yet. Later on, I'm going to be the murderer. It's one of those things I've always wanted to be. Hullo! that sounds like the racket beginning."

A series of heavy thumps testified to Dalziel's conscientious attack on Campbell's door.

"Carry on, Ferguson," said Wimsey.

Ferguson, his face a little set and pale in the light of the petrol-gas lamp, moved across to the window and drew back the curtain. "Who's that?" he shouted. "For God's sake stop making that filthy row. Oh, it's you, Farren. What's the matter?"

"Whaur's that —— —— Campbell?" roared the Sergeant at the top of his lungs. "Beggin' yer pardon, sir, but my orders is tae reprojuice the conversation as reported. Where's Campbell gone?"

"Campbell? I haven't seen him all day. I haven't the faintest idea where he is. What do you want him for?"

"I'm wantin' tae twist his guts oot," yelled the Sergeant with relish. "I'll no have the b—— hangin' roond after my wife. Jist yew show me whaur tae find the lousy—— an' I'll blow his bloody brains out."

"You're drunk," said Ferguson.

"I may be drunk an' I may no be drunk," retorted Dalziel with spirit, "it's no matter to you. I'm not too drunk tae ken a dirty—— when I find him makin' love tae my wife. Where is the bastard?"

"Don't be a fool, Farren. You know perfectly well Campbell's not doing anything of the sort. Pull yourself together and forget it. Go and sleep it off."

"Go an' so-and-so yerself," vociferated the Sergeant. "Leastways, that's what it's set doon for me tae say. Ye're a couple o' what's-his-names, the baith o' ye!"

"Oh, go and hang yourself!" said Ferguson.

"Ay, that's jist what I'm goin' tae do," said Dalziel. "I'm away tae hang masel' jist noo, but I'll ha'e the life oot o' Campbell first."

"Oh, right-oh! hang yourself by all means, but don't come making that bloody row. Go and do it somewhere else, for Christ's sake."

There was a pause. Ferguson remained at the window. Then a plaintive voice inquired from outside:

"What'll I do now, sir? My directions is tae hang aboot a bit."

"You kick the door violently," said Ferguson, "and walk round to the back and make a noise there. Then you come back and let off a lot of foul language and go off on your bicycle."

"Is that right, sir?"

"Just about right," said Ferguson. "An excellent performance. I congratulate you."

"Will I go away, now?"

"Put the bicycle in its place," said Wimsey, joining Ferguson at the window, "and then come back here."

"Verra gude," said Dalziel. His red tail-lamp moved away to the gate and vanished behind the hedge.

"The worthy Sergeant is enjoying himself," said Ferguson. "His choice of language is not quite as good as Farren's though."

"Our presence probably cramped his style a bit," said Wimsey. "Eight-fifteen. The next act doesn't take place till after ten. What shall we do, Fiscal? Play cards or tell stories? Or would you like me to read aloud to you? Ferguson has a fine collection of detective novels." He strolled over to the shelves. "Hullo, Ferguson, where's that thing of Connington's, *The Two Tickets Puzzle?* I was going to recommend that to the Fiscal. I think he'd like it."

"I've lent it to the padre at the Anwoth," replied Ferguson.

"What a pity! Never mind. Here's an Austin Freeman. He's always sound and informative. Try this one, *The Eye of Osiris.* Great stuff. All about a mummy. Or Kennedy's *Corpse on the Mat*—that's nice and light and cheerful, like its title. Or if you're fed up with murders, try the new Cole, *Burglars in Bucks.*"

"Thank you," said the Fiscal, in an austere voice, belied by the twinkle behind his glasses. "I have brought the latest number of *Blackwood* to while away the time."

"Crushed again!" said Wimsey. "Ah! here's Dalziel. Come on, Sergeant. I'll take you on at dominoes for ha'penny points. I'm a great dab at dominoes."

Ferguson took up a book and sat down by the fire. Wimsey produced a box of dominoes from his pocket and slung them out on the table. The Sergeant pulled a chair in beside him. The Fiscal turned over the pages of *Blackwood.*

The silence became oppressive. The flutter of leaves, the click of the dominoes, and the ticking of the clock sounded unnaturally loud. Nine o'clock struck. Wimsey paid the Sergeant fourpence and the game went on.

Ten o'clock struck.

"This is where you start getting ready for bed, isn't it, Ferguson," said Wimsey without taking his eyes from the table.

"Yes." Ferguson pushed back his chair and got up. He wandered round the room, putting away a newspaper here and a book there.

Once or twice he dropped things and had to pick them up. He walked over to the shelf and selected a book, then poured out a glass of whiskey and soda. He drank this slowly, standing by the mantelpiece.

"Do I put out the light?" he asked, when he had finished.

"Did you put out the light?"

"Yes."

"Put it out then."

Ferguson turned off the petrol-gas. The light dimmed and sank. The mantle glowed redly for a moment or two, and faded gradually out.

"Do I go to bed?" came the voice from the dark.

"Did you go to bed?"

"Yes."

"Go to bed then."

Ferguson's footsteps passed slowly out of the door and up the stairs.

"My God," said Wimsey, softly. "I had my revolver ready. Listen!"

The hum of a car came down the lane. It drew nearer, louder. The car was turning in at the gate. The headlights flashed across the window and passed. Wimsey got up.

"Do you hear that, Ferguson?" he called up the stair.

"Yes."

"What is it?"

"Campbell's car."

"Can you see it?"

"I'm not looking at it. But I know the sound of the engine."

Wimsey went out into the yard. The engine was still running noisily, and the driver appeared to be finding some difficulty in backing into the shed.

"What the bloody hell are you doing, Campbell?" shouted Wimsey. "Mind where you're going, you drunken ass. You'll have that wall down again."

The reply was an outburst of very military language. Wimsey retorted, and a handsome slanging-match ensued. Sergeant Dalziel, stealing up the stairs in his stockinged feet, found Ferguson hanging with head and shoulders out of the bedroom window.

The voices of the men wrangling below came up loudly. Then there was a leap and a scuffle. Two dark bodies swayed backwards and forwards. Then came a crash and a heavy fall, followed by a most realistic groan.

"Was that the way it was, Mr. Ferguson?"

Ferguson turned so sharply that he hit his head a crash against the window-frame.

"How you startled me!" he said. "No, not in the least. I heard nothing of that kind. Nothing like that happened at all."

"Och, weel," said the Sergeant philosophically. "We'll maybe be mistaken. An' by the way, Mr. Ferguson, I was tae ask ye no tae gae tae yer bed jist noo, because we'll be wantin' the room for the pairpose of observation."

"What am I to do then?"

"Ye'll jist come doon an' sit wi' the Fiscal in the back room."

"I don't know what you're getting at," said Ferguson, yielding to the Sergeant's clutch upon his arm, "but you've got it all wrong, you know. And if I'm not to get any rest to-night, I think I'd better go over and ask for a bed at the Anwoth."

"That's no a bad idea, sir," replied the Sergeant, "but we'll ask ye tae bide here till 12 o'clock. I'll jist run over tae the hotel an' tell them tae expect ye."

"Oh, I can do that, Sergeant."

"I'll no be pittin' ye tae the trouble, sir," replied Dalziel, politely. He had used his torch to guide them down the stair and now led his victim into the studio, where the Fiscal was once more placidly reading *Blackwood* by the light of a candle.

"Sit ye doon, sir," he urged, pleasantly. "I'll be back in a crack. Ah! here's Inspector Macphairson comin' in wi' the observation car. He'll be company for ye."

In a very few moments the Inspector came in.

"Whit's happened?" asked the Sergeant, eagerly.

"His lordship is carryin' on terrible over the corp," said the Inspector with a grin, "tryin' tae revive it wi' whuskey."

"Will ye bide here a moment, Inspector, while I rin over tae the Anwoth tae bespeak a room for Mr. Ferguson?"

Macpherson glanced from the frail figure of the Fiscal to Ferguson, kneading his handkerchief into a ball between his clammy hands. Then he nodded. The Sergeant went out. There was a long silence.

Sergeant Dalziel went no farther than the gate, where he flashed his torch. The bulky form of Constable Ross rose silently out of the hedge. Dalziel dispatched him to the hotel with a whispered message, and then went to see what was happening in the yard.

Here he found the Chief Constable extended flat on the ground, apparently receiving frantic first aid from Wimsey.

"Is he deid yet?" asked Dalziel sympathetically.

"As mutton," replied the murderer, sadly. "I daresay we ought to have spun the riot out a bit longer, but the great thing is that he's dead. What's the time? Half-past ten. That's good enough. He breathed stertorously for a few minutes, and then, you know, he died. How did Ferguson take it?"

"Badly," replied the Sergeant, "but he denies it."

"Naturally he would."

"He's away tae the Anwoth for a quiet night."

"Then I hope he'll sleep well. But we shall want him here till 12."

"Ay, I've settled that."

"Good. Carry on now. I'm supposed to be thinking out my plan of escape."

The Sergeant waited for the return of P. C. Ross, and then went back to Ferguson's house to announce that all was well.

"How did your bit go, sir?" he asked the Inspector.

"Fine—the time worked out beautifully. We allowed five minutes for the struggle and five for the hair-cuttin' business."

"Did anyone pass ye?"

"Not a solitary soul."

"That was gude luck. Weel, I'll away tae his lordship."

"Ay."

"But this is all wrong, you know, Inspector," protested Ferguson. "A thing like that couldn't have happened without my hearing it."

"It'll maybe have taken place in the road," said the Inspector, diplomatically, "but it's mair convenient tae du't in private."

"Oh, I see."

The Sergeant returned to the yard to find Wimsey laboriously hoisting the Chief Constable on his back. He carried the inert body into the garage and dumped it on the floor, rather heavily. "Hi!" said the corpse. "You shut up," said Wimsey, "you're dead, sir. I couldn't drag you. It might leave marks."

He stood looking down on the body.

"No blood," he said, "thank God there's no blood. I'll do it. I must do it. I must think, that's all. Think. I might pretend to be out fishing. But that's no good. I've got to have a witness. Suppose I just leave him here and pretend that Farren did it. But Farren may have gone home. He'll be able to prove he wasn't here. Besides, I don't want to get Farren into trouble if I can help it. Can't I make it look like an accident?"

He went out to the car.

"Better put this in," he said, "Farren might come back. If he does, I've got him. Or he's got me. One or the other. No, that won't do. Anyway, I can't count on it. The accident's the thing. And an alibi. Wait!"

He backed the car into the garage and switched the lights out.

"Whiskey's the next move, I think," said he. He picked up the bottle from where he had left it. "Probably, Dalziel, I did my think-ing in the cottage, but just for the moment I'll do it in the garage. I'll just fetch a couple of glasses and the water-jug."

A smothered shout from the garage indicated at this point that the corpse was growing restive.

"All right, corpse," yelled Wimsey, cheerfully, "I'm getting drinks."

He fetched the glasses and the water, Dalziel moving dog-like at his heels, and brought the whole consignment back to the garage.

"We'll all have a drink," he said. "Corpse, you may sit up. Now, listen. It's difficult for me to think this plan out aloud now, be-cause I know beforehand what it's going to be. But I know that when I was detecting it, it took me about an hour to hit on the general outline of it, and a bit more to fill in the details. So we'll give Ferguson all that time to play with. At about half-past eleven I shall begin to get to work. Meanwhile I think I'll make out a list of the things I've got to do. It would be fatal to forget anything."

He switched on the lights again, then switched them off.

"Better not do that. Can't run the risk of letting the batteries run down. Lend me your torch, Dalziel. I don't want to do it at the cottage, under Ferguson's nose. He might, of course, betray himself and confess, but he might not. Besides, I'd rather he didn't really. I've set my heart on this reconstruction."

He pulled a notebook out of his pocket and began to write. The Chief Constable and the Sergeant passed the whiskey bottle from hand to hand and conversed in whispers. Eleven o'clock struck from the church tower. Wimsey went on writing. At a quarter-past eleven he read his notes through very carefully and stowed them away in his pocket. After ten minutes more, he stood up.

"I'm supposed to have made my plans now," he said, "more or less, that is. Now I've got to start work. I've got to sleep in two beds to-night, so I'll start with Ferguson's. Dalziel, you must be getting ready to be Strachan."

The Sergeant nodded.

"And the corpse had better stay here. Cheerio, folks. Leave a drink or two in the bottle for me."

The corpse and the Sergeant stood for a moment at the door and watched Wimsey's dark figure cross the yard. It was dark, but not pitch-dark, and they saw him slip through the door. Presently the light of a candle flickered in the bed-room. Dalziel moved away, got into the observation car and started it up.

"Ferguson!"

Wimsey's voice sounded a little hoarse. Ferguson rose and went to the foot of the stairway.

"Come up here."

Ferguson went up rather reluctantly, and found Wimsey with his shoes off, and in his shirt-sleeves standing by the bed.

"I'm going to lie down and have a rest. I want you to wait here with me till something happens."

"This is a silly game."

"It is, rather, I'm afraid. But you'll soon be out of it."

Wimsey got into bed and drew the clothes over him. Ferguson took a chair by the window. Presently the noise of an approaching car was heard. It stopped at the gate, and footsteps passed hurriedly across the yard.

Knock, knock, knock.

Wimsey consulted his watch. Ten minutes after midnight. He got out of bed and stood close behind Ferguson, almost touching him.

"Look out of window, please."

Ferguson obeyed. A dark form stood on Campbell's threshold. It knocked again, stepped back and looked up at the windows, walked round the house and came round to the door again. Then it moved aside and seemed to fumble behind the window shutter.

Then came the scrape of a key being fitted into a lock. The door opened, and the figure went in.

"Is that right?"

"Yes."

They watched again. There came a flash of light on the side window of the downstairs room. Then it passed away and presently appeared in the bedroom, the window of which faced Campbell's. It moved as though it were being flashed about the room; then vanished. After a little time it reappeared downstairs and remained stationary.

"Is that right?"

"Not quite. It was matches, not a torch."

"I see. How did you know that, by the way? I thought you only heard this person come and didn't see anything."

He heard the hiss of Ferguson's breath. Then:—

"Did I say that? I didn't mean to give quite that impression. I heard the door open and saw the light upstairs. But I didn't actually see the person who came."

"And you didn't see him come out again?"

"No."

"And you had no idea who it was?"

"No."

"And you saw nobody else that night?"

"Nobody."

"And you saw Campbell go off in his car at 7.30 next morning?"

"Yes."

"Right. Then you can hop it now, if you want to."

"Well, I think I will. . . . I say, Wimsey!"

"Yes?"

"Oh, nothing! Good night!"

"Good night."

"He nearly told me then," said Wimsey. "Poor devil!"

Ferguson went out of the house and out of the gate. Two stealthy shadows crept out from the hedge and followed him.

Wimsey waited at the window till he saw Dalziel leave the next-door cottage and carefully lock the door behind him, replacing the key in its hiding-place. When the hum of the car had died away in the distance, he ran hastily down the stairs, and across to the garage.

"Corpse!" he cried.

"Yessir!" said the corpse, smartly.

"While that ghastly blighter was nosing round—I—in my rôle as murderer, you understand—had an awful thought. All this time you're getting stiff. If I leave you like that I shall never be able to pack you into the back of the car. Come out, sir, and be arranged in a nice hunched-up position."

"Don't you dump me in the car earlier?"

"No, or you wouldn't look natural. I lay you out on the floor to set. Now, where's that blighter Dalziel? I hope he hasn't buzzed zealously off to Falbae. No. Here he comes. Dalziel, help me to arrange the corpse exactly as it looked when it was found. It had the arms folded round in front, I think, and the head tucked down on them—no! not as far as that—we mustn't cover up the bruise on the temple. That's here. Now the legs bundled up sideways. Right. Hold that. That's beautiful."

"Do I stay like this all night?" asked Sir Maxwell, dolefully.

"No—but remember the pose. We shall want it to-morrow. We'll consider that done. Now we lock the garage door and take the key, for fear of other visitors. Now we go across to Campbell's place. Hullo, Fiscal! come to see the fun? And Macpherson? That's the ticket.

"Now we find the key and open the door, locking it, I think, behind us. We shut the shutters and light up. My God! what's this? A note. *Look out for F.* Great Jehoshaphat!— Oh, no, of course, it doesn't mean me—it means Farren. Now—do we use that or destroy it? Better destroy it. It's an accident we're staging, not a murder. We don't want the slightest suggestion of violence. Besides —must be decent to Farren. Campbell is alive till 7.30 to-morrow, so he found this and read it. When did he come in, though? After 12, of course, since Strachan can say he wasn't here earlier. Yes, but how do I know how many people saw him come in at 10.15? Must say one thing or the other. Better suggest he came in and then went out again while I was asleep. On foot, perhaps, so that I didn't hear the car. Damn Strachan! What did he want to come poking his nose in for, anyhow?

"Well, now—Campbell's bed and Campbell's pyjamas. I don't think we put on the pyjamas. We shake them out—Tuesday's wash-day, so they've had a week's use, and we've only got to sprawl them

about on the floor to make 'em look natural. Basin—dirty water—
wash the hands and face. That does that and leaves the towel untidy. Bed. Must get into that. Horrid business, lying in bed when
you can't and mustn't sleep, but it's got to be done. And one can
think.

"One can read, too. I've provided some literature. Got it out of
Ferguson's place just now. L.M.S. Time-table. Great work of
literature. Style slightly telegraphic, but packed with interest. Road-
map, too, also from next-door. Does the bed look sufficiently tousled
yet? No. I'll give it half an hour—rather a restless half-hour, I'm
afraid."

The restless half-hour over, the murderer crawled out of bed,
dragging half the clothes with him.

"I think that's fairly convincing. Now. Throw dirty water into
slop-pail and dirty a fresh lot. Shaving brush? Toothbrush? Damn
it, no. Must do them later on, or they'll dry up. But I can go down
and pack up the painting kit and lay two breakfast-tables. And meanwhile, you know, I can still be thinking out my plan. There's a
horrible hole in it at present, and one place where I simply must trust
rather to luck. By the way, my present intention, I may tell you, is
to catch the 12.35 at Barrhill. But that absolutely depends on my
getting away in good time from the Minnoch. Let's pray there
won't be many people about."

"But ye didna gae tae Barrhill."

"No; I think something happened to make me change my mind."
Wimsey was busily sorting out crockery. "You'll remember that
my overmastering necessity is to get to Glasgow somehow. I have
announced my intention of going, and I shall be feeling morbidly
nervous about making any change of plan. If you only knew how
my brain is spinning at the moment. There! there's Campbell's
breakfast all laid out ready: tea-pot, cup and saucer, two plates,
knife, fork, bread, butter, sugar. Milk! I must remember to take
Campbell's milk in in the morning, by the way; I know when to
expect it, you see. Eggs, rasher and frying-pan laid out in the
kitchen. Now, over to my own house. Same business here. I believe I had kippers for breakfast actually, but it doesn't matter. For
my own convenience I will make it a boiled egg."

He chattered on as he laid the breakfast-materials out. Then sud-

denly, as though struck by a sudden thought, he dropped the sauce-
pan on the kitchen floor.

"Curse it! I was nearly forgetting. All this alibi depends on my
going by train from Gatehouse. But I told a whole lot of people
yesterday that I was going to drive to Dumfries and take the 7.35
train from there. Why should I change my mind? It will look so
funny. The car. Something wrong with the car. Something the local
people can't be supposed to put right in a hurry. Of course—mag.
trouble. Yes—I can work that, and it'll probably help my alibi, too.
Steady, old man. Loads of time. Be sure you finish one thing properly
before you start another. Right. Breakfast's ready. Now then. I've
done my bed, but I haven't done the water and things. Do that now.
Pyjamas—there! One lot dirty water. Two lots dirty water. Happy
thought. Clean socks and shirt to go to Glasgow in, and respectable
suit. You must imagine that I'm doing all this. Must be a gray flannel suit, to match those bags of Campbell's. Here it is, as a matter
of fact, hanging up. I won't put it on, but we might have a look
at the pockets. Hullo, Macpherson, here you are! See the smear of
white paint on the lining of the left-hand jacket pocket? Careless,
careless. A little benzine rids us of this guilt. Well, well, well."

He went swiftly through the motions of changing his garments,
while the police, with satisfaction, examined the grey flannel jacket.
Play-acting was all very well, but this had the appearance of solid
evidence.

Presently Wimsey indicated that the change of clothes was supposed to be accomplished.

"I am spending the night in Glasgow," he went on, "so I must
pack an attaché-case. Here it is. Clean pyjamas, shaving-tackle,
toothbrush. Better shave now, to save time. Five minutes for a shave.
In they go. What else? Oh, a burberry. Absolutely essential. But
I shall want to use that first. And a soft felt hat. *Voilà!* a clean
collar, no doubt. There it is. And the magneto will have to go in.
That will just about fill the case. Now we go over the way again."

He led them back to Campbell's cottage, where, after putting on
a pair of thin gloves, he carefully checked and repacked all the
articles contained in Campbell's painting-outfit, which had been
brought over by Dalziel from the police-station for that purpose.

"Campbell would take some grub with him," observed the murderer thoughtfully. "I'd better cut some. Here is a ham in the cup-

board. Bread, butter, ham, mustard. And a small whiskey-flask, considerately left in full view. I think I shall be right in filling it up. Splendid. Now we go out and detach the mag. from our own car. Gently does it. Up she comes. Now we've got to damage her somewhere. I won't do it really, but we'll suppose it done. Wrap her up neatly in brown paper. Careful man, Ferguson. Always keeps odd bits of string and paper and stationery handy in case they're wanted. Right. Now we'll put this in the attaché-case so that we don't forget it. We shall want an extra cap for when we cease to be Campbell. We'll put that in the pocket of Campbell's cloak. Oh, yes. And this pair of spectacles will be a good aid to disguise. They're Campbell's, but happily they are just sun-glare glasses with plain lenses so that's O.K. We'll put those in our pocket. Now then, we're all fit and ready.

"Now comes the moment when we have to trust to a stroke of luck. We've got to go out and find a bicycle. It may take a bit of time, but the odds are that if it isn't down one close it'll be down the next. Put out the lights. Lock both doors and take the keys away. We can't risk any more Strachans paying visits while we're away."

Suiting the action to the words, Wimsey left the cottages and walked briskly away down the road, closely followed by his observers. "I told you there'd be walking exercise," said Wimsey. "You people had better take the car. I shall have the bike to come back on."

As the cortège arrived opposite the Anwoth Hotel, a bulky form came cautiously up to meet it.

"He's in there, all right," said P. C. Ross. "Duncan's watching the other entrance and we've got the Gatehouse policeman sittin' in the back garden tae see that he doesna get oot by the windows. Here's your bicycle, my lord."

"Wonderful!" said Wimsey. "Hit it the very first shot. Anybody'd think it had been left there on purpose. No"—as the constable obligingly struck a match. "No lights. I'm supposed to be stealing this, my dear man. Good night—or rather, good morning. Wish us luck."

It was a little after two when Wimsey got back to the cottages with the bicycle.

"Now," he said, when he had deposited the bicycle in the garage, "we can have a rest. Nothing further happens till about 5 o'clock."

The conspirators accordingly rolled themselves up in rugs and coats and disposed themselves on chairs and hearth-rugs, the couch being voted to the Fiscal in the right of seniority.

The Chief Constable, being an old soldier, slept promptly and soundly. He was awakened a little before five by a clashing of pots and pans.

"Breakfast for the observers is served in the kitchen," said Wimsey's voice in his ear. "I am going up to finish off the bedrooms."

At a quarter-past five this job was finished, Campbell's toothbrush and shaving-brush and both sets of soap and towels left wet and the proper appearances produced. Wimsey then came in to cook and eat his solitary eggs and bacon in Campbell's front room. The tea-pot was left on the hob to keep warm.

"I don't know," said Wimsey, "whether he left the fires going or re-lit them. He did one or the other, and it doesn't matter a hoot. Now, corpse, it's time I packed you into the car. I probably did it earlier, but you'd have been so uncomfortable. Come and take up your pose again, and remember you're supposed to be perfectly rigid by now."

"This may be fun to you," grumbled Sir Maxwell, "but it's death to me."

"So it is," said Wimsey. "Never mind. Ready? Up you go!"

"Eh!" said Macpherson, as Wimsey seized the Chief Constable's cramped and reluctant body and swung it into the back seat of the Morris, "but your lordship's wonderful strong for your size."

"It's just a knack," said Wimsey, ruthlessly ramming his victim down between the seat and the floor. "I hope you aren't permanently damaged, sir. Can you stick it?" he added, as he pulled on his gloves.

"Carry on," said the corpse, in a muffled voice.

Wimsey slung in the painting outfit—stool, satchel and easel—followed it with Campbell's cloak and hat, and piled the bicycle on top, securing it with a tow-rope which he produced from a corner of the garage, and tucking a large rug round and over his awkward load.

"We'll let the easel stick out a bit," he remarked. "It looks innocent and explains the rest of the load. Is that right? What's the time?"

"A quarter to six, my lord."

"Right; now we can start."

"But ye've no eaten Ferguson's breakfast, my lord."

"No; that comes later. Wait a bit. We'd better lock the doors again. Right-ho!"

He drew a cloth cap closely down upon his head, muffled himself unrecognisably in a burberry and muffler, and climbed into the driving-seat.

"Ready? Right. Let her go!"

The car with its burden moved gently out into the pale light of the morning. It bore round to the right at the end of the lane and took the direction of Gatehouse Station. The observation car swung in behind and followed it.

Upwards the road climbed steadily, mounting triumphantly past the wooded beauty of Castramont, ever higher over the lovely valley of the Fleet. Through the trees and out on to the lofty edge of the moor, with the rolling hills lifting their misty heads upon the right. Past the quarry and up still farther to the wide stretch of heather and pasture. Sheep stared at them from the roadside, and scurried foolishly across their path. Partridges, enjoying their last weeks of security, rose whirring and clattering from among the ling. Over to the northeast, white in the morning, the graceful arches of the Fleet viaduct gleamed pallidly. And ahead, grim and frowning, stood the great wall of the Clints of Dromore, scarred and sheer and granite-grey, the gate of the wilderness and guardian-barrier of the Fleet.

The little cottage by the level crossing seemed still asleep and the gates stood open. The cars passed over the line and, avoiding the station entrance, turned sharp away to the left, along the old road to Creetown. Here, for some distance, the way was flanked on either side by a stone wall, but, after a few hundred yards, the walls came to a stop. Wimsey held up a warning hand, stopped, turned his car, with some bumping, over the grass, and drove it well behind the shelter of the wall on the left. The police-car halted in the middle of the road.

"What noo?" asked Macpherson.

Wimsey alighted and peered cautiously under the rug.

"Still alive, Sir Maxwell?"

"Only just."

"Well, I think you might come out now and have a stretch. You won't be needed again till 9 o'clock. Sit down comfortably with the Fiscal and have a smoke."

"And what do the others do?"

"They walk back with me to Gatehouse," said Wimsey, with a grim smile.

"Mayn't we bring the car?" said Macpherson, mournfully.

"You can if you like, but it would be more sporting to cheer me with a little pleasant conversation. Damn it! I've *got* to walk."

Eventually it was arranged that Macpherson should walk with Lord Peter, while Dalziel brought the car along behind in case the station-omnibus proved to be crowded. Telling the Fiscal to see that the corpse behaved itself, Wimsey waved a cheerful hand and started off with Macpherson to trudge the six-and-a-half miles back to Gatehouse.

The last mile was the most awkward, for the road was getting busy, and they had to be continually diving over walls and under hedges to avoid observation. At the last moment they were nearly caught in the lane by the paper-boy, who passed, whistling, within a foot of them while they crouched behind a convenient hawthorn-bush.

"Damn the paper-boy," said Wimsey. "Ferguson, of course, would have been expecting him. In any case, he probably did all this earlier, but I didn't want to keep the corpse out all night. A quarter to eight. We've cut it rather fine. Never mind. Here goes."

They took the remainder of the lane at a run, unlocked Campbell's door, hid the key, performed the motions of taking in the milk and emptying part of it down the sink, took in and opened letters and newspapers, and dashed back to Ferguson's cottage. Here Wimsey took in Ferguson's milk, boiled his egg and made his tea, and sat down to his breakfast with an air of simple enjoyment.

At 8 o'clock, the rotund form of Mrs. Green was seen waddling down the lane. Wimsey looked out of the window and waved a friendly hand to her.

"Better warn her, Macpherson," he said. "If she goes into Campbell's place, she'll have a fit."

Macpherson hurried out, and was seen to vanish into the next-door cottage with Mrs. Green. Presently he returned, smiling broadly.

"Verra gude, my lord," he said, "she's tellt me it a' luiks fine; jist precisely as it did the mornin' Campbell was missin'."

"Good," said Wimsey. He finished his breakfast, packed the burberry into the attaché-case, and made a tour of inspection round the house, to make sure that nothing looked suspicious. With the exception of the mysterious remains of four extra breakfasts in the kitchen, everything seemed normal. He strolled out, met Mrs. Green in the front of the cottages, had a word with her, mentioned that he was catching the station 'bus and strolled down to the end of the lane.

Shortly after 8.30, the pant of the omnibus was heard coming along the road. Wimsey flagged it and got in. The police car followed on behind, much to the interest of the other passengers in the omnibus.

At 9 o'clock, or a little after, 'bus and car drew up in the station yard. Wimsey alighted and came across to the car.

"I want you, Inspector, to come across to the train with me. When the train has gone, come out and join Dalziel here. Then get out on to the road and pick up the other car."

The two officers nodded, and Wimsey strolled into the station with the Inspector at his heels. He spoke to the station-master and booking-clerk and bought a first-class return to Glasgow. After a few minutes, the train was signalled, and a general exodus took place to the opposite platform. The station-master marched across, carrying the staff under his arm; the signalman came down from his lofty perch and crossed also, to perform the duties of a porter. The passengers from the 'bus streamed across the line, followed by the 'bus-conductor on the lookout for return passengers with parcels. The booking-clerk retired into his office and took up a paper. Wimsey and the Inspector crossed over with the other passengers.

The train came in. Wimsey wrung the Inspector's hand affectionately, as though he were not going to see him again for a month, and stepped into the first-class compartment which the porter was holding open for him. The station-master exchanged staffs and a pleasantry or two with the guard. A crate of poultry was wheeled along and dumped into the van. It suddenly occurred to Macpherson that this was all wrong. He ought to have been travelling with Wimsey. He darted to the carriage-window and looked in. The compartment was empty. The whistle blew. The guard waved his flag. The porter, with great bustle, urged Macpherson to "stand away." The train moved out. Macpherson, left gazing up and down the line, perceived that it was empty.

"By God!" said Macpherson, slapping his thigh. "In at one side and oot at t'ither. The auldest dodge in the haill bag o' tricks."

He ran precipitately across the line and joined Dalziel.

"The cunning wee b——!" he exclaimed affectionately. "He's did it! Did ye see him come across?"

Dalziel shook his head.

"Is that what he did? Och, the station buildin's is between us. There's a path through the station-master's garden. He'll ha' come by that. We'll best be movin'."

They passed up the station entrance and turned along the road. In front of them went a small grey figure, walking briskly. It was then ten minutes past nine.

CHAPTER XXVIII

LORD PETER WIMSEY

THE corpse was repacked into the car. Wimsey put on Campbell's hat and cloak, again wrapping a muffler closely about his chin so that very little of his features was visible beneath the flapping black brim. He backed the car out on to the road and drove gently away towards Creetown. The road was stony, and Wimsey knew that his tyres were a good deal worn. A puncture would have been fatal. He kept his speed down to a cautious twenty miles an hour. He thought as he drove how maddening this slow progress must have been to Ferguson, to whom time had been so precious. With a real corpse in the back seat, it must have been a horrible temptation to go all out, at whatever risk.

The road was completely deserted, except for the wee burn which chuckled along placidly beside them. Once he had to get down to open a gate. The burn, deserting the right-hand side of the road, ran under a small bridge and reappeared on their left, glimmering down over stones to meander beneath a clump of trees. The sun was growing stronger.

Between twenty and twenty-five minutes past nine they came down at the head of the steep little plunge into Creetown, opposite the clock-tower. Wimsey swung the car out to the right into the main road, and encountered the astonished gaze of the proprietor of the Ellangowan Hotel, who was talking to a motorist by the petrol-pump. For a moment he stared as though he had seen a ghost—then he caught sight of Macpherson and Dalziel, following in the second car with the Fiscal, and waved his hand with an understanding smile.

"First incident not according to schedule," said Wimsey. "It's odd that Ferguson shouldn't have been seen at this point—especially as he would quite probably have liked to be seen. But that's life. If you want a thing, you don't get it."

He pressed his foot on the accelerator and took the road at a good thirty-five miles an hour.

Five miles farther on, he passed the turn to the New Galloway road. It was just after half-past nine.

"Near enough," said Wimsey to himself. He kept his foot down and hurried along over the fine new non-skid surface which had just been laid down and was rapidly making the road from Cree-town to Newton-Stewart one of the safest and finest in the three kingdoms. Just outside Newton-Stewart, he had to slow down to pass the road-engine and workers, the road-laying having now advanced to that point. After a brief delay, bumping over the new-laid granite, he pushed on again, but instead of following the main road, turned off just before he reached the bridge into a third-class road running parallel to the main road through Minnigaff, and following the left bank of the Cree. It ran through a wood and past the Cruives of Cree, through Longbaes and Borgan, and emerged into the lonely hill-country, swelling with green mound after green mound, round as the hill of the King of Elfland; then a sharp right-hand turn and he saw his goal before him—the bridge, the rusty iron gate, and the steep granite wall that overhung the Minnoch.

He ran the car up upon the grass and got out. The police-car drew up into the shelter of a little quarry on the opposite side of the road. When the observers came up with him, Wimsey was already rolling back the rug and pulling out the bicycle.

"Ye've made verra gude time," observed the Inspector. "It's jist on 10 o'clock."

Wimsey nodded. He ran up on to the higher ground and surveyed the road and the hills to left and right. Not a soul was to be seen—not so much as a cow or a sheep. Though they were only just off a main road and a few hundred yards from a farm, the place was as still and secret as the heart of a desert. He ran down again to the car, flung the painting-kit upon the grass, opened the door of the tonneau and clutched ruthlessly the huddled form of the Chief Constable, who, more dead than alive after his disagreeable journey, hardly needed to feign the stiffness which was cramping him in every limb. Hoisted in a dismal bundle on Wimsey's back, he made the last lurching stage of his progress, to be dumped with a heavy thud on the hard granite, at the edge of the incline.

"Wait there," said Wimsey, in a menacing tone, "and don't move, or you'll fall into the river."

The Chief Constable dug his fingers into a bunch of heather and prayed silently. He opened his eyes, saw the granite sloping sharply away beneath him, and shut them again. After a few minutes, he felt himself enveloped in a musty smother of rug. Then came another pause, and the sound of voices and heartless laughter. Then he was deserted again. He tried to imagine what was happening and guessed, rightly, that Wimsey was secreting the bicycle somewhere. Then the voices came back, and a few muttered curses suggested that somebody was setting up an easel with unpractised hands. More laughter. Then the rug was twitched from his head and Wimsey's voice announced, "You can come out now."

Sir Maxwell retreated cautiously on hands and knees from the precipice, which, to his prejudiced eyes, appeared to be about two hundred feet in depth, rolled over and sat up.

"Oh, God!" he said, rubbing his legs. "What have I done to deserve all this?"

"I'm sorry, sir," said Wimsey. "If you had been really dead, you know, you wouldn't have noticed it. But I didn't like to go as far as that. Well, now we've got an hour and a half. I ought to paint the picture, but, as that is beyond me, I thought we might have a little picnic. There's some grub in the other car. They're just bringing it up."

"I could do with something to drink," said Sir Maxwell.

"You shall have it. Hullo! Somebody's coming. We'll give them a start. Get under the rug again, sir."

The distant clack of a farm-lorry was making itself heard in the distance. The Chief Constable hurriedly snatched up the rug and froze. Wimsey sat down before the easel and assumed brush and palette.

Presently the lorry loomed into sight over the bridge. The driver, glancing across with natural interest at the spot where the tragedy had taken place, suddenly caught sight of the easel, the black hat and the conspicuous cloak. He gave vent to one fearful yell and rammed his foot down on the accelerator. The lorry went leaping and crashing forward, scattering the stones right and left in its mad progress. Wimsey laughed. The Chief Constable sprang up to see what was happening and laughed too. In a few minutes the rest of the party joined them, so agitated with laughter that they could scarcely hold the parcels they were carrying.

"Och, mon!" said Dalziel, "but that was grand! That was young Jock. Did ye hear the skelloch he let oot? He's away noo tae tell the folks at Clauchaneasy that auld Campbell's ghaist is sittin' up pentin' pictures at the Minnoch."

"I trust the poor lad will come to no harm with his lorry," observed the Fiscal. "He appeared to me to be driving at a reckless pace."

"Never mind him," said the Chief Constable. "Lads like that have nine lives. But I'm dying of hunger and thirst, if you are not. Half-past five is a terrible hour for breakfast."

The picnic was a cheerful one, though it was a little disturbed by the return of Jock, supported by a number of friends, to view the phenomenon of a ghost in broad daylight.

"This is getting rather public," said Wimsey.

Sergeant Dalziel grunted, and strode down to warn the spectators off, his stalwart jaws still champing a wedge of veal and ham pie. The hills returned to their wonted quiet.

At 11.25 Wimsey rose regretfully.

"Corpse-time," he said. "Here, Sir Maxwell, is the moment when you go bumpety-bump into the water."

"Is it?" said the Chief Constable. "I draw the line there."

"It would make you rather a wet-blanket on the party," said Wimsey. "Well, we'll suppose it done. Pack up, you languid aristocrats, and return to your Rolls-Royce, while I pant and sweat upon this confounded bicycle. We had better take away the Morris and the rest of the doings. There's no point in leaving them."

He removed Campbell's cloak and changed the black hat for his own cap, then retrieved the bicycle from its hiding-place, and strapped the attaché-case to the carrier. With a grunt of disgust he put on the tinted spectacles, threw his leg across the saddle and pedalled furiously away. The others packed themselves at leisure into the two cars. The procession wound out upon the Bargrennan road.

Nine and a half miles of crawling in the wake of the bicycle brought them to Barrhill. Just outside the village, Wimsey signalled a halt.

"Look here," said he. "Here's where I have to guess. I guess that Ferguson meant to catch the 12.35 here, but something went wrong. It's 12.33 now, and I could just do it. The station is just down that side-road there. But he must have started late and missed it. I don't know why. Listen! There she comes!"

As he spoke, the smoke of the train came in view. They heard her draw up into the station. Then, in a few minutes, she panted away again.

"Well, on time," said Wimsey. "Anyway, we've missed her now. She's a local as far as Girvan. Then she turns into an express, only stopping at Maybole before she gets to Ayr. Then she becomes still more exalted by the addition of a Pullman Restaurant Car, and scorns the earth, running right through to Paisley and Glasgow. Our position is fairly hopeless, you see. We can only carry on through the village and wait for a miracle."

He remounted and pedalled on, glancing back from time to time over his shoulder. Presently the sound of an overtaking car made itself heard. An old Daimler limousine, packed with cardboard dress-boxes, purred past at a moderate twenty-two or three miles an hour. Wimsey let it pass him, then, head down and legs violently at work, swung in behind it. In another moment, his hand was on the ledge of the rear window, and he was free-wheeling easily in its wake. The driver did not turn his head.

"A-ah!" said Macpherson. "It's our friend Clarence Gordon, by Jove! And him tellin' us he'd passed the man on the road. Ay, imph'm, an' he wad be tellin' nae mair nor less than the truth. We'll hope his lordship's no killt."

"He's safe enough," said the Chief Constable, "providing his tyres hold out. That's a very long-headed young man, for all his blether. At this rate, we'll be beating the train all right. How far is it to Girvan?"

"Aboot twelve miles. We ought tae pass her at Pinmore. She's due there at 12.53."

"Let's hope Clarence Gordon keeps his foot down. Go gently, Macpherson. We don't want to overtake him."

Clarence Gordon was a careful driver, but acted nobly up to expectation. He positively put on a spurt after passing Pinwherry, and as they attacked the sharp rise to Pinmore, they caught sight of the black hinder-end of the train labouring along the track that ran parallel and close to the road. As they topped the hill, and left the train behind them, Wimsey waved his hat. They span merrily along, bearing to the left and winding down towards the sea. At five minutes past one, the first houses of Girvan rose about them. The pursuers' hearts beat furiously as the train now caught them up again on their right and rushed past them towards Girvan Station. At the end of the town, Wimsey let go his hold on the car, sprinting away for dear life to the right down the station road. At eight minutes past he was on the platform, with three minutes to spare. The police force, like the ranks of Tuscany, could scarce forbear to cheer. Leaving Dalziel to arrange for the safe keeping of the cars, Macpherson ran to the booking office and took three first-class tickets to Ayr. As he passed Wimsey on the platform, he saw him unstrapping the attaché-case and heard him cry to the porter in an exaggerated Oxford accent: "Heah! portah! label this bicycle for Ayr." And as he turned away from the booking-window, the porter's urgent voice came right in his ear:

"One first and a bicycle-ticket to Ayr, and make it quick, laddie. I must be gettin' back tae my gentleman."

They tumbled out on to the platform. The bicycle was being bundled into the rear van. They leapt for their carriage. The whistle blew. They were off.

"Gosh!" said Wimsey, wiping his face. And then: "Damn this thing, it's like a fly-paper."

In his left hand, concealed by the hat which he had removed for the sake of coolness, he held something which he now displayed with a grin. It was a luggage-label for Euston.

"Simple as shelling peas," he said, laughing. "I pinched it while he was wheeling the bike off to the van. All ready gummed, too. They do things handsomely on the L.M.S. Fortunately the pigeonhole was labelled, so I didn't have to hunt for it. Well, that's that. Now we can take a breather. There's nothing else till we get to Ayr."

After a stop at Maybole to collect the tickets, the train ran merrily along to Ayr. Almost before it drew up at the platform, Wimsey was out of the train. He ran back to the rear van, with Macpherson hurrying at his heels.

"Let me have that bicycle out, quick," he said to the guard. "You'll see it there. Labelled to Ayr. Here's the ticket."

The guard, who was the same man whom Ross had interviewed previously, stared at Wimsey, and appeared to hesitate.

"It's a' richt, guard," said Macpherson. "I'm a police officer. Let this gentleman have what he wants."

The guard, with a puzzled look, handed out the bicycle, receiving the ticket in exchange. Wimsey pressed a shilling into his hand and hurried with the bicycle along the platform to a point near the station entrance where the end of the bookstall masked him from the view both of the guard and of the booking-clerk. Dalziel, seeing that Macpherson was involved in explanations with the guard, followed Wimsey quietly, and was in time to see him moisten the Euston luggage-label with an expansive lick and clap it on to the bicycle over the Ayr label. This done, Wimsey marched briskly out, attaché-case in hand, and plunged down the little side-street and into the public convenience. In less than a minute he was out again, minus spectacles, his cap exchanged for the soft felt hat, and wearing the burberry. Passengers were now dashing through the booking-hall to catch the Glasgow train. Wimsey joined them and purchased a third-class ticket to Glasgow. Dalziel, panting on his heels, purchased four. By the time he had paid for them, Wimsey was gone. The Chief Constable and the Fiscal, waiting near the hoarding at the head of the side-bays, received a cheerful wink from Wimsey as he strolled up and planted the bicycle against the hoarding. They were probably the only people who noticed this manœuvre, for the Pullman Car had by now been attached to the train, and the platform was filled with passengers, porters and luggage. Wimsey, his hands before his face lighting his cigarette, wandered away towards the head of the train. Doors slammed. Dalziel and Macpherson skipped into a compartment. Wimsey followed. The Chief Constable and the Fiscal did likewise. The guard shouted "Right away!" and the train moved out again. The whole business had occupied exactly six minutes.

"There's another good bicycle gone west," said Wimsey.

"No," said Macpherson. "I saw what ye'd be after an' I warned a porter tae send it back to Gatehoose. It belongs tae the constable, and he wad not care tae be wantin' it," he added, thriftily.

"Splendid. I say—it's all gone rather prettily so far, don't you think!"

"Charmingly," said the Fiscal, "but you're not forgetting, Lord Peter, that this train doesn't get into St. Enoch till 2.55, and that, according to these motor-people—er—Sparkes & Crisp—Mr. Ferguson was in their show-rooms at ten minutes to three?"

"That's what they say," replied Wimsey, "but Ferguson didn't say that. He said 'About three.' I fancy, with luck, we may be able to reconcile those two statements."

"And how about that other ticket you've got there?" put in Sir Maxwell. "That's the thing that's been worrying me. The ticket from Gatehouse to Glasgow."

"It doesn't worry *me*," said Wimsey, confidently.

"Oh, well," said the Chief Constable, "if you're pleased, we're pleased."

"I have not enjoyed anything so much for a long time," said the Fiscal, who seemed quite unable to get over his delight in the excursion. "I ought to be sorry to see the net closing round this poor Mr. Ferguson, but I must admit that I find myself a prey to excitement."

"Yes—I'm sorry for Ferguson too," answered Wimsey. "I wish you hadn't reminded me, sir. But it can't be helped. I'd be sorrier still if it was Farren, for instance. Poor beggar! This business will tie him by the leg for ever, I'm afraid. Opportunity doesn't come twice. No; the only thing that's really worrying me is the possibility of this train's getting in late."

The train, however, ran most creditably to time, and drew into St. Enoch at 2.55 to the minute. Wimsey was out of it at once and led his party along the platform at a great pace.

As they passed the entrance to the station hotel, he turned to Sir Maxwell.

"I suggest," he said, "though I don't absolutely know, that it was at this point that Ferguson caught sight of Miss Cochran and Miss Selby and their party. They were probably just emerging from their lunch, and he guessed that their friends had come along to meet their train at Glasgow."

He broke off to wave frantically to a taxi. The whole five of them crammed into it, and Wimsey directed the driver to set him down in the street where Messrs. Sparkes & Crisp had their show-rooms.

"And drive like blazes," he added.

At five minutes past three he tapped on the glass. The driver pulled up and they all scrambled out on to the pavement. Wimsey paid off the taxi and headed off at a brisk pace for the motor show-rooms a few yards away.

"Don't let's all go in in a bunch," he said. "Come with me, Sir Maxwell, and the others can drift in afterwards."

Messrs. Sparkes & Crisp possessed the usual kind of establishment, filled with tall show-cases exhibiting motoring gadgets. On the right was a counter, where a lad was earnestly discussing with a customer the rival merit of two different brands of shock-absorber. Through an archway appeared a glittering array of motor-cycles and side-cars. A frosted-glass door on the left appeared to lead to an inner office.

Wimsey darted silently in with Sir Maxwell and disappeared behind a show-case. The lad and the customer continued their dis-cussion. After about a minute, Wimsey emerged again and strode wrathfully to the counter.

"See here, sonnie," he said, peremptorily, "do you want to do any business to-day, or don't you? I've got an appointment and I can't wait here all afternoon." He looked at his watch. "I've been hanging about here for the last ten minutes."

"Very sorry, sir. What can I do for you?"

Wimsey brought out his brown-paper parcel from the attaché-case.

"You're agents for these magnetos?"

"Yes, sir. That will be our Mr. Saunders. Excuse me one minute, sir. Call him down, sir."

The youth dashed to the frosted-glass door, leaving Wimsey to endure the furious stare of the specialist in shock-absorbers.

"Will you come this way, sir?"

Wimsey, attaching his party to him with a glance, plunged through the door and was conducted to a small office where "our Mr. Saunders" sat, in company with a typist.

Mr. Saunders was a fresh-faced young man with the Eton-and-Oxford manner. He greeted Wimsey like one welcoming an old school-friend after many years' absence. Then he glanced beyond him to Sergeant Dalziel, and his breezy gusto seemed to suffer a slight diminution.

"Look here, old horse," said Wimsey, "you've seen this magneto before, I fancy?"

Mr. Saunders looked at the magneto and its number rather helplessly, and said:

"Yes, yes, oh, yes, to be sure. Quite, Number XX/47302. Yes.
When did we have Number XX/47302 through our hands, Miss
Madden?"

Miss Madden referred to a card-index file.

"It came in for repairs a fortnight ago, Mr. Saunders. It belongs to Mr. Ferguson of Gatehouse. He brought it in himself. Defect in armature winding. Returned to him the day before yesterday."

"Yes—exactly. Our fellows at the shops reported a defect in the
armature winding. Quite. I hope it is quite O.K. now, Mr.—
er——"

"After that," said Wimsey, "you may remember getting a visit
from my friend here, Sergeant Dalziel."

"Oh, absolutely," said Mr. Saunders. "Quite so. You're very
well, I hope, Sergeant?"

"You told him then," said Wimsey, "that Mr. Ferguson came in
here about ten minutes to three."

"Did I? Oh, yes—I remember. Mr. Crisp called me in. You
remember, Miss Madden? Yes. But I didn't say that. Birkett said
that—the young man in the show-room, don't you know. Said the
customer had been waiting ten minutes. Yes. I didn't see the chappie
when he came in, you know. I found him waiting when I got
back from lunch. I was a little late that day, I think. Yes. Lunching
with a customer. Business, and all that sort of thing. Yes. Mr.
Crisp rather hauled me over the coals, I remember. Ha, ha!"

"When exactly *did* ye come in, Mr. Saunders?" asked the Inspector, grimly.

"Oh, well—must have been about three o'clock, I'm afraid. Yes.
Half an hour late. Business, of course. Mr. Crisp——"

"Wull ye no speak the truth, mon?" said Inspector Macpherson,
irritated.

"Eh? Oh—well—as a matter of fact, I may have been a minute
or two later. I—I rather avoided looking at the clock, I'm afraid.
What time did I come in, Miss Madden?"

"A quarter past three, Mr. Saunders," said Miss Madden con-
cisely. "I remember the occasion perfectly."

"By Jove, was it? Well, I thought it must have been somewhere about three or a little after. What a memory you've got, Miss Madden."

Miss Madden smiled faintly.

"There you are, Inspector," said Wimsey. "Difference between five minutes to and five minutes past. All the difference, isn't it?"

"Ye may have tae swear tae this in a court of law, Mr. Saunders," said the Inspector, sourly. "So I'll trouble ye no tae forget it again."

"Oh, I say, really?" said Mr. Saunders, in some alarm. "Look here, shall I have to say who I was lunching with? Because, as a matter of fact, it wasn't exactly business. At least, it was private business."

"That will be your own concern, Mr. Saunders. Ye may like tae know that we're investigatin' a case o' murder."

"Oh, I *say!* Of course, I didn't know that. Mr. Crisp just asked me when I came in. I said, about three—because it really was that, you know, more or less. Of course, if I'd known, I should have asked Miss Madden. She has such a wonderful memory for details."

"Ay," said the Inspector, "and I wad advise ye tae cultivate the same yersel'. Gude mornin' tae ye."

The investigators were shown out by Mr. Saunders, who burbled unconvincingly all down the passage.

"It's not much good questioning this fellow Birkett, I suppose," said Sir Maxwell. "He probably spoke in perfect good faith. He'd be ready to swear to-day that he'd kept you waiting, Wimsey."

"Probably. Well, now, we've got to be up at the Exhibition at four. Not much time. However, I noticed a jobbing printer's on the way up here. I daresay we shall find what we want there."

He led them at a quick pace along the street, and darted into a small printing-works.

"I want to buy a few metal types," he said. "Rather like these. Must be this size, and as near in character as you can supply them." He produced a sheet of paper.

The foreman scratched his head.

"That'll be 5 point," he said. "The nearest thing to it wad be Clarendon caps. Ay, we can gi'e ye that, if ye wasn't wantin' a great weight o't."

"Oh, dear, no. I only want five letters—S—M and L—A and D, and a complete set of figures."

"Will monotype castings do ye?"

"I'd rather have foundry-metal if you have it. I want to use them as punches for a small piece of leather-work."

"Verra gude." The foreman went to a case of type, extracted the required letters and figures and wrapped them up in a screw of paper, mentioning a small price.

Wimsey paid for them and put the parcel in his pocket.

"By the way," he said, "did you have a gentleman in here, asking for the same thing, a fortnight ago?"

"No, sir. I wad mind it weel eneugh. Na, na, it wad be a rather uncommon transaction. I havena been askit for sic a thing since I cam' tae this business, an' that's twa year next January."

"Oh, well, it doesn't matter. Thanks awfully. Good morning."

"Better get a trade directory, Inspector, and count out all the printers. And—yes—wait—the people who sell book-binding materials. Ferguson must have got these—unless, of course, he brought them with him, which isn't very likely."

Dalziel departed on this errand, while the rest took a taxi and hurried away to the Exhibition, which they reached a few minutes before four. Here they dallied till half-past four, making a hasty tour of all the rooms, and noting one or two striking pictures in each.

"There," said Wimsey, as they passed the turnstile again. "Now, if we were to meet any inquisitive friends on the doorway, we could persuade them that we had visited the whole show and used our brains. And now we had better make tracks for a quiet place. I suggest a hotel bedroom."

CHAPTER XXIX

LORD PETER WIMSEY

IN A remote bedroom in one of Glasgow's principal hotels, Wimsey unwrapped his little parcel of types, together with Ferguson's safety-razor, and a small hammer, which he had purchased on the way.

Then, gathering his audience about him, he brought out from his pocket the outward half of his first-class ticket from Gatehouse to Glasgow.

"Now, gentlemen," said he, "we come to the crucial point of our investigation.

"If you had read that excellent work of Mr. Connington's, to which I drew your attention, you would have found that it contained an account of how a gentleman forged a clip-mark on his railway ticket, by means of a pair of nail-scissors.

"That was on an English line. Now, the Scottish railway authorities, possibly out of sheer tiresomeness, and possibly with the laudable idea of making the way of the ticket-forger hard, are not content with a single triangular clip.

"The other day I travelled—at great inconvenience to myself—from Gatehouse to Glasgow by the 9.8 a. m. train. I found that the brutal ticket-collectors actually inflicted three ferocious punches on my poor little half-ticket. The first was at Maxwelltown, where they produced a horrible set of indented letters and numerals, thus: LMS 42D. At Hurlford, they were content to take a large bite out of the ticket—not a simple triangular snip, but a disgusting thing like a squat figure 1. Ferguson would probably often have seen these marks, and having the artist's eye and a remarkable visual memory, would no doubt be able to reproduce these things from memory. Personally, I took the precaution of drawing the mark left by the clipper. Here it is: Then, at Mauchline, they went all cautious again, and disfigured the ticket with another cipher-code, LMS 23A . Now, gentlemen, with your permission and these instruments, we will proceed to forge the punch-marks on this ticket."

He took up the safety-razor, detached the blade, and, laying the ticket down on the marble-topped washstand, proceeded to cut the Hurlford clip-mark out of the pasteboard.

This done, he laid the ticket on the blotting-pad provided by the hotel, placed the type-metal figure 2 carefully just above the edge of the ticket, and delivered a smart tap with the hammer. The figure appeared, when the type was lifted, sharply incised on the face of the ticket, which, on being turned over, showed a thicker and blunter version of the figure in relief on the reverse.

"Eh, mon!" exclaimed Macpherson, "but ye're ower clever tae be an honest mon."

Wimsey added the figure 3 and an A, taking care to keep the feet of the letters parallel—a task easily accomplished by setting the beard of the type in line with the edge of the pasteboard. Then, with careful attention to spacing and uprightness, he punched in the letters LMS over the 23A. This completed the Mauchline punch-mark. In a third place he forged the **LMS 42D** for the Maxwelltown mark, and laid his tools aside with a sigh of satisfaction.

"It's a wee bit groggy here and there," he said, "but it would probably pass on a casual inspection. Now, there's only one thing to do, and that is, to get it back into the hands of the railway-company. I'd better take only one witness to this. We don't want to create a sensation."

The Inspector was chosen to accompany him, and, taking a taxi, they bustled down to St. Enoch Station. Here Wimsey inquired, in a fussy manner, for the collector who had been on duty when the 2.16 came in from Dumfries. The man was pointed out to him at one of the barriers. Wimsey, wreathing his features into a kind of peevish smile, approached him with an air of worried kindliness.

"Oh, good evening. I think you were at the barrier when I came in on the 2.16 this afternoon. Now, do you know that you let me get past without giving up my ticket? Yes, yes, he-he! I might have been defrauding the company and all that. I really think you ought to be more careful. Yes. I'm a shareholder on this line, and my cousin is a director, and I *do* think it's dreadfully careless. There'd be an inquiry when they found a ticket short at the audit-office, of course, but you know, he-he, I could have escaped by that time, couldn't I? Tut, tut—no wonder dividends go down. But I don't want to get you into trouble, my good fellow, so I've brought you the ticket, and if I were you I'd just slip it in with the others and say no more about it. But you'll be more careful in future, won't you?"

During this harangue, which was poured out all in one breath, allowing no time for reply, the ticket-collector's face changed gradually from weary courtesy to astonishment and from astonishment to anger.

"Eh, sir," said the man, the moment he could get a word in edgeways, "I dinna ken what ye'll be up to, but I'll no be had twice that way within the fortnight."

Inspector Macpherson here intervened.

"My mon," said he, "I'm a police officer, an' I'll trouble ye tae attend tae me. Have ye had this same thing happen tae ye before?"

The ticket-collector, now thoroughly alarmed, excused himself, stammered and then let out the whole story.

He had been on duty just about this time exactly a fortnight earlier. A gentleman had come, just as Wimsey had done, and produced a ticket, explaining that he had somehow slipped through the barrier without having to give it up. He (the collector) had examined the ticket, and seen that it had been properly clipped at Maxwelltown, Hurlford and Mauchline, and he had seen no reason to doubt the passenger's story. Not wishing to be reprimanded for negligence, he had thanked the gentleman, taken the ticket and carried it to the clerk who was making up that day's tickets for dispatch to the audit-office. The clerk had obligingly added the ticket to the appropriate bundle, and no more had been heard about it. The collector was sorry, but in view of the fact that the ticket appeared perfectly in order in every way, he had not thought he could be doing any harm. On being shown the photograph of Ferguson, the collector rather tentatively identified him as the passenger who had brought back the ticket.

The clerk confirmed the collector's story, and all that remained was to visit the audit-office and obtain a view of the ticket itself. This, owing to the fact that there had already been one police inquiry about it, was fortunately still in existence. A careful examination showed a slight difference between the form of the lettering and that of the correctly-punched tickets in the same bunch, and also that, whereas the figures purporting to have been punched on it at Mauchline were $\frac{LMS}{23A}$ the other tickets bore the cipher $\frac{LMS}{23B}$.

It was explained that in each case the letter following the numerals denoted the particular collector who clipped the tickets on that train, each man having his own pair of clippers. The Mauchline numbers ranged from 23A to 23G. Therefore, while in itself the punch-mark $\frac{LMS}{23A}$ was perfectly correct and in order, it was suspicious that collector A should have punched only that one ticket out of all the tickets punched on that train. The previous inquiry had, of course, merely been directed to ascertain that the ticket had actually reached Glasgow, and therefore no special attention was paid to the punch-marks. Now, however, it was evident enough that the punch-marks were forgeries, very neatly executed.

On their return to the hotel, Wimsey and the Inspector were met by Dalziel, with additional confirmation. A man corresponding to Ferguson's description had, on the Tuesday in question, visited a firm that sold book-binders' tools, and purchased a set of letter-punches, similar in character and size to the letter on the tickets. He had explained that he was doing a little amateur book-binding, and wanted the punches for the spines of a set of volumes, which were to be labelled SAMUEL, 1, 2, 3 and 4—this series containing all the letters and numbers necessary for faking the ticket-punches. The case against Ferguson was complete.

· · · · · · ·

Wimsey was rather silent as they took the last train back from Glasgow.

"You know," he said, "I rather liked Ferguson, and I couldn't stick Campbell at any price. I rather wish——"

"Can't be helped, Wimsey," said the Chief Constable. "Murder is murder, you know."

"Not always," said Wimsey.

· · · · · · ·

They came back to find Ferguson under arrest. He had endeavoured to take out his car—had found the magneto missing and had then attempted to make a bolt for the railway-station. Ross and Duncan had then thought it time to intervene. He had made no reply when arrested and cautioned, and was then in the Newton-

Stewart police-station, awaiting examination. On being confronted with the forged ticket, he gave in, and, despite the warnings of the police, decided to tell his story.

"It wasn't murder," he said. "I swear to God it wasn't murder. And I told you the truth when I said that it didn't happen in the least like your reconstruction.

"Campbell came back at 10.15, just as I said. He barged into my place and began boasting about what he had done to Gowan and what he was going to do to Farren. He had been drinking again after he came in. He used filthy expressions to me and told me he was going to have it out with me, once and for all. He was damnably offensive. I tell you, it wasn't murder. It was Campbell's night to howl, and he got what was coming to him.

"I told him to get out of my house. He wouldn't go, and I tried to push him out. He attacked me, and there was a struggle. I'm stronger than I look, and he wasn't sober. There was a rough and tumble, and I got a heavy punch in on his jaw. He went over and caught his head on the rounded top of the studio stove. When I went to pick him up, he was dead. That was at 11 o'clock.

"Well, I was frightened. I knew I'd often threatened to do him in, and I'd got no witnesses. Here he was, in my house, dead, and I had certainly used force to him first.

"Then I began to think that I might make it look like an accident. I needn't go into the details. You seem to know them all. My plan worked perfectly, with one exception, and I got over that, and as a matter of fact, it did me good. I meant to start from Barrhill, but I missed the train, and then I hung on to old Ikey-Mo, which made my alibi much better, because it didn't look, on the face of it, as though I could have got to Girvan in time, especially when I'd heard from Jock Graham that you knew I couldn't have started from the Minnoch before 11.30.

"It was bad luck, of course, that the body was found quite so soon. I knew there might be trouble over that *rigor mortis* business. Was that what put you on to the idea of murder in the first place?"

"No," said Wimsey. "It was your habit of putting paints in your pocket. Did you realise that you had carried off Campbell's flake white?"

"I didn't notice it till I got back home. But it never occurred to me that anybody would spot that. I suppose you were the intelligent sleuth, Wimsey. I'd have taken it up to the Minnoch and dropped it somewhere, only that you had seen it the day you came to the studio. That was the first real fright I got. But afterwards I thought I could rely on the alibi. I was rather proud of that ticket-forgery. And I hoped you would overlook the possibilities of Ikey-Mo."

"There's only one thing I don't understand," said the Chief Constable; "why didn't you start out earlier from the Minnoch? There wasn't any need to do such a lot to the painting."

Ferguson smiled faintly.

"That was a big bloomer. You reconstructed the events of the night, and you know what a lot I had to do? Well—I forgot one thing. I forgot to wind up my watch, which I usually do at bed-time. I was going to pack up my painting things, after I'd done a goodish bit, when I heard a lorry coming along. I waited for that to go by and looked at my watch. It said half-past ten. I thought I could easily give it another half-hour. I didn't want to hang about at Barrhill for fear of being recognised. I estimated another half-hour, and looked at my watch again. It was still half-past ten.

"That put me into a panic. I booted the body over the bank and packed up as though the devil was after me. That must have been how I came to overlook the flake white. I scorched away as fast as I could, but that bicycle I borrowed was too small for me and geared rather low. A beast. I missed the train by a hair's-breadth—it was just moving out of the station as I got to the station turn. I rode on in a kind of desperation—and then that car came along and I thought I was saved. But apparently I wasn't.

"I'm sorry. I didn't mean to kill Campbell. And I still say, and say again, it was not murder."

Wimsey got up.

"Look here, Ferguson," he said. "I'm damned sorry, and I always thought it couldn't really be murder. Will you forgive me?"

"I'm glad," said Ferguson. "I've felt like hell ever since. I'd really rather stand my trial. I'd like to tell everybody that it wasn't murder. You do believe that, don't you?"

"I do," said Wimsey, "and if the jury are sensible people, they'll bring it in self-defence or justifiable homicide."

The jury, after hearing of Mr. Gowan's experiences, took a view mid-way between murder and self-defence. They brought it in man-slaughter, with a strong recommendation to mercy, on the ground that Campbell was undoubtedly looking for trouble, and the beard of Samson was not sacrificed altogether in vain.

THE END